The Tale of the Years,

From the Coming of the Valar to the Kingdom of Arda until the end of the first age of the Children of Ilúvatar

Of the beginning of Time and its Reckoning

Time indeed began with the beginning of Eä, and in that beginning the Valar came into the world. But the measurement which the Valar made of the ages of their labours is not known to any of the Children of Ilúvatar, until the first flowering of Telperion in Valinor. Thereafter the Valar counted time by the ages of Valinor, whereof each age contained one hundred of the years of the Valar; but each such year was longer than are now nine years under the Sun. *Thus spake Quennar Onótimo concerning this matter:*

Now measured by the flowering of the Trees there were twelve hours in each Day of the Valar, and one thousand of such days the Valar took to be a year in their realm. It is supposed indeed by the Loremasters that the Valar so devised the hours of the Trees that one hundred of such years so measured should be in duration as one fifth of an Age of the Valar, as those ages were in the days of their labours before the foundation of Valinor; whereas each Age of the Valar is one exact part, how great or how small they alone know, of the whole history of Eä from its beginning to the End that shall be. But these things are not certainly known even to Vanyar.

As for the Years of the Trees in comparison with those that came after: one such year was longer than nine such as are now. For there were in each Year of the Trees twelve thousand hours. Yet the hours of the Trees were each seven times as long as is one hour of a full day upon Middle-earth from sunset unto sunset beside the Shores of the Great Sea. Therefore each Day of

THE HISTORY OF MIDDLE-EARTH III

Works by J.R.R. Tolkien
THE HOBBIT
LEAF BY NIGGLE
ON FAIRY-STORIES
FARMER GILES OF HAM
THE HOMECOMING OF BEORHTNOTH
THE LORD OF THE RINGS
THE ADVENTURES OF TOM BOMBADIL
THE ROAD GOES EVER ON (WITH DONALD SWANN)
SMITH OF WOOTTON MAJOR

Works published posthumously
SIR GAWAIN AND THE GREEN KNIGHT, PEARL AND SIR ORFEO*
THE FATHER CHRISTMAS LETTERS
THE SILMARILLION*
PICTURES BY J.R.R. TOLKIEN*
UNFINISHED TALES*
THE LETTERS OF J.R.R. TOLKIEN*
FINN AND HENGEST
MR BLISS
THE MONSTERS AND THE CRITICS & OTHER ESSAYS*
ROVERANDOM
THE CHILDREN OF HÚRIN*
THE LEGEND OF SIGURD AND GUDRÚN*
THE FALL OF ARTHUR*
BEOWULF: A TRANSLATION AND COMMENTARY*
THE STORY OF KULLERVO
THE LAY OF AOTROU AND ITROUN
BEREN AND LÚTHIEN*
THE FALL OF GONDOLIN*
THE NATURE OF MIDDLE-EARTH
THE FALL OF NÚMENOR

The History of Middle-earth – by Christopher Tolkien
I THE BOOK OF LOST TALES, PART ONE
II THE BOOK OF LOST TALES, PART TWO
III THE LAYS OF BELERIAND
IV THE SHAPING OF MIDDLE-EARTH
V THE LOST ROAD AND OTHER WRITINGS
VI THE RETURN OF THE SHADOW
VII THE TREASON OF ISENGARD
VIII THE WAR OF THE RING
IX SAURON DEFEATED
X MORGOTH'S RING
XI THE WAR OF THE JEWELS
XII THE PEOPLES OF MIDDLE-EARTH

* Edited by Christopher Tolkien

TOLKIEN

The History of Middle-earth III

X Morgoth's Ring
XI The War of the Jewels
XII The Peoples of Middle-earth

CHRISTOPHER TOLKIEN

HarperCollins*Publishers*

HarperCollins*Publishers* Ltd
1 London Bridge Street,
London SE1 9GF

HarperCollins*Publishers*
Macken House, 39/40 Mayor Street Upper,
Dublin 1, D01 C9W8, Ireland

www.tolkien.co.uk
www.tolkienestate.com

This edition published by HarperCollins*Publishers* 2002

15

First published by HarperCollins*Publishers* 2000

Morgoth's Ring first published in Great Britain by
HarperCollins*Publishers* 1993
The War of the Jewels first published in Great Britain by
HarperCollins*Publishers* 1994
The Peoples of Middle-earth first published in Great Britain by
HarperCollins*Publishers* 1996

Copyright © The Tolkien Estate Limited and C.R. Tolkien
1993, 1994 and 1996
This edition Copyright © HarperCollins*Publishers* 2002

ISBN 978-0-00-714917-9

 ® and 'Tolkien'® are registered trade marks of
The Tolkien Estate Limited

Set in Sabon

Printed and bound in Italy by ROTOLITO S.p.A.

All rights reserved. No part of this publication may be reproduced,
stored in a retrieval system, or transmitted in any form or by any means,
electronic, mechanical, photocopying, recording or otherwise,
without the prior permission of the publishers.

This book is produced from independently certified FSC™ paper
to ensure responsible forest management.
For more information visit: www.harpercollins.co.uk/green

MORGOTH'S RING

J. R. R. TOLKIEN

Morgoth's Ring

The Later Silmarillion
PART ONE
The Legends of Aman

Christopher Tolkien

CONTENTS

Foreword *page* vii

PART ONE

AINULINDALË 1

PART TWO

THE ANNALS OF AMAN 45

PART THREE

THE LATER *QUENTA SILMARILLION*

I   THE FIRST PHASE   141
  1 Of the Valar   143
  2 Of Valinor and the Two Trees   152
  3 Of the Coming of the Elves   158
  4 Of Thingol and Melian   171
  5 Of Eldanor and the Princes of the Eldalië   173
  6 Of the Silmarils and the Darkening of Valinor   184
  7 Of the Flight of the Noldor   193
  8 Of the Sun and Moon and the Hiding of Valinor   197

II   THE SECOND PHASE   199
  The Valaquenta   199
  The Earliest Version of the Story of Finwë and
    Míriel   205

Laws and Customs among the Eldar	207
Later versions of the Story of Finwë and Míriel	254
Of Fëanor and the Unchaining of Melkor	271
Of the Silmarils and the Unrest of the Noldor	273
Of the Darkening of Valinor	282
Of the Rape of the Silmarils	292
Of the Thieves' Quarrel	295

PART FOUR

ATHRABETH FINROD AH ANDRETH	301

PART FIVE

MYTHS TRANSFORMED	367
Appendix: Synopsis of the Texts	432
Index	434

FOREWORD

The *Quenta Silmarillion*, with the *Ainulindalë*, the *Annals of Valinor*, and the *Annals of Beleriand*, as they stood when my father began *The Lord of the Rings* at the end of 1937, were published six years ago in *The Lost Road and Other Writings*. That was the first great break in the continuous development of *The Silmarillion* from its origins in *The Book of Lost Tales*; but while one may indeed regret that matters fell out as they did just at that time, when the *Quenta Silmarillion* was in sight of the end, it was not in itself disastrous. Although, as will be seen in Part One of this book, a potentially destructive doubt had emerged before my father finished work on *The Lord of the Rings*, nonetheless in the years that immediately followed its completion he embarked on an ambitious remaking and enlargement of all the Matter of the Elder Days, without departure from the essentials of the original structure.

The creative power and confidence of that time is unmistakable. In July 1949, writing to the publishers on the subject of a sequel to *Farmer Giles of Ham*, he said that when he had finally achieved *The Lord of the Rings* 'the released spring may do something'; and in a letter to Stanley Unwin of February 1950, when, as he said, that goal had been reached at last, he wrote: 'For me the chief thing is that I feel that the whole matter is now "exorcized", and rides me no more. I can turn now to other things...' It is very significant also, I believe, that at that time he was deeply committed to the publication of *The Silmarillion* and *The Lord of the Rings* 'in conjunction or in connexion' as a single work, 'one long Saga of the Jewels and the Rings'.

But little of all the work begun at that time was completed. The new *Lay of Leithian*, the new tale of Tuor and the Fall of Gondolin, the *Grey Annals* (of Beleriand), the revision of the *Quenta Silmarillion*, were all abandoned. I have little doubt that despair of publication, at least in the form that he regarded as essential, was the prime cause. The negotiations with Collins to publish both works had collapsed. In June 1952 he wrote to Rayner Unwin:

As for *The Lord of the Rings* and *The Silmarillion*, they are where they were. The one finished (and the end revised), and the other still unfinished (or unrevised), and both gathering dust. I have been both off and on too unwell, and too burdened to do much about them, and too downhearted. Watching paper-shortages and costs mounting against me. But I have rather modified my views. Better something than nothing! Although to me all are one, and the 'Lord of the Rings' would be better far (and eased) as part of the whole, I would gladly consider the publication of any part of this stuff. Years are becoming precious ...

Thus he bowed to necessity, but it was a grief to him.

This second break was destructive – in the sense, that *The Silmarillion* would never now be finally achieved. In the years that followed he was overwhelmed: the demands of his position in the University, and the necessity of moving house, led him to declare that the preparation of *The Lord of the Rings* for publication, which should have been 'a labour of delight', had been 'transformed into a nightmare'. Publication was followed by a huge correspondence of discussion, explanation, and analysis, of which the examples retrieved and published in the volume of his letters provide abundant evidence. It seems not to have been until the end of the 1950s that he turned again seriously to the *Silmarillion* narrative (for which there was now an insistent demand). But it was too late. As will be seen in the latter part of this book, much had changed since (and, as I incline to think, in direct relation to) the publication of *The Lord of the Rings* and its immediate aftermath. Meditating long on the world that he had brought into being and was now in part unveiled, he had become absorbed in analytic speculation concerning its underlying postulates. Before he could prepare a new and final *Silmarillion* he must satisfy the requirements of a coherent theological and metaphysical system, rendered now more complex in its presentation by the supposition of obscure and conflicting elements in its roots and its tradition.

Among the chief 'structural' conceptions of the mythology that he pondered in those years were the myth of Light; the nature of Aman; the immortality (and death) of the Elves; the mode of their reincarnation; the Fall of Men and the length of their early history; the origin of the Orcs; and above all, the power and significance of Melkor-Morgoth, which was enlarged to become the ground and source of the corruption of

FOREWORD

Arda. For this reason I have chosen *Morgoth's Ring* as the title of this book. It derives from a passage in my father's essay 'Notes on motives in the *Silmarillion*' (pp. 394 ff.), in which he contrasted the nature of Sauron's power, concentrated in the One Ring, with that of Morgoth, enormously greater, but dispersed or disseminated into the very matter of Arda: 'the whole of Middle-earth was Morgoth's Ring'.

Thus this book and (as I hope) its successor attempt to document two radically distinct 'phases': that following the completion of *The Lord of the Rings*, and that following its publication. For a number of reasons, however, I have found it more satisfactory in presentation to divide the material, not according to these two 'phases', but by separating the narrative into two parts. While this division is artificial, I have been able to include in this book a high proportion of all that my father wrote in the years after *The Lord of the Rings* was finished, both in narrative and discussion (to which must be added of course all the material in the volume of letters), concerning the Elder Days before the Hiding of Valinor. The next volume will contain, according to my intention, all or at any rate most of the original texts relating to the legends of Beleriand and the War of the Jewels, including the full text of the *Grey Annals* and a major narrative remaining unpublished and unknown, *The Wanderings of Húrin*.

The publication of the texts in this book makes it possible to relate, if not at all points or in every detail, the first eleven chapters (with the exception of Chapter II 'Of Aulë and Yavanna' and Chapter X 'Of the Sindar') of the published *Silmarillion* to their sources. This is not the purpose of the book, and I have not discussed the construction of the published text at large; I have presented the material in terms of its evolution from earlier forms, and in those parts that concern the revision and rewriting of the *Quenta Silmarillion* I have retained the paragraph numbers from the pre-*Lord of the Rings* text given in Volume V, so that comparison is made simple. But the (inevitably complex) documentation of the revised *Quenta Silmarillion* is intended to show clearly its very curious relationship to the *Annals of Aman*, which was a major consideration in the formation of the text in the first part of the published work.

I am much indebted to Mr Charles Noad, who has once again undertaken the onerous task of reading the text in proof independently and checking all references and citations with scrupulous care, to its great improvement.

I am very grateful for the following communications concerning Volume IX, *Sauron Defeated*. Mr John D. Rateliff has pointed out an entry in the diary of W. H. Lewis for 22 August 1946 (*Brothers and Friends: The Diaries of Major Warren Hamilton Lewis*, ed. C. S. Kilby and M. L. Mead, 1982, p. 194). In this entry Warnie Lewis recorded that at the Inklings meeting that evening my father read 'a magnificent myth which is to knit up and conclude his Papers of the Notions [*sic*] Club.' The myth is of course the Drowning of Anadûnê. I was present on this occasion but cannot recall it (in this connection see *Sauron Defeated* p. 389).

Mr William Hicklin has explained why John Rashbold, the undergraduate member of the Notion Club who never speaks, should bear the second name Jethro. In the Old Testament Moses' father-in-law is named both *Jethro* and *Reuel* (Exodus 2:18 and 3:1); thus *John Jethro Rashbold = John Reuel Tolkien* (see *Sauron Defeated* pp. 151, 160).

I was unable to explain the reference (pp. 277–8) to the retreat of the Danes from Porlock in Somerset to 'Broad Relic', but Miss Rhona Beare has pointed out that 'Broad Relic' and 'Steep Relic' are in fact names used in manuscripts of the Anglo-Saxon Chronicle for the islands of Flatholme and Steepholme at the mouth of the river Severn (see *The Lost Road and Other Writings* p. 80); according to Earle and Plummer, *Two of the Saxon Chronicles Parallel* (1892; II.128), 'The name "Relic" may point to some Irish religious settlements on these islands; "relicc" (= reliquiae) is the regular Irish name for a cemetery.'

I take this opportunity to notice two important misprints that entered the text of *Sauron Defeated* at a late stage. The first is on p. 297, where line 45 of the poem *Imram* should read *We sailed then on till all winds failed*, etc. The second is on p. 475, where in Index II a line was dropped after the entry *Pharazîr*; the following should be restored: *Pillar of Heaven, The* 238, 241–2, 249, 302, 315, 317, 335, 353.

Lastly, I should mention that after the text of this book was in print I added a discussion of the significance of the star-names that appear on p. 160 to the head-note to the Index.

PART ONE

AINULINDALË

AINULINDALË

The evidence is clear that when *The Lord of the Rings* was at last completed my father returned with great energy to the legends of the Elder Days. He was working on the new version of the *Lay of Leithian* in 1950 (III.330); and he noted (V.294) that he had revised the *Quenta Silmarillion* as far as the end of the tale of Beren and Lúthien on 10 May 1951. The last page of the later *Tale of Tuor*, where the manuscript is reduced to notes before finally breaking off (*Unfinished Tales* p. 56), is written on a page from an engagement calendar bearing the date September 1951, and the same calendar, with dates in September, October, and November 1951, was used for riders to *Tuor* and the *Grey Annals* (the last version of the *Annals of Beleriand* and a close companion work to the *Annals of Aman*, the last version of the *Annals of Valinor*). The account, some ten thousand words long, of the 'cycles' of the legends, written to Milton Waldman of the London publisher Collins and given in part in *The Letters of J. R. R. Tolkien* (no.131), was very probably written towards the end of that year.

Until recently I had assumed without question that every element in the new work on the Elder Days belonged to the years 1950 and 1951; but I have now discovered unambiguous evidence that my father had in fact turned again to the *Ainulindalë* some years before he finished *The Lord of the Rings*. As will be seen, this is no mere matter of getting the textual history right, but is of great significance.

I had long been aware of extremely puzzling facts in the history of the rewriting of the *Ainulindalë*. The fine pre-*Lord of the Rings* manuscript, lettered 'B', was described and printed in V.155 ff.; as I noted there (p. 156) 'the manuscript became the vehicle of massive rewriting many years later, when great changes in the cosmological conception had entered.' So drastic was the revision (with a great deal of new material written on the blank verso pages) that in the result two distinct texts of the work, wholly divergent in essential respects, exist physically in the same manuscript. This new text I shall distinguish as 'C'.

But there is another text, a typescript made by my father, that was also directly based on *Ainulindalë* B of the 1930s; and in this there appears a much more radical – one might say a devastating – change in the cosmology: for in this version the Sun is already in existence from the beginning of Arda. I shall refer to this typescript as 'C*'.

A peculiarity of C* is that for a long stretch it proceeds in very close relationship to C, but yet constantly differs from it, though always in quite insignificant ways. In many cases my father later *wrote in the C reading* on the typescript. I will illustrate this by a single example, a passage in §25 (p. 15). Here C*, as typed, has:

> But when they clad themselves the Valar arrayed themselves in the form and temper some as of male and some as of female; and the choice that they made herein proceeded, doubtless, from that temper that each had from their uttermost beginning; for male and female are not matters only of the body any more than of the raiment.

The C text has here:

> But when they clad themselves the Valar arrayed them in the form some as of male and some as of female; for that difference of temper they had even from their beginning, and it is but bodied forth in the choice of each, not made by the choice; even as with us male and female may be shown by the raiment, but is not made thereby.

Now in C this passage was written at the same time as what precedes it and what follows it – it is all of a piece; whereas in C* the original typed passage was struck through and the C text substituted in pencil.

There seemed no other explanation possible but that C* preceded C; yet it seemed extraordinary, even incredible, that my father should have *first* made a clear new typescript version from the old B manuscript and *then* returned to that manuscript to cover it somewhat chaotically with new writing – the more so since C* and C are for much of their length closely similar.

When working on *The Notion Club Papers* I found among rough notes and jottings on the Adûnaic language a torn half-sheet of the same paper as carries a passage from the *Ainulindalë*, written in pencil in my father's most rapid hand. While not proof that he was working on the *Ainulindalë* so early as 1946 (the year to which I ascribe the development of Adûnaic, when *The Lord of the Rings* had been long halted and *The Return of the King* no more than begun: see IX.12–13, 147) this strongly suggested it; and as will be seen in a moment there is certain evidence that the text C* was in existence by 1948. Moreover in a main structural feature C* follows this bit of text, as C does not (see p. 42); it seemed very probable therefore that C* was typed from a very rough text of which the torn half-sheet is all that remains.

Here it must be mentioned that on the first page of C* my father wrote later 'Round World Version', and (obviously at the same time) on the title-page of B/C he wrote 'Old Flat World Version' – the word 'Old' being a subsequent addition. It would obviously be very interesting to know when he labelled them thus; and the answer is provided by the following evidences. The first is a draft for a letter, undated and with no indication of whom he was addressing:

These tales are feigned to be translated from the preserved works of
Ælfwine of England (c.900 A.D.), called by the Elves Eriol, who
being blown west from Ireland eventually came upon the 'Straight
Road' and found Tol Eressëa the Lonely Isle.

He brought back copies and translations of many works. I do not
trouble you with the Anglo-Saxon forms. (The only trace of these is
the use of *c* for *k* as in *Celeb*- beside *Keleb*-.)

All these histories are told by Elves and are not primarily
concerned with Men.

I have ventured to include 2 others.

(1) A 'Round World' version of the 'Music of the Ainur'.

(2) A 'Man's' version of the *Fall of Númenor* told from men's
point of view, and with names in a non-Elvish tongue. 'The
Drowning of Anadūnē'. This also is 'Round World'.[1]

The Elvish myths are 'Flat World'. A pity really but it is too
integral to change it.

On the back of the paper he wrote: 'For the moment I cannot find the
Tale called *The Rings of Power*', and referred again in much the same
terms to 'two other tales' that he was 'enclosing'.

There is another draft for this letter which, while again undated,
was written from Merton College and addressed to Mrs. Katherine
Farrer, the wife of Dr. Austin Farrer, theologian and at that time
Chaplain of Trinity College:

Dear Mrs. Farrer,

These tales are feigned (I do not include their slender framework)
to be translated from the preserved work of Ælfwine of England
(c.900 A.D.), who being blown west from Ireland eventually came
upon the 'straight road' and found the Lonely Isle, Tol Eressëa,
beyond the seas.

There he learned ancient lore, and brought back translations and
excerpts from works of Elvish lore. The specimen of the 'Anglo-
Saxon' original is not included.

NB All these histories are told by the Elves, and are not primarily
concerned with Men.

I have ventured to include, besides the 'Silmarillion' or main
chronicle, one or two other connected 'myths': 'The Music of the
Ainur', the Beginning; and the Later Tales:[2] 'The Rings of Power',
and 'The Fall of Númenor', which link up with Hobbit-lore of the
later or 'Third Age'.

Yours
JRRT

The end of this, from 'and the Later Tales', was struck out and marked
'not included'.

It cannot be doubted that these were drafts for the undated letter to

Katherine Farrer which is printed as no.115 in *The Letters of J. R. R. Tolkien*, for though there is not much left from these drafts in that form of it, it contains the words 'I am distressed (for myself) to be unable to find the "Rings of Power", which with the "Fall of Númenor" is the link between the *Silmarillion* and the Hobbit world.'

My father said in the first of the two drafts given above that he was including in the materials to be lent to Katherine Farrer 'two others', one of which was 'a "Round World" version of the "Music of Ainur"'; and this can be taken to mean that he was giving her two versions, 'Flat World' and 'Round World'. Now there is preserved a portion of a letter to him from Katherine Farrer, and on this my father pencilled a date: 'October 1948'. She had by this time received and read what he had given to her, and in the course of her illuminating and deeply enthusiastic remarks she said: 'I like the Flat Earth versions best. The hope of Heaven is the only thing which makes modern astronomy tolerable: otherwise there must be an East and a West and Walls: aims and choices and not an endless circle of wandering.'

It must have been when he was preparing the texts for her that he wrote the words 'Flat World Version' and 'Round World Version' on the texts B/C and C* of the *Ainulindalë*. Beyond this one can only go by guesswork; but my guess is that the 'Flat World Version' was the old B manuscript *before* it had been covered with the revisions and new elements that constitute version C. It may be that Katherine Farrer's opinion had some influence on my father in his decision to make this new version C on the old manuscript – deriving much of it from C*, and emending C* in conformity with new readings. Thus:

- *Ainulindalë* B, a manuscript of the 1930s. When lending this to Katherine Farrer in 1948 he wrote on it 'Flat World Version'.
- A new version, lost apart from a single torn sheet, written in 1946.
- A typescript, *Ainulindalë* C*, based on this text. When lending this in 1948 he wrote on it 'Round World Version'.
- *Ainulindalë* C, made after the return of the texts by covering the old B manuscript with new writing, and removing certain radically innovative elements present in C*.

It would in this way be entirely explicable how it came about that the typescript C* *preceded* the complicated and confusing revision (C) on the old manuscript – this being the precursor of the last version of the work that my father wrote, *Ainulindalë* 'D', made in all probability not long after C.

Ainulindalë C* was thus an experiment, conceived and composed, as it appears, before the writing of *The Return of the King*, and certainly before *The Lord of the Rings* was finished. It was set aside; but as will appear later in this book, it was by no means entirely forgotten.

C* should therefore in strict chronology be given first; but in view

AINULINDALË

of its peculiarities it cannot be made the base text. It is necessary therefore to change the chronological order, and I give first version C in full, following it with a full account of the development in the final text D, and postponing consideration of C* to the end of Part One.

Before giving the text of C, however, there is another brief document that has value for dating: this is a brief, isolated list of names and their definitions headed *Alterations in last revision 1951*.[3]

> *Atani* N[oldorin] *Edain* = Western Men or Fathers of Men
> *Pengoloð*[4]
> *Aman* name of land beyond Pelóri or mountains of Valinor, of which Valinor is part
> *Melkor*[5]
> *Arda* Elvish name of Earth = our world. Also *Kingdom of Arda* = fenced region. Field of Arda.
> *Illuin* Lamp of North = *Helkar*[6]
> *Ormal* Lamp of South = *Ringil*[6]
> *Isle of Almaren* in the Great Lake
> *Valaróma* = Horn of Oromë
> *Eru* = Ilúvatar
> *Ëa* = Universe of that which Is

Not all these names were newly devised at this time, of course: thus *Eru* and *Arda* go back to my father's work on *The Notion Club Papers* and *The Drowning of Anadûnê*, as also does *Aman* (where however it was the Adûnaic name of Manwë).

In *Ainulindalë* C appear *Arda*, *Melkor*, and *Pelóri*, but the Lamps are called *Foros* and *Hyaras*, not *Illuin* and *Ormal*, and the Isle in the Great Lake is *Almar*, not *Almaren*. The final text D, as originally written, has *Atani*, *Almaren* and *Aman*, but *Aman* did not mean the Blessed Realm; the Lamps are named *Forontë* and *Hyarantë*, and the Horn of Oromë is *Rombaras*. These differences from the '1951 list' show that *Ainulindalë* D was made before that time.

I give now the text of *Ainulindalë* C in full. Since despite radical changes in the structure and the addition of much new material a good deal of the old form does survive, it is not really necessary to do so, but to give it partly in the form of textual notes would make the development very difficult to follow; and *Ainulindalë* C is an important document in the history of the mythological conception of the created Universe. The remodelling that constituted C out of B was in fact done at different times, and is in places chaotic, full of changes and substitutions; I do not attempt to disentangle the different layers, but give the final form after all changes, with a few developments that took place while C was in the making recorded in the notes that follow the text (p. 22). I have numbered the paragraphs as a convenient means of reference subsequently.

On the title-page the original words 'This was written by Rúmil of Tûn' (V.156) were extended thus:

> This was written by Rúmil of Túna
> and was told to Ælfwine in Eressëa
> (as he records)
> by Pengoloð the Sage

The form *Túna* for *Tûn* as the name of the city came in with the earliest layer of emendation to QS (pre-*Lord of the Rings*, see V.225, §39). Since the city is *Tirion* in *The Lord of the Rings* it might be thought that this extension of the title was made in the earlier period; but in a later version of the title-page (p. 30) my father retained 'Rúmil of Túna', and in the *Annals of Aman* he frequently used *Túna* (beside *Tirion*) in general reference to 'the city on the hill' (see p. 90, §67).

It is not said in any of the title-pages to the texts of the earlier period that Pengoloð (Pengolod) actually instructed Ælfwine himself; he is cited as the author of works which Ælfwine saw and translated.[7]

The Music of the Ainur
and the Coming of the Valar

These are the words that Pengoloð[8] spake to Ælfwine concerning the beginning of the World.

§1   There was Ilúvatar, the All-father, and he made first the Ainur, the Holy Ones, that were the offspring of his thought, and they were with him before aught else was made. And he spoke to them, propounding to them themes of music, and they sang before him, and he was glad. But for a long while they sang only each alone, or but few together, while the rest hearkened; for each comprehended only that part of the mind of Ilúvatar from which he came, and in the understanding of their brethren they grew but slowly. Yet ever as they listened they came to deeper understanding, and increased in unison and harmony.

§2   And it came to pass that Ilúvatar called together all the Ainur, and declared to them a mighty theme, unfolding to them things greater and more wonderful than he had yet revealed; and the glory of its beginning and the splendour of its end amazed the Ainur, so that they bowed before Ilúvatar and were silent.

§3   Then said Ilúvatar: 'Of the theme that I have declared to you, I will now that ye make in harmony together a Great Music. And since I have kindled you with the Flame Imperishable, ye shall show forth your powers in adorning this theme, each with his own thoughts and devices, if he will. But I will sit and hearken and be glad that through you great beauty has been wakened into song.'

§4 Then the voices of the Ainur, like unto harps and lutes, and pipes and trumpets, and viols and organs, and like unto countless choirs singing with words, began to fashion the theme of Ilúvatar to a great music; and a sound arose of endless interchanging melodies, woven in harmony, that passed beyond hearing into the depths and into the heights, and the places of the dwelling of Ilúvatar were filled to overflowing, and the music and the echo of the music went out into the Void, and it was not void. Never since have the Ainur made any music like to this music, though it has been said that a greater still shall be made before Ilúvatar by the choirs of the Ainur and the Children of Ilúvatar after the end of days.[9] Then shall the themes of Ilúvatar be played aright, and take Being in the moment of their utterance, for all shall then understand his intent in their part, and shall know the comprehension of each, and Ilúvatar shall give to their thoughts the secret fire, being well pleased.

§5 But now Ilúvatar sat and hearkened, and for a great while it seemed good to him, for in the music there were no flaws. But as the theme progressed, it came into the heart of Melkor to interweave matters of his own imagining that were not in accord with the theme of Ilúvatar; for he sought therein to increase the power and glory of the part assigned to himself. To Melkor among the Ainur had been given the greatest gifts of power and knowledge, and he had a share in all the gifts of his brethren; and he had gone often alone into the void places seeking the Imperishable Flame. For desire grew hot within him to bring into Being things of his own, and it seemed to him that Ilúvatar took no thought for the Void, and he was impatient of its emptiness. Yet he found not the Fire, for it is with Ilúvatar. But being alone he had begun to conceive thoughts of his own unlike those of his brethren.

§6 Some of these thoughts he now wove into his music, and straightway discord arose about him, and many that sang nigh him grew despondent and their thought was disturbed and their music faltered; but some began to attune their music to his rather than to the thought which they had at first. Then the discord of Melkor spread ever wider, and the melodies that had been heard at first foundered in a sea of turbulent sound. But Ilúvatar sat and hearkened, until it seemed that about his throne there was a raging storm, as of dark waters that made war one upon the other in an endless wrath that would not be assuaged.

§7 Then Ilúvatar arose, and the Ainur perceived that he smiled; and he lifted up his left hand, and a new theme began amid the storm, like and yet unlike to the former theme, and it gathered power and had new beauty. But the discord of Melkor arose in uproar and contended with it, and there was again a war of sound more violent than before, until many of the Ainur were dismayed and played no longer, and Melkor had the mastery. Then again Ilúvatar arose, and the Ainur perceived that his countenance was stern; and he lifted up his right hand; and behold, a third theme grew amid the confusion, and it was unlike the others. For it seemed at first soft and sweet, a mere rippling of gentle sounds in delicate melodies, but it could not be quenched, and it grew, and it took to itself power and profundity. And it seemed at last that there were two musics progressing at one time before the seat of Ilúvatar, and they were utterly at variance. One was deep and wide and beautiful, but slow and blended with an immeasurable sorrow, from which its beauty chiefly came. The other had now achieved a unity of its own; but it was loud, and vain, and endlessly repeated, and it had little harmony, but rather a clamorous unison as of many trumpets braying upon a few notes. And it essayed to drown the other music by the violence of its voice, but it seemed that its most triumphant notes were taken by the other and woven into its own solemn pattern.

§8 In the midst of this strife, whereat the halls of Ilúvatar shook and a tremor ran out into the silences yet unmoved, Ilúvatar arose a third time, and his face was terrible to behold. Then he raised up both his hands, and in one chord, deeper than the Abyss, higher than the Firmament, more glorious than the Sun, piercing as the light of the eye of Ilúvatar, the Music ceased.

§9 Then Ilúvatar spoke, and he said: 'Mighty are the Ainur, and mightiest among them is Melkor; but that he may know, and all the Ainur, that I am Ilúvatar, those things that ye have sung and played, lo! I will show them forth, that ye may see what ye have done. And thou, Melkor, shalt see that no theme may be played that has not its uttermost source in me, nor can any alter the music in my despite. For he that attempteth this shall be but mine instrument in the devising of things more wonderful, which he himself hath not imagined.'

§10 Then the Ainur were afraid, and they did not yet

comprehend the words that were said to them; and Melkor was filled with shame, of which came secret anger. But Ilúvatar arose in splendour, and he went forth from the fair regions that he had made for the Ainur; and the Ainur followed him.

§11   But when they were come into the Void, Ilúvatar said to them: 'Behold your Music!' And he showed to them a vision, giving to them sight where before was only hearing; and they saw a new World made visible before them, and it was globed amid the Void, and it was sustained therein, but was not of it. And as they looked and wondered this World began to unfold its history, and it seemed to them that it lived and grew.

§12   And when the Ainur had gazed for a while and were silent, Ilúvatar said again: 'Behold your Music! This is your minstrelsy; and each of you that had part in it shall find contained there, within the design that I set before you, all those things which it may seem that he himself devised or added. And thou, Melkor, wilt discover all the secret thoughts of thy mind, and wilt perceive that they are but a part of the whole and tributary to its glory.'

§13   And many other things Ilúvatar spoke to the Ainur at that time, and because of their memory of his words, and the knowledge that each has of the music which he himself made, the Ainur know much of what was, and is, and is to come, and few things are unseen by them. Yet some things there are that they cannot see, neither alone nor taking counsel together (as thou shalt hear, Ælfwine); for to none but himself has Ilúvatar revealed all that he has in store, and in every age there come forth things that are new and have no foretelling, for they do not spring from the past. And so it was that, as this vision of the World was played before them, the Ainur saw that it contained things which they had not thought. And they saw with amazement the coming of the Children of Ilúvatar, and the habitation that was prepared for them; and they perceived that they themselves in the labour of their music had been busy with the preparation of this dwelling, and yet knew not that it had any purpose beyond its own beauty. For the Children of Ilúvatar were conceived by him alone; and they came with the Third Theme,[10] and were not in the theme which Ilúvatar propounded at the beginning, and none of the Ainur had part in their making. Therefore when they beheld them, the more did they love them, being things other than themselves, strange and free, wherein they saw the mind of Ilúvatar reflected anew and learned yet a little more of his wisdom, which otherwise had been hidden even from the Holy Ones.

§14 Now the Children of Ilúvatar are Elves and Men, the Firstborn and the Followers. And amid all the splendours of the World, its vast halls and spaces, and its wheeling fires, Ilúvatar chose a place for their habitation in the Deeps of Time and in the midst of the innumerable Stars. And this habitation might seem a little thing to those who consider only the majesty of the Ainur, and not their terrible sharpness – as who should take the whole field of the Sun as the foundations of a pillar and so raise it until the cone of its summit was more bitter than a needle – or who consider only the immeasurable vastness of the World, which still the Ainur are shaping, and not the minute precision to which they shape all things therein. But thou must understand, Ælfwine, that when the Ainur had beheld this habitation in a vision and had seen the Children of Ilúvatar arise therein, then many of the most mighty of the Holy Ones bent all their thought and their desire towards that place. And of these Melkor was the chief, even as he was in the beginning the greatest of the Ainur who took part in the Music. And he feigned, even to himself at first, that he desired to go thither and order all things for the good of the Children of Ilúvatar, controlling the turmoils of the heat and the cold that had come to pass through him. But he desired rather to subdue to his will both Elves and Men, envying the gifts with which Ilúvatar promised to endow them; and he wished himself to have subjects and servants, and to be called Lord, and to be a master over other wills.

§15 But the other Ainur looked upon this habitation in the Halls of Aman,[11] which the Elves call Arda, the Earth, and looking upon light they were joyful, and their eyes seeing many colours were filled with gladness; but because of the roaring of the sea they felt a great unquiet. And they observed the winds and the air, and the matters whereof the Middle-earth was made,[12] of iron and stone and silver and gold and many substances; but of all these water they most greatly praised. And it is said by the Eldar that in water there lives yet the echo of the Music of the Ainur, and many of the Children of Ilúvatar hearken still unsated to the voices of the sea, and yet know not for what they listen.

§16 Now to water had that Ainu whom we call Ulmo most turned his thought, and of all most deeply was he instructed by

Ilúvatar in music. But of the airs and winds Manwë most had pondered, who was the noblest of the Ainur. Of the fabric of Earth had Aulë thought, to whom Ilúvatar had given skill and knowledge scarce less than to Melkor; but the delight and pride of Aulë was in the deed of making, and in the thing made, and not in possession nor in himself, wherefore he became a maker and teacher, and none have called him lord.

§17 Now Ilúvatar spake to Ulmo and said: 'Seest thou not here in this little realm in the Deeps of Time and in the midst of the innumerable Stars how Melkor hath made war upon thy province? He hath bethought him of bitter cold immoderate, and yet hath not destroyed the beauty of thy fountains, nor of thy clear pools. Behold the snow, and the cunning work of frost! Behold the towers and mansions of ice! Melkor hath devised heats and fire without restraint, and hath not dried up thy desire, nor utterly quelled the music of the sea. Behold rather the height and glory of the clouds, and the everchanging mists and vapours, and listen to the fall of rain upon the Earth! And in these clouds thou art drawn yet nearer to Manwë, thy friend whom thou lovest.'

§18 Then Ulmo answered: 'Yea, truly, Water is become now fairer than my heart imagined, neither had my secret thought conceived the snow-flake, nor in all my music was contained the falling of the rain. Lo! I will seek Manwë, that he and I may make melodies for ever and ever to thy delight!' And Manwë and Ulmo have from the beginning been allied, and in all things have served most faithfully the purpose of Ilúvatar.

§19 But behold! even as Ulmo spoke, and while the Ainur were yet gazing upon this vision, it was taken away and hidden from their sight; and it seemed to them that in that moment they perceived a new thing, Darkness, which they had not known before, except in thought. But they had become enamoured of the beauty of the vision, and engrossed in the unfolding of the World which came there to being, and their minds were filled with it; for the history was incomplete and the circles not full-wrought when the vision was taken away, and there was unrest among them.

§20 Therefore Ilúvatar called to them and said: 'I know the desire of your minds that what ye have seen should verily be, not only in your thought, but even as ye yourselves are, and yet other. Therefore I say: Let these things Be! And I will send forth the flame imperishable into the Void, and it shall be at the heart of the World, and the World shall Be; and those of you that will may go down into it.' And suddenly the Ainur saw afar off a light, as it were a cloud with a living heart of flame; and they knew that this was no vision only, but that Ilúvatar had made a new thing.

§21 Thus it came to pass that of the Holy Ones some abode still with Ilúvatar beyond the confines of the World; but others, and among them many of the greatest and most fair, took the leave of Ilúvatar and descended into it. But this condition Ilúvatar made, or it is the necessity of their love, that their power should henceforth be contained and bounded in the World, and be within it for ever, so that they are its life and it is theirs. And therefore, Ælfwine, we name them the Valar, the Powers of the World.

§22 But behold! when the Valar entered into the World they were at first astounded and at a loss, for it was as if naught was yet made which they had seen in vision, and all was but on point to begin, and yet unshapen; and it was dark. For the Great Music had been but the growth and flowering of thought in the Timeless Halls, and the Vision only a foreshowing; but now they had entered in at the beginning of Time, and the Valar perceived that the World had been but foreshadowed and foresung, and they must achieve it.

§23 So began their great labours in wastes unmeasured and unexplored, and in ages uncounted and forgotten, until in the Deeps of Time and in the midst of the vast halls of the World there came to be that hour and that place where was made the habitation of the Children of Ilúvatar. And in this work the chief part was taken by Manwë and Aulë and Ulmo. But Melkor, too, was there from the first, and he meddled in all that was done, turning it, if he might, to his own desires and purposes; and he kindled great fires. When therefore Earth was young and full of flame Melkor coveted it, and he said to the Valar: 'This shall be my own kingdom! And I name it unto myself!'

§24 But Manwë was the brother of Melkor in the mind of Ilúvatar, and he was the chief instrument of the second Theme that Ilúvatar had raised up against the discord of Melkor; and he called unto himself others of his kin and many spirits both greater and less, and they went down into the Halls of Aman and aided Manwë, lest Melkor should hinder the fulfilment of their labour for ever, and the Earth should wither ere it flowered. And Manwë said unto Melkor: 'This kingdom thou shalt not take for thine own, wrongfully, for many others have laboured here no less than thou.' And there was strife between Melkor and the Valar, and for a time Melkor departed and withdrew to other regions and did there what he would, but the Earth he could not put from his heart. For he was alone, without friend or companion, and he had as yet but small following; since of those that had attuned their music to his in the beginning not all had been willing to go down with him into the World, and few that had come would yet endure his servitude.

§25 But the Valar now took to themselves shape and form; and because they were drawn thither by love for the Children of Ilúvatar, for whom they hoped, they took shape after that manner which they had beheld in the Vision of Ilúvatar; save only in majesty and splendour, for they are mighty and holy. Moreover their shape comes of their knowledge and desire of the visible World, rather than of the World itself, and they need it not, save only as we use raiment, and yet we may be naked and suffer no loss of our being. Therefore the Valar may walk unclad, as it were, and then even the Eldar cannot clearly perceive them, though they be present. But when they clad themselves the Valar arrayed them in the form some as of male and some as of female; for that difference of temper they had even from their beginning, and it is but bodied forth in the choice of each, not made by the choice; even as with us male and female may be shown by the raiment, but is not made thereby. And Manwë and Ulmo and Aulë were as Kings; but Varda was the Queen of the Valar, and the spouse of Manwë, and her beauty was high and terrible and of great reverence. Yavanna was her sister, and Yavanna espoused Aulë; but Nienna dwells alone, even as does Ulmo. And these with Melkor are the Seven Great Ones of the Kingdom of Arda.[13] But think not, Ælfwine, that the shapes wherein the Great Ones array themselves are at all times like unto the shapes of kings and queens of the Children of Ilúvatar; for at whiles they may clothe them in their own thought, made visible in forms terrible and wonderful. And I myself, long years agone, in the land of the Valar[14] have seen Yavanna in the likeness of a Tree; and the beauty and majesty of that form could not be told in words, not unless all the things that grow in the earth, from the least unto the greatest, should sing in choir together, making unto their queen an offering of song to be laid before the throne of Ilúvatar.

§26 And behold! the Valar drew unto them many companions, some less, some well-nigh as great as themselves, and they laboured in the ordering of the Earth, and the curbing of its tumults. Then Melkor saw what was done, and that the Valar walked upon Earth as powers visible, clad in the raiment of the World, and were lovely and glorious to see, and blissful; and that Earth was become as a garden for them, for its turmoils were subdued. His envy grew then the greater within him; and he also took visible form, but because of his mood, and the malice that increased in him, that form was dark and terrible. And he descended upon Earth in power and majesty greater than any other of the Valar, as a mountain that wades in the sea and has its head above the clouds and is clad in ice and crowned with fire and smoke; and the light of his eyes was like a flame that withers with heat and pierces with a deadly cold.

§27 Thus began the first battle of the Valar and Melkor for the dominion of Arda; and of those tumults we know but little; for know thou, Ælfwine, what I have declared unto thee is come from the Valar themselves, with whom we of the Eldalië spoke in the land of Valinor, and we were instructed by them; but little would they ever tell of the days of war ere the coming of the Elves. But this we know: that the Valar endeavoured ever, in despite of Melkor, to rule the Earth and to prepare it for the coming of the Children; and they built lands, and Melkor destroyed them; valleys they delved and Melkor raised them up; mountains they carved and Melkor threw them down; seas they hollowed and Melkor spilled them; and naught might come to peace or lasting growth, for as surely as the Valar began a labour so would Melkor undo it or corrupt it. And yet their labour was not vain, and slowly the Earth was shaped and made firm.

§28 But of all such matters, Ælfwine, others shall tell thee, or thou shalt read in other lore; for it is not my part at this time to instruct thee in the history of the Earth. And now behold! here is the habitation of the Children of Ilúvatar established at the last in the deeps of Time and amidst the innumerable stars. And here are the Valar, the Powers of the World, contesting for the possession of the jewel of Ilúvatar; and thus thy feet are on the beginning of the road.

Words of Pengolod[15]

§29 And when he had ended the *Ainulindalë*, such as Rúmil had made it, Pengolod the Sage paused a while; and Ælfwine said to him: Little, you say, would the Valar tell to the Eldar of the days before their coming: but do not the wise among you know more of those ancient wars than Rúmil has here set forth? Or will you not tell me more of the Valar as they were when first your kindred beheld and knew them?

§30 And Pengoloð answered: Much of what I know or have learned from the elders in lore, I have written; and what I have written thou shalt read, if thou wilt, when thou hast learned better the tongue of the Noldor and their scripts. For these matters are too great and manifold to be spoken or to be taught in speech within the brief patience and heedfulness of those of mortal race. But some little more I may tell to thee now, since thou askest it of me.

§31 This tale I have heard also among the loremasters of the Noldor in ages past. For they tell us that the war began before Arda was full-shaped, and ere yet there was anything that grew or walked upon earth, and for long Melkor had the upper hand. But in the midst of the war a spirit of great strength and hardihood came to the aid of the Valar, hearing in the far heaven that there was battle in the Little World. And he came like a storm of laughter and loud song, and Earth shook under his great golden feet. So came Tulkas, the Strong and the Merry, whose anger passeth like a mighty wind, scattering cloud and darkness before it. And Melkor was shaken by the laughter of Tulkas, and fled from the Earth; and there was peace for a long age. And Tulkas remained and became one of the Valar of the kingdom of Arda; but Melkor brooded in the outer darkness, and his hate was given to Tulkas for ever after. In that time the Valar brought order to the seas and the lands and the mountains, and they planted seeds; and since, when the fires had been subdued or buried beneath the primeval hills, there was need of Light they wrought two mighty lamps for the enlightening of the Middle-earth which they had built amid the Encircling Seas, and they set the lamps upon high pillars, loftier far than any of the mountains of the later days. And one they raised near to the North of Middle-earth, and it was named Foros; and the other they raised in the South, and it was called Hyaras.[16] And the light of the lamps of the Valar went out over the Earth so that all was lit as it were in a changeless day. Then the seeds that the Valar had planted began swiftly to sprout and to burgeon, and there arose a multitude of growing things great and small, grasses, and flowers of many colours, and trees whose blossom was like snow upon the mountains[17] but whose feet were wrapped in the shadow of their mighty limbs. And beasts and birds came forth and dwelt in the green plains or in the rivers and the lakes, or walked in the darkness of the woods. And richest was the growth of plant and beast in the midmost parts of the Earth where the lights of both lamps met and were blended. And there upon the isle of Almar[18] in a great lake was the first dwelling of the gods, when all things were new, and green was yet a marvel in the eyes of the makers.

§32 But at length Melkor returned in secret, and far in the North where the light of Foros was only dim he made a hidden dwelling. And he sent forth his power and turned again to evil much that had been well begun, so that fens became rank and poisonous and forests perilous and full of fear, and beasts became monsters of horn and ivory and dyed the Earth with blood. And when he saw his time he revealed himself and made war again on the Valar, his brethren; and he threw down the lamps, and a new darkness fell on the Earth, and all growth ceased; and in the fall of the lamps (which were very great) the seas were lifted up in fury, and many lands were drowned. And the Valar at that time had long dwelt upon an island in the midst of the Earth,[19] but now they were forced to depart again; and they made their home in the uttermost West,[20] and they fortified it; and they built many mansions in that land upon the borders of the World which is called Valinor; and to fence that land from the East they built the Pelóri Valion,[21] the Mountains of Valinor that were the highest upon Earth. Thence they came with war against Melkor; but he had grown in stature and malice, so that they could not at that time either overcome him or take him captive, and he escaped from their wrath and built himself a mighty fortress in the North of Middle-earth, and delved great caverns underground, and gathered there many lesser powers that seeing his greatness and growing strength were now willing to serve him; and the name of that strong and evil place was Utumno.

§33 Thus it was that Earth lay wrapped in darkness again, save in Valinor, as the ages drew on to the hour appointed for the coming of the Firstborn of the Children of Ilúvatar. And in the darkness Melkor dwelt, and still often walked abroad in Middle-earth; and he wielded cold and fire, from the tops of the mountains to the deep furnaces that are beneath them, and whatsoever was violent or cruel or deadly in those days was laid to his charge.

§34 And in Valinor dwelt the Valar and all their kin and folk, and because of the bliss and beauty of that land they came seldom to Middle-earth. Yet Yavanna, to whom all things that grow are dear, forsook not the Earth[22] utterly, and leaving the house of Aulë and the light of Valinor she would come at times and heal the hurts of Melkor; and returning she would ever urge the Valar to that war with his evil power that they must surely wage ere the coming of the Firstborn. And Oromë also, the hunter, rode at whiles in the darkness of the unlit forests, sounding his mighty horn, whereat the shadows of Utumno, and even Melkor himself, would flee away.

§35 In the midst of the Blessed Realm Aulë dwelt, and laboured long, for in the making of all things in that land he had the chief part; and he wrought there many fair and shapely things both openly and in secret. Of him comes the love and knowledge of the Earth and of all those things that it contains, whether the lore of those who do not make but seek only for the understanding of what is, studying the fabric of the Earth and the blending and mutation of its elements, or the lore of all craftsmen: the tiller and the husbandman, the weaver, the shaper of wood, or the forger of metals. [And Aulë we name the Friend of the Noldor, for of him they learned much in after days, and they are the wisest and most skilled of the Elves. And in their own fashion, according to their own gifts which Ilúvatar gave to them, they added much to his teaching, delighting in tongues and alphabets and in the figures of broidery, of drawing, and of carving. And the Noldor it was who achieved the invention of gems, which were not in the world before their coming; and the fairest of all gems were the Silmarils, and they are lost.][23]

§36 But Manwë Súlimo, highest and holiest of the Valar, sat upon the borders of the West, forsaking not in his thought the Outer Lands. For his throne was set in majesty upon the pinnacle of Taniquetil, which was the highest of the mountains of the world, standing upon the margin of the Seas. Spirits in the shape of hawks and eagles flew ever to and from his halls; and their eyes could see to the depths of the sea and could pierce the hidden caverns under the world, and their wings could bear them through the three regions of the firmament beyond the lights of heaven to the edge of Darkness. Thus they brought word to him of well nigh all that passed in Aman:[24] yet some things were hidden even from the eyes of Manwë, for where Melkor sat in his dark thought impenetrable shadows lay. With Manwë dwelt Varda the most beautiful, whom the Noldor name Elbereth, Queen of the Valar; she it was who wrought the stars. And the children of Manwë and Varda are Fionwë Úrion their son, and Ilmarë their daughter;[25] and these were the eldest of the children of the Valar. They dwelt with Manwë, and with them were a great host of fair spirits in great blessedness. Elves and Men revere Manwë most of all the Valar, for he has no thought for his own honour, and is not jealous of his power, but ruleth all to peace. [The Lindar he loved most of all the Elves, and of him they received song and poesy. For poesy is the delight of Manwë, and the song of words is his music.][26] Behold, the raiment of Manwë is blue, and blue is the fire of his eyes, and his sceptre is of sapphire which the Noldor wrought for him; and he is King of the world of gods and elves and men, and the chief defence against Melkor.

§37 But Ulmo was alone, and he abode not in Valinor, but dwelt from the beginning of Arda in the Outer Ocean, as he still does; and thence he governed the flowing of all waters, and the courses of all rivers, the replenishment of springs and the distilling of rain and dew throughout the world. In the deep places he gives thought to music great and terrible; and the echo thereof runs through all the veins of the Earth,[27] and its joy is as the joy of a fountain in the sun whose springs are in the wells of unfathomed sorrow at the foundations of the world. The Teleri learned much of him, and for this reason their music has both sadness and enchantment. Salmar came with him, who made the conches of Ulmo; and Ossë and Uinen, to whom he gave control of the waves and of the inner seas; and many other spirits beside. And thus even under the darkness of Melkor life coursed still through many secret lodes, and the Earth did not die; and ever afterward to all who were lost in that darkness or wandered far from the light of the Valar the ear of Ulmo was open, nor has he ever forsaken Middle-earth, and whatsoever may since have befallen of ruin or change he has not ceased to take thought for it, nor will until the end.[28]

§38 After the departure of the Valar there was silence for an age, and Ilúvatar sat alone in thought. Then Ilúvatar spake, and he said: 'Behold I love the world, and it is a mansion for Elves and Men. But the Elves shall be the fairest of earthly creatures, and they shall have and shall conceive more beauty than all my children, and they shall have greater bliss in this world. But to Men I will give a new gift.'

§39 Therefore he willed that the hearts of Men should seek beyond the world and find no rest therein; but they should have a virtue to fashion their life, amid the powers and chances of the world, beyond the Music of the Ainur, which is as fate to all things else. And of their operation everything should be, in shape and deed, completed, and the world fulfilled unto the last and smallest. Lo! even we, Elves, have found to our sorrow that Men have a strange power for good or ill, and for turning things aside from the purpose of Valar or of Elves; so that it is said among us that Fate is not master of the children of Men; yet are they blind, and their joy is small, which should be great.

§40 But Ilúvatar knew that Men, being set amid the turmoils of the powers of the world, would stray often, and would not use their gift in harmony; and he said: 'These too, in their time, shall find that all they do redounds at the end only to the glory of my work.' Yet the Elves say that Men are often a grief even unto Manwë, who knows most of the mind of Ilúvatar. For Men resemble Melkor most of all the Ainur, and yet he hath ever feared and hated them, even those who served him.[29] It is one with this gift of freedom that the children of Men dwell only a short space in the world alive, and yet are not bound to it, and depart whither we know not. Whereas the Eldar remain until the end of days, and their love of the world is deeper, therefore, and more sorrowful. But they die not, till the world dies, unless they are slain or waste in grief – for to both these seeming deaths they are subject – nor does age subdue their strength, unless one grow weary of ten thousand centuries; and dying they are gathered in the halls of Mandos in Valinor, whence often they return and are reborn in their children. But the sons of Men die indeed, and leave the World; wherefore they are called the Guests, or the Strangers. Death is their fate, the gift of Ilúvatar unto them, which as Time wears even the Powers shall envy. But Melkor hath cast his shadow upon it, and confounded it with darkness, and brought forth evil out of good, and fear out of hope. Yet it is said that they will join in the Second Music of the Ainur, whereas Ilúvatar has not revealed what he purposes for Elves and Valar after the World's end; and Melkor has not discovered it.

NOTES

1. It was not until after the publication of *Sauron Defeated* that I remembered the existence of this reference to *The Drowning of Anadûnê* as 'a "Man's" version of the *Fall of Númenor* told from men's point of view', and the description of it as 'Round World': see IX.394–5, 406.
2. The first page of the third version of *The Fall of Númenor* (IX.331) is headed 'The Last Tales', and the tale itself numbered '1'.
3. I have referred to this list before, in V.294 and 338. In the latter passage I took the 'revision' to be that of the *Quenta Silmarillion*; but since not all the names in the list occur in it the reference may be more general.
4. *Pengoloð*: i.e. not *Pengolod*. See note 15.
5. *Melkor*: i.e. not *Melko*; see V.338.
6. The names *Helkar* and *Ringil* were struck through at the time of writing; this was a shorthand, meaning '*Illuin* and *Ormal* replace *Helkar* and *Ringil*, which are rejected.' See note 16.
7. On Ælfwine in Tol Eressëa see my summary in IX.279–80.
8. Rúmil in *Ainulindalë* B (V.156).
9. See V.164 note 2.
10. There was no suggestion in the earlier versions that the Children of Ilúvatar entered the Music with the Third Theme.
11. Here and in §24 my father wrote *the Halls of Anar*, changing *Anar* to *Aman* later (cf. notes 13 and 24). On the use of these names see pp. 28, 44.
12. See V.164 note 9.
13. *Kingdom of Arda* replaced *Kingdom of Anar* at the time of writing; cf. note 11.
14. Pengoloð refers to the time before the Flight of the Noldor.
15. These words were pencilled lightly on the manuscript. The name is clearly spelt *Pengolod* here and in the paragraph that follows, but *Pengoloð* in §30.
16. In the *Ambarkanta* the northern lamp was *Helkar*, the southern *Ringil*; see p. 7 and note 6, and IV.256.
17. In the *Quenta Silmarillion* §38 (V.222), repeating the words of the *Quenta* (IV.87), it was said that 'the first flowers that ever were east of the Mountains of the Gods' bloomed on the western shores of Tol Eressëa in the light of the Trees that came through the Pass of Kalakilya.
18. The name of the isle was first written *Eccuilë*, changed at once to

Version C AINULINDALË

Eremar, which was subsequently altered to *Almar* (*Almaren* in the list of alterations made in 1951, p. 7).
19 The concluding sentence of §31 concerning the dwelling of the Valar on 'the isle of Almar in a great lake' was an addition to the main body of the new text; hence the repetition here.
20 My father first wrote here: 'in the uttermost parts of Andúnë'.
21 The name *Pelóri (Valion)* first occurs here; it is found also (under *Aman*) in the list of alterations made in 1951 (p. 7).
22 My father first wrote here 'world', changing it at once to 'earth', which I have capitalised – as also at two other occurrences: capitalisation is inconsistent in *Ainulindalë* C, partly owing to the retention of passages from the original text B.
23 The square brackets enclosing this passage (developed from *Ainulindalë* B, V.162) probably imply its proposed exclusion.
24 The words *in Aman* were added later, at the same time as the change of *the Halls of Anar* to *the Halls of Aman* in §§15, 24 (see note 11).
25 See V.165 note 20.
26 As note 23.
27 *Ainulindalë* B has 'all the veins of the world': this was changed to 'of the Earth', I think simply to avoid repetition, since the sentence ends with 'the foundations of the world'.
28 From this point there is no indication on the manuscript of my father's intention, but in view of the next version D it seems clear that we are to continue with the concluding portion of the old B text (from 'After the departure of the Valar ...', V.163). In D, however, there is an intervening passage (see pp. 35–6) that makes the conclusion more integral with what precedes. – These final paragraphs (§§38–40) were left largely unchanged (though with significant alterations in §40) from the text of B, but I give it in full in order to provide a complete text at this point.
29 This was changed from the B version 'For Men resemble Melko most of all the Ainur, and yet have ever feared and hated him.'

Commentary on the Ainulindalë text C

The revision C introduces a radical re-ordering of the original matter of the *Ainulindalë*, together with much that is new; and it is easiest to show this in the form of a table. This table is in no sense a synopsis of the content, but simply a scheme to show the structural interrelations.

B	C

The playing of the Music
    Discord of Melko, the Three Themes
	The playing of the Music
	    Discord of Melkor, the Three Themes

Declaration of Ilúvatar to the Ainur: *the Music has been given Being*; the things that Melko has introduced into the Design	Declaration of Ilúvatar to the Ainur: 'I will show forth the things that you have played'
The Ainur see the World made real	The Ainur see the World in vision; they see the coming of the Children of Ilúvatar
	Elves and Men made by Ilúvatar alone; the love of the Ainur for them
	Desire of the Ainur for the World, and the desire of Melkor to have dominion in it
Joy of the Ainur in the elements of the Earth	Joy of the Ainur in the elements of the Earth
Ulmo's concern with waters, Manwë's with the airs, Aulë's with the fabric of the Earth	Ulmo's concern with waters, Manwë's with the airs, Aulë's with the fabric of the Earth
Desire of the Ainur for the World, and the desire of Melko to have dominion in it	
Elves and Men made by Ilúvatar alone; nature of the Children and their relations with the Ainur	
	The vision of the World taken away; unrest of the Ainur
	Ilúvatar gives Being to the vision
Entry of the Ainur into the World	Entry of the Ainur into the World
Melko walked alone; Ulmo dwelt in the Outer Ocean; Aulë in Valinor; Manwë with Varda on Taniquetil. Relations with the Teleri, Noldor, Lindar	
The forms taken by the Valar, some male, some female	
	The World unshaped; agelong labours of the Valar
	Strife between Melkor and the Valar; withdrawal of Melkor from the Earth
	The forms taken by the Valar, some male, some female: 'I have seen Yavanna'

Version C AINULINDALË

> Melkor's return; first battle of the Valar for the dominion of Arda; elemental strife
>
> *End of the Ainulindalë of Rúmil told to Ælfwine by Pengoloð*
>
> *Words of Pengoloð*
>
> Question of Ælfwine and reply of Pengoloð:
>
> Coming of Tulkas and rout of Melkor
>
> Building of the Lamps. Earth illumined; arising of birds and beasts and flowers
>
> Dwelling of the Valar on the island in the great lake
>
> Secret return of Melkor; blight and monstrosity spread from his hidden dwelling in the North; he cast down the Lamps
>
> Retreat of the Valar into the West and foundation of Valinor
>
> The Valar came with war against Melkor but could not overcome him; Melkor built Utumno
>
> Melkor walked abroad in Middle-earth
>
> The Valar came seldom to Middle-earth save Yavanna and Oromë
>
> Aulë dwelt in Valinor; Manwë with Varda on Taniquetil; Ulmo in the Outer Ocean. Relations with the Noldor, Lindar, Teleri

After the departure of the Valar, Ilúvatar's silence, and then his declaration concerning Elves and Men: the gift of freedom and death to Men; nature of the immortality of the Elves

End of the Ainulindalë spoken by Rúmil to Ælfwine

The central shift in the myth of the Creation lies of course in the fact that in the old form, when the Ainur contemplate the World and find joy in its contemplation and desire it, the World has been given Being by Ilúvatar, whereas in C it is a Vision that has not been given Being. With this may be compared my father's words in the account of his works written for Milton Waldman in 1951 (*Letters* no.131, p. 146):

> They [the Valar] are 'divine', that is, were originally 'outside' and existed 'before' the making of the world. Their power and wisdom is derived from their Knowledge of the cosmogonical drama, which they perceived first as a drama (that is as in a fashion we perceive a story composed by someone else), and later as a 'reality'.

In the Vision, moreover, in which the Ainur see the unfolding of the history of the World as yet unmade, they see the arising within it of the Children of Ilúvatar (§13); and when the Vision is made real and the Ainur descend into the World, it is their knowledge and love of the Children of Ilúvatar who are to be that directs their shape and form when they make themselves visible (§25). Several passages in letters of my father from the years 1956–8 bear closely on these conceptions (see *Letters* nos.181, 200, 212).

But the nature and extent of the *Ainulindalë* is also greatly changed; it contains now the first battle of Melkor with the Valar for the dominion of Arda, but it does not contain the original concluding passage concerning Ilúvatar's Gift to Men, nor the accounts of Manwë, Ulmo and Aulë: these latter, together with much new material concerning the first wars in Arda, are placed in a sort of Appendix, the Words of Pengoloð to Ælfwine. This is reminiscent of the original *Music of the Ainur* in *The Book of Lost Tales*, with Ælfwine (Eriol) appearing in person as questioner.

In the pre-*Lord of the Rings* texts Melko's part in the beginning of Earth's history was conceived far more simply. As late as the *Ambarkanta* (IV.238) the story was that

> the Valar coming into the World descended first upon Middle-earth at its centre, save Melko who descended in the furthest North. But the Valar took a portion of land and made an island and hallowed it, and set it in the Western Sea and abode upon it, while they were busied in the exploration and first ordering of the World. As is told they desired to make lamps, and Melko offered to devise a new substance of great strength and beauty to be their pillars. And he set up these great pillars north and south of the Earth's middle yet nearer to it than the chasm; and the Gods placed lamps upon them and the Earth had light for a while.

In the *Quenta Silmarillion* (V.208) and the *Later Annals of Valinor* (V.110–11) there is no suggestion that Melko departed from the Earth after the first coming of the Valar, and indeed the cosmology described in the *Ambarkanta* could not allow of it: as I said in my commentary (IV.253):

> It is not indeed explained in the *Ambarkanta* how the Valar entered the world at its beginning, passing through the impassable Walls,

and perhaps we should not expect it to be. But the central idea at this time is clear: from the Beginning to the Great Battle in which Melko was overthrown, the world with all its inhabitants was inescapably bounded; but at the very end, in order to extrude Melko into the Void, the Valar were able to pierce the Walls by a Door.

The far more complex account in the new work of the movements of Melkor and of his strife with the Valar is an indication at once, therefore, that shifts have taken place in the cosmology.

In the *Ainulindalë* proper it is now told that Melkor entered the World with the other Ainur at the beginning – he 'was there from the first', and claimed Earth for his own (§23); but he was alone, and unable to resist the Valar, and he 'withdrew to other regions' (§24). There followed the labours of the Valar 'in the ordering of the Earth, and the curbing of its tumults', and Melkor saw from afar that 'Earth was become as a garden for them'; then in envy and malice he 'descended upon Earth' to begin 'the first battle of the Valar and Melkor for the dominion of Arda' (§§26–7). The words 'Earth was become as a garden for them' are not to be interpreted as a reference to the 'Spring of Arda', for the description of this follows in the Words of Pengoloð; where appears also the wholly new element that Tulkas was not one of the Ainur who entered the World at the beginning, but came only when 'in the far heaven' he heard of the war 'in the Little World' (§31).

Then follows the building of the Lamps and the Spring of Arda; for Melkor had fled from the Earth a second time, routed by Tulkas, and 'brooded in the outer darkness'. At the end of 'a long age' he came back in secret to the far North of Middle-earth, whence his evil power spread, and whence he came against the Valar in renewed war, and cast down the Lamps (§32). Then the Valar departed from the island of Almar in the great lake and made their dwelling in the uttermost West; and from Valinor they came against Melkor again. But they could not defeat him; and at that time he built Utumno. There are thus four distinct periods of strife between Melkor and the Valar, and he departed out of Arda and returned to it twice.

We are brought therefore to the forbidding problem of the underlying conception of the World in this phase of my father's later work. In the original *Music of the Ainur* in *The Book of Lost Tales* Ilúvatar 'fashioned [for the Ainur] dwellings in the void, and dwelt among them' (I.52); at the end of the Music he 'went forth from his dwellings, past those fair regions he had fashioned for the Ainur, out into the dark places' (I.55); and 'when they reached the midmost void they beheld a sight of surpassing beauty and wonder where before had been emptiness': 'the Ainur marvelled to see how the world was globed amid the void and yet separated from it' (I.55–6). This may not be a simple conception, but it is pictorially simple. In *Ainulindalë* B it was not changed (V.159). In the *Ambarkanta* 'the World' *(Ilu)* is 'globed' within the invisible, impassable Walls of the World *(Ilurambar)*, and 'the World is set amid Kúma, the Void, the Night without form or time' (IV.235–7). I take these accounts to be in agreement. 'The World' comprises 'the Earth' *(Ambar)*, the region of the heavenly bodies that pass over it, and the Outer Sea *(Vaiya)*, 'more like to sea below the Earth and more like to air above the Earth', which enfolds or 'englobes' all (IV.236).

In C, likewise, Ilúvatar 'went forth from the fair regions that he had made for the Ainur', and they came into the Void (§§10–11). There Ilúvatar showed them a Vision, 'and they saw a new World ... globed amid the Void, and it was sustained therein, but was not of it' (repeating the words of B, though they were here written out anew). But then it is said in C (§14) that 'amid all the splendours of the World, its vast halls and spaces, and its wheeling fires, Ilúvatar chose a place for their habitation [i.e. the habitation of the Children of Ilúvatar] in the Deeps of Time and in the midst of the innumerable Stars.' This habitation is 'Arda, the Earth', which is 'in the Halls of Aman' (§15). When Ilúvatar gave Being to the Vision, he said (§20): 'Let these things Be! And I will send forth the flame imperishable into the Void, and it shall be at the heart of the World, and the World shall Be; and those of you that will may go down into it.' Some of the Ainur 'abode still with Ilúvatar beyond the confines of the World' (§21); but those who 'entered into the World' (§22) are the Valar, the Powers of the World, and they laboured 'in wastes unmeasured and unexplored ... until in the Deeps of Time and in the midst of the vast halls of the World there came to be that hour and that place where was made the habitation of the Children of Ilúvatar' (§23). It is also said (§24) that the lesser spirits who aided Manwë 'went down into the Halls of Aman'. It is clear that 'the Halls of Aman' are equivalent to 'the World' (and indeed in the following text D the reading of C in §23 'the vast halls of the World' becomes 'the vast halls of Aman'). I am unable however to cast any light on the use of the name *Aman* in the later *Ainulindalë* texts. In *The Drowning of Anadûnê*, where it first appeared, it was the Adûnaic name of Manwë, but that meaning is surely not present here.

It emerges then that the word 'World' is explicitly used in a new sense. In the *Ambarkanta* diagram I (IV.243) Ilu *is* 'the World', the Earth and Sky, two halves of a globe itself globed within Vaiya. In C Arda, the Earth, the habitation of Elves and Men, is *within* 'the World', 'the Halls of Aman'. The evident fact that my father also used 'World' in another sense in C (the clearest case being 'that land upon the borders of the World which is called Valinor', §32) does not make matters any easier, but does not contradict this distinction.

In order to understand the implications of this change, it must first be asked: What can be said of the nature of *Arda* in this new conception?

In the *Ambarkanta* diagram I my father long afterwards changed the title-word *Ilu* to *Arda* (IV.242). He would scarcely have done this if the conceptions behind the two names did not continue to bear a substantial resemblance to each other. *Arda*, then, retains major characteristics of the image of *Ilu*, and this is shown by what is said in the text of C itself: as that Ulmo 'dwelt from the beginning of Arda in the Outer Ocean' and the echo of his music 'runs through all the veins of the Earth' (§37), or that the spirits flying from Manwë's halls in the shape of hawks and eagles were borne by their wings *'through the three regions of the firmament'* (§36).

On this basis it may be said that the major difference in the new conception is that while Arda is physically the same as Ilu, it is no longer 'the World globed amid the Void': for Arda is within 'the World' – which is itself 'globed amid the Void' (§11).

But we at once meet with a serious difficulty – and there was no second *Ambarkanta* to help in resolving it. For 'the World', 'the Halls of Aman', which surrounds Arda, is not the Void: though Arda 'might seem a little thing to those ... who consider only the immeasurable vastness of the World' (§14), the World is spatially defined ('globed', §11), and it contains 'splendours ... and wheeling fires'; and Ilúvatar chose the habitation of the Children, which is Arda, 'in the midst of the innumerable Stars'. How can this possibly be brought into agreement with the idea (IV.241, 243) of the Tinwë-mallë, the path of the stars, which is the 'middle air' of Ilmen, the second region of the firmament of Ilu? Yet in C (§36) the spirits that fly from Taniquetil pass through 'the three regions of the firmament *beyond the lights of heaven to the edge of Darkness*'. Since this derives without change from B (V.162), and since C is a reworking of the actual B manuscript, it might be thought that this passage was retained unintentionally; but in fact it comes in a part of the text that was written entirely anew, not emended on the original manuscript (much of C was written anew even when the old text was being largely followed).

It has been seen (p. 27) that the greatly enlarged history of Melkor and the Valar in the beginning depends in part on the changed cosmology, for he twice departed out of Arda. This raises the question of the passage of the Walls of the World, and indeed of the form which that conception now took: for, as will be seen, the idea of the Walls had not been abandoned. But I postpone further discussion of this baffling topic until subsequent texts that bear on it are reached.

Ainulindalë D

This next version of the *Ainulindalë* is a manuscript of unusual splendour, with illuminated capitals and a beautiful script, in which for a part of its length my father made use of Anglo-Saxon letter-forms – even to the extent of using old abbreviations, as the letter 'thorn' with a stroke across the stem for 'that'. This feature at once associates it closely with *Ainulindalë* C, where in the long passages of new text written on the old manuscript he did the same here and there. There can in any case be little question that this new version belongs closely in time with C, which was a very difficult and chaotic text and had to be given more lucid form; and it shares the common characteristic of the various series of my father's manuscripts of beginning as a close (indeed in this case almost an exact) copy of the exemplar but diverging more and more markedly as it proceeds. In this case I give the full text only for certain passages, and for the rest list the changes (other than a small number of slight stylistic changes of a word or two without significance for the conception) by reference to the paragraphs of C.

The text of D was subsequently emended, though not very heavily, in several 'layers', the earlier made with care, the later roughly; where of any importance these are shown as such in the textual representation that follows.

D has a fine separate title-page, with *Ainulindalë* in tengwar, and then:

Ainulindalë
The Music of the
Ainur

This was made by Rúmil of Túna in the Elder
Days. It is here written as it was spoken in
Eressëa to Ælfwine by Pengoloð the Sage. To it
are added the further words that Pengoloð
spoke at that time concerning the Valar, the
Eldar and the Atani; of which more is said
hereafter

The first page of the text is headed *Ainulindalë* (written also in tengwar), and is then as in C (p. 8), with the following added subsequently: 'First he recited to him the Ainulindalë as Rúmil made it.'

§13 '(as thou shalt hear, Ælfwine)' omitted.

§14 'the whole field of the Sun'; D 'the whole field of Arda'

§15 'the Halls of Aman' as in C; not subsequently emended (see p. 37).

§16 As written, D retained the reading of C: 'and not in possession nor in himself, wherefore he became a maker and teacher, and none have called him Lord.' This was emended to: 'and neither in possession nor in his own mastery; wherefore he gives and hoards not, and is free from care, passing ever on to some new work.' The new text being in the present tense conflicts with 'the delight ... of Aulë was in the deed of making' just preceding.

§17 'Behold the towers and mansions of ice!' omitted, perhaps inadvertently.

§19 After 'when the vision was taken away' there is a footnote that seems to have been an early addition:
And some have said that the Vision ceased ere the fulfilment of the Dominion of Men and the fading of the Firstborn; wherefore, though the Music is over all, the Valar have not seen as with sight the Later Ages or the ending of the World. Quoth Pengoloð.

§20 Before 'Let these things Be!' the word *'Ea!'* was added subsequently; and after 'Ilúvatar had made a new thing' was added 'Ea, the World that Is.'

§23 'in the midst of the vast halls of the World'; D 'in the midst of the vast halls of Aman'; 'Aman' here later emended to 'Ea' (see note 15 above, and p. 37).

§24 'they went down into the Halls of Aman'; D 'they came down into the fields of Arda'

'but the Earth he could not put from his heart'; D 'but he did not put the desire of the kingdom of Arda from his heart'

The concluding passage of this paragraph, from 'For he was alone, without friend or companion ...', omitted.

§25 'shape and form'; 'form' emended in D to 'hue'.

§27 'But this we know:'; D 'But this said Rúmil in the end of the *Ainulindalë* which I have recounted to thee:'

'the coming of the Children'; D 'the coming of the Firstborn'

'And yet their labour was not vain, and slowly the Earth was shaped and made firm'; D 'And yet their labour was not all in vain; and though nowhere and in no work was their will and purpose wholly fulfilled, and all things were in hue and shape other than the Valar had at first intended, slowly nonetheless the Earth was fashioned and made firm.'

Heading before §29: 'Words of Pengolod'; D 'Here are the words of Pengoloð to Ælfwine'

§29 'Pengolod'; D 'Pengoloð' (but 'Pengoloð' in C §30)

§31 'the loremasters of the Noldor'; D 'the loremasters'

'the Little World'; D 'the Little Kingdom'

After the passage about the coming of Tulkas in §31 the text of D shows so many changes from C that I give the next part in full.

In that time the Valar brought order to the seas and the lands and the mountains, and Yavanna planted at last the seeds that she had long devised. And since, when the fires had been subdued or buried beneath the primeval hills, there was need of light, Aulë wrought two mighty lamps for the enlightenment of the Middle-earth which he had built amid the Encircling Seas. Then Varda filled the lamps and Manwë hallowed them, and the Valar set them upon high pillars, more lofty far than are any mountains of the later days. One lamp they raised near to the North of Middle-earth, and it was named [Forontë >] Illuin; and the other was raised in the South, and it was named [Hyarantë >] Ormal; and the light of the Lamps of the Valar flowed out over the Earth, so that all was lit as it were in a changeless Day.

Then the seeds that Yavanna had sown began swiftly to sprout and to burgeon, and there arose a multitude of growing things great and small, [grasses, and flowers of many hues, and trees whose blossom was like snow upon the mountains, so tall were they, >] mosses and grasses, and great ferns, and trees whose tops were crowned with cloud as they were living mountains, / but whose feet were wrapped in a green twilight. And beasts [*struck out:* and birds] came forth and dwelt in the grassy plains, or in the rivers and the lakes, or walked in the shadow of the woods. [And richest was the growth of plant and beast in the midmost >] As yet no flower had bloomed nor any bird had sung, for these things waited still their time in the bosom of Palúrien; but wealth there was of her imagining, and nowhere more rich than in the midmost / parts of the Earth, where the light of both the Lamps met and blended. And there upon the Isle of Almaren in the Great Lake was the first dwelling of the gods when all things were young, and new-made green was yet a marvel in the eyes of the [makers. >] makers; and they were long content.

§32 But at length Melkor returned in secret, and far in the North, where the beams of [Forontë >] Illuin were cold and dim, he made a hidden dwelling. Thence he sent forth his power and turned again to evil much that had been well begun; so that green things fell sick and rotted, and rivers were choked with weeds and slime, and fens were made, rank and poisonous, and the breeding place of flies; and forests grew dark and perilous, the haunts of fear; and beasts became monsters of horn and ivory and dyed the earth with blood. And when he saw his time,

Melkor revealed himself, and he made war again on the Valar his brethren; and he threw down the Lamps, and a new darkness fell, and all growth ceased. And in the fall of the Lamps, which were very great, the seas were lifted up in fury, and many lands were drowned. Then the Valar were driven from their abode in Almaren, and they removed from the Middle-earth, and made their home in the uttermost West, [*added:*] in Aman the Blessed, / and they fortified it against the onslaught of Melkor. Many mansions they built in that land upon the borders of the world which is since called Valinor, whose western marges fall into the mists of the Outer Sea, and whose fences against the East are the [Pelóri >] Pelóre Valion, the Mountains of Valinor, highest upon Earth.

Thence they came at last with a great host against Melkor, to wrest from him the rule of the Middle-earth; but he now had grown in malice and in strength and was master of many monsters and evil things, so that they could not at that time overcome him utterly, nor take him captive; and he escaped from their wrath, and lay hid until they had departed. Then he returned to his dwelling in the North, and there built for himself a mighty fortress, and delved great caverns underground secure from assault, and he gathered to him many lesser powers that seeing his greatness and growing strength were now willing to serve him; and the name of that evil fastness was Utumno.

§33 Thus it was that the Earth lay darkling again, save only in Valinor, as the ages drew on to the hour appointed by Ilúvatar for the coming of the Firstborn. And in the darkness Melkor dwelt, and still often walked abroad, in many shapes of power and fear; and he wielded cold and fire, from the tops of the mountains to the deep furnaces that are beneath them; and whatsoever was cruel or violent or deadly in those days is laid to his charge.

§34 But in Valinor the Valar dwelt with all their kin and folk, and because of the beauty and bliss of that realm they came seldom now to Middle-earth, but gave to the Land beyond the Mountains their chief care and love.

D omits the remainder of C §34 concerning the visits of Yavanna and Oromë to Middle-earth (see p. 35), and continues from the beginning of C §35: 'And in the midst of the Blessed Realm were the mansions of Aulë, and there he laboured long.' From this point D becomes again much closer to C, and the differences can be given in the form of notes.

§35   'Of him comes the love and knowledge of the Earth'; D 'Of him comes the lore ...' (both readings certain).

'the fabric of the Earth'; D 'the fabric of the world'

'the tiller and the husbandman, the weaver, the shaper of wood, or the forger of metals'; D 'the weaver, the shaper of wood, and the worker in metals; and the tiller and the husbandman also. Though these last and all that deal with things that grow and bear fruit must look also to the spouse of Aulë, Yavanna Palúrien.'

The passage concerning the Noldor, bracketed in C, was retained in D, with change of 'and they are the wisest and most skilled of the Elves' to 'and they are the most skilled of the Elves'

§36   'all that passed in Aman' retained in D (cf. note to §23 above).

'from the eyes of Manwë'; D 'from the eyes of Manwë and the servants of Manwë'

'she it was who wrought the Stars' altered (late) in D to 'she it was who wrought the Great Stars'

Immediately following this a passage in D is very heavily inked out, so that it is totally illegible; but it was obviously the passage that follows here in C: 'And the children of Manwë and Varda are Fionwë Úrion their son, and Ilmarë their daughter; and these were the eldest of the children of the Valar. They dwelt with Manwë'. A semi-colon was placed after 'Stars', and D as emended continues with 'and with them were a great host of fair spirits', &c.

The passage concerning the Lindar, bracketed in C, was retained in D, with a late change of 'Lindar' to 'Vanyar'.

'and the chief defence against Melkor'; D 'the vicegerent of Ilúvatar, and the chief defence against the evil of Melkor.'

From the beginning of §37 I give the text of D in full to the end of the work.

§37 . But Ulmo was alone, and he abode not in Valinor, nor ever came thither unless there was need for a great council: he dwelt from the beginning of Arda in the Outer Ocean, and still he dwells there. Thence he governed the flowing of all waters, and the ebbing, the courses of all rivers and the replenishment of springs, the distilling of all dews and rain in every land beneath the sky. In the deep places he gives thought to musics great and terrible; and the echo thereof runs through all the veins of the world in sorrow and in joy; for if joyful is the fountain that rises in the sun, its springs are in the wells of sorrow unfathomed at the foundations of the Earth. The Teleri learned much of Ulmo, and for this reason their music has both sadness and enchantment. Salmar came with him to Arda, he who made the conches of Ulmo that none may ever forget who once has heard them; and Ossë and Uinen also, to whom he gave the government of the waves and the movements of the Inner Seas, and many other spirits beside. And thus it was [*added:*] by the power of Ulmo / that even under the darkness of Melkor life coursed still through many secret lodes, and the Earth did not die; and to all who were lost in that darkness or wandered far from the light of the Valar the ear of Ulmo was ever open; nor has he ever forsaken Middle-earth, and whatso may since have befallen of ruin or of change he has not ceased to take thought for it, and will not until the end of days.

The following passage concerning Yavanna and Oromë derives from §34 in C; it was omitted at that point in D (p. 33).

[§34] And in that time of dark Yavanna also was unwilling utterly to forsake the outer lands; for all things that grow are dear to her, and she mourned for the works that she had begun in Middle-earth but Melkor had marred. Therefore leaving the house of Aulë and the flowering meads of Valinor she would come at times and heal the hurts of Melkor; and returning she would ever urge the Valar to that war with his evil dominion that they must surely wage ere the coming of the Firstborn. And Oromë tamer of beasts would ride too at whiles in the darkness of the unlit forests; as a mighty hunter he came with spear and bow [pursuing to the death the monsters and fell creatures of the kingdom of Melkor. Then borne upon his tireless steed with shining mane and golden hoof, he would sound the great horn Rombaras, whereat >] upon his tireless steed with shining mane and golden hoof, pursuing to the death the monsters and fell creatures of the kingdom of Melkor. Then in the twilight of the world he would sound his great horn, the Valaróma, upon the plains of Arda, whereat / the mountains echoed and the shadows of Utumno fled away, and even the heart of Melkor himself was shaken, foreboding the wrath to come.

The following paragraph, after Pengoloð's address to Ælfwine (not in C), takes up a passage in *Ainulindalë* B, V.160–1 (itself not greatly modified from the original *Music of the Ainur* in *The Book of Lost Tales*, I.57), which was not used in C:

Now all is said to thee, Ælfwine, for this present, concerning the manner of the Earth and its rulers in the time before days and ere the world became such as the Children have known it. Of these thou hast not asked, but a little I will say and so make an end. For Elves and Men are the Children; and since they understood not fully that theme by which they entered into the Music, none of the Ainur dared to add anything to their fashion. For which reason the Valar are to these kindreds rather their elders and their chieftains than their masters; and if ever in their dealings with Elves and Men the Ainur have endeavoured to force them when they would not be guided, this has seldom turned to good, howsoever good the intent. The dealings of the Ainur have been mostly with the Elves, for Ilúvatar made the Eldar more like in nature to the Ainur, though less in might and stature, whereas to Men he gave strange gifts.

§38 For it is said that after the departure of the Valar there was silence and for an age Ilúvatar sat alone in thought. Then he spoke, and he said: 'Behold I love the Earth, which shall be a mansion for the Eldar and the Atani! But the Eldar shall be the fairest of all earthly creatures, and they shall have and shall conceive and bring forth more beauty than all my children; and they shall have the greater bliss in this world. But to the Atani (which are Men) I will give a new gift.'

§39 Therefore he willed that the hearts of Men should seek beyond the world and should find no rest therein; but they should have a virtue to shape their life, amid the powers and chances of the world, beyond the Music of the Ainur, which is as fate to all things else; and of their operation everything should be, in form and deed, completed, and the world fulfilled unto the last and smallest. [*The following passage struck out:* Lo! even we of the Eldalië have found to our sorrow that Men have a strange power for good or for ill, and for turning things aside from the purpose of Valar or of Elves; so that it is said among us that Fate is not the master of the children of Men; yet they are blind, and their joy is small, which should be great.]

§40 But Ilúvatar knew that Men, being set amid the turmoils of the powers of the world, would stray often, and would not use their gifts in harmony; and he said: 'These too in their time shall find that all that they do redounds at the end only to the glory of my work.' Yet we of the Eldar believe that Men are often a grief to Manwë, who knows most of the mind of Ilúvatar. For it seems to us that Men resemble Melkor most of all the Ainur, and yet he has ever feared and hated them, even those that served him.

It is one with this gift of freedom that the children of Men dwell only a short space in the world alive, and are not bound to it, and depart soon whither we know not. Whereas the Eldar remain until the end of days, and their love of the Earth and all the world is more single and poignant, therefore, and as the years lengthen ever more sorrowful. Memory is our burden. For the Eldar die not till the world dies, unless they are slain or waste in grief (and to both these seeming deaths they are subject); neither does age subdue their strength, unless one grow weary of ten thousand centuries; and dying they are gathered in the halls of Mandos in Valinor, whence often they return and are reborn among their children. But the sons of Men die indeed, and leave the World (it is said); wherefore they are called the Guests, or the Strangers. Death is their fate, the gift of Ilúvatar, which as Time wears even the Powers shall envy. But Melkor has cast his shadow upon it, and confounded it with darkness, and brought forth evil out of good, and fear out of hope. Yet of old the Valar said unto us that Men shall join in the Second Music of the Ainur, whereas Ilúvatar has not revealed what he purposes for the Elves after the World's end, and Melkor has not discovered it.

Commentary on the Ainulindalë text D

It will be seen that this text, which can only in part be called a new version, does not extend, contradict, or clarify the 'new cosmology' in any respect – that is to say, as D was originally written. The alteration in §24 of 'they went down into the Halls of Aman' to 'they came down into the fields of Arda' only makes this particular passage more coherent: for Arda had now been established, and it was to the conflict in Arda that those other spirits came. The change in §23 of 'in the midst of the vast halls of the World' to 'in the midst of the vast halls of Aman' is presumably not significant, since the one is clearly equivalent to the other (see p. 28).

With additions and corrections to the text, however, a new element enters: *Ea*. This was the word that Ilúvatar spoke at the moment of the Creation of the World: '*Ea!* Let these things Be!'; and the Ainur knew that 'Ilúvatar had made a new thing, Ea, the World that Is' (§20). In §23, where the reading of C 'the vast halls of the World' had become in D 'the vast halls of Aman', 'Aman' was replaced by 'Ea'. The failure to change 'the Halls of Aman' to 'the Halls of Ea' in §15 was obviously an oversight. The later meaning of 'Aman', the Blessed

Realm, appears in an addition to the text in §32.

There can be no doubt that *Ea*, the Word of Creation that is also the word for the World Created, functions here as did *Aman*; the 'Being' that the word contained and brought forth was the 'new World ... globed amid the Void' that the Ainur had seen in vision (§11), and which now they saw as a light far off, 'as it were a cloud with a living heart of flame' (§20), and into which those of them who wished descended.

But it is perfectly explicit that the Ainur, created by Ilúvatar (§1), dwelt in 'fair regions' that Ilúvatar had made for them (§10); some of them remained 'beyond the confines of the World' (§21) – and Tulkas heard 'in the far heaven' of the War in Arda. How then can the word *Ea* be defined in the list of '1951 alterations' (p. 7) as 'Universe of that which Is'? This expression can surely not be made equivalent to 'the World that Is' (§20). Must not the '*Universe* of that which Is' contain '*Ea*, the World', and the Ainur who saw it created?

Other points arising from differences between C and D, and from emendations made to D, are referred to under the paragraphs in which they occur:

§31 The omission of the words 'of the Noldor' after 'loremasters' was probably made because Pengoloð is expressly a Noldo: cf. §36, where D has 'whom we Noldor name Elbereth'.

In the substantially revised latter part of this paragraph (p. 32; C text p. 17) the names of the Lamps are changed again, from *Foros* and *Hyaras* to *Forontë* and *Hyarantë*; and by early emendation they reach at last the final forms *Illuin* and *Ormal* (as given in the list of '1951 alterations', p. 7). Now it is specifically Yavanna who planted seeds in Middle-earth; and it is Aulë who made the Lamps – but this was told in both the earlier and later *Annals of Valinor* (IV.263, V.110), and indeed goes back to the original *Music of the Ainur* (I.69).

In the correction made to the passage about the first growth in Arda under the light of the Lamps the narrative is brought back to the older tradition concerning the first flowers (yet 'grasses' already appeared); see p. 22 note 17.

'Almaren in the Great Lake', as in the 1951 list (p. 7), now replaces 'Almar in a great lake'.

§32 *Aman*, in an addition to the manuscript, now acquires its later meaning. – The account of the assault on Melkor by the Valar coming forth from Valinor is slightly extended in D: they came 'with a great host', and Melkor 'lay hid until they had departed', then 'returned to his dwelling in the North', where he built Utumno.

§36 The late change of 'she it was who wrought the Stars' to 'she it

Version D   AINULINDALË   39

was who wrought the Great Stars' is notable: the suggestion must be that Varda *only* made the Great Stars. See p. 376 and note 4.

§34 (p. 35; passage omitted at its place in C). The name *Rombaras* for the Horn of Oromë is found uniquely here; the name that replaces it in the revision of the passage, *Valaróma*, appears in the 1951 list (p. 7).

D was the last version of the *Ainulindalë*. A typescript was made of it, but this is an amanuensis text of no significance, save for a few notes that my father made on it. This text was taken from D when most, but not all, the corrections had been made to it. At the top of the first page he pencilled the following (unfortunately not entirely legible) note:

The World should be equivalent to Arda (the realm) = our planet. Creation the Universe (........ universe) should be Ea, What Is.

This raises again, and again inconclusively, the question discussed on pp. 37–8. The note is at least clear to this extent, that 'the World' is no longer to be the 'new World ... globed amid the Void' which the Ainur saw (§11), but is to be applied to Arda – and this is of course a reversion, so far as the word is concerned, to the stage of the *Ambarkanta*, where *Ilu* (Arda) is 'the World' (see p. 28). But the difficulty with the definition of *Ea* as the 'Universe of that which Is' in the 1951 list, or as 'Creation the Universe' in the present note, remains – remains, that is, if the conception of a 'World globed amid the Void' and separate from the Void remained. It looks, indeed, rather as if my father were thinking in quite different terms: Arda, the World, is set within an indefinite vastness in which all 'Creation' is comprehended; but there is no way of knowing when this note was written. See further pp. 62–4.

Another pencilled note on the first page of the typescript reads: 'Ilúvatar All-father (*ilúve* "the whole")'; cf. the *Etymologies* (V.361): stem IL 'all', ILU 'universe', Quenya *ilu, ilúve; Ilúvatar*. For the original etymology of *Ilúvatar* ('Sky-father') see I.255.

On the title-page of the typescript my father wrote: '*Atani* (Second) Followers = Men'. *Atani* (which is listed among the 1951 alterations) is not found in *Ainulindalë* C, but appears in D (title-page and §38).

Ainulindalë C*

I have already discussed the relationship of this very remarkable version to *Ainulindalë* C, and shown that it preceded C and was composed before *The Lord of the Rings* was finished (see pp. 3–6). I have noted also that when lending the typescript C* to Katherine Farrer in 1948 my father labelled it 'Round World Version', and that he gave her also the old B manuscript (in all probability before he covered it with new writing to form version C), which he labelled 'Flat World Version'.

There are only two details to be observed in the first part of this version. In §15 C* had, as did C, 'the Halls of Anar', and again as in C this was later emended to 'the Halls of Aman'. This emendation was made at the same time on both texts; but on C* my father added a footnote: '*Anar* = the Sun' (see p. 44). And in §19, whereas both C and D have 'for the history was incomplete and the circles not full-wrought when the vision was taken away', C* has 'the circles of time' (this reading was adopted in the published *Silmarillion*, p. 20).

But from part way through §23 to the end of §24 C* develops the B text quite differently from C:

§23 So began their great labours [*rejected immediately:* in the beginning of Time and in the immeasurable ages forgotten] in wastes unmeasured and unexplored, and in ages uncounted and forgotten, until in the Deeps of Time and in the midst of the vast halls of the World there came to be that hour and that place where was made the habitation of the Children of Ilúvatar. And many of the Valar repaired thither from the uttermost parts of heaven. But the first of these was Melkor. And Melkor took the Earth, while it was yet young and full of fire, to be his own kingdom.

§24 But Manwë was the brother of Melkor, and he was the chief instrument of the second Theme that Ilúvatar had raised up against the discord of Melkor. And he called unto himself others of his brethren and many spirits both greater and less, and he said to them: 'Let us go to the Halls of Anar [*not emended*], *where the Sun of the Little World is kindled*, and watch that Melkor bring it not all to ruin!'

And they went thither, Manwë and Ulmo and Aulë, and others of whom thou shalt yet hear, Ælfwine, and behold! Melkor was before them; but he had little company, save a few of those lesser spirits that had attuned their music to his; and he walked alone; and the Earth was in flames. The coming of the Valar was not indeed welcome to Melkor, for he desired not friends but servants, and he said: 'This is my kingdom, which I have named unto myself.' But the Valar answered that this he could not lawfully do, for in making and governance they had all their part. And there was strife between the Valar and Melkor; and for a time Melkor departed and *withdrew beyond the arrows of the Sun*, and brooded on his desire.

Version C* AINULINDALË 41

On the two sentences which I have italicised see pp. 43–4. The narrative in this version differs from that of C, since here Melkor preceded the other Ainur, and Manwë's summons was not made out of Arda to other spirits that had not yet come, but was an invitation to enter Arda with him.

From the beginning of §25 C* reverts to the common text (more accurately, from this point C follows C*); the expression 'Kingdom of Anar' in §25 was later emended to 'Kingdom of Arda' (in C this change was made in the act of writing, p. 22 note 13). But near the end of §27 C* diverges again:

... for as surely as the Valar began a labour so would Melkor undo it or corrupt it; so that forests became fierce and rank and poisonous, and beasts became monsters of horn and ivory, and they fought, and dyed the earth with blood.

In C this passage comes in later (§32), and the corruption described is that worked by Melkor on the living things that came to being in the light of the Lamps; but in C*, as will be seen, the story of the Lamps had been abandoned (p. 43).

C* then jumps from the end of §27 to §31, which in C is a part of the words of Pengolod (Pengoloð) after the end of the *Ainulindalë* proper, and proceeds as follows:

§31 And this tale also I have heard among the sages of the Noldor in ages past: that in the midst of the War, and before yet there was any thing that grew or walked on Earth, there was a time when the Valar came near to the mastery; for a spirit of great strength and hardihood came to their aid, hearing in the far heaven that there was battle in the Little World. And he came like a storm of laughter and loud song, and the Earth shook under his great golden feet. So came Tulkas, the Strong and the Merry, whose anger passeth like a mighty wind, scattering cloud and darkness before it. And Melkor was shaken by the laughter of Tulkas and fled from the Earth. Then he gathered himself together and summoned all his might and his hatred, and he said: 'I will rend the Earth asunder, and break it, and none shall possess it.'

But this Melkor could not do, for the Earth may not be wholly destroyed against its fate; nevertheless Melkor took a portion of it, and seized it for his own, and reft it away; and he made it a little earth of his own, and it wheeled round about in the sky, following the greater earth wheresoever it went, so that Melkor could observe thence all that happened below, and could send forth his malice and trouble the seas and shake the lands. And still there is rumour among the Eldar of the war in which the Valar assaulted the stronghold of Melkor, and cast him out, and removed it further from the Earth, and it remains in the sky, Ithil whom Men call the Moon. There is both blinding heat and cold intolerable, as might be looked for in any work of Melkor, but now at least it is clean, yet utterly barren; and nought liveth there, nor ever hath, nor shall. And herein is revealed again the words of Ilúvatar; for Ithil has become a mirror to the greater Earth, catching the light of the Sun, when she is invisible; and because of malice silver has been made of gold, and moonlight of sunlight, and Earth in its anguish and loss has been greatly enriched.

But of all such matters, Ælfwine, others shall tell thee ...

These last words are the beginning of §28 in C, the end of the *Ainulindalë* proper, and the paragraph appears in C* in almost exactly the same form. After this C* ends abruptly with the concluding passage, C §§38–40, in which however there are some notable differences. §38 reads thus in C*:

But out beyond the World in the Timeless Halls after the departure of the Valar there was silence, and Ilúvatar sat in thought, and the Holy Ones that stood nigh moved not. Then Ilúvatar spoke and he said: 'Verily I love the World and am glad that it Is. And my thought is bent to that place where are the mansions of the Elves and of Men. Behold! the Eldar shall be the fairest of Earthly creatures, and they shall have and shall conceive more beauty than all other offspring of my thought; and they shall have the greater bliss in the World. But to Men I will give a new gift.'

It is to be noted that the scrap of manuscript found with the Adûnaic papers, discussed on p. 4, has precisely the structure of C*: it begins with 'But of all such matters, Ælfwine ...' and continues to the end of the paragraph '... and thus thy feet are on the beginning of the road', following this with 'But out beyond the World in the Timeless Halls ...'

§39 is virtually the same in both texts; but §40, after the opening sentence (Ilúvatar's words concerning Men), continues thus to the end:

Yet the Eldar know that Men have often been a grief to the Valar that love them, not least to Manwë, who knows most of the mind of Ilúvatar. For Men resemble Melkor most of all the

Ainur; and yet he hath ever feared and hated them, even those that serve him.

It is one with this gift of freedom that the Children of Men dwell only a short space in the world alive, and yet are not bound to it, nor shall perish utterly for ever. Whereas the Eldar remain until the end of days, and therefore their love of the world is deeper and more joyous, save that when evil is done to it, or its beauty is despoiled, then they are grieved bitterly, and the sorrow of the Elves for that which might have been fills now all the Earth with tears that Men hear not. But the sons of Men die indeed and leave what they have made or marred. Yet the Valar say that Men shall join in the Second Music of the Ainur, but Manwë alone knoweth what Ilúvatar hath purposed for the Elves after the World's end: the Elves know not, and Melkor hath not discovered it.

The concluding section §§38–40 was struck through, and against it my father wrote a question, whether to place it 'in The Silmarillion' or to insert it 'in modified form' earlier in the present text.

The fundamental difference between C* and C lies in this, that in C* the Sun is already present from the beginning of Arda (see the italicised passages in §24 on p. 40), and the origin of the Moon, similarly 'de-mythologised' by removal from all association with the Two Trees, is placed in the context of the tumults of Arda's making. It seems strange indeed that my father was prepared to conceive of the Moon – the Moon, that cherishes the memory of the Elves (V.118, 240) – as a dead and blasted survival of the hatred of Melkor, however beautiful its light. In consequence, the old legend of the Lamps was also abandoned: whence the different placing of the passage about Melkor's perversion of living things, p. 41.

There is no indication whatsoever of how the myth of the Two Trees was to be accommodated to these new ideas. But for that time the 'de-mythologising' version C* was set aside; and the D text followed from C without a trace of them. The *Annals of Aman*, certainly later than the end of the *Ainulindalë* series, contains a full account of the Making of the Sun and Moon; and in my father's long letter to Milton Waldman, written almost certainly in 1951, the old myth is fully present and its significance defined (*Letters* no.131):

> There was the Light of Valinor made visible in the Two Trees of Silver and Gold. These were slain by the Enemy out of malice, and Valinor was darkened, though from them, ere they died utterly, were derived the lights of Sun and Moon. (A marked difference here between these legends and most others is that the Sun is not a divine

symbol, but a second-best thing, and the 'light of the Sun' (the world under the sun) become terms for a fallen world, and a dislocated imperfect vision).

In conclusion, there remains the perplexing question of the name *Anar* in C* and C, to which I can find no satisfactory solution. *Anar* occurred first in §15, where the reference is to the 'habitation in *the Halls of Anar* which the Elves call Arda, the Earth'; and here in both texts my father later emended 'Anar' to 'Aman', while in C* he added a footnote: '*Anar* = the Sun'. In §24 the spirits whom Manwë summoned to his aid 'went down into the Halls of Anar', and here again 'Anar' was later changed to 'Aman' in C; in C* the reading is somewhat different, and in this text 'Anar' was left to stand: Manwë said to the other spirits 'Let us go to the Halls of Anar where the Sun of the Little World is kindled'. The retention of 'Anar' in C* seems however to be no more than an oversight. Finally, in §25 are named 'the Seven Great Ones of the Kingdom of Anar', changed subsequently in C* but in the act of writing in C to 'the Kingdom of Arda'.

The name *Anar* (*Anor*) = 'the Sun' goes back a long way – to *The Lost Road*, the *Quenta Silmarillion*, and the *Etymologies* (see the Index to Vol.V), and had been repeated in *The Notion Club Papers* (IX.302–3, 306), beside *Minas Anor*, *Anárion*, *Anórien* in *The Lord of the Rings*. It seems therefore at first sight very probable that *Anar* means 'the Sun' in these texts of the *Ainulindalë*. On this assumption the footnote to §15 in C* was no more than an explanatory gloss; while 'the Kingdom of Anar' in §25 = 'the Kingdom of the Sun' ('the Sun of the Little World'): cf. the change in D §14 (p. 30) of 'the whole field of the Sun' to 'the whole field of Arda'. The fact that in C, in which the myth of the Making of the Sun and Moon is implicitly present, my father wrote 'the Kingdom of Anar' would be explicable on the basis that he had C* before him, and wrote 'Anar' inadvertently before immediately changing it to 'Arda'.

There is however a radical objection to this explanation. In §§15, 24 'the Halls of Anar' is the name given to 'the vast halls of the World' with their 'wheeling fires', in which Ilúvatar chose a place for the habitation of Elves and Men; and subsequently *Anar* > *Aman* > *Ea* (p. 31, §23). Here the interpretation of *Anar* as 'the Sun' seems impossible. It may be therefore that my father's note to C* §15 '*Anar* = the Sun' (made at the same time as he changed 'Anar' to 'Aman' in the body of the text) implies that he had been using the name in another sense, but was now asserting that this and no other was the meaning of *Anar*.

PART TWO

THE
ANNALS
OF
AMAN

THE ANNALS OF AMAN

The second version (pre-*Lord of the Rings*) of the *Annals of Valinor* (**AV 2**) has been given in V.109 ff. I mentioned there that the first part of AV 2 was – years later – covered with emendation and new writing, and that this new work was the initial drafting of the *Annals of Aman*. In this case I shall spend no time on the original draft, apart from some points arising in it which are mentioned in the notes. It does not extend very far – not even so far as the bringing forth of the Two Trees, and so far as it goes it is extremely close to the *Annals of Aman*; but my father evidently very soon decided to embark on a wholly new text.

Of the *Annals of Aman*, which I shall refer to throughout by the abbreviation '**AAm**', there is a good clear manuscript, with a fair amount of correction in different 'layers'. Emendations belonging to the time of composition, or soon after, were carefully made; and the manuscript gives the impression of being a 'fair copy', a second text. But while passages of drafting may have been lost, I very much doubt that a complete 'first text' of the *Annals* existed (see further p. 121 note 17). The work undoubtedly belongs with the large development and recasting of the Matter of the Elder Days that my father undertook when *The Lord of the Rings* was finished (see p. 3), and it stands in close relationship to the revision at that time of the corresponding parts of the *Quenta Silmarillion* (V.204–43, referred to throughout as QS), the text that had been abandoned at the end of 1937. Equally clearly it followed the last text of the *Ainulindalë* (D).

There is an amanuensis typescript of AAm bearing some late emendations and notes, together with its carbon copy bearing a very few, but different, emendations; I am inclined to date this text to 1958, although the evidence for this is a matter of inference and suggestion (see pp. 141–2, 300). There is also an interesting, divergent typescript of the early part of the work, made by my father (pp. 64–8, 79–80).

I give the whole text of the *Annals* narrative, incorporating the emendations made to it; where earlier readings are of interest they are recorded in the notes. I number the paragraphs for subsequent reference, and since the text is long I have divided it for convenience into six sections. The sections are followed by numbered textual notes (not in the case of section 2), and then by a commentary referenced to the paragraph-numbers.

The dates of the annals of the Years of the Trees were changed very frequently – in some cases there are as many as six substitutions – and I give only the final form. Since the continual changing of the dates seems in no case to be associated with changes in the actual narrative, and since the final articulation of the dates seems to have been achieved before the completion of the manuscript, I think it is sufficient to notice that my father at first allowed a longer span of years from the arising of the Trees to their destruction. Thus at first the Silmarils were achieved by Fëanor in the Year of the Trees 1600 (later 1450), and Tulkas was sent to lay hands on Melkor in 1700 (later 1490) – though other dates were proposed and rejected as well as these. From this point the revised dating (1490–1500) is the only one, but here too the dates were much altered in detail, and the final result is not at all points perfectly clear.

First section of the Annals of Aman

The first page of AAm is extant in two forms, both fine manuscripts, all but identical in text but differing in title and in the brief preamble. The first has the title *The Annals of Valinor*, and opens thus: 'Here begin the Annals of Valinor, and speak of the coming of the Valar to Arda'; beside the title was added: 'These were written by Quennar i Onótimo who learned much, and borrowed much also, from Rúmil; but they were enlarged by Pengoloð.' This last was struck out, and the title and preamble emended to the form they have on the second copy, as given below, with *Valinor* > *Aman* and the addition of the words 'which Rúmil wrote (made)'. I imagine that my father recopied the page because he wished it to look well, and had spoiled it by these changes. The title *Annals of Aman* came in at this point, therefore, and very possibly the final meaning of the name *Aman* also: it occurs once in *Ainulindalë* D, but as an addition to the text (p. 33, §32).

THE ANNALS OF AMAN

Here begin the Annals of Aman, which Rúmil made, and speak of the coming of the Valar to Arda:

§1 At the Beginning Eru Ilúvatar made Ëa, the World that is,[1] and the Valar entered into it, and they are the Powers of Ëa. These are the nine chieftains of the Valar that dwelt in Arda: Manwë, Ulmo, Aulë, Oromë, Tulkas, Ossë, Mandos, Lorien,[2] and Melkor.

§2 Of these Manwë and Melkor were most puissant and were brethren. Manwë is lord of the Valar, and holy; but Melkor turned to lust of power and pride, and became evil and violent, and his name is accursed, and is not spoken; he is named Morgoth. Oromë and Tulkas were younger in the thought of Eru ere the devising of the World, and Tulkas came last to the kingdom of Arda. The queens of the Valar are seven: Varda, Yavanna, Niënna, Vairë, Vana, Nessa, and Uinen. No less in might and majesty are they than the chieftains, and they sit ever in the councils of the Valar.

§3 Varda was Manwë's spouse from the beginning, but Aulë espoused Yavanna, her sister, in Ëa.[3] Vana the fair, her younger sister, is the wife of Oromë; and Nessa, the sister of Oromë, is Tulkas' wife; and Uinen, lady of the seas, is the spouse of Ossë. Vairë the Weaver dwells with Mandos. No spouse hath Ulmo, nor Melkor. No lord hath Niënna the sorrowful, queen of shadow, Manwë's sister and Melkor's. The wife of Lorien is Estë the pale, but she goes not to the councils of the Valar and is not accounted among the rulers of Arda, but is the chief of the Maiar.

§4 With these great powers came many other spirits of like kind but less might and authority; these are the Maiar, the Beautiful,[4] the folk of the Valar. And with them are numbered also the Valarindi, the offspring of the Valar, their children begotten in Arda, yet of the race of the Ainur who were before the World; they are many and fair.

At this point my father wrote in: *This is drawn from the work of Quennar Onótimo*. These words refer not to what precedes but to the following passage, headed *Of the Beginning of Time and its Reckoning* (although in the preamble – struck through – of the rejected first page of AAm Quennar i Onótimo is said to have been the author of the *Annals* as a whole, p. 48).

The entire section on the subject of the Reckoning of Time was later marked in pencil: 'Transfer to the Tale of Years'. *The Tale of Years*, a chronological list of the same sort as that in Appendix B to *The Lord of the Rings*, exists in different forms, associated with the earlier and later *Annals*; the later form, closely associated with AAm and its companion the *Grey Annals (Annals of Beleriand)*, is perhaps the most complex and difficult text of all that my father left behind him. This need not concern us here; but associated with it are two very fine manuscripts (one of them, the later of the two, among the most beautiful that he made: see the frontispiece) giving in almost identical form the same text *Of the Beginning of Time and its Reckoning* as is found here in AAm, but placing it as the opening of *The Tale of Years* and the prelude to the chronological list of events. These two manuscripts are of course later than the text in AAm, and some readings in which they differ from it are given in the notes. AAm continues:

This is drawn from the work of Quennar Onótimo.[5]

Of the Beginning of Time and its Reckoning

§5 Time indeed began with the beginning of Ëa, and in that beginning the Valar came into the World. But the measurement which the Valar made of the ages of their labours is not known to any of the Children of Ilúvatar, until the first flowering of Telperion in Valinor. Thereafter the Valar counted time by the ages of Valinor, whereof each age contained *one hundred* of the Years of the Valar; but each such year was longer than are *nine* years under the Sun.[6]

§6 Now measured by the flowering of the Trees there were *twelve* hours in each Day of the Valar, and *one thousand* of such days the Valar took to be a year in their realm. It is supposed indeed by the Lore-masters that the Valar so devised the hours of the Trees that *one hundred* of such years so measured should be in duration as one age of the Valar[7] (as those ages were in the days of their labours before the foundation of Valinor).[8] Nonetheless this is not certainly known.

§7 But as for the Years of the Trees and those that came after,[9] one such Year was longer than nine such years as now are. For there were in each such Year *twelve thousand* hours. Yet the hours of the Trees were each *seven* times as long as is *one* hour of a full-day upon Middle-earth from sun-rise to sun-rise, when light and dark are equally divided.[10] Therefore each Day of the Valar endured for *four and eighty* of our hours, and each Year for *four and eighty thousand*: which is as much as *three thousand and five hundred* of our days, and is somewhat more than are *nine and one half* of our years (nine and one half and eight hundredths and yet a little).[11]

§8 It is recorded by the Lore-masters that this is not rightly as the Valar designed at the making and ordering[12] of the Moon and Sun. For it was their intention that *ten* years of the Sun, no more and no less, should be in length as one Year of the Trees had been; and it was their first device that each year of the Sun should contain *seven hundred* times of sunlight and moonlight, and each of these times should contain *twelve* hours, each in duration one *seventh* of an hour of the Trees. By that reckoning each Sun-year would contain *three hundred and fifty* full days of divided moonlight and sunlight, that is *eight thousand and four hundred* hours, equalling *twelve hundred* hours of the Trees, or *one tenth* of a Valian Year. But the Moon and Sun proved more wayward and slower in their passage than the Valar had intended, as is hereafter told,[13] and a year of the Sun is somewhat longer than was one tenth of a Year in the Days of the Trees.

§9 The shorter year of the Sun was so made[14] because of the greater speed of all growth, and likewise of all change and withering, that the Valar knew should come to pass after the death of the Trees. And after that evil had befallen the Valar reckoned time in Arda by the years of the Sun, and do so still, even after the Change of the World and the hiding of Aman; but ten years of the Sun they account now as but one year,[15] and one thousand but as a century. This is drawn from the Yénonótië of Quennar: quoth Pengoloð.[16]

§10 It is computed by the lore-masters that the Valar came to the realm of Arda, which is the Earth, five thousand Valian Years ere the first rising of the Moon, which is as much as to say forty-seven thousands and nine hundred and one of our years. Of these, three thousand and five hundred (or thirty-three thousand five hundred and thirty of our reckoning) passed ere the measurement of time first known to the Eldar began with the flowering of the Trees. Those were the Days before days. Thereafter one thousand and four hundred and five and ninety Valian Years (or fourteen thousand of our years and three hundred and twenty-two) followed during which the Light of the Trees shone in Valinor. Those were the Days of Bliss. In those days, in the Year one thousand and fifty of the Valar, the Elves awoke in Kuiviénen and the First Age of the Children of Ilúvatar began.[17]

1 The First Year of the Valar in Arda

§11 After ages of labour beyond knowledge or reckoning in the great halls of Ëa the Valar descended into Arda in the beginning of its being, and they began there their labour fore-ordained for the shaping of its lands and its waters, even from the foundations to the highest towers of the Air.

§12 But their labours were frustrated and turned aside from their design, for Melkor coveted the dominion of Arda, and he claimed the kingship and was at strife with Manwë. And Melkor wrought great ruin with fire and deadly cold and marred all that the other Valar made.

1500

§13 It came to pass that hearing afar of the war in Arda Tulkas the Strong came thither out of distant regions of Eä to the aid of Manwë. Then Arda was filled with the sound of his laughter, but he turned a face of anger towards Melkor; and Melkor fled before his wrath and his mirth, and forsook Arda, and there was a long peace.

§14 Now the Valar began their labours anew; and when the lands and the waters were ordered the Valar had need of light, that the seeds of Yavanna's devising might grow and have life. Aulë therefore wrought two great lamps, as it were of silver and of gold and yet translucent, and Varda filled them with hallowed fire, to give light to the Earth. Illuin and Ormal they were named. 1900 And they were set upon mighty pillars as mountains in the midst of Arda, to the northward and the southward.

§15 Then the Valar continued their labours until all the kingdom of Arda was ordered and made ready, and there was great growth of trees and herbs, and beasts and birds came forth and dwelt in the plains and in the waters, and the mountains were green and fair to look upon. And the Valar made their dwelling upon a green isle in the midst of a lake; and that lake was between Illuin and Ormal in the midmost of Arda; and there in the Isle of Almaren, because of the blending of the lights, all things were richest in growth and fairest of hue. But the Valar were seldom there gathered in company, for ever they would fare abroad in Arda, each in his own business.

§16 And it came to pass that at last the Valar were content, and they were minded to rest a while from labour and watch the growth and unfolding of the things that they had devised and begun. Therefore Manwë ordained a great feast, and summoned all the Valar and the queens of the Valar unto Almaren, together with all their folk. And they came at his bidding; but Aulë, it is said, and Tulkas were weary; for the craft of Aulë and the strength of Tulkas had been at the service of all without ceasing in the days of their labour.

§17 Now Melkor knew of all that was done; for even then he had secret friends and spies among the Maiar whom he had converted to his cause, and of these the chief, as after became known, was Sauron, a great craftsman of the household of Aulë. And afar off in the dark places Melkor was filled with hatred, being jealous of the work of his peers, whom he desired to make subject to himself. Therefore he gathered to himself spirits out of the voids of Eä that he had perverted to his service, and he deemed himself strong. And seeing now his time he drew near again unto Arda, and looked down upon it, and the beauty of the Earth in its Spring filled him the more with hate.

3400

§18 Now therefore the Valar were gathered upon Almaren and feasted and made merry, fearing no evil, and because of the light of Illuin they did not perceive the shadow in the North that was cast from afar by Melkor; for he was grown dark as the Night of the Void.[18] And it is sung that in that feast of the Spring of Arda Tulkas espoused Nessa the sister of Oromë, and Vana robed [her] in her flowers, and she danced before the Valar upon the green grass of Almaren.

§19 Then Tulkas slept, being weary and content, and Melkor deemed that his hour had come. And he passed, therefore, over the Walls of the Night[19] with his host, and he came to Middle-earth in the North; and the Valar were not aware of him.

§20 Now Melkor began the delving and building of a vast fortress deep under Earth, beneath dark mountains where the light of Illuin was dim.[20] That stronghold was named Utumno. And though the Valar knew nought of it as yet, nonetheless the evil of Melkor and the blight of his hatred flowed out thence, and the Spring of Arda was marred, and living things became sick and rotted, or were corrupted to monstrous forms.

3450

§21 Then the Valar knew indeed that Melkor was at work again, and they sought for his hiding-place. But Melkor, trusting in the strength of Utumno and the might of his servants, came forth suddenly to war, and struck the first blow, ere the Valar were prepared. And he assailed the lights of Illuin and Ormal, and he cast down their pillars, and broke their lamps. Then in the overthrow of the mighty pillars lands were broken and seas arose in tumult; and when the lamps were spilled destroying flame was poured out over the Earth. And the shape of Arda and the symmetry of its waters and its lands was marred in that time, so that the first designs of the Valar were never after restored.

§22 In the confusion and the darkness Melkor escaped, though fear fell upon him; for above the roaring of the seas he heard the voice of Manwë as a mighty wind, and the earth trembled beneath the feet of Tulkas. But he came to Utumno ere Tulkas could overtake him; and there he lay hid. And the Valar could not at that time overcome him, for the greater part of their strength was needed to restrain the tumults of the Earth, and to save from ruin all that could be saved of their labour; and afterward they feared to rend the Earth again, until they knew where the Children of Ilúvatar were dwelling, who were yet to come in a time that was hidden from the Valar.

§23 Thus ended the Spring of Arda. And the dwelling of the Valar upon Almaren was utterly destroyed, and the gods had no abiding place upon the face of the earth. Therefore they removed from Middle-earth and went to the Land of Aman, which was westernmost of all lands upon the borders of the world; for its west shores looked upon the Outer Sea that encircled the kingdom of Arda, and beyond were the Walls of the Night.[21] But the east-shores of Aman are the uttermost end of the Great Sea of the West; and since Melkor had returned to Middle-earth, and they could not yet overcome him, the Valar fortified their dwelling, and upon the shores of the Sea they raised the Pelóri, the Mountains of Aman, highest upon earth. And above all the mountains of the Pelóri was that height which was called Taniquetil, upon whose summit Manwë set his throne. But behind the walls of the Pelóri the Valar established their mansions and their domain in that region which is called Valinor. There in the Guarded Realm they gathered great store of light and all the fairest things that were saved from the ruin; and many others yet fairer they made anew, and Valinor became more beautiful even than Middle-earth in the Spring of Arda; and it was blessed and holy, for the gods dwelt there, and there nought faded nor withered, neither was there any stain upon flower or leaf in that land, nor any corruption or sickness in anything that lived; for the very stones and waters were hallowed.

§24 Therefore the Valar and all their folk were joyful again, and for long they were well content, and they came seldom over the mountains to the Outer Lands; and Middle-earth lay in a twilight beneath the stars that Varda had wrought in the ages forgotten of her labours in Eä.

3500

§25 And it came to pass that, after Valinor was full-wrought and the mansions of the Valar were established and their gardens and woodlands were arrayed, the Valar built their city in the midst of the plain beyond the Pelóri. That city they named Valmar the Blessed. And before its western gate there was a green mound, and it was bare save for a sward of unfading grass.

§26 Then Yavanna and Niënna came to that Green Mound; and Yavanna hallowed it, and sat there long upon the green grass and sang a song of great power, in which was set all her thought of things that grow in the earth. But Niënna thought in silence, and watered the mould with tears. Then all the Valar were gathered together to hearken to the song of Yavanna; and the mound was in the midst of the Ring of Doom before the gates of Valmar, and the Valar sat round about in silence upon their thrones of council, and their folk were set before their feet. And as the gods watched, behold! upon the mound there sprang two green saplings, and they grew and became fair and tall, and they came to blossom.

§27 Thus there awoke in the world the Two Trees of Valinor, of all growing things the fairest and most renowned, whose fate is woven with the fate of Arda. The elder of the Trees was named Telperion, and its blossoms were of shining white, and a dew of silver light was spilled from them. Laurelin the younger Tree was called; its green leaves were edged with gold, and its flowers were like to clusters of yellow flame, and a rain of gold dripped from them to the ground. From those Trees there came forth a great light, and all Valinor was filled with it. Then the bliss of the Valar was increased; for the light of the Trees was holy and of great power, so that, if aught was good or lovely or of worth, in that light its loveliness and its worth were fully revealed; and all that walked in that light were glad at heart.

§28 But the light that was spilled from the Trees endured long, ere it was taken up into the airs or sank into the earth for their enrichment. Therefore of its abundance Varda was wont to gather great store, and it was hoarded in mighty vats nigh to the Green Mound. Thence the Maiar would draw it and bring it to frith and field, even those far removed from Valmar, so that all regions of Valinor were nourished and waxed ever fairer.

§29 Thus began the Days of the Bliss of Valinor, and thus began also the count of Time. For the Trees waxed to full bloom and light, and waned again, unceasingly, without change of speed or fullness. Telperion came first to flower, and a little ere he ceased to shine Laurelin began to bud; and again ere Laurelin had grown dim Telperion awoke once more. Therefore the Valar took the time of the flowering, first of Telperion and then of Laurelin, to be for them a Day in Valinor; and the time when each Tree was flowering alone they divided into five hours, each equal to the time of the mingling of their lights, twice in each Day. There were thus twelve such hours in every Day of the Valar; and one thousand of those Days was held to be a Year, for then the Trees would put forth a new branch and their stature would increase.

The opening section of the *Annals of Aman* ends here; it is followed by a heading *Here begins a new Reckoning in the Light of the Trees*, with dates beginning at Y.T.1, the First Year of the Trees.

NOTES

1 The definition of *Ëa* as 'the World that Is' is found also at the appearance of the name in an addition to the text of *Ainulindalë* D, p. 31, §20. I give it throughout in the form that it has in the texts, *Ea, Ëa, Eä*.
2 The original form of the name was *Lórien*, but this was changed to *Lŏrien* on the QS manuscript.
3 AV 2 had here (V.110) 'Yavanna, whom Aulë espoused after in the world, in Valinor'; in the later rewriting of the AV 2 manuscript that led directly to AAm (p. 47) this became 'Yavanna, whom Aulë espoused in Arda', where AAm has 'in Ëa'.
4 AV 2 had here (V.110) 'these are the Vanimor, the Beautiful', changed in the later rewriting (see note 3) to 'these are the Mairi...', and then to 'these are the Maiar...' This was probably where the word *Maiar* first arose.
5 In the earlier (only) of the two manuscripts of the opening of *The Tale of Years* the heading *Of the Beginning of Time and its Reckoning* was subsequently extended by the addition of *From the work of Quennar Onótimo*; see note 6.
6 As this sentence was first written in the draft text for the beginning of AAm (the rewriting of AV 2) it read: 'each such year is in length even as are ten years of the Sun that is now'; i.e., my father still retained the old much simpler computation going back through AV 2 (V.110) to AV 1 (IV.263). This was changed on the draft text to 'each such year is longer than are nine years of

the Sun that is now'. In the earlier of the *Tale of Years* versions the words 'as it now is' were pencilled in after 'nine years under the Sun', while the second reads 'than are now nine years under the Sun'.

The second *Tale of Years* version, which does not refer to Quennar Onótimo in the heading *Of the Beginning of Time and its Reckoning* (note 5), has here: 'Thus spake Quennar Onótimo concerning this matter'. What follows from this point is in all three texts in markedly smaller script, so that the reference to Quennar seems most appropriate here.

7   The later (only) of the *Tale of Years* versions has 'one fifth of an age of the Valar' for 'one age of the Valar'.

8   The earlier of the *Tale of Years* versions adds here: 'whereas each age of the Valar is one exact part (how great or small they alone know) of the whole history of Ëa. But these things are not certainly known even to the Eldar'; the later begins the additional passage in the same way, but ends: '... of the whole history of Ëa from its beginning to the End that shall be. But these things are not certainly known even to [the] Vanyar.'

9   The *Tale of Years* versions have here: 'As for the Years of the Trees in comparison with those that came after', which makes the meaning clear.

10 In the earlier *Tale of Years* version 'from sun-rise to sun-rise' was changed in pencil to 'from sunset to sunset', and the following sentence 'at such times as light and dark are equally divided' was bracketed. The second version has a different reading: 'from sunset unto sunset beside the Shores of the Great Sea'.

11 In the *Tale of Years* versions the words '(nine and one half and eight hundredths and yet a little)' are omitted.

12 In the *Tale of Years* versions the words 'and ordering' are omitted.

13 For 'as is hereafter told' (which refers to the account of the Sun and Moon later in AAm) the *Tale of Years* versions have 'as is elsewhere told'.

14 For 'was so made' the *Tale of Years* versions have 'was appointed by the Valar'.

15 'but one year' becomes in the *Tale of Years* versions 'but one year unto themselves'.

16 The *Tale of Years* versions have here 'Thus speaketh the *Yénonótië* of Quennar'. With *Yénonótië* cf. *Yénië Valinóren* 'Annals of Valinor' in the title-pages of QS (V.202), and the name *Onótimo* itself; see the *Etymologies*, stems NOT 'count', YEN 'year' (V.378, 400).

17 Paragraph §10 had this form in the draft text for the beginning of AAm:

It hath been computed by the Masters of Lore that the Valar

came to the Kingdom of Arda, which is this Earth, five and forty thousand years of our time ere the first rising of the Moon. And of these thirty thousand passed ere the measurement of Time began with the flowering of the Trees. These were the Days before Days. And fifteen thousand years followed after during which the Light of the Trees yet lived, and nigh on six hundred more of the New Sun and Moon after the slaying of the Trees. And these are called the Elder Days, and with their ending ended the First Age of Time, and Melkor was thrust from the world.

Thus whereas in AV 1 and AV 2 the reckoning was thus (V.Y. = Valian Year(s), S.Y. = Sun Year(s)):
V.Y. 1000 = S.Y. 10000   First flowering of the Trees
V.Y. 3000 = S.Y. 30000   Rising of the Moon
this first revision gives:
S.Y. 30000   First flowering of the Trees
S.Y. 45000   Rising of the Moon
This reckoning was then replaced again:
V.Y. 3500 = S.Y. 33530   First flowering of the Trees
V.Y. 5300 = S.Y. 50775   Rising of the Moon
These figures show a ratio of 1 V.Y. = 9·58 S.Y. (see the commentary on §§5–10, pp. 59–60). This last reckoning was the form in AAm as first written, which was then changed many times to give the text printed.

18 The text as written had 'dark as the night that was before Ea', changed later to 'dark as the Night of the Void'.
19 The text as first written had 'over the borders of Ëa'; this was changed later to 'over the Walls of the Night upon the borders of Arda', and then 'upon the borders of Arda' was struck out.
20 The text was first written 'far from the light of Illuin'.
21 The text as written had 'which is westernmost of all lands' and 'look upon the Outer Sea that encircles the kingdom of Arda'; the changes to the past tense were perhaps made at the time of writing, since the next phrase, 'and beyond were the Walls of the Night', had the past tense as written. On the other hand, the following sentence has the present tense ('But the east shores of Aman are the uttermost end of the Great Sea of the West'), where *are* was allowed to stand.

Commentary on the first section of the Annals of Aman

§§1–3   On the occurrence of the name *Eru* see p. 7. The account of the interrelations of the Valar and the queens of the Valar remains closely based on that in AV 2 (V.110), and retains old phrases (as 'Manwë and Melkor were most puissant and were brethren') going back to the original *Annals* (IV.263). There are however some developments in this opening section. On the phrase in §2, 'Oromë and Tulkas were younger in the thought of Eru ere the devising of the World', see V.120. That Tulkas came last to Arda derives from the rewritten *Ainulindalë* (§31).

It is not said now, as it was in AV 2, that Oromë was the son of Yavanna. On the other hand, it is now said, as in the *Quenta* (Q) and QS, that Vana was the sister of Yavanna (and Varda), whereas this was not said in AV 2. These differences are perhaps connected; for if both accounts are combined Oromë's wife is the sister of his mother. But this may be to take too conventional a view of the divine relations.

The statements that Estë 'goes not to the councils of the Valar and is not accounted among the rulers of Arda', and that she is the chief of the Maiar (see note 4 above), are entirely new.

§4 The passage concerning the 'lesser spirits' shows no significant development from that in AV 2 (V.110) except for the replacement of *Vanimor* by *Maiar* (translated 'the Beautiful' as *Vanimor* had been); the *Valarindi*, Children of the Valar, 'begotten in Arda' and numbered among the Maiar, remain. On the earlier history of these conceptions see V.120–1; and see further p. 69.

§5 *Telperion* first appeared in QS §16 (V.209), but not as the primary name of the Elder Tree, which remained *Silpion*. *Telperion*, used in *The Lord of the Rings*, now became the primary name.

§§5–10 The account of the Reckoning of Time is at first sight somewhat baffling, but it can be clarified.

(i) According to the reckoning by the Trees
12 hours (a full flowering of both Trees) = 1 day
1000 days (12000 hours) = 1 year
100 years = 1 age of the Valar (as the Valar reckoned the ages before the Trees, according to a supposition of the Loremasters of the Elves; see notes 7 and 8 to the text)

(ii) Relation of the reckoning by the Trees to the reckoning by the Sun
1 hour of the Trees = 7 hours of our time
1 day of the Trees = (7 × 12) 84 hours of our time
1 year of the Trees = (7 × 12000) 84000 hours of our time
There are (365·25 × 24) 8766 hours in a Sun Year, and thus:
1 year of the Trees = (84000 ÷ 8766) 9·582 Sun Years*

---

* Cf. the text (§7): 'nine and one half and eight hundredths and *yet a little*'.

(iii) Original intention of the Valar for the new reckoning by the Sun and Moon

12 hours of moonlight ⎱ 24 hours = 1 full day
12 hours of sunlight ⎰
700 times of sunlight and moonlight = 350 full days = 1 Sun Year
1 hour = $\frac{1}{7}$ of 1 hour of the Trees

Therefore:
1 Sun Year would have (24 × 350) 8400 hours = (8400 ÷ 7)
1200 hours of the Trees = $\frac{1}{10}$ of a Valian Year (see (i) above); thus 1 Valian Year would = 10 Sun Years

The matter can be expressed more concisely thus:
1 year of the Trees = (7 × 12000) 84000 hours of our time
84000 ÷ (350 × 24) 8400 = 10
but
84000 ÷ (365·25 × 24) 8766 = 9·582

(iv) The dates of the first flowering of the Trees and the first rising of the Moon (§10)

The Trees first flowered after 3500 Valian Years had passed, which is said to be equal to 33530 Sun Years (this presupposes an equivalence of 9·58; 9·582 gives 33537).

The Moon first rose after 5000 Valian Years had passed, which is said to be equal to 47901 Sun Years (this presupposes an equivalence of 9·5802; if the equivalence is 9·582 the number of Sun Years would be 47910, if 9·58 the number would be 47900).

The Trees shone for 1495 Valian Years, which is said to be equal to 14322 Sun Years (this presupposes an equivalence of almost exactly 9·58).

§§11–29 The great expansion of the pre-*Lord of the Rings* narrative (QS, AV 2) is in part derived from the later *Ainulindalë* (that AAm followed the last version, D, of that work is shown by various details, as for instance the names *Ëa*, *Illuin*, and *Ormal*, the first of these entering D by later addition, and those of the Lamps replacing *Forontë* and *Hyarantë* by emendation). But there is much that is entirely new: as that Manwë held a great feast on the Isle of Almaren, where Tulkas espoused Nessa; that Sauron was 'a great craftsman of the household of Aulë'; that the Valar were unable to overcome Melkor at that time because of the need to subdue the turmoil of the Earth and to preserve what they might of what they had achieved; and other features mentioned below. – The question of the cosmology is discussed at the end of this commentary.

§15 The statement that under the light of the Lamps 'there was great growth of trees and herbs, and beasts and birds came forth' (cf.

also §18, where Vana robed Nessa in flowers at the feast on Almaren) belongs with the *Ainulindalë* (§31): 'flowers of many hues, and trees whose blossom was like snow upon the mountains ... beasts and birds came forth' – where however the text was corrected ('As yet no flower had bloomed nor any bird had sung'). See p. 22 note 17, and p. 38, §31.

§20 A structural difference between AAm and the *Ainulindalë* is that in the latter Melkor did not begin the delving of Utumno until *after* the overthrow of the Lamps and his escape from the Valar (§32) – a story that goes back through the texts to the old 'Sketch of the Mythology'. In AAm, on the other hand, Melkor built Utumno, or was at least far advanced in the work, before the Valar were aware of him, and it was from Utumno that the blight and corruption proceeded; the Valar then perceived his presence in Arda and 'sought for his hiding-place', and it was this (as it appears) that led to Melkor's sudden emergence in open war and the casting down of the Lamps.

§22 The attack on Melkor by the Valar returning out of Valinor, described in the *Ainulindalë* (§32), is not mentioned in AAm, which says only that they 'could not at that time overcome him', taking up the words of QS §12 (V.208). That the idea had been abandoned is seen subsequently, p. 78, §47.

§23 That all life in Aman was free from any fading or withering, and free of blight and sickness, had not actually been said in previous texts.

§24 Whereas in the texts of the 1930s the old idea of the *Lost Tales* that the stars were created in two separate acts (I.69, 113–14, 133) had been abandoned, it now reappears: Varda wrought stars 'in the ages forgotten of her labours in Ëa', and later in AAm (p. 71, §35) it is told that 'she made stars newer and brighter' before the awakening of the Elves. This is presumably to be associated with the conception in the later *Ainulindalë* (§§14, 28) of the establishment of Arda 'in the midst of the innumerable stars'.

§§25–6 That the Trees grew on a green mound in the Ring of Doom is a new detail, though the implication of QS §14 (V.209) is that the Trees were in the Ring. The Ring and the Mound are here said to have been before the western gate of Valmar; in the *Lost Tales* the Trees were to the north of the city, and were moreover 'leagues asunder' from each other (I.71, 143).

§28 This account of the light that spilled from the Trees being drawn by Maiar from the wells of Varda to 'water' all the lands of Valinor has its roots in the old idea that the Trees 'must needs be *watered* with light to have sap and live' (I.73).

§29 At the end of this paragraph is a remarkable new detail, that after a thousand days the Trees put out a new branch; and that this was why a Valian Year was so constituted. It is apparent – and is stated here expressly – that the Valian day had twelve hours because the period of mingled light was exactly five times shorter than the period of full light-flowering of either Telperion or Laurelin; if it had been three times shorter the day would have had eight hours, and so on. The Valian day was therefore *of the Trees' nature*. We now learn that the Valian year of 1000 days was also *due to the Trees' nature*, since after that time the Trees would put out a new branch.

There is no suggestion here that the further calculation that a hundred years constituted a Valian Age (which goes back to the earliest *Annals*, IV.263) was related to the inner structure of the Trees; but it is said in the section *Of the Beginning of Time and its Reckoning* (§6) that the Lore-masters supposed 'that the Valar *so devised* the hours of the Trees that one hundred of such years so measured should be in duration as one age of the Valar *(as those ages were in the days of their labours before the foundation of Valinor)*' – i.e., before the Trees. Since the two passages are only separated by a few pages in the same manuscript the presumption is that they are not contradictory; and taken together the meaning can only be that the periods of the Trees, which were of their nature, were nonetheless related to a mode of measurement of time before the Trees came into existence. That in turn seems to demand that the Valar knew, and had 'devised', before ever Yavanna and Nienna came to the Green Mound, the periodic nature of the Trees' light.

The cosmological problem is here provided with new evidences. The relevant statements in this first section of AAm are these:

§1 Ëa is 'the World that is'; the Valar are 'the Powers of Ëa'.
§11 After ages of labour 'in the great halls of Ëa the Valar descended into Arda in the beginning of its being'.
§13 Tulkas came to Arda 'out of distant regions of Ëa'.
§17 Melkor gathered spirits 'out of the voids of Ëa'; and he 'drew near again unto Arda, and looked down upon it'.
§18 The Valar did not perceive the dark shadow 'cast from afar by Melkor'.
§19 Melkor 'passed over the borders of Ëa' > 'passed over the Walls of the Night upon the borders of Arda' > 'passed over the Walls of the Night' (note 19).
§23 The Outer Sea 'encircled the kingdom of Arda, and beyond were the Walls of the Night'.

The Walls of the Night have not been named elsewhere: but it is hard to see, especially in view of the sentence cited from §23, how they can not be equated with the Walls of the World. I have said (p. 29) that the departure of Melkor from Arda in the *Ainulindalë* – the new story that came in after *The Lord of the Rings* – raises the question of the passage of the Walls of the World and of the form which that conception now took. The idea of such a passage in fact appeared, and most puzzlingly, in the earlier period, at the end of Q, where it is said that some believe that Melko at times returns to the world, and that he 'creeps back surmounting the Walls' (IV.164, 253). The passage in AAm §19 (as emended) is unequivocal: Melkor *passed over* the Walls of the Night. We have returned to the earliest imagination of the Walls: cf. my remark in I.227, 'the implication seems clear that the Walls were originally conceived like the walls of terrestrial cities, or gardens – walls with a top: a "ring-fence".' Thus, we may suppose, Melkor could 'look down upon Arda' (§17); thus his vast shadow could be cast even before he passed over the Walls (§18); and thus Tulkas (§13) and the spirits summoned by Melkor (§19) could enter the 'fenced region' (as *Arda* is defined, p. 7).

But the phrase 'he passed over the Walls of the Night' was an emendation of what my father first wrote: 'he passed over the borders of Ëa'. Can this mean anything other than that on entering Arda Melkor left Ëa? In this connection one may turn back to the two *Ambarkanta* diagrams of 'Ilu' (IV.242–5), on which much later (perhaps about this time) my father made pencilled corrections to *Ilurambar* 'the Walls of the World', changing this to *Ëarambar* ('the Walls of Ëa'). (Of course, if the Walls are no longer conceived as a spherical shell – whence the expression 'globed amid the Void' as used in the early *Ainulindalë* versions – but as a surmountable rampart, the *Ëarambar* cannot be taken as the same conception as the *Ilurambar*, but only as a new name for the Walls, now differently conceived; and the substitution of the new name on the old diagrams is therefore to that extent misleading.) It is likewise hard to see what *Ëarambar* can mean but 'the Walls that *fence out* the dark wastes of "the voids of Ëa"' (an expression used in §17), in contrast to *Ilurambar* 'the Walls that *fence in* Ilu.'

The difficulty with this, of course, is that Ëa is elsewhere defined as the 'Universe of that which Is' (p. 7), 'Creation the Universe' (p. 39), and Ëa therefore necessarily comprehends Arda; it is in any case abundantly clear from all the texts of the later period that Arda is within Ëa. But it may be that Arda can nonetheless be regarded as separate from Ëa when Ëa is regarded as 'Space'.

Amid all the ambiguities (most especially, in the use of the word 'World'), the testimony seems to be that in these texts the *Ambarkanta* world-image survived at least in the conception of the Outer Sea extending to the Walls of the World, now called the Walls of the Night – though the Walls have come to be differently conceived (see also p. 135, §168). Now in the revision of 'The Silmarillion' made in 1951 the phrase in QS §12 (V.209) 'the Walls of the World fence out the Void and the Eldest Dark' – a phrase in perfect agreement of course with the

Ambarkanta – was retained (p. 154). This is a central difficulty in relation to the *Ainulindalë*, where it is made as plain as could be wished that Eä came into being *in the Void*, it was *globed amid the Void* (§§11, 20, and see pp. 37–8); how then can the Walls of Arda 'fence out the Void and the Eldest Darkness'?

A possible explanation, of a sort, may be hinted at in the words cited above from AAm §17: Melkor gathered spirits *out of the voids of Eä*. It may be that, although AAm is not far distant in time from the last version (D) of the *Ainulindalë*, my father's conception did not in fact now accord entirely with what he had written there; that (as I suggested, p. 39) he was now thinking of Arda as being 'set within an indefinite vastness in which all "Creation" is comprehended', rather than of a bounded Eä itself set 'amid the Void'. Then, beyond the Walls of the Night, the bounds of Arda, stretch 'the voids of Eä'. But this suggestion does not, of course, clear up all the problems, ambiguities, and apparent contradictions in the cosmology of the later period, which have been discussed earlier.

★

I have mentioned (p. 47) that there exists a typescript of the early part of AAm that is quite distinct from the amanuensis typescript of the whole work. I was unaware of its existence when the text of *The Silmarillion* was prepared for publication. It was taken directly from and closely based upon the AAm manuscript, and was certainly made by my father, who introduced changes from the manuscript as he typed. It has in fact a great many such changes, mostly minor or very minor, but also some important alterations and additions; and it does not include the section *Of the Beginning of Time and its Reckoning*. None of these changes appear in the emendations made to the amanuensis typescript or its carbon copy, except the removal of the section on the Reckoning of Time (p. 68).

I will refer to this text as '**AAm***'. There seems no way to determine with certainty when it was made, and I can only record my feeling that it belongs with the writing of the AAm manuscript rather than to some later time. At any rate my father soon abandoned it (see p. 80). It may be that having set it aside he forgot about it, or lost it; and when the opportunity arose to have the work typed by a secretary who was a trained typist (as appears to be the case) he simply handed over the AAm manuscript as it stood (including therefore the section on the Reckoning of Time, although in AAm* he had cut this out).

I give now the noteworthy changes in AAm* (which extends a short way beyond the point reached in this first section; for the remainder of the text see pp. 79–80).

The preamble

Here begin the 'Annals of Aman'. Rúmil made them in the Elder

Days, and they were held in memory by the Exiles. Those parts which we learned and remembered were thus set down in Númenor before the Shadow fell upon it.

This is especially interesting since it shows a different mode of transmission from the 'Pengoloð – Ælfwine' tradition: the *Annals* are conceived as a written work made in Númenor, deriving from the 'Exiles', the Noldor in Middle-earth, who themselves derived it from the work of Rúmil. The idea that Númenor was an essential element in the transmission of the legends of the Elder Days will reappear (see especially pp. 370, 373–4, 401–2).

§1 For 'chieftains of the Valar' AAm* has 'lords of the Valar', and subsequently. *Lorien* was changed in pencil on the typescript to *Lorion* (but not in the passage cited under §3 below).

§2 In AAm the old phrase 'Manwë and Melkor were most puissant and were brethren' was preserved, but AAm* has here:

> Melkor and Manwë were brethren in the thought of Eru, and the eldest of their kind, and their power was equal and greater than that of all others who dwelt in Arda. Manwë is King of the Valar...

It is said in the later *Ainulindalë* (§§5, 9) that Melkor was the mightiest of the Ainur, and this in fact goes back to the pre-*Lord of the Rings* text B of the *Ainulindalë* (see V.164 note 4 for the different statements made on this subject). Later in AAm (p. 97, §102) Fëanor 'shut the doors of his house in the face of the mightiest of all the dwellers in Ëa'.

This text has 'Oromë and Tulkas were the youngest in the thought of Eru' where AAm has 'younger'.

§3 There is a strange mixture of present and past tenses in this passage: thus 'Vána the fair is the wife of Oromë', 'Vairë the Weaver dwells with Mandos', but 'No spouse had Ulmo, nor Melkor', 'No lord had Nienna', 'the wife of Lorien was Estë the Pale'. On this question see pp. 204–5.

It is not now said that Vana (marked Vána at the first occurrence but not subsequently) was the sister of Yavanna (see p. 59).

As typed, the passage beginning 'No lord had Nienna' (spelt thus, not Niënna, at all occurrences in AAm*) ran thus:

> No lord had Nienna, queen of Shadow, Manwë's sister. The wife of Tulkas was Nessa the Young; and the wife of Lorien was Estë the Pale. These do not sit in the councils of the Valar but are the highest among the Maiar.

In AAm it is said of Estë alone that 'she goes not to the councils of the Valar', and her name does not appear in the list of the queens of the Valar: she is 'the chief of the Maiar'. In the present text, despite the exclusion of Nessa also from the councils, and the statement that she and Estë 'are the highest among the Maiar', her name still stands in the list of the queens. Contemporary emendations to the typescript produced this remarkable change:

> No lord had Nienna, Manwë's sister; nor Nessa the Evermaid. The wife of Tulkas was Lëa the Young; and the wife of Lorien was Estë the Pale ...

The text then continues as before, so that the two who do not sit in the councils of the Valar and are 'the highest among the Maiar' become Lëa and Estë. There is no trace of this development in any other text, but Lëa appears again in AAm* as the text was typed (see under §18 below).

§4 This paragraph was substantially extended:

> With these great powers came many other spirits of the same kind, begotten in the thought of Eru before the making of Eä, but having less might and authority. These are the Maiar, the people of the Valar; they are beautiful, but their number is not known and few have names among Elves or Men.
>
> There are also those whom we call the Valarindi, who are the Children of the Valar, begotten of their love after their entry into Eä. They are the elder children of the World; and though their being began within Eä, yet they are of the race of the Ainur, who were before the world, and they have power and rank below that of the Valar only.

§12 At the end of this paragraph AAm* adds: 'So passed many years of the Valar in strife.'

§14 The date V.Y.1900 of the setting up of the Lamps is omitted in AAm*.

§15 AAm* retains the words of AAm, 'and there was great growth of trees and herbs, and beasts and birds came forth ...' See the commentary on this passage, p. 60: the reference to the appearance of birds and flowers at this time was removed from *Ainulindalë* D by what looks to be a fairly early change in the text, and there is in this a suggestion that the two versions of the opening of the *Annals of Aman* belong fairly closely together (see p. 64).

§17 This paragraph underwent several modifications:

> Now Melkor knew all that was done; for even then he had secret friends among the Maiar, whom he had converted to his cause, whether in the first playing of the Ainulindalë or afterwards in Eä. Of these the chief, as afterwards became known, was Sauron, a great craftsman of the household of Aulë. Thus far off in the dark places of Eä, to which he had retreated, Melkor was filled with new hatred, being jealous of the work of his peers, whom he desired to make subject

to himself. Therefore he had gathered to himself spirits out of the voids of Eä who served him, until he deemed that he was strong; and seeing now his time he drew near to Arda again; and he looked down upon it, and the beauty of the Earth in its Spring filled him with wonder, but because it was not his, he resolved to destroy it.

§18 Here Tulkas' wife Lëa the Young appears again, in the text as typed and not by emendation (see under §3 above), named now Lëa-vinya ('Lëa the Young'):

It is told that in that feast of the Spring of Arda Tulkas espoused Lëa-vinya, fairest of the maidens of Yavanna, and Vana robed her in flowers that came then first to their opening; and she danced before the Valar ...

On the reference to the first flowers see under §15 above.

§19 AAm* has 'the Walls of Night' for 'the Walls of the Night', and again in §23.

§20 Now Melkor began the delving and building of a vast fortress deep under the Earth, [*struck out:* beneath the roots of] far from the light of Illuin; and he raised great mountains above his halls. That stronghold was after called Utumno the Deep-hidden; and though the Valar for a long time knew nothing of it ...

In AAm Utumno was delved 'beneath dark mountains'; the new text, in which Melkor raised mountains above it (as Thangorodrim above Angband), arose in the act of typing.

§21 Where AAm has 'And he assailed the lights of Illuin and Ormal' AAm* has:

He came down like a black storm from the North, and he assailed the lights of Illuin and Ormal.

§22 The conclusion of this paragraph in AAm, 'who were yet to come in a time that was hidden from the Valar', is omitted in AAm*.

§23 The word 'gods' was removed in AAm* at both occurrences: at the beginning of the paragraph 'the gods had no abiding place' becomes 'they had', and near the end 'for the gods dwelt there' becomes 'for the Servants of Ilúvatar dwelt there'.

The Land of Aman was 'upon the borders of the ancient world' (i.e. the world before the Cataclysm); 'upon the borders of the world' AAm. The passage concerning Taniquetil was changed to read thus:

But above all the mountains of the Pelóri was that height which was named Taniquetil Oiolossë, the gleaming peak of Everwhite, upon whose summit Manwë set his throne, before the doors of the domed halls of Varda.

§25 In AAm it is said that 'the Valar built their city'; AAm* has:

... in the midst of the plain west of the Pelóri Aulë and his people built for them a fair city. That city they named Valimar the Blessed.

This reappears from the *Lost Tales*; cf. I.77: 'Now have I recounted the manner of the dwellings of all the great Gods which Aulë of his craftsmanship raised in Valinor.' – This is the first occurrence of the form *Valimar* (again in §§26, 28 of this text).

§26 After the words 'But Nienna sat silent in thought, and her tears fell upon the mould' there is a footnote in the new version:

For it is said that even in the Music Nienna took little part, but listened intent to all that she heard. Therefore she was rich in memory, and farsighted, perceiving how the themes should unfold in the Tale of Arda. But she had little mirth, and all her love was mingled with pity, grieving for the harms of the world and for the things that failed of fulfilment. So great was her ruth, it is said, that she could not endure to the end of the Music. Therefore she has not the hope of Manwë. He is more farseeing; but Pity is the heart of Nienna.

On this passage see p. 388 and note 2. The statement here that Nienna 'could not endure to the end of the Music', and that 'therefore she has not the hope of Manwë', is very striking; but it is not said in what Manwë's hope lies. It may possibly be relevant to recall the Pengoloð footnote to *Ainulindalë* D, §19 (p. 31):

And some have said that the Vision ceased ere the fulfilment of the Dominion of Men and the fading of the Firstborn; wherefore, though the Music is over all, the Valar have not seen as with sight the Later Ages or the ending of the World.

§28 For 'hoarded in mighty vats' AAm* has 'hoarded in deep pools'.

★

It remains to consider the very few emendations made to the amanuensis typescript of AAm in this opening section, and those (almost entirely different) made to the carbon copy. These changes were hasty, and casual, in no sense a real revision of the work. They were made at some later time which I am unable to define; but they have the effect of bringing the opening of AAm into agreement with the latest form of the other tradition, proceeding from QS chapter 1 'Of the Valar' and ultimately issuing in the short independent work *Valaquenta*.

On the top copy of the typescript not only was the section on the Reckoning of Time struck through (see p. 64) but also the compressed account of the Valar at the beginning: a note on the covering page of the text directs that the *Annals* are to start at the First Year of the Valar in Arda (§11 in this book). But pencilled changes had been made to §§1–4 before this:

§1 'nine chieftains' > 'seven chieftains'; Ossë and Melkor were struck from the list. On the removal of Ossë see p. 91, §70.

§2 The word 'also' added in 'The queens of the Valar are also seven'; Estë added, and Uinen removed, so that the list becomes 'Varda, Yavanna, Nienna, Estë, Vairë, Vana, and Nessa'.

§3 'Varda was Manwë's spouse from the beginning' > 'Varda was Manwë's spouse from the beginning of Arda'

'and Uinen, lady of the seas, is the spouse of Ossë' was struck out (a consequence simply of Ossë's being no longer numbered among the 'chieftains').

'Manwë's sister and Melkor's' (of Nienna) was struck out.

'but she goes not to the councils of the Valar and is not accounted among the rulers of Arda, but is the chief of the Maiar' (of Estë) was struck out (a consequence of Estë's now being included in the 'queens').

§4 'And with them are numbered also the Valarindi ...' to the end of the paragraph was struck out (see below).

§28 'mighty vats' > 'shining wells' (cf. the change made in AAm*, p. 68).

Quite distinct changes were made on the carbon copy in this section on the Valar. In §3 'the wife of Oromë' and 'Tulkas' wife' were changed to 'the spouse of Oromë' and 'Tulkas' spouse'; 'No lord hath Nienna' was changed to 'No companion hath Nienna'; and in the margin against these changes my father wrote:

Note that 'spouse' meant only an 'association'. The Valar had no bodies, but could assume shapes. After the coming of the Eldar they most often used shapes of 'human' form, though taller (*not* gigantic) and more magnificent.

At the same time the passage concerning the Valarindi, the Children of the Valar, at the end of §4 was struck out (as it was also on the top copy), since this note is a most definitive statement that any such conception was out of the question.

A few other pencillings were made at subsequent points in the carbon copy:

§20 Against *Utumno* is pencilled: 'Utupnŭ √TUI? cover over, hide'; with this cf. AAm* §20 (p. 67): 'that stronghold was after called Utumno the Deep-hidden', and see the *Etymologies* (V.394), stem TUB, where the original form of the name is given as *Utubnu.

§23 Where the word 'gods' was replaced by 'the Servants of Ilúvatar' in AAm* (p. 67) my father corrected it on the carbon copy of the typescript to 'the Deathless'. At the occurrence of 'gods' at the beginning of the paragraph he made the same change (to 'they') as in AAm*.

§25 After 'a green mound' is added *Ezellohar*; and in §26 *Ezellohar* replaces 'that Green Mound'.

Second section of the Annals of Aman

Here begins a new Reckoning in the Light of the Trees

1*

§30 For one thousand years of the Trees the Valar dwelt in bliss in Valinor beyond the Mountains of Aman, and all Middle-earth lay in a twilight under the stars. Thither the Valar seldom came, save only Yavanna and Oromë; and Yavanna often would walk there in the shadows, grieving because all the growth and promise of the Spring of Arda was checked. And she set a sleep upon many fair things that had arisen in the Spring, both tree and herb and beast and bird, so that they should not age but should wait for a time of awakening that yet should be. But Melkor dwelt in Utumno, and he slept not, but watched, and laboured; and the evil things that he had perverted walked abroad, and the dark and slumbering woods were haunted by monsters and shapes of dread. And in Utumno he wrought the race of demons whom the Elves after named the Balrogs. But these came not yet from the gates of Utumno, because of the watchfulness of Oromë.

§31 Now Oromë dearly loved all the works of Yavanna, and he was ever ready to her bidding. And for this reason, and because he desired at whiles to ride in forests greater and wider than the friths of Valinor, he would often come also to Middle-earth, and there go a-hunting under the stars. Then his white horse, Nahar, shone like silver in the shadows; and the sleeping earth trembled at the beat of his golden hooves. And Oromë would blow his mighty horn, whereat the mountains shook, and things of evil fled away; but Melkor quailed in Utumno and dared not venture forth. For it is said that even as his malice grew, and the strength of his hatred, so the heart of Melkor failed; and with all his knowledge and his might and his many servants he became craven, giving battle only to those of little strength, tormenting the weak, and trusting ever to his slaves and creatures to do his evil work. Yet ever his dominion spread southward over Middle-earth, for even as Oromë passed the servants of Melkor would gather again; and the Earth was full of shadows and deceit.

* Pencilled beside '1' is 'YT' (Year of the Trees), and also 'YV 3501' (i.e. Year of the Valar). – The 'YT' dates were very frequently changed on the manuscript, and it is in places very difficult to interpret the changes; I give only the final forms (see pp. 47–8).

1000

§32 It came to pass that the Valar held council, for they became troubled by the tidings that Yavanna and Oromë brought from the Outer Lands. And Yavanna spoke before the Valar, and foretold that the coming of the Children of Ilúvatar was drawing nigh, albeit the hour and the place of that coming was known only to Ilúvatar. And Yavanna besought Manwë to give light to Middle-earth, for the stay of the evils of Melkor and the comfort of the Children; and Oromë and Tulkas spoke likewise, being eager for war with Utumno.

§33 But Mandos spoke and said that though the Coming was prepared it should not yet be for many Years; and the Elder Children should come in the darkness and look first upon the Stars. For so it was ordained.

§34 Then Varda went forth from the council, and she looked out from the height of Taniquetil, and beheld the darkness of the Earth beneath the innumerable stars, faint and far. Then she began a great labour, the greatest of all the works of the Valar since their coming unto Arda.

1000–1050

§35 Now Varda took the light that issued from Telperion and was stored in Valinor and she made stars newer and brighter. And many other of the ancient stars she gathered together and set as signs in the heavens of Arda. The greatest of these was Menelmakar, the Swordsman of the Sky. This, it is said, was a sign of Túrin Turambar, who should come into the world, and a foreshowing of the Last Battle that shall be at the end of Days.

1050

§36 Last of all Varda made the sign of bright stars that is called the Valakirka, the Sickle of the Gods, and this she hung about the North as a threat unto Utumno and a token of the doom of Melkor.

§37 In that hour, it is said, the Quendi, the Elder Children of Ilúvatar, awoke: these Men have named the Elves, and many other names. By the Waters of Awakening, Kuiviénen, they rose from the sleep of Ilúvatar and their eyes beheld first of all things the stars of heaven. Therefore they have ever loved the starlight, and have revered Varda Elentárië above all the Valar.

§38   In the changes of the world the shapes of lands and of seas have been broken and remade; rivers have not kept their courses, neither have mountains remained steadfast; and to Kuiviénen there is no returning. But it is said among the Quendi that it lay far off in Middle-earth, eastward of Endon (which is the midmost point) and northward; and it was a bay in the Inland Sea of Helkar. And that sea stood where aforetime the roots of the mountain of Illuin had been ere Melkor overthrew it. Many waters flowed down thither from heights in the East, and the first sound that was heard by the ears of the Elves was the sound of water flowing, and the sound of water falling over stone.

§39   Long the Quendi dwelt in their first home by the water under stars and they walked the Earth in wonder; and they began to make speech and to give names to all things that they perceived. And they named themselves the Quendi, signifying those that speak with voices; for as yet they had met no other living things that spoke or sang.

§40   At this time also, it is said, Melian, fairest of the Maiar, desiring to look upon the stars, went up upon Taniquetil; and suddenly she desired to see Middle-earth, and she left Valinor and walked in the twilight.

1085

§41   And when the Elves had dwelt in the world five and thirty Years of the Valar (which is like unto three hundred and thirty-five of our years) it chanced that Oromë rode to Endon in his hunting, and he turned north by the shores of Helkar and passed under the shadows of the Orokarni, the Mountains of the East. And on a sudden Nahar set up a great neighing and then stood still. And Oromë wondered and sat silent, and it seemed to him that in the quiet of the land under the stars he heard afar off many voices singing.

§42   Thus it was that the Valar found at last, as it were by chance, those whom they had so long awaited. And when Oromë looked upon them he was filled with wonder, as though they were things unforeseen and unimagined; and he loved the Quendi, and named them Eldar, the people of the stars.

The original manuscript page was interpolated at this point, a passage being written in the margin as follows:

Yet by after-knowledge the masters of lore say sadly that Oromë was not, mayhap, the first of the Great Ones to look upon the Elves. For Melkor was on the watch, and his spies were many. And it is thought that lurking near his servants had led astray some of the Quendi that ventured afield, and they took them as captives to Utumno, and there enslaved them. Of these slaves it is held came the Orkor that were afterward chief foes of the Eldar. And Melkor's lies were soon abroad, so that whispers were heard among the Quendi, warning them that if any of their kindred passed away into the shadows and were seen no more, they must beware of a fell huntsman on a great horse, for he it was that carried them off to devour them. Hence it was that at the approach of Oromë many of the Quendi fled and hid themselves.

The original text then continues, with a new date 1086, 'Swiftly Oromë rode back to Valinor and brought tidings to the Valar' (see §46 below). But the interpolated passage just given was subsequently replaced on a new page by the following long and important passage §§43–5 (found in the typescript as typed):

§43 Yet many of the Quendi were adread at his coming. This was the doing of Melkor. For by after-knowledge the masters of lore say that Melkor, ever watchful, was first aware of the awakening of the Quendi, and sent shadows and evil spirits to watch and waylay them. So it came to pass, some years ere the coming of Oromë, that if any of the Elves strayed far abroad, alone or few together, they would often vanish and never return; and the Quendi said that the Hunter had caught them, and they were afraid. Even so, in the most ancient songs of our people, of which some echoes are remembered still in the West, we hear of the shadow-shapes that walked in the hills about Kuiviénen, or would pass suddenly over the stars; and of the dark Rider upon his wild horse that pursued those that wandered to take them and devour them. Now Melkor greatly hated and feared the riding of Oromë, and either verily he sent his dark servants as riders, or he set lying whispers abroad, for the purpose that the Quendi should shun Oromë, if ever haply they met.

§44 Thus it was that when Nahar neighed and Oromë indeed came among them, some of the Quendi hid themselves, and some fled and were lost. But those that had the courage to stay perceived swiftly that the Great Rider was noble and fair and no shape out of Darkness; for the Light of Aman was in his face, and all the noblest of the Quendi were drawn towards it.

§45 But of those hapless who were ensnared by Melkor little

is known of a certainty. For who of the living hath descended into the pits of Utumno, or hath explored the darkness of the counsels of Melkor? Yet this is held true by the wise of Eressëa: that all those of the Quendi that came into the hands of Melkor, ere Utumno was broken, were put there in prison, and by slow arts of cruelty and wickedness were corrupted and enslaved. Thus did Melkor breed the hideous race of the Orkor in envy and mockery of the Eldar, of whom they were afterwards the bitterest foes. For the Orkor had life and multiplied after the manner of the Children of Ilúvatar; and naught that had life of its own, nor the semblance thereof, could ever Melkor make since his rebellion in the Ainulindalë before the Beginning: so say the wise. And deep in their dark hearts the Orkor loathed the Master whom they served in fear, the maker only of their misery. This maybe was the vilest deed of Melkor and the most hateful to Eru.

1086

§46 Oromë tarried a while among the Quendi, and then swiftly he rode back to Valinor and brought the tidings to the Valar. And he spoke of the shadows that troubled Kuiviénen. Then the Valar sat in council and debated long what it were best to do for the guarding of the Quendi; but Oromë returned at once to Middle-earth and abode with the Elves.

1090

§47 Manwë sat long in thought upon Taniquetil, and he resolved at the last to make war upon Melkor, though Arda should receive yet more hurts in that strife. For the first time, therefore, the Valar assailed Melkor, not he the Valar, and they came forth to war in all their might, and they defeated him utterly. This they did on behalf of the Elves, and Melkor knew it well, and forgot it not.

1090–2

§48 Melkor met the onset of the Valar in the North-west of Middle-earth, and all that region was much broken. But this first victory of the hosts of the West was swift and easy, and the servants of Melkor fled before them to Utumno. Then the Valar marched over Middle-earth, and they set a guard over Kuiviénen; and thereafter the Quendi knew naught of the Great War of the Gods, save that the Earth shook and groaned beneath them, and the waters were moved; and in the North there were lights as of mighty fires. But after two years the Valar passed into the far North and began the long siege of Utumno.

1092–1100

§49 That siege was long and grievous, and many battles were fought before its gates of which naught but the rumour is known to the Quendi. Middle-earth was sorely shaken in that time, and the Great Sea that sundered it from Aman grew wide and deep. And the lands of the far North were all made desolate in those days, and so have ever remained; for there Utumno was delved exceeding deep, and its pits and caverns reached out far beneath the earth, and they were filled with fires and with great hosts of the servants of Melkor.

1099

§50 It came to pass that at last the gates of Utumno were broken and its halls unroofed, and Melkor took refuge in the uttermost pit. Thence, seeing that all was lost (for that time), he sent forth on a sudden a host of Balrogs, the last of his servants that remained, and they assailed the standard of Manwë, as it were a tide of flame. But they were withered in the wind of his wrath and slain with the lightning of his sword; and Melkor stood at last alone. Then, since he was but one against many, Tulkas stood forth as champion of the Valar and wrestled with him and cast him upon his face, and bound him with the chain Angainor. Thus ended the first war of the West upon the North.

Commentary on the second section of the
Annals of Aman

(There are no textual notes to this section of the text.) In the portion given above the *Annals of Aman* correspond to the opening of Chapter 3 *Of the Coming of the Elves* in the other or 'Silmarillion' tradition (QS §§18–21, V.211–13). Contemporary (more or less) with the writing of the *Annals of Aman* was the major revision of the *Quenta Silmarillion*, but here comparison must obviously be restricted to the pre-*Lord of the Rings* text, together with AV 2, annals V.Y.1000–1990 (V.111–12).

§30   In AAm there is now recounted the laying by Yavanna of a sleep on living things that had awoken in the Spring of Arda, of which there is no trace in QS (or in the later rewritings).
      The making of the Balrogs is then mentioned; and while in AAm (§17) the account of Melkor's 'host', spirits 'out of the

voids of Ëa' and 'secret friends and spies among the Maiar', is fuller than in the other tradition at any stage, the Balrogs are still firmly stated to be *demons of his own making*, and moreover to have been made in Utumno at this time. On the conception of Balrogs in AAm see further under §§42–5, 50 in this commentary, and especially p. 79, §30.

§31 That Oromë's horse was white and shod with gold is stated in QS (§24) and Q (§2), but this is the first appearance of the horse's name *Nahar*. Oromë is here represented as a guardian presence in Middle-earth, to such an extent even that the Balrogs did not issue from Utumno on account of him (§30); cf. AV 2 (V.111) 'Morgoth withdrew before his horn'.

§§34–6 On the two star-makings see p. 61, §24. There is here the remarkable statement that *Menelmakar* (Orion) was 'a sign of Túrin Turambar, who should come into the world, and a foreshowing of the Last Battle that shall be at the end of Days.' This is a reference to the Second Prophecy of Mandos (in the *Quenta*, IV.165):

Then shall the last battle be gathered on the fields of Valinor. In that day Tulkas shall strive with Melko, and on his right shall stand Fionwë and on his left Túrin Turambar, son of Húrin, Conqueror of Fate, coming from the halls of Mandos; and it shall be the black sword of Túrin that deals unto Melko his death and final end; and so shall the children of Húrin and all Men be avenged.

The Quenya name *Menelmacar* is mentioned in Appendix E (I) to *The Lord of the Rings*; in *The Fellowship of the Ring* (p. 91) appears the Sindarin form: 'the Swordsman of the Sky, Menelvagor with his shining belt'.

§37 That the Elves awoke at the first shining of the Sickle of the Gods is told in AV 2 (V.111); 'at the opening of the first stars' QS §20.

§38 The reference to the site of Kuiviénen is interesting. Of this no more is said in the other tradition than that it lay 'in the East of the Middle-earth' (QS §20, preserved throughout the later texts). In AAm Kuiviénen lay N.E. of Endon, the midmost point. In the list of names accompanying the *Ambarkanta* (IV.241) appears '*ambar-endya* or Middle Earth of which *Endor* is the midmost point', and *Endor* is written over the centre of the middle-land in the *Ambarkanta* diagrams (IV.243, 245) – on the map (IV.248–9) it is marked as a point: 'Endor Earth-middle', and here it was corrected to *Endon*, the form in the present passage of AAm, though later changed back again to *Endor* (so also on the typescript of AAm my father corrected *Endon* to *Endor* here and in §41, p. 80). See IV.254–5.

In AAm Kuiviénen was 'a bay in the Inland Sea of Helkar'; in QS it is 'the starlit mere' (so also in Q), which was retained in the later texts. On the *Ambarkanta* map it is shown to the N.E. of Endor (Endon), and is marked at the eastern side of the Sea of Helkar; in the text it is 'beside the waters of Helkar' (IV.239). It is not clear whether these various statements show one and the same conception. Here in AAm is the first reference to the Sea of Helkar (formed after the fall of the northern Lamp) since the *Ambarkanta* – in which text the Lamp itself was called *Helkar*; see IV.256.

§39 Cf. QS §20: 'For a while [Oromë] abode with them, and taught them the language of the Gods, from whence afterwards they made the fair Elvish speech', and the *Lhammas* (V.168): 'of [Oromë] they learned after their capacity the speech of the Valar; and all the tongues that have been derived thence may be called Oromian or Quendian'. It is now said in AAm that the Quendi had achieved language, and that they gave names 'to all things that they perceived', before ever Oromë came upon them (which was 335 Years of the Sun since their awakening). Cf. *Gilfanon's Tale* in *The Book of Lost Tales* (I.232): 'Now the Eldar or Qendi had the gift of speech direct from Ilúvatar'.

§40 This paragraph was interpolated into the manuscript; it appears in the typescript as typed. The placing of Melian's departure at this time derives from the *Annals of Valinor* (IV.264, V.111); in QS (§31) it is said that she 'often strayed from Valinor on long journey into the Hither Lands'. The meaning of the words of AAm, that Melian, 'desiring to look upon the stars, went up upon Taniquetil', is presumably that she climbed on Taniquetil's eastern slopes, where the light of the Trees was hidden.

§41 As noted in IV.256, the statement that Oromë 'turned north by the shores of Helkar and passed under the shadows of the Orokarni, the Mountains of the East' agrees perfectly with the *Ambarkanta* map (IV.249; on the map the Orokarni are named Red Mountains).

'He heard afar off many voices singing': cf. QS §20: 'But Oromë came upon them ... while they dwelt yet silent beside the starlit mere, Kuiviénen'. See under §39 above.

§42 QS (§20) has here the extraordinary statement that 'Oromë looking upon the Elves was filled with love and wonder; for their coming was not in the Music of the Ainur, and was hidden in the secret thought of Ilúvatar'; see my discussion of this passage, V.216–17.

On the history of the meaning of the name *Eldar* see the references to this given under the entry *Eldar* in the Index to Vol.V.

§§42-5 *The origin of the Orcs.* The first appearance of the idea that their origin was connected with the Elves is in QS §18, and later in QS (§62) it is said that *when Morgoth returned to Middle-earth* after the destruction of the Trees

> he brought into being the race of the Orcs, and they grew and multiplied in the bowels of the earth. These Orcs Morgoth made in envy and mockery of the Elves, and they were made of stone, but their hearts of hatred.

(For my father's changing views concerning the time of the origin of the Orcs in the chronology of the Elder Days see IV.314, V.238.) In the interpolation into the manuscript of AAm and its subsequent rewriting and extension (pp. 72-4) there appears, together with the story of the Rider who was rumoured to carry off the Quendi if they strayed, the theory that Melkor *bred* the Orcs (here called *Orkor*) 'in envy and mockery of the Eldar' *from Quendi enslaved in the east of Middle-earth* before ever Oromë came upon them. It is explicit (§45) that Melkor could *make* nothing that had life of its own since his rebellion; but this is in sharp contradiction to §30, where it is said that 'in Utumno he *wrought* the race of demons whom the Elves after named the Balrogs'. I do not think that the interpolation in which the former of these statements appears was made after any very long interval: my father's views on this subject seem to have been changing swiftly, and a different account of the origin of the Balrogs is found in the soon abandoned typescript which I have called AAm* (see p. 79, §30). The retention of the statement in §30, despite its contradiction to that in §45, was no doubt due to oversight, and both appear in the main typescript of AAm. – See further on the question of the origin of the Orcs p. 123, §127, and pp. 408 ff.

§47   The words 'For the first time, therefore, the Valar assailed Melkor, not he the Valar' show that the story in the *Ainulindalë* that the Valar came against him out of Valinor after the fall of the Lamps had been abandoned (p. 61, §22).

§49   On the changes in the Earth at the time of the Great War of the Gods as described in the *Ambarkanta* see IV.239. While the two texts are not necessarily contradictory, it is curious that it should be said in AAm that at this time 'the Great Sea that sundered [Middle-earth] from Aman grew wide and deep'; for in the *Ambarkanta* (*ibid.*, and see the map, IV.249) the much greater width of the Western Sea than that of the Eastern came about at the time of the foundation of Valinor:

> For their further protection the Valar thrust away Middle-earth at the centre and crowded it eastward, so that it was bended, and the great sea of the West is very wide in the middle, the widest of all waters of the Earth. The shape of the

Earth in the East was much like that in the West, save for the narrowing of the Eastern Sea, and the thrusting of the land thither.

§50 It is notable that the Balrogs were still at this time, when *The Lord of the Rings* had been completed, conceived to have existed in very large numbers (Melkor sent forth 'a host of Balrogs'); see p. 80, §50.

★

The typescript text (AAm*) which my father began but soon abandoned continues for a little way beyond the point reached in the first section (p. 68). Significant differences from AAm are as follows:

§30   ... But Melkor dwelt in Utumno, and he did not sleep, but watched and laboured; and whatsoever good Yavanna worked in the lands he undid if he could, and the evil things that he had perverted walked far abroad, and the dark and slumbering woods were haunted by monsters and shapes of dread. And in Utumno he multiplied the race of the evil spirits that followed him, the Úmaiar, of whom the chief were those demons whom the Elves afterwards named the Balrogath. But they did not yet come forth from the gates of Utumno because of their fear of Oromë.

The latter part of this passage is of much interest as showing a marked development from the idea that Melkor 'made' the Balrogs at this time (see p. 78). They now become 'evil spirits (*Úmaiar*) that followed him' – but he could 'multiply' them. The term *Úmaiar*, not met before, stands to *Maiar* as *Úvanimor* to *Vanimor* (see IV.293, footnote).

§31   ... and there would go a-hunting under the stars. He had great love of horses and of hounds, but all beasts were in his thought, and he hunted only the monsters and fell creatures of Melkor. If he descried them afar or his great hounds got wind of them, then his white horse, Nahar, shone like silver as it ran through the shadows, and the sleeping earth trembled at the beat of his golden hooves. And at the mort Oromë would blow his great horn, until the mountains shook ...

mort: the horn-call blown at the kill.

... and trusting ever to his slaves to do his evil work. [his slaves and creatures, AAm]

§32   It came to pass that Manwë summoned the Valar to council, for they were troubled by the tidings that Yavanna and Oromë brought from the Outer Lands, saying that if Melkor were left longer to work his will unhindered, all Middle-earth would fall into ruin irretrievable; and Manwë knew moreover that the coming of the Children of Ilúvatar was now drawing near, although the very hour and place of their coming was known only to Ilúvatar himself. And Manwë spoke of this to the Valar; and Yavanna besought him to give light to Middle-earth, for the stay of the evils of Melkor and the comfort of the Children; and

Here the typescript AAm* ends, at the foot of a page. Once again, what began as a copy was changing with gathering speed into a new version. But I see no reason to think that any more of it ever existed.

★

It remains to record a very few late scribbled changes and notes made on one or other copy of the typescript of the whole text.

§§38, 41   *Endon* > *Endor* (see p. 76, §38).

§42   'and named them Eldar, the people of the stars' > 'and called them the people of the stars'. In the margin my father wrote (i.e. with reference to the original text): 'but he could not − [?as this] was later Quenya.'

§43   Against the middle portion of this paragraph is a note in the margin: 'Alter this. Orcs are not Elvish.' See pp. 408 ff.

§50   'a host of Balrogs, the last of his servants that remained' > 'his Balrogs, the last of his servants that remained faithful to him'. In the margin my father wrote: 'There should not be supposed more than say 3 or at most 7 ever existed.' See p. 79, §50.

Third section of the Annals of Aman

1100

The Chaining of Melkor

§51   Then the Valar returned to the Land of Aman, and Melkor was led captive, bound hand and foot and blindfold; and he was brought to the Ring of Doom. There he lay upon his face before the feet of Manwë, and he sued for pardon and freedom, recalling his kinship with Manwë. But his prayer was denied, and it is said that in that hour the Valar would fain have put him to death. But death none can deal to any of the race of the Valar, neither can any, save Eru only, remove them from Eä, the World that is, be they willing or unwilling. Therefore Manwë cast Melkor into prison, and he was shut in the fastness of Mandos, whence none can escape.

§52   And the Valar doomed Melkor there to abide for three ages of Valinor, ere he should come forth again to be tried by his peers, and sue once more for terms of pardon. And this was done, and peace returned to the kingdom of Arda; and this was the Noontide of the Blessed Realm. Yet many evil things yet lingered in Middle-earth that had fled away from the wrath of the Lords of the West, or lay hidden in the deeps of the earth. For the vaults of Utumno were many, and hidden with deceit, and not all were discovered by the Valar.

1101

§53 Now the Valar sat again in council and debated what they should do for the comfort and guidance of the Children of Ilúvatar. And at length, because of the great love that the Valar had for the Quendi, they sent a summons to them, bidding them to remove and dwell in bliss in Aman and in the Light of the Trees. And Oromë bore the message of the Valar to Kuiviénen.

1102

§54 The Quendi were dismayed by the summons of the Valar, and they were unwilling to depart from Middle-earth. Therefore Oromë was sent again to them, and he chose from among them ambassadors who should go to Valinor and speak for their people. And three only of the chieftains of the Quendi were willing to adventure the journey: Ingwë, Finwë, and Elwë, who afterward were kings.

§55 The three Elf-lords were brought, therefore, to Valmar, and there spoke with Manwë and the Valar; and they were filled with awe, but the beauty and splendour of the land of Valinor overcame their fear, and they desired the Light of the Trees.

1104

§56 And after they had dwelt in Valinor a while, Oromë brought them back to Kuiviénen, and they spoke before their people and counselled them to heed the summons of the Valar and remove into the West.

1105

§57 Then befell the first sundering of the Elvenfolk. For the kindred of Ingwë, and the most part of the kindreds of Finwë and Olwë, were swayed by the words of their lords, and were willing to depart and follow Oromë. And these were known ever after as the Eldar, by the name that Oromë gave to them in their own tongue. But the kindreds of Morwë and Nurwë were unwilling and refused the summons, preferring the starlight and the wide spaces of the Earth to the rumour of the Trees. Now these dwelt furthest from the waters of Kuiviénen, and wandered in the hills, and they had not seen Oromë at his first coming, and of the Valar they knew no more than shapes and rumours of wrath and power as they marched to war. And mayhap the lies of Melkor concerning Oromë and Nahar (that above were recalled) lived still among them, so that they feared him as a demon that would devour them.[1] These are the Avari, the Unwilling, and they were sundered in that time from the Eldar, and met never again until many ages were past.

§58 The Eldar now prepared for their Great March, and they went in three hosts. First came the Vanyar, the most eager for the road, the people of Ingwë. Next came the Noldor, a greater host (though some remained behind), the people of Finwë. Last came the Teleri, and they were the least eager. Yet their host that began the March was greatest of all, and they had therefore two lords: Elwë Singollo, and Olwë his brother. And when all was made ready Oromë rode before them upon Nahar, white in the starlight. And they began their long journey and passed by the Sea of Helkar ere they bent somewhat westward.[2] And it is said that before them great clouds hung still black in the North above the ruins of war, and the stars in that region were hidden. Then not a few grew afraid and repented and turned back and are forgotten.

1115

§59 Long and slow was the March of the Eldar into the West, for the leagues of Middle-earth were uncounted, and weary and pathless. Nor did the Eldar desire to hasten, for they were filled with wonder at all that they saw, and by many lands and rivers they would fain abide; and though all were yet willing to wander, not a few rather feared their journey's end than hoped for it. Therefore, whenever Oromë departed, as at times he would, having other matters to heed, they halted and went forward no more until he returned to guide them.

§60 And it came to pass that after ten Years of journeying in this manner (which is to say in such a time as we now should reckon well nigh a century of our years) the Eldar passed through a forest, and came to a great river, wider and broader than any that they yet had seen, and beyond it were mountains whose sharp horns seemed to pierce the realm of the stars.[3]

§61 This river, it is said, was even that river that was after called Anduin the Great, and was ever the frontier of the Westlands of Middle-earth. But the mountains were the Hithaeglir, the Towers of Mist upon the borders of Eriador; yet they were taller and more terrible in those days, and they were reared by Melkor to hinder the riding of Oromë.[4] Now the Teleri abode long on the east-bank of the River and wished to remain there, but the Vanyar and the Noldor passed the River with the aid of Oromë, and he led them to the passes of the mountains.[5] And when Oromë was gone forward the Teleri looked upon the shadowy heights and were afraid.

§62 Then one arose in the host of Olwë, which was ever hindmost on the march, and his name was Nano (or Dân in the tongue of his own people). And he forsook the westward march, and led away a numerous folk, and they went south down the River, and passed out of the knowledge of the Eldar until long years were over. These were the Nandor.

1125

§63 And when again ten years had passed, the Vanyar and Noldor came at length over the mountains that stood between Eriador and the westernmost land of Middle-earth, that the Elves after named Beleriand. And the foremost companies passed over the Vale of Sirion and came to the shores of the Great Sea. Then great fear came upon them, and many repented sorely of their journey and withdrew into the woods of Beleriand. And Oromë returned to Valinor to seek the counsel of Manwë.

1128

§64 Now the host of the Teleri came at last to Beleriand and dwelt in the eastward region beyond the River Gelion. And they came unwillingly, being urged by Elwë their king; for he was eager indeed to return to Valinor and the light that he had beheld (though his doom forbade it); and he wished not to be sundered from the Noldor, for he had great friendship with Finwë their lord.

1130

§65 At this time Elwë strayed in the woods of Beleriand and was lost, and his people sought him long in vain. For as he journeyed homeward from a meeting with Finwë, he passed by the borders of Nan Elmoth. There he heard the nightingales singing, and he was spell-bound, for they were the birds of

Melian the Maia, who came from the gardens of Lorien in the Blessed Realm. And Elwë followed the birds deep into Nan Elmoth, and there he saw Melian standing in a glade open to heaven, and a starlit mist was about her. Thus began the love of Elwë Greymantle and Melian the fair; and he took her hand, and it is said that thus they stood while the stars measured out the courses of many Years, and the trees of Nan Elmoth grew tall and dark about them.

1132

§66 Now Ulmo, by the counsel of the Valar, came to the shores of Middle-earth and spoke with the Eldar; and because of his words and the music which he made for them upon his conches their fear of the Sea was turned rather to desire. Therefore Ulmo and his servants took an island which long had stood alone amidst the Sea, since the tumults of the fall of Illuin, and they moved it, and brought it to the grey bay of Balar, as it were a mighty ship. And the Vanyar and the Noldor embarked upon the isle, Eressëa, and were drawn over the Sea, and came at last to the land of Aman.[6] But the Teleri remained still in Middle-earth; for many dwelt in East Beleriand and heard not the summons of Ulmo until too late; and many searched yet for Elwë Singollo, their king, and would not depart without him. But when the Teleri learned that Ingwë and Finwë and their peoples were gone, they pressed on to the shore, and there dwelt in longing for their friends that had departed. And they took Olwë, Elwë's brother, to be their king. And Ossë and Uinen came to them and befriended them and taught them all manner of sea-lore and sea-music. Thus it came to be that the Teleri, who were from the beginning lovers of water, and the fairest singers of the Elvenfolk, were after enamoured of the seas, and their songs were filled with the sound of the waves upon the shore.

1133

§67 In this Year the Vanyar and the Noldor came to Aman, and the cleft of the Kalakiryan[7] was made in the Pelóri; and the Elves took possession of Eldamar, and began the building of the green hill of Túna in sight of the Sea. And upon Túna they raised the white walls of the Watchful City, Tirion the Hallowed.

1140

§68 In this year Tirion was full-wrought, and the Tower of

Ingwë was built, Mindon Eldaliéva, and its silver lamp was kindled. But Ingwë and many of the Vanyar yearned for the Light of the Trees, and he and many of his household departed and went to Valinor, and dwell forever with the people of Manwë. And though others of the Vanyar dwelt still in Tirion in fellowship with the Noldor, the sundering of those kindreds and of their tongue was begun; for ever and anon yet more of the Vanyar would depart.

1142

§69 In this year Yavanna gave to the Noldor the White Tree, Galathilion, image of the Tree Telperion, and it was planted beneath the Mindon and grew and flourished.

1149

§70 In this year Ulmo hearkened to the prayers of Finwë and went again to Middle-earth to bring Elwë and his people to Aman, if they would come. And most of them proved now willing indeed; but Ossë was grieved. For his care was for the seas of Middle-earth and the shores of the Outer Lands, and he came seldom to Aman, unless summoned to council; and he was ill-pleased that the fair voices of the Teleri should be heard no more in Middle-earth. Some therefore he persuaded to remain, and those were the Eldar that long abode on the coasts of Beleriand, the first mariners upon earth and the first makers of ships. Their havens were at Brithombar and Eglarest. Cirdan the Shipwright was their lord.

1150

§71 The kinsfolk and friends of Elwë also were unwilling to depart; but Olwë would be gone, and at last Ulmo took all who would embark upon Eressëa and drew them over the deeps of the Sea. And the friends of Elwë were left behind, and they called themselves, therefore, in their own tongue the Eglath, the Forsaken People. And they sought still for Elwë in sorrow. But it was not his doom ever to return to the Light of the Trees, greatly though he had desired it. Yet the Light of Aman was in the face of Melian the fair, and in that light he was content.

1151

§72 Now Ossë followed after the Teleri, and when they were come nigh to the Bay of Eldamar he called to them, and they knew his voice, and they begged Ulmo to stay their voyage.

And Ulmo granted this, and at his bidding Ossë made fast the island and rooted it in the foundations of the Sea; and there the Teleri abode as they wished still under the stars of heaven, and yet within sight of Aman and the deathless shore; and they could see from afar the Light of the Trees as it passed through the Kalakiryan, and touched the dark waves to silver and gold.

§73 Ulmo did this the more readily, for that he understood the hearts of the Teleri, and in the council of the Valar he had chiefly spoken against the summons, deeming that it were better for the Quendi to remain in Middle-earth. But the Valar were little pleased to learn what he had done; and Finwë grieved when the Teleri came not, and yet more when he learned that Elwë was forsaken, and knew that he should not see him again, unless it were in the halls of Mandos.

1152

§74 At this time Elwë Singollo, it is said, awoke from his trance, and he dwelt with Melian in the woods of Beleriand. But he was a great lord and noble, tallest in stature of all the Children of Ilúvatar, and like unto a lord of the Maiar; and a high doom was before him. For he became a king renowned, and his folk were all the Eldar of Beleriand; the Sindar they were named, the Grey-elves, the Elves of the Twilight, and King Greymantle was he, Elu Thingol in the tongue of the Sindar. And Melian was his Queen, wiser than any child of Middle-earth; and of the love of Thingol and Melian there came into the world the fairest of all the Children of Ilúvatar that was or ever shall be.

1161

§75 It came to pass that after the Teleri had dwelt for one hundred years of our reckoning upon the Lonely Isle their hearts were changed, and they were drawn towards the Light that flowed out from Aman. Therefore Ossë[8] taught them the craft of shipbuilding, and when their ships were made ready he brought them, as his parting gift, many strong-winged swans. And the swans drew the white ships of the Teleri over the windless sea. Thus at last and latest they came to Aman and the shores of Eldamar; and there the Noldor welcomed them with joy.

1162

§76 In this year Olwë lord of the Teleri, with the aid of

Finwë and the Noldor, began the building of Alqualondë, the Swanhaven, upon the coast of Eldamar, north of the Kalakiryan.

1165

§77 In this year the last of the Vanyar departed from Tirion, and the Noldor dwelt there alone, and their converse and friendship thereafter was rather with the Teleri.

NOTES

1 This sentence is an interpolation in the manuscript, and is itself rewritten from an earlier interpolation:
    And this, maybe, was also one of the first-fruits of the lies of Melkor for the deceit of the Quendi, that despite his sojourn among them many still feared him and Nahar his steed.
The typescript has the form given in the text.
2 This is an emendation from 'went north until Helkar was passed and then north-west'; the typescript has the emended sentence.
3 My father added hastily here, using a ball-point pen and so apparently much later (see p. 102, §78):
    Here they dwelt for a year, and here Indis wife of Finwë bore him a son, eldest of all the second generation of the Eldar. He was first named Minyon First-begotten, but afterwards Curufinwë or Fëanor.
This was struck out, perhaps as soon as written; see note 5.
4 'and they were reared by Melkor to hinder the riding of Oromë' is a pencilled addition that appears in the typescript as typed.
5 Added to the manuscript here at the same time and in the same way as the passage given in note 3 (and struck out at the same time as that):
    Here Indis wife of Finwë was lost, and fell from a great height. And her body was found in a deep gorge, and there buried. And when Finwë would not go forward, and wished to remain there, Oromë spoke to him of the fate of the Quendi, and how they could return again, if they would, after a while. For their spirits do not die, and yet do not leave Arda, and by the command of Eru a dwelling place is made for them in Aman. Then Finwë was eager to go forward.
6 After this there stood in the manuscript: 'and Ingwë and his household passed into Valinor, and dwell forever with the people of Manwë.' This was struck out and is not in the typescript, but it reappears in the annal for 1140.
7 *Kalakiryan* is a pencilled emendation from *Kalakirya*, and at subsequent occurrences (but at the very end of the *Annals*, p. 133, §180, *Kalakiryan* is the form in the manuscript as written).

8   *Ulmo* in the manuscript as first written, changed early to *Ossë*.

Commentary on the third section of the
Annals of Aman

This section of AAm corresponds to QS Chapter 3 *Of the Coming of the Elves* (including 3(b) *Of Thingol* and 3(c) *Of Kôr and Alqualondë*) from §22 to §39 and elements of §§43–5; and to AV 2, Valian Years 1980–2111. These texts are found in V.213 ff., 112–13.

A cursory comparison shows that an enormous extension at large and in detail has taken place; and while concurrent development had proceeded in the 'Silmarillion' tradition also (with which AAm has not a few phrases in common), AAm is a very distinct narrative, with a large number of features absent from the other tradition and some actual divergences. Here, as before, I observe the more important developments in AAm in relation to the pre-*Lord of the Rings* narratives; and in many cases I restrict myself to a simple reference to the new elements that have entered the legends, it being implied in such cases that the matter in question is wholly new.

§51   Melkor sued for pardon in the Ring of Doom; the Valar wished to put him to death, but none can slay any of Valarin race, nor remove them from Eä, save Eru only.

§52   Melkor was condemned to Mandos for three ages (three hundred Valian Years); in AV 2, and in QS (§47), he was condemned for seven ages.

§54   Elwë, the third of the 'ambassadors', is now Thingol himself, whereas in QS he was Thingol's brother; see V.217 §23, and cf. AV 2 (V.112): 'Thingol, brother of Elwë, lord of the Teleri'. The brother of Elwë-Thingol now becomes Olwë (§58).

§57   Only 'the most part' of the kindreds of Finwë and Olwë were willing to depart. The *Avari* were the kindreds of Morwë and Nurwë (and presumably those of the other kindreds who would not go); and an explanation is given of their not going: they dwelt furthest from Kuiviénen and had not seen Oromë at his first coming.

§58   The First Host now bears the name *Vanyar*, not as previously *Lindar* (cf. p. 34, §36). The Third Host, the Teleri, had two lords, the brothers Elwë and Olwë; and Elwë is now called *Singollo* ('Greymantle', §65; in QS *Sindo* 'the Grey', §30). – The route taken by the Eldar on the Great March is described (and it agrees well with the track shown on the *Ambarkanta* map, IV.249). Many turned back in fear at the great clouds still hanging in the North.

§59   The slowness of the journey is described: the wonder of the Elves, the reluctance of many to complete the journey, the long halts. The journey took twenty Valian Years; in AV 1 it took ten (IV.272), and apparently also in AV 2.

§§ 60–1 Important names enter from *The Lord of the Rings*: *Anduin*, *Eriador*, *Hithaeglir* ('the Towers of Mist'); the forest east of the river is not named, but is of course Mirkwood. The origin of the Hithaeglir is told: they were raised by Melkor to hinder the riding of Oromë. I noticed (IV.256–7) in connection with the *Ambarkanta* map that there is no trace there of the Misty Mountains or of Anduin (which first appeared, as did Mirkwood, in *The Hobbit*, where the river is called the Great River of Wilderland).

The Teleri remained on the eastern bank of Anduin when the Vanyar and the Noldor crossed the river and went up into the passes of the Misty Mountains.

§ 62 It was at this point on the Great March that the Nandor broke off, and they went south down Anduin; they were of the Teleri (from the host of Olwë), and their leader's name was *Nano*, or *Dân* in the speech of his own people. In QS (§ 28) and AV 2 these people were of the Noldor, and in QS they were called in their own tongue *Danas*, after their first leader Dân; similarly in the *Lhammas* (V.175–6). The name *Nandor* does not appear in these works, but see the *Etymologies*, stems DAN and NDAN (V.353, 375), and also V.188.

§ 63 The fear of the Sea among the Vanyar and Noldor caused many to withdraw from the shores into the woods of Beleriand; and Oromë returned to Valinor to seek Manwë's counsel.

§ 64 The Teleri came reluctantly into Beleriand, urged on by Elwë, and dwelt at first in the east, beyond the River Gelion. Elwë had great friendship with Finwë.

§ 65 Elwë was journeying home from a meeting with Finwë when he entered Nan Elmoth. This name first emerged in the post-*Lord of the Rings* rewriting of the *Lay of Leithian* (III.346–7, 349). In QS (§ 32) it is not said where the meeting of Thingol and Melian took place; in AV 2 'Melian enchanted him in the woods of Beleriand'. The trance into which Elwë fell endured for many Valian Years (annals 1130, 1152: that is for more than two centuries measured by the Sun).

§ 66 Ulmo made music for the Elves and turned their fear of the Sea into desire. The Teleri came to the shores of the Sea when they heard that the Vanyar and the Noldor had departed, and took Olwë to be their king.

§ 67 The name *Kalakilya* 'Pass of Light' is found in QS and the *Lhammas*; cf. Quenya *kilya* 'cleft, pass between hills, gorge', in the *Etymologies*, stem KIL (V.365). The form in AAm, *Kalakiryan*, replaced earlier *Kalakirya* (note 7 above).

'The Elves took possession of Eldamar, and began the building of the green hill of Túna'; cf. also §§75–6 'the shores, coast, of Eldamar'. This contradicts the footnote to QS §39 (never subsequently changed, p. 176), where *Eldamar* is a name of the Elvish city itself and *Eldanor* or *Elendë* the region where the Elves dwelt (earlier, on the *Ambarkanta* map (IV.249), Elvenhome was named *Eldaros*). The usage here (found also in the rewritten *Lay of Leithian*) is in fact a reversion to the earliest meaning of *Eldamar*; see I.251.

The city is now Tirion upon Túna, not Túna upon Kôr; see QS §39 and commentary, and also I.258 (*Kortirion*). But my father continued to use *Túna* also as the name of the city: e.g. p. 97, §101, where Melkor speaks of Fëanor's words 'in Túna'. Tirion is called here *Tirion the Hallowed*, as it was in Bilbo's song at Rivendell (VII.93, 98, 101).

§68 The Tower of Ingwë (*Ingwemindon* in QS) is now *Mindon Eldaliéva*. – In AAm Ingwë and 'many of his household' removed from Tirion only seven Valian Years after the coming of the Vanyar and the Noldor to Aman, and in the year of the completion of Tirion and the kindling of Ingwë's lamp; and the departure of the rest of the Vanyar is represented as a long drawn out movement over 25 Valian Years (see §77). In QS (§45) a different impression is given, for it is said that '*As the ages passed* the Lindar grew to love the land of the Gods and the full light of the Trees, and they forsook the city of Túna'.

§69 In QS (§16) *Galathilion* is the Gnomish name of Silpion (Telperion), and there is no mention of an 'image' of the Elder Tree being given by Yavanna to the Noldor of Tirion (see IX.58).

§70 Ulmo's return to the shores of Middle-earth was on account of the prayers of Finwë. The statement that Ossë 'came seldom to Aman, unless summoned to council' reflects the preservation in AAm (p. 48, §1) of his old status as one of the Valar. The southern Haven of the Falas now reverts to the form *Eglarest*, which preceded *Eglorest* of QS and AV 2. Cirdan the Shipwright, lord of the Havens, appears from *The Lord of the Rings*.

§71 While it is not said in QS that any others of the Teleri, beside the Elves of the Falas, remained in Middle-earth when Ulmo returned, but only that the people of Thingol 'looked for him in vain' (§32), it is told in the *Lhammas* §6 (V.174) that Thingol was 'king in Beleriand of the many Teleri who ... remained on the Falassë, and of others that went not because they tarried searching for Thingol in the woods.' In AAm 'the kinsfolk and friends of Elwë also were unwilling to depart', and they were left behind, and called themselves *Eglath*, the Forsaken People.

§§72–3 Ulmo granted readily the request of the Teleri, for he had opposed the summoning of the Quendi to Valinor, and Ossë rooted Tol Eressëa to the sea-bottom at Ulmo's command; but the Valar were displeased, and Finwë was grieved (most of all for the knowledge that Elwë Singollo his friend was not in Tol Eressëa). The final form of the legend is thus now present: see QS §37 and commentary.

§74 Thingol's people were 'all the Eldar of Beleriand', and they were named the *Sindar*, the Grey-elves. This is the first time that we meet the name in the texts (as here presented); it does not occur in *The Lord of the Rings* apart from the Appendices. The Sindarin name of Elwë Singollo is *Elu Thingol* (see II.50).

§75 The Teleri dwelt for 100 years of the Sun in Tol Eressëa; in QS (§43) and in AV 2 they dwelt there for 100 Valian Years (see p. 183, §43).

It was Ossë, not as in QS Ulmo, who taught the Teleri the craft of shipbuilding; but as the text was written (note 8 above) it was Ulmo who did so, and it was Ulmo too who gave them the swans (Ossë in QS).

§76 The Teleri had the aid of Finwë and the Noldor in the building of Alqualondë.

The two passages concerning Indis wife of Finwë, roughly written in against §§60 and 61 (notes 3 and 5 above) and then struck out, are notable as the first indications of what would become a major further development in the Valinorian legend, though the stories told here bear no relation to the later narrative. These briefly sketched ideas may have been merely passing, rejected as soon as jotted down; but they show my father's concern with Fëanor, feeling that the greatness of his powers and formidable nature were related to a singularity of origin – he was *the first-born of the Eldar*: that is to say, he did not 'waken' by Kuiviénen, but had a father and mother, and was born in Middle-earth. The idea that Finwë was bereaved also appears; and this is the first appearance of Fëanor's name *Curufinwë*.

★

Finally, I record a few very late notes on one or other of the typescript texts (top copy and carbon) of the *Annals of Aman*:
§65 'the trees of Nan Elmoth' > 'the sapling trees of Nan Elmoth'
§66 Against the word 'conches': 'pipes of shell horns', with a query.
§70 Against the first sentence my father wrote 'Needs revising'; but I do not know in what respect he intended to do so. Against 'summoned to council' he wrote an X and 'he [Ossë] was not a Vala, but a chief of the Maiar, servant of Ulmo.' He had been removed from the Valar by emendation to the typescript in §1 (p. 69).

Fourth section of the Annals of Aman

[This section of the *Annals* has a good many changes made at the time of writing, and also various alterations and additions – some substantial – that seem certainly to belong to much the same time. These are incorporated into the text given here, with details of the more important alterations recorded in the notes that follow it. A few short additions that are decidedly later are placed in the notes.]

1179

§78 Fëanor, eldest son of Finwë, was born in Tirion upon Túna. His mother was Byrde Míriel.[1]

§79 Now the Noldor[2] took delight in all lore and all crafts, and Aulë and his folk came often among them. Yet such skill had Ilúvatar granted to them that in many matters, especially such as needed adroitness and fineness of handiwork, they soon surpassed their teachers. It is said that about this time the masons of the House of Finwë quarrying in the mountains for stone for their building (for they delighted in the building of high towers) first discovered the earth-gems, in which the Land of Aman was indeed surpassingly rich. And their craftsmen devised tools for the cutting and shaping of the gems, and carved them in many forms of bright beauty; and they hoarded them not but gave them freely to all who desired them, and all Valinor was enriched by their labour.[3]

§80 In this year Rúmil, most renowned of the masters of the lore of speech, first devised letters and began recording in writing the tongues of the Eldar and their songs and wisdom.[4]

1190

§81 In this year was born Fingolfin son of Finwë, who after was King of the Exiles.

1230

§82 Finrod Finwë's son was born.

1250

§83 In this time began the flowering of the skill of Fëanor son of Finwë, who was of all the Noldor the greatest maker and craftsman. And he took thought and devised new letters, bettering the devices of Rúmil, and those letters the Eldar have used ever since that day. This was but the beginning of the works of Fëanor. Greatly he loved gems, and he began to study how by the skill of his hand and mind he could make others greater and brighter than those hidden in the earth.[5]

§84 [In this time also, it is said among the Sindar, the Naugrim[6] whom we also name the Nornwaith (the Dwarves) came over the mountains into Beleriand and became known to the Elves. Now the Dwarves were great smiths and masons, being indeed (it is believed) brought into being by Aulë; yet of old small beauty was in their works. Therefore each people had great profit of the other, though their friendship was ever cool. But at that time no griefs lay between them, and King Thingol welcomed them; and the Longbeards of Belegost aided him in the delving and building of the great halls of Menegroth, where he after dwelt with Melian, his Queen. Thus saith Pengoloð.][7]

1280

§85 In this year Finrod Finwë's son wedded Ëarwen King Olwë's daughter of Alqualondë, and there was a great feast in the land of the Teleri. Thus the children of Finrod, Inglor and Galadriel, were the kin of King Thingol Greymantle in Beleriand.

1350

§86 [At this time a part of the lost Elves of the people of Dân after long wanderings came up into Beleriand from the South. Their leader was Denethor son of Dân, and he brought them to Ossiriand where seven rivers flow down from the Mountains of Lindon. These are the Green-elves. They had the friendship of Thingol. Quoth Pengoloð.][8]

1400

§87 Now it came to pass that Melkor had dwelt alone in the duress of Mandos for the three ages that were doomed by the Valar, and he came before their conclave to be tried. And Melkor sued for pardon at the feet of Manwë, and humbled himself, and swore to abide his rule, and to aid the Valar in all ways that he could, for the good of Arda, and the profit of Valar and of Eldar, if so he should be granted freedom, and a place as the least of all the folk of Valinor.

§88 And Nienna aided his prayer (because of her kinship), and Manwë granted it, for being himself free of all evil he saw not the depths of the heart of Melkor, and believed in his oaths. But Mandos was silent, and Ulmo's heart misgave him.

1410

§89 Then Melkor dwelt for a while in a humble house in Valmar under vigilance, and was not yet suffered to walk abroad alone. But since in that time all his words and works were fair, and he became in outward form and seeming even as the Valar his brethren, Manwë gave him his freedom within Valinor. Yet Tulkas' mirth was clouded whenever he saw Melkor pass by, and the nails of his fingers bit into the palms of his hands, for the restraint that he put upon himself.

§90 And indeed Melkor was false and betrayed the clemency of Manwë, and used his freedom to spread lies abroad and poison the peace of Valinor. Thus a shadow fell upon the Blessed Land and its golden Noon passed; yet it was long ere the lies of Melkor bore fruit, and still the Valar dwelt long in bliss.

§91 Now in his heart Melkor most hated the Eldar, both because they were fair and joyful and because in them he saw the reason for the arising of the Valar and his own downfall and subjection. Therefore all the more did he feign love for them, and sought their friendship, and offered them the service of his lore and labour in any great deed that they would do. And many of the Noldor, because of their desire of all knowledge, hearkened to him and took delight in his teaching. But the Vanyar would have no part with him.

1449

§92 In this Year Fëanor began that labour of his which is renowned above all the works of the Eldalië; for his heart conceived the Silmarils, and he made much study and many essays ere their fashioning could begin. And though Melkor said after that Fëanor had his instruction in that work, he lied in his lust and his envy; for Fëanor was driven by the fire of his own heart only, and was eager and proud, working ever swiftly and alone, asking no aid and brooking no counsel.

1450

The Silmarilli of Fëanor are made

§93 In this year the Silmarils were full-wrought, the wonder of Arda. As three great jewels they were in form. But not until the End, when Fëanor shall return who perished when the Sun was young and sitteth now in the Halls of Awaiting and comes no more amongst his kin; not until Sun passeth and the Moon falls shall it be known of what substance they were made. Like the crystal of diamonds it appeared and yet was more strong than adamant, so that no violence within the walls of this world could mar it or break it. Yet that crystal was to the Silmarils but as is the body to the Children of Ilúvatar: the house of its inner fire, that is within it and yet in all parts of it, and is its life. And the inner fire of the Silmarils Fëanor made of the blended Light of the Trees of Valinor which lives in them yet, though the Trees have long withered and shine no more. Therefore even in the uttermost darkness the Silmarils of their own radiance shone like the stars of Varda; and yet, as were they indeed living things, they rejoiced in light and received it, and gave it back in hues more lovely than before.

§94 And all the folk of Valinor were amazed at the handiwork of Fëanor, and were filled with wonder and delight, and Varda hallowed the Silmarils, so that thereafter no mortal flesh nor any evil or unclean thing might touch them, but it was scorched and burned with unendurable pain. And Melkor lusted for the Silmarils and the very memory of their radiance was like a gnawing fire in his heart.[9]

1450–1490

§95 Therefore, though he still dissembled his purposes with great cunning, Melkor sought now ever more eagerly how he should destroy Fëanor, and end the friendship of Valar and Eldar. Long was he at work; and slow at first and barren was his labour. But he that sows lies in the end shall not lack of a harvest, and soon he may rest from toil indeed, while others reap and sow in his stead. Ever Melkor found some ears that would heed him, and some tongues that would enlarge what they had heard. For the lies of Melkor take root by the truth that is in them.

§96 Thus it was that whispers arose in Eldamar that the Valar had brought the Eldar to Valinor being jealous of their beauty and skill, and fearing that they should grow too strong to be governed in the free lands of the East. And then Melkor foretold the coming of Men, of which the Valar had not yet spoken to the Elves, and again it was whispered abroad that the gods purposed to reserve the kingdoms of Middle-earth for the younger and weaker race whom they might more easily sway, defrauding the Elves of the inheritance of Ilúvatar.

§97 Then at last the princes of the Noldor began to murmur

against the Valar, and many became filled with pride, forgetting all that the Valar had taught to them and given to them. And in that time (having now awakened anger and pride) Melkor spoke to the Eldar concerning weapons, which they had not before possessed or known; for the armouries of the Valar after the chaining of Melkor were shut. But now the Noldor began the smithying of swords and axes and spears; and shields they made displaying the tokens of many houses and kindreds that vied one with another.

§98 A great smith was Fëanor in those days, and a proud and masterful prince, jealous of all that he had; and Melkor kept watch on him. For still he lusted after the Silmarils; but Fëanor now brought them seldom to light, and kept them locked rather in the darkness of the treasury of Túna; and he began to begrudge the sight of them to all save to his sire and to his seven sons. Therefore Melkor set new lies abroad that Fingolfin was plotting to supplant Fëanor and his father in the favour of the Valar, and was like to succeed, for the Valar were ill-pleased that the Silmarils were not committed to their keeping. Of those lies quarrels arose among the proud children of Finwë and Melkor was well-pleased; for all now went to his design. And suddenly ere the Valar were aware the peace of Valinor was broken and swords were drawn in Eldamar.

1490

§99 Then the Gods were wroth, and they summoned Fëanor before them. And they laid bare all the lies of Melkor; but because it was Fëanor that had first broken the peace and threatened violence in Aman he was by their judgement banished for twenty[10] years from Tirion. And he went forth and dwelt northward in Valinor near to the halls of Mandos, and built a new treasury and stronghold at Formenos; and great wealth of gems he laid there in hoard, but the Silmarils were shut in a chamber of iron. And thither came Finwë, because of the love that he bore to Fëanor; and Fingolfin ruled the Noldor of Túna. Thus the lies of Melkor were made true in seeming, and the bitterness that he had wrought endured long between the sons of Fingolfin and Fëanor.

§100 Straight from the Ring of Doom Tulkas went in haste to lay hands upon Melkor, but Melkor knowing that his devices were bewrayed[11] had hidden himself from the sight of eyes, and a cloud was about him; and it seemed to the folk of Valinor that the light of the Trees was become dimmer than its wont, and the shadows were darker and longer.

1492

§101 And it is said that Melkor was not seen again for a while; but suddenly he appeared before the doors of the house of Finwë and Fëanor at Formenos, and sought to speak with them. And he said to them: 'Behold the truth of all that I have spoken, and how you are indeed banished unjustly. And think not that the Silmarils lie safe in any treasury within the realm of the gods. But if the heart of Fëanor is yet free and bold as his words were in Túna, then I will aid you, and bring you far from this narrow land. For am I not Vala as are they? Yea, and more than they, and have ever been a friend to the Noldor, most skilled and valiant of all the folk of Arda.'

§102 Then the heart of Fëanor was increased in bitterness and filled with fear for the Silmarils, and in that mood he endured. But Melkor's words touched too deep, and awoke a fire more fierce than he intended; and Fëanor looked upon him with blazing eyes, and lo! he saw through the semblance of Melkor and pierced the cloaks of his mind, perceiving there the lust for the Silmarils. Then hate overcame all fear and he cursed Melkor and bade him begone. 'Get thee from my gate, thou gangrel,[12] jail-crow of Mandos,' said he, and he shut the doors of his house in the face of the mightiest of all the dwellers in Ea.

§103 And at that time, being himself in peril, Melkor departed, consumed with wrath, and bitter vengeance he plotted for his shame. But Finwë was filled with great fear, and in haste he sent messengers to Manwë in Valmar.

§104 Then Oromë and Tulkas set out in pursuit of Melkor, but ere they had ridden far messengers came from Eldamar, telling that Melkor had fled through the Kalakiryan,[13] passing by the hill of Túna in wrath as a thunder cloud. And with the flight of Melkor the shadow was lifted from Valinor, and for a while all the land was fair again. But the gods sought in vain for tidings of their enemy, and doubt lay heavy upon their hearts what new evil he might attempt.

§105 It is told that Melkor came to the dark region of Arvalin. Now that narrow land lay south of the Bay of Eldamar, but east of the mountains of the Pelóri, and its long and mournful shores stretched away into the South of the world, lightless and unexplored. There, between the sheer walls of the mountains and the cold dark Sea, the shadows were deepest in the world. And there secretly Ungoliantë had made her abode. Whence she came none of the Eldar know, but maybe she came to the South out of the darkness of Eä, in that time when Melkor destroyed the lights of Illuin and Ormal, and because of his dwelling in the North the heed of the Valar was turned most thither and the South was long forgotten. Thence she crept towards the realm of the light of the Valar. For she hungered for light and hated it. In a deep cleft of the mountains she dwelt, and took shape as it were a spider of monstrous form, sucking up all such light as she could find, or that strayed over the walls of Valinor, and she spun it forth again in black webs of strangling gloom, until no light more could come to her abode, and she was famished.

§106 It may well be that Melkor, if none other, knew of her being and her abode, and that she was in the beginning one of those that he had corrupted to his service. And coming at length to Arvalin, he sought her out, and demanded her aid in his revenge. But she was loath to dare the perils of Valinor and the great wrath of the gods, and would not stir from her hiding until Melkor had vowed to render her a reward that should heal the gnawing of her hunger and hatred.

1495

§107 At last having well laid their plans Melkor and Ungoliantë set forth. A great darkness was about them that Ungoliantë wove, and black ropes also she span and made fast among the rocks, and so after long labour, from web to web, she climbed at last to the summit of Hyarantar, which is the highest pinnacle of the mountains south of Taniquetil. There indeed (save for that watch-tower of the South) the Pelóri were less lofty, and less was the vigilance of the Valar, for they had ever been on guard rather against the North.

§108 Now Ungoliantë wrought a ladder of ropes and cast it down, and Melkor climbed upon it, and so came to that high place, whence he could look down upon the Guarded Realm. And below lay the wild green-wood of Oromë, and west-away shimmered the fields and pastures of Yavanna, pale gold beneath the tall wheat of the gods. But Melkor looked north, and saw afar the shining plain, and the silver domes of Valmar gleaming in the mingling of the lights of Telperion and Laurelin. Then Melkor laughed aloud, and leapt swiftly down the long western slopes; and Ungoliantë was at his side and her darkness covered them.

§109   Now it was a time of festival, as Melkor well knew. For though all tides and seasons were at the will of the Valar, and there was in Valinor no winter of death, nonetheless the gods dwelt then in the kingdom of Arda, and that was but a small realm in the halls of Ëa, whose life is Time, which flows ever from the first note to the last chord of Eru. And it was then the pleasure of the Valar (as is told in the *Ainulindalë*) to clothe themselves in the forms of the Children of Ilúvatar; and they ate and they drank and gathered the fruits of Yavanna, and drew strength from the Earth which under Eru they had made.

§110   Therefore Yavanna set times for the flowering and the ripening of all growing things: upspringing, blooming, and seed-time. And at each first gathering of fruits Manwë made a high-tide for the praising of Eru, and all the folk of Valinor poured forth their joy in music and song. Such now was the hour; but Manwë, hoping that indeed the shadow of Melkor was removed from the land, and fearing no worse than maybe a new war with Utumno and a new victory to end all, had decreed that this feast should be more glorious than any that had been held since the coming of the Eldar. He designed moreover to heal the evil that had arisen among the Noldor, and they all were bidden, therefore, to come to him and mingle with the Maiar in his halls upon Taniquetil, and there put aside all the griefs that lay between their princes and forget utterly the lies of their Enemy.

§111   There came the Vanyar, and there came the Noldor, and the Maiar were gathered together, and the Valar were arrayed in their beauty and majesty; and they sang before Manwë in his lofty halls, or played upon the green slopes of Taniquetil that looked west to the Trees. In that day the streets of Valmar were empty and the stairs of Túna were silent; only the Teleri beyond the mountains still sang upon the shores of the Sea, for they recked little of seasons or times, and gave no thought to the cares of the Rulers of Arda or to the shadow that had fallen upon Valinor, for it had not touched them, as yet.

§112   One thing only marred the design of Manwë. Fëanor indeed came, for him alone Manwë had commanded to come; but Finwë came not nor any others of the Noldor of Formenos. For said Finwë: 'While the ban lasts upon Fëanor my son, that he may not go to Túna, I hold myself unkinged, and will not meet my people, nor those that rule in my stead.' And Fëanor came not in raiment of festival, and he wore no ornament, neither silver nor gold nor any gem; and he denied the sight of the Silmarils to Eldar and Valar, and left them locked in darkness in their chamber of iron. Nonetheless, he met Fingolfin before the throne of Manwë, and was reconciled in words, and Fingolfin set at nought the unsheathing of the sword.

§113 It is said that even as Fëanor and Fingolfin stood before Manwë, and it was the Mingling of the Lights and both Trees were shining and the silent city of Valmar was filled with radiance as of silver and gold, in that hour Melkor and Ungoliantë came over the plain and stood before the Green Mound. Then Melkor sprang up, and with his black spear he smote each Tree to its core, a little above the roots, and their sap poured forth, as it were their blood, and was spilled upon the ground. But Ungoliantë sucked it up, and going then from Tree to Tree she plied her foul lips to their wounds, till they were drained; and the poison that was in her passed into their tissues and withered them; and they died. And still Ungoliantë thirsted, and going to the Vats of Varda she drank them dry; but Ungoliantë belched forth black vapours as she drank, and swelled to a shape so vast and hideous that even Melkor was adread.

§114 Then Darkness fell upon Valinor. Of the deeds of that day much is said in the *Aldudénië* (the Lament for the Trees) that Elemírë of the Vanyar made and is known to all the Eldar. Yet no song or tale could hold all the grief and terror that then befell. The Light failed; and that was woe enough, but the Darkness that followed was more than loss of light. In that hour was made the Dark which seems not lack but a thing with being of its own: for it was indeed made by malice out of Light, and it had the power to pierce the eye, and to enter heart and mind, and strangle the very will.

§115 Varda looked down from the Holy Mountain, and beheld the Shadow soaring up in sudden towers of gloom; Valmar had foundered in a deep sea of night. Soon Taniquetil stood alone, as a last island of light in a world that was drowned. All song ceased. There was silence in Valinor, and no sound could be heard, save only from afar there came on the wind through the pass of the mountains the wailing of the Teleri like the cold cry of gulls. For it blew chill from the East in that hour, and the vast shadows of the Sea were rolled against the walls of the shore.

§116 But Manwë from his high seat looked out, and his eyes alone pierced through the gloom, and he saw afar off how a Darkness beyond dark moved north over the land, and he knew that Melkor was there. Then the pursuit was begun, and the earth shook beneath the horses of the host of Oromë, and the fire that was stricken from the hooves of Nahar was the first light that returned to Valinor. But so soon as any came up with the Cloud of Ungoliantë, the riders of the Valar were blinded and dismayed, and they were scattered, and went they knew not whither; and the sound of the Valaróma faltered and failed. And Tulkas was as a man caught in a black net at night, and he stood powerless and beat the air in vain. And when the Darkness had passed, it was too late: Melkor had gone whither he would, and his vengeance was full-wrought.

NOTES

1 This annal is an early replacement; the original annal, concerning the marriage of Finrod and Ëarwen Olwë's daughter, reappears in very similar form in the manuscript as originally written under the year 1280. Later, in ball-point pen, my father changed the date of this annal to 1169, and added new annals for 1170, 'Míriel falls asleep and passes to Mandar' (on *Mandar* see p. 205), and 1172 'Doom of Manwë concerning the espousals of the Eldar.' On these matters see pp. 205 ff., and see note 4 below. The new annals appear in the typescript as typed.

2 The name *Noldor* is here written with a tilde, *Ñoldor* (representing the back nasal, the *ng* of *king*; see IV.174). This becomes the normal form in all my father's later writings, though often casually omitted (none of his typewriters possessed this sign); it is not represented in the spelling of the name *Noldor* in this book.

3 The latter part of this passage, concerning gems, is very largely an addition. As first written, all that was said on the subject was:

It is said that about this time the craftsmen of the House of Finwë (of whom Fëanor his eldest son was the most skilful) first devised gems; and all Valinor was enriched by their labour.

See note 5.

4 A new annal was added here at the same time as those given in note 1: '1185 Finwë weds Indis of the Vanyar.'

5 This sentence ('Greatly he loved gems ...') is an addition going

with the change and expansion referred to in note 3.
6 *Naugrim* was written in pencil above the original reading *Nauglath* (which however was not struck out), and the word 'also' (in 'whom we also name') added at the same time.
7 This Beleriandic interpolation by Pengoloð, bracketed in the original, was an addition to the manuscript; cf. note 8. Against it my father later pencilled: 'Transfer to A[nnals of] B[eleriand]'.
8 This bracketed interpolation by Pengoloð was an addition to the manuscript; and like that referred to in note 7 it was marked later for transfer to the *Annals of Beleriand*. The name of the leader of the Nandor was first written *Enadar*, changed immediately to *Denethor* (the name in AV 2, QS, and the *Lhammas*).
   Later my father added here in pencil a new annal, for 1362: 'Here was born Isfin Fingolfin's daughter, the White Lady of the Noldor' (see note 9).
9 A hasty addition in ink, subsequently struck out, gives an annal for 1469: 'Here was born the first daughter of Fingolfin, the White Lady of the Noldor' (see note 8). It is not said elsewhere that Fingolfin had any daughter but Isfin.
10 The manuscript has 'three' > 'ten' > 'twenty' (Valian Years).
11 *bewrayed*: 'revealed', 'betrayed'.
12 *gangrel* ('vagabond') replaced *beggarman* (see p. 191).
13 My father first wrote *Kalakilya*, the old form, but changed it at once to *Kalakirya*; *-n* was added later (see p. 89, §67).

Commentary on the fourth section of the
Annals of Aman

This section of the *Annals* corresponds in content to QS Chapter 4 *Of the Silmarils and the Darkening of Valinor* (V.227–31), and to AV 2 annals 2500 to the beginning of 2990 (V.113–14). The account in AAm bears no comparison with the cursory AV 2, and represents a wholly different impulse; indeed, in this section we see the annal form disappearing as a fully-fledged narrative emerges. As was often the case in my father's work, the story took over and expanded whatever restrictions of form he had set for it. The new narrative is double the length of that in QS, to which it is closely related in structure. In expression it is almost entirely new; and yet comparison between them will show that AAm tends rather to a greater definition of the narrative than to significant change in the structure or marked new additions – though both are present. The following comments are in no way intended as an analysis of all the differences of emphasis, suggestion, and detail between AAm and QS.

§78 Earlier in AAm, under the year 1115, appear rejected insertions (see p. 87, notes 3 and 5) in which are recorded the birth of Fëanor to Finwë's wife Indis in Middle-earth in the course of the

Great Journey, and her subsequent death in a fall in the Misty Mountains. Written in ball-point pen these insertions would appear to be relatively late; here on the other hand, in what seems to be an early addition (written carefully in ink, and see note 1 above), Fëanor was born in Tirion, and his mother was Míriel, called Byrde Míriel (Old English *byrde*, 'broideress'; see pp. 185, 192). In late insertions (notes 1 and 4 above) it is recorded that in 1170 Míriel 'fell asleep' and passed to Mandos, and in 1185 Finwë married Indis of the Vanyar.

§79 At an earlier point in QS (§40) it is said that the Noldor 'contrived the fashioning of gems'; similarly in AV 2 (V.113) they 'invented gems', and again in *Ainulindalë* B (V.162). This idea is found in all the earlier texts, going back to the elaborate account in the old tale of *The Coming of the Elves* (see I.58, 127). In the later period it survived in the final version D of the *Ainulindalë* (§35, see pp. 19 and 34), and was still present at first in AAm (see note 3 above). The rewriting of this passage rejects the idea of 'invention': the gems of the Noldor were mined in Aman.

§80 The association of the Noldor with alphabetic script goes back to the *Lost Tales*, where this art is ascribed primarily to Aulë (I.58); 'in those days Aulë aided by the Gnomes contrived alphabets and scripts' (I.141). In *Ainulindalë* B (V.162) the Noldor 'added much to [Aulë's] teaching and delighted much in tongues and alphabets', and this survived in the later versions. Now Rúmil and (in §83) Fëanor emerge as the great inventors. Cf. *The Lord of the Rings*, Appendix E (II):

> The Tengwar ... had been developed by the Noldor, the kindred of the Eldar most skilled in such matters, long before their exile. The oldest Eldarin letters, the Tengwar of Rúmil, were not used in Middle-earth. The later letters, the Tengwar of Fëanor, were largely a new invention, though they owed something to the letters of Rúmil.

If Rúmil were the author of the *Annals of Aman*, as is said in the preamble (p. 48), he is here describing himself in the words 'most renowned of the masters of the lore of speech'.

§82 *Finrod*: earlier name of Finarfin (Finarphin).

§84 The form *Nauglath* (see note 6, p. 102) is, curiously, a reversion to the original Gnomish name of the Dwarves in the *Lost Tales* (see I.261), although *Naugrim* occurs as an original form in QS at a later point in the narrative (§122). [The entry *Naugrim* was inadvertently dropped from the index to Vol. V. The references are 273, 277, 405.] – On the name *Sindar* see p. 91, §74.

On earlier references to the Dwarves in Beleriand see IV.336; as I noted there, the statement in the second version of the earliest *Annals of Beleriand* (IV.332) that the Dwarves had 'of old' a road into Beleriand is the first sign of the later idea that the Dwarves had been active in Beleriand long before the Return of the Noldor. But the present passage is the first reference to the Dwarves' aiding of Thingol in the delving and building of Menegroth. – The legend of Aulë's making of the Dwarves is referred to in the texts of the earlier period: AB 2 (V.129), the *Lhammas* (V.178 and commentary), and QS (§123 and commentary).

§85 Here appears the important development whereby the princes of the Third House of the Noldor became close kin to Thingol of Doriath (Elwë Singollo, brother of Olwë of Alqualondë, §58); and Galadriel enters from *The Lord of the Rings*. Cf. Appendix F (I, *Of the Elves*): 'The Lady Galadriel of the royal house of Finrod, father of Felagund, Lord of Nargothrond' (a statement that was changed in the Second Edition of *The Lord of the Rings*, when Finrod had become Finarphin and Inglor had become Finrod (Felagund)).

§86 In AV 2 (V.112, also in an interpolation by Pengolod) and in QS (§115) the Elves under Denethor did not come into Beleriand 'from the South', but came over the Blue Mountains; the meaning here is probably that they crossed the mountains in a region to the south of Ossiriand. There were not seven rivers flowing down from the mountains, but six: the seventh river of Ossiriand was the great river Gelion, into which the six flowed.

§88 *because of her kinship*: in AAm §3 (as in AV 2 and in QS §9) Nienna was 'Manwë's sister and Melko(r)'s'. In AAm* (p. 65) she is named only Manwë's sister.

§92 In AV 2 two ages passed (V.Y.2500–2700) between the making of the Silmarils and the release of Melkor; similarly in QS (§§46–7). In AAm the relation of the two is reversed, with the release of Melkor placed under Year of the Trees 1400 and the final achievement of the Silmarils under 1450.

§93 With what is said here concerning the fate of Fëanor cf. QS §88: 'so fiery was his spirit that his body fell to ash as his spirit sped; and it has never again appeared upon earth nor left the realm of Mandos.'

§97 On the Elves' ignorance of weapons see p. 106, §97.

§98 No mention is made in QS (§52) of the dissensions reaching the point of drawn swords. In AAm §112 'Fingolfin set at nought the unsheathing of the sword'; and in the margin of the typescript text at this point my father wrote: 'refers to what?' A later expansion of the chapter in QS, close in time to the writing of AAm, tells that Fëanor menaced Fingolfin with drawn sword (p. 189, §52); and in view of §112 it seems probable that this was inadvertently omitted here.

§99 The term of Fëanor's banishment (see note 10 above) is not stated in the older texts. – The name *Formenos* now enters, in an addition to the text.

§102 *the mightiest of all the dwellers in Ëa*: see p. 65, §2.

§105 The time of Ungoliantë's coming to Arda is placed (as a surmise) with the entry of Melkor and his host before the overthrow of the Lamps (see p. 53, §19). With 'maybe she came to the South out of the darkness of Ëa' cf. QS §55: 'from the Outer Darkness, maybe, that lies beyond the Walls of the World'.

§106 Though again put as a surmise, Ungoliantë's origin is now found in her ancient corruption by Melkor, and it is suggested that he went to Arvalin of set purpose to find her.

§107 The high mountain in the southern range of the Pelóri now receives a name, *Hyarantar* (later replaced by *Hyarmentir*, see p. 285).

§109–10 In the *Lost Tales* the occasion of the great festival was commemoration of the coming of the Eldar to Valinor (I.143), but in later texts its occasion is not specified. Now a new and remarkable account of it is given, with a reference to the passage in the *Ainulindalë* (§25) where the visible shapes taken by the Valar in Arda are described; and here the idea of these 'shapes' is extended (as it appears) to the point where the great spirits might eat, and drink, and 'draw strength from the Earth'. Wholly new also in this passage is the element of Manwë's purpose to achieve concord among the Noldor.

§112 In QS (§60) Fëanor was present at the festival on Taniquetil; now enters the story that he came alone from Formenos, being commanded so to do by Manwë, in sombre garments, that Finwë refused to come while his son lived in banishment, and that Fëanor was reconciled 'in words' with Fingolfin before Manwë's throne. At this stage, of course, Fëanor and Fingolfin were still full brothers.

§114 There is no trace of the work *Aldudénië* among my father's papers. With the passage concerning the Darkness that came with the extinction of the Light of the Trees cf. the *Ainulindalë* §19: 'and it seemed to [the Ainur] that in that moment they perceived a new thing, Darkness, which they had not known before, except in thought.'

§116 On Oromë's horn *Valaróma* see *Ainulindalë* D, §34 (pp. 35 and 39).

There are a good many notes and changes made on the typescript, some added by the typist under my father's direction; but only a few of them need be recorded.

§78 The two new annal entries given in note 1 above, and that in note 4, are present in the typescript as typed.

§81 After the entry for 1190 a new entry was added for the year 1200: 'Lúthien born' (with a query).

§84 A blank is left in the typescript where the manuscript has *Naugrim* written above *Nauglath*, possibly because the typist did not know which form to put (see note 6). The blank was not filled in, but the name *Nornwaith* that follows was struck through.

§85 After the annal for 1280 the following Beleriandic entries were added:
1300 Daeron, loremaster of Thingol, contrives the Runes.
      Turgon, son of Fingolfin, and Inglor, son of Finrod, born.
1320 The Orcs first appear in Beleriand.

§86 After the annal for 1350 two entries were added:
1362 Galadriel, daughter of Finrod, born in Eldamar.
      Isfin, White Lady of the Noldor, born in Tirion.
The second of these appears also as a pencilled addition to the manuscript (note 8).

§97 Against the words 'Melkor spoke to the Eldar concerning weapons, which they had not before possessed or known' my father wrote on the typescript: 'No! They must have had weapons on the Great Journey.' Cf. the passage in QS on this subject (footnote to §49): 'The Elves had before possessed only weapons of the chase, spears and bows and arrows.'

§99 The term of Fëanor's banishment was changed yet again (see note 10), from 'twenty' to 'twelve'.

§113 After 'the Green Mound' was added: 'of Ezellohar'. This name was added to the typescript at earlier occurrences: p. 69, §25. – 'The Vats of Varda' become 'The Wells of Varda'; see p. 69, §28.

§114 The typist misread *Elemírë*, and my father corrected the error to the form *Elemmírë*.

I do not know what intention lay behind the introduction of the Beleriandic entries given under §§81, 85 above.

Fifth section of the Annals of Aman

§117 Thus it came to pass that after a while a great concourse of folk was gathered about the Ring of Doom; and the gods sat in shadow, for it was night. But now night only as it may be in some land of the world, when the stars peer fitfully through the wrack of great clouds, and cold fogs drift in from a sullen shore of the sea. Then Yavanna stood upon the Green

Mound, and it was bare now and black; and she gazed upon the Trees and they were both dead and dark. Then many voices were lifted in lamentation; for it seemed to those that mourned that they had drained to the dregs the cup of woe that Melkor had filled for them. But it was not so.

§118 For Yavanna spoke before the Valar, saying: 'The Light of the Trees hath gone hence, and liveth now only in the jewels of Fëanor. Foresighted was he. Lo! for those even who are mightiest there is some deed that they may accomplish once, and once only. The Light of the Trees I brought into being, and can do so never again within Eä. Yet had I but a little of that Light, I could recall life to the Trees, ere their roots die; and then our hurt should be healed, and the malice of Melkor be confounded.'

§119 And Manwë spoke, and said: 'Hearest thou, Fëanor, the words of Yavanna? Wilt thou grant what she would ask?'

And there was a long silence, but Fëanor answered no word.

Then Tulkas cried: 'Speak, O Noldo, yea or nay! But who shall deny Yavanna? And did not the light of the Silmarils come from her work in the beginning?'

But Aulë the Maker[1] said: 'Be not hasty! We ask a greater thing than thou knowest. Let him have peace yet a while.'

§120 But Fëanor spoke then, and cried bitterly: 'Verily for the less even as for the greater there is some deed that he may accomplish but once only. And in that deed his heart shall rest. Mayhap I can unlock my jewels, but never again shall I make their like; and if they be broken, then broken will be my heart, and I shall die: first of all the Children of Eru.'

§121 'Not the first,' quoth Mandos, but they understood not his word; and again there was silence, while Fëanor brooded in the dark. And it seemed to him that he was beset in a ring of enemies, and the words of Melkor returned to him, saying that the Silmarils were not safe, if the Valar would possess them. 'And is he not Vala as are they,' said his thought, 'and understandeth their hearts? Yea, a thief shall reveal thieves.' Then he cried aloud: 'Nay, this thing I will not do of free will. But if the Valar will constrain me, then verily shall I know that Melkor is of their kindred.'

§122 'Thou hast spoken,' quoth Mandos; then all sat in silence, while Nienna wept upon Korlairë and mourned for the bitterness of the world. And even as she mourned, messengers came from Formenos, and they were Noldor, and bore new tidings of evil. For they told now how a blind Darkness came northward, and in the midst walked some power for which there was no name, and the Darkness issued from it. But Melkor also was there, and he came to the house of Fëanor, and there he slew Finwë, king of the Noldor, before the doors, and spilled the first blood of the Children of Ilúvatar. For Finwë alone had not fled from the horror of the Dark. But the stronghold of Formenos Melkor had broken, and had utterly destroyed, and all the wealth of gems he had taken; and the Silmarils were gone.

§123 Then Fëanor rose up and cursed Melkor, naming him *Morgoth*;[2] and he cursed also the summons of Manwë, and the hour in which he came to Taniquetil, thinking in his folly that had he been at Formenos, his strength would have availed more than to be slain also, as Melkor had hoped.[3] But now Fëanor ran from the concourse and fled into the night, as one mad both with wrath and with grief: for his father was dearer to him than the Light of Valinor or the peerless works of his hands; and who among sons, of Elves or of Men, have held their fathers of greater worth?

§124 And those who beheld Fëanor depart grieved sorely for him; but Yavanna was dismayed, fearing now that the Great Darkness would swallow the last rays of Light for ever. For though the Valar did not yet understand fully what had befallen, they perceived that Melkor had called upon some aid that came from Without. The Silmarils had passed away, and all one it may seem, therefore, whether Fëanor would have said[4] yea or nay at the last; yet had he said yea at the first and so cleansed his heart ere the dread tidings came, his after deeds maybe had been other than they were. But now the doom of the Noldor drew nigh.

§125 Meanwhile, it is told, Morgoth escaping from the pursuit of the Valar came to the waste-land of Araman, that northward, as Arvalin to the south, lay between the walls of the Mountains and the Great Sea. Thus he passed to the Helkaraxë where the Strait between Araman and Middle-earth is filled with grinding ice; and he crossed over and came back to the North of the world. Then so soon as they set foot there and were escaped from the land of the Valar, Ungoliantë summoned Morgoth to deliver to her her reward. The half of her fee was the sap of the Trees; the other half was to be a full share in all the jewels they should take. Morgoth yielded these grudgingly, one by one, until she had devoured all and their beauty perished from the earth, and then huger and darker grew Ungoliantë, and yet she hungered for more.

§126 But Morgoth would give her no part in the Silmarils: these he named unto himself for ever. Thus there befell the first thieves' quarrel, and the fear of Yavanna came not to pass: that the Darkness should swallow the last rays of the Light. But Ungoliantë was wroth, and so great had she become that Morgoth could not master her; and she enmeshed him in her strangling webs, and his dreadful cry echoed through the world. Then there came to his aid the Balrogs, who endured still in deep places in the North where the Valar had not discovered them. With their whips of flame they smote her webs asunder, and they drove Ungoliantë away, and she went down into Beleriand and dwelt awhile beneath Ered Orgoroth in that valley which after was named Nan Dungorthin, because of the fear and horror that she bred there. But when she had healed her hurts and spawned there a foul brood she passed away out of the Northlands, and returned into the South of the world, where she abides yet for all that the Eldar have heard.

§127 Then Morgoth being freed gathered again all his servants that he could find, and he delved anew his vast vaults and his dungeons in that place which the Noldor after called Angband, and above them he reared the reeking towers of Thangorodrim. There countless became the hosts of his beasts and his demons; and thence there now came forth in hosts beyond count the fell race of the Orkor, that had grown and multiplied in the bowels of the earth like a plague. These creatures Morgoth bred in envy and mockery of the Eldar. In form[5] they were like unto the Children of Ilúvatar, yet foul to look upon; for they were bred[6] in hatred, and with hatred they were filled; and he loathed the things that he had wrought, and with loathing they served him. Their voices were as the clashing of stones, and they laughed not save only at torment and cruel deeds. The *Glamhoth*, host of tumult, the Noldor called them. (Orcs we may name them; for in days of old they were strong and fell as demons. Yet they were not of demon kind, but children[7] of earth corrupted by Morgoth, and they could be slain or destroyed by the valiant with weapons of war. [But indeed a darker tale some yet tell in Eressëa, saying that the Orcs were verily in their beginning of the Quendi themselves, a kindred of the Avari unhappy whom Morgoth cozened, and then made captive, and so enslaved them, and so brought them utterly to ruin.* For, saith Pengoloð, Melkor could never since the *Ainulindalë* make of his own aught that had life or the semblance of life, and still less might he do so after his treachery in Valinor and the fullness of his own corruption.]⁸ Quoth Ælfwine.)

§128 Dark now fell the shadow on Beleriand, as elsewhere is told; but in Angband Morgoth forged for himself a great crown of iron; and he called himself King of the World.⁹ In token of which he set the Silmarils in his crown. His evil hands were burned black by the touch of those hallowed jewels, and black they have been ever since; and he was never again free from the pain of the burning. The crown he never took from his head, though its weight became a weariness unto torment; and never but once only, while his realm lasted, did he depart for a while secretly from his domain in the North.¹⁰ And once only also did he himself wield weapon, until the Last Battle. For now, more than in the days of Utumno ere his pride was humbled, his hatred devoured him, and in the domination of his servants and the inspiring of them with lust of evil, he spent his spirit. Nonetheless his majesty as one of the Valar long remained, though turned to terror, and before his face all save the mightiest sank into a dark pit of fear.

Of the Speech of Fëanor upon Túna

§129 When it was known that Morgoth had escaped from Valinor and pursuit was unavailing, the Valar remained long seated in darkness in the Ring of Doom, and the Maiar and the Vanyar stood by them and wept; but the Noldor for the most part returned sadly to Túna. Dark now was the fair city of Tirion, and fogs drifted in from the Shadowy Seas, and mantled its towers. The lamp of the Mindon burned pale in the gloom.

§130 Then suddenly Fëanor appeared in the city and called on all to come to the high Court of the King upon the summit of Túna. The doom of banishment that had been laid upon him was not yet lifted, and he rebelled against the Valar. A great multitude gathered swiftly, therefore, to hear what he would say, and the hill and all the streets, and the stairs that climbed to

---

* [footnote to the text] In the Annals of Beleriand it is said that this he did in the Dark ere ever the Quendi were found by Oromë.

the Court were thronged with the many torches that all bore in hand as they came.

§131 Fëanor was a master of words, and his tongue had great power over hearts when he would use it. Now he was on fire, and that night he made a speech before the Noldor which they have ever remembered. Fierce and fell were his words, and filled with anger and pride; and they moved the people to madness like the fumes of hot wine. His wrath and his hate were most given to Morgoth, and yet well nigh all that he said came from the very lies of Morgoth himself. He claimed now the kingship of all the Noldor, since Finwë was dead, and he scorned the decrees of the Valar.

§132 'Why, O my people,' he cried, 'why should we longer serve these jealous gods, who cannot keep us, nor their own realm even, secure from their Enemy? And though he be now their foe, are not they and he of one kin? Vengeance calls me hence, but even were it otherwise, I would not dwell longer in the same land with the kin of my father's slayer and the thief of my treasure. Yet I am not the only valiant in this valiant people. And have ye not all lost your king? And what else have ye not lost, cooped here in a narrow land between the jealous mountains and the harvestless Sea? Here once was light, that the Valar begrudged to Middle-earth, but now dark levels all. Shall we mourn here deedless for ever, a shadow-folk, mist-haunting, dropping vain tears in the salt thankless Sea? Or shall we go home? In Kuiviénen sweet ran the waters under unclouded stars, and wide lands lay about where a free folk might walk. There they lie still and await us who in our folly forsook them. Come away! Let the cowards keep this city. But by the blood of Finwë! unless I dote, if the cowards only remain, then grass will grow in the streets. Nay, rot, mildew, and toadstool.'

§133 Long he spoke, and ever he urged the Noldor to follow him and by their own prowess to win freedom and great realms in the lands of the East ere it was too late; for he echoed the lies of Melkor that the Valar had cozened them and would hold them captive so that Men might rule Middle-earth; and many of the Eldar heard then for the first time of the Aftercomers. 'Fair shall the end be,' he cried, 'though long and hard shall be the road! Say farewell to bondage! But say farewell also to ease! Say farewell to the weak! Say farewell to your treasures – more still shall we make! Journey light. But bring with you your swords! For we will go further than Tauros, endure longer than Tulkas: we will never turn back from pursuit. After Morgoth to the ends of the Earth! War shall he have and hatred undying. But when we have conquered and have regained the Silmarils that he stole, then behold! We, we alone, shall be the lords of the unsullied Light, and masters of the bliss and the beauty of Arda! No other race shall oust us!'[11]

§134 Then Fëanor swore a terrible oath. Straightway his seven sons leaped to his side and each took the selfsame oath; and red as blood shone their drawn swords in the glare of the torches.

'Be he foe or friend, be he foul or clean,
brood of Morgoth or bright Vala,
Elda or Maia or Aftercomer,
Man yet unborn upon Middle-earth,
neither law, nor love, nor league of swords,
dread nor danger, not Doom itself,
shall defend him from Fëanor, and Fëanor's kin,
whoso hideth or hoardeth, or in hand taketh,
finding keepeth or afar casteth
a Silmaril. This swear we all:
death we will deal him ere Day's ending,
woe unto world's end! Our word hear thou,
Eru Allfather! To the everlasting
Darkness doom us if our deed faileth.
On the holy mountain hear in witness
and our vow remember, Manwë and Varda!'

Thus spoke Maidros and Maglor, and Celegorn, Curufin and Cranthir, Damrod and Díriel, princes of the Noldor. But by that name none should swear an oath, good or evil, nor in anger call upon such witness, and many quailed to hear the fell words. For so sworn, good or evil, an oath may not be broken, and it shall pursue oathkeeper or oathbreaker to the world's end.

§135 Fingolfin, and his son Turgon, therefore spoke against Fëanor, and fierce words awoke, so that once again wrath came near to the edge of swords. But Finrod, who was skilled also in words, spoke softly, as his wont was, and sought to calm the Noldor, persuading them to pause and ponder ere deeds were done that could not be undone. But of his own sons Orodreth alone spoke in like manner; for Inglor was with Turgon his friend,[12] whereas Galadriel, the only woman of the Noldor to stand that day tall and valiant among the contending princes, was eager to be gone. No oaths she swore, but the words of

Fëanor concerning Middle-earth had kindled her heart, and she yearned to see the wide untrodden lands and to rule there a realm maybe at her own will. For youngest of the House of Finwë she came into the world west of the Sea, and knew yet nought of the unguarded lands. Of like mind was Fingon Fingolfin's son, being moved also by Fëanor's words, though he loved him little;[13] and with Fingon as ever stood Angrod and Egnor, sons of Finrod. But these held their peace and spoke not against their fathers.

§136 In the end after long debate Fëanor prevailed, and the greater part of the Noldor there assembled he set aflame with the desire of new things and strange countries. Therefore when Finrod spoke yet again for heed and delay, a great shout went up: 'Nay, let us be gone! Let us be gone!' And straightway Fëanor and his sons began to prepare for the marching forth.

§137 Little foresight could there be for those who dared to take so dark a road. Yet all was done in over-haste; for Fëanor drove them on, fearing lest in the cooling of hearts his words should wane and other counsels yet prevail. And for all his proud words he did not forget the power of the Valar. But from Valmar no message came, and Manwë was silent. He would not yet either forbid or hinder Fëanor's purpose; for the Valar were aggrieved that they were charged with evil intent to the Eldar, or that any were held captive by them against their will. Now they watched and waited, for they did not yet believe that Fëanor could hold the host of the Noldor to his will.

§138 And indeed when Fëanor began the marshalling of the Noldor for their setting out, then at once dissension arose. For though he had brought the assembly in a mind to depart, by no means all were of a mind to take Fëanor as king. Greater love was given to Fingolfin and his sons, and his household and the most part of the dwellers in Tirion refused to renounce him, if he would go with them. Thus at the last the Noldor set forth divided in two hosts. Fëanor and his following were in the van; but the greater host came behind under Fingolfin. And he marched against his wisdom, because Fingon his son so urged him, and because he would not be sundered from his people that were eager to go, nor leave them to the rash counsels of Fëanor. With Fingolfin went Finrod also and for like reason; but most loath was he to depart.

§139 It is recorded that of all the Noldor in Valinor, who were grown now to a great people, but one tithe refused to take the road: some for the love that they bore to the Valar (and to Aulë not least), some for the love of Tirion and the many things that they had made; none for fear of peril by the way. For they were indeed a valiant people.

§140 But even as the trumpet sang and Fëanor issued from the gates of Tirion a messenger came at last from Manwë, saying: 'Against the folly of Fëanor shall be set my counsel only. Go not forth! For the hour is evil, and your road leads to sorrows that ye do not foresee. No aid will the Valar lend you in this emprise; but lo! they will not hinder you; for this ye shall know: as ye came hither freely, freely shall ye depart. But thou Fëanor Finwë's son by thine oath art exiled. The lies of Melkor thou shalt unlearn in bitterness. Vala he is, thou saist. Then thou hast sworn in vain, for none of the Valar canst thou overcome now or ever within the halls of Eä,[14] not though Eru whom thou namest had made thee thrice greater than thou art.'[15]

§141 But Fëanor laughed, and spoke not to the herald, but to the Noldor, saying: 'So! Then will this valiant people send forth the heir of their King alone into banishment with his sons only, and return to their bondage? But if any will come with me, to them I say: Is sorrow foreboded to you? Verily in Aman we have seen it. In Aman we have come through bliss to woe. The other now we will try: through sorrow to find joy. Or at the least: freedom!'

§142 Then turning to the herald he cried: 'Say this to Manwë Sulimo, High-king of Arda: If Fëanor cannot overthrow Morgoth, at least he delays not to assail him, and sits not idle in grief. And Eru, mayhap, has set in me a fire greater than thou knowest. Such hurt, at the least, will I do the Foe of the Valar that even the mighty in the Ring of Doom shall wonder to hear it. Yea, in the end they shall follow me. Farewell!'

§143 In that hour the voice of Fëanor grew so great and so potent that even the herald of the Valar bowed before him as one full-answered, and departed; and the Noldor were overruled. Therefore they continued their march; and the House of Fëanor hastened before them along the coasts of Elendë: and not once did they turn their eyes backward to Tirion upon Túna. Slower and less eagerly came the host of Fingolfin after them. Of these Fingon was the foremost; but at the rear went Finrod and Inglor, and many of the fairest and wisest of the Noldor; and often they looked behind them to see their fair city, until the lamp of the Mindon Eldaliéva was lost in the night. More than any others of the exiles they carried thence memories of the bliss that they had forsaken, and some even of the fair things that they had made there they took with them: a solace and a burden on the road.

Of the First Kin-slaying and the Doom of the Noldor

§144 Now Fëanor led the Noldor northward, because his first purpose was to follow Morgoth. Moreover, Túna beneath Taniquetil was set nigh to the girdle of Arda, and there the Great Sea was immeasurably wide, whereas ever northward the sundering seas grew narrower, as the waste-land of Araman and the coasts of Middle-earth drew together. But the hosts had not gone far, ere it came to the mind of Fëanor, over late, that all these great companies, both of the full-grown and war-high and many others, and great store of goods withal, would never overcome the long leagues to the North, nor cross the seas at the last, save with the aid of ships.

§145 Therefore Fëanor now resolved to persuade the Teleri, ever friends of the Noldor, to join with them; for thus he thought to diminish the wealth of Valinor yet further and to increase his own power of war. Thus also he would get ships swiftly. For it would need great time and toil to build a great fleet, even if the Noldor had skill and timber in plenty for such craft, as indeed they had not. He hastened then to Alqualondë, and spoke to the Teleri as he had spoken in Tirion.

§146 But the Teleri were unmoved by aught that he could say. They were grieved indeed at the going of their kinsfolk and long friends, but would rather dissuade them than aid them; and no ship would they lend, nor help in the building, against the will of the Valar. As for themselves they desired now no other home but the strands of Eldamar, and no other lord than Olwë, prince of Alqualondë. And he had never lent ear to Morgoth, nor welcomed him to his land, and he trusted still that Ulmo and the other great among the Valar would redress the hurts of Morgoth, and that the night would pass yet to new dawn.

§147 Then Fëanor grew wroth, for he still feared delay; and he spoke hotly to Olwë. 'Thou renouncest thy friendship, even in the hour of our need,' said he. 'Yet fain were ye of our aid when ye came at last to these shores, fainthearted loiterers, and wellnigh emptyhanded. In huts on the beaches would ye dwell still, had not the Noldor carved out your haven and toiled on your walls.'

§148 But Olwë answered: 'Nay, we renounce no friendship. But it may be the hard part of a friend to rebuke a friend's folly. And when your folk welcomed us and gave us aid, otherwise then ye spoke: in the land of Aman we were to dwell for ever, as brothers whose houses stand side by side. But as for our white ships: those ye gave us not. That craft we learned not from the Noldor, but from the Lords of the Sea; and the white timbers we wrought with our own hands and the white sails were woven by our fair wives and maidens. Therefore we will neither give them nor sell them for any league or friendship. For I say to thee, Fëanor, these are to us as are the gems of the Noldor: the work of our hearts, whose like we shall not make again.'

§149 Thereupon Fëanor left him, and sat beyond the walls brooding darkly, until his host was assembled. When he deemed that his strength was enough he went to the Haven of the Swans and began to man the ships that were anchored there and to take them away by force. But the Teleri withstood him stoutly, and they cast many of the Noldor into the sea. Then swords were drawn, and a bitter fight was fought upon the ships, and about the lamplit quays and piers of the Haven, and even upon the great arch of its gate. Thrice the folk of Fëanor were driven back, and many were slain upon either side; but the vanguard of the Noldor were succoured by Fingon with the foremost people of Fingolfin. These coming up found a battle joined and their own kin falling, and they rushed in ere they knew rightly the cause of the quarrel: some deemed indeed that the Teleri had sought to waylay the march of the Noldor, at the bidding of the Valar.

§150 Thus at last the Teleri were overcome, and a great part of their mariners that dwelt in Alqualondë were wickedly slain. For the Noldor were become fierce and desperate, and the Teleri had less strength, and were armed mostly with light bows only. Then the Noldor drew away their white ships, and manned their oars as best they might, and rowed them north along the coast. And Olwë called upon Ossë, but he came not; for he had been summoned to Valmar to the vigil and council of the gods; and it was not permitted by the Valar that the Flight of the Noldor should be hindered by force. But Uinen wept for the mariners of the Teleri; and the sea rose in wrath against the slayers, so that many of the ships were wrecked and those in them drowned. Of the Kin-slaying at Alqualondë more is told in that lament which is named *Noldolantë*,[16] The Fall of the Noldor, which Maglor made ere he was lost.

1496

§151 Nonetheless the greater part of the Noldor escaped, and when the storm was over they held on their course, some by ship, some by land; but the way was long and ever more evil as they went forward. After they had marched for a great while in the unmeasured night they came at length to the north of the Guarded Realm upon the borders of the empty waste of Araman, which were mountainous and cold. There they beheld suddenly a dark figure standing upon a high rock that looked down upon the shore. Some say that it was Mandos himself and no lesser herald of Manwë. And they heard a loud voice, solemn and terrible, that bade them stand and give ear.[17]

§152 All halted and stood still, and from end to end of the hosts of the Noldor the voice was heard speaking the Prophecy of the North and the Doom of the Noldor. 'Turn back! Turn back! Seek the pardon of the Valar lest their curse fall upon you!' So the voice began, and many woes it foretold in dark words, which the Noldor understood not until the woes indeed after befell them. 'Tears unnumbered ye shall shed; but if ye go further, be assured that the Valar will fence Valinor against you, and shut you out, so that not even the echo of your lamentation shall pass over the mountains.

§153 'Lo! on the House of Fëanor the wrath of the gods lieth from the West into the uttermost East, and upon all that will follow them it shall be laid also. Their Oath shall drive them, and yet betray them, and ever snatch away the very treasures that they have sworn to pursue. To evil end shall all things turn that they begin well; and by the treason of kin unto kin, and the fear of treason, shall this come to pass. The Dispossessed shall they be for ever.

§154 'Behold! Ye have spilled the blood of your kindred unrighteously and have stained the land of Aman. For blood ye shall render blood, and beyond Aman ye shall dwell in Death's shadow. For know now that though Eru appointed unto you to die not in Eä, and no sickness may assail you, yet slain may ye be, and slain ye shall be: by weapon and by torment and by grief; and your houseless spirits shall come then to Mandos. There long shall ye abide and yearn for your bodies and find little pity though all whom ye have slain should entreat for you. And those that endure in Middle-earth and come not to Mandos, they shall grow weary of the world as with a great burden, and shall wane, and become as shadows of regret before the younger race that cometh after. The Valar have spoken.'

§155 Then many quailed. But Fëanor hardened his heart and said: 'We have sworn, and not lightly. This Oath we will keep. And lo! we are threatened with many evils, and treason not least; but one thing is not said: that we shall suffer from cravens; from cowardice or the fear of cowardice among us. Therefore I say we will go on, and this doom I add: the deeds that we do shall be the matter of song until the last days of Arda.' And the doom of Fëanor was true-spoken also.

§156 But in that hour Finrod forsook the march, and turned back, being filled with grief, and with bitterness against the house of Fëanor, because of his kinship with Olwë of Alqualondë; and many of his people went with him, retracing their steps in sorrow, until they beheld once more the far beam of the Mindon upon Túna still shining in the night, and so came at last to Valinor. There they received the pardon of the Valar, and Finrod was set to rule the remnant of the Noldor in the Blessed Realm. But his sons were not with him, for they would not forsake the sons of Fingolfin; and all Fingolfin's folk went forward still, feeling the constraint of their kinship and the will of Fëanor, and fearing to face the doom of the gods, since not all of them had been guiltless of the kinslaying at Alqualondë. Moreover Fingon and Turgon were bold and fiery of heart and loath to abandon any task to which they had put their hands until the bitter end, if bitter it must be. So the main host held on, and swiftly the evil that was forespoken began its work.

1497

§157 The Noldor came at last far into the North of Arda, and they saw the first teeth of the ice that floated in the sea, and knew that they were drawing nigh to the Helkaraxë. For between the West-land of Aman that in the north curved eastward and the east-shores of Endar (which is Middle-earth) that bore westward there was a narrow strait, through which the chill waters of the Encircling Sea and the waves of the Great Sea flowed together, and there were vast fogs and mists of deathly cold, and the sea-streams were filled with clashing hills of ice and the grinding of ice deep-sunken. Such was the Helkaraxë, and there none yet had dared to tread save the Valar only and Ungoliantë.

§158 Therefore Fëanor halted and the Noldor debated what course they should now take. But soon they began to suffer anguish from the cold, and the clinging mists through which no gleam of star could pierce; and many of them repented of the road and began to murmur, especially those that followed Fingolfin, cursing Fëanor, and naming him as the cause of all the woes of the Eldar. But Fëanor, knowing all that was said, took counsel with his sons. Two courses only they saw to escape from Araman and come unto Endar: by the straits or by ship. But the Helkaraxë they deemed impassable, whereas the ships were too few. Many had been lost upon their long journey and there remained now not enough to bear across all the great host together; yet none were willing to abide upon the west-coast while others were ferried first: already the fear of treachery was awake among the Noldor.

§159 Therefore it came into the hearts of Fëanor and his sons to seize all the ships and depart suddenly; for they had retained the mastery of the fleet since the battle of the Haven, and it was manned only by those who had fought there and were bound unto Fëanor. And lo! as though it came at his call there sprang up a wind from the north-west, and Fëanor slipped away[18] secretly with all whom he deemed true to him, and went aboard, and put out to sea, and left Fingolfin in Araman. And since the sea was there narrow, steering east and somewhat south he passed over without loss, and first of all the Noldor set foot once more upon the shores of Middle-earth. And the landing of Fëanor was at the mouth of that firth which was called Drengist, and ran into Dor-lómin.[19]

§160 But when they were landed, Maidros the eldest of his sons (and on a time a friend of Fingon ere Morgoth's lies came between) spoke to Fëanor, saying: 'Now what ships and men wilt thou spare to return, and whom shall they bear hither first? Fingon the valiant?'

§161 Then Fëanor laughed as one fey, and his wrath was unleashed: 'None and none!' he cried. 'What I have left behind I count now no loss: needless baggage on the road it has proved. Let those that cursed my name, curse me still! And whine their way back to the cages of the Valar, if they can find no other! Let the ships burn!'

§162 Then Maidros alone stood aside, but Fëanor and his sons set fire in the white ships of the Teleri. So in that place which was called Losgar at the outlet of the Firth of Drengist[20] ended in a great burning bright and terrible the fairest vessels that ever sailed the sea.[21] And Fingolfin and his people saw the light afar off red beneath the clouds. This was the first-fruits of the Kinslaying and the Doom of the Noldor.

§163 Then Fingolfin knew that he was betrayed, and left to perish in misery or go back in shame. And his heart was bitter, but desired now as never before to come by some way into Middle-earth, and meet Fëanor again. And he and his host wandered long and wretchedly; but their valour and endurance grew greater with hardship; for they were yet a mighty folk, the elder children undying of Eru Ilúvatar, but new-come from the Blessed Realm, and not yet weary with the weariness of Earth; and the fire of their hearts was young. Therefore led by Fingolfin and his sons, and by Inglor and Galadriel the valiant and fair, they dared to pass into the untrodden North, and finding no other way they endured at last the terror of the Helkaraxë and the cruel hills of ice. Few of the deeds of the Noldor thereafter surpassed that desperate crossing in hardihood or in woe. Many there perished, and it was with a lessened host that Fingolfin set foot at last upon the Northlands of Endar. Little love for Fëanor or his sons had those that then marched behind him, and blew their trumpets in Middle-earth at the first rising of the Moon.

 Here the Noldor passed out of Aman and
 the Annals of Aman tell of them no more

NOTES

1 'Aulë the Maker' replaced 'Ulmo'.
2 Struck out here, probably at once: '(the Dark Enemy)'.
3 Struck out here (later): 'not a second time would the Black Foe of Arda be dismissed with proud words of scorn.'
4 This passage is a replacement of the original text:
 but Yavanna was dismayed, for now the Light of the Trees had passed utterly into a great Darkness, which though the Valar did not yet understand they perceived that it must come from some aid that Morgoth had called from Without, and they feared that it was lost beyond the End. Therefore all was one, whether Fëanor said ...
5 This passage was emended from the original text, which read thus:

> There countless became the hosts of his beasts and his demons; and he brought now into being the fell race of the Orkor, and they grew and multiplied in the bowels of the earth like a plague. These creatures Morgoth made in envy and mockery of the Eldar. Therefore in form ...

6 'bred' is an emendation of 'made'.
7 'children' is an emendation of 'a spawn'.
8 This passage, from 'But indeed a darker tale ...' and including the footnote, was struck out at a later time than the changes given in notes 5–7 and perhaps in revision of the text before the making of the typescript, in which it does not appear. The whole addition by Ælfwine is enclosed within brackets as originally written.
9 The original text was 'Aran Endór, King of Middle-earth.' *Aran Endór* was then corrected to *Tarumbar*; finally the reading 'King of the World' was substituted.
10 The text as originally written read here: 'and never but once only did he come forth from the deeps that he had dug, while his realm lasted.' When my father corrected this to the text printed he added all that follows to the end of the paragraph.
11 In this paragraph the passage from 'ere it was too late' as far as 'many of the Eldar heard then for the first time of the Aftercomers', and the final sentence 'No other race shall oust us', were later additions.
12 The associations of the Noldorin princes were different as this passage was first written: 'Fingolfin and his sons Fingon and Turgon spoke against Fëanor', and 'of [Finrod's] own sons Inglor alone spoke in like manner, for Angrod and Egnor were with Fingon, and Orodreth stood aside; whereas Galadriel ...' But the changes that give the text printed appear to have been made immediately, since the passage at the end of the paragraph belongs to the original writing of the text.
13 Struck out here: 'and his sons less' (cf. the passage in §160 where Fingon's friendship with Maidros is referred to).
14 *Eä* is so spelt here, and again in §154, but in the last two occurrences in the text it is spelt *Ëa*.
15 Struck out here: 'and Melkor least of all, who is mightiest save one.'
16 The name *Noldolantë* was added in the margin. It does not appear in the typescript.
17 The page beginning here and carrying §§152–4 is much more roughly written than the rest of the manuscript, and my father struck it through and replaced it. It might be thought at first sight that this is the only place where a first draft of AAm survives, but this is not the case. The rough 'draft' page was written on the reverse of that carrying §§149–51, and that is in the same good

clear script as elsewhere (with a number of changes made in the act of composition). It is plain then that the rejected page did not begin as 'rough draft' (and the handwriting bears this out), but degenerated into it; and this instance is, if anything, rather evidence against the idea of a lost first draft of the *Annals of Aman* (see p. 47).

The first text originally began, following QS §71, 'Once again he warned the Noldor to return and seek pardon, or in the end they should return at last only after bitter sorrow and woes unspeakable.' The Doom of the Noldor in the final form was in fact only changed from the draft by a rearrangement of its parts and in many details of phrasing. Two points may be noted. After '... over the mountains' at the end of §152 stood 'Ye shall be free of them and they of you'; and the sentence in §154 beginning 'There long shall ye abide...' read 'There long shall ye abide, and be not set free until those ye have slain entreat for you.'

18 This sentence replaced the following: 'Waiting then but a little for a north wind that brought a deep mist upon the host he slipped away...'
19 The last sentence of §159 was a later addition.
20 The passage 'in that place ... the Firth of Drengist' was a later addition.
21 Changed from 'the fairest vessels of the Elder Days'.

Commentary on the fifth section of the
Annals of Aman

This section of the *Annals* corresponds in content to QS Chapter 5 *Of the Flight of the Noldor* (V.232-8), and to AV 2 annals 2990-2994 (V.114-17). After the opening paragraphs the narrative of the *Annals* is again closely related in structure to the chapter in QS, and from §125 onwards many phrases are retained from it (more in fact than appears from the text printed, since in some cases my father adopted phrases without change from QS and then altered them). On the other hand, the narrative is greatly expanded in scope.

§§117-24 There now enters a new and subtle articulation in the story, with the assertion of Yavanna that with the holy light regained from the Silmarils she could rekindle the Trees before their roots died, the demand made upon Fëanor, and his refusal — before the news came from Formenos.
§121 Mandos said 'Not the first' because he knew that Finwë had been murdered. See further p. 127, §120.
§122 *Korlairë*: the first occurrence of this name (see p. 127, §122). — A new element in the narrative is that 'Finwë alone had not fled from the horror of the Dark.' In QS (§60) and AV 2 Morgoth

slew many others beside. Where Fëanor's sons were, or where they went (for Fëanor came to the festival alone, §112), is not told (see pp. 293–4).

§123 It is now first said that it was Fëanor who named Melkor *Morgoth* ('the Dark Enemy', note 2 above). In AAm (unlike QS) *Melkor* is always so named until this point, but after this almost invariably *Morgoth*.

§125 *Araman*: QS *Eruman*. The change had appeared previously on the *Ambarkanta* map V (IV.250–1), where it was put in many years after the making of the map.

§126 In QS (§62) no more is said of Ungoliantë's fate than that the Balrogs drove her away 'into the uttermost South, where she long remained'; now appears the story that she dwelt first in Nan Dungorthin, and only afterwards, after spawning there, did she retreat into the South of the world. But the spiders of Nan Dungorthin 'of the fell race of Ungoliantë' are referred to later in QS, in the story of Beren's flight from Dorthonion (see V.299, and the published *Silmarillion* p. 164).

§127 *The origin of the Orcs*. In QS (§62) the idea had already arisen that the Orcs originated in mockery of the Elves, but not yet that the Orcs were in any other way associated with them: they were a 'creation' of Morgoth's own, 'made of stone', and he brought them into being *when he returned to Middle-earth*. As AAm was first written (see notes 5–7 above) this view still held; the word 'made' was still used – though not the words 'made of stone'. But in Ælfwine's note that follows (and which was written continuously with what precedes) they are called 'a spawn of earth corrupted by Morgoth'; and the 'darker tale' told in Eressëa – that the Orcs were in their beginning enslaved and corrupted Elves (Avari) – is certainly the first appearance of this idea, contradicting what precedes, or perhaps rather at this stage presenting an alternative theory. It is ascribed to Pengoloð; and Pengoloð argues to Ælfwine that Melkor could actually *make* nothing that had life, but could only corrupt what was already living. The implication of this second theory would probably, though not necessarily, be that the Orcs came into being much earlier, before the Captivity of Melkor; and that this implication is present is suggested by the footnote reference to the *Annals of Beleriand* – meaning the last version of these Annals, the *Grey Annals*, companion to the *Annals of Aman*: 'it is said that this he did in the Dark ere ever the Quendi were found by Oromë.'

At this point my father went back to an earlier part of AAm (p. 72, §42) and interpolated the passage 'Yet by afterknowledge ...', where the idea of the capture of wandering

Quendi in their earliest days is filled out, though it remains only a supposition of the 'masters of lore'. Perhaps at the same time he emended the present passage, changing 'he brought now into being' to 'thence there now came forth in hosts beyond count', 'made' to 'bred', and 'a spawn of earth' to 'children of earth'. He then (as I conjecture) developed the interpolation at the earlier point much more fully (§§43–5), where the idea becomes less a supposition than a certainty of history: the powerlessness of Melkor to make living things is a known fact ('so say the wise'). Finally, at a later time (see note 8), he cut out the whole passage at the end of §127 beginning 'But indeed a darker tale some yet tell in Eressëa ...' – either because he only then observed that it had been superseded by §§43–5 and was in any case not in the appropriate place, or because he rejected this theory of the origin of the Orcs. See further p. 127, §127.

The word *for* in 'Orcs we may name them; *for* in days of old they were strong and fell as demons. Yet they were not of demon kind' (an observation of Ælfwine's) suggests that *Orcs* is Old English (cf. *orc-nēas* in *Beowulf* line 112), conveniently similar to the Elvish word. This would explain why Ælfwine said, in effect, 'We may call them Orcs, because they were strong and fell as demons, even though they were not in fact *demons*.' In a letter of my father's written on 25 April 1954 (*Letters* no.144) he said that the word *Orc* 'is as far as I am concerned actually derived from Old English *orc* "demon", but only because of its phonetic suitability' (and also: 'Orcs ... are nowhere clearly stated to be of any particular origin. But since they are servants of the Dark Power, and later of Sauron, neither of whom could, or would, produce living things, they must be "corruptions"').

§128 The final reading here 'King of the World' (see note 9) returns to that of QS (§63), which goes back to Q (IV.93). – On the subject of Morgoth's departures from Angband QS has: 'it was never his wont to leave the deep places of his fortress', and there is no mention of his one absence.

§§132–3 The report of Fëanor's speech is greatly extended from that in QS (§§66–7).

§133 *Tauros*: Oromë; cf. QS §8: 'He is a hunter, and he loves all trees; for which reason he is called Aldaron, and by the Gnomes Tauros, the lord of forests'; also the *Etymologies*, stem TÁWAR (V.391): 'N[oldorin] *Tauros* "Forest-Dread", usual N by-name of Oromë (N Araw)'. It is notable that Fëanor should use this name (see p. 146, §8). In the typescript, for no very clear reason, the typist left a blank here, in which my father later pencilled *Oromë*.

§135 As AAm was first written (see note 12 above) the alignments of the Noldorin princes were already changed from the account in QS (§68), since Angrod and Egnor were now opposed to Fëanor – and Galadriel now has a part in the matter, being eager to leave Aman. As rewritten, a more subtle alignment is portrayed: for Fingon now independently urges departure, and Angrod and Egnor move with him. Of Fingolfin's sons Turgon alone now supports his father, but Inglor stands with him; and Orodreth moves into Inglor's place as the only one of his sons to support Finrod.

The close friendship of Turgon with Felagund (Inglor) had appeared already in the earliest *Annals of Beleriand* (IV.296); in a late addition to the AAm typescript (p. 106, §85) they were born in the same Year of the Trees.

The statement that Galadriel, 'youngest of the House of Finwë', 'came into the world west of the Sea, and knew yet nought of the unguarded lands', is strange, because all the progeny of Finwë were born in Aman (AAm §§78, 81–2).

§136 The Noldor were moved by 'the desire of new things and strange countries'; in QS they were 'filled with desire for the Silmarils'.

§137 The march from Tirion was undertaken with too little preparation and in too great haste; cf. AV 2 (annal 2992): 'The great march of the Gnomes was long preparing.'

§139 Only one tenth of the Noldor remained behind in Tirion.

§§140–2 The words of Manwë's messenger are given, and the episode is much expanded. The herald does not say, as in QS (§68), that the Valar forbade the march, but it is now said that Fëanor had exiled himself through the very fact of his oath; and Fëanor in his reply accuses the Valar of sitting idle and making no move against Morgoth.

§143 *Elendë* (Elvenhome, Elfland): see p. 90, §67.

§§145–8 Fëanor himself (not as in QS §70 messengers) went to Olwë at Alqualondë, and their words together are fully recounted. In §147 Fëanor speaks of the building of the Haven by the Noldor, which is mentioned earlier in AAm (§76).

§§149–50 The account in AAm of the battle at Alqualondë and its aftermath follows QS §70 closely and retains much of its phrasing; but in §149 it is now told that those of the second host who joined in the battle mistook its cause.

§150 On the weapons of the Teleri see p. 106, §97. – The song of the Flight of the Gnomes (QS §70) is now called *Noldolantë*, the Fall of the Noldor, 'which Maglor made ere he was lost.'

§§152–4 The Prophecy of the North, now called 'the Prophecy of the North and the Doom of the Noldor', is significantly developed: by the warning that such of the Noldor as may be slain afterwards shall remain long in Mandos 'yearning for their bodies', and that those who endure in Middle-earth shall grow weary of the world and shall *wane*. In this AAm looks back to AV 2 (annal 2993, V.116; almost the same in AV 1, IV.267):

> A measure of mortality should visit the Noldor, and they should be slain with weapons, and with torments, and with sorrow, and in the long end they should fade upon Middle-earth and wane before the younger race.

I have discussed these passages in IV.278–9. See further pp. 265 ff.

§156 As in AV (both texts), many of Finrod's people returned with him to Valinor; in QS (§72) only 'a few of his household' turned back. A new element in Finrod's motive for return is his kinship with Olwë of Alqualondë, for his wife was Eärwen Olwë's daughter (§85).

§157 Endar 'Middle-earth'. The form *Endon* was used earlier in AAm of 'the midmost point' of Middle-earth (§38), where it was changed on the typescript to *Endor* (p. 80). These forms *Endon* and *Endor* had appeared in the *Ambarkanta* and maps (see p. 76, §38). In *The Lord of the Rings* Quenya *Endórë*, Sindarin *Ennor*, means not the midmost point but Middle-earth itself, and in a letter of 1967 (*Letters* no.297, p. 384) my father referred to Q. *Endor*, S. *Ennor* = Middle-earth, with the etymology *en(ed)* 'middle' and *(n)dor* 'land (mass)'; cf. also *Aran Endór* 'King of Middle-earth', note 9 above. But in the present passage the form *Endar* is perfectly clear, as also again in §§158, 163. The typist however in each case, for some reason, typed *Endor*, and my father did not alter it. On the other hand, in the title of the next section in AAm (p. 129) the typist put *Endar* as in the manuscript, and again my father let this stand. In the published *Silmarillion* (p. 89) I printed, hesitantly, the form *Endor*.

This passage concerning the Helkaraxë derives not from QS but from AV 2 (annal 2994, almost the same in AV 1), and it is very notable that it remains in complete congruence with the cosmography of the *Ambarkanta* (see IV.238, 254).

§159 The story that Angrod and Egnor came to Middle-earth in the ships with the Fëanorians is now abandoned, with the loss of the story that they were close friends of the sons of Fëanor, and especially of Celegorn and Curufin (QS §§42, 72–3).

§160–2 Maidros takes no part in the burning of the ships, and remembers Fingon, his former friend. Fëanor's motive in this act is sufficiently explained in the older texts, but in AAm the insane pride and fury that drove him is far more strongly conveyed; he was indeed 'fey'.

§162 The addition (note 20 above) of the name *Losgar* of the place of the burning of the ships is derived from its sole occurrence in the earlier texts, at the beginning of the later *Annals of Beleriand* (AB 2, V.125 and commentary).

§163 On the difference between the final sentence from that in QS ('and came unto Beleriand at the rising of the sun') see V.239, commentary on §73.

Among the notes and corrections written by my father on the typescript in this section of AAm, not all of which need be recorded, there are several indicating proposed extensions of the narrative.

§120 'I shall die' > 'I shall be slain'; 'first of all the Children of Eru' underlined; and a note in the margin against the words 'Not the first' (at the beginning of §121): 'X This no longer fits even the Eldar of Valinor. Finwë Fëanor's father was first to be slain of the High-elves, Míriel Fëanor's mother the first to die.' It is to be remembered that when AAm was written the history of Míriel had not yet been devised; the entries that state that Míriel 'fell asleep and passed to Mandos' and that Finwë afterwards wedded Indis (p. 101, notes 1 and 4) were later additions (found in the typescript as typed). See further pp. 268–9.

§122 The typist left a blank for *Korlairë*, which my father filled with the form *Korolairë*. Later he underlined this in pencil and wrote *Ezellohar* against it (see p. 106, §113).

§126 *Ered Orgoroth* > *Ered Gorgorath*; *Nan Dungorthin* > *Nan Dungortheb*. See V.298–9.

§127 Against the opening of this paragraph my father wrote: 'The making of this fortress as a guard against a landing from the West should come earlier. See p. 156, §12.

In the typescript the passage concerning the Orcs ran as it stands in the text printed from the manuscript on p. 109 only as far as 'they could be slain or destroyed by the valiant with weapons of war'; the remainder of the paragraph had been struck out in the manuscript (note 8, p. 121), apart from the words 'Quoth Ælfwine' at the end (which the typist did not notice and omitted, ending the paragraph at 'weapons of war' without closing the brackets). Against the first part of the passage my father wrote an X on the typescript and a brief illegible direction of which the first word might be 'cut', with a reference to the passage on the subject in §45. It is not clear what precisely was to be cut (if I read the word correctly), but seeing that he noted on the typescript against the earlier passage (p. 80, §43): 'Alter this. Orcs are not Elvish', it seems likely that the same objection applied here (see further pp. 408 ff.). – He rectified the typist's error in omitting the words 'Quoth Ælfwine' by cutting out the words '(Orcs we may name them; for', so that the text reads: 'The *Glamhoth*, host of tumult, the Noldor called them. In days of old they were strong and fell as demons ...' This was perhaps done without consulting the manuscript.

§132 In 'the salt thankless Sea' the word *salt* was struck out.

§134 Marginal note against the names of the Sons of Fëanor: 'X Names will be revised.' In the text *Cranthir* > *Caranthir*, *Damrod* and *Díriel* struck out (but no other names substituted), and the *n* of *Celegorn* underlined.

§135 Marginal note against the opening of this paragraph: 'Names and relations now altered.' In the text *Finrod* > *Finarphin* (and subsequently), and *Inglor* > *Finrod* (and subsequently); also *Orodreth* underlined and marked with an X.

§137 Against the sentence 'He [Manwë] would not yet either forbid or hinder Fëanor's purpose' is the marginal note: 'Manwë and the Valar could not – sc. were not permitted to hinder the Noldor except by counsel – *not* by force.'

§149 Marginal note against the passage describing the involvement of the second host in the fighting: 'Finrod and Galadriel (whose husband was of the Teleri) fought *against* Fëanor in defence of Alqualondë.' On this see the very late note (1973) of my father's concerning Galadriel's conduct at the time of the rebellion of the Noldor in *Unfinished Tales*, pp. 231–2: 'In Fëanor's revolt that followed the Darkening of Valinor Galadriel had no part: indeed she with Celeborn fought heroically in defence of Alqualondë against the assault of the Noldor ...'

§162 'Fëanor and his sons set fire in' was changed to 'Fëanor caused fire to be set to'. A marginal note at the end of the paragraph reads: 'Tragedy of the burning of one of Fëanor's [*added:* 2 younger] sons, who had returned to sleep in his ship.' Another note at the same place reads: 'Fëanor's youngest sons were twins'; this is followed by a bracketed word which was struck out, probably '(unlike)'. It was said in QS (§41) that Damrod and Díriel were 'twin brethren alike in mood and face'.

§163 Marginal note against 'Many there perished' (i.e. in the crossing of the Helkaraxë): 'Turgon's wife was lost and he had then only one daughter and no other heir. Turgon was nearly lost himself in attempts to rescue his wife – and he had less love for the Sons of Fëanor than any other.'

Sixth and last section of the Annals of Aman

1495–1500

Of the Moon and the Sun. The Lighting of Endar, and the Hiding of Valinor

§164 It is told that the Valar sat long unmoved upon their thrones in the Ring of Doom, but they were not idle as Fëanor said in the folly of his heart. For the gods may work many things with thought rather than with hands, and without voices in silence they may hold council one with another. Thus they held vigil in the night of Valinor, and their thought passed back beyond Eä and forth to the End; yet neither power nor wisdom assuaged their grief, and the knowing of evil in the hour of its being. Neither did they mourn more for the death of the Trees than for the marring of Fëanor: of all Melkor's works the most wicked.

§165 For Fëanor was made the mightiest in all parts of body and mind: in valour, in endurance, in beauty, in understanding, in skill, in strength and subtlety alike: of all the Children of Eru, and a bright flame was in him. The works of wonder for the glory of Arda that he might otherwise have wrought only Manwë might in some measure conceive. And the Vanyar who held vigil with the Valar have recorded that when the messengers reported to Manwë the answers of Fëanor to his heralds Manwë wept and bowed his head. But at that last word of Fëanor: that at the least the Noldor should do deeds to live in song for ever: he raised his head, as one that hears a voice afar off, and he said: 'So shall it be! Dear-bought those songs shall be accounted, and yet shall be well-bought. For the price could be no other. Thus, even as Eru spoke to us, shall beauty not before conceived be brought into Eä, and evil yet be good to have been.'

'And yet remain evil,' quoth Mandos. 'To me shall Fëanor come soon.'

§166 But when at last the Valar learned that the Noldor had indeed passed out of Aman and were come back into Middle-earth, they arose and began to set forth in deeds those counsels they had taken in thought for the redress of the evils of Melkor.

§167 Then Manwë bade Yavanna and Nienna to put forth all their powers of growth and healing; and they put forth all their powers upon the Trees. But the tears of Nienna availed not to heal their mortal wounds; and for a long while Yavanna sang alone in the shadows. Yet even as hope failed and her song faltered, behold! Telperion bore at last upon a leafless bough one great flower of silver, and Laurelin a single fruit of gold.

§168 These Yavanna took, and then the Trees died, and their lifeless stems stand yet in Valinor, a memorial of vanished joy. But the flower and fruit Yavanna gave to Aulë, and Manwë hallowed them; and Aulë and his folk made vessels to hold them and preserve their radiance, as is said in the *Narsilion*, the Song of the Sun and Moon. These vessels the gods gave to Varda, that they might become lamps of heaven, outshining the ancient stars, being nearer to Arda; and she gave them power to traverse the lower regions of Ilmen, and set them to voyage upon appointed courses above the girdle of the Earth from the West unto the East, and to return.

§169 These things the Valar did, recalling in their twilight the darkness of the lands of Arda; and they resolved now to illumine Middle-earth and with light to hinder the deeds of Morgoth. For they remembered the Quendi, the Avari that had remained by the waters of their awakening, and did not utterly forsake the Noldor in exile; and Manwë knew also that the hour of the coming of Men was drawn nigh.

§170 Indeed it is said that, even as the Valar made war upon Melkor on behalf of the Quendi, so now for that time they forbore on behalf of the Hildi, the Aftercomers, younger children of Eru. For grievous had been the hurts of Middle-earth in the war upon Utumno, and the Valar feared lest even worse should now befall; whereas the Hildi should be mortal, and weaker than the Quendi to withstand fear and tumult. Moreover it was not revealed to Manwë where the beginning of Men should be, north, south, or east. Therefore the Valar sent forth light, but made strong the land of their dwelling.

§171 Isil the Sheen the Vanyar of old named the Moon, flower of Telperion in Valinor; and Anar the Fire-golden, fruit of Laurelin, they named the Sun. But the Noldor named them Rána the wayward, and Vása the consumer; for the Sun was set as a sign for the awakening of Men and the waning of the Elves, but the Moon cherishes their memory.

§172 The maiden whom the Valar chose from among the Maiar to guide the vessel of the Sun was named Arien, and he that steered the island of the Moon was Tilion.* In the days of

* Marginal notes against *Arien* and *Tilion*: 'dægred Æ' and 'hyrned Æ'.

the Trees Arien had tended the golden flowers in the gardens of Vana and refreshed them with the bright dews of Laurelin. Tilion was a young hunter of the company of Oromë, and he had a silver bow. He was a lover of silver, and when he would rest he forsook the woods of Oromë and went unto Lorien and lay adream by the pools of Estë in the flickering beams of Telperion; and he begged to be given the task of tending ever the last Flower of Silver. Arien the maiden was mightier than he, and she was chosen because she had not feared the heats of Laurelin, and was unhurt by them, being from the beginning a spirit of fire, whom nonetheless Melkor had not deceived nor drawn to his service. Fair indeed was Arien to behold, but too bright were her eyes for even the Eldar to look on, and leaving Valinor she forsook the form and raiment which, like the Valar, she had there worn, and she was as a naked flame, terrible in the fullness of her splendour.

1500

§173 Isil was first wrought and made ready, and first rose into the realm of the stars, and was the elder of the new lights, as was Telperion of the Trees. Then for a while the world had moonlight, and many things stirred and woke that had waited long in the sleep of Yavanna. The servants of Morgoth were amazed, but the dark-elves looked up in delight; and it is told that Fingolfin set foot upon the Northern Lands with the first moon-rise, and the shadows of his host were long and black. Tilion had traversed the heavens seven times, and was thus in the furthest East when the vessel of Arien was made ready. Then Anar arose in glory, and the snow upon the mountains glowed as with fire, and there was heard the sound of many waterfalls; but the servants of Morgoth fled to Angband and cowered in fear, and Fingolfin unfurled his banners.

§174 Now Varda purposed that the two vessels should journey in Ilmen and ever be aloft, but not together: each should pass from Valinor into the East and return, the one issuing from the West as the other turned from the East. Thus the first of the new days were reckoned after the manner of the Trees from the mingling of the lights when Arien and Tilion passed in their courses, above the middle of the Earth. But Tilion was wayward and uncertain in speed, and held not to his appointed path; and he sought to come near to Arien, being drawn by the splendour of her beauty, though the flame of Anar scorched him, and the island of the Moon was darkened.

§175 Because of the waywardness of Tilion, therefore, and yet more because of the prayers of Lorien and Estë, who said that sleep and rest had been banished from the Earth, and the stars were hidden, Varda changed her counsel, and allowed a time wherein the world should still have shadow and half-light. Anar rested, therefore, a while in Valinor, lying upon the cool bosom of the Outer Sea; and Evening, which was the time of the descent and resting of the Sun, was the hour of greatest light and joy in Aman. But soon the Sun was drawn down by the servants of Ulmo, and went then in haste under the Earth, and came so unseen to the East and there mounted the heaven again, lest night should be over-long and evil walk under the Moon. But by Anar the waters of the Outer Sea were made hot and glowed with coloured fire, and Valinor had light for a while after the passing of Arien. Yet as she journeyed under the Earth and drew towards the East the glow faded and Valinor was dim, and the Valar mourned then most for the death of Laurelin. At dawn the shadows of their Mountains of Defence lay heavy on the land of the Valar.

§176 Varda commanded the Moon to journey in like manner, and passing under Earth to arise in the East, but only after the Sun had descended from heaven. But Tilion went with uncertain pace, as yet he goes, and was still drawn towards Arien, as he shall ever be; so that oft both may be seen above the Earth together, or at times it will chance that he comes so nigh that his shadow cuts off her brightness, and there is a darkness amid the day.

§177 Therefore by the coming and going of Anar the Valar reckoned the days thereafter until the Change of the World. For Tilion tarried seldom in Valinor, but more oft would pass swiftly over the westland of Aman, over Arvalin, or Araman, or Valinor, and plunge in the chasm beyond the Outer Sea, pursuing his way alone amid the grots and caverns at the roots of Arda. There he would oft wander long, and late would return.

§178 Still therefore, after the Long Night, the light of Valinor was greater and fairer than upon Middle-earth; for the Sun rested there, and the lights of heaven drew nearer to Earth in that region. But neither the Sun nor the Moon can recall the light that was of old, that came from the Trees ere they were touched by the poison of Ungoliantë. That light lives now in the Silmarils alone, and they are lost.

§179 But Morgoth hated the new lights and was for a while confounded by this unlooked-for stroke of the Valar. Then he assailed Tilion, sending spirits of shadow against him, and there was strife in Ilmen beneath the paths of the stars, and Tilion was the victor: as he ever yet hath been, though still the pursuing darkness overtakes him at whiles. But Arien Morgoth feared with a great fear, and dared not to come nigh her, having indeed no longer the power. For as he grew in malice, and sent forth from himself the evil that he conceived in lies and creatures of wickedness, his power passed into them and was dispersed, and he himself became ever more earth-bound, unwilling to issue from his dark strongholds. With shadow therefore he hid himself and his servants from Arien, the glance of whose eyes they could not long endure, and the lands nigh his dwelling were shrouded in fumes and great clouds.[1]

§180 But seeing the assault upon Tilion the Valar were in doubt, fearing what the malice and cunning of Melkor might yet contrive against them. Being unwilling, as hath been said, yet to make war upon him in Middle-earth, they remembered nonetheless the ruin of Almaren and resolved that the like should not befall Valinor. Therefore at this time they fortified Valinor anew; and they raised up the mountain-walls of the Pelóri to sheer and dreadful heights, east, north, and south. Their outer sides were dark and smooth, without foothold or ledge,[2] and they fell in great precipices with faces hard as glass, and they rose up to towers with crowns of white ice. A sleepless watch was set upon them. No pass led through them – save only at the Kalakiryan[3] wherein still stood forsaken the green hillof Túna. This pass the Valar did not close because of the Eldar that were faithful: for all those of elven-race, even the Vanyar and Ingwë their lord, must breathe at whiles the outer air and the wind that comes over the Sea from the lands of their birth; and the gods would not sunder the Teleri wholly from their kin. Therefore in the Kalakiryan they set strong towers and many sentinels; and at its issue upon the plains of Valmar a host was encamped; for the armouries of the Valar were opened, and the Maiar and the Sons of the Valar were arrayed as for war. Neither bird nor beast nor Elf nor Man, nor any other creature beside that dwelt in Middle-earth, could pass that leaguer.

§181 And in that time also, which songs call *Nurtalë Valinóreva*, the Hiding of Valinor, the Enchanted Isles were set, and all the seas about them were filled with shadows and bewilderment; and these isles were strung as a net in the Shadowy Seas[4] from north unto south, before Tol Eressëa, the Lonely Isle, is reached by one sailing west. Hardly might any vessel pass between them: for in the dangerous sounds the waves sighed for ever upon dark rocks shrouded in mist. And in the twilight a great weariness came upon mariners and a loathing of the Sea; but all that ever set foot upon the islands were there entrapped, and slept until the Change of the World. Thus it was that, as Mandos foretold to them in Araman, the Blessed Realm was shut against the Noldor, and of the many messengers that in after-days they sent into the West none came ever to Valinor – save one only: the mightiest mariner of song.

Here with the Hiding of Valinor
end
The Annals of Aman

NOTES

1 This paragraph, from 'Then he assailed Tilion ...', was first written thus:
   Tilion indeed he assailed, sending dark spirits of shadow against him, which still pursue him, though ever yet Tilion has overcome them. But Arien he feared with a great fear and dared not to trouble, and neither he nor any of his creatures could look upon her, nor long endure the glance of her eyes. In shadows he hid their wickedness from her, and sent forth fumes and dark clouds, so that the lands near his dwelling were drear and shrouded in glooms, though far above bright Anar might sail in blue heaven. For as he grew in malice and let issue forth from him the evil that he conceived in lies and creatures of ill-
   At this point my father stopped, struck out what he had written, and replaced it with the text printed.
2 As first written this phrase read: 'without ledge or foothold even for birds', corrected immediately to the text given (QS has 'without ledge or foothold for aught save birds').
3 *Kalakiryan* was here so written (and again below); see p. 87, note 7.
4 'the Shadowy Seas' (as in QS) emended from 'the Great Sea'.

Commentary on the sixth and last section of the
Annals of Aman

This account of the Making of the Sun and Moon was the last that my father wrote. He was following QS Chapter 8 *Of the Sun and Moon and the Hiding of Valinor* (V.239–43) very closely, but with many changes and notably many omissions. I indicate here most of the developments, some much more significant than others.

§164 With the silent communion of the Valar among themselves, not in QS, cf. what is said in *The Return of the King* VI.6 'Many Partings' of the speech of Celeborn and Galadriel, Gandalf and Elrond in Eregion:

> If any wanderer had chanced to pass, little would he have seen or heard, and it would have seemed to him only that he saw grey figures, carved in stone, memorials of forgotten things now lost in unpeopled lands. For they did not move or speak with mouth, looking from mind to mind; and only their shining eyes stirred and kindled as their thoughts went to and fro.

Perhaps to be compared also are Michael Ramer's remarks in *The Notion Club Papers*, IX.202.

§165 The praise of Fëanor, and Manwë's thought concerning his words, are not in QS, nor the foretelling of Mandos that Fëanor will soon come to him.

§167 In QS Nienna is not named with Yavanna in the attempt to heal the Trees.

§168 The QS text 'lamps of heaven, outshining the ancient stars; and she gave them power to traverse the region of the stars' is changed to 'lamps of heaven, outshining the ancient stars, *being nearer to Arda*; and she gave them power to traverse *the lower regions* of Ilmen'. AAm here moves in fact closer to the *Ambarkanta*, where it was told (IV.237) that the Sun 'sails from East to West *through the lower Ilmen*'. I have said earlier (p. 63) that 'the testimony seems to be that in these texts [i.e. AAm and the *Ainulindalë*] the *Ambarkanta* world-image survived at least in the conception of the Outer Sea extending to the Walls of the World'; now it is seen that the region of Ilmen, in which the Sun and Moon have their courses, survived also. Is it to be understood that Ilmen was also still the region of the stars? This is not a necessary presumption from the wording of the new text at this point; however, in §173 it is said that 'Isil ... rose *into the realm of the stars*'. In the *Ainulindalë* the problem has been encountered that 'the three regions of the firmament' are retained together with the irreconcilable conception of Arda as set 'in the midst of the innumerable stars' of Ëa: see p. 29.

With 'the girdle of the Earth' (not in QS) cf. AAm §144: 'Túna beneath Taniquetil was set nigh to the girdle of Arda, and there the Great Sea was immeasurably wide'.

§170 It is not said in QS that the Valar forbore to make war upon Morgoth on account of the coming of Men that was at hand, fearing great destruction and being ignorant of the place where Mankind should arise.

§171 In QS *Isil* and *Úrin* are names given by the Gods to Moon and Sun, and *Rana* and *Anar* the Eldarin names (§75 and commentary). In AAm *Isil* and *Anar* become Vanyarin names, and *Rána* and *Vása* Noldorin; so also in *The Lost Road* (V.41) and *The Notion Club Papers* (IX.306) the 'Eressëan' or 'Avallonian' (i.e. Quenya) names are *Isil* and *Anar*.

§172 One of the Old English glosses by Ælfwine, *hyrned* 'horned' of Tilion, is found already in QS (marginal note to §75); the other word, *dægred*, of Arien, meant 'daybreak, dawn'.

It is not now said that Tilion loved Arien (and for this reason forsook the woods of Oromë and dwelt in the gardens of Lórien), though in §174 Tilion 'sought to come near to Arien, being drawn by the splendour of her beauty'. The description of the fire-spirit Arien, who ceased to clothe herself in any form but became 'as a naked flame', is not in QS; the original story of Urwendi in the *Lost Tales* may be compared (I.187).

§173 'Isil... rose into the realm of the stars': see under §168 above. The idea of the stars fleeing 'affrighted' from Tilion, who wandered from his path pursuing them, is abandoned (as is also subsequently the mythical explanation of shooting stars – stars that had fled to the roots of the Earth and now flee again from Tilion into the upper air, QS §78).

§§175–8 The account of the motions of the Sun and Moon is put entirely into the past tense, where QS uses the present.

§175 Estë takes the place of Nienna as complaining against the new lights. – The name *Vaiya* is not used of the Outer Sea in AAm.

§177 'Therefore by the coming and going of Anar the Valar reckoned the days thereafter *until the Change of the World*': there is nothing corresponding to this in QS (§78). – The passage in QS (and very similarly in the *Ambarkanta*, IV.237) concerning the coming at times of both Arien and Tilion together above Valinor is abandoned.

In QS Tilion 'plunges into the chasm between the shores of the earth and the Outer Sea', and similarly in the *Ambarkanta* he plunges into the chasm of Ilmen. In AAm, on the other hand, he would 'plunge in the chasm *beyond the Outer Sea*'. As I have said previously (IV.254, second footnote) I am at a loss to explain this, though I retained it in the published *Silmarillion* which here derives from AAm. But in view of the fact that in AAm it is said expressly (§23) that the Outer Sea encircled the Kingdom of Arda, and beyond the Outer Sea were the Walls of the Night, I am now inclined to think that the sentence in AAm was a slip, that whatever my father intended it was not what he wrote. For even if we suppose that the relations of Ilmen, the Chasm, the Outer Sea, and the Walls were now in some way differently conceived, it remains that Tilion after plunging in the chasm *came to the roots of Arda*: he must therefore still be *within* the Outer Sea, which encompasses Arda.

§178 The idea of the storing by the Valar of the radiance of the Sun in vessels, vats, and pools (QS §79) is omitted in AAm.

The last words of this paragraph, 'and they are lost', are not in QS, but are in fact derived from the *Ainulindalë*: 'the fairest of all gems were the Silmarils, and they are lost', which first appeared in the original *Music of the Ainur* (I.58) and survived through the later texts (V.162, and in this book p. 19, §35).

§§179–80 The prophecy of the rekindling of the Trees is omitted (and this ancient feature finally lost, see IV.20, 49–50), as is the foretelling by Ulmo concerning Men; but there now appears the assault on Tilion by Morgoth, his great fear of Arien, and the account of his loss of power through dispersion among his slaves. The phrase in §179 'though still the pursuing darkness overtakes him at whiles' evidently refers to eclipses of the Moon.

The further fortification of Valinor still of course arises from the fear of the Valar of 'the might and cunning of Morgoth' (QS), but Morgoth's attack on the Moon is now the mainspring of their fear: 'But seeing the assault upon Tilion the Valar were in doubt, fearing what the malice and cunning of Melkor might yet contrive against them.'

§180 The hill of Túna is said to be forsaken; it is not said in the account of Finrod's return (§156) that he ruled thereafter in Tirion, but only (as in QS, §72) that he 'was set to rule the remnant of the Noldor in the Blessed Realm.' In QS §79, however, 'the remnant of the Gnomes dwelt ever in the deep cleft of the mountains.'

'the Maiar and the Sons of the Valar': see p. 59, §4.

§181 The Hiding of Valinor is called *Nurtalë Valinóreva*. – In QS mariners who set foot upon the Enchanted Isles 'are there entrapped and wound in everlasting sleep'; in AAm they 'were there entrapped, and slept until the Change of the World.' With the reference to the Change of the World cf. under §177 above; and with the change from present to past tense cf. under §§175–8.

My father scribbled a few hasty notes on the typescript, but those that arose from his later rejection of the essentials of the cosmogonic myth are not given here. The following may however be recorded:

§169 The words 'utterly forsake' were underlined, with a marginal note: 'They *forbade* return and made it impossible for Elves or Men to reach Aman – since that experiment had proved disastrous. But they would not give the Noldor *aid* in fighting Melkor. Manwë however sent Maia spirits in Eagle form to dwell near Thangorodrim and keep watch on all that Melkor did and assist the Noldor in extreme cases. Ulmo went to Beleriand and took a secret but active part in Elvish resistance.' On the Eagles as Maiar see pp. 409–11.

§170 Beside this paragraph (and evidently arising from the words 'it was not revealed to Manwë where the beginning of Men should be') my father noted on the typescript that Manwë told the other Valar that he had been visited by the mind of Eru, and warned that Men might not be taken living from Middle-earth.

§176 Against the last sentence of this paragraph my father wrote: 'What then causes eclipses of the Moon?' See the commentary on §§179–80 above.

PART THREE

THE LATER
QUENTA SILMARILLION

THE LATER *QUENTA SILMARILLION*

(I) THE FIRST PHASE

In this book, as explained in the Foreword, my account of the development of *The Silmarillion* in the years following the completion of *The Lord of the Rings* is restricted to the 'Valinorian' part of the narrative – that is to say, to the part corresponding to the *Annals of Aman*.

As with the *Annals of Valinor (Aman)* (p. 47), my father did not begin revision of the *Quenta Silmarillion* as a new venture on blank sheets, but took up again the original QS manuscript and the typescript (entitled *'Eldanyárë'*) derived from it (see V.199–201) and covered them with corrections and expansions. As already seen (p. 3), he noted that the revision had reached the end of the tale of Beren and Lúthien on 10 May 1951. The chapters were very differently treated, some being much more developed than others and running to several further texts.

An amanuensis typescript was then made, providing a reasonably clear and uniform text from the now complicated and difficult materials. This was made by the same person as made the typescript of *Ainulindalë* D (p. 39) and seems to have been paginated continuously on from it. I shall call this typescript 'LQ 1' (for 'Later Quenta 1', i.e. 'the first continuous text of the later *Quenta Silmarillion*'). It seems virtually certain that it was made in 1951(–2).

LQ 1 was corrected, at different times and to greatly varying extent. A new typescript, in top copy and carbon, was professionally made later, incorporating all the alterations made to LQ 1. This text I shall call 'LQ 2'. In a letter to Rayner Unwin of 7 December 1957 (*Letters* no.204) my father said:

> I now see quite clearly that I must, as a necessary preliminary to 'remoulding',[*] get copies made of all copyable material. And I shall put that in hand as soon as possible. But I think the best way of dealing with this (at this stage, in which much of the stuff is in irreplaceable sole copies) is to install a typist in my room in college, and not let any material out of my keeping, until it is multiplied.

---

[*] This word refers to a letter from Lord Halsbury, who had said: 'I can quite see that there is a struggle ahead to re-mould it into the requisite form for publication' (cited earlier in my father's letter to Rayner Unwin).

It seems likely that it was soon after this that LQ 2 was made. It is noteworthy that it was typed on the same machine as was used for the typescript of the *Annals of Aman* (also extant in top copy and carbon), and both texts may well belong to the same time – say 1958. LQ 2 (like LQ 1) has naturally no textual value in itself, but it received careful emendation in Chapter 1 *Of the Valar* (thereafter, however, only scattered jottings).

Finally, my father turned to new narrative writing in the Matter of the First Age before the Hiding of Valinor. The first chapter, *Of the Valar*, much altered at this time, became separated off from the *Quenta Silmarillion* proper under the title *Valaquenta*; while the sixth chapter, *Of the Silmarils and the Darkening of Valinor* (numbered 4 in QS, V.227), and a part of the seventh, *Of the Flight of the Noldor* (numbered 5 in QS), were very greatly enlarged and gave rise to new chapters with these titles:

Of Finwë and Míriel
Of Fëanor and the Unchaining of Melkor
Of the Silmarils and the Unrest of the Noldor
Of the Darkening of Valinor
Of the Rape of the Silmarils
Of the Thieves' Quarrel

This new work exemplifies the 'remoulding' to which my father looked forward in the letter to Rayner Unwin cited above. It represents (together with much other writing of a predominantly speculative nature) a second phase in his later work on *The Silmarillion*. The first phase included the new version of the *Lay of Leithian*, the later *Ainulindalë*, the *Annals of Aman* and the *Grey Annals*, the later *Tale of Tuor*, and the first wave of revision of the *Quenta Silmarillion*, much of this work left unfinished. The years 1953–5 saw the preparation and publication of *The Lord of the Rings*; and there seems reason to think that it was a good while yet before he turned again to *The Silmarillion*, or at least to its earlier chapters.

In these substantially rewritten chapters of the 'second phase' he was moving strongly into a new conception of the work, a new and much fuller mode of narrative – envisaging, as it appears, a thoroughgoing 're-expansion' from the still fairly condensed form (despite a good deal of enlargement in the 1951 revision) that went back through QS and Q to the 'Sketch of the Mythology' of 1926, which had made a brief summary from the amplitude of *The Book of Lost Tales* (on this evolution see IV.76).

It has been difficult to find a satisfactory method of presentation for the later evolution of *The Silmarillion*. In the first place, the chapters must obviously be treated separately, since the extent of the later development, and the textual history, varies so widely. Equally clearly, a complete documentation of every alteration from start to finish (that is, detailing the precise sequence of change through successive texts) is out of the question. After much experimentation the plan I have followed is based on this consideration: seeing that a great deal of the development can be ascribed to a relatively short time (the '1951 revision'), it seems best to take LQ 1, marking the end of that stage, as the 'common text'. But while I print LQ 1 in full as it was typed (as far as Chapter 5: Chapters 6–8 are differently treated), I also include in the text the corrections and expansions made to it subsequently, indicated as such. This gives at once a view of the state of the work in both LQ 1, at the end of the 'first phase', and in LQ 2, at the beginning of the 'second phase' some seven years later. Beyond this, the treatment of each chapter varies according to the peculiarities of its history. The late expanded versions of certain chapters belonging to the 'second phase' are treated separately (pp. 199 ff.).

Particular difficulties are encountered in the later work on *The Silmarillion*, in that so much of the typescript material was not made by my father, and he seems often to have corrected these texts without going back to the earlier ones from which they were taken; while when there were both top copy and carbon copy he often kept them in different places (for fear of loss), and one copy is often emended differently from the other, or one is not emended when the other is. Moreover he was liable to emend a text *after* later texts had been derived from it.

★

1 OF THE VALAR

In my edition of 'QS' in Volume V of this history the text of the first chapters (1, 2, 3(a), 3(b), 3(c)) is taken from the typescript which my father made from the QS manuscript in (as I have argued, V.200) December 1937–January 1938, and which incorporated certain revisions made to the opening chapters on the manuscript. This text I will refer to as 'the QS typescript'. Both manuscript and typescript were used for the '1951 revision', but it was the latter that was the copy from which LQ 1 was made, there being some fourteen years between them. As already explained, the changes made subsequently to LQ 1 are shown as such in the text.

There is now no title-page to LQ 1 (see p. 200), which begins with Ælfwine's note (with the Old English verses) and the Translator's note in an almost exact copy of the old QS typescript (V.203–4), the only difference being *Pengoloth* for *Pengolod* (at the first occurrence changed to *Pengolodh*, representing voiced 'th'). The page, like that of the QS typescript, is headed *Eldanyarë* (History of the Elves).

The paragraph numbers are those of QS (V.204–7), with '10a' and '10b' used to indicate the passages additional to the text of QS, and belonging to different times, at the end of the chapter.

Here begins the Silmarillion or History of the Silmarils

1. Of the Valar

§1 In the beginning Eru, [*added:* the One,] who in Elvish tongue is named Ilúvatar, made the Ainur of his thought; and they made a great music before him. Of this Music the World was made; for Ilúvatar made visible the song of the Ainur, and they beheld it as a light in the darkness. And many of the mightiest among them became enamoured of its beauty and of its history which they saw beginning and unfolding as in a Vision. Therefore Ilúvatar gave to their vision Being, and set it amid the Void, and the Secret Fire was sent to burn at the heart of the World.

Then those of the Ainur who would entered into the World at the beginning of Time, and behold! it was their task to achieve it and by their labour to fulfill the Vision which they had seen. Long they laboured in the regions of Eä, which are vast beyond the thought of Elves and Men, until in the time appointed was made Arda, the Kingdom of Earth. Then they put on the raiment of Earth and descended into it and dwelt therein; and they are therein.

§2 These spirits the Elves name the Valar, which is the Powers, and Men have often called them gods. Many lesser spirits of their own kind they brought in their train, both great and small; and some of these Men have confused with the Elves, but wrongfully [*read* wrongly], for they were made before the World, whereas Elves and Men awoke first on Earth, after the coming of the Valar. Yet in the making of Elves and of Men, and in the giving to each of their especial gifts, none of the Valar had any part. Ilúvatar alone was their author; wherefore they are called the Children of Ilúvatar [> Eru].

§3 The chieftains of the Valar were nine. These were the names of the Nine Gods [> gods] in the Elvish tongue as it was spoken in Valinor; though they have other or altered names in the speech of the Gnomes [> Sindar], and their names among Men are manifold: Manwë and Melkor, Ulmo, Aulë, Mandos, Lorien [> Lorion], Tulkas, Ossë, and Oromë.

§4 Manwë and Melkor were brethren in the thought of Ilúvatar / and mightiest of those Ainur who came into the World. But Manwë is the lord of the gods, and prince of the airs and winds, and ruler of the sky. With him dwells as wife Varda the maker of the stars [> The mightiest of those Ainur who came into the World was Melkor; but Manwë was dearest to the heart of Ilúvatar and understood most clearly his purposes. He was appointed to be, in the fullness of time, the first of all kings: lord of the realm of Arda and ruler of all that dwell therein. And there his delight is in the winds of the world and in all the regions of the air. With him in Arda dwells as spouse Varda kindler of the stars], immortal lady of the heights, whose name is holy. Fionwë and Ilmarë are their son and daughter [*this sentence struck out*]. Next in might and closest in friendship to Manwë is Ulmo, lord of waters. He dwells alone in the Outer Seas, but has the government of all waters, seas, and rivers, fountains and springs, throughout the earth. Subject to him is Ossë, the master of the seas about the lands of Men; and his wife is Uinen the lady of the sea. Her hair lies spread through all the waters under skies.

§5 Aulë has might but little less [> little less] than Ulmo. He is a smith and a master of crafts; and his spouse is Yavanna, the giver of fruits and lover of all things that grow. In majesty she is next to Varda, her sister, among the queens of the Valar. She is fair and tall, and often the Elves name her Palúrien, the Lady of the Wide Earth.

§6 The Fanturi [> Fëanturi] were brethren, and are named Mandos and Lorien [> Lorion]. Yet these are not their right names, and are the names rather of the places of their abiding. For their right names are seldom spoken save in secret: which are Námo and Irmo. Quoth Rúmil. Nurufantur the elder was also called, [> which are Námo and Irmo. Námo, the elder, is] the master of the houses of the dead, and the gatherer of the spirits of the slain. He forgets nothing, and knows all that shall be, save only what Ilúvatar has hidden; but he speaks only at the command of Manwë. He is the doomsman of the Valar. Vairë the weaver is his wife, who weaves all things that have been in time in her storied webs, and the halls of Mandos that ever widen as the ages pass are clothed therewith. Olofantur the younger of these brethren was also named, [> Irmo, the younger of these brethren, is] the master of visions and of dreams. His gardens in the land of the gods are the fairest of all places in the world, and filled with many spirits. Estë the pale is his wife, who walks not by day, but sleeps on an island in the dark lake of Lorien [> Lorion]. Thence her fountains bring refreshment to the folk of Valinor; yet she comes not to the councils of the Valar, and is not reckoned among their queens.

§7   Strongest of limb, and greatest in deeds of prowess, is Tulkas, who is surnamed Poldórëa the Valiant. He is unclothed in his disport, which is much in wrestling; and he rides no steed, for he can outrun all things that go on feet, and he is tireless. His hair and beard are golden, and his flesh ruddy; his weapons are his hands. He recks little of either past or future, and is of small avail as a counsellor, but a hardy friend. He has great love for Fionwë, son [> Ëonwë, herald] of Manwë. His wife is Nessa, sister of Oromë; she is lissom of limb and fleet of foot, and dances in Valinor upon lawns of never-fading green.

§8   Oromë is a mighty lord, and little less than Tulkas in strength, or in wrath, if he be aroused. He loved the lands of Earth, while they were still dark, and he left them unwillingly and came last to Valinor; and he comes even yet at times east over the mountains. Of old he was often seen upon the hills and plains. He is a hunter, and he loves all trees; for which reason he is called Aldaron, and by the Gnomes [> Sindar] Tauros [> Tauron], the lord of forests. He delights in horses and in hounds, and his horns are loud in the friths and woods that Yavanna planted in Valinor; but he blows them not upon the Middle-earth since the fading of the Elves, whom he loved. Vána is his wife, the ever-young, the queen of flowers, who has the beauty both of heaven and of earth upon her face and in all her works; she is the younger sister of Varda and Palúrien.

§9   But mightier than she is Niënna, Manwë's sister and Melkor's. She dwells alone. Pity is in her heart, and mourning and weeping come to her; shadow is her realm and her throne hidden. For her halls are west of West, nigh to the borders of the World and Darkness [*read* the Darkness]; and she comes seldom to Valmar, the city of the gods, where all is glad. She goes rather to the halls of Mandos, which are nearer and yet more northward; and all those who go to Mandos cry to her. For she is a healer of hurts, and turns pain to medicine and sorrow to wisdom. The windows of her house look outward from the walls of the World.

§10   Last do all name Melkor. But the Gnomes [> Noldor], who suffered most from his evil deeds, will not speak his name, and they call him Morgoth, the black god [> the Black Foe], and Bauglir, the Constrainer. Great might was given to him by Ilúvatar, and he was coëval with Manwë, and part he had of all the powers of the other Valar; but he turned them to evil uses.

He coveted the world and all that was in it, and desired the lordship of Manwë and the realms of all the gods; and pride and jealousy and lust grew ever in his heart, till he became unlike his brethren. Wrath consumed him, and he begot violence and destruction and excess. In ice and fire was his delight. But darkness he used most in all his evil works, and turned it to fear and a name of dread among Elves and Men.

§10a Thus it may be seen that there are nine Valar, and Seven queens of the Valar of no less might; for whereas Melkor and Ulmo dwell alone, so also doth Nienna, while Estë is not numbered among the Rulers. But the Seven Great Ones of the Realm of Arda are Manwë and Melkor, Varda, Ulmo, Yavanna, Aulë, and Nienna; for though Manwë is their chief [> king], in majesty they are peers, surpassing beyond compare all others whether of the Valar and their kin, or of any other order that Ilúvatar has conceived [> caused to be].

§10b [*All the following was added to the typescript in ink:* With the Valar were other spirits whose being also began before the world: these are the *maiar*, of the same order as the Great but of less might and majesty. Among them Eönwë the herald of Manwë, and Ilmarë handmaid of Varda were the chief. Many others there are who have no names among Elves or Men, for they appear seldom in forms visible. But great and fair was Melian of the people of Yavanna, who [*struck out:* on her behalf] tended once the gardens of Estë, ere she came to Middle-earth. And wise was Olórin, counsellor of Irmo: secret enemy of the secret evils of Melkor, for his bright visions drove away the imaginations of darkness.

Of Melian much is later told; but of Olórin this tale does not speak. In later days he dearly loved the Children of Eru, and took pity on their sorrows. Those who hearkened to him arose from despair; and in their hearts the desire to heal and to renew awoke, and thoughts of fair things that had not yet been but might yet be made for the enrichment of Arda. Nothing he made himself and nothing he possessed, but kindled the hearts of others, and in their delight he was glad.

But not all of the *maiar* were faithful to the Valar; for some were from the beginning drawn to the power of Melkor, and others he corrupted later to his service. Sauron was the name by which the chief of these was afterwards called, but he was not alone.]

★

All the changes shown in the text of LQ 1 given above were taken up into the second complete and continuous typescript LQ 2, made some seven years later (pp. 141–2), which introduced a few errors. It cannot be said when the alterations were made to LQ 1, though most of them look as if they were made at the same time.

The typescript LQ 2 was much more fully and carefully emended in this chapter than in any subsequent one, though in many cases only on one of the two copies. I give here a list of these alterations:*

§1 After 'the Secret Fire was sent to burn at the heart of the World' was added: 'and it was called Eä', with 'Let it be!' in a footnote (struck out on the top copy).

§2 'and some of these Men have confused with the Elves, but wrongfully' > 'these are the *Maiar*, whom Men have often confounded with the Elves, but wrongly' ('wrongfully' was an error on the part of the typist of LQ 1).

§3 On the form *Lorien* with short vowel see p. 56 note 2. The typist did not understand my father's corrections of the name on LQ 1, which were unclear, and typed at the three occurrences (§§3, 6) *Lorien, Lorin, Lorion*. At the first two my father corrected the name to *Lorinen*, but struck this out, probably at once; his final form on LQ 2 was *Lóriën* (so marked).

§4 'in all the regions of the air.' > '... air; therefore he is surnamed Súlimo.'

The typist of LQ 2 omitted the word 'kindler' after 'Varda', so producing 'Varda of the stars'; my father changed 'stars' to 'Stars', showing that he had not observed the error.

§5 In 'she [Yavanna] is next to Varda, her sister,' the words 'her sister' were struck out (cf. under §8 below).

§6 The opening of the paragraph was again rewritten, to read: 'The Fëanturi were brethren, and are called most often Mandos and Lóriën. Yet these are rightly the names of the places of their abiding; for their true names are Námo and Irmo. Námo, the elder, dwells in Mandos, and is the keeper of the Houses of the Dead'

'(Vairë the weaver is his) wife' > 'spouse'

'His gardens in the land of the gods are the fairest' > 'In Lórien are his gardens in the land of the gods, and they are the fairest'

'(Estë the pale is his) wife' > 'spouse' (top copy only)

'an island in the dark lake of Lorion' > 'an island in the tree-shadowed lake of Lórellin'

---

* No doubt many of the corrections to LQ 1 as a whole belong to the 'second phase' of revision (p. 142), while LQ 2 and the corrections made to it are constituent elements in that phase; but it is obviously far more convenient and clear to set them all out together in relation to the primary text LQ 1.

§7 'Poldórëa' > 'Astaldo'
'His wife is Nessa' > 'His spouse is Nessa'

§8 The earlier part of this paragraph was substantially altered, but almost all of the new text appears on the carbon copy only:

He loved the lands of Middle-earth, and he left them unwillingly and came last to Valinor; and oft of old he passed back east over the mountains, and returned with his host to the hills and plains. He is a hunter of monsters and fell beasts, and delights in horses and hounds, and all trees he loves; and Tauron the Sindar called him, the lord of the forests. The Valaróma was the name of his great horn, the sound of which was like the upgoing of the Sun in scarlet, and the sheer lightning cleaving the clouds. Above all the horns of his host it was heard in the woods that Yavanna brought forth in Valinor; for there he would train his folk and his beasts for the pursuit of the evil creatures of Melkor. But the Valaróma is blown no more upon the Middle-earth since the change of the world and the fading of the Elves, whom he loved.

'she [Vána] is the younger sister of Varda and Palúrien' > 'she is the younger sister of Yavanna' (top copy only)

§9 'Nienna, Manwë's sister and Melkor's' > 'sister of Námo' (top copy only)

§10 'Bauglir' > 'Baugron' (top copy only)
'the lordship of Manwë' > 'the kingship of Manwë' (top copy only)

§10b 'With the Valar were other spirits' > 'With the Valar, as has been said, were other spirits' (top copy only)

'these are the *maiar*' > 'the *Maiar*' (top copy only); *maiar* > *Maiar* again at end.

I have shown all these changes in unnecessary detail since they serve to indicate the nature of much of the material constituting 'the later Silmarillion'.

Commentary on Chapter 1, 'Of the Valar'

§1 The new opening of *The Silmarillion* came in with the first phase of the revision, and it is obvious that it followed and was dependent on the new version of the *Ainulindalë*, with its new conception of the Creation of the World:

Ilúvatar *made visible the song of the Ainur* ... [The Ainur saw the history of the World] *unfolding as in a Vision*. Therefore Ilúvatar *gave to their vision Being* ... *it was their task to achieve it* and by their labour *to fulfill the Vision which they had seen.*

The first form of the new opening, written on the QS manuscript, had 'Long they laboured in the regions of Aman', using that name in the sense that it bore in the later *Ainulindalë* texts ('the Halls of Aman', the World); on the QS typescript (see p. 143) *Aman* was emended to *Eä* (which therefore appears in LQ 1).

§2 The name *Maiar*, introduced in the addition made at the end of LQ 1 (§10b) and appearing in this paragraph in LQ 2, is first found in the preliminary drafting for the *Annals of Aman* (*Mairi* > *Maiar*, p. 49 and note 4). See further under §10b below.

§3 The passing change of *Lorien* to *Lorion* is found also in AAm* (the second, abandoned version of the opening of AAm), p. 65, §1.

§4 On the change to LQ 1 whereby Melkor becomes 'the mightiest of those Ainur who came into the World' (and not possessing only powers equal to those of Manwë) see p. 65, §2.

On the loss of the original sentence 'Fionwë and Ilmarë are their son and daughter', heavily inked out on LQ 1, see under §10b below. So also in the final text D of the *Ainulindalë* the reference to Fionwë and Ilmarë as the son and daughter of Manwë and Varda was strongly blacked out (p. 34, §36).

§5 On the striking out on LQ 2 of the statement that Yavanna was the sister of Varda see under §8 below.

§6 In the earliest phase of the revision a marginal note was added against the names Mandos and Lorien, which as entered on the QS typescript read:

Yet these are not their right names, and are the names rather of the places of their abiding. For their right names are seldom spoken save in secret: which are Núr and Lís. Quoth Rúmil.

(In the *Lost Tales* Mandos is the name of the God, and also the name of his halls; it is also said (I.76) that Vefántur (Mandos) called his halls by his own name, Vê.) *Núr* and *Lís* were then corrected to *Námo* and *Irmo*. The typist of LQ 1 took this up into the body of the text, which was obviously not my father's intention. This typist did the same elsewhere, and my father then restored the passage to its original status as a marginal note; but in this case he left it to stand, getting rid of the words 'Quoth Rúmil' (and of the old name *Nurufantur*; similarly with *Olofantur* subsequently).

At the foot of the page carrying this passage in the carbon copy of LQ 2 he pencilled the following (referring to the names *Námo* and *Irmo*): 'Judgement (of what is)   Desire (of what might be or should be)'.

What is said at the end of the paragraph about Estë is found in AAm (p. 49, §3), where it is also told that she was 'the chief of the Maiar'. This was repeated in AAm* (p. 65, §3), where Nessa is added to Estë as 'the highest among the Maiar'.

The change of 'wife' to 'spouse' was made on LQ 2 in the

accounts of Vairë, Estë, and Nessa (§§6–7); in that of Vána (§8) it was merely overlooked, while Varda had become Manwë's 'spouse' in a change made to LQ 1 (§4), and Yavanna was already Aulë's 'spouse' in QS (§5). The same change was made on the typescript of AAm (p. 69), and its significance is seen from the accompanying marginal comment: 'Note that "spouse" meant only an "association". The Valar had no bodies, but could assume shapes.' At this time the passage in AAm concerning the Children of the Valar was removed (see under §10b below).

§8 In AAm (§133, pp. 111, 124) the form was still *Tauros* (in Fëanor's speech on the summit of Túna), and was not corrected.

The name *Valaróma* (appearing in the expanded passage on LQ 2) occurs in AAm (p. 101, §116) and by emendation of *Rombaras* in *Ainulindalë* D (p. 35, §34).

The statement in §5 that Yavanna is the sister of Varda does not appear in QS, but it was merely derived from that in QS §8, that Vana is 'the younger sister of Varda and Palúrien'. This goes back to Q (IV.79, 167), but no further. Varda and Yavanna were still sisters in AAm (p. 49, §3), but the idea was abandoned in corrections to LQ 2.

§9 That Niënna was the sister of Manwë and Melkor ('brethren in the thought of Ilúvatar') goes back to the earliest *Annals of Valinor* (IV.263), and remained in AAm (p. 49, §3; cf. p. 93, §88, where Niënna aided the prayer of Melkor for pardon 'because of her kinship'). With the change in LQ 2 whereby she becomes 'sister of Námo', omitting Irmo his brother, cf. AAm* (p. 65, §3), where she is named only 'Manwë's sister', omitting Melkor.

§10 The name *Baugron* (changed from *Bauglir* in LQ 2) is found nowhere else. It was not adopted in the published *Silmarillion*.

§10a The meaning of the passage is more evident from a table; the names italicised are 'the Seven Great Ones of the Realm of Arda'.

Manwë..................*Varda*
Melkor
Ulmo
Aulë....................*Yavanna*
                         Niënna
Mandos..................Vairë
Lorien..(Estë)
Tulkas..................Nessa
Ossë....................Uinen
Oromë..................Vána

§10b Fionwë and Ilmarë were removed from §4 as the children of Manwë and Varda, and in §7 Fionwë becomes Ëonwë, 'herald of Manwë'; here Ilmarë becomes 'handmaid of Varda'. This is an aspect of an important development in the conception of the Powers of Arda, the abandonment of the old and long-rooted idea of 'the Children of the Valar, the Sons of the Valar'. It was still present in AAm (p. 49, §4), where the Valarindi, 'the offspring of the Valar', were 'numbered with' the Maiar (but in AAm* they are distinguished from the Maiar, p. 66, §4). On the typescript text of AAm the conception of the Children of the Valar was struck out (see under §6 above).

Melian is a Maia (as in AAm §40), and she is 'of the people of Yavanna' (in QS §31 'she was akin, before the World was made, unto Yavanna'). And here Olórin (Gandalf), as 'counsellor of Irmo', enters *The Silmarillion*.

In AAm (p. 52, §17) Sauron ('a great craftsman of the household of Aulë') is likewise said to have been the chief of the Maiar who turned to Melkor.

It may be that the (relatively) heavy correction carried out on the LQ 2 text of this chapter was the preliminary to its final, enlarged form called the *Valaquenta* (pp. 199 ff.).

2 OF VALINOR AND THE TWO TREES

The textual situation in this chapter differs from that in Chapter 1, in that here, after the alterations made to the original pre-*Lord of the Rings* texts (the QS manuscript and derived QS typescript) there followed two typescripts made by my father before LQ 1 was made, and in the first of these the opening of the chapter was greatly changed from its form in QS. I shall not however distinguish the 'layers' in the textual history before the amanuensis typescript LQ 1 was reached, although some particular points are recorded in the commentary.

The further development of this chapter from QS was effectively confined to the 1951 revision, since late rewriting and expansion corresponding to the development of the *Valaquenta* out of Chapter 1 *Of the Valar* was not undertaken in this case. It is conceivable, I think, that (while there is no evidence one way or the other) having remade Chapter 1 as the *Valaquenta* my father postponed the rewriting of Chapter 2 because his views on the treatment of the myth of the Two Trees in the light of the later cosmology were too uncertain.

There follows now the text of LQ 1, with the (very few) subsequent changes made to it shown as such. The paragraph numbers correspond to those in QS (V.208–10).

2. Of Valinor and the Two Trees

§11 Now in the beginning of the Kingdom of Arda Melkor contested with his brother Manwë and the Valar for the

Chapter 2 THE LATER *QUENTA SILMARILLION* (I) 153

overlordship, and all that they wrought he hindered or marred, if he might. But he fled before the onset of Tulkas, and there was peace. But since Melkor had perverted light to a destroying flame, when he was gone and his fires were subdued the Valar perceived that the Earth was dark, save for the glimmer of the innumerable stars which Varda had made in the ages unrecorded of the labours of Eä. Aulë, therefore, at the prayer of Yavanna, wrought two mighty Lamps [*added:* Illuin and Ormal] for the lighting of Arda; and the Valar set them upon lofty pillars northward and southward in Middle-earth, and in the light of the Lamps they ordered all their realm, and the desire of Yavanna had fruit, and living things came forth and grew abundantly.

In those days the dwelling of the Valar was upon an isle in a great lake in the midst of the Middle-earth that Aulë had built. There the light of the Lamps mingled and growth was swiftest and fairest; and behold! in the blending of Illuin and Ormal there came forth Greenness, and it was new; and Middle-earth rejoiced, and the Valar praised the name of Yavanna. But Melkor hearing of these works, and being filled with wrath and envy, returned secretly to Arda out of the Darkness and gathered his strength in the North, and he marred the labours of Yavanna, so that the growth of Earth was corrupted and many monstrous things were born. Then coming with war against the Valar suddenly, he cast down the Lamps, and night returned, and in the fall of the pillars of Illuin and Ormal the seas arose and many lands were drowned.

§12 In the darkness and the confusion of the seas the Valar could not at that time overcome Melkor; for his strength had increased with his malice, and he had now gathered to his service many other spirits, and many evil things also of his own making. Thus he escaped from the wrath of the Valar, and far in the North he built himself a fortress, and delved great caverns underground, and deemed that he was secure from assault for ever. But the gods removed into the uttermost West and there made their home and fortified it; and they built many mansions in that land upon the borders of the World, which is called Valinor. And Valinor was bounded upon the hither side by the

---

* [footnote to the text – see page 154] Which is Gársecg: quoth Ælfwine. [This note was mistakenly placed in the text by the typist, and subsequently reinstated as a footnote.]

Great Sea of the West,* and eastward upon its shores the Valar built the Pelóri, the Mountains of Aman, that are highest upon Earth. But on the further side lay the Outer Sea, which encircles the Kingdom of Arda, and is called by the Elves Vaiya. How wide is that sea none know but the gods, and beyond it are the Walls of the World to fence out the Void and the Eldest Darkness.

§13 Now in that guarded land the Valar gathered all light and all fair things; and there are their houses, their gardens, and their towers. In the midst of the plain beyond the Mountains was the City of the Gods [> their city], Valmar the beautiful of many bells. But Manwë and Varda had halls upon the loftiest of the Mountains of Aman, whence they could look out across the Earth even into the furthest East. Taniquetil the Elves name that holy mountain, and Oiolossë Everlasting Whiteness, and Elerína [> Elerrína] Crowned with Stars, and many names beside. But the Gnomes [> Sindar] spoke of it in their later tongue as Amon Uilos.**

§14 In Valinor Yavanna hallowed the mould with mighty song, and Nienna watered it with tears. In that time the gods [> Valar] were gathered together, and they sat silent upon their thrones of council in the Ring of Doom nigh unto the golden gates of Valmar the Blessed; and Yavanna Palúrien sang before them and they watched.

§15 From the earth there came forth two slender shoots; and silence was over all the world in that hour, nor was there any other sound save the slow chanting of Palúrien. Under her song two fair trees uprose and grew. Of all things which the gods [> she] made they have most renown, and about their fate all the tales of the Elder World are woven. The one had leaves of dark green that beneath were as shining silver; and he bore white blossoms like unto a cherry-tree, were it surpassing great and fair; and from each of his countless flowers a dew of silver light was ever falling, but the earth beneath was dappled with

---

* [footnote to the text – see page 153]
** [footnote to the text] In the language of this island of Men *Heofonsýl* was its name among those few that ever descried it afar off. Yet in error [> So I wrote in error], as the Eldar teach me; for that is rightly the name only of the mountain of Númenor, the Meneltarma, which has foundered for ever: quoth Ælfwine. [This note was also mistakenly placed in the text by the typist. See the commentary on §13.]

the dancing shadows of his fluttering leaves. The other bore leaves of a young green like the new-opened beech; their edges were of glittering gold. Flowers swung upon her branches like clusters of yellow flame, formed each to a glowing horn that spilled a golden rain upon the ground; and from the blossom of that tree there came forth warmth and a great light.

§16 Telperion the one was called in Valinor, and Silpion, and Ninquelótë, and many names in song beside; but the Gnomes name him [> but in the Sindarin tongue he was called] Galathilion. Laurelin was the other [> the other was] called, and Malinalda, and Kulúrien, and many other names; but the Gnomes name her [> but the Sindar named her] Galadlóriel.

§17 In seven hours the glory of each tree waxed to full and waned again to naught; and each awoke once more to life an hour before the other ceased to shine. Thus in Valinor twice every day there came a gentle hour of softer light when both Trees were faint and their gold and silver beams were mingled. Telperion was the elder of the Trees and came first to full stature and to bloom; and that first hour in which he shone alone, the white glimmer of a silver dawn, the gods reckoned not into the tale of hours, but named it the Opening Hour, and counted therefrom the ages of their reign in Valinor. Therefore at the sixth hour of the First Day, and of all the joyous days thereafter until the Darkening, Telperion ceased his time of flower; and at the twelfth hour Laurelin her blossoming. And each day of the gods in Valinor [> Aman] contained twelve hours, and ended with the second mingling of the lights, in which Laurelin was waning but Telperion was waxing.* And the dews of Telperion and the spilth of Laurelin Varda let hoard in great vats, like

* [footnote to the text] Other names of Laurelin among the Noldor [> in the Sindarin tongue] are [> were] *Glewellin* (which is the same as *Laurelin*, song of gold), *Lasgalen* green of leaf, and *Melthinorn* tree of gold; and her image in Gondolin was named *Glingal*. [*Struck out*: Of old among the Noldor] The Elder Tree was named also *Silivros* glimmering [> sparkling] rain, *Celeborn* tree of silver, and *Nimloth* pale blossom. But in after days *Galathilion the Less* was the name of the White Tree of Túna, and his seedling was named *Celeborn* in Eressëa, and *Nimloth* in Númenor, the gift of the Eldar. The image of Telperion that Turgon made in Gondolin was *Belthil*. Quoth Pengolod. [Like the previous ones this footnote was put into the body of the text by the typist of LQ 1, but afterwards reinstated in its proper place.]

[*struck out:* unto] shining lakes, that were to all the land of the Valar as wells of water and of light.

Commentary on Chapter 2, 'Of Valinor and the Two Trees'

The final typescript (LQ 2) of this chapter received very few corrections, and those only on the top copy (such as were made are recorded in the commentary that follows). Thus the LQ 1 text given above, with the corrections shown, is virtually the final text of the chapter.

§§11–12   This chapter underwent little change from the text of QS (V.208–10) apart from the greatly expanded opening – in which most of the new material derives from the later *Ainulindalë*. That the much fuller story in AAm (see p. 60, commentary on §§11–29) was written after the revision of the *Silmarillion* chapter can be seen from various points. Thus the old story that Melkor only began the delving of Utumno *after* the fall of the Lamps is still present (see p. 61, §20). The phrase in LQ §11 concerning the first star-making of Varda was first written in the form '... the ages unrecorded of the labours of the Great in Aman' (for *Aman* > *Eä* see p. 149, §1), which shows it to be earlier than the closely similar phrase in AAm (§24): 'Middle-earth lay in a twilight beneath the stars that Varda had wrought in the ages forgotten of her labours in Eä' – where it is used in a distinct context, of the darkness *after* the fall of the Lamps.

§12   The footnote to QS §12 giving the name *Utumno* of Melko's original fortress survived at first in the revised version, but was lost from one of the typescripts and not reinstated.

On the final text LQ 2 my father pencilled a hasty footnote after 'deemed that he was secure from assault for ever':

> The chief of his fortresses was at Utumno in the North of Middle-earth; but he made also a fortress and armoury not far from the northwestern shores of the Sea, to resist any assault from Aman. This was called Angband and was commanded by Saùron, lieutenant of Melkor.

In QS (§§62, 105) the story was that Morgoth, when he returned from Valinor, built Angband on the ruins of Utumno; in AAm (§127, p. 109) this may well have been still present, but the statement of QS §62 that 'Morgoth came back to his ancient habitation' is lacking. Now there enters the story that Melkor built both strongholds in the ancient days – and also that Sauron was the commander of Angband; cf. the late note written on the typescript of AAm (p. 127, §127): 'The making of this fortress [Angband] as a guard against a landing from the West should come earlier.'

The original passage in QS concerning Vaiya, the Outer Sea,

beyond which 'the Walls of the World fence out the Void and the Eldest Dark', reflecting the contemporary *Ambarkanta*, survived in the revision almost unchanged, except that it is now said that none but the Valar know how wide is the Outer Sea (in contrast to the *Ambarkanta* and its diagrams). On the great difficulty of interpreting this passage in the light of the later world-image see pp. 62–4.

On LQ 2 my father emended *Vaiya* to *Ekkaia* (whence its occurrence in the published *Silmarillion*). The Outer Sea is given no Elvish name in AAm.

§13 In the first texts of the 1951 revision the sentence 'and in the language of this island of Men *Heofonsýl* was its name among those few that ever descried it afar off' was part of the text (as it was in QS, with *Tindbrenting* for *Heofonsýl*), and the footnote began at 'Yet in error, as the Eldar teach me ...' This seems the natural arrangement. The typist of LQ 1, as often elsewhere, put the footnote into the body of the text; but my father when correcting LQ 1 put the whole passage into a footnote – in contrast to what he did in a similar case in the first chapter (p. 150, §6), where he left the footnote in the text. It certainly seems clear in these cases that he did not refer back to the texts preceding LQ 1 (see p. 143). – The Old English name *Heofonsýl* 'Pillar of Heaven' occurs in *The Notion Club Papers* of the Meneltarma (IX.314).

§14 *Palúrien* > *Kementári* by a pencilled change on LQ 2. This was as it were a casual change, not made in §15 (nor in §5). *Kementári* occurs in the *Valaquenta* (p. 202).

§16 *Telperion* (not *Silpion*) is the primary name in AAm (first appearing in §5, pp. 50, 59); in the *Silmarillion* tradition it became the primary name by emendation to the first typescript text of the 1951 revision.

§17 With the reference (in the footnote on the names of the Two Trees) to *Galathilion the Less*, the White Tree of Túna, cf. AAm §69 (annal 1142, p. 85): 'In this year Yavanna gave to the Noldor the White Tree, Galathilion, image of the Tree Telperion'.

In the last sentence the word 'vats' was changed to 'wells' on LQ 2 (cf. 'mighty vats' in AAm §28, changed on the typescript to 'shining wells' (p. 69); in AAm* 'deep pools' (p. 68)).

On the carbon copy of LQ 2, which otherwise received no emendations, my father added the following note to the word *spilth* in the last sentence:

meant to indicate that Laurelin is 'founded' on the laburnum. 'jocund spilth of yellow fire' Francis Thompson – who no doubt got the word from Timon of Athens (his vocabulary was largely derived from Elizabethan English)

The reference is to Francis Thompsons's *Sister Songs*, The Proem:

> Mark yonder, how the long laburnum drips
> Its jocund spilth of fire, its honey of wild flame!

Cf. the original description of Laurelin in the *Lost Tales* (I.72): 'all its boughs were hidden by long swaying clusters of gold flowers like a myriad hanging lamps of flame, and light spilled from the tips of these and splashed upon the ground with a sweet noise.' In the earlier versions (from Q through to the first typescript of the 1951 revision) Laurelin was expressly likened to 'those trees Men now call Golden-rain' – that being a name of the laburnum, and the words 'a golden rain' are used in the final form of the passage (§15). – The reference to *Timon of Athens* is to Act II, Scene 2, 'our vaults have wept / With drunken spilth of wine'.

3   OF THE COMING OF THE ELVES

The textual situation here is similar to that in the previous chapter but more complicated. After very substantial revision carried out on the old pre-*Lord of the Rings* texts there followed a typescript made by my father; but after LQ 1 had been taken from it he made further changes to it (mostly very minor, but a major alteration in §20), which were 'lost', since LQ 2 was a straight copy of LQ 1 and he clearly never compared the texts in detail. This typescript I shall refer to for the purposes of this section as 'Text A'. For some reason it ceases to be a typescript at the words 'counselled the Elves to remove' (near the end of §23), which stand at the foot of a page, and becomes a manuscript on the following page with the words 'into the West'. The manuscript portion is in two forms, the first heavily emended, and the second written out fair.

There follows now the text of LQ 1 (the 'lost' alterations made to Text A are given in the commentary). The system of paragraph-numbering in this chapter, and elsewhere, needs a word of explanation. As generally, I have retained the numbers of QS, introducing 'sub-paragraph numbers' (as §18a) where QS has nothing corresponding. Where the revised text expands a QS paragraph into more than one, or several (as in §§20, 23) only the first is numbered.

3.   Of the Coming of the Elves

§18   In all this time, since Melkor overthrew the Lamps, the Middle-earth east of the Mountains was without light. While the Lamps had shone, growth began there which now was checked, because all was again dark. But already the oldest living things had arisen: in the sea the great weeds, and on the earth the shadow of great trees; and in the valleys of the night-clad hills there were dark creatures old and strong. In those lands and forests Oromë would often hunt; and there too at times Yavanna came, singing sorrowfully; for she was grieved at the darkness of Middle-earth and ill content that it was forsaken. But the other Valar came seldom thither; and in the North Melkor built his strength, and gathered his demons about him. These were the first made of his creatures: their hearts were of fire, but they were cloaked in darkness, and terror went before them; they had whips of flame. Balrogs they were named by the Noldor in later days. And in that dark time Melkor made many other monsters of divers shapes and kinds that long troubled the world; yet the Orcs were not made until he had looked upon the Elves, and he made them in mockery of the Children of Ilúvatar. His realm spread now ever southward over the Middle-earth.

§18a It came to pass that the Valar held council, and Yavanna spoke before them, saying: 'Behold, ye mighty of Arda, the Vision of Eru was brief and soon taken away, so that maybe we cannot guess within a narrow count of days the hour appointed. Yet be sure of this: the hour approaches, and within this age our hope shall be revealed, and the Children shall awake. But it is not in Aman that they shall awaken. Shall we then leave the lands of their dwelling desolate and full of evil? Shall they walk in darkness while we have light? Shall they call Melkor lord while Manwë sits upon the Holy Hill?'

And Tulkas cried aloud: 'Nay! Let us make war swiftly! Have we not rested from strife over-long, and is not our strength now renewed? Shall one alone contest with us for ever?'

But at the bidding of Manwë Mandos spoke and he said: 'In this age the Children shall come indeed, but they come not yet. Moreover it is doom that the First Children should come in the darkness and should look first upon the Stars. Great light shall be for their waning. To Varda ever shall they call at need.'

§19 And Varda said naught, but departing from the council she went to the mountain of Taniquetil and looked forth; and she beheld the darkness and was moved.

Then Varda took the silver dews from the vats of Telperion, and therewith she made new stars and brighter against the coming of the First-born. Wherefore she whose name out of the deeps of time and the labours of Eä was Tintallë, the Kindler, was called after by the Elves Elentári, the Queen of the Stars. Karnil and Luinil, Nénar and Lumbar, Alkarinquë and Elemmíre she wrought in that time, and other of her works of old she gathered together and set as signs in Heaven that the gods may read: Wilwarin, Telumendil, Soronúmë, and Anarríma; and Menelmakar with his shining belt that forebodes the Last Battle that shall be. And high in the North as a challenge unto Melkor she set the crown of seven mighty stars to swing, the Valakirka, the Sickle of the Gods and sign of doom. Many names have these stars been given; but in the North in the Elder Days Men called them the Burning Briar: quoth Pengolod [> (quoth Pengoloð)].

§20 It is told that even as Varda ended her labours, and they were long, when first Menelmakar strode up the sky and the blue fire of Helluin flickered in the mists above the borders of the world, in that hour the Children of the Earth awoke, the First-born of Ilúvatar. Themselves they named the Quendi, whom we call Elves (quoth Ælfwine); but Oromë named them in their own tongue Eldar, people of the stars, and that name has since been borne by all that followed him upon the westward road. In the beginning they were stronger and greater than they have since become; but not more fair, for though the beauty of the Quendi in the days of their youth was beyond all other beauty that Ilúvatar has caused to be, it has not perished, but lives in the West, and sorrow and wisdom have enriched it.

And Oromë looking upon the Elves was filled with love and wonder, as though they were beings sudden and marvellous and unforetold. For [so] it shall ever be even with the Valar. From without the world, though all things may be forethought in music or foreshown in vision from afar, to those who enter verily into Eä each in its time shall be met at unawares as something new and strange.

Thus it was that Oromë came upon the Quendi by chance in his wandering, while they dwelt yet silent upon [*read* beside] the star-lit mere, Kuiviénen, Water of Awakening, in the East of Middle-earth. For a while he abode with them and aided them in the making of language; for that was their first work of craft upon Earth, and ever most dear to their hearts, and the fair Elvish speech was sweet in the ears of the Valar. Then swiftly Oromë rode back over land and sea to Valinor, filled with the thought of the beauty of the Elves, and he brought the tidings to Valmar. And the gods rejoiced, and yet were amazed at what he told; but Manwë sat long upon Taniquetil deep in thought, and he sought the counsel of Ilúvatar. And coming then down to Valmar he called a conclave of the Great, and thither came even Ulmo from the Outer Sea.

And Manwë said to the Valar: 'This is the counsel of Ilúvatar in my heart: that we should take up again the mastery of Arda, at whatsoever cost, and deliver the Quendi from the shadows of Melkor.' Then Tulkas was glad; but Aulë was grieved, and it is said that he (and others of the Valar) had before been unwilling to strive with Melkor, foreboding the hurts of the world that must come of that strife.

§21 But now the Valar made ready and came forth from Aman in the strength of war, resolving to assault the fortress of Melkor in the North and make an end. Never did Melkor forget that this war was made on behalf of the Elves and that they were the cause of his downfall. Yet they had no part in those deeds; and little do they know of the riding of the power of the West against the North in the beginning of their days, and of the fire and tumult of the Battle of the Gods. In those days the shape of Middle-earth was changed and broken and the seas were moved. Tulkas it was who at the last wrestled with Melkor and overthrew him, and he was bound with the chain Angainor that Aulë had wrought, and led captive; and the world had peace for a great age. Nonetheless the fortress of Melkor at Utumno had many mighty vaults and caverns hidden with deceit far under earth, and these the Valar did not all discover nor utterly destroy, and many evil things still lingered there; and others were dispersed and fled into the dark and roamed in the waste places of the world, awaiting a more evil hour.

§22 But when the Battle was ended and from the ruin of the North great clouds arose and hid the stars, the Valar drew Melkor back to Valinor bound hand and foot and blindfold, and he was cast into prison in the halls of Mandos, from whence none have ever escaped save by the will of Mandos and Manwë, neither Vala, nor Elf, nor mortal Man. Vast are those halls and strong, and they were built in the north of the land of Aman. There was Melkor doomed to abide for seven [> three] ages long, ere his cause should be tried again, or he should sue for pardon.

§23 Then again the gods were gathered in council and were divided in debate. For some (and of these Ulmo was the chief) held that the Quendi should be left free to walk as they would in

Middle-earth, and with their gifts of skill to order all the lands and heal their hurts. But the most part feared for the Quendi in the dangerous world amid the deceits of the starlit dusk; and they were filled moreover with the love of the beauty of the Elves and desired their fellowship. At the last, therefore, the Valar summoned the Quendi to Valinor, there to be gathered at the knees of the gods in the light of the blessed Trees for ever. And Mandos who had spoken not at all in the debate broke silence and said: 'So it is doomed.' For of this summons came many woes that after befell; yet those who hold that the Valar erred, thinking rather of the bliss of Valinor than of the Earth, and seeking to wrest the will of Ilúvatar to their own pleasure, speak with the tongues [*read* tongue] of Melkor.

Nonetheless the Elves were at first unwilling to hearken to the summons, for they had as yet seen the Valar only in their wrath as they went to war, save Oromë alone, and they were filled with dread. Therefore Oromë was sent again to them, and he chose from among them three ambassadors; and he brought them to Valmar. These were Ingwë and Finwë and Elwë, who after were kings of the Three Kindreds of the Eldar; and coming they were filled with awe by the glory and majesty of the Valar and desired greatly the light and splendour of the Trees. Therefore they returned and counselled the Elves to remove into the West, and the greater part of the people hearkened to their counsel. This they did of their free will, and yet were swayed by the majesty of the gods, ere their own wisdom was full grown. The Elves that obeyed the summons and followed the three kings are called the Eldar, by the name that Oromë gave them; for he was their guide and led them at the last unto Valinor. Yet there were many who preferred the starlight and the wide spaces of the Earth to the rumour of the glory of the Trees, and they remained behind. These are called the Avari, the Unwilling.

§24 The Eldar prepared now a great march from their first homes in the East. When all was made ready, Oromë rode at their head upon Nahar, his white horse shod with gold; and behind him the Eldalië were arrayed in three hosts.

§25 The smallest host and the first to set forth was led by Ingwë, the most high lord of all the Elvish race. He entered into Valinor and sits at the feet of the Powers, and all Elves revere his name; but he has never returned nor looked again upon Middle-earth. The Lindar [> Vanyar] were his folk, fairest of

Chapter 3 THE LATER *QUENTA SILMARILLION* (I)

the Quendi; they are the High Elves, and the beloved of Manwë and Varda, and few Men have spoken with them.

§26 Next came the Noldor, a name of wisdom.* They are the Deep Elves, and the friends of Aulë. Their lord was Finwë, wisest of all the children of the world. His kindred are renowned in song, for they fought and laboured long and grievously in the northern lands of old.

§27 The greatest host came last, and they are named the Teleri, for they tarried on the road, and were not wholly of a mind to pass from the dusk to the light of Valinor. In water they had great delight, and those that came at last to the west shores were enamoured of the Sea. The Sea-elves therefore they became in Valinor, the Soloneldi [> Falmari], for they made music beside the breaking waves. Two lords they had, for their numbers were very great: Elwë Singollo, which signifies Greymantle, and Olwë his brother. The hair of Olwë was long and white, and his eyes were blue; but the hair of Elwë was grey as silver, and his eyes were as stars; he was the tallest of all the Elven-folk.

[§28 The paragraph concerning the people of Dân who left the Great March and turned south was displaced to follow §29; see the Commentary.]

§29 These are the chief peoples of the Eldalië, who passing at length into the uttermost West in the days of the Two Trees are called the Kalaquendi, the Elves of the Light. But others of the Eldar there were who set out indeed upon the Westward March, but became lost upon the long road, or turned aside, or lingered on the shores of Middle-earth. They dwelt by the sea, or wandered in the woods and mountains of the world, yet their hearts were ever turned towards the West. These the Kalaquendi call the Alamanyar [> Úmanyar], since they came never to the Land of Aman and the Blessed Realm. But the Alamanyar [> Úmanyar] and the Avari alike they name the Moriquendi, Elves of the Darkness, for they never beheld the light before the Sun and Moon.

The Alamanyar [> Úmanyar] were for the most part of the

* [footnote to the text] The Gnomes they may be called in our tongue, quoth Ælfwine. (The word that he uses is *Witan*. More is said of this matter in the Tenth Chapter where the tale speaks of the Edain.) [See the commentary on §26.]

race of the Teleri. For the hindmost of that people, repenting of the journey, forsook the host of Olwë, and Dân was their leader; and they turned southward and wandered long and far; and they became a folk apart, unlike their kin, save that they loved water, and dwelt most beside falls and running streams. They had greater lore of living things, tree and herb, bird and beast, than all other Elves. The Nandor they are called. It was Denethor son of Dân who turning again west at last led a part of that people over the mountains into Beleriand ere the rising of the Moon.

§30 Others there were also of the Teleri that remained in Middle-earth. These were the Elves of Beleriand in the west of the Northern lands. They came from the host of Elwë the Grey. He was lost in the woods and many of his folk sought him long in vain; and thus when their kindred departed over Sea they were left behind and went not into the West. Therefore they are called the Sindar, the Grey Elves, but themselves they named Eglath, the Forsaken. Elwë after became their king, mightiest of all the Alamanyar [*correction to* Úmanyar *missed*]. He it was who was called Thingol in the language of Doriath.

[Other names in song and tale are given to these peoples. The Vanyar are the Blessed Elves, and the Spear-elves, the Elves of the Air, the friends of the Gods, the Holy Elves and the Immortal, and the Children of Ingwë; they are the Fair Folk and the White.

The Noldor are the Wise, and the Golden, the Valiant, the Sword-elves, the Elves of the Earth, the Foes of Melkor, the Skilled of Hand, the Jewel-wrights, the Companions of Men, the Followers of Finwë.

The Teleri are the Foam-riders, the Singers of the Shore, the Free, and the Swift, and the Arrow-elves; they are the Elves of the Sea, the Ship-wrights, the Swanherds, the Gatherers of Pearl, the Blue Elves, the people of Olwë. The Nandor are the Host of Dân, the Wood-elves, the Wanderers, the Axe-elves, the Green Elves and the Brown, the Hidden People; and those that came at last to Ossiriand are the Elves of the Seven Rivers, the Singers Unseen, the Kingless, the Weaponless, and the Lost Folk, for they are now no more. The Sindar are the Lemberi, the Lingerers; they are the Friends of Ossë, the Elves of the Twilight, the Silvern, the Enchanters, the Wards of

Melian, the Kindred of Lúthien, the people of Elwë. Quoth Pengoloð.]

Commentary on Chapter 3, 'Of the Coming of the Elves'

LQ 1 is here again, as in the previous chapter, virtually the final text, for the later typescript LQ 2 was scarcely touched, and there was no further enlargement or expansion.

§18 In AAm §30 (p. 70) it is said that Melkor 'wrought' the Balrogs in Utumno during the long darkness after the fall of the Lamps; but in an interpolation to AAm there enters the view that Melkor, after his rebellion, could make nothing that had life of its own (§45, see pp. 74, 78), and in AAm*, the second version of the opening of AAm (p. 79, §30), the Balrogs become the chief of 'the evil spirits that followed him, the Umaiar', whom at that time he *multiplied*. The statement in QS §18 that the Balrogs were 'the first made of his creatures' survived through all the texts of the later revision of the *Quenta*, but in the margin of one of the copies of LQ 2 my father wrote: 'See *Valaquenta* for true account.' This is a reference to the passage which appears in the published *Silmarillion* on p. 31:

> For of the Maiar many were drawn to his splendour in the days of his greatness, and remained in that allegiance down into his darkness; and others he corrupted afterwards to his service with lies and treacherous gifts. Dreadful among these spirits were the Valaraukar, the scourges of fire that in Middle-earth were called the Balrogs, demons of terror.

The actual text of LQ 2 my father emended at this time very hastily to read:

> These were the (*ëalar*) spirits who first adhered to him in the days of his splendour, and became most like him in his corruption: their hearts were of fire, but they were cloaked in darkness, and terror went before them; they had whips of flame. Balrogs they were named by the Noldor in later days. And in that dark time Melkor bred many other monsters of divers shapes and kinds that long troubled the world; and his realm spread now ever southward over the Middle-earth. But the Orks, mockeries and perversions of the Children of Eru, did not appear until after the Awakening of the Elves.

There is a footnote to the word *ëalar* in this passage:

> 'spirit' (not incarnate, which was *fëa*, S[indarin] *fae*). *ëala* 'being'.

On the origin of the Orcs in AAm (and especially with respect to the word 'perversions' in the passage just given) see pp. 78, 123–4. *Orks* was my father's late spelling.

§18a Of Yavanna's words before the Valar, and the words of Tulkas and Mandos, there has been no previous suggestion in the *Quenta* tradition; but cf. AV 2 (V.111, annal 1900): 'Yavanna often reproached the Valar for their neglected stewardship'. This was extended in AAm §§32–3 (p. 71), where most of the elements of the present passage appear, though more briefly expressed.

§19 Here the two star-makings are expressly contrasted, and Varda's names *Tintallë* 'the Kindler' and *Elentári* 'Queen of the Stars' differentiated in their bearing. The second star-making is described also in AAm §§35–6 (p. 71), but far more briefly, and though the 'gathering together of the ancient stars' to form signs in the heavens is mentioned there also, only the constellations *Menelmakar* (Orion) and *Valakirka* are named. That Menelmakar forebodes the Last Battle is said in both sources, but LQ does not name it as a sign of Túrin Turambar.

The name 'Burning Briar' for the Great Bear still survives in the *Quenta* tradition. This observation was made into a footnote in Text A (on which see p. 158), with the addition 'quoth Pengolod', but the typist of LQ 1 put it as usual into the body of the text, where my father left it.

In Text A, in which the names of the great stars and the constellations first entered, *Wilwarin*, *Karnil*, and *Alkarinquë* were typed *Vilvarin*, *Carnil*, and *Alcarinquë* and then altered to the forms in LQ 1. By a later change to Text A *Elentári* > *Elentárië*, not found in LQ 1 and LQ 2. – The name *Elemmírë* has appeared in AAm §114 (pp. 100, 106) as that of the Vanyarin Elf who made the *Aldudénië*.

§20 Although in Text A my father added the words 'quoth Ælfwine' to 'whom we call Elves' (deriving from QS) he retained this in the body of the text, and only on the final typescript LQ 2 wrote a direction that it should be a footnote.

The aberrant idea in QS that the coming of the Elves was not in the Music of the Ainur (see V.217) is now displaced by a much more subtle explanation of Oromë's astonishment. The detailed statement of the place of Kuiviénen in AAm §38 (p. 72) is absent here.

The history of the passage concerning Oromë and the Quendi (from 'For a while he abode with them ...') is curious and complex. In text A as he typed it my father followed QS exactly in saying that Oromë 'taught them the language of the gods, from whence afterwards they made the fair Elvish speech', and that afterwards he returned to Valinor and brought tidings of the Awakening of the Quendi to Valmar. He then altered this to the text found in LQ 1 above (he 'aided them in the making of language; for that was their first work of craft upon Earth ...'), and at the same time added at the beginning of §20 the words 'in their own tongue' ('but Oromë named them in their own tongue Eldar, people of the stars'). In this form the passage survived into LQ 2 without further change.

On Text A, however, my father struck out the passage beginning 'For a while he abode with them ...' and replaced it with the following on a slip pinned to the typescript:

Then swiftly he rode back over land and sea to Valinor, filled with the thought of the beauty of the long-awaited, and he brought the tidings to Valmar. And the gods rejoiced, and yet were in doubt amid their mirth, and they debated what counsel it were best now to take to guard the Elves from the shadow of Melkor. At once Oromë returned to Kuiviénen, and he abode there long among the Elves, and aided them in the making of language; for that was their first work of craft upon Earth, and ever the dearest to their hearts, and sweet was the Elven-tongue on the ears of the Valar. But Manwë sat alone upon Taniquetil ...

This further revision makes Oromë return *at once* to Valinor, and *then* come back to Kuiviénen, where he aided the Elves in the making of language. It does not appear in LQ 1 and LQ 2 because, as I have said, this and other alterations were made to Text A after LQ 1 had been taken from it.

In AAm §39 (p. 72) the story is different: there the Quendi 'began to make speech and to give names to all things that they perceived' long before Oromë came upon them (335 Sun Years after the Awakening); and nothing is said of his playing any part in the evolution of Elvish speech.

In the sentence 'while they dwelt yet silent *upon* the star-lit mere' Text A has *beside*; *upon* in LQ 1 (and LQ 2) was clearly an error introduced by the typist (and similarly with the omission of *so* earlier in this paragraph and *tongues* for *tongue* in §23).

§21 On LQ 2 my father changed 'the fortress of Melkor' in the first sentence to 'the fortresses of Melkor', and at the end of the paragraph 'the fortress of Melkor at Utumno' to 'the fortresses of Melkor'. In this case he made the changes on LQ 1 also, but I have not included them in the text printed, since they were very late, and belonged with the changed story of the origin of Angband: see the commentary on Chapter 2, §12 (p. 156).

On Text A 'little do they know of the riding of the power of the West' was changed to 'they know little', but this, like the major change made to §20, was made after LQ 1 had been taken from Text A.

There reappears here for the first time since the *Lost Tales* the story that Aulë made the chain Angainor (elaborately recounted in *The Chaining of Melko*, I.100–1, where the form was *Angaino*; in *The Tale of Tinúviel*, II.19, there is a reference to 'the chain Angainu that Aulë and Tulkas made').

§22 Changes were also made in this paragraph after LQ 1 had been made: 'from whence' > 'whence', and 'Vast are those halls and strong' > 'Vast and strong are those halls'.

In AAm §52 Melkor was condemned to Mandos for three ages (pp. 80, 88).

§23 That there were differing counsels of the Valar on the Summoning of the Quendi was not even hinted in the *Quenta* tradition till now. In AAm §53 (p. 81) there is mention of a debate, and in §73 (p. 86) it is told that in the council of the Valar Ulmo 'had chiefly spoken against the summons, deeming that it were better for the Quendi to remain in Middle-earth.' The belief that the Valar erred is not here imputed to them as an error 'with good intent' (QS, V.214), and to this extent is harshly repudiated.

The passage concerning the three ambassadors remains virtually unchanged from QS, but in the course of the revision (see under §27 below) there came to be an internal change of reference – when Elwë became Thingol, whereas previously he had been Thingol's brother (see V.217, §23). Probably the sentences 'These were Ingwë and Finwë and Elwë, who after were kings of the Three Kindreds of the Eldar' and 'The Elves that obeyed the summons and followed the three kings' should have been modified when that transformation took place, and when the Third Host came to have two lords.

There is no mention in LQ of the kindreds of Morwë and Nurwë, who refused the summons (AAm §57, p. 81).

Another very minor change was made to Text A after LQ 1 was made: 'And Mandos who had spoken not at all' > 'And Mandos who had not spoken'.

§25 The name *Lindar* was altered to *Vanyar* by a late change made to the final text of the *Ainulindalë* (p. 34, §36); in AAm §58 (p. 82) *Vanyar* appears in the text as written. – By a pencilled change to LQ 2 'High Elves' was changed to 'Fair Elves' (see V.218, §25).

§26 In Text A the opening sentence of this paragraph read: 'Next came the Noldor, a name of wisdom, and the Gnomes they may be called in our tongue', with 'Quoth Ælfwine. (The word that he uses ...' placed in a footnote. The typist of LQ 1 placed all this in the body of the text; but my father directed that it should all go into a footnote, as is done in the text printed. In the Old English versions of the 1930s *Witan* was not used, but *Noldelfe*, *Noldielfe* (see also IV.212). On one copy of LQ 2 my father struck out 'Gnomes' and wrote above 'Enquirers'; this occurs nowhere else.

Chapter 3 THE LATER *QUENTA SILMARILLION* (I) 169

At the end of the paragraph he added to Text A: 'Dark is their hue and grey are their eyes'; this did not get into the later typescripts. See I.44.

§27 By the end of the revision, represented by LQ 1, the final position had been reached, as in AAm §§58, 74: Elwë Singollo (Greymantle) – who is Elu Thingol King of Doriath – and his brother Olwë, the two lords of the host of the Teleri on the Great March until Elwë was lost. The stages passed through to reach this can be observed in the earlier version of the end of Text A (see p. 158). First came the idea that there were two lords, because the numbers were very great: Elwë and his brother Sindo ('the locks of Sindo were as grey as silver ... but the hair of Elwë was long and white, and he was the tallest of all the Elven-race'). Then *Elwë* was changed to *Solwë*, and *Sindo* to *Elwë*; at this stage, probably, Elwë (the Grey) became one of the three original ambassadors, displacing his brother (now Solwë) in this at the same time as he took his name (and became in his stead 'the tallest of all the Elven-folk').

§28 In the first stage of the 1951 revision, carried out on the original QS typescript, the people of Dân, still from the host of the Noldor, were thus described:

They are not counted among the Eldar, nor yet among the Avari. The [Nandar >] Nandor who turn back they were called, and akin was the name of their first leader Nano, who in their tongue was called Dân. His son was Denethor, who led them into Beleriand ere the rising of the Moon. The *Danathrim*, Danians, they were named in that land.

The term *Pereldar* 'Half-eldar' used in QS had now disappeared, and in this passage is clearly the first occurrence of the name *Nandor* (which appears subsequently in AAm §62: see pp. 83, 89).

In the next stage (Text A) the paragraph was removed from its former place and set at the end of §29. At this stage the Nandor, also called the *Laiquendi* or Green-elves, became Telerin Elves from the host of Sindo the Grey, and were placed with the other Teleri (followers of Sindo) who remained behind in Beleriand under the name *Ekelli* (first written *Ecelli*), 'the Forsaken'. See further under §§29–30.

§§29–30 In the first stage of the revision the form *Lembi* 'Lingerers' – the Elves of the Great Journey who 'were lost upon the long road' – became *Lemberi*, classed with the Avari as *Moriquendi*, Dark Elves. The term *Kalaquendi*, Light Elves, also appeared in the account (though found much earlier, together with *Moriquendi*, in the table associated with the *Lhammas*, V.197, and also in the *Etymologies*). At this stage the old subdivision *Ilkorindi* (comprising Lembi and Pereldar or Danas, see the table given in V.219) is not present, and the place of the Nandor is not defined.

In the next stage (Text A) the term *Lemberi* was not used, and there emerged the short-lived term *Ekelli (Ecelli)* used (like the old *Ilkorindi*) of all the 'lost Eldar', including the Nandor (see under §28); *Ekelli* was the name given to them by the Elves of Valinor, and meant 'the Forsaken, their kin that were left behind'. Thus:

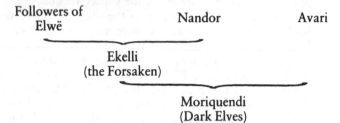

Ekelli was then replaced by *Alamanyar* ('since they came never to the Land of Aman'), and the Nandor became Elves from the host of Olwë; while those who sought in vain for Elwë Singollo (Thingol) are 'therefore' called *Sindar*, the Grey Elves, 'but themselves they named *Eglath*, the Forsaken.' Thus:

It was here, undoubtedly, that the name *Sindar* arose: occurrences earlier in LQ were inserted later, and that in AAm (§74, see p. 91) was later also. With the change of *Alamanyar* to *Úmanyar* on LQ 1 the final form (as shown in the table in the published *Silmarillion*, p. 309) was reached.

Thus some important developments in the narrative emerged in the course of the 1951 revision of the end of this chapter. The original Elwë, who in QS (§30) was Thingol's brother, became Olwë, while the name Elwë was transferred to Thingol – who became one of the three Elvish 'ambassadors' taken by Oromë to Valinor, in the place of his brother; and both Olwë and Elwë were leaders of the Telerin host on the Great March from Kuiviénen. The story that the Eldar of Beleriand (the Sindar) did not pass over the Sea because they were left behind seeking for Elwë Singollo takes up a passage in the *Lhammas* (V.174, cited on p. 90, §71); in QS there was no suggestion that the Elves of

Doriath were specifically those of Thingol's following who would not abandon the search for him.

In AAm the whole matter is treated from a different point of view: there, the events and geography of the Great Journey are a central element, but the complexities of naming and classification are not. It is clear however that AAm was not written until the revision of the *Quenta* tradition concerning the Sundering of the Elves was virtually complete: for in AAm the Nandor are from the host of Olwë (§62), and the followers of Elwë who were left behind called themselves *Eglath*, the Forsaken People (§71).

The passage recounting the names used in poetry for the Elvish peoples, which goes back to QS, and which forms an integral part of Text A, was for some reason omitted from LQ 1; my father wrote it onto the typescript subsequently (with *Vanyar* for *Lindar* of Text A).

Later changes made to Text A altered 'Axe-elves' to 'Staff-elves' as a name of the Nandor, and introduced 'Axe-elves' as a name of the Sindar (following 'the Friends of Ossë'); but these were 'lost' and do not appear in LQ 1 and LQ 2. – The name Lemberi 'Lingerers' (see under §§29–30 above) reappears as one of the by-names of the Sindar; and 'the Green Elves and the Brown' re-emerge from the old *Tale of the Nauglafring* (II.237, etc.).

It remains to notice lastly that on LQ 2 my father changed the title of the chapter to *Of the Coming of the Elves and the Captivity of Melkor*, which was followed in the published *Silmarillion*; and also that on one copy of this typescript, against the first occurrence of *Úmanyar* (§29), he wrote *Alamanyar* in the margin, as if he were considering a return to the earlier name.

4 OF THINGOL AND MELIAN

Of Thingol and Melian was not a separate chapter in the QS manuscript and the derived QS typescript, although in both there was a sub-heading (and in *The Lost Road*, V.220, I treated it as separate, numbering it 3(b)). The first text of the 1951 revision was a manuscript that continued on from the manuscript ending of 'Text A' of *The Coming of the Elves* (see p. 158), and here my father may have intended it as a separate chapter, although there is no number. From 'Text A', as in the preceding chapter, LQ 1 was taken, and the final text was LQ 2 (in which the chapter is numbered '4').

The first paragraph remained almost unchanged from QS, but the remainder was much expanded.

Of Thingol and Melian

§31 Thus it came to pass that Elu-thingol [> Elwë Singollo] and many of his folk abode in Beleriand and went not to Valinor.

Melian was a *maia*, of the race of the Valar. She dwelt in the gardens of Olofantur, and among all his fair folk there was none more beautiful than she, nor more wise, nor more skilled in songs of enchantment. It is told that the gods would leave their business, and the birds of Valinor their mirth, that the bells of Valmar were silent and the fountains ceased to flow, when at the mingling of the lights Melian sang in Lorien. Nightingales went always with her, and she taught them their song. She loved the deep shadow of great trees; but she was akin, before the world was made, unto Yavanna herself, and on a time she departed from Valinor on a long journey into the Hither Lands, and there she filled the silence of Arda before the dawn with her voice and with the voices of her birds.

§32 Now it came to pass that when their journey was near its end the folk of Elwë rested long and dwelt in Beleriand beyond Gelion; and King Elwë went often through the great woods, for he had friendship with the Noldor who lay to the westward, and with Finwë their lord. And it chanced on a time that he came alone to the starlit wood of Nan Elmoth, and there on a sudden he heard the song of nightingales. Then an enchantment fell upon him, and he stood still; and afar off beyond the voices of the *lómelindi** he heard the voice of Melian, and it filled all his heart with wonder and desire. He forgot then utterly all his folk and all the purposes of his mind, and following the birds under the shadows of the trees he passed deep into Nan Elmoth and was lost. But he came at last to a glade open to the stars, and there Melian stood; and out of the darkness he beheld her with hands outstretched, and the light of Aman was in her face.

No word she spoke; but being filled with love Elwë came to her and took her hand; and straightway a spell was laid on him, so that they stood thus, hand in hand, while long years were measured by the wheeling stars above them; and the trees of Nan Elmoth grew tall and dark ere they spoke any word one to another.

* [footnote to the text] *lómelindi*: 'dusk-singers' = nightingales.

§33 Thus Elwë's folk who sought him found him not, and Olwë took the kingship of the Teleri and departed; but Elwë Singollo came never again across the sea to Valinor; and Melian returned not thither while their realm together lasted; and of her a strain of the [*read:* of the race of the] immortal gods came among both Elves and Men, as hereafter shall be told. In after days Melian and Elwë became Queen and King of Grey Elves, and their hidden halls were in Menegroth, the Thousand Caves, in Doriath; and as Thingol Greymantle he was known in the [*read:* to all in the] tongue of that land. Great power Melian lent to Thingol her spouse, who was in himself great among the Eldar; for he alone of all the Forsaken had seen with his own eyes the Trees in the day of their flowering, and king though he were [> was] of Alamanyar [> Úmanyar], he was not accounted among the Moriquendi, but with the Elves of the Light, mighty upon Middle-earth.

Commentary on Chapter 4, 'Of Thingol and Melian'

§31 The form 'Elu-thingol' here first appeared. — *Olofantur* was corrected to *Lórien* on one copy of LQ 2 (see p. 150, §6).

§32 With the mention of the long sojourn of the Teleri in the lands beyond Gelion cf. AAm §64 (p. 83). The story of Elwë's journey to visit Finwë his friend is told also in AAm (§§64–5); and the phrase 'the trees of Nan Elmoth grew tall and dark' is found in both sources. In AAm Elwë's trance lasted for more than two centuries measured by the Sun (p. 89, §65).

§33 It now becomes explicit, and not merely implied, that Thingol had been to Valinor, as one of the three ambassadors (see pp. 168–9, §§23, 27). — The readings in LQ 1 'a strain of the immortal gods' and 'he was known in the tongue of that land' were clearly mere errors of omission on the part of the typist; the readings proposed are found in my father's manuscript Text A (see p. 158). A late change to Text A made after LQ 1 was copied from it was 'Grey Elves' to 'the Grey Elves'.

5 OF ELDANOR AND THE PRINCES OF THE ELDALIË

My father did less revision and rewriting of this chapter than on those preceding, and in fact did not himself make a wholly new text: the revision of 1951 was very largely restricted to emendation of the old QS typescript, and it was from this that LQ 1 was taken. In the QS typescript this was not a separate chapter, but a 'sub-chapter' entitled

Of Kôr and Alqualondë (in *The Lost Road* numbered 3(c); V.221–5); after which that typescript was abandoned, and for the remainder of the work there is only the QS manuscript from the pre-*Lord of the Rings* period.

Emendation to the QS typescript was carried out at different times, and three important passages of rewriting (see the commentary on §§40, 43) were 'lost' and not taken up into the later texts.

Of Eldanor and the Princes of the Eldalië

§34 In time the hosts of the Eldalië came to the last western shores of the Hither Lands. In the North these shores, in the ancient days after the battle of the gods, sloped ever westward, until in the northernmost parts of the earth only a narrow sea divided the Outer Land of Aman, upon which Valinor was built, from the Hither Lands; but this narrow sea was filled with grinding ice, because of the violence of the frosts of Melkor. Therefore Oromë did not lead the Eldar into the far North, but brought them to the fair lands about the River Sirion that afterwards were named Beleriand; and from those shores whence first the hosts of the Eldar looked in fear and wonder on the sea there stretched an ocean, wide and dark and deep, between them and the Mountains of Aman.

§35 There they waited and gazed upon the dark waves. But Ulmo came from the Valar; and he uprooted a half-sunken island, which now long had stood alone amid the sea, far from either shore; and with the aid of his servants he moved it, as it were a mighty ship, and anchored it in the bay into which Sirion pours his water.* Thereon he embarked the Lindar [> Vanyar] and the Noldor, for they had already assembled. But the Teleri were behind, being slower and less eager upon the march, and they were delayed also by the loss of Thingol and their fruitless search; and they did not come until Ulmo had departed.

§36 Therefore Ulmo drew the Lindar [> Vanyar] and the Noldor over the sea to the long shores beneath the Mountains of Valinor, and they entered the land of the gods and were welcomed to its bliss. But the Teleri dwelt long by the coasts of

---

* [footnote to the text] And some have told that the great isle of Balar, that lay of old in that bay, was the eastern horn of the Lonely Isle, that broke asunder and remained behind, when Ulmo removed that land again into the West. Quoth Rúmil. [Placed in the body of the text by the typist of LQ 1 but subsequently reinstated as a footnote.]

the western sea, awaiting Ulmo's return; and they grew to love the sound of the waves, and they made songs filled with the music of water. Ossë heard them, and came thither; and he loved them, delighting in the music of their voices. Sitting upon a rock nigh to the margin of the sea he spoke to them and instructed them. Great therefore was his grief when Ulmo returned at length to bear them away to Valinor. Some he persuaded to remain on the beaches of the Middle-earth, and these were the Elves of the Falas that in after days had dwellings at the havens of Brithombar and Eglorest in Beleriand; but most of the Teleri embarked upon the isle and were drawn far away.

§37 Ossë followed them, and when they were come near to their journey's end, he called to them; and they begged Ulmo to halt for a while, so that they might take leave of their friend and look their last upon the sky of stars. For the light of the Trees that filtered through the passes of the hills filled them with awe. And Ulmo understood well their hearts, and granted their request; and at his bidding Ossë made fast the island and rooted it in the foundations of the sea. Then Ulmo returned to Valinor and made known what had been done, and the Valar for the most part were ill-pleased; but the island could not again be moved without great hurt, or without peril to the Teleri who dwelt thereon; and it was not moved, but stood there alone for many an age. No other land lay near it, and it was called Tol Eressëa, the Lonely Isle.* There the Teleri long had their home, and Ossë was often among them, and they learned of him strange musics and sea-lore; and he brought to them sea-birds, the gift of Yavanna, for their delight. By this long sojourn of the Teleri apart in the Lonely Isle was caused the sundering of their speech from the language of the Lindar [> Vanyar] and the Noldor.

§38 To these the Valar had given a land and dwelling-places. Even among the radiant flowers of the Tree-lit gardens of the gods they longed still to see the stars at times. Therefore a gap was made in the great walls of the Pelóri, and there in a deep valley that ran down to the sea the Eldar raised a high green hill: Túna it was called. From the West the light of the

---

* [footnote to the text] *Avallónë* also it was after called, signifying the isle that lies nighest unto the Valar in Valinor. Quoth Ælfwine. [Placed in the body of the text by the typist of LQ 1 but subsequently reinstated as a footnote.]

Trees fell upon it, and its shadow lay ever eastward; and to the East it looked towards the Bay of Elvenhome, and the Lonely Isle, and the Shadowy Seas. Then through the Kalakiryan, the Pass of Light, the radiance of the Blessed Realm streamed forth, kindling the waves with gleams of gold and silver, and it touched the Lonely Isle, and its western shore grew green and fair. There bloomed the first flowers that ever were east of the mountains of the gods.

§39 Upon the crown of Túna, the green hill, the city of the Elves was built, the white walls and terraces of Tirion; and the highest of the towers of that city was the Tower of Ingwë, the Mindon, Mindon Eldaliéva, whose silver lamp shone far out into the mists of the sea. Few are the ships of mortal Men that have seen its slender beam. In Tirion* the Lindar [> Vanyar] and the Noldor dwelt long time in fellowship. And since of all things in Valinor they loved most the White Tree, Yavanna made for them a tree in all things like a lesser image of Telperion, save that it did not give light of its own being; and this tree was planted in the courts beneath the Tower and there flourished, and its seedlings were many in Eldanor. Of which one was after planted in Eressëa, and prospered. Thence came in the fullness of time, as is later told, the White Tree of Númenor.

§40 Manwë and Varda loved most the Lindar [> Vanyar], the High Elves, and holy and immortal were all their deeds and songs. The Noldor were beloved of Aulë, and of Mandos the wise; and great became their knowledge and their skill. Yet ever greater was their thirst for more knowledge, and their desire to make things wonderful and new. They were changeful in speech, for they had great love of words, and sought ever to find names more fit for all things that they knew or imagined. In Valinor they first contrived the fashioning of gems, and they made them in countless myriads of many kinds and hues; and they filled all Elendë with them, and the halls of the gods in Valinor were enriched.

---

* [footnote to the text] That is the Watchful City. *Eldamar* (that is Elvenhome) it was also called; but the regions where the Elves dwelt, and whence the stars could be seen, were called *Elendë*, or *Eldanor* (that is Elvenland): quoth Ælfwine. [Placed in the body of the text by the typist of LQ 1 but subsequently reinstated as a footnote.]

§41 The Noldor afterwards came back to Middle-earth, and this tale tells mostly of their deeds; therefore the names and kinship of their princes may here be told in that form which these names after had in the tongue of the Gnomes as it was [> the Elves] in Beleriand upon the Middle-earth. Finwë was king of the Noldor. His sons were Fëanor, Fingolfin, and Finrod [> Finarphin]. Of these Fëanor was the mightiest in skill of word and hand, more learned in lore than his brethren; in his heart his spirit burned as flame. Fingolfin was the strongest, the most steadfast, and the most valiant. Finrod [> Finarphin] was the fairest, and the most wise of heart; and afterwards he was a friend of the sons of Olwë, lord of the Teleri, and had to wife Eärwen, the swan-maiden of Alqualondë, Olwë's daughter. The seven sons of Fëanor were Maidros [> Maedhros] the tall; Maglor a musician and a mighty singer, whose voice was heard far over land and sea; Celegorn [> Celegorm] the fair, and Cranthir [> Caranthir] the dark; and Curufin the crafty, who inherited most of his father's skill of hand; and the youngest Damrod and Díriel [> Amrod and Amras], who were twin brothers alike in mood and face. They afterwards were great hunters in the woods of Middle-earth. A hunter also was Celegorn [> Celegorm], who in Valinor was a friend of Oromë and followed oft the great god's horn.

§42 The sons of Fingolfin were Fingon, who was after king of the Gnomes [> Noldor] in the North of the World; and Turgon of Gondolin; and their sister was Isfin [> Írith] the White. [*Added:* She was younger in the years of the Eldar than her brethren; and when she was grown to full stature and beauty she was greater and stronger than woman's wont, and she loved much to ride on horse and to hunt in the forests, and there was often in the company of her kinsmen, the sons of Fëanor; but to none was her heart's love given. She was called the White Lady of the Noldor; for though her hair was dark, she was pale and clear of hue, and she was ever arrayed in silver and white.] The sons of Finrod [> Finarphin] were Inglor [> Finrod] the faithful (who afterwards was named Felagund, Lord of Caves), [*struck out:* and Orodreth,] and Angrod, and Egnor [> Aegnor]. And these four [> three] were as close in friendship with the sons of Fingolfin as though they were all brethren together. A sister they had, Galadriel, the fairest lady of the house of Finwë, and the most valiant. Her hair was lit with gold as though it had caught in a mesh the radiance of Laurelin.

§43 Here must be told how the Teleri came at last to Valinor. For nigh on one hundred of the years of Valinor, which were each as ten of the years of the Sun that were after made, they dwelt in Tol Eressëa. But slowly their hearts were moved, and were drawn towards the light that flowed out over the sea unto their isle; and they were torn between the love of the music of the waves upon their shores, and desire to see again their kindred and to look upon the splendour of the gods. Yet in the end desire of the light was the stronger. Therefore Ulmo taught them the craft of ship-building; and Ossë, submitting to Ulmo, brought them as his farewell gift the strong-winged swans. These they harnessed to their fleet of white ships, and thus they were drawn without the help of the winds to Valinor.

§44 There they dwelt upon the long shores of Elvenhome [> Elvenland], and if they wished they could see the light of the Trees, and could visit the golden streets of Valmar and the crystal stairs of Tirion upon the Green Hill. But most it was their wont to sail in their swift ships upon the waters of the Bay of Elvenhome, or to walk in the waves upon the shore with their long hair gleaming like foam in the light beyond the hill. Many jewels the Noldor gave them, opals and diamonds and pale crystals, which they strewed upon the shores and scattered in the pools. Marvellous were the beaches of Elendë in those days. And many pearls they won for themselves from the sea, and their halls were of pearl, and of pearl were the mansions of Elwë [> Olwë] at the Haven of the Swans, lit with many lamps. For Alqualondë, the Haven of the Swans, was their chief town, and the harbour of their ships; and these were fashioned in the likeness of swans, white, and their beaks were of gold with eyes of gold and jet. The gate of that harbour was an arch of living rock sea-carven, and it lay upon the confines of the Elvenland, north of Kalakiryan, where the light of the stars was bright and clear.

§45 As the ages passed the Lindar [> Vanyar] grew to love the land of the gods and the full light of the Trees, and they forsook the city upon Túna, and dwelt upon the mountain of Manwë, or about the plains and woods of Valinor, and became sundered from the Noldor. But remembrance of the Earth under the Stars remained in the hearts of the Gnomes [> Noldor], and they abode in the Kalakiryan, and in the hills and valleys within sound of the western sea; and though many of them went oft about the land of the gods [> Valar], making far journeys in search of the secrets of land and water and all living things, [*struck out:* yet their intercourse was more with the Teleri than with the Lindar (> Vanyar); and] the tongues [> peoples] of Túna and of Alqualondë drew together in those days. Finwë was king of Túna and Elwë [> Olwë] of Alqualondë; but Ingwë was ever held the high-king of all the Elves. He dwelt thereafter at the feet of Manwë upon Taniquetil. Fëanor and his sons abode seldom in one place for long. They travelled far and wide upon [*read:* within] the confines of Valinor, going even to the borders of the Dark and the cold shores of the Outer Sea, seeking the unknown. Often they were guests in the halls of Aulë; but Celegorn [> Celegorm] went rather to the house of Oromë, and there he got great knowledge of all birds and beasts, and all their tongues he knew. For all living things that are or have been in the Kingdom of Arda, save only the fell and evil creatures of Melkor, lived then in Valinor; and there also were many other creatures beautiful and strange that have not yet been seen upon the Middle-earth, and perchance never now shall be, since the fashion of the World was changed.

Commentary on Chapter 5, 'Of Eldanor and the Princes of the Eldalië'

§35 The identification of the isle of the Gods' first dwelling with the isle of the Elves' ferrying (see IV.45) was abandoned when the isle of the Gods amid the seas became an isle (Almaren) in a great lake in the midst of Middle-earth. Tol Eressëa has now no significant origin. Cf. AAm §66 (p. 84): 'an island which long had stood alone amidst the Sea, since the tumults of the fall of Illuin'. The old story was still present in a draft narrative associated with *The Drowning of Anadûnê* (IX.402 and note 11).

§36 The form *Eglorest* was retained from QS presumably through oversight and not changed to *Eglarest* as in AAm (§70).

§37 The changed story of the rooting of Tol Eressëa to the bottom of the sea appears also in AAm (§§72–3 and commentary); with 'Ulmo understood well their hearts' cf. LQ §23 (p. 161: Ulmo's belief that the Quendi should be left in Middle-earth).

In Ælfwine's note *Avallónë* appears as a name of Tol Eressëa, not, as in the published *Silmarillion*, of a haven in the isle; cf. the *Akallabêth* (p. 260): 'there is in that land a haven that is named Avallónë, for it is of all cities the nearest to Valinor.' In the third version of *The Fall of Númenor* (IX.332), as here, Tol Eressëa 'was named anew Avallon: for it is hard by Valinor and within sight of the Blessed Realm'; while on the other hand in the narrative sketches associated with *The Drowning of Anadûnê* the name '*Avallon(de)*' already appears as the name of the eastern haven (IX.399, 403 and note 12).

§38 'The Bay of Elvenhome': in the footnote to §39, as in its forerunner in QS, 'Elvenhome' is the name of the city, translating *Eldamar*, while 'Elvenland' is the name of the regions where the Elves dwelt, translating *Eldanor*; in §44 of this chapter QS 'shores of Elvenhome' was changed in the revision to 'shores of Elvenland', but 'the Bay of Elvenhome' was allowed to stand in §§38, 44. In AAm *Eldamar* is the name of the region: see p. 90, §67.

The form *Kalakiryan*, for earlier *Kalakirya*, arose in the course of the composition of AAm (p. 87 note 7).

On 'the first flowers that ever were east of the mountains of the gods' see p. 60, §15, and the references given there.

§39 *Tirion* upon *Túna*, replacing *Túna* upon *Kôr*, and *Mindon Eldaliéva* replacing *Ingwemindon*, are found also in AAm §§67–8 (pp. 84–5, 90). – On LQ 2 'the Mindon, Mindon Eldaliéva' (the original emendation to the QS typescript, not an error) the repetition of 'Mindon' was bracketed for exclusion.

'In Tirion the Vanyar and the Noldor dwelt long time in fellowship': this is scarcely in accord with AAm (see p. 90, §68). LQ retained also the old phrase in §45: 'As the ages passed the Vanyar grew to love the land of the gods ... and they forsook the city upon Túna'.

The gift of Yavanna to the people of Tirion of an 'image' of Telperion is recorded also in AAm §69 (p. 85), where it is named *Galathilion* and is a gift to the Noldor. In LQ §16 *Galathilion* is the Sindarin name of Telperion, and in the footnote to LQ §17 on the names of the Trees the White Tree of Túna is *Galathilion the Less*. The Trees of Eressëa and Númenor are referred to in that note also, and given the names *Celeborn* and *Nimloth* (both of which were names of Telperion).

§40 'High Elves' > 'Fair Elves' by a late change to LQ 2, as in Chapter 3 (p. 168, §25).

On one copy of LQ 2 my father revised the paragraph thus:

Manwë and Varda loved most the Vanyar, the High Elves, and all their deeds and songs were holy and immortal. The Noldor were beloved of Aulë, and of Mandos the wise; and their knowledge and skill became great. Yet ever greater grew their thirst for more knowledge, and their desire to make things new and wonderful. They were changeful in speech, for they had great love of words, and were never weary of devising names more fitting for all the things that they knew or imagined.

This is strange, and I cannot really explain it; it seems as if he were experimenting (but casually, and only in this and one other passage) with a stylistic 'reduction', especially in respect of the characteristic 'inversions'. Comparison with the text as it stood (which is that of QS) shows how flat the opening sentences had become.

After LQ 1 had been made my father returned to the original QS typescript, and wrote in a substantial new passage on the subject of the jewels of the Noldor; this was not entered on LQ 1 and so was 'lost', since he never rediscovered it, and the final typescript LQ 2 still retained the old text in which the Noldor 'contrived the fashioning of gems'. The new passage read (following the words 'all things that they knew or imagined.'):

> And in all crafts of hand they delighted also; and their masons built many towers tall and slender, and many halls and houses of marble. Thus it came to pass that, quarrying in the hills after stone, the Noldor first discovered gems, in which the Land of Aman was indeed surpassing rich, and they brought them forth in countless myriads of many kinds and hues; and they carved and fashioned them in shapes of bright beauty, and they filled all Elendë with them, and the halls of the gods in Valinor were enriched.

In fact, a closely similar change (including the phrase 'carved them in many forms of bright beauty') was made to AAm §79 (p. 92 with note 3 and p. 103).

§§41–2 In Appendix F to *The Lord of the Rings* is found in the First Edition (published in October 1955): 'the Lady Galadriel of the royal house of Finrod, father of Felagund'; in the Second Edition (1966) this became 'the Lady Galadriel of the royal house of Finarphin and sister of Finrod Felagund'. Since as late as September 1954 (*Letters* no.150) my father was apologising to Allen and Unwin for not having as yet 'any copy to send in for the Appendices', it is clear that *Finrod* > *Finarphin* and *Inglor* > *Finrod* cannot have been entered on LQ 1 until after this time. On the typescript text of AAm (p. 128, §134) he noted that the names of the Sons of Fëanor 'will be revised', and on the text he changed *Cranthir* to *Caranthir*, underlined the *n* of *Celegorn*, and struck out *Damrod* and *Díriel* without replacing them. LQ 2 has the altered names. I have suggested that the typescripts of AAm and LQ 2 belong to much the same time (perhaps about 1958): see pp. 141–2.

It is characteristic of the textual puzzles that abound in my father's later work on *The Silmarillion* that the regular change of *Lindar* > *Vanyar* was undoubtedly made on LQ 1 in this chapter at the same time as these other changes of name; yet AAm has *Vanyar* as first written. It may be that a good deal of the correction to LQ 1 was actually carried out a long time after that text was typed.

§41 The marriage of Finrod (= Finarphin) to Eärwen Olwë's daughter is recorded under the Valian Year 1280 in AAm §85 (p. 93). – By a late change to LQ 2 *Maglor* > *Maelor*; *Maelor* occurs in the later *Lay of Leithian*, III.353.

§42 The passage describing the White Lady of the Noldor was added on a slip to the original QS typescript, and this slip is a page from a used engagement calendar dated October 1951. At that stage her name was still *Isfin*. A rejected draft for this rider on the same slip began thus:

She was younger in the years of the Eldar than her brethren, for she awoke in Valinor [not upon Middle-earth >] after the making of the Silmarils, and even as the first shadow fell upon the Blessed Realm; and when she was grown to full stature ...

The words 'She was younger in the years of the Eldar than her brethren, for she awoke in Valinor not upon Middle-earth' are not in accord with AAm, where Fingolfin their father was himself born in Aman (§81).

The rider was not taken up into LQ 1 as typed, which still had the name *Isfin*, as in AAm (see p. 102 notes 8 and 9: the first birth-date for Isfin (1469) makes her born after the making of the Silmarils in 1450, but the second (1362) before). But later *Isfin* was changed to *Írith* on LQ 1 (at the same time as the corrections of *Finrod* to *Finarphin*, etc.), and the same rider was attached on a slip, identical in wording to that attached to the old QS typescript, but with the name *Írith*. This is presumably a case where a 'lost' change was recovered.

In QS Angrod and Egnor were friends of the sons of Fëanor, while Inglor and Orodreth were friends of the sons of Fingolfin, Fingon and Turgon. Now the association of Angrod and Egnor with the Fëanorians (which led to their being allowed passage in the ships at the time of the crossing to Middle-earth, QS §73) was abandoned (as it was also in AAm, §135, pp. 113, 125), and all four of Finarphin's sons become the bosom friends of Fingon and Turgon. 'And these four' was changed to 'And these three' on LQ 1 when Orodreth was finally ejected entirely from the third generation of the Noldorin princes (see III.91, 246, and *Unfinished Tales* p. 255 note 20).

Here Galadriel enters the *Quenta* tradition; for Galadriel in AAm see §§85, 135 and commentary. On one copy of LQ 2 my father noted: 'In High-elvish her name was *Altariellë* "Lady with garland of sunlight", *galata-rīg-elle* = S[indarin] *Galadriel*. It was thus mere accident that her name resembled *galað* (Silvan *galad* "tree").' Cf. the Appendix to *The Silmarillion* p. 360, entry *kal-*.

§43 In this paragraph my father made two narrative changes that (like the passage concerning the jewels of the Noldor referred to under §40 above) were 'lost', since they were made to the QS typescript after LQ 1 had been copied from it. The first concerns the sentence 'For nigh on one hundred of the years of Valinor, which were each as ten of the years of the Sun that were after made' (the text of QS, preserved in LQ 1 and 2); here the following was substituted:

> For well-nigh one hundred of the years of our time (though that be but ten of the Years of the Valar) they dwelt in Tol Eressëa.

The reduction of the time during which the Teleri dwelt apart in Tol Eressëa from 1000 to 100 years of the Sun was clearly made for linguistic reasons. A thousand years would introduce such changes as to make the tongues of the Noldor (a people in any case 'changeful in speech', §40) and the Teleri into different languages, which could not conceivably 'draw together' again (§45). In AAm (§§72, 75) the 'lost' reckoning of only 100 years of the Sun is present.

On one copy of LQ 2 my father emended the original passage anew, and produced: 'They dwelt in Tol Eressëa for nearly one hundred of the years of Valinor (which were each as ten of the later years of the Sun in Middle-earth).' Since this does not alter the sense in any way it must have been made to reduce the archaic element (cf. the passage given under §40 above). Thus the revision made to the QS typescript for reasons of likelihood in linguistic history was forgotten; on the other hand, the change on LQ 1 of 'tongues' to 'peoples' in 'the tongues of Túna and of Alqualondë drew together in those days' was very probably made for the same reason, though resolving the difficulty in a different way.

The second of the 'lost' emendations in this paragraph changed the story that it was Ulmo who taught the Teleri the craft of ship-building:

> Therefore Ulmo, submitting to the will of the Valar, sent unto them Ossë their friend, and he, albeit in grief, taught them the craft of ship-building; and when their ships were built he brought to them as his farewell gift the strong-winged swans.

In AAm §75 Ulmo as teacher was likewise corrected to Ossë (p. 86 and note 8). This shift is an aspect of the changed story of the rooting of Tol Eressëa to the sea-bottom; where in QS Ossë submitted to Ulmo, Ulmo now submits to the will of the Valar.

§44 *Kalakiryan* was corrected on one copy of LQ 2 to *the Calaciryan*, and the same change of spelling in §45. – It is at first sight puzzling that LQ 1 has *Olwë* in §41 but *Elwë* in §§44–5, but the reason is simply that the correction in the latter two places was missed on the QS typescript.

6 OF THE SILMARILS AND THE DARKENING OF VALINOR

The textual history of this chapter is entirely different from that of any of the preceding ones. In the first stage of revision, only few and slight changes were made to the QS manuscript (the old QS typescript text having stopped at the end of the previous chapter), and these were taken up into LQ 1. But *after* LQ 1 had been made, my father returned to the old manuscript, and on the verso pages began a new version – rather oddly, paginating it on from the end of the QS typescript, and retaining the chapter number 4. This was clearly an element in the revision of 1951. At first this version is virtually continuous (as far as part way through §50), and if retaining the old text he wrote it out anew; but after this point he made use of the actual QS manuscript text, though emending it and interpolating it very heavily. At '... came into that region that is called Arvalin' (§55) the new work effectively ceases. My father scarcely touched LQ 1: he made a couple of changes on the first page of the typescript, including *Lindar* > *Vanyar*, but then stopped: a later occurrence of *Lindar* was left to stand. Here therefore LQ 1 ceases to be of use, and the text printed is the new text of the chapter written on the QS manuscript: it will be convenient to refer to this simply as 'LQ'.

The new writing was itself emended and interpolated subsequently, in red ink; I give the text in its final form, but in a few cases where the distinction between earlier and later readings is of interest I record the earlier in notes following the text. The title given to the new version was *Of the Silmarilli and the Darkening of Valinor*, but this was changed to (apparently – the intention is not perfectly clear) *Of Fëanor and the Silmarilli, and the Darkening of Valinor*. For the QS version (in which it is numbered Chapter 4) see V.227–31. There is no text of the chapter extant in the LQ 2 series.

§46 From this time, when the Three Kindreds of the Eldar were gathered at last in Valinor, and Melkor was chained, began the Noontide of the Blessed Realm and its fullness of glory and bliss, long in tale of years, but in memory too brief. In those days the Eldar became full-grown in stature of body and of mind, and the Noldor advanced ever in skill and knowledge; and the long years were filled with their joyful labours, in which many new things fair and wonderful were devised.

§46a Then it was that the Noldor first bethought them of letters, and Rúmil of Túna was the name of that lore-master who first made fitting signs for the recording of speech and song, some for graving upon metal or in stone, others for drawing with brush or with pen.

§46b In that time was born in Eldamar in the house of the king, in Tirion upon the crown of Túna, Fëanor the eldest of the sons of Finwë, and the most beloved. Míriel was the name of his mother. Silver was her hair and dark were her eyes, but her hands were more skilled to fineness than any hands even of the Noldor. By her was the craft of needles devised; and were but one fragment of the broideries of Míriel to be seen in Middle-earth it would be held dearer than a king's realm, for the richness of her devices and the fire of their colours were as manifold and as bright as the glory of leaf and flower and wing in the fields of Yavanna. Therefore she was named Míriel Serende.*

§46c And Fëanor grew swiftly as if a secret fire were kindled within him, and he was tall and fair of face and masterful, and he became of all the Noldor the most subtle of heart and of mind, and the most skilled of hand. He it was that in his youth, bettering the work of Rúmil, made those letters which bear his name, and which ever since the Eldar have used; yet this was the least of his works. For he it was that first of the Noldor discovered how gems greater and brighter than those of the Earth might be made with skill. And the first gems that Fëanor devised were white and colourless, but being set under starlight they would blaze with blue and white fires brighter than Helluin. And other crystals he made, wherein things far away could be seen small but clear, as with the eyes of the Eagles of Manwë. Seldom were the hand and mind of Fëanor at rest.[1]

§47 Now at length the Noontide of Valinor drew to its close. For it came to pass that Melkor, as the Valar decreed, had dwelt for three ages in the duress of Mandos, alone. And when he had suffered that bondage, as the Valar had promised, he was brought again before them in conclave. He looked then upon the bliss and glory of the Valar, and malice was in his heart; he looked upon the fair Children of Ilúvatar that sat at the feet of the gods, and hatred filled him; he looked upon the wealth of bright gems and lusted for them; but he hid his thoughts and postponed his vengeance.

* [footnote to the text] That is Byrde Míriel (the Broideress): quoth Ælfwine.

§48 Before the gates of Valmar Melkor abased himself at the feet of Manwë and sued for pardon, promising that, if he might be made but the least of the free folk of Valinor, he would aid the Valar in all their deeds, and most of all in the healing of the many hurts that he had wrought and now would work no more. And Niënna aided his prayer, but Mandos was silent. Then Manwë granted him pardon; but the Valar would not yet suffer him to depart from their sight and vigilance. He was given, therefore, a humble dwelling within the gates of the city, and put on trial; and he was not permitted to go more than one league from Valmar, save by the leave of Manwë and with a guardian at his side. But fair-seeming were all the words and deeds of Melkor in that time, and both Valar and Eldar had much profit from his aid. Wherefore in a while he was allowed to go freely about the land, and it seemed to Manwë that his evil was cured. For he himself was free from the evil and could not comprehend it, and he knew that in the beginning, in the thought of Eru, Melkor had been even as he. Yet it is said that Ulmo's heart misgave him, and Tulkas clenched his hands whenever he saw Melkor, his foe, go by. For if Tulkas is slow to wrath, slow is he also to forget.

§49 Most fair of all was Melkor to the Eldar, and he aided them in many works, if they would let him. The Vanyar, indeed, the people of Ingwë, held him in suspicion; for Ulmo had warned them, and they heeded his words. But the Noldor took delight in the many things of hidden knowledge that he could reveal to them, and some hearkened to words that it would have been better that they should never have heard.

§49a It has been said indeed that Fëanor learned much of Melkor in secret, but that doubtless is but one of the many lies of Melkor himself, envying the skill of Fëanor and desiring to claim part in his deeds. For certain it is that, snared though he might be (as others) by the lies of Melkor, none of all the Eldalië ever hated Melkor more than Fëanor son of Finwë, who first named him *Morgoth*.

§49b And in that time there was done the deed most renowned of all the works of the Elvenfolk. For Fëanor, being now come to his full might, was filled with a new thought, or maybe some shadow of foreknowledge came to him of the doom that should be; and he pondered how the Light of the Trees, the glory of the Blessed Realm, might be preserved imperishable. Then he began a long and marvellous labour; and he summoned all his lore, and his power, and his subtle craft, for he purposed now to make things more fair than any of the Eldar had yet made, whose beauty should last beyond the End.

Three jewels he made, and named them *Silmarils*. A living fire burned within them that was blended of the Light of the Two Trees. Of their own radiance they shone, even in the dark of the deepest treasury; yet all lights that fell upon them, however faint, they received and returned again in marvellous hues to which their own inner fire gave a surpassing loveliness. No mortal flesh, nor flesh unclean, nor any thing of evil will could touch them, but it was scorched and withered; neither could they be hurt or broken by any strength in all the kingdom of Arda. These jewels the Elves prized beyond all their works, and Varda hallowed them, and Mandos foretold that the fates of Arda, earth, sea, and air, lay locked within them. And the heart of Fëanor was fast bound to these things that he himself had made.

§50* But the heart of Melkor also desired these fairest of jewels; and from that time with desire the malice of Melkor grew ever greater, though nought of it could be seen in the semblance that he wore, or in the fair form that he assumed after the manner of the Valar his brethren. And when he saw his chances he sowed a seed of lies and hints of evil among all who were open to his converse. Bitterly did the people of the Noldor atone for their folly in the days to come. Coming often among them he would speak ever words of greatest praise, sweet but poisoned honey; for amid all the fair words others were ever subtly woven. Visions he would conjure in their hearts of the mighty realms they might have ruled at their own will, in power and freedom in the East. And then he would whisper, to any that leaned towards him, that the gods had brought the Eldar to Valinor because of their jealousy, fearing that the beauty of the Quendi, and the makers' power that Ilúvatar had bequeathed to them, would grow too great for the Valar to govern, as the Elves waxed and spread over the wide lands of the world.

In those days, moreover, though the Valar knew indeed of the coming of Men that were to be,[2] the Elves knew yet nought of it; for the gods had not revealed it, and the time was not yet near. But Melkor spake to the Elves in secret of Mortal Men,

---

* The beginning of this paragraph corresponds in content to the end of QS §49.

though he knew little of the truth. Manwë alone knew aught clearly of the mind of Ilúvatar concerning Men, and he has ever been their friend. Yet Melkor whispered that the gods kept the Eldar captive, so that Men coming should defraud them of the kingdoms of Middle-earth; for the weaker and short-lived race the Valar saw would be more easily swayed by them. Small truth was there in this, and little have the Valar ever prevailed to sway the wills or fates of Men, and least of all to good. But many of the Noldor believed, or half-believed, the evil words. [It is told, also, that at this time Melkor would speak to the Eldar of weapons and armour, and of the power that they give to him that is armed to defend his own (as he said). The Eldar had before possessed no weapons, and since the chaining of Melkor the armouries of the gods had been shut. But the Noldor now learned the fashioning of swords of tempered steel, and the making of bows and of arrows and of spears; and they made shields in those days and emblazoned them with devices of silver and gold and gems. Thus it was that the Noldor were armed in the days of their Flight. Thus too, as oft was seen, the evil of Melkor was turned against him; for the swords of the Gnomes did him more hurt than anything under the gods upon this earth. Yet they had little joy of Melkor's teaching; for all the sorrows of the Gnomes they wrought with their own swords, as later shall be seen. Quoth Pengoloð.]

§51 Thus, ere the gods were aware, the peace of Valinor was poisoned. The Noldor began to murmur against the Valar and their kindred; and many became filled with vanity, forgetting all that the gods had given them and taught to them. Fiercest burned the flame in the eager heart of Fëanor, and Melkor laughed in his secrecy; for to that mark above all had his lies been addressed, and Fëanor he most hated, lusting all the while for the Silmarils. Yet never could he come nigh them; for though at great feasts Fëanor would wear them, blazing upon his brow, at other times they were guarded close, locked in the deep hoards of Túna. There were no thieves in Valinor, as yet; but Fëanor loved the Silmarils with a greedy love, and he began to grudge the sight of them to all save to his sire and to his sons.

§52 High princes were Fëanor and Fingolfin, the elder sons of Finwë; but they grew proud and jealous each of his right, and his possessions. And lo! Melkor set new lies abroad, and whispers came to Fëanor that Fingolfin and his sons, Fingon and Turgon, were plotting to usurp the leadership of Finwë and of the elder house of Fëanor, and to supplant them by leave of the Valar – for the Valar were ill-pleased that the Silmarils lay in Túna, and were not given to their keeping. Of these lies quarrels were born among the proud children of Finwë, and of these quarrels came the end of the high days of Valinor and the evening of its ancient glory; for Fëanor spake words of rebellion against the Valar, crying aloud that he would depart from Valinor back to the world without, and deliver, as he said, the Gnomes from thraldom, if they would follow him. And when Fingolfin sought to restrain him Fëanor drew his sword upon him.[3] For the lies of Melkor, though he knew not clearly their source, had taken root in the pride of his heart.

§53 Then the Valar were wroth and dismayed, and[4] Fëanor was summoned to answer in the Ring of Doom; and there the lies of Melkor were laid bare for all those to see who had the will. By the judgement of the gods Fëanor was banished for twenty years[5] from Túna, since he had disturbed its peace. But with him went Finwë his father, who loved him more than his other sons, and many other Gnomes also. Northward in Valinor, in the hills near to the halls of Mandos, they built a strong place and a treasury at Formenos;[6] and they gathered there a multitude of gems. But Fingolfin ruled the Noldor in Túna; and thus Melkor's words seemed justified (though Fëanor had wrought their fulfilment by his own deeds), and the bitterness that Melkor had sown endured, even though the lies were revealed, and long afterwards it lived still between the sons of Fëanor and Fingolfin.

§54 Straight from the midst of their council the Valar sent Tulkas to lay hands on Melkor and bring him again to judgement, but Melkor hid himself, and none could discover whither he had gone; and the shadows of all standing things seemed to grow longer and darker in that time. It is said that for two years[7] none saw Melkor, until he appeared privily to Fëanor, feigning friendship with cunning argument, and urging him to his former thought of flight. But his cunning overreached his aim; for knowing that the jewels held the heart of Fëanor in thrall, he said at the last: 'Here is a strong place and well guarded, but think not that the Silmarils will lie safe in any treasury within reach of the Valar!'

Then the fires of the heart of Fëanor were kindled, and his eyes blazed, and his sight burned through all the fair-semblance of Melkor to the dark depths of his mind, and perceived there his fierce lust for the Silmarils. Then hate overcame Fëanor's fear, and he spoke shamefully to Melkor, saying: 'Get thee gone, gangrel! Thou jail-crow of Mandos!' And he shut the doors of his house upon the mightiest of all the dwellers in Eä, as though he were a beggar.

And Melkor departed in shame, for he was himself in peril, and saw not his time yet for revenge; but his heart was black with anger. And Finwë was filled with dread, and sent messengers in haste to the Valar.

§55 Now the gods were sitting in council before their gates, fearing the lengthening of the shadows, when the messenger came from Finwë, but ere Tulkas could set forth others came that brought tidings from Eldanor. For Melkor had fled through the Kalakirya, and from the hill of Túna the Elves saw him pass in wrath as a thunder-cloud. Thus Melkor departed, and for a while the Trees shone again unshadowed, and still Valinor was fair; yet as a cloud far off that looms ever higher, borne upon a slow cold wind, a doubt now marred the mirth of all the dwellers in Aman, dreading they knew not what evil might yet come. And the Valar sought ever for news of Melkor, in vain. But he passed from Eldanor and[8] came into that region that is called Arvalin, which lies south of the Bay of Elendë, and is a narrow land beneath the eastern feet of the Mountains of Aman. There the shadows were deepest and thickest in the World. In that land, secret and unknown, dwelt in spider's form Ungoliantë, weaver of dark webs. It is not told whence she came; from the Outer Darkness, maybe, that lies in Eä beyond the walls of the World. In a ravine she lived, and spun her webs in a cleft of the mountains; for she sucked up light and shining things to spin them forth again in black nets of choking gloom and clinging fog. She hungered ever for more food.

§56 Melkor met Ungoliantë in Arvalin, and with her he plotted his revenge; but she demanded a great and terrible reward, ere she would dare the perils of Valinor and the power of the gods. Then, when Melkor had vowed to give all that she lusted for, she wove a great darkness about her for their protection, and black ropes she span, and cast from rocky peak to peak; and in this way she scaled at last the highest pinnacle of the mountains, far south of Taniquetil. In that region the vigilance of the Valar was less, because the wild woods of Oromë lay in the south of Valinor, and the walls of the mountains looked there eastward upon the untrodden land and empty seas; and the gods held guard rather against the North where of old Melkor had delved his fortress and deep throne.

For §§57–9 see the end of the commentary on this chapter, p. 193.

NOTES

1 This passage concerning the gems devised by Fëanor (following 'yet this was the least of his works') was a secondary addition (see p. 184). See the commentary on §46c.
2 From this point the virtually continuous newly written text changes to a heavily emended and interpolated treatment of the QS manuscript (p. 184).
3 'drew his sword upon him' was changed from 'menaced him with his sword'.
4 'Then the Valar were wroth and dismayed, and' was a secondary addition.
5 'twenty years' was changed from 'ten years'.
6 'at Formenos' was a secondary addition.
7 'two years' was changed from 'a great while'.
8 From this point the new work on the chapter effectively ceases, and the few differences from QS belong to the earlier layer of emendation that was taken up into LQ 1; but I give the text to the end of §56 in order to take in the majority of these earlier changes.

Commentary on Chapter 6, 'Of the Silmarils and the Darkening of Valinor'

A comparison will show that the new writing in LQ stands in close relation to the corresponding part of AAm. New elements in LQ appear also in AAm, such as Fëanor's mother Míriel (§78, p. 92), the devising of letters by Rúmil and Fëanor (§§80, 83), or the placing of the making of the Silmarils after the release of Melkor (p. 104, §92). There are constant similarities of wording and many actual identities of phrase (notably in the encounter of Fëanor with Melkor at Formenos, LQ §54, AAm §102).

Can precedence be established between the two? It is scarcely possible to demonstrate it one way or the other, for individual details tell in both ways. Thus Fëanor's word to Melkor, 'gangrel', was that first written in LQ, whereas in AAm it replaced 'beggarman'; but 'the Valar were wroth and dismayed' is an addition to LQ (note 4), whereas 'the Gods were wroth' in AAm (§99) was not. The change in LQ of 'ten years' to 'twenty years' as the term of Fëanor's banishment from Tirion (note 5) is a change also in AAm (§99 and note 10), and the name Formenos is an addition in both. I think in fact that the two texts were closely contemporary. It will be seen that after the revision in LQ has come to an end AAm continues on (from §105) in the same larger and more expansive fashion obviously based structurally on the *Quenta* tradition: and it may be therefore that the LQ text petered out because the 'Annals' (scarcely 'Annals' any more) had become my father's preference.

How he conceived the relation between the two at this time seems impossible to say. As I have said (p. 102), 'we see the annal form disappearing as a fully-fledged narrative emerges'; and the AAm narrative, while differing in every sentence from the *Silmarillion* version, is nonetheless very obviously 'the same'. Certainly too similar to it to be regarded as the representation of a separate tradition of learning and memory, or even of the work of a different 'loremaster'. There are only the most minor variations in the two narratives (for example, in LQ the messengers came to Valinor telling that Melkor had fled through the Kalakirya before Tulkas had set out in pursuit (§55), whereas in AAm the messengers came 'ere Oromë and Tulkas had ridden far' (§104)); and there is constant echoing of vocabulary and phrasing. See further on this topic pp. 289–91.

§46b *Byrde Míriel* (in the footnote to the text): cf. AAm §78 (p. 92), where Fëanor's mother (in a replacement entry) is given, rather oddly, the Old English 'surname' *Byrde*, not *Serende*, in the text itself and without reference to Ælfwine.

§46c The passage in AAm §83 (p. 92 and note 5) concerning Fëanor's study of the making of gems by skill was an addition, as was that in the present text (note 1 above); the idea is associated with the change from the devising of gems by the Noldor to their obtaining them from the ground of Aman (see LQ §40 and commentary).

With the mention of the 'crystals... wherein things far away could be seen small but clear' (not referred to in AAm) cf. Gandalf's words in *The Two Towers* (III.11): 'The *palantíri* came from beyond Westernesse, from Eldamar. The Noldor made them. Fëanor himself, maybe, wrought them, in days so long ago that the time cannot be measured in years.'

§49a Cf. AAm §123 (p. 108): 'Then Fëanor rose up and cursed Melkor, naming him *Morgoth*'. In AAm *Melkor* is used throughout until the time when Fëanor named him Morgoth (p. 123, §123); so also in the revision of QS the use of *Morgoth* before this point in the narrative was changed to *Melkor*.

§49b The passage concerning the Silmarils corresponds in content to the latter part of QS §46; for, as in AAm, the making of the Silmarils now comes after the release of Melkor.

§50 The passage on the arming of the Elves is no longer given as a footnote, and is moved to a different place from that in QS (§49); but it is enclosed within brackets and attributed to Pengoloð. The text is at this point in any case extremely

Chapter 6 THE LATER *QUENTA SILMARILLION* (I) 193

  disordered, since it consists partly of new writing and partly of passages retained from the original QS text. The old note was largely written out afresh, though it was not greatly changed from the earlier form: the chief difference being that whereas it was said in QS that the Elves had previously possessed 'weapons of the chase, spears and bows and arrows' it is now told (as in AAm, p. 96, §97) that they had no weapons before this time. See further p. 281.

§52 On Fëanor's drawing his sword on Fingolfin see p. 104, §98. – It is curious that (despite §46b 'in Tirion upon the crown of Túna') here 'the Silmarils lay *in Túna*', and again in §53 'Fingolfin ruled the Noldor *in Túna*'. The same is found in AAm (p. 90, §67), and much later (see p. 282).

§55 The words 'in Eä', not found in LQ 1, belong with the later work on the QS manuscript as presented in the text given above (see note 8). On the words 'the Outer Darkness... that lies in Eä beyond the walls of the World' see pp. 62–4.

§§57–9 In the last paragraphs of the chapter, not given in the text (p. 191), changes made to QS were:

  §57: *Morgoth* > *Melkor*, and at all subsequent occurrences.

  §58: *Tûn* > *Túna*; *the shores of Elvenhome* > *the shores of Eldamar*; *Silpion* > *Telperion*; *protected by fate* omitted; *With his black spear* > *Suddenly with his black spear*; *leaf and branch and root* > *root and leaf and bough*; and at the end of the paragraph (after *she swelled to monstrous form*) was added: *but still she was athirst. She drank therefore also of the vats of Varda, and drained them utterly.*

  §59: *their feet* > *the feet of the hunters*; *escaped the hunt* > *escaped them*.

  I have noticed earlier (p. 142) that much later (after the publication of *The Lord of the Rings*) my father turned to new narrative writing within the body of the *Quenta Silmarillion*: beginning with Chapter 1, which became the *Valaquenta*, and then jumping to the present chapter, 6. A new story of ramifying implications, that of the death of Fëanor's mother Míriel and Finwë's second marriage to Indis of the Vanyar, had now entered; but this further and final development is here postponed (see pp. 205 ff.).

7 OF THE FLIGHT OF THE NOLDOR

The textual history of this chapter is relatively simple (for the late rewriting just referred to, which extends some little way into it, see pp. 292 ff.). The original chapter in QS (V.232–8, where it is numbered 5) was corrected, not very extensively, at the time of the 1951 revision, and as corrected was typed in the amanuensis text LQ 1. This received no corrections at all, but on the later amanuensis typescript LQ 2 my father made a few changes, mostly the regular alteration of names. In this case I do not give the revised text, but record individually the significant changes made to QS. Various small changes of wording are not mentioned, nor are regular name-changes as *Melko* > *Melkor*, *Tûn* > *Túna* or *Tirion*, *Kôr* > *Túna*, *the pass of Kôr* > *the pass of Kalakiryan*, *Elwë* > *Olwë*. In §69 *western land* > *Westland* and *Helkaraksë* > *Helkaraxë* (so spelt in AAm), in §70 *strands of Elvenhome* > *strands of Eldanor*, and in §71 *Eruman* > *Araman* (cf. AAm §125, pp. 108, 123).

§60 At the first three occurrences 'Morgoth' > 'Melkor', and at the end of the paragraph, after 'the violence of Morgoth', was added: 'for such was his name from that day forth among the Gnomes'; thereafter 'Morgoth' was retained. At the foot of the page my father noted: 'In more ancient form *Moringotto*'. It was here that the story entered that Melkor received the name *Morgoth* at this time, though there was no suggestion yet that it was Fëanor who gave it to him. That entered in AAm (§123) and in the contemporary rewriting of Chapter 6 (p. 186, §49a); no doubt at the same time my father struck out on the QS manuscript the addition just given and substituted: 'So Fëanor called him in that hour: the Black Foe, and that name he bore among the Noldor ever after.' *Morgoth* was translated 'the Dark Enemy' in the AAm passage, but for some reason this was rejected (p. 120, note 2).

The sentence in §60 'a thing before unseen that in the gathering night had seemed to be a spider of monstrous form' was changed to 'a thing before unseen for which no word was known, a vast shape of darkness black in the gathering night'; cf. AAm §122. The Valar are to be wholly ignorant of the nature of the aid that Melkor had summoned (cf. AAm §124), and the Darkness (or 'Unlight') of Ungoliantë becomes a central idea of the legend.

§62 The passage concerning the Orcs, from 'he brought into being the race of the Orcs' to the end of the paragraph, was rewritten as follows:

he brought into being the race of the Orkor,* and they grew and multiplied in the bowels of the earth. These creatures Morgoth made in envy and mockery of the Elves. Therefore in form they were like unto the Children of Ilúvatar, yet foul to look upon; for they were made in hatred, and with hatred

they were filled. Their voices were as the clashing of stones, and they laughed not, save only at torment and cruel deeds. *Glamhoth*, the hosts of tumult, the Noldor called them.
* [footnote to the text] In Gnomish speech this name is *orch* of one, *yrch* of many. Orcs we may name them, for in the ancient days they were strong and fell as demons; yet they were of other kind, a spawn of earth corrupted by the power of Morgoth, and they could be slain or destroyed by the valiant: quoth Ælfwine.

This is closely related to AAm §127, as that was first written (see pp. 120–1, notes 5–7, and commentary p. 123), and contains the same conjunction of two apparently different theories, that the Orcs were 'made' by Morgoth and that they were 'a spawn of earth' corrupted by him.

My father then altered the passage by cutting out Ælfwine's footnote to the word *Orkor* but adding a closely similar passage in the body of the text, thus:
Glamhoth, the hosts of tumult, the Noldor called them. Orcs we may name them;* for in ancient days they were strong and fell as demons. Yet they were not of demon-kind, but a spawn of earth corrupted by Morgoth, and they could be slain or destroyed by the valiant with weapons of war.
* [footnote to the text] Quoth Ælfwine.

This rearrangement is puzzling, for Ælfwine's contribution can hardly be limited to the words 'Orcs we may name them' (see p. 124); but perhaps by placing the asterisk at this point my father meant to indicate that all that follows it was added by Ælfwine. On the LQ typescript he changed it again, putting the whole passage from 'Orcs we may name them' into a footnote.

On the QS manuscript he scribbled later, against the first part of the passage, concerning the making of the Orcs: 'Alter this. See *Annals*.' This refers to the change introduced into AAm whereby the Orcs had been bred from captured Quendi many ages before: see the commentary on AAm §127 (p. 123).

§67 'masters of the enchanted light' > 'masters of the unsullied Light'; cf. AAm §133 'lords of the unsullied Light'.

§68 'But of his own sons Inglor alone spake with him [Finrod]; Angrod and Egnor took the part of Fëanor, and Orodreth stood aside' > 'But of his own children Inglor alone spoke in like manner; for Angrod and Egnor and Galadriel were with Fingon, whereas Orodreth stood aside and spoke not.' As AAm was first written the same account of the associations of the Noldorin princes was given, but it was changed immediately: see AAm §135 (pp. 112, 125), and p. 121, note 12.

'and with Fingolfin were Finrod and Inglor' > 'and with Fingolfin were Finrod and his house'

§72 The whole of this paragraph was rewritten as follows:

Then Finrod turned back, being filled with grief, and with bitterness against the house of Fëanor because of his kinship with Olwë of Alqualondë; and many of his people went with him, retracing their steps in sorrow, until they beheld once more the far beam of the Mindon upon Túna, still shining in the night, and so came at last to Valinor again. And they received the pardon of the Valar, and Finrod was set to rule the remnant of the Noldor in the Blessed Realm. But his sons were not with him, for they would not forsake the sons of Fingolfin; and all Fingolfin's folk went forward still, fearing to face the doom of the gods, since not all of them had been guiltless of the kinslaying at Alqualondë. Moreover Fingon and Turgon, though they had no part in that deed, were bold and fiery of heart and loath to abandon any task to which they had put their hands until the bitter end, if bitter it must be. So the main host held on, and all too swiftly the evil that was foretold began its work.

This is almost word for word the same as AAm §156, the only real difference being the mention here that Fingon and Turgon had no part in the kinslaying. That the rewriting of QS preceded the passage in AAm, however, is shown by the fact that *Olwë* is here a later change from *Elwë*.

§73 'and they took with them only such as were faithful to their house, among whom were Angrod and Egnor' was left unchanged, through oversight, and survived into the typescript LQ 2. The association of Angrod and Egnor with the Fëanorians (so that they were given passage to Middle-earth in the ships) had been abandoned in the rewritings of QS §§68, 72 given above.

'a great burning, terrible and bright' > 'a great burning, terrible and bright, at the place that was after called Losgar, at the outlet of the Firth of Drengist'. The same addition was made to AAm (§162, pp. 120, 127, and p. 122 note 20).

'Therefore led by Fingolfin, and Fingon, Turgon, and Inglor' > 'Therefore led by Fingolfin and his sons, and by Inglor and Galadriel the fair and valiant'; this is virtually the text of AAm (§163, p. 120).

'and came unto Beleriand at the rising of the sun' > 'and came unto Middle-earth at the rising of the Moon'; cf. AAm §163 (pp. 120, 127).

Emendations made to one or other of the copies of the typescript LQ 2 give the later names or name-forms of certain of the Noldorin princes, as in Chapter 5 (pp. 177, 181, §§41–2): Finrod > Finarphin and Finarfin, Inglor > Finrod, Egnor > Ægnor (as emended in Chapter 5 spelt Aegnor). — In 'his ancient fortress, Utumno in the North' (§62) Utumno > Angband; this reflects the late story that both Utumno and Angband were built in the ancient days (see p. 156, §12) – and it was of course to the western fortress, Angband, that Melkor returned and which he rebuilt from its ruins.

Against the passage in §68 'The greater part marched behind Fingolfin, who with his sons yielded to the general voice against their wisdom, because they would not desert their people' my father noted on a copy of LQ 2: 'also because of the promise made by Fingolfin (above)'. This refers to a passage in the final rewriting of the previous chapter (p. 287, §58c), where Fingolfin said to Fëanor before Manwë: 'Thou shalt lead and I will follow.' The word 'above' means that the final text was in being and had been incorporated into the LQ 2 typescript.

8 OF THE SUN AND MOON AND THE HIDING OF VALINOR

The textual situation here is the simplest so far: we have the chapter in QS (V.239–43), and emendations made to QS in 1951, taken up into the typescript LQ 1, which was not emended subsequently. (A few lightly pencilled alterations were not incorporated in LQ 1, either because the typist could not interpret them or because they were entered on the manuscript subsequently.) As with Chapter 6 (p. 184) the later typescript LQ 2 is not extant. The history of this chapter in *The Silmarillion* therefore ends with the few changes made to QS in 1951; there is also the account in AAm §§164–81, which was itself closely derived from QS, with changes and omissions. In this case again I give the significant changes made to QS and not the whole text. Regular changes of name are (§79) *Kalakilya* > *Kalakiryan, the mound of Kôr* > *the mound of Túna*.

§74 The passage beginning 'And Manwë bade Yavanna ...' was changed to a form almost identical with AAm §167 (p. 129):
And Manwë bade Yavanna and Nienna to put forth all their powers of growth and healing; and they put forth all their powers upon the Trees, but the tears of Nienna availed not to heal their mortal wounds; and for a long while Yavanna sang on alone in the shadows. Yet even as hope failed and her song faltered in the dark, lo! Telperion bore at last upon a leafless bough one great flower of silver, and Laurelin a single golden fruit.

§75 The passage giving the names of the Sun and Moon was changed to a form intermediate between QS and AAm §171:

> Isil the Sheen the gods of old named the Moon in Valinor, and Anar Fire-golden they named the Sun; but the Eldar named them also Rána the wayward, the giver of visions, and [Úrin >] Naira, the heart of flame, that awakens and consumes.

Thus *Úrin* > *Anar* (with changed meaning, 'Fire-golden'), as in AAm, but this and *Isil* remain names given by the Gods, not by the Vanyar; *Úrin* was at first changed about with *Anar* and made the Eldarin name of the Sun, but was then replaced by *Naira* (*Vása* in AAm). *Rána* (replacing *Rǎna*) and *Naira* remain Eldarin names, whereas in AAm *Rána* and *Vása* are Noldorin.

'The maiden chosen from among their own folk by the Valar' > 'The maiden whom the Valar chose from among the Maiar' (agreeing with AAm §172).

Pencilled in the margin against *Arien* (above the original marginal gloss by Ælfwine *hyrned* 'horned' to the name Tilion, V.240, footnote) is the unrecorded Old English word *Dægbore* ('Day-bearer', feminine). In AAm (§172, marginal notes) the Old English words supplied by Ælfwine are *hyrned* and *dægred* (daybreak, dawn).

'the pools lit by the flickering light of Silpion' > 'the pools of Estë in Telperion's flickering beams' (agreeing with AAm §172). *Silpion* > *Telperion* subsequently (see p. 59, §5).

§76 'Rǎna was first wrought' > 'Isil was first wrought' (as AAm §173).

'Melko' > 'Morgoth', because he is to be known as *Morgoth* from the point in the narrative where he is given that name (p. 194, §60).

§77 'the prayers of Lórien and Nienna' > 'the prayers of Lorien and Estë' (as AAm §175).

'Varda changed her design' > 'Varda changed her counsel' (as AAm §175).

The entire passage beginning at 'is the hour of greatest light' and continuing to §79 'the Valar store the radiance of the Sun in many vessels' was put into the past tense (cf. AAm §§175–8).

§78 *Eruman* > *Aruman* (not *Araman*). Since *Eruman* was changed to *Araman* in the revision made at this time to an earlier page in QS (§71) *Aruman* here is no doubt merely an incomplete alteration.

§79 Rewriting of the passage in QS beginning 'That light lives now only in the Silmarils' removed at last the ancient idea of the 'rekindling' of 'the Elder Sun and Moon, which are the Trees' (for the history of this see II.285–6, IV.20, 49, 98), or at least restricted it to a foretelling of the recovery of the Silmarils; but

Chapter 8 THE LATER *QUENTA SILMARILLION* (I)   199

the strange prophecy of Ulmo that this would only come to pass through the aid of Men was retained. To none of this is there anything corresponding in AAm. The changed passage reads:

That light lives now only in the Silmarils; though there shall yet come a time, maybe, when they are found again and their fire released, and the ancient joy and glory return. Ulmo foretold to the Valar...'

The sentence (not in AAm, §180) 'the fleet of the Teleri kept the shore' was changed to 'rebuilt with Ossë's aid, the fleet of the Teleri kept the shore'.

§80 'the Bay of Elvenhome' > 'The Bay of Eldanor'.

It seems to me very probable that my father made these changes to QS before he wrote the section on the Sun and Moon in the *Annals of Aman*; in any case they were doubtless closely contemporary.

(II) THE SECOND PHASE

An acute problem of presentation arose in the treatment of the late expanded version of Chapter 6 *Of the Silmarils and the Darkening of Valinor* (see pp. 142, 184 ff.), in that the first part of the new text was based on and developed in stages from a major independent disquisition concerning the nature of the Eldar. Arising out of an account of their marriage laws and customs, this discussion extends into a lengthy analysis of the meaning of death, immortality and rebirth in respect of the Elves. I found that to give the late narrative text of Chapter 6 immediately following the text of the 'first phase' version, postponing the long and remarkable essay from which it derives, was extremely confusing; while to introduce the essay into the series of 'first phase' chapters made matters worse. For this reason I have divided this part of the book into two sections, and give here separately the late narrative versions of Chapters 1, 6, and a part of 7 together with the essay on the Eldar. To date these writings (and those given in Part Four) with any real precision seems impossible on the evidence that I know of, but such as there is points clearly in most cases to the late 1950s and not much later (for detailed discussion see p. 300).

★

THE VALAQUENTA

Of the final, enlarged form of the old Chapter 1, the *Valaquenta* (abbreviated Vq), there are two texts, both of them typescripts made by my father (Vq 1 and Vq 2). Vq 1 begins as a copy of LQ 2, but very soon diverges, and with the introduction of much new matter becomes in several parts entirely distinct. Though typewritten it is very much a draft text, confused and (at any rate as it exists now) incomplete. It was followed, I would think immediately, by the finished text Vq 2.

Vq 1 is headed like the preceding versions, 'QUENTA SILMARIL-LION. Here begins the *Silmarillion*, or the History of the Silmarils. I. Of the Valar.' Vq 2, on the other hand, is headed 'VALAQUENTA. Here is the Account of the Valar and Maiar according to the Lore of the Eldar.' That the original first chapter of *The Silmarillion* had become a separate entity like the *Ainulindalë* is shown, apart from the new title, by the fact that to the final text (LQ 2) of the next chapter, *Of Valinor and the Two Trees*, a title-page (together with a page carrying the preamble, Ælfwine's note, and the Translator's note) was attached, and the chapter numbered '1'. This title-page is virtually the same as that in the old QS typescript (see V.202), with the heading '*Eldanyárë*' and beneath '*Quenta Silmarillion*', the division into three parts, and the forms *Pennas Silevril, Yénie Valinóren, Inias Valannor* (where however the old typescript was changed to *Balannor*), and *Inias Beleriand*. The fact that it was taken from the original '*Eldanyárë*' text suggests that it really belonged to LQ 1 (whose title-page is missing, p. 143). It is true that it was typed at the same time as the rest of LQ 2, but I imagine that (having decided to separate off the *Valaquenta*) my father at this time gave the title-page of LQ 1 to the typist of LQ 2 to copy, after which it was mislaid and lost. It seems odd that he should have done this; at least one might have expected him to change the second element from *The Annals of Valinor* to *The Annals of Aman*. He did indeed make some pencilled emendations to it: *Yénie Valinóren* to *Yénie Valinóreo* (and beneath this *Valinóre Yénie*), and *Inias Valannor* to *Ínias Dor-Rodyn*.

Essentially, Vq 1 was the innovating version, and Vq 2 refined stylistically on the new material, although in any given case it is possible that Vq 1 was as LQ 2 and that Vq 2 introduced the new text; however, I treat this detail as largely immaterial. In what follows I comment on notable features arising from a comparison between the *Valaquenta* and LQ (that is, the corrected text of LQ 1 given on pp. 144–7, referred to by the numbered paragraphs, together with the emendations made to its copy LQ 2 given on pp. 148–9). The text of the *Valaquenta* is found in the published *Silmarillion* (references are to the original hardback edition, 1977). Since a number of editorial changes were made to the text of the *Valaquenta* I notice certain points of substance in which they differ.

§1   The words 'Let it be!' were not included in the Vq texts (see p. 148, §1).

§2   Nearly all of this paragraph concerning the Maiar and the confusion with Elves (as emended in LQ 2) still survived in Vq 1, but was eliminated in Vq 2 (the first part of it reappearing, rewritten, at the beginning of the section 'Of the Maiar'). The end of the paragraph, concerning the making of the Children of Eru, was eliminated in Vq 2 and does not reappear.

§3 Vq 1 as typed followed LQ exactly in the list of the 'chieftains of the Valar' (with *Lóriën* as in LQ 2 for earlier *Lorien*), but a list of the seven queens (*Valier*) was also given: Varda, Yavanna, Niënna, Vána, Vairë, Nessa, Uinen (agreeing with the table given on p. 151). In Vq 1 the nine 'chieftains' became by emendation seven: Melkor and Ossë were removed (and Oromë's place changed, so that he stands after Aulë); this is the number and order of 'the Lords of the Valar' in Vq 2 and in the published work (p. 25). Also by emendation to Vq 1 the queens lose Uinen but gain Estë, who is placed after Niënna, and Vána is set after Vairë; this again was the final form. These changes, both to Valar and Valier, were made also to the typescript of AAm (p. 69, §§1–2). The names *Vána* and *Niënna* are given thus in Vq 2.

The sentence in LQ 'though they have other or altered names in the speech of the Sindar' was retained in Vq 1 with the addition of 'in Middle-earth', but changed in Vq 2 to 'though they have other names in the speech of the Elves in Middle-earth.'

§4 (*Varda*) The history of the phrase 'With Manwë dwells Varda' (*The Silmarillion* p. 26) is curious. QS §4 has 'With him dwells as wife Varda ...'; by emendation to LQ 1 it became 'With him *in Arda* dwells as spouse Varda ...'; and in Vq it is 'With Manwë *now* dwells as spouse Varda ...' In 1975, when the main work on the text of the published *Silmarillion* was done, being then much less clear than I have since become about certain dates and textual relations (and ignorant of the existence of some texts), I did not see that this 'now' could have any significance, and moreover it contributed to the problem of tense in the *Valaquenta*, which is discussed below; I therefore omitted it. It is however undoubtedly significant. In AAm it is said (p. 49, §3): 'Varda was Manwë's spouse *from the beginning*', in contrast to the later 'union' of Yavanna and Aulë 'in Ëa' (on which see under §5 below). But the typescript text of AAm was emended (p. 69, §3) to 'Varda was Manwë's spouse *from the beginning of Arda*', which shows that some complex conception was present (though never definitively expressed) concerning the time of the 'union' of the great spirits.

In the new, much extended passage concerning Varda, Vq 1 has 'She speaks seldom in words, save to Manwë', where Vq 2 followed by the published text (p. 26) has 'Manwë and Varda are seldom parted, and they remain in Valinor.'

(*Ulmo*) The long new passage concerning Ulmo entered in Vq 1, which has some interesting differences from the final form: it is said that Ulmo 'had less need of the light of the Trees or of any resting-place', and that 'his counsels grew ever away from the mind of Manwë (whom nonetheless he obeyed)': cf. the *Ainulindalë* (p. 13, §18), 'Manwë and Ulmo have from the beginning been allied, and in all things have served most faithfully the purpose of Ilúvatar'. In both Vq texts his horns are called *Falarombar*, changed on the Vq 2 typescript to *Ulumúri*; cf. the original name of the horn of Oromë, *Rombaras* (p. 35, §34), and the *Etymologies*, V.384, stem ROM.

(Ossë and Uinen) The passage concerning Ossë and Uinen, much enlarged, now appears in the section 'Of the Maiar', since they have ceased to be numbered among the Valar (see under §3 above).

§5 *(Aulë)* In the words (referring to Melkor and Aulë) 'Both, also, desired to make things of their own that should be new and unthought of by others' (*The Silmarillion* p. 27) there is very probably a reflection of the legend of Aulë's making of the Dwarves.

(Yavanna) Here again, as with Varda (§4 above), I wrongly changed the text concerning Yavanna's union with Aulë. Both Vq texts have 'The spouse of Aulë *in Arda* is Yavanna', and the words 'in Arda' are certainly significant (see V.120).

'Some there are who have seen her standing like a tree under heaven' recalls the later versions of the *Ainulindalë*, where it is Pengoloð himself who declares to Ælfwine that he has so seen her 'long years agone, in the land of the Valar' (p. 15, §25).

The name *Kementári* is found as a correction of *Palúrien* in LQ 2, Chapter 2 (p. 157, §14).

§6 *(Mandos)* The editorial change of 'northward' to 'westward' in 'Námo the elder dwells in Mandos, which is northward in Valinor' in the published text (p. 28) is a regrettable error, which I have explained in I.82. – It may be noted here that in the passage in §9 concerning Nienna the change of 'the halls of Mandos, which are nearer and yet more northward' (found from QS to LQ 2) to 'the halls of Mandos, which are near to her own' is not editorial, but is found in the Vq texts.

§7 *(Tulkas)* The sentence 'He came last to Arda, to aid the Valar in the first battles with Melkor' only entered with Vq 2, but derives from the later *Ainulindalë* (§31).

§8 *(Oromë)* In emendation to one copy only of LQ 2 the name *Aldaron* of Oromë was lost (see p. 149, §8), and it does not appear in either text of Vq. It should not have been reintroduced into the published text (p. 29). The sentence *(ibid.)* 'by the Sindar Tauron' derives from LQ 2 and Vq 1, but was in fact changed in Vq 2 to 'Tauron he is called in Middle-earth'; cf. under §3 above, where 'Sindar' was also removed in Vq 2. The translation of *Tauron* should be 'the Lord of the Forests'.

The name *Nahar* of Oromë's horse first appears in AAm §31 (p. 70). – After the words 'for the pursuit of the evil creatures of Melkor' (*The Silmarillion* p. 29) the Vq texts have 'But the Valaróma is not blown, and Nahar runs no more upon the Middle-earth since the change of the world and the waning of the Elves, whom he loved.' This sentence goes back through the versions to QS (though the Valaróma does not appear in it till LQ 2 and Nahar not till Vq), and I regret its exclusion from *The Silmarillion*.

§9 (*Nienna*) The account of Nienna appears at an earlier point in Vq (following the Fëanturi, to whom she is now 'akin') than it had in previous versions. The words 'sister of the Fëanturi' were changed editorially from Vq 'sister of Námo' (see p. 151, §9).

At the end of the account of the Valar and Valier appears the name and conception of the *Aratar*, the High Ones of Arda, of whom there are eight after the removal of Melkor. This contrasts with the conception of 'the Seven Great Ones of the Realm of Arda' (p. 147, §10a), among whom Melkor is numbered, but not Oromë, nor Mandos.

§§10a, b *Of the Maiar*. The words in the published text (p. 30) concerning Eönwë, 'whose might in arms is surpassed by none in Arda', were an editorial addition, made in order to prepare for his leadership of the hosts of the West at the Great Battle (*The Silmarillion* pp. 251–2). For the end of the Elder Days there is scarcely any material from the period following *The Lord of the Rings*.

(*Melian*) In LQ 2 Melian was said to be 'of the people of Yavanna'; see p. 147, §10b.

(*Olórin*) At the end of the account of Olórin is scribbled on the typescript Vq 1: 'He was humble in the Land of the Blessed; and in Middle-earth he sought no renown. His triumph was in the uprising of the fallen, and his joy was in the renewal of hope.' This appears in Vq 2, but my father subsequently placed inverted commas round it. It was wrongly omitted from *The Silmarillion* (p. 31).

Of the Enemies. In this almost entirely new section appears the conception that the Balrogs (*Valaraukar*) were powerful spirits from before the World; so also in AAm* (p. 79, §30) the Balrogs are described as the chief of 'the evil spirits that followed [Melkor], the Úmaiar'. See further p. 165, §18.

The *Valaquenta* texts end thus, and speak of the Marring of Arda, the underlying concern of many of the writings given subsequently in this book:

Here ends *The Valaquenta*. If it has passed from the high and beautiful to darkness and ruin, that was of old the fate of Arda

Marred; and if any change shall come and the Marring be amended, Manwë and Varda may know; but they have not revealed it, and it is not declared in the dooms of Mandos.

The Second Prophecy of Mandos (V.333) had now therefore definitively disappeared. This passage was used to form a conclusion to the published *Silmarillion* (p. 255).

In my foreword to *The Silmarillion* I wrote that in the *Valaquenta* 'we have to assume that while it contains much that must go back to the earliest days of the Eldar in Valinor, it was remodelled in later times; and thus explain its continual shifting of tense and viewpoint, so that the divine powers seem now present and active in the world, now remote, a vanished order known only to memory.'

The problem of tense in this work is certainly very difficult. Already in Q (IV.78–9) the shifting from past to present tense appears, where Ossë and Uinen and Nienna are described in the present, in contrast to all the others, while Ulmo 'was' next in might to Manwë, but he 'dwells' alone in the Outer Seas. In QS (see V.208) the present tense is used, almost though not exclusively – but 'Tulkas *had* great love for Fionwë' early became '*has*', and 'Oromë *was* a mighty lord' became 'Oromë *is*' in the 1951 revision.

With the additions and alterations made in the course of that revision the variations continue. In LQ §10a, for instance, 'there *are* nine Valar', contrasting with the original passage in §3, 'The chieftains of the Valar *were* nine', which goes back through QS to Q; or in the passage about the Maiar in §10b 'Among them Eönwë ... and Ilmarë ... *were* the chief', but 'Many others there *are*' (altered from '*were*'). The same mixture of present and past is found in AAm* (p. 65, §3).

The situation remains the same in the Vq texts, and in preparing the *Valaquenta* for publication I altered (with misgiving and doubt) some of the tenses. The readings of the published work which were altered from those in Vq are:

p. 25: 'The Lords of the Valar *are* seven; and the Valier ... *are* seven also'; 'The names of the Lords in due order *are*'; 'the names of the Queens *are*'

p. 26: 'Manwë *is* dearest to Ilúvatar and *understands* most clearly his purposes'; 'he *hated* her, and *feared* her'

p. 27: 'Ulmo *loves* both Elves and Men'

p. 28: 'The Fëanturi ... *are* brethren'

p. 30: 'it *is* otherwise in Aman'; 'Chief among the Maiar ... *are* Ilmarë ... and Eönwë'

In all these cases, except 'he hated her, and feared her' on p. 26, the tense was changed from past to present. The change on p. 28 seems in any case mistaken (cf. p. 26, 'Manwë and Melkor were brethren in the thought of Ilúvatar'); and to make any of them was probably a misjudgement. But the problem is real. A leading consideration in the preparation of the text was the achievement of coherence and consistency; and a fundamental problem was uncertainty as to the mode by which in my father's later thought the 'Lore of the Eldar' had been transmitted. But I now think that I attached too much importance to the aim of consistency, which may be present when not evident, and was too ready to deal with 'difficulties' simply by eliminating them.

★

THE EARLIEST VERSION OF THE STORY OF FINWË AND MÍRIEL

The story of Finwë and Míriel, which would assume an extraordinary importance in my father's later work on *The Silmarillion*, began as a rider in manuscript to the 'first phase' revision of Chapter 6, *Of the Silmarils and the Darkening of Valinor*; it was inserted after the account of the marvellous skill of Míriel, called *Serendë* 'the Broideress', mother of Fëanor, at the end of LQ §46b (p. 185). I shall refer to this rider as 'FM 1' (i.e. the first text treating of the story of Finwë and Míriel in the *Quenta Silmarillion*).

A curious feature of this text is the presence of marginal dates; and three late insertions to the *Annals of Aman* (p. 101, notes 1 and 4) are closely associated with it. The entry in AAm for the Valian Year 1179 (p. 92) gave the birth of Fëanor in Tirion and his mother's name *Byrdë Míriel*. Afterwards my father changed this date to 1169, and at the same time added these new annals:

1170 Míriel falls asleep and passes to Mandar.
1172 Doom of Manwë concerning the espousals of the Eldar.
1185 Finwë weds Indis of the Vanyar.

In the present rider to LQ the dates, which were a good deal changed, are the same, or the same to within a year or two. It is obvious that the insertions to AAm and the rider to LQ are contemporary; and while my father probably only put in the dates in the latter as a guide to his thought (they are absent from the subsequent texts of *Finwë and Míriel*), the fact that he did so seems a testimony to the closeness that the two 'modes' now had for him.

The text FM 1 was subsequently emended in ball-point pen; the changed readings are shown in the text that now follows. It may be noted here that at the first three occurrences of the name my father wrote *Mandar*, changing it before the text was completed to *Mandos*. The inserted entry in AAm for the year 1170, cited above, also has *Mandar*. Thus even this very long-established name, going back to the earliest form of the legends, was still susceptible of change; but it was a passing movement and does not appear again.

Now it is told that in the bearing of her son Míriel was

consumed in spirit and body; and that after his birth she yearned for rest from the labour of living. And she said to Finwë: 'Never again shall I bear a child; for strength that would have nourished the life of many has gone forth into Fëanáro.'*
Then Manwë granted the prayer of Míriel. And she went to Lorien, and laid her down to sleep upon a bed of flowers [> beneath a silver tree]; and there her fair body remained unwithered in the keeping of the maidens of Estë. But her spirit passed to rest in the halls of Mandos.

Finwë's grief was great, and he gave to his son all the love that he had for Míriel; for Fëanáro was like his mother in voice and countenance. Yet Finwë was not content, and he desired to have more children. He spoke, therefore, [> After some years, therefore, he spoke] to Manwë, saying: 'Lord, behold! I am bereaved; and alone among the Eldar I am without a wife, and must hope for no sons save one, and no daughter. Whereas Ingwë and Olwë beget many children in the bliss of Aman. Must I remain ever so? For I deem that Míriel will not return again ever from the house of Vairë.'

Then Manwë considered the words of Finwë; and after a time he summoned all the counsellors of the Eldar, and in their hearing Mandos spoke this doom: 'This is the law of Ilúvatar for you [> This is the way of life that Ilúvatar hath ordained for you], his children, as you know well: the First-born shall take one spouse only and have no other in this life, while Arda endureth. But this law takes no account [> But herein no account is taken] of Death. This doom is therefore now made, by the right of lawgiving that Ilúvatar committed to Manwë: that if the spirit of a spouse, husband or wife, forsaking the body, shall for any cause pass into the keeping of Mandos, then the living shall be permitted to take another spouse. But this can only be, if the former union be dissolved for ever. Therefore the one that is in the keeping of Mandos must there remain until the end of Arda, and shall not awake again or take bodily form. For none among the Quendi shall have two spouses at one time alive and awake. But since it is not to be thought that the living shall, by his or her will alone, confine the spirit of the other to Mandos, this disunion shall come to pass only by the consent of

---

* [footnote to the text] Thus she named her son: *Spirit-of-Fire*: and by that name he was known among the Eldar. [*Fëanáro* is so spelt here, but *Feänáro* subsequently.]

both. And after the giving of the consent ten years of the Valar shall pass ere Mandos confirms it. Within that time either party may revoke this consent; but when Mandos has confirmed it, and the living spouse has wedded another, it shall be irrevocable until the end of Arda. This is the doom of Námo in this matter.'

It is said that Míriel answered Mandos saying: 'I came hither to escape from the body, and I do not desire ever to return to it'; and after ten years the doom of disunion was spoken. [*Added*: And Míriel has dwelt ever since in the house of Vairë, and it is her part to record there the histories of the kin of Finwë and all the deeds of the Noldor.] And in the years following [> But when three years more had passed] Finwë took as second spouse Indis of the Vanyar, of the kin [> sister] of Ingwë; and she bore five fair children of whom her two sons are most renowned in the histories of the Noldor. But her eldest child was a daughter, Findis, and she bore also two other daughters: Írimë and Faniel [> Faniel and Írimë].

The wedding of the father was not pleasing to Feänáro; and though the love between them was not lessened, Feänáro had no great love for Indis or her children, and as soon as he might he lived apart from them, being busy from early childhood upon the lore and craft in which he delighted, and he laboured at many tasks, being in all pursuits eager and swift.

There is a direction here to return to LQ (at the beginning of §46c, p. 185) with the words 'For he grew swiftly ...'

★

LAWS AND CUSTOMS AMONG THE ELDAR

As I have explained (p. 199), I have found that the best method of presenting the material is to give at this point the long essay concerning the nature and customs of the Eldar, although of course it cannot be said to be a part of the *Quenta Silmarillion*.

This work is extant in two versions, a completed manuscript ('**A**') and a revision of this in a typescript ('**B**') made by my father that was abandoned when somewhat less than halfway through. The two texts bear different titles, and since both are long I shall use an abbreviated form, *Laws and Customs among the Eldar* (in references later, simply *Laws and Customs*). From the existence of the two versions arises a difficulty of presentation frequently encountered in my father's work. The typescript B, so far as it goes, follows the manuscript A pretty closely for the most part – too closely to justify printing them both in full, even if space allowed. On the other hand there are many points in which B differs significantly from A. The options are therefore to give A in full with important divergences in B in textual notes, or to give B as far as it goes with A's divergences in notes, and then the remainder from A. Since B is a clearer and improved text I have decided on the latter course.

It is not easy to say from what fictional perspective *Laws and Customs among the Eldar* was composed. There is a reference to the Elves who linger in Middle-earth 'in these after-days' (p. 223); on the other hand the writer speaks as if the customs of the Noldor were present and observable ('Among the Noldor it may be seen that the making of bread is done mostly by women', p. 214) – though this cannot be pressed. It is clear in any case that it is presented as the work, not of one of the Eldar, but of a Man: the observation about the variety of the names borne by the Eldar, 'which ... may to us seem bewildering' (p. 216; found in both texts, in different words) is decisive. Ælfwine is indeed associated with the work, but in an extremely puzzling way. He does not appear at all in A as that was originally written; but among various corrections and alterations made in red ball-point pen (doubtless as a preliminary to the making of the typescript) my father wrote 'Ælfwine's Preamble' in the margin against the opening of the text – without however marking where this 'preamble' ended. In B the first two paragraphs are marked 'Ælfwine's Preamble' and placed within ornate brackets, and this very clearly belongs with the making of the typescript, although it is by no means obvious why the opening should be thus set apart; while later in B (p. 224) there is a long observation, set within similar brackets, that ends with the words 'So spoke Ælfwine' – but this passage is absent in any form from A.

There are no initial drafts or rough writings extant, and if none existed the manuscript text is remarkably clear and orderly, without much correction at the time of composition, though a good deal changed subsequently. It may be that it had been substantially composed, the product of long thought, before it was first written down; at the same time, my impression is that my father had not fully planned its structure when he began. This is suggested by the curious way in which the judgement of Mandos in the case of Finwë and Míriel precedes the actual story of what led to the judgement (pp. 225–6, 236–9); while after the account of Finwë's marriage to Indis there follows the Debate of the Valar, although that was held before 'the Statute of Finwë and Míriel' was promulgated. It is hard to believe that my father can have intended this rather confusing structure, and the view that the work evolved as he wrote seems borne out by the title in A:

> Of the marriage laws and customs of the
> Eldar, their children, and other
> matters touching thereon

At the same time as the words 'Ælfwine's Preamble' and other corrections in red ball-point pen were made to the manuscript (see above) he wrote in bold letters beneath the title: 'The Statute of Finwë and Míriel' – almost as if this was to be the new title of the work as a whole, although the original one was not struck out.

The typescript B has the long title given at the beginning of the text below; the text in this version ends before the story of Finwë and Míriel and the Debate of the Valar is reached. Why my father abandoned it I cannot say; perhaps he was merely interrupted by some external cause, perhaps he was dissatisfied by its form.

But all these questions are very secondary to the import of the work itself: a comprehensive (if sometimes obscure, and tantalising in its obscurity) declaration of his thought at that time on fundamental aspects of the nature of the Quendi, distinguishing them from Men: the power of the incarnate *fëa* (spirit) in relation to the body; the 'consuming' of the body by the *fëa*; the destiny of Elvish spirits, ordained by Eru, 'to dwell in Arda for all the life of Arda'; the meaning of death for such beings, and of existence after death; the nature of Elvish re-birth; and the consequences of the Marring of Arda by Melkor.

There follows now the typescript version B so far as it goes. At the end of the text (pp. 228 ff.) are notes largely limited to the textual relations of the two versions; these are necessarily very selective, and do not record the very many changes of wording in B that modify or improve the expression without altering the sense of the original text in any important way. B itself was scarcely changed after it had been typed; but a pencilled note on the first page reads 'For *hrondo* read *hröa*', and this change was carried out in the greater part of the text. The word used in A for the body was *hrôn*, which became *hrondo* in the course of the writing of the manuscript.

OF THE LAWS AND CUSTOMS AMONG THE ELDAR PERTAINING TO MARRIAGE AND OTHER MATTERS RELATED THERETO: TOGETHER WITH THE STATUTE OF FINWË AND MÍRIEL AND THE DEBATE OF THE VALAR AT ITS MAKING

Ælfwine's Preamble

[The Eldar grew in bodily form slower than Men, but in mind more swiftly. They learned to speak before they were one year old; and in the same time they learned to walk and to dance, for their wills came soon to the mastery of their bodies. Nonetheless there was less difference between the two Kindreds, Elves and Men, in early youth; and a man who watched elf-children at play might well have believed that they were the children of Men, of some fair and happy people. For in their early days elf-children delighted still in the world about them, and the fire of their spirit had not consumed them, and the burden of memory was still light upon them.[1]

This same watcher might indeed have wondered at the small limbs and stature of these children, judging their age by their skill in words and grace in motion. For at the end of the third year mortal children began to outstrip the Elves, hastening on to a full stature while the Elves lingered in the first spring of childhood. Children of Men might reach their full height while Eldar of the same age were still in body like to mortals of no more than seven years.[2] Not until the fiftieth year did the Eldar attain the stature and shape in which their lives would afterwards endure, and for some a hundred years would pass before they were full-grown.]

The Eldar wedded for the most part in their youth and soon after their fiftieth year. They had few children, but these were very dear to them. Their families, or houses, were held together by love and a deep feeling for kinship in mind and body; and the children needed little governing or teaching.[3] There were seldom more than four children in any house, and the number grew less as ages passed; but even in days of old, while the Eldar were still few and eager to increase their kind, Fëanor was renowned as the father of seven sons, and the histories record none that surpassed him.[4]

The Eldar wedded once only in life, and for love or at the least by free will upon either part. Even when in after days, as the histories reveal, many of the Eldar in Middle-earth became corrupted, and their hearts darkened by the shadow that lies upon Arda, seldom is any tale told of deeds of lust among them.[5]

Marriage, save for rare ill chances or strange fates, was the natural course of life for all the Eldar. It took place in this way. Those who would afterwards become wedded might choose one another early in youth, even as children (and indeed this happened often in days of peace); but unless they desired soon to be married and were of fitting age, the betrothal awaited the judgement of the parents of either party.

In due time the betrothal was announced at a meeting of the two houses concerned,[6] and the betrothed gave silver rings one to another. According to the laws of the Eldar this betrothal was bound then to stand for one year at least, and it often stood for longer. During this time it could be revoked by a public return of the rings, the rings then being molten and not again used for a betrothal. Such was the law; but the right of revoking was seldom used, for the Eldar do not err lightly in such choice. They are not easily deceived by their own kind; and their spirits being masters of their bodies, they are seldom swayed by the desires of the body only, but are by nature continent and steadfast.

Nonetheless among the Eldar, even in Aman, the desire for marriage was not always fulfilled. Love was not always returned; and more than one might desire one other for spouse. Concerning this, the only cause by which sorrow entered the bliss of Aman, the Valar were in doubt. Some held that it came from the marring of Arda, and from the Shadow under which the Eldar awoke; for thence only (they said) comes grief or disorder. Some held that it came of love itself, and of the freedom of each *fëa*, and was a mystery of the nature of the Children of Eru.

After the betrothal it was the part of the betrothed to appoint the time of their wedding, when at least one year had passed. Then at a feast, again[7] shared by the two houses, the marriage was celebrated. At the end of the feast the betrothed stood forth, and the mother of the bride and the father of the bridegroom joined the hands of the pair and blessed them. For this blessing there was a solemn form, but no mortal has heard it; though the Eldar say that Varda was named in witness by the mother and Manwë by the father; and moreover that the name of Eru was spoken (as was seldom done at any other time). The betrothed then received back one from the other their silver rings (and treasured them); but they gave in exchange slender rings of gold, which were worn upon the index of the right hand.

Among the Noldor also it was a custom that the bride's mother should give to the bridegroom a jewel upon a chain or collar; and the bridegroom's father should give a like gift to the bride. These gifts were sometimes given before the feast. (Thus the gift of Galadriel to Aragorn, since she was in place of Arwen's mother, was in part a bridal gift and earnest of the wedding that was later accomplished.)

But these ceremonies were not rites necessary to marriage; they were only a gracious mode by which the love of the parents was manifested,[8] and the union was recognized which would join not only the betrothed but their two houses together. It was the act of bodily union that achieved marriage, and after which the indissoluble bond was complete. In happy days and times of peace it was held ungracious and contemptuous of kin to forgo the ceremonies, but it was at all times lawful for any of the Eldar, both being unwed, to marry thus of free consent one to another without ceremony or witness (save blessings exchanged and the naming of the Name); and the union so joined was alike indissoluble. In days of old, in times of trouble, in flight and exile and wandering, such marriages were often made.[9]

As for the begetting and bearing of children: a year passes between the begetting and the birth of an elf-child, so that the days of both are the same or nearly so, and it is the day of begetting that is remembered year by year. For the most part these days come in the Spring. It might be thought that, since the Eldar do not (as Men deem) grow old in body, they may bring forth children at any time in the ages of their lives. But this is not so. For the Eldar do indeed grow older, even if slowly: the limit of their lives is the life of Arda, which though long beyond the reckoning of Men is not endless, and ages also. Moreover their body and spirit are not separated but coherent. As the weight of the years, with all their changes of desire and thought, gathers upon the spirit of the Eldar, so do the impulses and moods of their bodies change. This the Eldar mean when they speak of their spirits consuming them; and they say that ere Arda ends all the Eldalië on earth will have become as spirits invisible to mortal eyes, unless they will to be seen by some among Men into whose minds they may enter directly.[10]

Also the Eldar say that in the begetting, and still more in the bearing of children, greater share and strength of their being, in mind and in body, goes forth than in the making of mortal children. For these reasons it came to pass that the Eldar brought forth few children; and also that their time of generation was in their youth or earlier life, unless strange and hard fates befell them. But at whatever age they married, their children were born within a short space of years after their wedding.* For with regard to generation the power and the will

---

* Short as the Eldar reckoned time. In mortal count there was often a long interval between the wedding and the first child-birth, and even longer between child and child.

are not among the Eldar distinguishable. Doubtless they would retain for many ages the power of generation, if the will and desire were not satisfied; but with the exercise of the power the desire soon ceases, and the mind turns to other things.[11] The union of love is indeed to them great delight and joy, and the 'days of the children', as they call them, remain in their memory as the most merry in life; but they have many other powers of body and of mind which their nature urges them to fulfil.

Thus, although the wedded remain so for ever, they do not necessarily dwell or house together at all times; for without considering the chances and separations of evil days, wife and husband, albeit united, remain persons individual having each gifts of mind and body that differ. Yet it would seem to any of the Eldar a grievous thing if a wedded pair were sundered during the bearing of a child, or while the first years of its childhood lasted. For which reason the Eldar would beget children only in days of happiness and peace if they could.

In all such things, not concerned with the bringing forth of children, the *neri* and *nissi*[12] (that is, the men and women) of the Eldar are equal – unless it be in this (as they themselves say) that for the *nissi* the making of things new is for the most part shown in the forming of their children, so that invention and change is otherwise mostly brought about by the *neri*. There are, however, no matters which among the Eldar only a *nér* can think or do, or others with which only a *nís* is concerned. There are indeed some differences between the natural inclinations of *neri* and *nissi*, and other differences that have been established by custom (varying in place and in time, and in the several races of the Eldar). For instance, the arts of healing, and all that touches on the care of the body, are among all the Eldar most practised by the *nissi*; whereas it was the elven-men who bore arms at need. And the Eldar deemed that the dealing of death, even when lawful or under necessity, diminished the power of healing, and that the virtue of the *nissi* in this matter was due rather to their abstaining from hunting or war than to any special power that went with their womanhood. Indeed in dire straits or desperate defence, the *nissi* fought valiantly, and there was less difference in strength and speed between elven-men and elven-women that had not borne child than is seen among mortals. On the other hand many elven-men were great healers and skilled in the lore of living bodies, though such men abstained from hunting, and went not to war until the last need.

As for other matters, we may speak of the customs of the Noldor (of whom most is known in Middle-earth). Among the Noldor it may be seen that the making of bread is done mostly by women; and the making of the *lembas* is by ancient law reserved to them. Yet the cooking and preparing of other food is generally a task and pleasure of men. The *nissi* are more often skilled in the tending of fields and gardens, in playing upon instruments of music, and in the spinning, weaving, fashioning, and adornment of all threads and cloths; and in matters of lore they love most the histories of the Eldar and of the houses of the Noldor; and all matters of kinship and descent are held by them in memory. But the *neri* are more skilled as smiths and wrights, as carvers of wood and stone, and as jewellers. It is they for the most part who compose musics and make the instruments, or devise new ones; they are the chief poets and students of languages and inventors of words. Many of them delight in forestry and in the lore of the wild, seeking the friendship of all things that grow or live there in freedom. But all these things, and other matters of labour and play, or of deeper knowledge concerning being and the life of the World, may at different times be pursued by any among the Noldor, be they *neri* or *nissi*.

OF NAMING

This is the manner in which the naming of children was achieved among the Noldor. Soon after birth the child was named. It was the right of the father to devise this first name,[13] and he it was that announced it to the child's kindred upon either side. It was called, therefore, the father-name, and it stood first, if other names were afterwards added. It remained unaltered,* for it lay not in the choice of the child.

But every child among the Noldor (in which point, maybe, they differed from the other Eldar) had also the right to name himself or herself. Now the first ceremony, the announcement of the father-name, was called the *Essecarmë* or 'Name-making'. Later there was another ceremony called the *Essecilmë* or 'Name-choosing'. This took place at no fixed date after the

---

* Save for such changes as might befall its spoken form in the passing of the long years; for (as is elsewhere told) even the tongues of the Eldar were subject to change.

Essecarmë, but could not take place before the child was deemed ready and capable of *lámatyávë*, as the Noldor called it: that is, of individual pleasure in the sounds and forms of words. The Noldor were of all the Eldar the swiftest in acquiring word-mastery; but even among them few before at least the seventh year had become fully aware of their own individual *lámatyávë*, or had gained a complete mastery of the inherited language and its structure, so as to express this *tyávë* skilfully within its limits. The *Essecilmë*, therefore, the object of which was the expression of this personal characteristic,* usually took place at or about the end of the tenth year.

In elder times the 'Chosen Name', or second name, was usually freshly devised, and though framed according to the structure of the language of the day, it often had no previous significance. In later ages, when there was a great abundance of names already in existence, it was more often selected from names that were known. But even so some modification of the old name might be made.[14]

Now both these names, the father-name and the chosen name, were 'true names', not nicknames; but the father-name was public, and the chosen name was private, especially when used alone. Private, not secret. The chosen names were regarded by the Noldor as part of their personal property, like (say) their rings, cups, or knives, or other possessions which they could lend, or share with kindred and friends, but which could not be taken without leave. The use of the chosen name, except by members of the same house (parents, sisters, and brothers), was a token of closest intimacy and love, when permitted. It was, therefore, presumptuous or insulting to use it without permission.**[15]

Since, however, the Eldar were by nature immortal within Arda, but were by no means changeless, after a time one might wish for a new name.†[16] He might then devise for himself a new chosen name. But this did not abrogate the former name, which

---

*This *lámatyávë* was held a mark of individuality, and more important indeed than others, such as stature, colour, and features of face.

**This sentiment had thus nothing to do with 'magic' or with taboos, such as are found among Men.

†The Eldar hold that, apart from ill chances and the destruction of their bodies, they may in the course of their years each exercise and

remained part of the 'full title' of any Noldo: that is the sequence of all the names that had been acquired in the course of life.[17]

These deliberate changes of chosen name were not frequent. There was another source of the variety of names borne by any one of the Eldar, which in the reading of their histories may to us seem bewildering. This was found in the *Anessi*: the given (or added) names. Of these the most important were the so-called 'mother-names'.[18] Mothers often gave to their children special names of their own choosing. The most notable of these were the 'names of insight', *essi tercenyë*, or of 'foresight', *apacenyë*. In the hour of birth, or on some other occasion of moment, the mother might give a name to her child, indicating some dominant feature of its nature as perceived by her, or some foresight of its special fate.[19] These names had authority, and were regarded as true names when solemnly given, and were public not private if placed (as was sometimes done) immediately after the father-name.

All other 'given names' were not true names, and indeed might not be recognized by the person to whom they were applied, unless they were actually adopted or self-given. Names, or nicknames, of this kind might be given by anyone, not necessarily by members of the same house or kin, in memory of some deed, or event, or in token of some marked feature of body or mind. They were seldom included in the 'full title', but when they were, because of their wide use and fame, they were set at the end in some form such as this: 'by some called Telcontar' (that is Strider); or 'sometimes known as Mormacil' (that is Blacksword).

enjoy all the varied talents of their kind, whether of skill or of lore, though in different order and in different degrees. With such changes of 'mind-mood' or *inwisti* their *lámatyáver* might also change. But such changes or progressions were in fact seen most among the *neri*, for the *nissi*, even as they came sooner to maturity, remained then more steadfast and were less desirous of change. [According to the Eldar, the only 'character' of any person that was not subject to change was the difference of sex. For this they held to belong not only to the body *(hrondo)* [> *(hröa)*] but also to the mind *(inno)* [> *(indo)*] equally: that is, to the person as a whole. This person or individual they often called *essë* (that is 'name'), but it was also called *erdë*, or 'singularity'. Those who returned from Mandos, therefore, after the death of their first body, returned always to the same name and to the same sex as formerly.]

The *amilessi tercenyë*, or mother-names of insight, had a high position, and in general use sometimes replaced, both within the family and without, the father-name and chosen name, though the father-name (and the chosen among those of the Eldar that had the custom of the *essecilmë*) remained ever the true or primary name, and a necessary part of any 'full title'. The 'names of insight' were more often given in the early days of the Eldar, and in that time they came more readily into public use, because it was then still the custom for the father-name of a son to be a modification of the father's name (as *Finwë* / *Curufinwë*) or a patronymic (as *Finwion* 'son of Finwë'). The father-name of a daughter would likewise often be derived from the name of the mother.

Renowned examples of these things are found in the early histories. Thus Finwë, first lord of the Noldor, first named his eldest son *Finwion*;[20] but later when his talent was revealed this was modified to *Curufinwë*.[21] But the name of insight which his mother Míriel gave to him in the hour of birth was *Fëanáro* 'Spirit of Fire';* and by this name he became known to all, and he is so called in all the histories. (It is said that he also took this name as his chosen name, in honour of his mother, whom he never saw.)[22] Elwë, lord of the Teleri, became widely known by the *anessë* or given name *Sindicollo* 'Greycloak', and hence later, in the changed form of the Sindarin tongue, he was called *Elu Thingol*. *Thingol* indeed was the name most used for him by others, though *Elu* or *Elu-thingol* remained his right title in his own realm.

OF DEATH AND THE SEVERANCE OF FËA AND HRONDO [> HRÖA][23]

It must be understood that what has yet been said concerning Eldarin marriage refers to its right course and nature in a world unmarred, or to the manners of those uncorrupted by the Shadow and to days of peace and order. But nothing, as has been said, utterly avoids the Shadow upon Arda or is wholly unmarred, so as to proceed unhindered upon its right courses. In the Elder Days, and in the ages before the Dominion of Men, there were times of great trouble and many griefs and evil

---

* Though the form *Fëanor* which it took later in the speech of Beleriand is more often used. [> *(later)* Though the form *Fëanor*, which is more often used, was a blend of Q[uenya] *Fëanáro* and S[indarin] *Faenor*.]

chances; and Death[24] afflicted all the Eldar, as it did all other living things in Arda save the Valar only: for the visible form of the Valar proceeds from their own will and with regard to their true being is to be likened rather to the chosen raiment of Elves and Men than to their bodies.

Now the Eldar are immortal within Arda according to their right nature. But if a *fëa* (or spirit) indwells in and coheres with a *hrondo* [> *hröa*] (or bodily form) that is not of its own choice but ordained, and is made of the flesh or substance of Arda itself,[25] then the fortune of this union must be vulnerable by the evils that do hurt to Arda, even if that union be by nature and purpose permanent. For in spite of this union, which is of such a kind that according to unmarred nature no living person incarnate may be without a *fëa*, nor without a *hrondo* [> *hröa*], yet *fëa* and *hrondo* [> *hröa*] are not the same things; and though the *fëa* cannot be broken or disintegrated by any violence from without, the *hrondo* [> *hröa*] can be hurt and may be utterly destroyed.

If then the *hrondo* [> *hröa*] be destroyed, or so hurt that it ceases to have health, sooner or later it 'dies'. That is: it becomes painful for the *fëa* to dwell in it, being neither a help to life and will nor a delight to use, so that the *fëa* departs from it, and its function being at an end its coherence is unloosed, and it returns again to the general *hrón* [> *orma*] of Arda.[26] Then the *fëa* is, as it were, houseless, and it becomes invisible to bodily eyes (though clearly perceptible by direct awareness to other *fëar*).

This destruction of the *hrondo* [> *hröa*], causing death or the unhousing of the *fëa*, was soon experienced by the immortal Eldar, when they awoke in the marred and overshadowed realm of Arda. Indeed in their earlier days death came more readily; for their bodies were then less different[27] from the bodies of Men, and the command of their spirits over their bodies less complete.

This command was, nonetheless, at all times greater than it has ever been among Men. From their beginnings the chief difference between Elves and Men lay in the fate and nature of their spirits. The *fëar* of the Elves were destined to dwell in Arda for all the life of Arda, and the death of the flesh did not abrogate that destiny. Their *fëar* were tenacious therefore of life 'in the raiment of Arda', and far excelled the spirits of Men in power over that 'raiment', even from the first days[28] protecting their bodies from many ills and assaults (such as disease), and healing them swiftly of injuries, so that they recovered from wounds that would have proved fatal to Men.

As ages passed the dominance of their *fëar* ever increased, 'consuming' their bodies (as has been noted).[29] The end of this process is their 'fading', as Men have called it; for the body becomes at last, as it were, a mere memory held by the *fëa*; and that end has already been achieved in many regions of Middle-earth, so that the Elves are indeed deathless and may not be destroyed or changed.[30] Thus it is that the further we go back in the histories, the more often do we read of the death of the Elves of old; and in the days when the minds of the Eldalië were young and not yet fully awake death among them seemed to differ little from the death of Men.

What then happened to the houseless *fëa*? The answer to this question the Elves did not know by nature. In their beginning (so they report) they believed, or guessed, that they 'entered into Nothing', and ended like other living things that they knew, even as a tree that was felled and burned. Others guessed more darkly that they passed into 'the Realm of Night' and into the power of the 'Lord of Night'.[31] These opinions were plainly derived from the Shadow under which they awoke; and it was to deliver them from this shadow upon their minds, more even than from the dangers of Arda marred, that the Valar desired to bring them to the light of Aman.

It was in Aman that they learned of Manwë that each *fëa* was imperishable within the life of Arda, and that its fate was to inhabit Arda to its end. Those *fëar*, therefore, that in the marring of Arda suffered unnaturally a divorce from their *hrondor* [> *hröar*] remained still in Arda and in Time. But in this state they were open to the direct instruction and command of the Valar. As soon as they were disbodied they were summoned to leave the places of their life and death and go to the 'Halls of Waiting': Mandos, in the realm of the Valar.

If they obeyed this summons different opportunities lay before them.[32] The length of time that they dwelt in Waiting was partly at the will of Námo the Judge, lord of Mandos, partly at their own will. The happiest fortune, they deemed, was after the Waiting to be re-born, for so the evil and grief that they had suffered in the curtailment of their natural course might be redressed.

OF RE-BIRTH AND OTHER DOOMS OF THOSE THAT GO TO MANDOS[33]

Now the Eldar hold that to each elf-child a new *fëa* is given, not akin to the *fëar* of the parents (save in belonging to the same order and nature); and this *fëa* either did not exist before birth, or is the *fëa* of one that is re-born.

The new *fëa*, and therefore in their beginning all *fëar*, they believe to come direct from Eru and from beyond Ëa. Therefore many of them hold that it cannot be asserted that the fate of the Elves is to be confined within Arda for ever and with it to cease. This last opinion they draw from their own thought, for the Valar, having had no part in the devising of the Children of Eru, do not know fully the purposes of Eru concerning them, nor the final ends that he prepares for them.

But they did not reach these opinions at once or without dissent. In their youth, while their knowledge and experience were small and they had not yet received the instruction of the Valar (or had not yet fully understood it), many still held that in the creation of their kind Eru had committed this power to them: to beget children in all ways like to themselves, body and indwelling spirit; and that therefore the *fëa* of a child came from its parents as did its *hrondo*.[34]

Yet always some dissented, saying: 'Indeed a living person may resemble the parents and be perceived as a blending, in various degrees, of these two; but this resemblance is most reasonably related to the *hrondo*. It is strongest and clearest in early youth, while the body is dominant and most like the bodies of its parents.' (This is true of all elf-children.)[35] 'Whereas in all children, though in some it may be more marked and sooner apparent, there is a part of character not to be understood from parentage, to which it may indeed be quite contrary. This difference is most reasonably attributed to the *fëa*, new and not akin to the parents; for it becomes clearer and stronger as life proceeds and the *fëa* increases in mastery.'

Later when the Elves became aware of re-birth this argument was added: 'If the *fëar* of children were normally derived from the parents and akin to them, then re-birth would be unnatural and unjust. For it would deprive the second parents, without consent, of one half of their parentage, intruding into their kin a child half alien.'

Nonetheless, the older opinion was not wholly void. For all

the Eldar, being aware of it in themselves, spoke of the passing of much strength, both of mind and of body, into their children, in bearing and begetting. Therefore they hold that the *fëa*, though unbegotten, draws nourishment from the parents before the birth of the child: directly from the *fëa* of the mother while she bears and nourishes the *hrondo*, and mediately but equally from the father, whose *fëa* is bound in union with the mother's and supports it.

It was for this reason that all parents desired to dwell together during the year of bearing, and regarded separation at that time as a grief and injury, depriving the child of some part of its fathering. 'For,' said they, 'though the union of the *fëar* of the wedded is not broken by distance of place, yet in creatures that live as spirits embodied *fëa* communes with *fëa* in full only when the bodies dwell together.'

A houseless *fëa* that chose or was permitted to return to life re-entered the incarnate world through child-birth. Only thus could it return.* For it is plain that the provision of a bodily house for a *fëa*, and the union of *fëa* with *hrondo*, was committed by Eru to the Children, to be achieved in the act of begetting.

As for this re-birth, it was not an opinion, but known and certain. For the *fëa* re-born became a child indeed, enjoying once more all the wonder and newness of childhood; but slowly, and only after it had acquired a knowledge of the world and mastery of itself, its memory would awake; until, when the re-born elf was full-grown, it recalled all its former life, and then the old life, and the 'waiting', and the new life became one ordered history and identity. This memory would thus hold a double joy of childhood, and also an experience and knowledge greater than the years of its body. In this way the violence or grief that the re-born had suffered was redressed and its being

---

* Save in rare and strange cases: that is, where the body that the *fëa* had forsaken was whole, and remained still coherent and incorrupt. But this could seldom happen; for death unwilling could occur only when great violence was done to the body; and in death by will, such as at times befell because of utter weariness or great grief, the *fëa* would not desire to return, until the body, deserted by the spirit, was dissolved. This happened swiftly in Middle-earth. In Aman only was there no decay. Thus Míriel was there rehoused in her own body, as is hereafter told.

was enriched. For the Re-born are twice nourished, and twice parented,* and have two memories of the joy of awaking and discovering the world of living and the splendour of Arda. Their life is, therefore, as if a year had two springs and though an untimely frost followed after the first, the second spring and all the summer after were fairer and more blessed.

The Eldar say that more than one re-birth is seldom recorded. But the reasons for this they do not fully know. Maybe, it is so ordered by the will of Eru; while the Re-born (they say) are stronger, having greater mastery of their bodies and being more patient of griefs. But many, doubtless, that have twice died do not wish to return.[36]

Re-birth is not the only fate of the houseless *fëar*. The Shadow upon Arda caused not only misfortune and injury to the body. It could corrupt the mind; and those among the Eldar who were darkened in spirit did unnatural deeds, and were capable of hatred and malice. Not all who died suffered innocently. Moreover, some *fëar* in grief or weariness gave up hope, and turning away from life relinquished their bodies, even though these might have been healed or were indeed unhurt.†[37] Few of these latter desired to be re-born, not at least until they had been long in 'waiting'; some never returned. Of the others, the wrong-doers, many were held long in 'waiting', and some were not permitted to take up their lives again.

For there was, for all the *fëar* of the Dead, a time of Waiting, in which, howsoever they had died, they were corrected, instructed, strengthened, or comforted, according to their needs or deserts. *If they would consent to this.* But the *fëa* in its nakedness is obdurate, and remains long in the bondage of its memory and old purposes (especially if these were evil).

Those who were healed could be re-born, if they desired it:

---

* In some cases a *fëa* re-born might have the same parents again. For instance, if its first body had died in early youth. But this did not often happen; neither did a *fëa* necessarily re-enter its own former kin, for often a great length of time passed before it wished or was permitted to return.

† Though the griefs might be great and wholly unmerited, and death (or rather the abandonment of life) might be, therefore, understandable and innocent, it was held that the refusal to return to life, after repose in Mandos, was a fault, showing a weakness or lack of courage in the *fëa*.

none are re-born or sent back into life unwilling. The others remained, by desire or command, *fëar* unbodied, and they could only observe the unfolding of the Tale of Arda from afar, having no effect therein. For it was a doom of Mandos that only those who took up life again might operate in Arda, or commune with the *fëar* of the Living, even with those that had once been dear to them.[38]

Concerning the fate of other elves, especially of the Dark-elves who refused the summons to Aman, the Eldar know little. The Re-born report that in Mandos there are many elves, and among them many of the Alamanyar,[39] but that there is in the Halls of Waiting little mingling or communing of kind with kind, or indeed of any one *fëa* with another. For the houseless *fëa* is solitary by nature, and turns only towards those with whom, maybe, it formed strong bonds of love in life.

The *fëa* is single, and in the last impregnable. It cannot be brought to Mandos. It is summoned; and the summons proceeds from just authority, and is imperative; yet it may be refused. Among those who refused the summons (or rather invitation) of the Valar to Aman in the first years of the Elves, refusal of the summons to Mandos and the Halls of Waiting is, the Eldar say, frequent. It was less frequent, however, in ancient days, while Morgoth was in Arda, or his servant Sauron after him; for then the *fëa* unbodied would flee in terror of the Shadow to any refuge – unless it were already committed to the Darkness and passed then into its dominion. In like manner even of the Eldar some who had become corrupted refused the summons, and then had little power to resist the counter-summons of Morgoth.

But it would seem that in these after-days more and more of the Elves, be they of the Eldalië in origin or be they of other kinds, who linger in Middle-earth now refuse the summons of Mandos, and wander houseless in the world,* unwilling to leave it[40] and unable to inhabit it, haunting trees or springs or hidden places that once they knew. Not all of these are kindly or

---

* For only those who willingly go to Mandos may be re-born. Re-birth is a grace, and comes of the power that Eru committed to the Valar for the ruling of Arda and the redress of its marring. It does not lie in the power of any *fëa* in itself. Only those return whom, after Mandos has spoken the doom of release, Manwë and Varda bless.

unstained by the Shadow. Indeed the refusal of the summons is in itself a sign of taint.

It is therefore a foolish and perilous thing, besides being a wrong deed forbidden justly by the appointed Rulers of Arda, if the Living seek to commune with the Unbodied, though the houseless may desire it, especially the most unworthy among them. For the Unbodied, wandering in the world, are those who at the least have refused the door of life and remain in regret and self-pity. Some are filled with bitterness, grievance, and envy. Some were enslaved by the Dark Lord and do his work still, though he himself is gone. They will not speak truth or wisdom. To call on them is folly. To attempt to master them and to make them servants of one own's will is wickedness. Such practices are of Morgoth; and the necromancers are of the host of Sauron his servant.

Some say that the Houseless desire bodies, though they are not willing to seek them lawfully by submission to the judgement of Mandos. The wicked among them will take bodies, if they can, unlawfully. The peril of communing with them is, therefore, not only the peril of being deluded by fantasies or lies: there is peril also of destruction. For one of the hungry Houseless, if it is admitted to the friendship of the Living, may seek to eject the *fëa* from its body; and in the contest for mastery the body may be gravely injured, even if it be not wrested from its rightful habitant. Or the Houseless may plead for shelter, and if it is admitted, then it will seek to enslave its host and use both his will and his body for its own purposes. It is said that Sauron did these things, and taught his followers how to achieve them.

[Thus it may be seen that those who in latter days hold that the Elves are dangerous to Men and that it is folly or wickedness to seek converse with them do not speak without reason. For how, it may be asked, shall a mortal distinguish the kinds? On the one hand, the Houseless, rebels at least against the Rulers, and maybe even deeper under the Shadow; on the other, the Lingerers, whose bodily forms may no longer be seen by us mortals, or seen only dimly and fitfully. Yet the answer is not in truth difficult. Evil is not one thing among Elves and another among Men. Those who give evil counsel, or speak against the Rulers (or if they dare, against the One), are evil, and should be shunned whether bodied or unbodied. Moreover, the Lingerers are not houseless, though they may seem to be. They do not desire bodies, neither do they seek shelter, nor strive for mastery over body or mind. Indeed they do not seek converse with Men at all, save maybe rarely, either for the doing of some good, or because they perceive in a Man's spirit some love of things ancient and fair. Then they may reveal to him their forms (through his mind working outwardly, maybe), and he will behold them in their beauty. Of such he may have no fear, though he may feel awe of them. For the Houseless have no forms to reveal, and even if it were within their power (as some Men say) to counterfeit elvish forms, deluding the minds of Men with fantasies, such visions would be marred by the evil of their intent. For the hearts of true Men uprise in joy to behold the true likenesses of the First-born, their elder kindred; and this joy nothing evil can counterfeit. So spoke Ælfwine.][41]

OF THE SEVERANCE OF MARRIAGE

Much has now been said concerning death and re-birth among the Elves. It may be asked: of what effect were these upon their marriage?

Since death and the sundering of spirit and body was one of the griefs of Arda Marred, it came inevitably to pass that death at times came between two that were wedded. Then the Eldar were in doubt, since this was an evil unnatural. Permanent marriage was in accordance with elvish nature, and they never had need of any law to teach this or to enforce it; but if a 'permanent' marriage was in fact broken, as when one of the partners was slain, then they did not know what should be done or thought.

In this matter they turned to Manwë for counsel, and, as is recorded in the case of Finwë, Lord of the Noldor, Manwë delivered his ruling through the mouth of Námo Mandos, the Judge.

'Marriage of the Eldar,' he said, 'is by and for the Living, and for the duration of life. Since the Elves are by nature permanent in life within Arda, so also is their unmarred marriage. But if their life is interrupted or ended, then their marriage must be likewise. Now marriage is chiefly of the body, but it is nonetheless not of the body only but of the spirit and body together, for it begins and endures in the will of the *fëa*. Therefore when one of the partners of a marriage dies the marriage is not yet ended, but is in abeyance. For those that were joined are now sundered; but their union remains still a union of will.

'How then can a marriage be ended and the union be dissolved? For unless this be done, there can be no second marriage. By the law of the nature of the Elves, the *neri* and the *nissi* being equal, there can be union only of one with one.[42] Plainly an end can be made only by the ending of the will; and this must proceed from the Dead, or be by doom. By the ending of the will, when the Dead are not willing ever to return to life in the body; by doom, when they are not permitted to return. For a union that is for the life of Arda is ended, if it cannot be resumed within the life of Arda.

'We say that the ending of will must proceed from the Dead, for the Living may not for their own purposes compel the Dead to remain thus, nor deny to them re-birth, if they desire it. And it must be clearly understood that this will of the Dead not to return, when it has been solemnly declared and is ratified by Mandos, shall then become a doom: the Dead will not be permitted ever to return to the life of the body.'

The Eldar then asked: 'How shall the will or doom be known?' It was answered: 'Only by recourse to Manwë and by the pronouncement of Námo. In this matter it shall not be lawful for any of the Eldar to judge his own case. For who among the Living can discern the thoughts of the Dead, or presume the dooms of Mandos?'

Upon this pronouncement of Mandos, which is called the 'Doom of Finwë and Míriel'[43] for reasons to be told, there are many commentaries that record the explanation of points arising from its consideration, some given by the Valar, some later reasoned by the Eldar. Of these the more important are here added.

1. It was asked: 'What is meant by the saying that marriage is chiefly of the body, and yet is both of spirit and body?'

It was answered: 'Marriage is chiefly of the body, for it is achieved by bodily union, and its first operation is the begetting of the bodies of children, even though it endures beyond this and has other operations. And the union of bodies in marriage is unique, and no other union resembles it. Whereas the union of *fëar* in marriage differs from other unions of love and friendship not so much in kind as in its closeness and permanence, which are derived partly from the bodies in their union and in their dwelling together.

'Nonetheless marriage concerns also the *fëar*. For the *fëar* of the Elves are of their nature male and female, and not their *hrondor*[44] only. And the beginning of marriage is in the affinity of the *fëar*, and in the love arising therefrom. And this love includes in it, from its first awakening, the desire for marriage, and is therefore like to but not in all ways the same as other motions of love and friendship, even those between Elves of male and female nature who do not have this inclination. It is therefore true to say that, though achieved by and in the body, marriage proceeds from the *fëa* and resides ultimately in its will. For which reason it cannot be ended, as has been declared, while that will remains.'

2. It was asked: 'If the Dead return to the Living, are the sundered spouses still wedded? And how may that be, if marriage is chiefly of the body, whereas the body of one part of the union is destroyed? Must the sundered be again married, if they wish? Or whether they wish it or no?'

It was answered: 'It has been said that marriage resides ultimately in the will of the *fëar*. Also the identity of person resides wholly in the *fëa*,[45] and the re-born is the same person as the one who died. It is the purpose of the grace of re-birth that the unnatural breach in the continuity of life should be redressed; and none of the Dead will be permitted to be re-born until and unless they desire to take up their former life and continue it. Indeed they cannot escape it, for the re-born soon recover full memory of all their past.

'If then marriage is not ended while the Dead are in the Halls of Waiting, in hope or purpose to return, but is only in abeyance, how then shall it be ended, when the *fëa* is again in the land of the living?

'But herein there is indeed a difficulty, that reveals to us that death is a thing unnatural. It may be amended, but it cannot, while Arda lasts, be wholly undone or made as if it had not been. What shall come to pass as the Eldar grow older cannot be wholly foreseen. But perceiving their nature, as we now do, we hold that the love of the

---

Here the typescript version B breaks off, with much of the content of the essay as declared in the title unfulfilled (see p. 209). The text ends at the foot of a page, but I think it virtually certain that this was where my father abandoned it.

NOTES

1 In A the opening paragraph ended: 'the fire of their spirit had not consumed them, nor their minds turned inwards', subsequently changed to the text of B.
2 Added here later in A: 'Yet the Elf-child would have more knowledge and skill.' This was not taken up in B.
3 A: 'They had few children, but these were dear to them beyond all else that they possessed. (Though no Elf would speak of possessing children; he would say: "three children have been added unto me", or "are with me", or "are in my house"; for their families were held together ...' (the brackets being closed at the words 'or teaching').
4 A: '... while the Eldar were still few, and eager to increase their kind, before the weight of years lay on them, there is no record of any number more than seven', with 'seldom' written later above 'no'.
5 For this paragraph A has:
   The Eldar wedded once for all. Many, as the histories reveal, could become estranged from good, for nothing can wholly escape from the evil shadow that lies upon Arda. Some fell into pride, and self-will, and could be guilty of deeds of malice, enmity, greed and jealousy. But among all these evils there is no record of any among the Elves that took another's spouse by force; for this was wholly against their nature, and one so forced would have rejected bodily life and passed to Mandos. Guile or trickery in this matter was scarcely possible (even if it could be thought that any Elf would purpose to use it); for the Eldar can read at once in the eyes and voice of another whether they be wed or unwed.
6 The original reading in A was 'at a [feast >] repast shared by the two "houses" concerned', changed later to 'at a meeting' as in B. See note 7.
7 The word 'again' in 'again shared by the two houses' depends on the original reading in A given in note 6.
8 A: 'and were only a gracious recognition of the change of state'.
9 Added here in A, probably very much later: '[Thus Beren and Tinúviel could lawfully have wedded, but for Beren's oath to Thingol.]'
10 This paragraph ends in A: 'This the Eldar mean when they speak of their spirits consuming them; and they say that ere Arda ends all the Elf-folk will have become spirits no less than those in Mandos, invisible to mortal eyes, unless they will to be seen.' The words 'no less than those in Mandos' stood in B as typed, but were heavily struck out.

Laws B THE LATER *QUENTA SILMARILLION* (II) 229

11 For the passage in B 'For with regard to generation ...' A has: 'For, whether the Eldar retain their power of generation (as is likely if we speak of days of old when all the Eldalië were young) or in time lose it (as some say those that remain on Earth have now lost it), at all times they lose the desire and will with the exercise of that power.'

12 For *neri* and *nissi* in B (see the *Etymologies* in Vol.V, entries NĒR, NIS) A has *quendor* and *quender*, changed later to *quendur* and *quendir*. For the singulars *nér* and *nís* occurring subsequently A has *quendo* and *quende*, changed to *quendu* and *quendi*. The substance of this passage concerning the difference in characteristic activity among men and women of the Eldar is essentially the same in A, but no reference is made to the Noldor.

13 It is said in A that it was the right of the father, not to 'devise' the first name, but to 'announce' it, and this is followed by a note: 'Though the name was often the mother's choice. But it was held to be the right of the father to devise the name of [the first son >] his sons, if he would, and of the mother to devise the name of [the first daughter >] her daughters. But in any case the father proclaimed the name.' To the words 'This name was thus called the "father-name" or first name' was added later in A: 'It always had a meaning and was made of known words.'

14 At this point there is a footnote in B (deriving closely from A) which was later struck through:
    It will be observed in the histories how seldom the same name recurs for different persons. This is because, both in *Essecarmë* and in *Essecilmë*, there was usually an attempt to mark individuality; and names were regarded as the property of those who first bore them.

15 The footnote here reads thus in A:
    This feeling had nothing to do with 'magic' or taboo. The Eldar did indeed believe in a special relation between a name of a person and his life and individuality; but this concerned both first and second name (alone or together), which they might conceal from enemies.

16 The latter part of the footnote here, which I have enclosed in square brackets, is found typed on a separate page belonging with the B typescript, but with no direction for its insertion (see note 37). It is found however in closely similar words in the A version of the footnote, following 'their *lámatyávë* might also change' (A does not have the conclusion of the note in B, 'But such changes or progressions ...').
    In the A version of the note the Elvish word of which 'mind-mood' is a translation was first written *ingil*-[?*weidi*, very uncertain], changed to *inwaldi*, and later to *inwisti*, as in B. In A the Elvish word for the body is *rhōn* (changed later to *hrondo*, the

word used in B), and for the mind *īn*, *indo* (the latter changed later to *inno*, whereas B has *inno* > *indo*).

17 A has a different account here: 'They might then devise a new "Chosen Name", but this replaced the former, and became the Second Name. Identity was preserved by the permanence for all formal and legal purposes of the First Name or father's name.'

18 A has: 'this was the *Anessi*, the given names, or "nick-names"' (with reference to the original meaning of *nick-name*, changed from *(an) eke-name*, meaning an additional or added name).

19 The passage following this in A reads thus:

Later, when the character and gifts of the child were revealed, as it grew, she might also give a similar name to it (or modify its father-name). But this latter branch of 'mother-names' differed in authority only rather than in kind from general given or nick-names. These were given to persons by anyone (not necessarily even members of their 'house' or kin), in memory of some deed, or event, or some striking peculiarity. Though these names had no authority and were not 'true names', they often became widely known and used, and were sometimes recognized by the persons themselves and their families.

The 'mother-names of insight' had an intermediate position. They had parental authority and the authority of maternal *terken* [*added:* insight], and were often used instead of either father-name or chosen name, or might replace them both – replaced them, that is, in actual usage. The 'true' or primary *Essë* of any person remained the father-name. The 'names of insight', though at no time frequent, were more frequent in the early days of the Eldar ...

20 In A it is said that 'Finwë originally named his eldest son *Finwë*'.

21 *Curufinwë*: the name has been met in the rejected addition to AAm where appear my father's first thoughts on the story of Fëanor's birth (when his mother was named Indis): see p. 87 note 3.

22 A has here a passage that was omitted in B:

Finwë then named his second son (by another mother, Indis) also *Finwë*, modifying it later to *Nolofinwë*. But the mother-name which Indis gave to him was *Ingoldo*, signifying that he was partly of both the Ingar (people of Ingwë), her own kin, and of the Noldor. By this name he also became generally known; though after the rule of the Noldor was committed to him by Manwë (in the place of his elder brother and his father) he took the name of *Finwë*, and was in fact usually called *Ingoldo-finwë*. Similarly the third son was *Arafinwë* and also *Ingalaurë* (because he had the golden hair of his mother's kin).

As in the name *Noldor* throughout the later texts, *Nolofinwë* is

written with a tilde over the N. – On this passage see further p. 265 note 10.
23 In A there is no subtitle here, but before 'It must be understood...' there stands the following:
In what has been said concerning names it will be noted that for Finwë, first lord of the Noldor, two wives are named: Míriel and Indis; though it was said that the marriage of the Eldar is permanent and indissoluble.
24 After 'and Death' there followed in B 'in its Elvish mode', derived from A; but this was rejected as soon as typed.
25 A: 'and is made also as it were of the *hrōn* (or flesh and substance) of Arda'; cf. *rhōn* 'body', note 16. The word *hrōn* was left unchanged in A here (see note 26); subsequently where B has *hrondo* (> *hröa*) A has *hrōn*, *hrón*, and *hrôn* (> *hrondo*), until later in the text *hrondo* appears in A as first written (note 34).
26 The words 'and it returns again to the general *hrôn* of Arda' were added to the A-text at the same time as other occurrences of *hrôn* were changed to *hrondo* (note 25); thus *hrôn* here in B (subsequently > *orma*) represents a distinction between *hrôn* (of the 'body' of Arda) and *hrondo*. At a later point in the A manuscript there is the following hastily pencilled note, which was struck through:
√s-ron 'flesh, substance, matter'. Q. *hrōn*, *hrŏm-* 'matter', the substance of Arda, hence *hrondo* 'physical body, "the flesh"'.
27 B as typed had 'little different', as does A, but 'little' was at once changed to 'less'.
28 Where B has 'even from the first days' A has 'even at first'.
29 'as has been noted' (not said in A): the previous references are on pp. 210 ('Ælfwine's Preamble') and 212.
30 In A the first part of this paragraph reads:
As ages passed their spirits became more dominant, and 'consumed' their bodies – the end of this process (now achieved), they said, was that the body should become as it were a mere memory of the spirit – though it never became changeable like raiment.
31 A: 'Others guessed that they passed into the realm of Dark and the power of the Dark Lord (as they called him).'
32 A: '(The *fëar* of the Eldar, with rare exceptions, at once obeyed that summons.) After that different opportunities lay before them.'
33 There is no subtitle here in A.
34 Here and subsequently *hrondo* (not *hrôn*) appears in the A-text as written (see notes 25 and 44). Purely coincidentally, as it seems, here and subsequently *hrondo* was not changed to *hröa* in B.
35 This bracketed statement derives from an addition made to A:

'This is true of all Elf-children, whatever may be the case with Men, in whom the body is ever more dominant.'

36 This paragraph is absent from A.
37 This footnote is not in the B-text, but is found typed separately on the same page as the passage referred to in note 16, and like that passage without direction for its insertion. It derives fairly closely from a footnote found at this point in A; this however ends: '... was held a fault or weakness, needing correction or cure if that could be achieved.'
38 From 'The others remained' to the end of the paragraph the A-text as first written read thus:
    Others, freed from desire of life and of doing, yet not from operations of the mind in observing or reflexion, might remain as spirits, *fëar* unbodied, and yet be permitted to go forth from Mandos, and to return thither or not, as they would. As ages passed, the numbers of these increased, the Eldar say. With the minds of the Living they can commune, if the Living remember them or open their minds to receive them. This the Eldar call 'communing with the *fëar* (or the Unliving)', and in the latter days it has become easier and more frequent. But they could only observe what passed or was done as the Tale of Arda unfolded. They could
    The passage was struck out when this point was reached and replaced by the text that stands here in B. Cf. the subsequent passage (p. 224), found both in A and in B: 'It is therefore a foolish and perilous thing, besides being a wrong deed forbidden justly by the appointed Rulers of Arda, if the Living seek to commune with the Unbodied ...'
39 On *Alamanyar* see pp. 170–1.
40 A sets the opening of this paragraph in the past tense: 'But in after days more and more of the Elves that lingered in Middle-earth refused the summons of Mandos, and wandered houseless in the world, unwilling to leave it ...'
41 This paragraph, attributed to Ælfwine and bracketed in the same way as is the opening 'Preamble', is absent from A, which continues on from 'These things it is said that Sauron did, and taught his chief followers how to achieve them' as follows:
    In this account the lives and customs of the Eldar have been considered mainly in their natural courses in days untroubled, and in accordance with their true nature unmarred. But, as has been said, the Eldar did not escape the Shadow upon Arda, that caused both misfortunes and misdeeds to afflict them.
    This was replaced by the sentence beginning 'Now much has been said concerning death and rebirth among the Eldar ...' as in B, but without the subtitle 'Of the Severance of Marriage'.
42 This sentence is absent from A, and so there appear here no

equivalents of the words *neri* and *nissi* in B (see note 12).
43 A has 'the "Statute of Finwë and Míriel"', as in the title of the B-text.
44 A had here *hróni*, changed to *hrondor*: see note 34.
45 From here to the point where it breaks off B diverges altogether from A, and I take up the presentation of the A-text in full from the beginning of this second response.

I give now the remainder of the work from the original manuscript A, taking it up shortly before the point where the typescript B breaks off (see note 45 above). Alterations and additions are mostly noted as such.

In A the actual tale of Finwë, Míriel, and Indis reappears (pp. 236–9); it is easily shown that this version followed FM 1 (the rider to LQ chapter 6, *Of the Silmarils and the Darkening of Valinor*, pp. 205–7), but I think at no long interval: the manuscript style of the two texts is notably similar.

It was answered: It has been said that marriage resides ultimately in the will of the *fëa*. Also the identity of person resides in the *fëa*; and the Dead that return [*struck out:* will] in time recover full memory of the past; what is more, though the body is more than raiment and the change of body [will not be of no effect >] will certainly have effect upon the reborn, the *fëa* is the master, and the reborn will come to resemble their former self so closely that all who knew them before Death will recognize them, soonest and most readily the former spouse. Nonetheless, since marriage is also of the body and one body has perished, they must be married again, if they will. For they will have returned, as it were, to that state in their former life when by the motions of their *fëar* they desired to be married. There will be no question of desiring this or not desiring it. For by the steadfastness of the *fëar* of the Eldar uncorrupted they will desire it; and none of the Dead will be permitted by Mandos to be reborn, until and unless they desire to take up life again in continuity with their past. For it is the purpose of the time in Waiting in Mandos that the unnatural breach in the continuity of the life of the Eldar should be healed, though it cannot be undone or made of no effect in Arda. It follows, therefore, also that the Dead will be reborn in such place and time that the meeting and recognition of the sundered shall surely come to pass, and there shall be no hindrance to their marriage.

Upon this the Eldar comment: 'By this is meant that the Reborn Spouse will not appear among the close kindred of the Living Spouse, and in fact the Reborn appear as a rule amongst their own former kin, unless in the chances of Arda things have so changed that the meeting of the sundered would thus be unlikely. [*Added:* For the first purpose of the *fëa* that seeks rebirth is to find its spouse, and children, if it had these in life.] The Reborn that were unwedded always return to their own kin.' For the marriages of the Eldar do not take place between 'close kin'. This again is a matter in which they needed no law or instruction, but acted by nature, though they gave reasons for it later, declaring that it was due to the nature of bodies and the processes of generation; but also to the nature of *fëar*. 'For,' they said, '*fëar* are also akin, and the motions of love between them, as say between a brother and sister, are not of the same kind as those that make the beginning of marriage.' By 'close kin' for this purpose was meant members of one 'house', especially sisters and brothers. None of the Eldar married those in direct line of descent, nor children of the same parents, nor the sister or brother of either of their parents; nor did they wed 'half-sisters' or 'half-brothers'. Since as has been shown only in the rarest events did the Eldar have second spouses, *half-sister* or *half-brother* had for them a special meaning: they used these terms when both of the parents of one child were related to both of the parents of another, as when two brothers married two sisters of another family, or a sister and a brother of one house married a brother and sister of another: things which often occurred. Otherwise 'first cousins', as we should say, might marry, but seldom did so, or desired to do so, unless one of the parents of each were far-sundered in kin.

Hardly otherwise shall it be when both spouses are slain or die: they will marry again in due time after rebirth, unless they desire to remain together in Mandos.

It was asked: Why must the Dead remain in Mandos for ever, if the *fëa* consents to the ending of its marriage? And what is this Doom of which Mandos speaks?

It was answered: The reasons are to be found in what has been said already. Marriage is for life, and cannot, therefore, be ended, save by the interruption of death without return. While there is hope or purpose of return it is not ended, and the Living cannot therefore marry again. If the Living is permitted to marry again, then by doom Mandos will not permit the Dead to return. For, as has been declared, one reborn is the same person as before death and returns to take up and continue his or her former life. But if the former spouse were re-married, this would not be possible, and great grief and doubt would afflict all three parties. To speak of the dooms of Mandos: these are of three kinds. He utters the decisions of Manwë, or of the Valar in conclave, which become binding upon all, even the Valar, when they are so declared: for which reason a time passes between the decision and the doom. In similar manner he utters the decisions and purposes of others who are under his jurisdiction, who are the Dead, in grave matters that affect justice and the right order of Arda; and when so spoken these decisions become 'laws' also, though pertaining only to particular persons or cases, and Mandos will not permit them to be revoked or broken: for which reason again a time must pass between decision and doom.* And lastly there are the dooms of Mandos that proceed from Mandos himself, as judge in matters that belong to his office as ordained from the beginning. He is the judge of right and of wrong, and of innocence or guilt (and all the degrees and mingling of these) in the mischances and misdeeds that come to pass in Arda. All those who come to Mandos are judged with regard to innocence or guilt, in the matter of their death and in all other deeds and purposes of their lives in the body; and Mandos appoints to each the manner and the length of their time of Waiting according to this judgement. But his dooms in such matters are not uttered in haste; and even the most guilty are long tested, whether they may be healed or corrected, before any final doom is given (such as never to return again among the Living). Therefore it was said: 'Who among the Living can presume the dooms of Mandos?'

> Upon this the Eldar comment: 'Innocence or guilt in the matter of death is spoken of, because to be in any way culpable in incurring this evil (whether by forcing others to slay one in their defence against unjust violence, or by foolhardiness or the making good of rash vaunts, or by slaying oneself or wilfully withdrawing the *fëa* from the body) is held a fault. Or at the least, the withdrawal from life is held a good reason, unless the will of the *fëa* be changed, for the *fëa* to remain among the Dead and not to return. As for guilt in other matters little is known of the dealings of Mandos with the Dead. For several reasons: Because those who have done great evil (who are few) do not return. Because those who have been under the correction of Mandos will not speak of it, and indeed, being healed, remember little of it; for they have returned to their natural courses,

---

* In the case of a decision never to return to life by a *fëa* of the Dead, the least time of interval appointed by Mandos was ten Valian years. During this period the decision could be revoked.

and the unnatural and perverted is no longer in the continuity of their lives. Because also, as has been said, though all that die are summoned to Mandos, it is within the power of the *fëar* of the Elves to refuse the summons, and doubtless many of the most unhappy, or most corrupted spirits (especially those of the Dark-elves) do refuse, and so come to worse evil, or at best wander unhoused and unhealed, without hope of return. Not so do they escape judgement for ever; for Eru abideth and is over all.

This judgement is known as the 'Statute of Finwë and Míriel', for theirs was the first case, and it was on behalf of Finwë that Manwë's counsel was sought in this matter. Now Finwë, first Lord of the Noldor, had to wife Míriel who was called the *Serindë*, because of her surpassing skill in weaving and sewing, and their love was great for one another. But in the bearing of her first son Míriel was consumed in spirit and body, so that wellnigh all strength seemed to have passed from her. This son was Curufinwë, most renowned of all the Noldor as Feänáro (or Feänor),[1] Spirit-of-fire, the name which Míriel gave to him at birth; he was mighty in body and in all the skills of the body, and supreme among the Eldar in eagerness and strength and subtlety of mind. But Míriel said to Finwë: 'Never again shall I bear child; for strength that would have nourished the life of many has gone forth into Feänáro.'

Then Finwë was greatly grieved, for the Noldor were in the youth of their days and dwelt in the bliss of the Noontide of Aman, but were still few in number, and he desired to bring forth many children into that bliss. He said, therefore: 'Surely there is healing in Aman? Here all weariness can find rest.'

Therefore Finwë sought the counsel of Manwë, and Manwë delivered Míriel to the care of Irmo in Lórien.[2] At their parting (for a little while as he deemed) Finwë was sad, for it seemed a thing unhappy that the mother should depart and miss the beginning at least of the childhood days of her son. 'Unhappy it is indeed,' said Míriel, 'and I would weep if I were not so weary. But hold me blameless in this, and in aught that may come after. Rest now I must. Farewell, dear lord.' No clearer than this did she speak, but in her heart she yearned not only for sleep and rest, but for release from the labour of living. She went then to Lórien and laid her down to sleep beneath a silver tree, but though she seemed to sleep indeed her spirit departed from her body and passed in silence to the halls of Mandos; and the maidens of Estë tended her fair body so that it remained unwithered, yet she did not return.

Finwë's grief was great, and he went often to the gardens of Lorien and sitting beneath the silver willows beside the body of his wife he called her by her names. But it was of no avail, and he alone in all the Blessed Realm was bereaved and sorrowful. After a while he went to Lorien no more, for it did but increase his grief. All his love he gave to his son; for Fëanáro was like his mother in voice and countenance, and Finwë was to him both father and mother, and there was a double bond of love upon their hearts. Yet Finwë was not content, being young and eager, and desiring to have more children to bring mirth into his house. [He spoke, therefore, to Manwë >] When, therefore, ten years had passed, he spoke to Manwë, saying: 'Lord, behold! I am bereaved and solitary. Alone among the Eldar I have no wife, and must hope for no sons save one, and no daughter. Must I remain ever thus? [For I believe not that Míriel will return again >] For my heart warns me that Míriel will not return again from the house of Vairë while Arda lasts. Is there not healing of grief in Aman?'

Then Manwë took pity upon Finwë, and he considered his plea, and when Mandos had spoken his doom as has been recorded,[3] Manwë called Finwë to him, and said: 'Thou hast heard the doom that has been declared. If Míriel, thy wife, will not return and releases thee, your union[4] is dissolved, and thou hast leave to take another wife.'

It is said that Míriel answered Mandos, saying: 'I came hither to escape from the body, and I do not desire ever to return to it. My life is gone out into Feänáro, my son. This gift I have given to him whom I loved, and I can give no more. Beyond Arda this may be healed, but not within it.'

Then Mandos adjudged her innocent, deeming that she had died under a necessity too great for her to withstand. Therefore her choice was permitted, and she was left in peace; and after ten years the doom of disunion was spoken. [In the year following >] And after three years more Finwë took as second spouse Indis the fair; and she was in all ways unlike Míriel. She was not of the Noldor, but of the Vanyar, [of the kin >] sister of Ingwë; and she was golden-haired, and tall, and exceedingly swift of foot. She laboured not with her hands, but sang and made music, and there was ever light and mirth about her while the bliss of Aman endured. She loved Finwë dearly, for her heart had turned to him long before, while the people of Ingwë dwelt still with the Noldor in Túna.⁵ In those days she had looked upon the Lord of the Noldor, dark-haired and white-browed, eager of face and thoughtful-eyed, and he seemed to her fairest and noblest among the Eldar, and his voice and mastery of words delighted her. Therefore she remained unwedded, when her people departed to Valinor, and she walked often alone in the fields and friths of the Valar, [turning her thought to things that grow untended >] filling them with music. But it came to pass that Ingwë, hearing of the strange grief of Finwë, and desiring to lift up his heart and withdraw him from vain mourning in Lorien, sent messages bidding him to leave Túna for a while and the reminders of his loss, and to come and dwell in the light of the Trees. This message Finwë did not answer, until after the doom of Mandos was spoken; but then deeming that he must seek to build his life anew and that the bidding of Ingwë was wise, he arose and went to the house of Ingwë upon the west of Mount Oiolossë. His coming was unlooked for, but welcome; and when Indis saw Finwë climbing the paths of the mountain (and the light of Laurelin was behind him as a glory) without forethought she sang suddenly in great joy, and her voice went up as the song of a *lirulin* in the sky.⁶ And when Finwë heard that song falling from above he looked up and saw Indis in the golden light, and he knew in that moment that she loved him and had long done so. Then his heart turned at last to her, and he believed that this chance, as it seemed, had been granted for the comfort of them both. 'Behold!' he said. 'There is indeed healing of grief in Aman!'

In this way came to pass ere long the wedding of Finwë and Indis, sister of Ingwë. In Indis was proved true indeed the saying that 'the loss of one may be the gain of another.' But this also she found true: 'the house remembers the builder, though others may dwell in it after.' For Finwë loved her well, and was glad, and she bore him children in whom he rejoiced,*⁷ yet the shadow of Míriel did not depart from his heart, and Fëanáro had the chief share of his thought. The wedding of his father was not pleasing to Fëanáro, and though it did not lessen his

---

* Five children she bore, three daughters and two sons, in this order: Findis, Nolofinwë, Faniel, Arafinwë, and Írimë. Concerning the naming of the sons we have spoken above.

love for his father, he had little love for Indis or her children, least of all for his half-brethren. As soon as he might (and he was wellnigh fullgrown ere Nolofinwë was born) he left his father's house and lived apart from them, giving all his heart and thought to the pursuit of lore and the practice of crafts. In those unhappy things which afterward came to pass and in which Feanáro was a leader, many saw the effects of this breach in the house of Finwë, judging that if Finwë had endured his loss and been content with the fathering of his mighty son, the courses of Feanáro would have been otherwise, and much sorrow and evil would never have been.

Thus it is that the cases in which remarriage of the Eldar can take place are rare, but rarer still are those who do this, even when it is permissible. For the sorrow and strife in the house of Finwë is graven in the memory of the Eldar.

[It is recorded by the Eldar that the Valar found this matter of Finwë strange, and debated much concerning it. For Finwë they could not accuse of any guilt, and the Statute that had been made for Finwë and Míriel was just and reasonable. Yet it was clear that many evils would have been avoided, [if either Míriel had been less faint, or Finwë more patient >] if it had not been made, or at least had not been used. *This passage was later replaced as follows:*] It is recorded by the Eldar that the Valar debated long the case of Finwë and Míriel, after the Statute was made, but not yet declared. For they perceived that this was a grave matter, and a portent, in that Míriel had died even in Aman, and had brought sorrow to the Blessed Realm, things which they before had believed could not come to pass. Also, though the Statute seemed just, some feared that it would not heal the death of grief, but perpetuate it. And Manwë spoke to the Valar, saying: 'In this matter ye must not forget that you deal with Arda Marred – out of which ye brought the Eldar. Neither must ye forget that in Arda Marred *Justice* is not *Healing*. Healing cometh only by suffering and patience, and maketh no demand, not even for Justice. Justice worketh only within the bonds of things as they are, accepting the marring of Arda, and therefore though Justice is itself good and desireth no further evil, it can but perpetuate the evil that was, and doth not prevent it from the bearing of fruit in sorrow. Thus the Statute was just, but it accepted Death and the severance of Finwë and Míriel, a thing unnatural in Arda Unmarred, and therefore with reference to Arda Unmarred it was unnatural and fraught with Death. The liberty that it gave was a lower road that, if it led not still downwards, could not again ascend. But Healing must retain ever the thought of Arda Unmarred, and if it cannot ascend, must abide in patience. This is Hope which, I deem, is before all else the virtue most fair in the Children of Eru, [but cannot be commanded to come when needed: patience must often long await it.]'[8]

Then Aulë, friend of the Noldor [*added:* and lover of Fëanor], spake. 'But did this matter indeed arise out of Arda Marred?' he asked. 'For it seemeth to me that it arose from the bearing of Feanáro. Now Finwë and all the Noldor that followed him were never in heart or thought swayed by [Morgoth >] Melkor, the Marrer; how then did this strange thing come to pass, even in Aman the Unshadowed? That the bearing of a child should lay such a weariness upon the mother that she desired life no longer. This child is the greatest in gifts that hath arisen or shall arise among the Eldar. But the Eldar are the first Children of Eru, and belong to him directly. Therefore the greatness of the child must proceed from his will directly, and be intended for the good of the Eldar and of all Arda. What then of the cost of the birth? Must it not be thought that the greatness and the cost come not from Arda, Marred or Unmarred, but from beyond Arda? For this we know to be true, and as the ages pass it shall often be manifest (in small matters and in great) that all the Tale of Arda was not in the Great Theme, and that things shall come to pass in that Tale which cannot be foreseen, for they are new and are not begotten by the past that preceded them.'[9] [*Added:* Thus Aulë spake being unwilling to believe that any taint of the Shadow lay upon Fëanor, or upon any of the Noldor. He had been the most eager to summon them to Valinor.][10]

But Ulmo answered: 'Nonetheless Míriel died. [And is not death for the Eldar an evil, that is a thing unnatural in Arda Unmarred, which must proceed therefore from the marring? Or if the death of Míriel doth not so, but cometh from beyond Arda, how shall death that is unnatural and evil be known from that which is a new thing and hath no reason in the past, unless the latter cause neither sorrow nor doubt? But the death of Míriel has brought both into Aman. *This passage was later replaced as follows:*] And death is for the Eldar an evil, that is a thing unnatural in Arda Unmarred, which must proceed therefore from the marring. For if the death of Míriel was otherwise, and came from beyond Arda (as a new thing having no cause in the past) it would not bring grief or doubt. For Eru is Lord of All, and moveth all the devices of his creatures, even the malice of the Marrer, in his final purposes, but he doth not of his prime motion impose grief upon them. But the death of Míriel has brought sorrow to Aman. / The coming of Feänáro must proceed certainly from the will of Eru; but I hold that the marring of his birth comes of the Shadow, and is a portent of evils to come. For the greatest are the most potent also for evil. Have a care, my brethren, thinking not that the Shadow is gone for ever, though it is beaten down. Doth it not dwell even now in Aman, though you deem the bonds to be unbreakable?' [For Ulmo had dissented >] Thus Ulmo spake, who had dissented from the counsels of the Valar, when they brought Melkor the Marrer to Mandos after his defeat.[11] [*Added:* Also he loved the Elves (and Men afterwards), but otherwise than Aulë, believing that they should be left free, however perilous that might seem. Thus afterwards it was seen, that though he loved Feänor and all the Noldor more coolly, he had more mercy for their errors and misdeeds.]

Then Yavanna spoke, and though she was the spouse of Aulë she leaned rather to Ulmo. 'My lord Aulë errs,' she said, 'in that he speaks of Finwë and Míriel as being free in heart and thought from the Shadow, as if that proved that naught that befell them could come from the Shadow or from the marring of Arda. But even as the Children are not as we (who came from beyond Arda wholly and in all our being) but are both spirit and body, and that body is of Arda and by Arda was nourished: so the Shadow worketh not only upon spirits, but has marred the very *hrón* of Arda, and all Middle-earth is perverted by the evil of Melkor, who has wrought in it as mightily as any one among us here. Therefore none of those who awoke in Middle-earth, and there dwelt before they came hither, have come here wholly free. The failing of the strength of the body of Míriel may then be ascribed, with some reason, to the evil of Arda Marred, and her death be a thing unnatural. And that this should appear in Aman seemeth to me as to Ulmo a sign to be heeded.'[12]

Then Nienna spoke, who came to Valmar seldom, but sat now upon the left hand of Manwë. 'In the use of Justice there must be Pity, which is the consideration of the singleness of each that cometh under Justice. Which of you Valar, in your wisdom, will blame these Children, Finwë and Míriel? For the Children are both strong and without might. Mandos you hold to be the strongest of all that are in Arda, being the least moved, and therefore you have dared to commit even the Marrer himself to his keeping. Yet I say to you that each *fëa* of the Children is as strong as he; for it hath the strength of its singleness impregnable (which cometh to it from Eru as to us): in its nakedness it is obdurate beyond all power that ye have to move it if it will not. Yet the Children are not mighty: in life they are little, and can effect little; and they are young, and they know Time only. Their minds are as the hands of their babes, little in grasp, and even that grasp is yet unfilled. How shall they perceive the [?end] of deeds, or forgo the desires which arise from their very nature, the indwelling of the spirit in [the] body which is their right condition? Have ye known the weariness of Míriel, or felt the bereavement of Finwë?

'Míriel, I deem, died by necessity of body, in suffering [for] which she was blameless or indeed to be praised, and yet was not given power to resist it: the cost of so great a child-bearing. And herein I think that Aulë perceiveth a part of the truth. The severance of the *fëa* was in Míriel a thing special. Death is indeed death and within the Great Theme cometh from the Marrer and is grievous; but Eru in this death had a purpose of immediate good, and it need not have borne any bitter fruit; whereas Death that comes from the Marrer only is intended for evil, and its healing must await in Hope only, even until the End. But Finwë not understanding death (as how should he?) called Míriel, and she did not return, and he was bereaved, and his natural life and expectation was impaired. Justly he cried: "Is there not healing in Aman?" That cry could not be unheeded, and what could be done we have done. Wherefore should this be grudged?'

But Ulmo answered her saying: 'Nay! Though I do not condemn, yet still I will judge. Herein I perceive not only the direct will of Eru, but fault in his creatures. Not guilt, yet a failing from the highest which is the Hope of which the King hath spoken. And I doubt not that the taking of the higher road, an ascent that though hard was not impossible, was part of that purpose of immediate good of which Nienna speaketh.[13] For the *fëa* of Míriel may have departed by necessity, but it departed in the will not to return. Therein was her fault, for this will was not under compulsion irresistible; it was a failure in hope by the *fëa*, acceptance of the weariness and weakness of the body, as a thing beyond healing, and which therefore was not healed. But this resolve entailed not only abandoning her own life, but also the desertion of her spouse, and the marring of his. The justification which she urged is insufficient; for by the gift of a child however great, nor indeed by the gift of many children, the union of marriage is not ended, having further purpose. For one thing, Feänáro will be deprived of the mother's part in his nurture. Moreover, if she would return she need bear no more, unless by the renewal of rebirth her weariness were healed.

'Thus Finwë was aggrieved and claimed justice. But when he called her and she did not return, in only a few years he fell into despair. Herein lay his fault, and failing in Hope. But also he founded his claim mainly upon his desire for children, considering his own self and his loss more than the griefs that had befallen his wife: that was a failing in full love.

'The *fëar* of the Eldar, as Niënna hath said, cannot be broken or forced,* and the motion of their will cannot therefore be predicted with certainty. Yet it seemeth to me that there was hope still that after repose in Mandos the *fëa* of Míriel should return of itself to its nature, which is to desire to inhabit a body. This strange event should issue, rather than in dissolving their union, in the use by Finwë of the patience of full love, and the learning of Hope; and in the return of Míriel, wider in mind, and renewed in body. Thus together they might foster their great son with joined love, and his right nurture be assured. But the *fëa* of Míriel hath not been left in peace, and by importuning its will hath been hardened; and in that resolve it must remain without change while Arda lasteth, if the Statute is declared. Thus the impatience of Finwë will close the door of life upon the *fëa* of his spouse. This is the greater fault. For it is more unnatural that one of the Eldar should remain for ever as *fëa* without body than that one should remain alive wedded but bereaved. A trial was imposed upon Finwë (not by Míriel only), and he hath asked for justice, and relief.'

---

* By this is meant primarily the *fëar* naked and unhoused. Living, the *fëar* can be deluded; and they can be dominated by fear (of one of great power such as Melkor) and so enslaved. But these things are wicked and tyrannous and are done by Melkor alone among the Valar. They beget only hatred and loathing in the enslaved (which is the sign of inmost and ultimate dissent). To no good purpose can such means be used, for they render all purposes evil.

'Nay!' said Vairë suddenly. 'The *fëa* of Míriel is with me. I know it well, for it is small. But it is strong; proud and obdurate. It is of that sort who having said: *this I will do*, make their words a doom irrevocable unto themselves. She will not return to life, or to Finwë, even if he waiteth until the ageing of the world. Of this he is aware, I deem, as his words show. For he did not found his claim on his desire for children only, but he said to the King: *my heart warns me that Míriel will not return while Arda lasts*. Of what sort the knowledge or belief may be that he would thus express, and whence it came to him, I know not. But *fëa* perceiveth *fëa* and knoweth the disposition of the other, in marriage especially, in ways that we cannot fully understand. We cannot probe all the mystery of the nature of the Children. But if we are to speak of Justice, then Finwë's belief must be taken into account; and if, as I judge, it is well-founded, not a fantasy of his own inconstancy, but against his will and desire, we must otherwise assess the faults of these two. When one of the Queens of the Valar, Varda or Yavanna, or even I, departeth for ever from Arda, and leaveth her spouse, will he or nill he,[14] then let that spouse judge Finwë, if he will, remembering that Finwë cannot follow Míriel without doing wrong to his nature, nor without forsaking the duty and bond of his fatherhood.'

When Vairë had spoken, the Valar sat long in silence, until at length Manwë spoke again. 'There is reason and wisdom in all that has been said. Truly, in the matter of the Children we approach mysteries, and the key to their full understanding was not given to us. In part the Children are indeed one, or maybe the chief, of those "new things" of which Aulë hath spoken.* Yet they came into Arda Marred, and were destined to do so, and to endure the Marring, even though they came in their beginning from beyond Eä. For these "new things", manifesting the finger of Ilúvatar, as we say: they may have no past in Arda and be unpredictable before they appear, yet they have thereafter future operations which may be predicted, according to wisdom and knowledge, since they become at once part of Eä, and part of the past of all that followeth. We may say, therefore, that the Elves are destined to know "death" in their mode, being

---

* Meaning that though they appeared in the Great Theme, they were introduced by Eru himself, not mediated by any of the Ainur; and even so they were not fully revealed to the Ainur.

sent into a world which contains "death", and having a form for which "death" is possible. For though by their prime nature, unmarred, they rightly dwell as spirit and body coherent, yet these are two things, not the same, and their severance (which is "death") is a possibility inherent in their union.

'Aulë and Nienna err, I deem; for what each saith in different words meaneth this much: that Death which cometh from the Marrer may be one thing, and Death as an instrument of Eru be another thing and discernible: the one being of malice, and therefore only evil and inevitably grievous; the other, being of benevolence, intending particular and immediate good, and therefore not evil, and either not grievous or easily and swiftly to be healed. For the evil and the grief of death are in the mere severance and breach of nature, which is alike in both (or death is not their name); and both occur only in Arda Marred, and accord with its processes.

'Therefore I deem that Ulmo is to be followed rather, holding that Eru need not and would not desire as a special instrument of his benevolence a thing that is evil. Wherefore, indeed, should he intrude death as a "new thing" into a world that suffereth it already? Nonetheless, Eru is Lord of All, and will use as instruments of his final purposes, which are good, whatsoever any of his creatures, great or small, do or devise, in his despite or in his service. But we must hold that it is his will that those of the Eldar who serve him should not be cast down by griefs or evils that they encounter in Arda Marred; but should ascend to a strength and wisdom that they would not otherwise have achieved: that the Children of Eru should grow to be daughters and sons.

'For Arda Unmarred hath two aspects or senses. The first is the Unmarred that they discern in the Marred, if their eyes are not dimmed, and yearn for, as we yearn for the Will of Eru: this is the ground upon which Hope is built. The second is the Unmarred that shall be: that is, to speak according to Time in which they have their being, the Arda Healed, which shall be greater and more fair than the first, because of the Marring: this is the Hope that sustaineth. It cometh not only from the yearning for the Will of Ilúvatar the Begetter (which by itself may lead those within Time to no more than regret), but also from trust in Eru the Lord everlasting, that he is good, and that his works shall all end in good. This the Marrer hath denied, and in this denial is the root of evil, and its end is in despair.

'Therefore, notwithstanding the words of Vairë, I abide by

that which I said first. For though she speaketh not without knowledge, she uttereth opinion and not certainty. The Valar have not and must not presume certainty with regard to the wills of the Children. Nor, even were they certain in this one case concerning the *fëa* of Míriel, would that unmake the union of love that once was between her and her spouse, or render void the judgement that constancy to it would in Finwë be a better and fairer course, more in accord with Arda Unmarred, or with the will of Eru in permitting this thing to befall him. The Statute openeth the liberty of a lower road, and accepting death, countenanceth death, and cannot heal it. If that liberty is used, the evil of the death of Míriel will continue to have power, and will bear fruit in sorrow.

'But this matter I now commit to Námo the Judge. Let him speak last!'

Then Námo Mandos spoke, saying: 'All that I have heard I have considered again; though naught pertinent to judgement hath been brought forward that was not already considered in the making of the Statute. Let the Statute stand, for it is just.

'It is our part to rule Arda, and to counsel the Children, or to command them in things committed to our authority. Therefore it is our task to deal with Arda Marred, and to declare what is just within it. We may indeed in counsel point to the higher road, but we cannot compel any free creature to walk upon it. That leadeth to tyranny, which disfigureth good and maketh it seem hateful.

'Healing by final Hope, as Manwë hath spoken of it, is a law which one can give to oneself only; of others justice alone can be demanded. A ruler who discerning justice refuseth to it the sanction of law, demanding abnegation of rights and self-sacrifice, will not drive his subjects to these virtues, virtuous only if free, but by unnaturally making justice unlawful, will drive them rather to rebellion against all law. Not by such means will Arda be healed.

'It is right, therefore, that this just Statute should be proclaimed, and those that use it shall be blameless, whatsoever followeth after. Thus shall the Tale of the Eldar, within the Tale of Arda, be fashioned.

'Hearken now, O Valar! To me foretelling* is granted no less

---

* By which was meant prophecy concerning things which neither reason upon evidence, nor (for the Valar) knowledge of the Great

than doom, and I will proclaim now to you things both near and far. Behold! Indis the fair shall be made glad and fruitful, who might else have been solitary. For not in death only hath the Shadow entered into Aman with the coming of the Children destined to suffer; there are other sorrows, even if they be less. Long she hath loved Finwë, in patience and without bitterness. Aulë nameth Fëanor the greatest of the Eldar, and in potency that is true. But I say unto you that the children of Indis shall also be great, and the Tale of Arda more glorious because of their coming. And from them shall spring things so fair that no tears shall dim their beauty; in whose being the Valar, and the Kindreds both of Elves and of Men that are to come shall all have part, and in whose deeds they shall rejoice. So that, long hence when all that here is, and seemeth yet fair and impregnable, shall nonetheless have faded and passed away, the Light of Aman shall not wholly cease among the free peoples of Arda until the End.

'When he that shall be called Eärendil setteth foot upon the shores of Aman, ye shall remember my words. In that hour ye will not say that the Statute of Justice hath borne fruit only in death; and the griefs that shall come ye shall weigh in the balance, and they shall not seem too heavy compared with the rising of the light when Valinor groweth dim.'

'So be it!' said Manwë.[15]

Therefore the Statute was proclaimed, and the meeting of Indis and Finwë took place, as has been told.

But after a while Nienna came to Manwë, and she said: 'Lord of Aman, it is now made clear that the death of Míriel was an evil of Arda Marred, for with the coming hither of the Eldar the Shadow hath found an entrance even into Aman. Nonetheless Aman remaineth the Realm of the Valar, wherein thy will is paramount. Though the death of severance may find out the Eldar in thy realm, yet one thing cometh not to it, and shall not:* and that is deforming and decay. Behold then! The body of Míriel lieth unmarred, even as a fair house that awaiteth its mistress, who hath gone upon a journey. In this at least,

Theme, could discover or swiftly perceive. Only rarely and in great matters was Mandos moved to prophecy.

* Yet after the slaying of the Trees it did so while Melkor remained there; and the body of Finwë, slain by Melkor, was withered and passed into dust, even as the Trees themselves had withered.

therefore, her death differeth from death in Middle-earth: that for the houseless *fëa* a fair body is still ready, and rebirth is not the only gate by which it may return to life, if thou wilt grant her leave and give her thy blessing. Moreover the body has lain long now in repose in the peace of Lorien; and must not the rulers of Arda have respect even to bodies and all fair forms? Why should it lie idle and untenanted, when doubtless it would not now afflict the *fëa* with weariness, but rejoice it with hope of doing?'

But this Mandos forbade. 'Nay,' said he, 'if Míriel were rehoused, she would be again among the Living, and Finwë would have two spouses alive in Aman. Thus would the Statute be contravened, and my Doom set at naught. And injury would be done also to Indis, who used the liberty of the Statute, but would now by its breach be deprived, for Finwë would desire to return to his former spouse.'

But Nienna said to Mandos: 'Nay! Let Míriel have the joy of her body and of the use of its skills in which she delighted, and dwell not for ever remembering only her brief life before, and its ending in weariness! Can she not be removed from the Halls of Waiting, and taken into the service of Vairë? If she cometh never thence, nor seeketh to walk among the Living, why shouldst thou hold the Doom set at naught, or fear for griefs that might arise? Pity must have a part in Justice.'

But Mandos was unmoved. And the body of Míriel lay at rest in Lorien, until the escape of Melkor the Marrer and the Darkening of Valinor. In that evil time Finwë was slain by the Marrer himself, and his body was burned as by lightning stroke and was destroyed. Then Míriel and Finwë met again in Mandos, and lo! Míriel was glad of the meeting, and her sadness was lightened; and the will in which she had been set was released.

And when she learned of Finwë all that had befallen since her departure (for she had given no heed to it, nor asked tidings, until then) she was greatly moved; and she said to Finwë in her thought: 'I erred in leaving thee and our son, or at the least in not soon returning after brief repose; for had I done so he might have grown wiser. But the children of Indis shall redress his errors and therefore I am glad that they should have being, and Indis hath my love. How should I bear grudge against one who received what I rejected and cherished what I abandoned. Would that I might set all the Tale of our people and of thee and thy children in a tapestry of many colours, as a memorial brighter than memory! For though I am cut off now from the world, and I accept that Doom as just, I would still watch and record all that befalls those dear to me, and their offspring also. [*Added:* I feel again the call of my body and its skills.]'

And Finwë said to Vairë: 'Dost thou hear the prayer and desire of Míriel? Why will Mandos refuse this redress of her griefs, that her being may not be void and without avail? Behold! I instead will abide with Mandos for ever, and so make amends. For surely, if I remain unhoused, and forgo life in Arda, then his Doom will be inviolate.'

'So thou may deem,' answered Vairë; 'yet Mandos is stern, and he will not readily permit a vow to be revoked. Also he will consider not only Míriel and thee, but Indis and thy children, whom thou seemest to forget, pitying now Míriel only.'

'Thou art unjust to me in thy thought,' said Finwë. 'It is unlawful to have two wives, but one may love two women, each differently, and without diminishing one love by another. Love of Indis did not drive out love of Míriel; so now pity for Míriel doth not lessen my heart's care for Indis. But Indis parted from me without death. I had not seen her for many years, and when the Marrer smote me I was alone. She hath dear children to comfort her, and her love, I deem, is now most for Ingoldo.[16] His father she may miss; but not the father of Fëanáro! But above all her heart now yearns for the halls of Ingwë and the peace of the Vanyar, far from the strife of the Noldor. Little comfort should I bring her, if I returned; and the lordship of the Noldor hath passed to my sons.'[17]

But when Mandos was approached he said to Finwë: 'It is well that thou desirest not to return, for this I should have forbidden, until the present griefs are long passed. But it is better still that thou hast made this offer, to deprive thyself, of thy free will, and out of pity for another. This is a counsel of healing, out of which good may grow.'

Therefore when Nienna came to him and renewed her prayer for Míriel, he consented, accepting the abnegation of Finwë as her ransom. Then the *fëa* of Míriel was released and came before Manwë and received his blessing; and she went then to Lorien and re-entered her body, and awoke again, as one that cometh out of a deep sleep; and she arose and her body was refreshed. But after she had stood in the twilight of Lorien a long while in thought, remembering her former life, and all the tidings that she had learned, her heart was still sad, and she had no desire to return to her own people. Therefore she went to the doors of the House of Vairë and prayed to be admitted; and this prayer was granted, although in that House none of the Living dwelt nor have others ever entered it in the body.[18] But Míriel was accepted by Vairë and became her chief handmaid; and all tidings of the Noldor down the years from their beginning were brought to her, and she wove them in webs historial, so fair and skilled that they seemed to live, imperishable, shining with a light of many hues fairer than are known in Middle-earth. This labour Finwë is at times permitted to look upon. And still she is at work, though her name has been changed. For now she is named *Fíriel*,* which to the Eldar signifies 'She that died',[19] and also 'She that sighed'. As fair as the webs of *Fíriel* is praise that is given seldom even to works of the Eldar.

* For before the passing of Míriel the Eldar of Valinor had no word for 'dying' in this manner, though they had words for being destroyed (in body) or being slain. But *fírë* meant to 'expire', as of one sighing or releasing a deep breath; and at the passing of Míriel she had sighed a great sigh, and then lay still; and those who stood by said *fírië*, 'she hath breathed forth'. This word the Eldar afterwards used of the death of Men. But though this sigh they take to be a symbol of release, and the ceasing of the body's life, the Eldar do not confound the breath of the body with the spirit. This they call, as hath been seen, *fëa* or *fairë*, of which the ancient significance seems to be rather 'radiance'. For though the *fëa* in itself is not visible to bodily eyes, it is in light that the Eldar find the most fitting symbol in bodily terms of the indwelling spirit, 'the light of the house' or *cöacalina* as they also name it. And those in whom the *fëa* is strong and untainted, they say, appear even to mortal eyes to shine at times translucent (albeit faintly), as though a lamp burned within.

At the end of the manuscript of *Laws and Customs among the Eldar* are several pages of roughly written 'Notes', and I append here a portion of this material.

(i)

This debate of the Valar not wholly feigned. For the Eldar were permitted to attend all conclaves, and many did so (especially those that so deeply concerned them, their fate, and their place in Arda, as did this matter). Reference is made to things that had not at that time happened (is it ..... prophecy?), but that is partly due to later commentators. For the 'Statute of Finwë and Míriel' was among the documents of lore most deeply studied and pondered. And as has been seen many questions and answers arising were appended.

[?Thus] questions were also asked concerning the fate and death of Men. All [?*read* Also] concerning other 'speaking', and therefore 'reasonable', kinds: Ents, Dwarves, Trolls, Orcs – and the speaking of beasts such as Huan, or the Great Eagles.

Later my father commented against the beginning of this note that the Eldar would not be present at this debate ('certainly not Finwë!'), and that the Valar would have informed the loremasters of the Eldar concerning it.

(ii)

[The] 'Fate of Men' was also later discussed by the Eldar, when they had met Men and knew them. But they had little evidence, and therefore did not know or assert, but 'supposed' or 'guessed'. One such supposition was that Elves and Men will become one people. Another is that some Men, if they desire it, will be permitted to join the Elves in New Arda, or to visit them there – though it will not be the *home* of Men. The most widely held supposition is that the fate of Men is wholly different, and that they will not be concerned with Arda at all.

At the end of this note my father wrote subsequently: 'But see full treatment of this later in *Athrabeth Finrod ah Andreth*.' This work constitutes Part Four in this book.

(iii)

Fate of 'Immortal' Elves: ? to inhabit New Arda (or Arda Healed). Probably not, in a physical sense. Since what is meant by 'The Tale of Arda' seems to be this. The World and its Time appears to *begin* and *end* simply because it is bounded, neither infinite nor eternal. Its finite 'story' when complete will be, like a work of art, beautiful and good (as a whole), and from outside, sc. not *in* Time or its Time, it can be contemplated with wonder and delight – especially by those who have taken part in its 'Tale'. Only in that sense will Elves (or Men) *inhabit* Arda Complete. But New Arda or Arda Unmarred (Healed) would imply a continuance, beyond the End (or Completion). Of that nothing can be surmised. Unless it be this. Since the Elves (and Men) were made *for* Arda, the satisfaction of their nature will require Arda (without the malice of the Marrer): therefore *before the Ending* the Marring will be wholly undone or healed (or absorbed into good, beauty, and joy). In that region of Time and Place the Elves will dwell as their home, but not be confined to it. But no blessed spirits from what is still to us the future can intrude into our own periods of Time. For to contemplate the Tale of Arda the Blessed must (in spirit or whole being) leave the Time of Arda. But others use another analogy, saying that there will indeed be a New Arda, rebuilt from the beginning without Malice, and that the Elves will take part in this from the beginning. It will be in Ëa, say they – for they hold that all Creation of any sort must be in Ëa, proceeding from Eru in the same way, and therefore being of the same Order. They do not believe in contemporaneous non-contiguous worlds except as an amusing fantasy of the mind. They are (say they) either altogether unknowable, even as to whether they are or are not, or else if there are any intersections (however rare) they are only provinces of one Ëa.

At the head of the page on which this note stands my father wrote: 'But see *Athrabeth*': see (ii) above.

NOTES

[These notes refer to the part of the text of *Laws and Customs among the Eldar* given from the manuscript A, pp. 233 ff.]

1 The spelling *Feänáro* is found also in the first text of the tale, FM 1 (see p. 206, footnote). The name is variously written subsequently in A (*Feänáro, Fëanáro, Feanáro*).
2 For the form *Lorien* with short vowel see p. 56 note 2 and p. 148, §3.
3 For the doom of Mandos (the 'Statute of Finwë and Míriel') in this work see pp. 225–6. In FM 1 the doom, in its earliest expression, is given at this point in the story (pp. 206–7).
4 *your union*: *your* is plural, and not inconsistent with *thy, thee, thou* in the same sentence.
5 *in Túna*: see p. 193, §52, and p. 282.
6 My father first wrote 'an *aimenel*' (> *aimenal*), but changed it immediately to 'a *lirulin*', writing 'lark' in the margin.
7 The reference in the footnote here is to the passage in A (omitted in B) which is given in note 22 on p. 230. As in that passage the name *Nolofinwë* is written with a tilde over the *N*. The order of the names of the daughters of Finwë and Indis is as in the

emended text of FM 1, p. 207. See further p. 262 and note 10.
8 The brackets are in the original.
9 Cf. the *Ainulindalë* §13 (p. 11): 'Yet some things there are that [the Ainur] cannot see ...; for to none but himself has Ilúvatar revealed all that he has in store, and in every age there come forth things that are new and have no foretelling, for they do not spring from the past.'
10 It is not told elsewhere that Aulë was the most eager among the Valar that the Elves should be summoned to Valinor. Cf. what is said earlier in *Laws and Customs* (p. 219, found in both texts, but not elsewhere) concerning the motive of the Valar in bringing the Elves to Aman.
11 As with the reference to Aulë mentioned in note 10, it is not told elsewhere that Ulmo dissented from the decision of the Valar to bring Melkor to Mandos. Cf. the passage in the first text of the *Valaquenta*, lost in the final form: '[Ulmo's] counsels grew ever away from the mind of Manwë' (p. 202).
12 At this point there originally followed: 'Then when others had spoken Manwë answered: 'There is reason in all that hath been said ...' Manwë's speech was apparently abandoned after a few lines, and the speeches of Nienna, Ulmo, and Vairë introduced; after which Manwë's speech reappears (p. 244).
13 This sentence ('And I doubt not ...') was subsequently placed in brackets.
14 *nill* is the old negative verb 'will not': thus 'will he or nill he' means 'whether he wills it or wills it not' (surviving as *willy-nilly*).
15 The text stops here, not at the foot of a page. It takes up again on a new sheet, in a rougher script that continues to the end of the work; but my father paginated this further text continuously with the preceding.
16 *Ingoldo:* the mother-name of Fingolfin (p. 230 note 22).
17 In the account of the marriage of Finwë and Indis in the present work (p. 238) there is no mention of this estrangement, or at least separation. In the final work on Chapter 6 of the *Quenta Silmarillion*, however, it is implied that Indis did not depart with Finwë to Formenos, because it is told that Fëanor's wife Nerdanel would not go with him into banishment and 'asked leave to abide with Indis' (p. 279, §53d).
18 On Míriel's entry into the House of Vairë see p. 263 note 9.
19 *Fíriel*: see the *Etymologies* in Vol.V, p. 381, stem PHIR.

★

LATER VERSIONS OF THE STORY OF FINWË AND MÍRIEL IN THE *QUENTA SILMARILLION*

The next version of the story was a short typescript derived closely for the most part from that in *Laws and Customs among the Eldar* (pp. 236–9); it is entitled *Of Finwë and Míriel*, and begins: 'Finwë, first lord of the Noldor, had to wife Míriel, who was called the *Serindë*...' (cf. p. 236). There is no indication that it was intended to stand in the text of the *Quenta Silmarillion*, but there can scarcely be any question that my father did so intend it; I will refer to it therefore as 'FM 2'.

The most important divergence in FM 2 from the text in *Laws and Customs* is at the words (p. 237): 'Then Manwë took pity upon Finwë, and he considered his plea, and when Mandos had spoken his doom as has been recorded, Manwë called Finwë to him...' For the purpose of the inclusion of the story in the narrative of the *Quenta Silmarillion* the judgement of Mandos had obviously to be given at this point (as it had been in the original version, FM 1, p. 206); and in FM 2 the judgement was preceded by a reference to the Debate of the Valar and some indication of the nature of their concern. The word 'Statute' is used here in a wider and a narrower sense: as a name for the record made by the Eldar of all matters relevant to the judgement of Mandos, as well as the title of the actual judgement.

> Then Manwë was moved with pity for Finwë, and he considered his plea. But because this seemed to him a great matter and not lightly to be judged, he summoned the Valar in Council. Of the long debate that they held the Elves wrote a record, for their chieftains were permitted to be present.[1] This was called 'The Statute of Finwë and Míriel' and was preserved among the chief of their books of law; for in the debate, before the Statute was at last established by the doom of Námo Mandos, many matters concerning the Eldar, their fate in Arda, their death and re-birth and the nature of their marriage, were examined and judged. And the Valar were greatly concerned to see that all their labour for the guarding of Valinor was of no avail, to keep out evil and the shadow of Melkor, if any thing, living or unliving, was brought thither out of Middle-earth and left free or unguarded; and they perceived at last how great was the power of Melkor in Arda, in the making of which as it was*

---

* *Arda Hastaina*, or 'Arda Marred', as they named it. For *Arda*, or in full *Arda Alahasta*, the 'Unmarred', they named the thought which they had, each severally, or as a Council under Manwë, of that Arda in which Melkor had no part.

his part was such that all things, save in Aman alone, had an inclination to evil and to perversion from their right forms and courses. Wherefore those whose being began in Arda, and who moreover were by nature a union of spirit and body, drawing the sustenance of the latter from Arda Marred, must ever be, in some degree, liable to grief, to do or to suffer things unnatural; and though dwelling in Aman might be a guard against this evil, it was not a full cure, unless in long ages. And with this thought a shadow passed over the hearts of the Valar, even in the noon-tide of the Blessed Realm, presage of the sorrows which the Children should bring into the world.

Now this was the doom of Námo in this case, and in all cases where a marriage of the Eldar might be sundered by the death of one only of the partners. 'Marriage among the Eldar is by and for the Living...'

The doom of Mandos in FM 2 differs from the form in *Laws and Customs* (pp. 225–6) only in detail of expression and not at all in substance, except for some expansion at the very end.

'... For it must be clearly understood that, when this will not to return has been solemnly declared and ratified by Mandos, then the living partner may take another spouse lawfully. For it is contrary to the nature of the Eldar to live unwedded, and the Dead may not compel the Living to remain solitary against their will. If therefore the Living take another partner, the will of the Dead shall not be revoked, but shall be a doom of Mandos. For he will permit none of the Eldar to walk alive in the body who has two spouses living also.'

This in brief was the Doom of Mandos, that was after called the *Statute of Finwë and Míriel*. And when Mandos had spoken as the Mouth of Manwë, the Eldar that heard him asked: 'How shall the will or doom be known?'; and it was answered: 'Only by recourse to Manwë and the pronouncement of Mandos. In this matter it shall not be lawful for any of the Eldar to judge his own case. For who among the Living can discover the thoughts of the Dead or presume the judgements of Mandos?'

Then Manwë called Finwë to him...

Other divergences from the text of *Laws and Customs* in FM 2 were taken up into the final text (FM 4), which is given in full on pp. 256 ff., and need not be set out here, or if lost from the final text are given in the notes to it.

FM 2 was followed by a further typescript, 'FM 3', made on a different machine (see p. 300). This is expressly a chapter of the *Quenta Silmarillion*, with the title as typed *Of Fëanor and the Darkening of Valinor*, changed later to *Of Finwë and Míriel*. This version was a good deal reduced by omissions, and my father evidently found it unsatisfactory, for he went on to make a further and much more substantial version, 'FM 4', with which the textual history of the story of Finwë and Míriel comes to an end.

It is clear that when making FM 3 and FM 4 he had the preceding texts in front of him, and that he selected variously from them as he sought to achieve a satisfactory form. To set out all the detail of this development would take much space but serve little purpose, since very little was in fact omitted from the final, 're-expanded' text FM 4; and I give this text here in full.

FM 4 has a general heading *Of the Silmarils and the Darkening of Valinor*, with a subtitle *Of Finwë and Míriel* (the typescript then continues with further 'sub-chapters', to which however my father subsequently gave numbers as chapters in their own right: see p. 299). The paragraph numbers provided for reference do not relate to any numbers previously used, since after the opening the text is entirely different; for the 'LQ' (1951) version of the opening of the chapter see pp. 184–5, §§46, 46a–b.

OF THE SILMARILS AND THE DARKENING OF VALINOR

OF FINWË AND MÍRIEL

§1   Now the three kindreds of the Eldar were gathered at last in Valinor, and Melkor was chained. This was the Noontide of the Blessed Realm, the fullness of its glory and bliss, long in tale of years, but in memory too brief. In those days the Eldar became full-grown in stature of body and of mind, and the Noldor advanced ever in skill and knowledge; and the long years were filled with their joyful labours, in which many new things fair and wonderful were devised. It was in this time that the Noldor first made letters, and Rúmil of Túna was the name of the lore-master who first achieved fitting signs for the recording of speech and song, some for graving upon metal or in stone, others for drawing with brush or with pen.

§2   It came to pass that in Eldamar, in the house of the King in Tirion, there was born the eldest of the sons of Finwë, and the most beloved. Kurufinwë was his name, but by his mother he was called Fëanor,* Spirit of Fire, by which title he is remembered in all the tales of the Noldor.

§3 Míriel was the name of his mother. Her hair was like silver; and she was slender as a white flower in the grass. Soft and sweet was her voice, and she sang as she worked, like rippling water, in music without words. For her hands were more skilled to make things fine and delicate than any other hands even among the Noldor. By her the craft of needles was devised; and if but one fragment of the broideries of Míriel were seen in Middle-earth it would be held dearer than a king's realm; for the richness of her devices and the fire of their colours were as manifold and as bright as the wealth of leaf and flower and wing in the fields of Yavanna. Therefore she was called *Serinde*.†

§4 The love of Finwë and Míriel was great and full of joy, for it began in the Blessed Realm and in days of mirth. But in the bearing of her son she was consumed in spirit and body, so that almost all strength seemed to have passed from her; and when she had named him[2] she said to Finwë: 'Never again shall I bear a child, for strength that would have nourished the life of many has gone forth into Fëanor.'

§5 Finwë was greatly grieved, for the Noldor were in the youth of their days, but were still few in number, and he desired to bring forth many children into the bliss of Aman. He said therefore: 'Surely there is healing in Aman? Here all weariness can find rest.'

§6 But when Míriel still languished, Finwë sought the counsel of Manwë, and Manwë delivered her to the care of Irmo in Lorien.[3] At their parting (for a little while as he thought) Finwë was sad, for it seemed an unhappy chance that the mother should depart and miss the beginning at least of the childhood days of her son.

§7 'Unhappy it is indeed,' said Míriel, 'and I would weep, if I were not so weary. But hold me blameless in this, and in all that may come after. Rest now I must. Farewell, dear lord!'

§8 She spoke no clearer than this at that time, but in her heart she yearned not only for sleep and rest but release from

---

* [footnote to the text] *Fëanáro* in the form of the speech of those days.

† [footnote to the text] *Míriel Serinde*: that is *Byrde Míriel* (Míriel the Broideress): quoth Ælfwine.

the labour of living. She went then to Lorien and laid her down to sleep beneath a silver tree; but though she seemed to sleep, her spirit indeed departed from her body and passed in silence to the keeping of Mandos, and abode in the house of Vairë.[4] The maidens of Estë tended her fair body so that it remained unwithered, but she did not return.

§9 Finwë lived in sorrow; and he went often to the gardens of Lorien, and sitting beneath the silver willows beside the body of his wife he called her by her names. But it was of no avail, and Finwë alone in all the Blessed Realm was bereaved of joy. After a while he went to Lorien no more, for it increased his grief to see the fair form of Míriel that would not hear his call. All his love he gave now to his son; for Fëanor in childhood was like his mother in voice and countenance, and Finwë was to him both father and mother and there was a double bond of love upon them.

§10 Yet Finwë was not content, being young and eager; and he still desired to have more children to bring mirth into his house. When, therefore, twelve years had passed he went again to Manwë. 'My Lord,' he said, 'behold! I am bereaved. Alone among the Eldar I have no wife, and must hope for no sons save one, and for no daughter. Whereas Ingwë and Olwë beget many children in the bliss of Aman. Must I remain ever so? For my heart warns me that Míriel will not return again ever from the house of Vairë.'

§11 Then Manwë was moved with pity for Finwë; but because this seemed to him a great matter, and the coming of death (albeit of free will) into the Blessed Realm a grave portent not lightly to be judged, he summoned the Valar in Council, and bade the chieftains and loremasters of the Eldar also to be present. Of the long debate of the Valar the Eldar wrote a record. This they called *Namna Finwë Míriello*, the Statute of Finwë and Míriel,[5] and it was preserved among the books of their Law; for in the debate many matters concerning the Eldar, their fate in Arda, and their death and re-birth, were examined and judged. For the Valar were greatly concerned to see that their labour for the guarding of Valinor was unavailing, if any thing, living or unliving, was brought thither out of Middle-earth, and they perceived now more clearly how great was the hurt that Melkor of old had done to the substance of Arda, so that all those who were incarnate and drew the sustenance of their bodies from Arda Marred, must ever be liable to grief, to do or to suffer things unnatural in Arda Unmarred. And this marring could not now be wholly undone, not even by Melkor repentant; for power had gone forth from him and could not be recalled, but would continue to work according to the will that had set it in motion. And with this thought a shadow passed over the hearts of the Valar, presage of the sorrows which the Children should bring into the world.

§12 But when all was said, Manwë commanded Mandos to speak and announce his judgement. Then Mandos stood upon the Doom-hill and said:

'It is the way of Life that Ilúvatar hath ordained for you, his children, as ye know well, that the life of the Quendi shall not end until the end of Arda; and that they shall take each one spouse only and have no other in their life, while Arda endureth. But herein no account is taken of Death, which cometh from the marring of Arda. This doom is, therefore, now made by the right of lawgiving that Ilúvatar committed to Manwë.

When the spirit of a spouse, husband or wife, shall for any cause pass into the keeping of Mandos, then the living may be permitted lawfully to take another spouse, if the former union be dissolved for ever.

§13 'How shall a marriage be ended for ever? By the will of the Dead, or by the doom of Mandos. By the will of the Dead, if they refuse ever to return to the life of the body; by the doom of Mandos, if he will not permit them to return. For a union that was for the life of Arda is ended, if it cannot be resumed within the life of Arda.

§14 'We say "by the will of the Dead", for it would be unjust that the Living should for their own purposes confine the Dead in Mandos, denying to them all hope of return. It is also unjust that the Dead by refusal of life should compel the Living to remain solitary until the End; and therefore we have declared that in such case the Living may take another spouse. But understand well that if this be done, then the refusal of life by the Dead shall be irrevocable, and they shall never again return to life in the body. For none among the Quendi shall have two spouses at one time awake and alive.

'This is the doom of Námo Mandos in this matter.'

§15 When Mandos had spoken thus, the Eldar who were present asked: 'How then shall the will or the doom be known?'

It was answered: 'Only by recourse to Manwë, and by the pronouncement of Mandos. For who among the Living can discover the will of the Dead, or presume the judgements of Mandos?'

§16 Then Manwë called Finwë to him, and said: 'Thou hast heard the doom that has been declared. If Míriel, thy wife, will not return, your[6] marriage is ended, and thou hast leave to take another wife. But this is permission, not counsel. For the severance cometh from the marring of Arda; and those who accept this permission accept the marring, whereas the bereaved who remain steadfast belong in spirit and will to Arda Unmarred. This is a grave matter upon which the fate of many may depend. Be not in haste!'

§17 Finwë answered: 'I am in no haste, My Lord, and my heart has no desire, save the hope that when this doom is made clear to Míriel, she may yet relent and set a term to my bereavement.'

§18 Vairë with whom Míriel dwelt made known to her the doom,[7] and spoke also of the sorrow of Finwë. But Míriel answered: 'I came hither to escape from the body, and I do not desire ever to return to it. My life has gone out into Fëanor, my son. That gift I have given to him whom I loved. I can give no more. Beyond Arda this may be healed, but not within it.'

§19 Then Vairë said to Mandos: 'The spirit of Míriel hath dwelt with me, and I know it. It is small, but it is strong and obdurate: one of those who having said *this will I do* make their words a law irrevocable unto themselves. Unless constrained, she will not return to life or to Finwë, not though he should wait until the ageing of the world.'[8]

§20 But Mandos said: 'It is not lawful for the Valar to constrain the Dead to return'; and he summoned the spirit of Míriel to appear before him. 'Thy will must rule in this matter, spirit of Míriel, once wife of Finwë,' he said. 'In Mandos thou shalt abide. But take heed! Thou art of the Quendi, and even if thou refuse the body, thou must remain in Arda and within the time of its history. The Eldar are not as the Valar. Their spirits are less strong to stand than thou deemest. Do not wonder, then, if thy will should change in time, and this doom which thou takest upon thyself become grievous to thee. Yea, and to many others!'

§21 But the spirit of Míriel remained silent. Mandos therefore accepted her choice, and she went then to the Halls of

Waiting appointed to the Eldar and was left in peace.*⁹ Nonetheless Mandos declared that a space of twelve years should pass between the declaration of the will of the Dead and the pronouncement of the doom of disunion.

§22 During that time Fëanor dwelt in the care of his father. Soon he began to show forth the skills in hand and mind of both Finwë and Míriel. As he grew from childhood he became ever more like Finwë in stature and countenance, but in mood he resembled Míriel rather. His will was strong and determined, and he pursued all his purposes both eagerly and steadfastly. Few ever changed his courses by counsel, none by force.

§23 It came to pass that after three years more Finwë took as second wife Indis the fair. She was in all ways unlike Míriel. She was not of the Noldor but of the Vanyar, being the sister of Ingwë; and she was golden-haired and tall and exceedingly swift of foot. She did not labour with her hands, but made music and wove words into song; and there was ever light and mirth about her while the bliss of Aman lasted.

§24 She loved Finwë dearly; for her heart had turned to him long before, while the Vanyar still dwelt with the Noldor in Túna. In those days she had looked upon the Lord of the Noldor, and he seemed to her fairest and noblest of the Eldar, dark-haired and white of brow, eager of face but with eyes full of thought; and his voice and mastery of words delighted her. Therefore she remained unwedded when her people removed to Valinor, and she walked often alone in the friths and fields of the Valar, filling them with music.

§25 Now Ingwë, hearing of the strange grief of Finwë, and desiring to lift up his heart and withdraw him from vain mourning in Lorien, had sent messages bidding him to leave Túna for a while, and to come and dwell for a season in the full light of the Trees. Finwë thanked him but did not go, while there was yet hope that Míriel would return. But when the doom of Mandos was spoken, it came into his heart that he must seek to build his life anew. 'Maybe, there is healing in the light of Laurelin and hope in the blossom of Telperion,' he said. 'I will take the counsel of Ingwë.'

* [footnote to the text] But it is said that after a time she was permitted to return to the house of Vairë, and there it was her part to record in web and broidery all the histories of the Kin of Finwë and the deeds of the Noldor.

§26 Therefore one day, when Fëanor was far abroad walking in the mountains in the strength of his youth, Finwë arose and went forth from Túna alone, and he passed through the Kalakiryan, and went towards the house of Ingwë upon the west slopes of Oiolossë. His coming was unheralded and unforeseen; and when Indis saw Finwë climbing the paths of the Mountain, and the light of Laurelin was behind him as a glory, without forethought she sang suddenly in great joy, and her voice went up as a song of the *lirulin** in the sky. Then Finwë heard that song falling from above, and he looked up and saw Indis in the golden light, and he knew in that moment that she loved him and had long done so. Then his heart turned at last to her; and he believed that this chance, as it seemed, had been granted for the comfort of them both. 'Behold!' he said. 'There is indeed healing of grief in Aman!'

§27 In one year from their meeting upon the Mountain Finwë, King of the Noldor, wedded Indis, sister of Ingwë; and the Vanyar and Noldor for the most part rejoiced. In Indis was first proved true the saying: The loss of one may be the gain of another; but this saying also she found true: The house remembers the builder, though others may dwell in it after. For Finwë loved her dearly, and was glad again; and she bore him five children whom he loved;†[10] yet the shadow of Míriel did not depart from the house of Finwë, nor from his heart; and of all whom he loved Fëanor had ever the chief share of his thought.

§28 The wedding of the father was not pleasing to Fëanor; and though it did not lessen the love between them, Fëanor had no great love for Indis or her children. As soon as he might he lived apart from them, exploring the land of Aman, or busying himself with the lore and the crafts in which he delighted. In those unhappy things which later came to pass, and in which Fëanor was the leader, many saw the effect of this breach in the house of Finwë, judging that if Finwë had endured his loss and had been content with the fathering of his mighty son, the courses of Fëanor would have been otherwise, and great sorrow and evil might have been prevented. Yet the children of Indis

---

* [footnote to the text] The lark.

† [footnote to the text] Findis, Fingolfin, Finvain, [Finarphin >] Finarfin and Faniel: three daughters, and two sons (Fingolfin and Finarfin).

were great and glorious, and their children also; and if they had not lived, the history of the Eldar would have been the poorer.[11]

NOTES

1 See Note (i) following *Laws and Customs* and my father's comment on it, pp. 250–1.
2 In FM 2 it is said, following *Laws and Customs* p. 236, that Míriel gave the name Fëanáro to her son 'at birth', and at this point a long footnote is added on the subject of name-giving:
   According to the custom of the Eldar. In addition to their 'true names', which were their father-name and their chosen name, they often received other or 'added names'. Of these the most important were the mother-names. Mothers often gave to their children special names of their own choosing, the most notable of which were 'names of insight'. In the hour of birth, or on some other occasion of moment, a mother might give to her child a name that referred to dominant features of its nature as she perceived it, or that came of foresight and referred to its special fate. Names of this kind might become more widely used than the father-name (which was often only the name of the father repeated or modified); and if the child adopted a mother-name as a 'chosen name', then it became also a 'true name'. Curufinwë took Fëanáro as his chosen name. Fëanor is the form that this name took in the later speech of the Exiled Noldor.
   This represents an extreme compression of the section on *Naming* in *Laws and Customs*, pp. 214 ff.
3 *Lorien* was still the form in *Laws and Customs* and in the texts FM 2 and FM 3; in the present text FM 4 my father typed *Lórien*, but then altered it back to *Lorien*.
4 *and abode in the house of Vairë*: these words first appear in the present text; see note 9.
5 On the application of the term 'Statute' here see p. 254.
6 See p. 252, note 4.
7 FM 2 as typed had here, expanding the passage in *Laws and Customs*, p. 237: 'But Mandos summoned Míriel, and made known to her the Doom ...' This was later emended to read: 'Vairë, with whom Míriel dwelt, made known to her the Doom ...'
8 These words of Vairë's are derived from her intervention in the Debate of the Valar in *Laws and Customs*, p. 244.
9 The footnote at this point is derived from *Laws and Customs* (pp. 249–50), although Míriel's entry into the house of Vairë stands there at the end of a long account recording the coming of Finwë to the halls of Mandos, his renunciation of re-birth, and the

re-entry of the *fëa* of Míriel into her body that still lay in Lorien. In FM 2 there is no mention of Míriel after the words 'she went then to the Halls of Waiting appointed to the Eldar and was left in peace.' In FM 3 the text at this point is very compressed, and reads (in place of FM 4 §§18–23, all of which is present in FM 2 apart from the present footnote):

... 'I came hither to escape from the body, and I will not return to it'; and after ten years had passed the doom of disunion was spoken. And Míriel has dwelt ever since in the house of Vairë, and it is her part to record there the histories of the Kin of Finwë and all the deeds of the Noldor.

It came to pass that after three more years Finwë took as second wife Indis the Fair ...

These texts are thus altogether inconsistent on the subject of the ultimate fate of Míriel. In particular the references to the House of Vairë are confusing. It was told in AAm (p. 49, §3) that 'Vairë the Weaver dwells with Mandos', and the same is implied in QS §6 (V.205, retained almost unchanged in the *Valaquenta*): 'Vairë the weaver is his wife, who weaves all things that have been in time in her storied webs, and the halls of Mandos ... are clothed therewith.' In *Laws and Customs* (p. 236) the spirit of Míriel departed from her body in Lorien 'and passed in silence *to the halls of Mandos*', and Finwë said to Manwë 'my heart warns me that Míriel will not return again *from the house of Vairë*'; in the debate of the Valar before the proclamation of the 'Statute' Vairë said that 'the *fëa* of Míriel is with me' (p. 244). But afterwards Nienna asked of Mandos that Míriel should be 'removed from the Halls of Waiting, and taken into the service of Vairë' (p. 248); this was refused, and when Finwë was slain their *fëar* encountered each other '*in Mandos*'. Thereafter the *fëa* of Míriel was 'released', and re-united with her body 'she went to the doors of the House of Vairë and prayed to be admitted; and this prayer was granted, although in that House none of the Living dwelt nor have others ever entered it in the body.' Thus within the same text 'the house of Vairë' is both equated with 'the halls of Mandos' and distinguished from them.

In FM 4 (§8) the spirit of Míriel 'passed in silence to the *keeping* of Mandos, and abode *in the house of Vairë*' (see note 4 above); and in §18 'Vairë with whom Míriel dwelt made known to her the doom.' After Míriel's refusal of return 'she went then to the Halls of Waiting appointed to the Eldar and was left in peace' (§21), but (according to the footnote to this paragraph) 'after a time she was permitted to *return* to the house of Vairë.' Thus in this final text it seems certain that Vairë in some sense dwelt apart.

Very curiously, my father subsequently bracketed the footnote and wrote against it 'Omit', commenting beside it: 'Alter this. What happened when Finwë came to Mandos?' Yet he had already answered this question very fully in *Laws and Customs*, where indeed it was the very fact of the coming of Finwë to the halls of Mandos that led to the release of Míriel and her admission to the house of Vairë.

10 In FM 2 the footnote on the names of the children of Indis read thus:

> Three daughters and two sons, in this order: Findis, Nolofinwë, Faniel, Arafinwë, and Írimë. The mother-name of Nolofinwë was Ingoldo, signifying that he came of both the kin of the Ingar and of the Noldor. The mother-name of Arafinwë was Ingalaurë, for he had the golden hair of his mother's people, and that endured in his line afterwards.

This was derived from a passage in the A-text of *Laws and Customs* (p. 230 note 22) which was omitted in B; in that however the daughters were not mentioned. The name *Írimë* (for later *Finvain*) goes back to the original text FM 1 (p. 207). In the note in FM 3 the names are as in FM 4, but those of the sons are spelt *Fingolphin* and *Finarphin*, and this comment is added: 'These names are given in the forms of the later tongue in Middle-earth (save Findis and Faniel who did not leave Valinor).'

In a very late essay (1968 or later; referred to in IV.174) my father said that the mother-name of Finrod Felagund was *Ingoldo*, but he gave to it a wholly different significance. The term *Ingar* ('people of Ingwë') occurring in *Laws and Customs* text A (p. 230 note 22) and here, has not been found before.

11 FM 2 ends differently after 'might have been prevented':

> Thus it is that the cases in which the Eldar can marry again or desire to do so are rare; and rarer still are those who do this even when it is lawful; for the sorrow and strife in the house of Finwë are graven in the memory of the Noldor Elves.

This derives from *Laws and Customs*, p. 239. In FM 3 the conclusion is as in FM 4, but after 'and great sorrow and evil might have been prevented' it continues: 'But this judgement was but a guess. Certain it is that the children of Indis were great and glorious ...' The later ending derives in its thought from the prophecy of Mandos in *Laws and Customs* (p. 247) at the final proclamation of the 'Statute of Finwë and Míriel'.

A note on certain conceptions in the story of Finwë and Míriel

The nature of Elvish 'immortality' and 'death' had been stated very long before in *The Book of Lost Tales* (I.76):

Thither [i.e. to Mandos] in after days fared the Elves of all the clans who were by illhap slain with weapons or did die of grief for those that were slain – and only so might the Eldar die, and then it was only for a while. There Mandos spake their doom, and there they waited in the darkness, dreaming of their past deeds, until such time as he appointed when they might again be born into their children, and go forth to laugh and sing again.

And in the original *Music of the Ainur* (I.59) it is said of the Elves that 'dying they are reborn in their children, so that their number minishes not, nor grows.'

In the *Quenta* (IV.100, deriving from the 'Sketch of the Mythology', IV.21) the idea of rebirth is qualified:

Immortal were the Elves, and their wisdom waxed and grew from age to age, and no sickness or pestilence brought them death. But they could be slain with weapons in those days, even by mortal Men, and some waned and wasted with sorrow till they faded from the earth. Slain or fading their spirits went back to the halls of Mandos to wait a thousand years, or the pleasure of Mandos according to their deserts, before they were recalled to free life in Valinor, or were reborn, it is said, into their own children.

In QS the corresponding passage (§85, V.246) was much enlarged:

Immortal were the Elves, and their wisdom waxed from age to age, and no sickness nor pestilence brought death to them. Yet their bodies were of the stuff of earth and could be destroyed, and in those days they were more like to the bodies of Men, and to the earth, since they had not so long been inhabited by the fire of the spirit, which consumeth them from within in the courses of time. Therefore they could perish in the tumults of the world, and stone and water had power over them, and they could be slain with weapons in those days, even by mortal Men. And outside Valinor they tasted bitter grief, and some wasted and waned with sorrow, until they faded from the earth. Such was the measure of their mortality foretold in the Doom of Mandos spoken in Eruman. But if they were slain or wasted with grief, they died not from the earth, and their spirits went back to the halls of Mandos, and there waited, days or years, even a thousand, according to the will of Mandos and their deserts. Thence they are recalled at length to freedom, either as spirits, taking form according to their own thought, as the lesser folk of the divine race; or else, it is said, they are at times re-born into their own children, and the ancient wisdom of their race does not perish or grow less.

At the end of the *Ainulindalë* it is said (I cite the final text D, p. 37, but the passage goes back almost unchanged to the pre-*Lord of the Rings* version, V.163):

For the Eldar die not till the world dies, unless they are slain or waste in grief (and to both these seeming deaths they are subject);

neither does age subdue their strength, unless one grow weary of ten thousand centuries; and dying they are gathered in the halls of Mandos in Valinor, whence often they return and are reborn among their children.

And in the Doom of the Noldor as it appears in AAm (§154, p. 117) it was declared:

> For know now that though Eru appointed unto you to die not in Eä, and no sickness may assail you, yet slain may ye be, and slain ye shall be: by weapon and by torment and by grief; and your houseless spirits shall come then to Mandos. There long shall ye abide and yearn for your bodies and find little pity though all whom ye have slain should entreat for you.

The meaning of this, I feel sure, is: It is contrary indeed to the 'right nature' of the Elves that they should die, but nonetheless death may come to them.

The testimony of all these passages (and others not cited), early and late, is that Elvish 'death' (or 'seeming death', in the words of the *Ainulindalë*) was always a possible fate, deriving from their nature as incarnate beings. But there is a constant threat of ambiguity imposed by the words that must be used. The Elves cannot 'die' in the sense that Men 'die', since Men (by the Gift of Ilúvatar) depart from the 'world' never to return, whereas the Elves cannot depart from it so long as it lasts. In the legend of Beren and Lúthien Mandos offered her a choice: and the doom that she chose was that the destiny decreed by her nature should be changed. 'So it was that *alone of the Eldalië she has died indeed*, and left the world long ago' (*The Silmarillion* p. 187). But the Elves can nonetheless suffer the severance of spirit from body, which is 'death'. Thus it may be said that the essential distinction between the (possible) death of Elves and the (inevitable) death of Men is a difference of *destiny after death*. See V.304; and cf. *Laws and Customs*, p. 218: 'From their beginnings the chief difference between Elves and Men lay in the fate and nature of their spirits. The *fëar* of the Elves were destined to dwell in Arda for all the life of Arda, and the death of the flesh did not abrogate that destiny.'

In a draft for a letter written in October 1958 (see p. 300) my father discussed the meaning of the 'immortality' of the Elves (*Letters* no. 212):

> In this mythical 'prehistory' *immortality*, strictly longevity coextensive with the life of Arda, was part of the given nature of the Elves; beyond the End nothing was revealed. *Mortality*, that is a short life-span having no relation to the life of Arda, is spoken of as the given nature of Men ...
> In the Elvish legends there is record of a strange case of an Elf (Míriel mother of Fëanor) that tried to *die*, which had disastrous results, leading to the 'Fall' of the High-elves. The Elves were not

subject to disease, but they could be 'slain': that is their bodies could be destroyed, or mutilated so as to be unfit to sustain life. But this did not lead naturally to 'death': they were rehabilitated and reborn and eventually recovered memory of all their past: they remained 'identical'. But Míriel wished to abandon being, and refused rebirth. 'But Míriel wished to *abandon being*': this is a dark saying. There is nothing in any of the accounts to suggest that she desired annihilation, the ending of her existence in any form. In *Laws and Customs* (p. 222) my father wrote that 'some *fëar* in grief or weariness gave up hope, and turning away from life relinquished their bodies, even though these might have been healed or were indeed unhurt. Few of these ... desired to be re-born, not at least until they had been long in "waiting"; some never returned.' This surely accords with what is told of the death of Míriel.

It seems, at any rate, that when my father said here that Míriel 'tried to *die*' he meant that she sought a 'true death': not a 'seeming death', but a departure for ever out of Arda. Yet this could not be: for death in this sense was contrary to 'the given nature of the Elves', appointed by Ilúvatar; and indeed, in *Of Finwë and Míriel* (§20) Mandos spoke to the *fëa* of Míriel, saying: 'In Mandos thou shalt abide. But take heed! Thou art of the Quendi, and even if thou refuse the body, *thou must remain in Arda and within the time of its history.*'

But the 'seeming death' to which the Elves are subject had never yet appeared in Aman in all the long years since the Vanyar and the Noldor came to Eldamar. In the *Annals of Aman*, written before the story of Míriel had arisen, Fëanor spoke before the Valar after the Death of the Trees (§§120–1, p. 107):

'... Mayhap I can unlock my jewels, but never again shall I make their like; and if they be broken, then broken will be my heart, and I shall die: first of all the Children of Eru.'

'Not the first,' quoth Mandos, but they understood not his word ...

Mandos knew that Morgoth had murdered Finwë at Formenos, 'and spilled the first blood of the Children of Ilúvatar' (§122).

Against the words of Mandos my father afterwards noted on the AAm typescript (p. 127, §120): 'This no longer fits even the Eldar of Valinor. Finwë Fëanor's father was first to be slain of the High-elves, Míriel Fëanor's mother the first to die', and on the text itself he changed Fëanor's 'I shall die' to 'I shall be slain'. It might seem that a distinction is made here between 'dying' and 'being slain', but I do not think that this is the case. What is meant is simply that Míriel was the first to die, and Finwë was the second to die – but the first to be slain. After the story of Míriel had entered Fëanor could no longer say 'I shall die: first of all the Children of Eru'; my father therefore, wishing to retain the pregnant words of Mandos 'Not the first', altered Fëanor's to 'I shall be slain'.

Much later, this passage in AAm was used again in the new work on the *Quenta Silmarillion* (see p. 293), taking this form:

'... and I shall be slain, first of all the Children of Eru.'

'Not the first,' quoth Mandos, but they did not understand his words, thinking that he spoke of Míriel.

The meaning here seems to be that those who heard the words of Mandos (speaking of the murder of Finwë as yet unknown to them) thought that he spoke of Míriel, because she was the only one of the Eldar whom they knew to have died; but since Míriel had not been *slain* 'they did not understand his words'. Even so, it cannot be supposed that Finwë was the first to be slain of the Children of Eru; cf. my father's note on the AAm typescript 'This no longer fits *even* the Eldar of Valinor', and the passage in *Laws and Customs*, p. 218: 'This destruction of the *hröa*, causing death or the unhousing of the *fëa*, was soon experienced by the immortal Eldar, when they awoke in the marred and overshadowed realm of Arda.'

It is made plain in *Laws and Customs* and in the new 'sub-chapter' of the *Quenta Silmarillion* that the primary significance of the death of Míriel is that it was the first appearance of Death in Aman; and the debate was concerned with this *unlooked-for event*, and its implications for the laws that governed the life of deathless Aman. In *Laws and Customs* (p. 241) Yavanna declared that 'the Shadow ... has marred the very *hrón* of Arda, and all Middle-earth is perverted by the evil of Melkor ... Therefore none of those who awoke in Middle-earth, and there dwelt before they came hither, have come here wholly free. The failing of the strength of the body of Míriel may then be ascribed, with some reason, to the evil of Arda Marred, and her death be a thing unnatural.' In FM 2 (p. 254) this thought, represented as a new perception on the part of the Valar, takes this form:

And the Valar were greatly concerned to see that all their labour for the guarding of Valinor was of no avail, to keep out evil and the shadow of Melkor, if any thing, living or unliving, was brought thither out of Middle-earth and left free or unguarded; and they perceived at last how great was the power of Melkor in Arda, in the making of which as it was his part was such that all things, *save in Aman alone*, had an inclination to evil and to perversion from their right forms and courses. Wherefore those whose being began in Arda, and who moreover were by nature a union of spirit and body, drawing the sustenance of the latter from Arda Marred, must ever be, in some degree, liable to grief, to do or to suffer things unnatural; and though dwelling in Aman might be a guard against this evil, it was not a full cure, unless in long ages.

This was largely retained in the final text FM 4 (p. 258, §11), though without the references to Aman; and Mandos expressly declared that

Death (i.e. of the Firstborn) is a consequence of the Marring of Arda (§12).

In the draft letter of 1958 cited above in reference to the death of Míriel my father continued:

I suppose a difference between this Myth and what may be perhaps called Christian mythology is this. In the latter the Fall of Man is subsequent to and a consequence (though not a necessary consequence) of the 'Fall of the Angels': a rebellion of created free-will at a higher level than Man; but it is not clearly held (and in many versions is not held at all) that this affected the 'World' in its nature: evil was brought in from outside, by Satan. In this Myth the rebellion of created free-will precedes creation of the World (Eä); Eä has in it, subcreatively introduced, evil, rebellious, discordant elements of its own nature already when the *Let it Be* was spoken. The Fall or corruption, therefore, of all things in it and all inhabitants of it, was a possibility if not inevitable.

In *Of Finwë and Míriel* all this is presented as a new perception, or at least as a greatly sharpened perception, by the Valar; and 'with this thought a shadow passed over the hearts of the Valar, presage of the sorrows which the Children should bring into the world.' One might wonder that it needed the death of Míriel to bring the Powers of Arda to this perception. One might wonder also how it should be that even in Aman none of the Eldar were drowned in the sea or missed their footing in the mountains and fell from a great height. This latter consideration is indeed countered to some degree by what is told of the corporeal nature of the Elves. Their bodies are described as closely analogous to those of mortal Men, but against this is to be set the following passage from *Laws and Customs* (p. 218):

The *fëar* of the Elves were destined to dwell in Arda for all the life of Arda, and the death of the flesh did not abrogate that destiny. Their *fëar* were tenacious therefore of life 'in the raiment of Arda', and far excelled the spirits of Men in power over that 'raiment', even from the first days protecting their bodies from many ills and assaults (such as disease), and healing them swiftly of injuries, so that they recovered from wounds that would have proved fatal to Men.

This, however, while diminishing the physical vulnerability of the Elves as compared with Men, does not alter the fact that the actual destruction of such bodies by violence is an inherent possibility in the nature of Arda: 'though the *fëa* cannot be broken or disintegrated by any violence from without, the *hröa* can be hurt and may be utterly destroyed' (*ibid.*). Very explicit are the words of Manwë in his final address to the Valar before the proclamation of the Statute (p. 244):

[The Elves] came into Arda Marred, and were destined to do so, and to endure the Marring, even though they came in their beginning from beyond Eä. ... We may say, therefore, that the Elves are destined to know 'death' in their mode, being sent into a world which contains 'death', and having a form for which 'death' is possible. For though by their prime nature, unmarred, they rightly dwell as spirit and body coherent, yet these are two things, not the same, and their severance (which is 'death') is a possibility inherent in their union.

But it is made plain that while, on the one hand, this possibility of 'death' for the Elves was a consequence of the Marring of Arda by Melkor, on the other hand the death of Míriel so gravely disquieted the Valar because it was the first that had taken place in Aman. Is it to be supposed, then, that until this time the Valar had been deluded, believing falsely that the incarnate Elves, *by the fact of their dwelling in Aman*, were protected from all possibility of the severance of spirit and body, in any of the ways that such severance might come about in Middle-earth – believing indeed that the Marring of Arda and the possibility of death for the incarnate had effect only east of the Great Sea, and only now discovering the falsity of this belief when Míriel died? (See the passage from 'text VII' on p. 400.)

The 'immortality' of the Elves (co-extensive with the 'life' of Arda), their deaths and rebirths, were deep-laid and fundamental elements in my father's conception. At this time he was subjecting these ideas to an elaborate analysis, and extending that analysis to the ideas of 'deathless Aman' and the significance of Melkor in the perversion of Creation as it had been expounded to the Ainur by Ilúvatar in the Beginning. This analysis is, in part, presented as a debate among the Valar themselves, in which they reach new perceptions concerning the nature of Arda; but the theoretical discussion of moral and natural laws is given an immediate dimension from its arising out of the strange story of the griefs of Finwë and Míriel. That story was retained in the published *Silmarillion*, but with no intimation of its implications for the Rulers of Arda and the loremasters of the Elves.

In these writings is seen my father's preoccupation in the years following the publication of *The Lord of the Rings* with the philosophical aspects of the mythology and its systemisation. Of the deliberations of the Gods the sages of the Eldar preserved a record among the books of their law. How far away from these grave Doctors seems the 'hornéd moon' that rode over Ælfwine's ship off the coasts of the Lonely Isle (II.321), as 'the long night of Faërie held on'! Ælfwine is still present as communicator and commentator; but there have been great changes in Elfinesse.

★

OF FËANOR AND THE UNCHAINING OF MELKOR

The previous 'sub-chapter' *Of Finwë and Míriel* has reached only, in terms of the earlier Chapter 6, to the end of §46b (p. 185). For the next section there are only two late texts, continuing straight on in the typescripts that I have called FM 3 and FM 4 (pp. 255–6): from this point it is convenient to call them 'A' and 'B'. A, though a finished text, is in effect a draft for the second typescript (B) that clearly followed it immediately, and need not be further considered beyond noting that it does not contain the new passage about Fëanor's wife, and that the title is *Of Fëanor and the Silmarils and the Darkening of Valinor*: this text makes no further subdivisions.

In this section my father did not greatly alter (except by the addition concerning Fëanor's wife) the text of LQ, §§46c–48, and the changes can be recorded without giving the whole text again. Very minor differences are not mentioned.

§46c The only difference here from LQ is that Fëanor's hair is said to have been 'raven-dark'. But at the end of the paragraph, after 'Seldom were the hand and mind of Fëanor at rest', the following passage was added:

> While still in early youth Fëanor wedded Nerdanel, a maiden of the Noldor; at which many wondered, for she was not among the fairest of her people. But she was strong, and free of mind, and filled with the desire of knowledge. In her youth she loved to wander far from the dwellings of the Noldor, either beside the long shores of the Sea or in the hills; and thus she and Fëanor had met and were companions in many journeys. Her father, Mahtan, was a great smith, and among those of the Noldor most dear to the heart of Aulë. Of Mahtan Nerdanel learned much of crafts that women of the Noldor seldom used: the making of things of metal and stone. She made images, some of the Valar in their forms visible, and many others of men and women of the Eldar, and these were so like that their friends, if they knew not her art, would speak to them; but many things she wrought also of her own thought in shapes strong and strange but beautiful.
>
> She also was firm of will, but she was slower and more patient than Fëanor, desiring to understand minds rather than to master them. When in company with others she would often sit still listening to their words, and watching their gestures and the movements of their faces. Her mood she bequeathed in part to some of her sons, but not to all. Seven sons she bore to Fëanor, and it is not recorded in the histories of old that any others of the Eldar had so many

children. With her wisdom at first she restrained Fëanor when the fire of his heart burned too hot; but his later deeds grieved her and they became estranged.

Now even while Fëanor and the craftsmen of the Noldor wrought with delight, foreseeing no end to their labours, and while the sons of Indis grew to manhood, the Noontide of Valinor was drawing to its close.

The text then continues as in LQ §47 (p. 185). – The name *Nerdanel* of Fëanor's wife was an emendation: the original name as typed was *Istarnië*.

§47 LQ 'at the feet of the gods' becomes 'at the feet of the Mighty'.
§48 'and most of all in the healing of the many hurts that he had done to the world. His prayer Nienna aided, but the others were silent.'

From LQ 'Wherefore in a while he was allowed to go freely about the land' the text was changed:

Therefore after a time Manwë gave him leave to go freely about the land. The evil that Melkor had wrought of old in wrath and malice was beyond full healing [cf. p. 259, §11], but his aid, if he would truly give it, would do more than aught else to amend the world. For Melkor was in his beginning the greatest of the Powers, and Manwë believed that if he were repentant he would regain in great part his first might and wisdom. On this path he judged that Melkor was now set, and would persevere if he were treated without grudge. Jealousy and rancour Manwë was slow to perceive, for he knew them not in himself; and he did not understand that all love had departed from the mind of Melkor for ever.

Ulmo, it is said, was not deceived; and Tulkas clenched his hands whenever he saw Melkor his foe go by, for if Tulkas is slow to wrath, he is slow also to forget. But they obeyed the ruling of Manwë; for those who will defend authority against rebellion must not themselves rebel.

OF THE SILMARILS AND THE UNREST OF THE NOLDOR

This chapter-heading is present only in the second of the two late typescripts (B), and it was there written in subsequently. The first of the texts (A) was still fairly close to LQ §§49–54; though many changes were introduced they are for the most part of slight if any narrative significance. Here again it was effectively a draft for the second text and need not be further considered. The second text, however, was much altered and expanded in the latter part of the 'sub-chapter'.

§49 Most fair of all was Melkor's countenance to the Eldar, and he aided them in many works, if they would let him. The Vanyar indeed held him in suspicion, for they dwelt in the light of the Trees and were content; and to the Teleri he gave little heed, deeming them of little worth, tools too weak for his designs. But the Noldor took delight in the hidden knowledge that he could reveal to them; and some hearkened to words that it would have been better for them never to have heard.

§49a In after days Melkor indeed declared that Fëanor had learned much art from him in secret; but that was only one of the many lies of Melkor, envying the skill of Fëanor and desiring to claim part in his works. For none of the Eldalië ever hated Melkor more than Fëanor son of Finwë, and though he was snared in the webs of Melkor's malice against the Valar, he held no converse with him in person, and he took no counsel from him. Indeed he sought the counsel of none that dwelt in Aman, great or small, save only and for a little while of Nerdanel the wise, his wife.

§49b In that time, but before Melkor was given his freedom within the land of Aman, those things were wrought that afterwards were the most renowned of all the works of the Elvenfolk. For Fëanor, being now come to his full might, was filled with a new thought, or maybe some shadow of foreboding came to him of the doom that drew near; and he pondered how the Light of the Trees, the glory of the Blessed Realm, might be preserved imperishable. Then he began a long and secret labour, and he summoned all his lore, and his power, and his subtle craft, for the making of jewels more marvellous than any that had yet been devised, whose beauty should last beyond the End.

Three jewels he made, and named them the Silmarils. A living fire burned within them that was blended of the Light of the Two Trees. Of their own radiance they shone, even in the dark of the deepest treasury; yet all lights that fell upon them, however faint, they received and returned again in marvellous hues to which their own inner fire gave a surpassing loveliness. No mortal flesh, nor hands unclean, nor anything of evil will could touch them, but it was scorched and withered; neither could they be broken by any strength within the Kingdom of Arda. The Silmarils the Eldar prized beyond all other treasures in Aman or upon Earth; and Varda hallowed them, and Mandos foretold that the fates of Arda, earth, sea, and air, lay locked within them. The heart of Fëanor was fast bound to these things that he himself had made.

§50 Then Melkor lusted also for the Silmarils; and from that time inflamed by this desire the malice of his heart grew greater, though naught of it could yet be seen in the semblance that he wore, or in the fair form that he assumed, after the manner of the Valar, his brethren.

Therefore, whenever he saw his chances, he began to sow a seed of falsehood and hints of evil among all who were open to his converse. But he did this with cunning, so that few who heard these lies ever took them from his own lips: they passed from friend to friend, as secrets the knowledge of which proves the teller wise; and in the telling they grew and spread, like weeds running up rank in shady places. Bitterly the people of the Noldor atoned for the folly of their open ears in days to come.

When he saw that many leaned towards him, Melkor would often walk among them, speaking ever words of greatest praise, sweet but poisoned honey; for amid all the fair words others were woven, so subtly that many who heard them believed in recollection that they arose from their own thought. Visions he would conjure up in their hearts of the mighty realms that they could have ruled at their own will in power and freedom in the East; and then whispers went abroad that the Valar had brought the Eldar to Aman because of their jealousy, fearing that the beauty of the Quendi and the makers' power that Ilúvatar had bequeathed to them would grow too great for the Valar to govern, as the Elvenfolk waxed and spread over the wide lands of the world.

In those days, moreover, though the Valar knew indeed of the coming of Men that were to be, the Elves as yet knew naught of it; for Manwë had not revealed it to them, and the time was not yet near. But Melkor spoke to them in secret of Mortal Men, seeing how the silence of the Valar might be twisted to evil. Little he knew yet concerning Men, for engrossed with his own thought in the Music he had paid small heed to the Second Theme of Ilúvatar; but now the whisper went among the Elves that Manwë held them captive, so that Men might come and supplant them in the dominions of the Middle-earth. For the Valar saw that this weaker and short-lived race would be more easily swayed by them. Alas! little have the Valar ever prevailed to sway the wills of Men; but many of the Noldor believed, or half believed, these evil words.

§51 Thus ere the Valar were aware, the peace of Valinor was poisoned. The Noldor began to murmur against them and all their kindred; and many became filled with vanity, forgetting how much of what they had and knew came to them in gift from the Valar. Fiercest burned the new flame of desire for freedom and wider realms in the eager heart of Fëanor; and Melkor laughed in his secrecy, for to that mark his lies had been addressed, hating Fëanor above all, and lusting ever for the Silmarils. But these he was not suffered to approach. For though at great feasts Fëanor would wear them blazing upon his brow, at other times they were guarded close, locked in the deep chambers of his hoard in Túna. There were no thieves in Valinor as yet; but Fëanor began to love the Silmarils with a greedy love, and grudged the sight of them to all, save to his father or to his sons. Seldom he remembered now that the light with which they were lit was not his own.

§52 High princes were Fëanor and Fingolfin, the elder sons of Finwë, honoured by all in Aman; but now they grew proud and jealous each of his rights and his possessions. And lo! Melkor then set new lies abroad, and whispers came to Fëanor that Fingolfin and his sons were plotting to usurp the leadership of Finwë and of the elder line of Fëanor, and to supplant them by the leave of the Valar: for the Valar were ill pleased that the Silmarils lay in Túna and were not given to their keeping. But to Fingolfin and Finarfin it was said: 'Beware! Small love has the proud son of Míriel ever had for the children of Indis. Now he has become great, and he has his father in his hand. It will not be long before he drives you forth from Túna!'

§52a It is told also that when Melkor saw that these lies were smouldering he began to speak, first to the sons of Fëanor, and at other times to the sons of Indis, concerning weapons and armour, and of the power that they give to him that has them to defend his own (as he said). Now the Quendi had possessed weapons in Middle-earth, but not of their own devising. They had been made by Aulë and sent as gifts by the hand of Oromë, when it became known to the Valar that the Quendi were beset by prowling evils that had discovered the places of their dwelling beside Cuiviénen; and more were sent later for the defence of the Eldar upon the Great March to the shores of the Sea. But all these were long unused, and lay in hoard as memorials of old days half-forgotten; and since the chaining of Melkor the armouries of the Valar also had been shut.

§52b But now the lords of the Noldor took out their swords and spears and sharpened them, re-strung their bows and filled their quivers with arrows. And they made shields in those days and emblazoned them with devices of silver and gold and gems. These only they wore abroad, and of other weapons they did not speak, for each believed that he alone had received the warning. But when Fëanor got wind of what was being done, he made for himself a secret forge, of which not even Melkor was aware; and there he wrought fell swords of tempered steel for himself and for his seven sons, and tall helms with plumes of red. Bitterly Mahtan rued the day when he had taught to the husband of Nerdanel, his daughter, all the lore of metal work that he learned of Aulë.

§52c Thus with lies and evil whisperings and false counsel Melkor kindled the hearts of the Noldor to strife; and of their quarrels came at length the end of the high days of Valinor and the evening of its ancient glory. For Fëanor now began openly to speak words of rebellion against the Valar, crying aloud that he would depart from Valinor back to the world without, and would deliver the Noldor from thraldom (as he said), if they would follow him.

§52d Then there was great unrest in Túna, and Finwë was troubled, and he summoned all his lords to council. But Fingolfin hastened to his halls and stood before him, saying: 'King and father, wilt thou not restrain the pride of our brother, Curufinwë, who is called the Spirit of Fire, all too truly? By what right does he speak for all our people, as were he king? Thou it was who long ago spoke before the Quendi, bidding them accept the guesting of the Mighty in Aman. Thou it was that led the Noldor upon the long road through the perilous Earth to the light of Eldanor. If this does not now repent thee, two sons at least thou hast to honour thy words!'

§52e But even as he spoke, suddenly Fëanor appeared, and he strode into the chamber tall and threatening. A fire of anger was in his eyes, and he was fully armed: his high helm upon his head, and at his side a mighty sword. 'So it is, even as I guessed,' he said: 'my half-brother would be before me with my father, in this as in all other matters. He would not wait for the council, where all words would be heard by all, and answered. He would speak against me in secret. This I will not brook!' he cried, turning upon Fingolfin. 'Get thee gone, and take thy due place!' Then as a flash of flame he drew his sword. 'Get thee gone and dare my wrath no longer!'

§52f Then Fingolfin bowed before Finwë, and without word or glance at Fëanor he went from the chamber. But Fëanor followed him, and at the door of the king's house he stayed him. The point of his bright sword he set against Fingolfin's breast. 'See, half-brother!' he said. 'This is sharper than thy tongue. Try but once more to usurp my place and the love of my father, and maybe it will rid the Noldor of a would-be master of thralls.'

§52g These words were heard by many, for the house of Finwë was in the great square beneath the Mindon, and many people were gathered there. But Fingolfin again made no answer, and passing through the throng in silence he went to seek Finarfin his brother.

§52h The unrest of the Noldor was not indeed hidden from the Valar; but its seed had been sown in the dark; and therefore, since Fëanor first spoke openly against the Valar, they deemed that he was the mover of discontent, being eminent in self-will and arrogance, though all the Noldor had become proud. It was, maybe, the nature of the Children that as they grew they should become wilful, and should desire to escape from tutelage, remembering it with little gratitude. Therefore Manwë was grieved, but he watched and said no word. The Valar had brought the Eldar to their land freely, to dwell or to depart; and though they might judge departure to be folly, it would not be lawful to restrain them from it, if wise counsel did not suffice.

§53 But now the deeds of Fëanor could not be passed over, and the Valar were wroth; and dismayed also, perceiving that more was at work than the wilfulness of youth. Therefore Manwë summoned Fëanor to appear before the Valar to answer for all his words and deeds, and he was brought to the gates of Valmar. Thither also were summoned all others who had any part in the matter, or any knowledge thereof, or any grievance of their own to declare.

§53a Then Mandos set Fëanor before him in the Ring of Doom and bade him answer to all that was asked of him. Great must be the power and will of any who would lie to Mandos, or even refuse his questioning. But Fëanor had no thought of it. He was so besotted with the lies of Melkor that had taken root in his proud heart (though he did not yet clearly perceive their source) that he judged himself justified in all points, and other judgement he scorned.

§53b But when all was said, and all the testimonies were spoken, and words and deeds were brought out of the dark into the light, then at last the root was laid bare: the malice of Melkor was revealed, and his lies and half-lies made plain for all to recognize who had the will to see. Straightway Tulkas was sent from the council to lay hands on Melkor and bring him again to judgement. But Fëanor was not held wholly guiltless in himself. For he had forged secret swords, and had drawn one in anger unjustified, threatening the life of his kinsman.

§53c Therefore Mandos said to him: 'Thou speakest of thraldom. If thraldom it be, thou canst not escape it. For Manwë is King of Arda, and not of Aman only. And this deed was unlawful, whether in Aman or not in Aman. Though more insolent in Aman, for it is a hallowed land. Therefore this doom is now made: for twelve years thou shalt leave Túna where this threat was uttered. In that time take counsel with thyself, and remember who and what thou art. But after that time this matter shall be set in peace and held redressed, if others will release thee.'

§53d Then Fingolfin rose and said: 'I will release my brother.' But Fëanor spoke no word in answer; and when he had stood silent before the Valar for a while, he turned and left the council and departed from Valmar. At once he returned to Túna, and before the term of seven days that was set, he gathered his goods and his treasures and left the city and went far away. With him went his sons, and Finwë his father, who would not be parted from him, in fault or guiltless, and some others also of the Noldor. But Nerdanel would not go with him, and she asked leave to abide with Indis, whom she had ever esteemed, though this had been little to the liking of Fëanor. Northward in Valinor, in the hills near to the halls of Mandos, Fëanor and his sons made a strong place and a treasury at Formenos, and they laid in hoard a multitude of gems, and weapons also: they did not put aside the swords that Fëanor had made. But Fingolfin now ruled the Noldor in Túna; and thus the very words of Melkor seemed to be fulfilled (though it was Fëanor who had by his own deeds brought this thing to pass);

and the bitterness that Melkor had sown endured, even though his lies had been made manifest. Long afterward it lived still between Fëanor and the sons of Indis.

§54 Worse now befell. In vain Tulkas sought for Melkor. For Melkor, knowing that his devices were revealed, hid himself and passed from place to place as a cloud in the hills. And though none could discover whither he had gone, it seemed that the light of Valinor was dimmed, and the shadows of all standing things grew longer and darker in that time. It is said that for two years no one in Valinor saw Melkor again, nor heard any rumour of him, until suddenly he sought out Fëanor. Secretly he came to Formenos, in guise as a traveller that seeks for lodging; and he spoke with Fëanor before his door. Friendship he feigned with cunning argument, urging him to his former thought of flight from the trammels of the Valar.

'Behold the truth of all that I have spoken, and how thou art banished unjustly,' he said. 'But if the heart of Fëanor is still undaunted, as it was in Túna, then I will aid him and bring him far from this narrow land. For am I not Vala also? Yea, and more than those who sit here in pride. I have ever been a friend of the Noldor, knowing their worth: the most skilled and the most valiant of all the folk of Arda.'

Now Fëanor's heart was still bitter at his humiliation before Mandos, and for a moment he paused and looked at Melkor in silence, wondering if indeed he might trust him so far at least as to aid his escape. But Melkor's cunning overreached his aim, and seeing Fëanor hesitate, and knowing that the Silmarils held his heart in thrall, he said at the last: 'Here is a strong place well guarded, but think not that the Silmarils will lie safe in any treasury within the realm of the Valar!'

Then the fires of the heart of Fëanor were kindled, and his eyes blazed; and his sight burned through all the fair-semblance of Melkor to the dark depths of his mind, perceiving there his fierce lust for the Silmarils. Then hate overcame Fëanor's fear, and he spoke shamefully to Melkor, saying: 'Get thee from my gate, gangrel! Thou jail-crow of Mandos!' And he shut the door of his house in the face of the mightiest of all the dwellers in Eä.

Then Melkor departed in shame, for he was himself in peril, and he saw not his time yet for revenge; but his heart was black with anger. And Finwë was filled with great dread, and in haste he sent messengers to Manwë in Valmar.

Commentary

In the first part of this 'sub-chapter' *Of the Silmarils and the Unrest of the Noldor* the story as it was told in LQ (pp. 184 ff.) was scarcely changed even in detail, despite the many changes of wording introduced in this last version – except in the matter of the weapons of the Eldar (§§52a,b). In QS, where the matter first entered (V.228, note by Pengoloð to §49), it was said that 'the Elves had before possessed only weapons of the chase, spears and bows and arrows', but that now, under the influence of Melkor, the Noldor 'learned the fashioning of swords of tempered steel, and the making of mail' and shields. This was rewritten in LQ §50 (p. 188), still as an observation made by Pengoloð, to read that the Elves had originally possessed *no* weapons, and that now they learned the making of all kinds of arms, swords, spears, bows and arrows. Similarly in AAm §97 (p. 96): 'Melkor spoke to the Eldar concerning weapons, which they had not before possessed or known'; but my father afterwards noted on the typescript of AAm (p. 106, §97): 'No! They must have had weapons on the Great Journey.' Feeling a need to explain how the Quendi survived 'amid the deceits of the starlit dusk', and concluding that they must have been armed in Middle-earth, he adopted the (to my mind) somewhat mechanical narrative device introduced here (§52a).

Explanations in such a world may prompt unneeded reflections. The passage of Oromë on his horse Nahar from Aman to Middle-earth is never described, nor (I would say) need it be, nor should it be; the movements of the great Valar (and indeed of the lesser divine, as Melian) are a mystery that we do not seek to penetrate. They are from beyond Arda and do not derive from it. In the (very old) story of the transportation of the three original Elvish 'ambassadors' from Kuiviénen to Valinor we might wonder with more right, perhaps, how they journeyed, for the Elves, whatever their powers, are Children of Earth, and must live and move in the physical world of Arda. My father never said any more about that; and we may suppose, if we will, that they passed over the Grinding Ice, borne upon Nahar.* But that he perceived a need to respond, at a certain level, to speculation of this kind is apparent from this story of Oromë's bringing to the Eldar a great store of weapons made in Valinor – for the store must have been great to be useful in the protection of such a host.

In the latter part of the new version the story is greatly developed, and yet not in such a way as to contradict the earlier versions – which can be read as a synopsis of the latest. It may indeed be that the story

---

* Cf. the story referred to in the old 'Sketch of the Mythology', that 'Lúthien went even over the Grinding Ice, aided by the power of her divine mother, Melian, to Mandos' halls' (IV.25, 55).

of Fëanor's fierce encounter with Fingolfin in the house of Finwë was present to my father's mind already when he wrote LQ (end of §52), though he did not actually recount it till much later.

It is worth remarking that in writing the new version he also had an eye to AAm; thus in §54 he took up the words of Melkor to Fëanor at Formenos in AAm §101 (p. 97) – though removing the sentence 'And think not that the Silmarils lie safe in any treasury within the realm of the gods' from its place in AAm and using it as it was used in LQ, the sudden clue for Fëanor of Melkor's true intention.

There remain a few isolated points. In both texts of the last version occurs the phrase in §49b: 'The Silmarils the Eldar prized beyond all other treasures *in Aman or upon Earth*'. This usage goes back a long way (see the Index to Vol.IV, entries *Earth* and *World*), unsuitable as it may seem to the world in which Aman was physically approachable across the Sea. But the Earth is Middle-earth: it is not the equivalent of Arda; cf. also §52d: 'Thou it was that led the Noldor upon the long road through the perilous Earth to the light of Eldanor.'

It is also curious that *Túna* is now used at every occurrence, not *Tirion*; see p. 90, §67, and p. 193, §52.

In §50 it is said of Melkor that 'Little he knew yet concerning Men, for engrossed with his own thought in the Music he had paid small heed to the Second Theme of Ilúvatar'. Compare the *Ainulindalë* (both the C and D texts) §13: the Children of Ilúvatar 'came with the Third Theme', and §24: Manwë 'was the chief instrument of the second Theme that Ilúvatar had raised up against the discord of Melkor.' See further p. 358 note 10.

The names *Fingolfin* and *Finarfin* are thus spelt in B, but in A *Fingolphin* and *Finarphin* (see p. 265 note 10). In the Second Edition of *The Lord of the Rings* (1966) *Finarphin* was spelt thus, later changed on my suggestion to *Finarfin* (Appendix F, *Of the Elves*).

OF THE DARKENING OF VALINOR

The first of the two late typescripts (A) comes to an end after a few lines of this next 'sub-chapter', in which LQ §55 was followed virtually word for word; and it ends at exactly the same point as does the LQ rewriting of QS (see p. 190 and note 8). For the next part of the narrative, therefore, we have on the one hand the text of QS (§§55-9), with the very few revisions that had been made to it in the revision of 1951, and on the other the much later and very greatly expanded version that follows here, extant throughout almost all its length only in the one typescript B. There is also a single typescript page, intermediate between A and B, which extends a short way further than does A; and much extremely rough working for the chapter in its late form which is for the most part scarcely legible.

Much of this final version of the story of Melkor and Ungoliantë and the destruction of the Trees stands in such close relationship to AAm that it would be possible, for some sections of the text, to be content with reference to AAm and notes of the differences; nonetheless I give the text in full, for these reasons. First, because despite the closeness to AAm there is also a major transformation of the legend; and second, because the relation between the two traditions, *The Silmarillion* and the *Annals*, here takes a new turn, and this is important for the understanding of the nature of the published *Silmarillion*, and its justification. It would be less easy to follow these interesting developments if part of the text appeared only in notes referring to another text.

§55 Now the Valar were sitting in council before the gates of Valmar, fearing the lengthening of the shadows, when the messengers came from Finwë. At once Oromë and Tulkas sprang up, but even as they set out in pursuit other messengers brought tidings from Eldanor. Melkor had fled through the Kalakiryan, and from the hill of Túna the Elves had seen him pass in wrath as a thunder-cloud. 'Then,' said they, 'he turned northward, and our kinsfolk in Alqualondë report that his Shadow went by their haven towards Araman.'

Thus Melkor departed from Valinor, and for a while the Two Trees shone again unshadowed and the land was filled with light; yet as a cloud far off that looms ever higher, borne upon a slow cold wind, a doubt now marred the joy of all the dwellers in Aman, dreading they knew not what evil that yet might come.

§55a When Manwë heard of the ways that Melkor had taken, it seemed plain to him that Melkor purposed to escape to his old strongholds in the North of Middle-earth, as was indeed his most likely course. Though there was little hope in this, Oromë and Tulkas with many of their folk went with all speed northward, seeking to overtake him if they might; but they found no trace or rumour of him beyond the shores of the Teleri, and in the unpeopled wastes that draw near to the Ice they could hear no tidings even from the birds. Therefore at length they returned, but the watch was redoubled along all the northern fences of Aman.

§55b This indeed Melkor had expected; but he had other things to do before he would return to Middle-earth, and ere the pursuit set out, indeed ere the messengers came to Valmar, he had turned back and in great secrecy passed away far to the

South. For Melkor was yet as one of the Valar, and he could still (though with pain) change his form, or walk unclad, as could his brethren; though that power he was soon to lose for ever.

§55c Thus unseen he came at last to the region that once was called Avathar,* beneath the eastern feet of the Pelóri; a narrow land it had become, eaten away by the Sea, and was long forsaken. There the shadows were deepest and thickest in the world. In Avathar, secret and unknown save to Melkor, dwelt Ungoliantë, and she had taken spider's form, and was a weaver of dark webs. It is not known whence she came, though among the Eldar it was said that in ages long before she had descended from the darkness that lies about Arda, when Melkor first looked down in envy upon the light in the kingdom of Manwë. But she had disowned her Master, desiring to be mistress of her own lust, taking all things to herself to feed her emptiness. To the South she had fled, and so had escaped the assaults of the Valar and the hunters of Oromë, for their vigilance had ever been to the North, and the South was long unheeded. Thence she had crept towards the light of the Blessed Realm; for she hungered for light and hated it.

§55d In a ravine she lived and wove her black webs in a cleft of the mountains. All light she sucked up and spun it forth in dark nets of gloom. But now she was famished, and in great torment; for all living things had fled far away, and her own webs shut out from her all light that could come to her dwelling, whether through passes in the walls of Aman, or from the heavens above. Yet she had no longer the strength or will to depart.

§56 Now Melkor sought for her, and he put on again the form that he had worn as the tyrant of Utumno: a dark Lord, tall and terrible. In that form he remained ever after. And when Ungoliantë saw him coming she was afraid, knowing his hatred for all who tried to escape from him. She shrank into her deepest lair, and tried to shroud herself in new shadow; but such darkness as in her famine she could weave was no defence against the eyes of Melkor, Lord of Utumno and Angband.

§56a 'Come forth!' he said. 'Thrice fool: to leave me first, to dwell here languishing within reach of feasts untold, and now to shun me, Giver of Gifts, thy only hope! Come forth and see! I have brought thee an earnest of greater bounty to follow.' But

---

* [footnote to the text] The Shadows (in ancient Quenya).

Ungoliantë made no answer, and retreated deeper into the cloven rock. Then Melkor was angered, for he was in haste, having reckoned his times to a nicety. 'Come out!' he cried. 'I have need of thee and will not be denied. Either thou wilt serve me, or I will bury thee here and under black stone thou shalt wither into naught.' Then suddenly he held up in his hands two shining gems. They were green, and in that lightless place they reflected the dreadful light of his eyes, as if some ravening beast had come hunting there. Thus the great Thief set his lure for the lesser.

§56b Slowly Ungoliantë came forth; but as she drew near Melkor withheld the lure. 'Nay, nay,' he said. 'I do not bring thee these Elvish sweets in love or in pity; they are to strengthen thee, when thou hast agreed to do my bidding.' 'What is your bidding, Master?' she said, and her eyes gloated upon the gems.

§56c There in the black shadows, beyond the sight even of Manwë in his highest halls, Melkor with Ungoliantë plotted his revenge. But when Ungoliantë understood his purpose, she was torn between great lust and great fear. She would not dare the perils of Aman, or the power of the dreadful Lords, without a great reward; for she feared the eyes of Manwë and Varda more even than the wrath of Melkor. Therefore Melkor said to her: 'Do as I bid, and if thou art still hungry when we meet again, then, I vow, I will give to thee whatsoever thy lust may demand. Yea, with both hands!' Lightly he made this vow (as he ever did), thinking little of its fulfilment, and he laughed in his heart; for if she achieved his design, he would have no need, he thought, to appease her, or any one else in Arda, great or small.

§56d 'Come then!' he said. 'Here is the earnest!' And he delivered the gems to her, not only the first two but many others that he had stolen in Valinor. Then swiftly Ungoliantë began to grow again and to find new strength. A cloak of darkness she wove about herself: an unlight, in which things seemed to be no more, and which eyes could not pierce, for it was void. Then slowly she wrought her webs: rope by rope from cleft to cleft, from jutting rock to pinnacle of stone, ever climbing upwards, crawling and clinging, until at last she achieved the very summit of Mount Hyarmentir, the highest mountain in that region of the world, far south of great Taniquetil. There the Valar were not vigilant; for west of the Pelóri was an empty land in twilight, until northward one came to the tall fences of the woods of Oromë; and eastward the mountains looked out, save for forgotten Avathar, only upon the dim waters of the pathless Sea.

§57 But now upon the mountain-top dark Ungoliantë lay. For a while she rested, and with eyes faint from labour she saw the glimmer of the stars in the dome of Varda and the radiance of Valmar far away. Slowly her eyes wakened and took fire, and her lust increased until it overcame her fear. She began in stealth to creep down into the Blessed Realm.

§57a Still in the dark depths Melkor stood, gnawing his mind, between evil hope and doubt; but when he had stood, revolving his chances, as long as his urgency allowed, he turned away and went down to the shore. There he cursed the Sea, saying: 'Slime of Ulmo! I will conquer thee yet, shrivel thee to a stinking ooze. Yea, ere long Ulmo and Ossë shall wither, and Uinen crawl as a mud-worm at my feet!' With that suddenly he passed from Avathar and went to do his will.

§58 [see AAm §§109–10] Now it was a time of festival, as Melkor knew well. In Aman all tides and seasons were at the will of the Valar, and there was no winter of death; but even as it was the delight of the Valar to clothe themselves in the forms of the Children of Ilúvatar,* so also they would eat and drink and gather the fruits of Yavanna, and share the bounty of the Earth which under Eru they had made. Therefore Yavanna set times for the flowering and the ripening of all growing things in Valinor: upspringing, blooming, and seed-time. And after the coming of the First-born Children, the Eldar, at these times they made feasts, at which all the dwellers in Aman would assemble in mirth. The greatest of the feasts was at the first gathering of fruits, and this was held upon Taniquetil; for Manwë decreed that at this time all should join in the praise of Eru Ilúvatar, and the peoples of Valinor, Valar, Maiar, and Eldar, poured forth their joy in music and song.

§58a This day had now come once more, and Manwë prepared a feast greater than any that had been held since the entry of the Eldar into Aman. For though the escape of Melkor portended toils and sorrows to come, and indeed none could tell what further hurts would be done to Arda, ere he could be subdued again, at this time Manwë desired to unite all his people once more in joy, healing all that was amiss, and

---

* [footnote to the text] As is told in the *Ainulindalë*. [The same reference to the *Ainulindalë* (§25) is made in AAm §109.]

strengthening them with the blessing of Eru to hold ever in heart the hope of Arda Unmarred. He bade all come who would, but the Noldor above all; for he hoped that there they would put aside the griefs that lay between their lords, and forget utterly the lies of their Enemy. Therefore he sent a messenger to Formenos, saying: 'Fëanor son of Finwë, come and do not deny my bidding! In my love thou remainest and wilt be honoured in my hall.'

§58b [*see* AAm §111] There came the Vanyar, and there came the Noldor of Túna, and the Maiar were gathered together, and the Valar were arrayed in their beauty and majesty; and they sang before Manwë and Varda in the halls of Taniquetil, or played and danced upon the green slopes of the Mountain that looked west to the Trees. In that day the streets of Valmar were empty, and the stairs of Túna were silent, and all the land lay sleeping in peace. Only the Teleri beyond the mountains still sang upon the shores of the Sea; for they recked little of seasons or times, and gave no thought to the cares of the King of Arda, or to the shadow that had fallen upon Valinor; for it had not touched them, as yet.

§58c [*see* AAm §112] One thing only marred the hope of Manwë. Fëanor came indeed, for he read the message of Manwë as a command; but Finwë would not come and remained in Formenos, and with him were the sons of Fëanor. For said Finwë: 'While the ban lasts upon Fëanor, my son, that he may not go to Túna, I hold myself unkinged, and I will not meet my people.' And Fëanor did not come in raiment of festival, and he wore no ornament, neither silver nor gold nor any gem; and he denied the sight of the Silmarils to the Valar and the Eldar, and left them in Formenos, locked in a chamber of iron.

Nonetheless he met Fingolfin before the throne of Manwë, and was reconciled in word. For Fingolfin held forth his hand, saying: 'As I promised, I do now. I release thee, and remember no grievance.'

Then Fëanor took his hand in silence; but Fingolfin said: 'Half-brother in blood, full brother in heart I will be. Thou shalt lead and I will follow. May no new grief divide us!'

'I hear thee,' said Fëanor. 'So be it!' But they did not know then the full meaning that their words would bear.

§58d [*see* AAm §113] It is told that even as Fëanor and Fingolfin stood before Manwë, there came the Mingling of the Lights, and both Trees were shining, and the silent city of

Valmar was filled with a radiance of silver and gold. And in that very hour Ungoliantë came hastening over the fields of Valinor. Hunger and thirst now drove her. No longer she crept but ran, as the shadow of a black cloud upon the wind fleets over the sunlit earth. Now she came to the Green Mound of the Corolairë, and her Unlight rose up even to the roots of the Trees. Then with her black beak she pierced their rind, wounded them deep; and their juices gushed forth and she drank them up. But when no more flowed she set her mouth to the wounds, and sucked them dry, and the poison of Death that was in her went into their tissues and withered them, root, branch, and leaf, and they died. And still Ungoliantë thirsted; and she went to the great Wells of Varda and drained them dry. And as she drank, she belched forth vast vapours, and in their midst she swelled to a shape more huge and hideous than even her most lustful dream had hoped ever to achieve. At last, knowing that the time was short, she hastened away, north, to the tryst that Melkor had made with her, and did not mean to keep.

§58e Outside he had lurked, until the failing of the Light announced that Ungoliantë had done her work. Then through the Kalakiryan, now only a dim ravine in walls of shadow, he came striding back, Lord of Utumno, a black shape of hate, visiting the places of his humiliation with revenge. All the land fell swiftly through grey twilight into night as Melkor stood within the Ring of Doom and cursed it; and he defiled the judgement seat of Manwë and threw down the thrones of the Valar.

§58f Then he went on to his second mark, which he had kept secret in his mind; but Ungoliantë was aware of him, and turning swiftly she overtook him on his road. Aghast indeed was Melkor to see her, monstrous, grown to a lust and power that he could not master without aid. He could not contend with her, even if time allowed; and he could not escape. She took him into her Unlight, and they went on together to the one place in the land of the Valar that he would have hidden from her.

§59 [see AAm §114] So the great Darkness came upon Valinor. Of the deeds of that time much is told in the *Aldudénië*** that Elemmírë of the Vanyar made and is known to all the Eldar. Yet no song or tale could contain all the grief and terror

---

* [footnote to the text] The Lament for the Two Trees.

that then came upon the Blessed Realm. The Light went out; but the Darkness that followed was more than loss. In that hour the dwellers in Aman knew the Unlight, and it seemed not lack, but a thing with being of its own, that made by malice out of Light had the power to pierce the eye, to enter heart and mind and strangle the very will.

§59a [*see* AAm §115]   Varda looked down from the Holy Mountain, and she beheld the Shadow soaring up in sudden towers of gloom. Valmar was blotted out, and all the land foundered in a deep sea of night. Soon Taniquetil stood alone, a last island in a drowned world. All song ceased. There was silence in Valinor, and no sound could be heard, save only from afar there came on the wind through the pass of the mountains the wailing of the Teleri like the cold cry of gulls. For it blew chill from the East in that hour, and the vast shadows of the Sea were rolled against the walls of the shore.

§59b [*see* AAm §116]   Then Manwë went up to his high seat upon the mountain-top, and he looked out, and his eyes pierced through the night, until they saw within the dark a Darkness which they could not penetrate, huge but far away, moving now northward with great speed; and he knew that Melkor had come and gone. Then the Valar began their pursuit; and soon the earth shook beneath the horses of the host of Oromë, and the fire that was stricken from the hooves of Nahar was the first light that returned to Valinor. But when the riding of the wrath of the Valar came up with the Cloud of Ungoliantë all were blinded and dismayed, and the host was scattered, and they went this way and that, they knew not whither. In vain Oromë wound his horn, for the Valaróma was choked and gave no sound. Tulkas was as a man caught in a black net at night, and he stood powerless and beat the air in vain. And when the Cloud had passed, it was too late. Melkor had gone whither he would, and his vengeance was achieved.

Commentary

Leaving for a moment the remarkable narrative shift in this 'subchapter' *Of the Darkening of Valinor*, the new version introduces many elements lacking in the old story: among the most important being the origin of Ungoliantë; the account of the festival in Valinor, with the 'investing' of the Valar in the form of the Children of Ilúvatar and their partaking of the physical celebration of the harvest; Manwë's purpose to achieve concord among the Noldor; Finwë's refusal to leave Formenos while Fëanor was banished from Tirion; and the reconciliation of Fëanor with Fingolfin before Manwë's throne. But all these are present in the *Annals of Aman*, and largely in the same words. My father, very obviously, had AAm in front of him; as has been seen (pp. 191–2), LQ and AAm were very close in the earlier part of the now replaced Chapter 6, and while LQ ceases at the point where Melkor goes to Arvalin AAm does not, but continues on (§§105–16) in the same larger fashion, expanding the old story while retaining the structure of the *Quenta* tradition.

Now, however, in this final version of the *Quenta*, my father returned to the *Annals* and used them for the further expansion of the other – increasingly hard to differentiate – 'tradition'. Schematically:

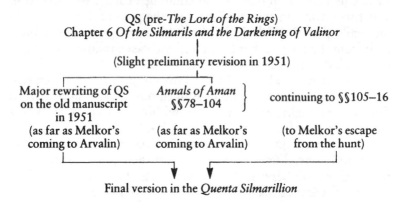

That in the pre-*The Lord of the Rings* period the *Annals of Valinor* and the *Annals of Beleriand* constituted distinct entities, forming with the *Quenta Silmarillion* a tripartite work, is very clear (see IV.284); and a list of the constituent parts of the Matter of Middle-earth associated with the long letter to Milton Waldman (see p. 3) shows that this was still the case, in theory at least, in 1951.

Yet we have seen how close the versions did in fact become in the course of the 1951 revision; and now, in the last phase of his work on the actual narratives, when (as I have suggested, p. 142) my father was envisaging a 're-expansion' of the whole, a new conception of *The Silmarillion*, a new and much fuller mode of narrative, he derived entire passages from the *Annals* with scarcely any significant change. I have said (p. 192) that AAm and the rewriting (LQ) of the first part of Chapter 6, as I think clearly contemporary, are too similar in every aspect, if continually different in actual wording, to be regarded as the product of a separate tradition of learning and memory, or even as the product of two different 'loremasters'; but the relation of this last version of the *Silmarillion* tradition to AAm on which it draws seems to show that my father had now ceased to regard them as different works. It may be, though I have no other evidence for it, that if he had continued this last version he would have 'cannibalised' the *Annals* wherever he chose to, regarding the latter now as no more than a constituent draft text for the sole work that was to emerge: *The Silmarillion*.

To turn now to the major departure from the old legend – which goes back to the original tale of *The Theft of Melko and the Darkening of Valinor* (I.152–3): *Melkor was not present at the destruction of the Trees*. When Ungoliantë climbs Mount Hyarmentir he stays for a while beside her lair; goes down then to the shores of Avathar and curses the Sea; lurks outside the Pelóri until the great darkness falls; then hastens through the pass to Valmar to desecrate the Ring of Doom. Why was this done? Not, surely, to bring in the casting down by Melkor of the thrones of the Valar – for this could have been achieved without altering the story, or at any rate without altering it so radically. The reason for the change, I think, was that my father found it unacceptable that Melkor should have risked allowing Ungoliantë to come anywhere near the Silmarils. In the new story, Melkor's plan was to wait until she had destroyed the Trees and then go alone in the darkness to Formenos. The tryst 'that Melkor had made with her, and did not mean to keep' (§58d) was not at Formenos – that being 'his second mark, which he had kept secret in his mind' (§58f); that is why it is said that Ungoliantë 'turned swiftly' and overtook him. Then 'they went on together to the one place in the land of the Valar that he would have hidden from her.'

Other features of this text are discussed under individual paragraphs.

§§55, 55b There now appears the story that after Melkor was seen from the hill of Túna passing through the Kalakiryan he turned northwards up the coast into Araman; but this was a feint, and he turned back southwards in secret and came into Avathar to find Ungoliantë. (I suggested (I.157), perhaps too positively, that the germ of this northward movement on the part of Melkor is to be found in the old *Tale* (I.145), where Melko originally 'purposed to get to northward over the passes nigh to Mandos', but thought better of it. There is indeed no trace of the idea in any intervening version; but features apparently long lost do undoubtedly emerge again.)

§55a 'Melkor purposed to escape to *his old strongholds* in the North of Middle-earth': i.e. Utumno and Angband. See p. 156, §12.

§55c Here first appears the name *Avathar*, and the ancient name *Arvalin* at last disappears. In the short intermediate typescript referred to on p. 282 the name is not *Avathar* but *Vastuman* (typed over *Arvalin*). *Vastuman* is not translated.

§56d *Hyarmentir* replaces *Hyarantar* of AAm §107.

§57 'The glimmer of the stars in the dome of Varda': on the Dome of Varda see pp. 385–8.

§58d *Corolairë*: see AAm §122 (pp. 107, 127). – *The Wells of Varda*: see p. 157, §17.

§59 The *Aldudénië* of *Elemmírë* is named also in AAm §114 (*Elemírë*; later *Elemmírë*, p. 106).

Entirely new are the statements that Melkor 'could still (though with pain) change his form, or walk unclad', but that at the time of his meeting with Ungoliantë he appeared as the Dark Lord of Utumno, and never again changed from that appearance afterwards (§§55b, 56). He is now explicitly the Master of Ungoliantë (§§56a, b); cf. AAm §106: 'It may well be that ... she was in the beginning one of those that he had corrupted to his service.' The narrative is greatly expanded by the account of his persuasion of Ungoliantë and his luring of her by gems stolen in Valinor – giving her strength also to dare the deed: for the great spider was weak through famine of light (§55d).

THE LATER DEVELOPMENT OF CHAPTER 7

The late typescript B follows straight on from 'Melkor had gone whither he would, and his vengeance was achieved' at the end of the 'sub-chapter' *Of the Darkening of Valinor* (p. 289), with no more than a space, but my father afterwards wrote in a heading [*Of*] *The Rape of the Silmarils*; further on there is a typed heading *Of the Thieves' Quarrel*.

As in the preceding 'sub-chapter', the end of which corresponds to the end of the former Chapter 6 (QS Chapter 4), he again turned to the *Annals of Aman*, and in this case he adopted substantial parts of the older text so closely that the new is almost an exact copy, with only a word or two changed here and there (on the implications of his thus amalgamating the two 'traditions' see pp. 289–91). But he also introduced a new element into the narrative: the attack by Melkor on Formenos reported by Maedros (as his name is here spelt: in a late emendation to LQ Chapter 5 *Maedhros*, p. 177, §41). Only now do the sons of Fëanor play a part in this story: see p. 123, §122.

I do not give the text in the sections where it becomes scarcely distinct from that of AAm. The paragraph numbers here begin a new series, since they cannot be usefully related to those of QS.

OF THE RAPE OF THE SILMARILS

§1 When the Trees should have flowered for yet one more day, but time was blind and unmeasured, the Valar returned to the Ring of Doom. They sat upon the ground, for their thrones were defiled, and they were in dark raiment of grief. About them was a great concourse of folk, hardly to be seen; for it was night. But the stars of Varda now glimmered overhead, and the air was clean. The winds of Manwë had driven the vapours of death far away and rolled back the shadows of the Sea. Now Yavanna arose and stood upon the Green Mound, but it was bare and black. She laid her hands upon the Trees, but they were dead and dark; and each branch that she touched broke and fell lifeless at her feet. Then the voices of all the host were lifted in lamentation; and it seemed to those that mourned that they had drained to the dregs the cup of woe that Melkor had filled for them. But it was not so.

§§2–3 *For Yavanna spoke before the Valar, saying* ... These paragraphs, in which the demand is made upon Fëanor that the light of the Silmarils be released for the saving of the Trees, are almost identical to AAm §§118–19 (p. 107), with only a very few changes of no significance, as 'Fëanor answered no word': 'Fëanor made no answer'.

§§4–5 *But Fëanor spoke then, and cried bitterly* ... These paragraphs are virtually identical to AAm §§120–1, except at the end of §120 and the beginning of §121. In AAm Fëanor declared that he would be the first to die 'of all the Children of Eru', but on the typescript of AAm, after the emergence of the story of Míriel, my father corrected 'I shall die' to 'I shall be slain', and this change was taken up here. The form of the passage in the new version has been given and discussed on pp. 268–9.

§6 'Thou hast spoken,' said Mandos. Then again there was silence, and thought was stilled. But after a while Nienna arose, and she went up onto the Mound; and she cast back her grey hood, and her eyes shone like stars in the rain, for her tears were poured out, and she washed away the defilements of Ungoliantë. And when she had wept she sang slowly, mourning for the bitterness of the world and all hurts of the Marring of Arda.

§7 But even as she mourned, there was heard the sound of feet hastening in the night. Then through the throng came the sons of Fëanor, flying from the North, and they bore new tidings of evil. Maedros spoke for them. 'Blood and darkness!' he cried. 'Finwë the king is slain, and the Silmarils are gone!'

Then Fëanor fell upon his face and lay as one dead, until the full tale was told.

§8 'My lord,' said Maedros to Manwë, 'it was the day of festival, but the king was heavy with grief at the departure of my father, a foreboding was on him. He would not go from the house. We were irked by the idleness and silence of the day, and we went riding towards the Green Hills. Our faces were northward, but suddenly we were aware that all was growing dim. The Light was failing. In dread we turned and rode back in haste, seeing great shadows rise up before us. But even as we drew near to Formenos the darkness came upon us; and in the midst was a blackness like a cloud that enveloped the house of Fëanor.

§9 'We heard the sound of great blows struck. Out of the cloud we saw a sudden flame of fire. And then there was one piercing cry. But when we urged on our horses they reared and cast us to the ground, and they fled away wild. We lay upon our faces without strength; for suddenly the cloud came on, and for a while we were blind. But it passed us by and moved away north at great speed. Melkor was there, we do not doubt. But not he alone! Some other power was with him, some huge evil: even as it passed it robbed us of all wit and will.

§10 'Darkness and blood! When we could move again we came to the house. There we found the king slain at the door. His head was crushed as with a great mace of iron. We found no others: all had fled, and he had stood alone, defiant. That is plain; for his sword lay beside him, twisted and untempered as if by lightning-stroke. All the house was broken and ravaged. Naught is left. The treasuries are empty. The chamber of iron is torn apart. The Silmarils are taken!'

§11 [see AAm §123] Then suddenly Fëanor rose, and lifting up his hand before Manwë he cursed Melkor, naming him Morgoth, the Black Foe of the world.* And he cursed also the summons of Manwë and the hour in which he came to Taniquetil, thinking in the madness of his grief that had he been at Formenos, his strength would have availed more than to be slain also, as Morgoth had purposed. Then with a cry he ran from the Ring of Doom and fled into the night, distraught; for his father was dearer to him than the Light of Valinor or the peerless works of his hands: and who among sons, of Elves or of Men, have held their fathers of greater worth?

* [footnote to the text] By that name only was he known to the Eldar ever after. (In the ancient form used by Fëanor it was *Moriñgotho*.) [Cf. the note added in LQ to QS §60 (p. 194), where the ancient form is *Moringotto*.]

§12 [see AAm §124]   After him Maedros and his brethren went in haste, dismayed, for they had not known that he was present when Maedros spoke; and now they feared that he might slay himself. All those who saw Fëanor's anguish grieved for him and forgave all his bitterness. But his loss was not his alone. Yavanna wept even as Nienna, in dread lest the Darkness should now swallow the last rays of the Light of Valinor for ever. For though the Valar did not yet understand fully what had befallen, they perceived that Melkor had called upon some aid that came from beyond Arda.

The Silmarils had passed away, and all one it may seem whether Fëanor had said yea or nay to Yavanna. Yet, had he said yea at the first, and so cleansed his heart ere the dreadful tidings came, his after-deeds would have been other than they proved. But now the doom of the Noldor drew near.

OF THE THIEVES' QUARREL

§13   Meanwhile, it is told, Morgoth escaping from the pursuit of the Valar came to the wastes of Araman. This land lay northward between the Mountains of the Pelóri and the Great Sea, as Avathar lay to the south. But Araman was a wider land, and between the shores and the mountains were long and dreary plains without hindrance to passage, but bleak, and ever colder as the Ice drew nearer.

§14   Through this dim land Morgoth and Ungoliant passed in haste, and so through the great mists of Oiomúrë came to the Helkaraxë, where the strait between Araman and Middle-earth was filled with grinding ice; and they crossed over and came back at last to the North of the Outer World. Together they went on, for Morgoth could not elude Ungoliant, and her cloud was still about him, and all her eyes were upon him. But when they had come to that region that was after called Lammoth, north of the Firth of Drengist, Morgoth grew more hopeful, for they were drawing near to the ruins of Angband where his great western stronghold had been. But Ungoliant perceived his mood and guessed that he would soon try to escape and defraud her, if he could. Therefore she stayed him, and demanded that he should now fulfill his promise.

§15   'Black-heart!' she said (calling him 'Master' no longer). 'I have done your bidding. But I hunger still.'

'What wouldst thou have more?' said Morgoth. 'All the

world for thy belly? I did not vow to give thee that. I am its Lord.'

'Not so much,' said she. 'But there was a great treasury, of which you said naught to me, and would have said naught even now, if I had not watched you. I will have all that. Yea, with both hands you shall give it!'

'Thou hast had the half already,' said Morgoth. For when she was with him (against his will) at the sack of Formenos, he had let her feast awhile upon the gems of Fëanor, so that she should not come to the chamber of iron.

'I hunger,' she said. 'I will have the other half!'

Then perforce Morgoth surrendered to her the gems that he bore with him, one by one and grudgingly; and she devoured them, and their beauty perished from the world. Then her strength was renewed, but her lust unsated.

'With one hand you give,' she said, 'with the left only. Open your right hand!'

§16   In his right hand Morgoth held close the Silmarils that he had taken from the chamber of iron; and though they were locked in a crystal casket, they had begun to burn him, and his hand was clenched in pain. But he would not open it. 'Nay!' he said. 'These things thou shalt not have, nor see. I name them unto myself for ever. Thou hast had already more than thy due. For with my power that I put into thee thy work was accomplished. I need thee no more. Go, filth! Gnaw thy lust in some hole far away, or I will put a fire in thy maw that shall burn thee for ever!'

§17   But Ungoliant was not daunted. She had grown great, and he less by the power that had gone out of him. Now she rose against him, and her cloud closed about him, and she cast upon him a hideous web of clinging thongs to strangle him. Then Morgoth sent forth a terrible cry that echoed in the mountains. Therefore that region was called Lammoth;* for the echoes of his voice dwelt there ever after, so that any who cried aloud in that land awoke them, and all the waste between the hills and the sea was filled with a clamour as of voices in anguish.

§18   But the cry of Morgoth in that hour was the greatest and most dreadful that was ever heard in the northern world: the mountains shook, and the earth trembled, and rocks were

---

* [footnote to the text] The Great Echo.

riven asunder. Deep in forgotten places that cry was heard. Far beneath the halls of Angband, in vaults to which the Valar in the haste of their assault had not descended, the Balrogs lurked still, awaiting ever the return of their lord. Swiftly they arose, and they passed with winged speed over Hithlum, and they came to Lammoth as a tempest of fire.

§19 Then Ungoliant quailed, and she turned to flight, belching black vapours to cover her; but the Balrogs pursued her with whips of flame into the Mountains of Shadow,* until Morgoth recalled them. Then her webs were shorn asunder, and Morgoth was released, and he returned to Angband.

§20 But Ungoliant went into Beleriand, and there dwelt for a time beneath the Eryd Orgoroth [> Gorgoroth], in the dark valley that was after called Nan Dungorthep† because of the horror that she bred there. But when she had healed her hurts as best she could, and had spawned there a foul brood, she passed away. For there were other evil creatures of spider-form that had dwelt there since the days of the delving of Angband; and she mated with them and devoured them. But whither she went after no tale tells. It is said that she ended long ago, when in her uttermost famine she devoured herself at last.

§21 Thus ended the Thieves' Quarrel; and the fear of Yavanna that the Silmarils would be swallowed up and fall into nothingness did not come to pass. But they remained in the power of Morgoth.

The new version ends here in the typescript; but among the pages of very rough draft material there is the following abandoned passage that continues the narrative for a short distance:

Now Morgoth, having achieved his malice against Valinor, and escaped from bondage, gathered again all his servants that he could find; and through all the North ran the news that he had returned. From near and far, from the ruins of Utumno, and from deep dales and shadows under the mountains and from all dark and hidden places they crept back to him.

Then swiftly they began to delve anew the vast vaults of Angband and to uplift its pillared halls of stone amid smoke and fire, and above them were reared the reeking towers of Thangorodrim.

* [footnote to the text] Eryd Wethrin on the borders of Beleriand.
† [footnote to the text] The Valley of Dreadful Death.

Here the writing was abandoned. After 'Thangorodrim' my father added later: '(The Mountains of Oppression)'. In terms of the pre-*Lord of the Rings* narrative, the new version extends only to halfway through the third paragraph (§62) of the chapter *Of the Flight of the Noldor* in QS (V.233).

Commentary

§10 With 'His head was crushed as with a great mace of iron' compare *Laws and Customs* p. 248, where it is said that the body of Finwë 'was burned as by a lightning stroke and was destroyed.' But the accounts may not be altogether contradictory, for in the present text Maedros speaks of seeing a sudden flame out of the Cloud of Ungoliantë, followed by 'one piercing cry', and of finding Finwë's sword 'twisted and untempered as if by lightning-stroke'.

§14 From this point the name has the form *Ungoliant* (as in *The Lord of the Rings*), not *Ungoliantë* as hitherto. – Here appears the name *Lammoth* (cf. 'the Echoing Mountains of Lammoth' in the later *Tale of Tuor*, *Unfinished Tales* p. 23); see under §17 below.

'the ruins of Angband': cf. the change made to LQ 2, p. 197: 'To his aid there came the Balrogs that lived yet in the deepest places of his ancient fortress, [Utumno >] Angband in the North.'

§15 Ungoliant no longer calls Morgoth 'Master', but she continues to address him as a superior, using 'you', whereas Morgoth calls her 'thou' as previously.

There is here a difference in the narrative. In the earlier sources it had been the compact between them that half of the fee of Ungoliant was the sap of the Trees, and the other half 'a full share in all the jewels they should take' (AAm §125). The story is now that the sap of the Trees was her reward for destroying them; for it had not been any part of Morgoth's intention that she should go to Formenos, and so there could now be no question of 'the other half of her fee' in jewels to be plundered there. The 'half' that Morgoth speaks of now refers to the jewels that Ungoliant devoured at Formenos because he was unable to prevent her; and she attempts to force him to yield up 'the other half', the jewels that Morgoth had acquired there for himself.

'with both hands' refers to Morgoth's words to Ungoliant in Avathar (p. 285, §56c): 'Do as I bid, and if thou art still hungry when we meet again, then, I vow, I will give to thee whatsoever thy lust may demand. Yea, with both hands!'

§17 The great cry of Morgoth when Ungoliant enmeshed him goes back to Q (IV.93), but only now appears the story of its echo that could always be wakened. On the echoes of Lammoth see *Unfinished Tales* pp. 23, 52.

§19 Here (in the footnote) first appears *Eryd Wethrin* (for earlier *Eredwethion*).

§20 *Ered Orgoroth* was changed to *Ered Gorgorath* on the AAm typescript, and *Nan Dungorthin* to *Nan Dungortheb* (p. 127, §126). 'Valley of Dreadful Death' is the first translation given of the latter name since *Nan Dumgorthin* was rendered 'land of the dark idols' in the old *Tale of Tinúviel* (see II.62-3).

The story that Ungoliant went to Nan Dungorthin and spawned a brood there appears also in AAm (§126, pp. 109, 123); but it is said there that she 'returned into the South of the world, where she abides yet for all that the Eldar have heard.'

★

I have treated all this new writing in the typescript B as a series of 'subchapters', in view of the general heading at the beginning (p. 256), *Of the Silmarils and the Darkening of Valinor*; but on a covering page to the typescript my father wrote very hastily:

This [is] a specimen of the new revised and enlarged (final?) form and so is not entirely consistent with the remainder. It contains:
    V   Of Finwë and Míriel
    VI   Of Fëanor and the Unchaining of Melkor
    VII Of the Silmarils and the Unrest of the Noldor
    VIII The Darkening of Valinor
    IX   The Thieves' Quarrel

These chapter numbers were later pencilled in against the subheadings in the typescript; but the general title *Of the Silmarils and the Darkening of Valinor* was not removed. *The Rape of the Silmarils* (p. 292) was not included in this list and did not receive a number in the text; maybe it was added after the list was made.

The original Chapter 1 *Of the Valar* had been separated off as the *Valaquenta*, and the original Chapter 2 *Of Valinor and the Two Trees* had become Chapter 1 (see p. 200). Since *Of Finwë and Míriel* is here numbered 5, Chapters 2, 3 and 4 were evidently to be *Of the Coming of the Elves*, *Of Thingol and Melian*, and *Of Eldanor and the Princes of the Eldalië*.

Lastly, it must be mentioned that my father wrote the chapter number 'X' against the title *The Flight of the Noldor* on the LQ 2 typescript (following from 'IX *The Thieves' Quarrel*' in the list given above), and 'XI' against the title of the next extant chapter in the LQ 2 series, *Of Men*. Against the words in the latter (QS §82, V.245) 'At the first rising of the Sun above the earth the younger children of the world awoke' he wrote on LQ 2: 'This depends upon an old version in which the Sun was first made after the death of the Trees (described in a chapter omitted).' The significance of this will appear in Part Five.

Note on Dating

It is convenient to collect here the evidence, such as it is, bearing on the date of this late rewriting, and the texts associated with it.

I have mentioned that in a letter of December 1957 my father told Rayner Unwin that it was his intention to 'get copies made of all copyable material', with a view to 'remoulding' *The Silmarillion*; and I have suggested that the amanuensis typescript LQ 2 of *The Silmarillion* and that of the *Annals of Aman*, which were made on the same typewriter and probably belong to the same time, may therefore be tentatively ascribed to about 1958 (see pp. 141–2).

If this dating is accepted for the moment, then the annals inserted into the manuscript of AAm concerning the death of Míriel, the 'Doom of Manwë concerning the espousals of the Eldar', and the marriage of Finwë to Indis must have preceded 1958 or belong to that year, since they appear in the typescript of AAm as typed (p. 101 notes 1 and 4, p. 127, §120); while the rider FM 1 to LQ concerning Finwë and Míriel is certainly contemporary with the AAm insertions (p. 205). The story of Finwë and Míriel in the manuscript (A) of *Laws and Customs among the Eldar* certainly followed FM 1, but the two texts were probably close in time (p. 233). It is thus notable that in the letter written by my father in October 1958 (see pp. 267, 270) this story and its implications were in the forefront of his mind.

The second text of the story of Finwë and Míriel (FM 2, p. 254) intended for inclusion in *The Silmarillion* very probably preceded the typescript (B) of *Laws and Customs among the Eldar*, since this latter was typed on a new typewriter with a rather distinctive typeface. Also typed on this machine were the *Valaquenta* and the texts of the late rewriting of Chapter 6(–7). The first letter of my father's that I know of to be typed on the new typewriter is dated January 1959.

There is no actual proof of date in any of this, of course, but taken together it points clearly, I think, to the late 1950s as the time when the story of Finwë and Míriel arose and *Laws and Customs among the Eldar* was written. Further evidence is provided by the *Athrabeth Finrod ah Andreth* (see pp. 304, 360).

PART FOUR

ATHRABETH
FINROD
AH
ANDRETH

ATHRABETH FINROD AH ANDRETH

While this very remarkable and hitherto unknown work, 'The Debate of Finrod and Andreth', is set at a later time in the history of the Elder Days than is otherwise reached in this book, it should clearly be given here on account of its association, both in date and content, with the writings and revisions of the 'Second Phase' of the post-*Lord of the Rings* history of *The Silmarillion*. I have thought it best to let it stand as a separate Part in this book rather than include it with the miscellaneous writings in Part Five, since unlike those it is a major and finished work, and is referred to elsewhere as if it had for my father some 'authority'.

The textual situation, so far as the actual narrative of the 'Debate' is concerned, is simple. There is one manuscript ('**A**'), very similar in style and appearance to that of *Laws and Customs among the Eldar*, and like it clear and fluent – although in this case there are some pages of drafting extant, with clear indications that others existed (see pp. 350 ff.). There are also two amanuensis typescripts, taken independently from the manuscript after all emendation had been made to it. One of these ('**B**'), probably the first to be made, is of slight value: it has many errors, and was looked through very cursorily by my father with scarcely any emendation. The other ('**C**'), extant also in a carbon copy, is a better text though not without errors; this he read more carefully and introduced a number of minor changes, but missed some errors through not checking it against the manuscript. The text printed here is therefore established from the manuscript, taking up emendations made to the typescripts.

Neither of the typescripts of the *Athrabeth* has any title; both begin with the words 'Now it chanced that on a time of spring ...' (p. 307). The manuscript, on the other hand, bears the title *Of Death and the Children of Eru, and the Marring of Men* (with another title or sub-title added later, *The Converse of Finrod and Andreth*), and two pages of introductory text precede the sentence with which the typescripts open. This introduction to the 'Converse' was in fact the continuation of an essay which my father removed and let stand separately: see pp. 424 ff., where this work, entitled *Aman*, is given.

This introductory section was subsequently typed by my father, with a carbon copy, on the new typewriter (see p. 300), and attached to the beginning of the copies of the amanuensis typescript C. It has no title or heading. In typing it he substantially recast it; but the actual matter of the manuscript version was largely retained, so that only a few differences need be noted (see pp. 305–6).

As to the date of the work: that it was written after the completion of the manuscript of *Laws and Customs among the Eldar* is seen from my father's comments on the latter, 'But see full treatment of this later in *Athrabeth Finrod ah Andreth*' and 'But see *Athrabeth*' (pp. 251–2). It is evident also that it followed the typescript B of *Laws and Customs*, since the word *hröa(r)* is used, a term which only replaced *hrondo(r)* in that typescript by hasty later correction (p. 209). The text and the very elaborate Commentary (typed on the new typewriter) appended to it are preserved in folded newspapers of January 1960; and it is clear from what is written on the newspapers (see p. 329) that the material was complete when they were used for this purpose. It is true of course that January 1960 is not thereby proved to be a *terminus ad quem*, because it could have been indefinitely later that the newspaper was so used; but that, I think, is very unlikely, and I would therefore place the work in 1959. The only evidence that can be set against this is the fact that the small quantity of original draft material is all written on slips made from documents of the year 1955; but if my father had a store of such paper, as is likely enough, this would show no more than that initial work on the *Athrabeth* belongs to that year or later. At the same time it must be allowed to be perfectly possible that he was working on it at intervals over a substantial period of time.

There follows now the introductory text in the typescript version.

Now the Eldar learned that, according to the lore of the Edain, Men believed that their *hröar* were not by right nature short-lived, but had been made so by the malice of Melkor. It was not clear to the Eldar whether Men meant: by the general marring of Arda (which they themselves held to be the cause of the waning of their own *hröar*); or by some special malice against Men as Men that was achieved in the dark ages before the Edain and the Eldar met in Beleriand; or by both. But to the Eldar it seemed that, if the mortality of Men had come by special malice, the nature of Men had been grievously changed from the first design of Eru; and this was a matter of wonder and dread to them, for, if it were indeed so, then the power of Melkor must be (or have been in the beginning) far greater than even the Eldar had understood; whereas the original nature of Men must have been strange indeed and unlike that of any others of the dwellers in Arda.

Concerning these things it is recorded in the ancient lore of the Eldar that once Finrod Felagund and Andreth the Wise-woman conversed in Beleriand long ago. This tale, which the Eldar call *Athrabeth Finrod ah Andreth*, is here given in one of the forms that have been preserved.

Finrod (son of Finarfin, son of Finwë) was the wisest of the exiled Noldor, being more concerned than all others with matters of thought (rather than with making or with skill of hand); and he was eager moreover to discover all that he could concerning Mankind. He it was that first met Men in Beleriand and befriended them; and for this reason he was often called by the Eldar *Edennil*, 'the Friend of Men'. His chief love was given to the people of Bëor the Old, for it was these that he had first found in the woods of eastern Beleriand.

Andreth was a woman of the House of Bëor, the sister of Bregor father of Barahir (whose son was Beren One-hand the renowned). She was wise in thought, and learned in the lore of Men and their histories; for which reason the Eldar called her *Saelind*, 'Wise-heart'.

Of the Wise some were women, and they were greatly esteemed among Men, especially for their knowledge of the legends of ancient days. Another Wise-woman was Adanel, sister of Hador Lorindol at one time Lord of the People of Marach, whose lore and traditions, and their language also, were different from those of the People of Bëor. But Adanel was married to a kinsman of Andreth, Belemir of the House of Bëor: he was grandsire of Emeldir, mother of Beren. In her youth Andreth had dwelt long in Belemir's house, and so had learned from Adanel much of the lore of the People of Marach, besides the lore of her own folk.

In the days of the peace before Melkor broke the Siege of Angband, Finrod would often visit Andreth, whom he loved in great friendship, for he found her more ready to impart her knowledge to him than were most of the Wise among Men. A shadow seemed to lie upon them, and there was a darkness behind them, of which they were loth to speak even among themselves. And they were in awe of the Eldar and would not easily reveal to them their thought or their legends. Indeed the Wise among Men (who were few) for the most part kept their wisdom secret and handed it on only to those whom they chose.

The chief difference between the manuscript and typescript versions of this introductory piece concerns the expanded genealogy of the

House of Bëor, for here the manuscript gives some additional information concerning Adanel:

> Another wise-woman, though of a different House and different tradition, was Adanel sister of Hador. She married Belemir of the House of Bëor, grandson of Belen second son of Bëor the Old, to whom the wisdom of Bëor (for Bëor himself had been one of the wise) was chiefly transmitted. And there had been great love between Belemir and Andreth his younger kinswoman (the daughter of his second cousin Boromir), and she dwelt long in his house, and so learned much of the lore also of the 'people of Marach' and the House of Hador from Adanel.

If to the genealogical references in the published *Silmarillion* (pp. 142, 148, and the Index s.v. *Emeldir*) is added this information from the introduction to the *Athrabeth* the following tree can be derived (the new names are printed in italics):

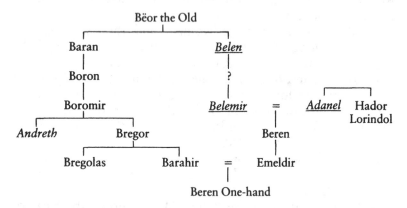

Most of the genealogical information about the House of Bëor in the published *Silmarillion* is derived of course from post-*Lord of the Rings* work on the text: in QS and the *Annals of Beleriand* (AB 2) Beren's father Barahir was the son of Bëor the Old, and the People of Marach had not emerged.

Other differences in the manuscript version of the introduction are the statements that Andreth 'learned also all that she could hear of the Eldar', and that Finrod was often called by the Eldar '*Atandil* (or *Edennil*)' (see the 'Glossary' to the *Athrabeth*, p. 349).

In the first footnote to the opening of the narrative proper the date of the *Athrabeth* is given as 'about 409 during the Long Peace (260–455)'. In the year 260 Glaurung first emerged from the gates of Angband, and in 455 befell the Dagor Bragollach or Battle of Sudden

Flame, when the Siege of Angband was broken. According to the older chronology (see V.130, 274; still preserved in the *Grey Annals* of c.1951) Finrod Felagund had encountered Bëor in the foothills of the Blue Mountains in the year 400, but the date of that meeting had now been set back by ninety years, to 310 (third footnote to the text).

There follows now 'The Debate of Finrod and Andreth', which as already noted has no title in the typescripts (B and C), and which in the original manuscript (A) runs on continuously without new heading from the introduction.

Now it chanced that on a time of spring* Finrod was for a while a guest in the house of Belemir; and he fell to talking with Andreth the Wise-woman concerning Men and their fates. For at that time Boron, Lord of the folk of Bëor, had but lately died soon after Yule, and Finrod was grieved.

'Sad to me, Andreth,' he said, 'is the swift passing of your people. For now Boron your father's father is gone; and though he was old, you say, as age goes among Men,** yet I had known him too briefly. Little while indeed it seems to me since I first saw† Bëor in the east of this land, yet now he is gone, and his sons, and his son's son also.'

'More than a hundred years it is now,' said Andreth, 'since we came over the Mountains; and Bëor and Baran and Boron each lived beyond his ninetieth year. Our passing was swifter before we found this land.'

'Then are you content here?' said Finrod.

'Content?' said Andreth. 'No heart of Man is content. All passing and dying is a grief to it; but if the withering is less soon then that is some amendment, a little lifting of the Shadow.'

'What mean you by that?' said Finrod.

'Surely you know well!' said Andreth. 'The darkness that is now confined to the North, but once'; and here she paused and her eyes darkled, as if her mind were gone back into black years best forgot. 'But once lay upon all Middle-earth, while ye dwelt in your bliss.'

* [footnote to the text] This would be about 409 during the Long Peace (260–455). At that time Belemir and Adanel were old in the reckoning of Men, being some 70 years of age; but Andreth was in full vigour, being not yet 50 (48). She was unwed, as was not uncommon for Wise-women of Men.

** [footnote to the text] He was 93.

† [footnote to the text] In 310, about 100 years before this.

'It was not concerning the Shadow that I asked,' said Finrod. 'What mean you, I would say, by the lifting of it? Or how is the swift fate of Men concerned with it? Ye also, we hold (being instructed by the Great who know), are Children of Eru, and your fate and nature is from Him.'

'I see,' said Andreth, 'that in this ye of the High-elves do not differ from your lesser kindred whom we have met in the world, though they have never dwelt in the Light. All ye Elves deem that we die swiftly by our true kind. That we are brittle and brief, and ye are strong and lasting. We may be "Children of Eru", as ye say in your lore; but we are children to you also: to be loved a little maybe, and yet creatures of less worth, upon whom ye may look down from the height of your power and your knowledge, with a smile, or with pity, or with a shaking of heads.'

'Alas, you speak near the truth,' said Finrod. 'At least of many of my people; but not of all, and certainly not of me. But consider this well, Andreth, when we name you "Children of Eru" we do not speak lightly; for that name we do not utter ever in jest or without full intent. When we speak so, we speak out of knowledge, not out of mere Elvish lore; and we proclaim that ye are our kin, in a kinship far closer (both of *hröa* and *fëa*) than that which binds together all other creatures of Arda, and ourselves to them.

'Other creatures also in Middle-earth we love in their measure and kind: the beasts and birds who are our friends, the trees, and even the fair flowers that pass more swiftly than Men. Their passing we regret; but believe it to be a part of their nature, as much as are their shapes or their hues.

'But for you, who are our nearer kin, our regret is far greater. Yet, if we consider the briefness of life in all Middle-earth, must we not believe that your brevity is also part of your nature? Do not your own people believe this too? And yet from your words and their bitterness I guess that you think that we err.'

'I think that you err, and all who think likewise,' said Andreth; 'and that that error itself comes of the Shadow. But to speak of Men. Some will say this and some that; but most, thinking little, will ever hold that what is in their brief span in the world has ever been so, and shall so ever remain, whether they like it or no. But there are some that think otherwise; men call them "Wise", but heed them little. For they do not speak with assurance or with one voice, having no sure knowledge such as ye boast of, but perforce depending upon "lore", from which truth (if it can be found) must be winnowed. And in every winnowing there is chaff with the corn that is chosen, and doubtless some corn with the chaff which is rejected.

'Yet among my people, from Wise unto Wise out of the darkness, comes the voice saying that Men are not now as they were, nor as their true nature was in their beginning. And clearer still is this said by the Wise of the People of Marach, who have preserved in memory a name for Him that ye call Eru, though in my folk He was almost forgotten. So I learn from Adanel. They say plainly that Men are *not* by nature short-lived, but have become so through the malice of the Lord of the Darkness whom they do not name.'

'That I can well believe,' said Finrod: 'that your bodies suffer in some measure the malice of Melkor. For you live in Arda Marred, as do we, and all the matter of Arda was tainted by him, before ye or we came forth and drew our *hröar* and their sustenance therefrom: all save only maybe Aman before he came there.[1] For know, it is not otherwise with the Quendi[2] themselves: their health and stature is diminished. Already those of us who dwell in Middle-earth, and even we who have returned to it, find that the change[3] of their bodies is swifter than in the beginning. And that, I judge, must forebode that they will prove less strong to last than they were designed to be, though this may not be clearly revealed for many long years.

'And likewise with the *hröar* of Men, they are weaker than they should be. Thus it comes to pass that here in the West, to which of old his power scarcely extended, they have more health, as you say.'

'Nay, nay!' said Andreth. 'You do not understand my words. For you are ever in one mind, my lord: the Elves are the Elves, and Men are Men, and though they have a common Enemy, by whom both are injured, still the ordained interval remains between the lords and the humble, the firstcomers high and enduring, the followers lowly and of brief service.

'That is not the voice that the Wise hear out of the darkness and from beyond it. Nay, lord, the Wise among Men say: "We were not made for death, nor born ever to die. Death was imposed upon us." And behold! the fear of it is with us always, and we flee from it for ever as the hart from the hunter. But for myself I deem that we cannot escape within this world, nay, not even if we could come to the Light beyond the Sea, or that

Aman of which ye tell. In that hope we set out and have journeyed through many lives of Men; but the hope was vain. So said the Wise, but that did not stay the march, for as I have said, they are little heeded. And lo! we have fled from the Shadow to the last shores of Middle-earth, to find only that it is here before us!'

Then Finrod was silent; but after a while he said: 'These words are strange and terrible. And you speak with the bitterness of one whose pride has been humiliated, and seeks therefore to wound those to whom she speaks. If all the Wise among Men speak so, then well I can believe that ye have suffered some great hurt. But not by my people, Andreth, nor by any of the Quendi. If we are as we are, and ye are as we find you, that is not by any deed of ours, nor of our desire; and your sorrow does not rejoice us nor feed our pride. One only would say otherwise: that Enemy whom you do not name.

'Beware of the chaff with your corn, Andreth! For it may be deadly: lies of the Enemy that out of envy will breed hate. Not all the voices that come out of the darkness speak truth to those minds that listen for strange news.

'But who did you this hurt? Who imposed death upon you? Melkor, it is plain that you would say, or whatever name you have for him in secret. For you speak of death and his shadow, as if these were one and the same; and as if to escape from the Shadow was to escape also from Death.

'But these two are not the same, Andreth. So I deem, or death would not be found at all in this world which he did not design but Another. Nay, *death* is but the name that we give to something that he has tainted, and it sounds therefore evil; but untainted its name would be good.'[4]

'What do ye know of death? Ye do not fear it, because ye[5] do not know it,' said Andreth.

'We have seen it, and we fear it,' answered Finrod. 'We too may die, Andreth; and we have died. My father's father was cruelly slain, and many have followed him, exiles in the night, in the cruel ice, in the insatiable sea. And in Middle-earth we have died, by fire and by smoke, by venom and the cruel blades of battle. Fëanor is dead, and Fingolphin was trodden under the feet of the Morgoth.[6]

'For what end? To overthrow the Shadow, or if that may not be, to keep it from spreading once more over all Middle-earth –

to defend the Children of Eru, Andreth, all the Children and not the proud Eldar only!'

'I had heard,' said Andreth, 'that it was to regain your treasure that your Enemy had stolen; but maybe the House of Finarphin is not at one with the Sons of Fëanor. Nonetheless for all your valour, I say again: "what know ye of death?" To you it may be in pain, it may be bitter and a loss – but only for a time, a little taken from abundance, unless I have been told untruth. For ye know that in dying you do not leave the world, and that you may return to life.

'Otherwise it is with us: dying we die, and we go out to no return. Death is an uttermost end, a loss irremediable. And it is abominable; for it is also a wrong that is done to us.'

'That difference I perceive,' said Finrod. 'You would say there are two deaths: the one is a harm and a loss but not an end, the other is an end without redress; and the Quendi suffer only the first?'

'Yes, but there is another difference also,' said Andreth. 'One is but a wound in the chances of the world, which the brave, or the strong, or the fortunate, may hope to avoid. The other is death ineluctable; death the hunter who cannot in the end be escaped. Be a Man strong, or swift, or bold; be he wise or a fool; be he evil, or be he in all the deeds of his days just and merciful, let him love the world or loathe it, he must die and must leave it – and become carrion that men are fain to hide or to burn.'

'And being thus pursued, have Men no hope?' said Finrod.

'They have no certainty and no knowledge, only fears, or dreams in the dark,' answered Andreth. 'But hope? Hope, that is another matter, of which even the Wise seldom speak.' Then her voice grew more gentle. 'Yet, Lord Finrod of the House of Finarphin, of the high and puissant Elves, perhaps we may speak of it anon, you and I.'

'Anon we may,' said Finrod, 'but as yet we walk in the shadows of fear. Thus far, then, I perceive that the great difference between Elves and Men is in the speed of the end. In this only. For if you deem that for the Quendi there is no death ineluctable, you err.

'Now none of us know, though the Valar may know, the future of Arda, or how long it is ordained to endure. But it will not endure for ever. It was made by Eru, but He is not in it. The One only has no limits. Arda, and Eä itself, must therefore be bounded. You see us, the Quendi, still in the first ages of our being, and the end is far off. As maybe among you death may seem to a young man in his strength; save that we have long years of life and thought already behind us. But the end will come. That we all know. And then we must die; we must perish utterly, it seems, for we belong to Arda (in *hröa* and *fëa*).[7] And beyond that what? "The going out to no return," as you say; "the uttermost end, the irremediable loss"?

'Our hunter is slow-footed, but he never loses the trail. Beyond the day when he shall blow the mort,[8] we have no certainty, no knowledge. And no one speaks to us of hope.'

'I did not know this,' said Andreth; 'and yet...'

'And yet at least ours is slow-footed, you would say?' said Finrod. 'True. But it is not clear that a foreseen doom long delayed is in all ways a lighter burden than one that comes soon. But if I have understood your words thus far, you do not believe that this difference was designed so in the beginning. You were not at first doomed to swift death.

'Much could be said concerning this belief (be it a true guess or no). But first I would ask: how do ye say that this has come about? By the malice of Melkor I guessed, and you have not denied it. But I see now that you do not speak of the diminishment that all in Arda Marred suffer; but of some special stroke of enmity against your people, against Men as Men. Is that so?'

'It is indeed,' said Andreth.

'Then this is a matter of dread,' said Finrod. 'We know Melkor, the Morgoth, and know him to be mighty. Yea, I have seen him, and I have heard his voice; and I have stood blind in the night that is at the heart of his shadow, whereof you, Andreth, know nought save by hearsay and the memory of your people. But never even in the night have we believed that he could prevail against the Children of Eru. This one he might cozen, or that one he might corrupt; but to change the doom of a whole people of the Children, to rob them of their inheritance: if he could do that in Eru's despite, then greater and more terrible is he by far than we guessed; then all the valour of the Noldor is but presumption and folly – nay, Valinor and the Mountains of the Pelóri are builded on sand.'

'Behold!' said Andreth. 'Did I not say that ye do not know death? Lo! when you are made to face it in thought only, as we know it in deed and in thought all our lives, at once you fall into a despair. We know, if ye do not,[9] that the Nameless is Lord of this World, and your valour, and ours too, is a folly; or at least it is fruitless.'

'Beware!' said Finrod. 'Beware lest you speak the unspeakable, wittingly or in ignorance, confounding Eru with the Enemy who would fain have you do so. The Lord of this World is not he, but the One who made him, and his Vicegerent is Manwë, the Elder King of Arda who is blessed.

'Nay, Andreth, the mind darkened and distraught; to bow and yet to loathe; to flee and yet not to reject; to love the body and yet scorn it, the carrion-disgust: these things may come from the Morgoth, indeed. But to doom the deathless to death, from father unto son, and yet to leave to them the memory of an inheritance taken away, and the desire for what is lost: could the Morgoth do this? No, I say. And for that reason I said that if your tale is true, then all in Arda is vain, from the pinnacle of Oiolossë to the uttermost abyss. For I do not believe your tale. None could have done this save the One.

'Therefore I say to you, Andreth, what did ye do, ye Men, long ago in the dark? How did ye anger Eru? For otherwise all your tales are but dark dreams devised in a Dark Mind. Will you say what you know or have heard?'

'I will not,' said Andreth. 'We do not speak of this to those of other race. But indeed the Wise are uncertain and speak with contrary voices; for whatever happened long ago, we have fled from it; we have tried to forget, and so long have we tried that now we cannot remember any time when we were not as we are – save only legends of days when death came less swiftly and our span was still far longer, but already there was death.'

'Ye cannot remember?' said Finrod. 'Are there no tales of your days before death, though ye will not tell them to strangers?'

'Maybe,' said Andreth. 'If not among my folk, then among the folk of Adanel, perhaps.' She fell silent, and gazed at the fire.

'Do you think that none know save yourselves?' said Finrod at last. 'Do not the Valar know?'

Andreth looked up and her eyes darkened. 'The Valar?' she said. 'How should I know, or any Man? Your Valar do not trouble us either with care or with instruction. They sent no summons to us.'

'What do you know of them?' said Finrod. 'I have seen them and dwelt among them, and in the presence of Manwë and Varda I have stood in the Light. Speak not of them so, nor of anything that is high above you. Such words came first out of the Lying Mouth.

'Has it never entered into your thought, Andreth, that out there in ages long past ye may have put yourselves out of their care, and beyond the reach of their help? Or even that ye, the Children of Men, were not a matter that they could govern? For ye were too great. Yea, I mean this, and do not only flatter your pride: too great. Sole masters of yourselves within Arda, under the hand of the One. Beware then how you speak! If ye will not speak to others of your wound or how ye came by it, take heed lest (as unskilled leeches) ye misjudge the hurt, or in pride misplace the blame.

'But let us turn now to other matters, since you will not say more of this. I would consider your first state before the wound. For what you say of that is also to me a wonder, and hard to understand. You say: "we were not made for death, nor born ever to die." What do you mean: that ye were as we are, or otherwise?'

'This lore takes no account of you,' said Andreth, 'for we knew nothing of the Eldar. We considered only dying and not-dying. Of life as long as the world but no longer we had not heard; indeed not until now has it entered my mind.'

'To speak truly,' said Finrod, 'I had thought that this belief of yours, that ye too were not made for death, was but a dream of your pride, bred in envy of the Quendi, to equal or surpass them. Not so, you will say. Yet long ere ye came to this land, ye met other folk of the Quendi, and by some were befriended. Were ye not then already mortal? And did ye never speak with them concerning life and death? Though without any words they would soon discover your mortality, and ere long you would perceive that they did not die.'

'"Not so" I say indeed,' answered Andreth. 'We may have been mortal when first we met the Elves far away, or maybe we were not: our lore does not say, or at least none that I have learned. But already we had our lore, and needed none from the Elves: we knew that in our beginning we had been born *never to die*. And by that, my lord, we meant: *born to life everlasting, without any shadow of any end*.'

'Then have the Wise among you considered how strange is the true nature that they claim for the Atani?' said Finrod.

'Is it so strange?' said Andreth. 'Many of the Wise hold that in their true nature no living things would die.'

'In that the Eldar would say that they err,' said Finrod. 'To us your claim for Men is strange, and indeed hard to accept, for two reasons. You claim, if you fully understand your own words, to have had imperishable bodies, not bounded by the limits of Arda, and yet derived from its matter and sustained by it. And you claim also (though this you may not have perceived) to have had *hröar* and *fëar* that were from the beginning out of harmony. Yet harmony of *hröa* and *fëa* is, we believe, essential to the true nature unmarred of all the Incarnate: the *Mirröanwi*[10] as we call the Children of Eru.'

'The first difficulty I perceive,' said Andreth, 'and to it our Wise have their own answer. The second, as you guess, I do not perceive.'

'Do you not?' said Finrod. 'Then you do not see yourselves clearly. But it may often happen that friends and kinsmen see some things plainly that are hidden from their friend himself.

'Now we Eldar are your kinsmen, and your friends also (if you will believe it), and we have observed you already through three lives of Men with love and concern and much thought. Of this then we are certain without debate, or else all our wisdom is vain: the *fëar* of Men, though close akin indeed to the *fëar* of the Quendi, are yet not the same. For strange as we deem it, we see clearly that the *fëar* of Men are not, as are ours, confined to Arda, nor is Arda their home.

'Can you deny it? Now we Eldar do not deny that ye love Arda and all that is therein (in so far as ye are free from the Shadow) maybe even as greatly as do we. Yet otherwise. Each of our kindreds perceives Arda differently, and appraises its beauties in different mode and degree. How shall I say it? To me the difference seems like that between one who visits a strange country, and abides there a while (but need not), and one who has lived in that land always (and must). To the former all things that he sees are new and strange, and in that degree lovable. To the other all things are familiar, the only things that are, his own, and in that degree precious.'

'If you mean that Men are the guests,' said Andreth.

'You have said the word,' said Finrod: 'that name we have given to you.'

'Lordly as ever,' said Andreth. 'But even if we be but guests in a land where all is your own, my lords, as you say, tell me what other land or things do we know?'

'Nay, tell me!' said Finrod. 'For if you do not know, how can we? But do you know that the Eldar say of Men that they look at no thing for itself; that if they study it, it is to discover something else; that if they love it, it is only (so it seems) because it reminds them of some other dearer thing? Yet with what is this comparison? Where are these other things?

'We are both, Elves and Men, in Arda and of Arda; and such knowledge as Men have is derived from Arda (or so it would appear). Whence then comes this memory that ye have with you, even before ye begin to learn?

'It is not of other regions in Arda from which ye have journeyed. We also have journeyed from afar. But were you and I to go together to your ancient homes east away I should recognize the things there as part of my home, but I should see in your eyes the same wonder and comparison as I see in the eyes of Men in Beleriand who were born here.'

'You speak strange words, Finrod,' said Andreth, 'which I have not heard before. Yet my heart is stirred as if by some truth that it recognizes even if it does not understand it. But fleeting is that memory, and goes ere it can be grasped; and then we grow blind. And those among us who have known the Eldar, and maybe have loved them, say on our side: "There is no weariness in the eyes of the Elves". And we find that they do not understand the saying that goes among Men: *too often seen is seen no longer*. And they wonder much that in the tongues of Men the same word may mean both "long-known" and "stale".

'We have thought that this was so only because the Elves have lasting life and undiminished vigour. "Grown-up children" we, the guests, sometimes call you, my lord. And yet – and yet, if nothing in Arda for us holds its savour long, and all fair things grow dim, what then? Does it not come from [the] Shadow upon our hearts? Or do you say that it is not so, but this was ever our nature, even before the wound?'

'I say so, indeed,' answered Finrod. 'The Shadow may have darkened your unrest, bringing swifter weariness and soon turning it to disdain, but the unrest was ever there, I believe. And if this is so, then can you not now perceive the disharmony that I spoke of? If indeed your Wisdom had lore like to ours, teaching that the *Mirröanwi* are made of a union of body and mind, of *hröa* and *fëa*, or as we say in picture the House and the Indweller.

'For what is the "death" that you mourn but the severing of

these two? And what is the "deathlessness" that you have lost but that the two should remain united for ever?

'But what then shall we think of the union in Man: of an Indweller, who is but a guest here in Arda and not here at home, with a House that is built of the matter of Arda and must therefore (one would suppose) here remain?

'At least one would not hope for this House a life longer than Arda of which it is part. Yet you claim that the House too was immortal, do you not? I would rather believe that such a *fëa* of its own nature would at some time of its own will have abandoned the house of its sojourn here, even though the sojourn might have been longer than is now permitted. Then "death" would (as I said) have sounded otherwise to you: as a release, or return, nay! as going home! But this you do not believe, it seems?'

'Nay, I do not believe this,' said Andreth. 'For that would be contempt of the body, and is a thought of the Darkness unnatural in any of the Incarnate whose life uncorrupted is a union of mutual love. But the body is not an inn to keep a traveller warm for a night, ere he goes on his way, and then to receive another. It is a house made for one dweller only, indeed not only house but raiment also; and it is not clear to me that we should in this case speak only of the raiment being fitted to the wearer rather than of the wearer being fitted to the raiment.

'I hold then that it is not to be thought that the severance of these two could be according to the true nature of Men. For were it "natural" for the body to be abandoned and die, but "natural" for the *fëa* to live on, then there would indeed be a disharmony in Man, and his parts would not be united by love. His body would be a hindrance at best, or a chain. An imposition indeed, not a gift. But there is one who imposes, and who devises chains, and if such were our nature in the beginning, then we should derive it from him – but that you say should not be spoken.

'Alas! Out in the darkness men do say this nonetheless, but not the Atani as thou knowest, not now. I hold that in this we are as ye are, truly Incarnates, and that we do not live in our right being and its fullness save in a union of love and peace between the House and the Dweller. Wherefore death, which divides them, is a disaster to both.'

'Ever more you amaze my thought, Andreth,' said Finrod. 'For if your claim is true, then lo! a *fëa* which is here but a traveller is wedded indissolubly to a *hröa* of Arda; to divide them is a grievous hurt, and yet each must fulfil its right nature without tyranny of the other. Then this must surely follow: the *fëa* when it departs must take with it the *hröa*. And what can this mean unless it be that the *fëa* shall have the power to uplift the *hröa*, as its eternal spouse and companion, into an endurance everlasting beyond Eä, and beyond Time? Thus would Arda, or part thereof, be healed not only of the taint of Melkor, but released even from the limits that were set for it in the "Vision of Eru" of which the Valar speak.

'Therefore I say that if this can be believed, then mighty indeed under Eru were Men made in their beginning; and dreadful beyond all other calamities was the change in their state.

'Is it, then, a vision of what was designed to be when Arda was complete – of living things and even of the very lands and seas of Arda made eternal and indestructible, for ever beautiful and new – with which the *fëar* of Men compare what they see here? Or is there somewhere else a world of which all things which we see, all things that either Elves or Men know, are only tokens or reminders?'

'If so it resides in the mind of Eru, I deem,' said Andreth. 'To such questions how can we find the answers, here in the mists of Arda Marred? Otherwise it might have been, had we not been changed; but being as we are, even the Wise among us have given too little thought to Arda itself, or to other things that dwell here. We have thought most of ourselves: of how our *hröar* and *fëar* should have dwelt together for ever in joy, and of the darkness impenetrable that now awaits us.'

'Then not only the High Eldar are forgetful of their kin!' said Finrod. 'But this is strange to me, and even as did your heart when I spoke of your unrest, so now mine leaps up as at the hearing of good news.

'This then, I propound, was the errand of Men, not the followers, but the heirs and fulfillers of all: to heal the Marring of Arda, already foreshadowed before their devising; and to do more, as agents of the magnificence of Eru: to enlarge the Music and surpass the Vision of the World![11]

'For that Arda Healed shall not be Arda Unmarred, but a third thing and a greater, and yet the same.[12] I have conversed with the Valar who were present at the making of the Music ere the being of the World began. And now I wonder: Did they hear the end of the Music? Was there not something in or beyond the final chords of Eru which, being overwhelmed thereby, they did not perceive?[13]

'Or again, since Eru is for ever free, maybe he made no Music and showed no Vision beyond a certain point. Beyond that point we cannot see or know, until by our own roads we come there, Valar or Eldar or Men.

'As may a master in the telling of tales keep hidden the greatest moment until it comes in due course. It may be guessed at indeed, in some measure, by those of us who have listened with full heart and mind; but so the teller would wish. In no wise is the surprise and wonder of his art thus diminished, for thus we share, as it were, in his authorship. But not so, if all were told us in a preface before we entered in!'

'What then would you say is the supreme moment that Eru has reserved?' Andreth asked.

'Ah, wise lady!' said Finrod. 'I am an Elda, and again I was thinking of my own people. But nay, of all the Children of Eru. I was thinking that by the Second Children we might have been delivered from death. For ever as we spoke of death being a division of the united, I thought in my heart of a death that is not so: but the ending together of both. For that is what lies before us, so far as our reason could see: the completion of Arda and its end, and therefore also of us children of Arda; the end when all the long lives of the Elves shall be wholly in the past.[14]

'And then suddenly I beheld as a vision Arda Remade; and there the Eldar completed but not ended could abide in the present for ever,[15] and there walk, maybe, with the Children of Men, their deliverers, and sing to them such songs as, even in the Bliss beyond bliss, should make the green valleys ring and the everlasting mountain-tops to throb like harps.'

Then Andreth looked under her brows at Finrod: 'And what, when ye were not singing, would ye say to us?' she asked.

Finrod laughed. 'I can only guess,' he said. 'Why, wise lady, I think that we should tell you tales of the Past and of Arda that was Before, of the perils and great deeds and the making of the Silmarils! We were the lordly ones then! But ye, ye would then be at home, looking at all things intently, as your own. Ye would be the lordly ones. "The eyes of Elves are always thinking of something else," ye would say. But ye would know then of what we were reminded: of the days when we first met, and our hands touched in the dark. Beyond the End of the World we shall not change; for in memory is our great talent, as shall be seen ever more clearly as the ages of this Arda pass: a heavy burden to be, I fear; but in the Days of which we now speak a great wealth.' And then he paused, for he saw that Andreth was weeping silently.

'Alas, lord!' she said. 'What then is to be done now? For we speak as if these things are, or as if they will assuredly be. But Men have been diminished and their power is taken away. We look for no Arda Remade: darkness lies before us, into which we stare in vain. If by our aid your everlasting mansions were to be prepared, they will not be built now.'

'Have ye then no hope?' said Finrod.

'What is hope?' she said. 'An expectation of good, which though uncertain has some foundation in what is known? Then we have none.'

'That is one thing that Men call "hope",' said Finrod. '*Amdir* we call it, "looking up". But there is another which is founded deeper. *Estel* we call it, that is "trust". It is not defeated by the ways of the world, for it does not come from experience, but from our nature and first being. If we are indeed the *Eruhin*, the Children of the One, then He will not suffer Himself to be deprived of His own, not by any Enemy, not even by ourselves. This is the last foundation of *Estel*, which we keep even when we contemplate the End: of all His designs the issue must be for His Children's joy. *Amdir* you have not, you say. Does no *Estel* at all abide?'

'Maybe,' she said. 'But no! Do you not perceive that it is part of our wound that *Estel* should falter and its foundations be shaken? Are we the Children of the One? Are we not cast off finally? Or were we ever so? Is not the Nameless the Lord of the World?'

'Say it not even in question!' said Finrod.

'It cannot be unsaid,' answered Andreth, 'if you would understand the despair in which we walk. Or in which most Men walk. Among the Atani, as you call us, or the Seekers as we say: those who left the lands of despair and the Men of darkness and journeyed west in vain hope: it is believed that healing may yet be found, or that there is some way of escape. But is this indeed *Estel*? Is it not *Amdir* rather; but without reason: mere flight in a dream from what waking they know: that there is no escape from darkness and death?'

'*Mere flight in a dream* you say,' answered Finrod. 'In dream many desires are revealed; and desire may be the last flicker of

Estel. But you do not mean *dream*, Andreth. You confound *dream* and *waking* with *hope* and *belief*, to make the one more doubtful and the other more sure. Are they asleep when they speak of escape and healing?'

'Asleep or awake, they say nothing clearly,' answered Andreth. 'How or when shall healing come? To what manner of being shall those who see that time be re-made? And what of us who before it go out into darkness unhealed? To such questions only those of the "Old Hope" (as they call themselves) have any guess of an answer.'

'*Those of the Old Hope?*' said Finrod. 'Who are they?'

'A few,' she said; 'but their number has grown since we came to this land, and they see that the Nameless can (as they think) be defied. Yet that is no good reason. To defy him does not undo his work of old. And if the valour of the Eldar fails here, then their despair will be deeper. For it was not on the might of Men, or of any of the peoples of Arda, that the old hope was grounded.'

'What then was this hope, if you know?' Finrod asked.

'They say,' answered Andreth: 'they say that the One will himself enter into Arda, and heal Men and all the Marring from the beginning to the end. This they say also, or they feign, is a rumour that has come down through years uncounted, even from the days of our undoing.'[16]

'They say, they feign?' said Finrod. 'Are you then not one of them?'

'How can I be, lord? All wisdom is against them. Who is the One, whom ye call Eru? If we put aside the Men who serve the Nameless, as do many in Middle-earth, still many Men perceive the world only as a war between Light and Dark equipotent. But you will say: nay, that is Manwë and Melkor; Eru is above them. Is then Eru only the greatest of the Valar, a great god among gods, as most Men will say, even among the Atani: a king who dwells far from his kingdom and leaves lesser princes to do here much as they will? Again you say: nay, Eru is One, alone without peer, and He made Eä, and is beyond it; and the Valar are greater than we, but yet no nearer to His majesty. Is this not so?'

'Yes,' said Finrod. 'We say this, and the Valar we know, and they say the same, all save one. But which, think you, is more likely to lie: those who make themselves humble, or he that exalts himself?'

'I do not doubt,' said Andreth. 'And for that reason the saying of Hope passes my understanding. How could Eru enter into the thing that He has made, and than which He is beyond measure greater? Can the singer enter into his tale or the designer into his picture?'

'He is already in it, as well as outside,' said Finrod. 'But indeed the "in-dwelling" and the "out-living" are not in the same mode.'

'Truly,' said Andreth. 'So may Eru in that mode be present in Eä that proceeded from Him. But they speak of Eru Himself *entering into Arda*, and that is a thing wholly different. How could He the greater do this? Would it not shatter Arda, or indeed all Eä?'

'Ask me not,' said Finrod. 'These things are beyond the compass of the wisdom of the Eldar, or of the Valar maybe. But I doubt that our words may mislead us, and that when you say "greater" you think of the dimensions of Arda, in which the greater vessel may not be contained in the less.

'But such words may not be used of the Measureless. If Eru wished to do this, I do not doubt that He would find a way, though I cannot foresee it. For, as it seems to me, even if He in Himself were to enter in, He must still remain also as He is: the Author without. And yet, Andreth, to speak with humility, I cannot conceive how else this healing could be achieved. Since Eru will surely not suffer Melkor to turn the world to his own will and to triumph in the end. Yet there is no power conceivable greater than Melkor save Eru only. Therefore Eru, if He will not relinquish His work to Melkor, who must else proceed to mastery, then Eru must come in to conquer him.

'More: even if Melkor (or the Morgoth that he has become) could in any way be thrown down or thrust from Arda, still his Shadow would remain, and the evil that he has wrought and sown as a seed would wax and multiply. And if any remedy for this is to be found, ere all is ended, any new light to oppose the shadow, or any medicine for the wounds: then it must, I deem, come from without.'

'Then, lord,' said Andreth, and she looked up in wonder, 'you believe in this Hope?'

'Ask me not yet,' he answered. 'For it is still to me but strange news that comes from afar. No such hope was ever spoken to the Quendi. To you only it was sent. And yet through you we may hear it and lift up our hearts.' He paused a while, and then looking gravely at Andreth he said: 'Yes, Wise-woman, maybe it was ordained that we Quendi, and ye Atani, ere the world grows old, should meet and bring news one to another, and so we should learn of the Hope from you: ordained, indeed, that thou and I, Andreth, should sit here and speak together, across the gulf that divides our kindreds, so that while the Shadow still broods in the North we should not be wholly afraid.'

'*Across the gulf that divides our kindreds!*' said Andreth. 'Is there no bridge but mere words?' And then she wept again.

'There may be. For some. I do not know,' he said. 'The gulf, maybe, is between our fates rather, for else we are close akin, closer than any other creatures in the world. Yet perilous is it to cross a gulf set by doom; and should any do so, they will not find joy upon the other side, but the griefs of both. So I deem.

'But why dost thou say "mere words"? Do not words overpass the gulf between one life and another? Between thee and me surely more has passed than empty sound? Have we not drawn near at all? But that is, I think, little comfort to thee.'

'I have not asked for comfort,' said Andreth. 'For what do I need it?'

'For the doom of Men that has touched thee as a woman,' said Finrod. 'Dost thou think that I do not know? Is he not my brother dearly loved? Aegnor:[17] *Aikanár*, the Sharp-flame, swift and eager. And not long are the years since you first met, and your hands touched in this darkness. Yet then thou wert a maiden, brave and eager, in the morning upon the high hills of Dorthonion.'[18]

'Say on!' said Andreth. 'Say: who art now but a wise-woman, alone, and age that shall not touch him has already set winter's grey in thy hair! But say not *thou* to me, for so he once did!'[19]

'Alas!' said Finrod. 'That is the bitterness, beloved *adaneth*, woman of Men, is it not? that has run through all your words. If I could speak any comfort, you would deem it lordly from one on my side of the sundering doom. But what can I say, save to remind you of the Hope that you yourself have revealed?'

'I did not say that it was ever my hope,' answered Andreth. 'And even were it so, I would still cry: why should this hurt come here and now? Why should we love you, and why should ye love us (if ye do), and yet set the gulf between?'

'Because we were so made, close kin,' said Finrod. 'But we did not make ourselves, and therefore we, the Eldar, did not set the gulf. Nay, *adaneth*, we are not lordly in this, but pitiful.[20] That word will displease thee. Yet pity is of two kinds: one is of kinship recognized, and is near to love; the other is of difference of fortune perceived, and is near to pride. I speak of the former.'

'Speak of neither to me!' said Andreth. 'I desire neither. I was young and I looked on his flame, and now I am old and lost. He was young and his flame leaped towards me, but he turned away, and he is young still. Do candles pity moths?'

'Or moths candles, when the wind blows them out?' said Finrod. '*Adaneth*, I tell thee, *Aikanár* the Sharp-flame loved thee. For thy sake now he will never take the hand of any bride of his own kindred, but live alone to the end, remembering the morning in the hills of Dorthonion. But too soon in the North-wind his flame will go out! Foresight is given to the Eldar in many things not far off, though seldom of joy, and I say to thee thou shalt live long in the order of your kind, and he will go forth before thee and he will not wish to return.'

Then Andreth stood up and stretched her hands to the fire. 'Then why did he turn away? Why leave me while I had still a few good years to spend?'

'Alas!' said Finrod. 'I fear the truth will not satisfy thee. The Eldar have one kind, and ye another; and each judges the others by themselves – until they learn, as do few. This is time of war, Andreth, and in such days the Elves do not wed or bear child;[21] but prepare for death – or for flight. Aegnor has no trust (nor have I) in this siege of Angband that it will last long; and then what will become of this land? If his heart ruled, he would have wished to take thee and flee far away, east or south, forsaking his kin, and thine. Love and loyalty hold him to his. What of thee to thine? Thou hast said thyself that there is no escape by flight within the bounds of the world.'

'For one year, one day, of the flame I would have given all: kin, youth, and hope itself: *adaneth* I am,' said Andreth.

'That he knew,' said Finrod; 'and he withdrew and did not grasp what lay to his hand: *elda* he is. For such barters are paid for in anguish that cannot be guessed, until it comes, and in ignorance rather than in courage the Eldar judge that they are made.

'Nay, *adaneth*, if any marriage can be between our kindred and thine, then it shall be for some high purpose of Doom. Brief it will be and hard at the end. Yea, the least cruel fate that could befall would be that death should soon end it.'

'But the end is always cruel – for Men,' said Andreth. 'I

would not have troubled him, when my short youth was spent. I would not have hobbled as a hag after his bright feet, when I could no longer run beside him!'

'Maybe not,' said Finrod. 'So you feel now. But do you think of him? He would not have run before thee. He would have stayed at thy side to uphold thee. Then pity thou wouldst have had in every hour, pity inescapable. He would not have thee so shamed.

'Andreth *adaneth*, the life and love of the Eldar dwells much in memory; and we (if not ye) would rather have a memory that is fair but unfinished than one that goes on to a grievous end. Now he will ever remember thee in the sun of morning, and that last evening by the water of Aeluin in which he saw thy face mirrored with a star caught in thy hair – ever, until the North-wind brings the night of his flame. Yea, and after that, sitting in the House of Mandos in the Halls of Awaiting until the end of Arda.'

'And what shall I remember?' said she. 'And when I go to what halls shall I come? To a darkness in which even the memory of the sharp flame shall be quenched? Even the memory of rejection. That at least.'

Finrod sighed and stood up. 'The Eldar have no healing words for such thoughts, *adaneth*,' he said. 'But would you wish that Elves and Men had never met? Is the light of the flame, which otherwise you would never have seen, of no worth even now? You believe yourself scorned? Put away at least that thought, which comes out of the Darkness, and then our speech together will not have been wholly in vain. Farewell!'

Darkness fell in the room. He took her hand in the light of the fire. 'Whither go you?' she said.

'North away,' he said: 'to the swords, and the siege, and the walls of defence – that yet for a while in Beleriand rivers may run clean, leaves spring, and birds build their nests, ere Night comes.'

'Will he be there, bright and tall, and the wind in his hair? Tell him. Tell him not to be reckless. Not to seek danger beyond need!'

'I will tell him,' said Finrod. 'But I might as well tell thee not to weep. He is a warrior, Andreth, and a spirit of wrath. In every stroke that he deals he sees the Enemy who long ago did thee this hurt.

'But you are not for Arda. Whither you go may you find light. Await us there, my brother – and me.'

NOTES

1. Perhaps to be compared with this is a passage in the Debate of the Valar in *Laws and Customs* (p. 247), where Nienna said to Manwë: 'Though the death of severance may find out the Eldar in thy realm, yet one thing cometh not to it, and shall not: and that is deforming and decay'; to which is added in a footnote: 'Yet after the slaying of the Trees it did so while Melkor remained there; and the body of Finwë, slain by Melkor, was withered and passed into dust, even as the Trees themselves had withered.'
2. Here and at several, but by no means all, subsequent occurrences *Quendi* was emended to *Elves* on the typescript C.
3. *change* was an emendation to the typescript B (only); the manuscript has *growth*.
4. Cf. the words of Pengoloð to Ælfwine at the end of the *Ainulindalë* (p. 37), of the mortality of Men: 'Death is their fate, the gift of Ilúvatar, which as Time wears even the Powers shall envy. But Melkor has cast his shadow upon it, and confounded it with darkness, and brought forth evil out of good, and fear out of hope.'
5. The manuscript has here: 'What do ye know of death? Ye do not fear it, because you do not know it.' The typist of C replaced the first *ye* by *you*; my father let this stand, but corrected the original occurrence of *you* to *ye*. On the opening page of the typescript he noted that *ye* is used for the plural only, and that *you* 'represents the Elvish pronoun of polite address', while *thou, thee* 'represent the familiar (or affectionate) pronoun'. This distinction is not always maintained in the manuscript; but in a number of cases *you*, where *ye* might be expected, may be intended, and I have only corrected the forms where error seems certain.
6. This is a strange error. Fingolfin died in 456, the year after the Dagor Bragollach (V.132, repeated in the *Grey Annals*): see p. 306.
7. Cf. *Laws and Customs*, p. 220: 'The new *fëa*, and therefore in their beginning all *fëar*, they [the Eldar] believe to come direct from Eru and from beyond Ëa. Therefore many of them hold that it cannot be asserted that the fate of the Elves is to be confined within Arda for ever and with it to cease.'
8. *mort*: the note sounded on a horn at the death of the quarry.
9. The distinction between *ye* (plural) and *you* (singular) is presumably intended (see note 5).
10. The manuscript has *Mirruyainar*, followed in both typescripts. On B my father emended the name to *Mirroyainar* here but not at the second occurrence (p. 316); on C he changed it to *Mirröanwi*

at both occurrences. See the 'Glossary' to the *Athrabeth*, p. 350.

11 In the margin of the manuscript, repeated in the typescript C, is written against this paragraph: 'In the Music of Eru Men only entered after the discords of Melkor.' Of course this was true of the Elves also. See Author's Note 1 to the Commentary on the *Athrabeth* and note 10 (p. 358).

12 Cf. the words of Manwë at the end of the Debate of the Valar in *Laws and Customs* (p. 245): 'For Arda Unmarred hath two aspects or senses. The first is the Unmarred that they [the Eldar] discern in the Marred...: this is the ground upon which Hope is built. The second is the Unmarred that shall be: that is, to speak according to Time in which they have their being, the Arda Healed, which shall be greater and more fair than the first, because of the Marring: this is the Hope that sustaineth.'

13 It is said in the *Ainulindalë* (p. 13, §19) that 'the history was incomplete and the circles not full-wrought when the vision was taken away', to which in the final text D (p. 31) was added a footnote, attributed to Pengoloð:

And some have said that the Vision ceased ere the fulfilment of the Dominion of Men and the fading of the Firstborn; wherefore, though the Music is over all, the Valar have not seen as with sight the Later Ages or the ending of the World.

In the 'lost' typescript AAm* of the opening of the *Annals of Aman* (p. 64) it is said that Nienna could not endure to the end of the Music, and that 'therefore she has not the hope of Manwë' (p. 68).

14 See p. 312 and note 7.

15 On the conception of Arda Complete see note (iii) at the end of *Laws and Customs* (p. 251).

16 It was of course fundamental to the whole conception of the Elder Days that Men awoke in the East at the first Sunrise, and that they had existed for no more than a few hundred years when Finrod Felagund came upon Bëor and his people in the foothills of the Blue Mountains. There have been suggestions earlier in the *Athrabeth* that Andreth was looking much further back in time to the awakening of Men (thus she speaks of 'legends of days when death came less swiftly and our span was still far longer', p. 313); in her words here, 'a rumour that has come down through years uncounted', a profound alteration in the conception seems plain. The chronology of the Years of the Sun is however maintained in the *Athrabeth*, with the dating of the meeting of Finrod and Andreth as 'about 409 during the Long Peace (260–455)' (see p. 306). See further p. 378.

17 Both here and on p. 324 the name was written *Egnor* in the manuscript, subsequently changed to *Aegnor*; cf. p. 177 (§42) and p. 197.

18 Cf. QS §117 (V.264): 'Angrod and Egnor watched Bladorion from the northern slopes of Dorthonion' (during the Siege of Angband), and §129 (V.276): 'Barahir [son of Bëor the Old] dwelt mostly on the north marches with Angrod and Egnor.'
19 The sentence 'But say not *thou* to me, for so he once did' was an addition to the manuscript; Finrod has begun to address Andreth as *thou* from shortly before this point. But from here to the end of the text the usage is very confused, inconsistent in the manuscript and with inconsistent emendation to the typescript (both *thou* to *you* and *you* to *thou*); it seems that my father was in two minds as to which forms Finrod should employ, and I have left the text as it stands.
20 *pitiful*: i.e. filled with pity, compassionate.
21 Cf. *Laws and Customs*, p. 213: 'it would seem to any of the Eldar a grievous thing if a wedded pair were sundered during the bearing of a child, or while the first years of its childhood lasted. For which reason the Eldar would beget children only in days of happiness and peace if they could.'

★

The *Athrabeth Finrod ah Andreth* perhaps marks the culmination of my father's thought on the relation of Elves and Men, in Finrod's exalted vision of the original design of Eru for Mankind; but his central purpose was to explore fully for the first time the nature of 'the Marring of Men'. In the long account of his work that he wrote for Milton Waldman in 1951 (*Letters* no.131, pp. 147–8) he had said:

The first fall of Man ... nowhere appears – Men do not come on the stage until all that is long past, and there is only a rumour that for a while they fell under the domination of the Enemy and that some repented.

In the *Athrabeth* Finrod approaches this 'rumour' directly: 'Therefore I say to you, Andreth, *what did ye do, ye Men, long ago in the dark? How did ye anger Eru?* ... Will you say what you know or have heard?' He is met by a blank refusal: '"I will not," said Andreth. "We do not speak of this to those of other race"'; but to Finrod's subsequent question 'Are there no tales of your days before death, though ye will not tell them to strangers?' Andreth replies: 'Maybe. If not among my folk, then among the folk of Adanel, perhaps.' The legend of the Fall of Man preserved among certain of the Edain was (as will be seen shortly) about to enter.

Presenting the fundamental differences of destiny, nature, and experience between Elves and Men in the form of a philosophical debate between Finrod Lord of Nargothrond and Andreth descendant of Bëor the Old, the argument is nonetheless conducted with an increasing intensity, and bitterness on the part of Andreth, the bearing of which (though known to both speakers independently) is only revealed at the end. But to this passionate work my father appended a long discursive and critical commentary in a very different vein, which follows here.

The newspapers in which the *Athrabeth* and the commentary were preserved (see p. 304) bear the inscription:

Addit. Silmarillion

Athrabeth Finrod ah Andreth

Commentary

On one of these wrappers my father added: 'Should be last item in an appendix' (i.e. to *The Silmarillion*).

This commentary he typed himself, in top copy and carbon, with a few subsequent emendations almost identical in both. Following the commentary are numbered notes that bulk much larger than the commentary itself, since some of them constitute short essays. I distinguish these from my own numbered notes to the text (pp. 357ff.) by the words 'Author's Note'.

Very rough drafting for the commentary is extant, and that this followed the making of the amanuensis typescripts of the *Athrabeth* itself is seen from the occurrence in it of the word *Mirröanwi* (see note 10 above).

ATHRABETH FINROD AH ANDRETH
The Debate of Finrod and Andreth

This is not presented as an argument of any cogency for Men in their present situation (or the one in which they believe themselves to be), though it may have some interest for Men who start with similar beliefs or assumptions to those held by the Elvish king Finrod.

It is in fact simply part of the portrayal of the imaginary world of the *Silmarillion*, and an example of the kind of thing that enquiring minds on either side, the Elvish or the Human, must have said to one another after they became acquainted. We see here the attempt of a generous Elvish mind to fathom the relations of Elves and Men, and the part they were designed to play in what he would have called the *Oienkarmë Eruo* (The One's perpetual production), which might be rendered by 'God's management of the Drama'.

There are certain things in this world that have to be accepted as 'facts'. *The existence of Elves:* that is of a race of beings closely akin to Men, so closely indeed that they must be regarded as physically (or biologically) simply branches of the same race.[1] The Elves appeared on Earth earlier, but not (mythologically or geologically) much earlier;[2] they were 'immortal', and did not 'die' except by accident. Men, when they appeared on the scene (that is, when they met the Elves), were, however, much as they now are: they 'died', even if they escaped all accidents, at about the age of 70 to 80. *The existence of the Valar:* that is of certain angelic Beings (created, but at least as powerful as the 'gods' of human mythologies), the chief of whom still resided in an actual physical part of the Earth. They were the agents and vice-gerents of Eru (God). They had been for nameless ages engaged in a demiurgic labour[3] completing to the design of Eru the structure of the Universe (Eä); but were now concentrated on Earth for the principal Drama of Creation: the war of the *Eruhín* (The Children of God), Elves and Men, against Melkor. Melkor, originally the most powerful of the Valar,[4] had become a rebel, against his brethren and against Eru, and was the prime Spirit of Evil.

With regard to King Finrod, it must be understood that he starts with certain basic beliefs, which he would have said were derived from one or more of these sources: his created nature; angelic instruction; thought; and experience.

1. There exists Eru (The One); that is, One God Creator, who made (or more strictly designed) the World, but is not Himself the World. This world, or Universe, he calls *Eä*, an Elvish word that means 'It is', or 'Let It Be'.

2. There are on Earth 'incarnate' creatures, Elves and Men: these are made of a union of *hröa* and *fëa* (roughly but not exactly equivalent to 'body' and 'soul'). This, he would say, was a *known fact* concerning Elvish nature, and could therefore be deduced for human nature from the close kinship of Elves and Men.

3. *Hröa* and *fëa* he would say are wholly distinct in kind, and not on the 'same plane of derivation from Eru', *(Author's Note 1, p. 336)* but were designed each for the other, to abide in perpetual harmony. The *fëa* is indestructible, a unique identity which cannot be disintegrated or absorbed into any other identity. The *hröa*, however, can be destroyed and dissolved: that is a fact of experience. (In such a case he would describe the *fëa* as 'exiled' or 'houseless'.)

4. The separation of *fëa* and *hröa* is 'unnatural', and proceeds

not from the original design, but from the 'Marring of Arda', which is due to the operations of Melkor.

5. Elvish 'immortality' is bounded within a part of Time (which he would call the History of Arda), and is therefore strictly to be called rather 'serial longevity', the utmost limit of which is the length of the existence of Arda. *(Author's Note 2, p. 337)* A corollary of this is that the Elvish *fëa* is also limited to the Time of Arda, or at least held within it and unable to leave it, while it lasts.

6. From this it would follow in thought, if it were not a fact of Elvish experience, that a 'houseless' Elvish *fëa* must have the power or opportunity to return to incarnate life, if it has the desire or will to do so. (Actually the Elves discovered that their *fëar* had not this power in themselves, but that the opportunity and means were provided by the Valar, by the special permission of Eru for the amendment of the unnatural state of divorce. It was not lawful for the Valar to force a *fëa* to return; but they could impose conditions, and judge whether return should be permitted at all, and if so, in what way or after how long.) *(Author's Note 3, p. 339)*

7. Since Men die, without accident, and whether they will to do so or not, their *fëar* must have a different relation to Time. The Elves believed, though they had no certain information, that the *fëar* of Men, if disembodied, left Time (sooner or later), and never returned. *(Author's Note 4, p. 340)*

The Elves observed that all Men died (a fact confirmed by Men). They therefore deduced that this was 'natural' to Men (sc. was by the design of Eru), and supposed that the brevity of human life was due to this character of the human *fëa*: that it was not designed to stay long in Arda. Whereas their own *fëar*, being designed to remain in Arda to its end, imposed long endurance on their bodies; for they were (as a fact of experience) in far greater control of them. *(Author's Note 5, p. 341)*

Beyond the 'End of Arda' Elvish thought could not penetrate, and they were without any specific instruction. *(Author's Note 6, p. 341)* It seemed clear to them that their *hröar* must then end, and therefore any kind of re-incarnation would be impossible. *(Author's Note 7, p. 342)* All the Elves would then 'die' at the End of Arda. What this would mean they did not know. They said therefore that Men had a shadow behind them, but the Elves had a shadow before them.

Their dilemma was this: the thought of existence as *fëar* only was revolting to them, and they found it hard to believe that it was natural or designed for them, since they were essentially 'dwellers in Arda', and by nature wholly in love with Arda. The alternative: that their *fëar* would also cease to exist at 'the End', seemed even more intolerable. Both absolute annihilation, and cessation of conscious identity, were wholly repugnant to thought and desire. *(Author's Note 8, p. 343)*

Some argued that, although integral and unique (as Eru from whom they directly proceeded), each *fëa*, being created, was finite, and might therefore be also of finite duration. It was not destructible within its appointed term, but when that was reached it ceased to be; or ceased to have any more experience, and 'resided only in the Past'.

But they saw that this did not provide any escape. For, even if an Elvish *fëa* was able 'consciously' to dwell in or contemplate the Past, this would be a condition wholly unsatisfying to its desire. *(Reference to Author's Note 8)* The Elves had (as they said themselves) a 'great talent' for memory, but this tended to regret rather than to joy. Also, however long the History of the Elves might become before it ended, it would be an object of too limited range. To be perpetually 'imprisoned in a tale' (as they said), even if it was a very great tale ending triumphantly, would become a torment.[5] For greater than the talent of memory was the Elvish talent for *making*, and for discovery. The Elvish *fëa* was above all designed to make things in co-operation with its *hröa*.

Therefore in the last resort the Elves were obliged to rest on 'naked *estel*' (as they said): the trust in Eru, that whatever He designed beyond the End would be recognized by each *fëa* as wholly satisfying (at the least). Probably it would contain joys unforeseeable. But they remained in the belief that it would remain in intelligible relation with their present nature and desires, proceed from them, and include them.

For these reasons the Elves were less sympathetic than Men expected to the lack of hope (or *estel*) in Men faced by death. Men were, of course, in general entirely ignorant of the 'Shadow Ahead' which conditioned Elvish thought and feeling, and simply envied Elvish 'immortality'. But the Elves were on their part generally ignorant of the persistent tradition among Men that Men were also by nature immortal.

As is seen in the *Athrabeth*, Finrod is deeply moved and amazed to discover this tradition. He uncovers a concomitant tradition that the change in the condition of Men from their original design was due to a primeval disaster, about which human lore is unclear, or Andreth is at least unwilling to say much. *(Author's Note 9, p. 343)* He remains, nonetheless, in the opinion that the condition of Men before the disaster (or as we might say, of unfallen Man) cannot have been the same as that of the Elves. That is, their 'immortality' cannot have been the longevity within Arda of the Elves; otherwise they would have been simply Elves, and their separate introduction later into the Drama by Eru would have no function. He thinks that the notion of Men that, unchanged, they would not have died (in the sense of leaving Arda) is due to human misrepresentation of their own tradition, and possibly to envious comparison of themselves to the Elves. For one thing, he does not think this fits, as we might say, 'the observable peculiarities of human psychology', as compared with Elvish feelings towards the visible world.

He therefore guesses that it is the fear of death that is the result of the disaster. It is feared because it now is combined with severance of *hröa* and *fëa*. But the *fëar* of Men must have been designed to leave Arda willingly or indeed by desire – maybe after a longer time than the present average human life, but still in a time very short compared with Elvish lives. Then basing his argument on the axiom that severance of *hröa* and *fëa* is unnatural and contrary to design, he comes (or if you like jumps) to the conclusion that the *fëa* of unfallen Man would have taken with it its *hröa* into the new mode of existence (free from Time). In other words, that 'assumption' was the natural end of each human life, though as far as we know it has been the end of the only 'unfallen' member of Mankind.[6] He then has a vision of Men as the agents of the 'unmarring' of Arda, not merely undoing the marring or evil wrought by Melkor, but by producing a third thing, 'Arda Re-made' – for Eru never merely undoes the past, but brings into being something new, richer than the 'first design'. In Arda Re-made Elves and Men will each separately find joy and content, and an interplay of friendship, a bond of which will be the Past.

Andreth says that in that case the disaster to Men was appalling; for this re-making (if indeed it was the proper function of Men) cannot now be achieved. Finrod evidently remains in the hope that it will be achieved, though he does not say how that could be. He now sees, however, that the power of Melkor was greater than had been understood (even by the Elves, who had actually seen him in incarnate form): if he had been able to change Men, and so destroy the plan.[7]

More strictly speaking, he would say that Melkor had not 'changed' Men, but 'seduced' them (to allegiance to himself) very early in their history, so that Eru had changed their 'fate'. For Melkor could seduce individual minds and wills, but he could not make this heritable, or alter (contrary to the will and design of Eru) the relation of a whole people to Time and Arda. But the power of Melkor over material things was plainly vast. The whole of Arda (and indeed probably many other parts of Eä) had been marred by him. Melkor was not just a local Evil on Earth, nor a Guardian Angel of Earth who had gone wrong: he was the Spirit of Evil, arising even before the making of Eä. His attempt to dominate the structure of Eä, and of Arda in particular, and alter the designs of Eru (which governed all the operations of the faithful Valar), had introduced evil, or a tendency to aberration from the design, into all the physical matter of Arda. It was for this reason, no doubt, that he had been totally successful with Men, but only partially so with Elves (who remained as a people 'unfallen'). His power was wielded over matter, and through it. *(Author's Note 10, p. 344)* But by nature the *fëar* of Men were in much less strong control of their *hröar* than was the case with the Elves. Individual Elves might be seduced to a kind of minor 'Melkorism': desiring to be their own masters in Arda, and to have things their own way, leading in extreme cases to rebellion against the tutelage of the Valar; but not one had ever entered the service or allegiance of Melkor himself, nor ever denied the existence and absolute supremacy of Eru. Some dreadful things of this sort, Finrod guesses, Men must have done, as a whole; but Andreth does not reveal what were Men's traditions on this point. *(Reference to Author's Note 9)*

Finrod, however, sees now that, as things were, no created thing or being in Arda, or in all Eä, was powerful enough to counteract or heal Evil: that is to subdue Melkor (in his present person, reduced though that was) *and* the Evil that he had dissipated and sent out from himself into the very structure of the world.

Only Eru himself could do this. Therefore, since it was unthinkable that Eru would abandon the world to the ultimate triumph and domination of Melkor (which could mean its ruin and reduction to chaos), Eru Himself must at some time come to oppose Melkor. But Eru could not enter *wholly* into the world and its history, which is, however great, only a finite Drama. He must as Author always remain 'outside' the Drama, even though that Drama depends on His design and His will for its beginning and continuance, in every detail and moment. Finrod therefore thinks that He will, when He comes, have to be both 'outside' and inside; and so he glimpses the possibility of complexity or of distinctions in the nature of Eru, which nonetheless leaves Him 'The One'. *(Author's Note 11, p. 345)*

Since Finrod had already guessed that the redemptive function was originally specially assigned to Men, he probably proceeded to the expectation that 'the coming of Eru', if it took place, would be specially and primarily concerned with Men: that is to an imaginative guess or vision that Eru would come incarnated in human form. This, however, does not appear in the *Athrabeth*.

The argument is not, of course, presented in the *Athrabeth* in these terms, or in this order, or so precisely. The *Athrabeth* is a conversation, in which many assumptions and steps of thought have to be supplied by the reader. Actually, though it deals with such things as death and the relations of Elves and Men to Time and Arda, and to one another, its real purpose is dramatic: to exhibit the generosity of Finrod's mind, his love and pity for Andreth, and the tragic situations that must arise in the meeting of Elves and Men (in the ages of the youth of the Elves). For as eventually becomes plain, Andreth had in youth fallen in love with Aegnor, Finrod's brother; and though she knew that he returned her love (or could have done so if he had deigned to), he had not declared it, but had left her – and she believed that she was rejected as too lowly for an Elf. Finrod (though she was not aware of this) knew about this situation. For this reason he understood and did not take offence at the bitterness with which she spoke of the Elves, and even of the Valar. He succeeded in the end in making her understand that she was not 'rejected' out of scorn or Elvish lordliness; but that the departure of Aegnor was for motives of 'wisdom', and cost Aegnor great pain: he was an equal victim of the tragedy.

In the event Aegnor perished soon after this conversation,[8] when Melkor broke the Siege of Angband in the ruinous Battle of Sudden Flame, and the destruction of the Elvish realms in Beleriand was begun. Finrod took refuge in the great southern stronghold of Nargothrond; but not long after sacrificed his life to save Beren One-hand. (It is probable, though nowhere stated, that Andreth herself perished at this time, for all the northern realm, where Finrod and his brothers, and the People of Bëor, dwelt was devastated and conquered by Melkor. But she would then be a very old woman.)[9]

Finrod thus was slain before the two marriages of Elves and Men had taken place, though without his aid the marriage of Beren and Lúthien would not have come to pass. The marriage of Beren certainly fulfilled his prediction that such marriages would only be for some high purpose of Doom, and that the least cruel fate would be that death should soon end them.

Author's Notes on the 'Commentary'

Note 1

Because *fëar* were held to be directly created by Eru, and 'sent into' Eä; whereas Eä was achieved mediately by the Valar.

According to the *Ainulindalë* there were five stages in Creation. a. The creation of the Ainur. b. The communication by Eru of his Design to the Ainur. c. The Great Music, which was as it were a rehearsal, and remained in the stage of thought or imagination. d. The 'Vision' of Eru, which was again only a foreshowing of possibility, and was incomplete. e. The Achievement, which is still going on.

The Eldar held that Eru was and is free at all stages. This freedom was shown in the Music by His introduction, after the arising of the discords of Melkor, of the two new themes, representing the coming of Elves and Men, which were not in His first communication.[10] He may therefore in stage 5 introduce things directly, which were not in the Music and so are not achieved through the Valar. It remains, nonetheless, true in general to regard Eä as achieved through their mediation.

The additions of Eru, however, will not be 'alien'; they will be accommodated to the nature and character of Eä and of those that dwell in it; they may enhance the past and enrich its purpose and significance, but they will contain it and not destroy it.

Thus the 'newness' of the themes of the Children of Eru, Elves and Men, consisted in the association of *fëar* with, or 'housing' them in, *hröar* belonging to Eä, in such a way that either were incomplete without the others. But the *fëar* were not spirits of a wholly different kind to the Ainur; whereas the bodies were of a kind closely akin to the bodies of living things already in the primary design (even if adapted to their new function, or modified by the indwelling *fëar*).

Note 2

Arda, or 'The Kingdom of Arda' (as being directly under the kingship of Eru's vice-gerent Manwë) is not easy to translate, since neither 'earth' nor 'world' are entirely suitable. Physically Arda was what we should call the Solar System.[11] Presumably the Eldar could have had as much and as accurate information concerning this, its structure, origin, and its relation to the rest of Eä (the Universe) as they could comprehend. Probably those who were interested did acquire this knowledge. Not all the Eldar were interested in everything; most of them concentrated their attention on (or as they said 'were in love with') the Earth.

The traditions here referred to have come down from the Eldar of the First Age, through Elves who never were directly acquainted with the Valar, and through Men who received 'lore' from the Elves, but who had myths and cosmogonic legends, and astronomical guesses, of their own. There is, however, nothing in them that seriously conflicts with present human notions of the Solar System, and its size and position relative to the Universe. It must be remembered, however, that it does not necessarily follow that 'True Information' concerning Arda (such as the ancient Eldar might have received from the Valar) must agree with Men's present theories. Also, the Eldar (and the Valar) were not overwhelmed or even principally impressed by notions of size and distance. Their interest, certainly the interest of the *Silmarillion* and all related matter, may be termed 'dramatic'. Places or worlds were interesting or important because of what happened in them.

It is certainly the case with the Elvish traditions that the principal part of Arda was the Earth (*Imbar* 'The Habitation'),[12] as the scene of the Drama of the war of the Valar and the Children of Eru with Melkor: so that loosely used Arda often seems to mean the Earth: and that from this point of view the function of the Solar System was to make possible the existence of Imbar. With regard to the relation of Arda to Eä, the assertion that the principal demiurgic Ainur (the Valar), including the originally greatest of all, Melkor, had taken up their 'residence' in Arda,[13] ever since its establishment, also implies that however minute Arda was dramatically the chief point in Eä.

These views are not mathematical or astronomical, or even biological, and so cannot be held necessarily to conflict with the theories of our physical sciences. We cannot say that there 'must' be elsewhere in Eä other solar systems 'like' Arda, still less that, if there are, they or any one of them must contain a parallel to Imbar. We cannot even say that these things are mathematically very 'likely'. But even if the presence elsewhere in Eä of biological 'life' was demonstrable, it would not invalidate the Elvish view that Arda (at least while it endures) is the dramatic centre. The demonstration that there existed elsewhere Incarnates, parallel to the Children of Eru, would of course modify the picture, though not wholly invalidate it. The Elvish answer would probably be: 'Well, that is another Tale. It is not our Tale. Eru can no doubt bring to pass more than one. Not everything is adumbrated in the *Ainulindalë*; or the *Ainulindalë* may have a wider reference than we knew: other dramas, like in kind if different in process and result, may have gone on in Eä, or may yet go on.' But they would certainly add: 'But they are not going on now. The drama of Arda is the present concern of Eä.' Actually it is plainly the view of the Elvish tradition that the Drama of Arda is unique. We cannot at present assert that this is untrue.

The Elves were of course primarily and deeply (more deeply than Men) concerned with Arda, and Imbar in particular. They appear to have held that the physical universe, Eä, had a beginning and would have an end: that it was limited and finite in all dimensions. They certainly held that all things or 'makings', that is constructed (however simply and incipiently) from basic 'matter', which they called *erma*,[14] were impermanent, within Eä. They were therefore much concerned with 'The End of Arda'. They knew themselves to be limited by Arda; but the length of its existence they do not seem to have known. Possibly the Valar did not know. More probably, they were not informed by the will or design of Eru, who appears in the Elvish tradition to demand two things from His Children (of either Kindred): belief in Him, and proceeding from that, hope or trust in Him (called by the Eldar *estel*).

But in any case, whether adumbrated in the Music or not, the

End could be brought about by Eru at any time by intervention, so that it could not be certainly foreseen. (A minor and as it were foreshadowing intervention of this sort was the catastrophe in which Númenor was obliterated, and the physical residence of the Valar in Imbar was ended.) The Elvish conception of the End was in fact *catastrophic*. They did not think that Arda (or at any rate Imbar) would just run down into lifeless inanition. But this conception was not embodied by them in any myth or legend. See Note 7.

Note 3

In Elvish tradition their re-incarnation was a special permission granted by Eru to Manwë, when Manwë directly consulted Him at the time of the debate concerning Finwë and Míriel.[15] (Míriel 'died' in Aman by refusing to live any longer in the body, and so raised the whole question of the unnatural divorce of an Elvish *fëa* and its *hröa*, and of the bereavement of Elves that still lived: Finwë, her husband, was left solitary.) The Valar, or Mandos as the mouthpiece of all commands and in many cases their executor, were given power to summon, with full authority, all houseless *fëar* of Elves to Aman. There they were given the choice to remain houseless, or (if they wished) to be re-housed in the same form and shape as they had had.[16] Normally they must nonetheless remain in Aman.[17] Therefore, if they dwelt in Middle-earth, their bereavement of friends and kin, and the bereavement of these, was not amended. Death was not wholly healed. But as Andreth saw, this certitude concerning their immediate future after death, and the knowledge that at the least they would again if they wished be able as *incarnates* to do and make things and continue their experience of Arda, made death to the Elves a totally different thing from death as it appeared to Men.

They were given a choice, because Eru did not allow their free will to be taken away. Similarly the houseless *fëar* were *summoned*, not brought, to Mandos. They could refuse the summons, but this would imply that they were in some way tainted, or they would not wish to refuse the authority of Mandos: refusal had grave consequences, inevitably proceeding from the rebellion against authority.

They 'normally remained in Aman'. Simply because they were, when rehoused, again in actual physical bodies, and return to Middle-earth was therefore very difficult and perilous.

Also during the period of the Exile of the Noldor the Valar had for the time being cut all communications (by physical means) between Aman and Middle-earth. The Valar could of course have arranged for the transference, if there was sufficiently grave reason. Bereavement of friends and kin was, apparently, not considered a sufficient reason. Probably under instruction of Eru. In any case, as far as the Noldor were concerned, these had, as a people, cut themselves off from mercy; they had left Aman demanding absolute freedom to be their own masters, to carry on their war against Melkor with their own unaided valour, and to face death and its consequences. The only case of a special arrangement recorded in the Histories is that of Beren and Lúthien. Beren was slain soon after their marriage, and Lúthien died of grief. They were both re-housed and sent back to Beleriand; but both became 'mortal' and died later according to the normal human span. The reasons for this, which must have been done by an express permission of Eru, were not fully apparent until later, but were certainly of unique weight. The grief of Lúthien was so great that according to the Eldar it moved the pity of even Mandos the Unmoved. Beren and Lúthien together had achieved the greatest of all the deeds against Melkor: regaining one of the Silmarils. Lúthien was not of the Noldor but daughter of Thingol (of the Teleri), and her mother Melian was 'divine', a *maia* (one of the minor members of the spirit-race of the Valar). Thus from the union of Lúthien and Beren which was made possible by their return, the infusion of a 'divine' and an Elvish strain into Mankind was to be brought about, providing a link between Mankind and the Elder World, after the establishment of the Dominion of Men.

Note 4

Sooner or later: because the Elves believed that the *fëar* of dead Men also went to Mandos (without choice in the matter: their free will with regard to death was taken away). There they waited until they were surrendered to Eru. The truth of this is not asserted. No living Man was allowed to go to Aman. No *fëa* of a dead Man ever returned to life in Middle-earth. To all such statements and decrees there are always some exceptions (because of the 'freedom of Eru'). Eärendil reached Aman, even in the time of the Ban; but he bore the Silmaril recovered by his ancestress Lúthien,[18] and he was 'half-elven': he was not allowed to return to Middle-earth. Beren returned to actual life, for a short time; but he was not actually seen again by living Men.

The passing 'oversea' to Eressëa (an isle within sight of Aman) was permitted to, and indeed urged upon, all Elves remaining in Middle-earth after the downfall of Morgoth in Angband. This really marked the beginning of the Dominion of Men, though there was (in our view) a long twilight period between the downfall of Morgoth and the final overthrow of Sauron: lasting, that is, through the Second and Third Ages. But at the end of the Second Age came the great Catastrophe (by an intervention of Eru that foreshadowed, as it were, the End of Arda): the annihilation of Númenor, and the 'removal' of Aman from the physical world. The passing 'oversea', therefore, of Mortals after the Catastrophe – which is recorded in *The Lord of the Rings* – is not quite the same thing. It was in any case a special grace. An opportunity for dying according to the original plan for the unfallen: they went to a state in which they could acquire greater knowledge and peace of mind, and being healed of all hurts both of mind and body, could at last surrender themselves: die of free will, and even of desire, in *estel*. A thing which Aragorn achieved without any such aid.

Note 5

They were thus capable of far greater and longer physical exertions (in pursuit of some dominant purpose of their minds) without weariness; they were not subject to diseases; they healed rapidly and completely after injuries that would have proved fatal to Men; and they could endure great physical pain for long periods. Their bodies could not, however, survive vital injuries, or violent assaults upon their structure; nor replace missing members (such as a hand hewn off). On the reverse side: the Elves could die, and did die, by their will; as for example because of great grief or bereavement, or because of the frustration of their dominant desires and purposes. This wilful death was not regarded as wicked, but it was a fault implying some defect or taint in the *fëa*, and those who came to Mandos by this means might be refused further incarnate life.

Note 6

Because the Valar had no information; or because information was withheld. See Note 2 [fifth paragraph].

Note 7

See Note 2. The Elves expected the End of Arda to be catastrophic. They thought that it would be brought about by the dissolution of the structure of Imbar at least, if not of the whole system. The End of Arda is not, of course, the same thing as the end of Eä. About this they held that nothing could be known, except that Eä was ultimately finite. It is noteworthy that the Elves had no myths or legends dealing with the end of the world. The myth that appears at the end of the *Silmarillion* is of Númenórean origin;[19] it is clearly made by Men, though Men acquainted with Elvish tradition. All Elvish traditions are presented as 'histories', or as accounts of what once was.

We are here dealing with Elvish thought at an early period, when the Eldar were still fully 'physical' in bodily form. Much later, when the process (already glimpsed by Finrod) called 'waning' or 'fading' had become more effective, their views of the End of Arda, so far as it affected themselves, must have been modified. But there are few records of any contacts of Elvish and Human thought in such latter days. They eventually became housed, if it can be called that, not in actual visible and tangible *hröar*, but only in the memory of the *fëa* of its bodily form, and its desire for it; and therefore not dependent for mere existence upon the material of Arda.[20] But they appear to have held, and indeed still to hold, that this desire for the *hröa* shows that their later (and present) condition is not natural to them, and they remain in *estel* that Eru will heal it. 'Not natural', whether it is due wholly, as they earlier thought, to the weakening of the *hröa* (derived from the debility introduced by Melkor into the substance of Arda upon which it must feed), or partly to the inevitable working of a dominant *fëa* upon a material *hröa* through many ages. (In the latter case 'natural' can refer only to an ideal state, in which unmarred matter could for ever endure the indwelling of a perfectly adapted *fëa*. It cannot refer to the actual design of Eru, since the Themes of the Children were introduced after the arising of the discords of Melkor. The 'waning' of the Elvish *hröar* must therefore be part of the History of Arda as envisaged by Eru, and the mode in which the Elves were to make way for the Dominion of Men. The Elves find their supersession by Men a mystery, and a cause of grief; for they say that Men, at least so largely governed as they are by the evil of Melkor, have less and less *love* for Arda in itself, and are largely busy in destroying it in the attempt to dominate it. They still believe that Eru's healing of all the griefs of Arda will come now by or through Men; but the Elves' part in the healing or redemption will be chiefly in the restoration of the *love* of Arda, to which their memory of the Past and understanding of what might have been will contribute. Arda they say will be destroyed by wicked Men (or the wickedness in Men); but healed through the goodness in Men. The wickedness, the domineering lovelessness, the Elves will offset. By the holiness of good men – their direct attachment to Eru, before and above all Eru's works[21] – the Elves may be delivered from the last of their griefs: sadness; the sadness that must come even from the unselfish love of anything less than Eru.)

Note 8

Desire. The Elves insisted that 'desires', especially such fundamental desires as are here dealt with, were to be taken as indications of the true natures of the Incarnates, and of the direction in which their unmarred fulfilment must lie. They distinguished between *desire of the fëa* (perception that something right or necessary is not present, leading to desire or hope for it); *wish*, or *personal wish* (the feeling of the lack of something, the force of which primarily concerns oneself, and which may have little or no reference to the general fitness of things); *illusion*, the refusal to recognize that things are not as they should be, leading to the delusion that they are as one would desire them to be, when they are not so. (The last might now be called 'wishful thinking', legitimately; but this term, the Elves would say, is quite illegitimate when applied to the first. The last can be disproved by reference to facts. The first not so. Unless desirability is held to be *always* delusory, and the sole basis for the hope of amendment. But *desires of the fëa* may often be shown to be reasonable by arguments quite unconnected with personal wish. The fact that they *accord* with 'desire', or even with personal wish, does not invalidate them. Actually the Elves believed that the 'lightening of the heart' or the 'stirring of joy' (to which they often refer), which may accompany the hearing of a proposition or an argument, is not an indication of its falsity but of the recognition by the *fëa* that it is on the path of truth.)

Note 9

It is probable that Andreth was actually unwilling to say more.

Partly by a kind of loyalty that restrained Men from revealing to the Elves all that they knew about the darkness in their past; partly because she felt unable to make up her own mind about the conflicting human traditions. Longer recensions of the *Athrabeth*, evidently edited under Númenórean influence, make her give, under pressure, a more precise answer. Some are very brief, some longer. All agree, however, in making the cause of disaster the acceptance by Men of Melkor as King (or King and God). In one version a complete legend (compressed in time-scale) is given explicitly as a Númenórean tradition, for it makes Andreth say: *This is the Tale that Adanel of the House of Hador told to me.* The Númenóreans were largely, and their non-Elvish traditions mainly, derived from the People of Marach, of whom the House of Hador were the chieftains.[22] The legend bears certain resemblances to the Númenórean traditions concerning the part played by Sauron in the downfall of Númenor. But this does not prove that it is entirely a fiction of post-downfall days. It is no doubt mainly derived from actual lore of the People of Marach, quite independent of the *Athrabeth*. [*Added note:* Nothing is hereby asserted concerning its 'truth', historical or otherwise.] The operations of Sauron naturally and inevitably resembled or repeated those of his master. That a people in possession of such a legend or tradition should have later been deluded by Sauron is sad but, in view of human history generally, not incredible. Indeed if fish had fish-lore and Wise-fish, it is probable that the business of anglers would be very little hindered.[23]

The 'Tale of Adanel' is attached [pp. 345–9].

Note 10

'Matter' is not regarded as evil or opposed to 'Spirit'. Matter was wholly good in origin. It remained a 'creature of Eru' and still largely good, and indeed self-healing, when not interfered with: that is, when the latent evil intruded by Melkor was not deliberately roused and used by evil minds. Melkor had concentrated his attention on 'matter', because spirits could only be dominated completely by fear; and fear was most easily exerted through matter (especially in the case of the Incarnates, whom he most desired to subjugate). For example by fear that material things that were loved might be destroyed, or the fear (in Incarnates) that their bodies might be hurt. (Melkor also used and perverted for his purposes the 'fear of Eru', fully or vaguely understood. But this was more difficult and perilous and required more cunning. Lesser spirits might be lured by love or admiration of himself and his powers, and so led at last into a posture of rebellion against Eru. Their fear of Him might then be darkened, so that they adhered to Melkor, as a captain and protector, becoming at last too terrified to return to the allegiance of Eru, even after they had discovered Melkor and had begun to hate him.)

Note 11

This is actually already glimpsed in the *Ainulindalë*, in which reference is made to the 'Flame Imperishable'. This appears to mean the Creative activity of Eru (in some sense distinct from or within Him), by which things could be given a 'real' and independent (though derivative and created) existence. The Flame Imperishable is sent out from Eru, to dwell in the heart of the world, and the world then Is, on the same plane as the Ainur, and they can enter into it. But this is not, of course, the same as the re-entry of Eru to defeat Melkor. It refers rather to the mystery of 'authorship', by which the author, while remaining 'outside' and independent of his work, also 'indwells' in it, on its derivative plane, below that of his own being, as the source and guarantee of its being.

[*The 'Tale of Adanel'*]

Then Andreth being urged by Finrod said at last: 'This is the tale that Adanel of the House of Hador told to me:'

Some say the Disaster happened at the beginning of the history of our people, before any had yet died. The Voice had spoken to us, and we had listened. The Voice said: 'Ye are my children. I have sent you to dwell here. In time ye will inherit all this Earth, but first ye must be children and learn. Call on me and I shall hear; for I am watching over you.'

We understood the Voice in our hearts, though we had no words yet. Then the desire for words awoke in us, and we began to make them. But we were few, and the world was wide and strange. Though we greatly desired to understand, learning was difficult, and the making of words was slow.

In that time we called often and the Voice answered. But it seldom answered our questions, saying only: 'First seek to find the answer for yourselves. For ye will have joy in the finding, and so grow from childhood and become wise. Do not seek to leave childhood before your time.'

But we were in haste, and we desired to order things to our will; and the shapes of many things that we wished to make awoke in our minds. Therefore we spoke less and less to the Voice.

Then one appeared among us, in our own form visible, but greater and more beautiful; and he said that he had come out of pity. 'Ye should not have been left alone and uninstructed,' he said. 'The world is full of marvellous riches which knowledge can unlock. Ye could have food more abundant and more delicious than the poor things that ye now eat. Ye could have dwellings of ease, in which ye could keep light and shut out the night. Ye could be clad even as I.'

Then we looked and lo! he was clad in raiment that shone like silver and gold, and he had a crown on his head, and gems in his hair. 'If ye wish to be like me,' he said, 'I will teach you.' Then we took him as teacher.

He was less swift than we had hoped to teach us how to find, or to make for ourselves, the things that we desired, though he had awakened many desires in our hearts. But if any doubted or were impatient, he would bring and set before us all that we wished for. 'I am the Giver of Gifts,' he said; 'and the gifts shall never fail as long as ye trust me.'

Therefore we revered him, and we were enthralled by him; and we depended upon his gifts, fearing to return to a life without them that now seemed poor and hard. And we believed all that he taught. For we were eager to know about the world and its being: about the beasts and birds, and the plants that grew in the Earth; about our own making; and about the lights of heaven, and the countless stars, and the Dark in which they are set.

All that he taught seemed good, for he had great knowledge. But ever more and more he would speak of the Dark. 'Greatest of all is the Dark,' he said, 'for It has no bounds. I came out of the Dark, but I am Its master. For I have made Light. I made the Sun and the Moon and the countless stars. I will protect you from the Dark, which else would devour you.'

Then we spoke of the Voice. But his face became terrible; for he was angry. 'Fools!' he said. 'That was the Voice of the Dark. It wishes to keep you from me; for It is hungry for you.'

Then he went away, and we did not see him for a long time,

and without his gifts we were poor. And there came a day when suddenly the Sun's light began to fail, until it was blotted out and a great shadow fell on the world; and all the beasts and birds were afraid. Then he came again, walking through the shadow like a bright fire.

We fell upon our faces. 'There are some among you who are still listening to the Voice of the Dark,' he said, 'and therefore It is drawing nearer. Choose now! Ye may have the Dark as Lord, or ye may have Me. But unless ye take Me for Lord and swear to serve Me, I shall depart and leave you; for I have other realms and dwelling places, and I do not need the Earth, nor you.'

Then in fear we spoke as he commanded, saying: 'Thou art the Lord; Thee only we will serve. The Voice we abjure and will not hearken to it again.'

'So be it!' he said. 'Now build Me a house upon a high place, and call it the House of the Lord. Thither I will come when I will. There ye shall call on Me and make your petitions to Me.'

And when we had built a great house, he came and stood before the high seat, and the house was lit as with fire. 'Now,' he said, 'come forth any who still listen to the Voice!'

There were some, but for fear they remained still and said naught. 'Then bow before Me and acknowledge Me!' he said. And all bowed to the ground before him, saying: 'Thou art the One Great, and we are Thine.'

Thereupon he went up as in a great flame and smoke, and we were scorched by the heat. But suddenly he was gone, and it was darker than night; and we fled from the House.

Ever after we went in great dread of the Dark; but he seldom appeared among us again in fair form, and he brought few gifts. If at great need we dared to go to the House and pray to him to help us, we heard his voice, and received his commands. But now he would always command us to do some deed, or to give him some gift, before he would listen to our prayer; and ever the deeds became worse, and the gifts harder to give up.

The first Voice we never heard again, save once. In the stillness of the night It spoke, saying: 'Ye have abjured Me, but ye remain Mine. I gave you life. Now it shall be shortened, and each of you in a little while shall come to Me, to learn who is your Lord: the one ye worship, or I who made him.'

Then our terror of the Dark was increased; for we believed that the Voice was of the Darkness behind the stars. And some of us began to die in horror and anguish, fearing to go out into the Dark. Then we called on our Master to save us from death, and he did not answer. But when we went to the House and all bowed down there, at last he came, great and majestic, but his face was cruel and proud.

'Now ye are Mine and must do My will,' he said. 'I do not trouble that some of you die and go to appease the hunger of the Dark; for otherwise there would soon be too many of you, crawling like lice on the Earth. But if ye do not do My will, ye will feel My anger, and ye will die sooner, for I will slay you.'

Thereafter we were grievously afflicted, by weariness, and hunger, and sickness; and the Earth and all things in it were turned against us. Fire and Water rebelled against us. The birds and beasts shunned us, or if they were strong they assailed us. Plants gave us poison; and we feared the shadows under trees.

Then we yearned for our life as it was before our Master came; and we hated him, but feared him no less than the Dark. And we did his bidding, and more than his bidding; for anything that we thought would please him, however evil, we did, in the hope that he would lighten our afflictions, and at the least would not slay us.

For most of us this was in vain. But to some he began to show favour: to the strongest and cruellest, and to those who went most often to the House. He gave gifts to them, and knowledge that they kept secret; and they became powerful and proud, and they enslaved us, so that we had no rest from labour amidst our afflictions.

Then there arose some among us who said openly in their despair: 'Now we know at last who lied, and who desired to devour us. Not the first Voice. It is the Master that we have taken who is the Darkness; and he did not come forth from it, as he said, but he dwells in it. We will serve him no longer! He is our Enemy.'

Then in fear lest he should hear them and punish us all, we slew them, if we could; and those that fled we hunted; and if any were caught, our masters, his friends, commanded that they should be taken to the House and there done to death by fire. That pleased him greatly, his friends said; and indeed for a while it seemed that our afflictions were lightened.

But it is told that there were a few that escaped us, and went away into far countries, fleeing from the shadow. Yet they did not escape from the anger of the Voice; for they had built the House and bowed down in it. And they came at last to the land's end and the shores of the impassable water; and behold! the Enemy was there before them.

Together with the *Athrabeth* papers there is a *Glossary* (as my father termed it), a brief index of names and terms with definitions and some etymological information. This is confined to the *Athrabeth* itself, and so from the nature of the work is not large, but there are a few omissions (as *Athrabeth*, *Andreth*, and names of the People of Bëor). Written in manuscript, it was made after the amanuensis typescripts of the *Athrabeth* had been taken from the manuscript and emended, as the entry *Mirröanwi* shows (see p. 326 note 10). It seems curious that my father should have provided this, since most of the definitions or explanations would be unnecessary to one who had read *The Silmarillion*, and taken with the explanations of fundamental conceptions that appear in the Commentary may suggest that he conceived it as an independent work – although on one of the newspaper wrappers of the *Athrabeth* papers (p. 329) he noted that it should be the last item in an Appendix (to *The Silmarillion*).

Most of the information provided is readily found elsewhere, and I give only a selection of the entries, in whole or in part, with very slight editing for purposes of clarity.

Adaneth   Sindarin, 'woman, mortal woman'.
Arda   'kingdom', sc. the 'kingdom of Manwë'. The 'Solar System', or Earth as the *dramatic* centre of this, as the scene of the war of the 'Children of Eru' against Melkor.
Edennil   (Quenya *Atandil*) 'devoted to the *Atani*, Men'; name given to Finrod.
[Extracted from entry *Eldar*:]   But only part of the Eldar actually reached Aman. A large part of the Third Host (*Lindar* 'Singers', also called *Teleri* 'Those Behind') remained in the West of Middle-earth. These are the *Sindar* 'Grey-elves'. ... The Elves who were in or who ever had dwelt in Aman were called the High-elves *(Tareldar)*.[24]
fëa   'spirit': the particular 'spirit' belonging to and 'housed' in any one *hröa* of the Incarnates. It corresponds, more or less, to 'soul'; and to 'mind', when any attempt is made to distinguish between mentality, and the mental processes of Incarnates, conditioned and limited by the co-operation of the physical organs of the *hröa*. It was thus in its being (apart from its experience) the impulse and power to think: enquire and reflect, as distinct from the means of acquiring data. It was conscious and self-aware: 'self' however in Incarnates included the *hröa*. The *fëa* was said by the Eldar to retain the impress or memory of the *hröa* and of all the combined experiences of itself and its body. (Quenya *fëa* (dissyllabic) is from older **phāya*. Sindarin *faer*, of the same meaning, corresponds to Quenya *fairë* 'spirit (in general)', as opposed to matter (*erma*) or 'flesh' (*hrávë*).)

Finarphin / Finarfin [the name is given thus in alternative spellings]

hröa See *fëa*. (The Quenya form is derived from older **srawā*. The Sindarin form of *hröa* and *hrávë* (*srāwē*) was *rhaw*: cf. *Mirröanwi*.)

Mandos [extract] (The name *Mandos* (stem *mandost-*) means approximately 'castle of custody': from *mbandō* 'custody, safekeeping', and *osto* 'a strong or fortified building or place'. The Sindarin form of *mbandō*, Quenya *mando*, was *band*, occurring in *Angband* 'Iron-gaol', the name given to Morgoth's dwelling, Quenya *Angamando*.)

Melkor (also Melko) [extract] (*Melkor*, in older form *Melkórë*, probably means 'Mighty-rising', sc. 'uprising of power'; *Melko* simply 'the Mighty One'.)[25]

Mirröanwi Incarnates; those (spirits) 'put into flesh'; cf. *hröa*. (From **mi-srawanwe*.)

Ñoldor The name means 'lore-masters' or those specially devoted to knowledge. (The most ancient form was *ngolodō*, Quenya *noldo*, Sindarin *golodh*: in the transcription *ñ* = the Fëanorian letter for the back nasal, the *ng* of *king*.)[26] The Quenya word *ñólë* meant 'lore, knowledge', but its Sindarin equivalent *gûl*, owing to its frequent use in such combinations as *morgul* (cf. *Minas Morgul* in *The Lord of the Rings*) was only used for evil or perverted knowledge, necromancy, sorcery. This word *gûl* was also used in the language of Mordor.

Valar [extract] (The name) means 'those with power, the Powers'. But it should more strictly be translated 'the Authorities'. The 'power' of the Valar resided in the 'authority' they had from Eru. They had sufficient 'power' for their functions – that is, vast or godlike power over, and knowledge of, the physical structure of the Universe, and understanding of the designs of Eru. But they were forbidden to use *force* upon the Children of Eru. The stem *melk-*[27] (seen in *Melkor*) on the other hand means 'power' as force and strength.

I have referred (p. 303) to the existence of original draft material for the *Athrabeth*. The chief element in this is a small bundle of slips made from Merton College documents of 1955 and written very rapidly in ball-point pen; but it is plain that my father was following an earlier text, no longer extant, which he could not read at all points: words are marked with queries, dots are put in for missing phrases (some of which were filled in doubtfully afterwards), and some sentences do not seems to be correct. This draft, which I will call 'A', corresponds to the section in the final text from Finrod's words 'But what then shall we think of the union in Man' on p. 317 to 'then Eru must come in to conquer him' on p. 322; but the one is in certain respects extraordinarily different from the other. I give here two extracts to illustrate this. The first takes up from Finrod's questions (p. 318) 'Or is there somewhere else a world of which all things which we see, all things that either Elves or Men know, are only tokens or reminders?':

'If so it resides only in the mind of Eru,' said Andreth. 'But to such questions I know no answer. This much only can I say: that among us some hold that our errand here was to heal the Marring of Arda, and by making the *hröa* partake in the life of the *fëa* to put it beyond any marring of Melkor or any other spirit of malice for ever. But that "Arda Healed" (or Remade) shall not be "Arda Unmarred", but a third thing and a greater. And that third thing maybe is in the mind of Eru, and is in his answer. You have spoken to me of the Music and you have conversed with the Valar who were present at its making ere the world began. Did they hear the end of the Music? Or was there not something beyond the final chords of Eru, which (being overwhelmed thereby) the Valar did not hear? Or again maybe, since Eru is for ever free, He made no music and showed no Vision beyond a certain point. Beyond that point (which neither Valar nor Eldar . . .) we cannot see or know, until, each by our own roads, we come there.'

'In what did Melkor's malice show itself?'

Darkness lies over that. Saelon (sc. Andreth)[28] has little to answer. 'Some men say that he blasphemed Eru, and denied His existence, or His power, and that our fathers assented, and took Melkor to be a Lord and God; and that thereby our *fëar* denied their own true nature, and so became darkened and weakened almost to the death (if that be possible for *fëar*). And through the weakness of the *fëar* our *hröar* fell into unhealth, and lay open to all evils and disorders of the world. And others say that Eru himself spoke in wrath, saying: "If the Darkness be your God, little here shall you have of Light, but shall leave it soon and come before Me, to learn who lieth: Melkor or I Who made him."'[29]

The second passage corresponds in its placing to that beginning at Andreth's words in the final text (p. 321) 'Asleep or awake, they say nothing clearly':

'... Some say that ... Eru will find a way of healing that will heal both our fathers and ourselves and those that shall follow us. But how that shall come to pass, or to what manner of being this healing will make us, only those of the Hope (as we say) can guess; none can clearly assert.

'But there are among us a few (of whom I am one) who have the Great Hope, as we call it, and believe that His secret has been handed down from the days before our wounding. This is the Great Hope: that Eru will himself enter into Arda and heal Men and all the Marring.'

'But this is a strange thing! Do you claim to have known of Eru before ever we met? What is his name?'

'As it is with you, but different only in form of sound: The One.'

'But still this passes my understanding,' said Finrod. 'For how could Eru enter into the thing that He has made, and than which He is infinitely greater? Can the poet enter his story or the designer enter his picture?'

'He is already in it, and outside it,' said Saelon, 'though not in the same mode.'

'Yea verily,' said Finrod, 'and so is Eru in that mode / sense in Arda. But you speak of Eru *entering* into Arda, which is surely another matter. How could he do so, who is infinitely greater: would it not shatter Arda, or indeed Eä?'

'He could find a way, I doubt not,' said Saelon, 'though indeed I cannot conceive the way. But whatever you think, that is the Great Hope of Men. And I do not see – so to speak with humility – what else could be done; since Eru will surely not suffer Melkor to triumph and abandon His own work. But there is nothing more powerful that is conceivable than Melkor, save Eru only. Therefore Eru, if he will not relinquish his work to Melkor, who is ...., Eru must come in to conquer him.

At this point the draft text A ends. It will be seen in the first of these passages that the large vision of Finrod in the final form of the *Athrabeth* concerning 'Arda Remade', which arises in his mind from the words of Andreth, was originally a belief held by certain of the Atani, and it is Andreth who proposes the idea that this vision was absent from the end of the Music of the Ainur, or was not perceived by them; while in the second passage Andreth names herself as one of those who entertains 'the Great Hope', and to Finrod's incredulity that Eru could enter into Arda she provides those same speculative answers that are given to Finrod in the final text. It is thus apparent that my father's ideas concerning not only the structure and tenor of the 'Converse of Finrod and Andreth' but the very nature of the beliefs of the first Men in Beleriand underwent a major development as he worked on the *Athrabeth*.

An isolated page ('B') written, like draft A, on a Merton College document of 1955, carries an interesting passage that was not used in the final version.

'What says the wisdom of Men concerning the nature of the *Mirruyaina*?' said Finrod. 'Or what do you hold, Andreth, who know also much of the teaching of the Eldar?'

'Men say various things, be they Wise or no,' said Andreth. 'Many hold that there is but a single thing: the body, and that we are one of the beasts, though the latest come and the most cunning. But others hold that the body is not all, but contains some other thing. For often we speak of the body as a "house", or as "raiment", and that implies an indwelling, though of what we speak in uncertainty.[30]

'Among my folk men speak mostly of the "breath" (or the "breath of life"), and they say that if it leaves the house, it may by seeing eyes be seen as a *wraith*, a shadowy image of the living thing that was.'

'That is but a guess,' said Finrod, 'and long ago we said things similar, but we know now that the Indweller is not "breath"[31] (which the *hröa* uses), and that seeing eyes cannot see one that is houseless, but that the living eyes may draw from the *fëa* within an image which the houseless conveys to the housed: the memory of itself.'

'Maybe,' said Andreth. 'But among the people of Marach men speak rather of the "fire", or the "fire on the hearth", from whose burning the house is warmed, and from which arise the heats of the heart, or the smokes of wrath.'

'That is another guess,' said Finrod, 'and holds also some truth, I believe.'

'Doubtless,' said Andreth. 'But those who speak thus, of the "breath" or of the "fire", do not think of it as belonging to Men only, but as the life of all living things. As Men have their houses, but beasts also have their dwellings in holes or in nests, so both have a life within that may grow cold or go forth.'

'Then in what way do Men differ from beasts in such lore?' said Finrod. 'How can they claim ever to have had a life indestructible?'

'The Wise have considered this,' said Andreth. 'And among them are some that speak more after the manner of the Eldar. But they speak rather of three things: the *earth* and the *fire* and the *Dweller*. By which they intend the stuff of which the body is built, which of itself is inert and does not grow or move; and the life which grows and takes to itself increase; and the *Indweller* who dwells there, and is master both of house and of hearth – or once was.'

'And wishes never to leave them – and once need never do so? It was then the Indweller who suffered the wound?' said Finrod.

'Not so,' said Andreth. 'Clearly not so; but Man, the whole: house, life, and master.'

'But the Master must have been the one that was wronged (as you say), or did wrong (as I guess); for the house might suffer for the folly of the Master, but hardly the Master for the misdeeds of the house! But let that be, for you do not desire to speak of it. Do you yourself hold this belief?'

'It is not a belief,' said Andreth. 'For we do not know enough for any certainty concerning *earth* or *growth* or *thought*, and maybe never shall; for if they were designed by the One, then doubtless they will ever hold for us some mystery inscrutable, however much we learn. But it is a guess that is near, I hold.'

Here this text ends. Finally, there is another isolated slip ('C'), again taken from a document dated 1955, as follows:

> Query: Is it not right to make Andreth refuse to discuss any traditions or legends of the 'Fall'? Already it is (if inevitably) too like a parody of Christianity. Any legend of the Fall would make it completely so?
>
> Originally instead of refusal to talk of it Andreth was made (under pressure) to say something of this sort:
>
> It is said that Melkor looked fair in ancient days, and that when he had gained Men's love he blasphemed Eru, denying his existence and claiming that he was the Lord, and Men assented and took him as Lord and God. Thereupon (say some) our spirits having denied their own true nature at once became darkened and weakened; and through this weakness they lost the mastery of their bodies, which fell into unhealth. Others say that Eru Himself spoke in wrath, saying: 'If the Darkness be your god, little shall ye have here of Light [*later* > on earth ye shall have little Light], and shall leave it soon and come before Me to learn who lieth: your god or I who made him.' And these are the most afraid of death.

This is very difficult to interpret. My father's initial question must mean (in view of the following sentences): 'It is surely right to make Andreth refuse ...', implying 'as is now the case, as the text stands'. But he then proceeded to write a passage in which Andreth did not refuse to say something of such traditions, but consented 'under pressure' (I do not know how to interpret the word 'Originally' in 'Originally instead of refusal to talk of it'); and this was evidently where the germ of what would become the 'Tale of Adanel', the legend of the Fall, first appeared. But this sketch of what Andreth said to Finrod about the Fall of Man is very close to, indeed largely the same as, what she said in the draft text A (p. 351); and that draft was itself derived from a previous writing now lost (p. 350). It seems then that that lost writing contained no account of the Fall, and it was presumably to this that my father's question referred: 'Is it not right to make Andreth refuse to discuss any traditions or legends of the "Fall"?'

The remarks with which text C begins are evidence that he was in some way concerned about these new developments, these new directions, in the underlying 'theology' of Arda, or at any rate their so explicit expression. Certainly, if one looks back to earlier writings of his, one must become aware of a significant shift. In the account written for Milton Waldman in 1951 (*Letters* no.131, p. 147) he had said:

> The Doom (or the Gift) of Men is mortality, freedom from the

circles of the world. Since the point of view of the whole cycle is the Elvish, mortality is not explained mythically: it is a mystery of God of which no more is known than that 'what God has purposed for Men is hidden': a grief and an envy to the immortal Elves. ...

In the cosmogony there is a fall: a fall of Angels we should say. Though quite different in form, of course, to that of Christian myth. These tales are 'new', they are not directly derived from other myths and legends, but they must inevitably contain a large measure of ancient wide-spread motives or elements. After all, I believe that legends and myths are largely made of 'truth', and indeed present aspects of it that can only be received in this mode; and long ago certain truths and modes of this kind were discovered and must always reappear. There cannot be any 'story' without a fall – all stories are ultimately about the fall – at least not for human minds as we know them and have them.

So, proceeding, the Elves have a fall, before their 'history' can become storial. (The first fall of Man, for reasons explained, nowhere appears – Men do not come on the stage until all that is long past, and there is only a rumour that for a while they fell under the domination of the Enemy and that some repented.)

'The first fall of Man, *for reasons explained*, nowhere appears.' What were those reasons? My father must have been referring to the beginning of this letter, where he wrote of the Arthurian legend that 'it is involved in, and explicitly contains the Christian religion', and went on:

For reasons which I will not elaborate, that seems to me fatal. Myth and fairy-story must, as all art, reflect and contain in solution elements of moral and religious truth (or error), but not explicit, not in the known form of the primary 'real' world.

Some years before the time of that letter, however, in one of the curious 'Sketches' associated with *The Drowning of Anadûnê*, he had referred briefly to the original Fall of Men, and there it was accompanied by a very strange speculation on God's original design for mankind (IX.401):

Men (the Followers or Second Kindred) came second, but it is guessed that in the first design of God they were destined (after tutelage) to take on the governance of all the Earth, and ultimately to become Valar, to 'enrich Heaven', Ilúve. But Evil (incarnate in Melekō) seduced them, and they fell.

A little later in the same text (IX.402) he wrote:

Though all Men had 'fallen', not all remained enslaved. Some repented, rebelled against Melekō, and made friends of the Eldar, and tried to be loyal to God.

There is certainly a belief expressed here (whatever weight was to be attached to it – for by whom was it 'guessed'?) that the Fall introduced a change incalculably vast in the nature and destiny of Men, a change brought about by the 'Spirit of Evil', Melkor.

But in 1954 he was saying, in the draft of a long letter to Peter Hastings that was not sent (*Letters* no.153):

... my *legendarium*, especially the 'Downfall of Númenor' which lies immediately behind *The Lord of the Rings*, is based on my view: that Men are essentially mortal and must not try to become 'immortal' in the flesh.

To this he added a footnote:

Since 'mortality' is thus represented as a special gift of God to the Second Race of the Children (the *Eruhíni*, the Children of the One God) and not a punishment for a Fall, you may call that 'bad theology'. So it may be, in the primary world, but it is an imagination capable of elucidating truth, and a legitimate basis of legends.

And again, in another letter of 1954, to Father Robert Murray (*Letters* no.156, footnote to p. 205) he wrote:

But the view of the myth [of the Downfall of Númenor] is that Death – the mere shortness of human life-span – is not a punishment for the Fall, but a biologically (and therefore also spiritually, since body and spirit are integrated) inherent part of Man's nature.

It seems to me therefore that there are problems in the *Athrabeth Finrod ah Andreth* for the interpretation of my father's thought on these matters; but I am unable to resolve them. It is unfortunate that the questionings with which this slip of paper begins are so elliptically expressed, especially the words 'Already it is (if inevitably) too like a parody of Christianity.' Obviously, he was not referring to the legend of the Fall: he was saying clearly that the introduction of such a legend would make 'it' – presumably, the *Athrabeth* – altogether into 'a parody of Christianity'.

Was he referring then to the astonishing conception in the *Athrabeth* of 'the Great Hope of Men', as it is called in the draft A (p. 352), 'the Old Hope' as it is called in the final text (p. 321), that Eru himself will enter into Arda to oppose the evil of Melkor? In the Commentary (p. 335) this was further defined: 'Finrod ... probably proceeded to the expectation that "the coming of Eru", if it took place, would be specially and primarily concerned with Men: that is to an imaginative guess or vision that Eru would come *incarnated in human form*' – though my father noted that 'This does not appear in the *Athrabeth*'. But this surely is not parody, nor even parallel, but the extension – if only represented as vision, hope, or prophecy – of the 'theology' of Arda into specifically, and of course centrally, Christian belief; and a manifest challenge to my father's view in his letter of 1951 on the necessary limitations of the expression of 'moral and religious truth (or error)' in a 'Secondary World'.

NOTES

1 Cf. my father's draft letter of September 1954 (*Letters* no.153, p. 189): 'Elves and Men are evidently in biological terms one race, or they could not breed and produce fertile offspring – even as a rare event', and the following passage.
2 According to the chronology of the *Annals of Aman* the Elves awoke in the Year of the Trees 1050 (p. 71, §37), 450 of such Years before the rising of the Sun, or something more than 4300 years of our time (for the reckoning see p. 59); see p. 327 note 16.
3 *demiurgic labour*: the creative work of 'demiurges', in the sense of mighty but limited beings subordinate to God.
4 On Melkor as 'originally the most powerful of the Valar' see p. 65, §2. There are a number of references in the late writings to the supremacy of Melkor's power in the beginning, but see especially the essay *Melkor Morgoth* given on pp. 390 ff. It is curious that in his letter to Rhona Beare of October 1958 (*Letters* no.211) my father wrote: 'In the cosmogonic myth Manwë is said to be "brother" of Melkor, that is they were coëval and equipotent in the mind of the Creator.'
5 Cf. Finrod's words in the *Athrabeth*, p. 319: 'Beyond the End of the World we shall not change; for in memory is our great talent, as shall be seen ever more clearly as the ages of this Arda pass: a heavy burden to be, I fear; but in the Days of which we now speak a great wealth.'
6 The reference is to the Virgin Mary. See the footnote (*Letters* p. 286) to the draft continuation of the letter referred to in note 4.
7 This analysis does not adhere strictly to the actual course of the *Athrabeth*, and (as is expressly stated, p. 335) was not intended to do so. Thus it was in fact Finrod who said that 'the disaster to Men was appalling' ('dreadful beyond all other calamities was the change in their state', p. 318); and his recognition that 'the power of Melkor was greater than had been understood' comes much earlier in the debate ('to change the doom of a whole people of the Children, to rob them of their inheritance: if he could do that in Eru's despite, then greater and more terrible is he by far than we guessed', p. 312).
8 'Aegnor perished soon after this conversation': in fact, 46 years later (see note 9).
9 In the *Grey Annals* (and in the published *Silmarillion*) Finrod is clearly represented as ruling his great realm from the stronghold of Nargothrond (founded centuries before) during the Siege of Angband, and at the Battle of Sudden Flame he is said to have been 'hastening from the south' (*The Silmarillion* p. 152). At the end of the *Athrabeth*, on the other hand, he tells Andreth that he is leaving for the North, 'to the swords, and the siege, and the

walls of defence' (p. 325), and in the present passage it is said that he and his brothers and the People of Bëor dwelt in 'the northern realm' and that when the Siege was broken he 'took refuge' in Nargothrond.

The last sentence of the paragraph 'But she would then be a very old woman' was a late addition. Against it my father pencilled 'about 94'; cf. the footnote to the opening sentence of the *Athrabeth*, p. 307: Andreth was 48 years old at the time of the conversation with Finrod, stated to have taken place about the year 409, and thus 'about 94' in 455, the year of the Battle of Sudden Flame.

10   In the *Ainulindalë* (p. 11, §13) it was expressly stated that the Children of Ilúvatar '*came with the Third Theme*, and were not in the theme which Ilúvatar propounded at the beginning'. Of the Second Theme it is said in the *Ainulindalë* (p. 14, §24) that 'Manwë ... was the chief instrument of the Second Theme that Ilúvatar had raised up against the discord of Melkor.'

It is perhaps possible that by 'the two new themes' in the present passage my father was thinking of the introduction of Elves and Men into the Music as allied 'themes' that in the *Ainulindalë* were described as 'the Third Theme', but it seems to me more probable that a different conception of the Music had entered. In this connection, in a passage in the final rewriting and elaboration of QS Chapter 6 (p. 275, §50) it is told that Melkor spoke secretly to the Eldar in Aman concerning Men, although he knew little about them, 'for engrossed with his own thought in the Music he had paid small heed to the Second Theme of Ilúvatar'. If this was not simply an inadvertence, it might support the view that the Second and Third Themes had become those that introduced Elves and Men – although it would surely be in the Second Theme that the Elves entered, and Men in the Third. It may be noted also that in the draft continuation of the letter to Rhona Beare of October 1958 (*Letters* no.212), to which I have several times referred, my father wrote: 'Their "themes" were introduced into the Music by the One, when the discords of Melkor arose'; and there is a further reference to 'the Themes of the Children' in Author's Note 7 (p. 342).

11   Against the opening sentences of Note 2 is written in the margin: '*Arda* means Realm'. With the statement here that 'Physically Arda was what we should call the Solar System', and in the third paragraph of this Note that 'the principal part of Arda was the Earth (*Imbar* "The Habitation")', though 'loosely used Arda often seems to mean the Earth', cf. the list of names associated with the revision of the *Quenta Silmarillion* in 1951 (p. 7): '*Arda*   Elvish name of Earth = our world. Also *Kingdom of Arda* = fenced region'. The statements in this Note imply of

12. The term *Imbar* has not occurred before; but cf. *Ambar* 'the Earth' (IV.235 ff., and the *Etymologies*, V.372, 'Quenya *a-mbar* "oikoumenē", Earth'; also *Ambar-metta* 'the ending of the world' in Aragorn's words at his coronation, *The Return of the King* p. 245).

course a radical transformation of the cosmological myth, a recrudescence of the abandoned ideas seen in the *Ainulindalë* text C* of the later 1940s (pp. 3–6, 43). Much further writing on this subject will be found in texts given in Part Five (see especially Texts I and II, pp. 370, 375 ff.).

13. 'the principal demiurgic Ainur ... had taken up their "residence" in Arda': cf. the *Ainulindalë* (p. 14, §21): 'Thus it came to pass that of the Holy Ones some abode still with Ilúvatar beyond the confines of the World; but others, and among them many of the greatest and most fair, took the leave of Ilúvatar and descended into it.' — On the word 'demiurgic' see note 3 above.

14. *erma*: in the typescript B of *Laws and Customs* appears the word *orma*, a later pencilled alteration of the word *hrón* ('the general *hrón* [> *orma*] of Arda'), p. 218.

15. This is a reference to a conception not yet met: see the Appendix to this Part, pp. 361 ff.

16. The possibility of return to incarnate life through childbirth is no longer countenanced: see note 15.

17. 'Normally they must nonetheless remain in Aman': the reasons for this are explained later in this Note. See further pp. 364–5.

18. Lúthien was not the ancestress of Eärendil, son of Tuor and Idril Celebrindal of Gondolin; she was the grandmother of Elwing, wife of Eärendil.

19. 'The myth that appears at the end of the *Silmarillion*': in so far as the reference is to any actual written text, this is the conclusion of QS (V.333, §§31–2), the Prophecy of Mandos.

20. Cf. *Laws and Customs* (typescript text B, p. 219):
    As ages passed the dominance of their *fëar* ever increased, 'consuming' their bodies ... The end of this process is their 'fading' ...; for the body becomes at last, as it were, a mere memory held by the *fëa*; and that end has already been achieved in many regions of Middle-earth, so that the Elves are indeed deathless and may not be destroyed or changed.

21. 'before and above all Eru's works'; i.e. 'before and above the *works* of Eru, of whatever kind'.

22. For previous references to the People of Marach see pp. 305–6, 309, 344.

23. Another version of Note 9 is extant, the opening of which reads thus:
    It is probable that Andreth was actually unwilling to say more. She may also have felt unable to make up her mind about the

conflicting human traditions on the point. Longer recensions of the *Athrabeth*, which appear to have been 'edited' under Númenórean influence (the Númenóreans were mainly derived from the People of Marach, who had more specific traditions concerning what we should call the Fall), make her give, under pressure, a more precise answer. Briefly this:

Some say the disaster happened very early in the history of our people; some say in the first generation. The Voice of the One had spoken to us, some say by a Messenger, some by a Voice only, some that it was by a knowledge in our hearts which we had from the beginning. But we were few and the world seemed very wide; and we wondered much at all that we saw, but we were ignorant, and yet desired greatly to know, and we were in haste to make things, the shapes of which grew in our minds.

Then one came among us, in our own shape, but greater and more beautiful ...

From this point the text differs from the 'Tale of Adanel' (p. 346) only in very minor details of wording; but it stops (not at the foot of a page) at the words 'we would hear his voice, and receive his commands' (the 'Tale of Adanel' p. 347).

This first version was rejected and set aside, and at some later stage my father noted on the typescript: 'The rest of the notes and the conclusion of the legend of Melkor's Deception seems lost. The full copy was sent to Mrs. E. J. Neave (my aunt) in Wales not long before her death. It seems never to have come back. Lost – or destroyed by her hasty executors?' Then afterwards he noted against this that the complete text of the Notes and the legend (the 'Tale of Adanel') had been found. The keeping of his papers in separate places for fear of loss led to such distresses in his later years. – Jane Neave died in 1963; see the *Note on Dating*, p. 300.

24 With the names *Lindar* 'Singers' of the Teleri and *Tareldar* 'High-elves' cf. the Index to *The Silmarillion*, entries *Teleri*, *Eldar*.

25 It is notable that the old form *Melko* is given here as an alternative form.

26 See p. 101 note 2.

27 *melk-*: this stem was first written with two vowels, perhaps *melek-*, but the second vowel seems to have been inked out.

28 *Saelon*: replaced by *Saelind* ('Wise-heart'), p. 305.

29 Cf. the words of the Voice of Eru in the 'Tale of Adanel', p. 347.

30 The meaning is: 'though we speak in uncertainty of what it is that "indwells"'.

31 Cf. the footnote at the end of *Laws and Customs*, p. 250.

APPENDIX

'The Converse of Manwë and Eru'
and later conceptions of Elvish reincarnation

The statement at the beginning of Note 3 (p. 339) that 'in Elvish tradition their re-incarnation was a special permission granted by Eru to Manwë, when Manwë directly consulted Him at the time of the debate concerning Finwë and Míriel' seems very strange in the light of *Laws and Customs among the Eldar*, where it was stated very explicitly (p. 221) that 'A houseless *fëa* that chose or was permitted to return to life *re-entered the incarnate world through child-birth. Only thus could it return*' (to which such 'a rare and strange case' as that of Míriel, who was 'rehoused in her own body', is noted as the only exception). In *Laws and Customs* it is a presupposition of the whole matter that Míriel might in the nature of things return from death if she would; thus Ulmo said in the Debate of the Valar that 'the *fëa* of Míriel may have departed by necessity, but it departed *in the will not to return*', and that '*therein was her fault*' (p. 242). It cannot be thought that *Laws and Customs* was written on the basis that rebirth was only 'granted as a special permission' by Eru to Manwë 'at the time of the debate concerning Finwë and Míriel', an idea of which there is no hint or suggestion in that work.

The explanation of this is that after the writing of *Laws and Customs* my father's views concerning the fate of Elves who had died underwent a radical change, and the passage cited from Note 3 to the Commentary on the *Athrabeth* does not in fact refer to 'rebirth' at all.

There exists a text entitled *The Converse of Manwë and Eru*, which followed *Laws and Customs* but preceded the Commentary on the *Athrabeth*. This work (in typescript) was planned as twofold, the first part being the questions of Manwë and the replies of Eru, and the second an elaborate philosophical discussion of the significance and implications; but it was abandoned before it was finished, and a second, more ample version of the 'Converse' was given up after only a couple of pages. I give the first part, the 'Converse', only, in the original shorter recension.

Manwë spoke to Eru, saying: 'Behold! an evil appears in Arda that we did not look for: the First-born Children, whom Thou madest immortal, suffer now severance of spirit and body. Many of the *fëar* of the Elves in Middle-earth are now houseless; and even in Aman there is one. The houseless we summon to Aman, to keep them from the Darkness, and all who hear our voice abide here in waiting. What further is to be done? Is there no means by which their lives may be renewed, to follow the courses which Thou hast designed? And what of the bereaved who mourn those that have gone?'

Eru answered: 'Let the houseless be re-housed!'

Manwë asked: 'How shall this be done?'

Eru answered: 'Let the body that was destroyed be re-made. Or let the naked *fëa* be re-born as a child.'

Manwë said: 'Is it Thy will that we should attempt these things? For we fear to meddle with Thy Children.'

Eru answered: 'Have I not given to the Valar the rule of Arda, and power over all the substance thereof, to shape it at their will under My will? Ye have not been backward in these things. As for my First-born, have ye not removed great numbers of them to Aman from the Middle-earth in which I set them?'

Manwë answered: 'This we have done, for fear of Melcor, and with good intent, though not without misgiving. But to use our power upon the flesh that Thou hast designed, to house the spirits of Thy Children, this seems a matter beyond our authority, even were it not beyond our skill.'

Eru said: 'I give you authority. The skills ye have already, if ye will take heed. Look and ye will find that each spirit of My Children retaineth in itself the full imprint and memory of its former house; and in its nakedness it is open to you, so that ye may clearly perceive all that is in it. After this imprint ye may make for it again such a house in all particulars as it had ere evil befell it. Thus ye may send it back to the lands of the Living.'

Then Manwë asked further: 'O Ilúvatar, hast Thou not spoken also of re-birth? Is that too within our power and authority?'

Eru answered: 'It shall be within your authority, but it is not in your power. Those whom ye judge fit to be re-born, if they desire it and understand clearly what they incur, ye shall surrender to Me; and I will consider them.'

It will be seen that wholly new dimensions to the question of the return of the Dead to the Living had now entered. My father had come to think that before the death of Míriel there had never been any 're-housing' of the *fëar* of the Dead, and that it was only in response to the appeal of Manwë that Eru decreed such a possibility and the modes by which it might be brought about. One such mode is the rebirth of the *fëa* as a child, but such of the Dead as desire it are to be surrendered to Eru to await His judgement in their case. The other mode is the making, by the Valar, of 'such a house in all particulars as it had ere evil befell it': the reincarnation of the Dead in a *hröa* identical to that which death had overtaken. The long discussion that follows the 'Converse' is very largely concerned with the ideas of 'identity' and 'equivalence' in relation to this form of reincarnation, represented as a commentary by Eldarin loremasters.

A hastily written manuscript on small slips of paper, entitled 'Reincarnation of Elves', seems to show my father's reflections on the subject between the abandonment of *The Converse of Manwë and Eru* and the Commentary on the *Athrabeth*. In this discussion he referred in rapid and elliptical expression to the difficulties at every level (including practical and psychological) in the idea of the reincarnation of the *fëa* as the newborn child of second parents, who as it grows up recaptures the memory of its previous life: 'the most fatal objection' being that 'it contradicts the fundamental notion that *fëa* and *hröa* were each *fitted* to the other: since *hröar* have a physical descent, the body of rebirth, having different parents, must be different', and this must be a condition of pain to the reborn *fëa*.

He was here abandoning, and for good, the long-rooted conception (see pp. 265–7) of rebirth as the mode by which the Elves might return to incarnate life: from his scrutiny of the mythical idea, questioning its validity in the terms he had adopted, it had come to seem to him a serious flaw in the metaphysic of Elvish existence. But, he said, it was a 'dilemma', for the reincarnation of the Elves 'seems an essential element in the tales'. 'The only solution,' he decided in this discussion, was the idea of the remaking in identical form of the *hröa* of the Dead in the manner declared by Eru in *The Converse of Manwë and Eru*: the *fëa* retains a memory, an imprint, of its *hröa*, its 'former house', so powerful and precise that the reconstruction of an identical body can proceed from it.

The idea of a 'Converse' between Manwë and Eru was not abandoned, and is indeed referred to in 'Reincarnation of Elves' (but the 'Converse' as given above must have been in existence, since in it Eru expressly declares rebirth to be a mode of reincarnation open to the 'houseless' *fëa*, whereas in the present discussion such an idea is firmly rejected and allowed no place in 'the only solution' to the 'dilemma'). The new conception proceeds, in outline, as follows. The Music of the Ainur had contained no prevision of the death of Elves and the existence of their 'houseless' *fëar*, since according to their nature they were to be immortal within the life of Arda. There were many such *fëar* of Elves who had died in Middle-earth gathered in the Halls of Mandos, but it was not until the death of Míriel in Aman that Manwë appealed directly to Eru for counsel. Eru 'accepted and ratified the position' – though making it plain to Manwë that the Valar should have contested Melkor's domination of Middle-earth far earlier, and that they had lacked *estel*: they should have trusted that in a legitimate war Eru would not have permitted Melkor so greatly to damage Arda that the Children could not come, or could not inhabit it (cf. LQ §20, p. 161: 'And Manwë said to the Valar: "This is the counsel of Ilúvatar in my heart: that we should take up again the mastery of Arda, at whatsoever cost, and deliver the Quendi from the shadows of Melkor." Then Tulkas was glad; but Aulë was grieved, and it is said that he (and others of the Valar) had before been unwilling to strive with Melkor, foreboding the hurts of the world that must come of that strife').

It is then said that 'the *fëar* of the Dead all go to Mandos in Aman: or rather they are now summoned thither by the authority given by Eru. A place is made for them.' This appears to mean that it was only now that Mandos was empowered to summon the spirits of the Dead to Aman; but the following words 'A place is made for them' are hard to understand, since they seem to deny even that the Halls of Waiting existed before Manwë spoke to Eru (despite the statement earlier in 'Reincarnation of Elves' that there were many houseless *fëar* gathered in Mandos before the 'Converse' took place).

The Valar are now given the authority to reincarnate the *fëar* of Elves who have died in *hröar* identical to those they have lost; and the text continues: 'The re-housed *fëa* will normally remain in Aman. Only in very exceptional cases, as Beren and Lúthien, will they be transported back to Middle-earth. ... Hence death in Middle-earth had much of the same sort of sorrow and sunderance for Elves and Men. But, as Andreth saw, the certainty of living again and *doing* things in incarnate form made a vital difference to death as a personal terror' (cf. the *Athrabeth* p. 311).

In what appears to be a second thought my father then asked whether it might not be possible that the 'houseless' *fëa* was itself allowed (being instructed) to rebuild its *hröa* from its memory (and this, as appears from very late writing on the subject of the reincarnation of Glorfindel of Gondolin, became his firm and stable view of the matter). He wrote here: 'Memory by a *fëa* of experience is evidently powerful, vivid, and complete. So the underlying conception is that "matter" will be taken up into "spirit", by becoming part of its *knowledge* – and so rendered timeless and under the spirit's command. As the Elves remaining in Middle-earth slowly "consumed" their bodies – or made them into raiments of memory? The resurrection of the body (at least as far as Elves were concerned) was in a sense incorporeal. But while it could pass physical barriers at will, it could at will oppose a barrier to matter. If you touched a resurrected body you felt it. Or if it willed it could simply elude you – disappear. Its position in space was at will.'

Neither in the passage on the subject of reincarnation in the Commentary on the *Athrabeth* (p. 331, §6) nor in the Note 3 that refers to it (p. 339) is there any mention of rebirth; while the latter very evidently echoes the words of 'Resurrection of Elves'. Thus it is strongly implied in Note 3, if not expressly stated, that it was only at the time of Manwë's speech with Eru that Mandos was given the power actually to summon the *fëar* of the Dead; and the passage that follows this in the Note is closely similar to what is said in 'Resurrection of Elves':

> They were given the choice to remain houseless, or (if they wished) to be re-housed in the same form and shape as they had had. Normally they must nonetheless remain in Aman. Therefore, if they dwelt in Middle-earth, their bereavement of friends and kin, and the bereavement of these, was not amended. Death was not wholly healed. But as Andreth saw, this certitude concerning their immediate future after death, and the knowledge that at the least they would again if they wished be able as *incarnates* to do and make things and continue their experience of Arda, made death to the Elves a totally different thing from death as it appeared to Men.

An interesting point in respect of the chronology of composition arises from the remark found both in 'Reincarnation of Elves' and in Note 3 to the Commentary that death for Elves and death for Men were very different things 'as Andreth saw'. Thus the *Athrabeth* was in existence when 'Reincarnation of Elves' was written; but the Commentary followed 'Reincarnation'. This seems clear evidence that there was an interval between the writing of the actual Debate of Finrod and Andreth and the writing of the Commentary on it.

One further passage in 'Reincarnation of Elves' should be mentioned. In a sort of aside from the course of his thoughts, moving more rapidly (even) than his pen, my father remarked that 'the exact nature of existence in Aman or Eressëa after their "removal" must be dubious and unexplained', as must the question of 'how "mortals" could go there at all'. On this he observed that Eru had 'long before' committed the Dead of mortals also to Mandos; cf. QS §86 (V.247): 'What befell their spirits after death the Elves know not. Some say that they too go to the halls of Mandos; but their place of waiting there is not that of the Elves; and Mandos under Ilúvatar alone save Manwë knows whither they go after the time of recollection in those silent halls beside the Western Sea.' 'The sojourn of Frodo' (he went on) 'in Eressëa – then on to Mandos? – was only an extended form of this. Frodo would eventually leave the world (desiring to do so). So that the sailing in ship was equivalent to death.'

With this may be contrasted what he wrote at the end of his account of *The Lord of the Rings* in his letter to Milton Waldman of 1951 (a passage omitted in *Letters* but printed in IX.132):

> To Bilbo and Frodo the special grace is granted to go with the Elves they loved – an Arthurian ending, in which it is, of course, not made

explicit whether this is an 'allegory' of death, or a mode of healing and restoration leading to a return.

In his letter to Naomi Mitchison of September 1954 (*Letters* no.154), however, he said:

> ... the mythical idea underlying is that for mortals, since their 'kind' cannot be changed for ever, this is strictly only a temporary reward: a healing and redress of suffering. They cannot abide for ever, and though they cannot return to mortal earth, they can and will 'die' – of free will, and leave the world. (In this setting the return of Arthur would be quite impossible, a vain imagining.)

And much later, in a draft letter of 1963 (*Letters* no.246), he wrote:

> Frodo was sent or allowed to pass over Sea to heal him – if that could be done, *before he died*. He would have eventually to 'pass away': no mortal could, or can, abide for ever on earth, or within Time. So he went both to a purgatory and to a reward, for a while: a period of reflection and peace and a gaining of a truer understanding of his position in littleness and in greatness, spent still in Time amid the natural beauty of 'Arda Unmarred', the Earth unspoiled by evil.

PART FIVE

MYTHS TRANSFORMED

MYTHS TRANSFORMED

In this last section of the book I give a number of late writings of my father's, various in nature but concerned with, broadly speaking, the reinterpretation of central elements in the 'mythology' (or *legendarium* as he called it) to accord with the imperatives of a greatly modified underlying conception. Some of these papers (there are notable exceptions) offer exceptional difficulty: fluidity of ideas, ambiguous and allusive expression, illegible passages. But the greatest problem is that there is very little firm indication of date external or relative: to order them into even an approximate sequence of composition seems impossible (though I believe that virtually all of them come from the years that saw the writing of *Laws and Customs among the Eldar*, the *Athrabeth*, and late revisions of parts of the *Quenta Silmarillion* – the late 1950s, in the aftermath of the publication of *The Lord of the Rings*).

In these writings can be read the record of a prolonged interior debate. Years before this time, the first signs have been seen of emerging ideas that if pursued would cause massive disturbance in *The Silmarillion*: I have shown, as I believe, that when my father first began to revise and rewrite the existing narratives of the Elder Days, before *The Lord of the Rings* was completed, he wrote a version of the *Ainulindalë* that introduced a radical transformation of the astronomical myth, but that for that time he stayed his hand (pp. 3–6, 43). But now, as will be seen in many of the essays and notes that follow, he had come to believe that such a vast upheaval was a necessity, that the cosmos of the old myth was no longer valid; and at the same time he was impelled to try to construct a more secure 'theoretical' or 'systematic' basis for elements in the *legendarium* that were not to be dislodged. With their questionings, their certainties giving way to doubt, their contradictory resolutions, these writings are to be read with a sense of intellectual and imaginative stress in the face of such a dismantling and reconstitution, believed to be an inescapable necessity, but never to be achieved.

The texts, arranged in a very loose 'thematic' sequence, are numbered in Roman numerals. Almost all have received very minor editing (matters of punctuation, insertion of omitted words, and suchlike). Numbered notes (not present in all cases) follow the individual texts.

I

I give first a short statement written on two slips found pinned to one of the typescripts of the *Annals of Aman*, which would date it to 1958 or later (if my general conclusions about dating are correct, p. 300).

This descends from the oldest forms of the mythology – when it was still intended to be no more than another primitive mythology, though more coherent and less 'savage'. It was consequently a 'Flat Earth' cosmogony (much easier to manage anyway): the Matter of Númenor had not been devised.

It is now clear to me that in any case the Mythology must actually be a 'Mannish' affair. (Men are really only interested in Men and in Men's ideas and visions.) The High Eldar living and being tutored by the demiurgic beings must have known, or at least their writers and loremasters must have known, the 'truth' (according to their measure of understanding). What we have in the *Silmarillion* etc. are traditions (especially personalized, and centred upon *actors*, such as Fëanor) handed on by *Men* in Númenor and later in Middle-earth (Arnor and Gondor); but already far back – from the first association of the Dúnedain and Elf-friends with the Eldar in Beleriand – blended and confused with their own Mannish myths and cosmic ideas.

At that point (in reconsideration of the early cosmogonic parts) I was inclined to adhere to the Flat Earth and the astronomically absurd business of the making of the Sun and Moon. But you can make up stories of that kind when you live among people who have the same general background of imagination, when the Sun 'really' rises in the East and goes down in the West, etc. When however (no matter how little most people know or think about astronomy) it is the general belief that we live upon a 'spherical' island in 'Space' you cannot do this any more.

One loses, of course, the dramatic impact of such things as the first 'incarnates' waking in a starlit world – or the coming of the High Elves to Middle-earth and unfurling their banners at the *first* rising of the Moon.

I have given this first, because – though jotted down at great speed – it is an express statement of my father's views at this time, in three major respects. The astronomical myths of the Elder Days cannot be regarded as a record of the traditional beliefs of the Eldar in any pure form, because the High-elves of Aman cannot have been thus ignorant; and the cosmological elements in *The Silmarillion* are essentially a record of mythological ideas, complex in origin, prevailing among Men.[1] In this note, however, my father appears to have accepted that these ideas do not in themselves necessarily lead to great upheaval in the essential 'world-structure' of *The Silmarillion*, but on the contrary provide a basis for its retention ('At that point ... I was inclined to adhere to the Flat Earth'). The conclusion of this brief statement appears then to be a further and unconnected step: that the cosmological myth of *The Silmarillion* was a 'creative error' on the part of its maker, since it could have no imaginative truth for people who know very well that such an 'astronomy' is delusory.

As he stated it, this may seem to be an argument of the most doubtful nature, raising indeed the question, why is the myth of the Two Trees (which so far as record goes he never showed any intention to abandon) more acceptable than that of the creation of the Sun and the Moon from the last fruit and flower of the Trees as they died? Or indeed, if this is true, how can it be acceptable that the Evening Star is the Silmaril cut by Beren from Morgoth's crown?

It is at any rate clear, for he stated it unambiguously enough, that he had come to believe that the art of the 'Sub-creator' cannot, or should not attempt to, extend to the 'mythical' revelation of a conception of the shape of the Earth and the origin of the lights of heaven that runs counter to the known physical truths of his own days: 'You cannot do this any more'. And this opinion is rendered more complex and difficult of discussion by the rise in importance of the Eldarin 'loremasters' of Aman, whose intellectual attainments and knowledge must preclude any idea that a 'false' astronomy could have prevailed among them. It seems to me that he was devising – from within it – a fearful weapon against his own creation.

In this brief text he wrote scornfully of 'the astronomically absurd business of the making of the Sun and Moon'. I think it possible that it was the actual nature of this myth that led him finally to abandon it. It is in conception beautiful, and not absurd; but it is exceedingly 'primitive'. Of the original 'Tale of the Sun and Moon' in *The Book of Lost Tales* I wrote (I.201):

As a result of this fullness and intensity of description, the origin of the Sun and Moon in the last fruit and last flower of the Trees has less of mystery than in the succinct and beautiful language of *The Silmarillion*; but also much is said here to emphasize the great size of the 'Fruit of Noon', and the increase in the heat and brilliance of the Sunship after its launching, so that the reflection rises less readily that if the Sun that brilliantly illumines the whole Earth was but one fruit of Laurelin then Valinor must have been painfully bright and hot in the days of the Trees. In the early story the last outpourings of life from the dying Trees are utterly strange and 'enormous', those of Laurelin portentous, even ominous; the Sun is astoundingly bright and hot even to the Valar, who are awestruck and disquieted by what has been done (the Gods knew 'that they had done a greater thing than they at first knew'); and the anger and distress of certain of the Valar at the burning light of the Sun enforces the feeling that in the last fruit of Laurelin a terrible and unforeseen power has been released.

As the *Quenta Silmarillion* evolved and changed the myth had been diminished in the scale and energy of its presentation; indeed in the final form of the chapter, and in the *Annals of Aman*, the description of the actual origin of the Sun and Moon is reduced to a few lines.

> Yet even as hope failed and her song faltered, behold! Telperion bore at last upon a leafless bough one great flower of silver, and Laurelin a single fruit of gold.
>
> These Yavanna took, and then the Trees died, and their lifeless stems stand yet in Valinor, a memorial of vanished joy. But the flower and fruit Yavanna gave to Aulë, and Manwë hallowed them; and Aulë and his folk made vessels to hold them and preserve their radiance, as is said in the *Narsilion*, the Song of the Sun and Moon. These vessels the gods gave to Varda, that they might become lamps of heaven, outshining the ancient stars...

The grave and tranquil words cannot entirely suppress a sense that there emerges here an outcropping, as it were, uneroded, from an older level, more fantastic, more bizarre. As indeed it does: such was the nature of the work, evolved over so many years. But it did not stand in the work as an isolated myth, a now gratuitous element that could be excised; for bound up with it was the myth of the Two Trees ('the Elder Sun and Moon'), giving light through long ages to the land of Valinor, while Middle-earth lay in darkness, illumined only by the stars in the firmament of Arda. In that darkness the Elves awoke, the People of the Stars; and after the death of the Trees the ancient Light was preserved only in the Silmarils. In 1951 my father had written (*Letters* no.131, p. 148):

> There was the Light of Valinor made visible in the Two Trees of Silver and Gold. These were slain by the Enemy out of malice, and Valinor was darkened, though from them, ere they died utterly, were derived the lights of Sun and Moon. (A marked difference here between these legends and most others is that the Sun is not a divine symbol, but a second-best thing, and the 'light of the Sun' (the world under the sun) become terms for a fallen world, and a dislocated imperfect vision.)

But: 'You cannot do this any more.' In the following pages will be seen how, driven by this conviction, he attempted to undo what he had done, but to retain what he might. It is remarkable that he never at this time seems to have felt that what he said in this present note provided a resolution of the problem that he believed to exist:

Text I MYTHS TRANSFORMED 373

What we have in the *Silmarillion* etc. are traditions... handed on by Men in Númenor and later in Middle-earth (Arnor and Gondor); but already far back – from the first association of the Dúnedain and Elf-friends with the Eldar in Beleriand – *blended and confused with their own Mannish myths and cosmic ideas.*

It is tempting to suppose that when my father wrote that 'in reconsideration of the early cosmogonic parts' he was 'inclined to adhere to the Flat Earth and the astronomically absurd business of the making of the Sun and Moon', he was referring to *Ainulindalë* C and the *Annals of Aman*. If this were so, it might account for the developments in *Ainulindalë* C discussed on pp. 27–9, where Arda becomes a small world within the vastness of Eä – but retains the 'Flat Earth' characteristics of Ilu from the *Ambarkanta* and before.

In connection with my father's statement that the legends of *The Silmarillion* were traditions handed on by Men in Númenor and later in the Númenórean kingdoms in Middle-earth, this is a convenient place to give an entirely isolated note carefully typed (but not on his later typewriter) on a small slip and headed 'Memorandum'.

The three Great Tales must be Númenórean, and derived from matter preserved in Gondor. They were part of the *Atanatárion* (or the Legendarium of the Fathers of Men). ?Sindarin *Nern in Edenedair* (or *In Adanath*).

They are (1) *Narn Beren ion Barahir* also called *Narn e·Dinúviel* (Tale of the Nightingale)
                (2) *Narn e·mbar Hador* containing (a) *Narn i·Chîn Húrin* (or *Narn e·'Rach Morgoth* Tale of the Curse of Morgoth); and (b) *Narn en·Êl* (or *Narn e·Dant Gondolin ar Orthad en·Êl*)
Should not these be given as Appendices to the *Silmarillion*?

In the question with which this ends my father was presumably distinguishing between long and short forms of the tales. – Two further notes on this slip, typed at the same time as the above, refer to 'the Tale of Túrin' and suggest that he was working on it at that time.[2] I do not know of any precise evidence to date the great development of the 'Túrin Saga', but it certainly belongs to an earlier period than the writings given in the latter part of this book.

The idea that the legends of the Elder Days derived from Númenórean tradition appears also in the abandoned typescript (AAm*) of the *Annals of Aman* that my father made himself (p. 64).[3] In this text the preamble states:

Here begin the 'Annals of Aman'. Rúmil made them in the Elder Days, and they were held in memory by the Exiles. Those parts which we learned and remembered were thus set down in Númenor before the Shadow fell upon it.

NOTES

1 Very similar remarks are made in Note 2 to the Commentary on the *Athrabeth* (p. 337):

> Physically Arda was what we should call the Solar System. Presumably the Eldar could have had as much and as accurate information concerning this, its structure, origin, and its relation to the rest of Eä as they could comprehend.

A little further on in this same Note it is said:

> The traditions here referred to have come down from the Eldar of the First Age, through Elves who never were directly acquainted with the Valar, and through Men who received 'lore' from the Elves, but who had myths and cosmogonic legends, and astronomical guesses, of their own. *There is, however, nothing in them that seriously conflicts with present human notions of the Solar System, and its size and position relative to the Universe.*

The sentence which I have italicised suggests an assured commitment, at the least, to the re-formation of the old cosmology. – For references in the Commentary on the *Athrabeth* to the Númenórean part in the transmission of legends of the Elder Days see pp. 342, 344, 360.

2 These are a proposal that Níniel (Nienor) should 'in her looks and ways' remind Túrin of Lalaeth, his sister who died in childhood (see *Unfinished Tales* p. 147 note 7), and another, marked with a query, that Túrin should think of the words of Saeros, the Elf of Doriath, when he finds Níniel naked in the eaves of the Forest of Brethil (*Unfinished Tales* pp. 80, 122).

On the back of this slip my father wrote (in a furious scribble in ball-point pen):

> The cosmogonic myths are Númenórean, blending Elven-lore with human myth and imagination. A note should say that the Wise of Númenor recorded that the making of stars was not so, nor of Sun and Moon. For Sun and stars were all older than Arda. But the placing of Arda amidst stars and under the [?guard] of the Sun was due to Manwë and Varda before the assault of Melkor.

I take the words 'the Wise of Númenor recorded that the making of stars was not so, nor of Sun and Moon' to mean that the making of the Sun, Moon and stars was not derived from 'Elven-lore'. It is to be noted that *Arda* here means 'the Earth', not 'the Solar System'.

3 I have said (p. 64) that I would be inclined to place AAm* with the

writing of the original manuscript of the *Annals* rather than to some later time, but this is no more than a guess.

II

This is a text of a most problematic nature, a manuscript in ink that falls into two parts which are plainly very closely associated: a discussion, with proposals for the 'regeneration' of the mythology; and an abandoned narrative. Neither has title or heading.

The Making of the Sun and Moon *must* occur long before the coming of the Elves; and *cannot* be made to be after the death of the Two Trees – if that occurred in any connexion with the sojourn of the Noldor in Valinor. The time allowed is too short. Neither could there be woods and flowers &c. on earth, if there had been no light since the overthrow of the Lamps![1]

But how can, nonetheless, the Eldar be called the 'Star-folk'?

Since the Eldar are supposed to be wiser and have truer knowledge of the history and nature of the Earth than Men (or than Wild Elves), *their* legends should have a closer relation to the knowledge now possessed of at least the *form* of the Solar System (= Kingdom of Arda);[2] though it need not, of course, follow any 'scientific' theory of its making or development.

It therefore seems clear that the cosmogonic mythology should represent Arda as it is, more or less: an island in the void 'amidst the innumerable stars'. The Sun should be coeval with Earth, though its relative size need not be considered, while the apparent revolution of the Sun about the Earth will be accepted.*

The Stars, therefore, in general will be other and remoter parts of the Great Tale of Eä, which do not concern the Valar of Arda. Though, even if not explicitly, it will be an underlying assumption that the Kingdom of Arda is of *central* importance, selected amid all the immeasurable vast of Eä as the scene for the main drama of the conflict of Melkor with Ilúvatar, and the Children of Eru. Melkor is the *supreme* spirit of Pride and Revolt, *not* just the chief Vala of the Earth, who has turned to evil.[3]

---

* [marginal note] It is or would be in any case a 'fact of life' for any intelligence that chose the Earth for a place of life and labour. [There is no indication where this is to go, but nowhere else on the page seems suitable.]

Varda, therefore, as one of the great Valar of Arda, cannot be said to have 'kindled' the stars, as an original subcreative act – not at least the stars in general.[4]

The Story, it seems, should follow such a line as this. The entry of the Valar into Eä at the beginning of Time. The choosing of the Kingdom of Arda as their chief abiding place (? by the highest and noblest of the Ainur,[5] to whom Ilúvatar had intended to commit the care of the *Eruhíni*). Manwë and his companions elude Melkor and begin the ordering of Arda, but Melkor seeks for them and at last finds Arda,[6] and contests the kingship with Manwë.

This period will, roughly, correspond to supposed primeval epochs before Earth became habitable. A time of fire and cataclysm. Melkor disarrayed the Sun so that at periods it was too hot, and at others too cold. Whether this was due to the state of the Sun, or alterations in the orbit of Earth, need not be made precise: both are possible.

But after a battle Melkor is driven out from Earth itself. (The First Battle?) He finds he can only come there in great secrecy. At this time he begins first to turn most to cold and darkness. His first desire (and weapon) had been fire and heat. It was in the wielding of *flame* that Tulkas (? originally Vala of the Sun) defeated him in the First Battle. Melkor therefore comes mostly *at night* and especially to the North in winter. (It was after the First Battle that Varda set *certain stars* as ominous signs for the dwellers in Arda to see.)

The Valar to counteract this make the Moon. Out of earth-stuff or Sun? This is to be a subsidiary light to mitigate night* (as Melkor had made it), and also a 'vessel of watch and ward' to circle the world.[7] But Melkor gathered in the Void spirits of cold &c. and suddenly assailed it, driving out the Vala Tilion.[8] The Moon was thereafter long while steerless and vagrant and called *Rana* (neuter).[9]

[*If* Tulkas came from the Sun, then *Tulkas* was the form this Vala adopted on Earth, being in origin *Auron* (masculine). But the Sun is feminine; and it is better that the Vala should be *Áren*, a maiden whom Melkor endeavoured to make his spouse (or ravished);[10] she went up in a flame of wrath and anguish and

---

* [marginal note] But not to drive it away. It was necessary to have an alternation, 'because in Eä according to the Tale nothing can endure endlessly without weariness and corruption.'

her spirit was released from Eä, but Melkor was blackened and burned, and his form was thereafter dark, and he took to darkness. (The Sun itself was *Anar* neuter or *Úr*, cf. *Rana, Ithil*.)]

The Sun remained a Lonely Fire, polluted by Melkor, but after the death of the Two Trees Tilion returned to the Moon, which remained therefore an enemy of Melkor and his servants and creatures of night – and so beloved of Elves later &c.

After the capture of the Moon Melkor begins to be more bold again. He establishes permanent seats in the North deep underground. From thence proceeds the secret corruption which perverts the labours of the Valar (especially of Aulë and Yavanna).

The Valar grow weary. At length discovering Melkor and where he dwells they seek to drive him out again, but Utumno proves too strong.

Varda has preserved some of the Primeval Light (her original chief concern in the Great Tale). The Two Trees are made. The Valar make their resting place and dwellings in Valinor in the West.

Now one of the objects of the Trees (as later of the Jewels) was the healing of the hurts of Melkor, but this could easily have a *selfish* aspect: the staying of history – not going on with the Tale. This effect it had on the Valar. They became more and more enamoured of Valinor, and went there more often and stayed there longer. Middle-earth was left too little tended, and too little protected against Melkor.

Towards the end of the Days of Bliss, the Valar find the tables turned. They are driven out of Middle-earth by Melkor and his evil spirits and monsters; and can only themselves come there secretly and briefly (Oromë and Yavanna mainly).

This period must be *brief*. Both sides know that the coming of the Children of God is imminent. Melkor desires to dominate them at once with fear and darkness and enslave them. He *darkens the world* [*added in margin:* for 7 years?] cutting off all vision of the sky so far as he can, and though far south (it is said) this was not effective. From the far North (where [they are] dense) to the middle (Endor)[11] great clouds brood. Moon and stars are invisible. Day is only a dim twilight at full. Only light [is] in Valinor.

Varda arises in her might and Manwë of the Winds and strive with the Cloud of Unseeing. But as fast as it is rent Melkor closes the veil again – at least over Middle-earth. Then came the Great Wind of Manwë, and the veil was rent. The stars shine out clear even in the North (*Valakirka*) and after the long dark seem terribly bright.

It is in the *dark* just before that the Elves awake. The first thing they see in the dark is the stars. But Melkor brings up glooms out of the East, and the stars fade away west. Hence they think from the beginning of light and beauty in the West.

The Coming of Oromë.

The Third Battle and the captivity of Melkor. The Eldar go to Valinor. The clouds slowly disperse after the capture of Melkor though Utumno still belches. It is darkest eastward, furthest from the breath of Manwë.

The March of the Eldar is through great Rains?

Men awake in an Isle amid the floods and therefore welcome the Sun which seems to come out of the East. Only when the world is drier do they leave the Isle and spread abroad.

It is only Men that met Elves and heard the rumours of the West that go that way. For the Elves said: 'If you delight in the Sun, you will walk in the path it goes.'

The coming of Men will therefore be much further back.[12] This will be better; for a bare 400 years is quite inadequate to produce the variety, and the advancement (e.g. of the Edain) at the time of Felagund.[13]

Men must awake while Melkor is still in Arda? – because of their Fall.[14] Therefore in some period during the Great March.

This text ends here. There follows now the associated narrative, identical in appearance to the foregoing discussion (both elements are written in the same rather unusual script).

After the Valar, who before were the Ainur of the Great Song, entered into Eä, those who were the noblest among them and understood most of the mind of Ilúvatar sought amid the immeasurable regions of the Beginning for that place where they should establish the Kingdom of Arda in time to come. And when they had chosen that point and region where it should be, they began the labours that were needed. Others there were, countless to our thought though known each and numbered in the mind of Ilúvatar, whose labour lay elsewhere and in other regions and histories of the Great Tale, amid stars remote and worlds beyond the reach of the furthest thought. But of these others we know nothing and cannot know, though the Valar of Arda, maybe, remember them all.

Chief of the Valar of Arda was he whom the Eldar afterwards

named Manwë, the Blessed: the Elder King, since he was the first of all kings in [Arda >] Eä. Brother to him was Melkor, the Potent, and he had, as has been told, fallen into pride and desire of his own dominion. Therefore the Valar avoided him, and began the building and ordering of Arda without him. For which reason it is said that whereas there is now great evil in Arda and many things therein are at discord, so that the good of one seemeth to be the hurt of another, nonetheless the foundations of this world are good, and it turns by nature to good, healing itself from within by the power that was set there in its making; and evil in Arda would fail and pass away if it were not renewed from without: that is: that comes from wills and being [sic] that are other than Arda itself.

And as is known well, the prime among these is Melkor. Measureless as were the regions of Eä, yet in the Beginning, where he could have been Master of all that was done – for there were many of the Ainur of the Song willing to follow him and serve him, if he called – still he was not content. And he sought ever for Arda and Manwë, his brother, begrudging him the kingship, small though it might seem to his desire and his potency; for he knew that to that kingship Ilúvatar designed to give the highest royalty in Eä, and under the rule of that throne to bring forth the Children of God. And in his thought which deceived him, for the liar shall lie unto himself, he believed that over the Children he might hold absolute sway and be unto them sole lord and master, as he could not be to spirits of his own kind, however subservient to himself. For they knew that the One Is, and must assent to Melkor's rebellion of their own choice; whereas he purposed to withhold from the Children this knowledge and be for ever a shadow between them and the light.

As a shadow Melkor did not then conceive himself. For in his beginning he loved and desired light, and the form that he took was exceedingly bright; and he said in his heart: 'On such brightness as I am the Children shall hardly endure to look; therefore to know of aught else or beyond or even to strain their small minds to conceive of it would not be for their good.' But the lesser brightness that stands before the greater becomes a darkness. And Melkor was jealous, therefore, of all other brightnesses, and wished to take all light unto himself. Therefore Ilúvatar, at the entering in of the Valar into Eä, added a theme to the Great Song which was not in it at the first Singing, and he called one of the Ainur to him. Now this was that Spirit which afterwards became Varda (and taking female form became the spouse of Manwë). To Varda Ilúvatar said: 'I will give unto thee a parting gift. Thou shalt take into Eä a light that is holy, coming new from Me, unsullied by the thought and lust of Melkor, and with thee it shall enter into Eä, and be in Eä, but not of Eä.' Wherefore Varda is the most holy and revered of all the Valar, and those that name the light of Varda name the love of Eä that Eru has, and they are afraid, less only to name the One. Nonetheless this gift of Ilúvatar to the Valar has its own peril, as have all his free gifts: which is in the end no more than to say that they play a part in the Great Tale so that it may be complete; for without peril they would be without power, and the giving would be void.

When therefore at last Melkor discovered the abiding place of Manwë and his friends he went thither in great haste, as a blazing fire. And finding that already great labours had been achieved without his counsel, he was angered, and desired to undo what was done or to alter it according to his own mind.

But this Manwë would not suffer, and there was war therefore in Arda. But as is elsewhere written Melkor was at that time defeated with the aid of Tulkas (who was not among those who began the building of Eä) and driven out again into the Void that lay about Arda. This is named the First Battle; and though Manwë had the victory, great hurt was done to the work of the Valar; and the worst of the deeds of the wrath of Melkor was seen in the Sun. Now the Sun was designed to be the heart of Arda, and the Valar purposed that it should give light to all that Realm, unceasingly and without wearying or diminution, and that from its light the world should receive health and life and growth. Therefore Varda set there the most ardent and beautiful of all those spirits that had entered with her into Eä, and she was named *Ar(i)*,[15] and Varda gave to her keeping a portion of the gift of Ilúvatar so that the Sun should endure and be blessed and give blessing. The Sun, the loremasters tell us, was in that beginning named *Âs* (which is as near as it can be interpreted Warmth, to which are joined Light and Solace), and that the spirit therefore was called *Āzië* (or later *Ārië*).

But Melkor, as hath been told, lusted after all light, desiring it jealously for his own. Moreover he soon perceived that in Âs there was a light that had been concealed from him, and which had a power of which he had not thought. Therefore, afire at once with desire and anger, he went to Âs [*written above:* Asa], and he spoke to Árië, saying: 'I have chosen thee, and thou shalt be my spouse, even as Varda is to Manwë, and together we shall wield all splendour and mastery. Then the kingship of Arda shall be mine in deed as in right, and thou shalt be the partner of my glory.'

But Árië rejected Melkor and rebuked him, saying: "Speak not of right, which thou hast long forgotten. Neither for thee nor by thee alone was Eä made; and thou shalt not be King of Arda. Beware therefore; for there is in the heart of Ás a light in which thou hast no part, and a fire which will not serve thee. Put not out thy hand to it. For though thy potency may destroy it, it will burn thee and thy brightness will be made dark.'

Melkor did not heed her warning, but cried in his wrath: 'The gift which is withheld I take!' and he ravished Árië, desiring both to abase her and to take into himself her powers. Then the spirit of Árië went up like a flame of anguish and wrath, and departed for ever from Arda;* and the Sun was bereft of the Light of Varda, and was stained by the assault of Melkor. And being for a long while without rule it flamed with excessive heat or grew too cool, so that grievous hurt was done to Arda and the fashioning of the world was marred and delayed, until with long toil the Valar made a new order.† But even as Árië foretold, Melkor was burned and his brightness darkened, and he gave no more light, but light pained him exceedingly and he hated it.

Nonetheless Melkor would not leave Arda in peace; and above all he begrudged to the Valar their dwelling on Earth, and desired to injure their labours there, or bring them to naught, if he could. Therefore he returned to Earth, but for fear of the might of the Valar and of Tulkas more than all he came now in secret. And in his hatred of the Sun he came to the North at night in winter. At first he would depart when the long day of summer came; but after a time, becoming bolder again, and desiring a dwelling place of his own, he began the delving

---

* [marginal note] Indeed some say that it was released from Eä.

† [marginal note] Also some of the Wise have said that the ordering of Arda, as to the placing and courses of its parts, was disarrayed by Melkor, so that the Earth was at times drawn too near to the Sun, and at others went too far off.

underground of his great fortress in the far North, which was afterwards named *Utumno* (or *Udûn*).

The Valar therefore, when they became aware by the signs of evil that were seen upon Earth that Melkor had stolen back, sought in vain for him, though Tulcas and Oromë went wide over Middle-earth even to the uttermost East. When they perceived that Melkor would now turn darkness and night to his purposes, as he had aforetime sought to wield flame, they were grieved; for it was a part of their design that there should be change and alteration upon Earth, and neither day perpetual nor night without end.* For by Night the Children of Arda should know Day, and perceive and love Light; and yet Night should also in its kind be good and blessed, being a time of repose, and of inward thought; and a vision also of things high and fair that are beyond Arda, but are veiled by the splendour of Anar. But Melkor would make it a time of peril unseen, of fear without form, an uneasy vigil; or a haunted dream, leading through despair to the shadow of Death.

Therefore Manwë took counsel with Varda, and they called Aulë to their aid. And they resolved to alter the fashion of Arda and of Earth, and in their thought they devised Ithil, the Moon. In what way and with what labours they wrought in deed this great device of their thought, who shall say: for which of the Children hath seen the Valar in the uprising of their strength or listened to their counsels in the flower of their youth? Who hath observed their labour as they laboured, who hath seen the newness of the new?

Some say that it was out of Earth[16] itself that Ithil was made, and thus Ambar[17] was diminished; others say that the Moon was made of like things to the Earth and of that which is Eä itself as it was made in the Tale.[18]

Now when the Moon was full-wrought it was set above Ambar, and directed to go ever round and about, bringing a light to dark places from which the Sun had departed. But it was a lesser light, so that moonlight was not the same as sunlight, and there was still change of light upon the Earth; moreover

---

* [footnote to the text] For it is indeed of the nature of Eä and the Great History that naught may stay unchanged in time, and things which do so, or appear to do so, or endeavour to remain so, become a weariness, and are loved no longer (or are at best unheeded).

there was still also night under the stars, for the Moon and the Sun were at certain times and seasons both absent.

This at least is what came after to be by that doom spoken by Ilúvatar ..... the evil of Melkor should in its own despite bring forth things more fair than the devising of his ..... For some have held that the Moon was at first aflame, but was later made [?strong] and life .....: later but while Arda was unfashioned and still in the turmoils of Melkor.

So much is known to the Wise, that Tilion — [*sic*] and that Melkor was filled with new wrath at the rising of the Moon. Therefore for a while he left Ambar again and went out into the Outer Night, and gathered to him some of those spirits who would answer his call.

A page of rough and disconnected notes obviously preceded this text, but must belong to much the same time: ideas found in the discussion and synopsis preceding the narrative are found also here, such as the 'great darkness of shadow' created by Melkor that blotted out the Sun. In these notes my father was still asking himself whether he should 'keep the old mythological story of the making of the Sun and Moon, or alter the background to a "round earth" version', and observing that in the latter case the Moon would be a work of Melkor's to provide 'a safe retreat' — thus returning to the idea of the origin of the Moon found years before in text C* of the *Ainulindalë* (p. 41, §31). Doubt and lack of certain direction are very strongly conveyed, as he wrestled with the intractable problems posed by the presence of the Sun in the sky under which the Elves awoke, which was lit only by the stars.[19]

There are features in the present text that clearly associate it with the Commentary on the *Athrabeth* (see notes 2 and 3 below), among them the use of the name *Arda* to mean the Solar System; but while the Earth itself is in the Commentary named *Imbar* it has here the older name *Ambar* (see note 17). There can be no doubt, I think, that the present text was the earlier of the two. On the other hand, no more finished or complete presentation of the new conceptions at large, the 'new mythology', is found; and it seems at any rate arguable that while committed in mind to the abandonment of the old myth of the origin of the Sun and Moon my father left in abeyance the formulation and expression of the new. It may be, though I have no evidence on the question one way or the other, that he came to perceive from such experimental writing as this text that the old structure was too comprehensive, too interlocked in all its parts, indeed its roots too deep, to withstand such a devastating surgery.

NOTES

1 In AAm §15 (p. 52) 'there was great growth of trees and herbs, and beasts and birds came forth' in the light of the Lamps: that was the Spring of Arda. But after the destruction of the Lamps Yavanna 'set a sleep upon many fair things that had arisen in the Spring, both tree and herb and beast and bird, so that they should not age but should wait for a time of awakening that yet should be' (§30, p. 70).

2 On the astronomical knowledge to be presumed among the High-elves cf. Note 2 to the Commentary on the *Athrabeth* (p. 337) – where as here *Arda* is equated with the Solar System – and Text I (p. 370).

3 The thought of this paragraph is closely paralleled in Note 2 to the Commentary on the *Athrabeth* (p. 337), and the final sentence is very similar to what is said in the Commentary itself, p. 334 ('Melkor was not just a local Evil on Earth...').

4 In AAm §24 (p. 54) it is told that after the Fall of the Lamps 'Middle-earth lay in a twilight beneath the stars that Varda had wrought in the ages forgotten of her labours in Eä', and in §34 (p. 71) Varda looked out from Taniquetil 'and beheld the darkness of the Earth beneath the innumerable stars, faint and far', before she began the making of new and brighter stars; so also in the revised *Quenta Silmarillion* (p. 159, §19): 'Then Varda ... made new stars and brighter against the coming of the First-born. Wherefore she whose name out of the deeps of time and the labours of Eä was Tintallë, the Kindler, was called after by the Elves Elentári, the Queen of the Stars.' But if she can still perhaps be called *Elentári*, she can no longer be called *Tintallë* (see however p. 388 and note 3).

In a late emendation to the final text D of the *Ainulindalë* (p. 34, §36) the words concerning Varda 'she it was who wrought the Stars' were changed to 'she it was who wrought the Great Stars'; and it seems possible that this was done in the light of the ideas presented here.

5 Cf. Note 2 to the Commentary on the *Athrabeth* (p. 337), with note 13 to that passage.

6 This is of course altogether different from the form of the legend in the *Ainulindalë* (p. 14, §23): 'But Melkor, too, was there from the first, and he meddled in all that was done'; while in the text C* (p. 40) Melkor entered Arda before the other Ainur.

7 The legend in *Ainulindalë* C* that Melkor himself made the Moon so that he 'could observe thence all that happened below' (p. 41, §31) had been abandoned (but see p. 383).

8 In AAm (p. 131, §172) and in QS (§75) Tilion was no Vala, but 'a young hunter of the company of Oromë'. In AAm §179

Text II   MYTHS TRANSFORMED   385

    appears the story that Morgoth assailed Tilion, 'sending spirits of shadow against him', but unavailingly.

9   On names of the Sun and Moon see QS §75 and commentary (V.241, 243) and the later revision of the passage (p. 198); also AAm §171 and commentary (pp. 130, 136).

10   In AAm (p. 133, §179) it was told that 'Arien Morgoth feared with a great fear, and dared not to come nigh her'.

11   On the name *Endor* see AAm §38 (pp. 72, 76).

12   See p. 327 note 16.

13   'at the time of Felagund': i.e. at the time when Finrod Felagund encountered Men, first of the High-elves to do so (p. 307).

14   'Men must awake while Melkor is still in Arda?': 'Arda' must be an error for 'Middle-earth' (i.e. before his captivity in Aman).

15   An *s* is pencilled over the *r* of *Ār(i)*.

16   Above *Earth* my father wrote Ambar, then struck it out, and wrote '*Mar* = House'. See the next note.

17   In Note 2 to the Commentary on the *Athrabeth* (p. 337, and see note 12 to that passage) appears *Imbar*, translated 'the Habitation', = Earth, 'the principal part of Arda' (= the Solar System).

18   From this point the manuscript becomes very rough, in places illegible, and soon peters out.

19   In other scribbled notes (written at the same time as text II and constituting a part of that manuscript) my father wrote that Varda gave the holy light received in gift from Ilúvatar (see p. 380) not only to the Sun and to the Two Trees but also to 'the significant Star'. The meaning of this is nowhere explained. Beside it he wrote *Signifer*, and many experimental Elvish names, as *Taengyl, Tengyl, Tannacolli* or *Tankol, Tainacolli*; also a verbal root *tana* 'show, indicate'; *tanna* 'sign'; and *kolla* 'borne, worn, especially a vestment or cloak', with the note '*Sindikoll-o* is masculinized'.

III

This very brief and hasty statement was found in a small collection of such notes folded in a newspaper of April 1959. It was written on a slip of paper torn from a bill from Merton College dated in June 1955; a similar bill of October 1955 was used for a passage of drafting for the *Athrabeth* (p. 352). I have noticed (p. 304) that the use of such documents of the year 1955 might suggest that the *Athrabeth* was not the work of a single concentrated period, although if my father had prepared a supply of such slips for brief notes or passages of drafting and other purposes the date would be misleading.

What happened in Valinor after the Death of the Trees? Aman was 'unveiled' – it had been covered with a *dome* (made by

Varda) of mist or cloud down through which no sight would pierce nor light. This dome was lit by stars – in imitation of the great Firmament of Eä. This now rendered Valinor dark except for starlight [i.e. after the death of the Trees]. It was removed and Aman was lit by the Sun – its blessing was thus removed. (Melkor's defilement of the Sun must thus precede the Two Trees which had light of Sun and Stars before Melkor [?tainted] it – or the Trees [?could ?would] be lit by light before the [?Turbulence] of Melkor.)

I do not feel altogether certain of the meaning of the extremely elliptical concluding sentence in brackets, but it should perhaps be interpreted thus – as the statement of a problem arising from what has been said. The Dome of Varda must have been contrived after the ravishing of Árië by Melkor, in order to keep out the Sun's polluted light;[1] and Aman was lit beneath the Dome by the Two Trees. But on the other hand, it is an essential idea that the light of the Trees was derived from the Sun before it was 'tainted'. A resolution of this conflict may be found (reading 'could', not 'would', in the last phrase) in the idea that the light of the Trees was an unsullied light preserved by Varda from a time before the assaults of Melkor.

In the initial discussion in text II it is made clear that the Sun had been defiled before the Two Trees came into being: 'Now one of the objects of the Trees ... was the healing of the hurts of Melkor' (p. 377); but it is also said that 'Varda has preserved some of the Primeval Light ... The Two Trees are made.' This appears to be the solution to which my father came in the present text, thus suggesting that it preceded text II. On the other hand, there is no suggestion of the Dome of Varda in text II, and that text gives the impression that my father was beginning a new story, working it out as he went. It is probably vain to try to establish a clear sequence of composition from these papers, since he might return to the same problem and find what appears to be the same resolution at different times.

It is a notable fact that the Dome of Varda appears in my father's final work on the narrative text of the *Quenta Silmarillion* Chapter 6 (p. 286, §57). Where in AAm (p. 98, §108) it was told that Melkor, with Ungoliantë beside him, looked out from the summit of Mount Hyarantar and 'saw afar ... the silver domes of Valmar gleaming in the mingling of the lights of Telperion and Laurelin', in the *Quenta Silmarillion* Ungoliantë (now, in the changed story, lying on the summit alone) 'saw *the glimmer of the stars in the dome of Varda* and the radiance of Valmar far away.' Thus when later in the final rewriting ('The Rape of the Silmarils', p. 293, §1) it is told that above the Valar sitting in the Ring of Doom 'the stars of Varda now glimmered overhead', it must be the stars of the Dome that were glimmering.²

NOTES

1 But in text IV (p. 388) it is said that the Dome of Varda was made 'to keep out any spirits or spies of Melkor'.
2 In the corresponding passage in the *Annals of Aman* (p. 106, §117) it is said: 'the gods sat in shadow, for it was night. But now night only as it may be in some land of the world, when the stars peer fitfully through the wrack of great clouds, and cold fogs drift in from a sullen shore of the sea.' In the published *Silmarillion* the final text ('the stars of Varda now glimmered overhead') was used; this does not indeed introduce any difficulty within the narrative, but I did not at that time perceive the significance of the words.

IV

There is a further statement about the Dome of Varda in a manuscript to which I have several times referred (VI.466; VIII.20; IX.73), an analysis (in intention) of all fragments of other languages found in *The Lord of the Rings*. The passage that I quote here comes from a long note on the song to Elbereth at the end of the chapter 'Many Meetings'. It may be mentioned incidentally that my father noted on the word *menel*: 'the heavens, the apparent dome of the sky. (Probably a Quenya word introduced into Sindarin. It was opposed to *kemen* "the Earth" as an apparent flat floor under *menel*. But these were "pictorial" words, as the lore of the Eldar and the Númenóreans knew much astronomy.)'

The passage concerning the Dome arises from the statement that *Elbereth* has *el-* 'star' prefixed (with the note 'But since *b* is not mutated the name is probably to be referred to *elen-barathi > elmbereth*').

The mythological association of Varda with the stars is of twofold origin. In the 'demiurgic period', before the establishment of Arda 'the Realm', while the Valar in general (including an unnamed host of others who never came to Arda)¹ were labouring in the general construction of Eä (the World or Universe), Varda was in Eldarin and Númenórean legend said to have designed and set in their places most of the principal stars; but being (by destiny and desire) the future Queen of Arda, in which her ultimate function lay, especially as the lover and protectress of the Quendi, she was concerned not only with the great Stars in themselves, but also in their relations to Arda, and their appearance therefrom (and their effect upon the Children to come). Such forms and major patterns, therefore, as we call (for instance) *the Plough*, or *Orion*, were said to be her designs. Thus the *Valacirca* or 'Sickle of the Gods', which was one of the Eldarin names for the Plough, was, it was said, intended later to be a sign of menace and threat of vengeance over the North in which Melkor took up his abode (Varda was the most foresighted of all the Valar, possessing the clearest memory of the Music and Vision in which she had played only a small part as actor or player, but had listened most attentively).[2]

Later, when the Valar took refuge from Melkor, and the imminent ruin of Arda, and built and fortified Valinor in Aman, it was Varda who made the great dome above Valinor, to keep out any spirits or spies of Melkor. It was made as a simulacrum of the true firmament *(Tar-menel)*, and the patterns were therein repeated, but with apparent stars (or 'sparks' : *tinwi*) of greater relative size to the total visible area. So that the lesser firmament of Valinor *(Nur-menel)* was very brilliant.

From this work (chiefly: but also her original demiurgic labours were included) she was called 'Star-kindler'. Note that *Velen* properly referred to the real stars of Eä (but could also naturally be transferred to their *imagines*). The words *tinwë*, *ñillë* (√*tin* 'spark', √*ngil* 'silver glint') and Sindarin *tim*, *gil* referred properly to the Valinorian *imagines*. Hence Quenya *Tintallë* from *tinta* 'cause to sparkle', but also *Elentári* 'Queen of Stars'; Sindarin *Elbereth*, but also *Gilthoniel*.[3]

This note on Elbereth ends with a slightly jumbled and obscure statement to the effect that *Gilthoniel* is derived from the stems √*ngil* and √*thăn / thān* 'kindle, set light to'; *iel* a feminine suffix corresponding to male -*we*.

These remarks on Varda seem to raise further questions. In text II (pp. 375–6) my father declared that 'the cosmogonic mythology should represent Arda as it is, more or less: an island in the void "amidst the innumerable stars"'; that 'the Stars, therefore, in general will be other and remoter parts of the Great Tale of Eä, which do not concern the Valar of Arda'; and that 'Varda, therefore, as one of the great Valar of Arda, cannot be said to have "kindled" the stars, as an original subcreative act – not at least the stars in general.' I have taken this to mean (p. 384 note 4) that the 'star-making' of Varda was to be confined to (at most) the making of the 'Great Stars' before the Awakening of the Elves. In the present text, on the other hand, appears the remarkable conception that the 'demiurgic' work of Varda was the making and disposition of certain 'principal' stars, which should in ages to come, after the establishment of the Earth, be visible in its skies as figures significant of its history – the 'dramatic centre' of Eä.

While I think it certain that this text comes from the late 1950s, there seems no way in which to date it more precisely either externally or in relation to other writings.

NOTES

1 Cf. text II (p. 378): 'Others there were, countless to our thought ..., whose labour lay elsewhere and in other regions and histories of the Great Tale, amid stars remote and worlds beyond the reach of the furthest thought.'
2 It is a curious point that what is said here of Varda's part in the Music of the Ainur is largely repeated from what is told of Nienna in the 'lost' typescript of the beginning of the *Annals of Aman* (AAm*, p. 68, §26). There it is told of her that she 'took little part' in the Music, but 'listened intent to all that she heard. Therefore she was rich in memory, and farsighted, perceiving how the themes should unfold in the Tale of Arda.'
3 It is interesting to compare what is said here about the names of Varda with what my father said on the subject in a note dated 3 February 1938 (V.200): '*Tintallë* Kindler can stand – but *tinwë* in Quenya only = spark (*tinta-* to kindle). Therefore *Tinwerína* > *Elerína*, *Tinwerontar* > *Elentári*'.

V

This brief comment, entitled 'Sun The Trees Silmarils', is found on a single sheet, together with other more substantial writings similar in appearance, preserved in a folded newspaper of November 1958.

The making of the Sun after the Death of the Trees is not only impossible 'mythology' now – especially since the Valar must be supposed to know the truth about the structure of Eä (and not make mythical guesses like Men) and to have communicated this to the Eldar (and so to Númenóreans!) – it is also impossible chronologically in the Narrative.

The Sun existed as part of the Kingdom of Arda. In so far as there was darkness (and diminishment of growth in Arda consequently) when the Valar removed to Aman it was due to obscurations devised by Melkor: clouds and smokes (a volcanic era!).

The Sun was the immediate source of the light of Arda. The Blessedness of the Trees (as compared with other growing things later) was that they were kindled and illumined with the light of the Sun and Moon *before these were tainted*. The attack of Melkor on the Sun (and Moon) must therefore be subsequent to the establishment of Valinor, and be Melkor's effort to produce darkness.

Since the Silmarils were kindled from the Trees after the Death of the Trees, this 'light of the Unmarred Sun' remained only in them.

In text III, my father's note on the removal of the Dome of Varda after the death of the Trees, he was confronted by the problem (if my analysis of his meaning is correct, p. 386) that 'Melkor's defilement of the Sun must *precede* the Two Trees', whereas the light of the Trees was derived from the unsullied light of the Sun and Moon. Here he concludes that 'the attack of Melkor on the Sun (and Moon) must be *subsequent to* the establishment of Valinor'.

The word *after* in the concluding sentence is no more than a slip in extremely rapid writing.

VI

This text, entitled *Melkor* with *Morgoth* written beneath, is from the same collection as is text III (found in a newspaper dated April 1959), and was written on four slips made from further copies of the same Merton College documents dated June 1955 as is the draft A of the *Athrabeth* (pp. 350–2). The slip on which text III is written carries also preliminary drafting for the present essay on Melkor.

It is notable that text VI begins with a reference to 'Finrod and Andreth', which was therefore in existence, at least in some form.

Melkor Morgoth

Melkor must be made *far more powerful* in original nature (cf. 'Finrod and Andreth'). The greatest power under Eru (sc. the greatest created power).[1] (He was to make / devise / begin; Manwë (a little less great) was to improve, carry out, complete.)

Later, he must *not* be able to be controlled or 'chained' by all the Valar combined. Note that in the early age of Arda he was alone able to drive the Valar out of Middle-earth into retreat.

The war against Utumno was only undertaken by the Valar with reluctance, and without hope of real victory, but rather as a covering action or diversion, to enable them to get the Quendi out of his sphere of influence. But Melkor had already progressed some way towards becoming 'the Morgoth, a tyrant (or central tyranny and will), + his agents'.[2] Only the *total* contained the old power of the complete Melkor; so that if 'the Morgoth' could be reached or temporarily separated from his agents he was much more nearly controllable and on a power-level with the Valar. The Valar find that they can deal with his agents (sc. armies, Balrogs, etc.) piecemeal. So that they come at last to Utumno itself and find that 'the Morgoth' has no longer for the moment sufficient 'force' (in any sense) to shield himself from direct personal contact. Manwë at last faces Melkor again, as he has not done since he entered Arda. Both are amazed: Manwë to perceive the *decrease* in Melkor as a *person*; Melkor to perceive this also from his own point of view: he has now less personal force than Manwë, and can no longer daunt him with his gaze.

Either Manwë must tell him so or he must himself suddenly realize (or both) that this has happened: he is 'dispersed'. But the lust to have creatures under him, dominated, has become habitual and necessary to Melkor, so that even if the process was reversible (possibly was by absolute and unfeigned self-abasement and repentance only) he cannot bring himself to do it.* As with all other characters there must be a *trembling moment* when it is in the balance: he nearly repents – and does not, and becomes much wickeder, and more foolish.

Possibly (and he thinks it possible) he could now *at that moment* be humiliated against his own will and 'chained' – if and before his dispersed forces reassemble. So – as soon as he has mentally rejected repentance – he (just like Sauron afterwards on this model) makes a mockery of self-abasement and repentance. From which actually he gets a kind of perverted pleasure as in desecrating something holy – [for the mere contemplating of the possibility of genuine repentance, if that did not come specially then as a direct grace from Eru, was at least one last flicker of his true primeval nature.][3] He *feigns* remorse and repentance. He actually kneels before Manwë and surrenders – in the first instance to avoid being chained by the Chain Angainor, which once upon him he fears would not ever be able to be shaken off. But also suddenly he has the idea of

---

* [footnote to the text] One of the reasons for his self-weakening is that he has given to his 'creatures', Orcs, Balrogs, etc. *power of recuperation and multiplication*. So that they will gather again without further specific orders. Part of his native creative power has gone out into making an independent evil growth out of his control.

penetrating the vaunted fastness of Valinor, and ruining it. So he offers to become 'the least of the Valar' and servant of them each and all, to help (in advice and skill) in repairing all the evils and hurts he has done. It is this offer which seduces or deludes Manwë – Manwë must be shown to have his own inherent fault (though not sin):* he has become engrossed (partly out of sheer fear of Melkor, partly out of desire to control him) in amendment, healing, re-ordering – even 'keeping the status quo' – to the loss of all creative power and even to weakness in dealing with difficult and perilous situations. Against the advice of some of the Valar (such as Tulkas) he grants Melkor's prayer.

Melkor is taken back to Valinor going last (save for Tulkas† who follows bearing Angainor and clinking it to remind Melkor).

But at the council Melkor is not given immediate freedom. The Valar in assembly will not tolerate this. Melkor is remitted to Mandos (to stay there in 'reclusion' and meditate, and complete his repentance – and also his plans for redress).[4]

Then he begins to doubt the wisdom of his own policy, and would have rejected it all and burst out into flaming rebellion – but he is now absolutely isolated from his agents and in enemy territory. He cannot. Therefore he swallows the bitter pill (but it greatly increases his hate, and he ever afterward accused Manwë of being faithless).

The rest of the story, with Melkor's release, and permission to attend the Council sitting at the feet of Manwë (after the pattern of evil counsellors in later tales, which it could be said derive from this primeval model?), can then proceed more or less as already told.

In this short essay it is seen that in his reflections on the nature of Melkor, the vastness of his primeval power and its 'dispersion', my

* [footnote to the text] Every finite creature must have some weakness: that is some inadequacy to deal with some situations. It is not sinful when not willed, and when the creature does his best (even if it is not what should be done) as he sees it – with the conscious intent of serving Eru.

† [footnote to the text] Tulkas represents the good side of 'violence' in the war against evil. This is an absence of all compromise which will even face apparent evils (such as war) rather than parley; and does not (in any kind of pride) think that any one less than Eru can redress this, or rewrite the tale of Arda.

father had been led to propose certain important alterations in the narrative of the legends as told in the *Quenta Silmarillion* (pp. 161, 186) and in the *Annals of Aman* (pp. 75, 80, 93). In the narrative as it stood, and as it remained,[5] there was no suggestion that Melkor feigned repentance when (no longer able to 'daunt him with his gaze') he faced Manwë in Utumno – already harbouring 'the idea of penetrating the vaunted fastness of Valinor, and ruining it'. On the contrary, 'Tulkas stood forth as the champion of the Valar and wrestled with him and cast him upon his face, and bound him with the chain Angainor'[6] (an ancient element, going back to the richly pictorial and 'primitive' account in the story of 'The Chaining of Melko' in *The Book of Lost Tales*, I.100–4). Moreover, in the present text it was now, defeated at Utumno, that Melkor offered to become 'the least of the Valar', and to aid them in the redress of all the evils that he had brought to pass, whereas in the narratives he did this when he came before the Valar after he had endured the ages of his incarceration in Mandos and sued for pardon. Of Manwë it was said, when Melkor was allowed to go freely about Valinor, that he believed that his evil was cured: 'for he himself was free from the evil and could not comprehend it'. No such flaw or 'inherent fault' in Manwë as is described in this essay was suggested;[7] although it was told that Ulmo, and Tulkas, doubted the wisdom of such clemency (and this too is an element that goes back to *The Book of Lost Tales*: 'Such was the doom of Manwë... albeit Tulkas and Palúrien thought it merciful to peril' (I.105)).

NOTES

1 Cf. Finrod's words in the *Athrabeth* (p. 322): 'there is no power conceivable greater than Melkor save Eru only'.
2 The earliest reference to the idea of the 'dispersion' of Melkor's original power is found in the *Annals of Aman* §179 (p. 133):
> For as he grew in malice, and sent forth from himself the evil that he conceived in lies and creatures of wickedness, his power passed into them and was dispersed, and he himself became ever more earth-bound, unwilling to issue from his dark strongholds.

Cf. also *Annals* §128 (p. 110). – The expression 'the Morgoth' is used several times by Finrod in the *Athrabeth*.
3 The square brackets were put in after the writing of the passage.
4 'his plans for redress': i.e. redress of the evils he has brought about.
5 The second passage in QS, in which the pardon of Melkor is recounted (p. 186, §48), was changed in the final rewriting of Chapter 6: see p. 273, §48. But though the changed text introduced the ideas that any complete reversal of the evils brought about by Melkor was impossible, and that he was 'in his beginning

the greatest of the Powers', the narrative was not altered in respect of changes envisaged in this essay (see note 7).

6   Alteration to the old story of the encounter at Utumno might have entered if QS Chapter 3 (in which this is recounted) had formed a part of the late rewriting that transformed the old Chapter 6; but see note 7.

7   In the final rewriting of QS Chapter 6 (p. 273, §48) this remained the case (note 5); and the original story was also retained that it was in Valinor after his imprisonment, not at Utumno, that Melkor made his promises of service and reparation. This might suggest that the present essay was written *after* the new work on QS (almost certainly dating from the end of the 1950s, p. 300), supporting the idea that the date of the documents on which the essay was written (1955) is misleading (see p. 385).

VII

This essay is found in two forms. The earlier ('A') is a fairly brief text of four pages in manuscript, titled 'Some notes on the "philosophy" of the *Silmarillion*'; it is rapidly expressed and does not have a clear ending. The second ('B') is a greatly expanded version of twelve pages, also in manuscript, of far more careful expression and beginning in fine script, but breaking off unfinished, indeed in the middle of a sentence. This is titled 'Notes on motives in *the Silmarillion*'.

The relation between the two forms is such that for most of its length there is no need to give any of the text of A, for all of its content is found embedded in B. From the point (p. 401) where the Valar are condemned for the raising of the Pelóri, however, the texts diverge. In B my father introduced a long palliation of the conduct of the Valar, and the essay breaks off before the matter of the concluding section of A was reached (see note 6); this is therefore given at the end of B.

The text of B was subsequently divided and lettered as three distinct sections, here numbered (i), (ii), and (iii).

Notes on motives in the Silmarillion

(i)

Sauron was 'greater', effectively, in the Second Age than Morgoth at the end of the First. Why? Because, though he was far smaller by natural stature, he had not yet fallen so low. Eventually he also squandered his power (of being) in the endeavour to gain control of others. But he was not obliged to expend so much of himself. To gain domination over Arda, Morgoth had let most of his being pass into the *physical* constituents of the Earth – hence all things that were born on

Earth and lived on and by it, beasts or plants or incarnate spirits, were liable to be 'stained'. Morgoth at the time of the War of the Jewels had become permanently 'incarnate': for this reason he was afraid, and waged the war almost entirely by means of devices, or of subordinates and dominated creatures.

Sauron, however, inherited the 'corruption' of Arda, and only spent his (much more limited) power on the Rings; for it was the *creatures* of earth, in their *minds and wills*, that he desired to dominate. In this way Sauron was also wiser than Melkor-Morgoth. Sauron was not a beginner of discord; and he probably knew more of the 'Music' than did Melkor, whose mind had always been filled with his own plans and devices, and gave little attention to other things. The time of Melkor's greatest power, therefore, was in the physical beginnings of the World; a vast demiurgic lust for power and the achievement of his own will and designs, on a great scale. And later after things had become more stable, Melkor was more interested in and capable of dealing with a volcanic eruption, for example, than with (say) a tree. It is indeed probable that he was simply unaware of the minor or more delicate productions of Yavanna: such as small flowers.*

Thus, as 'Morgoth', when Melkor was confronted by the existence of other inhabitants of Arda, with other wills and intelligences, he was enraged by the mere fact of their existence, and his only notion of dealing with them was by physical force, or the fear of it. His sole ultimate object was their destruction. Elves, and still more Men, he despised because of their 'weakness': that is their lack of physical force, or power over 'matter'; but he was also afraid of them. He was aware, at any rate originally when still capable of rational thought, that he could not 'annihilate'** them: that is, destroy their being; but their physical 'life', and incarnate form became increasingly to his mind the only thing that was worth considering.† Or he

* [footnote to the text] If such things were forced upon his attention, he was angry and hated them, as coming from other minds than his own.

** [bracketed note inserted into the text] Melkor could not, of course, 'annihilate' anything of matter, he could only ruin or destroy or corrupt the forms given to matter by other minds in their sub-creative activities.

† [footnote without indication of reference in the text] For this

became so far advanced in Lying that he lied even to himself, and pretended that he could destroy them and rid Arda of them altogether. Hence his endeavour always to break wills and subordinate them to or absorb them into his own will and being, before destroying their bodies. This was sheer nihilism, and negation its one ultimate object: Morgoth would no doubt, if he had been victorious, have ultimately destroyed even his own 'creatures', such as the Orcs, when they had served his sole purpose in using them: the destruction of Elves and Men. Melkor's final impotence and despair lay in this: that whereas the Valar (and in their degree Elves and Men) could still love 'Arda Marred', that is Arda with a Melkor-ingredient, and could still heal this or that hurt, or produce from its very marring, from its state as it was, things beautiful and lovely, Melkor could do nothing with Arda, which was not from his own mind and was interwoven with the work and thoughts of others: even left alone he could only have gone raging on till all was levelled again into a formless chaos. And yet even so he would have been defeated, because it would still have 'existed', independent of his own mind, and a world in potential.

Sauron had never reached this stage of nihilistic madness. He did not object to the existence of the world, so long as he could do what he liked with it. He still had the relics of positive purposes, that descended from the good of the nature in which he began: it had been his virtue (and therefore also the cause of his fall, and of his relapse) that he loved order and co-ordination, and disliked all confusion and wasteful friction. (It was the apparent will and power of Melkor to effect his designs quickly and masterfully that had first attracted Sauron to him.) Sauron had, in fact, been very like Saruman, and so still understood him quickly and could guess what he would be likely to think and do, even without the aid of *palantíri* or of spies; whereas Gandalf eluded and puzzled him. But like all minds of this cast, Sauron's love (originally) or (later) mere understanding of other individual intelligences was correspondingly weaker; and though the only real good in, or rational motive for, all this ordering and planning and organization was the good of all inhabitants of Arda (even admitting Sauron's

reason he himself came to fear 'death' – the destruction of his assumed bodily form – above everything, and sought to avoid any kind of injury to his own form.

right to be their supreme lord), his 'plans', the idea coming from his own isolated mind, became the sole object of his will, and an end, the End, in itself.*

Morgoth had no 'plan': unless destruction and reduction to *nil* of a world in which he had only a *share* can be called a 'plan'. But this is, of course, a simplification of the situation. Sauron had not served Morgoth, even in his last stages, without becoming infected by his lust for destruction, and his hatred of God (which must end in nihilism). Sauron could not, of course, be a 'sincere' atheist. Though one of the minor spirits created before the world, he knew Eru, according to his measure. He probably deluded himself with the notion that the Valar (including Melkor) having failed, Eru had simply abandoned Eä, or at any rate Arda, and would not concern himself with it any more. It would appear that he interpreted the 'change of the world' at the Downfall of Númenor, when Aman was removed from the physical world, in this sense: Valar (and Elves) were removed from effective control, and Men under God's curse and wrath. If he thought about the *Istari*, especially Saruman and Gandalf, he imagined them as emissaries from the Valar, seeking to establish their lost power again and 'colonize' Middle-earth, as a mere effort of defeated imperialists (without knowledge or sanction of Eru). His cynicism, which (sincerely) regarded the motives of Manwë as precisely the same as his own, seemed fully justified in Saruman. Gandalf he did not understand. But certainly he had already become evil, and therefore stupid, enough to imagine that his different behaviour was due simply to weaker intelligence and lack of firm masterful purpose. He was only a rather cleverer Radagast – cleverer, because it is more profitable (more productive of power) to become absorbed in the study of people than of animals.

Sauron was not a 'sincere' atheist, but he preached atheism, because it weakened resistance to himself (and he had ceased to fear God's action in Arda). As was seen in the case of Ar-Pharazôn. But there was seen the effect of Melkor upon Sauron: he spoke of Melkor in Melkor's own terms: as a god, or even as God. This may have been the residue of a state which

---

* [footnote to the text] But his capability of corrupting other minds, and even engaging their service, was a residue from the fact that his original desire for 'order' had really envisaged the good estate (especially physical well-being) of his 'subjects'.

was in a sense a shadow of good: the ability once in Sauron at least to admire or admit the superiority of a being other than himself. Melkor, and still more Sauron himself afterwards, both profited by this darkened shadow of good and the services of 'worshippers'. But it may be doubted whether even such a shadow of good was still sincerely operative in Sauron by that time. His cunning motive is probably best expressed thus. To wean one of the God-fearing from their allegiance it is best to propound another *unseen* object of allegiance and another hope of benefits; propound to him a Lord who will sanction what he desires and not forbid it. Sauron, apparently a defeated rival for world-power, now a mere hostage, can hardly propound himself; but as the former servant and disciple of Melkor, the worship of Melkor will raise him from hostage to high priest. But though Sauron's whole true motive was the destruction of the Númenóreans, this was a particular matter of revenge upon Ar-Pharazôn, for humiliation. Sauron (unlike Morgoth) would have been content for the Númenóreans to exist, *as his own subjects*, and indeed he used a great many of them that he corrupted to his allegiance.

(ii)

No one, not even one of the Valar, can read the mind of other 'equal beings':* that is one cannot 'see' them or comprehend them fully and directly by simple inspection. One can *deduce* much of their thought, from general comparisons leading to conclusions concerning the nature and tendencies of minds and thought, and from particular knowledge of individuals, and special circumstances. But this is no more reading or inspection of another mind than is deduction concerning the contents of a closed room, or events taken place out of sight. Neither is so-called 'thought-transference' a process of mind-reading: this is but the reception, and interpretation by the receiving mind, of the impact of a thought, or thought-pattern, emanating from another mind, which is no more the mind in full or in itself than is the distant sight of a man running the man himself. Minds can exhibit or reveal themselves to other minds by the action of their

* [marginal note] All rational minds / spirits deriving direct from Eru are 'equal' – in order and status – though not necessarily 'coëval' or of like original power.

own wills (though it is doubtful if, even when willing or desiring this, a mind can actually reveal itself wholly to any other mind). It is thus a temptation to minds of greater power to govern or constrain the will of other, and weaker, minds, so as to induce or force them to reveal themselves. But to force such a revelation, or to induce it by any lying or deception, even for supposedly 'good' purposes (including the 'good' of the person so persuaded or dominated), is absolutely forbidden. To do so is a crime, and the 'good' in the purposes of those who commit this crime swiftly becomes corrupted.

Much could thus 'go on behind Manwë's back': indeed the innermost being of all other minds, great and small, was hidden from him. And with regard to the Enemy, Melkor, in particular, he could not penetrate by distant mind-sight his thought and purposes, since Melkor remained in a fixed and powerful will to withhold his mind: which physically expressed took shape in the darkness and shadows that surrounded him. But Manwë could of course use, and did use, his own great knowledge, his vast experience of things and of persons, his memory of the 'Music', and his own far sight, and the tidings of his messengers.

He, like Melkor, practically never is seen or heard of outside or far away from his own halls and permanent residence. Why is this? For no very profound reason. The Government is always in Whitehall. King Arthur is usually in Camelot or Caerleon, and news and adventures come there and arise there. The 'Elder King' is obviously not going to be finally defeated or destroyed, at least not before some ultimate 'Ragnarök'[1] – which even for us is still in the future, so he can have no real 'adventures'. But, if you keep him *at home*, the issue of any particular event (since it cannot then result in a final 'checkmate') can remain in literary suspense. Even to the final war against Morgoth it is Fionwë son of Manwë who leads out the power of the Valar. When we move out Manwë it will be the last battle, and the end of the World (or of 'Arda Marred') as the Eldar would say.

[Morgoth's staying 'at home' has, as described above, quite a different reason: his fear of being killed or even hurt (the literary motive is not present, for since he is pitted against the Elder King, the issue of any one of his enterprises is always in doubt).]

Melkor 'incarnated' himself (as Morgoth) permanently. He did this so as to control the *hroa*,[2] the 'flesh' or physical matter, of Arda. He attempted to identify himself with it. A vaster, and more perilous, procedure, though of similar sort to the operations of Sauron with the Rings. Thus, outside the Blessed Realm, all 'matter' was likely to have a 'Melkor ingredient',[3] and those who had bodies, nourished by the *hroa* of Arda, had as it were a tendency, small or great, towards Melkor: they were none of them wholly free of him in their incarnate form, and their bodies had an effect upon their spirits.

But in this way Morgoth lost (or exchanged, or transmuted) the greater part of his original 'angelic' powers, of mind and spirit, while gaining a terrible grip upon the physical world. For this reason he *had* to be fought, mainly by physical force, and enormous material ruin was a probable consequence of any direct combat with him, victorious or otherwise. This is the chief explanation of the constant reluctance of the Valar to come into open battle against Morgoth. Manwë's task and problem was much more difficult than Gandalf's. Sauron's, relatively smaller, power was *concentrated*; Morgoth's vast power was *disseminated*. The whole of 'Middle-earth' was Morgoth's Ring, though temporarily his attention was mainly upon the North-west. Unless swiftly successful, War against him might well end in reducing all Middle-earth to chaos, possibly even all Arda. It is easy to say: 'It was the task and function of the Elder King to govern Arda and make it possible for the Children of Eru to live in it unmolested.' But the dilemma of the Valar was this: Arda could only be liberated by a physical battle; but a probable result of such a battle was the irretrievable ruin of Arda. Moreover, the final eradication of Sauron (as a power directing evil) was achievable by the destruction of the Ring. No such eradication of Morgoth was possible, since this required the complete disintegration of the 'matter' of Arda. Sauron's power was not (for example) in gold as such, but in a particular form or shape made of a particular portion of total gold. Morgoth's power was disseminated throughout Gold, if nowhere absolute (for he did not create Gold) it was nowhere absent. (It was this Morgoth-element in matter, indeed, which was a prerequisite for such 'magic' and other evils as Sauron practised with it and upon it.)

It is quite possible, of course, that certain 'elements' or conditions of matter had attracted Morgoth's special attention (mainly, unless in the remote past, for reasons of his own plans). For example, all gold (in Middle-earth) seems to have had a specially 'evil' trend – but not silver. Water is represented as being almost entirely free of Morgoth. (This, of course, does not mean that any particular sea, stream, river, well, or even vessel of water could not be poisoned or defiled – as all things could.)

(iii)

The Valar 'fade' and become more impotent, precisely in proportion as the shape and constitution of things becomes more defined and settled. The longer the Past, the more nearly defined the Future, and the less room for important change (untrammelled action, on a physical plane, that is not destructive in purpose). The Past, once 'achieved', has become part of the 'Music in being'. Only Eru may or can alter the 'Music'. The last major effort, of this demiurgic kind, made by the Valar was the lifting up of the range of the Pelóri to a great height. It is possible to view this as, if not an actually bad action, at least as a mistaken one. Ulmo disapproved of it.[4] It had one good, and legitimate, object: the preservation incorrupt of at least a part of Arda. But it seemed to have a selfish or neglectful (or despairing) motive also; for the effort to preserve the Elves incorrupt there had proved a failure if they were to be left free: many had refused to come to the Blessed Realm, many had revolted and left it. Whereas, with regard to Men, Manwë and all the Valar knew quite well that they could not come to Aman at all; and the longevity (co-extensive with the life of Arda) of Valar and Eldar was expressly not permitted to Men. Thus the 'Hiding of Valinor' came near to countering Morgoth's possessiveness by a rival possessiveness, setting up a private domain of light and bliss against one of darkness and domination: a palace and a pleasaunce[5] (well-fenced) against a fortress and a dungeon.[6]

This appearance of selfish *fainéance* in the Valar in the mythology as told is (though I have not explained it or commented on it) I think only an 'appearance', and one which we are apt to accept as the truth, since we are all in some degree affected by the shadow and lies of their Enemy, the Calumniator. It has to be remembered that the 'mythology' is represented as being two stages removed from a true record: it is based first upon Elvish records and lore about the Valar and their own dealings with them; and these have reached us (fragmentarily) only through relics of Númenórean (human) traditions, derived from the Eldar, in the earlier parts, though for later times supplemented by anthropocentric histories and tales.[7] These, it is true, came down through the 'Faithful' and their descendants in Middle-earth, but could not altogether escape the darkening of the picture due to the hostility of the rebellious Númenóreans to the Valar.

Even so, and on the grounds of the stories as received, it is possible to view the matter otherwise. The closing of Valinor against the rebel Noldor (who left it voluntarily and after warning) was in itself just. But, if we dare to attempt to enter the mind of the Elder King, assigning motives and finding faults, there are things to remember before we deliver a judgement. Manwë was the spirit of greatest wisdom and *prudence* in Arda. He is represented as having had the greatest knowledge of the Music, as a whole, possessed by any one finite mind; and he alone of all persons or minds in that time is represented as having the power of *direct* recourse to and communication with Eru. He must have grasped with great clarity what even we may perceive dimly: that it was the essential mode of the process of 'history' in Arda that evil should constantly arise, and that out of it new good should constantly come. One especial aspect of this is the strange way in which the evils of the Marrer, or his inheritors, are turned into weapons against evil. If we consider the situation after the escape of Morgoth and the reëstablishment of his abode in Middle-earth, we shall see that the heroic Noldor were the best possible weapon with which to keep Morgoth at bay, virtually besieged, and at any rate fully occupied, on the northern fringe of Middle-earth, without provoking him to a frenzy of nihilistic destruction. And in the meanwhile, Men, or the best elements in Mankind, shaking off his shadow, came into contact with a people who had actually seen and experienced the Blessed Realm.

In their association with the warring Eldar Men were raised to their fullest achievable stature, and by the two marriages the transference to them, or infusion into Mankind, of the noblest Elf-strain was accomplished, in readiness for the still distant, but inevitably approaching, days when the Elves would 'fade'.

The last intervention with physical force by the Valar, ending in the breaking of Thangorodrim, may then be viewed as not in fact reluctant or even unduly delayed, but timed with precision. The intervention came before the annihilation of the Eldar and the Edain. Morgoth though locally triumphant had neglected most of Middle-earth during the war; and by it he had in fact been *weakened*: in power and prestige (he had lost and failed to recover one of the Silmarils), and above all in mind. He had become absorbed in 'kingship', and though a tyrant of ogre-size and monstrous power, this was a vast fall even from his former wickedness of hate, and his terrible nihilism. He had fallen to *like* being a tyrant-king with conquered slaves, and vast obedient armies.[8]

The war was successful, and ruin was limited to the small (if beautiful) region of Beleriand. Morgoth was thus actually *made captive in physical form*,[9] and in that form taken as a mere criminal to Aman and delivered to Námo Mandos as judge – and executioner. He was judged, and eventually taken out of the Blessed Realm and *executed*: that is *killed* like one of the Incarnates. It was then made plain (though it must have been understood beforehand by Manwë and Námo) that, though he had 'disseminated' his power (his evil and possessive and rebellious will) far and wide into the matter of Arda, he had lost direct control of this, and all that 'he', as a surviving remnant of integral being, retained as 'himself' and under control was the terribly shrunken and reduced spirit that inhabited his self-imposed (but now beloved) body. When that body was destroyed he was weak and utterly 'houseless', and for that time at a loss and 'unanchored' as it were. We read that he was then thrust out into the Void.[10] That should mean that he was put outside Time and Space, outside Eä altogether; but if that were so this would imply a direct intervention of Eru (with or without supplication of the Valar). It may however refer inaccurately* to the extrusion or flight of his spirit from Arda.

In any case, in seeking to absorb or rather to infiltrate himself throughout 'matter', what was then left of him was no longer powerful enough to reclothe itself. (It would now remain *fixed* in the *desire* to do so: there was *no* 'repentance' or possibility of it: Melkor had abandoned for ever all 'spiritual' ambitions, and existed almost solely as a desire to possess and dominate matter, and Arda in particular.) At least it could not *yet* reclothe itself. We need not suppose that Manwë was deluded into supposing that this had been a war to end war, or

---

* [footnote to the text] Since the minds of Men (and even of the Elves) were inclined to confuse the 'Void', as a conception of the state of Not-being, outside Creation or Eä, with the conception of vast *spaces* within Eä, especially those conceived to lie all about the enisled 'Kingdom of Arda' (which we should probably call the Solar System).

even to end Melkor. Melkor was not Sauron. We speak of him being 'weakened, shrunken, reduced'; but this is in comparison with the great Valar. He had been a being of immense potency and life. The Elves certainly held and taught that *fëar* or 'spirits' may grow of their own life (independently of the body), even as they may be hurt and healed, be diminished and renewed.[11] The dark spirit of Melkor's 'remainder' might be expected, therefore, eventually and after long ages to increase again, even (as some held) to draw back into itself some of its formerly dissipated power. It would do this (even if Sauron could not) because of its relative greatness. It did not repent, or turn finally away from its obsession, but retained still relics of wisdom, so that it could still seek its object indirectly, and not merely blindly. It would rest, seek to heal itself, distract itself by other thoughts and desires and devices – but all simply to recover enough strength to return to the attack on the Valar, and to its old obsession. As it grew again it would become, as it were, a dark shadow, brooding on the confines of Arda, and yearning towards it.

Nonetheless the breaking of Thangorodrim and the extrusion of Melkor was the end of 'Morgoth' as such, and for that age (and many ages after). It was thus, also, in a sense the end of Manwë's prime function and task as Elder King, until the End. He had been the Adversary of the Enemy.

It is very reasonable to suppose that Manwë knew that before long (as he saw 'time') the Dominion of Men must begin, and the making of history would then be committed to them: for their struggle with Evil special arrangements had been made! Manwë knew of Sauron, of course. He had commanded Sauron to come before him for judgement, but had left room for repentance and ultimate rehabilitation. Sauron had refused and had fled into hiding. Sauron, however, was a problem that Men had to deal with finally: the first of the many concentrations of Evil into definite power-points that they would have to combat, as it was also the last of those in 'mythological' personalized (but non-human) form.

It may be noted that Sauron's first defeat was achieved by the Númenóreans alone (though Sauron was not in fact overthrown personally: his 'captivity' was voluntary and a trick). In the first overthrow and disembodiment of Sauron in Middle-earth (neglecting the matter of Lúthien)[12]

Here the long version B breaks off, at the foot of a page. I give now the conclusion of version A from the point where the texts diverge (see p. 394 and note 6), beginning with the sentence corresponding to B (p. 401) 'The last major effort, of this demiurgic kind, made by the Valar...'

The last effort of this sort made by the Valar was the raising up of the Pelóri – but this was not a good act: it came near to countering Morgoth in his own way – apart from the element of selfishness in its object of preserving Aman as a blissful region to live in.

The Valar were like architects working with a plan 'passed' by the Government. They became less and less important (structurally!) as the plan was more and more nearly achieved. Even in the First Age we see them after uncounted ages of work near the end of their time of work – not wisdom or counsel. (The wiser they became the less power they had to *do* anything – save by counsel.)

Similarly the Elves faded, having introduced 'art and science'.[13] Men will also 'fade', *if* it proves to be the plan that things shall still go on, when they have completed their function. But even the Elves had the notion that this would not be so: that the end of Men would somehow be bound up with the end of history, or as they called it 'Arda Marred' (*Arda Sahta*), and the achievement of 'Arda Healed' (*Arda Envinyanta*).[14] (They do not seem to have been clear or precise – how should they be! – whether *Arda Envinyanta* was a permanent state of achievement, which could therefore only be enjoyed 'outside Time', as it were: surveying the Tale as an englobed whole; or a state of unmarred bliss within Time and in a 'place' that was in some sense a lineal and historical descent of our world or 'Arda Marred'. They seem often to have meant both. 'Arda Unmarred' did not actually exist, but remained in thought – Arda without Melkor, or rather without the effects of his becoming evil; but is the source from which all ideas of order and perfection are derived. 'Arda Healed' is thus both the completion of the 'Tale of Arda' which has taken up all the deeds of Melkor, but must according to the promise of Ilúvatar be seen to be good; and also a state of redress and bliss beyond the 'circles of the world'.)[15]

Evil is fissiparous. But itself barren. Melkor could not 'beget', or have any spouse (though he attempted to ravish Arien, this was to destroy and 'distain'[16] her, not to beget fiery offspring). Out of the *discords* of the Music – sc. not directly out of either of the themes,[17] Eru's or Melkor's, but of their dissonance with regard one to another – evil things appeared in Arda, which did not descend from any direct plan or vision of Melkor: they were *not* 'his children'; and therefore, since all evil hates, hated him too. The progeniture of things was corrupted. Hence *Orcs*? Part of the Elf-Man idea gone wrong. Though as for Orcs, the Eldar believed Morgoth had actually 'bred' them by capturing Men (and Elves) early and increasing to the utmost any corrupt tendencies they possessed.

Despite its incomplete state (whether due to the loss of the conclusion of the fully developed form of the essay or to its abandonment, see note 6) this is the most comprehensive account that my father wrote of how, in his later years, he had come to 'interpret' the nature of Evil in his mythology; never elsewhere did he write any such exposition of the nature of Morgoth, of his decline, and of his corruption of Arda, nor draw out the distinction between Morgoth and Sauron: 'the whole of Middle-earth was Morgoth's Ring'.

To place this essay in sequential relation to the other 'philosophical' or 'theological' writings given in this book with any certainty seems scarcely possible, though 'Fionwë son of Manwë' on p. 399 (for 'Eönwë herald of Manwë') may suggest that it stands relatively early among them (see pp. 151–2). It shows a marked likeness in tone to the many letters of exposition that my father wrote in the later 1950s, and indeed it seems to me very possible that the correspondence which followed the publication of *The Lord of the Rings* played a significant part in the development of his examination of the 'images and events' of the mythology.[18]

NOTES

1 *Ragnarök*: 'the Doom of the Gods' (Old Norse): see IX.286.
2 *hroa*: so written here and at the second occurrence below (and in text A), not as elsewhere always *hröa*, where it means the body of an incarnate being. The word used for 'physical matter' in *Laws and Customs* was *hrón*, later changed to *orma* (p. 218 and note 26); in the Commentary on the *Athrabeth* and in the 'Glossary' of names the word is *erma* (pp. 338, 349).
3 On this sentence see p. 271.
4 Overt condemnation, strongly expressed, of the Valar for the Hiding of Valinor is found in the story of that name in *The Book of Lost Tales* (I.208–9), but disappears in the later versions. Of the old story I noted (I.223) that 'in *The Silmarillion* there is no vestige of the tumultuous council, no suggestion of a disagreement among the Valar, with Manwë, Varda and Ulmo actively

disapproving the work and holding aloof from it', and I commented:
> It is most curious to observe that the action of the Valar here sprang essentially from indolence mixed with fear. Nowhere does my father's early conception of the *fainéant* Gods appear more clearly. He held moreover quite explicitly that their failure to make war upon Melko then and there was a deep error, diminishing themselves, and (as it appears) irreparable. In his later writing the Hiding of Valinor remained indeed, but only as a great fact of mythological antiquity; there is no whisper of its condemnation.

The last words refer to the actual *Silmarillion* narratives. Ulmo's disapproval now reappears, and is a further evidence of his isolation in the counsels of the Valar (see p. 253 note 11); cf. his words to Tuor at Vinyamar (having spoken to him, among other things, of 'the hiding of the Blessed Realm', though what he said is not told): 'Therefore, though in the days of this darkness I seem to oppose the will of my brethren, the Lords of the West, that is my part among them, to which I was appointed ere the making of the World' (*Unfinished Tales* p. 29).

5   *pleasaunce* (= *pleasance*): a 'pleasure-garden'. My father used this word several times in *The Book of Lost Tales* (see I.275, *pleasance*), for example of the gardens of Lórien.

6   At this point my father wrote on the manuscript later: 'See original short form on Fading of Elves (and Men)'. See p. 394. This seems a clear indication that B was not completed, or that if it was its conclusion was early lost.

7   Cf. the statement on this subject in the brief text I, p. 370.

8   Since this discussion is introduced in justification of the Hiding of Valinor, the bearing of the argument seems to be that the history of Middle-earth in the last centuries of the First Age would not have been possible of achievement had Valinor remained open to the return of the Noldor.

9   As, of course, had happened to Melkor long before, after the sack of Utumno.

10 Cf. the conclusion of QS (V.332, §29): 'But Morgoth himself the Gods thrust through the Door of Night into the Timeless Void, beyond the Walls of the World'.

11 The following was added marginally after the page was written:
> If they do not sink below a certain level. Since no *fëa* can be annihilated, reduced to zero or not-existing, it is no[t] clear what is meant. Thus Sauron was *said* to have fallen below the point of ever recovering, though he had previously recovered. What is probably meant is that a 'wicked' spirit becomes fixed in a certain desire or ambition, and if it cannot repent then this desire becomes virtually its whole being. But the desire may be

wholly beyond the weakness it has fallen to, and it will then be unable to withdraw its attention from the unobtainable desire, even to attend to itself. It will then remain for ever in impotent desire or memory of desire.

12 A reference to the legend of the defeat of Sauron by Lúthien and Huan on the isle of Tol-in-Gaurhoth, where Beren was imprisoned (*The Silmarillion* pp. 174–5).

13 Cf. *Letters* no.181 (1956): 'In this mythological world the Elves and Men are in their incarnate forms kindred, but in the relation of their "spirits" to the world in time represent different "experiments", each of which has its own natural trend, and weakness. The Elves represent, as it were, the artistic, aesthetic, and purely scientific aspects of the Humane nature raised to a higher level than is actually seen in Men.'

14 In the text FM 2 of 'Finwë and Míriel' (p. 254, footnote) 'Arda Marred' is *Arda Hastaina*. *Arda Envinyanta*, at both occurrences, was first written *Arda Vincarna*.

15 With this passage in brackets cf. especially note (iii) at the end of *Laws and Customs* (p. 251); also pp. 245, 254 (footnote), 318.

16 *distain*: an archaic verb meaning 'stain', 'discolour', 'defile'.

17 The Three Themes of Ilúvatar in the Music of the Ainur are here treated as a single theme, in opposition to the discordant 'theme' of Melkor.

18 In a letter of June 1957 (*Letters* no.200) he wrote:

> I am sorry if this all seems dreary and 'pompose'. But so do all attempts to 'explain' the images and events of a mythology. Naturally the stories come first. But it is, I suppose, some test of the consistency of a mythology as such, if it is capable of some sort of rational or rationalized explanation.

VIII

In the last sentence of the original short version of text VII (p. 406) my father wrote that the Eldar believed that Morgoth bred the Orcs 'by capturing Men (and Elves) early' (i.e. in the early days of their existence). This indicates that his views on this subject had changed since the *Annals of Aman*. For the theory of the origin of the Orcs as it stood, in point of written record in the narratives,[1] at this time see AAm §42–5 (pp. 72–4, and commentary p. 78), and §127 (pp. 109–10, and commentary pp. 123–4). In the final form in AAm (p. 74) 'this is held true by the wise of Eressëa':

> all those of the Quendi that came into the hands of Melkor, ere Utumno was broken, were put there in prison, and by slow arts of cruelty and wickedness were corrupted and enslaved. Thus did

Text VIII   MYTHS TRANSFORMED   409

Melkor breed the hideous race of the Orkor in envy and mockery of the Eldar, of whom they were afterwards the bitterest foes. For the Orkor had life and multiplied after the manner of the Children of Ilúvatar; and naught that had life of its own, nor the semblance thereof, could ever Melkor make since his rebellion in the Ainulindalë before the Beginning: so say the wise.

On the typescript of AAm my father noted against the account of the origin of the Orcs: 'Alter this. Orcs are not Elvish' (p. 80).

The present text, entitled 'Orcs', is a short essay (very much a record of 'thinking with the pen') found in the same small collection gathered in a newspaper of 1959 as texts III and VI. Like them it was written on Merton College papers of 1955; and like text VI it makes reference to 'Finrod and Andreth' (see pp. 385, 390).

Orcs

Their nature and origin require more thought. They are not easy to work into the theory and system.

(1) As the case of Aulë and the Dwarves shows, only Eru could make creatures with independent wills, and with reasoning powers. But Orcs seem to have both: they can try to cheat Morgoth / Sauron, rebel against him, or criticize him.

(2) ? Therefore they must be *corruptions* of something pre-existing.

(3) But Men had not yet appeared, when the Orcs already existed. Aulë constructed the Dwarves out of his memory of the Music; but Eru would not sanction the work of Melkor so as to allow the independence of the Orcs. (Not unless Orcs were ultimately remediable, or could be amended and 'saved'?)

It also seems clear (see 'Finrod and Andreth') that though Melkor could utterly corrupt and ruin individuals, it is not possible to contemplate his absolute perversion of a whole people, or group of peoples, and *his making that state heritable*.[2] [*Added later:* This latter must (if a fact) be an act of Eru.]

In that case Elves, as a source, are very unlikely. And are Orcs 'immortal', in the Elvish sense? Or trolls? It seems clearly implied in *The Lord of the Rings* that trolls existed in their own right, but were 'tinkered' with by Melkor.[3]

(4) What of talking beasts and birds with reasoning and speech? These have been rather lightly adopted from less 'serious' mythologies, but play a part which cannot now be excised. They are certainly 'exceptions' and not much used, but

sufficiently to show they are a recognized feature of the world. All other creatures accept them as natural if not common.

But true 'rational' creatures, 'speaking peoples', are all of human / 'humanoid' form. Only the Valar and Maiar are intelligences that can assume forms of Arda at will. Huan and Sorontar could be Maiar – emissaries of Manwë.[4] But unfortunately in *The Lord of the Rings* Gwaehir and Landroval are said to be *descendants* of Sorontar.[5]

In any case is it likely or possible that even the least of the Maiar would become Orcs? Yes: both outside Arda and in it, before the fall of Utumno. Melkor had corrupted many spirits – some great, as Sauron, or less so, as Balrogs. The least could have been primitive (and much more powerful and perilous) Orcs; but by practising when embodied procreation they would (cf. Melian) [become] more and more earthbound, unable to return to spirit-state (even demon-form), until released by death (killing), and they would dwindle in force. When released they would, of course, like Sauron, be 'damned': i.e. reduced to impotence, infinitely recessive: still hating but unable more and more to make it effective physically (or would not a very dwindled dead Orc-state be a poltergeist?).

But again – would Eru provide *fëar* for such creatures? For the Eagles etc. perhaps. But not for Orcs.[6]

It does however seem best to view Melkor's corrupting power as always starting, at least, in the moral or theological level. Any creature that took him for Lord (and especially those who blasphemously called him Father or Creator) became soon corrupted in all parts of its being, the *fëa* dragging down the *hröa* in its descent into Morgothism: hate and destruction. As for Elves being 'immortal': they in fact only had enormously long lives, and were themselves physically 'wearing out', and suffering a slow progressive weakening of their bodies.

In summary: I think it must be assumed that 'talking' is not necessarily the sign of the possession of a 'rational soul' or *fëa*.[7] The Orcs were *beasts* of humanized shape (to mock Men and Elves) deliberately perverted / converted into a more close resemblance to Men. Their 'talking' was really reeling off 'records' set in them by Melkor. Even their rebellious critical words – he knew about them. Melkor taught them *speech* and as they bred they inherited this; and they had just as much independence as have, say, dogs or horses of their human masters. This talking was largely echoic (cf. parrots). In *The*

Text VIII   MYTHS TRANSFORMED   411

Lord of the Rings Sauron is said to have *devised a language* for them.[8]

The same sort of thing may be said of Húan and the Eagles: they were taught language by the Valar, and raised to a higher level – but they still had no *fëar*.

But Finrod probably went too far in his assertion that Melkor *could not* wholly corrupt any work of Eru, or that Eru would (necessarily) interfere to abrogate the corruption, or to end the being of His own creatures because they had been corrupted and fallen into evil.[9]

It remains therefore terribly possible there was an Elvish strain in the Orcs.[10] These may then even have been mated with beasts (sterile!) – and later Men. Their life-span would be diminished. And dying they would go to Mandos and be held in prison till the End.

The text as written ends here, but my father subsequently added the following passage. The words with which it opens are a reference to text VI, *Melkor Morgoth* (p. 390).

See 'Melkor'. It will there be seen that the *wills* of Orcs and Balrogs etc. are part of Melkor's power 'dispersed'. Their spirit is one of hate. But hate is non-coöperative (except under direct fear). Hence the rebellions, mutinies, etc. when Morgoth seems far off. Orcs are beasts and Balrogs corrupted Maiar. Also (n.b.) Morgoth not Sauron is the source of Orc-wills. Sauron is just another (if greater) agent. Orcs can rebel against him without losing their own irremediable allegiance to evil (Morgoth). *Aulë* wanted love. But of course had no thought of dispersing his power. Only Eru can give *love and independence*. If a finite sub-creator tries to do this he really wants absolute loving obedience, but it turns into robotic servitude and becomes evil.

NOTES

1   In a long letter to Peter Hastings of September 1954, which was not sent (*Letters* no.153), my father wrote as follows on the question of whether Orcs 'could have "souls" or "spirits"':
    ... since in my myth at any rate I do not conceive of the making of souls or spirits, things of an equal order if not an equal power to the Valar, as a possible 'delegation', I have represented at least the Orcs as pre-existing real beings on whom the Dark Lord has exerted the fullness of his power in remodelling and corrupting them, not making them. ... There might be other

'makings' all the same which were more like puppets filled (only at a distance) with their maker's mind and will, or ant-like operating under direction of a queen-centre.

Earlier in this letter he had quoted Frodo's words to Sam in the chapter 'The Tower of Cirith Ungol': 'The Shadow that bred them can only mock, it cannot make: not real new things of its own. I don't think it gave life to the orcs, it only ruined them and twisted them'; and he went on: 'In the legends of the Elder Days it is suggested that the Diabolus subjugated and corrupted some of the earliest Elves ...' He also said that the Orcs 'are fundamentally a race of "rational incarnate" creatures'.

2 In the *Athrabeth* (p. 312) Finrod declared:

> But never even in the night have we believed that [Melkor] could prevail against the Children of Eru. This one he might cozen, or that one he might corrupt; but to change the doom of a whole people of the Children, to rob them of their inheritance: if he could do that in Eru's despite, then greater and more terrible is he by far than we guessed ...

3 In *The Lord of the Rings* Appendix F (I) it is said of Trolls:

> In their beginning far back in the twilight of the Elder Days, these were creatures of dull and lumpish nature and had no more language than beasts. But Sauron had made use of them, teaching them what little they could learn, and increasing their wits with wickedness.

In the long letter of September 1954 cited in note 1 he wrote of them:

> I am not sure about Trolls. I think they are mere 'counterfeits', and hence (though here I am of course only using elements of old barbarous mythmaking that had no 'aware' metaphysic) they return to mere stone images when not in the dark. But there are other sorts of Trolls beside these rather ridiculous, if brutal, Stone-trolls, for which other origins are suggested. Of course ... when you make Trolls *speak* you are giving them a power, which in our world (probably) connotes the possession of a 'soul'.

4 See p. 138. – At the bottom of the page bearing the brief text V (p. 389) my father jotted down the following, entirely unconnected with the matter of the text:

> Living things in Aman. As the Valar would robe themselves like the Children, many of the Maiar robed themselves like other lesser living things, as trees, flowers, beasts. (Huan.)

5 'There came Gwaihir the Windlord, and Landroval his brother, greatest of all the Eagles of the North, mightiest of the descendants of old Thorondor' ('The Field of Cormallen' in *The Return of the King*).

Text VIII   MYTHS TRANSFORMED   413

6   At this point there is a note that begins 'Criticism of (1) (2) (3) above' (i.e. the opening points of this text, p. 409) and then refers obscurely to the 'last battle and fall of Barad-dûr etc.' in *The Lord of the Rings*. In view of what follows my father was presumably thinking of this passage in the chapter 'Mount Doom':
> From all his policies and webs of fear and treachery, from all his stratagems and wars his mind shook free; and throughout his realm a tremor ran, his slaves quailed, and his armies halted, and his captains suddenly steerless, bereft of will, wavered and despaired. For they were forgotten.

The note continues:
> They had little or no *will* when not actually 'attended to' by the mind of Sauron. Does their cheating and rebellion pass that possible to such animals as dogs etc.?

7   Cf. the end of the passage cited from the letter of 1954 in note 3.
8   Appendix F (I): 'It is said that the Black Speech was devised by Sauron in the Dark Years'.
9   See the citation from the *Athrabeth* in note 2. Finrod did not in fact assert the latter part of the opinion here attributed to him.
10 The assertion that 'it remains therefore terribly possible there was an Elvish strain in the Orcs' seems merely to contradict what has been said about their being no more than 'talking beasts' without advancing any new considerations. In the passage added at the end of the text the statement that 'Orcs are beasts' is repeated.

IX

This is another and quite separate note on the origin of the Orcs, written quickly in pencil, and without any indication of date.

This suggests – though it is not explicit – that the 'Orcs' were of Elvish origin. Their origin is more clearly dealt with elsewhere. One point only is certain: Melkor could not 'create' living 'creatures' of independent wills.

He (and all the 'spirits' of the 'First-created', according to their measure) could assume bodily shapes; and he (and they) could dominate the minds of other creatures, including Elves and Men, by force, fear, or deceits, or sheer magnificence.

The Elves from their earliest times invented and used a word or words with a base *(o)rok* to denote anything that caused fear and/or horror. It would originally have been applied to 'phantoms' (spirits assuming visible forms) as well as to any independently existing creatures. Its application (in all Elvish tongues) specifically to the creatures called *Orks* – so I shall spell it in *The Silmarillion* – was later.

Since Melkor could not 'create' an independent species, but had immense powers of corruption and distortion of those that came into his power, it is probable that these *Orks* had a mixed origin. Most of them plainly (and biologically) were corruptions of Elves (and probably later also of Men). But always among them (as special servants and spies of Melkor, and as leaders) there must have been numerous corrupted minor spirits who assumed similar bodily shapes. (These would exhibit terrifying and demonic characters.)

The Elves would have classed the creatures called 'trolls' (in *The Hobbit* and *The Lord of the Rings*) as Orcs – in character and origin – but they were larger and slower. It would seem evident that they were corruptions of primitive human types.

At the bottom of the page my father wrote: 'See *The Lord of the Rings* Appendix p. 410'; this is the passage in Appendix F concerning Trolls.

It seems possible that his opening words in this note 'This suggests – though it is not explicit – that the "Orcs" were of Elvish origin' actually refer to the previous text given here, VIII, where he first wrote that 'Elves, as a source, are very unlikely', but later concluded that 'it remains therefore terribly possible there was an Elvish strain in the Orcs'. But if this is so, the following words 'Their origin is more clearly dealt with elsewhere' must refer to something else.

He now expressly asserts the earlier view (see p. 408 and note 1) that the Orcs were in origin corrupted Elves, but observes that 'later' some were probably derived from Men. In saying this (as the last paragraph and the reference to *The Lord of the Rings* Appendix F suggest) he seems to have been thinking of Trolls, and specifically of the *Olog-hai*, the great Trolls who appeared at the end of the Third Age (as stated in Appendix F): 'That Sauron bred them none doubted, though from what stock was not known. Some held that they were not Trolls but giant Orcs; but the Olog-hai were in fashion of body and mind quite unlike even the largest of Orc-kind, whom they far surpassed in size and power.'

The conception that among the Orcs 'there must have been numerous corrupted minor spirits who assumed similar bodily shapes' appears also in text VIII (p. 410): 'Melkor had corrupted many spirits – some great, as Sauron, or less so, as Balrogs. The least could have been primitive (and much more powerful and perilous) Orcs'.

X

I give here a text of an altogether different kind, a very finished essay on the origin of the Orcs. It is necessary to explain something of the relations of this text.

There is a major work, which I hope to publish in *The History of Middle-earth*, entitled *Essekenta Eldarinwa* or *Quendi and Eldar*. It is extant in a good typescript made by my father on his later typewriter, both in top copy and carbon; and it is preceded in both copies by a manuscript page which describes the content of the work:

> Enquiry into the origins of the Elvish names for Elves and their varieties clans and divisions: with Appendices on their names for the other Incarnates: Men, Dwarves, and Orcs; and on their analysis of their own language, Quenya: with a note on the 'Language of the Valar'.

With the appendices *Quendi and Eldar* runs to nearly fifty closely typed pages, and being a highly finished and lucid work is of the utmost interest.

To one of the title pages my father subjoined the following:

> To which is added an abbreviation of the *Ósanwe-kenta* or 'Communication of Thought' that Pengolodh set at the end of his *Lammas* or 'Account of Tongues'

This is a separate work of eight typescript pages, separately paginated, but found together with both copies of *Quendi and Eldar*. In addition, and not referred to on the title-pages, there is a further typescript of four pages (also found with both copies of *Quendi and Eldar*) entitled *Orcs*; and this is the text given here.

All three elements are identical in general appearance, but *Orcs* stands apart from the others, having no linguistic bearing; and in view of this I have thought it legitimate to abstract it and print it in this book together with the other discussions of the origin of the Orcs given as texts VIII and IX.

As to the date of this complex, one of the copies is preserved in a folded newspaper of March 1960. On this my father wrote: '"Quendi and Eldar" with Appendices'; beneath is a brief list of the Appendices, the items all written at the same time, which includes both *Ósanwe* and *Origin of Orcs* (the same is true of the cover of the other copy of the *Quendi and Eldar* complex). All the material was thus in being when the newspaper was used for this purpose, and although, as in other similar cases, this does not provide a perfectly certain *terminus ad quem*, there seems no reason to doubt that it belongs to 1959–60 (cf. p. 304).

Appendix C to *Quendi and Eldar*, 'Elvish Names for the Orcs', is primarily concerned with etymology, but it opens with the following passage:

It is not here the place to debate the question of the origin of the Orcs. They were bred by Melkor, and their breeding was the most wicked and lamentable of his works in Arda, but not the most terrible. For clearly they were meant in his malice to be a mockery of the Children of Ilúvatar, wholly subservient to his will, and nursed in an unappeasable hatred of Elves and Men.

The Orcs of the later wars, after the escape of Melkor-Morgoth and his return to Middle-earth, were neither spirits nor phantoms, but living creatures, capable of speech and of some crafts and organization, or at least capable of learning such things from higher creatures or from their Master. They bred and multiplied rapidly whenever left undisturbed. It is unlikely, as a consideration of the ultimate origin of this race would make clearer, that the Quendi had met any Orcs of this kind, before their finding by Oromë and the separation of Eldar and Avari.

But it is known that Melkor had become aware of the Quendi before the Valar began their war against him, and the joy of the Elves in Middle-earth had already been darkened by shadows of fear. Dreadful shapes had begun to haunt the borders of their dwellings, and some of their people vanished into the darkness and were heard of no more. Some of these things may have been phantoms and delusions; but some were, no doubt, shapes taken by the servants of Melkor, mocking and degrading the very forms of the Children. For Melkor had in his service great numbers of the Maiar, who had the power, as had their Master, of taking visible and tangible shape in Arda.

No doubt my father was led from his words here 'It is unlikely, as a consideration of the ultimate origin of this race would make clearer, that the Quendi had met any Orcs of this kind, before their finding by Oromë' to write that 'consideration' which follows here. It will be seen that one passage of this initial statement was re-used.

Orcs

The origin of the Orcs is a matter of debate. Some have called them the *Melkorohíni*, the Children of Melkor; but the wiser say: nay, the slaves of Melkor, but not his children; for Melkor had no children.[1] Nonetheless, it was by the malice of Melkor that the Orcs arose, and plainly they were meant by him to be a mockery of the Children of Eru, being bred to be wholly subservient to his will and filled with unappeasable hatred of Elves and Men.

Text X   MYTHS TRANSFORMED   417

Now the Orcs of the later wars, after the escape of Melkor-Morgoth and his return to Middle-earth, were not 'spirits', nor phantoms, but living creatures, capable of speech and some crafts and organization; or at least capable of learning these things from higher creatures and from their Master. They bred and multiplied rapidly, whenever left undisturbed. So far as can be gleaned from the legends that have come down to us from our earliest days,[2] it would seem that the Quendi had never yet encountered any Orcs of this kind before the coming of Oromë to Cuiviénen.

Those who believe that the Orcs were bred from some kind of Men, captured and perverted by Melkor, assert that it was impossible for the Quendi to have known of Orcs before the Separation and the departure of the Eldar. For though the time of the awakening of Men is not known, even the calculations of the loremasters that place it earliest do not assign it a date long before the Great March began,[3] certainly not long enough before it to allow for the corruption of Men into Orcs. On the other hand, it is plain that soon after his return Morgoth had at his command a great number of these creatures, with whom he ere long began to attack the Elves. There was still less time between his return and these first assaults for the breeding of Orcs and for the transfer of their hosts westward.

This view of the origin of the Orcs thus meets with difficulties of chronology. But though Men may take comfort in this, the theory remains nonetheless the most probable. It accords with all that is known of Melkor, and of the nature and behaviour of Orcs – and of Men. Melkor was impotent to produce any living thing, but skilled in the corruption of things that did not proceed from himself, if he could dominate them. But if he had indeed attempted to make creatures of his own in imitation or mockery of the Incarnates, he would, like Aulë, only have succeeded in producing puppets: his creatures would have acted only while the attention of his will was upon them, and they would have shown no reluctance to execute any command of his, even if it were to destroy themselves.

But the Orcs were not of this kind. They were certainly dominated by their Master, but his dominion was by fear, and they were aware of this fear and hated him. They were indeed so corrupted that they were pitiless, and there was no cruelty or wickedness that they would not commit; but this was the corruption of independent wills, and they took pleasure in their deeds. They were capable of acting on their own, doing evil deeds unbidden for their own sport; or if Morgoth and his agents were far away, they might neglect his commands. They sometimes fought [> They hated one another and often fought] among themselves, to the detriment of Morgoth's plans.

Moreover, the Orcs continued to live and breed and to carry on their business of ravaging and plundering after Morgoth was overthrown. They had other characteristics of the Incarnates also. They had languages of their own, and spoke among themselves in various tongues according to differences of breed that were discernible among them. They needed food and drink, and rest, though many were by training as tough as Dwarves in enduring hardship. They could be slain, and they were subject to disease; but apart from these ills they died and were not immortal, even according to the manner of the Quendi; indeed they appear to have been by nature short-lived compared with the span of Men of higher race, such as the Edain.

This last point was not well understood in the Elder Days. For Morgoth had many servants, the oldest and most potent of whom were immortal, belonging indeed in their beginning to the Maiar; and these evil spirits like their Master could take on visible forms. Those whose business it was to direct the Orcs often took Orkish shapes, though they were greater and more terrible.[4] Thus it was that the histories speak of Great Orcs or Orc-captains who were not slain, and who reappeared in battle through years far longer than the span of the lives of Men.*[5]

Finally, there is a cogent point, though horrible to relate. It became clear in time that undoubted Men could under the domination of Morgoth or his agents in a few generations be reduced almost to the Orc-level of mind and habits; and then they would or could be made to mate with Orcs, producing new breeds, often larger and more cunning. There is no doubt that long afterwards, in the Third Age, Saruman rediscovered this, or learned of it in lore, and in his lust for mastery committed this, his wickedest deed: the interbreeding of Orcs and Men,

---

* [footnote to the text] *Boldog*, for instance, is a name that occurs many times in the tales of the War. But it is possible that *Boldog* was not a personal name, and either a title, or else the name of a kind of creature: the Orc-formed Maiar, only less formidable than the Balrogs.

producing both Men-orcs large and cunning, and Orc-men treacherous and vile.

But even before this wickedness of Morgoth was suspected the Wise in the Elder Days taught always that the Orcs were not 'made' by Melkor, and therefore were not in their origin evil. They might have become irredeemable (at least by Elves and Men), but they remained within the Law. That is, that though of necessity, being the fingers of the hand of Morgoth, they must be fought with the utmost severity, they must not be dealt with in their own terms of cruelty and treachery. Captives must not be tormented, not even to discover information for the defence of the homes of Elves and Men. If any Orcs surrendered and asked for mercy, they must be granted it, even at a cost.* This was the teaching of the Wise, though in the horror of the War it was not always heeded.

It is true, of course, that Morgoth held the Orcs in dire thraldom; for in their corruption they had lost almost all possibility of resisting the domination of his will. So great indeed did its pressure upon them become ere Angband fell that, if he turned his thought towards them, they were conscious of his 'eye' wherever they might be; and when Morgoth was at last removed from Arda the Orcs that survived in the West were scattered, leaderless and almost witless, and were for a long time without control or purpose.

This servitude to a central will that reduced the Orcs almost to an ant-like life was seen even more plainly in the Second and Third Ages under the tyranny of Sauron, Morgoth's chief lieutenant. Sauron indeed achieved even greater control over his Orcs than Morgoth had done. He was, of course, operating on a smaller scale, and he had no enemies so great and so fell as were the Noldor in their might in the Elder Days. But he had also inherited from those days difficulties, such as the diversity of the Orcs in breed and language, and the feuds among them; while in many places in Middle-earth, after the fall of Thangorodrim and during the concealment of Sauron, the Orcs recovering from their helplessness had set up petty realms of their own and

---

* [footnote to the text] Few Orcs ever did so in the Elder Days, and at no time would any Orc treat with any Elf. For one thing Morgoth had achieved was to convince the Orcs beyond refutation that the Elves were crueller than themselves, taking captives only for 'amusement', or to eat them (as the Orcs would do at need).

had become accustomed to independence. Nonetheless Sauron in time managed to unite them all in unreasoning hatred of the Elves and of Men who associated with them; while the Orcs of his own trained armies were so completely under his will that they would sacrifice themselves without hesitation at his command.* And he proved even more skilful than his Master also in the corruption of Men who were beyond the reach of the Wise, and in reducing them to a vassalage, in which they would march with the Orcs, and vie with them in cruelty and destruction.

It is thus probably to Sauron that we may look for a solution of the problem of chronology. Though of immensely smaller native power than his Master, he remained less corrupt, cooler and more capable of calculation. At least in the Elder Days, and before he was bereft of his lord and fell into the folly of imitating him, and endeavouring to become himself supreme Lord of Middle-earth. While Morgoth still stood, Sauron did not seek his own supremacy, but worked and schemed for another, desiring the triumph of Melkor, whom in the beginning he had adored. He thus was often able to achieve things, first conceived by Melkor, which his master did not or could not complete in the furious haste of his malice.

We may assume, then, that the idea of breeding the Orcs came from Melkor, not at first maybe so much for the provision of servants or the infantry of his wars of destruction, as for the defilement of the Children and the blasphemous mockery of the designs of Eru. The details of the accomplishment of this wickedness were, however, left mainly to the subtleties of Sauron. In that case the conception in mind of the Orcs may go far back into the night of Melkor's thought, though the beginning of their actual breeding must await the awakening of Men.

When Melkor was made captive, Sauron escaped and lay hid in Middle-earth; and it can in this way be understood how the breeding of the Orcs (no doubt already begun) went on with increasing speed during the age when the Noldor dwelt in Aman; so that when they returned to Middle-earth they found it already infested with this plague, to the torment of all that dwelt

---

* [footnote to the text] But there remained one flaw in his control, inevitable. In the kingdom of hate and fear, the strongest thing is hate. All his Orcs hated one another, and must be kept ever at war with some 'enemy' to prevent them from slaying one another.

there, Elves or Men or Dwarves. It was Sauron, also, who secretly repaired Angband for the help of his Master when he returned;[6] and there the dark places underground were already manned with hosts of the Orcs before Melkor came back at last, as Morgoth the Black Enemy, and sent them forth to bring ruin upon all that was fair. And though Angband has fallen and Morgoth is removed, still they come forth from the lightless places in the darkness of their hearts, and the earth is withered under their pitiless feet.

This then, as it may appear, was my father's final view of the question: Orcs were bred from Men, and if 'the conception in mind of the Orcs may go far back into the night of Melkor's thought' it was Sauron who, during the ages of Melkor's captivity in Aman, brought into being the black armies that were available to his Master when he returned.

But, as always, it is not quite so simple. Accompanying one copy of the typescript of this essay are some pages in manuscript for which my father used the blank reverse sides of papers provided by the publishers dated 10 November 1969. These pages carry two notes on the 'Orcs' essay: one, discussing the spelling of the word *orc*, is given on p. 422; the other is a note arising from something in the essay which is not indicated, but which is obviously the passage on p. 417 discussing the puppet-like nature inevitable in creatures brought into being by one of the great Powers themselves: the note was intended to stand in relation to the words 'But the Orcs were not of this kind'.

The *orks*, it is true, sometimes appear to have been reduced to a condition very similar, though there remains actually a profound difference. Those *orks* who dwelt long under the immediate attention of his will – as garrisons of his strongholds or elements of armies trained for special purposes in his war-designs – would act like herds, obeying instantly, as if with one will, his commands even if ordered to sacrifice their lives in his service. And as was seen when Morgoth was at last overthrown and cast out, those *orks* that had been so absorbed scattered helplessly, without purpose either to flee or to fight, and soon died or slew themselves.

Other originally independent creatures, and Men among them (but neither Elves nor Dwarves), could also be reduced to a like condition. But 'puppets', with no independent life or will, would simply cease to move or do anything at all when the will of their maker was brought to nothing. In any case the number of *orks* that were thus 'absorbed' was always only a small part of their total. To hold them in absolute servitude required a great expense of will. Morgoth though in origin possessed of vast power was finite; and it was this expenditure upon the *orks*, and still more upon the other far more formidable creatures in his service, that in the event so dissipated his powers of mind that Morgoth's overthrow became possible. Thus the greater part of the *orks*, though under his orders and the dark shadow of their fear of him, were only intermittently objects of his immediate thought and concern, and while that was removed they relapsed into independence and became conscious of their hatred of him and his tyranny. Then they might neglect his orders, or engage in

Here the text breaks off. But the curious thing is that rough drafting for the second paragraph of this note (written on the same paper bearing the same date) begins thus:

But Men could (and can still) be reduced to such a condition. 'Puppets' would simply cease to move or 'live' at all, when not set in motion by the direct will of their maker. In any case, though the number of orks at the height of Morgoth's power, and *still after his return from captivity*, seems to have been very great, those who were 'absorbed' were always a small part of the total.

The words that I have italicised deny an essential conception of the essay.

The other note reads thus:

Orcs

This spelling was taken from Old English. The word seemed, in itself, very suitable to the creatures that I had in mind. But the Old English *orc* in meaning – so far as that is known – is not suitable.[7] Also the spelling of what, in the later more organized linguistic situation, must have been a Common Speech form of a word or group of similar words should be *ork*. If only because of spelling difficulties in modern English: an adjective *orc* + *ish* becomes necessary, and *orcish* will not do.[8] In any future publication I shall use *ork*.

In text IX (the brief writing in which my father declared the theory of Elvish origin to be certain) he spelt the word *Orks*, and said 'so I shall spell it in *The Silmarillion*'. In the present essay, obviously later than text IX, it is spelt *Orcs*; but now, in 1969 or later, he asserted again that it must be *Orks*.

NOTES

1 See text VII, p. 406. – On one copy of the text my father pencilled against this sentence the names *Erusēni, Melkorsēni*.
2 'legends that have come down to us from our earliest days': this purports then to be an Elvish writing. Sauron is spoken of subsequently as a being of the past ('This servitude to a central will ... was seen even more plainly in the Second and Third Ages under the tyranny of Sauron', p. 419); but in the last sentence of the essay the Orcs are a plague that still afflicts the world.
3 The time of the Awakening of Men is now placed far back; cf. text II (p. 378): 'The March of the Eldar is through great Rains? Men awake in an Isle amid the floods'; 'The coming of Men will therefore be much further back'; 'Men must awake while Melkor is still in [Middle-earth] – because of their Fall. Therefore in some period during the Great March' (see p. 385 note 14). In the chronology of the *Annals of Aman* and the *Grey Annals* the Great March began in the Year of the Trees 1105 (p. 82), and the foremost companies of the Eldar came to the shores of the Great Sea in 1125; Men awoke in Hildórien in the year of the first rising of the Sun, which was the Year of the Trees 1500. Thus if the Awakening of Men is placed even very late in the period of the Great March of the Eldar it will be set back by more than 3500 Years of the Sun. See further p. 430 note 5.
4 Cf. text IX, p. 414: 'But always among them [Orcs] (as special servants and spies of Melkor, and as leaders) there must have been numerous corrupted minor spirits who assumed similar bodily shapes'; also text VIII, p. 410.
5 The footnote at this point, stating that '*Boldog*, for instance, is a name that occurs many times in the tales of the War', and was perhaps not a personal name, is curious. *Boldog* appears several times in the *Lay of Leithian* as the name of the Orc-captain who led a raid into Doriath (references in the Index to *The Lays of Beleriand*); he reappears in the *Quenta* (IV.113), but is not mentioned thereafter. I do not know of any other reference to an Orc named *Boldog*.
6 On the later story that Angband was built by Melkor in the ancient days and that it was commanded by Sauron see p. 156, §12. There has been no reference to the repairing of Angband against Morgoth's return, and cf. the last narrative development in the *Quenta Silmarillion* of the story of his return (p. 295, §14): Morgoth and Ungoliant 'were drawing near to the ruins of Angband where his great western stronghold had been.'
7 See p. 124.
8 '*orcish* will not do': because it would be pronounced 'orsish'. The

Orkish language was so spelt in The Lord of the Rings from the First Edition.

XI

This concluding text, entitled *Aman*, is a clear manuscript written with little hesitation or correction. I had regarded it as an independent essay, and in doubt where best to place it had left it to the end; but when this book had been fully completed and prepared for publication I realised that it stands in fact in very close relationship to the manuscript of *Athrabeth Finrod ah Andreth*.

That manuscript opens with an introductory section (given in the typescript version that my father subsequently made, pp. 304–5), beginning with the statement that some Men believed that their *hröar* were not by nature short-lived, but had become so by the malice of Melkor. I had not observed the significance of some lines at the head of this first page of the *Athrabeth*, which my father had struck through: these lines begin with the words 'the *hröa*, and it would live on, a witless body, not even a beast but a monster', and end '... Death itself, in either agony or horror, would with Men enter into Aman itself.' Now this passage is virtually identical to the conclusion of the present text, the last page of which begins at precisely the same point.

It is clear, therefore, that *Aman* originally led into the *Athrabeth*, but that my father removed it to stand alone and copied out the concluding passage on a separate sheet. At the same time, presumably, he gave the remainder (the *Athrabeth* and its introduction) the titles *Of Death and the Children of Eru, and the Marring of Men* and *The Converse of Finrod and Andreth*.[1]

It might have been preferable to place *Aman* with the *Athrabeth* in Part Four; but I thought it unnecessary at such a late stage to embark on a major upheaval of the structure of the book, and so left it to stand separately here.

Aman

In Aman things were far otherwise than in Middle-earth. But they resembled the mode of Elvish life, just as the Elves more nearly resemble the Valar and Maiar than do Men.

In Aman the length of the unit of 'year' was the same as it was for the Quendi. But for a different reason. In Aman this length was assigned by the Valar for their own purposes, and was related to that process which may be called the 'Ageing of Arda'. For Aman was within Arda and therefore within the Time of Arda (which was not eternal, whether Unmarred or Marred). Therefore Arda and all things in it must age, however slowly, as it proceeds from beginning to end. This ageing could be perceived by the Valar in about that length of time (proportionate to the whole of Arda's appointed span) which they called a Year; but not in a less period.[2]

But as for the Valar themselves, and the Maiar also in their degree: they could live at any speed of thought or motion which they chose or desired.*[3]

> *They could move backward or forward in thought, and return again so swiftly that to those who were in their presence they did not appear to have moved. All that was past they could fully perceive; but being now in Time the future they could only perceive or explore in so far as its design was made clear to them in the Music, or as each one of them was specially concerned with this or that part of Eru's design, being His agent or Subcreator. In this way of perception they could foresee none of the acts of the Children, Elves and Men, in whose conceiving and introduction into Ea none of the Valar had played any part at all; concerning the Children they could only deduce likelihood, in the same way as can the Children themselves, though from a far greater knowledge of facts and the contributory events of the past, and with far greater intelligence and wisdom. Yet there always remained an uncertainty with regard to the words and deeds of Elves and Men in Time not yet unfolded.

The unit, or Valian Year, was thus not in Aman related to the natural rates of 'growth' of any person or thing that dwelt there. Time in Aman was actual time, not merely a mode of perception. As, say, 100 years went by in Middle-earth as part of Arda, so 100 years passed in Aman, which was also a part of Arda. It was, however, the fact that the Elvish speed of 'growth' accorded with the unit of Valian time† that made it possible for the Valar to bring the Eldar to dwell in Aman. In one Valian

> †Not by the design of the Valar, though doubtless not by chance. That is, it may be that Eru in designing the natures of Elves and Men and their relations one to another and to the Valar ordained that the 'growth' of the Elves should accord with the Valian perception of the progress or ageing of Arda, so that the Elves should be able to cohabit with the Valar and Maiar. Since the Children appeared in the Music, and also in the Vision, the Valar knew something or indeed much of the ordained natures of Elves and Men before they came into existence. They knew certainly that Elves should be 'immortal' or of very long life, and Men of brief life. But it was probably only during the sojourn of Oromë among the fathers of the Quendi that the Valar discovered

precisely what was the mode of their lives with regard to the lapse of Time.

year the Eldar dwelling there grew and developed in much the same way as mortals did in one year upon Middle-earth. In recording the events in Aman, therefore, we may as did the Eldar themselves use the Valian unit,[4] though we must not forget that within any such 'year' the Eldar enjoyed an immense series of delights and achievements which even the most gifted of Men could not accomplish in twelve times twelve mortal years.[5] Nonetheless the Eldar 'aged' at the same speed in Aman as they had done in their beginning upon Middle-earth.

But the Eldar were not *native* to Aman, which had not been, by the Valar, designed for them. In Aman, before their coming, there had dwelt only the Valar and their lesser kindred the Maiar. But for their delight and use there were in Aman also a great multitude of creatures, without *fëar*, of many kinds: animals or moving creatures, and plants that are steadfast. There, it is believed, were the counterparts of all the creatures that are or have been on Earth,[6] and others also that were made for Aman only. And each kind had, as on Earth, its own nature and natural speed of growth.

But since Aman was made for the Valar, that they might have peace and delight therein, all those creatures that were thither transplanted or were trained or bred or brought into being for the purpose of inhabitation in Aman were given a speed of growth such that one year of the life natural to their kinds on Earth should in Aman be one Valian Year.

For the Eldar this was a source of joy. For in Aman the world appeared to them as it does to Men on Earth, but without the shadow of death soon to come. Whereas on Earth to them all things in comparison with themselves were fleeting, swift to change and die or pass away, in Aman they endured and did not so soon cheat love with their mortality. On Earth while an elf-child did but grow to be a man or a woman, in some 3000 years, forests would rise and fall, and all the face of the land would change, while birds and flowers innumerable would be born and die in *löar* upon *löar* under the wheeling Sun.

But beside all this Aman is called also the Blessed Realm, and in this was found its blessedness: in health and joy. For in Aman no creatures suffered any sickness or disorder of their natures; nor was there any decay or ageing more swift than the slow ageing of Arda itself. So that all things coming at last to fullness of form and virtue remained in that state, blissfully, ageing and wearying of their life and being no swifter than the Valar themselves. And this blessing also was granted to the Eldar.

On earth the Quendi suffered no sickness, and the health of their bodies was supported by the might of the longeval *fëar*. But their bodies, being of the stuff of Arda, were nonetheless not so enduring as their spirits; for the longevity of the Quendi was derived primarily from their *fëar*, whose nature or 'doom' was to abide in Arda until its end. Therefore, after the vitality of the *hröa* was expended in achieving full growth, it began to weaken or grow weary. Very slowly indeed, but to all the Quendi perceptibly. For a while it would be fortified and maintained by its indwelling *fëa*, and then its vitality would begin to ebb, and its desire for physical life and joy in it would pass ever more swiftly away. Then an Elf would begin (as they say now, for these things did not fully appear in the Elder Days) to 'fade', until the *fëa* as it were consumed the *hröa* until it remained only in the love and memory of the spirit that had inhabited it.

But in Aman, since its blessing descended upon the *hröar* of the Eldar, as upon all other bodies, the *hröar* aged only apace with the *fëar*, and the Eldar that remained in the Blessed Realm endured in full maturity and in undimmed power of body and spirit conjoined for ages beyond our mortal comprehension.

Aman and Mortal Men[7]

If it is thus in Aman, or was ere the Change of the World, and therein the Eldar had health and lasting joy, what shall we say of Men? No Man has ever set foot in Aman, or at least none has ever returned thence; for the Valar forbade it. Why so? To the Númenóreans they said that they did so because Eru had forbidden them to admit Men to the Blessed Realm; and they declared also that Men would not there be blessed (as they imagined) but accursed, and would 'wither even as a moth in a flame too bright'.

Beyond these words we can but go in guess. Yet we may consider the matter so. The Valar were not only by Eru forbidden the attempt, they *could not* alter the nature, or 'doom' of Eru, of any of the Children, in which was included the speed of their growth (relative to the whole life of Arda) and the length of their life-span. Even the Eldar in that respect remained unchanged.

Let us suppose then that the Valar had also admitted to Aman some of the Atani, and (so that we may consider a whole life of a Man in such a state) that 'mortal' children were there born, as were children of the Eldar. Then, even though in Aman, a mortal child would still grow to maturity in some twenty years of the Sun, and the natural span of its life, the period of the cohesion of *hröa* and *fëa*, would be no more than, say, 100 years. Not much more, even though his body would suffer no sickness or disorder in Aman, where no such evils existed. (Unless Men brought these evils with them – as why should they not? Even the Eldar brought to the Blessed Realm some taint of the Shadow upon Arda in which they came into being.)

But in Aman such a creature would be a fleeting thing, the most swift-passing of all beasts. For his whole life would last little more than one half-year, and while all other living creatures would seem to him hardly to change, but to remain steadfast in life and joy with hope of endless years undimmed, he would rise and pass – even as upon Earth the grass may rise in spring and wither ere the winter. Then he would become filled with envy, deeming himself a victim of injustice, being denied the graces given to all other things. He would not value what he had, but feeling that he was among the least and most despised of all creatures, he would grow soon to contemn his manhood, and hate those more richly endowed. He would not escape the fear and sorrow of his swift mortality that is his lot upon Earth, in Arda Marred, but would be burdened by it unbearably to the loss of all delight.

But if any should ask: why could not in Aman the blessing of longevity be granted to him, as it was to the Eldar? This must be answered. Because this would bring joy to the Eldar, their nature being different from that of Men. The nature of an Elvish *fëa* was to endure the world to the end, and an Elvish *hröa* was also longeval by nature; so that an Elvish *fëa* finding that its *hröa* endured with it, supporting its indwelling and remaining unwearied in bodily delight, would have increased and more lasting joy [*sic*]. Some indeed of the Eldar doubt that any special grace or blessing was accorded to them, other than admittance to Aman. For they hold that the failure of their *hröar* to endure in vitality unwearied as long as their *fëar* – a process which was not observed until the later ages – is due to the Marring of Arda, and comes of the Shadow, and of the taint of Melkor that touches all the matter (or *hröa*)[8] of Arda, if not indeed of all Eä.

So that all that happened in Aman was that this weakness of the Elvish *hröar* did not develop in the health of Aman and the Light of the Trees.

But let us suppose that the 'blessing of Aman' was also accorded to Men.* What then? Would a great good be done to them? Their bodies would still come swiftly to full growth. In the seventh part of a year a Man could be born and become full-grown, as swiftly as in Aman a bird would hatch and fly from the nest. But then it would not wither or age but would endure in vigour and in the delight of bodily living. But what of that Man's *fëa*? Its nature and 'doom' could not be changed, neither by the health of Aman nor by the will of Manwë himself. Yet it is (as the Eldar hold) its nature and doom under the will of Eru that it should *not* endure Arda for long, but should depart and go elsewhither, returning maybe direct to Eru for another fate or purpose that is beyond the knowledge or guess of the Eldar.

Very soon then the *fëa* and *hröa* of a Man in Aman would not be united and at peace, but would be opposed, to the great pain of both. The *hröa* being in full vigour and joy of life would cling to the *fëa*, lest its departure should bring death; and against death it would revolt as would a great beast in full life either flee from the hunter or turn savagely upon him. But the *fëa* would be as it were in prison, becoming ever more weary of all the delights of the *hröa*, until they were loathsome to it, longing ever more and more to be gone, until even those matters for its thought that it received through the *hröa* and its senses became meaningless. The Man would not be blessed, but accursed; and he would curse the Valar and Aman and all the things of Arda. And he would not willingly leave Aman, for that would mean rapid death, and he would have to be thrust forth with violence. But if he remained in Aman,[9] what should he come to, ere Arda were at last fulfilled and he found release? Either his *fëa* would be wholly dominated by the *hröa*, and he would become more like a beast, though one tormented within. Or else, if his *fëa* were strong, it would leave the *hröa*. Then one of two things would happen: either this would be accomplished only in hate,

---

* Or (as some Men hold) that their *hröar* are *not* by nature short-lived, but have become so through the malice of Melkor over and above the general marring of Arda, and that this hurt could be healed and undone in Aman.

by violence, and the *hröa*, in full life, would be rent and die in sudden agony; or else the *fëa* would in loathing and without pity desert the *hröa*, and it would live on, a witless body, not even a beast but a monster, a very work of Melkor in the midst of Aman, which the Valar themselves would fain destroy.

Now these things are but matters of thought, and might-have-beens; for Eru and the Valar under Him have not permitted Men as they are[10] to dwell in Aman. Yet at least it may be seen that Men in Aman would not escape the dread of death, but would have it in greater degree and for long ages. And moreover, it seems probable that death itself, either in agony or horror, would with Men enter into Aman itself.

At this point *Aman* as originally written (see p. 424) continued with the words 'Now some Men hold that their *hröar* are not indeed by nature short-lived ...', which became the beginning of the introductory passage to the *Athrabeth* (see p. 304).

NOTES

1. The number III and a further title *The Marring of Men* (the other titles remaining) was given to the second part, while *Aman* was numbered II. No writing numbered I is found.
2. It will be seen that, as a consequence of the transformation of the 'cosmogonic myth', a wholly new conception of the 'Valian Year' had entered. The elaborate computation of Time in the *Annals of Aman* (see pp. 49–51, 59–60) was based on the 'cycle' of the Two Trees that had ceased to exist in relation to the diurnal movement of the Sun that had come into being – there was a 'new reckoning'. But the 'Valian Year' is now, as it appears, a 'unit of perception' of the passage of the Time of Arda, derived from the capacity of the Valar to perceive at such intervals the process of the ageing of Arda from its beginning to its end. See note 5.
3. My father wrote the following passage ('They could move backward or forward in thought ...') in the body of the manuscript at this point, but in a small italic script, and I have preserved this form in the text printed; similarly with the following passage that interrupts the main text at the words 'the unit of Valian time'.
4. 'we may ... use the Valian unit': in other words, presumably, the old structure of dates in the chronicle of Aman may be retained, although the meaning of those dates in terms of Middle-earth will be radically different. See note 5.
5. There is now a vast discrepancy between Valian Years and 'mortal years'; cf. also 'his whole life would last little more than

one half-year' (p. 428), 'In the seventh part of a year a Man could be born and become full-grown' (p. 429). In notes not given in this book, in which my father was calculating on this basis the time of the Awakening of Men, he expressly stated that 144 Sun Years = 1 Valian Year (in this connection see Appendix D to *The Lord of the Rings*: 'It seems clear that the Eldar in Middle-earth ... reckoned in long periods, and the Quenya word *yén* ... really means 144 of our years'). Placing the event 'after or about the time of the sack of Utumno, Valian Year 1100' (see pp. 75, 80), a gigantic lapse of time could now be conceived between the 'arising' of Men and their first appearance in Beleriand.

6 For this use of 'Earth' in opposition to 'Aman', very frequent in this essay, see p. 282.
7 The sub-heading *Aman and Mortal Men* was a later addition.
8 With this use of the word *hröa* cf. text VII, p. 399: 'the *hroa*, the "flesh" or physical matter, of Arda'.
9 This passage, from 'And he would not willingly leave Aman ...', was a later addition. As the text was written, it continued on from 'all the things of Arda' to 'And what should he come to ...'
10 The words 'as they are' were a later addition of the same time as those referred to in notes 7 and 9.

APPENDIX

SYNOPSIS OF THE TEXTS

This list is intended as no more than a very concise statement of the manuscripts and typescripts referred to in this book (other than those in Part Five).

Ainulindalë

B   Manuscript, dating from the 1930s, given in V.155 ff.

C*   Author's typescript, introducing radical changes in the cosmology, in existence by 1948; see pp. 3–7, 39 ff.

C   Rewriting of B, using the old manuscript (see pp. 3, 7); given in full pp. 8 ff.

D   Fine manuscript, the last version of the *Ainulindalë*, developed from C; given in part pp. 29 ff.

Annals of Valinor

AV 1   'The Earliest Annals of Valinor', given in IV.262 ff.

AV 2   'The Later Annals of Valinor', given in V.109 ff.

–   For the rewriting of the opening of AV 2 preceding the *Annals of Aman* see p. 47.

Annals of Aman

AAm   Manuscript, dating from the early 1950s, given in full pp. 48 ff; divided editorially into six sections followed by notes and commentary.

AAm*   Author's typescript of the opening of AAm, with many departures from the manuscript (pp. 64–8, 79–80).

AAm typescript   Amanuensis typescript, dating from about 1958 (see pp. 141–2, 300). Annotations and alterations made to this are given at the end of the commentaries on each section of AAm.

Quenta Silmarillion

Q   'The Quenta' *(Qenta Noldorinwa)*, dating from 1930, given in IV.76 ff.

QS   *Quenta Silmarillion*, fine manuscript abandoned at the end of 1937, given in V.199 ff.

APPENDIX

QS typescript   Author's typescript; new text (entitled *Eldanyárë*) of the opening chapters, dating from December 1937–January 1938 (see p. 143).

LQ 1   'Later Quenta 1', amanuensis typescript of revised QS, made in 1951(–2); see p. 141.

LQ 2   'Later Quenta 2', amanuensis typescript incorporating all alterations made to LQ 1, made about 1958; see pp. 141–2.

LQ   For the uses of this abbreviation see pp. 184, 200.

Laws and Customs among the Eldar

A   Manuscript, given in full in its latter part (pp. 233 ff.), from the point where the typescript B breaks off (see pp. 207–8).

B   Author's typescript, unfinished, given in full pp. 209 ff.

Late recasting and development of parts of The Silmarillion

Vq 1   Author's typescript developed from LQ 2 Chapter 1 'Of the Valar' (see pp. 199–200).

Vq 2   Author's typescript following Vq 1, entitled *Valaquenta* (pp. 200 ff.).

FM 1   Manuscript rider to QS; the first text treating the story of Finwë and Míriel (pp. 205 ff.).

FM 2   Author's typescript, second text of the story of Finwë and Míriel in the *Silmarillion* narrative (pp. 254–5 ff.).

FM 3   Author's typescript, superseded by FM 4; see pp. 255–6.

FM 4   Author's typescript, final text of the story of Finwë and Míriel; given in full pp. 256 ff.

A   Author's typescript (continuation of FM 3), superseded by B; see pp. 271–2, 282.

B   Author's typescript (continuation of FM 4), the last, and extensively developed, text of the remainder of the original Chapter 6 and the beginning of Chapter 7 (pp. 272 ff.).

Athrabeth

A   Manuscript, given (with author's typescript version of the introductory section) in full pp. 304 ff.

B, C   Amanuensis typescripts (see p. 303).

Commentary   Author's typescript of the Commentary on the *Athrabeth*, with extensive notes; given in full pp. 329 ff.

INDEX

In this book certain names appear very frequently indeed throughout – in the most extreme cases, *Valar* and *Melkor*, the number of references is well over half the number of pages in the book. Such great blocks of numbers must be of doubtful utility, but I have in fact included all references in the index, apart from the occasional use as in previous volumes of the word *passim* to cover a long run of references from which only a single page is missing here and there. In some cases, as in *Melkor, Elves*, I have in addition listed references to certain central and recurrent topics. On pp. 470–1 will be found an appendix to the index in which I have collected separately the large number of words (many of them specialised terms) in the Elvish languages that occur in the book.

Names occurring in the titles of chapters and other headings are not normally indexed, nor are the names of the recipients of letters; and individual 'Lost Tales' are not given separate entries.

Star-names

The names of the stars and constellations that appear on p. 160 are mostly left unidentified in the index, despite much that has been written on the subject since the publication of *The Silmarillion*; and this is a convenient place to refer to a matter that I neglected to mention in the text of the book. This concerns an isolated manuscript page preserved with the texts of *The Lord of the Rings* at Marquette University; and I am very grateful to Mr Charles B. Elston of Marquette for his help on this question.

One side of this page carries primary drafting for a passage in Chapter 3 (*Of the Coming of the Elves*) of the *Quenta Silmarillion* (§§18a–19), and the other a second draft for the same passage, which though very roughly written almost reaches the text printed on pp. 159–60. I have noticed (p. 158) that in the case of Chapter 3 my father himself made a new text, intervening between the revision carried out on the old pre-*Lord of the Rings* texts and the amanuensis typescript LQ 1; it was in that version of the chapter ('Text A') that the new material in §§18a–19 entered (see p. 166, §19). The place of the Marquette page is thus very clearly defined; as drafting for the passage in Text A it belongs to the 1951 revision of *The Silmarillion*.

In the second, all but final, draft my father is seen in the act of devising the names of the constellations, with various experimental forms before those that appear in the final text were reached; but he set down the names of the stars without any hesitation, thus: *Karnil, Luinil, Nénar, Lumbar, Alkarinque, Elemmire.* Above *Karnil* he wrote 'M', above *Lumbar* 'S', above *Alkarinque* 'Jup', and above *Elemmire* again 'M'. No letter stands above *Luinil*, but above *Nénar* there is an 'N' which was struck out (Mr Elston informs me that this 'N' is perfectly clear in the original and that no other interpretation is possible).

Now if *Alkarinque* is Jupiter, then a great red star named *Karnil* and marked with 'M' must be Mars (cf. Michael Ramer's name *Karan* for Mars, IX.220) – which in turn leads to the identification of *Lumbar* ('S') with Saturn, and *Elemmire* ('M') with Mercury. In an article by Jorge Quiñonez and Ned Raggett, *Nólë i Meneldilo, Lore of the Astronomer*, published in the periodical *Vinyar Tengwar* no.12 (July 1990), the authors concluded that my father originally intended *Nénar* ('N') for the planet Neptune, but transferred the identification to *Luinil, Nénar* thus becoming Uranus. The six names, therefore, are the Elvish names of the planets other than Venus (*Eärendil*); and this conclusion appears to be no mere ingenious deduction but to derive from my father's own clear indications.

Nonetheless, I find it so extraordinary as to be altogether incredible. It is to be remembered that the six names appear in the context of the making by Varda of 'new stars *and brighter* against the coming of the First-born': they must be the names of very conspicuous objects in the heavens of Arda. That Mars and Jupiter, if not Saturn, should appear among them would seem inevitable, seeing that in my father's astronomical myth the planets were never distinguished from the 'fixed stars'; but how is it to be thought that *Nénar* and *Luinil*, self-evidently the names of great lights in the region of Ilmen, should refer to Uranus and Neptune, faint and minute among 'the innumerable stars', the one barely visible to the naked eye, and the other not at all? Reference in this connection to the extraordinary powers of sight possessed by the Elves is beside the point: because from the astronomical myth as presented in the *Annals of Aman* and in the first post-*Lord of the Rings* revision of the *Quenta Silmarillion* the entire conceptual basis of the astronomy by which the remote planets of the Solar System were discoverable must of very nature be absent. But what then is to be said of the letter 'N' written above the name *Nénar*?

It seems to me quite possible that the six names existed before the writing of the draft page now at Marquette, even if they were never written down, and further, that some of them did not possess specific identifications with our names – though *Karnil* was surely always Mars, and *Alkarinque* no doubt Jupiter. On this hypothesis, I could well imagine (it would not be uncharacteristic) that as he reflected on these names my father amused himself by extending the list to include all the planets (with the exception of the Evening Star – and Pluto!), and whimsically, as one might say, with a sense both of appropriateness (associating the stem *nen-* 'water' with the sea-god) and essential inappropriateness, wrote in the N of Neptune above *Nénar*.

This is not of course offered as a formal and precise proposal in explanation of this extremely puzzling fact, but it does seem to me that something on these lines is very much more probable than that he seriously intended the name *Nénar* to signify the planet Neptune.

Adanel Sister of Hador Lórindol; a 'Wise-woman'. 305–7, 309, 313, 328, 344–5; *Tale of Adanel* 344–9, 354, 360
Adûnaic 4, 7, 28, 42
Aegnor Son of Finarfin (=Finrod (1)). 177, 323–4, (325–6), 327, 335, 357; *Ægnor* 197; earlier form *Egnor* 113, 121, 125–6, 177, 182, 195–7, 327–8. See *Aikanár*.
Ælfwine Ælfwine of England, the Mariner. 5, 8, 11–12, 14–17, 22, 25–6, 30, 35–6, 40, 42, 65, 110, 121, 123–4, 127–8, 130, 136, 143, 153–4, (157), 160, 163, 166, 168, 175–6, 179, 185, 192, 195, 198, 200, 202, 208–9, 225, 231–2, 257, 271, 326. See *Eriol*.
Aeluin Tarn Aeluin, lake on Dorthonion. 325
Aftercomers Men. 111–12, 121, 130. See *Followers, Hildi*.
Aikanár 'Sharp-flame', Aegnor son of Finarfin. 323–4
Ainulindalë (not as title) 66, 74, 110, 409. See *Music of the Ainur*.
Ainur (not including *Music of the Ainur*) 8–14, 21, 23–8, 36–9, 41, 43, 49, 65–6, 105, 144–5, 149–50, 244, 253, 271, 336–8, 345, 352, 359, 376, 378–80, 384; singular *Ainu* 12; the Holy Ones 8, 12, 14, 42, 359
Akallabêth 179
Alamanyar Elves of the Great March who never reached Aman (Sindar and Nandor). 163–4, 170–1, 173, 223, 232. (Replaced *Ekelli*, replaced by *Úmanyar*.)
Aldaron Name of Oromë. 124, 146, 202. See *Tauron*.
Aldudénië The Lament for the Trees, made by Elemmírë. 100, 105, 166, 288, 292
Alkarinquë The planet Jupiter. 160, 166; *Alcarinquë* 166. See pp. 434–5.
All-father Ilúvatar. 8, 39; *Eru Allfather* 112
Almaren First abode of the Valar in Arda, an island in a great lake. 7, 23, 32–3, 38, 52–4, 60–1, 133, 179; earlier form *Almar* 7, 18, 23, (25), 27, 38. Earlier names *Eccuilë* 22, *Eremar* 23. See *Great Lake*.
Alqualondë 87, 91, 93, 104, 115–18, 125–6, 128, 177–9, 183, 196, 283. See *Haven of the Swans*.
Altariellë Galadriel. 182
Aman (1) Adûnaic name of Manwë. 7, 28. (2) The world, Eä (often *the Halls of Aman*) 7, 12, 14, 20, 22–3, 28–9, 30–1, 34, 37–8, 40, 44, 149–50, 156. (3) The Blessed Realm. 7, 33, 37–8, 48, 51, 54, 58, 61, 67, 73, 75, 78, 80–1, 84–7, 90, 92, 96, 103,

114, 116–18, 120, 125, 129, 132, 138, 155–6, 159, 161, 163, 170, 172, 174, 181–2, 190, 192, 204, 206, 211, 219, 221, 223, 236–42, 247–8, 253, 255, 257–8, 261–2, 268–71, 274–7, 279, 281–6, 289, 309–10, 339–41, 349, 358–9, 361–5, 370–1, 385–6, 388–9, 397, 401, 403, 405, 412, 420–1, 424–31; *Aman the Unshadowed* 240. See *Blessed Realm, Mountains of Aman.*

Ambar 'Earth'. 28, 359, 382–3, 385; *Ambar-endya* 'Middle-earth' 76; *Ambar-metta* 359. See *Imbar*.

Ambarkanta 22, 26, 28–9, 39, 63–4, 76–8, 88–90, 123, 126, 135–6, 157, 373

Amon Uilos 154. See *Taniquetil*.

Amrod and Amras Later names of Damrod and Díriel. 177. On the death of one of the brothers at Losgar see 128.

Anar (1) Of uncertain meaning (see 44): *Halls of Anar* 22–3, 40, 44, *Kingdom of Anar* 22, 41, 44. (2) The Sun. 40, 44, 130–2, 134, 136, 198, 377, 382 (*Fire-golden* 130, 198); *Anor* 44.

Anárion Son of Elendil. 44

Anarríma Name of a constellation. 160

Andreth 'Wise-woman' of the House of Bëor. 303–28, 333–6, 338, 343–5, 349, 351–4, 357–9, 364–5, 390. See *Saelind*.

Anduin 82, 89; *the River* 83; *the Great River of Wilderland* 89

Andúnë The West. 23

Angainor The chain with which Melkor was bound. 75, 161, 167, 391–3; earlier *Angaino, Angainu* 168

Angband 67, 109–10, 124, (127), 131, 156, 167, 197, 284, 291, 295, 297–8, 306, 341, 350, 419, 421, 423; *the Siege of Angband* 305, 307, 324(–5), 328, 336, 357(–8); Quenya *Angamando* 350

Anglo-Saxon 5, 30. See *Old English*.

Angrod Son of Finarfin (=Finrod (1)). 113, 121, 125–6, 177, 182, 195–6, 328

Annals of Aman For the relation of the *Annals* to the *Quenta* tradition see 102, 191–2, 205, 283, 289–91

Annals of Beleriand 3, 49, 102–3, 110, 123, 125, 127, 290, 306, and see *Grey Annals*.

Anórien 44

Arafinwë Finarfin. 230, 238, 265. See *Ingalaurë*.

Aragorn 211, 341, 359

Araman Wasteland beneath the Pelóri and the Sea, north of Taniquetil. 108, 115, 117, 119, 123, 132, 134, 194, 198, 283, 291, 295. (Replaced *Eruman*.)

Aran Endór 'King of Middle-earth' (Morgoth). 121, 126. See *Endor, Tarumbar, King of the World*.

Aratar The High Ones of Arda. 203. See *(The) Great Ones*.

Araw Oromë. 124

Arda (including many references to *the Kingdom, Realm, of Arda*) 3, 7, 12, 15–17, 20, 22, 25–31, 34–5, 37–9, 41, 43–4, 48–71 *passim*, 74–5, 80, 87, 93–4, 97, 99–100, 105, 112, 114–15, 118, 120, 129–30, 132, 135–7, 144–5, 147, 151–4, 159, 161, 172, 179, 187, 201–3, 206–7, 209–10, 212, 215, 217–20, 222–8, 231–5, 237, 240–55 *passim*, 258–60, 267–71, 275, 280–2, 284–6, 295, 304, 308–9, 311–22, 325–6, 331–43 *passim*, 349, 351–2, 354, 356–9, 361–5, 372–406 *passim*, 410, 416, 419, 424–31.

King of Arda, see *Manwë*; Queen of Arda, see *Varda*; Girdle of Arda 115, 135. For the Tale of Arda see *(The) Great Tale*; for Arda Marred, Arda Unmarred, etc. see *(The) Marring of Arda*; for the later meaning of Arda see references under *Solar System*; and see *(The) Earth, Rulers of Arda, Spring of Arda*.

Arien   The Sun-maiden. 130–4, 136–7, 198, 385, 405. Other, late names: *Áren* 376, *Ár(i)* 380, 385, *Ázië* 380, *Árië* 380–1, 386; Old English names *Dægred* 130, 136, *Dægbore* 198

Arnor   370, 373

Ar-Pharazôn   397–8

Arrow-elves   A name of the Teleri. 164

Arthur, King   366, 399; *Arthurian* 355, 365

Arvalin   Wasteland between the Pelóri and the Sea, south of Taniquetil. 97–8, 105, 108, 132, 184, 190, 290–1. (Replaced by *Vastuman, Avathar*.)

Arwen   211

Ás   The Sun. 380–1; *Asa* 381

Astaldo   Name of Tulkas. 149. (Replaced *Poldórëa*.)

Atanatárion   'Legendarium of the Fathers of Men'. 373

Atandil   'Friend of the Atani', name of Finrod Felagund. 306, 349. See *Edennil*.

Atani   The Followers, Men; Western Men. 7, 30, 36, 39, 314, 317, 320–1, 323, 349, 352, 428. See *Edain; (The) Seekers*.

Aulë   13–15, 19, 24–6, 31–5, 38, 40, 48–9, 52, 56, 60, 66–8, 92–3, 103–4, 107, 114, 120, 130, 144–5, 147, 151–3, 161, 163, 167–8, 176, 179–80, 201–2, 240–2, 244–5, 247, 253, 272, 276–7, 364, 372, 377, 382, 409, 411, 417; called *the Maker* 107, 120, *Friend of the Noldor* 19; *Friends of Aulë*, a name of the Noldor, 163. Aulë and the Dwarves 93, 104, 202, 409, 417

Auron   Tulkas (as Vala of the Sun). 376

Avallónë   (1) Tol Eressëa. 175, 179; *Avallon* 179.   (2) Haven in Tol Eressëa. 179; *Avallon(de)* 180

Avallonian   Quenya. 136. See *Eressëan*.

Avari   'The Unwilling', Elves who refused the Great March, 82, 88, 109, 123, 130, 162–3, 169–70, 416

Avathar   'The Shadows', later name of Arvalin. 284, 286, 291, 295, 298. See *Vastuman*.

Axe-elves   (1) A name of the Nandor. 164, 171.   (2) A name of the Sindar. 171

Baggins   See *Bilbo, Frodo.*
Balar   Bay of Balar 84, (174); *Isle of Balar* 174
Balrogs   70, 75–6, 78–80, 109, 123, 159, 165, 203, 297–8, 391, 410–11, 414, 418; *Balrogath* 79. See *Valaraukar,* and on their origin and number see especially 165 and 79–80.
Ban of the Valar   340
Barad-dûr   413
Barahir   Father of Beren One-hand. 305–6, 328, 373
Baran   Elder son of Bëor the Old. 306–7
Battle of Sudden Flame   306, 336, 357–8; *Dagor Bragollach* 306, 326
Battle of the Haven   119. See *Haven of the Swans.*
Battles of the Gods   The First Battle of the Valar for the dominion of Arda 16, 25–7, 376, 380; *the Battle of the Gods* (when Melkor was chained) 161, 174, *the Great War of the Gods* 74, 78, called *the Third Battle* 378; *the Last Battle* (1) the final overthrow of Melkor 110, called *the Great Battle* 27, 203, (2) the battle 'at the end of days' 71, 76, 160, 166, 399
Bauglir   Name of Morgoth. 146 *(the Constrainer),* 149, 151; *Baugron* 149, 151
Belegost   City of the Dwarves in the Blue Mountains. 93
Belemir   Husband of Adanel, grandson of Belen. 305–7
Belen   Second son of Bëor the Old. 306
Beleriand   83, 85–6, 89–91, 93, 103–4, 106, 109–10, 127, 138, 164, 169–70, 172, 174–5, 177, 196, 217, 297, 304–5, 316, 325, 336, 340, 352, 370, 373, 403, 431; *East(ern) Beleriand* 84, 305; *Beleriandic* (not of language) 102, 106
Belthil   Image of Telperion in Gondolin. 155
Bëor the Old   305–7, 327–8; *House of, People of, Bëor* 305–7, 327–8, 336, 349, 358
Beowulf   124
Beren   (1) Grandfather of Beren One-hand. 306.   (2) 'One-hand'. 3, 123, 141, 228, 267, 305–6, 336, 340, 364, 371, 373, 408
Bilbo   90, 365
Black Foe, The   Morgoth. 120, 146, 194, 294; *the Black God* 146. See *(The) Enemy.*
Black Speech   413
Blacksword   217; the black sword of Túrin 76. See *Mormacil, Túrin.*
Bladorion   The great northern plain *(Ard-galen).* 328
Blessed Elves   A name of the Vanyar. 164
Blessed Realm, The   7, 19, 33, 37, 84, 118, 120, 134, 137, 163, 176, 180, 182, 186, 196, 237, 239, 255–6, 258, 274, 284, 286, 289, 400–3, 407, 426–8; *the Blessed Land* 94, *Land of the Blessed* 203; *the Noon(tide) of,* 81, 94, 183, 236, 255–6. See *Aman.*
Blue Elves   A name of the Teleri. 164

Blue Mountains 104, 307, 327; *the Mountains* 83, 93, 164, 307. See *Mountains of Lindon*.
Boldog Orc-name. 418, 423; leader of a raid into Doriath 423
Book of Lost Tales, the Lost Tales (including references to individual tales, not separately indexed) 26–7, 35, 61, 68, 77, 103, 105, 136–7, 142, 150, 158, 167–8, 171, 265–6, 291, 299, 371, 393, 406–7
Boromir Father of Andreth and Bregor. 306
Boron Father of Boromir. 306–7
Bregolas Brother of Barahir. 306
Bregor Father of Bregolas and Barahir. 305–6
Brethil, Forest of 374
Brithombar The northern Haven of the Falas. 85, 175
Brown Elves A name of the Nandor. 164, 171
Burning Briar The constellation of the Great Bear. 160, 166

Calaciryan See *Kalakiryan*.
Caranthir Son of Fëanor, called 'the Dark'. 128, 177, 181; earlier form *Cranthir* 112, 128, 177, 181
Carnil See *Karnil*.
Cataclysm, The 67. *The Catastrophe* 341
Celeborn (1) 'Tree of silver', a name of Telperion, and also of the White Tree of Eressëa. 155, (176), 180. (2) Lord of Lothlórien. 128, 135
Celegorm Son of Fëanor, called 'the Fair'. 177, 179; earlier form *Celegorn* 112, 126, 128, 177, 179, 181
Change of the World 51, 132, 134, 136–7, 149, (179), 203, 397, 427
Chasm (of Ilmen) See *Ilmen*.
Children of Eru, Children of Ilúvatar (including many references to *the Children*, also *My Children*, etc.) 9, 11–12, 14–16, 18, 21–2, 24, 26, 28–9, 31, 36, 40, 50–1, 54, 71, 74, 79–81, 86, 95, 99, 107, 109, 127, 129–30, 144, 147, 159, 165, 185, 194, 201, 206, 211, 220–1, 240–2, 244–7, 255, 259, 268–70, 278, 282, 286, 289, 293, 308, 311–12, 315, 319–20, 336–8, 342, 345, 349–50, 356–8, 361–3, 375, 379, 382, 388, 400, 409, 412, 416, 420, 425, 427; *Children of God* 330, 356, 377, 379. See *Eruhíni, Mirröanwi*.
Children of (the) Earth, of the World 109, 124, 160, 163, 281, 299, *of Arda* 319, 382. *Elder Children, First(born) Children* 71, 120, 159, 286, 361; *Younger Children, Second (race of the) Children* 130, 299, 319, 356
Children of Húrin 76
Children of Ingwë A name of the Vanyar. 164
Children of Melkor 416. See *Melkorohíni*.
Children of the Valar 20, 34, 49, 59, 66, 69, 151–2; *Sons of the*

Valar 133, 137, 152; *elder children of the World* 66. See *Valarindi*.
Christianity 354, 356; *Christian* (religion, belief, myth) 270, 355–6
Chronology (1) within the narrative. 48, 306–7, 326–7, 357–8, 375, 378, 417, 420, 423. (2) of composition. 3–4, 6–7, 47, 60, 64, 66, 141–3, 181–2, 191, 199, 205, 233, 300, 304, 350, 352, 354, 360, 365, 370, 385, 389–90, 394, 409, 415, 421–2
Circles (of the world) 13, 327, 355, 405; *circles of time* 40
Cirdan the Shipwright 85, 90
Cloud of Unseeing 377
Common Speech 422
Companions of Men A name of the Noldor. 164
Corolairë See *Korolairë*.
Cosmology (discussed) 3–6, 26–9, 37–9, 43–4, 62–4, 135–6, 157, 358, 369–74, 383
Cranthir See *Caranthir*.
Cuiviénen See *Kuiviénen*.
Curufin Son of Fëanor, called 'the Crafty'. 112, 126, 177
Curufinwë Fëanor. 87, 91, 217, 230, 236, 263, 277; *Kurufinwë* 256

Daeron Minstrel of Doriath. 106 ('loremaster of Thingol')
Dagor Bragollach See *Battle of Sudden Flame*.
Damrod and Díriel Sons of Fëanor (twin brothers). 112, 128, 176, 181. See *Amrod and Amras*.
Dân Leader of the Nandor. 83, 89, 93, 163–4, 169. *The Host of Dân*, a name of the Nandor, 164. See *Nano*.
Danas The people of Dân. 89, 169. See *Nandor*.
Danathrim, Danians = Danas. 169
Dark Ages 304
Dark-elves 131, 169–70, 223, 236; *Elves of the Darkness* 163. See *Moriquendi, Wild Elves*.
Darkening of Valinor See *Valinor*.
Dark, (Great) Darkness (with various and often indeterminate reference, as of the Void, of Melkor, of Middle-earth, of the Darkness behind and before Men) 20, 29, 37, 74, 100–1, 105, 108–10, 112, 120, 122–3, 146–7, 153, 159, 165, 179, 190, 194, 223, 231, 284, 288–9, 291, 294–5, 305, 307, 309–10, 313, 317–18, 320–1, 323, 325–6, 328, 344, 346–8, 351, 354, 361, 372, 377–9, 382–4, 389–90, 399, 401. *Eldest Dark(ness)* 63–4, 154, 157; *Outer Darkness* 17, 27, 105, 190, 193; *Lord of the Darkness* 309
Dark Lord 224, 231, 284, 292, 411; *Dark Power* 124; and see *Dark*.
Dark Years 413
Days before Days (before the Two Trees) 51, 58; *Days of Bliss* (in the Light of the Trees) 51, 56, 377

Dead, The (of Elves) 222, 226–7, 233–5, 255, 259–61, 362–5; (of Men) 365
Death See entries *Elves, Men.*
Deathless, The The Valar. 69
Deep Elves A name of the Noldor. 163
Deeps of Time 12–14, 16, 28, 40, 159, 384. See *Time.*
Denethor Son of Dân; leader of the Green-elves. 93, 102, 104, 164, 169. Transient name *Enadar* 102
Díriel See *Damrod and Díriel.*
Dispossessed, The The House of Fëanor. 117
Dome of Varda 286, 292, 385–8, 390. See *Nur-menel*; and cf. *the domed halls of Varda* 67
Dominion of Men 31, 68, 217, 327, 340–2, 404
Doom 112, 160, 323–4, 336; Doom *of the Noldor*, see *Noldor.*
Doom-hill (of the Valar) 259
Door (of Night) 27, 407
Doriath 104, 164, 169, 171, 173, 374, 423
Dor-lómin 119
Dorthonion 123, 323–4, 328
Drama, The (of Arda, especially of the war against Melkor) 26, 329–30, 333, 335, 337–8, 375 (cf. also 349, 389)
Drengist, Firth of 119–20, 122, 196, 295
Drowning of Anadûnê, The (title) 5, 7, 22, 28, 179–80, 355
Dúnedain 370, 373
Dwarves 93, 103–4, 202, 251, 409, 415, 418, 421. See *Naugrim, Nornwaith; Aulë.*

Eä 7, 31, 37–9, 44, 48–54, 56–8, 60–7, 76, 80, 88, 97–9, 105, 107, 114, 117, 121, 129, 135, 144, 148, 150, 153, 156, 159–60, 190, 193, 201, 220, 244, 252, 267, 270, 280, 311, 318, 321–2, 326, 330, 334, 336–8, 342, 352, 373–82, 384, 386–9, 397, 403, 425, 428. See *(The) Great Tale, (The) Universe.*
Eagles 185 (of Manwë), 412; the nature of the Great Eagles 138, 251, 410–11. See *Gwaehir, Landroval, Sorontar, Thorondor.*
Eärambar The Walls of Eä. 63
Eärendil (134), 247, 340, 359
Earth (The) 7, 12–20, 23–9, 31–7, 40–4, 51–4, 58, 60, 67, 70–2, 74, 78–9, 81, 85, 99, 104–5, 112, 120, 131–2, 136, 144–6, 153–4, 160, 162, 166–7, 174, 178, 185, 188, 212, 229, 266, 275, 277, 281–2, 286, 299, 330, 334, 337, 345–9, 355, 358–9, 366, 371, 374–6, 381–5, 387, 389, 394–5, 421, 426–8, 431; *Earthly* 42. For use in sense 'Middle-earth', excluding Aman, see 282, 431.

    Girdle of the Earth 130, 135; *Kingdom of Earth* 144. See *Arda, Ambar, Imbar.*

INDEX 443

Eärwen Olwë's daughter, wife of Finarfin (=Finrod (1)). 93, 101, 126, 177 *(the swan-maiden of Alqualondë)*, 182
East, The   18, 33, 72, 76, 79, 95, 100, 111, 117, 130–2, 135, 154, 160, 162, 176, 187, 275, 289, 327, 370, 378, 382. See *Mountains of the East*.
Eastern Sea   78–9
Eccuilë   See *Almaren*.
Echoing Mountains   298. See *Lammoth*.
Edain   7, 163, 304, 328, 378, 402, 418. See *Atani*.
Edennil   'Friend of Men', name of Finrod Felagund. 305–6, 349. See *Atandil*.
Eglarest   The southern Haven of the Falas. 85, 90, 179; earlier form *Eglorest* 90, 175, 179
Eglath   'The Forsaken People', name given to themselves by the Sindar. 85, 90, 164, 170–1. See *Ekelli*.
Egnor   Son of Finarfin; see *Aegnor*.
Ekelli, Ecelli   'The Forsaken', name given by the Elves of Valinor to the Sindar and Nandor; replaced by *Alamanyar*. 169–70
Ekkaia   The Outer Sea. 157. See *Vaiya*.
Elbereth   'Queen of the Stars', Varda. 20, 38, 387–8; etymology 387. See *Elentári, Tinwerontar*.
Eldalië   The People of the Elves. 16, 36, 94, 162–3, 174, 186, 212, 219, 223, 229, 267, 274. See *Elvenfolk*.
Eldamar   'Elvenhome', land of the Eldar in Aman, and also a name of their city (Tirion). 84, 90, 95–7, 106, 176, 180, 185, 192, 256, 268; *Bay of Eldamar* 85, 97, *coast, shores, strands of Eldamar* 86–7, 90, 115, 193. See *Eldanor, Elendë, Elvenhome, Elvenland*, and for the relations of the names see 90, 176, 180.
Eldanor   'Elvenland', land of the Eldar in Aman. 90, 176, 180, 190, 277, 282–3; *Bay of Eldanor* 199, *strands of Eldanor* 194. See *Eldamar*.
Eldanyárë   'History of the Elves' (title). 141, 143, 200
Eldar   (and singular *Elda*) 12, 15, 17, 21, 30, 36–7, 42–3, 51, 57, 69, 72–4, 77–8, 80–8, 91–6, 98–101, 103, 105–6, 109, 111–13, 119, 121, 127, 131, 133, 154–5, 157, 160, 162–3, 167–70, 173–5, 177, 182–8, 198–200, 204–40 *passim*, 243, 245, 247, 250–1, 254–78 *passim*, 281, 284, 286–8, 294, 299–300, 304–6, 311, 314–28 *passim*, 336–8, 340, 342, 349, 351–3, 355, 358, 370, 373–5, 378, 387, 389, 399, 401–2, 406, 408–9, 416–17, 423, 426–9, 431
   People of the Stars (name given by Oromë) 72, 80, (81), 160, (162), 167, 372, *Star-folk* 375; *High Eldar* 318, 370
Eldarin   103, 136, 198, 217, 363, 371, 387–8
Eldaros   Elvenhome (land of the Elves). 90
Elder Days   3, 30, 47, 58, 64–5, 78, 122, 160, 203, 217, 303, 327, 369–70, 373–4, 412, 418–20, 427; *Elder World* 154, 340

Elder King Manwë. 313, 379, 399–400, 402, 404
Elder Tree Telperion. 59, 90, 155
Eldest Dark(ness) See *Dark*.
Elemmírë (1) Vanyarin Elf, maker of the *Aludénië*. 106, 166, 288, 292; *Elemírë* 100, 106, 292. (2) Name of a bright star (the planet Mercury?). 160. See pp. 434–5.
Elendë Land of the Eldar in Aman. 90, 114, 125, 176, 178, 180; *Bay of Elendë* 190. See *Eldamar*, *Eldanor*.
Elentári 'Queen of the Stars', Varda. 160, 166, 384, 388–9; *Elentárië* 71, 166. See *Tintallë*.
Elerrína 'Crowned with stars', Taniquetil. 154; *Elerína* 154, 389. See *Tinwerína*.
Elf-friends 370, 373; *Elf-lords* 81; *Elf-child(ren)* 209–10, 212, 220, 228, 232, 426; *Elf-strain* 402
Elfinesse 271
Elrond 135
Elu Thingol See *Elwë* (2), *Thingol*.
Elvenfolk 81, 84, 163, 169, 186, 274–5; *Elf-folk* 228. See *Eldalië*.
Elvenhome Land of the Eldar in Aman, and also a name of their city. 90, 125, 176, 180; *Bay of Elvenhome* 176, 178, 180, 199, *shores, strands of Elvenhome* 178, 180, 193–4. See *Eldamar*.
Elvenland Land of the Eldar in Aman. 176, 180; *shores of Elvenland* 178, 180; *Elfland* 125. See *Eldamar*, *Eldanor*.
Elven- *lore* 374; *men, women* 199; *race* 133, 169; *tongue* 167
Elves (and *Elf*) 5, 12, 16, 19–22, 24–5, 28, 34, 36–7, 42–4, 51, 59, 61, 66, 70–4, 76–9, 83–4, 88–90, 93, 95, 104, 106, 108, 123, 130, 133, 138, 144–9, 154, 159–80 *passim*, 187, 190, 192–4, 199–201, 203–4, 208–10, 218–21, 223–8, 232, 236, 241, 244, 247, 251–4, 265–8, 270–1, 275, 281, 283, 294, 308–9, 311, 314, 316, 318–19, 324–44, 349, 351, 355, 357–9, 361, 363–5, 372, 374–5, 377–8, 383–4, 388, 395–7, 401–21 *passim*, 424–5, 427. See *Quendi*.

The 'fading' or 'waning' of the Elves, the 'consuming' of the body by the spirit 31, 68, 118, 126, 130, 146, 149, 203, 209–10, 212, 219, 228, 231, 266–7, 304, 327, 342, 359, 364, 402, 405, 407, 410, 427; immortality and death of the Elves 21, 37, 87, 117, 126, 206, 209, 218–19, 221–2, 225, 227, 231, 233, 242, 244–5, 247–8, 250, 254, 258–9, 266–71, 310–12, 319, 330–2, 339–41, 359, 361, 363–5, 410, 425, 427; rebirth, reincarnation 21, 37, 80, 104, 209, 219–23, 226–7, 233–4, 248, 254, 263, 266–8, 331, 339–40, 359, 361–4

Elves of the Air (Vanyar) 164; *Elves of the Darkness* 163 (see *Dark-Elves*, *Moriquendi*); *Elves of the Earth* (Noldor) 164; *Elves of the Falas* 90, 175; *Elves of the Light* 163, 173 (see *Light Elves*, *Kalaquendi*); *Elves of the Sea* (Teleri) 164; *Elves of the Seven*

Rivers (the Nandor of Ossiriand) 164; *Elves of the Twilight* (Sindar) 86, 164

Elvish (of language) 5, 7, 77 (origin of Elvish speech), 124, 144, 157, 160, 166–7, 229, 326, 330, 358, 385, 413, 415; (with other reference) 5, 80, 90, 127, 138, 162, 170–1, 209, 225, 231, 265, 267, 281, 285, 308, 329–33, 335–40, 342, 344, 355, 361, 363, 401, 409, 411, 413–14, 422–5, 428–9

Elwë (1) Brother of Thingol (later *Olwë*). 88, 168–70, 178–9, 183, 194, 196. See *Solwë*. (2) Thingol of Doriath, called *Singollo* 'Greymantle'. 81–6, 88–91, 104, 162–4, 168–173, 217; *Elwë the Grey* 164, 169; *the People of Elwë*, a name of the Sindar, 165. *Elu Thingol* (*Elu-thingol*), his name in Sindarin, 86, 91, 169, 172–3, 217; *Elu* 217. See *Greymantle, Sindo, Singollo, Thingol*.

Elwing 359

Emeldir Mother of Beren One-hand. 305–6

Enadar See *Denethor*.

Enchanted Isles 133–4, 137

Enchanters, The A name of the Sindar. 164

Encircling Sea(s) 17, 32, 118

Endar Middle-earth. 118–20, 126, 129. See *Endor*.

Endor (1) Midmost point of Middle-earth. 76–7, 80, 126, 377, 385; also *Endon* 72, 76–7, 80, 126. (2) Middle-earth. 126; Quenya *Endórë*, Sindarin *Ennor*, 126; and see *Aran Endór*.

End, The 94, 120, 129, 187, 242, 247, 251–2, 259, 267, 274, 319–20, 332, 339, 404, 411; *the End of Arda* 259, 331, 338, 341–2, (405), 430; *the Ending of the World, the World's End* 22, 31, 37, 43, 68, 112, 319, 327, 357, 399, 428; *the End of Eä* 57, 342; *end of days* 9, 21, 35, 37, 71, 76; *Ambar-metta* 'the ending of the world' 359

Enemy, The 43, 99, 111, 287, 309–11, 313, 320, 325, 328, 348–9, 355, 372, 399, 401, 404; *the Dark Enemy* 120, 123, 194, *the Black Enemy* 421; *the Enemies* 203; *Foe of the Valar* 114

Enquirers Term used to replace *Gnomes*. 168

Ents 251

Eönwë Herald of Manwë. 146–7, 151, 203–4, 406. (Replaced *Fionwë*, son of Manwë.)

Eregion Hollin. 135

Eremar See *Almaren*.

Eressëa See *Tol Eressëa*.

Eressëan Quenya. 136. See *Avallonian*.

Eriador 83, 89

Eriol 5, 26. See *Ælfwine*.

Eru 7, 48–9, 58–9, 65–6, 74, 80, 87–8, 99, 114, 117, 129, 138, 144, 159, 186, 209, 211(–12), 220–3, 236, 241–2, 244–6, 252,

267–8, 286–7, 304, 309, 311–13, 318–19, 321–2, 326–8, 330–45, 350–2, 354, 356–7, 359–65, 380, 390–3, 397–8, 401–3, 406, 409–11, 420, 425, 427, 429–30; *Eru Allfather, Eru Ilúvatar* 48, 112, 120, 286; *the Voice (of Eru)* 345–8, 360. See *Children of Eru, God, Ilúvatar, Lord of All, (The) One.*

Eruhín Children of Eru. 320, 330; *Eruhíni* 356, 376; *Eruséni* 423

Eruman Earlier name of *Araman.* 123, 194, 198, 266

Eryd (Ered) Orgoroth The Mountains of Terror. 109, 127, 297, 299; *Eryd Gorgoroth* 297, *Ered Gorgorath* 127, 299

Eryd Wethrin The Mountains of Shadow. 297, 299; earlier *Eredwethion* 299

Estë Called 'the Pale'. 49, 59, 65–6, 69, 131–2, 136, 145, 147–8, 150–1, 198, 201, 206, 237, 258. On the status of Estë see 49, 59, 65–6, 69, 146–7, 201

Etymologies, The In Vol.V, *The Lost Road.* 39, 44, 57, 69, 89, 124, 169, 202, 229, 253, 359

Evening Star 371

Everwhite Taniquetil. 67. See *Oiolossë.*

Exiles, The The Noldor in Middle-earth. 65, 92, 115, 373; *Exiled Noldor* 263, 305; *the Exile* 103, 340

Eye of Morgoth 419

Ezellohar The Mound of the Two Trees. 69, 106, 127. See *Green Mound, Corolairë.*

Fading of the Elves See *Elves.*

Faërie 271

Fair Elves The Vanyar (replacing *High Elves*) 168, 180; *Fair Folk* 164

Faithful, The (of Númenor) 402

Falarombar The horns of Ulmo. 202. (Replaced by *Ulumúri.*)

Falas The coasts of Beleriand. 90, 175; *Falassë* 90. See *Havens.*

Fall of Númenor (title) 5–6, 22, 179

Fall, The (of Men) 270, 328, 333–4, 344–5, 351, 354–6, 360, 378, 423; legend of the Fall *(Tale of Adanel)* 345–9; (of the Elves) 267, 355; (of the Angels) 270, 355; (in general sense) 270, 355; *fallen world* 372

Falmari A name of the Teleri of Valinor. 163. (Replaced *Soloneldi.*)

Faniel Daughter of Finwë and Indis. 207, 238, 262, 265

Fanturi See *Fëanturi.*

Farrer, Katherine 5–6, 39

Fathers of Men 7, 373. See *Atanatárion.*

Fëanor 48, 65, 87, 90–2, 94–129 *passim*, 135, 151, 177, 179, 185–95, 197, 205, 210, 217, 230, 236, 240–1, 247(–8), 253, 257–8, 260–3, 267–8, (269), 272–80, 282, 287, 290, 293–6, 310, 370; *Fëanáro* 'Spirit-of-Fire' 206–7, 217, 236–41, 243, 249, 252, 257, 263; *Faenor* (Sindarin) 217; *House of Fëanor* 114,

INDEX

117–18, 189, 196. See *Curufinwë, Finwë* (2), *Finwion, Minyon; Sons of Fëanor.*

Fëanorians 126, 182, 196; *Fëanorian* (of letters) 350; Oath of the Fëanorians 112, 114, 117–18, 125

Fëanturi Mandos (Námo) and Lórien (Irmo). 145, 148, 203–4; earlier form *Fanturi* 145

Felagund 'Lord of Caves' 177; see *Inglor, Finrod* (2).

Fellowship of the Ring, The (title) 76

Finarfin 103, 197, (207), 262, 276, 278, 282, 305, 350; *Finarphin* 103–4, 128, 177, 181–2, 197, 262, 265, 276, 282, 305, 350; House of *Finarphin* 311. (Replaced *Finrod* (1).) See *Arafinwë, Ingalaurë, Finrod* (1).

Findis Daughter of Finwë and Indis. 207, 238, 262, 265

Fingolfin 92, 96, 100, 102, 104–6, 112–14, 116, 118–21, 125, 131, 177, 182, 188–9, 193, 196–7, (207), 253, 262, 276–9, 282, 287, 290, 326; *Fingolphin* 265, 282, 310. See *Nolofinwë, Ingoldo* (1), *Finwë* (2).

Fingon 113–14, 116, 118–19, 121, 125–6, 177, 182, 188, 195–6

Finrod (1) Earlier name of Finarfin. 92–3, 101, 103–4, 106, 112–14, 118, 121, 125–6, 128, 137, 177, 181–2, 195–7

Finrod (2) Later name of *Inglor*; references include also *Finrod Felagund* and *Felagund* used alone. 104, 125, 128, 177, 181, 197, 265, 303–25, 327–30, 333–6, 342, 345, 349–54, 356–8, 365, 378, 385, 390, 393, 411–13. See *Atandil, Edennil.*

Finvain Daughter of Finwë and Indis. 262, 265. (Replaced *Írimë*.)

Finwë (1) 81–93, 96–7, 99, 101–3, 105, 108, 111, 114, 122, 125, 127, 162–3, 168, 172–3, 177, 179, 185–6, 188–90, 193, 205–9, 217, 225, 230–1, 233, 236–65 *passim*, 268–9, 271, 274, 276–80, 282–3, 287, 289, 293(–4), 298, 300, 305, (310), 326, 339, 361; House, Kin of Finwë 92, 101, 113, 125, 177, 207, 239, 261–2, 264–5; Followers of Finwë, a name of the Noldor, 164. See *Statute of Finwë and Míriel.*

Finwë (2) Original name both of Fëanor and of Fingolfin. 230

Finwion 'Son of Finwë', original name of Fëanor. 217

Fionwë Son of Manwë. 76, 145–6, 150–1, 204, 399, 406; *Fionwë Úrion* 20, 34. See *Eönwë.*

Fíriel Later name of Míriel. 250, 253

First Age 51, 58, 142, 337, 374, 394, 405, 407

First Battle See *Battles of the Gods.*

Firstborn, The The Elves. 12, 18–19, 31, 33, 35, 68, 159–60, 206, 225, 270, 286, 327, 361–2, 384. *Firstcomers* 309

First-created, The 413

Flame Imperishable, The 8–9, 13, 28, 345. See *(The) Secret Fire.*

Flat World 4–6, 40; *Flat Earth* 6, 370–1, 373

Foam-riders A name of the Teleri. 164

Foes of Melkor A name of the Noldor. 164

Followers 12, 309, 318, 355. See *Aftercomers, Atani, Hildi.*
Followers of Finwë See *Finwë.*
Formenos Stronghold of the Fëanorians in the north of Valinor. 96–7, 99, 105, 107–8, 122, 189, 191, 253, 268, 279–80, 282, 287, 289–92, 294, 296, 298
Forontë The Northern Lamp. 7, 32, 38, 60. (Replaced *Foros*; replaced by *Illuin.*)
Foros The Northern Lamp. 7, 17–18, 38. (Replaced *Helkar.*)
Forsaken (People), The 85, 90, 164, 169–71, 173. See *Eglath, Ekelli.*
Free, The A name of the Teleri. 164
Friend of the Noldor See *Aulë.*
Friends of Aulë See *Aulë; Friends of Ossë*, see *Ossë; Friends of the Gods*, see *Gods.*
Frodo 365–6, 412; and see 341.

Galadlóriel (Gnomish >) Sindarin name of Laurelin. 155
Galadriel 93, 104, 106, 112, 120–1, 125, 128, 135, 177, 181–2, 195–6, 211; etymology of the name 182
Galathilion (1) (Gnomish >) Sindarin name of Telperion. 90, 155, 180. (2) The White Tree of Túna (Tirion), image of Telperion. 85, 90, 155, 157, (176), 180; called *Galathilion the Less* 155, 157, 180
Gandalf 135, 152, 192, 396–7, 400. See *Olórin.*
Gársecg (Old English) The Great Sea. 153
Gatherers of Pearl A name of the Teleri. 164
Gelion, River 83, 89, 104, 172–3
gems, jewels, of the Noldor 19, 92–3, 96, 101, 103, 108, 116, 176, 178, 181, 183, 185, 189, 191–2, 279, 285, 292, 296, 298
Gift of Ilúvatar, The (of Man's mortality) 21, 26, 36–7, 42–3, 267, 326, 354, 356; (of Light to the Valar) 380, 385
Gilthoniel Varda. 388
Glamhoth 'Host(s) of tumult', Orcs. 109, 128, 195
Glaurung 306
Glewellin 'Song of gold', (Noldorin >) Sindarin name of Laurelin. 155
Glingal Image of Laurelin in Gondolin. 155
Glorfindel of Gondolin 364
Gnomes 103, 124–5, 137, 146, 154–5, 163, 168, 177–8, 188–9, 194; language of 144, 177; *Song of the Flight of the Gnomes* 125
Gnomish (language) 90, 103, 195
God 329–30, 355, 357, 397; *Children of God* 330, 356, 377, 379, 398. See *Eru, Children of Eru, (The) One.*
God(s) 18, 20, 26, 32, 54–5, 67–9, 95–9, 106, 111, 116–18, 129–30, 133, 136, 144, 147, 150, 153–5, 160–2, 167, 172–3, 175–9, 181, 185, 187–91, 196, 198, 271, 273, 282, 321, 372, 387, 407; of Melkor as 'God' 344, 351, 354, 397. *City of the*

Gods 146, 154; *Land of the Gods* 90, 145, 148, 174, 178, 180; *Mountains of the Gods* 22, 176, 180; *language of the Gods* 77, 166; *Sickle of the Gods*, see *Valakirka*; *Friends of the Gods*, a name of the Vanyar, 164; *the Black God* 146; *the Nine Gods* 144; and see *Battles of the Gods, Valar.*
Golden Elves A name of the Noldor. 164
Gondolin 155, 177, 359, 364, 373
Gondor 370, 373
Great Battle See *Battles of the Gods.*
Great Bear (constellation) 166. See *(The) Plough, Burning Briar, Valakirka.*
Great Journey 103, 106, 169, 171, 281. See *Great March.*
Great Lake 7, 18, 23, 25, 27, 32, 38, 52, 153, 179. See *Almaren.*
Great March (of the Eldar from Kuiviénen; including references to the March, the Westward March) 82–3, 88–9, 162–3, 169–70, 277, 378, 417, 423. See *Great Journey.*
Great Music, Great Song See *Music of the Ainur.*
Great Ones, The 15, 73; *the Great* (115), 147, 156, 161, 308; *the Seven Great Ones* 15, 44, 147, 151. See *Aratar.*
Great River of Wilderland 89
Great Sea 57, 75, 78, 83, 108, 115, 118, 134–5, 271, 295, 423; *Great Sea of the West* 54, 58, 78, 154. See *(The) Sea, Western Sea, Gársecg.*
Great Stars 34, 39, 384, 387–8
Great Tales 373
Great Tale, The 377–8, 380, 389, ~ *of Eä* 375, 388; *the Great History* 382; *the Tale* 377, 382, 405; *the Tale of Arda* 68, 223, 232, 240, 246–7, 251–2, 389, 392, 405; *the Tale of the Eldar* 246. See also 332, 338
Great Theme The Great Music. 240, 242, 244, 246–7
Great War of the Gods See *Battles of the Gods.*
Green-elves 93, 164, 169, 171. See *Laiquendi, Nandor.*
Green Hill The hill of Túna. 178
Green Hills In the north of Valinor. 294
Green Mound The Mound of the Two Trees. 55, 61–2, 69, 100, 106–7, 288, 293. See *Ezellohar, Korolairë.*
Grey Annals The final version of the *Annals of Beleriand*. 3, 49, 123, 142, 307, 326, 357, 423
Grey-elves 86, 91, 164, 170, 173, 349. See *Sindar.*
Greymantle Translation of *Singollo*, Thingol (Elwë). 84, 88, 93, 163, 169, 173; *King Greymantle* 86; *Greycloak* 217
Grinding Ice 108, 174, 281, 295; *the Ice* 283, 295, 310. See *Helkaraxë.*
Guarded Realm, The Valinor. 54, 98, 117
Guests, The An Elvish name for Men. 21, 37, 315–16
Gwaehir 410; *Gwaihir the Windlord* 412

Hador 306, 373, *Hador Lorindol* 305–6; *House of Hador* 306, 344–5
Half-elven 340; *Half-eldar*, see *Pereldar*.
Halls of Waiting (Awaiting) 94, 219, 223, 227, 248, 260–1, 264, 325, 364; other references to the 'waiting' of the Dead 219, 221–2, 233, 235, 266, 268; the *place of waiting* of Men 365
Haven of the Swans 116, 178; *Swanhaven* 86; *the Haven* 116, 125; *Battle of the Haven* 119
Havens of the Falas 90; *Lord of the Havens* 90. See *Brithombar, Eglarest*.
Heaven(s) 40, 71, 84, 86, 130, 132, 134, 146, 160, 202, 284, 346, 355, 371–2, 387; *the far heaven* 17, 27, 38, 41. See *Ilúvë*.
Helkar (1) The Northern Lamp. 7, 22, 77. See *Foros, Forontë, Illuin*. (2) The Inland Sea of Helkar. 72, 77, 82, 87
Helkaraxë 108, 118–20, 126, 128, 194, 295; *Helkaraksë* 194. See *Grinding Ice*.
Helluin The star Sirius. 160, 185
Heofonsýl (Old English) 'Pillar of Heaven'; with reference both to Taniquetil and the Meneltarma. 154, 157
Hidden People, The A name of the Nandor. 164
Hiding of Valinor See *Nurtalë Valinóreva, Valinor*.
High Eldar 318, 370
High-elves (1) Name of the (Lindar >) Vanyar (see *Fair Elves*). 163, 168, 176, 180. (2) The Elves of the West. 127, 267–8, 308, 349, 360, 370, 384–5; *High-elvish* (speech) 182. See *Tareldar*.
Hildi Men. 130. See *Aftercomers, Followers*.
Hildórien Land of the awakening of Men. 423
Hithaeglir 'Towers of Mist'. (82), 83, 89. See *Misty Mountains*.
Hither Lands Middle-earth. 77, 172, 174
Hithlum 297
Hobbit, The 89, 414. *Hobbit world, Hobbit-lore* 5–6
Holy Elves A name of the Vanyar. 164
Holy Mountain Taniquetil. 100, 112, 154, 289; *Holy Hill* 159
Holy Ones See *Ainur*.
Hope 245, 311, 320, 322–3, 327, 332, 338; *the Hope* 351, *the Great Hope* 351–2, 356; *the Old Hope* 321, 356. See *amdir, estel* in the Index of Elvish terms, p. 470
Horn of Oromë 7, 39, 70, 76, 202, and see *Rombaras, Valaróma*.
Host of Dân See *Dân*.
Houses of the Dead 145, 148
House, The (1) As image of the body. 362–3; *the House and the Indweller* 316–17, 352–3; *houseless* (of the Dead) 218–19, 221–5, 232, 248, 330–1, 339, 353, 361–5, 403 (of Melkor); *housed, unhoused, rehoused*, etc. 218, 221, 236, 243, 248–9, 269, 337, 339–40, 342, 349, 353, 361–5
House, The (2) Of Melkor in the *Tale of Adanel*. 347–8

INDEX 451

Huan The Hound of Valinor. 251, 408, 410–12
Húrin 76, 373; *Children of Húrin* 76; *Narn i Chîn Húrin* 373
Hyarantar Earlier name of Mount Hyarmentir. 98, 105, (190), 291, 386
Hyarantë The Southern Lamp. 7, 32, 38, 60. (Replaced *Hyaras*, replaced by *Ormal*.)
Hyarmentir Highest peak of the southern Pelóri. 105, 285, 291. (Replaced *Hyarantar*.)
Hyaras The Southern Lamp. 7, 17, 38. (Replaced *Ringil*, replaced by *Hyarantë*.)

Ice, The See *Grinding Ice, Helkaraxë*.
Idril Celebrindal Daughter of Turgon. (128), 359
Ilkorindi Elves 'not of Kôr', used in the sense of the 'lost Eldar'. 169–70
Illuin The Northern Lamp. 7, 22, 32, 38, 52–3, 58, 60, 67, 72, 84, 98, 153, 179. See *Helkar, Foros, Forontë*.
Ilmarë (1) Daughter of Manwë and Varda. 20, 34, 145, 150–1. (2) 'The handmaid of Varda'. 147, 152, 204
Ilmen Region of the firmament in which the Sun, Moon, and Stars have their courses. 29, 130–1, 133, 135, 137; *Chasm (of Ilmen)* 26, 132, 136–7
Ilu The World, as described in the *Ambarkanta*. 28–9, 39, 63, 373
Ilurambar The Walls of the World. 28, 63. See *Eärambar*.
Ilúvatar 7–16, 19, 21, 24–9, 31, 33–4, 36–40, 42–4, 48, 71, 77, 80, 92, 95, 144–7, 149, 151, 160–2, 187–8, 202, 204, 206, 244–5, 253, 259, 268, 271, 275, 282, 358–9, 362, 364–5, 375–6, 378–80, 383, 385, 405, 408; *Eru Ilúvatar* 48, 120, 286; *Servants of Ilúvatar*, the Valar, 67, 69. See *Children of Eru, Eru, Gift of Ilúvatar; All-father*.
Ilúvë 'Heaven'. 355
Imbar 'The Habitation'; the Earth as 'the principal part of Arda' (see 337). 337–9, 342, 358–9, 383, 385. See *Ambar*.
Immortal Elves A name of the Vanyar. 164
Indis (1) Wife of Finwë, mother of Fëanor. 87, 91, 102, 230. (2) Second wife of Finwë, mother of Fingolfin and Finarfin; called 'the Fair'. 101, 103, 127, 193, 205, 207–8, 230–1, 233, 237–9, 247–9, 252–3, 261–2, 264–5, 273, 276, 279–80, 300
Ingalaurë Mother-name of Finarfin (Arafinwë). 230, 265
Ingar The people of Ingwë. 230, 265
Inglor Earlier name of Finrod (2); references include also *Felagund*. 93, 104, 106, 112, 114, 120–1, 125, 128, 177, 181–2, 195–7
Ingoldo (1) Mother-name of Fingolfin (Nolofinwë). 230, 249, 253, 265, *Ingoldo-Finwë* 230. (2) Mother-name of Finrod Felagund. 265
Ingwë King of the Vanyar, and *High-king of all the Elves* (179).

81–2, 84–5, 87, 90, 133, 162, 168, 176, 179, 186, 206–7, 230, 237–8, 249, 258, 261–2, 265. See *Children of Ingwë, Ingwemindon.*
Ingwemindon 90, 180; *Tower of Ingwë* 84–5, 90, 176. See *Mindon Eldaliéva.*
Inias Beleriand The Annals of Beleriand. 200; *Inias Valannor (Balannor), Ínias Dor-Rodyn* 200
Inner Seas 20, 35, (145)
Ireland 5
Írimë Daughter of Finwë and Indis. 207, 238, 265. (Replaced by *Finvain.*)
Írith Daughter of Fingolfin, called 'the White'. 177, 182. See *Isfin, White Lady of the Noldor.*
Irmo True name of the Vala Lórien. 145, 147–8, 150–2, 236, 257; rendered 'Desire' 150. See *Olofantur, Lís.*
Iron Crown of Morgoth 110, (371)
Isfin Earlier name of Írith. 102, 106, 177, 182
Isil 'The Sheen', name of the Moon. 130–1, 135–6, 198. See *Ithil.*
Istari The Wizards. 397
Istarnië See *Nerdanel.*
Ithil The Moon. 42, 377, 382

Jewels, The The Silmarils. 107, 268, 377; *War of the Jewels* 395. See *gems, jewels, of the Noldor*
Jewel-wrights A name of the Noldor. 164

Kalakiryan The Pass of Light. 84, 86–7, 89, 97, 102, 133–4, 176, 178, 180, 183, 194, 197, 262, 283, 288(–9), 291, *Calaciryan* 183. Earlier forms *Kalakirya* 87, 89, 102, 180, 190, 192, *Kalakilya* 22, 89, 102, 197
Kalaquendi Elves of the Light. 163, 169. See *Light Elves.*
Karnil The planet Mars. 160, 166; *Carnil* 166. See pp. 434–5.
Kementári Name of Yavanna. 157, 202. (Replaced *Palúrien.*)
Kindred of Lúthien A name of the Sindar. 165
Kindreds *Three Kindreds of the Eldar* 162, 168, 184, 256; *Two Kindreds* (Elves and Men) 209, (247, 338), and see 308. See *Second Kindred.*
Kingless, The A name of the Nandor of Ossiriand. 164
Kinslaying, The At Alqualondë. 115, 117–18, 120, 196
Kôr 90, 180, 194, 197; *the Pass of Kôr* 194
King of the World Name taken by Morgoth. 110, 121, 124 (and see *Lord of the World* in entry *World*); *King of Middle-earth* 121, 126 (see *Aran Endór, Tarumbar*).
Korolairë The Mound of the Two Trees. 127, *Corolairë* 288; *Korlairë* 107, 122, 127. See *Ezellohar, Green Mound.*
Kuiviénen The Water(s) of Awakening. 51, 71–4, 76–7, 81–2, 88,

91, 111, (130), 160, 166–7, 170, 281, *Cuiviénen* 277, 417. On the site of Kuiviénen see 72, 76–7
Kulúrien A name of Laurelin. 155
Kúma 28. See *(The) Void*.
Kurufinwë See *Curufinwë*.

Laiquendi Green-elves. 169. See *Nandor*.
Lalaeth Sister of Túrin. 374
Lammoth Region north of the Firth of Drengist. 295–9; the Great Echo 296; Echoing Mountains of Lammoth 298
Lamps, The 7, 17–18, 25–7, 32–3, 38, 41, 43, 52–3, 60–1, 66, 78, 105, 153, 156, 158, 165, 375, 384. See *Forontë, Illuin; Hyarantë, Ormal*.
Land of the Blessed See *(The) Blessed Realm*.
Landroval Brother of Gwaihir the Windlord. 410, 412
Lasgalen 'Green of leaf', (Noldorin >) Sindarin name of Laurelin. 155
Last Battle, The See *Battles of the Gods*.
Later Ages 31, 68, 327
Later Tales 5. Last Tales 22
Laurelin 55–6, 62, 98, 130–2, 155, 157–8, 177, 197, 238, 261–2, 371–2, 386; 'founded on the laburnum' ('Golden-rain') 157
Lay of Leithian 3, 89, 142, 182, 423
Lëa the Young Wife of Tulkas. 66–7; *Lëa-vinya* 67
Lemberi 'The Lingerers'. (1) Name of the Eldar 'lost upon the long road'. 169. (2) A name of the Sindar. 164, 171
Lembi = *Lemberi* (1). 169
letters (devised by Rúmil, Fëanor) 92, 103, 184–5, 191, 256, 350. See *tengwar*.
Letters of J. R. R. Tolkien, The 3, 6, 26, 43, 124, 126, 141, 181, 267, 270, 290, 300, 328, 354, 356–8, 365–6, 372, 408, 411–13; other letters 5, 300
Lhammas, The 77, 89–90, 102, 104, 169–70; *Lammas* 415
Light (of various reference, not including those expressly to the Light of the Trees) 43, 73, 83, 85–6, 98, 100, 108–9, 111–12, 122, 132, 153–4, 158, 163, 178, 195, 198–9, 247, 250, 284, 288–9, 294–5, 308–9, 313, 321–2, 326, 346, 351, 354, 372, 379–80, 382, 389–90, 401; the *Primeval Light*, the Light of Varda, 377, 380–1, 385–6
Light Elves 169; Elves of the Light 163, 173. See *Kalaquendi*.
Lindar (1) Earlier name of the Vanyar. 20, 24–5, 34, 88, 90, 162, 168, 171, 174–6, 178–9, 181, 184. (2) A name of the Teleri. 349, 360
Lindon See *Mountains of Lindon*.
Lingerers (1) See *Lemberi*. (2) 'Faded' Elves in Middle-earth. 224
Lís True name of the Vala Lórien. 150. (Replaced by *Irmo*.)

Little World, Little Kingdom See *(The) World*.
Living, The (Elves) 206, 223–7, 232, 234–5, 248, 250, 255, 259–60, 264, 362
Lonely Isle 5, 86, 134, 174–6, 271. See *Tol Eressëa*.
Longbeards The Dwarves of Belegost. 93
Long Peace, The (305), 306–7, 327
Lord of All Eru. 241, 245; *Lord everlasting* 245
Lord of Night, of the Darkness, of the World See *Night*, etc.
Lord of the Rings, The (title) 3–4, 6, 8, 26, 39, 44, 47, 49, 59–60, 63, 65, 75–6, 79, 88–91, 103–4, 126, 141–2, 152, 158, 174, 181, 193, 203, 266, 271, 282, 290, 298, 303, 306, 341, 350, 356, 365, 369, 387, 406, 409–14, 424, 431
Lords of the Sea Ulmo and Ossë. 116
Lords of the West 81, 407; *the Lords* 285
Lórellin Lake in Lórien in Valinor. 148
Loremaster(s) 17, 31, 38, 50–1, 59, 62, 106, 184, 191, 251, 256, 258, 271, 290, 350, 363, 370–1, 380, 417; *masters of lore* 57, 72–3, 124, ~ *of the lore of speech* 92, 103
Lórien, Lorien The abode of the Vala Irmo, but used also as his name. 48–9, 56, 65–6, 84, 131–2, 136, 144–5, 148, 150–1, 172–3, 198, 201, 206, 236–8, 248–9, 252, 257–8, 261, 263–4, 407. Variant forms *Lorion* 65, 144–5, 148, 150, *Lorinen* 148; on *Lórien, Lorien* see 56, 148, 263. See *Irmo, Lís, Olofantur*.
Lorindol See *Hador*.
Losgar The place where Fëanor burned the ships of the Teleri. 120, 127, 196
Lost Folk A name of the Nandor of Ossiriand. 164. *Lost Elves of the people of Dân* 93
Lost Road, The 44, 136
Lost Tales See *Book of Lost Tales*.
Luinil Name of a bright star. 160. See pp. 434–5.
Lumbar Name of a bright star (the planet Saturn?). 160. See pp. 434–5.
Lúthien 3, (86), 106, 141, 267, 281, 336, 340, 359, 364, 404, 408; see *Kindred of Lúthien, Tinúviel*.

Maedros, Maedhros See *Maidros*.
Maglor Son of Fëanor. 112, 117, 125, 177, 182; *Maelor* 182
Mahtan Father of Fëanor's wife Nerdanel. 272, 277
Maiar (and singular *Maia*) 'The Beautiful' (49). 49, 52, 55–6, 59, 61, 65–6, 69, 72, 76, 79, 84, 86, 91, 99, 110, 112, 130, 133, 137–8, 147–50, 152, 165, 172, 198, 200, 203–4, 286–7, 340, 410–12, 416, 418, 424–6; original form *Mairi* 56, 150. See *Vanimor*.
Maidros Eldest son of Fëanor, called 'the Tall'. 112, 119–21, 126, 177; later forms *Maedros* 292–5, 298, *Maedhros* 177, 292
Malinalda Name of Laurelin. 155

INDEX

Mandar See *Mandos*.

Mandos The abode of the Vala Námo, but used also as his name. 21, 37, 48–9, 65, 71, 76, 80, 86, 88, 93, 96–7, 103–4, 107, 117–18, 122, 126–7, 129, 134–5, 144–6, 148, 150–1, 159, 161–2, 166, 168, 176, 180, 185–7, 189–90, 202–8, 216, 219, 222–6, 228, 232–8, 241–3, 246–9, 252–5, 258–61, 263–9, 275, 278–81, 291, 293, 325, 339–41, 350, 359, 363–5, 392–3, 403, 411; *Mandar* 101, 205

    Called *Námo Mandos* 225, 246, 254, 259, 403; *Doomsman of the Valar* 145, *the Mouth of Manwë* 255, *the Unmoved*, 340, *the Wise* 176, 'the strongest of all in Arda' 242. Prophecies of Mandos 76, 204, 246–7, 359; Doom of Mandos in Araman, see *Noldor*; etymology of the name 350. See *Námo, Núr, Nurufantur, Vê, Vefántur; Summons of Mandos*.

Mannish (of the beliefs and traditions of Men) 370, 373, and see 5, 22.

Manwë 7, 13–15, 19–21, 24–6, 28–9, 32, 34, 36, 40–4, 48–9, 51–4, 59–60, 65–9, 71, 74–5, 79–81, 83, 85, 87, 89, 93–4, 97, 99–101, 104–5, 107–8, 112–14, 117, 125, 128–30, 135, 137–8, 144–7, 149–52, 154, 159, 161, 163, 167, 176, 179–80, 185–6, 188, 197, 201–2, 204–6, 211, 219, 223, 225–6, 230, 235–7, 239, 241, 244, 246–7, 249, 253–5, 257–60, 264, 270, 273, 275–90 *passim*, 293–4, 300, 313, 321, 326–7, 337, 339, 349, 357–8, 361–5, 372, 374, 376–82, 390–3, 397, 399–404, 406, 410, 429

    Called *King of the World* 20, *of the Valar* 65, (147); *Lord of the Gods* 144; *(High-)King, Lord, of Arda* 114, 145, 279, 287, 313, *the King* 242, 244, *Lord of Aman* 247. *The Great Wind of Manwë* 377; *the Mouth of Manwë* (Mandos) 255. See *Elder King, Súlimo*.

Marach Leader of the third host of Men to enter Beleriand. *The people of Marach* 305–6, 309, 344, 353, 359–60

Marrer, The Melkor. 240–2, 245, 248–9, 252, 402

Marring of Arda, The 203–4, 209, 211, 219, 223, 239–41, 244–5, 252, 259–60, 270–1, 293, 304, 318, 321, 331, 351, 428–9

    Arda Marred 203–4, 219, 225, 239–41, 244–7, 254–5, 258, 269–70, 309, 312, 318, 327, 396, 399, 405, 408, 424, 428; *Arda Hasteina* 254, 408, *Arda Sahta* 405

    Arda Unmarred 239–40, 245–6, 251, 258, 260, 287, 318, 327, 351, 366, 405, 424; *Arda Alahasta* 254

    Arda Healed 245, 251, 318, 327, 351, 405; *Arda Vincarna* 408, *Arda Envinyanta* 405, 408; *Arda Remade* 319–20, 333, 351–2; *Arda Complete* 251, (318–19), 327; *New Arda* 251–2

    Other references to 'marring': 53, 217–18, 225, 232, 241, 243, 245, 247, 259, 269, 315, 333–4, 342–3, 351, 381, 390, 396; *the Marring of Men* 328 (see *(The) Fall*).

Melekō   See *Melko*.
Melian   72, 77, 84–6, 89, 93, 147, 152, 172–3, 203, 281, 340, 410. See *Wards of Melian*, and on Melian's relation to Yavanna see 147, 152, 172.
Melko   Earlier, or alternative, form for *Melkor* (see 350). 22–4, 26–7, 63, 76, 104, 156, 194, 198, 291, 350, 360, 407; *Melekō* 355
Melkor   7, 9–27, 29, 32–8, 40–3, 48–9, 51–4, 58–67, 69–75, 78–80, 82–3, 87–90, 93–101, 104–8, 110–11, 114, 121, 123–4, 129–31, 133, 138, 144–7, 149–53, 156, 158–62, 165, 167–8, 174, 179, 184–94, 197, 201–4, 209, 240–1, 243, 247–8, 253–4, 256, 258–9, 269, 271, 273–95 *passim*, 304–5, 309–10, 312, 318, 321–2, 326–7, 330–1, 333–8, 340, 342, 344–5, 349–52, 354, 356–8, 360, 362–4, 374–400, 403–24 *passim*, 428–30; unnamed, in the *Tale of Adanel*, 346–8, 360; spelt *Melcor* 362; *Melkórë* 350.

Etymology of the name 350; called *the Calumniator* 401, *the Diabolus* 412; *Melkorism* 334. See *(The) Marrer, Morgoth*.

The power of Melkor 9–10, 12, 48, 59, 65, 97, 121, 144–6, 150, 190, 254–5, 258, 269, 273, 280, 304, 312, 322, 330, 334, 352, 357, 375, 390, 392–4; his power 'dispersed' 110, 133, 137, 259, 296, 334, 390–5, 400, 403–4, 411, 422; his inability to make living things 74, 78, 110, 123–4, 165, 409, 413–14, 417; his bodily form 187, 275, 284, 292, 346, 377, 395–6, 399, 403
Melkorohíni   'Children of Melkor'. 416, and see 406; *Melkorséni* 423
Melthinorn   'Tree of gold', (Noldorin >) Sindarin name of Laurelin. 155
Men   (also *Man, Mankind*) 5, 12, 20–6, 28, 36–7, 39, 42–4, 66, 71, 76, 95, 108, 111–12, 130, 133, 135–8, 144–5, 147–8, 154, 157–8, 160–1, 163, 173, 176, 187–8, 199, 204, 208–10, 212, 215, 218–19, 224–5, 232, 241, 245, 250–1, 266–7, 270, 275–6, 282, 294, 304–5, 307–44 *passim*, 349–58, 364–5, 370, 373–5, 378, 385, 389, 395–7, 401–31 *passim*

The awakening or coming of Men 95, 130, 135, 138, 187, 275, 327, 378 ('in an Isle amid the floods'), 385, 409, 417, 420, 423, 431; the mortality and death of Men 21, 37, 43, 219, 250, 267, 304, 307–17, 326, 330–3, 339–41, 354–6, 365–6, 424–6, 429–30. See *Dominion of Men*.
Menegroth   'The Thousand Caves' in Doriath. 93, 104, 173
Menelmakar   'Swordsman of the Sky'. 71, 76, 160, 166; *Menelmacar* 76. See *Menelvagor, Orion*.
Meneltarma   154, 157; *the mountain of Númenor* 154. See *Heofonsýl*.
Menelvagor   Sindarin form for *Menelmakar*. 76
Men-orcs   419

Merton College 5, 350, 352, 385, 390, 409
Middle-earth (also *the Middle-earth*) 12, 17–20, 25–7, 32–3, 35, 38, 50, 53–4, 65, 70–86 *passim*, 90–1, 95, 102–3, 108, 111–13, 115, 118–21, 123, 126, 129–30, 132–3, 138, 146–7, 149, 153, 156, 158–65, 168, 173, 175, 177, 179, 182–3, 185, 188, 196, 201–3, 208, 210, 214, 219, 221, 223, 232, 241, 248, 250, 254, 257–8, 265, 269, 271, 276, 281–3, 290–1, 295, 307–10, 321, 339–41, 349, 359, 361–5, 370, 372–3, 377, 382, 384–5, 390, 397, 400, 402, 404, 406–7, 416–17, 419–20, 423–6, 430–1

Middle-earth as *Morgoth's Ring* 372, 377. See *Ambar*; *Endar*, *Endor*; *Hither Lands*, *Outer Lands*.
Mighty, The   The Valar. 273, 277
Minas Anor   44
Minas Morgul   350
Mindon Eldaliéva   (including references to *the Mindon*) 85, 90, 110, 115, 118, 176, 180, 196, 278. See *Ingwemindon*.
Minyon   'First-begotten', Fëanor. 87
Míriel   First wife of Finwë, mother of Fëanor. 92, 101, 103, 127, 185, 191–3, 205–9, 217, 221, 231, 233, 236, 238–44, 246–50, 253–71 *passim*, 276, 293, 300, 339, 361–3. Called *Byrde* (Old English) 92, 103, 185, 192, 205, 257; *Serendë* 185, 192, 205, *Serindë* 236, 254, 257. See *Fíriel*; *Statute of Finwë and Míriel*.
Mirkwood   (82), 89
Mirröanwi   Incarnate beings, Children of Eru. 315–16, 326, 329, 349–50. Earlier forms *Mirruyaina(r)* 326, 352, *Mirroyainar* 326
Misty Mountains   89, 103; *Towers of Mist*, reared by Melkor, 83, (87), 89. See *Hithaeglir*.
Moon, The   (41), 42–4, 50–1, 57–8, 60, 94, 120, 130–2, 134–8, 163–4, 169, 196, 198, 271, 346, 370–7, 382–5, 390; *island of the Moon* 130–1, *Flower of Silver* 131; *the Elder Moon* (the White Tree) 198, 372. See *Isil*, *Ithil*, *Rána*.
Mordor   350
Morgoth   48, 76, 78, 108–12, 114–15, 119–25, 130–1, 133–5, 137, 146, 156, 186, 192–5, 198–9, 223–4, 240, 268, 294–8, 341, 350, 371–3, 385, 394–7, 399–409, 411, 416–23; *the Morgoth* 310, 312–13, 322, 390–1, 393; *Moringotto* 194, 294, *Moriñgotho* 294; Melkor so first named by Fëanor 108, 186, 194, 294. See *(The) Black Foe*, *(The) Enemy*, *King of the World*.
Moriquendi   163, 169–70, 173. See *Dark-elves*.
Mormacil   'Blacksword', name of Túrin in Nargothrond. 216. (On the different forms of the name see the Index to Vol.IV, *Mormakil*.)
Morwë   Leader of a kindred of the Avari. 81, 88, 168
Mountain of Manwë   Taniquetil. 178
Mountains of Aman   The Pelóri. 54, 70, 154, 174, 190; *Mountains of Defence* 132; *Mountains of the Gods*, see *Gods*; *Mountains of*

Valinor 7, 18, 33, 174. For references to *the Mountains* see *Pelóri*.
Mountains of Lindon   93. See *Blue Mountains*.
Mountains of Shadow   297. See *Eryd Wethrin*.
Mountains of the East   72, 77. See *Orokarni*.
Mouth of Manwë, The   Mandos. 255, and see 339.
Music of the Ainur   (not as title; including references to *the Music*) 9–12, 15, 21–4, 27, 31, 36, (40), 68, 77, 144, (160), 166, 275, 282, 318–19, 327, 336, 338, 351–2, 358, 363, 388–9, 395, 399, 401–2, 405, 408–9, 425; *Music of Eru* (99), 327, (351); *Great Music* 8–9, 14, 144, 336; *Song of the Ainur* 144, 149, *the Song* 379, *the Great Song* 378–9; *Second Music of the Ainur* 21, 37, 43. See *Ainulindalë, Great Theme, Themes*.

Nahar   Orome's horse. (35), 70, 72–3, 76, 79, 82, 87, 101, 162, 203, 281, 289
Naira   The Sun. 198
Nameless, The   Andreth's reference to Melkor. 312, 320–1
Naming of the Eldar   214–17, 229–30, 263
Námo   'The Judge', true name of Mandos; often *Námo Mandos*. 145, 148–51, 202–3, 207, 219, 225–6, 246, 254–5, 259, 403. See *Nurufantur, Núr*.
Nandor   The people of Dân (Nano), who abandoned the Great March; the Green-elves of Ossiriand. 83, 89, 102, 164, 169–71; *Nandar* 169. See *Danas, Green-elves*.
Nan Dungortheb   'Valley of Dreadful Death' (297). 127, 297, 299; earlier *Nan Dungorthin* 109, 123, 127, 299, original form *Nan Dumgorthin* 299
Nan Elmoth   83–4, 89, 91, 172–3
Nano   Leader of the Nandor (Dân). 83, 89, 169
Nargothrond   104, 328, 336, 357–8
Narsilion   The Song of the Sun and Moon. 130, 372
Naugrim   The Dwarves. 93, 102–3, 106; earlier *Nauglath* 102–3, 106. See *Nornwaith*. [The entry *Naugrim* was omitted from the Index to Vol.V: see p. 103.]
Neave, Jane   360
Necromancers   224
Nénar   Name of a bright star. 160. See pp. 434–6.
Nerdanel   Wife of Fëanor, called 'the Wise' (274). 253, 272–4, 277, 279; rejected name *Istarnië* 273
Nessa   Sister of Oromë and wife of Tulkas, called 'the Young' (65). 49, 53, 60–1, 65–6, 69, 146, 149, 150–1, 201; said to be a Maia 65. When replaced by Lëa as wife of Tulkas (see *Lëa the Young*) called the *Ever-maid*, 66
New Arda   See *(The) Marring of Arda*.

Nienna (also *Nienna*) 15, 49, 55, 62, 65–6, 68–9, 93, 104, 107, 129, 135–6, 146–7, 149, 151, 154, 186, 197–8, 201–4, 241–3, 245, 247–9, 253, 264, 273, 293, 295, 326–7, 389; called *queen of Shadow* 65

Nienor Sister of Túrin. 374

Night (with reference to Melkor) 312, 376–7, 382; *Night of the Void* (28), 53, 58, *Outer Night* 383; *Lord, Realm, of Night* 219. See *Door (of Night), Walls of (the) Night.*

Nimloth 'Pale blossom', a name of Telperion, and also of the White Tree of Númenor. 155, (176), 180

Niniel Name given to Nienor. 374

Ninquelótë A name of Telperion. 155

Noldolantë 'The Fall of the Noldor', Maglor's lament. 117, 121, 125

Noldor (and singular *Noldo*) 17, 19–20, 22, 24–5, 31, 34, 38, 41, 65, 82–97 *passim*, 99, 101–20, 122, 125–6, 128–30, 134, 137–8, 146, 155, 157, 159, 163–5, 168–9, 172, 174–89 *passim*, 192–6, 207–8, 211, 214–17, 225, 229–31, 236–8, 240–1, 249–50, 254, 256–7, 261–5, 268, 272–82, 287, 289, 305, 312, 340, 350, 375, 402, 407, 419–20; Old English *Noldelfe, Noldielfe* 168 (and see *Witan*).

The Doom of the Noldor (Doom of Mandos) 108, 115, 117, 120, 122, 125, 266–7, 295; *The Prophecy of the North* 117, 125. On the spelling *Ñoldor* see 101, 350; etymology 350. See *Gnomes, White Lady of the Noldor.*

Noldorin (of language) 7, 125, 136, 198 (see *Gnomish*); with other reference 121, 125, 182, 195–6

Nolofinwë Fingolfin. 230, 238–9, 252, 265

Nornwaith The Dwarves. 93, 106. See *Naugrim.*

North, The 7, 17–18, 25–7, 32–3, 38, 53, 67, 71, 74–5, 82, 88, 98, 108–10, 115, 118, 120, 153, 156, 159–61, 174, 177, 191, 197, 283–4, 291, 293, 295, 297, 307, 323, 376–8, 381–2, 388, 412; *the Northlands* 109, ~ *of Endar* 120, *the Northern Lands* 131, 163–4, *the Northern World* 296; *the North-west* (of Middle-earth) 400. *The Prophecy of the North*, see *Noldor.*

Notion Club Papers, The 4, 7, 44, 135–6, 157

Númenor 65, 154–5, 176, 180, 370, 373–4; the destruction of Númenor 339, 341, 344, 356, 397. See *Meneltarma, Nimloth.*

Númenórean(s) 342, 344, 360, 373–4, 387, 389, 398, 401–2, 404, 427. Númenórean tradition in *The Silmarillion* 65, 342, 344, 360, 370, 373–4, 389, 401

Núr True name of Mandos. 150. (Replaced by *Námo*.)

Nur-menel The 'lesser firmament' of the Dome of Varda. 388

Nurtalë Valinóreva The Hiding of Valinor. 133, 137

Nurufantur Mandos. 145, 150.

Nurwë Leader of a kindred of the Avari. 81, 88, 168

Oiolossë 'Everlasting Whiteness' (154), Taniquetil. 67, 154, 238, 262, 313. See *Everwhite*.
Oiomúrë Region of mists near the Helkaraxë. 295
Old English (including names) 124, 130, 136, 143, 154, 157, 163, 168, 185, 192, 198, 205, 257, 422. See *Anglo-Saxon*.
Old Norse 406
Olofantur Lórien. 145, 150, 172–3
Olog-hai The great Trolls of the Third Age. 414
Olórin Gandalf. 147, 152, 203
Olwë 81–6, 88–9, 93, 101, 104, 115–16, 118, 125–6, 163–4, 169–70, 173, 177–9, 182–3, 194, 196, 206, 258; *People of Olwë*, a name of the Teleri, 164. See *Elwë* (1), *Solwë*.
One, The Eru. 144, 224, 311, 313–14, 320–1, 329–30, 335, 351, 353, 358, 360, 379–80; *the One God* 356, *the One Great* (of Melkor) 347
Onótimo See *Quennar (i) Onótimo*.
Orc-men 419. See *Men-orcs*.
Orcs 78, 80, 106, 109, 123–4, 127–8, 159, 165, 194–5, 251, 391, 396, 406, 408–23; *Great Orcs* 418; *Orks* 165, 414, 421–2; *Orkor* 73–4, 78, 109, 120, 194–5, 409; *Orkish* 418, 424; *orch*, *yrch* 195. Origin of the name 124, 422, and its spelling 414, 422–3; etymology 413. See *Glamhoth*.
Orion 76, 166, 388. See *Menelmakar*, *Menelvagor*.
Orkor, *Orks* See *Orcs*.
Ormal The Southern Lamp. 7, 22, 32, 38, 52–3, 60, 67, 98, 153. See *Ringil*, *Hyaras*, *Hyarantë*.
Orodreth Son of Finarfin. 112, 121, 125, 128, 177, 182, 195
Orokarni The Red Mountains, the Mountains of the East. 72, 77
Oromë 7, 19, 25, 33, 35, 39, 48–9, 53, 59, 65, 69–83 *passim*, 87–9, 97–8, 101, 105, 110, 123–4, 131, 136, 144, 146, (149), 151, 159–60, 162, 166–7, 170, 174, 177, 179, 190, 192, 201–4, 276, 281, 283–5, 289, 377–8, 382, 384, 416–17, 425. Called *the Hunter* 73, *the (Great) Rider* 73, 78. See *Aldaron*, *Araw*, *Tauron*; *Horn of Oromë*.
Oromian (languages) 77
Ossë 20, 35, 48–9, 69, 84–6, 88, 90–1, 116, 144–5, 151, 175, 178, 183, 199, 201–2, 204, 286. *Friends of Ossë*, a name of the Sindar, 164, 171
Ossiriand 93, 104, 164
Outer Darkness See *Dark*. *Outer Night*, see *Night*.
Outer Lands (1) Middle-earth. 19, 35, 54, 71, 79, 85; *Outer World* 295. (2) *Outer Land of Aman* 174
Outer Sea 28, 33, 54, 58, 62–3, 132, 135–7, 154, 156–7, 161, 179, *Outer Seas* 145, 204, *Outer Ocean* 20, 24–5, 29, 34. See *Ekkaia*, *Vaiya*.

INDEX

Palantíri (185), 192, 396
Palúrien 'Lady of the Wide Earth' (145). 32, 34, 145–6, 149, 151, 154, 157, 202, 393. (Replaced by *Kementári*.)
Pass of Light See *Kalakiryan*.
Pelóri 7, 18, 23, 33, 54–5, 67, 84, 97–8, 105, 133, 154, 175, 284–5, 291, 295, 312, 394, 401, 405; *Pelóri (Pelóre) Valion* 18, 23, 33; *the Mountains* 33, 54, 98–100, 108, 111, 117, 122, 137, 146, 149, 154, 158, 190, 284–5, 287, 289, 295. See *Mountains of Aman*.
Pengoloð (also *Pengoloth, Pengolodh*) 'The Sage' (of Gondolin). 7–8, 17, 22, 25–7, 30–1, 35, 38, 41, 48, 51, 65, 68, 93, 102, 110, 123, 143, 160, 165, 188, 192, 202, 281, 326–7, 415; *Pengolod* 8, 17, 22, 31, 41, 104, 143, 155, 160, 166, 281
Pennas Silevril = *Quenta Silmarillion*. 200
People of Elwë See *Elwë* (2). *People of Olwë*, see *Olwë*.
People of the Stars See *Eldar*.
Pereldar 'Half-eldar'. 169
Plough, The The constellation of the Great Bear. 388
Poldórëa 'The Valiant', Tulkas. 146, 149. (Replaced by *Astaldo*.)
Powers, The 21, 37, 144, 162, 273, 326, 350, 394, 421; *the Powers of Arda* 152, 270, *of Eä* 48, 62, *of the World* 14, 16, 28, 36
Prophecy of the North See *Noldor*; *Prophecies of Mandos*, see *Mandos*.

Quendi 71–5, 77–8, 81, 86–7, 91, 109–10, 123–4, 130, 160–3, 166–8, 179, 187, 195, 206, 209, 259–60, 268, 275–7, 281, 309–12, 314–15, 322–3, 326, 364, 387, 390, 408, 416–18, 424, 426–7; *Qendi* 77
Quendian (languages) 77
Quendi and Eldar (title of work also called *Essekenta Eldarinwa*) 415
Quennar (i) Onotimo Eldarin loremaster. 48–50, 56–7; *Quennar* 51, 57, *Onotimo* 57
Quenya 39, 76, 80, 89, 126, 136, 217, 231, 284, 349–50, 359, 387–9, 415, 431 See *Avallonian, Eressëan*.

Radagast 397
Ragnarök 399, 406
Ramer, Michael Member of the Notion Club. 135
Rána (also *Rana*) 'The Wayward', the Moon. 130, 136, 198, 376–7
Rebirth of the Elves, the Reborn See *Elves*.
Red Mountains 77. See *Orokarni*.
Return of the King, The (title) 4, 6, 135, 359, 412
Ringil The Southern Lamp. 7, 22. See *Hyaras, Hyarantë, Ormal*.
Ring of Doom The council-place of the Valar. 55, 61, 80, 88, 96, 106, 110, 114, 129, 154, 189, 278, 288, 291–2, 294, 386

Rings of Power, The (title) 5–6
Rings, The 395, 400; *the Ring* 400; *Morgoth's Ring*, Middle-earth, 400, 406
Rivendell 90
Rombaras The horn of Oromë. 7, 35, 39, 151, 202. (Replaced by *Valaróma*.)
Round World 4–6, 22, 39; *Round Earth* 383
Rulers of Arda, The 49, 99, 224, 232, 248, 271; *the Rulers* 147
Rúmil 8, 17, 22, 25, 30–1, 48, 64–5, 92, 103, 145, 150, 174, 184–5, 191, 256, 373
Runes (of Daeron) 106

Saelind 'Wise-heart', Andreth. 305, 360; earlier form *Saelon* 351–2, 360
Saeros Elf of Doriath, enemy of Túrin. 374
Salmar Companion of Ulmo. 20, 35
Sam Gamgee 412
Saruman 396–7, 418
Satan 270
Sauron 52, 60, 66, 124, 147, 152, 156, 223–4, 232, 341, 344, 391, 394–8, 400, 404, 406–14, 419–21, 423; see especially 394–8
Sea, The (5), 19, 54, 84–6, 89, 98–9, 101, 111, 113, 115–16, 119, 125, 128, 133–4, 156, 163–4, 170, 174–6, 178–9, (191), 272, 277, 282, 284, 286–7, 289, 291, 293, 296, 309–10, (349), 366. See *Great Sea, Shadowy Seas, Sundering Seas, Western Sea*.
Sea-elves The Teleri. 163; *Elves of the Sea* 164
Second Age 341, 394, 419, 423
Second Children See *Children of Eru*.
Second Kindred Men. 355
Second Theme See *Themes*.
Secret Fire, The 9, 144, 148; *the Fire* 9. See *(The) Flame Imperishable*.
Seekers, The Western Men. 320
Serendë, Serindë 'Broideress'. See *Míriel*.
Seven Great Ones, The See *(The) Great Ones*.
Seven Rivers (of Ossiriand) 93, 104; *Elves of the Seven Rivers*, see *Elves*.
Shadow, The (of Melkor, but used in different senses) 21, 37, 53, 65, 97, 99–100, 110, 167, 210–11, 217, (218), 219, 222–4, 228, 232, 240–1, 247, 254, 269, 283, 289, 305, 307–8, 310, 312, 315, 322–3, 326, 348, 374, 379, 401–2, 404, 412, 422, 428, and see 399; the Shadow upon Men 305, 316, 331
Shadowy Seas 110, 134, 176
Ship-wrights, The A name of the Teleri. 164
Sickle of the Gods 71, 76, 160, 388. See *Valakirka*.
Siege of Angband See *Angband*.

Silivros 'Sparkling rain', a name of Telperion. 155

Silmarillion, The (general references) 5–6, 43, 63, 75, 88, 141–4, 149, 152, 156–7, 181, 192, 197, 200, 205, 283, 290–1, 300, 303, 329, 337, 342, 349, 359, 369–71, 373, 394, 406–7, 414, 422; (references to the published work) 40, 64, 123, 126, 136, 151, 157, 165, 170–1, 179, 182, 200–4, 267, 271, 283, 306, 357, 360, 387, 408

Silmaril(s) 19, 48, 94–7, 100, 104, 107–10, 112, 122, 125, 132, 137, 144, 182, 187–93, 198–200, (268), 274–6, 280, 282, 287, 291, 293–7, 319, 340, 371–2, 390, 402; *Silmarilli* 94. See *(The) Jewels.*

Silpion The former common name of the White Tree of Valinor, later *Telperion.* 54, 90, 155, 157, 193, 198

Silvan (language) 182

Silvern Elves A name of the Sindar. 164

Sindar 86, 91, 93, 103, 146, 149, 154–5, 164, 170–1, 202, 349; language of the Sindar 86, 144, 201–2; first occurrence of the name 170. See *Grey-elves.*

Sindarin 76, 91, 126, 155, 165, 180, 182, 217, 349–50, 373, 387–8

Sindicollo See *Singollo.*

Sindo 'The Grey', Thingol. 88, 169. See *Elwë* (2).

Singers of the Shore A name of the Teleri. 164

Singers Unseen A name of the Nandor of Ossiriand. 164

Singollo 'Greymantle'. 82, 84, 86, 88, 91, 104, 163, 169–70, 172–3; *Sindicollo* 217, 385. See *Elwë* (2), *Greymantle.*

Sirion, River 174; *Vale of Sirion* 83

Skilled of Hand, The A name of the Noldor. 164

Solar System, The 337, (338, 342), 349, 358, 374–5, 383–5, 403

Soloneldi A name of the Teleri of Valinor. 163. (Replaced by *Falmari.*)

Solwë Name transitional between *Elwë* (1) and *Olwë.* 169

Sons of Fëanor 96, 112–14, 119–21, 123, 126, 128, 177, 179, 181–2, 188–9, 210, 272, 276–7, 279, 287, 292–3, 311

Sons of the Valar See *Children of the Valar.*

Sorontar King of Eagles. 410. See *Thorondor.*

Sorontúmë Name of a constellation. 160

South, The 7, 17, 32, 93, 97–8, 104–5, 109, 123, 284, 299, 377

Spear-elves A name of the Vanyar. 164

Spring of Arda (18), 27, (32), 53–4, 67, 70, 75, 384

Staff-elves A name of the Nandor. 171. (Replaced *Axe-elves* (1).)

Star-folk See Eldar.

Star-kindler Varda. 388. See *Tintallë.*

Star-making 20, 34, 38–9, 54, 61, 71, 156, 159–60, 166, 374, 376, 388

Stars 12–13, 16, 20, 28–9, 34, 38, 54, 61, 70–3, 76–7, 79, (81), 82–3, 86, 95, 106, 111, 130–3, 135–6, 145, 148, 153, 156,

159–61, (162), 166, 172, 175–6, 178, 346–7, (370), 372, 374–8, 382–4, 386–9; stars in the Dome of Varda *(tinwi)* 286, 292–3, 386–8; shooting stars 136; *the significant Star* 385. See *Great Stars; Eldar.*
Statute of Finwë and Míriel (including references to *the Statute*) 208–9, 233, 236, 239, 243, 246–8, 251–2, 254–5, 258, 263–5, 270; *Doom of ~* 226; *Namna Finwë Míriello* 258
Stone-trolls   412. See *Trolls.*
Straight Road, The   5
Strangers   An Elvish name for Men. 21, 37
Strider   216. See *Telcontar.*
Súlimo   Name of Manwë. 19, 114, 148; *Manwë of the Winds* 377
Summons of Mandos   219, 223–4, 232, 236, 339, 364–5
Sun, The   (not including references to *Sun Years, Years of the Sun*) 3, 10, 12, 30, 40, 42–4, 50–1, 58–60, 89, 94, 127, 129–30, 132, 134–7, 149, 163, 173, 196, 198–9, 299–300, 327, 346–7, 357, 370–86 *passim,* 389–90, 423, 426, 430; *the Fruit of Noon* 371; *the Sunship* 371; *the Elder Sun* (the Golden Tree) 198, 372; *the Unmarred Sun* 390. See *Anar* (2), *Âs, Naira, Úr, Úrin, Vása;* and *Reckoning of Time* in entry *Time.*
Sundering Seas   115
Swanhaven   87. See *Alqualondë, Haven of the Swans.*
Swanherds   A name of the Teleri. 164
Swift, The   A name of the Teleri. 164
Sword-elves   A name of the Noldor. 164

Tale, The; Tale of Arda   See *(The) Great Tale.*
Tale of Years, The   (title) 49, 56–7
Taniquetil   19, 24–5, 29, 54, 67, 71–2, 74, 77, 98–100, 105, 108, 115, 135, 154, 159, 161, 167, 179, 190, 285–7, 289, 294, 384; *the Mountain* 262, 287. See *Holy Mountain, Mountain of Manwë, Oiolossë.*
Tareldar   High-elves 349, 360
Tar-menel   The firmament. 388. See *Nur-menel.*
Tarumbar   'Lord of the Earth' (Morgoth). 121
Tauron   'Lord of the Forests', name of Oromë. 146, 149, 202; earlier form *Tauros* 111, 124, 146, 151. See *Aldaron.*
Telcontar   'Strider'. 216
Teleri   20, 24–5, 35, 82–91, 93, 99–100, 115–16, 120, 125, 128, 133, 163–4, 169, 173–5, 177–9, 183, 199, 217, 274, 283, 287, 289, 340, 349, 360
Telerin   (not of language) 169–70
Telperion   50, 55–6, 59, 62, 71, 85, 90, 98, 130–1, (154), 155, 157, 159, 176, 180, 193, 197–8, 261, 372, 386; *the White Tree* 176. See *Silpion.*
Telumendil   Name of a constellation. 160

tengwar 30, 103, (350). See *letters*.
Thangorodrim 67, 109, 138, 297–8, 402, 404, 419; the Mountains of Oppression 298
Themes (of the Music of the Ainur) The Three Themes 23, 408; the Second Theme (10), 14, 40, 275, 282, 358; the Third Theme 10–11, 22, 282, 358; Themes of the Children 336, 342, 358; a new theme 379; two Themes, those of Eru and Melkor, 406, 408. See especially 358, and *Great Theme*.
Thingol 86, 88–91, 93, 104, 106, 164, 168, 170–1, 173–4, 217, 228, 340. For *Elu Thingol* see *Elwë* (2).
Third Age 5, 341, 414, 418–19, 423
Third Battle See *Battles of the Gods*.
Third Host The Teleri. 168, 349
Third Theme See *Themes*.
Thompson, Francis 157–8
Thorondor King of Eagles. 412. See *Sorontar*.
Thousand Caves 173. See *Menegroth*.
Three Kindreds See *Kindreds*.
Tilion Steersman of the Moon. 130–4, 136–7, 198, 376–7, 383–5; called a Vala 376, 384; Old English name *Hyrned* 130, 136, 198
Time 14, 21, 28, 37, 40, 50–1, 56, 58, 99, 144, 219, 242, 245, 251–2, 292, 318, 326–7, 331, 333–5, 366, 376, 382, 403–5, 408, 424–6, 430, and see *Deeps of Time*; circles of time 40. Reckoning of Time 49–51, 56–62, 72, 82, 131–2, 155, 183, 425–6, 430–1
Timeless Halls 14, 42; *Timeless Void* 407
Timon of Athens 157–8
Tindbrenting Old English name of Taniquetil. 157
Tintallë 'The Kindler', Varda. 159, 166, 384, 388–9
Tinúviel 288; *Narn e·Dinúviel* 373. See *Lúthien*.
Tinwë-mallë 'Star-street', the path of the stars, Ilmen. 29
Tinwerína 'Crowned with stars', Taniquetil. 387. See *Elerrína*.
Tinwerontar 'Queen of Stars', Varda. 389
Tirion 8, 84–5, 87, 90, 92, 96, 103, 106, 110, 113–15, 125, 137, 176, 178, 180, 185, 191, 193–4, 205, 256, 282, 290; the Court of the King 110–11; called the Hallowed 84, 90, the Watchful City 84, 176. See *Túna*.
Tol Eressëa and *Eressëa* 5, 8, 22, 30, 74, 84–5, 91, 109, 123–4, 134, 155, 175–6, 178–9, 183, 341, 365, 408; the White Tree of Eressëa, see *Celeborn* (1). See *Lonely Isle*.
Tol-in-Gaurhoth 'Isle of Werewolves'. 408
Towers of Mist See *Misty Mountains*.
Trees, The See *(The) Two Trees*.
Trolls 251, 409, 412, 414; Stone-trolls 412. See *Olog-hai*.
Tulkas 17, 25, 27, 31, 38, 41, 48–9, 52–4, 59–60, 62–3, 65–7, 69, 71, 75–6, 94, 96–7, 101, 107, 112, 144, 146, 151, 153, 159, 161,

166, 168, 186, 189–90, 192, 202, 204, 273, 279–80, 283, 289, 364, 376, 380–1, 392–3, *Tulcas* 382. Latecomer to Arda 17, 27, 41, 52, and cf. 380; suggested origin as Vala of the Sun 376 (see *Auron*).

Tûn Old name of Tirion. 8, 193–4

Túna The hill on which Tirion was built, but also often used of the city itself (see 8, 90, 193, 282), and not in all cases distinguishable. 8, 30, 84, 90, 92, 96–7, 99, 110, 114–15, 118, 133, 135, 137, 151, 155, 157, 175–6, 178–80, 183–5, 188–90, 193–4, 196–7, 238, 252, 256, 261–2, 276–7, 279–80, 282–3, 287, 291; the White Tree of Túna (Tirion), see *Galathilion* (2).

Tuor 359, 407; *the Tale of Tuor* 3, 142, 298

Turgon 106, 112, 118, 121, 125, 128, 155, 177, 182, 188, 196; Turgon's wife (died in the Helkaraxë) 128

Túrin (Turambar) 71, 76, 166, 373–4; his black sword 76 (see *Mormacil*).

Two Kindreds See *Kindreds*.

Two Towers, The (title) 192

Two Trees, The (including references to *the Trees*) 22, 43, 47–8, 50–1, 55–62, 70, 77–8, 81, 85–6, 90, 95, 97, 99–100, 104–5, 107–8, 120, 122, 125, 129–32, 135, 137, 152, 154–5, 157, 162–3, 173, 175–6, 178, 180, 186–7, 190, 197–8, 201, 238, 247, 261, 268, 274, 283, 287–8, 291–3, 298, 300, 326, 371–2, 375, 377, 385–6, 389–90, 429–30; *the Elder Sun and Moon* 198, 372

Udûn Utumno. 382

Uinen 'Lady of the sea(s)'. 20, 35, 49, 69, 84, 116, 145, 151, 201–2, 204, 286

Ulmo 12–15, 20, 24–6, 29, 34–5, 40, 48–9, 65, 84–6, 88–91, 93, 115, 120, 132, 137–8, 144–5, 147, 151, 161, 168, 174–5, 178–9, 183, 186, 199, 201, 204, 240–2, 245, 253, 273, 286, 361, 393, 401, 406–7

Ulumúri The horns of Ulmo. 202. (Replaced *Falarombar*.)

Úmaiar Evil spirits that followed Melkor. 79, 165, 203

Úmanyar Later name of the *Alamanyar*. 163–4, 170–1, 173

Unbodied, The (Elves) See *(The) Unliving*.

Unfinished Tales 3, 128, 182, 298–9, 374, 407

Ungoliantë 98–101, 105, 108–9, 119, 123, 132, 190, (193), 194, 283–6, 288–9, 291–3, 298, 386; *Ungoliant* 295–6, 298–9, 423; *the Cloud of Ungoliantë* 101, 289, (294), 295–8; her origin 98, 105, 190, 284, and fate 109, 123, 297, 299

Universe, The 7, 38–9, 63, 330, 337–8, 350, 374, 387

Unlight 194, 285, 288–9

Unliving, The (Elves) 232. *The Unbodied* 224, 232

Unmarred See *(The) Marring of Arda*.

INDEX

Úr   The Sun. 377. *Úrin* 136, 198
Urwendi   Original name of the Sun-maiden. 136
Utumno   'The Deep-hidden' (67, 69). 18–19, 25, 27, 33, 35, 38, 53–4, 61, 67, 69–71, 73–6, 78–9, 81, 99, 110, 130, 156, 161, 165, 167, 197, 284, 288, 291–2, 297–8, 377–8, 382, 390–1, 393–4, 407–8, 410, 431. See *Udûn*.
Úvanimor   Evil creatures bred by Morgoth. 79. See *Vanimor*.

Vairë   'The Weaver', wife of Mandos. 49, 65, 69, 145, 148, 151, 201, 244–5, 248–50, 253, 260, 263–4; *the house of Vairë* 206–7, 237, 250, 253, 258, 261, 263–5
Vaiya   The Outer Sea. 28, 136, 154, 156. See *Ekkaia*.
Valakirka   The Sickle of the Gods. 71, 160, 166, 378, *Valacirca* 388. See *Great Bear, (The) Plough, Burning Briar*.
Valar   (and singular *Vala*) 4, 8, 14–43 *passim*, 48–62, 65–75, 77–82, 84, 86, 88, 90–1, 93–101, 105, 107–8, 110–20, 125, 128–33, 135–8, 144–7, 149, 152–4, 157, 159–62, 166–8, 172, 174–6, 178, 183, 185–91, 194, 196, 198–204, 211, 218–20, 223, 226, 235, 238–9, 241, 243–4, 246–7, 250–1, 253–5, 258–61, 268–93 *passim*, 295, 297, 311, 313, 318–19, 321–2, 327, 330–1, 334–41, 350–1, 355, 357, 362–4, 372, 374–82, 384, 386–94, 396–407, 410–12, 415–16, 424–30.
   The number of the Valar: nine 48, 69, 144, 147, 201, 204, seven 69, 201, 204, (and see *(The) Great Ones*); Queens of the Valar 49, 52, 58, 65–6, 69, 145–7, 201, 244 (see *Valier*). Their appearance, 'shapes', 4, 15, 69, 99, 105, 131, 144, 151, 218, 272, 284, 286, 289, 412; their 'errors' 162, 166, 168, 394, 401, 405, 407; 'fading' or impotence 401, 405; the Debate of the Valar 208–9, 239–46, 254, 258, 263–4, 269, 271, 326–7, 339, 361. Land of the Valar 15, 108, 132, 156, 202, 288, 291. See *Aratar, (The) Deathless, Gods, (The) Great Ones, (The) Mighty, (The) Powers, (The) Rulers of Arda; Children of the Valar*.
Valaraukar   Balrogs. 165, 203
Valarin   88
Valarindi   'Offspring of the Valar'. 49, 59, 66, 69, 152. See *Children of the Valar*.
Valaróma   The horn of Oromë. 7, 35, 39, 101, 105, 149, 151, 203, 289. (Replaced *Rombaras*.)
Valian Age, Valian Years   See *Years of the Valar*.
Valiant, The   A name of the Noldor. 164
Valier   The Queens of the Valar. 201, 203–4. See *Valar*.
Valimar   See *Valmar*.
Valinor   7, 16, 18–21, 24–5, 27–8, 33–5, 37–8, 43, 48, 50–1, 54–6, 61–2, 67–8, 70–4, 76–8, 80–1, 83, 85, 87, 89, 91–101, 105, 108–11, 113, 115, 117–18, 126–7, 129–34, 136–7, 144–6, 149, 152–6, 160–3, 166–7, 170, 172–9, 181–90, 192, 196, 198,

201–2, 204, 238, 240, 247, 250, 253–4, 256, 258, 261, 265–9, 276–7, 279–81, 283, 285–9, 292, 294–5, 297, 312, 371–2, 375, 377–8, 385–6, 388, 390, 392–4, 402, 407. See *Land of the Gods*, ~ *Valar* (in entries *Gods, Valar*); *Aman, (The) Blessed Realm, (The) Guarded Realm; Mountains of Aman*.

The Darkening of Valinor 128, 155, 248; the Hiding of Valinor 129, 133–4, 137, 142, 401, 406–7; the Noontide of Valinor 185, 273

Valinorian 91, 141, 388

Valmar City of the Gods, called 'the Blessed'. 55, 61, 81, 94, 97–100, 113, 116, 146, 154, 160–2, 166–7, 172, 178, 186, 241, 278–80, 283, 286–9, 291, 386; *Valimar* 68; *the plains of Valmar* 133. See *Gods*.

Vána (also Vana) 49, 53, 59, 61, 65, 67, 69, 131, 146, 149, 151, 201

Vanimor 'The Beautiful'; precursors of the Maiar. 56, 59, 79. See *Úvanimor*.

Vanyar 34, 57, 82–5, 87–90, 94, 99–101, 103, 110, 129–30, 133, 162, 164, 168, 171, 174–6, 178–81, 184, 186, 193, 198, 205, 207, 237, 249, 261–2, 268, 274, 287–8

Vanyarin 136, 166

Varda 15, 20, 24–5, 32, 34, 38–9, 49, 52, 54–5, 59, 61, 67, 69, 71, 95, 100, 106, 112, 130–2, (135), 144–52, 153–6, 159–60, 163, 166, 176, 180, 187, 193, 198, 201–2, 204, 211, 223, 244, 275, 285–8, 293, 313, 372, 374, 376–7, 379–82, 384–90, 406

Queen of the Valar 15, 20, 145, Queen of Arda 387; Queen of the Stars, see *Elbereth, Elentári, Tinwerontar*. The Vats or Wells of Varda 61, 100, 106, 193, 288, other references 55, 68–9, 155, 157, 159. See *Dome of Varda, Star-making, Tintallë*.

Vása 'The Consumer', the Sun. 130, 136, 198

Vastuman Name replacing *Arvalin* and replaced by *Avathar*. 291

Vê Original true name of Mandos; also *Vefántur*. 150

Vilvarin See *Wilwarin*.

Vinyamar Turgon's dwelling in Nevrast. 407

Virgin Mary, The 357

Vision, The (shown by Ilúvatar to the Ainur) 11–15, 24–6, 28, 31, 38, 40, 68, 144, 149, 159(–60), 318–19, 327, 336, 351, 388, 425

Voice (of Eru), The See *Eru*.

Void, The 9, 11, 13, 27–9, 38–9, 53, 58, 63–4, 144, 154, 157, 375–6, 380, 388, 403, 407; *the voids of Eä* 53, 62–4, 67, 76. See especially 403, and see *Outer Darkness* (in entry *Dark*), *Kúma*.

Walls of (the) Night 53–4, 58, 62–4, 67, 136–7

Walls (of the World) 26, 28–9, 62–3, 95, 107, 135, 146, 154, 157, 190, 193, 407; *Walls of Arda* 64. See *Eärambar, Ilurambar*.

Wanderers, The A name of the Nandor. 164

Waning of the Elves See *Elves*.

Wards of Melian   A name of the Sindar. 164–5
War of the Jewels   See *(The) Jewels.*
Waters of Awakening   See *Kuiviénen.*
Weaponless, The   A name of the Nandor of Ossiriand. 164
Wells of Varda   See *Varda.*
Westernesse   Númenor. 192
Western Men   7
Western Sea   26, 78, 175, 178, 365. See *(The) Sea.*
Westland   Aman. 118, 132, 194; *western land* 194. *West-lands of Middle-earth* 82–3
West, The   19, 25, 73, 75, 79, 81–2, 117, 127, 130–1, 134–5, 146, 156, 160–4, 167, 174–5, 370, 377–8; (of Middle-earth) 309, 349, 419; the *uttermost West* 18, 27, 33, 153, 163; *the hosts of the West* 74, 203. See *Great Sea, Lords of the West.*
White Lady of the Noldor   102, 106, 177, 182. See *Isfin, Írith.*
White Elves   A name of the Vanyar. 164
White Tree   Of Valinor, see *Telperion*; of Túna, see *Galathilion* (2); of Eressëa, see *Celeborn* (1); of Númenor, see *Nimloth.*
Wild Elves   Dark-elves. 375
Wilwarin   Name of a constellation. 160, 166; *Vilvarin* 166
Wise, The   381, 383, 419–20; the *Wise of Eressëa* 17, 74, 124, 408–9; among Men 305–6, 308–11, 313–15, 318, 352–3; the Wise of Númenor 374. A name of the Noldor, 164
Wise-women   (among Men) 305, 307; *Wise-woman* (of Adanel and Andreth) 304–7, 323
Witan   (Old English) The Gnomes. 163, 168
Wood-elves   A name of the Nandor. 164
World, The   7–8, 11–44 *passim*, 48–50, 54, 56, 58–9, 62–3, 66–8, 72, 76, 80, 95, 98, 106, 108–9, 118, 131, 144–50, 152–4, 160–3, 165, 176, 179, 186, 189–90, 203–4, 214, 223–4, 232, 244–5, 249, 251, 255, 259–60, 266–7, 270, 273, 275, 277, 284–5, 293–5, 299, 308–11, 314, 318–24, 329–30, 335, 337, 342, 345–7, 351, 355–6, 358–9, 364–6, 372–3, 376, 378–81, 387, 395–7, 399, 405, 407, 410, 428; and see *(The) End.*

The Little World 17, 27, 31, 40–1, 44, *Little Kingdom* 31; *Lord of the (this) World* 296, 312–13, 320. See *Change of the World, Circles (of the World), Walls (of the World).*

Yavanna   15, 19, 24–5, 32–5, 38, 49, 52, 55–6, 59, 62, 65, 67, 69–71, 75, 79–80, 85, 90, 98–9, 106–9, 120, 122, 129–31, 135, 145–54, 157, 159, 166, 172, 175–6, 180, 185, 197, 201–3, 241, 244, 257, 269, 286, 293, 295, 297, 372, 377, 384, 395. See *Palúrien, Kementári.*
Years of the Valar (Valian Years)   For references to the nature and computation of the Ages, Years and Days before the Sun see

Reckoning of Time in entry Time; for the later conception see 425–6, 430–1
Yénië Valinóren   'Annals of Valinor'. 57, 200
Yénonótië   The treatise of Quenna Onótimo. 51, 57
Yule   307

★

APPENDIX TO THE INDEX
Elvish words and terms

adaneth   mortal woman. 323–5, 349
aimenel, aimenal   lark. 252. See lirulin.
amdir   'looking up', hope. 320. See estel.
amilessi   mother-names. 217
anessë, pl. anessi   'given' or 'added' names. 216–17, 230
apacenyë   in essi apacenyë, names of foresight. 216
band   custody, prison. 350. See mando.
cöacalina   'light of the house', indwelling spirit. 250
ëala, pl. ëalar   being, spirit (not incarnate). 165
erdë   singularity. 216
erma   physical matter. 338, 349, 359, 406. See hrón (2), orma.
essë, pl. essi   name. 216, 230
essecarmë   name-making. 214–15, 229
essecilmë   name-choosing. 214–15, 217, 229
essekenta   In title Essekenta Eldarinwa. 415
estel   hope, trust. 320–1, 332, 338, 341–2, 363. See amdir.
fairë   spirit (in general); Sindarin faer. 250, 349
fëa, pl. fëar   (< *phăya) soul, indwelling spirit, of an incarnate being. 165, 209, 211, 218–27, 231–36, 242–4, 246, 248–50, 264, 267–70, 308, 312, 315–18, 326, 330–4, 336–7, 339–43, 349–51, 353, 359, 361–5, 404, 407, 410, 426–30
fírë   to sigh, breathe forth, 'expire'; fírië 'has breathed forth'. 250
galað   (Sindarin) tree. 182
*galata-rĭg-elle   'lady with garland of sunlight' (Galadriel). 182
gil   (Sindarin) silver glint. 388. See ñillë.
golodh   (Sindarin) Noldo (< *ngolodō). 350
gûl   (Sindarin) evil knowledge, sorcery. 350. See ñólë.
hrávë   flesh. 349. See rhaw.
hröa, pl. hröar   (1) body (of an incarnate being). 209, 216, 218–19, 231, 269–70, 304, 308–9, 312, 315–16, 318, 330–4, 337, 339, 342, 349–51, 353, 362–4, 406, 410, 424, 427–30. See hrón (1), hrondo.   (2) physical matter. 399–400, 406, 428, 431. See hrón (2).
hrón   (1) body (of an incarnate being); replaced by hrondo. 209, 231,

INDEX 471

pl. *hróni* 233. See *rhón*. (2) physical matter. 218, 231, 241, 269, 359, 406. See *erma, orma.*
hrondo, pl. *hrondor* body (of an incarnate being); replaced by *hröa*. 209, 216, 218–21, 227, 229, 231, 233, 304
ilúvë the whole. 39
ín, inno, indo mind. 216, 230
inwisti 'mind-mood'. 216, 229; earlier *inwaldi* 229
kemen the earth. 387
kilya cleft, gorge. 89
kolla vestment, cloak. 385
lámatyávë individual pleasure in wordforms. 215, 229, pl. *lámatyáver* 216; *tyávë* 215
lembas 214
lirulin lark. 238, 252, 262. See *aimenel.*
löa solar year; pl. *löar* (so spelt) 426
lómelindi 'dusk-singers', nightingales. 172
mando (< **mbandō*) custody. 350. See *band.*
menel the heavens. 387
namna (Finwë Míriello) the Statute (of Finwë and Míriel). 258
narn, pl. *nern* in titles of 'the Great Tales'. 373
nér, pl. *neri* (Elvish) man. 213–14, 216, 226, 229, 233. See *quendo.*
nís, pl. *nissi* (Elvish) woman. 213–14, 216, 226, 229, 233. See *quende.*
ñillë silver glint. 361. See *gil.*
ñólë lore, knowledge. 350. See *gûl.*
oienkarmë (Eruo) the perpetual production (of Eru). 329
orma physical matter. 218, 231, 359, 406. See *hröa* (2), *hrón* (2), *erma.*
ósanwe-kenta communication of thought. 415
*osto strong place, fortress. 350
quende, quendi, pl. *quender, quendir* (Elvish) woman. 229. See *nís.*
quendo, quendu, pl. *quendor, quendur* (Elvish) man. 229. See *nér.*
rhaw (Sindarin) flesh. 350. See *hrávë.*
rhón body. 229, 231. See *hrón* (1).
tana to show, indicate. 385
tanna sign. 385
terken insight. 230; *essi (amilessi) tercenyë*, names (mother-names) of insight, 216–17
tim (Sindarin) spark. 388
tinta to kindle, cause to sparkle. 388–9
tinwë, pl. *tinwi* spark. 388–9
tyávë See *lámatyávë.*
yén year equivalent to 144 Sun-years. 431

THE WAR OF THE JEWELS

J. R. R. TOLKIEN

The War of the Jewels

The Later Silmarillion
PART TWO
The Legends of Beleriand

Christopher Tolkien

CONTENTS

Foreword *page* vii

PART ONE

THE GREY ANNALS 1

PART TWO

THE LATER *QUENTA SILMARILLION*

9	Of Men	173
10	Of the Siege of Angband	175
11	Of Beleriand and its Realms	180
12	Of Turgon and the Building of Gondolin	198
13	Concerning the Dwarves	201
14	Of the Coming of Men into the West	215
15	Of the Ruin of Beleriand and the Fall of Fingolfin	238
	The Last Chapters	243

PART THREE

THE WANDERINGS OF HÚRIN
AND OTHER WRITINGS NOT FORMING PART OF
THE *QUENTA SILMARILLION*

I	The Wanderings of Húrin	251
II	Ælfwine and Dírhaval	311
III	Maeglin	316

| IV | Of the Ents and the Eagles | 340 |
| V | The Tale of Years | 342 |

PART FOUR

QUENDI AND ELDAR 357

Index 425

FOREWORD

The War of the Jewels is a companion to and continuation of *Morgoth's Ring*, Volume 10 in *The History of Middle-earth*. As I explained in that book, the two together contain virtually all of my father's narrative writing on the subject of the Elder Days in the years after *The Lord of the Rings*, but the division into two is made 'transversely': between the first part of 'The Silmarillion' ('the Legends of Aman') and the second ('the Legends of Beleriand'). I use the term 'Silmarillion', of course, in a very wide sense: this though potentially confusing is imposed by the extremely complex relationship of the different 'works' – especially but not only that of the *Quenta Silmarillion* and the *Annals*; and my father himself employed the name in this way. The division of the whole corpus into two parts is indeed a natural one: the Great Sea divides them. The title of this second part, *The War of the Jewels*, is an expression that my father often used of the last six centuries of the First Age: the history of Beleriand after the return of Morgoth to Middle-earth and the coming of the Noldor, until its end.

In the foreword to *Morgoth's Ring* I emphasised the distinction between the first period of writing that followed in the early 1950s the actual completion of *The Lord of the Rings*, and the later work that followed its publication; in this book also, therefore, two distinct 'phases' are documented.

The number of new works that my father embarked upon in that first 'phase', highly creative but all too brief, is astonishing. There were the new *Lay of Leithian*, of which all that he wrote before he abandoned it was published in *The Lays of Beleriand*; the *Annals of Aman* and new versions of the *Ainulindalë*; the *Grey Annals*, abandoned at the end of the tale of Túrin; the new *Tale of Tuor and the Fall of Gondolin* (published in *Unfinished Tales*), abandoned before Tuor actually entered the city; and all the new tale of Túrin and Nienor from Túrin's return to Dor-lómin to their deaths in Brethil (see p. 144 in this book). There were also an abandoned prose saga of Beren and Lúthien (see V.295); the story of Maeglin; and an extensive revision of the *Quenta Silmarillion*, the central work of the last period before *The Lord of the Rings*, interrupted near the beginning of the tale of Túrin in 1937 and never concluded.

I expressed the view in the foreword to *Morgoth's Ring* that 'despair of publication, at least in the form that he regarded as essential' (i.e. the conjunction of *The Silmarillion* and *The Lord of the Rings* in a single work) was the fundamental cause of the collapse of this new endeavour; and that this break destroyed all prospect that what may be called 'the older Silmarillion' would ever be completed. In *Morgoth's Ring* I have documented the massive upheaval, in the years that followed, in his conception of the old myths: an upheaval that never issued in new and secure form. But we come now to the last epoch of the Elder Days, when the scene shifts to Middle-earth and the mythical element recedes: the High-elves return across the Great Sea to make war upon Morgoth, Dwarves and Men come over the mountains into Beleriand, and bound up with this history of the movement of peoples, of the policies of kingdoms, of momentous battles and ruinous defeats, are the heroic tales of Beren One-hand and Túrin Turambar. Yet in *The War of the Jewels* the record is completed of all my father's further work on that history in the years following the publication of *The Lord of the Rings*; and even with all the labour that went into the elaboration of parts of 'the Saga of Túrin' it is obvious that this bears no comparison with his aims or indeed his achievements in the early 1950s.

In Part Two of this book it will be seen that in this later phase of his work the *Quenta Silmarillion* underwent scarcely any further significant rewriting or addition, other than the introduction of the new chapter *Of the Coming of Men into the West* with the radically altered earlier history of the Edain in Beleriand; and that (the most remarkable fact in the whole history of *The Silmarillion*) the last chapters (the tale of Húrin and the dragon-gold of Nargothrond, the Necklace of the Dwarves, the ruin of Doriath, the fall of Gondolin, the Kinslayings) remained in the form of the *Quenta Noldorinwa* of 1930 and were never touched again. Only some meagre hints are found in later writings.

For this there can be no simple explanation, but it seems to me that an important element was the centrality that my father accorded to the story of Húrin and Morwen and their children, Túrin Turambar and Niënor Níniel. This became for him, I believe, the dominant and absorbing story of the end of the

Elder Days, in which complexity of motive and character, trapped in the mysterious workings of Morgoth's curse, sets it altogether apart. He never finally achieved important passages of Túrin's life; but he extended the 'great saga' (as he justly called it) into 'the Wanderings of Húrin', following the old story that Húrin was released by Morgoth from his imprisonment in Angband after the deaths of his children, and went first to the ruined halls of Nargothrond. The dominance of the underlying theme led to a new story, a new dimension to the ruin that Húrin's release would bring: his catastrophic entry into the land of the People of Haleth, the Forest of Brethil. There were no antecedents whatsoever to this tale; but antecedents to the manner of its telling are found in parts of the prose 'saga' of the Children of Húrin (*Narn i Chîn Húrin*, given in *Unfinished Tales*), of which 'Húrin in Brethil' is a further extension. That 'saga' went back to the foundations in *The Book of Lost Tales*, but its great elaboration belongs largely to the period after the publication of *The Lord of the Rings*; and in its later development there entered an immediacy in the telling and a fullness in the recording of event and dialogue that must be described as a new narrative impulse: in relation to the mode of the 'Quenta', it is as if the focus of the glass by which the remote ages were viewed had been sharply changed.

But with Húrin's grim and even it may seem sardonic departure from the ruin of Brethil and dying Manthor this impulse ceased – as it appears. Húrin never came back to Nargothrond and Doriath; and we are denied an account, in this mode of story-telling, of what should be the culminating moment of the saga after the deaths of his children and his wife – his confrontation of Thingol and Melian in the Thousand Caves.

It might be, then, that my father had no inclination to return to the *Quenta Silmarillion*, and its characteristic mode, until he had told on an ample scale, and with the same immediacy as that of his sojourn in Brethil, the full tale of Húrin's tragic and destructive 'wanderings' – and their aftermath also: for it is to be remembered that his bringing of the treasure of Nargothrond to Doriath would lead to the slaying of Thingol by the Dwarves, the sack of Menegroth, and all the train of events that issued in the attack of the Fëanorians on Dior Thingol's heir in Doriath and, at the last, the destruction of the Havens of Sirion. If my father had done this, then out of it might have come, I suppose, new chapters of the *Quenta Silmarillion*, and a return to that quality in the older writing that I attempted to describe in my foreword to *The Book of Lost Tales*: 'The compendious or epitomising form and manner of *The Silmarillion*, with its suggestion of ages of poetry and "lore" behind it, strongly evokes a sense of "untold tales", even in the telling of them ... There is no narrative urgency, the pressure and fear of the immediate and unknown event. We do not actually see the Silmarils as we see the Ring.'

But this is entirely speculative, because none of it came about: neither the 'great saga' nor the *Quenta Silmarillion* were concluded. Freely as my father often wrote of his work, he never so much as hinted at his larger intentions for the structure of the whole. I think that it must be said that we are left, finally, in the dark.

'The Silmarillion', again in the widest sense, is very evidently a literary entity of a singular nature. I would say that it can only be defined in terms of its history; and that history is with this book largely completed ('largely', because I have not entered further into the complexities of the tale of Túrin in those parts that my father left in confusion and uncertainty, as explained in *Unfinished Tales*, p. 6). It is indeed the only 'completion' possible, because it was always 'in progress'; the published work is not in any way a completion, but a construction devised out of the existing materials. Those materials are now made available, save only in a few details and in the matter of 'Túrin' just mentioned; and with them a criticism of the 'constructed' *Silmarillion* becomes possible. I shall not enter into that question; although it will be apparent in this book that there are aspects of the work that I view with regret.

In *The War of the Jewels* I have included, as Part Four, a long essay of a very different nature: *Quendi and Eldar*. While there was no possibility of making *The History of Middle-earth* a history of the languages as well, I have not wished to eschew them altogether even when not essential to the narrative (as Adunaic is in *The Notion Club Papers*); I have wished to give at least some indication at different stages of the presence of this vital and evolving element, especially in regard to the meaning of names – thus the appendices to *The Book of Lost Tales* and the *Etymologies* in *The Lost Road*. *Quendi and Eldar* illustrates perhaps more than any other writing of my father's the significance of names, and of linguistic change affecting names, in his histories. It gives also an account of many things found nowhere else, such as the gesture-language of the Dwarves, and all that will ever be known, I believe, of Valarin, the language of the Valar.

I take this opportunity to give the correct text of a passage in *Morgoth's Ring*. Through an error that entered at a late stage and was not observed a line was dropped and a line repeated in note 16 on page 327; the text should read:

> There have been suggestions earlier in the *Athrabeth* that Andreth was looking much further back in time to the awakening of Men (thus she speaks of 'legends of days when death came less swiftly and our span was still far longer', p. 313); in her words here, 'a rumour that has come down through years uncounted', a profound alteration in the conception seems plain.

I have received a communication from Mr Patrick Wynne concerning Volume IX, *Sauron Defeated*, which I would like to record here. He has pointed out that several of the names in Michael Ramer's account of his experiences to the Notion Club are 'not just Hungarian in style but actual Hungarian words' (Ramer was born and spent his early childhood in Hungary, and he refers to the influence of Magyar on his 'linguistic taste', *Sauron Defeated* pp. 159, 201). Thus the world of the story that he wrote and read to the Club was first named *Gyönyörü* (*ibid.* p. 214, note 28), which means 'lovely'. His name for the planet Saturn was first given as *Gyürüchill* (p. 221, note 60), derived from Hungarian *gyürü* 'ring' and *csillag* 'star' (where *cs* is pronounced as English *ch* in *church*); *Gyürüchill* was then changed to *Shomorú*, probably from Hungarian *szomorú* 'sad' (though that is pronounced '*somorú*'), and if so, an allusion to the astrological belief in the cold and gloomy temperament of those born under the influence of that planet. Subsequently these names were replaced by others (*Emberü*, and *Eneköl* for Saturn) that cannot be so explained.

In this connection, Mr Carl F. Hostetter has observed that the Elvish star-name *Lumbar* ascribed to Saturn (whether or not my father always so intended it, see *Morgoth's Ring* pp. 434–5) can be explained in the same way as Ramer's *Shomorú*, in view of the Quenya word *lumbë*, 'gloom, shadow', recorded in the Elvish Etymologies (*The Lost Road and Other Writings*, p. 170).

Mr Hostetter has also pointed out that the name *Byrde* given to Finwë's first wife Míriel in the *Annals of Aman* (*Morgoth's Ring*, pp. 92, 185) is not, as I said (p. 103), an Old English word meaning 'broideress', for that is not found in Old English. The name actually depends on an argument advanced (on very good evidence) by my father that the word *byrde* 'broideress' must in fact have existed in the old language, and that it survived in the Middle English *burde* 'lady, damsel', its original specific sense faded and forgotten. His discussion is found in his article *Some Contributions to Middle-English Lexicography* (*The Review of English Studies* I.2, April 1925).

I am very grateful to Dr Judith Priestman for her generous help in providing me with copies of texts and maps in the Bodleian Library. The accuracy of the intricate text of this book has been much improved by the labour of Mr Charles Noad, unstintedly given and greatly appreciated. He has read the first proof with extreme care and with critical understanding, and has made many improvements; among these is an interpretation of the way in which the narrow path, followed by Túrin and afterwards by Brandir the Lame, went down through the woods above the Taeglin to Cabed-en-Aras: an interpretation that justifies expressions of my father's that I had taken to be merely erroneous (pp. 157, 159).

There remain a number of writings of my father's, other than those that are expressly philological, that I think should be included in this *History of Middle-earth*, and I hope to be able to publish a further volume in two years' time.

PART ONE

THE
GREY ANNALS

THE GREY ANNALS

The history of the *Annals of Beleriand* began about 1930, when my father wrote the earliest version ('**AB 1**') together with that of the *Annals of Valinor* ('**AV 1**'). These were printed in Vol.IV, *The Shaping of Middle-earth*; I remarked there that 'the *Annals* began, perhaps, in parallel with the *Quenta* as a convenient way of driving abreast, and keeping track of, the different elements in the ever more complex narrative web.' Second versions of both sets of *Annals* were composed later in the 1930s, as part of a group of texts comprising also the *Lhammas* or Account of Tongues, a new version of the *Ainulindalë*, and the central work of that time: a new version of 'The Silmarillion' proper, the unfinished *Quenta Silmarillion* ('**QS**'). These second versions, together with the other texts of that period, were printed in Vol.V, *The Lost Road and Other Writings*, under the titles *The Later Annals of Valinor* ('**AV 2**') and *The Later Annals of Beleriand* ('**AB 2**').

When my father turned again, in 1950–1, to the Matter of the Elder Days after the completion of *The Lord of the Rings*, he began new work on the *Annals* by taking up the AV 2 and AB 2 manuscripts from some 15 years earlier and using them as vehicles for revision and new writing. In the case of AV 2, correction of the old text was limited to the opening annals, and the beginnings of a new version written on the blank verso pages of this manuscript likewise petered out very quickly, so that there was no need to take much account of this preliminary work (X.47). In AB 2, on the other hand, the preparatory stages were much more extensive and substantial.

In the first place, revision of the original AB 2 text continues much further – although in practice this can be largely passed over, since the content of the revision appears in subsequent texts. (In some cases, as noted in V.124, it is not easy to separate 'early' (pre-*Lord of the Rings*) revisions and additions from 'late' (those of the early 1950s).) In the second place, the beginning of a new and much fuller version of the *Annals of Beleriand* on the blank verso pages of AB 2 extends for a considerable distance (13 manuscript pages) – and the first part of this is written in such a careful script, before it begins to degenerate, that it may be thought that my father did not at first intend it as a draft. This is entitled 'The Annals of Beleriand', and could on that account be referred to as '**AB 3**', but I shall in fact call it '**GA 1**' (see below).

The final text is a good clear manuscript bearing the title 'The Annals of Beleriand or the Grey Annals'. I have chosen to call this work the *Grey Annals*, abbreviated '**GA**', in order to mark its distinctive nature in relation to the earlier forms of the *Annals of Beleriand* and its close association with the *Annals of Aman* ('**AAm**'), which also bears a title different from that of its predecessors. The abandoned first version just mentioned is then more suitably called 'GA 1' than 'AB 3', since for most of its length it was followed very closely in the final text, and is to be regarded as a slightly earlier variant: it will be necessary to refer to it, and to cite passages from it, but there is no need to give it in full. Where it is necessary to distinguish the final text from the aborted version I shall call the former 'GA 2'.

There is some evidence that the *Grey Annals* followed the *Annals of Aman* (in its primary form), but the two works were, I feel certain, closely associated in time of composition. For the structure of the history of Beleriand the *Grey Annals* constitutes the primary text, and although much of the latter part of the work was used in the published *Silmarillion* with little change I give it in full. This is really essential on practical grounds, but is also in keeping with my intention in this 'History', in which I have traced the development of the Matter of the Elder Days from its beginning to its end within the compass of my father's actual writings: from this point of view the published work is not its end, and I do not treat his later writing primarily in relation to what was used, or how it was used, in '*The Silmarillion*'. – It is a most unhappy fact that he abandoned the *Grey Annals* at the death of Túrin – although, as will be seen subsequently (pp. 251 ff.), he added elements of a continuation at some later time.

I have not, as I did in the case of the *Annals of Aman*, divided the *Grey Annals* into sections, and the commentary, referenced to the numbered paragraphs, follows the end of the text (p. 103). Subsequent changes to the manuscript, which in places were heavy, are indicated as such.

At the top of the first page of the old AB 2 text, no doubt before he began work on the enormously enlarged new version, my father scribbled these notes: 'Make these the Sindarin Annals of Doriath and leave out most of the ...' (there are here two words that probably read 'Nold[orin] stuff'); and 'Put in notes about Denethor, Thingol, etc. from AV'.

Two other elements in the complex of papers constituting the *Grey Annals* remain to be mentioned. There are a number of disconnected rough pages bearing the words 'Old material of Grey Annals' (see p. 29); and there is an amanuensis typescript in top copy and carbon that clearly belongs with that of the *Annals of Aman*, which I tentatively dated to 1958 (X.47).

THE ANNALS OF BELERIAND
OR
THE GREY ANNALS

§1 These are the Annals of Beleriand as they were made by the Sindar, the Grey Elves of Doriath and the Havens, and enlarged from the records and memories of the remnant of the Noldor of Nargothrond and Gondolin at the Mouths of Sirion, whence they were brought back into the West.

§2 Beleriand is the name of the country that lay upon either side of the great river Sirion ere the Elder Days were ended. This name it bears in the oldest records that survive, and it is here retained in that form, though now it is called Belerian. The name signifies in the language of that land: the country of Balar. For this name the Sindar gave to Ossë, who came often to those coasts, and there befriended them. At first, therefore, this name was given to the land of the shores, on either side of Sirion's mouths, that face the Isle of Balar, but it spread until it included all the ancient coast of the North-west of Middle-earth south of the Firth of Drengist and all the inner land south of Hithlum up to the feet of Eryd Luin (the Blue Mountains). But south of the mouths of Sirion it had no sure boundaries; for there were pathless forests in those days between the unpeopled shores and the lower waters of Gelion.

VY 1050

§3 Hither, it is said, at this time came Melian the Maia from Valinor, when Varda made the great stars. In this same time the Quendi awoke by Kuiviénen, as is told in the Chronicle of Aman.

1080

§4 About this time the spies of Melkor discovered the Quendi and afflicted them.

1085

§5 In this year Oromë found the Quendi, and befriended them.

1090

§6 At this time the Valar came hither from Aman for their assault upon Melkor, whose stronghold was in the North beyond Eryd Engrin (the Iron Mountains). In these regions, therefore, were fought the first battles of the Powers of the West and the North, and all this land was much broken, and it took then that shape which it had until the coming of Fionwë. For the Great Sea broke in upon the coasts and made a deep gulf to the southward, and many lesser bays were made between the Great Gulf and Helkaraxë far in the North, where Middle-earth and Aman came nigh together. Of these bays the Bay of Balar was the chief; and into it the mighty river Sirion flowed down from the new-raised highlands northwards: Dorthonion and the mountains about Hithlum. At first these lands upon either side of Sirion were ruinous and desolate because of the War of the Powers, but soon growth began there, while most of Middle-earth slept in the Sleep of Yavanna, because the Valar of the Blessed Realm had set foot there; and there were young woods under the bright stars. These Melian the Maia fostered; and she dwelt most in the glades of Nan Elmoth beside the River Celon. There also dwelt her nightingales.

1102–5

§7 Ingwë, Finwë, and Elwë were brought to Valinor by Oromë as ambassadors of the Quendi; and they looked upon the Light of the Trees and yearned for it. Returning they counselled the Eldar to go to the Land of Aman, at the summons of the Valar.

1115

§8 Even as the Valar had come first to Beleriand as they went eastward, so later Oromë leading the hosts of the Eldar westwards towards Aman brought them to the shores of Beleriand. For there the Great Sea was less wide and yet free from the perils of the ice that lay further north. In this year of the Valar, therefore, the foremost companies of the Vanyar and Noldor passed through the vale of Sirion and came to the sea-coast between Drengist and the Bay of Balar. But because of their fear of the Sea, which they had before neither seen nor imagined, the Eldar drew back into the woods and highlands. And Oromë departed and went to Valinor and left them there for a time.

1128

§9 In this year the Teleri, who had lingered on the road,

came also at last over Eryd Luin into northern Beleriand. There they halted and dwelt a while between the River Gelion and Eryd Luin. At that time many of the Noldor dwelt westward of the Teleri, in those regions where afterwards stood the forests of Neldoreth and Region. Finwë was their lord, and with him Elwë lord of the Teleri had great friendship; and Elwë was wont often to visit Finwë in the dwellings of the Noldor.

1130

§10   In this year King Elwë Singollo of the Teleri was lost in the wilderness. As he journeyed home from a meeting with Finwë, he passed by Nan Elmoth, and he heard the nightingales of Melian the Maia, and followed them deep into the glades. There he saw Melian standing beneath the stars, and a white mist was about her, but the Light of Aman was in her face. Thus began the love of Elwë Greymantle and Melian of Valinor. Hand in hand they stood silent in the woods, while the wheeling stars measured many years, and the young trees of Nan Elmoth grew tall and dark. Long his people sought for Elwë in vain.

1132

§11   Now Ulmo, at the command of the Valar, came to the shores of Beleriand and summoned the Eldar to meet him; and he spoke to them, and made music upon his conches, and changed the fear of all who heard him into a great desire for the Sea. Then Ulmo and Ossë took an island, which stood far out in the Sea, and they moved it, and brought it, as it were a mighty ship, into the Bay of Balar; and the Vanyar and Noldor embarked thereon, and were drawn over Sea, until they came at last to the Land of Aman. But a part of that island which was deep-grounded in the shoals off the mouths of Sirion was broken away and remained; and this was the Isle of Balar to which afterward Ossë often came.

§12   For the Teleri had not embarked, but remained behind. Many indeed were dwelling at that time afar off in eastern Beleriand and heard the summons of Ulmo too late; and many others searched still for Elwë their king, and were not willing to depart without him. But when the Teleri learned that their kinsfolk, the Vanyar and the Noldor, were gone, the most part hastened to the shore and dwelt thereafter nigh the mouths of Sirion, in longing for their friends that had left them. And they took Olwë, Elwë's brother, for their lord. Then Ossë and Uinen came to them, and dwelt in the Isle of Balar, and became the friends of the Teleri and taught them all manner of sea-lore and sea-music.

1149–50

§13 In this year Ulmo returned to Beleriand. To this he was most moved by the prayers of the Noldor and of Finwë their king, who grieved at their sundering from the Teleri, and besought Ulmo to bring Elwë and his people to Aman, if they would come. And all those who followed Olwë were now willing to depart; but Ossë was sad at heart. For he went seldom to the shores of Aman, and loved the Teleri, and he was ill-pleased that their fair voices should be heard no longer by the strands of Middle-earth, which were his domain.

§14 Ossë therefore persuaded many to remain in Beleriand, and when King Olwë and his host were embarked upon the isle and passed over the Sea they abode still by the shore; and Ossë returned to them, and continued in friendship with them. And he taught to them the craft of shipbuilding and of sailing; and they became a folk of mariners, the first in Middle-earth, and had fair havens at Eglarest and Brithombar; but some dwelt still upon the Isle of Balar. Cirdan the Shipwright was the lord of this people, and all that shoreland between Drengist and Balar that he ruled was called the Falas. But among the Teleri were none yet so hardy of heart, and of their ships none so swift and strong that they might dare the deeps of the Great Sea or behold even from afar the Blessed Realm and the Light of the Trees of Valinor. Wherefore those that remained behind were called Moriquendi, Elves of the Dark.

1150

§15 The friends and kinsfolk of Elwë also remained; but they would fain have departed to Valinor and the Light of the Trees (which Elwë indeed had seen), if Ulmo and Olwë had been willing to tarry yet longer while they sought still for Elwë. But when Ulmo had tarried a full Year (and a Year of the Valar is in length well nigh as are ten of the years that now are) he departed, and the friends of Elwë were left behind. Therefore they called themselves the Eglath, the Forsaken People; and though they dwelt in the woods and hills rather than by the Sea, which filled them with sorrow, their inmost hearts yearned ever Westward.

1152

§16 At this time, it is told, Elwë Singollo awoke from his long trance. And he came forth from Nan Elmoth with Melian, and they dwelt thereafter in the woods in the midst of the land; and though Elwë had greatly desired to see again the light of the Trees, in the face of Melian the fair he beheld the Light of Aman as in an unclouded mirror, and in that light he was content. Then his folk gathered about him in joy; and they were amazed, for fair and noble as he had been, now he appeared as it were a lord of the Maiar, tallest of all the Children of Ilúvatar, his hair as grey silver, and his eyes like unto stars. King of the Eglath he became, and Melian was his Queen, wiser than any daughter of Middle-earth.

1200

§17 It is not known to any among Elves or Men when Lúthien, only child of Elwë and Melian, came into the World, fairest of all the Children of Ilúvatar that were or shall be. But it is held that it was at the end of the first age of the Chaining of Melkor, when all the Earth had great peace and the glory of Valinor was at its noon, and though Middle-earth for the most [part] lay in the Sleep of Yavanna, in Beleriand under the power of Melian there was life and joy and the bright stars shone like silver fires. In the Forest of Neldoreth it is said that she was born and cradled under the stars of heaven, and the white flowers of *niphredil* came forth to greet her, as stars from the earth.

1200–50

§18 In this time the power of Elwë and Melian reached over all Beleriand. Elu Thingol he was called in the tongue of his people, King Greymantle, and all the Elves of Beleriand from the mariners of Círdan to the wandering huntsmen of the Blue Mountains took him for lord. And they are called, therefore, the Sindar, the Grey Elves of starlit Berleriand. And albeit they were Moriquendi, under the lordship of Thingol and the teaching of Melian they became the fairest and the most wise and skilful of all the Elves of Middle-earth.

1250

§19 In this year the Norn-folk came first over the mountains into Beleriand. This people the Noldor after named the Naugrim, whom some Men call Dwarves. Their most ancient dwellings were far to the East, but they had delved for themselves great halls and mansions, after the manner of their kind, on the east-side of Eryd Luin, north and south of Mount Dolmed, in those places which the Eldar named Belegost and Nogrod (but they Gabilgathol and Tumunzahar). Thence they now came forth and made themselves known to the Elves; and the Elves were amazed, for they had deemed themselves to be the only living things in Middle-earth that spoke with words or wrought with hands; and that all others were beasts and birds only.

§20 Nonetheless they could understand no word of the tongue of the Naugrim, which to their ears was cumbrous and unlovely; and few ever of the Eldar have achieved the mastery of it. But the Dwarves were swift to learn (after a fashion), and indeed were more willing to learn the Elven-tongue than to teach to aliens their own; and soon there was much parley between the peoples. Ever cool was their friendship, though much profit they had one of the other. But at that time those griefs that lay between them had not yet come to pass, and they were welcomed by King Thingol.

§21 How the Dwarves came into the world the Eldar know not for certain, though the loremasters have elsewhere recorded the tales of the Naugrim themselves (such as they would reveal) concerning their beginning. They say that Aulë the Maker, whom they call Mahal, brought them into being; and however that may be, certain it is that they were great smiths and masons, though of old there was little beauty in their works. Iron and copper they loved to work more than silver or gold, and stone more than wood.

1300

Of the building of Menegroth

§22 Now Melian had after the manner of the Maiar, the people of Valinor, much foresight. And when two of the ages of the Chaining of Melkor had passed, she counselled Thingol that the Peace of Arda would not last for ever; and he therefore bethought him how he should make for himself a kingly dwelling, and a place that should be strong, if evil were to awake again in Middle-earth. He called therefore upon the Enfeng, the Longbeards of Belegost, whom he had befriended, and sought their aid and counsel. And they gave it willingly, for they were unwearied in those days, and eager for new works.

And though the Dwarves ever demanded a price for all that they did, whether with delight or with toil, at this time they held themselves paid. For Melian taught them much wisdom, which they were eager to get; whereas Thingol rewarded them with many fair pearls. These Cirdan gave to him, for they were got in great number in the shallow waters about the Isle of Balar; but the Naugrim had not before seen their like, and they held them dear. And one there was great as a dove's egg, and its sheen was as the starlight upon the foam of the sea; Nimphelos it was named, and the chieftain of the Enfeng prized it above a mountain of wealth.

§23 Therefore the Naugrim laboured long and gladly for Thingol, and devised for him mansions after the fashion of their folk, delved deep in the earth. Where the River Esgalduin flowed down, dividing Neldoreth from Region, there was in the midst of the forest a rocky hill, and the river ran at its feet. There they made the gates of the halls of Thingol, and they built a bridge of stone over the river, by which alone the gates could be entered. But beyond the gates wide passages ran down to high halls and chambers far below that were hewn in the living stone, so many and so great that that dwelling was named Menegroth, the Thousand Caves.

§24 But the Elves also had part in that labour, and Elves and Dwarves together, each with their own skills, there wrought out the visions of Melian, images of the wonder and beauty of Valinor beyond the Sea. The pillars of Menegroth were hewn in the likeness of the beeches of Oromë, stock, bough, and leaf, and they were lit with lanterns of gold. The nightingales sang there as in the gardens of Lorien; and there were fountains of silver, and basins of marble, and floors of many-coloured stones. Carven figures of beasts and of birds there ran upon the walls, or climbed upon the pillars, or peered among the branches entwined with many flowers. And as the years passed Melian and her maidens filled the halls with webs of many hues, wherein could be read the deeds of the Valar, and many things that had befallen in Arda since its beginning, and shadows of things that were yet to be. That was the fairest dwelling of any king that hath ever been east of the Sea.

1300-50

§25 After the building of Menegroth was achieved, there was peace in the realm of Thingol. The Naugrim would come ever and anon over the mountains and visit Menegroth and go in traffick about the land, though they went seldom to the Falas, for they hated the sound of the Sea and feared to look on it; but otherwise there came to Beleriand no rumour or tidings of the world without. But it came to pass that the Dwarves were troubled, and they spoke to King Thingol, saying that the Valar had not rooted out utterly the evils of the North, and now the remnant, having long multiplied in the dark, were coming forth once more and roaming far and wide. 'There are fell beasts,' said they, 'in the land east of the mountains, and the dark-elves that dwell there, your ancient kindred, are flying from the plains to the hills.'

1330

§26 And ere long (in the year 1330 according to the annals that were made in Doriath) the evil creatures came even to Beleriand, over passes in the mountains, or up from the south through the dark forests. Wolves there were, or creatures that walked in wolf-shapes, and other fell beings of shadow.

§27 Among these were the Orkor indeed, who after wrought ruin in Beleriand; but they were yet few and wary and did but smell out the ways of the land, awaiting the return of their Lord. Whence they came, or what they were, the Elves knew not then, deeming them to be Avari, maybe, that had become evil and savage in the wild. In which they guessed all too near, it is said.

§28 Therefore Thingol bethought [him] of arms, which before his folk had not needed, and these at first the Naugrim smithied for him. For they were greatly skilled in such work, though none among them surpassed the craftsmen of Nogrod, of whom Telchar the Smith was the greatest in renown. A warlike race of old were all the Naugrim, and they would fight fiercely with whomsoever aggrieved them: folk of Melkor, or Eldar, or Avari, or wild beasts, or not seldom with their own kin, Dwarves of other mansions and lordships. Their smith-craft indeed the Sindar soon learned of them; yet in the tempering of steel alone of all crafts the Dwarves were never outmatched even by the Noldor, and in the making of mail of linked rings (which the Enfeng first contrived) their work had no rival.

§29 At this time therefore the Sindar were well armed, and

they drove off all creatures of evil, and had peace again; but Thingol's armouries were stored with axes (the chief weapons of the Naugrim, and of the Sindar), and with spears and swords, and tall helms, and long coats of bright mail: for the hauberks of the Enfeng were so fashioned that they rusted not and shone ever as were they new-burnished. This proved well for Thingol in the time that was to come.

1350

The coming of Denethor

§30 Now as is elsewhere recounted, one Dân of the host of Olwë forsook the march of the Eldar at that time when the Teleri were halted by the shores of the Great River upon the borders of the westlands of Middle-earth. And he led away a numerous people and went south down the river, and of the wanderings of that people, the Nandor, little is now known. Some, it is said, dwelt age-long in the woods of the Vale of the Great River, some came at last to the mouths of Anduin, and there dwelt by the Sea, and others passing by the White Mountains came north again and entered the wilderness of Eriador between Eryd Luin and the far Mountains of Mist. Now these were a woodland folk and had no weapons of metal, and the coming of the fell beasts of the North affrayed them sorely, as the Naugrim reported. Therefore Denethor, the son of Dân, hearing rumour of the might of Thingol and his majesty, and of the peace of his realm, gathered such host of his scattered folk as he could and led them over the mountains into Beleriand. There they were welcomed by Thingol, as kin long lost that return, and they dwelt in Ossiriand in the south of his kingdom. For it was a great country, and yet little peopled; and it was so named, the Land of Seven Rivers, because it lay between the mighty stream of Gelion and the mountains, from which there flowed into Gelion the swift rivers: Ascar, Thalos, Legolin, Brilthor, Duilwen, and Adurant. In that region the forests in after days were tall and green, and the people of Denethor there dwelt warily and seldom seen, because of their raiment of the colour of leaves; and they were called therefore the Green-elves.

§31 Of the long years of peace that followed after the coming of Denethor there is little tale; for though in this time Dairon the minstrel, it is said, who was the chief loremaster of the kingdom of Thingol, devised his Runes,* [*added later in margin:* Cirth] they were little used by the Sindar for the keeping of records, until the days of the War, and much that was held in memory has perished in the ruin of Doriath. Yet verily of bliss and glad life there is little to be said, ere it endeth; as works fair and wonderful, while still they endure for eyes to see, are their own record, and only when they are in peril or broken for ever do they pass into song. In Beleriand in those days the Elves walked, and the rivers flowed, and the stars shone, and the night-flowers gave forth their scents; and the beauty of Melian was as the noon, and the beauty of Lúthien was as the dawn in spring. In Beleriand King Thingol upon his throne was as the sons of the Valar, whose power is at rest, whose joy is as an air that they breathe in all their days, whose thought flows in a tide untroubled from the heights to the deeps. In Beleriand still at whiles rode Oromë the great, passing like a wind over the mountains, and the sound of his horn came down the leagues of the starlight, and the Elves feared him for the splendour of his countenance and the great noise of the onrush of Nahar; but when the Valaróma echoed in the hills, they knew well that all evil things were fled far away.

1495

§32 It came to pass at last that the end of Bliss was at hand, and the noontide of Valinor was drawing to its twilight. For as is known to all, being written elsewhere in lore and sung in many songs, Melkor slew the Trees of the Valar with the aid of Ungoliantë, and escaped and came back to the north of Middle-earth. And hereafter he shall be known by that name that Fëanor gave him, the Dark Foe, Morgoth the Accursed.

§33 Far to the North befell the strife of Morgoth and Ungoliantë; but the great cry of Morgoth echoed through Beleriand, and all its folk shrank for fear; for though few knew what it foreboded, they heard then the herald of death.

§34 Soon after, indeed, Ungoliantë fled from the North and came into the realm of King Thingol, and a terror of darkness

---

* These, it is said, he contrived first ere the building of Menegroth, and after bettered them. The Naugrim, indeed, that came to Thingol learned the Runes of Dairon, and were well-pleased with the device, esteeming Dairon's skill higher than did the Sindar, his own folk; and by the Naugrim they [*later* > the Cirth] were taken east over the mountains and passed into the knowledge of many peoples.

was about her. But by the power of Melian she was stayed, and entered not into Neldoreth, but abode long while under the shadow of the precipices in which Dorthonion fell southward. Therefore they became known as Eryd Orgoroth, the Mountains of Terror, and none dared go thither, or pass nigh to them; for even after Ungoliantë herself departed and went whither she would back into the forgotten South of the world, her foul offspring dwelt there in form as spiders and wove there their hideous webs. There light and life were strangled, and there all waters were poisoned.

§35 Morgoth, however, came not himself to Beleriand, but went to the Iron Mountains, and there with the aid of his servants that came forth to meet him he delved anew his vast vaults and dungeons. These the Noldor after named Angband: the Iron Prison; and above their gates Morgoth reared the vast and threefold peaks of Thangorodrim, and a great reek of dark smoke was ever wreathed about them.

1497

§36 In this year Morgoth made his first assault upon Beleriand, which lay south of Angband. Indeed it is said that the gates of Morgoth were but one hundred and fifty leagues distant from the bridge of Menegroth; far and yet all too near.

§37 Now the Orcs that had multiplied in the bowels of the earth grew strong and fell, and their dark lord filled them with a lust of ruin and death; and they issued from Angband's gates under the clouds that Morgoth sent forth, and passed silently into the highlands of the north. Thence on a sudden a great army came to Beleriand and assailed King Thingol. Now in his wide realm many Elves wandered free in the wild or dwelt at peace in small kindreds of quiet folk far sundered. Only about Menegroth in the midst of the land, and along the Falas in the country of the mariners were there numerous peoples; but the Orcs came down upon either side of Menegroth, and from camps in the east between Celon and Gelion, and west in the plains between Sirion and Narog, they plundered far and wide; and Thingol was cut off from Cirdan at Eglarest.

§38 Therefore he called upon Denethor, and the Elves came in force from Region over Aros and from Ossiriand, and fought the first battle in the Wars of Beleriand. And the eastern host of the Orcs was taken between the armies of the Eldar, north of the Andram and midway between Aros and Gelion, and there they were utterly defeated, and those that fled north from the great slaughter were waylaid by the axes of the Naugrim that issued from Mount Dolmed: few indeed returned to Angband.

§39 But the victory of the Elves was dearbought. For the Elves of Ossiriand were light-armed, and no match for the Orcs, who were shod with iron and iron-shielded and bore great spears with broad blades. And Denethor was cut off and surrounded upon the hill of Amon Ereb; and there he fell and all his nearest kin about him, ere the host of Thingol could come to his aid. Bitterly though his fall was avenged, when Thingol came upon the rear of the Orcs and slew them aheaps, the Green-elves lamented him ever after and took no king again. After the battle some returned to Ossiriand, and their tidings filled the remnant of their folk with great fear, so that thereafter they came never forth in open war, but kept themselves by wariness and secrecy. And many went north and entered the guarded realm of Thingol and were merged with his folk.

§40 And when Thingol came again to Menegroth he learned that the Orc-host in the west was victorious and had driven Cirdan to the rim of the Sea. Therefore he withdrew all his folk that his summons could reach within the fastness of Neldoreth and Region, and Melian put forth her power and fenced all that dominion round about with an unseen wall of shadow and bewilderment: the Girdle of Melian, that none thereafter could pass against her will or the will of King Thingol (unless one should come with a power greater than that of Melian the Maia). Therefore this inner land which was long named Eglador was after called Doriath, the guarded kingdom, Land of the Girdle. Within it there was yet a watchful peace; but without there was peril and great fear, and the servants of Morgoth roamed at will, save in the walled havens of the Falas.

Of the Coming of the Noldor

§41 But new tidings were at hand, which none in Middle-earth had foreseen, neither Morgoth in his pits nor Melian in Menegroth; for no news came out of Aman, whether by messenger, or by spirit, or by vision in dream, after the death of the Trees and the hiding of Valinor. In this same year of the Valar (but some seven years after in the later reckoning of time) Fëanor came over Sea in the white ships of the Teleri, and landed in the Firth of Drengist, and there burned the ships at Losgar.

§42 Now the flames of that burning were seen not only by Fingolfin, whom Fëanor had deserted, but also by the Orcs and the watchers of Morgoth. No tale hath told what Morgoth thought in his heart at the tidings that Fëanor his bitterest foe had brought a host out of the West. Maybe he feared him little, for he had not yet had proof of the swords of the Noldor, and soon it was seen that he purposed to drive them back into the Sea.

§43 Drengist is a long firth which pierces the Echoing Hills of Eryd Lómin that are the west-fence of the great country of Hithlum. Thus the host of Fëanor passed from the shores into the inner regions of Hithlum, and marching about the northern end of the Mountains of Mithrim they encamped in that part which was named Mithrim and lay about the great lake amid the mountains that bore the same name.

§44 But the host of Melkor, orcs and werewolves, came through the passes of Eryd-wethrin and assailed Fëanor on a sudden, ere his camp was fullwrought or put in defence. There now on the grey fields of Mithrim was fought the second battle of the Wars of Beleriand, and the first meeting of the might of Morgoth with the valour of the Noldor. *Dagor-nuin-Giliath* it is named, the Battle under the Stars, for the Moon had not yet risen. In that battle, albeit outnumbered and taken at unawares, the Noldor were swiftly victorious. Strong and fair were they yet, for the light of Aman was not yet dimmed in their eyes; swift they were, and deadly in wrath, and long and terrible were their swords. The Orcs fled before them, and they were driven forth from Mithrim with great slaughter, and hunted over that great plain that lay north of Dorthonion, and was then called Ardgalen. There the armies that had passed south into the vales of Sirion and had beleaguered Cirdan came up to their succour, and were caught in their ruin. For Celegorn Fëanor's son, having news of them, waylaid them with a part of the Elven-host, and coming down upon them out of the hills nigh Eithel Sirion drove them into the Fen of Serech. Evil indeed were the tidings that came at last unto Angband, and Morgoth was dismayed. Ten days that battle endured, and from it returned of all the hosts that he had prepared for the conquest of the kingdoms of the Eldar no more than a handful of leaves.

§45 Yet cause he had for great joy, though it was hidden from him for a while. For the heart of Fëanor, in his wrath against the Enemy, blazed like a fire, and he would not halt, but pressed on behind the remnant of the Orcs, thinking, it is said, so to come at Morgoth himself. And he laughed aloud as he wielded his sword, and rejoiced that he had dared the wrath of the Valar and the evils of the road that he might see that hour of his vengeance. He knew naught of Angband or the great strength of defence that Morgoth had so swiftly prepared; but had he known, it would not have deterred him, for fey he was, consumed by the flame of his own wrath. Thus it was that he drew far ahead of the van of his host, and seeing this the servants of Morgoth turned to bay, and there issued from Angband Balrogs to aid them. There upon the confines of Dor Daedeloth, the land of Morgoth, Fëanor was surrounded, with few friends about him. Soon he stood alone; but long he fought on, and laughed undismayed, though he was wrapped in fire and wounded with many wounds. But at the last Gothmog,* Lord of the Balrogs, smote him to the ground, and there he would have perished, but Maidros and three other of his sons in that moment came up with force to his aid, and the Balrogs fled back to Angband.

§46 Then his sons raised up their father and bore him back towards Mithrim. But as they drew near to Eithel Sirion and were upon the upward path to the pass over the mountains, Fëanor bade them halt. For his wounds were mortal, and he knew that his hour was come. And looking out from the slopes of Eryd-wethrin with his last sight he beheld afar the peaks of Thangorodrim, mightiest of the towers of Middle-earth, and knew with the foreknowledge of death that no power of the Noldor would ever overthrow them; but he cursed the name of Morgoth, and laid it upon his sons to hold to their oath, and to avenge their father. Then he died; but he had neither burial nor tomb, for so fiery was his spirit that, as it passed, his body fell to ash and was borne away like a smoke, and his likeness has never again appeared in Arda, neither has his spirit left the realm of Mandos. Thus ended the mightiest of the Noldor, of whose deeds came both their greatest renown and their most grievous woe.

§47 Tidings of these great deeds came to Menegroth and to Eglarest, and the Grey-elves were filled with wonder and with hope, for they looked to have great help in their defence against

* [*Marginal note:*] whom Ecthelion afterward slew in Gondolin.

Morgoth from their mighty kindred that thus returned unlooked-for from the West in their very hour of need, believing indeed at first that they came as emissaries of the Valar to deliver their brethren from evil. Now the Grey-elves were of Telerian race, and Thingol was the brother of Olwë at Alqualondë, but naught yet was known of the kinslaying, nor of the manner of the exile of the Noldor, and of the oath of Fëanor. Yet though they had not heard of the Curse of Mandos, it was soon at work in Beleriand. For it entered into the heart of King Thingol to regret the days of peace when he was the high lord of all the land and its peoples. Wide were the countries of Beleriand and many empty and wild, and yet he welcomed not with full heart the coming of so many princes in might out of the West, eager for new realms.

§48 Thus there was from the first a coolness between him and the sons of Fëanor, whereas the closest friendship was needed, if Morgoth were to be withstood; for the [House >] sons of Fëanor were ever unwilling to accept the overlordship of Thingol, and would ask for no leave where they might dwell or might pass. When, therefore, ere long (by treachery and ill will, as later is told) the full tale of the deeds in Valinor became known in Beleriand, there was rather enmity than alliance between Doriath and the House of Fëanor; and this bitterness Morgoth eagerly inflamed by all means that he could find. But that evil lay as yet in the days to come, and the first meeting of the Sindar and the Noldor was eager and glad, though parley was at first not easy between them, for in their long severance the tongue of the Kalaquendi in Valinor and the Moriquendi in Beleriand had drawn far apart.

Excursus on the languages of Beleriand

I interrupt the text here since the complex variant material that follows in the two manuscripts cannot well be accommodated in the commentary.

In place of GA 2 §48 just given, GA 1 (making no reference to the active hostility that developed between Thingol and the Fëanorians) has only the following (after the words 'eager for new realms'):

Moreover in their long severance the tongues of the Sindar and the Noldor had drawn apart, and at first parley was not easy between them.

This is followed by a long 'excursus' (marked on the manuscript as an intrusion into the main text) on the development and relations of

Noldorin and Sindarin in Beleriand, the end of which is also the end of GA 1. This discussion reappears, rewritten, in GA 2, and then this revised form was itself substantially altered. It seems desirable to give all the versions of this passage, of central importance in the linguistic history of Middle-earth. The numbered notes to this section are found on p. 28.

The original version in GA 1 reads as follows.

It was indeed at the landing of Fëanor three hundred and sixty-five long years of the Valar[1] since the Noldor had passed over the Sea and left the Teleri behind them. Now that time was in length well nigh as three thousand and five hundred years of the Sun. In such an age the tongues of mortal Men that were far sundered would indeed change out of knowledge, unless it were as written records of song and wisdom. But in Valinor in the days of the Trees change was little to be perceived, save that which came of will and design, while in Middle-earth under the Sleep of Yavanna it was slow also, though before the Rising of the Moon all things had been stirred from slumber in Beleriand, as has before been told.[2] Therefore, whereas the tongue of the Noldor had altered little from the ancient tongue of the Eldar upon the march – and its altering had for the most part come in the making of new words (for things old and new) and in the softening and harmonizing of the sounds and patterns of the Quendian tongue to forms that seemed to the Noldor more beautiful – the language of the Sindar had changed much, even in unheeded growth as a tree may imperceptibly change its shape: as much maybe as an unwritten mortal tongue might change in five hundred years or more.[3] It was already ere the Rising of the Sun a speech greatly different to the ear from the Noldorin, and after that Rising all change was swift, for a while in the second Spring of Arda very swift indeed. To the ear, we say, because though Dairon the minstrel and loremaster of Menegroth had devised his Runes already by V.Y. 1300 (and after greatly bettered them), it was not the custom of the Sindar to write down their songs or records, and the Runes of Dairon (save in Menegroth) were used chiefly for names and brief inscriptions cut upon wood, stone, or metal. (The Naugrim[4] learned the Runes of Dairon from Menegroth, being well-pleased with the device and esteeming Dairon higher than [did] his own folk; and by the Naugrim they were brought east over the Mountains.)[5]

Soon, however, it came to pass that the Noldor in daily use

took on the Sindarin tongue, and this tongue enriched by words and devices from Noldorin became the tongue of all the Eldar in Beleriand (save in the country of the Green[-elves]) and the language of all the Eldar, either in Middle-earth, or that (as shall be told) went back from exile into the West and dwelt and dwell now upon Eressëa. In Valinor the ancient Elven-speech is maintained, and the Noldor never forsook it; but it became for them no longer a cradle-tongue, a mother-tongue, but a learned language of lore, and of high song and noble and solemn use. Few of the Sindar learned it, save in so far as they became, outside Doriath, merged in one people with Noldor and followed their princes; as indeed ere long happened indeed except for few scattered companies of Sindar in mountainous woods, and except also for the lordship of Cirdan, and the guarded kingdom of Thingol.

Now this change of tongue among the Noldor took place for many divers reasons. First, that though the Sindar were not numerous they far outnumbered the hosts of Fëanor and Fingolfin, such as in the end survived their dreadful journeys and reached Beleriand. Secondly and no less: that the Noldor having forsaken Aman themselves began to be subject to change undesigned while they were yet upon the march, and at the Rising of the Sun this change became swift – and the change in their daily tongue was such that, whether by reason of the like clime and soil and the like fortunes, whether by intercourse and mingling of blood, it changed in the same ways as did the Sindarin, and the two tongues grew towards one another. Thus it came that words taken from Noldorin into Telerin entered not in the true forms of High Speech but as it were altered and fitted to the character of the tongue of Beleriand. Thirdly: because after the death of Fëanor the overlordship of the Exiles (as shall be recounted) passed to Fingolfin, and he being of other mood than Fëanor acknowledged the high-kingship of Thingol and Menegroth, being indeed greatly in awe of that king, mightiest of the Eldar save Fëanor only, and of Melian no less. But though Elu-Thingol, great in memory, could recall the tongue of the Eldar as it had been ere riding from Finwë's camp he heard the birds of Nan Elmoth, in Doriath the Sindarin tongue alone was spoken, and all must learn it who would have dealings with the king.

It is said that it was after the Third Battle Dagor Aglareb[6] that the Noldor first began far and wide to take the Sindarin as they settled and established realms in Beleriand; though maybe the Noldorin survived (especially in Gondolin) until Dagor Arnediad[7] or until the Fall of Gondolin – survived, that is, in the spoken form that it had in Beleriand as different both from the Quenya (or Ancient Noldorin) and from the Sindarin: for the Quenya never perished and is known and used still by all such as crossed the Sea ere the Trees were slain.

This is the first general linguistic statement since the *Lhammas*, written long before, and there have been major shifts from the earlier theory. The third version of the *Lhammas*, '*Lammasethen*', the latest and shortest of the three, gives a clear statement of what is more diffusely expressed in the longer versions, and I cite a part of it (from V.193–4):

> Now ancient Noldorin, as first used, and written in the days of Fëanor in Tûn, remained spoken by the Noldor that did not leave Valinor at its darkening, and it abides still there, not greatly changed, and not greatly different from Lindarin. It is called *Kornoldorin*, or *Finrodian* because Finrod and many of his folk returned to Valinor and did not go to Beleriand. But most of the Noldor went to Beleriand, and in the 400 years of their wars with Morgoth their tongue changed greatly. For three reasons: because it was not in Valinor; because there was war and confusion, and much death among the Noldor, so that their tongue was subject to vicissitudes similar to those of mortal Men; and because in all the world, but especially in Middle-earth, change and growth was very great in the first years of the Sun. Also in Beleriand the tongue and dialects of the Telerian Ilkorins was current, and their king Thingol was very mighty; and Noldorin in Beleriand took much from Beleriandic especially of Doriath. Most of the names and places in that land were given in Doriathrin form. Noldorin returned, after the overthrow of Morgoth, into the West, and lives still in Toleressëa, where it changes now little; and this tongue is derived mainly from the tongue of Gondolin, whence came Eärendel; but it has much of Beleriandic, for Elwing his wife was daughter of Dior, Thingol's heir; and it has somewhat of Ossiriand, for Dior was son of Beren who lived long in Ossiriand.

There was also the book-tongue, 'Elf-Latin', Quenya, concerning which the *Lammasethen* gives a different account from that in the other versions (see V.195). The 'Elf-Latin', it is said (V.172), was brought to Middle-earth by the Noldor, it came to be used by all the Ilkorindi, 'and all Elves know it, even such as linger still in the Hither Lands'.

Thus in the *Lhammas* account we are concerned essentially with three tongues in Beleriand after the Return of the Noldor:

Quenya, the high language and book-tongue, brought from Valinor by the Noldor;

Noldorin, the language of the Noldor in Kôr, greatly changed in Beleriand and much influenced by the Ilkorin speech especially that of Doriath. (It is said in the *Lhammas*, V.174, that the Noldorin tongue of Kôr, *Korolambë* or *Kornoldorin*, was itself much changed from ancient times through the peculiar inventiveness of the Noldor.)

Beleriandic, the Ilkorin tongue of Beleriand, which had become in long ages very different from the tongues of Valinor.

The Noldorin speech of Gondolin was the language that survived in Tol Eressëa after the end of the Elder Days, though influenced by other speech, especially the Ilkorin of Doriath during the sojourn at Sirion's Mouths (see V.177–8).

In GA 1 we have still the conception that the language of the Noldor in Valinor was changed by Noldorin inventiveness, though it is emphasized that it had altered little 'from the ancient tongue of the Eldar upon the march'; and the profound difference between the Noldorin of the new-come Exiles out of Valinor and the ancient Telerian tongue of Beleriand (now called Sindarin) likewise remains – indeed it is the remark that at first communication between Noldor and Sindar was not easy that leads to this excursus. But in GA 1 it is said that, while the Sindarin tongue was 'enriched by words and devices from Noldorin', *Sindarin nevertheless became the language of all the Eldar of Middle-earth and was the language of Tol Eressëa after the Return*; while Noldorin of Valinor became a 'learned' tongue – equivalent in status to the 'Elf-Latin' or Quenya of the *Lhammas*, but learned by few among the Sindar; and indeed the 'Ancient Noldorin' is equated with Quenya (p. 22, at the end of the text). Among the reasons given for this development is that spoken Noldorin in Beleriand and Sindarin 'grew towards' each other, and it is made clear in the last paragraph of the text that there was at the end of the Elder Days a profound difference between the spoken Noldorin of Beleriand, where it survived, and 'Ancient Noldorin' or Quenya.

The statement that Fingolfin as 'overlord' of the Exiles 'acknowledged the high-kingship of Thingol and Menegroth', being 'greatly in awe of that king', is notable (cf. QS §121: 'and mighty though the Kings of the Noldor were in those days ... the name of Thingol was held in awe among them'). This is indeed one of the reasons given for the adoption of Sindarin by the Noldor in Beleriand – for in Thingol's domain only Sindarin might be used; but it is clear that as yet the idea of an actual ban on the use of the Noldorin speech among the Sindar had not arisen.

At the end of this linguistic passage in GA 1 my father wrote in rapid pencil:

Alter this. Let Sindar and Noldor speak much the same tongue owing (a) to changelessness in Valinor (b) to slow change in Middle-earth (c) to long memories of the Elves. But there were of course differences – new words in Noldorin and Sindarin. In both cases more by invention than involuntary. But after Rising of Sun change was sudden and swift – and the Noldor brought a special curse of changefulness with them (designed to cut them off from converse with Valinor?). The two tongues there changed and grew alike. Generally in Beleriand a Noldorized (slightly) Sindarin was spoken. In Doriath less Noldorin if any. [?Ossiriand] to be like Beleriandic.

The difference here from the primary text lies in a denial of any very significant difference between the language of Beleriand and the language of the incoming Noldor, with the subsequent history (as it appears, from the brief and hasty words) being rather one of the coalescence of the languages than of the abandonment of Noldorin.

The excursus on languages in GA 2, written in a much smaller script than that of the main body of the text, reads as follows.

It was indeed at the landing of Fëanor three hundred and sixty-five long years of the Valar since the Noldor had passed over the Sea and left the Sindar behind. Now that time was in length well nigh as three thousand and five hundred years of the Sun. In such an age the tongues of Men that were far sundered would indeed change out of knowledge, save such as were written down in records of song and wisdom. But in Valinor in the days of the Trees change was little to be perceived, save that which came of will and design, while in Middle-earth under the Sleep of Yavanna the change of growth was slow also. Nonetheless in Beleriand the Sleep before the coming of the Sun had been stirred (as elsewhere is told) and the language of the Sindar had in the long years changed much, even in unheeded growth, as a tree may imperceptibly change its shape: as much, maybe, as an unwritten tongue of the later days woud change in five hundred years or more. Whereas the Noldorin tongue, albeit still far nearer in most ways to the ancient common speech of the Eldar, had been altered by will (to forms that seemed to those in Aman more sweet upon the tongue or in the ear) and by the invention of many new words unknown to the Sindar. But speech between the two kindreds became easy and free in this wise. First that after the Rising of the Sun the change of all things in Arda was sudden and swift, and in the days of the Wars both the tongue of the Noldor and that of the Sindar changed greatly: moreover, whether by reason of the like clime, and soil, and the like fortunes, whether by intercourse and the mingling of the peoples, the two tongues changed in similar ways and drew together again. Secondly because in time it came to pass that most of the Noldor indeed forsook their own tongue in daily use and took the tongue of Beleriand instead, though they enriched it with many words of their own. Only in Gondolin, which was early peopled (by Noldor alone)[8] and cut off from intercourse with others, did the Noldorin tongue endure unto the end of the city; whereas in Doriath only was the Sindarin tongue maintained untouched by the Noldorin and less changed than the language of those without. Now this change in the speech of the Noldor came about in this wise. First: though the Sindar were not numerous they much outnumbered the hosts of Fëanor and Fingolfin, such as survived their dreadful journey. Secondly: because of the mingling of the peoples, whereby in all the countries save only in Doriath though the princes of the Noldor were the kings their followers were largely Sindarin by race. Thirdly: because after the death of Fëanor the overlordship of the Exiles passed to Fingolfin (save among the followers of Fëanor's sons), and he acknowledged the high-kingship of Thingol, being indeed in awe of that king, mightiest of the Eldar save Fëanor, and of Melian no less. But Thingol, because of the grievance of the Teleri against the Noldor, would not speak the Noldorin tongue and forbade his subjects to do so. Moreover it came to pass that the Noldor, having of their own will forsaken Aman in rebellion, became subject to change undesigned in a measure beyond even that of the Sindar, and their own tongue in daily use swiftly became unlike the high tongue of Valinor. But the Noldor, being loremasters, retained that high tongue in lore, and ceased not to use it for noble purposes and to teach it to their children. Therefore the form of their speech in daily use came to be held as debased, and the Noldor would use either the High Tongue as a learned language, or else in daily business and in all matters that concerned all the Eldar of Beleriand in general they would use rather the tongue of that land. It is said that it was after the Third Battle, Dagor Aglareb, that the Noldor first began far and wide to take the Sindarin tongue, as they settled and established their realms in Beleriand.

   This restructuring and partial rewriting of the text does not change very substantially the ideas expressed in the earlier form of it: my father did not take up his pencilled note of projected alterations given on p. 24. The passage concerning Dairon and the Runes is omitted, but that had been introduced earlier in GA 2 (§31). It is now emphasized that the Sindarin of Doriath was to some degree archaic, and 'untouched' by Noldorin: this is not stated in GA 1, though it is said there that 'in Doriath the Sindarin tongue alone was spoken'. The acknowledgement by Fingolfin of Thingol's 'high-kingship' is retained (with the reservation 'save among the followers of Fëanor's sons'), but there now appears the ban on the Noldorin tongue imposed by Thingol on his subjects when he learned of the Kinslaying at Alqualondë as one of the reasons for the abandonment of their own tongue by the Noldor. Noldorin is now said to have changed even more rapidly in Middle-earth after the Rising of the Sun than Sindarin, and this is associated with their rebellion in Aman (cf. the words in the pencilled comments at the end of the GA 1 text, p. 24: 'the Noldor brought a special curse of changefulness with them'); while the opinion coming to be held among the Noldor themselves that their spoken tongue was debased provides a further explanation of its abandonment.

My father then (probably after no long interval) rejected the whole of this second text after the words 'and by the invention of many new words unknown to the Sindar' (p. 24) and replaced it as follows:

But it came to pass ere long that the Exiles took up the tongue of Beleriand, as the language of daily use, and their ancient tongue was retained only as a high speech and a language of lore, especially in the houses of the Noldorin lords and among the wise. Now this change of speech was made for many reasons. First, the Noldor were fewer in number than the Sindar, and, save in Doriath [*struck our later:* and Gondolin],[9] the peoples soon became much mingled. Secondly, the Noldor learned the Sindarin tongue far more readily than the Sindar could learn the ancient speech; moreover, after the kinslaying became known, Thingol would hold no parley with any that spake in the tongue of the slayers at Alqualondë, and he forbade his folk to do so. Thus it was that the common speech of Beleriand after the Third Battle, Dagor Aglareb, was the speech of the Grey-elves, albeit somewhat enriched by words and devices drawn from Noldorin (save in Doriath where the language remained purer and less changed by time). [*Struck out later:* Only in Gondolin did the tongue of the Noldor remain in daily use until the end of that city; for it was early peopled by Turgon with Noldor only, from the North-west of the land, and was long hidden and cut off from all converse with others.[10] *The following replacement passage was written in the margin:*]

but the Noldor preserved ever the High-speech of the West as a language of lore, and in that language they would still give names to mighty men or to places of renown. / But all the days of the Wars of Beleriand, [wellnigh >] more than six hundred years, were times of great change, not only because of the labours and troubles of those years, but because in the first years of the Sun and the second Spring of Arda the growth and change of all living things was sudden and swift. Far other at the end of the Wars were [both the Sindarin and Noldorin tongues *later* >] the tongues of Beleriand[11] than they were at the landing of Fëanor, and only the High Speech being learned anew from letters remained unaltered. But these histories were made after the Last Battle and the end of the Elder Days, and therefore they were made in the tongue of the remnant of the Elves as it then was, ere it passed again into the West, and the names of those that they record and of the places that are remembered have for the most part that form which they had in the spoken speech at the last.

Here ends that part which was drawn mainly from the Grey Annals, and there follows matter drawn in brief from the *Quenta Noldorinwa*, and mingled with the traditions of Doriath.[12]

In this revised version, nothing is said about Sindarin and Noldorin 'drawing together' again, and there is no suggestion that the later tongue of the Noldor came to be regarded as 'debased'; spoken Noldorin endured (as the passage was originally written) in the wholly Noldorin city of Gondolin until its fall. The whole conception becomes in fact far simpler: the Noldor retained their own tongue as a High Speech, but Sindarin became their language of daily use (and this was because of the numerical inferiority of the Noldor and the mingling of the peoples outside Doriath, the difficulty that the Sindar found in acquiring the High Speech, and the ban imposed by Thingol). Sindarin received 'loanwords' from Noldorin, but not in Doriath, where the language remained somewhat archaic. By later changes to the text (see notes 8–11) the idea that Noldorin remained in daily use in Gondolin was abandoned.

It is interesting to read, at the end of this last version, that 'these histories' were made '*after* the Last Battle and the end of the Elder Days, and therefore they were made in the tongue of the remnant of the Elves as it then was, *ere* it passed again into the West.'

NOTES

1 365 years of the Valar: 1132–1497 (see GA §11).
2 On the awakening of Beleriand from the Sleep of Yavanna see §§6, 17, and the commentary on §§6, 10.
3 A rough draft of this passage is extant, and this has here:
   Therefore whereas the tongue of the Noldor had changed for the most part only in the making of new words (for things new and old), and in the wilful altering of the ancient tongue of the Quendi to forms and patterns that seemed to the Eldar more beautiful – in which Vanyar, Noldor, and Teleri differed and drew apart – the tongue of the Sindar had changed as living things change by growth – yet only so as in the later world might pass in 400 years.
4 Earlier in GA 1 the form is *Nauglath*: see the commentary on §19.
5 On this passage concerning the Runes of Dairon see §31 and commentary.
6 *Dagor Aglareb*, the Glorious Battle, was formerly the Second Battle (see commentary on §§36 ff.).
7 *Dagor Arnediad*: the Battle of Unnumbered Tears (*Nírnaith Arnediad*).
8 This represents my father's original view that there were no Grey-elves among the people of Gondolin; see note 9.
9 The removal of the words 'and Gondolin' shows the entry of the later conception (see note 8) that many Sindar dwelling in Nivrost at the coming of the Noldor took Turgon to be their lord, and that there were in fact more Elves of Sindarin origin than of Noldorin in the people of Gondolin; see §§107, 113 and commentary.
10 This passage was removed at the same time and for the same reason as the words 'and Gondolin' earlier in this revised text (note 9).
11 The change of 'both the Sindarin and Noldorin tongues' to 'the tongues of Beleriand' was made later than the changes referred to in notes 9 and 10, but presumably for the same reason, since the reference was to the spoken Noldorin of Gondolin. The plural 'tongues' in the revised wording is rather puzzling; perhaps my father was thinking of the speech of the Green-elves of Ossiriand, or possibly he meant the varieties (dialects) of Sindarin.
12 The term *Quenta Noldorinwa* appears in the title of Q (IV.77). I cannot say what conception my father had formed of the historical tradition when he wrote these concluding words.

THE GREY ANNALS

As I have said, the manuscript GA 1 does not continue after the end of the discussion of the languages, but for the next section of GA 2 there is a text on loose pages which may be regarded as a continuation of GA 1. It constitutes part of the material labelled 'Old material of Grey Annals' referred to on p. 4. This text runs from the (second) beginning of the annal 1497 ('Now Morgoth being dismayed ...') to the end of annal YS 20 (and for the annals 6 and 7 there is a very rough preliminary draft as well). To this text the GA 2 manuscript is very close indeed, and is scarcely more than a fine copy of it with changes of wording here and there; a few interesting points of difference are noticed in the commentary.

I return now to the text of GA 2, which need not now be distinguished by a number.

1497

§49 Now Morgoth being dismayed by the rout of his armies and the unlooked-for valour of the Noldor, and desiring time for new designs, sent emissaries to Maidros, and feigned that he was willing to treat with him. And Maidros feigned that he for his part was also willing, and either purposed evil to the other. Therefore against covenant each came with great force to the parley, but Morgoth with the more, and Maidros was defeated and taken captive.

§50 Then Morgoth held Maidros as a hostage, and swore only to release him, if the Noldor would march away, either to Valinor, or else far from Beleriand into the South of the world; and if they would not do this, then he would put Maidros to torment. But the other sons of Fëanor knew that Morgoth would betray them, and would not release Maidros, whatsoever they might do; and they were constrained also by their oath, and might not for any cause forsake the war against their Enemy.

1498

§51 Therefore Morgoth took Maidros, and setting a band of hellwrought steel about his right wrist hung him thereby above a precipice upon the west-tower of Thangorodrim, where none could reach him. But his brethren drew back and fortified a great camp in Hithlum.

1500

§52 In this time Fingolfin and those that followed him crossed the grinding ice of Helkaraxë, and so came at last with great woe and loss into the North of Endar; and their hearts were filled with bitterness. And even as they set foot upon Middle-earth, the ages of the Stars were ended, and the time of the Sun and Moon was begun, as is told in the Chronicle of Aman.

YS 1

§53 Here the Moon and the Sun, wrought by the Valar after the death of the Trees, rose new in the heaven. First the Moon came forth, and even as it rose above the darkness in the West Fingolfin let blow his silver trumpets, and began his march into Middle-earth; and the shadows of his host went long and black before them.

§54 The Elves of Middle-earth looked up with hope and delight at this new thing; but the servants of Morgoth were amazed; and Morgoth sent spirits of darkness to assail Tilion, the guardian of the moon, and there was strife in heaven. But soon after there came the first Dawn of the Sun, and it was like a great fire upon the towers of the Pelóri, and the clouds of Middle-earth were kindled, and all the mists of the world smoked and glowed like gold. Then Fingolfin unfurled his blue and silver banners, and flowers awoke from the Sleep of Yavanna and sprang up beneath the feet of his host.

§55 Then indeed Morgoth was dismayed, and he descended into the uttermost depths of Angband, and withdrew his servants, sending forth great reek and dark cloud to hide his land from the light of the Daystar. Therefore Fingolfin marched from the North unopposed through the fastness of the realm of Morgoth, and he passed over Dor-Daedeloth, and his foes hid beneath the earth; but the Elves smote upon the gates of Angband, and the challenge of their trumpets shook the towers of Thangorodrim. And Maidros heard them amid his torment and cried aloud, but his voice was lost in the echoes of the stone.

§56 From this time are reckoned the Years of the Sun. Swifter and briefer are they than the long Years of the Trees in Valinor. Lo! in that time the growth and the changing and ageing of all things was hastened exceedingly; and all living things spread and multiplied in the Second Spring of Arda, and the Eldar increased, and Beleriand grew green and fair.

§57 At the first Sunrise, it is said, Men, the younger children of Ilúvatar, awoke in Hildórien in the midmost regions of the world. The Atani they were named; but the Eldar called them also the Hildi, the Followers. Into the tale of Beleriand they came ere the end.

2

§58 Now Fingolfin, being of other temper than Fëanor, and wary of the wiles of Morgoth, after sounding his challenge withdrew from Dor-Daedeloth and turned towards Mithrim, for he had heard tidings that there he should find the sons of Fëanor, and he desired also to have the shield of the mountains, while his folk rested and grew strong; for he had seen the strength of Angband and deemed not that it would fall to the sound of trumpets only. Therefore coming at length to Hithlum he made his first camp and dwelling by the north-shore of Lake Mithrim.

§59 But no love was there in the hearts of Fingolfin and his folk for the people of Fëanor; and though Fingolfin learned that Fëanor was dead, he held his sons the accomplices of their father, and there was peril of war between the two hosts. Grievous as were their losses upon the road, the people of Fingolfin and Inglor son of Finrod were still more numerous than the followers of Fëanor; wherefore they withdrew before Fingolfin and removed their dwelling to the south-shore, and the Lake lay between the peoples.

§60 Many indeed of Fëanor's folk repented them sorely of the deed at Losgar, and were astounded at the valour which had brought the friends that they abandoned over the Ice of the North, and they would have welcomed them humbly had they dared for shame. Thus because of the curse that lay on them the Noldor achieved nothing, while Morgoth was dismayed and his servants still cowed by the sudden light. And Morgoth let make vast smokes and vapours in the pits of Angband, and they came forth from the reeking tops of the Iron Mountains, and the east wind bore them over Hithlum and darkened the new sun, and they fell, coiling about field and hollow, and lying upon the waters of Mithrim, drear and poisonous.

5

§61 Here Fingon the Valiant resolved to heal the feud that divided the Noldor, ere their Enemy should be ready for war; for the earth trembled in the north-lands with the thunder of the forges of Morgoth. Moreover the thought of his ancient friendship with Maiðros stung his heart with grief (though he knew not yet that Maidros had not forgotten him at the burning of the ships). Therefore he dared a deed which is justly renowned among the feats of the princes of the Noldor: alone, and without the counsel of any, he set forth in search of Maidros; and aided by the very darkness that Morgoth had made he came unseen into the fastness of his foes. In the *Quenta* it is told how at the last he found Maidros, by singing a song of Valinor alone in the dark mountains, and was aided by Thorondor the Eagle, who bore him aloft unto Maidros; but the bond of steel he could in no wise release and must sever the hand that it held. Thus he rescued his friend of old from torment, and their love was renewed; and the hatred between the houses of Fingolfin and Fëanor was assuaged. Thereafter Maidros wielded his sword in his left hand.

6

§62 Now the Noldor, being again united, set a watch upon the borders of Dor-Daedeloth, and held their main force in the north of the land, but they sent forth messengers far and wide to explore the countries of Beleriand and to treat with the folk that dwelt there.

§63 Beyond the Girdle of Melian those of Finrod's house were suffered to pass, for they could claim close kinship with King Thingol himself (their mother Ëarwen being his brother's daughter). Now Angrod was the first of the Exiles to come to Menegroth, as messenger of Inglor, and he spoke long with the King, telling him of the deeds of the Noldor in the north, and their numbers, and the ordering of their force; but being true and wisehearted and deeming all griefs now forgiven, he spoke naught of the deeds of Fëanor save his valiant death.

§64 And King Thingol hearkened, and he said to Angrod ere he went: 'Thus thou shalt speak for me to those that sent thee. In Hithlum indeed the Noldor have leave to do as they will, and in Dor Thonion they may dwell, and in the countries east of Doriath even to the feet of the mountains of Eryd Luin there is room and to spare. But elsewhere there are many of my folk, and I would not have them restrained of their freedoms, still less ousted from their homes. Beware therefore how ye princes of the West bear yourselves, for I am the Lord of Beleriand and all who seek to dwell there shall hear my word.

Into Doriath none shall come to abide there, but only such as I call as guests, or who seek me in great need.'

7

§65 Now the Noldor held council in Mithrim to ponder all such matters, and to resolve how they should deal in friendship with the Grey-elves, and yet best gather force and dispose it for the war upon Morgoth. For that cause they had come to Middle-earth; yet to many the northlands seemed chill and the south countries fairer, and they desired greatly new homes where their folk might increase in peace far from the camps of war in the highlands.

§66 To this council came Angrod out of Doriath bearing the words of King Thingol, and their welcome seemed cold to the Noldor. The sons of Fëanor indeed were wroth thereat; and Maidros laughed, saying: 'He is a king that can hold his own, or else his title is vain. Thingol does but grant us lands where his power does not run. Indeed Doriath only would be his realm this day, but for the coming of the Noldor. Therefore in Doriath let him reign, and be glad that he hath the sons of Finwë for neighbours, not the Orcs of Morgoth that we found. Elsewhere it shall go as seems good to us.'

§67 But Cranthir, who loved not the sons of Finrod, and was the harshest of the brethren and the most quick to anger, cried aloud: 'Yea more! Let not the sons of Finrod run hither and thither with their tales to this Dark-elf in his caves! Who made them our spokesmen to deal with him? And though they be come indeed to Beleriand, let them not so swiftly forget that their father was a lord of the Noldor, though their mother was of other kin.'

§68 Then Angrod was exceedingly wroth and went forth from the council. Maidros indeed rebuked Cranthir; but the greater part of the Noldor, of both followings, hearing his words were troubled in heart, fearing the fell spirit of the sons of Fëanor that, it seemed, would ever be like to burst forth in rash word or violence.

§69 Therefore when the council came to the choosing of one to be the overlord of the Exiles and the head of all their princes, the choice of all save few fell on Fingolfin. And even as the choice was made known, all those that heard it recalled the words of Mandos that the House of Fëanor should be called the Dispossessed for ever. None the less ill for that did the sons of

Fëanor take this choice, save Maidros only, though it touched him the nearest. But he restrained his brethen, saying to Fingolfin: 'If there lay no grievance between us, lord, still the choice would come rightly to thee, the eldest here of the house of Finwë, and not the least wise.'

§70 But the sons of Fëanor departed then from the council, and soon after they left Mithrim and went eastward to the countries wide and wild between Himring and Lake Helevorn under Mount Rerir. That region was named thereafter the March of Maidros; for there was little defence there of hill or river against assault from the North; and there Maidros and his brethren kept watch, gathering all such folk as would come to them, and they had little dealings with their kinsfolk westward, save at need.

§71 It is said, indeed, that Maidros himself devised this plan, to lessen the chances of strife, and because he was very willing that the chief peril of assault (as it seemed) should fall upon himself; and he remained for his part in friendship with the houses of Fingolfin and Finrod, and would come among them at whiles for common counsel. Yet he also was bound by the Oath, though it slept now for a time.

20

§72 In this year Fingolfin, King of the Noldor, called a great council and made a high feast, that was long after remembered as Mereth Aderthad, the Feast of Reuniting. And it was held nigh the fair pools of Ivrin (whence the swift Narog arose), for there the lands were green and fair at the feet of the mountains that shielded them from the North. Thither came many of the chieftains and people of Fingolfin and Inglor; and of the sons of Fëanor Maidros and Maglor with warriors of the March; and there they were joined by Cirdan and many folk of the Havens, and great concourse of the Grey-elves from woods and fields far and near, and even from Ossiriand there came some of the Nandor on behalf of their folk. But Thingol came not himself from Doriath, and sent but two messengers, Dairon and Mablung, bringing his greetings. At Mereth Aderthad many counsels were taken in good will, and oaths were sworn of league and friendship, and there was much mirth and good hope; and indeed there followed after a fair time of peace, of growth and blossoming, and all the land was glad, though still the Shadow brooded in the North.

§73 (At this feast it is recorded that the tongue of the Grey-elves was most spoken even by the Noldor, for whereas the Noldor readily learned the speech of the land, the Sindar were slow to master the tongue of Aman.)

50

§74 Here after long peace, as Inglor and Turgon journeyed together, and lay by night near the Twilight Meres, Ulmo laid a deep sleep upon them and troubled them in dreams. And thereafter each sought separately for places of strength and refuge in the land, lest Morgoth should burst from Angband as their dreams foreboded. [*Added later:* But Turgon found not what he sought, and returned to Nivrost.]

52

§75 In this year Inglor and his sister Galaðriel were long the guests of Thingol their kinsman. And Inglor was filled with wonder at the beauty and strength of Menegroth, and he desired greatly to make for himself a strong place in like manner. Therefore he opened his heart to Thingol, telling him of his dreams; and Thingol spoke to him of the caves under the High Faroth on the west-bank of Narog, and when he departed gave him guides to lead him to that place of which few yet knew. Thus Inglor came to the Caverns of Narog and began there to establish deep halls and armouries, after the manner of Menegroth; and that stronghold was called Nargothrond. Wherefore the Noldor named him Felagund, Lord of Caves, and that name he bore until his end. But Galaðriel did not depart [*added later:* from Doriath], and remained long with Melian, for there was much love between them.

53

§76 [Turgon journeying alone, by the favour of Ulmo *later* >] In this year Ulmo appeared to Turgon upon the shores of Nivrost, and at his bidding went forth alone, and by the favour of Ulmo he / discovered that hidden vale amid the encircling mountains where afterwards Gondolin was built. Of this he spoke to none yet, but began secretly to devise the plan of a city after the manner of Tirion upon Túna, for which his heart now yearned in exile.

60
The Third Battle

§77 Here Morgoth, believing the report of his spies that the lords of the Eldar were wandering abroad with little thought of war, made trial of the strength and watchfulness of his enemies. Once more, with little warning, his might was stirred, and suddenly there were earthquakes in the North, and fires came from fissures in the earth, and the Iron Mountains vomited flame; and an army of Orcs thrust down the Vale of Sirion and attempted to pierce to the heart of Beleriand. But Fingolfin and Maidros were not sleeping, and gathering swiftly great force of both Noldor and Sindar they destroyed all the scattered bands of the Orcs that had stolen into the land; but the main host they repelled, and drove out onto the fields of Ardgalen, and there surrounded it and destroyed it, to the least and last, within sight of Angband. This was the Third Battle of the Wars, and was called *Dagor Aglareb*, the Glorious Battle.

§78 A victory it was, and yet a warning; and the chieftains took heed of it, and thereafter drew closer their leaguer, and strengthened and ordered their watch, setting the Siege of Angband, which lasted wellnigh four hundred years. And Fingolfin boasted that (save by treason among themselves) Morgoth could never again burst from the leaguer of the Eldar. Yet neither could the Noldor take Angband nor regain the Silmarils. And war never wholly ceased in all that time of the Siege; for Morgoth was secretly forging new weapons, and ever and anon he would make trial of his enemies. Moreover, he was not encircled upon the uttermost north; and though the ice and snow restrained his enemies from keeping watch in the frozen wilderness, it hindered not his spies and messengers from secret going and coming.

> The following passage as the text was originally written began thus: 'At this time also Morgoth began a new evil. He bade his servants to take alive any of the Eldar ...' This was replaced by the long rider (written on a separate page) that follows here (§§79–81), returning to the original text at 'He now bade the Orkor to take alive any of the Eldar', the second sentence of §81.

§79 Nor himself, an he would go. Indeed we learn now in Eressëa from the Valar, through our kin that dwell still in Aman, that after Dagor-nuin-Giliath Melkor was so long in assailing the Eldar with strength for he himself had departed from

Angband, for the last time. Even as before at the awakening of the Quendi, his spies were watchful, and tidings soon came to him of the arising of Men. This seemed to him so great a matter that secretly under shadow he went forth into Middle-earth, leaving the command of the War to Sauron his lieutenant. Of his dealings with Men the Eldar knew naught at that time, and know little now, for neither the Valar nor Men have spoken to them clearly of these things.

§80 But that some darkness lay upon the hearts of Men (as the shadow of the kinslaying and the doom of Mandos lay upon the Noldor) the Eldar perceived clearly even in the fair folk of the Elf-friends that they first knew. To corrupt or destroy whatsoever arose new and fair was ever the chief desire of Morgoth; but as regards the Eldar, doubtless he had this purpose also in his errand: by fear and lies to make Men their foes, and bring them up out of the East against Beleriand. But this design was slow to ripen, and was never wholly achieved, for Men (it is said) were at first very few in number, whereas Morgoth grew afraid of the tidings of the growing power and union of the Eldar and came back to Angband, leaving behind at that time but few servants, and those of less might and cunning.

§81 Certain it is that at this time (which was the time of his return, if the aforesaid account be true, as we must believe) Morgoth began a new evil, desiring above all to sow fear and disunion among the Eldar in Beleriand. He now bade the Orkor to take alive any of the Eldar that they could and bring them bound to Angband. For it was his intent to use their lore and skill under duress for his own ends; moreover he took pleasure in tormenting them, and would besides by pain wring from them at times tidings of the deeds and counsels of his enemies. Some indeed he so daunted by the terror of his eyes that they needed no chains more, but walked ever in fear of him, doing his will wherever they might be. These he would unbind and let return to work treason among their own kin. In this way also was the curse of Mandos fulfilled, for after a while the Elves grew afraid of those who claimed to have escaped from thraldom, and often those hapless whom the Orcs ensnared, even if they broke from the toils would but wander homeless and friendless thereafter, becoming outlaws in the woods.

§82 And though it was long ere all these evils began to appear, it is said that even after the victory of the Third Battle some of the Eldar (either caught by robber bands in the woods, or over rash in pursuit of the foe) were thus seized and taken to Morgoth. And thus he learned much of all that had befallen since the rebellion of Fëanor, and rejoiced seeing therein the seed of many dissensions among his foes. But thus also it became known to the Eldar that the Silmarils yet lived, and were set in the Iron Crown that Morgoth wore upon his dark throne. For the Noldor were a mighty race yet, and few of them could he so daunt that they would do his will, but escaping they became oft his deadliest foes.

§83 In the *Quenta Noldorinwa* it is recounted in what manner after Dagor Aglareb the lords of the Noldor and Sindar ordered the land, during the Siege of Angband. Here it suffices to say that [*added:* westernmost at first Turgon abode in Nivrost south of Drengist between Eryd Lómin and the Sea; but] Fingolfin and Fingon held Hithlum and had their abode and chief fortress at Eithel Sirion; and they had horsemen also that rode upon the fields of Ardgalen, for from few their horses had increased swiftly, and the grass of Ardgalen was yet rich and green. Of those horses many of the sires came from Valinor, and were given to Fingolfin by Maidros in atonement of his losses, for they had been carried by ship to Losgar.

§84 The sons of Finrod held the land from Hithlum unto the eastern end of Dorthonion. Inglor and Orodreth held the pass of Sirion, but Angrod and Egnor held the north slopes of Dorthonion as far as Aglon where began the March of Maidros aforesaid.

§85 Behind this leaguer from the Sea to Eryd Luin the wide countries of Beleriand, west and east of Sirion, were held in this wise. Though Fingolfin of Hithlum was overlord of all the Noldor, Inglor, well-beloved of all Elves, became indeed the greatest prince in the land. For King Felagund he was in Nargothrond, whereas his brothers Angrod and Egnor were lords of Dorthonion and his vassals; and he had also a fort and place of battle in the north, in the wide pass between Eredwethrin and Dorthonion through which Sirion flowed south. There stood an isle amid the river, and upon it Inglor built a mighty watchtower: Minnas-tirith: and there, when Nargothrond was made, he set Orodreth as warden. But upon either side of Narog all the folk of either race that dwelt in the lands took him for their lord, as far south as the Mouths of Sirion, and from

Nenning in the West to the borders of Doriath eastward. But in Eglarest, and west of Nenning to the Sea, Cirdan the Shipwright was lord, yet ever he was close in friendship with Nargothrond.

§86 Doriath in the midst of the land was the realm of King Thingol; and east the wide countries south of the March of Maidros, even to the borders of Ossiriand were held to be the domain of the sons of Fëanor. But few dwelt there save hunters and Grey-elves wandering, and there Damrod and Díriel abode and came seldom northward while the Siege lasted. Thither other of the Elven-lords would ride at whiles, even from afar, to hunt in the green-woods; but none ever passed east over Eryd Luin or looked upon Eriador, save the Green-elves only, who had kindred that dwelt yet in the further lands. Thus little news and late came to Beleriand of what passed in the regions of the East.

60–445

§87 For the most part the time of the Siege of Angband was a time of gladness, and the earth had peace under the new light, while the swords of the Noldor restrained the malice of Morgoth, and his thought being bent on their ruin he gave the less heed to aught else in Middle-earth. In this time therefore Men waxed and multiplied, [and they had converse with the Dark-elves of the Eastlands >] and among them were some that had converse with the Elves of Middle-earth, / and learned much of them. [From them it is said that they took the first beginnings of the many tongues of Men. Thus they heard rumour of the Blessed Realms [*sic*] of the West and of the Powers that dwelt there, and many of the Fathers of Men, the *Atanatári*, in their wanderings moved ever westward. *This passage was rewritten to read:*] From them it is said that they took the first beginnings of the western tongues of Men; and from them also they heard rumour of the Blessed Realms of the West and of the Powers of Light that dwelt there. Therefore many of the Fathers of Men, the *Atanatári*, in their wanderings moved ever westward, fleeing from the darkness that had ensnared them. For these Elf-friends were Men that had repented and rebelled against the Dark Power, and were cruelly hunted and oppressed by those that worshipped it, and its servants.

64

§88 Now the unquiet that Ulmo set in his heart returned to Turgon in Nivrost, and he gathered therefore his folk together, even to a third part of the Noldor of Fingolfin's people (nor were any of the Sindar among them), and with their wives and their goods they departed secretly along the south of Ered-wethrin, and few knew whither they were gone. But Turgon came to Gondolin, and there his folk pressed on with the building of the city that he had devised in his heart; and they set a guard upon it that none might come upon it from without.
[*This annal was later changed to read:*]
§89 Now the unquiet that Ulmo set in his heart returned to Turgon in Nivrost, and he gathered therefore many of his most skilled folk together and led them secretly to Gondolin, and there they began the building of the strong city that Turgon had devised in his heart; and they set a guard upon it that none might come upon their work from without.

65

§90 Here with the aid of the Noldor (whose skill far surpassed that of the Sindar) Brithombar and Eglarest were walled about with great walls, and fair towns were raised within, and harbours with quays and piers of stone. And the Tower of Ingildon was set up upon the cape west of Eglarest to watch the Sea; though needlessly, as it proved. For at no time ever did Morgoth essay to build ships or to make war by sea. Water all his servants shunned, and to the Sea none would willing go nigh, save in dire need.

66

§91 Now Galaðriel Finrod's daughter, as hath been told, dwelt with Melian, and was dear to her. And at times they would speak together of Valinor and the bliss of old; but beyond the dark hour of the death of the Trees Galaðriel would not go, but fell ever silent.

§92 And on a time Melian said: 'There is some woe that lies upon thee and thy kin. That I can see in thee, but all else is hidden from me; for by no vision or thought can I perceive aught that passed or passes in the West: a shadow lies over all the Land of Aman, and reaches far out over the Sea. [Wilt thou not >] Why wilt thou not tell me more?'

'For that woe is past,' answered Galaðriel; 'and I would take what joy is here left untroubled by memory. And maybe there is woe enough yet to come, though still hope may seem bright.'

§93 Then Melian looked in her eyes, and said: 'I believe not that the Noldor came forth as messengers of the Valar, as was said at first: not though they came in the very hour of our need. For lo! they speak never of the Valar, nor have their high lords brought any message to Thingol, whether from Manwë, or Ulmo, or even from Olwë the king's brother and his own folk that went over the Sea. For what cause, Galaðriel, were the high people of the Noldor driven forth as exiles from Aman? Or what evil lies on the sons of Fëanor that they are so haughty and fell? Do I not strike near the truth?'

§94 'Near, lady,' answered Galadriel, 'save that we were not driven forth, but came of our own will, and against that of the Valar. And through great peril and in despite of the Valar for this purpose we came: to take vengeance upon Morgoth, [or >] and regain what he stole.' Then Galaðriel spoke to Melian of the Silmarils, and of the slaying of King Finwë. But still she said no word of the Oath, nor of the Kinslaying, nor of the burning of the ships.

§95 But Melian, who looked still in her eyes as she spoke, said: 'Now much thou tellest me, and yet more I perceive. A darkness thou wouldst cast still over the long road from Tirion, but I see evil there, which Thingol should learn for his guidance.'

'Maybe,' said Galaðriel, 'but not of me.'

§96 And Melian spoke then no more of these matters with Galaðriel; but she told to King Thingol all that she had heard of the Silmarils. 'This is a great matter,' said she, 'a greater indeed than the Noldor themselves understand. For lo! the Light of Aman and the fate of Arda lie now locked in these things, the work of Fëanor, who is gone. They shall not be recovered, I foretell, by any power of the Eldar; and the world shall be broken in battles that are to come, ere they are wrested from Morgoth. See now! Fëanor they have slain (and many another I guess); but first of all the deaths they have brought and yet shall bring was Finwë thy friend. Morgoth slew him, ere he fled from Aman.'

§97 Then Thingol was silent a while with grief and foreboding; but at length he said: 'Now at last I understand the coming of the Noldor out of the West, at which I wondered much before. Not to our aid came they (save by chance); for those that remain upon Middle-earth the Valar will leave to their own devices, until the uttermost need. For vengeance and redress of their loss the Noldor came. Yet all the more sure shall they be as allies against Morgoth, with whom it is not now to be thought that they shall ever make treaty.'

§98 But Melian said: 'Truly for these causes they came; but for others also. Beware of the sons of Fëanor! The shadow of the wrath of the Gods lies upon them; and they have done evil, I perceive, both in Aman and to their own kin. A grief but lulled to sleep lies between the princes of the Noldor.'

§99 And Thingol said: 'What is that to me? Of Fëanor I have heard but report, which maketh him great indeed. Of his sons I hear little to my pleasure; yet they are likely to prove the deadliest foes of our foe.'

'Their words and their counsels shall have two edges,' said Melian; and afterward they spake no more of this matter.

67

§100 It was not long ere whispered tales began to pass among the Sindar concerning the deeds of the Noldor ere they came to Beleriand. Whence they came is now clear (though it was not so then), and as may well be thought, the evil truth was enhanced and poisoned with lies. Morgoth chose the Sindar for this first assault of his malice, because they knew him not, and were yet unwary and trustful of words. Therefore Cirdan, hearing these dark tales, was troubled. Wise he was, and perceived swiftly that, true or false, these tales were put about at this time with malice; but the malice he deemed was that of the princes of the Noldor because of the jealousy of their houses. Therefore he sent messengers to Thingol to tell all that he had heard.

§101 And it chanced that at that time the sons of Finrod were again the guests of Thingol, for they wished to see their sister Galaðriel. Then Thingol, being greatly moved, spake in ire to Inglor, saying: 'Ill hast thou done to me, kinsman, to conceal so great matters from me. For behold! I have learned of all the evil deeds of the Noldor.'

§102 But Inglor answered: 'What ill have I done thee, lord? Or what evil deed have the Noldor done in all thy realm to grieve thee? Neither against thy kingship nor against any of thy folk have they thought evil or done evil.'

§103 'I marvel at thee, son of Eärwen,' said Thingol, 'that thou wouldst come to the board of thy kinsman thus redhanded from the slaying of thy mother's kin, and yet say nought in defence, nor yet seek any pardon!'

§104 And Inglor was sorely troubled, but he was silent, for he could not defend himself, save by bringing charges against the other princes of the Noldor; and this he was loath to do before Thingol. But in Angrod's heart the memory of the words of Cranthir welled up again with bitterness, and he cried: 'Lord, I know not what lies thou hast heard, nor whence. But we come not redhanded. Guiltless we came forth, save maybe of folly, to listen to the words of fell Fëanor, and become as folk besotted with wine, and as briefly. No evil did we do on our road, but suffered ourselves great wrong. And forgave it. For which we are named tale-bearers to thee and treasonable to the Noldor. Untruly as thou knowest, for we have of our loyalty been silent before thee, and thus earned thy anger. But now these charges are not longer to be borne, and the truth thou shalt know.' Then he spake bitterly against the sons of Fëanor, telling of the blood at Alqualondë, and the doom of Mandos, and the burning of the ships at Losgar. 'Wherefore should we that endured the Grinding Ice bear the names of kinslayers and traitors?' he cried.

§105 'Yet the shadow of Mandos lies on you also,' said Melian. But Thingol was long silent ere he spoke. 'Go now!' he said. 'For my heart is hot within me. Later ye may return, if you will. For I will not shut my doors for ever against you my kin, that were ensnared in an evil that ye did not aid. With Fingolfin and his folk also I will keep friendship, for they have bitterly atoned for such ill as they did. And in our hatred of the Power that wrought all this woe our griefs shall be lost.

§106 'But hear this! Never again in my ears shall be heard the tongue of those who slew my folk in Alqualondë! Nor in all my realm shall that tongue be openly spoken, while my power endureth. All the Sindar shall hear my command that they shall neither speak with the tongue of the Noldor nor answer to it. And all such as use it shall be held slayers of kin and betrayers of kin unrepentant.'

§107 Then the sons of Finrod departed from Menegroth with heavy hearts, perceiving how the words of Mandos would ever be made true, and that none of the Noldor that followed after Fëanor could escape from the shadow that lay upon his house. And it came to pass even as Thingol had spoken; for the Sindar heard his word and thereafter throughout Beleriand they refused the tongue of the Noldor, and shunned those that spoke it aloud; but the Exiles took the Sindarin tongue in all their daily uses, [save only in Gondolin where Noldor dwelt unmingled, but that was yet hidden. >] and the High Speech of the West was spoken only by the lords of the Noldor among themselves, yet it lived ever as a language of lore wherever any of that folk dwelt.

102

§108 About this time it is recorded that Nargothrond was full-wrought, and Finrod's sons were gathered there to a feast and Galadriel came from Doriath and dwelt there a while. Now King Inglor Felagund had no wife, and Galadriel asked him why this was; but foresight came upon Felagund as she spoke, and he said: 'An oath I too shall swear, and must be free to fulfill it and go into darkness. Nor shall anything of all my realm endure that a son should inherit.'

§109 But it is said that not until that hour had such cold thoughts ruled him; for indeed she whom he had loved was Amárië of the Vanyar, and she was not permitted to go with him into exile.

116

§110 In this year according to the records of that city Gondolin was full-wrought, in fifty years after the coming of Turgon from Nivrost. But no tidings of this came over the mountains, nor were any of Turgon's kin bidden to a feast. [*This annal was later struck out and replaced by the following rider, §§111–13:*]

§111 In this year Gondolin was full-wrought, after fifty [*added:* and 2] years of secret toil. Now therefore Turgon prepared to depart from Nivrost, and leave his fair halls in Vinyamar beneath Mount Taras; and then [for the last time Ulmo himself came to him >] Ulmo came to him a second time / and said: 'Now thou shalt go at last to Gondolin, Turgon; and I will set my power in the Vale of Sirion, so that none shall mark thy going, nor shall any find there the hidden entrance to thy land against thy will. Longest of all the realms of the Eldalië shall Gondolin stand against Melkor. But love it not too well, and remember that the true hope of the Noldor lieth in the West and cometh from the Sea.'

§112   And Ulmo warned Turgon that he also lay under the Doom of Mandos, which Ulmo had no power to remove. 'Thus it may come to pass,' he said, 'that the curse of the Noldor shall find thee too ere the end, and treason shall awake within thy walls. Then shall they be in peril of fire. But if this peril draweth nigh, then even from Nivrost one shall come to warn thee, and from him beyond ruin and fire hope shall be born for Elves and Men. Leave, therefore, in this house arms and a sword, that in years to come he may find them, and thus shalt thou know him and be not deceived.' And Ulmo showed to Turgon of what kind and stature should be the mail and helm and sword that he left behind.

§113   Then Ulmo returned to the Sea; and Turgon sent forth all his folk (even to a third part of the Noldor of Fingolfin's House, and a yet greater host of the Sindar), and they passed away, company by company, secretly, under the shadows of Eryd Wethion, and came unseen with their wives and goods to Gondolin, and none knew whither they were gone. And last of all Turgon arose and went with his lords and household silently through the hills and passed the gates in the mountains, and they were shut. But Nivrost was empty of folk and so remained until the ruin of Beleriand.

150

§114   The people of Cranthir Fëanor's son dwelt beyond the upper waters of Gelion, about Lake Helevorn under the shadow of the Blue Mountains. At this time it is said that they first climbed into the mountains and looked eastward, and wide and wild it seemed to them was Middle-earth. Thus it was that Cranthir's folk first came upon the Naugrim, who after the onslaught of Morgoth and the coming of the Noldor had ceased their traffick into Beleriand. Now, though either people loved skill and was eager to learn, there was little love between the Noldor and the Dwarves. For the Dwarves were secret and quick to resentment, whereas Cranthir was haughty and scarce concealed his scorn for the unloveliness of the Naugrim, and his folk followed their lord. Nonetheless, since both peoples feared and hated Morgoth they made alliance, and had of it great profit. For the Naugrim learned many secrets of craft in those days, so that the smiths and masons of Nogrod and Belegost became renowned among their kin; but the Noldor got great wealth of iron, and their armouries became filled with store of weapons and harness of war. Moreover thereafter, until the power of Maidros was overthrown, all the traffick of the dwarf-mines passed first through the hands of Cranthir, and thus he won great riches.

155

§115 Here after long quiet Morgoth endeavoured to take Fingolfin at unawares (for he knew of the vigilance of Maidros); and he sent forth an army into the white north, and it turned then west and again south and came by the coasts to the firth of Drengist, and so would enter into the heart of the realm of Hithlum. But it was espied in time and taken in a trap among the hills at the head of the firth, and the most of the Orcs were driven into the sea. This was not reckoned among the great battles, and was but the most dangerous of the many trials and thrusts that Angband would make ever and anon against the leaguer. Thereafter there was peace for many years, and no open assault; for Morgoth perceived now that the Orcs unaided were no match for the Noldor, save in such numbers as he could not yet muster. Therefore he sought in his heart for new counsel, and he bethought him of dragons.

260

§116 Here Glaurung, the first of the *Urulóki*, the fire-drakes of the North, came forth from Angband's gate by night. He was yet young and scarce half-grown (for long and slow is the life of those worms), but the Elves fled before him to Erydwethrin and to Dorthonion in dismay; and he defiled the fields of Ardgalen. Then Fingon, prince of Hithlum, rode against him with archers upon horseback, and hemmed him round with a ring of swift riders. And Glaurung in turn was dismayed, for he could not endure their darts, being not yet come to his full armoury; and he fled back to hell, and came not forth again for many years. But Morgoth was ill pleased that Glaurung had disclosed himself over soon; and after his defeat there was the long peace of wellnigh two hundred years. In that time there was naught but affrays on the north-marches, and all Beleriand prospered and grew rich, and the Noldor built many towers and fair dwellings and made many things of beauty, and many poesies and histories and books of lore. And in many parts of the land the Noldor and Sindar became welded into one folk and spoke the same tongue; though ever this difference remained between them, that the Noldor of purer race had the greater power of mind and body, being both the mightier warriors and sages, and they built with stone, and loved rather the hill-slopes and open lands. Whereas the Sindar had the fairer voices and were more skilled in music (save only Maglor son of Fëanor), and loved the woods and riversides, and some still would wander far and wide without settled abode, and they sang as they went.

[*Isfin and Ëol*]

At this point in the manuscript my father inserted an annal entry for the year 316 concerning Isfin and Ëol, replacing the annal that stood in the manuscript under 471, which was struck out. He wrote the new annal on the back of a page from an engagement calendar for November 1951; and on the same page he added two further annals on the same subject, for the years 320 and 400. It is clearest and most convenient to give all four annals (i.e. the original one for 471 and the three later ones) together here.

§117 [*Rejected annal for the year 471*] In this year Isfin the White, sister of Turgon, wearying of the city, and desiring to look again upon Fingon her brother, went from Gondolin against the will and counsel of Turgon; and she strayed into Brethil and was lost in the dark forest. There Ëol, the Dark-elf, who abode in the forest, found her and took her to wife. In the depths of the wood he lived and shunned the sun, desiring only the starlight of old; for so he had dwelt since the first finding of Beleriand, and took no part in all the deeds of his kin.

316

§118 Here Isfin the White, sister of Turgon, wearying of the city, went from Gondolin against the [will >] wish of Turgon. And she went not to Fingon, as he bade, but sought the ways to the East, to the land of Celegorm and his brethren, her friends of old in Valinor. But she strayed from her escort in the shadows of Nan Dungorthin, and went on alone; and she came at last to Nan Elmoth. There she came into the enchantments of Ëol the Dark-elf, who abode in the wood and shunned the sun, desiring only the starlight of old. And Ëol took her to wife, and she abode with him, and no tidings of her came to any of her kin; for Ëol suffered her not to stray far, nor to fare abroad save in the dark or the twilight.

320

§119 Here Isfin the White bore a son in Nan Elmoth to Ëol the Dark-elf; and she would name him (?) Fingol [*added:* dur], but Ëol named him Glindûr [*later* > Maeglin]; for that was the name of the metal of Ëol, which he himself devised, and it was dark, supple, and yet strong; and even so was his son.

400

§120 Here Isfin and her son Glindûr [*later* > Maeglin] fled from Ëol the Dark-elf in Nan Elmoth, and came to Gondolin, and they were received with joy by Turgon, who had deemed his sister dead or lost beyond finding. But Ëol, following them with stealth, found the Hidden Way, and was brought by the Guard to Turgon. Turgon received him well, but he was wroth and filled with hatred of the Noldor, and spoke evilly, and demanded to depart with his son. And when that was denied to him he sought to slay Glindûr [*not emended*] with a poisoned dart, but Isfin sprang before her son, and was wounded, and died in that day. Therefore Ëol was doomed to death, and cast from the high walls of Gondolin; and he cursed his son as he died, foreboding that he should die a like death. But Glindûr [*later* > Maeglin] abode in Gondolin and became great among its lords.

370

§121 Here Bëor, eldest of the Fathers of Men of the West, was born east of the mountains.

388

§122 Here Haleth the Hunter was born in Eriador.

390

§123 Here also in Eriador was born Hador the Golden-haired, whose house was after the most renowned of all the kindreds of the Elf-friends.

400

§124 Here King Inglor Felagund went a-hunting in the eastern woods, as is told in the *Quenta*, and he passed into Ossiriand, and there came upon Bëor and his men, that were new-come over the mountains. Bëor became a vassal of

Felagund, and went back with him into the west-country, and dwelt with him until his death. There was great love between them. In eastern Beleriand was born Bregolas son of Bëor.

402

§125 Here there was fighting on the north-marches, more bitter than there had been since the routing of Glaurung; for the Orcs attempted to pierce the pass of Aglon. There Maidros and Maglor were aided by the sons of Finrod, and Bëor was with them, the first of Men to draw sword in behalf of the Eldar. In this year Barahir son of Bëor was born, who after dwelt in Dorthonion.

413

§126 Hundor son of Haleth was born.

417

§127 Galion the Tall, son of Hador, was born [beneath the shadows of Eryd Lindon >] in Eriador.

419

§128 Gundor son of Hador was born beneath the shadows of Eryd Lindon.

420

§129 In this year Haleth the Hunter came into Beleriand out of Eriador. Soon after came also Hador the Goldenhaired with great companies of Men. Haleth remained in Sirion's vale, and his folk wandered much in hunting, owning allegiance to no prince; but their dwellings were deep in the forest of Brethil between Taiglin and Sirion, where none before had dwelt because of the greatness and darkness of the trees. Hador hearing that there was room and need of folk in Hithlum, and being come of a northland people, became a vassal of Fingolfin; and he strengthened greatly the armies of the king, and he was given wide lands in Hithlum in the country of Dor-Lómin. There was ever great love between the Eldar and the house of Hador, and the folk of Hador were the first of Men to forsake their own tongue and speak the elven-tongue of Beleriand.

§130 It is said that in these matters none save Inglor took counsel with King Thingol. And he was ill pleased, for that reason and because he was troubled with dreams concerning the coming of Men, ere ever the first tidings of them were heard. Therefore he commanded that Men should take no lands to dwell in save in the north, in Hithlum and Dorthonion, and that the princes whom they served should be answerable for all that they did. And he said: 'Into Doriath shall no Man come while my realm lasts, not even those of the house of Bëor who serve Inglor the beloved.'

§131 Melian said naught to him at that time, but she said after to Galadriel: 'Now the world runs on swiftly to great tidings. And lo! one of Men, even of Bëor's house, shall indeed come, and the Girdle of Melian shall not restrain him, for doom greater than my power shall send him; and the songs that shall spring from that coming shall endure when all Middle-earth is changed.'

422

§132 Here at the prayer of Inglor Thingol granted to Haleth's people to live in Brethil; for they were in good friendship with the woodland Elves.

§133 In this time, the strength of Men being added to the Noldor, their hope rose high, and Morgoth was more straitly enclosed; for the folk of Hador, being hardy to endure cold and long wandering, feared not at times to go far into the North and keep watch on any movements of the Enemy. Now Fingolfin began to ponder an assault upon Angband; for he knew that they lived in danger while Morgoth was free to labour in his deep mines, devising what evils none could foretell ere he should reveal them. But because the land was grown so fair most of the Eldar were content with matters as they were and slow to begin an assault in which many must surely perish, were it in victory or defeat. Therefore his designs were delayed and came in the end to naught.

§134 The Men of the Three Houses now grew and multiplied; and they learned wisdom and craft and fair speech of the Eldar, and became more like to them than any other race have been, yet they were gladly subject to the Elf-lords and loyal; and there was as yet no grief between the two kindreds.

§135 The men of Bëor were dark or brown of hair, but fair of face, with grey eyes; of shapely form, having courage and endurance, yet they were no greater in stature than the Eldar of that day. For the Noldor indeed were tall as are in the latter days men of great might and majesty. But the people of Hador were of yet greater strength and stature, mighty among the Children of Eru, ready in mind, bold and steadfast. Yellowhaired they were for the most part and blue-eyed* and their women were tall and fair. Like unto them were the woodmen of Haleth, yet somewhat broader and less high.

423

§136   Hador's folk entered Dorlómin. [*This annal was a late pencilled addition.*]

[425 >] 424

§137   Baragund son of Bregolas son of Bëor was born in Dorthonion.

428

§138   Belegund his brother was born.

432

§139   Beren son of Barahir son of Bëor was born in Dorthonion, who was after named *Erchamion* the One-handed and *Camlost* the Emptyhanded. His mother was Emeldir the Manhearted.

436

§140   Hundor son of Haleth wedded Glorwendil daughter of Hador.

441

§141   Húrin the Steadfast son of Galion son of Hador was born in Hithlum. In the same year was born Handir son of Hundor.

[445 >] 443

§142   Morwen Eleðwen, the Elf-sheen, was born, daughter of Baragund. She was the fairest of all mortal maidens of the Elder Days.

444

§143   Huor brother of Húrin was born.

---

* Not so was Túrin, but his mother was of Bëor's house.

450

§144 Rían daughter of Belegund, mother of Tuor the Blessed, was born. In this year Bëor the Old, father of Men, died of [old age >] age. The Eldar saw then for the first time [the death of weariness, without wound or sickness; *by late pencilled change >*] the swift waning of the life of Men and the coming of death without wound or grief; and they wondered at the fate of Men, grieving greatly at the short span that was allotted to them. Bregolas then ruled the people of Bëor.

455

§145 *The Fell Year.* Here came an end of peace and mirth. In the winter, at the year's beginning, Morgoth unloosed at last his long-gathered strength, and he sought now to break with one great blow the leaguer of Angband, and to overthrow the Noldor and destroy Beleriand utterly. The Battle began suddenly on the night of mid-winter, and fell first and most heavily upon the sons of Finrod. This is named the *Dagor Bragollach*, the Battle of Sudden Flame. Rivers of fire ran down from Thangorodrim, and Glaurung, Father of Dragons, came forth in his full might. The green plains of Ardgalen were burned up and became a drear desert without growing thing; and thereafter they were called *Anfauglith*, the Gasping Dust.

§146 In the assault upon the defences of Dorthonion Angrod and Egnor, sons of Finrod, fell, and with them Bregolas was slain and a great part of the warriors of Bëor's folk. But Barahir his brother was in the fighting further westward nigh the passes of Sirion. There King Inglor Felagund, hastening from the south, was defeated and was surrounded with small company in the Fen of Serech. But Barahir came thither with the doughtiest of his men, and broke the leaguer of the Orcs and saved the Elven-king. Then Inglor gave to Barahir his ring, an heirloom of his house, in token of the oath that he swore unto Barahir to render whatsoever service was asked in hour of need to him or to any of his kin. Then Inglor went south to Nargothrond, but Barahir returned to Dorthonion to save what he could of the people of Bëor.

§147 Fingolfin and Fingon had marched indeed from Hithlum to the aid of the sons of Finrod, but they were driven back to the mountains with grievous loss. Hador, now aged [*later >* old *and* '65' *added*], fell defending his lord at Eithel

Sirion, and with him fell Gundor his [*added later:* younger] son, pierced with many arrows. Then Galion the Tall took the lordship of the House of Hador.

§148 Against the March of Maidros there came also a great army and the sons of Fëanor were overwhelmed. Maidros and Maglor held out valiantly upon the Hill of Himring, and Morgoth could not yet take the great fortress that they had there built; but the Orcs broke through upon either side, through Aglon and between Gelion and Celon, and they ravaged far into East Beleriand driving the Eldar before them, and Cranthir and Damrod and Díriel fled into the south. Celegorn and Curufin held strong forces behind Aglon, and many horsed archers, but they were overthrown, and Celegorn and Curufin hardly escaped, and passed westward along the north borders of Doriath with such mounted following as they could save, and came thus at length to the vale of Sirion.

§149 Turgon was not in that battle, nor Haleth, nor any but few of Haleth's men. [*The following passage, to the end of §150, was struck out later:* It is said that in the autumn before the Sudden Flame, Húrin son of Galion was dwelling as fosterson (as the custom was among the northern men) with Haleth, and Handir and Húrin, being of like age, went much together; and hunting in Sirion's vale they found [by chance or fate *later* >] by fate or the will of Ulmo / the hidden entrance into the valley of Tumladin where stood Gondolin the guarded city. There they were taken by the watch and brought before Turgon, and looked upon the city of which none that dwelt outside yet knew aught, save Thorondor King of Eagles. But Turgon welcomed them, for [messages and dreams sent by Ulmo, Lord of Waters, up the streams of Sirion had warned him that a time of grief approached in which he would have need of the help of Men. >] Ulmo, Lord of Waters, had warned him to look kindly upon the folk of the House of Hador, from whom great help should come to him at need.

§150 It is said that Turgon had great liking for the boy Húrin, and wished to keep him in Gondolin; but Thorondor brought dread tidings of the great battle, and Handir and Húrin wished to depart to share the troubles of their folk. Therefore Turgon let them go, but they swore to him oaths of secrecy and never revealed Gondolin; yet at this time Húrin learned something of the counsels of Turgon, though he kept them hidden in his heart.]

§151 When [*later* > But when] Turgon learned of the breaking of the leaguer of Angband, he sent secret messengers to the mouths of Sirion and to the Isle of Balar and there they [*the following passage was struck out and replaced at the time of writing:* built many swift ships. Thence many set sail upon Turgon's errand, seeking for Valinor, to ask for pardon and for aid of the Valar, but none came ever to the West and few returned.

§152 Now it seemed to Fingolfin, King of the Noldor, that he beheld the utter ruin of his people, and the defeat beyond redress of all their houses, and he was filled with wrath and despair. Then he rode forth alone to the gates of Angband] endeavoured to build ships that might sail into the uttermost West on Turgon's errand, seeking for Valinor, there to ask for pardon and the aid of the Valar. But the Noldor had not the art of shipbuilding, and all the craft that they built foundered or were driven back by the winds. But Turgon ever maintained a secret refuge upon the Isle of Balar, and the building of ships was never wholly abandoned.

§153 [*Original date here* 456 *struck out at the time of writing*] Morgoth learning now of the defeat of the sons of Finrod, and the scattering of the people of Fëanor, hemmed Fingolfin in Hithlum and sent a great force to attack the westward pass into the vales of Sirion; and Sauron his lieutenant (who in Beleriand was named *Gorsodh*) led that assault, and his hosts broke through and besieged the fortress of Inglor, Minnas-tirith upon Tolsirion. And this they took after bitter fighting, and Orodreth the brother of Inglor who held it was driven out. There he would have been slain, but Celegorn and Curufin came up with their riders, and such other force as they could gather, and they fought fiercely, and stemmed the tide for a while; and thus Orodreth escaped and came to Nargothrond. Thither also at last before the might of Sauron fled Celegorn and Curufin with small following; and they were harboured in Nargothrond gratefully, and the griefs that lay between the houses of Finrod and Fëanor were for that time forgotten.

§154 But Sauron took Minnas-tirith and made it into a watch-tower for Morgoth, and filled it with evil; for he was a sorcerer and a master of phantoms and terror. And the fair isle of Tolsirion became accursed and was called *Tol-in-Gaurhoth*, Isle of Werewolves; for Sauron fed many of these evil things.

456

§155 Now Fingolfin, King of the Noldor, beheld (as him seemed) the utter ruin of his people, and the defeat beyond redress of all their houses, and he was filled with wrath and despair. Therefore he did on his silver arms, and took his white helm, and his sword Ringil, and his blue shield set with a star of crystal, and mounting upon Rochallor his great steed he rode forth alone and none might restrain him. And he passed over the Anfauglith like a wind amid the dust, and all that beheld his onset fled in amaze, deeming that Oromë himself was come, for a great madness of ire was upon him, so that his eyes shone like the eyes of the Valar. Thus he came alone to Angband's gate and smote upon it once again, and sounding a challenge upon his silver horn he called Morgoth himself to come forth to combat, crying: 'Come forth, thou coward king, to fight with thine own hand! Den-dweller, wielder of thralls, liar and lurker, foe of Gods and Elves, come! For I would see thy craven face.'

§156 Then Morgoth came. For he could not refuse such a challenge before the face of his captains. But Fingolfin withstood him, though he towered above the Elven-king like a storm above a lonely tree, and his vast black shield unblazoned overshadowed the star of Fingolfin like a thundercloud. Morgoth fought with a great hammer, Grond, that he wielded as a mace, and Fingolfin fought with Ringil. Swift was Fingolfin, and avoiding the strokes of Grond, so that Morgoth smote only the ground (and at each blow a great pit was made), he wounded Morgoth seven times with his sword; and the cries of Morgoth echoed in the north-lands. But wearied at last Fingolfin fell, beaten to the earth by the hammer of Angband, and Morgoth set his foot upon his neck and crushed him.

§157 In his last throe Fingolfin pinned the foot of his Enemy to the earth with Ringil, and the black blood gushed forth and filled the pits of Grond. Morgoth went ever halt thereafter. Now lifting the body of the fallen king he would break it and cast it to his wolves, but Thorondor coming suddenly assailed him and marred his face, and snatching away the corse of Fingolfin bore it aloft to the mountains far away and laid it in a high place north of the valley of Gondolin; there the eagles piled a great cairn of stones. There was lamentation in Gondolin when Thorondor brought the tidings, for [the people of the hidden city were all *later* >] many of the people of the hidden city were / Noldor of Fingolfin's house. Now Rochallor had stayed beside the king until the end, but the wolves of Angband assailed him, and he escaped from them because of his great swiftness, and ran at last to Hithlum, and broke his heart and died. Then in great sorrow Fingon took the lordship of the house of Fingolfin and the kingdom of the Noldor. [*Late pencilled addition*: But his young son (?Findor) [*sic*] Gilgalad he sent to the Havens.]

§158 Now Morgoth's power overshadowed the north-lands, but [*struck out:* still] Barahir would not retreat and defended still the remant of his land and folk in Dorthonion. But Morgoth hunted down all that there remained of Elves or Men, and he sent Sauron against them; and all the forest of the northward slopes of that land was turned into a region of dread and dark enchantment, so that it was after called *Taur-nu-Fuin*, the Forest under Nightshade.

§159 At last so desperate was the case of Barahir that Emeldir the Manhearted his wife (whose mind was rather to fight beside her son and husband than to flee) gathered together all the women and children that were still left, and gave arms to those that would bear them, and led them into the mountains that lay behind, and so by perilous paths, until they came with loss and misery at last to Brethil. And some were there received into Haleth's folk, and some passed on to Dorlómin and the people of Galion Hador's son. (Among these were Morwen Eledhwen daughter of Baragund, and Rían daughter of Belegund.) But none ever again saw the menfolk that they had left. For these were slain one by one, or fled, until at last only Barahir and Beren his son, and Baragund and Belegund sons of Bregolas, were left, and with them [eight >] nine desperate men whose names were long remembered in song: Dagnir and Ragnor, Raðhruin and Dairuin and Gildor, Urthel and Arthad and Hathaldir, and Gorlim Unhappy. Outlaws without hope they became, for their dwellings were destroyed, and their wives and children slain or taken or fled with Emeldir. No help came to them and they were hunted as wild beasts.

458

§160 Here Haleth and his men fought with the Orcs that came down Sirion. In this battle they had help out of Doriath (for they dwelt upon its west-march), and Beleg the Bowman chief of the march-wards of Thingol brought great strength of the Eglath armed with axes into Brethil; and issuing from the deeps of the forest they took an Orc-legion at unawares and destroyed it. Thus for a while the black tide out of the North was stemmed in that region and the Orcs did not dare to cross the Taiglin for many years after.

> At this point my father inserted into the manuscript an extensive rider, replacing the rejected passage in annal 455 (§§149–50). This rider was written on the backs of two sheets from the engagement calendar for 1951 (see p. 47), covering weeks in August–September and December of that year.

§161 It is said that at this time Húrin and Huor, the sons of Galion, were dwelling with Haleth [*added later:* their kinsman] as fostersons (as the custom then was among northern Men); and they went both to battle with the Orcs, even Huor, for he would not be restrained, though he was but thirteen years in age. And being with a company that was cut off from the rest, they were pursued to the ford of Brithiach; and there they would have been taken or slain, but for the power of Ulmo, which was still strong in Sirion. Therefore a mist arose from the river and hid them from their enemies, and they escaped into Dimbar, and wandered in the hills beneath the sheer walls of the Crisaegrim. There Thorondor espied them, and sent two Eagles that took them and bore them up and brought them beyond the mountains to the secret vale of Tumladen and the hidden city of Gondolin, which no man else had yet seen.

§162 Then they were led before King Turgon, and he welcomed them, for Ulmo had counselled him to deal kindly with the House of Hador, whence great help should come to him at need. And Húrin and Huor dwelt as his guests for well nigh a year; and it is said that at this time Húrin learned something of the counsels and purposes of Turgon. For Turgon had great liking for Húrin, and for Huor his brother, and spoke much with them; and he wished to keep them in Gondolin, out of love and not for his law only. Now it was the law of the king that no stranger who found the way in, or looked on the guarded realm, should ever depart again until such time as the king should [come forth from hiding >] open the leaguer and the hidden people should come forth.

§163 But Húrin and Huor desired to return to their own kin, and share in the wars and griefs that now beset them. And

Húrin said to Turgon: 'Lord, we are but mortal men, and unlike the Eldar. They may endure long years, awaiting battle with their enemies in some far distant day. But for us time is short, and our hope and strength soon withereth. Moreover we found not the road hither, and indeed we know not surely where this city standeth; for we were brought in fear and wonder by the high ways of the air, and in mercy our eyes were veiled.'

§164 Then Turgon yielded to their prayer, and said: 'By the way that ye came ye have leave to depart, if Thorondor is willing. I grieve at this parting, yet in a little while, as the Eldar account it, we may meet again.'

§165 But it is said that [Glindûr *later* >] Maeglin, the king's sister-son, grieved not at all at their going, [save only *later* >] though he begrudged it/ that in this the king showed them favour, for he loved not the kindred of Men; and he said: 'Your grace is greater than ye know, and the law is become less stern than aforetime, or else no choice would be given you but to abide here to your life's end.'

§166 'The king's grace is great indeed,' answered Húrin; 'but if we have not thy trust then oaths we will take.' And the brethren swore never to reveal the counsels of Turgon and to keep secret all that they had seen in his realm. Then they took their leave, and the Eagles coming bore them away and set them down in Dor Lómin; and their kinsfolk rejoiced to see them, for messages from Brethil had reported that they were slain or taken by the Orcs. But though they told that they had dwelt a while in honour in the halls of King Turgon, to none, kin or stranger, would they ever speak of the manner of his land, or its ordering, or where upon earth it might be found. Nonetheless the strange fortune of the sons of Galion, and their friendship with Turgon, became known far and wide, and reached the ears of the servants of Morgoth.

The rider ends here, and I return to the original text of the *Annals*.

460

§167 The forest of Dorthonion rose southward into mountainous moors. There lay a lake, Tarn-aeluin, in the east of those highlands, and wild heaths were about it, and all that land was pathless and untamed; for even in the days of the Long Peace none had dwelt there. But the waters of Tarn-aeluin were held in reverence; for they were clear and blue by day and by night were a mirror for the stars. Melian herself, it was said, had hallowed that water in days of old. Thither Barahir and his outlaws withdrew, and there made their lair, and Morgoth could not discover it. But the rumour of the deeds of Barahir and his twelve men went far and wide, and enheartened those that were under the thraldom of Morgoth; and he therefore commanded Sauron to find and destroy the rebels speedily. Elsewhere in the *Quenta* and the *Lay of Leithian* is much told of this, and how Sauron ensnared Gorlim by a phantom of his wife Eilinel, and tormented him and cozened him, so that he betrayed the hidings of Barahir. Thus at last the outlaws were surrounded and all slain, save Beren son of Barahir. For Barahir his father had sent him on a perilous errand to spy upon the ways of the Enemy, and he was far afield when the lair was taken, and returned only to find the bodies of the slain.

§168 Then Beren pursued the Orcs that had slain his father, and coming upon their camp, at Rivil's Well above Serech, he entered it and slew the captain even as he boasted that he was the slayer of Barahir; and he snatched from him the hand of Barahir that had been cut off as a token for Sauron. Thus he regained the Ring of Felagund that his father had worn.

§169 Thereafter escaping from the Orcs Beren dwelt still in those lands as a solitary outlaw for four years, and did such deeds of single-handed daring that Morgoth put a price on his head no less than upon the head of Fingon King of the Noldor.

462

§170 Here Morgoth renewed his assaults, seeking to advance further into Beleriand and secure his hold southwards. For great though his victory had been in the Bragollach, and he had done grievous damage then and in the year after to his enemies, yet his own loss had been no less. And now the Eldar had recovered from their first dismay and were slowly regaining what they had lost. Dorthonion he now held and had established Sauron in the pass of Sirion; but in the east he had been foiled. Himring stood firm. The army that had driven into East Beleriand had been broken by Thingol on the borders of Doriath, and part had fled away south never to return to him, part retreating north had been stricken by a sortie of Maidros, while those that ventured near the mountains were hunted by the Dwarves. And still upon his flank Hithlum stood firm.

§171 He resolved, therefore, now to send force against

Hithlum; for in the eastward war he hoped ere long to have new help unforeseen by the Eldar. The assault upon Hithlum was bitter, but it was repelled from the passes of Erydwethrin. There, however, in the siege of the fortress of Eithel Sirion Galion was slain, for he held it on behalf of King Fingon. Húrin his son was but then new come to manhood, but he was mighty in heart and strength, and he defeated the Orcs and drove them with loss from the walls into the sands of Anfauglith. Thereafter he ruled the House of Hador. [*Added subsequently:*] Of less stature was he than his father (or his son after him), but tireless and enduring in body; lithe and swift he was, after the manner of his mother's kin, the daughter of Haleth.

§172 But King Fingon with most of the Noldor was hard put to it to hold back the army of Angband that came down from the north. Battle was joined upon the very plains of Hithlum, and Fingon was outnumbered; but timely help came from Cirdan. His ships in great strength sailed into Drengist and there landed a force that came up in the hour of need upon the west flank of the enemy. Then the Eldar had the victory and the Orcs broke and fled, pursued by the horsed archers even to the Iron Mountains.

463

§173 In this year new tidings came to Beleriand: the Swarthy Men came out of Eriador, and passing north about the Eryd Luin entered into Lothlann. Their coming was not wholly unlooked-for, since the Dwarves had warned Maidros that hosts of Men out of the further East were journeying towards Beleriand. They were short and broad, long and strong in the arm, and grew much hair on face and breast; their locks were dark as were their eyes, and their skins were sallow or swart. But they were not all of one kind, in looks or in temper, or in tongue. Some were not uncomely and were fair to deal with; some were grim and ill-favoured and of little trust. Their houses were many, and there was little love among them. They had small liking for the Elves, and for the most part loved rather the Naugrim of the mountains; but they were abashed by the lords of the Noldor, whose like they had not before encountered.

§174 But Maidros, knowing the weakness of the Noldor and the Elf-friends, whereas the pits of Angband seemed to hold store inexhaustible and ever renewed, made alliance with these new-come Men, and gave them dwellings both in Lothlann north of the March, and in the lands south of it. Now the two chieftains

> From this point there are two parallel versions of the text (the remainder of the annal concerning the Swarthy Men and the story of Beren and Lúthien); on the manuscript a secretary wrote 'Version I' (the first and much shorter version) and 'Version II' (much longer), and similarly on the typescript of the *Grey Annals*, where both forms are given. There can be no doubt at all that Version II was written second (even though it has the earlier form *Borthandos* while Version I has the later *Borthand*), for Version I is integral with the whole text of the *Annals*, whereas Version II ends before the bottom of a page. I give first the whole text of Version I, continuing from the point in the annal for 463 on the Swarthy Men where the text was broken off above.

that had the greatest followings and authority were named Bór and Ulfang. The sons of Bór were Borlas and Boromir and Borthand, and they followed Maidros and were faithful. The sons of Ulfang the swart were Ulfast and Ulwarth and Uldor the Accursed; and they followed Cranthir and swore allegiance to him and were faithless.*

464

§175 In the beginning of this year Beren was pressed so hard that at last he was forced to flee from Dorthonion. In time of winter and snow, therefore, he forsook the land and grave of his father and climbed into the Eryd Orgorath, and thence found a way down into Nan Dungorthin, and so came by paths that no Man nor Elf else dared to tread to the Girdle of Melian. And he passed through, even as Melian had foretold, for a great doom lay on him. In this year, in the spring, Húrin Galion's son of the House of Hador wedded Morwen Elfsheen daughter of Baragund of the House of Bëor [*this sentence was later marked for transposition to the beginning of the annal*]. [*Later insertion:*] In this year Túrin son of Húrin was born in Dorlómin.

§176 In this year at the mid-summer Beren son of Barahir met Lúthien Thingol's daughter in the forest of Neldoreth, and

---

* It was after thought that the people of Ulfang were already secretly in the service of Morgoth ere they came to Beleriand. Not so the people of Bór, who were worthy folk and tillers of the earth. Of them, it is said, came the most ancient of the Men that dwelt in the north of Eriador in the Second Age and [? *read* in] after-days.

because of her great beauty and his love a spell of dumbness was laid on him, and he wandered long in the woods of Doriath.

465

§177　In this year at the first spring Beren was released from his spell, and spoke to Lúthien, calling her *Tinúviel*, the Nightingale. Thus began the love of Beren the most renowned and Lúthien the most fair of which the *Lay of Leithian* was made.

§178　Beren was brought before King Thingol, who scorned him, and desiring to send him to death, said to him in mockery that he must bring a Silmaril from the crown of Morgoth as the bride-price of Lúthien. But Beren took the quest upon himself and departed, and came to Nargothrond and sought the aid of King Felagund. Then Felagund perceived that his oath had returned to bring him to death, but he was willing to lend to Beren all the aid of his kingdom, vain though it must prove.

§179　[Celegorm >] Celegorn and Curufin however hindered the quest, for their Oath was roused from slumber, and they swore that even should the quest be achieved they would slay any that kept the Silmaril or gave it to any hands but their own. And because of their fell words great fear fell on the folk of Nargothrond, and they withheld their aid from the king.

§180　King Inglor Felagund and Beren set forth, with ten companions only, and went northward; but they were waylaid by Sauron and cast into a pit in Tol-in-Gaurhoth. There they were devoured one by one by wolves; but Felagund fought the wolf that was sent to devour Beren, and slew it, and was slain. Thus perished from Middle-earth the fairest of the children of Finwë, and returned never again; but dwells now in Valinor with Amárië.

§181　Lúthien desired to follow Beren, but was held captive by her father, until she escaped and passed into the wild. There she was found by Celegorn and Curufin, and taken to Nargothrond. And evil entered into the hearts of the brethren, and they designed to seize the kingship of Nargothrond, and wed Lúthien to Celegorn and compel Thingol to alliance, and so make the sons of Fëanor the greatest House of the Noldor again.

§182　But Lúthien escaped them and came to Sauron's isle and with the aid of Húan the Hound of Valinor overthrew the werewolves and Sauron himself, and rescued Beren. And when these tidings were heard in Nargothrond Orodreth took the crown of Felagund and drove forth Celegorn and Curufin. And they riding east in haste found Beren and Lúthien near the borders of Doriath, and would seize Lúthien. But they were foiled, and rode away; yet Beren was sorely wounded.

§183 When Beren was healed he led Lúthien to her own land and there left her sleeping and went forth alone on his quest, but Lúthien following overtook him upon the borders of the Anfauglith.

[*Added:*] In the winter of this year, Túrin son of Húrin was born with omens of sorrow. [*Written against this later*: Place in 464]

466

§184 In disguise Beren and Lúthien came to Angband, and Lúthien cast Carcharoth the Wolf-warden of the gate into a slumber; and they descended to Morgoth's throne. There Lúthien laid her spell even upon Morgoth, so that he fell asleep against his will, and the Iron Crown rolled from his head.

§185 Lúthien and Beren bearing a Silmaril were waylaid at the gate by Carcharoth, and Carcharoth bit off the hand of Beren that held the jewel, and being filled with madness fled away. Then Thorondor and his eagles lifted up Beren and Lúthien, and bore them away and set them within the borders of Doriath. Long Lúthien fought with death, until Beren was again healed. And in the spring of the year she led him back to Menegroth. And when Thingol heard all that had befallen them, his mood was softened, for he was filled with wonder at the love of Lúthien and Beren, and perceived that their doom might not be withstood by any power of the world. For thus was it appointed that the two kindreds, the elder and the younger children of Eru, should be joined. Then Beren took the hand of Lúthien before the throne of her father.

§186 But soon after Carcharoth by the power of the Silmaril burst into Doriath, and the Wolf-hunt of Carcharoth was made. In that hunt were King Thingol, and Beren of the One Hand, and Beleg and Mablung and Húan the Hound of Valinor. And Carcharoth hurt Beren to the death, but Húan slew him and then died. From the belly of the Wolf Mablung cut the Jewel and Beren took it and gave it to Thingol, and said 'Now the Quest is achieved', and afterwards spoke no more. But ere he died Lúthien bade him farewell before the gates of

Menegroth, and said to him: 'Await me beyond the Western Sea.'
Thus ended the Quest of the Silmaril.

As has been seen (p. 61), 'Version II' takes up at a point in annal 463 concerning the Swarthy Men, following the words 'Now the two chieftains'; my father copied out the end of that annal simply because it stood at the head of the page on which the story of Beren and Lúthien began, as originally written. He inevitably introduced some differences, however, and I give the second text in full.

(Conclusion of annal 463 in Version II)
[Now the two chieftains] that had the greatest followings and authority were named Bór and Ulfang. The sons of Bór were Borlas and Boromir and Borthandos, and they were goodly men, and they followed Maidros and Maglor and were faithful. The sons of Ulfang the Swart were Ulfast and Ulwarth and Uldor the Accursed; and they followed Cranthir and swore allegiance to him, and were faithless. (It was after thought that the people of Ulfang were already secretly in the service of Morgoth ere they came to Beleriand.)*

464

§187 In the beginning of this year Beren was pressed so hard that at last, [in the winter >] soon after the mid-winter, he was forced to choose between flight and capture. He forsook then Dorthonion and passed into the Eryd Orgorath and found a way down into Nan Dungorthin, and so came by paths that neither Man nor Elf else ever dared to tread to the Girdle of Doriath. And he passed through, even as Melian had foretold to Galadriel; for a great doom lay on him.

In this year in the spring Húrin of the House of Hador wedded Morwen Elfsheen of the people of Bëor [*this sentence was later marked for transposition to the beginning of the annal, as in §175*].

§188 In this year at the midsummer Beren son of Barahir met Lúthien Thingol's daughter in the forest of Neldoreth, and becoming enamoured of her wandered long in the woods of Doriath, for a spell of dumbness was upon him. [*Later insertion, as in §175:*] Túrin son of Húrin was born in Dor Lómin.

* Of the people of Bór, it is said, came the most ancient of the Men that dwelt in the north of Eriador afterwards in the Second Age.

465

§189 In this year at the first spring Beren was released from his spell and spoke to Lúthien, calling her *Tinúviel*, the Nightingale (for he knew not her name yet, nor who she was). Thus began the love of Beren the blessed and Lúthien the most fair, of which the *Lay of Leithian* was made. Their meetings were espied by Dairon the minstrel (who also loved Lúthien) and were bewrayed to King Thingol. Then Thingol was wroth indeed, but Lúthien brought Beren to Menegroth, and Beren showed to him the ring of Inglor his kinsman. But Thingol spoke in anger scorning mortal Men, saying that the service of Beren's father to another prince gave the son no claim to walk in Doriath, still less to lift his eyes to Lúthien. Then Beren being stung by his scorn swore that by no power of spell, wall or weapon should he be withheld from his love; and Thingol would have cast him into prison or put him to death, if he had not sworn to Lúthien that no harm should come to Beren. But, as doom would, a thought came into his heart, and he answered in mockery: 'If thou fearest neither spell, wall nor weapons, as thou saist, then go fetch me a Silmaril from the crown of Morgoth. Then we will give jewel for jewel, but thou shalt win the fairer: Lúthien of the First-born and of the Gods.' And those who heard knew that he would save his oath, and yet send Beren to his death.

§190 But Beren looked in the eyes of Melian, who spake not, and he took upon himself the Quest of the Silmaril, and went forth from Menegroth alone.

§191 Now Beren went west to Nargothrond, and sought out King Felagund. And when Felagund heard of the quest he knew that the oath he had sworn was come upon him for his death (as long before he had said to Galadriel). But he kept his oath, and would have mustered all his host for the service of Beren, vain though all his strength must be in such a venture.

§192 But Celegorn and Curufin were in Nargothrond (as was before told), and the quest roused from sleep the Oath of Fëanor. And the brethren spoke against Felagund, and with their words set such a fear in the hearts of the people of Nargothrond that they would not obey their king, neither for many years after would they go to any open war.

§193 Then [Finrod >] Inglor cast off his crown and made ready to go forth alone with Beren, but ten of his most faithful knights stood beside him, and Edrahil, their chief, lifted the crown and bade the king give it in keeping to Orodreth his brother. But Celegorn said: 'Know this: thy going is vain; for could ye achieve this quest it would avail nothing. Neither thee nor this Man should we suffer to keep or to give a Silmaril of Fëanor. Against thee would come all the brethren to slay thee rather. And should Thingol gain it, then we would burn Doriath or die in the attempt. For we have sworn our Oath.'

§194 'I also have sworn an oath,' said Felagund, 'and I seek no release from it. Save thine own, until thou knowest more. But this I will say to you, [son of Fëanor >] Celegorn the fell, by the sight that is given me in this hour, that neither thou nor any son of Fëanor shall regain the Silmarils ever unto world's end. And this that we now seek shall come indeed, but never to your hands. Nay, your oath shall devour you, and deliver to other keeping the bride-price of Lúthien.'

§195 Thus King Felagund and Beren and their companions went forth, and waylaying a company of Orcs beyond the Taiglin they passed towards [Tolsirion >] Tol-in-Gaurhoth, disguised as soldiers of Morgoth. There they were questioned and laid bare by Sauron, and cast into a pit.

§196 Now Lúthien resolved in heart to follow Beren, but seeking the counsel of Dairon (who was of old her friend) she was again bewrayed to Thingol, and he in dismay set her in a prison high in the trees. But she escaped by arts of enchantment upon a rope of her own hair and passed into the wild. There she was found by Celegorn and Curufin, as they were a-hunting, and taken to Nargothrond, and there closely kept. For Celegorn being enamoured of her beauty resolved to wed her, and compel King Thingol's assent.

§197 But Lúthien with the aid of Húan, the hound of Valinor, who followed Celegorn but was won to the love of Lúthien, escaped from Nargothrond and came to Tol-in-Gaurhoth.

§198 There in the pits of Sauron one by one the twelve companions were slain and devoured by werewolves, until at last only Beren and Felagund remained. But none had betrayed them, and Sauron could not learn the errand upon which they went. He left the Elven-king to the last, for he knew who he was, and deemed that he was the mover in whatever venture was devised. But when the wolf came to Beren, Felagund with his last strength broke his bonds, and wrestled naked-handed with the wolf and slew it, and was slain.

§199 Thus perished Inglor Felagund son of Finrod, fairest and most beloved of the children of Finwë, and returned never again to Middle-earth. But it is said that released soon from Mandos, he went to Valinor and there dwells with Amárië.

§200 Beren sank down now into a darkness of sorrow and despair. In that hour Lúthien and Húan came to the bridge that led to Sauron's isle, and Lúthien sang a song of Doriath. Then Beren awoke from his darkness; and the towers of Sauron trembled, and he sent forth Draugluin the greatest of his werewolves. But Húan slew Draugluin, and when Sauron himself came forth in wolf-hame he overthrew him. Thus Sauron was constrained to yield up Tol-sirion, ere bereft of his bodily form he passed away as a black shadow into Taur-nu-Fuin.

§201 Thus Lúthien rescued Beren, and set free many hapless prisoners of Sauron. These prisoners Húan led back to Nargothrond, for his loyalty constrained him to return to Celegorn, his master. But when the tidings came to Nargothrond of the death of Felagund, and the great deeds of the Elf-maid, then Celegorn and Curufin were hated, and Orodreth took the crown of Nargothrond, and drove them forth; and they fled eastward to Himring.

§202 Lúthien and Beren wandered in the wild together in brief joy; and Beren led Lúthien back towards Doriath. Thus by ill chance Celegorn and Curufin came upon them as they rode to the north-borders with Húan. There Celegorn would ride Beren down, and Curufin seized Lúthien; but Beren overthrew Curufin, and took his horse and his knife, and was saved from death at the hands of Celegorn by Húan; who in that hour forsook his master and served Lúthien. Then Celegorn and Curufin rode away upon one horse, and Curufin shooting back smote Beren with an arrow and he fell.

466

§203 Lúthien and Húan guarded Beren in the woods, and Lúthien brought him back at last from the edge of death. But when he was healed, and they had passed into Doriath, Beren remembering his oath and proud words to Thingol, was unwilling to return to Menegroth, neither would he lead Lúthien upon his hopeless quest. Therefore in great grief he left her as she slept in a glade, and committing her to the care of Húan, rode away north upon his horse that he took from

Curufin. And since Tol-in-Gaurhoth was now destroyed he came at last to the north-slopes of Taur-nu-Fuin and looked across the Anfauglith to Thangorodrim and despaired.

§204   There he sent away his horse, and bade farewell to life and to the love of Lúthien, and prepared to go forth alone to death. But Lúthien was borne swiftly after him by Húan, and she came upon him in that hour, and would not be parted from him. Then with the aid of Húan and her arts, Lúthien disguised Beren as a wolf in the hame of Draugluin, and herself as the vampire Thuringwethil, and they passed over Anfauglith and came to Angband, but Húan abode in the woods.

§205   At Angband's gate Lúthien cast down the warden of the gate, Carcharoth mightiest of all wolves, into a deep slumber, and Beren and Lúthien came into the dreadful realm of Morgoth, and descended even into his uttermost hall and came before his throne. There Beren slunk in wolf-form beneath the very chair of Morgoth, but the disguise of Lúthien did not deceive Morgoth and she was revealed to him. Yet she eluded his foul grasp, and even as he watched her dancing, held as in a spell by her beauty, she set a deep slumber upon all the hall, and at last Morgoth himself was overcome and fell from his seat into a blind sleep, but the Iron Crown rolled from his head.

§206   Then Lúthien roused Beren and stripping off the wolf-hame he took the dwarf-knife of Curufin and cut from Morgoth's crown a Silmaril. But desiring suddenly to go beyond doom and rescue all the jewels he was betrayed by the knife which snapped, and a splinter smote Morgoth and disturbed his sleep.

§207   Then Beren and Lúthien fled, but at the gates they found Carcharoth once more awake, and he leaped upon Lúthien; and before she could use any art Beren sprang before and would daunt the wolf with the hand that held the Silmaril. But Carcharoth seized the hand and bit it off, and straightway the Silmaril burned him, and madness seized him and he fled away; but his howls roused all the sleepers in Angband. Then Lúthien knelt by Beren, as he lay in a swoon as it were of death, and all their quest seemed in ruin. But even as she drew forth the venom from Beren's wound with her lips, Thorondor came with Lhandroval and Gwaihir, his mightiest vassals, and they lifted up Lúthien and Beren and bore them south, high over Gondolin, and set them down on the borders of Doriath.

§208   There Húan found them and again they tended Beren

and won him from death, and as spring grew fair they passed into Doriath and came to Menegroth. Glad was their welcome in Doriath, for a spell of shadow and silence had lain upon all the land since Lúthien fled; and Dairon seeking her in sorrow had wandered far away and was lost.

§209 Thus once more Lúthien led Beren to the throne of her father, and he marvelled at him, but was not appeased; and he said to Beren: 'Didst thou not say that thou wouldst not return to me save with a jewel from the crown of Morgoth?' And Beren answered: 'Even now a Silmaril is in my hand.' And Thingol said: 'Show it to me!' But Beren said: 'That I cannot do; for my hand is not here.' And he held up his right arm; and from that hour he named himself *Camlost*.

§210 Then Thingol's mood was softened, for it seemed to him that this Man was unlike all others, and among the great in Arda, whereas the love of Lúthien was of a strength greater than all the kingdoms of West or East. And Beren took Lúthien's hand and laid it upon his breast before the throne of her father, and thus they were betrothed.

But now Carcharoth by the power of the Silmaril burst into Doriath.

> Here Version II breaks off abruptly, and not at the foot of a page. The page on which Version I ends, with the words 'Thus ended the Quest of the Silmaril' (p. 64), continues with the annal for 467.

467

§211 In this year at the first breaking of Spring Lúthien Tinúviel laid her body as a white flower on the grass and her spirit fled from Middle-earth, and she went unto Mandos, as it saith in the *Lay*. But a winter as it were the hoar age of mortal Men came upon Thingol.

468

§212 In this time Maidros began those counsels for the raising of the fortunes of the Eldar that are called the Union of Maidros. For new hope ran through the land, because of the deeds of Beren and Lúthien, and it seemed to many that Morgoth was not unconquerable, and that fear only gave him his power. Yet still the Oath of Fëanor lived and hindered all good, and not least the evil that Celegorn and Curufin had done because of it. Thus Thingol would lend no aid to any son of

Fëanor; and small help came from Nargothrond: there the Noldor trusted rather to defend their hidden stronghold by secrecy and stealth. But Maidros had the help of the Naugrim, both in armed force and in great store of weapons; and he gathered together again all his brethren and all the folk that would follow them; and the men of Bór and of Ulfang were marshalled and trained for war, and given fair arms, and they summoned yet more of their kinsfolk out of the East. And in Hithlum Fingon, ever the friend of Maidros, prepared for war, taking counsel with Himring. To Gondolin also the tidings came to the hidden king, Turgon, and in secret also he prepared for great battle. And Haleth gathered his folk in Brethil, and they whetted their axes; but he died of age ere the war came, and Hundor his son ruled his people.

469

§213 In the spring of this year Maidros made the first trial of his strength though his plans were not yet full-wrought. In which he erred, not concealing his stroke until it could be made suddenly with all strength, as Morgoth had done. For the Orcs indeed were driven out of Beleriand once more, and even Dorthonion was freed for a while, so that the frontiers of the Noldor were again as they were before the Bragollach, save that the Anfauglith was now a desert possessed by neither side. But Morgoth being warned of the uprising of the Eldar and the Elf-friends took counsel against them, and he sent forth many spies and workers of treason among them, as he was the better able now to do, for the faithless men of his secret allegiance were yet deep in the secrets of Fëanor's sons.

§214 In this year, it hath been [thought >] said, Beren and Lúthien returned to the world, for a while. For Lúthien had won this doom from Manwë that Beren might return to live again, and she with him; but only so that she too thereafter should be mortal as he, and should soon die indeed and lose the world and depart from the numbers of the Eldalië for ever. This doom she chose. And they appeared again unlooked for in Doriath, and those that saw them were both glad and fearful. But Lúthien went to Menegroth and healed the winter of Thingol with the touch of her hand; yet Melian looked in her eyes and read the doom that was written there, and turned away: for she knew that a parting beyond the end of the World had come between them, and no grief of loss hath been heavier than the grief of the heart of Melian Maia in that hour (unless only it were the grief of Elrond and Arwen). But Lúthien and Beren passed then out of the knowledge of Elves and Men, and dwelt a while alone by the green waters of Ossiriand in that land which the Eldar named therefore *Gwerth-i-guinar*, the land of the Dead that Live. Thereafter Beren son of Barahir spoke not again with any mortal Man.

470

§215 In this year was the birth of Dior Aranel the Beautiful in Gwerth-i-Guinar, who was after known as Dior Thingol's heir, father of the Halfelven.

The annal that follows now in GA, for 471, concerning Isfin and Ëol, was struck out; the revised version of the story appears on a rider inserted at an earlier point, under the year 316 (see §§117–18, where the rejected annal for 471 has been given). A new annal for 471 was added later in pencil:

471

§216 In this year Huor wedded Rían daughter of Belegund.

472

§217 *This is the Year of Lamentation.* At last Maidros resolved to assault Angband from east and from west. With the main host that he gathered, of Elves and Men and Dwarves, he purposed to march with banners displayed in open force from the east over Anfauglith. But when he had drawn forth, as he hoped, the armies of Morgoth in answer, then at a signal Fingon should issue from the passes of Hithlum with all his strength. Thus they thought to take the might of Morgoth as between anvil and hammer, and so break it to pieces.

§218 [Huor son of Galion wedded Rían daughter of Belegund upon the eve of battle, and marched with Húrin his brother in the army of Fingon. *Changed in pencil to read:*] Huor son of Galion wedded Rían daughter of Belegund in the first days of spring. But when he had been but two months wed, the summons came for the mustering of the hosts, and Húrin marched away with his brother in the army of Fingon.

§219 Here at midsummer was fought the Fifth Battle *Nírnaeth Arnediad*, Unnumbered Tears, upon the sands of the Anfauglith before the passes of Sirion. [*Struck out later:* The place of the chief slaughter was long marked by a great hill in which the slain were heaped, both Elves and Men: *Hauð-na-Dengin*, upon which alone in all Anfauglith the grass grew green.]

§220 In this battle Elves and Men were utterly defeated and the ruin of the Noldor was achieved. For Maidros was hindered at his setting out by the guile of Uldor the Accursed: first he gave false warning of an attack from Angband; then he must tarry for not all his men were willing to march. And the army in the West awaited the signal, and it came not, and they grew impatient, and there were whispers of treason among them.

§221 Now the army of the West contained the host of Hithlum, both Elves and Men, and to it was added both folk of the Falas, and a great company from Nargothrond [and many of the woodmen out of Brethil. *This was struck out and the following substituted:*] And many of the woodmen came also with Hundor of Brethil; and with him marched Mablung of Doriath with a small force of Grey-elves, some with axes, some with bows; for Mablung was unwilling to have no part in these great deeds, and Thingol gave leave to him to go, so long as he served not the sons of Fëanor. Therefore Mablung joined him to the host of Fingolfin [*read:* Fingon] and Húrin. / And lo! to the joy and wonder of all there was a sounding of great trumpets, and there marched up to war a host unlooked for. This was the army of Turgon that issued from Gondolin, ten thousand strong, with bright mail and long swords; and they were stationed southwards guarding the passes of Sirion.

§222 Then Morgoth, who knew much of what was done, chose his hour, and trusting in his servants to hold back Maidros and prevent the union of his foes, he sent forth a force seeming great (and yet but part of all that he had made ready) and marched them on Hithlum. Then hot of heart Fingon wished to assail them upon the plain, thinking he had the greater strength; but Húrin spoke against this, bidding him await the signal of Maidros, and let rather the Orcs break themselves against his strength arrayed in the hills.

§223 But the Captain of Morgoth in the West had been commanded to draw forth Fingon into open battle swiftly, by whatsoever means he could. Therefore when his van had come even to the inflowing of Rivil into Sirion and still none came forth to withstand him, he halted, and sent forth riders with tokens of parley; and they rode up close to the lines of their enemies upon the west-shore of Sirion at the feet of the mountains.

§224 Now they led with them Gelmir son of Guilin, a lord of Nargothrond, whom they had taken in the Bragollach and had blinded; and they showed him forth, crying: 'We have many more such at home, but ye must make haste, if ye would find them. For we shall slay them when we return, even so.' And they hewed off Gelmir's hands and feet, and his head last, within sight of the Elves.

§225 But by ill chance across the water stood Gwindor Guilin's son, and he indeed against the will of Orodreth had marched to the war with all the strength that he could muster because of his grief for his brother. Therefore his wrath [*struck out:* could no longer be restrained, but] was kindled to a flame, and the men of Nargothrond sprang over the stream and slew the riders, and drove then on against the main host. And seeing this all the host of the West was set on fire, and Fingon sounded his trumpets and leaped forth from the hills in sudden onslaught; and many also of the army of Gondolin joined in the battle ere Turgon could restrain them.

§226 And behold! the light of the drawing of the swords of the Noldor was like a fire in a field of reeds; and so fell was their onset that almost the designs of Morgoth went astray. Ere the army that he had sent westward could be strengthened, it was swept away; [and assailed from west and south it was hewn down as it stood, and the greatest slaughter of the Orcs was then made that yet had been achieved. >] and the banners of Fingolfin [? *read* Fingon] passed over Anfauglith and were raised before the walls of Angband. / Gwindor son of Guilin and the folk of Nargothrond were in the forefront of that battle, and they burst through the outer gates and slew the Orcs [even in the very tunnels of Morgoth >] within the very fortress of Morgoth, and he trembled upon his deep throne, hearing them beat upon his doors.

§227 But at the last Gwindor was taken and his men slain; for none had followed them, and no help came. By other secret doors in the mountains of Thangorodrim Morgoth had let forth his main host that was held in waiting, and Fingon was beaten back with great loss from the walls.

§228 Then in the plain of Anfauglith, on the [third >] fourth day of the war, began the *Nírnaeth Arnediad*, for no song can contain all its grief. The host of Fingon retreated over the sands of the desert, and there fell Hundor son of Haleth [*struck out:* in the rearguard] and most of the men of Brethil. But as night fell, and they were still far from [Ered-wethion >] Eryd-wethrin, the Orcs surrounded the army of Fingon, and they fought until day, pressed ever closer. Even so, all was not yet lost. In the morning were heard the horns of Turgon who brought up now his main host to the rescue [*struck out:* unlooked-for by the Orcs]; and the Noldor of Gondolin were strong and clad in mail, and they broke [the leaguer, and once again the might of Angband was defeated. >] through the ranks of the Orcs, and Turgon hewed his way to the side of Fingon, his brother. And it is said that the meeting of Turgon with Húrin who stood by his king was glad in the midst of the battle./

§229 And in that very day, at the third hour of morning, lo! at last the trumpets of Maidros were heard coming up from the east; and the banners of the sons of Fëanor assailed the enemy in the rear. It has been said that even then the Eldar might have won the day, had all their hosts proved faithful; for the Orcs wavered, and their onslaught was stayed, and already some were turning to flight.

§230 But even as the vanguard of Maidros came upon the Orcs, Morgoth loosed his last strength, and Angband was emptied. There came wolves, and wolfriders, and there came Balrogs a thousand, and there came worms and drakes, and Glaurung, Father of Dragons. And the strength and terror of the Great Worm were now grown great indeed, and Elves and Men withered before him; and he came between the hosts of Maidros and Fingon and swept them apart.

§231 Yet neither by wolf, balrog, nor dragon would Morgoth have achieved his end, but for the treachery of Men. In this hour the plots of Ulfang were revealed; for many of the Easterlings turned and fled, their hearts being filled with lies and fear; but the sons of Ulfang went over suddenly to the side of Morgoth and drove in upon the rear of the sons of Fëanor. And in the confusion that they wrought they came near to the standard of Maidros. They reaped not the reward that Morgoth promised them, for Maglor slew Uldor the Accursed, the leader in treason, and Bór and his sons slew Ulfast and Ulwarth ere they themselves were slain. But new strength of evil men came up that Uldor had summoned and kept hidden in the eastern hills, and the host of Maidros being assailed now on three sides, by the Orcs, and the beasts, and by the Swarthy Men, was dispersed and fled this way and that. Yet fate saved the sons of Fëanor, and though all were wounded, none were slain, for they drew together and gathering a remnant of Noldor and of the Naugrim about them they hewed a way out of the battle and escaped towards Mount Dolmed.

§232 Last of all the eastern force to stand firm were the Enfeng of [Nogrod >] Belegost, and thus won renown. Now the Naugrim withstood fire more hardily than either Elves or Men, and it was the custom moreover of the Enfeng to wear great masks [*struck out:* or vizors] in battle hideous to look upon, which stood them in good stead against the drakes. And but for them Glaurung and his brood would have withered all that was left of the Noldor. But the Naugrim made a circle about him when he assailed them, and even his mighty armour was not full proof against the blows of their great axes; and when in his rage he turned and struck down Azaghâl of Belegost and crawled over him, with his last stroke Azaghâl drove a knife into his belly and so wounded him that he fled the field and the beasts of Angband in dismay followed after him. Had Azaghâl but borne a sword great woe would have been spared to the Noldor that after befell [*added:*] but his knife went not deep enough. / But then the Enfeng raised up the body of Azaghâl and bore it away; and with slow steps they walked behind, singing a dirge in their deep voices, as it were a funeral pomp in their own country, and gave no heed more to their foes; and indeed none dared to stay them.

§233 But now in the western battle Fingon was surrounded by a tide of foes thrice greater than all that was left to him [*struck out:* and the Balrogs came against him]. There at last fell the King of the Noldor, and flame sprang from his helm when it was cloven. He was overborne by the Balrogs and beaten to the earth and his banners blue and silver were trodden into dust.

§234 The day was lost, but still Húrin and Huor with the men of Hador stood firm, and the Orcs could not yet win the passes of Sirion. Thus was the treachery of Uldor redressed; and the last stand of Húrin and Huor is the deed of war most renowned among the Eldar that the Fathers of Men wrought in their behalf. For Húrin spoke to Turgon saying: 'Go now, lord, while time is! For last art thou of the House of Fingolfin, and in thee lives the last hope of the Noldor. While Gondolin stands, strong and guarded, Morgoth shall still know fear in his heart.'

'Yet not long now can Gondolin be hidden, and being discovered it must fall,' said Turgon.

§235 'Yet [a while it must stand,' said Húrin; 'for out of Gondolin >] if it stands but a little while,' said [Húrin >] Huor, 'then out of [Gondolin *later* >] thy house / shall come the hope of Elves and Men. This I say to thee, lord, with the eyes of death; though here we part for ever, and I shall never look on thy white walls, from thee and me shall a new star arise. Farewell!'

§236 [*Struck out:* Then Turgon withdrew and all the Noldor of Gondolin went back down Sirion and vanished into the hills. But all the remnant of the host of the west gathered about the brethren and held the pass behind them.]

§237 [*Added subsequently:*] And [Glindûr *later* >] Maeglin, Turgon's sister-son, who stood by heard these words and marked them well, [*struck out later:* and looked closely at Huor,] but said naught.

§238 Then Turgon accepted the valiant words of the brethren, and summoning all that remained of the folk of Gondolin, and such of Fingon's host as could be gathered, he [withdrew >] fought his way southward,/ and escaped down Sirion, and vanished into the mountains and was hidden from the eyes of Morgoth. For Húrin and Huor held the pass behind him, so that no foe could follow him, and drew the remnant of the mighty men of Hithlum about them.

§239 Slowly they withdrew, until they came behind the Fen of Serech, and had the young stream of Sirion before them, and then they stood and gave way no more, for they were in the narrow gorge of the pass. Then all the host of Morgoth swarmed against them, and they bridged the stream with the dead, and encircled the remnant of Hithlum as a gathering tide about a rock.

§240 Huor fell pierced with a venomed arrow in the eye, and all the valiant men of Hador were slain about him in a heap, and the Orcs hewed their heads and piled them as a mound of gold; for the sun was shining on the [fourth >] sixth and last / day of the battle and their yellow locks shone amid the blood. Last of all Húrin stood alone. Then he cast aside his shield and wielded his axe two-handed; and it is sung that in that last stand he himself slew an hundred of the Orcs. But they took him alive at last, by the command of Morgoth, who thought thus to do him more evil than by death. Therefore his servants grappled him with their hands, which clung still to him though he hewed off their arms; and ever their numbers were renewed until at the last he fell buried beneath them. Then binding him they dragged him to Angband with mockery. Thus ended the *Nírnaeth Arnediad*, and the sun sank red over Hithlum, and there came a great storm on the winds of the West.

§241 Great indeed now was the triumph of Morgoth; and his design was accomplished in a manner after his own heart; for Men took the lives of Men, and betrayed the Eldar, and fear and hatred were aroused among those that should have been united against him. From that day indeed began the estrangement of Elves from Men, save only from those of the Three Houses of Bëor, Hador, and Haleth, and their children.

§242 The March of Maidros was no more. The fell sons of Fëanor were broken and wandered far away in the woods as leaves before the wind. The Gorge of Aglon was filled with Orcs, and the Hill of Himring was garrisoned by soldiers of Angband; the pass of Sirion was pierced and Tol-sirion retaken and its dread towers rebuilt. All the gates of Beleriand were in the power of Morgoth. The realm of Fingon was no more [*struck out:* for few ever of the host of Hithlum, Elves or Men, came ever back over the mountains to their land]. To Hithlum came back never one of Fingon's host, nor any of the Men of Hador, nor any tidings of the battle and the fate of their lords.

§243 Doriath indeed remained, and Nargothrond was hidden, and Cirdan held the Havens; but Morgoth gave small heed to them as yet, either for he knew little of them, or because their hour was not yet come in the deep purposes of his malice. But one thought troubled him deeply, and marred his triumph; Turgon had escaped the net, whom he most desired to take. For Turgon came of the great house of Fingolfin, and was now by right King of all the Noldor, [*struck out:* and from of old he hated him, scarce less than Fëanor, and feared him more. For never in Valinor would Turgon greet him, being a friend of Ulmo and of Tulkas; and moreover, ere yet darkness overwhelmed him and the blindness of malice, he looked upon Turgon and knew that from him should come, in some time that doom held, the end of all hope.] and Morgoth feared and hated most the house of Fingolfin, because they had scorned him in Valinor, and had the friendship of Ulmo, and because of the wounds that Fingolfin gave him in battle. Moreover of old his eye had lighted on Turgon, and a dark shadow fell on his heart, foreboding that, in some time that lay yet hidden in doom, from Turgon ruin should come to him.

§244 Therefore Húrin was brought before Morgoth, and defied him; and he was chained and set in torment. But Morgoth who would ever work first with lies and treachery, if they might avail, came to him where he lay in pain, and offered him freedom, and power and wealth as one of his great captains, if he would take service in his armies and lead a host against Turgon, or even if he would but reveal where that king had his stronghold. For he had learned that Húrin knew the secret counsels of Turgon. But again Húrin the Steadfast mocked him.

§245 Then Morgoth restrained his wrath and spoke of Húrin's wife and son now helpless in Hithlum [*written above later*: Dorlómin], and at his mercy to do what he would with them.

§246 'They know not the secrets of Turgon,' said Húrin. 'But an they did, thou shouldst not come at Turgon so; for they are of the houses of Hador and Bëor, and we sell not our troth for any price of profit or pain.'

§247 Then Morgoth cursed Húrin and Morwen and their offspring and set a doom upon them of sorrow and darkness; and taking Húrin from prison he set him in a chair of stone upon a high place of Thangorodrim. There he could see afar the land of Hithlum westward and the lands of Beleriand southward. There Morgoth standing beside him cursed him again, and set his power upon him so that he could not stray from that place, nor die, unless Morgoth released him.

§248 'Sit now there!' said Morgoth. 'Look upon the lands where the uttermost woe shall come upon those whom thou hast delivered unto me. Yea, verily! Doubt not the power of Melkor, Master of the fates of Arda! And with my eyes shalt thou see it, [*struck out*: and nought shall be hidden from thee, and all that befalls those thou holdest dear shall swiftly be told to thee] and with my ears shalt thou hear all tidings, and nought shall be hidden from thee!'

§249 And even so it came to pass; but it is not said that Húrin asked ever of Morgoth either mercy or death, for himself or for any of his kin.

§250 Now the Orcs in token of the great triumph of

Angband gathered with great labour all the bodies of their enemies that were slain, and all their harness and weapons, and they piled them, Elves and Men, in a great hill in the midst of the Anfauglith. [Hauð-na-D(engin) > Hauð-i-Nengin *later* >] Hauð-ina-Nengin was the name of that mound, and it was like unto a hill. But thither alone in all the desert the grass came, and grew again long and green, and thereafter no Orc dared tread upon the earth beneath which the swords of the Noldor crumbled into rust.

§251 Rían wife of Huor hearing no tidings of her lord went forth into the wild, and there gave birth to Tuor her son; and he was taken to foster by [the Dark-elves *later* >] Annael of the Grey-elves of Mithrim. But Rían went to [Hauð-i-Nengin *later* > Hauð-na-nDengin >] Hauð-in-nDengin and laid her there and died. And in Brethil Glorwendil, Hador's daughter, died of grief. But Morwen wife of Húrin abode in Hithlum, for she was with child.

§252 Morgoth now broke his pledges to the Easterlings that had served him, and denied to them the rich lands of Beleriand which they coveted, and he sent away these evil folk into Hithlum, and there commanded them to dwell. And little though they now loved their new king, yet they despised the remnant of the folk of Hador (the aged and the women and the children for the most part), and they oppressed them, and took their lands and goods, and wedded their women by force, and enslaved their children. And those of the Grey-elves that had dwelt there fled into the mountains, or were taken to the mines of the North and laboured there as thralls.

§253 Therefore Morwen unwilling that Túrin her son, being then seven years old, should become a slave, sent him forth with two aged servants, and bade them find if they could a way to Doriath, and there beg fostering for the son of Húrin, and kinsman of Beren (for her father was his cousin).

473

§254 In the [*added:*] first/beginning of this year was born to Morwen Elfsheen a maid-child, daughter of Húrin; and she was named Nienor, which is Mourning. And at about this time Túrin came through great perils to Doriath and was there received by Thingol, who took him to his own fostering, as he were king's son, in memory of Húrin. For Thingol's mood was now changed towards the houses of the Elf-friends.

§255 In this year Morgoth having rested his strength, and given heed to his own hurts and great losses, renewed the assault upon Beleriand, which now lay open to him; and the orcs and wolves passed far into the lands, even as far as the borders of Ossiriand upon one side, and Nan Tathren upon the other, and none were safe in field or wild.

§256 Many now fled to the Havens and took refuge behind Cirdan's walls, and the mariner folk passed up and down the coast and harried the enemy with swift landings. Therefore the first assault of Morgoth was against Cirdan; and ere the winter was come he sent great strength over Hithlum and Nivrost, and they came down the Rivers Brithon and Nenning, and ravaged all the Falas, and besieged the walls of Brithombar and Eglarest. Smiths and miners and masters of fire they brought with them, and set up great engines, and though they were stoutly resisted they broke the walls at last. Then the Havens were laid in ruin, and the Tower of Ingildon cast down, and all Cirdan's folk slain or enthralled, save those that went aboard and escaped by sea [*added:*] and some few that fled north to Mithrim.

§257 Then Cirdan took his remnant by ship, and they sailed to the Isle of Balar, [*struck out:* and mingled with Turgon's outpost there,] and made a refuge for all that could come thither. For they kept also a foothold at the mouths of Sirion, and there many light swift ships lay hid in the creeks and waters where the reeds were dense as a forest. [And seven ships at Turgon's asking Cirdan sent out into the West, but they never returned. >] And when Turgon heard of this he sent again his messengers to Sirion's Mouths, and besought the aid of Cirdan the Shipwright. And at his bidding Cirdan let build seven swift ships, and they sailed out into the West, and were never heard of again – save one and the last. Now the captain of this ship was Voronwë, and he toiled in the sea for many years, until returning at last in despair his ship foundered in a great storm within sight of land, and he alone survived, for Ulmo saved him from the wrath of Ossë, and the waves bore him up and cast him ashore in Nivrost./

481

§258 Túrin waxed fair and strong and wise in Doriath, but was marked with sorrow. In this his sixteenth year he went forth to battle on the marches of Doriath, and became the companion in arms of Beleg the Bowman. [*Later pencilled addition:*] Túrin donned the Dragon-helm of Galion.

484

§259　Here Túrin was a guest at Menegroth in honour for his deeds of valour. But he came from the wild, and was unkempt and his gear and garments were wayworn. And Orgof taunted him, and the people of Hithlum, and in his wrath he smote Orgof with a cup and slew him at the king's board. Then fearing the anger of Thingol he fled, and became an outlaw in the woods, and gathered a desperate band, of Elves and of Men [*struck out:* beyond the Girdle of Melian].

487

§260　Here Túrin's band captured Beleg and bound him; but Túrin returning released him, and they renewed their friendship. And Túrin learned of the king's pardon, but would not go back to Menegroth, and remained upon the marches. And since no foe yet could pass the Girdle of Melian, and he desired only to take vengeance on the Orcs, he made a lair in the woods between Sirion and Mindeb in the country of Dimbar.

> The following passage was rewritten several times and it is not possible to be perfectly certain of the detail of development at each stage. As first written it seems to have read:

§261　Here Tuor son of Huor, being now fifteen years of age, came to Hithlum seeking his kin, but they were no more, for Morwen and Niënor had been carried away to Mithrim and none remembered them.

> This seems to have been cancelled as soon as written, and a second form probably reads thus:

§262　Here Tuor son of Huor, being now fifteen years of age, came to Hithlum seeking his kin, but he found them not. For though the Elves that fostered him knew indeed their names, they knew not where they dwelt of old, or dwelt now in the change of the land. But Morwen and Niënor alone remained, and they dwelt still in Dor Lómin; therefore Tuor searched in Hithlum in vain, and the Easterlings seized him and enslaved him. But he escaped and became an outlaw in the wild lands about Lake Mithrim.

> In the final form of the passage the date 488 was added:

488

§263 Here Tuor son of Huor, being now sixteen years of age, seeking to escape from Dorlómin, was made captive and enslaved by Lorgan chief of the Easterlings; and he endured thraldom for [seven years *immediately* >] three years, ere he escaped and became an outlaw in the hills of Mithrim.

[*Struck out:* 488]

§264 Here Haldir Orodreth's son of Nargothrond was trapped and hung on a tree by Orcs. Thereafter the Elves of Nargothrond were yet more wary and secret, and would not suffer even Elves to stray in their lands.

489

§265 In this year Gwindor Guilin's son escaped from Angband. Blodren Ban's son was an Easterling, and being taken by Morgoth, and tormented because he was one of the faithful that withstood Uldor, entered the service of Morgoth and was released, and sent in search of Túrin. And he entered the hidden company in Dimbar, and served Túrin manfully for two years. But seeing now his chance he betrayed the refuge of Beleg and Túrin to the Orcs, as his errand was. Thus it was surrounded and taken, and Túrin was captured alive and carried towards Angband; but Beleg was left for dead among the slain. Blodren was slain by a chance arrow in the dark. [*Pencilled against this annal:* What happened to the Dragon-helm?]

§266 Beleg was found by Thingol's messengers, and taken to Menegroth and healed by Melian. At once he set forth in search of Túrin [*pencilled in margin:* bearing the Dragon-helm that Túrin had left in Menegroth]. He came upon Gwindor bewildered in Taur-na-Fuin (where Sauron now dwelt) and together they pursued the captors of Túrin. From an orc-camp on the edge of the desert they rescued him as he slept in drugged sleep, and carried him to a hidden dell. But Beleg as he laboured to unloose Túrin's fetters pricked his foot, and he was roused, and dreaming that he was surrounded by Orcs that would torment him, seized Beleg's sword and slew him ere he knew him. Gwindor buried Beleg, and led Túrin away, for a dumb madness of grief was on him.

490

§267 Through great perils Gwindor led Túrin towards Nargothrond, and they came to the pools of Ivrin, and there Túrin wept and was healed of his madness. Gwindor and Túrin came at last to Nargothrond, and were admitted; for Finduilas daughter of Orodreth, to whom Gwindor had been betrothed, alone of his people knew him again after the torments of Angband.

490–5

§268 During this time Túrin dwelt in Nargothrond, and became great in counsel and renown. The Noldor took Beleg's sword which Túrin had kept, and re-forged it, and it was made into a black sword with edges as of fire. Now Túrin [*added:*] had begged Gwindor to conceal his right name, for the horror he had of his slaying of Beleg and dread lest it were learned in Doriath; and he / had given out his name as *Iarwaeth* [*struck out:* the blood-stained], but now it was changed to *Mormegil* the Blacksword, because of the rumour of his deeds with that weapon in vengeance for Beleg; but the sword itself he named *Gurthang* Iron of Death. Then the heart of Finduilas was turned from Gwindor (who because of his pains in Angband was half crippled) and her love was given to Túrin; and Túrin loved her, but spoke not, being loyal to Gwindor. [*Added:*] Then Finduilas being torn in heart became sorrowful; and she grew wan and silent. / But Gwindor seeing what had befallen was bitter at heart, and cursed Morgoth, who could thus pursue his enemies with woe, whithersoever they might run. 'And now at last,' he said, 'I believe the tale of Angband that Morgoth hath cursed Húrin and all his kin.'

§269 And he spoke on a time to Finduilas, saying: 'Daughter of the House of Finrod, let no grief lie between us, for, though Morgoth hath laid my life in ruin, thee still I love. But go thou whither love leads thee! Yet beware! Not meet is it that the Elder Children should stoop to the Younger. Neither will fate suffer it, save once or twice only for some high cause of doom. But this Man is not Beren. A doom indeed lies on him, as seeing eyes may well read in him, but a dark doom. Enter not into it! And if thou wilt, then thy love shall betray thee to bitterness and death. For behold! this is not *Iarwaeth* nor *Mormegil*, but Túrin son of Húrin.'

§270 And Gwindor told how Húrin's torment and curse was known to all in Angband; and said: 'Doubt not the power of Morgoth Bauglir! Is it not written in me?' But Finduilas was silent.

§271 And later in like manner Gwindor spoke to Túrin; but Túrin answered: 'In love I hold thee for rescue and safe-keeping. And even were it not so, still I would do thee no hurt willingly, who hast suffered such great wrongs. Finduilas indeed I love, but fear not! Shall the accursed wed, and give as morrowgift his curse to one that he loves? Nay, not even to one of his own people. But now thou hast done ill to me, friend, to bewray my right name, and call my doom upon me, from which I had thought to lie hidden.'

§272 But when it became known to Orodreth [and the folk of Nargothrond that Iarwaeth was indeed the son of Húrin, then greater became his honour among them, and they would do >] that Iarwaeth was indeed the son of Húrin, he gave him great honour, and did / all that he counselled. And he being troubled by this new grief (for ever the love of Finduilas that he would not take grew greater) found solace only in war. And in that time the folk of Nargothrond forsook their secrecy, their war of ambush and hunting, and went openly to battle; and they [*struck out:* allied themselves with Handir of Brethil, and] built a bridge over the Narog from the great doors of Felagund for the swifter passage of their arms. And they drove the Orcs and beasts of Angband out of all the land between Narog and Sirion eastward, and westward to the Nenning and the borders of the desolate Falas. Thus Nargothrond was revealed to the wrath and malice of Morgoth, but still at Túrin's prayer his true name was not spoken, and rumour spoke only of Mormegil of Nargothrond.

The following entry, for the year 492, was struck out later. Its replacement, an inserted annal for the year 400, has been given earlier (§120).

§273 [*Rejected annal for the year 492*] Here Meglin son of Eöl was sent by his mother Isfin to Gondolin, and Turgon rejoiced to hear tidings of his sister whom he had deemed lost, and he received Meglin with honour as his sister-son. But it is said that Meglin, having been nurtured in the shadows of Brethil, was never wholly at ease in the light of Gondolin.

494

§274 In this time, when because of the deeds of Mormegil of Nargothrond the power of Morgoth was stemmed west of Sirion, Morwen and Niënor fled at last from Dor Lómin and came to Doriath, seeking tidings of Túrin. But they found him gone, and in Doriath no tidings had been heard of his name, since the Orcs took him, five years before. [*Added:*] Morwen and Niënor remained as guests of Thingol, and were treated with honour, but they were filled with sorrow, and yearned ever for tidings of Túrin. /

495

§275 Here [*added:*] Handir of Brethil was slain in the spring in fighting with Orcs that invaded his land. The Orcs gathered in the passes of Sirion. Late in the year having thus mustered great strength / Morgoth assailed Nargothrond. Glaurung the Urulókë passed [into Hithlum and there did great evil, and he came thence out of Dorlómin over the Erydwethrin >] over Anfauglith, and came thence into the north vales of Sirion and there did great evil, and he came thence under the shadows of the Erydwethrin / with a great army of Orcs in his train, and he defiled the Eithil Ivrin. Then he passed into the realm of Nargothrond, burning the Talath Dirnen, the Guarded Plain, between Narog and Sirion. Then Orodreth and Túrin [*struck out:* and Handir of Brethil; *added later:*] and Gwindor / went up against him, but they were defeated upon the field of Tum-halad; and Orodreth was slain [*struck out:* and Handir. *Added later:*] and Gwindor. [*Pencilled in margin:* Túrin in the battle wore the Dragon-helm.] Túrin bore Gwindor out of the rout, and escaping to a wood there laid him on the grass.

§276 And Gwindor said, 'Let bearing pay for bearing! But hapless was mine, and vain is thine. For now my body is marred, and I must leave Middle-earth; and though I love thee, son of Húrin, yet I rue the day I took thee from the Orcs. But for thy prowess, still I should have love and life, and Nargothrond should stand. Now if you love me, leave me! Haste thee to Nargothrond and save Finduilas. And this last I say to thee: she alone stands between thee and thy doom. If thou fail her, it shall not fail to find thee. Farewell!'

§277 Therefore Túrin sped now back to Nargothrond, mustering such of the rout as he met on the way. [*Added:*] And the leaves fell from the trees in a great wind as they went, for the autumn was passing to a dire winter. And one, Ornil, said: 'Even so fall the people of Nargothrond, but for them there shall come no Spring.' And Túrin hastened, / but Glaurung and his army were there before him (because of his succouring of Gwindor), and they came suddenly, ere those that were left on guard were aware of the defeat. In that day the bridge that Túrin let build over Narog proved an evil; for it was great and mightily made and could not swiftly be destroyed, and thus the enemy came readily over the deep river, and Glaurung came in full fire against the Doors of Felagund, and overthrew them, and passed within.

§278 And even as Túrin came up the ghastly sack of Nargothrond was wellnigh achieved. The Orcs had slain or driven off all that remained in arms, and they were even then ransacking all the great halls and chambers, plundering and destroying; but those of the women and maidens that were not burned or slain they had herded on the terrace before the doors, as slaves to be taken to Angband. Upon this ruin and woe Túrin came, and none could withstand him; or would not, though he struck down all before him, and passed over the bridge, and hewed his way towards the captives.

§279 And now he stood alone, for the few that had followed him had fled into hiding. But behold! in that moment Glaurung the fell issued from the gaping Doors of Felagund, and lay behind, between Túrin and the bridge. Then suddenly he spoke by the evil spirit that was in him, saying: 'Hail, son of Húrin. Well met!'

§280 Then Túrin sprang about, and strode against him, and fire was in his eyes, and the edges of Gurthang shone as with flame. But Glaurung withheld his blast, and opened wide his serpent-eyes and gazed upon Túrin. And without fear Túrin looked in those eyes as he raised up his sword, and lo! straightway he fell under the dreadful spell of the dragon, and was as one turned to stone. Thus long they stood unmoving, silent before the great Doors of Felagund. Then Glaurung spoke again, taunting Túrin. [*Pencilled against this paragraph:* For while he wore the Dragon-helm of Galion he was proof against the glance of Glaurung. Then the Worm perceiving this (*sic*)]

§281 'Evil have been all thy ways, son of Húrin,' said he. 'Thankless fosterling, outlaw, slayer of thy friend, thief of love, usurper of Nargothrond, captain foolhardy, and deserter of thy kin. [*Struck out:* How long wilt thou live to bring ruin upon all that love thee?] As thralls thy mother and sister live in Dorlómin, in misery and want. Thou art arrayed as a prince, but they go in rags. For thee they yearn, but thou reckest not of that. Glad may thy father be to learn that he hath such a son, as learn he shall.' And Túrin being under the spell of Glaurung, harkened to his words, and saw himself as in a mirror misshapen by malice, and loathed that which he saw. And while he was yet held by the eyes of Glaurung in torment of mind, and could not stir, at a sign from the dragon the Orcs drove away the herded captives, and they passed nigh to Túrin and went over the bridge. And behold! among them was Finduilas, and she held out her arms to Túrin, and called him by name. But not until her cries and the wailing of the captives was lost upon the northward road did Glaurung release Túrin, and he might not even stop his ears against that voice that haunted him after.

§282 Then suddenly Glaurung withdrew his glance, and waited; and Túrin stirred slowly as one waking from a hideous dream. Then coming to himself with a loud cry he sprang upon the dragon. But Glaurung laughed, saying: 'If thou wilt be slain, I will slay thee gladly. But small help will that be to Morwen and Nienor. No heed didst thou give to the cries of the Elf-woman. Wilt thou deny also the bond of thy blood?'

§283 But Túrin drawing back his sword stabbed at his eyes; and Glaurung coiling back swiftly towered above him, and said: 'Nay! At least thou art valiant. Beyond all whom I have met. And they lie who say that we of our part do not honour the valour of foes. Behold! I offer thee freedom. Go to thy kin, if thou canst. Get thee gone! And if Elf or Man be left to make tale of these days, then surely in scorn they will name thee, if thou spurnest this gift.'

§284 Then Túrin, being yet bemused by the eyes of the dragon, as were he treating with a foe that could know pity, believed the words of Glaurung, and turning away sped over the bridge. But as he went Glaurung spake behind him, saying in a fell voice: 'Haste thee now, son of Húrin, to Dorlómin! Or maybe the Orcs shall come before thee, once again. And if thou tarry for Finduilas, then never shalt thou see Morwen or Nienor again; and they will curse thee.' [*Pencilled in margin:* Glaurung taunts him with the Dragon-helm.]

§285 But Túrin passed away on the northward road, and Glaurung laughed once more, for he had accomplished the errand of his Master. Then he turned to his own pleasure, and sent forth his blast, and burned all about him. But all the Orcs that were busy in the sack he routed forth, and drove them away, and denied them their plunder even to the least thing of worth. The bridge then he broke down and cast into the foam of Narog, and being thus secure, he gathered all the hoard and riches of Felagund and heaped them, and lay then upon them in the innermost hall, and rested a while.

§286 Now Túrin hastened along the ways to the North, through the lands now desolate, between Narog and Taiglin, [*added:*] and the Fell Winter came down to meet him; for that year snow fell ere autumn was passed, and spring came late and cold. / Ever it seemed to him as he went that he heard the cries of Finduilas, calling his name by wood and by hill, and great was his anguish; but his heart being hot with the lies of Glaurung, and seeing ever in his mind the Orcs burning the house of Húrin or putting Morwen and Niënor to torment, he held on his way, turning never aside.

> There follows here a section of the text where the original writing was heavily emended, after which the greater part of the section was struck out and replaced. I give first the form as originally written. For the antecedents of the *Grey Annals* (other than the entries concerning Tuor) from this point to the end of the tale of Túrin (§349) see the commentary on §§287 ff.

§287 At last worn and hungry by long days of journey, as the sad autumn drew on he came to the pools of Ivrin, where before he had been healed. But they were broken and defiled, and he could not drink there again. An ill token it seemed to him.

§288 Thus he came through the passes into Dorlómin, and even as winter fell with snow from the North, he found again the land of his childhood. Bare was it and bleak. And Morwen was gone. Empty stood her house, broken and cold. It was more than a year since she departed to Doriath. Brodda the Easterling (who had wedded Morwen's kinswoman Airin) had plundered her house, and taken all that was left of her goods. Then Túrin's eyes were opened, and the spell of Glaurung was broken, and he knew the lies wherewith he had been cheated. And in his anguish and his wrath for the evils that his mother had suffered he slew Brodda in his own hall, and fled then out into the winter, a hunted man.

§289 Tidings came soon to Thingol in Doriath of the fall of Nargothrond; and [it was revealed now that Mormegil was indeed Túrin son of Húrin >] fear walked on the borders of the Hidden Kingdom.

§290 In this same year Tuor son of Huor was led by the sendings of Ulmo to a secret way that led from Mithrim, by a channel of water running under earth, and so came to the deep cleft at the head of Drengist, and passed out of the knowledge of the spies of Morgoth. Then journeying alone warily down the coasts he came through the Falas and the ruined Havens and so reached at the year's end the Mouths of Sirion. [*Added and then struck out*: In the spring of this year also Handir of Brethil was slain in fighting with the Orcs that ventured into Brethil.]

496

§291 Too late now Túrin sought for Finduilas, roaming the woods under the shadow of Eryd Wethion, wild and wary as a beast; and he waylaid all the roads that went north to the pass of Sirion. Too late. For all trails had grown old, or had perished in the winter. But thus it was that Túrin passing southwards down Taiglin came upon some of the folk of Haleth that dwelt still in the forest of Brethil. They were dwindled now by war to a small people, and dwelt for the most part secretly within a stockade upon the Amon Obel deep in the forest. Ephel Brandir was that place named; for Brandir son of Handir was now their lord since [Handir had not returned from the stricken field of Tum-halad. >] since Handir his father had been slain. And Brandir was no man of war, being lame by a misadventure in childhood; and he was gentle moreover in mood, loving wood rather than metal, and the knowledge of all things that grow in the earth rather than other lore.

At this point the rejected section of the narrative, beginning at §287, ends. The text that replaced it belongs to the time of the writing of the manuscript.

§292 At last worn by haste and the long road (for [eighty >] forty leagues had he journeyed without rest) he came with the first ice of winter to the pools of Ivrin, where before he had been healed. But they were now but a frozen mire, and he could not drink there again.

§293 Thus he came hardly by the passes of Dorlómin,

through bitter snows from the North, and found again the land of his childhood. Bare was it and bleak. And Morwen was gone. Empty stood her house, broken and cold, and no living thing now dwelt nigh.

§294 It so befell that Túrin came then to the hall of Brodda the Incomer, and learned of an old servant of Húrin that Brodda had taken to wife by force Airin Húrin's kinswoman, and had oppressed Morwen; and therefore in the year before she had fled with Nienor, none but Airin knew whither.

§295 Then Túrin strode to Brodda's table, and with threats learned from Airin that Morwen went to Doriath to seek her son. For said Airin: 'The lands were freed then from evil by the Blacksword of the South, who now hath fallen, they say.'

§296 Then Túrin's eyes were opened, and the last shreds of Glaurung's spell left him, and for anguish, and wrath at the lies that had deluded him, and hatred of the oppressors of Morwen, a black rage seized him, and he slew Brodda in his hall, and other Easterlings that were his guests, and then he fled out into the winter, a hunted man.

§297 But he was aided by some that remained of Hador's people and knew the ways of the wild, and with them he escaped through the falling snow and came to an outlaws' refuge in the southern mountains of Dorlómin. Thence Túrin passed again from the land of his childhood, and returned to Sirion's vale. His heart was bitter, for to Dorlómin he had brought only greater woe upon the remnant of his people, and they were glad of his going; and this comfort alone he had: that by the prowess of the Blacksword the ways to Doriath had been laid open to Morwen. And he said in his heart: 'Then those deeds wrought not evil to all! And where else might I have better bestowed my dear kin, even if I had come sooner? For if the Girdle of Melian is broken, then last hope is ended. Nay, it is better as it hath turned out. For behold! a shadow I cast wheresoever I come. Let Melian keep them! But I will leave them in peace unshadowed for a while.'

496

§298 Here Tuor son of Huor met Bronwë of the Noldor at the mouths of Sirion; and they began a journey northward along the great river. But as they dwelt in Nan Tathrin, and delayed because of the peace and beauty of that country in the spring, Ulmo himself came up Sirion and appeared to Tuor, and the yearning for the Great Sea was ever after in his heart. But now at Ulmo's command he went up Sirion, and by the power that Ulmo set upon them Tuor and Bronwë found the guarded entrance to Gondolin. There Tuor was brought before King Turgon, and spake the words that Ulmo had set in his mouth, bidding him depart and abandon the fair and mighty city that he had built, and go down to the Sea. But Turgon would not listen to this counsel; and [Meglin *later* >] Glindûr his sister-son spoke against Tuor. But Tuor was held in honour in Gondolin, for his kindred's sake.

> This annal was much emended and added to (and the date changed to 495), and then (since the text was now in a very confused state) struck out as far as 'bidding him depart' and replaced by the following version on a detached slip:

495

§299 Now Tuor Huor's son had lived as an outlaw in the caves of Androth above Mithrim for four years, and he had done great hurt to the Easterlings, and Lorgan set a price upon his head. But Ulmo, who had chosen him as the instrument of his designs, caused him to go by secret ways out of the land of Dorlómin, so that his going was hidden from all the servants of Morgoth; and he came to Nivrost. But there, becoming enamoured of the Sea, he tarried long; and in the autumn of the year Ulmo himself appeared to Tuor, and bade him to depart, and go to the hidden city of Turgon. And he sent to him Voronwë, last of the mariners of Turgon, to guide him; and Voronwë led Tuor eastward along the eaves of Eryd Wethion to Ivrin. (And there they saw Túrin pass, but spoke not with him.) And at the last by the power that Ulmo set upon them they came to the guarded gate of Gondolin. There Tuor was brought before the king, and spoke the counsel of Ulmo, bidding Turgon [*the following is the text already given in §298*] depart and abandon the fair and mighty city that he had built, and go down to the Sea. But Turgon would not listen to this counsel; and [Meglin *later* >] Glindûr his sister-son spoke against Tuor. But Tuor was held in honour in Gondolin, for his kindred's sake.

[496]

§300 Now Túrin coming down from Eryd Wethion sought for Finduilas in vain, roaming the woods under the shadow of the mountains, wild and wary as a beast; and he waylaid all the roads that went north to the passes of Sirion. Too late. For all the trails had grown old, or were washed away by the winter. But thus it was that, passing southwards down Taiglin, Túrin came upon some of the Men of Brethil, and delivered them from Orcs that had entrapped them. For the Orcs fled from Gurthang.

§301 He named himself Wildman of the Woods, and they besought him to come and dwell with them; but he said that he had an errand yet unachieved: to seek Finduilas Orodreth's daughter. Then Dorlas, leader of the woodmen, told the grievous tidings of her death. For the woodmen at the Crossings of Taiglin had waylaid the orc-host that led the captives of Nargothrond, hoping to rescue them; but the Orcs had at once cruelly slain their prisoners, and Finduilas they pinned to a tree with a spear. So she died, saying at the last: 'Tell the Mormegil that Finduilas is here.' Therefore they had laid her in a mound near that place, and named it *Hauð-en-Ellas*.

§302 Túrin bade them lead him thither, and there he fell down into a darkness of grief, and was near to death. Then Dorlas by his black sword, the fame whereof had come even into the deeps of Brethil, and by his quest of the king's daughter, knew that this Wildman was indeed the Mormegil of Nargothrond [added:] (whom rumour said was the son of Húrin of Dorlómin). The woodmen therefore lifted him up, and bore him away to their homes. These were set in a stockade upon a high place in the forest, Ephel Brandir upon Amon Obel; for the folk of Haleth were now dwindled by war to a small people, and Brandir son of Handir who ruled them was a man of gentle mood, and lame also from childhood, and he trusted rather in secrecy than in deeds of war to save them from the power of the North.

§303 Therefore he feared the tidings that Dorlas brought, and when he beheld the face of Túrin as he lay on the bier a cloud of foreboding lay on his heart. Nonetheless being moved by his woe, he took him into his own house and tended him; for he had skill in healing. And with the beginning of spring Túrin cast off his darkness, and grew hale again; and he arose, and he thought that he would remain in Brethil, hidden, and put his shadow behind him, forsaking the past. He took therefore a new name, *Turambar*, and besought the woodmen to forget that he was a stranger among them or ever bore any other name. Nonetheless he would not wholly leave deeds of war, for he could not endure that the Orcs should come to the Crossings of Taiglin or draw nigh Hauð-en-Ellas, and he made that a place of dread for them so that they shunned it. But he laid his black sword by, and used rather the bow.

§304 Now new tidings came to Doriath concerning Nargothrond, for some that had escaped from the defeat and the sack, and had survived the fell winter in the wild, came at last to Thingol, seeking refuge. But their tales were at variance, some saying that Nargothrond was empty, others that Glaurung abode there; some saying that all the lords and captains were slain, others that, nay, the Mormegil had returned to Nargothrond and there was made a prisoner under the spell of the dragon. But all declared that it was known to many in Nargothrond ere the end that the Mormegil was none other than Túrin Húrin's son. [*Pencilled addition:* And when she heard of the Dragonhelm Morwen knew this was true.]

§305 Then Morwen was distraught, and refusing the counsel of Melian, she rode forth alone into the wild to seek her son, or some true tidings of him. Thingol, therefore, sent Mablung after her, with many hardy march-wards, and some riders, to guard her, and to learn what news they might; but Nienor joined this company secretly in disguise, for she hoped that when Morwen saw that her daughter would go with her into peril, if she went on, then she would be willing to return to Doriath and leave the seeking of tidings to Mablung. But Morwen, being fey, would not be persuaded, and Mablung perforce led the ladies with him; and they passed out over the wide plain and came to Amon Ethir, a league before the bridge of Nargothrond. There Mablung set a guard of riders about Morwen and her daughter, and forbade them go further. But he, seeing from the hill no sign of any enemy, went down with his scouts to the Narog, as stealthily as they could go.

§306 But Glaurung was aware of all that they did, and he came forth in heat of wrath, and lay into the river; and a vast vapour and foul reek went up, in which Mablung and his company were blinded and lost. Then Glaurung passed east over Narog.

§307 Seeing the onset of Glaurung the guards upon Amon Ethir sought to lead the ladies away, and fly with them with all speed back eastwards; but the wind bore the blank mists upon them, and their horses were maddened by the dragon-stench, and were ungovernable, and ran this way and that, so that some were dashed against trees and slain, and others were borne far away. Thus the ladies were lost, and of Morwen indeed no sure tidings came ever to Doriath after. But Niënor, being thrown by her steed yet unhurt, groped her way back to Amon Ethir, there to await Mablung, and came thus above the reek into the sunlight. [Thus she came alone face to face with Glaurung himself, who had climbed up from the other side. >] And looking west she looked straight into the eyes of Glaurung, whose head lay upon the hill-top.

§308 Her will strove with him for a while, but he put forth his power, and having learned who she was (as indeed he guessed full well) he constrained her to gaze into his eyes, and laid a spell of utter darkness and forgetfulness, so that she could remember nothing that had ever befallen her, nor her own name, nor the name of any other thing; and for many days indeed she could neither hear, nor see, nor stir by her own will. Then Glaurung left her standing alone upon Amon Ethir, and he went back to Nargothrond.

§309 Now Mablung, who greatly daring had explored the halls of Felagund when Glaurung left them, fled from them at the approach of the dragon, and returned to Amon Ethir. The sun sank and night fell as he climbed the hill, and to his dismay he found none there, save Niënor standing alone under the stars as an image of stone. No word she spoke or heard, but would follow, if he took up her hand. Therefore in great grief he led her away, though it seemed to him vain; for they were both like to perish, succourless, in the wild.

§310 But they were found by three of Mablung's companions, and slowly they journeyed northward and eastward to the fences of Doriath where, nigh to the inflowing of Esgalduin, there was the secret gate by which those of its folk that returned from without were wont to enter. Slowly the strength of Niënor returned as they drew nearer to Doriath and further from Glaurung, but as yet she could not speak or hear, and walked blindly as she was led.

§311 But even as they drew near the fences at last she closed her wild staring eyes, and would sleep; and they laid her down and she slept; and they rested also, for they were utterly outworn. Being thus less heedful than was wise, they were there assailed by an Orc-band, such as now roamed often as nigh the fences of Doriath as they dared. But Niënor in that hour recovered hearing and sight, and being awakened by the cries of the Orcs, sprang up in terror as a wild thing, and fled ere they could come to her.

§312 Then the Orcs gave chase, and the Elves after; but though they overtook the Orcs indeed and slew them ere they could harm her, Niënor escaped them. For she fled as in a madness of fear, swifter than a deer, and tore off all her raiment as she ran, until she was naked [*bracketed later:*] but for a short kirtle. And she passed out of their sight, running northward, and though they sought her long they found her not, nor any trace of her. And at last Mablung in despair returned to Menegroth and told all his tidings. [*Added:* Greatly grieved were Thingol and Melian; but Mablung went forth and for three years sought in vain for tidings of Morwen and Niënor.]

§313 But Niënor ran on into the woods, until she was spent, and then fell and slept, and awoke; and behold it was a bright morning, and she rejoiced in light as it were a new thing, and all things else that she saw seemed new and strange, for she had no names for them. Nothing did she remember save a darkness that lay behind her, and a shadow of fear; therefore warily she went as a hunted beast, and became famished, for she had no food and knew not how to seek it. But coming at last to the Crossings of Taiglin she went over, seeking the shelter of the great trees of Brethil, for she was afraid, and it seemed to her that the darkness was overtaking her again from which she had fled.

§314 But it was a great storm of thunder that came up from the South, and in terror she cast herself down by the mound, Hauð-en-Ellas [*pencilled in margin:* Elleth], stopping her ears from the thunder, but the rain smote her and drenched her, and she lay like a wild beast that is dying.

§315 There Turambar found her, as he came to the Crossings of Taiglin, having heard a rumour of Orcs that roamed near. And seeing in a flare of lightning the body of a slain maiden (as it seemed) lying upon the mound of Finduilas, he was stricken [suddenly with fear >] to the heart. But the woodmen lifted her up, and Turambar cast his cloak about her, and they took her to a lodge nearby, and bathed her and warmed her and gave her food. And as soon as she looked upon Turambar she was comforted; for it seemed to her that she had found something at last that she long sought in her darkness; and she laid her hand in his and would not be parted from him.

§316 But when he asked her concerning her name and her kin and her misadventure, then she became troubled as a child that perceives that something is demanded but cannot understand what it be. And she burst into tears. Therefore Turambar said: 'Be not troubled! Doubtless thy tale is too sad yet to tell. It shall wait. But a name thou must have, and I will call thee *Níniel* (tear-maiden).' And at that name she shook her head, but said *Níniel*. That was the first word she spoke after her darkness, and it remained her name among the woodmen ever after.

§317 The next day they bore her towards Ephel Brandir, but at the falls of Celebros a great shuddering came upon her (wherefore afterwards that place was called Nen Girith), and ere she came to the home of the woodmen she was sick of a fever. She lay long in her sickness, but was healed by the skill of Brandir and the care of the leech-women of Brethil; and the women taught her language as to an infant. Ere autumn came she was hale again, and could speak, but remembered nothing before she was found by Turambar. Brandir loved her dearly, but all her heart was given to Turambar. All that year since the coming of Níniel there was peace in Brethil, and the Orcs did not trouble the woodmen.

497

§318 Turambar still remained at peace and went not to war. His heart turned to Níniel, and he asked her in marriage; but for that time she delayed in spite of her love. For Brandir foreboded he knew not what, and sought to restrain her, rather for her sake than his own or rivalry with Turambar; and he revealed to her that Turambar was Túrin son of Húrin, and though she knew not the name a shadow fell on her heart. This Turambar learned and was ill pleased with Brandir.

498

§319 In the spring of this year Turambar asked Níniel again, and vowed that he would now wed her, or go back to war in the wild. And Níniel took him with joy, and they were wedded at the mid-summer, and the Woodmen of Brethil made a great feast. But ere the end of the year Glaurung sent Orcs of his dominion against Brethil; and Turambar sat at home deedless, for he had promised Níniel that he would go to battle only if their home was assailed. But the woodmen were worsted, and Dorlas upbraided him that he would not aid the folk that he had taken for his own. Then Turambar arose and brought forth again his black sword, and he gathered a great force of the Men of Brethil, and they defeated the Orcs utterly. But Glaurung heard tidings that the Black Sword was in Brethil, and he pondered what he had heard, devising new evil.

499

§320 Níniel conceived in the spring of this year, and became wan and sad. At the same time there came to Ephel Brandir the first rumours that Glaurung had issued from Nargothrond. And Turambar sent out scouts far afield, for he now ordered things as he would, and few gave heed to Brandir.

§321 And as it drew near to summer Glaurung came to the borders of Brethil, and lay near the west-shore of Taiglin, and then there was great fear among the wood-folk, for it was now plain that the Great Worm would assail them and ravage their land, and not pass by, returning to Angband, as they had hoped. They sought therefore the counsel of Turambar. And he counselled them that it was vain to go against the Worm with all their force. Only by cunning and good fortune could they defeat him. He offered therefore himself to seek Glaurung on the borders of the land, and bade the rest of the people to remain at Ephel Brandir, but to prepare for flight. For if Glaurung had the victory, he would come first to the woodmen's homes to destroy them, and they could not hope to withstand him; but if they then scattered far and wide, then many might escape, for Glaurung would not take up his dwelling in Brethil and would return soon to Nargothrond.

§322 Then Turambar asked for companions willing to aid him in his peril, and Dorlas stood forth, but no others. Then Dorlas upbraided the people, and spoke scorn of Brandir who could not play the part of the heir of Haleth; and Brandir was shamed before his people, and was bitter at heart. But Torbarth [*pencilled above:* Gwerin] kinsman of Brandir asked his leave to go in his stead. Then Turambar said farewell to Níniel and she was filled with fear and foreboding, and their parting was sorrowful; but Turambar set out with his two companions and went to Nen Girith.

§323 Then Níniel being unable to endure her fear, and unwilling to wait in the Ephel tidings of Turambar's fortune, set forth after him, and a great company went with her. At this Brandir was filled more than ever before with dread, [*struck out*: but she heeded not his counsels] and he sought to dissuade her and the folk that would go with her from this rashness, but they heeded him not. Therefore he renounced his lordship, and all love for the people that had scorned him, and having naught left but his love for Níniel, he girt himself with a sword, and went after her; but being lame he fell far behind.

§324 Now Turambar came to Nen Girith at sundown and there learned that Glaurung lay on the brink of the high shores of the Taiglin, and was like to move when night fell. Then he called those tidings good; for the Worm lay at [Cabad-en-Aras >] Cabed-en-Aras, where the river ran in a deep and narrow gorge that a hunted deer might o'erleap, and Turambar deemed that he would seek no further, but would attempt to pass over the gorge. Therefore he purposed to creep down at dusk, and descend into the ravine under night, and cross over the wild water, and then climb up the further cliff (which was less sheer) and so come at the Worm beneath his guard.

§325 This counsel he then took, but the heart of Dorlas failed when they came to the races of Taiglin in the dark, and he dared not attempt the perilous crossing, but drew back and lurked in the woods burdened with shame. Turambar and Torbarth, nonetheless, crossed over in safety, for the loud roaring of the water drowned all other sounds, and Glaurung slept. But ere the middle-night the Worm roused, and with a great noise and blast cast his forward part across the chasm and began to draw his bulk after. Turambar and Torbarth were well-night overcome by the heat and the stench, as they sought in haste for a way up to come at Glaurung; and Torbarth was slain by a great stone that, dislodged from on high by the passage of the dragon, smote him upon the head and cast him into the River. So ended the last of the right kin of Haleth, and not the least valiant.

§326 Then Turambar summoned all his will and courage and climbed the cliff alone, and he thrust Gurthang into the soft belly of the Worm, even up to the hilts. But when Glaurung felt his death-pang he screamed, and in his dreadful throe he heaved up his bulk and hurled himself across the chasm, and there lay lashing and coiling in his agony. And he set all in a blaze about him, and beat all to ruin, until at last his fires died, and he lay still.

§327 Now Gurthang had been wrested from Turambar's

hand in the throe of Glaurung, and clave to the belly of the Worm. Turambar, therefore, crossed the water once more, desiring to recover his sword, and look on his foe. And he found him stretched at his length, and rolled upon one side; and the hilts of Gurthang stood in his belly. Then Turambar seized the hilts and set his foot upon the belly, and cried in mockery of the Worm and his words at Nargothrond: 'Hail, Worm of Morgoth! Well met again! Die now and the darkness have thee! Thus is Túrin son of Húrin avenged.'

§328 Then he wrenched out the sword, but a spout of black blood followed it, and fell on his hand, and the venom burned it. And thereupon Glaurung opened his eyes and looked upon Turambar with such malice, that it smote him as a blow; and by that stroke and the anguish of the venom he fell into a dark swoon, and lay as one dead, and his sword was beneath him.

§329 The yells of Glaurung rang in the woods and came to the folk that waited at Nen Girith; and when those that looked forth heard the scream of the Worm and saw from afar the ruin and burning that he made, they deemed that he had triumphed and was destroying those that assailed him. And Níniel sat and shuddered beside the falling water, and at the voice of Glaurung her darkness crept upon her again, so that she could not stir from that place of her own will.

§330 Even so Brandir found her, for he came to Nen Girith at last, limping wearily. And when he heard that the Worm had crossed the river and had beaten down his foes his heart yearned towards Níniel in pity. Yet he thought also: 'Turambar is dead, but Níniel lives. Now maybe she will come with me and I will lead her away and so we shall escape the Worm together.'

§331 After a while therefore he stood by Níniel and said: 'Come! It is time to go. If thou wilt, I will lead thee.' And he took her hand, and she arose silently, and followed him; and in the darkness none saw them go.

§332 But as they went down the path toward the Crossings the moon arose, and cast a grey light on the land, and Níniel said: 'Is this the way?' And Brandir answered that he knew no way, save to flee as they might from the Worm, and escape into the wild. But Níniel said: 'The Black Sword was my beloved and my husband. To seek him only do I go. What else couldst thou think?' And she sped on before him. Then she came towards the Crossings of Taiglin and beheld Hauð-en-Ellas in the white moonlight, and great dread came on her. Then with a cry she turned away, casting off her cloak, and fled southward along the river, and her white raiment shone in the moon.

§333 Thus Brandir saw her from the hill-side and turned to cross her path, but was still behind her, when she came to the ruin of Glaurung nigh the brink of [Cabad-en-Aras >] Cabed-en-Aras. There she saw the Worm lying, but heeded him not, for a man lay beside him; and she ran to Turambar and called his name in vain. Then, finding his hand that was burned, she laved it with tears and bound it about with a strip of her raiment, and kissed him and cried on him again to awake. Thereat Glaurung stirred for the last time ere he died, and he spoke with his last breath saying: 'Hail, Niënor daughter of Húrin. This is thy brother! Have joy of your meeting, and know him: Túrin son of Húrin, treacherous to foes, faithless to friends, and [a] curse unto his kin. And to thee worst of all, as now thou shalt feel!'

§334 Then Glaurung died, and the veil of his malice was taken from her, and she remembered all her life; and she sat as one stunned with horror and anguish. Then Brandir who had heard all, standing stricken upon the edge of the ruin, hastened towards her; but she leapt up and ran like a hunted deer, and came to [Cabad-en-Aras >] Cabed-en-Aras, and there cast herself over the brink, and was lost in the wild water.

§335 Then Brandir came and looked down into Cabad-en-Aras, and turned away in horror, and though he no longer desired life, he could not seek death in that roaring water. And thereafter no man looked ever again upon Cabad-en-Aras, nor would any beast or bird come there, nor any tree grow; and it was named Cabad Naeramarth, the Leap of Dreadful Doom.

§336 But Brandir now made his way back to Nen Girith, to bring tidings to the people; and he met Dorlas in the woods, and slew him (the first blood that ever he had spilled and the last). And he came to Nen Girith, and men cried to him: 'Hast thou seen her? Lo! Níniel is gone.'

§337 And he answered saying: 'Yea, Níniel is gone for ever. The Worm is dead, and Turambar is dead: and those tidings are good.' And folk murmured at these words, saying that he was crazed. But Brandir said: 'Hear me to the end! Níniel the beloved is also dead. She cast herself into the Taiglin desiring life no more. For she learned that she was none other than Niënor daughter of Húrin, ere her forgetfulness came upon her, and that Turambar was her brother, Túrin son of Húrin.'

§338   But even as he had ceased and the people wept, Túrin himself came before them. For when the Worm died, his swoon left him, and he fell into a deep sleep of weariness. But the cold of the night troubled him, and the hilts of Gurthang drove into his side, and he awoke. Then he saw that one had tended his hand, and he wondered much that he was left nonetheless to lie upon the cold ground; and he called and hearing no answer, he went in search of aid, for he was weary and sick.

§339   But when the people saw him they drew back in fear thinking that it was his unquiet spirit; and he said: 'Nay, be glad; for the Worm is dead, and I live. But wherefore have ye scorned my counsel, and come into peril? And where is Níniel? For her I would see. And surely ye did not bring her from her home?'

§340   Then Brandir told him that it was so and Níniel was dead. But the wife of Dorlas cried out: 'Nay, lord, he is crazed. For he came here saying that thou wert dead, and called it good tidings. But thou livest.'

§341   Then Turambar was wroth, and believed that all that Brandir said or did was done in malice towards himself and Níniel, begrudging their love; and he spoke evilly to Brandir, naming him Club-foot. Then Brandir reported all that he heard, and named Níniel Niënor daughter of Húrin, and cried out upon Turambar with the last words of Glaurung, that he was a curse unto his kin and to all that harboured him.

§342   Then Turambar fell into a fury, and charged Brandir with leading Níniel to her death, and publishing with delight the lies of Glaurung (if he devised them not himself indeed), and he cursed Brandir and slew him, and fled from the people into the woods. But after a while his madness left him, and he came to Hauð-en-Ellas and there sat and pondered all his deeds. And he cried upon Finduilas to bring him counsel; for he knew not whether he would do now more ill to go to Doriath to seek his kin, or to forsake them for ever and seek death in battle.

§343   And even as he sat there Mablung with a company of Grey-elves came over the Crossings of Taiglin, and he knew Túrin and hailed him, and was glad to find him living. For he had learned of the coming forth of Glaurung and that his path led to Brethil, and at the same time he had heard report that the Black Sword of Nargothrond now abode there. Therefore he came to give warning to Túrin and help if need be. But Túrin said: 'Too late thou comest. The Worm is dead.'

§344 Then they marvelled, and gave him great praise, but he cared nothing for it, and said: 'This only I ask: give me news of my kin, for in Dorlómin I learned that they had gone to the Hidden Kingdom.'

§345 Then Mablung was dismayed, but needs must tell to Túrin how Morwen was lost, and Niënor cast into a spell of dumb forgetfulness, and how she escaped them upon the borders of Doriath and fled northward. Then at last Túrin knew that doom had overtaken him, and that he had slain Brandir unjustly, so that the words of Glaurung were fulfilled in him. And he laughed as one fey, crying: 'This is a bitter jest indeed!' But he bade Mablung go, and return to Doriath, with curses upon it. 'And a curse too on thy errand!' he said. 'This only was wanting. Now comes the night!'

§346 Then he fled from them like the wind, and they were amazed, wondering what madness had seized him; and they followed after him. But Túrin far out-ran them, and came to Cabad-en-Aras, and heard the roaring of the water, and saw that all the leaves fell sere from the trees, as though winter had come. Then he cursed the place and named it Cabad Naeramarth, and he drew forth his sword, that now alone remained to him of all his possessions, and he said: 'Hail Gurthang! No lord or loyalty dost thou know, save the hand that wieldeth thee. From no blood wilt thou shrink. Wilt thou therefore take Túrin Turambar, wilt thou slay me swiftly?'

§347 And from the blade rang a cold voice in answer: 'Yea, I will drink thy blood gladly, that so I may forget the blood of Beleg my master, and the blood of Brandir slain unjustly. I will slay thee swiftly.'

§348 Then Túrin set the hilts upon the ground, and cast himself upon the point of Gurthang, and the black blade took his life. But Mablung and the Elves came and looked on the shape of the Worm lying dead, and upon the body of Túrin, and they were grieved; and when men of Brethil came thither, and they learned the reasons of Túrin's madness and death, they were aghast; and Mablung said bitterly: 'Lo! I also have been meshed in the doom of the Children of Húrin, and thus with my tidings have slain one that I loved.'

§349 Then they lifted up Túrin and found that Gurthang had broken asunder. But Elves and Men gathered then great store of wood and made a mighty burning, and the Worm was consumed to ashes. But Túrin they laid in a high mound where he had fallen, and the shards of Gurthang were laid beside him. And when all was done, the Elves sang a lament for the Children of Húrin, and a great grey stone was set upon the mound, and thereon was carven in the Runes of Doriath:

Here the manuscript comes to an end, at the foot of a page, and the typescript also. Later, and probably a good while later, since the writing is in ball-point pen, my father added in the margin of the manuscript:

> TURIN TURAMBAR DAGNIR
> GLAURUNGA

and beneath they wrote also:

> NIENOR NINIEL

But she was not there, nor was it ever known whither the cold waters of Taiglin had taken her. [Thus endeth the *Narn i Chîn Húrin*: which is the longest of all the lays of Beleriand, and was made by Men.]

It always seemed to me strange that my father should have abandoned the *Grey Annals* where he did, without at least writing the inscription that was carved on the stone; yet the facts that the amanuensis typescript ended at this point also, and that he added in the inscription in rough script on the manuscript at some later time, seemed proof positive that this was the case. Ultimately I discovered the explanation, which for reasons that will be seen I postpone to the beginning of Part Three (p. 251).

COMMENTARY

In this commentary the following abbreviations are used:

- **AV**   *Annals of Valinor* (see p. 3)
- **AAm** *Annals of Aman* (text with numbered paragraphs in Vol.X)
- **AB**   *Annals of Beleriand* (see p. 3). I use the revised dating of the annals in AB 2 (see V.124).
- **GA**   *Grey Annals* (**GA 1** abandoned opening, **GA 2** the final text when distinguished from GA 1: see pp. 3–4)
- **Q**   *The Quenta* (text in Vol.IV)
- **QS**   *Quenta Silmarillion* (text with numbered paragraphs in Vol.V)
- **NE**   The last part of the *Narn i Chîn Húrin*, given in *Unfinished Tales* (pp. 104–46), and referenced to the pages in that book; see pp. 144–5.

§1   This opening paragraph is absent from the abandoned version GA 1. Cf. the direction scribbled on the old AB 2 manuscript (p. 4) to 'make these the Sindarin Annals of Doriath'. For the beginning of the Annals in GA 1 see under §2 below.

§2 This is a much more definite statement of the development of the geographical concept of 'Beleriand' than that found in GA 1, where the Annals begin thus:

> The name Beleriand is drawn from the tongue of the Sindar, the Grey-elves that long dwelt in that country; and it signifies the land of Balar. For this name the Sindar gave to Ossë, who came much to those coasts, and there befriended them. In ancient days, ere the War of Utumno, it was but the northern shoreland of the long west-coast of Middle-earth, lying south of Eryd Engrin (the Iron Mountains) and between the Great Sea and Eryd Luin (the Blue Mountains).

This is in any case not easy to understand, since Beleriand 'in the ancient days' is defined as 'but' the northern shoreland of the west-coast of Middle-earth, yet extending south of the Iron Mountains and from the Great Sea to the Blue Mountains, an area in fact much greater than that described in GA 2 as its later extension of meaning. The latter agrees with the statement on the subject in QS §108, where 'Beleriand was bounded upon the North by Nivrost and Hithlum and Dorthonion'.

A possible explanation of the opening passage of GA 1 may be found, however, by reference to the *Ambarkanta* map IV (IV.249), where it will be seen that 'Beleriand' could well be described as 'but the northern shoreland of the long west-coast of Middle-earth, lying south of the Iron Mountains and between the Great Sea and the Blue Mountains'. The meaning of the opening of GA 1 may be, therefore, not that this geographical description was the original reference of the name 'Beleriand', but that before the War of Utumno (when Melkor was chained) Beleriand was 'but the northern shoreland of the long west-coast of Middle-earth', whereas in the ruin of that war there was formed the Great Gulf to the southward (referred to in GA §6, both texts; see *Ambarkanta* map V, IV.251), after which Beleriand could not be so described.

In the List of Names of the 1930s (V.404) 'Beleriand' was said as in GA 2 to have been originally the 'land about southern Sirion'; but is there said to have been 'named by the Elves of the Havens from Cape *Balar*, and Bay of *Balar* into which Sirion flowed'. In the *Etymologies* (V.350, stem BAL) *Beleriand* was likewise derived from (the isle of) *Balar*, and *Balar* in turn 'probably from *bálāre*, and so called because here Ossë visited the waiting Teleri.' At that time Ossë was a *Bala* (*Vala*).

On the later form *Belerian* see my father's note on Sindarin *Rochand* > *Rochan* (*Rohan*) in *Unfinished Tales* p. 318 (note 49 to *Cirion and Eorl*).

§3 Cf. the entry added to the annal for Valian Year 1050 in AAm

§40 (X.72, 77), concerning Melian's departure from Valinor. In the preceding annal 1000–1050 in AAm it is told that Varda 'made stars newer and brighter'.

§§3–5 The second sentence of the annal 1050 and the annals 1080 and 1085 were added to the manuscript subsequently. It is curious that there was no mention of the Awakening of the Elves in GA 1 nor in GA 2 as written; but among the rough draft pages referred to on p. 4 there is in fact a substantial passage beginning: 'In this same time the Quendi awoke by the waters of Kuiviénen: of which more is said in the Chronicles of Aman.' The text that follows in this draft is very close – much of it indeed virtually identical – to the long passage interpolated into AAm (§§43–5) on the fear of Oromë among the Quendi, the ensnaring of them by the servants of Melkor, and the breeding of the Orcs from those captured. There are no differences of substance between this text and the passage in AAm; and it is obvious that the latter followed, and was based on, the former, originally intended for inclusion in the *Grey Annals*.

In AAm the same dates are given for the Awakening of the Elves (1050) and for their discovery by Oromë (1085); no date is given in AAm for their discovery by Melkor, but it is said (AAm §43) that this was 'some years ere the coming of Oromë'.

§6 In GA 1 the sentence 'it took then that shape which it had until the coming of Fionwë' reads '... which it had until the Change of the World', using that expression not to refer to the World Made Round at the Drowning of Númenor but to the destruction of Beleriand in the final overthrow of Morgoth, at the end of the Elder Days.

The Great Gulf (shown and thus named on the *Ambarkanta* map V, IV.251) was referred to in QS §108: 'Beyond the river Gelion the land narrowed suddenly, for the Great Sea ran into a mighty gulf reaching almost to the feet of Eredlindon...' See under §2 above.

Unique to the *Grey Annals* is the statement that because the Valar had set foot in the lands about Sirion, when they came from Aman for the assault on Utumno, growth soon began there again 'while most of Middle-earth slept in the Sleep of Yavanna', and that Melian fostered the 'young woods under the bright stars'. See further under §10 below.

§7 This annal was a later addition to the manuscript; the date was first written 1102, then changed to 1102–5. AAm (§§54–6) has entries concerning the three ambassadors, their going in 1102 and their return to Kuiviénen in 1104.

§8 In AAm the dates were so often changed and became so confused that in rendering the text I gave only the final ones (see X.47–8); but in this part of AAm all the dates were in fact originally 100 Valian Years later – thus 1115, the year in which the Eldar reached the Anduin (X.82) was an emendation of 1215. Already in GA 1 the dates are in the 1100s as first written, showing that it followed AAm, if at no long interval. But it is curious that in GA (both texts) the coming of the Vanyar and Noldor to the Great Sea is placed in 1115; in AAm the march began in 1105, the Anduin was reached in 1115, and the Sea in 1125.

§10 This annal has close relations not only with that in AAm for the same year (§65) but also with the passage in the 'Silmarillion' tradition (X.172, §32).

With 'the young trees of Nan Elmoth' cf. the change made on one of the typescripts of AAm (X.91) of 'the trees of Nan Elmoth' to 'the sapling trees of Nan Elmoth', though this was made years later. The 'young trees' are no doubt to be connected with the phrase in GA §9 'where *afterwards stood* the forests of Neldoreth and Region'; and it seems clear that the trees were all young because, as is said in GA §6, 'the lands upon either side of Sirion were ruinous and desolate because of the War of the Powers, but soon growth began there, while most of Middle-earth slept in the Sleep of Yavanna, because the Valar of the Blessed Realm had set foot there; and there were young woods under the bright stars.'

The conception that there were trees in a world illumined only by starlight was a datum of the mythology (though years after the writing of the *Grey Annals* my father rejected it: 'Neither could there be woods and flowers &c. on earth, if there had been no light since the overthrow of the Lamps!', X.375); on the other hand, there appears in AAm (§30) the story, not present in the 'Silmarillion' tradition, that Yavanna 'set a sleep upon many fair things that had arisen in the Spring [i.e. before the fall of the Lamps], both tree and herb and beast and bird, so that they should not age but should wait for a time of awakening that yet should be.' In the other tradition (X.158, §18) 'While the Lamps had shone, growth began there which now was checked, because all was again dark. But already the oldest living things had arisen: in the sea the great weeds, and on the earth the shadow of great trees ... In those lands and forests Oromë would often hunt ...'

How these conceptions relate to each other is far from clear on the basis of these texts; but now, in the *Grey Annals* (§6), the peculiar nature of Beleriand is asserted, in that there alone growth began again under the stars on account of the passage of the Valar from Aman, and (§17) 'though Middle-earth for the most part lay in the Sleep of Yavanna, in Beleriand under the power of Melian there was life and joy and the bright stars shone like silver fires.'

§§11–12 This annal 1132 is very close to that in AAm (§66), largely identical in structure and near in phraseology; the only important feature in which it differs is the reference to the legend that a part of the island that became Tol Eressëa was broken off and became the

Isle of Balar. This story appears in a footnote to the next of QS §35 (V.221, X.174).

§§13-15 The annals 1149-50 and 1150 are again close to those in AAm (§§70-1), and were I think based on them (it may be noted that in GA 1, of which GA 2 is here for the most part scarcely more than a fair copy, my father first wrote in §15 'The friends and kinsfolk of Elwë also were unwilling to depart', as in AAm, but changed the last words in the act of writing to 'also remained').

§14 The whole extent of the coastal region from the Firth of Drengist south to Cape Balar is here named the Falas (cf. QS §109: 'the country of the Falas (or Coast), south of Nivrost'), and thus Cirdan is made the ruler of the shorelands of Nivrost (later Nevrast).

The last part of the annal 1149-50, concerning the fact that the Elves of the Havens did not cross the Great Sea (though there was no ban on their attempting to do so), is not in GA 1. It is indeed an answer to a question that has not emerged in any previous writing – though it becomes implicit from the first emergence of the sailing-elves of the Havens (Elves persuaded by Ossë to remain on the shores of Middle-earth are first mentioned in Q, IV.87).

§16 The annal 1152 is closely related to that in AAm (§74). The question arises why, if these Annals were the work of the Sindar (see §1), should they have such obvious affinity to those of Aman? Perhaps it should be supposed that both sets of Annals, as received, derive from the editorial work of Pengoloð in Tol Eressëa.

§17 There is nothing corresponding to the interesting annal 1200 in AAm. On the reference to the Sleep of Yavanna and the life and joy in Beleriand see under §10 above. Melian's power and presence in Beleriand is now given a greater significance. – Here *niphredil* appears from *The Lord of the Rings*.

§18 The idea of the 'higher culture' of the Dark-elves of Beleriand (the Sindar) goes back to the very early 'Sketch of the Mythology' (IV.21): 'Only in the realm of Doriath, whose queen was of divine race, did the Ilkorins equal the Koreldar'; this phrase with a slight modification survived through Q (IV.100) into QS (§85).

§19 Cf. the passage inserted into annal 1250 in AAm (§84), a Beleriandic interpolation by Pengoloð, against which my father later noted: 'Transfer to A[nnals of] B[eleriand]' (X.102, note 7). That passage (very greatly expanded here in GA) begins:

> In this time also, it is said among the Sindar, the Nauglath [*written above:* Naugrim] whom we also name the Nornwaith (the Dwarves) came over the mountains into Beleriand and became known to the Elves.

The present annal in GA 1 begins: 'In this year, it is recorded among the Sindar, the Nauglath came first over the mountains into

Beleriand. This people the Noldor after named the Norn-folk ...' In GA 2 the words 'it is recorded among the Sindar' are absent, and *Naugrim* replaces *Nauglath*.

In QS §124 the Dwarvish names of the cities in Eryd Luin were Gabilgathol (Belegost, the Great Fortress) and Khazaddûm (Nogrod, the Dwarfmine); Tumunzahar now first appears (also in QS revised, p. 206, §7).

§20 For statements in the *Lhammas* and in QS on the languages of the Dwarves see V.178–9, 273. – The concluding sentences of this paragraph ('Ever cool was their friendship ...') are very close to what is said in AAm (§84).

§21 This cautious and sceptical view of the story of the origin of the Dwarves – ascribing it entirely to the Dwarves themselves – seems to contrast with earlier texts, where it is said to be derived from 'the wise in Valinor' (V.129, 273). – The name *Mahal* of Aulë has not appeared before.

§22 *Enfeng, the Longbeards of Belegost.* In the old *Tale of the Nauglafring* the *Indrafangs* or Longbeards were the Dwarves of Belegost, while Dwarves of Nogrod were the *Nauglath* (see II.247). In Q the Indrafangs had become those of Nogrod (IV.104), and this reappears in QS (§124): 'those who dwelt in Nogrod they [the Gnomes] called Enfeng, the Longbeards, because their beards swept the floor before their feet.' In the passage in AAm (§84) the Longbeards, as here, are again the Dwarves of Belegost. – The conclusion of this paragraph is wholly different in GA 1:

> For Melian taught them much wisdom (which also they were eager to get), and she gave to them also the great jewel which alone she had brought out of Valinor, work of Fëanor, [*struck out but then ticked as if to stand:* for he gave many such to the folk of Lórien.] A white gem it was that gathered the starlight and sent it forth in blue fires; and the Enfeng prized it above a mountain of wealth.

This was an idea that did not fit the chronology, for Melian left Valinor in 1050, the year of the Awakening of the Elves, as stated both in AAm (see X.77) and GA (Fëanor was born more than a hundred Valian years later, AAm §78); and in GA 2 the story of the great pearl Nimphelos was substituted.

§§23–4 Thingol's early association with the Dwarves is mentioned in QS §122 (from their cities in the Blue Mountains the Dwarves 'journeyed often into Beleriand, and were admitted at times even into Doriath'), but the aid of the Longbeards of Belegost in the building of Menegroth did not appear until the interpolation in AAm (§84). That brief mention is here greatly expanded into a description of the Thousand Caves; cf. the *Lay of Leithian* (III.188–9, lines 980–1008), and for the earliest conception – before the rise of Thingol to his later wealth and majesty – see II.63, 128–9, 245–6.

§§25–9   In GA 1 the whole passage given here in the annals 1300–50 and 1330 is placed under 1320: the actual event in 1320 was the speaking of the Dwarves to Thingol concerning their fears ('In this year, however, the Dwarves were troubled ...', where GA 2 has 'But it came to pass that the Dwarves were troubled ...'), and it was 'not long thereafter' that 'evil creatures came even to Beleriand'. In a note to the year 1320 on the typescript of AAm (X.106, §85) my father added: 'The Orcs first appear in Beleriand'; in GA 2 (§26) the event is dated ten Valian Years later, in 1330.

§25   The Dwarves' hatred and fear of the Sea has not been mentioned before.

§26   GA 1 has 'over passes in the mountains, or up from the south where their heights fell away': probably referring to the region of the Great Gulf (*Ambarkanta* map V, IV.251).

§27   This paragraph was an addition to GA 1, though not long after the primary text was made. This is the later conception, introduced into AAm (see X.123, §127), according to which the Orcs existed before ever Oromë came upon the Elves, being indeed bred by Morgoth from captured Elves; the older tradition, that Morgoth brought the Orcs into being when he returned to Middle-earth from Valinor, survived unchanged in the final form of the *Quenta Silmarillion* (see X.194, §62). See further under §29 below.

§28   Telchar of Nogrod is not named here in GA 1. He goes back a long way in the history, appearing first in the second version of the *Lay of the Children of Húrin* (III.115), and in Q (IV.118) – where he is of Belegost, not Nogrod.

§29   Axes were 'the chief weapons of the Naugrim, and of the Sindar': cf. the name 'Axe-elves' of the Sindar, X.171. – Of the appearance of Orcs and other evil beings in Eriador and even in Beleriand long before (some 165 Valian Years) the return of Melkor to Middle-earth, and of the arming of the Sindar by the Dwarves, there has been no previous suggestion (see under §27 above).

§30   The coming of Denethor to Beleriand is more briefly recorded in an annal interpolated into AAm (§86) under the same date, 1350 – an interpolation by Pengoloð which (like that referred to under §19 above) was marked later for transfer to the *Annals of Beleriand*. With the mention of the halting of the Teleri on the shores of the Great River cf. the fuller account in AAm, annal 1115 (§§60–1). In GA 1 the name *Nandor* is interpreted, 'the Turners-back': this expression is found also in a note to one of the texts of the *Lhammas*, V.188.

   It has not (of course) been said before that the coming of Denethor over the Blue Mountains was brought about by the emergence of 'the fell beasts of the North'. The later history and divisions of the Nandor are now much more fully described: those who 'dwelt age-long' in the woods of the Vale of Anduin (the Elves of Lothlórien and Mirkwood, see *Unfinished Tales* p. 256), and those who went down Anduin, of whom some dwelt by the Sea, while others passed by the White Mountains (the first mention of Ered Nimrais in the writings concerned with the Elder Days) and entered Eriador. These last were the people of Denethor (of whom it is said in AAm that 'after long wanderings they came up into Beleriand from the South', see §86 and commentary, X.93, 104).

The words 'in after days' in 'In that region the forests in after days were tall and green' are perhaps significant: the association of green with the Elves of Ossiriand emerged after the rising of the Sun. See further under §44 below.

§31 The passage corresponding to this in GA 1 is very much briefer:
> Of the long years of peace that followed after the coming of Denethor there is no tale, save only that Oromë would come at whiles to the land, or pass over the mountains, and the sound of his horn came over the leagues of the starlight...

(concluding as in GA 2). But the passage in GA 2 concerning Dairon and his runes is largely derived from a later passage in GA 1 (absent in GA 2), for which see p. 20.

The word *Cirth* first appears here, though as a later addition to the manuscript (perhaps at the time when my father was preparing Appendix E to *The Lord of the Rings*). It is said in the footnote to the paragraph that Dairon contrived his runes 'ere the building of Menegroth' (begun in 1300, according to GA); so also in GA 1 'Dairon... had devised his Runes already by V.Y.1300'. An annal added to the typescript of AAm (X.106, §85) has '1300 Daeron, loremaster of Thingol, contrives the Runes.' For an earlier view of the origin of the Runes of Dairon (an invention of 'the Danian Elves of Ossiriand', elaborated in Doriath) see *The Treason of Isengard* pp. 453–5; there the name 'Alphabet of Dairon' is ascribed simply to the fact of 'the preservation in this script of some fragments of the songs of Dairon, the ill-fated minstrel of King Thingol of Doriath, in the works on the ancient Beleriandic languages by Pengolod the Wise of Gondolin'. See also my father's later statement concerning the Alphabet of Daeron at the beginning of Appendix E (II) to *The Lord of the Rings*.

§33 On the great cry of Morgoth see X.109, 296. Where GA 2 has 'few knew what it foreboded' GA 1 has 'few (save Melian and Thingol) knew what it foreboded'.

§34 So also in AAm (§126) and in the late *Quenta Silmarillion* text 'Of the Thieves' Quarrel' (X.297) Ungoliantë after her rout by the Balrogs went down into Beleriand and dwelt in Nan Dungorthin (Nan Dungortheb); but it is not said in those texts that the power of

Melian prevented her entry into the Forest of Neldoreth. In both it is said that that valley was so named because of the horror that she bred there, but the statement here that the Mountains of Terror came to be so called after that time is not found elsewhere. That Ungoliantë departed into the South of the world is said also in AAm, but in 'Of the Thieves' Quarrel' (X.297) 'whither she went after no tale tells'.

§35 The stage of development in the tradition of Morgoth's fortress is that of QS and AAm, in which Angband was built on the ruins of Utumno (see X.156, §12). – In GA 1 the name *Thangorodrim* is translated 'the Tyrannous Towers'; cf. the later translation 'the Mountains of Oppression' (X.298).

§§36 ff. This is the first full account of 'the First Battle of Beleriand' (a term previously applied to the Battle-under-Stars, which now becomes the Second Battle). In the pre-*Lord of the Rings* texts the first assault of the Orcs on Beleriand had been briefly described; thus in the second version (AV 2) of the *Annals of Valinor* it was said (V.114):

> Thingol with his ally Denithor of Ossiriand for a long while held back the Orcs from the South. But at length Denithor son of Dan was slain, and Thingol made his deep mansions in Menegroth, the Thousand Caves, and Melian wove magic of the Valar about the land of Doriath; and most of the Elves of Beleriand withdrew within its protection, save some that lingered about the western havens, Brithombar and Eglorest beside the Great Sea, and the Green-elves of Ossiriand who dwelt still behind the rivers of the East ...

In QS §115 the account ran thus:

> Of old the lord of Ossiriand was Denethor, friend of Thingol; but he was slain in battle when he marched to the aid of Thingol against Melko, in the days when the Orcs were first made and broke the starlit peace of Beleriand. Thereafter Doriath was fenced with enchantment, and many of the folk of Denethor removed to Doriath and mingled with the Elves of Thingol; but those that remained in Ossiriand had no king, and lived in the protection of their rivers.

§36 Between Menegroth and Thangorodrim on the second Silmarillion map (as drawn: not in my reproduction, V.409) the length is 14 cm, and the scale is stated to be 50 miles to 3·2 cm. (the length of the sides of the squares); the distance was therefore 218·75 miles, or just under 73 leagues (for my father's later interpretation of the scale in inches, not centimetres, see p. 332, but the difference has no significance here). The distance given here of 150 leagues (450 miles) from Menegroth to Angband's gate, more than doubling that shown on the second map, seems to imply a great extension of the northern plain. The geography of the far North is discussed in

V.270–2; but since it is impossible to say how my father came to conceive it I discreetly omitted all indication of the Iron Mountains and Thangorodrim from the map drawn for the published *Silmarillion*.

§38 GA 1 has here:
> Therefore he called on Denethor [*struck out*: and on the Enfengs] and the First Battle was fought in the Wars of Beleriand. And the Orcs in the east were routed and slain aheaps, and as they fled before the Elves they were waylaid by the axes of the Enfengs that issued from Mount Dolmed: few returned to the North.

In GA 2 'Region over Aros' refers to that part of the Forest of Region between the rivers Aros and Celon (see p. 183, square F 10). The implication of the sentence seems clearly to be that these Elves owed allegiance to Denethor; and this does not seem to be consistent with what is said in §39, that after the First Battle many of the Green-elves of Ossiriand 'went north and entered the guarded realm of Thingol and were merged with his folk'. Against this sentence in the typescript of GA my father wrote in the margin 'Orgol' and 'of the Guest-elves in Arthórien', marking these with carets to indicate that something should be said of them. In *Unfinished Tales*, p. 77, occurs the following passage:

> Saeros ... was of the Nandor, being one of those who took refuge in Doriath after the fall of their lord Denethor upon Amon Ereb, in the first battle of Beleriand. These Elves dwelt for the most part in Arthórien, between Aros and Celon in the east of Doriath, wandering at times over Celon into the wild lands beyond; and they were no friends to the Edain since their passage through Ossiriand and settlement in Estolad.

This was largely derived from an isolated note, very rapidly written and not at all points intelligible, among the *Narn* papers, but somewhat reduced. It is remarked in this note that 'the Nandor had turned away, never seen the Sea or even Ossë, and had become virtually Avari. They had also picked up various Avari before they came back west to Ossiriand.' Of those Nandor who took refuge in Doriath after the fall of Denethor it is said: 'In the event they did not mingle happily with the Teleri of Doriath, and so dwelt mostly in the small land Eglamar, Arthórien under their own chief. Some of them were "darkhearted", though this did not necessarily appear, except under strain or provocation.' 'The chief of the "Guest-elves", as they were called, was given a permanent place in Thingol's council'; and Saeros (in this note called in fact *Orgoph* or *Orgol*) was 'the son of the chief of the Guest-elves, and had been for a long time resident in Menegroth'.

I think it very probable that my father wrote 'Orgol' and 'of the Guest-elves in Arthórien' on the typescript of GA as the same time as he wrote this note.

Arthórien was entered on the second map (p. 183, square F 10). The application of the name *Eglamar* to Arthórien in this note is puzzling (see p. 189, §57).

The intervention of the Dwarves has not been referred to previously.

§40 The words 'unless one should come with a power greater than that of Melian the Maia' replaced at the time of writing 'unless haply some power greater than theirs should assail them'. – *Eglador*: my father pencilled this name under *Doriath* on the second map (see p. 186, §14).

§41 At the end of this paragraph the *Annals of Aman* cease to record the events in the *Grey Annals*, and comparison is with QS (V.248 ff.), together with the conclusion of AV 2 (V.117 ff.) and with AB 2 (V.125 ff.). In this commentary I do not generally refer to later developments in the *Quenta Silmarillion* tradition.

§44 For *Eryd-wethrin, the valour of the Noldor*, and *Dagor-nuin-Giliath* GA 1 has *Erydwethion, the valour of the Gnomes*, and *Dagor-nui-Ngiliath* (as in QS §88, marginal note).

This is the first occurrence of *Ardgalen* in the texts as here presented, replacing *Bladorion* as the original name of the great northern plain before its devastation. It is notable that *Ardgalen* 'the green region' is expressly stated to have been the name at this time before the rising of the Sun; cf. the change made long before to the passage in Q describing the Battle-under-Stars (when the battle was fought on the plain itself, not in Mithrim): 'yet young and green (it stretched to the feet of the tall mountains)' > 'yet dark beneath the stars' (IV.101, 103).

The Orc-hosts that passed southwards down the Vale of Sirion are not of course mentioned in previous accounts of the Battle-under-Stars. The attack on the Noldor in Mithrim is now taken up into a larger assault out of Angband, and the victory of the Noldor brought into relation with the newly-developed conception of the beleaguered Sindar.

In the account of the destruction of the western Orc-host by Celegorn is the first appearance of the Fen of Serech: this was first named in an addition to the second map the Fen of Rivil, subsequently changed to the Fen of Serech (p. 181, §3). Rivil was the stream that rising at Rivil's Well on Dorthonion made the fen at its inflowing into Sirion.

§45 In AV 2 (V.117) and QS (§88) the Balrogs were in the rearguard of Morgoth's host, and it was they who turned to bay. – Of the rescue of Fëanor GA 1 (following QS) has only: 'But his sons coming up with force rescued their father, and bore him back to Mithrim' (see under §46).

§46 The story of Fëanor's dying sight of Thangorodrim and his cursing of the name of Morgoth first appeared in Q (IV.101), where the Battle-under-Stars was fought on the plain of Bladorion (Ardgalen). In AV 1 and AV 2 (IV.268, V.117) the battle was fought in Mithrim, and Fëanor was mortally wounded when he advanced too far upon the plain, but he was brought back to Mithrim and died there; his sight of Thangorodrim and curse upon Morgoth do not appear. In QS (§88) my father combined the accounts: Fëanor died in Mithrim, but it is also told that he 'saw afar the peaks of Thangorodrim' as he died, and 'cursed the name of Morgoth thrice'; GA 1 follows this story (see under §45 above). It must have been the consideration that from Mithrim Thangorodrim was not visible on account of the heights of Eryd-wethrin that led to the story in GA 2 that Fëanor caused his sons to halt as they began the climb above Eithel Sirion, and that he died in that place.

§47 The initial misapprehension among the Grey-elves concerning the return of the Noldor is a wholly new element in the narrative, as is also the cold view taken by Thingol, seeing in it a threat to his own dominion. In the old versions his coolness does not appear until his refusal to attend the Feast of Reuniting (Mereth Aderthad) in the year 20 of the Sun, and arises rather from his insight into what the future might bring: 'Thingol came not himself, and he would not open his kingdom, nor remove its girdle of enchantment; for wise with the wisdom of Melian he trusted not that the restraint of Morgoth would last for ever' (QS §99, and very similarly in AB 2, V.126).

§49 The date 1497 is repeated from §36. – The Balrogs that constituted the force that Morgoth sent to the parley in QS (§89 and commentary) have disappeared.

§52 As in AAm §§157–8, 163 the form *Endar* ('Middle-earth') is clear, but here as there the typist put *Endor* (see X.126, §157).

§53 The paragraph opens in the manuscript with a large pointing hand.

§§54–5 In this passage, while there are echoes of the earlier texts, the writing is largely new, and there are new elements, notably the cry of Maidros on Thangorodrim.

§54 The story of Morgoth's assault on Tilion is told in AAm §179, where however it took place after both Sun and Moon were launched into the heavens. It is told in AAm that 'Tilion was the victor: as he ever yet hath been, though still the pursuing darkness overtakes him at whiles', evidently a reference to the eclipses of the Moon.

§57 On the placing of Hildórien see AV 2 (V.120, note 13) and QS §82 and commentary; also pp. 173–4. On the name *Atani* see X.7, 39.

§§58–60 While this annal for the second year of the Sun is obviously closely related to and in large part derived from QS §§92–3, it contains new elements, as the more explicit portrayal of Fingolfin's anger against the Fëanorians, and also the repentance of many of the latter for the burning of the ships at Losgar.

§61 The reference to the *Quenta* is to the much fuller account of the rescue of Maidros in QS §§94–7. In AAm (§160) it is told that Maidros was 'on a time a friend of Fingon ere Morgoth's lies came between', and (§162) that he alone stood aside at the burning of the ships. – The spelling *Maiðros*: at earlier occurrences in GA the name is spelt *Maidros*, and *Maidros* appears again in the following line; while in the draft text referred to on p. 29 the form is mostly *Maiðros* (cf. the later form *Maedhros*, X.177, adopted in the published *Silmarillion*, beside *Maedros* X.293, 295).

§§63–4 The content of this passage is largely new; there has been no previous mention of the coming of Angrod to Thingol and his silence about many matters in respect of the Return of the Noldor. The actual nature of Thingol's claim to overlordship, whereby he 'gave leave' to the princes of the Noldor to dwell in certain regions, is now specified (the acceptance by Fingolfin of Thingol's claim is referred to in the earlier forms of the linguistic excursus in GA, pp. 21, 25; cf. also the anticipatory words in §48, 'the sons of Fëanor were ever unwilling to accept the overlordship of Thingol, and would ask for no leave where they might dwell or might pass'). – The Telerin connection of the Third House of the Noldor through the marriage of Finrod (> Finarfin) to Eärwen Olwë's daughter appears in AAm §§85, 156, and see X.177.

§§65–71 The content of the annal for the year 7 is largely new, save that in QS (§98) there is told of the waiving of the high-kingship of the Noldor by Maidros, and the secret disavowal of this among some at least of his brothers ('to this his brethen did not all in their hearts agree'). In GA there is no mention of what is told in QS, that 'Maidros begged forgiveness for the desertion in Eruman, and gave back the goods of Fingolfin that had been borne away in the ships' (but see §83 and commentary); on the other hand we learn here of the scornful rejection of Thingol's claim by the Fëanorians (with no mention of Fingolfin's acceptance of it, see under §§63–4 above), of Cranthir's harsh disposition and his insulting speech at the council, of the *choosing* of Fingolfin as overlord of the Noldor, of the opinion that Maidros was behind the swift departure of the Fëanorians into the eastern lands (in order to lessen the chances of strife and to bear the brunt of the likeliest assault), and of his remaining in friendship with the other houses of the Noldor, despite the isolation of the Fëanorians.

§67 Curiously, the draft text has here and in §68 *Caranthir* (the later form), while the final text reverts to *Cranthir*. In the very rough initial draft for the annals 6 and 7 (see p. 29) the son of Fëanor who was 'the harshest and the most quick to anger' was Curufin, changed to Caranthir. On Caranthir's scornful reference to Thingol as 'this Dark-elf' see my note in the Index to the published *Silmarillion*, entry *Dark Elves*. – In the draft text Caranthir says 'let them not so quickly forget that they were Noldor!'

§72 In AB 2 (V.126) and QS (§99) Mereth Aderthad was held in Nan Tathren, the Land of Willows. GA is more specific concerning those who were present than are the earlier texts: Maidros and Maglor; Cirdan; and Dairon and Mablung as the only two representatives from Doriath (on Thingol's aloofness see §47 and commentary).

§73 That the Noldor learned Sindarin far more readily than the Sindar learned Noldorin has been stated already in the final form of the linguistic excursus, p. 26. It is stated in all three versions of the excursus that it was after Dagor Aglareb (in the year 60) that Sindarin became the common speech of Beleriand.

§74 In AB 2 (V.126) Turgon discovered the hidden vale of Gondolin in the same year (50) as Inglor Felagund discovered Nargothrond – the year of their dreams.

§75 This is the first mention (as the texts are presented) of Galadriel in Middle-earth in the Elder Days. The spelling *Galaðriel* is noteworthy, implying the association of her name with *galadh* 'tree' (*galað*): see X.182 and *Unfinished Tales* p. 267.

In AB 2 (V.126) and QS (§101) there is no suggestion that Inglor Felagund was aided by Thingol to his discovery of the caves where he established Nargothrond. In QS 'the High Faroth' are named, at a later point in the narrative, *Taur-na-Faroth* (see QS §112 and commentary). The great highlands west of Narog were originally called the Hills of the Hunters or the Hunters' Wold; see III.88, IV.225, and the *Etymologies* in V.387, stem SPAR.

The passage beginning 'Thus Inglor came to the Caverns of Narog' as far as 'that name he bore until his end' was an addition to the manuscript, but seems certainly to have been made at the time of the original writing. In view of the close relationship of this annal to the later development of the story in the QS tradition, where a very similar passage is found, I think that my father merely left it out inadvertently and at once noticed the omission (see pp. 177–8, §101).

§76 It is said in QS (§116) only that Gondolin was 'like unto Tûn of Valinor'. This idea perhaps goes far back: see II.208.

§77 *Dagor Aglareb*, the Glorious Battle, was originally the Second Battle in the Wars of Beleriand (see p. 21 and note 6).

§78 The Siege of Angband 'lasted wellnigh four hundred years': from 60 to 455 (see V.257–8).

§§79–81 This inserted passage, which returns to the original text near the beginning of §81, concerns Morgoth's departure from Angband and his attempt to corrupt the first Men in the East, and is of great interest. While in QS (§63) it was said of Morgoth that 'it was never his wont to leave the deep places of his fortress', in AAm

(§128, X.110) 'never but once only, while his realm lasted, did he depart for a while secretly from his domain in the North'; but it is not said or hinted for what purpose he went. (It is worth noting that a rough draft for the present rider in GA is found on the same page as a draft for the expansion of the passage in AAm, on which see X.121 note 10.)

The insertion is carefully written in the same style as the main text, and seems likely to belong to much the same time. It is notable that the reverse of the page used for it carries drafting for the final form of the insertion in AAm (§§43–5) concerning the ensnaring of the Quendi by the servants of Melkor in the lands about Kuiviénen (cf. the words in §79, 'Even as before at the awakening of the Quendi, his spies were watchful'). See further under §87 below.

§79 'Nor himself, an he would go': i.e., nor did the ice and snow hinder Morgoth himself, if he wished to go. – 'Indeed we learn now in Eressëa': cf. the end of the final version of the 'linguistic excursus' (p. 27): 'these histories were made after the Last Battle and the end of the Elder Days', and also the opening paragraph of the *Grey Annals* (p. 5).

§83 The reference to the *Quenta Noldorinwa* (see p. 27 and note 12) is to Chapter 9 'Of Beleriand and its Realms' in QS (V.258).

In QS §116 it is mentioned that 'many of the sires' of the horses of Fingolfin and Fingon came from Valinor. The horses are here said to have been '*given to* Fingolfin by Maidros *in atonement of* his losses, for they had been carried by ship to Losgar'. In an earlier passage in GA (see the commentary on §§65–71) the reference in QS §98 to the *return* of Fingolfin's goods that had been carried away in the ships is absent.

§85 *Eredwethrin*: earlier in GA the form is *Erydwethrin* (also *Eryd Lómin*, *Eryd Luin*); cf. under §113 below. – This is the first occurrence of the river-name *Nenning* for earlier *Eglor* (at whose mouth was the haven of Eglorest), named in AB 2 (V.128, 139) and on the second map (V.408). On the map my father later struck out *Eglor* and wrote in two names, *Eglahir* and *Nenning*, leaving both to stand (p. 187, §22).

In QS (§109) it is said that the Dark-elves of Brithombar and Eglorest 'took Felagund, lord of Nargothrond, to be their king'; see the commentary on this passage, V.267. My father seems to have been uncertain of the status of Cirdan: in a late change to the text of AB 2 (the passage given in V.146, note 13) he wrote that 'in the Havens the folk of the Falas were ruled by Cirdan of the Grey-elves; but he was ever close in friendship with Felagund and his folk' (agreeing with what is said here in GA), but he at once substituted: 'And in the west Cirdan the Shipwright who ruled the mariners of the Falas took Inglor also for overlord, and they were ever close in friendship.'

§87 The words '[Morgoth's] thought being bent on their ruin he gave the less heed to aught else in Middle-earth' seem hardly to agree with the inserted passage concerning Morgoth's departure from Angband (§§79–80). It may be suggested, however, that that passage is precisely concerned with the period *before* the attack on Beleriand in the year 60 (*Dagor Aglareb*) – which was postponed so long because of Morgoth's operations in the East, whence he returned in alarm at 'the growing power and union of the Eldar' (§80).

By alteration to the original passage in this annal concerning the beginning of the languages of Men a Dark-elvish origin is ascribed only to the 'western tongues'. I think that this represents a clarification rather than the entry of a new conception. It was said already in *Lhammas B* (V.179, §10):

> The languages of Men were from their beginning diverse and various; yet they were for the most part derived remotely from the language of the Valar. For the Dark-elves, various folk of the Lembi, befriended wandering Men in sundry times and places in the most ancient days, and taught them such things as they knew. But other Men learned also wholly or in part of the Orcs and of the Dwarves; while in the West ere they came into Beleriand the fair houses of the eldest Men learned of the Danas, or Green-elves.

The very interesting addition at the end of the annal belongs with the insertion about Morgoth's departure into the East. There it is said (§80): 'But that some darkness lay upon the hearts of Men ... the Eldar perceived clearly even in the fair folk of the Elf-friends that they first knew'; but the present passage is the first definite statement that Men in their beginning fell to the worship of Morgoth, and that the Elf-friends, repentant, fled west to escape persecution. In the long account of his works written for Milton Waldman in 1951, and so very probably belonging to the same period, my father had said: 'The first fall of Man ... nowhere appears – Men do not come on the stage until all that is long past, and there is only a rumour that for a while they fell under the domination of the Enemy and that some repented' (*Letters* no.131, pp. 147–8; see X.354–5).

§89 The new story in the revised form of the annal for 64, that Turgon at this time led only a part of his people – those skilled in such work – to Tumladen in order that they should begin the building of Gondolin, is extended further in a greatly expanded version of the annal for 116: see §§111–13.

§90 *The Tower of Ingildon*: this replaces the old name Tower of Tindobel (Tindabel), which survived in QS (§120) and AB 2 (V.129); see p. 197, §120. It is not said in GA as it was in QS that Inglor was the builder of the tower; this is perhaps to be connected with what is said in §85, that Cirdan was lord of the lands 'west of Nenning to the Sea'.

§§91–107 The entire content of the annals for 66 and 67 is new. Highly 'un-annalistic' in manner, with its long and superbly sustained discourse, this narrative is developed from the earlier passage in GA (§48) – or perhaps rather, reveals what my father had in mind when he wrote it:

> When, therefore, ere long (by treachery and ill will, as later is told) the full tale of the deeds in Valinor became known in Beleriand, there was rather enmity than alliance between Doriath and the House of Fëanor; and this bitterness Morgoth eagerly inflamed by all means that he could find.

A complete text of these annals is extant in a preliminary draft, but the form in GA followed this draft closely and the development was almost entirely stylistic. A few of the differences are worth noting:

§93 After 'not though they came in the very hour of our need' my father added to the draft text: 'The new lights of heaven are the sending of the Valar, not the Noldor, mighty though they be', and this was not taken up in GA.

§95 Draft text: '... over the long road from the Kalakiryan'. – After '"Maybe," said Galaðriel, "but not of me"' the draft continues:

> and being perplexed and recalling suddenly with anger the words of Caranthir she said ere she could set a guard on her tongue: 'For already the children of Finrod are charged with talebearing and treason to their kindred. Yet we at least were guiltless, and suffered evil ourselves.' And Melian spoke no more of these things with Galaðriel.

This passage was bracketed, and later in the draft the bitterness of the memory of Cranthir's words of sixty years before appears in Angrod's mouth, as in GA (§104). The draft has *Caranthir* in the first passage, *Cranthir* in the second; see under §67 above.

§105 In the draft Thingol says: 'for my heart is hot as the fire of Losgar'.

§107 After 'the words of Mandos would ever be made true' the draft has: 'and the curse that Fëanor drew upon him would darken all that was done after.'

On the spelling *Galaðriel* see under §75 above. In §94 appears *Galadriel*; the draft text begins with *Galaðriel* but then changes to *Galadriel*. This distinction is however probably artificial, since it is merely a question of the insertion or omission of the cross-line on the *d*, written in both cases in a single movement (a reversed 6).

§107 The revision at the end of the annal for 67 depends on the later story that the population of Gondolin was by no means exclusively Noldorin, and is similar to those made to the final version of the 'linguistic excursus' (see p. 26 and notes 9 and 10), a consequence of the rejection of the old conception that in Gondolin, and in Gondolin only, which was peopled by Noldor and cut off from intercourse with all others, the Noldorin tongue survived in daily use; see §113 and commentary.

§§108–9   The content of this annal, extended from the opening sentence recording the completion of Nargothrond (AB 2, V.129), is also entirely new. For the earlier story that Felagund did have a wife, and that their son was Gilgalad, see pp. 242–3.

§110   According to the chronology of the *Grey Annals* Turgon left Nivrost in the year 64 (§88), and thus the figure here of fifty years is an error for fifty-two. The error was repeated, but corrected, at the beginning of the revised annal for 116. Possibly my father had reverted in a momentary forgetfulness to the original dating, when the years were 52 and 102 (V.127, 129). See the commentary on §111.

§111   The change in the opening sentence of the new annal for 116 depends on the revised annal for 64 (§89), whereby Turgon did not definitively leave Vinyamar in that year but began the building of Gondolin. The erroneous fifty years, corrected to fifty-two, since the start of the work was presumably merely picked up from the rejected annal (see under §110).

§§111–12   Entirely new is the appearance of Ulmo to Turgon at Vinyamar on the eve of his departure, his warning, his prophecy, and his instruction to Turgon to leave arms in his house for one to find in later days (cf. II.208, where I suggested that the germ of this was already present in the original tale of *The Fall of Gondolin* – 'Thy coming was set in our books of wisdom'). But Ulmo's foretelling that Gondolin should stand longest against Morgoth goes back through Q (IV.136–7) to the *Sketch of the Mythology* (IV.34).

§113   The later story that there were many Sindar among Turgon's people has led to various changes already met in the text of GA: see the commentary on §107. – The reversion to the old form *wethion* in *Eryd Wethion* is curious (see commentary on §44).

At the foot of the page carrying the revised annal for 116 is the following rapidly pencilled note:

Set this rather in the *Silmarillion* and substitute a short notice:

'In this year as is said in the *Quenta* Gondolin was fully wrought, and Turgon arose and went thither with all his people, and Nivrost was emptied of folk and so remained. But the march of Turgon was hidden by the power of Ulmo, and none even of his kin in Hithlum knew whither he had gone.

Against this my father wrote 'Neglect this'; but since a new chapter was inserted into the *Quenta Silmarillion* which was largely based on the present rider (see pp. 198–9) this was presumably an instruction that was itself neglected.

§114   The date of this annal was first written 154, which was the revised date of the meeting of Cranthir's people with the Dwarves in

the Blue Mountains in AB 2 (V.129, and cf. QS §125). The passage describing the relations of Cranthir's folk with the Dwarves is new. It was stated in AB 2 (V.129–30) that the old Dwarf-road into Beleriand had become disused since the return of the Noldor, and in a late rewriting of that passage (precursor of the present annal) it is said:
> But after the coming of the Noldor the Dwarves came seldom any more by their old roads into Beleriand (until the power of Maidros fell in the Fourth Battle [i.e. the Dagor Bragollach in 455]), and all their traffic passed through the hands of Cranthir, and thus he won great riches.

The meaning is therefore that after the meeting of Cranthir's people with the Dwarves their renewed commerce with the Elves passed for three hundred years over the mountains much further north, into the northern parts of Thargelion about Lake Helevorn.

§115 The route of the Orc-army that departed from Angband 'into the white north' remains unchanged from AB 2 (V.130); cf. the account in QS §103, and my discussion of the geography in V.270–1.

§116 *Glaurung* here appears for earlier *Glómund*, together with *Urulóki* 'fire-serpents': cf. the original tale of *Turambar and the Foalókë* in *The Book of Lost Tales* (and 'this *lókë* (for so do the Eldar name the worms of Melko)', II.85).

In QS §104 it was not said that Morgoth was 'ill pleased' that the dragon 'had disclosed himself over soon', but on the contrary that Glómund issued from Angband 'by the command of Morgoth; for he was unwilling, being yet young and but half-grown.'

The content of the latter part of the annal has no antecedent in the old versions. I take the words 'the Noldor of purer race' to mean those Noldor who had no or little intermingling of Dark-elven character, with perhaps the implication that they were more faithful to their ancient nature as it had evolved in Aman.

§§117–20 The story, or rather the existence of a story, about Isfin and Eöl goes back to the beginning, and I shall briefly rehearse here what can be learnt of it before this time.

In the original tale of *The Fall of Gondolin* (II.165, 168) Isfin appears as Turgon's sister, and there is a reference to the 'tale of Isfin and Eöl', which 'may not here be told'. Meglin was their son.

In the fragmentary poem *The Lay of the Fall of Gondolin* Fingolfin's wife and daughter (Isfin) were seeking for him when Isfin was captured by Eöl 'in Doriath's forest'; and Isfin sent Meglin her son to Gondolin (III.146).

In the *Sketch of the Mythology* (IV.34–5) Isfin was lost in Taur-na-Fuin after the Battle of Unnumbered Tears and entrapped by Eöl; Isfin sent Meglin to Gondolin (which at that stage was not founded until after the Battle of Unnumbered Tears).

In Q (IV.136), similarly, Isfin was lost in Taur-na-Fuin after the Battle of Unnumbered Tears, and captured by Eöl; in addition, it is said that 'he was of gloomy mood, and had deserted the hosts ere the battle'. It is subsequently said (IV.140) that Isfin and Meglin came together to Gondolin at a time when Eöl was lost in Taur-na-Fuin.

In AB 1 (IV.301), in the year 171 (the year before the Battle of Unnumbered Tears), it is told that Isfin strayed out of Gondolin and was taken to wife by Eöl. [An error in the printed text of AB 1 here may be mentioned: 'Isfin daughter of Turgon' for 'Isfin sister of Turgon'.] In 192 'Meglin comes to Gondolin and is received by Turgon as his sister's child', without mention of Isfin. This was repeated in AB 2 (V.136, 139), with changed dates (271, 292, later > 471, 492), but now it is expressly stated that Meglin was sent to Gondolin by Isfin, and that he went alone (thus reverting to the story in the *Sketch of the Mythology*).

QS has no mention of the story.

§117 In GA as originally written the loss of Isfin is still placed in the year (471) before the Battle of Unnumbered Tears, but the motive is introduced that she left Gondolin in weariness of the city and wishing to see her brother Fingon; and she was lost in Brethil and entrapped by Eöl, who had lived there 'since the first finding of Beleriand' – which must mean that he withdrew into secrecy and solitude when the Elves of the Great March first entered Beleriand. The implication of the last words, 'took no part in all the deeds of his kin', is not explained.

§118 In the replacement annal 316 something more is suggested of Eöl's nature, and the element enters that disregarding Turgon's bidding Isfin went eastwards from Gondolin, seeking 'the land of Celegorm and his brethren, her friends of old in Valinor'. A description of Isfin on a page from an engagement calendar dated October 1951 (and so belonging to the same time as the new annals in GA discussed here) was attached to the account of the princes of the Noldor in QS (see X.177, 182), and in this account it is said that in Valinor Isfin 'loved much to ride on horse and to hunt in the forests, and there was often in the company of her kinsmen, the sons of Fëanor'. It is further told in the new annal for 316 that she became separated from her escort in Nan Dungorthin and came to Nan Elmoth, where Eöl's dwelling is now placed. She now leaves Gondolin long before the Battle of Unnumbered Tears.

§119 The name *Fingol* is not in fact written with a capital, but is preceded by an altered letter that I cannot interpret (it might possibly be intended as an O). As the annal was written *Glindûr* (replacing the primitive and long-enduring name *Meglin*) was primarily the name of the metal devised by Eöl, and with the later change of *Glindûr* to *Maeglin* this remained true of the name *Maeglin*.

§120 The story now reverts to that told in Q (IV.140): Isfin and Glindûr (Maeglin) came together to Gondolin; and the essential features of the final drama now appear. The original text (see pp. 316 ff.) of the fully told story of Isfin and Eöl and their son (Chapter 16 in the published *Silmarillion, Of Maeglin*) belongs to this period, and indeed it was already in existence when these new annals were written: they are a very condensed résumé. (For the rejected annal of which this is a replacement see §273 and commentary.)

§121 The date of Bëor's birth remains unchanged from that in AB 2 (as revised: 170 > 370, V.130), as do the dates of the following annals.

§122-3 The statements in the annals for 388 and 390 that Haleth and Hador were born in Eriador were not made in AB 2.

§124 The reference to the *Quenta* is to QS §§126 ff. – Against the first sentence of this annal my father afterwards pencilled an X, with a scribbled note: 'This is too late. It should be the date of the invitation of the [?Sires] of Men to come west'. This was struck through, apart from the first four words: these are the first indication of major changes in the chronology that would enter at a later time.

§125 This annal is substantially extended from that in AB 2, where no more was said than 'there was war on the East Marches, and Bëor was there with Felagund'.

§127 *Galion* replaces *Gumlin* of QS §127 (and AB 2 as early revised, V.146 note 20: originally in this text the names of the sons of Hador were in the reverse positions, Gundor being the elder). Later, the name *Galion* was replaced by *Galdor*. The change to 'in Eriador' was probably made for this reason: Hador entered Beleriand in 420; thus Galion was born while his father was somewhere in Eriador, in 417, but by the time of Gundor's birth in 419 Hador was already in the eastern foothills of the Blue Mountains (§128).

§129 The first paragraph of the annal for 420 is close to that in AB 2 (V.130-1), with some additions: that Brethil had never before been inhabited on account of the density of the forest, that Hador was the more ready to settle in Hithlum 'being come of a northland people', and that his lands in Hithlum were 'in the country of Dor-Lómin'. In the margin against this last my father later scribbled: '[427 >] 423 Hador's folk come to Dor-lómin', but struck this out; see §136 and commentary. The old view that the people of Hador abandoned their own language in Hithlum is retained (see V.149, annal 220).

§§130-2 The content of the latter part of the annal for 420 and the opening of that for 422 is wholly new: Thingol's dreams concerning Men before they appeared, his ban on their settlement save in the North and on the entry of any Man (even of Bëor's house) into Doriath, Melian's prophecy to Galadriel, and Thingol's permission to the people of Haleth to dwell in Brethil, despite his hostility to Men in general and his edict against their taking land so far south.

§133 This passage follows closely the annal in AB 2 (V.131), but with the interesting addition that the people of Hador would go far into the cold North to keep watch.

§135 With the notable sentence (not in AB 2) 'For the Noldor indeed were tall as are in the latter days men of great might and majesty' cf. the collected references to the relative stature of Men and Elves in the oldest writings, II.326. In the early texts it was said more than once that the first Men were smaller than their descendants, while the Elves were taller, and thus the two races were almost of a size; but the present passage is not clear in this respect.

As the last sentence but one of the paragraph was originally written it read: 'Yellowhaired they were and blue-eyed (not so was Túrin but his mother was of Bëor's house) and their women were tall and fair.' The words 'for the most part' were added; they had appeared in a closely similar passage in QS chapter 10 (V.276, §130).

§136 That Hador's folk were given lands in Dor-lómin was mentioned in the annal for 420, to which my father added afterwards, but then struck out, '[427 >] 423 Hador's folk come to Dor-lómin' (commentary on §129). The implication is presumably that for a few years they dwelt in some other part of Beleriand.

§139 Beren's mother Emeldir 'Manhearted' is not named in the earlier texts.

§142 In AB 2 the birth of Morwen was in 445. When the date was changed in GA to 443 the entry was moved.

§144 Tuor has not previously been given the title of 'the Blessed'.

§§145–7 In AB 2 (V.131–2) the Battle of Sudden Fire, recorded in the annal for 455, 'began suddenly on a night of mid-winter'; but the passage beginning 'Fingolfin and Fingon marched to the aid of Felagund' has a new date, 456. I suggested (V.150) that this was because the Battle of Sudden Fire began at midwinter of the year 455, i.e. at the end of the year. In GA, on the other hand, it is expressly stated (§145) that the assault out of Angband came 'at the year's beginning', 'on the night of mid-winter'; thus the new year began at the mark of mid-winter, and the battle was dated the first day of the year 455. See commentary on §147.

§145 There are here the first appearances of the names *Dagor Bragollach* (for *Dagor Vreged-úr* in QS, earlier *Dagor Húr-Breged* in AB 2) and *Anfauglith* (for *Dor-na-Fauglith*).

§147 In QS (V.282, §140) Hador, who was born in 390, is said to have been 'sixty and six years of age' at his death, not as here 65 (see commentary on §§145–7).

§§149–50 This passage, later struck from the manuscript apart from the opening sentence of §149, remained very close to that in AB 2 (V.132) with some influence in its structure from the story as told in QS (V.288), except in one important particular: Húrin's companion was not, as in AB 2 and QS, Haleth the Hunter himself, but Haleth's grandson Handir, born in the same year as Húrin. – The story of Húrin in Gondolin reappears in GA in a long rider to the annal 458 (§§161–6).

§§151–2 As this passage concerning Turgon's messengers was first written it followed closely that in AB 2 (V.132–3, and cf. the version in QS, V.288); as revised it introduces the ideas of the inability of the Noldor to build seaworthy ships, and of Turgon's nonetheless keeping a secret outpost and place of shipbuilding on the Isle of Balar thereafter.

§153 In the earlier accounts (AB 2 in V.132–3 with notes 25 and 29, and QS §141 and commentary) the story of how Celegorn and Curufin came to Nargothrond after their defeat in the east was shifting and obscure, but there was at any rate no suggestion that they played any part in the defence of Minnas-tirith on Tolsirion. My father made a note at this time on the AB 2 manuscript, suggesting a possible turn in the story: Celegorn and Curufin were driven west and helped manfully in the siege of Minnas-tirith, saving Orodreth's life: and so when Minnas-tirith was taken Orodreth could not help but harbour them in Nargothrond. He struck this out; but the story was now reintroduced and developed in the *Grey Annals*.

The date of the capture of Minnas-tirith was changed in the *Grey Annals*. In AB 2 the date was 457 (following the fall of Fingolfin in 456); so also in QS §143 'For nearly two years the Gnomes still defended the west pass ... and Minnastirith withstood the Orcs', and it was 'after the fall of Fingolfin' that Sauron came against Tolsirion. In GA the present passage, describing the assault on the Pass of Sirion, was first dated 456, but the date was struck out, so that these events fall within the Fell Year, 455; and the fall of Fingolfin follows (still dated 456).

§154 The later form *Tol-in-Gaurhoth* (for earlier *Tol-na-Gaurhoth*) now appears.

§§155–7 The story of Fingolfin's death in AB 2 (V.133) had been compressed into a few lines. Introducing a much extended account into the new *Annals*, my father drew largely upon the story as it had been told in QS (§§144–7 and commentary), with some regard also to Canto XII of the *Lay of Leithian* (on which the QS version was largely based). In content the differences are mostly small, but there enters here the great ride of Fingolfin across Anfauglith on his horse Rochallor, and the horse's flight from Angband and death in Hithlum. In AB 2 (as in AB 1 and Q) it was Thorondor who built

Fingolfin's cairn, whereas in QS it was Turgon (see the commentary on QS §147); now in the *Grey Annals* the building of the cairn is ascribed to 'the eagles'.

§157 The change of 'the people of the hidden city were all Noldor' to 'many of the people ... were Noldor' depends on the development whereby there were many Elves of Sindarin origin in Gondolin: see commentary on §107 and references given there.

In the late addition at the end of this paragraph (present in the GA typescript) appears the parentage of Gilgalad as adopted in the published *Silmarillion*; see further pp. 242–3.

§158 The form *Taur-nu-Fuin* (for earlier *Taur-na-Fuin*) now appears.

§159 In AB 2 (V.133), and in a closely similar passage in QS (§139), it was said that the wives of Baragund and Belegund were from Hithlum, and that when the Battle of Sudden Fire began their daughters Morwen and Rían were sojourning there among their kinsfolk – hence they were the only survivors. This story is now superseded and rejected: Emeldir Beren's mother led the surviving women and children of Bëor's people away over the mountains in the aftermath of the battle, and it was thus that Morwen and Rían came to Dor-lómin (by way of Brethil). It is not made clear whether their mothers were still women of Hithlum.

In AB 2 the full list of Barahir's band was not given, with a suggestion that only certain names were remembered, but it appears in QS (§139). The only name that differs in GA is *Arthad* for *Arthod*. *Radhruin* of QS is here written *Raðhruin* (*Radruin* by emendation of *Radros* in AB 2, V.147 note 31), but this may not be significant.

§160 This paragraph derives from the annal for 458 in AB 2 (V.133). In the story as told in QS (§152) Beleg came to the aid of Haleth 'with many archers'; cf. GA §29, 'Thingol's armouries were stored with axes (the chief weapons of the Naugrim, and of the Sindar)', and the name 'Axe-elves' of the Sindar (transferred from the Nandor), X.171. On the name *Eglath* ('The Forsaken') see X.85, 164, 170.

§161 Huor now at last appears as Húrin's companion in Gondolin, replacing Handir grandson of Haleth in the earlier, rejected passage in GA (§149).

Haleth was the kinsman of Húrin and Huor (as noticed in a late addition to the manuscript) through the marriage in 436 (§140) of Haleth's son Hundor to Glorwendil, daughter of Hador and sister of their father Galion. But the genealogy was further developed in the annal for 462 (see §171 and commentary) by the marriage of Galion to Haleth's daughter, so that Haleth was the grandfather of Húrin and Huor; and it seems very probable that this was the reason for the addition of the words 'their kinsman' here.

The story now becomes decisively different from the old version in AB 2 and QS, and still present in GA as originally written (§149); for Húrin and his companion (now his brother Huor) were not hunting in the Vale of Sirion before the Battle of Sudden Flame, but the fact of the fostering of Húrin (and now of his brother also) among the people of Haleth is brought into association with the defeat of the Orcs in 458 by the men of Brethil, aided by Elves out of Doriath, three years after the battle. There enters now also the story that Húrin and Huor were taken to Gondolin by the Eagles. – On the ford of Brithiach see p. 228, §28.

§§162–6 The story now reaches virtually its final form, with the major innovation of Maeglin's hostility to the young men but also of their being permitted to leave Gondolin despite the king's ban, here first stated in its full rigour, on departure from the city of any stranger who came there; and this permission was granted because of their ignorance of how it might be found. (The riders on the story of Isfin and Ëol, §§118–20, were written at the same time as the present one.)

§165 On the change of *Glindûr* to *Maeglin* see §119 and commentary.

§166 On the carbon copy of the typescript of GA my father wrote against the words 'But though they told that they had dwelt a while in honour in the halls of King Turgon': 'They did not reveal Turgon's name.' See p. 169.

§170 'The army that had driven into East Beleriand' must refer to the invasions of the year 455: cf. AB 2, annal 456; QS §142; and again in GA §148, in all of which the phrase 'far into East Beleriand' occurs. In AB 2, in the renewed assaults of the year 462 (V.134), 'the invasion of the Orcs encompassed Doriath, both west down Sirion, and east through the passes beyond Himling.' Of this there is no mention here in GA (nor in QS, §156); but there has also been no mention before the present passage of Thingol's victory after the Dagor Bragollach or indeed of the subsequent total destruction (as it appears) of the eastern invading force.

§171 The statement that 'in the eastward war [Morgoth] hoped ere long to have new help unforeseen by the Eldar' is a premonitory reference to the coming of the Swarthy Men; cf. QS §150, where, immediately before their entry into Beleriand, it is said that Morgoth 'sent his messengers east over the mountains', and that 'some were already secretly under the dominion of Morgoth, and came at his call'. In GA (§174, footnote) it is said that 'it was after thought that the people of Ulfang were already secretly in the service of Morgoth ere they came to Beleriand.' See further §§79–81 and commentary.

Of the assault on Hithlum no more was said in AB 2 (V.134) than that 'Morgoth went against Hithlum, but was driven back as yet'; in

QS (§156) it was Fingon, not Húrin, who 'drove [the Orcs] in the end with heavy slaughter from the land, and pursued them far across the sands of Fauglith.'

At the end of the paragraph, by later addition, is the first reference to the short stature of Húrin, and also to the 'double marriage' of Hador's son Galion and daughter Glorwendil to Haleth's daughter (unnamed) and son Hundor. It seems likely that this extension of the genealogy arose here, and was the basis of the addition of 'their kinsman' to the annal for 458 discussed in the commentary on §161.

§172 In QS (§156) there seems only to have been an assault on Hithlum from the east, from Fauglith, for it is said that 'the Orcs won many of the passes, and some came even into Mithrim'. In the present annal it seems that Galion and his son Húrin defeated the attack from the east, while Fingon attempted to defend Hithlum from the north (the intervention of Círdan is of course entirely new). On the puzzling question of the geographical configuration of the north of Hithlum see V.270–1 (and cf. what is said in GA of the route of the attack out of Angband in the year 155, §115 and commentary). The present passage does not clarify the matter, though the statement that the horsed archers of the Eldar pursued the Orcs 'even to the Iron Mountains' possibly suggests that Hithlum was to some degree open to the north. This would indeed be very surprising, since it would make Hithlum by far the most vulnerable of the territories of the Eldar, and Morgoth would have had little need to attempt to break through the vast natural defence of the Shadowy Mountains. But this is the merest speculation, and I know of no other evidence bearing on the matter.

§§173–4 New elements in this account of the Easterlings (cf. AB 2, V.134, and QS §151) are the explicit statement that they did not enter Beleriand over the Blue Mountains but passed to the north of them; the warning of the Dwarves to Maidros concerning their westward movement; the diversity of their tongues and their mutual hostility; their dwellings in Lothlann and south of the March of Maidros (in QS it is said only that they 'abode long in East Beleriand', §152). The form *Lothlann* appears for earlier *Lothland*; *Lothlann (Lhothlann)* is found in the *Etymologies* (stems LAD, LUS, V.367, 370).

§174 On the first sentence of the footnote to this paragraph see the commentary on §171. With the following remarks in the footnote concerning the descendants of the people of Bór in Eriador in the Second Age cf. QS chapter 16, §15 (V.310–11): 'From that day [Nírnaith Arnediad] the hearts of the Elves were estranged from Men, save only from those of the Three Houses, the peoples of Hador, and Bëor, and Haleth; for the sons of Bór, Boromir, Borlas, and Borthandos, who alone among the Easterlings proved true at need, all perished in that battle, and they left no heirs.' This suggests that the people of Bór ceased to be of any account after 472; but it is perhaps to be presumed in any case that these Men of Eriador were a branch of that people who never entered Beleriand.

§§175–210 I have described in V.295 how, after *The Lord of the Rings* was finished, my father began (on the blank verso pages of the manuscript of AB 2) a prose 'saga' of Beren and Lúthien, conceived on a large scale and closely following the revised *Lay of Leithian*; but this went no further than Dairon's betrayal to Thingol of Beren's presence in Doriath. Unless this work belongs to a time after the abandonment of the *Grey Annals*, which seems to me very improbable, the two versions of the tale that appear here in the *Annals* are the last of the many that my father wrote (for a full account of the complex history of the QS versions and drafts see V.292 ff.).

It will be seen that Version I is a précis of the narrative with no new elements, or elements inconsistent with the 'received tradition', apart from the reference to Amárië (see commentary on §180). Version II, if at the outset conceived on a fairly ample scale, again soon becomes another précis, though much fuller than Version I, and a great deal that is told in the completed QS text ('QS II', see V.292–3) is either not present or is treated much more cursorily: thus for example, nothing is said in GA of Húan's understanding of speech or speaking three times before his death, nor of his doom (*The Silmarillion* pp. 172–3), and much else that there is no need to detail here. But the structure of the two narratives remains very close.

It is curious to observe that the relation of the two versions in GA is the reverse of that between the two versions that my father made for the *Quenta Silmarillion*. The fuller form of the latter ('QS I') was very clearly an integral element in the QS manuscript as it proceeded, but he abandoned it and replaced it by the shorter form QS II because (as I have said, V.292) 'he saw that it was going to be too long, overbalancing the whole work. He had taken more than 4000 words to reach the departure of Beren and Felagund from Nargothrond'. In the case of the *Grey Annals*, on the other hand, it was the shorter form (Version I) that was integral to the text as written, while the fuller form (Version II) was intended to supplant it (though it was not finished).

For passages in the published *Silmarillion* derived from the *Grey Annals* see V.298–301.

§175 *Eryd Orgorath*: on the typescript of AAm *Ered Orgoroth* was changed to *Ered Gorgorath* (X.127, §126).

'And he passed through, even as Melian had foretold': see the words of Melian to Galadriel, §131.

In AB 2 (V.135) Húrin wedded Morwen in 464, as in GA, but Túrin was born in the winter of 465 'with sad omens'. This insertion in GA makes Túrin's birth in the year of his parents' marriage. See further the commentary on §183.

§178 The word 'bride-price' of the Silmaril demanded by Thingol had been used by Aragorn when he told the story on Weathertop.

§179 *Celegorm* was the original form, appearing in the *Lost Tales* (II.241). The name became *Celegorn* in the course of the writing of QS (V.226, 289), and this remained the form in AAm and GA; later it reverted to *Celegorm* (X.177, 179). The change of *m* to *n* here was made at the time of or very soon after the writing of this passage, and *Celegorm* was probably no more than a slip.

§180 With '[Felagund] dwells now in Valinor with Amárië' cf. QS I (V.300): 'But Inglor walks with Finrod his father among his kinsfolk in the light of the Blessed Realm, and it is not written that he has ever returned to Middle-earth.' In Version II (§199) it is said that 'released soon from Mandos, he went to Valinor and there dwells with Amárië.' It has been told in the annal for 102 (§109) that 'she whom [Felagund] had loved was Amárië of the Vanyar, and she was not permitted to go with him into exile.'

§183 Túrin's birth ('with sad omens') was likewise given in the year 465 in AB 2. The present entry was only inserted later, I think, because my father had inadvertently omitted it while concentrating on the story of Beren and Lúthien. Following the direction here 'Place in 464' a pencilled addition was made to the annal for that year in both versions (see §175 and commentary, §188).

§185 It appears from the penultimate sentence of this paragraph that the joining of the Two Kindreds is ascribed to the purpose of Eru. This is not in QS (I) (see *The Silmarillion* p. 184), nor in Version II of the story in the *Grey Annals* (§210).

§187 With the revised reading 'soon after the mid-winter' cf. the commentary on §§145-7.

§189 '[Thingol] answered in mockery': his tone is indeed less sombre and more briefly contemptuous than in QS (I) (*The Silmarillion* p. 167). In the *Lay of Leithian* (III.192, lines 1132-3) Thingol's warriors 'laughed loud and long' at his demand that Beren should fetch him a Silmaril; see my remarks on this, III.196.

§190 The detail of the glance passing between Melian and Beren at this juncture is not found in the other versions.

§191 The words 'as long before he had said to Galadriel' refer to Felagund's prophetic words in Nargothrond recorded in the annal for 102 (§108).

§193 The naming of Inglor 'Finrod' was perhaps no more than a slip without significance; but in view of the occurrence of 'Finrod Inglor the Fair' in a text associated with drafting for Aragorn's story on Weathertop (VI.187-8) it seems possible that my father had considered the shifting of the names (whereby Inglor became Finrod and Finrod his father became Finarfin) long before their appearance in print in the Second Edition of *The Lord of the Rings*.

§§193–4 In the long version QS (I), which ends at this point, when Felagund gave the crown of Nargothrond to his brother Orodreth 'Celegorm and Curufin said nothing, but they smiled and went from the halls' (*The Silmarillion* p. 170). The words of Celegorn and Felagund that follow here are a new element in the story.

The foresight of Felagund is undoubtedly intended to be a true foresight (like all such foresight, though it may be ambiguous). If full weight is given to the precise words used by Felagund, then it may be said that the conclusion of QS (V.331), where it is told that Maidros and Maglor did each regain a Silmaril for a brief time, is not contradicted.

§198 In QS (*The Silmarillion* p. 174) it is not said that Sauron 'left the Elven-king to the last, for he knew who he was', but only that he 'purposed to keep Felagund to the last, for he perceived that he was a Gnome of great might and wisdom.' See the *Lay of Leithian*, lines 2216–17 and 2581–2609 (III.231, 249).

§201 It is not told in other versions that Húan led the prisoners of Tolsirion back to Nargothrond; in QS it is said only that 'thither now returned many Elves that had been prisoners in the isle of Sauron' (*The Silmarillion* p. 176).

§203 The new year is placed at a slightly later point in the narrative in Version I, §184. In AB 2 all the latter part of the story of Beren and Lúthien, from their entry into Angband, was placed under the annal for the year 465 (V.135).

§204 The absence of any mention of the story that Húan and Lúthien turned aside to Tol-in-Gaurhoth on their way north, and clad in the wolfcoat of Draugluin and the batskin of Thuringwethil came upon Beren at the edge of Anfauglith (*The Silmarillion* pp. 178–9), is clearly due simply to compression. It was not said in QS (*ibid.* p. 179) that 'Húan abode in the woods' when Beren and Lúthien left him on their journey to Angband.

§207 It is not made clear in QS (*The Silmarillion* pp. 181–2) that it was the howls of Carcharoth that aroused the sleepers in Angband. – On the names Gwaihir and Lhandroval, which appear here in QS but not in the published *Silmarillion* (p. 182), see V.301 and IX.45.

§211 This annal is very close to a passage in QS (*The Silmarillion* p. 186).

§§212 ff. The text of QS is no longer the fine manuscript that was interrupted when it was sent to the publishers in November 1937, but the intermediate texts that my father wrote while it was away. These have been described in V.293–4: a rough but legible manuscript 'QS(C)' that completed the story of Beren and Lúthien, and extending through the whole of QS Chapter 16 *Of the Fourth Battle: Nírnaith Arnediad* was abandoned near the beginning of Chapter 17 (the story of Túrin); and a second manuscript 'QS(D)' which took up in the middle of Chapter 16 and extended somewhat further into Chapter 17, at which point the *Quenta Silmarillion* in that phase came to an end as a continuous narrative. From the beginning of Chapter 16 I began a new series of paragraph-numbers from §1 (V.306).

§212 In this annal (468) my father followed that in AB 2 (465-70, V.135) closely, and thus an important element in the 'Silmarillion' tradition is absent: the arrogant demand of the Fëanorians upon Thingol for the surrender of the Silmaril, followed by the violent menaces of Celegorn and Curufin against him, as the prime cause of his refusal to aid Maidros (see QS §6, and the passage in Q from which that derives, IV.116-17). In AB 2 Thingol's refusal is ascribed to 'the deeds of Celegorm and Curufin', and this is followed in GA. Again, the story in QS §7, absent in AB 2, that only a half of Haleth's people came forth from Brethil on account of 'the treacherous shaft of Curufin that wounded Beren', is not found in GA.

Notably, it is said in GA that Maidros had the help of the Dwarves 'in armed force' as well as in weapons of war; this was not said in AB 2 and was expressly denied in QS, where the Dwarves were represented as cynically engaged in the profitable enterprise of 'making mail and sword and spear for many armies' (see QS §3 and commentary).

§213 The annal in AB 2 from which this paragraph derives is dated 468. The present annal is much more explicit about the unwisdom of Maidros in revealing his power untimely than were the earlier accounts. – In QS (§3) it is said that at this time 'the Orcs were driven out of the northward regions of Beleriand', to which it is now added in GA that 'even Dorthonion was freed for a while'.

§214 The span of the second lives of Beren and Lúthien was said in the QS drafts to have been long, but the final text has 'whether the second span of his life was brief or long is not known to Elves or Men' (see V.305-6 on the development of the passage concerning the return of Beren and Lúthien and its form in the published *Silmarillion*). It seems possible that '[Lúthien] should *soon* die indeed' in the present text does not imply a short mortal span, but a mortal span in contrast to that of the Eldar.

The final text of QS says that Beren and Lúthien 'took up again their mortal form in Doriath', but the account here of their return to Thingol and Melian in Menegroth is entirely new (as also, of course, is the reference to Elrond and Arwen).

The land of the Dead that Live is named in QS(B) *Gwerth-i-Cuina* and in the final text of QS *Gyrth-i-Guinar* (V.305).

§215 In AB 2 the latter part of the legend of Beren and Lúthien, from their entry into Angband to their return from the dead, was placed under the year 465, whereas in GA it appears under 466, and the death of Lúthien in 467 (§211). The birth of Dior (whose name *Aranel* now appears) is here moved forward three years from the date in AB 2, 467.

§216 The wedding of Huor and Rían was given in AB 2 in the annal for 472, and was said to have taken place 'upon the eve of battle'. See §218 and commentary.

§§217 ff. In the very long account of the Nírnaeth Arnediad that follows my father made use both of the 'Silmarillion' and of the 'Annals' tradition, i.e. QS Chapter 16 and the account in AB 2. The QS chapter was itself largely derived from an interweaving of Q and AB 2 (see V.313). – A later version of the story of the battle, closely based on that in GA but with radical alterations, is given in Note 2 at the end of this commentary (pp. 165 ff.).

§218 This passage was not removed when the record of Huor's marriage to Rían was entered under 471 (§216); the typescript of GA, however, has only the later 471 entry.

§219 The Nírnaeth Arnediad, formerly the fourth battle in the wars of Beleriand, now becomes the fifth battle: see commentary on §§36 ff. The time of the year was not stated in the earlier accounts.

The placing of the passage on the subject of the Hill of Slain follows AB 2 (V.136); rejected here, it was replaced by another at the end of the story of the Nírnaeth Arnediad in GA (§250): cf. QS §19. On the name *Hauð-na-Dengin* see V.314, §19; also GA §§250–1.

§220 The actual nature of Uldor's machinations was not stated in the earlier accounts.

§221 'a great company from Nargothrond': earlier in GA (§212) it is said that 'small help came from Nargothrond' (cf. QS §5: 'only a small company'). – The addition concerning Mablung's presence, not in AB 2, comes from QS (§6), deriving from Q (IV.117); but in those texts Beleg ('who obeyed no man', 'who could not be restrained') came also to the battle. Thingol's qualified permission to Mablung is new in GA; in the *Quenta* tradition such permission was given by Orodreth to the company from Nargothrond. – The succession of Hundor on the death of his father, Haleth the Hunter, is recorded in the annal for 468 (§212). (Much later, when the genealogy of the People of Haleth was transformed, *Hundor* was replaced by '*Haldir* and *Hundar*'; on this see p. 236.)

On the unsatisfactory account of Turgon's emergence from Gondolin in QS, amalgamating the inconsistent stories in Q and AB 2, see V.313–15. In the *Grey Annals* the confusion is resolved. Turgon came up from Gondolin *before* battle was joined (in the AB story he and his host only came down from Taur-na-Fuin as Fingon's host withdrew southwards towards the Pass of Sirion, V.136–7), but only shortly before, and was stationed in the south guarding the Pass of Sirion.

§222   The story of the opening of the battle as told here differs from that in QS §10 (following Q), where Fingon and Turgon becoming impatient at the delay of Maidros sent their heralds into the plain of Fauglith to sound their trumpets in challenge to Morgoth.

§§224–5   There now appears the final link in this element of the narrative: the captured herald (see commentary on §222) slaughtered in provocation on the plain of Fauglith (QS §11) disappears and is replaced by Gelmir of Nargothrond, Gwindor's brother, who had been taken prisoner in the Battle of Sudden Flame. It was Gwindor's grief for his brother that had brought him from Nargothrond against the will of Orodreth the king, and his rage at the sight of Gelmir's murder was the cause of the fatal charge of the host of Hithlum. I have described the evolution of the story in IV.180.

§226   In §221 'the host of Fingolfin' is obviously a slip of the pen, for 'the host of Fingon', and so probably 'the banners of Fingolfin' here also: QS (§12) has 'the banners of Fingon'.

§228   'in the reargaurd', struck out in GA, is found both in AB 2 and in QS (§13). – It is not said either in AB 2 or in QS that the host of Hithlum was surrounded, only that the enemy came between them and Erydwethion, so that Fingon was forced to retreat towards the Pass of Sirion.

It seems clear that Turgon emerged from the Pass only a brief time before the coming of the decoy force out of Angband; therefore he had not yet actually encountered Húrin.

§230   The Balrogs were still at this time conceived to exist in large numbers; cf. AAm §50 (X.75): '[Melkor] sent forth on a sudden a host of Balrogs' – at which point my father noted on the typescript of AAm: 'There should not be supposed more than say 3 or at most 7 ever existed' (X.80).

§231   In AB 2 and in QS (§15) it was Cranthir, not Maglor, who slew Uldor the Accursed. It is not said in those texts that 'new strength of evil men came up that Uldor had summoned and kept hidden in the eastern hills', nor, of course, that the Fëanorians, fleeing towards Mount Dolmed, took with them a remnant of the Naugrim, for it was only with the *Grey Annals* that the Dwarves took part in the battle (commentary on §212).

§232   Earlier in GA (§22) the *Enfeng* are the Dwarves of Belegost, but there was a period (Q, QS) when they were those of Nogrod (see commentary on §22); this no doubt explains *Nogrod* here, which was struck out and replaced by *Belegost* as soon as written. – The entire paragraph, and all its detail, is original in GA.

§233   In QS (§17) the banners of Fingon were white. In the account in GA of the fall of Fingolfin (§155) his shield was blue set with a star of crystal, and his arms silver; this is found also in the QS version (§144).

§§234–5   The speeches between Turgon, Húrin, and Huor are

entirely new. In §235 one might expect Huor to have said: 'I shall never look on thy white walls *again*' (as he does in the published *Silmarillion*, p. 194), since he had been to Gondolin, fourteen years before; but see p. 169.

§§235-6 Virtually all the changes in these paragraphs were made at the time of the writing of the manuscript.

§237 The name *Glindûr* has appeared in other passages introduced into the primary text: §§119-20, 165.

§240 Original details in GA are the striking of Huor's eye by the venomed arrow, and the piling of the dead men of Hador's house 'as a mound of gold'.

§241 This paragraph is derived from passages in QS (§§15-16) that occur at an earlier point in the narrative; but there is no mention in GA of the sons of Bór (see commentary on §174).

§242 The statement here that 'Tol-sirion [was] retaken and its dread towers rebuilt', not previously made, is clearly in plain contradiction of what was said in QS (V.300): 'They buried the body of Felagund upon the hill-top of his own isle, and it was clean again, and ever after remained inviolate; for Sauron came never back thither.' In the published *Silmarillion* this passage in QS was changed.

§243 'Cirdan held the Havens' is of course an addition to the passage in QS (§20) which is here being closely followed. – The references to Morgoth's peculiar fear of Turgon, and to Ulmo's friendship towards the house of Fingolfin, who scorned Morgoth in Valinor, have no antecedents in earlier texts. It can be seen from the rejected lines (rough and with many changes in the manuscript) that my father was to some extent working out the thought as he wrote. The words 'from Turgon ruin should come to him' are a reference to Eärendil and his embassage to Valinor.

§§244-9 The encounter of Húrin with Morgoth as told in GA is based on and for the most part follows closely the story in QS (§§21-3), but with some expansions: Morgoth's words concerning Húrin's wife and son now helpless in Hithlum, Húrin's sight of Hithlum and Beleriand far off from his stone seat on Thangorodrim. See further p. 169.

§251 It is at this point in the narrative that the draft manuscripts QS(C) and QS(D), having concluded the 'Nírnaith' chapter with the setting of Húrin on Thangorodrim, give a new heading, in QS(C) 'Of Túrin the Hapless' and in QS(D) 'Of Túrin Turamarth or Túrin the Hapless'. This, which was to be the next chapter (17) in QS, begins with the birth of Tuor and the death of Rían on the Hill of Slain (to which the *Grey Annals* likewise now turn); but QS(C) goes only so far as Túrin's departure from Menegroth to go out to fight on the marches of Doriath wearing the Dragon-helm, and QS(D) continues beyond this point only to Túrin's self-imposed outlawry after the slaying of Orgof (GA §259).

The fostering of Tuor by Dark-elves was recorded both in AB 2 (V.137) and in QS (§24); rejected in GA, there appears instead the first mention of Annael and the Grey-elves of Mithrim (see commentary on §252). Glorwendil's death of grief for her husband Hundor son of Haleth is referred to in the course of the narrative of the Nírnaith Arnediad in QS (§13).

§252 In both AB 2 (V.138) and in QS (§19) it was recorded that 'the Elves of Hithlum' were enslaved in the mines of Morgoth at this time, such of them as did not escape into the wild, and one would naturally assume that this referred to Noldorin Elves of Fingolfin's people – although the very reference to Tuor's fostering by 'Dark-elves' shows that there were other Elves in Hithlum, and 'Grey-elves' may be simply a later term for the Dark-elves of Beleriand owning allegiance to Thingol. In his message to the new-come Noldor by the mouth of Angrod (GA §64) Thingol did not indeed suggest that there were any of his people (Grey-elves) in Hithlum: among the regions where the Noldor might dwell he named Hithlum, adding that 'elsewhere there are many of my folk, and I would not have them restrained of their freedoms, still less ousted from their homes.'

§253 At the end of this paragraph my father pencilled: '(September–Dec.)'; this clearly refers to the months of Túrin's journey from Hithlum to Doriath in the latter part of 472 (the Battle of Unnumbered Tears was fought at midsummer of that year, §219). According to the earlier dating (§183) he was born in the winter of 465; this was changed (§§175, 188) to 464, but without indication of the time of the year. If he were born in the winter of 464, he would still have been seven years old in the autumn of 472.

§256 The whole content of this paragraph is new to the history. In the sentence 'Smiths and miners and masters of fire' the published *Silmarillion* (p. 196), which derives from this passage, has 'makers of fire': this was a misreading of the manuscript.

§257 It was said earlier in GA (§§151–2) that after the Dagor Bragollach Turgon sent Elves of Gondolin to the mouths of Sirion and to the Isle of Balar to attempt shipbuilding (it is perhaps a question, why did he not approach Cirdan at that time?), and that he 'ever maintained a secret refuge upon the Isle of Balar'. But the phrase in the present passage 'and mingled with Turgon's outpost there' was struck out, and the subsequent 'when Turgon heard of this he sent again his messengers to Sirion's Mouths' suggests of itself that the idea of a permanent outpost from Gondolin on Balar had been abandoned.

Here, in an alteration to the text, Voronwë's story is extended back, and he appears in a new rôle as captain of the last of the seven ships sent out into the Western Ocean by Cirdan (it is not said that he was an Elf of Gondolin). In earlier texts he has of course played no such part. In Q (IV.141) Tuor at the mouths of Sirion met Bronweg (> Bronwë) who had been of old of the people of Turgon and had escaped from Angband. With §§256–7 cf. the story of Tuor in *Unfinished Tales*, pp. 34–5 and note 13.

§258 If Túrin were born in the winter of 464 (see commentary on §253) he would have been in his seventeenth year in 481; it seems therefore that the older date (465) for his birth is retained. The *Annals*, very cursory, do not mention the occasion of Túrin's going to war (the ceasing of all tidings out of Hithlum).

The scribbled note 'Túrin donned the Dragon-helm of Galion' is not in the typescript of GA. The Dragon-helm goes back to the old *Lay of the Children of Húrin*, and was described in Q (IV.118), in the context of Húrin's not having worn it at the Battle of Unnumbered Tears; in the *Lay* (not in Q) Túrin's taking it to war at this time is mentioned (III.16, line 377: 'then Húrin's son took the helm of his sire').

§259 It is here that QS came to an end as a continuous narrative (see V.321, 323).

§260 The first two sentences of this annal are derived from Q (IV.123) and AB 2 (V.138); but those texts do not give the place of Túrin's lair, here said to be in Dimbar.

§261 The first part of this follows AB 2 (on Tuor's 'coming to Hithlum' see V.151), but the statement that Morwen and Niënor 'had been carried away to Mithrim' seems altogether aberrant.

§263 The final form of the annal concerning Tuor, with the date changed to 488 and his age changed to sixteen, and the appearance of Lorgan chief of the Easterlings, is probably derived from the story in *Of Tuor and his Coming to Gondolin* (*Unfinished Tales* pp. 18–19): in the manuscript of that work the date 488 was inserted against the paragraph beginning 'Therefore Annael led his small people ...' (p. 18), and Tuor's age was changed from fifteen to sixteen in the same sentence. On the other hand that text has 'after three years of thraldom' (p. 19) as it was written, whereas in GA 'three' is a change from 'seven'.

§264 This is the original annal for 488. When the preceding passage on Tuor was given the date 488 the entry concerning Haldir of Nargothrond became a continuation of that year. The event was referred to in the *Lay of the Children of Húrin* (III.75, lines 2137–8), where Orodreth's son was named *Halmir*; *Halmir* in AB 2 was changed to *Haldir* (V.138 and note 38), which is the form in the *Etymologies* (explained as meaning 'hidden hero', stem SKAL^1, V.386).

§265 In Q Blodrin was a Gnome, with the later addition that he was a Fëanorian (IV.123 and note 5); the story told here that he was one of the faithful Easterlings who became a traitor after his capture by Morgoth is a new development. In Q his evil nature was ascribed to his having 'lived long with the Dwarves', and this was derived from the *Lay* (III.32). – On the pencilled query concerning the Dragon-helm see §266.

§266 In Q Thingol's messengers arrived on the scene because they had been sent to summon Túrin and Beleg to a feast (IV.123). – The attempt to develop the subsequent history of the Dragon-helm and weave it into the existing story was inherently very difficult. Here, the questions arise at once: (1) Why was the Dragon-helm in Menegroth? This may be answered by supposing that when Túrin came to Menegroth for the feast at which he slew Orgof (§259) he brought the Helm with him from Dimbar, and after the slaying he fled from the Thousand Caves without it; on this assumption, the Helm remained in Doriath during the following years (484–9). But (2) if this is granted, why should Beleg now carry it off into the wilds on what must have seemed an almost certainly vain search for Túrin, who had been captured by Orcs and haled off to Angband? In my father's later work on the Túrin legend he concluded finally that Túrin left the Dragon-helm in Dimbar when he went to Menegroth for the fatal feast, and that (in the later much more complex story) Beleg brought it from there when he came to Amon Rûdh in the winter snow: hence in the (extremely artificial) passage in the published *Silmarillion*, p. 204, 'he brought out of Dimbar the Dragon-helm of Dor-lómin'.

§267 In the *Lay*, likewise, it was Finduilas who asserted against the disbelief and suspicion in Nargothrond that it was indeed Flinding (Gwindor) who had returned (III.69–71).

§268 In this passage a new element enters the story: Túrin's assumption of a riddling name, *Iarwaeth* (cf. the later *Agarwaen* 'Bloodstained', *The Silmarillion* p. 210), and his asking Gwindor to conceal his true name 'for the horror he had of his slaying of Beleg and dread lest it were learned in Doriath'; and here also appears the final form of the name of the re-forged sword, *Gurthang* 'Iron of Death' for earlier *Gurtholfin* > *Gurtholf* (V.139 and note 39) 'Wand of Death' (*Gurthang* is a change on the manuscript from a rejected name that cannot be read: the second syllable is *tholf* but the first is not *Gur*, and the meaning given is probably 'Wand of Death'). The form *Mormegil* appears in the earliest *Annals* (AB 1), emended to *Mormael* (IV.304 and note 52); Q had *Mormaglir* and AB 2 *Mormael*.

§§269–72 The greater part of this narrative appears for the first time in the *Grey Annals*: Gwindor's revelation to Finduilas of Túrin's identity, his warning to her, and his assertion that all in Angband knew of the curse upon Húrin; Túrin's assurance to Gwindor concerning Finduilas and his displeasure with him for what he had done; the honour done to Túrin by Orodreth when he learned who he was and the king's acceptance of his counsels; Túrin's unhappy love for Finduilas leading him to seek escape from his trouble in warfare.

§271 *morrowgift*: the gift of the husband to the wife on the morning ('morrow') after the wedding.

§272 The alliance of the Elves of Nargothrond with Handir of Brethil goes back to the earliest *Annals* (IV.305); I do not know why this element in the story was removed. See further the commentary on §300. – The bridge over Narog is not said here to have been built on Túrin's counsel, but this appears subsequently (§277).

§273 This rejected annal for 492 adheres to the old story that Meglin was sent by Isfin to Gondolin (although the later story that Isfin and Meglin came together to Gondolin appeared long before in Q: see §120 and commentary), and there is no trace of the story of Ëol's pursuit, the death of Isfin from Ëol's dart aimed at Maeglin, and Ëol's execution and dying curse on his son.

§275 The somewhat later insertion at the beginning of the annal replaces the subsequent statement in this paragraph that Handir was slain in the battle of Tum-halad, which derives from AB 2 (V.139).

The removal of Glaurung's passage through Hithlum on his way to Nargothrond (recorded in AB 2) is a great improvement to the probabilities of the narrative. – *Eithil Ivrin*: formerly *Ivrineithel* (V.139), 'Ivrin's Well', source of the Narog. This is the first reference to the defiling of Ivrin by Glaurung.

The site of the battle is not made clear. In Q it was 'upon the Guarded Plain, north of Nargothrond' (IV.126), and in AB 2 (V.139) 'between Narog and Taiglin'. In later work on the *Narn* my father wrote in one of a series of narrative-outlines:

They contact the Orc-host which is greater than they knew (in spite of Túrin's boasted scouts). Also none but Túrin could withstand the approach of Glaurung. They were driven back and pressed by the Orcs into the Field of Tumhalad between Ginglith and Narog and there penned. There all the pride and host of Nargothrond withered away. Orodreth was slain in the forefront of battle, and Gwindor wounded to death. Then Túrin came to him and all fled him, and he lifted Gwindor and bore him out of battle and [*several words illegible*] he swam the Narog and bore Gwindor to [?a wood] of trees. But Glaurung went down east of Narog and hastened [?on ?in] to Nargothrond with a great number of Orcs.

This is, I believe, the only statement that the site of the battle was between Ginglith and Narog; but my father pencilled in the name *Tumhalad* between those rivers, towards their confluence, on the map (p. 182, square E 5). In GA Túrin's escape with Gwindor 'to a wood' is mentioned, but not his swimming of the Narog. This is a curious detail: presumably he swam the Narog to escape from the battle, and then went down the east bank of the river to the Bridge of Nargothrond.

But it is hard to know what to make of this late conception of the site of Tumhalad. It would seem that my father now conceived Glaurung and the Orc-host to have come south from Ivrin on the west side of Narog; but the text states that they 'went down east of Narog' to Nargothrond, and therefore they also must have crossed the river – by swimming, as Túrin had done? In the published *Silmarillion* (pp. 212–13) I was probably mistaken to follow this very hastily written and puzzling text, and on the map accompanying the book to mark the site of Tumhalad in accordance with it. But in any case I feel sure that the original site, in the plain east of Narog, was still present in GA.

With regard to the pencilled note 'Túrin in the battle wore the Dragon-helm', the Helm was last mentioned in these marginal notes on the subject when Beleg carried it with him from Menegroth on the journey in search of Túrin which led to his death (see §266 and commentary). My father must have supposed therefore that Gwindor and Túrin carried it with them to Nargothrond. This raises the obvious difficulty that the Helm would at once have revealed the identity of Túrin; but in *Unfinished Tales* (pp. 154–5) I have referred to an isolated piece of writing among the *Narn* material which 'tells that in Nargothrond Túrin would not wear the Helm again "lest it reveal him", but that he wore it when he went to the Battle of Tumhalad.' The passage in question reads:

> Beleg searching the orc-camp [in Taur-nu-Fuin] finds the dragon-helm – or was it set on Túrin's head in mockery by the Orcs that tormented him? Thus it was borne away to Nargothrond; but Túrin would not wear it again, lest it reveal him, until the Battle of Dalath Dirnen.

(*Dalath Dirnen*, the Guarded Plain, was the earlier form; the name was so spelt when entered on the map, but changed subsequently as in the texts to *Talath Dirnen* (p. 186, §17).)

§276 Against the first line of this paragraph my father wrote a date: 'Oct.13'; against the first line of §278 he wrote 'Oct.25'; and against the first line of §288 he wrote 'Nov.1'. These very uncharacteristic additions must refer to the actual days of his writing, in (as I presume) 1951.

In AB 2 all that is said here is that 'Gwindor died, and refused the succour of Túrin.' The same was said in Q (IV.126), and also that he died reproaching Túrin: as I noted (IV.184), 'the impression is given that the reproaches of Flinding (Gwindor) as he died were on account of Finduilas. There is indeed no suggestion here that Túrin's policy of open war was opposed in Nargothrond'. Here in GA appears the motive that Gwindor held his death and the ruin of Nargothrond against Túrin – or more accurately, reappears, since it is clearly present in the old *Tale of Turambar* (II.83–4). Gwindor's words in GA concerning Túrin and Finduilas are altogether different from those given to him in Q, and there now appears the idea of the supreme importance to Túrin of his choice concerning Finduilas: but this is again a reappearance, from the *Tale*, where his choice is explicitly condemned (II.87).

§277 It is a new element in the narrative that it was Túrin's rescue of Gwindor that allowed Glaurung and his host to reach Nargothrond before he did.

This is a convenient place to describe a text whose relation to the *Grey Annals* is very curious. The text itself has been given in *Unfinished Tales*, pp. 159–62: the story of the coming of the Noldorin Elves Gelmir and Arminas to Nargothrond to warn Orodreth of its peril, and their harsh reception by Túrin. There is both a manuscript (based on a very rough draft outline written on a slip) and a typescript, with carbon copy, made by my father on the typewriter that he seems to have used first about the end of 1958 (see X.300). The manuscript has no title or heading, but begins (as also does the rough draft and the typescript) with the date '495'. The top copy of the typescript has a heading added in manuscript: 'Insertion for the longer form of the *Narn*', while the carbon copy has the heading, also added in manuscript, 'Insertion to *Grey Annals*', but this was changed to the reading of the top copy.

The curious thing is that while the manuscript has no 'annalistic' quality apart from the date 495, the typescript begins with the annalistic word 'Here' (a usage derived from the *Anglo-Saxon Chronicle*):

Here Morgoth assailed Nargothrond. Túrin now commanded all the forces of Nargothrond, and ruled all matters of war. In the spring there came two Elves, and they named themselves Gelmir and Arminas...

Moreover, while the manuscript extends no further than the text printed in *Unfinished Tales*, ending with the words 'For so much at least of the words of Ulmo were read aright', the typescript does not end there but continues:

Here Handir of Brethil was slain in the spring, soon after the departure of the messengers. For the Orcs invaded his land, seeking to secure the crossings of Taiglin for their further advance; and Handir gave them battle, but the Men of Brethil were worsted and were driven back into their woods. The Orcs did not pursue them, for they had achieved their purpose for that time; and they continued to muster their strength in the passes of Sirion.

Late in the year, having [*struck out*: gathered his strength and] completed his design, Morgoth at last loosed his assault upon Nargothrond. Glaurung the Urulókë passed over the Anfauglith,

[§277]
and came thence into the north vales of Sirion, and there did great evil; and he came at length under the shadow of Eryd Wethian [*sic*], leading the great army of the Orcs in his train ...

The text then continues, almost exactly as in the *Grey Annals* §§275–6, concluding with Gwindor's words at the end of §276: 'If thou fail her, it shall not fail to find thee. Farewell!' The only significant difference from the text in the *Annals* is the statement that at the battle of Tum-halad 'Túrin put on the Dragon-helm of Hador'; this however had been said in a marginal note to GA §275.

This is very puzzling. So far as the content of the original manuscript of 'Gelmir and Arminas' is concerned, there seems nothing against the supposition that my father wrote it as an insertion to the *Grey Annals*, and indeed in appearance and style of script it could derive from the time when he was working on them, before the publication of *The Lord of the Rings*. The puzzle lies in my father's motive for making, years later, a typescript of the text and *adding to it* material taken directly from the *Grey Annals*, specifically reinforcing the place of 'Gelmir and Arminas' in the annalistic context – together with his uncertainty, shown in the headings to the carbon copy, as to what its place actually was to be. Subsequently, indeed, he bracketed on the typescript the date and opening words '495 Here Morgoth assailed Nargothrond', and struck out the words 'Here' and 'in the spring' at the beginning of the passage cited above, thus removing the obviously annalistic features; but the conclusion seems inescapable that when he made the typescript he could still conceive of the *Annals* as an ingredient in the recorded tradition of the Elder Days. (A curious relation is seen between a continuation of the *Annals* made after the main manuscript had been interrupted and the opening of the late work *The Wanderings of Hurin*: see pp. 251–4, 258–60.)

It should be mentioned that certain names in the text of 'Gelmir and Arminas' as printed in *Unfinished Tales* were editorial alterations made for the sake of consistency: in both manuscript and typescript Gelmir refers to Orodreth as 'Finrod's son', changed to 'Finarfin's son'; *Iarwaeth* was changed to *Agarwaen* (the later name found in the *Narn* papers); and *Eledhwen* was retained from the manuscript (*Eleðwen*) for the typescript *Eðelwen* (the form used in *The Wanderings of Húrin*).

§§278–85 This passage describing the fateful encounter of Túrin and Glaurung very greatly develops the bare narrative in Q (IV.126–7), but for the most part it is not at odds in essentials with the old version, and in places echoes it. On the other hand there is an important difference in the central motive. In Q (IV.126) the dragon offered him his freedom either 'to rescue his "stolen love" Finduilas, or to do his duty and go to the rescue of his mother and sister... But he must swear to abandon one or the other. Then Túrin in anguish and in doubt forsook Finduilas against his heart ...' In the story in the *Grey Annals*, on the other hand, Túrin had no choice: his will was under Glaurung's when Finduilas was taken away, and he was physically incapable of movement. The Dragon does indeed say at the end: 'And if thou tarry for Finduilas, then never shalt thou see Morwen or Niënor again; and they will curse thee'; but this is a warning, not the offering of a choice. In all this Glaurung appears as a torturer, with complete power over his victim so long as he chooses to exert it, morally superior and superior in knowledge, his pitiless corruption able to assume an air almost of benevolence, of knowing what is best: 'Then Túrin ... as were he treating with a foe that could know pity, believed the words of Glaurung'.

§280 The further pencilled note here on the subject of the Dragon-helm, observing that while Túrin wore it he was proof against Glaurung's eyes, can be somewhat amplified. I have given at the end of the commentary on §275 a note on the recovery of the Dragon-helm when Túrin was rescued from the Orcs in Taur-nu-Fuin, whence it came to Nargothrond. That note continues with an account of the meeting of Túrin with Glaurung before the Doors of Felagund (see *Unfinished Tales* p. 155). Here it is said that Glaurung desired to rid Túrin of the aid and protection of the Dragon-helm, and taunted him, saying that he had not the courage to look him in the face.

And indeed so great was the terror of the Dragon that Túrin dared not look straight upon his eye, but had kept the visor of his helmet down, shielding his face, and in his parley had looked no higher than Glaurung's feet. But being thus taunted, in pride and rashness he thrust up the visor and looked Glaurung in the eye.

At the head of the page my father noted that something should be said about the visor, 'how it protected the eyes from all darts (and from dragon-eyes)'.

This text, or rather the idea that it contains, is obviously behind the note in GA, and the last words of that note 'Then the Worm perceiving this' would no doubt have introduced some phrase to the effect that Glaurung taunted Túrin with cowardice in order to get him to remove it (cf. the note in the margin at §284 – which is scarcely in the right place). A further statement on the subject of the visor of the Helm is found in the *Narn* (*Unfinished Tales* p. 75, an expansion of the passage in QS Chapter 17, V.319): 'It had a visor (after the manner of those that the Dwarves used in their forges for the shielding of their eyes), and the face of one that wore it struck fear into the hearts of all beholders, but was itself guarded from dart and fire.' It is said here that the Helm was originally made for Azaghâl Lord of Belegost, and the history of how it came to Húrin is told.

In the published *Silmarillion* (p. 210) I adopted a passage from another text in the vast assemblage of the *Narn* papers, telling how Túrin found in the armouries of Nargothrond 'a dwarf-mask all gilded', and wore it into battle. It seems probable that this story arose at a stage when my father was treating the Dragon-helm as lost and out of the story (from the end of Dor-Cúarthol, the Land of Bow and Helm, when Túrin was taken by the Orcs), and I extended Túrin's wearing of it to the battle of Tumhalad (p. 212).

§§287 ff. From the Battle of Tumhalad to the end of the tale of Túrin the text of the *Grey Annals* was virtually the sole source of the latter part of Chapter 21 'Of Túrin Turambar' in the published *Silmarillion* (pp. 213–26). There now enters an element in the history, however, of which I was unaware, or more accurately misinterpreted, when I prepared the text of the *Narn* for publication in *Unfinished Tales*, and which must be made clear. At that time I was under the impression that the last part of the *Narn* (from the beginning of the section entitled *The Return of Túrin to Dor-lómin* to the end, *Unfinished Tales* pp. 104–46) was a relatively late text, belonging with all the other *Narn* material that (in terms of the narrative) precedes it; and I assumed that the story in the *Grey Annals* (to which the last part of the *Narn* is obviously closely related, despite its much greater length) preceded it by some years – that it was in fact an *elaboration* of the story in the *Annals*.

This view is wholly erroneous, and was due to my failure to study sufficiently closely the material (preserved in a different place) that preceded the final text of the story in the *Narn*. In fact, it soon becomes plain (as will be seen in the commentary that follows) that the long narrative in the *Grey Annals* was *based directly on* the final text of that in the *Narn*, and was a *reduction* of that text, congruent with it at virtually all points. The manuscript of this latter is very similar in appearance and style of script to that of the *Annals of Aman* and the *Grey Annals*, and undoubtedly belongs to the same period (presumptively 1951). Thus the massive development and enhancement of the final tragedy in Brethil is yet another major work of the prolific time that followed the completion of *The Lord of the Rings* (see *Morgoth's Ring*, pp. vii and 3).

The manuscript was headed (later) 'The Children of Húrin: last part', and at the top of the first page my father wrote 'Part of the "Children of Húrin" told in full scale'. I shall devote a good deal of the following commentary to showing how, in more important instances, my father developed the narrative in the *Narn*. It is to be remembered that the last version he had written was the very compressed story in the *Quenta* (Q) of 1930 (IV.127–30), behind which lay 'the earliest Silmarillion' or 'Sketch of the Mythology' (IV.30–1), and behind that the old *Tale of Turambar and the Foalókë* (II.88–112).

I shall not make a detailed comparison of the new narrative with the older forms, nor of the last part of the *Narn* with the *Grey Annals*. Since it is obviously out of the question to reprint the last part of the *Narn* in this book, I must refer to the text in *Unfinished Tales*, which is very close to the final form of the text in the manuscript, but introduces some unimportant changes in wording; the use of 'you' for 'thou' and 'thee' of the original; and some later forms of names. In order to avoid ambiguity I shall identify the last part of the *Narn* by the letters 'NE' (i.e. 'End of the *Narn*'); thus 'NE p. 132' is to be understood as meaning the text of the *Narn* in *Unfinished Tales* on p. 132. Where necessary I distinguish the actual manuscript, or manuscripts, from the printed text. There is also a later amanuensis typescript of NE.

§290 The addition concerning the death of Handir of Brethil, rejected here, reappears at the beginning of the annal for 495 (§275).

§291 The names *Amon Obel* and *Ephel Brandir* now first appear; they were marked in on the second map (see the redrawing on p. 182, square E 7). On the emendation concerning Handir of Brethil see §275 and commentary.

§292 The opening of NE (p. 104) is almost the same as that of the rewritten section in GA, rather than its original form (§287). This is to be explained, I think, on the supposition that my father was working (here at any rate) on the two versions at the same time. – In both texts 'eighty leagues' was changed to 'forty leagues'; the distance on the second map from Nargothrond to Ivrin measured in a straight line is 8 cm. or 41·6 leagues (see V.412).

§293 Against *Dorlómin* my father wrote in the margin the Quenya form *Lóminórë*, but he did not strike out *Dorlómin*.

§294 It is made clear in the later text from which the section *The Departure of Túrin* in the *Narn* is derived that Brodda forcibly wedded Húrin's kinswoman Aerin (later form for Airin) before Túrin left Dor-lómin (see *Unfinished Tales* p. 69); in GA Túrin only learns of it now, on his return, and this was certainly the case also in NE. Airin now becomes Húrin's kinswoman, not Morwen's, as she was in Q and QS, and still in the rejected form (§288) of the present passage.

It is seen from NE (p. 106) that the story of Túrin's childhood friendship with the lame Sador Labadal was already in being, although it had not yet been written (the parts of the *Narn* narrative preceding NE being unquestionably later); in GA there is no suggestion of this story, but I think it certain that this is due merely to the extreme condensation of the narrative here: the long conversation in NE between Túrin and Sador, and Sador's 'recognition', before ever Túrin entered Brodda's hall, is reduced to a few lines in the *Annals*. In that conversation and subsequently the text of

NE uses 'thou' and 'thee' throughout, but afterwards my father sometimes changed them to 'you' and sometimes not. It seems possible that where the changes were made it was because the speakers were using the 'polite plural' (as Sador to Túrin when he found out who he was); but in the published text I adopted 'you' throughout. – Where in NE (p. 105) Sador speaks of 'Húrin Galdor's son' the manuscript has 'Húrin Galion's son', *Galion* being still at that time the name of Húrin's father.

§§295–7   The whole episode in NE (pp. 106–9) following Túrin's entry into Brodda's hall, a massive development of the bare words of Q (IV.127 and note 9), is again greatly reduced in these paragraphs, and much is omitted: thus there is no mention of the general fighting, of Airin's firing of the hall, or of Asgon, the man of Dor-lómin (who will reappear).

§298   This annal concerning Tuor, dated 496, follows on from the entry about his departure from Mithrim at the end of the annal for 495 in the rejected section of the manuscript (§290). It is based on that in AB 2 (V.140), and adheres still to the old story that Tuor met Bronwë (Voronwë) at the mouths of Sirion; thus it was written before the addition was made to §257 whereby Voronwë became the sole survivor of the seven ships sent into the West and was cast ashore in Nivrost (see the commentary on that paragraph).

§299   Tuor was born in 472 (§251), was enslaved by Lorgan in 488 when he was sixteen years old and endured thraldom for three years, thus until 491 (§263), and in 495 had lived as an outlaw in the hills of Mithrim for four years.

This annal replaces both the preceding entries concerning Tuor (§§290, 298). Here the very old story of Tuor's going down to the mouths of Sirion is at last abandoned, and Ulmo appears to Tuor in Nivrost; Voronwë, cast ashore in Nivrost, now leads Tuor eastwards to Gondolin along the southern faces of the Shadowy Mountains. Here also appears the story that they saw Túrin at Ivrin on his journey northward from Nargothrond, and it may well be that this accounts for the change of date from 496 to 495; but the coming of Tuor to Turgon's ancient dwelling of Vinyamar and finding the arms left there long before at Ulmo's counsel is not referred to.

For the bidding of Ulmo to Turgon in Q, where it appears in two versions, see IV.142, 146–7, and my remarks IV.193–4. In GA there is no suggestion of Ulmo's counsel that Turgon should prepare for a great war against Morgoth and that Tuor should be his agent in the bringing of new nations of Men out of the East to his banners.

Elsewhere in GA the change is always *Glindûr* > *Maeglin*; *Meglin* > *Glindûr* here depends on the time of writing, for while my father was working on the *Annals* the series went *Meglin* > *Glindûr* > *Maeglin*.

§300 The manuscript has no date here, but it is clear that there should be (it is obviously 496 later in the annal, where 'with the beginning of spring Túrin cast off his darkness', §303); in the rejected version of the text the date 496 is given at this point (§291), and in the manuscript of NE also. The omission is due to the (second) rejected entry concerning Tuor (§298) having been dated 496.

The spelling *Taiglin* is found in NE also; *Teiglin* in both the published texts is an editorial alteration to a later form (see pp. 228, 309–10).

The story of Túrin's rescue of the men of Brethil from an attack by Orcs, derived from the lively account of the incident in NE (p. 110), is a new element in the narrative. It is to be noted, however, that as NE was first written there was no mention of it; the original text tells simply that when Túrin fell in with some of the folk of Haleth in Brethil

... the men that saw Túrin welcomed him, and even thus as a wild wanderer they knew him for the Mormegil, the great captain of Nargothrond, and the friend of Handir; and they marvelled that he had escaped, since they had heard that none had come out alive from the fortress of Felagund. Therefore they bade him come and rest among them for a while.

Following this is a brief preliminary passage in which Túrin's rescue of the men of Brethil from the Orc-attack is introduced, and finally the full account of the incident as it stands in NE. It is thus clearly seen that this story arose in the course of the writing of NE, as also did the motive that the woodmen *deduced* that the stranger was the Mormegil after Túrin had fallen into his swoon of grief. Both these elements are present in the GA version. This is one of many unquestionable evidences that the last part of the *Narn* preceded the *Grey Annals*.

It is also said in the rejected passage of NE that when Túrin told the woodmen of his quest for Finduilas

... they looked on him with grief and pity. 'Seek no more!' said one. 'For behold! the few of our men that escaped from Tum-halad brought us warning of an Orc-host that came from Nargothrond towards the crossings of Taiglin, marching slowly because of the number of their captives. ...'

In the final text the statement that the woodmen fought at Tumhalad disappears (and Dorlas says of their ambush of the Orc-host from Nargothrond 'we thought to deal our small stroke in the war', NE p. 111). This is to be related to the information in GA which was struck out, that the Elves of Nargothrond 'allied themselves with Handir' (§272 and commentary), and that Handir was slain at Tumhalad (§275 and commentary).

§§301–3 The narrative (condensed from that of NE, pp. 109–12)

greatly expands that of Q (IV.127): new elements are 'Wildman of the Woods', Dorlas, and the Hauð-en-Ellas where Finduilas was laid near the Crossings of Taiglin, which have not been named before; Dorlas' realisation that the stranger must be the Mormegil, rumoured to be Túrin son of Húrin (in Q there is no indication that the woodmen knew who he was until the end); Brandir's foreboding when he saw Túrin on the bier, and his healing of Túrin; Túrin's setting aside of the black sword. The old story in Q (IV.129) that Túrin became lord of the woodmen is now abandoned: Brandir, as will be seen later in the narrative (§323, NE p. 132), remained the titular ruler (and in NE, p. 129, at the council held before Túrin's setting out for the encounter with Glaurung, he 'sat indeed in the high-seat of the lord of the assembly, but unheeded').

§301 *Hauð-en-Ellas*: the later form *-Elleth* was pencilled in on both the NE and GA manuscripts, and *Haudh-en-Elleth* is found in a plot-sequence among the later *Narn* papers (p. 256); this was adopted in both NE and *The Silmarillion*. The translation 'Mound of the Elf-maid', not in GA, was introduced into *The Silmarillion* from NE (p. 112), and comparison of the texts will show a number of other instances, not recorded here, of this conflation.

§302 Against the name *Ephel Brandir* in NE (p. 110) my father wrote faintly on the amanuensis typescript that was made from the manuscript: *Obel Halad* and '.... of the chieftain'; the illegible word might be 'Tower', but looks more like 'Town'. 'Town of the Chieftain' is quite possibly the correct interpretation, if *town* is used in the ancient sense of 'enclosed dwelling-place' (see II.292, and my remarks on the name *Tavrobel* in V.412). On *Obel Halad* see pp. 258, 263.

§303 In GA Brandir's foreboding concerning Turambar came upon him after he had heard 'the tidings that Dorlas brought', and therefore knew who it was that lay on the bier; whereas in NE (p. 111) his foreboding is more prophetic and less 'rational' (see *Unfinished Tales* p. 111 and note 21). In NE Turambar 'laid his black sword by' in response to Brandir's warning (p. 112), but this is lost in GA.

§305 The new narrative is here further developed from Q (IV.128), where 'Thingol yielded so far to the tears and entreaties of Morwen that he sent forth a company of Elves toward Nargothrond to explore the truth. With them rode Morwen ...'; now she rides forth alone and the Elves are sent after her. Niënor's motive in joining the Elvish riders in disguise is now more complex; and Mablung, entirely absent from the story in Q (and AB 2), enters the narrative.

There is a very great reduction in GA of the elaborate story told in NE (pp. 112–16), but the narrative structure is the same (the flight of Morwen followed by the company led by Mablung). In NE

Thingol already had the idea of sending out a party to Nargothrond, independently of Morwen's wish to go.

In Q it seems certain that Niënor's presence was never revealed to the company, including Morwen (see my remarks, IV.185). The discovery of her at the passage of the Twilit Meres is not mentioned in GA, but that she was at some point revealed is implied by the words 'But Morwen ... would not be persuaded' (i.e. by the presence of Niënor); and Niënor was set with Morwen on the Hill of Spies. The condensation in the *Annals* of the story in NE here produces some obscurity, and in the passage in *The Silmarillion* (p. 217) corresponding to this paragraph I made use of both versions (and also Q), although at the time I misunderstood the relations between them.

The reference in NE (p. 114) to the hidden ferries at the Twilit Meres, not mentioned before, is lost in GA. In NE the sentence 'for by that way messengers would pass to and fro between Thingol and his kin in Nargothrond' continues in the manuscript 'ere the victory of Morgoth' (i.e. at Tumhalad), and these last words were changed to 'ere the death of Felagund'. This was omitted in the published text, in view of the later reference (*Unfinished Tales* p. 153) to the close relations of Orodreth with Menegroth: 'In all things [Orodreth] followed Thingol, with whom he exchanged messengers by secret ways'.

There appears here (in both versions) the Elvish name *Amon Ethir* of the Hill of Spies (the Spyhill, NE), and also (in NE only) its origin, which has never been given before: 'a mound as great as a hill that long ago Felagund had caused to be raised with great labour in the plain before his Doors'. In both versions it is a league from Nargothrond; in Q (IV.128) it was 'to the east of the Guarded Plain', but Morwen could see from its top the issuing of Glaurung. On the first map (following p. 220 in Vol.IV) it seems to be a long way east, or north-east, of Nargothrond (though 'Hill of Spies' is named on the map it is not perfectly clear where it is, IV.225); on the second map it is not named, but if it is the eminence marked on square F 6 (p. 182) it was likewise a long way from Nargothrond (about 15 leagues).

§306 'But Glaurung was aware of all that they did': where NE (p. 117) says of Glaurung that his eyes 'outreached the far sight of the Elves' a rejected form of the passage has the notable statement: 'Indeed further reached the sight of his fell eyes than even the eyes of the Elves (which thrice surpass those of Men).' Also, where it is said in NE that Glaurung 'went swiftly, for he was a mighty Worm, and yet lithe', there followed in the manuscript, but placed in brackets later, 'and he could go as speedily as a man could run, and tire not in a hundred leagues.'

§307 'Thus the ladies were lost, and of Morwen indeed no sure tidings came ever to Doriath after': so also in NE at a later point (p. 121): 'Neither then nor after did any certain news of her fate come to Doriath or to Dor-lómin', but against this my father wrote an X in the margin of the typescript. In NE the passage (p. 118) describing how one of the Elf-riders saw her as she disappeared into the mists crying *Nienor* replaced the following:

> After a while Morwen passed suddenly out of the mists, and near at hand there were two of the elf-riders; and whether she would or no her horse bore her with them swiftly away towards Doriath. And the riders comforted her, saying: 'You must go in our keeping. But others will guard your daughter. It is vain to tarry. Fear not! For she was mounted, and there is no horse but will make best speed away from the dragon-stench. We shall meet her in Doriath.'

This is another example of the precedence of NE as first written over GA; for this rejected text was apparently following the old story of Q (IV.128), that Morwen returned to Doriath. – In Q Nienor, whose presence was never revealed (see commentary on §305), did not go to the Hill of Spies with Morwen, but met with the Dragon on the banks of the Narog.

In the passage in NE (p. 118) describing the eyes of Glaurung when Nienor came face to face with him on the hill-top, the words 'they were terrible, being filled with the fell spirit of Morgoth, his master' contain an editorial alteration: the manuscript reads 'the fell spirit of Morgoth, who made him' (cf. IV.128). My father underlined the last three words in pencil, and faintly and barely legibly at the foot of the page he noted: 'Glaurung must be a demon [??contained in worm form].' On the emergence at this time of the view that Melkor could make nothing that had life of its own see X.74, 78.

§§309–12 There is a further great development in this passage (condensed from NE, pp. 119–21), following the enspelling of Nienor. There enters now Mablung's exploration of the deserted halls of Nargothrond; his discovery of Nienor on Amon Ethir in the early night; the meeting with the three other Elves of Mablung's company; the secret entrance into Doriath near the inflowing of Esgalduin; the attack by Orcs as they slept, and the slaying of the Orcs by Mablung and his companions; the flight of Nienor naked; and Mablung's return to Doriath and subsequent three-year-long search for Morwen and Nienor. In Q there is none of this; and it was Turambar with a party of the woodmen who slew the Orcs that pursued Nienor (IV.128–9).

§310 Where GA has 'the secret gate' into Doriath near the inflowing of Esgalduin into Sirion, NE (p. 120) has 'the guarded bridge'. A bridge is indeed more to be expected than a gate, for the Westmarch of Doriath, *Nivrim*, was within the Girdle of Melian (V.261–2).

§312 Similarly in the manuscript of NE, after 'until she went naked' (p. 121), the words 'but for the short elven-kirtle above the knee that she had worn in her disguise' were bracketed for exclusion.

§317 *The falls of Celebros.* In NE the passage beginning 'In the morning they bore Níniel towards Ephel Brandir' (pp. 122–3) replaced an earlier text, as follows:

In the morning they bore Níniel towards Ephel Brandir. Now there was a fair place on the way, a green sward amid white birches. There a stream leaping down from Amon Obel to find its way to the Taiglin went over a lip of worn stone, and fell into a rocky bowl far below, and all the air was filled with a soft spray, in which the sun would gleam with many colours. Therefore the woodmen called those falls *Celebros*, and loved to rest there a while.

The name *Celebros* first appeared in Q, 'the Falls of Silver-bowl' > 'the Falls of Celebros, Foam-silver', and the falls were in the Taiglin (see IV.129 and note 14). In GA the falls are still called *Celebros*, as in the passage just cited from NE from which it derives, but as in that passage my father would obviously have now placed them in the tributary stream falling down from Amon Obel towards the Taiglin.

In the NE manuscript, however, the passage was rewritten, and it is the rewritten text that stands in *Unfinished Tales* pp. 122–3: 'In the morning they bore Níniel towards Ephel Brandir, and the road went steeply upward towards Amon Obel until it came to a place where it must cross the tumbling stream of Celebros', &c. Thus *Celebros* becomes the name of the tributary stream, and in the continuation of this rewritten passage the falls themselves become *Dimrost*, the Rainy Stair. This change was not entered on the text of GA, but was incorporated in *The Silmarillion* (p. 220).

On the curious matter of the use in both versions of the name *Nen Girith* 'Shuddering Water' as if it were due to the fact of Níniel's fit of shuddering when she first came there, rather than to the prophetic nature of that shuddering whose meaning was not seen until she and Turambar were dead, see IV.186–7, where I discussed it fully.

§318 In Q (IV.129) it was said here that Brandir yielded the rule of the woodmen to Turambar (see commentary on §§301–3), and that 'he was ever true to Turambar; yet bitter was his soul when he might not win the love of Níniel.' This is not said in GA (or NE); but on the other hand there was nothing in Q about Níniel's delaying of the marriage, nor of Brandir's seeking to restrain her on account of his forebodings, nor yet of Brandir's revealing to her who Turambar was – indeed in Q, as I have mentioned (commentary on §§301–3), there is no indication that the woodmen knew his identity.

In NE, following the story in Q, the first draft of the passage begins: 'Turambar asked her in marriage, and she went to him gladly, and at the midsummer they were wed, and the woodmen made a great feast for them' (see NE pp. 124–5). In a second stage Brandir counselled Níniel to wait, but did not tell her that Turambar was Túrin son of Húrin: that entered with a further revision to the manuscript. GA has this final form. In NE (p. 125), however, Turambar's displeasure with Brandir was at his counsel of delay: in GA it was (apparently) at Brandir's revelation to Níniel of his identity. – The motive of Níniel's delaying of the marriage goes back to the *Tale* (II.102): 'she delayed him, saying nor yea nor no, yet herself she knew not why'.

§§322–5 Following the words in NE (p. 129) 'the tale of the scouts that had seen [Glaurung] had gone about and grown in the telling' the text as originally written continued:

> Then Brandir who stood [before his house in the open place of Ephel Brandir >] nigh spoke before them and said: 'I would fain come with thee, Captain Black Sword, but thou wouldst scorn me. Rightly. But

This was changed immediately to the text printed, with Dorlas' crying scorn on Brandir, who sat 'unheeded', 'in the high-seat of the lord of the assembly'.

Up to this point, drafting for the manuscript of NE consists of little more than scribbled slips. From here on, however, there are in effect two manuscripts: one (which I shall refer to as 'the draft manuscript') being the continuation of the original, which became so chaotic with rewriting that my father subsequently copied it out fair. The draft manuscript in this part of the narrative has much interest as showing my father's development of the story from the form it had reached in Q (IV.129–30).

The words given in NE to Brandir's kinsman Hunthor (Torbarth in GA) were given first to Brandir, speaking in self-defence:

> 'Thou speakest unjustly, Dorlas. How can it be said that my counsels were vain, when they were never taken? And I say to thee that Glaurung comes now to us, as to Nargothrond before, because our deeds have bewrayed us to him, as I feared. But the son of Handir asketh none to take his place at need. I am here and will gladly go. The less loss of a cripple unwedded than of many others. Will not some stand by me, who have also less care to leave behind?'

> Then five men came and stood by him. And Turambar said: 'That is enough. These five I will take. But, lord, I do not scorn thee, and any who do so are fools. But see! We must go in great haste ...'

[§§322-5]
This follows, in structure, the story in Q, where 'six of his boldest men begged to come with him'. In the draft manuscript 'Turambar with Dorlas and their five companions took horse and rode away in haste to Celebros'; and when later Turambar crossed the Taiglin (NE p. 133), 'in the deep dark he counted his following. They were four. "Albarth fell," said Dorlas, "and Taiglin took him beyond aid. The other two, I deem, were daunted, and skulk now yonder."' Albarth, who here first appears, seems to have been first written *Albard*.

The draft manuscript continues:

Then after a rest they that remained climbed, foot by foot, up the steep slope before them, till they came nigh the brink. There so foul grew the reek that their heads reeled, and they clung to the trees as best they could. The night was now passing, but there was a flicker above them as of smouldering fires, and a noise of some great beast sleeping; but if he stirred the earth quivered.

Dawn came slowly; and its glimmer came to Turambar as he strove with dark dreams of dread in which all his will had been given only to clinging and holding, while a great tide of blackness had sucked and gnawed at his limbs. And he woke and looked about in the wan light, and saw that only Dorlas remained by him.

'Seven wounds I hoped to give him,' he thought. 'Well, if it be two only, then they must go deep.'

But when day came indeed all passed as Turambar had hoped. For suddenly Glaurung bestirred himself, and drew himself slowly to the chasm's edge; and he did not turn aside, but prepared to spring over with his clawed forelegs and then draw his bulk after. Great was the horror of his coming, for he began the passage not right above Turambar, but many paces to the northward, and from under they could see his hideous head and gaping jaws as he peered over the brink. Then he let fly a blast, and the trees before him withered, and rocks fell into the river, and with that he cast himself forward and grappled the further bank and began to heave himself over the narrow chasm.

Now there was need of great haste, for though Turambar and Dorlas had escaped from the blast since they lay not right in Glaurung's path, they could not now come at him, and soon all the device of Turambar was in point to fail utterly. Heedless now of all else he clambered down, and Dorlas followed him. Then swiftly he came beneath the Worm; but there so deadly was the heat and the stench that he tottered and was almost blinded. And Dorlas because of the reek, or being daunted at last, clung to a tree by the water, and would not move   fell and lay as in a swoon [*sic; the sentence changed to:*] But Dorlas was overcome, and his

[§§322-5]
> will daunted at last, and he stumbled and fell and was engulfed in the water.
>   Then Turambar said aloud: 'Now thou art alone at the end, Master of Doom. Fail now or conquer!' And he summoned to him all his will, and all his hatred of the Worm and his Master, and climbed up, as one finding strength and skill beyond his measure; and lo! now the midmost parts of the dragon came above him...

I repeat here my remarks in IV.186:

> In the *Tale* (II.106) the band of seven clambered up the far side of the ravine in the evening and stayed there all night; at dawn of the second day, when the dragon moved to cross, Turambar saw that he had now only three companions, and when they had to climb back down to the stream-bed to come up under Glórund's belly these three had not the courage to go up again. Turambar slew the dragon by daylight... In Q the six all deserted Turambar during the first night... but he spent the whole of the following day clinging to the cliff; Glómund moved to pass over the ravine on the *second* night (my father clearly wished to make the dragon-slaying take place in darkness, but achieved this at first by extending the time Turambar spent in the gorge).

Curiously enough, in the text just given my father reverted, so far as the time-scale is concerned, to the story in the *Tale*, where Turambar spent the whole night in the ravine and the dragon moved to cross at the beginning of the next day (see further the commentary on §§329–32).

In the condensed account in Q nothing is said of the need to move along the river and then to climb up again to come under the dragon's belly ('The next evening... Glómund began the passage of the ravine, and his huge form *passed over Turambar's head*'); and here also it seems certain that my father went back to the *Tale*, where this is described in a way very similar to that in the draft manuscript of NE. In the *Tale* as in this draft there is no suggestion that the men had taken into account the possibility that the dragon might not cross at the point they had chosen (and therefore, in the final version, after attempting to climb they returned – as it must be assumed: it is not expressly stated – to the bottom of the ravine and waited); in both, they climbed up the far side of the gorge and clung beneath its brink, whence they had to climb down again to the water when the dragon moved. Dorlas' failure 'because of the reek' when he and Turambar came, in the riverbed, beneath the dragon corresponds to the failure of the three men in the *Tale*, who 'durst not climb the bank again' because 'the heat was so great and so vile the stench' (II.107).

[§§322-5]
The behaviour of Turambar's companions in the different versions can be set out thus:

The Tale
Three deserted during the night
The three others climbed down with Turambar to get beneath the dragon, but dared not climb up again

The Quenta
All six deserted during the (first) night (nothing is said of the need to change position)

Draft manuscript of NE
Two feared to cross the river and one (Albarth) was drowned in the crossing
Two more fled away during the night
The last (Dorlas) climbed down with Turambar to get beneath the dragon, but dared not climb up again

The revised and final story (NE pp. 133–4) is far better (and of course the version in GA, though very brief, is in agreement with it). By this time the passage in which Brandir defends himself against Dorlas (p. 152) had been emended to the final form (NE p. 129), except that Albarth (at first simply one of the five volunteers, but named because he fell and was drowned in the river) had become the kinsman of Brandir who rebukes Dorlas. There are now only two companions of Turambar, and the hard and boastful warrior Dorlas becomes the coward, while Albarth is the brave man who stays beside Turambar until he is struck by a falling stone. The development is a characteristic complex:

Brandir defends himself against Dorlas' scorn	Albarth defends Brandir against Dorlas' scorn
Turambar takes six companions	Turambar takes Dorlas and Albarth only as companions
One of these, Albarth, is drowned in the crossing; four flee; only Dorlas remains by Turambar	Dorlas flees Albarth remains by Turambar
Dorlas is drowned in the river	Albarth is drowned in the river

A curious detail in the final form of the story is worth remarking. In the new account, it occurs to Turambar that they are wasting their strength in climbing up the far side of the gorge *before* the dragon moves. It is not said that they descended from whatever point they had reached when he came to this realisation, and the passage concerning his dream 'in which all his will was given to

[§§322-5]

clinging' reappears from the earlier version (p. 153). But in the new story there was no need for them to cling: they could have, and surely would have, descended to the bottom and waited there. In fact, it is clear that this is what they did: it is said (NE p. 134) that when Glaurung moved to cross the ravine they were not standing right in his path, and Turambar at once 'clambered along the water-edge'. Thus the revised story still carries an unneeded trait from the earlier.

A draft slip, not fully legible, shows my father working out the new story:

Let Túrin slay dragon at nightfall. He reaches Nen Girith as sun is going down. He warns them that Glaurung will move in *dark*. He outlines his plan. They go down to Taiglin but there the heart fails his men, and they say: 'Lord, forgive us, but our hearts are not great enough for the venture. For [*illegible words*] the thought of those we have left.'

'What of me?' said Turambar. He dismissed them with scorn.

He goes on with Dorlas and Albarth.

This is an intermediate stage: there are other 'volunteers' beside Dorlas and Albarth, but they beg off before the crossing of the river. These others were abandoned.

This may seem much ado about a single episode, but it seems to me to illustrate in miniature the complex and subtle movement that is found in the history of the legends at large. It was, also, an episode of great importance: there are few 'monsters' to rival Glaurung, and my father strove to perfect the tale of how Túrin earned the title of *Dagnir Glaurunga*.

It remains to mention that in the final manuscript of NE *Albarth* was changed to *Torbarth*, the name in GA; but at all occurrences in NE of *Torbarth* it was changed later to *Hunthor*. In GA this further alteration was not made (it was of course adopted in *The Silmarillion*), but at the first occurrence only (§322) of *Torbarth* in GA my father pencilled above it *Gwerin*: on this name see further pp. 163–5.

§323 In the *Narn* (p. 132) it is told that Níniel and the people with her came to Nen Girith 'just at nightfall', but in the draft manuscript they reached the falls 'at the first breath of morning' (see commentary on §§329–32). In the draft manuscript, also, Brandir did not limp slowly after the others on his crutch, but 'took the small ambling horse that was trained to bear him, and he rode westward after Níniel and her companions. And many that saw him go had pity, for in truth he was well beloved by many.'

§324 As in GA, *Cabad-en-Aras* was corrected throughout, except where omitted by oversight, to *Cabed-en-Aras* on the final text of NE. The draft manuscript had *Mengas Dûr*, changed to *Cabad-en-*

Aras at the time of writing. In NE (p. 130) Turambar says of the ravine that over it, 'as you tell, a deer once leaped from the huntsmen of Haleth', and later (p. 140) Brandir says that Níniel 'leaped from the brink of the Deer's Leap'.

In NE (p. 130), when Turambar came to Nen Girith at sunset, he looked out over the falls, and seeing the spires of smoke rising by the banks of the Taiglin he said to his companions that this was good news, because he had feared that Glaurung would change his course and come to the Crossings, 'and so to the old road in the lowland'. I take this to be the old south road to Nargothrond, coming down from the Pass of Sirion and running through the western eaves of Brethil on its way to the Crossings; but the draft manuscript has here 'and so along the old road to Bar Haleth', against which my father wrote later: 'into deep Brethil'. *Bar Haleth* was written in above *Tavrobel* (struck out) on the map (see p. 186, §19). Beyond the fact that 'Tavrobel' was in the extreme east of Brethil it is not possible to be sure of its site. *Bar Haleth* was in turn crossed out. It seems certain therefore that this was a transient name for Ephel Brandir, which was marked in subsequently in the centre of Brethil; and 'the old road' in the draft manuscript distinct from that referred to in the final text.

§325 In NE it is told (p. 131) that from Nen Girith Turambar and his companions took the path to the Crossings, but 'before they came so far, they turned southward by a narrow track', and moved through the woods above the Taiglin towards Cabed-en-Aras. Mr Charles Noad has suggested that my sketch-map in *Unfinished Tales*, p. 149, should be modified, and the track shown to turn again *westward* to reach the Taiglin: thus 'The first stars glimmered in the East *behind* them'. See further p. 159, §333.

'So ended the last of the right kin of Haleth': 'right kin' must mean 'direct line'. But Torbarth was not the last, for Brandir, son of Handir son of Hundor son of Haleth, still lived.

§§329–32 The narrative of these paragraphs as first written in NE had many differences from the final text (pp. 135–7, beginning 'Now the screams of Glaurung came to the people at Nen Girith ...'), and I give the earlier text (which exists in two drafts); for the time-scale see commentary on §§322–5.

Now when the screams of Glaurung came to the folk at Nen Girith they were filled with terror; and the watchers beheld from afar the great breaking and burning that the Worm made in his throes, and deemed that he was trampling and destroying all those that had assailed him. Then those that had been most eager to come and see strange deeds were most eager to go, ere Glaurung should discover them. All therefore fled, either wild into the woods, or back towards Ephel Brandir.

[§§329–32]

But when Níniel heard the voice of the Worm, her heart died within her, and a shadow of her darkness fell on her, and she sat still, shuddering by Nen Girith.

The morning passed, and still she did not stir from the spot. So it was that Brandir found her. For he came at last to the bridge, spent and weary, having limped all the long way alone on his crutch; and it was seven leagues from Ephel Brandir. Fear had urged him on. For he met with some of those that fled back, and heard all that they had to tell. 'The Black Sword is surely dead, and all with him,' they said. But when he found that Níniel was not with them, and that they had left her behind in their terror, he cursed them and pressed on to Nen Girith, thinking to defend her or comfort her.

But now that he saw her still living, he found naught to say, and had neither counsel nor comfort, and stood silent looking on her misery with pity.

Time wore on, and the sun began to wester, and there came neither sound nor tidings. Brandir looking out could see no longer any smoke by the Taiglin. And suddenly he thought in his heart: 'Beyond doubt he is slain. But Níniel lives.' And he looked at her and his heart yearned towards her, and then he was aware that it was cold in that high place; and he went and cast his cloak about her, but she said naught to him. And he stood yet a while, and he could hear no sound but the voices of the trees and the birds and the water, and he thought: 'Surely the Worm is gone, and has passed into Brethil. He will overtake the hapless folk on the way.' But he pitied them no more: fools that had flouted his counsel. Nor his people waiting in Ephel Brandir: he had forsaken them. Thither Glaurung surely would go fast, and he would have time to lead Níniel away and escape. Whither he scarce knew, for he had never strayed beyond Brethil [*first draft only:* and though he knew of the Hidden Kingdom he knew little more than that its king loved not Men, and few were ever admitted]. But time was fleeting, and soon evening would come.

Then he went again to Níniel's side, and said: 'It groweth late, Níniel. What wouldst thou do?'

'I know not,' said she. 'For I am adread. But could I overcome my shuddering, I would arise and go, and seek my lord; though I fear that he is dead.'

Then Brandir knew not what to answer; and he said: 'All is strange. Who shall read the signs? But if he lives, would he not go to Ephel Brandir, where he left thee? And the bridge of Nen Girith doth not lie on the only road, or the straightest, thither from the place of battle.'

[§§329–32]
    Then Níniel was roused at last, and she stood up, crying: 'Towards tidings I came hither, and yet all tidings I miss! Hath some spell been laid on me that I linger here?' And she began to hasten down the path from the bridge. But Brandir called to her: 'Níniel! Go not alone. I will go with thee. Thou knowest not what thou may find. A healer thou mayest need. But if the dragon lies there, then beware! For the creatures of Morgoth die hard, and are dangerous in death.'

    But she heeded him not and went now as though her blood burned her, which before had been cold. And though he followed as he could, because of his lameness she passed away until she was out of his sight. Then Brandir cursed his fate and his weakness, but still he held on.

    Night fell and all the woods were still; and the moon rose away beyond Amon Obel, and the glades became pale. And Níniel ran on; but as she came down from the upland towards the river it seemed to her that she remembered the place, and feared it.

Thus Níniel passed the whole of the day at Nen Girith (in this earlier version she and the people with her had come there 'at the first breath of morning', commentary on §323, and Glaurung was slain in the morning); when Brandir perceived that it was cold and cast his cloak about her it was the second evening, whereas in the final story it was the night of Glaurung's death (and no long time can elapse between his death, Brandir's coming to Nen Girith, and Níniel's running down to Cabed-en-Aras). A further important divergence, among many other differences of detail, is that in the earlier all the people fled from Nen Girith, leaving Níniel alone. But from this point the draft manuscript and the final manuscript become closely similar.

§332 In NE (p. 136), as also at the end of the earlier version given in the commentary on §§329–32, 'the moon rose beyond Amon Obel'. The sketch-map in *Unfinished Tales* (p. 149) is not well oriented: as is seen from revisions made to the second map (and so reproduced on my map to the published *Silmarillion*), Amon Obel was almost due east of the Crossings of Taiglin.

§333 There are two points of detail to be mentioned in the text of NE corresponding to this paragraph. The words concerning the track that Brandir took to head off Níniel, 'went steeply down southward to the river' (p. 137), were an editorial change from the reading of the manuscript, which has 'went steeply down westward'. The change was made because it is expressly said here that it was the path that Turambar and his companions had taken earlier: cf. p. 131 'they turned southward by a narrow track'; but Mr Noad's clearly correct suggestion (see p. 157, §325) makes this emendation unnecessary. Secondly, in the words of Glaurung to Níniel at his death (p. 138) 'We meet again ere the end', 'ere the end' is a simple error for 'ere we end'.

§334 '[She] ran like a hunted deer, and came to Cabed-en-Aras': the name Cabed-en-Aras referred to the actual ravine in the Taiglin, and (as I suggested in *Unfinished Tales* p. 150, note 27) it may be supposed that the death-leap of Glaurung had carried him a good distance beyond the further cliff, so that Níniel had some way to run to the ravine. The wording of NE is clearer: 'Swiftly she came to the brink of Cabed-en-Aras'.

§335 *Cabad Naeramarth*: in an earlier form of this passage in NE (p. 138) the name was *Cabad Amarth* 'Leap of Doom'. In §§335, 346 *Cabad* was not corrected.

§§336–7 In Q there was no mention of Brandir's bringing the tidings to the waiting people. This was due to Q's compression, for it appears in the *Tale* (II.110); and his words in GA (deriving from NE) 'and those tidings are good' echo those in the *Tale*: 'and that is well; aye very well': in both, those who heard him thought that he was mad.

§§339–42 Q was here exceedingly compressed, saying only: 'he asked for Níniel, but none dared tell him, save Brandir. And Brandir distraught with grief reproached him; wherefore Túrin slew him ...' The complex scene in NE and GA goes back in a very general way to the *Tale* (II.111); there also Turambar calls Tamar (Brandir) 'Clubfoot', and it is this (as it appears) that leads him to tell all that he knows, which in turn incites Turambar to murder him, believing him to be lying out of malice.

§§346–7 In the *Tale* and Q the voice from the sword does not speak of Beleg or of Brandir. In NE as first written Turambar himself named them in his address to the sword: 'From no blood wilt thou shrink. Not from Beleg slain in madness, not from Brandir slain unjustly. That was a wicked deed, thou black sword. Do now a better and take Túrin Turambar! Wilt thou slay me swiftly?' And the voice from the blade replied: 'Thy blood will I gladly drink. For it is of the best, and sweeter will it seem than any that thou hast given me. Swift will I slay thee!' – echoing the words of Gurtholfin in the *Tale*, II.112; cf. also Q, IV.130.

§349 The sword was not broken in the *Tale* or in Q. – At the top of the manuscript page my father wrote hastily in pencil: 'Túrin should slay himself on Finduilas' tomb' (cf. *Unfinished Tales* p. 150, note 28).

The conclusion of NE (p. 146) in the manuscript actually reads: 'Thus endeth the tale of the Children of Húrin [*added:*] as it was told in the *Glaer nia* [later > *Narn i*] *Chîn Húrin*, the longest of all the lays of Beleriand.' The conclusion added afterwards to GA is thus almost exactly the same as that in NE, which does not however have the words 'and was made by Men'; with this cf. X.373.

NOTE 1

Variant forms at the end of the tale of the Children of Húrin

There are, first, some rough draft texts that sketch out ideas for the dénouement of the tragedy; there can be no doubt that they were all abandoned in favour of the actual ending in NE and GA. One of them, beginning as in NE p. 143 immediately after the slaying of Brandir, reads as follows:

> now cursing Middle-earth and all the life of Men, now calling upon Níniel. But when at last the madness left him, he walked still in the wild bent and haggard, and pondered all his life in his thought, and ever Níniel's image was before him. And now with opened eye he saw her, remembering his father: there in woman's form was his voice and his face and the bend of his brows, and his hair like to gold, even as Túrin had the dark hair and the grey eyes, the [?pale cheek] and [*illegible words*] of Morwen his mother of the House of Bëor. Doubt could not be. But how had it chanced? Where then was Morwen? Had they never reached the H[idden] K[ingdom]? How had they met Glaurung? But no, he dared never seek Morwen.

I believe that this was a soon abandoned idea that Túrin could come, through his own reflections, to a recognition that what Brandir had said was true. It was displaced by the story of the coming of Mablung to the Crossings of Taiglin and meeting Túrin there.

In two related passages my father entertained the idea that Túrin met Morwen before his end. The first is very brief:

> And as he sat like a beggar-man near the Crossings of Taiglin, an old woman came by bowed on a stick; ragged she was and forlorn and her grey hair blew wild in the wind. But she gave him good-day, saying: 'And good day it is, master, for the sun is warm, and then hunger gnaws less. These are evil days for our likes: for I see by your bearing that, as I and so many, you have seen prouder days. In the summer we can drag on our lives, but who dare look beyond winter?'
>
> 'Whither go you, lady?' he said, 'for so methinks you were once wont to be called.'
>
> 'Nowhither,' she answered. 'I have long since ceased to seek what I missed. Now I took for naught but what will keep me over night to the next grey dawn. Tell me, whither goes this green road? Do any still dwell in the deep forest? And are they as fell as wanderers' tales tell?'

'What say they?' he asked.

This is followed on the manuscript page by 'now cursing Middle-earth and all the life of Men' &c., leading into a draft of the final version, where Mablung appears at the Crossings.

The second of these passages is longer, but only barely legible and in places altogether illegible. It begins in the same way as that just given, but Morwen's second speech ends at 'I look for naught beyond what will keep me through the cold night to next dawn.' Then Túrin speaks:

'I seek not either,' said he. 'For what I had is now lost utterly and is gone from Middle-earth for ever. But what would you seek?'

'What would an old woman seek,' said she, 'out in the wild, but her children, even if all say they be dead. I sought for a son once, but he went long ago. Then I sought for my daughter, but 'tis five years since she was lost in the wild. Five years is a long time for one young and fair – if the Worm did not get her, the Orcs have [*illegible*], or the [?cold heedless] wild.'

Then suddenly T[úrin]'s heart stood still. 'What like was your daughter, lady? Or what maybe was her name?'

The old woman told him that her daughter was tall, with golden hair and blue eyes, fleet-footed, a lover of all things that grow;

'... Yet a little she leaped in her words, as her sire did also. Nienor daughter of Húrin she would have named herself, an you asked her. But maybe it would mean naught. For the name of Húrin was great [*illegible words*] All the realms [*illegible words*] are beaten down and mean folk or evil are lords. Yet you are of the older folk, I deem. I see by thy face that the old name meant somewhat to thee still.'

Túrin stared at her as a man that sees a ghost. 'Yea,' said he at last slowly. 'The name of Húrin of Hithlum and Morwen Baragund's daughter was known to me.

Of the remainder I can only read snatches:

and Morwen and her daughter went to the Hidden Kingdom [*illegible*] they say in Hithlum.' The old woman laughed bitterly. 'And what else did they say? That first Túrin went there and was used by the king in his border wars and lost, but came to Nargothrond and that Morwen went to seek him there with tardy aid of Thingol, but [*illegible words*] by the great drake Glaurung. [*illegible words*] Then she wept [*illegible words*]

This is clearly the beginning of another narrative route whereby Túrin might learn the truth, likewise abandoned before it was developed. – A pencilled note shows the entry of the 'Mablung-intervention':

Mablung searches and brings tidings to Thingol of Glaurung setting forth. This coincides with rumour (among orcs and wanderers) that the Black Sword has reappeared in Brethil. Mablung comes to Brethil (without orders from Thingol?) to warn Túrin and bring news of Nienor and Morwen.

Note 1   THE GREY ANNALS   163

Morwen should go back to Thingol and then depart as a beggar in the wild.

Lastly, and very remarkable, there is the following synopsis of the end of the story, written carefully on a slip, apparently over the same or similar text set down very roughly in pencil:

> Turambar sets out. Asks for two companions. Dorlas volunteers, and speaks scorn of Brandir. Gwerin kinsman of Brandir volunteers. Brandir is embittered. Turambar bids Níniel stay at home.
>
> When T[urambar] has gone Níniel insists on following. Brandir forbids but she takes no heed. Brandir appears to the Men of Brethil, but they will not obey him – they beg Níniel to remain, but as she will not, they will not restrain her by force. The wives of Dorlas and Gwerin go with her. Brandir follows after them.
>
> The slaying of the Dragon may be told more or less as already done. But when Níniel reaches Nen Girith shuddering again takes her, and she can go no further. The wives also are not willing to go on – for they meet the scouts at Nen Girith and learn how near the Worm is..... [*sic*]
>
> When Túrin draws his sword out of Glaurung's belly, Glaurung's blood burns his sword hand; *also* Glaurung speaks to him, and says that Níniel is his sister. Túrin falls into a swoon of pain and horror.
>
> The Dragon dies. Suddenly Níniel recovers her memory and all her past life is revealed to her. She sits aghast. Brandir sees her anguish, but believes that it is due to belief that Túrin has been slain – the dreadful cries of Glaurung have been heard at Nen Girith. Níniel gets up to flee, and Brandir thinking that she will really go in search of Túrin (while Glaurung is abroad) restrains her, saying *Wait!*
>
> She turns to him, crying that this was ever his counsel, and to her sorrow she did not take it. But he may give that counsel once too often!
>
> As indeed it proved. For at that moment Túrin appears. When the Dragon died his swoon also departed, but the anguish of the venom on his hand remained. He came, therefore, to Nen Girith for help, believing the scouts there. (It is Túrin that slays Dorlas on the way?)
>
> As Turambar appears, Níniel gives a wail, crying: 'Túrin son of Húrin! Too late have we met. The dark days are gone. But night comes after!' 'How know you that name?' 'Brandir told me, and behold! I am Niënor. Therefore we must part.' And with that, ere any could hold her, she leapt over the fall of Nen Girith, and so ended, crying 'Water, water, wash me clean! Wash me of my life!'
>
> Then the anguish of Túrin was terrible to see; and a mad fury took him, and he cursed Middle-earth and all the life of Men. And stooping over the falls, he cried in vain *Níniel, Níniel*. And he turned

in wrath upon all those that were there, against his command; and all fled away from him, save only Brandir, who for ruth and horror could not move. But Túrin turned to him and said: 'Behold thy work, limping evil! Had Níniel remained, as I left her, and hadst thou not told my name, she might have been restrained from death. I could have gone away and left her, and she might have mourned for Turambar only.'

But Brandir cursed him, saying that their wedding could not have been hid; and that it was Túrin who wrought all this grief. 'And me thou hast shorn of all that I had, and would have – for thou art reckless and greedy!'

Then Túrin slew Brandir in his wrath. And repenting, he slew himself (using same words to the sword).

Mablung comes with news, and is heart-stricken. The Elves help the Halethrim to build a mound or memorial for the Children of Húrin – but N[íniel] was not there, and her body could not be found: mayhap Celebros bore it to Taiglin and Taiglin to the Sea.

A further simplification would be to make Brandir willing to go with Níniel, to guard her – for he thought Túrin would die.

This last sentence presumably refers to Brandir's attempt to stop Níniel from following Turambar from Ephel Brandir.

It seems impossible actually to demonstrate at what point in the evolution of the legend this was written, but that it is anyway as late as the rewritten, final form of the last part of the *Narn* is clear from such a detail as that *Celebros* is the name of the stream (see commentary on §317). I think that it belongs with the other passages given in this Note, in that it represents another, though far more drastic, attempt to reach the dénouement of Túrin's 'recognition' – this time from Nienor herself, who has learned the truth through no intermediary, but simply from the removal of the spell on her memory by the Dragon's death. But Mablung appears, though now after Túrin's death, and so I suspect that it is the latest of these attempts, and may very probably have *succeeded* the final form of the text. *Gwerin* as the name of Brandir's kinsman (Albarth, Torbarth, Hunthor) has appeared once before, pencilled over the first occurrence of Torbarth in GA (§322).

That my father should even have contemplated, to the extent of roughing out a synopsis, breaking so violently the superb interlocking narrative structure represented by the final text of the last part of the *Narn* is extraordinary and hard to fathom. Did he feel that it had become too evidently a 'structure', too complex in those interlocking movements, reports, forebodings, chances? The concluding note ('A *further simplification* would be ...') may support this. But it seems to me most probable that he was primarily concerned with the coming of Mablung (or indeed Morwen) as a *deus ex machina* at that very moment, bearer of the irrefutable proof, which he felt to be a serious weakness.

However this may be, the result is, I think, and granting that it is only represented by a rapid synopsis written in a certain way, far weaker; and since, apart perhaps from the pencilled name *Gwerin* in the *Grey Annals*, there is no other trace of it, it may be that he thought likewise.

NOTE 2

A further account of the Battle of Unnumbered Tears

The text of Chapter 20 in the published *Silmarillion* was primarily derived from the story in the *Grey Annals*, but elements were introduced from the old Chapter 16 in QS (V.307–13), and also from a third text. This is a typescript made by my father, and to all appearance made *ab initio* on his typewriter; it was explicitly intended as a component in the long prose Tale of the Children of Húrin (the *Narn*), but he had the manuscript of the *Grey Annals* in front of him, and for much of its length the new version remained so close to the *Annals* text that it can be regarded as scarcely more than a variant, although unquestionably much later. For this reason, and also because some of its divergent (additional) features had in any case been incorporated in the *Silmarillion* chapter, I excluded it from the *Narn* in *Unfinished Tales* (see pp. 65–6 and note 2 in that book), except for its end. There is however a major divergence in the *Narn* account which altogether contradicts the previous versions, and this is a convenient place to record it, together with some other details.

The text opens as follows (the typescript was a good deal corrected in ink, I think almost certainly very soon after it had been made, and I adopt these corrections silently except in certain cases).

Many songs are yet sung, and many tales are yet told by the Elves of the Nirnaeth Arnoediad, the Battle of Unnumbered Tears, in which Fingon fell and the flower of the Eldar withered. If all were now retold a man's life would not suffice for the hearing. Here then shall be recounted only those deeds which bear upon the fate of the House of Hador and the children of Húrin the Steadfast.

Having gathered at length all the strength that he could Maedros appointed a day, the morning of Midsummer. On that day the trumpets of the Eldar greeted the rising of the Sun, and in the east was raised the standard of the Sons of Fëanor; and in the west the standard of Fingon, King of the Noldor.

Then Fingon looked out from the walls of Eithel Sirion, and

his host was arrayed in the valleys and woods upon the east borders of Eryd-wethion, well hid from the eyes of the Enemy; but he knew that it was very great. For there all the Noldor of Hithlum were assembled, and to them were gathered many Elves of the Falas and [*struck out at once:* a great company] of Nargothrond; and he had great strength of Men. Upon the right were stationed the host of Dor-lómin and all the valour of Húrin and Huor his brother, and to them had come Hundar of Brethil, their kinsman, with many men of the woods.

Then Fingon looked east and his elven-sight saw far off a dust and the glint of steel like stars in a mist, and he knew that Maedros had set forth; and he rejoiced. Then he looked towards Thangorodrim, and behold! there was a dark cloud about it and a black smoke went up; and he knew that the wrath of Morgoth was kindled and that their challenge would be accepted, and a shadow fell upon his heart. But at that moment a cry went up, passing on the wind from the south from vale to vale, and Elves and Men lifted up their voices in wonder and joy. For unsummoned and unlooked-for Turgon had opened the leaguer of Gondolin, and was come with an army, ten thousand strong, with bright mail and long swords and spears like a forest. Then when Fingon heard afar the great trumpet of Turgon, the shadow passed and his heart was uplifted, and he shouted aloud: *Utulie'n aurë! Aiya Eldalië ar Atanatarni, utulie'n aurë!* (The day has come! Lo, people of the Eldar and Fathers of Men, the day has come!) And all those who heard his great voice echo in the hills answered crying: *Auta i lómë!* (The night is passing!)

It was not long before the great battle was joined. For Morgoth knew much of what was done and designed by his foes and had laid his plans against the hour of their assault. Already a great force out of Angband was drawing near to Hithlum, while another and greater went to meet Maedros to prevent the union of the powers of the kings. And those that came against Fingon were clad all in dun raiment and showed no naked steel, and thus were already far over the sands before their approach became known.

Then the heart of Fingon [> the hearts of the Noldor] grew hot, and he [> their captains] wished to assail their foes on the plain; but Húrin [> Fingon] spoke against this.

'Beware of the guile of Morgoth, lords!' he said. 'Ever his strength is more than it seems, and his purpose other than he reveals. Do not reveal your own strength, but let the enemy spend his first in assault on the hills. At least until the signal of Maedros is seen.' For it was the design of the kings that Maedros should march openly over the Anfauglith with all his strength, of Elves and of Men and of Dwarves; and when he had drawn forth, as he hoped, the main armies of Morgoth in answer, then Fingon should come on from the west, and so the might of Morgoth should be taken as between hammer and anvil and be broken to pieces; and the signal for this was to be the firing of a great beacon in Dorthonion.

But the Captain of Morgoth in the west had been commanded to draw out Fingon from his hills by whatever means he could.

It is most remarkable that in this *Narn* version there is no reference whatever to the hindering of Maedros by the guile of Uldor the Accursed; while on the other hand there is here the entirely new statement that a second and greater force left Angband to intercept Maedros and 'prevent the union of the powers of the kings' (contrast GA §222, where it is said that Morgoth 'trusted in his servants to hold back Maidros and prevent the union of his foes' – referring of course to the machinations of Uldor). Later in this narrative, the passage corresponding to the opening of GA §228 reads:

Then in the plain of Anfauglith, on the fourth day of the war, there began the Nirnaeth Arnoediad, all the sorrow of which no tale can contain. Of all that befell in the eastward battle: of the routing of Glaurung the Drake by the Naugrim of Belegost; of the treachery of the Easterlings and the overthrow of the host of Maedros and the flight of the Sons of Fëanor, no more is here said. In the west the host of Fingon retreated over the sands ...

Here 'the eastward battle' is spoken of as if it were altogether separate from the fighting in the west: there is no suggestion here that the host of Maedros finally came up and fell upon the rear of the enemy (GA §229). Finally, where in GA the meeting of Turgon and Húrin in the midst of the battle is followed (§229) by the coming of the host of Maidros, the *Narn* version reads:

And it is said that the meeting of Turgon with Húrin who stood beside Fingon was glad in the midst of battle. For a while then the hosts of Angband were driven back, and Fingon again began his retreat. But having routed Maedros in the east Morgoth had now great forces to spare, and before Fingon and Turgon could come to the shelter of the hills they were assailed by a tide of foes thrice greater than all the force that was left to them.

With these last words the *Narn* version returns to the GA text at §233. Thus my father, for whatever reason, had expunged the entire element of 'the machinations of Uldor' in delaying Maedros, and radically altered the course of the Battle of Unnumbered Tears by introducing the defeat and rout of the eastern host before any junction of the forces was achieved.

In *The Silmarillion* I preserved (inevitably) the story as told in the *Grey Annals*, but incorporated certain elements from the *Narn*, as may be seen from a comparison of the opening of the latter (pp. 165–6) with *The Silmarillion* pp. 190–1: the cloud and smoke over Thangorodrim, the great cry of Fingon, the 'dun raiment' of the force from Angband that came towards Hithlum. Some other minor points in this passage may be mentioned. The 'great company from Nargothrond' (see §221 and commentary) is corrected (p. 166); and the name of the leader of the men of Brethil, in GA Hundor son of Haleth the Hunter, is changed to Hundar: later in the text his father is said to be Halmir – an aspect of the extremely complex refashioning of the genealogies of the Edain which need not be entered into here (see pp. 236–8).

In GA (§222), following QS (§11), it was Fingon who was all for attacking at once the force from Angband on the plain, and Húrin who opposed it; this was followed in the *Narn*, but then corrected to make it Fingon who opposed the rashness of his captains. The change was perhaps made for probability's sake: such prudence and experience of Morgoth should lie rather with Fingon King of the Noldor than with Húrin, a Man of no more than thirty-one years. – Húrin (> Fingon) urged that the western host should wait in its positions 'at least until the signal of Maedros is seen'. In GA (§217) the occasion of the signal of Maidros to Fingon (not particularised as a beacon in Dorthonion) was to be the moment when the march of Maidros in open force over Anfauglith had incited the host of Morgoth to come forth from Angband; and owing to Uldor the Accursed the signal did not come. In the *Narn* Fingon with his far sight had actually seen that Maedros had set out, and it is also told that great force was on its way from Angband to meet him; but it is not said that the beacon was fired.

Other features of the story as told in *The Silmarillion* that are not found in GA are derived from the *Narn*. In the latter there is a more detailed account of the confrontation between the two hosts, and the riders of Morgoth come to the walls of the fortress at Eithel Sirion (here called *Barad Eithel*): thus whereas in GA Gwindor saw the slaughter of his brother Gelmir 'across the water', in the *Narn* he was 'at that point in the outposts'. The account of the western battle is very close indeed to that in GA, but the death of Fingon is differently and more fully told (see *The Silmarillion* p. 193): with the coming of Gothmog 'high-captain of Angband' Fingon was cut off from Húrin and Turgon, who were driven towards the Fen of Serech. The speeches of Turgon, Húrin, and Huor were scarcely changed from their form in GA (§§234–5), but the needed change in Huor's words to 'I shall never look on thy white walls *again*' was made (see the commentary on §§234–5). Lastly, in the *Narn* it is said that Húrin 'seized the axe of an Orc-captain and wielded it two-handed', and again Gothmog appears (see *The Silmarillion* p. 195).

In the account of the Mound of the Slain the *Narn* version names it *Haudh-en-Ndengin*, subsequently changed to *Haudh-en-Nirnaeth*.

The *Narn* text concludes with a remarkable elaboration of the confrontation of Húrin and Morgoth on the basis of GA §§244–8 (itself an elaboration of QS §§21–3); this was the only part of the text included in *Unfinished Tales* (pp. 66–8). As the speeches were typed they were set entirely in the second person singular, 'thou wert', 'knowest thou', etc.; but my father went through it changing every 'thou' and 'thee' to 'you', and the equivalent verb-forms – and changing 'Knowest thou' to 'Do you know' rather than 'Know you' (also 'puissant' to 'mighty'). In this form, of course, the text was printed in *Unfinished Tales*.

NOTE 3

A further account of the coming of Húrin and Huor to Gondolin

As in the case of the story of the Battle of Unnumbered Tears described in Note 2 above, there is also a version of that of Húrin and Huor in Gondolin found as a component of the *Narn*. This is even more closely based on the story in the *Grey Annals* §§161–6: while there are many small variations in the precise wording, virtually none are of any moment in respect of the narrative, until the end is reached, where a significant difference appears. This story was excluded from the *Narn* in *Unfinished Tales*, but its existence noted: p. 146, note 1. Before the end the only point worth mentioning is that Maeglin's words (GA §165) are here much fiercer: 'The king's grace to you is greater than ye know; and some might wonder wherefore the strict law is abated for two knave-children of Men. It would be safer if they had no choice but to abide here as our servants to their life's end.'

According to the story in GA, Húrin and Huor told when they returned to Dor-lómin that 'they had dwelt a while in honour in the halls of King Turgon', even though they would say nothing else. Against this my father noted on the GA typescript (p. 127, §166): 'They did not reveal Turgon's name'; and in the *Narn* version they refused altogether to declare even to their father where they had been. This version was adopted in the published *Silmarillion* (p. 159), with only a change at the end. Here the *Narn* text has:

Then Galion [> Galdor] questioned them no more; but he and many others guessed at the truth. For both the oath of silence and the Eagles pointed to Turgon, men thought.

The conclusion of the passage in *The Silmarillion* ('and in time the strange fortune of Húrin and Huor reached the ears of the servants of Morgoth') was taken from the GA version.

On these two (otherwise so closely similar) texts of the story see further p. 314.

PART TWO

THE LATER
QUENTA SILMARILLION

THE LATER *QUENTA SILMARILLION*

In Part Two I shall trace the development of the *Quenta Silmarillion*, in the years following the completion of *The Lord of the Rings*, from the point reached in Vol.X, p. 199; but the history now becomes (for the most part) decidedly simpler: much of the development can be conveyed by recording individually all the significant changes made to QS, and there is no need to divide it into two 'phases', as was done in Vol.X. The basic textual series is QS (so far as it went before its abandonment); the early amanuensis typescript 'LQ 1' of 1951, for which see X.141–3; and the late amanuensis typescript 'LQ 2' of about 1958, for which see X.141-2, 300.

In this latter part of the history the chapter-numbers become rather confusing, but I think that it would be more confusing to have none, and therefore I continue the numbering used in Vol.X, where the last chapter treated, *Of the Sun and Moon and the Hiding of Valinor*, was given the number 8.

9 OF MEN

This chapter was numbered 7 in the QS manuscript (for the text see V.245–7, §§81–7). The difference is simply due to the fact that the three 'sub-chapters' in QS numbered in Vol.V 3(a), 3(b), and 3(c) were in Vol.X called 3, 4, and 5 (see X.299). Few changes were made to the QS manuscript in later revision, and those that were made were incorporated in LQ 1. That typescript received no alterations, and is of textual value in only a few respects; the typist of LQ 2 did not use it, but worked directly from the old manuscript.

§81   'The Valar sat now behind the mountains and feasted' > 'Thus the Valar sat now behind their mountains in peace'.

§82   The placing of Hildórien 'in the uttermost East of Middle-earth that lies beside the eastern sea' was changed to: 'in the midmost parts of Middle-earth beyond the Great River and the Inner Sea, in regions which neither the Eldar nor the Avari have known'.

Many phrases have been used of the site of Hildórien. In the 'Annals' tradition it was 'in the East of the world' (IV.269, V.118, 125), but this was changed on the manuscript of AV 2 to 'in the midmost regions of the world' (V.120, note 13). In the *Quenta* it was 'in the East of East' (IV.99), and in QS, as cited above, 'in the uttermost East of Middle-earth': in my commentary on QS (V.248) I suggested that this last was not in contradiction with the changed reading of AV 2: 'Hildórien was in the furthest east of *Middle-earth*, but it was in the middle regions of the world; see *Ambarkanta* map IV, on which Hildórien is marked (IV.249).'

In the texts of the post-*Lord of the Rings* period there is the statement in the *Grey Annals* (GA) §57 that it was 'in the midmost regions of the world', as in the emended reading of AV 2; and there is the new phrase in the revision of QS, 'in *the midmost parts of Middle-earth* beyond the Great River and the Inner Sea' (with loss of the mention in the original text of 'the eastern sea'). This last shows unambiguously that a change had taken place, but it is very hard to say what it was. It cannot be made to agree with the old *Ambarkanta* maps: one might indeed doubt that those maps carried much validity for the eastern regions by this time, and wonder whether by 'the Inner Sea' my father was referring to 'the Inland Sea of Rhûn' (see *The Treason of Isengard* pp. 307, 333) – but on the other hand, in the *Annals of Aman* (X.72, 82) from this same period the Great Journey of the Elves from Kuiviénen ('a bay in the Inland Sea of Helkar') is described in terms that suggest that the old conception was still fully present. Can the Sea of Rhûn be identified with the Sea of Helkar, vastly shrunken? – Nor is it easy to understand how Hildórien 'in the midmost parts of Middle-earth' could be 'in regions which neither the Eldar nor the Avari have known'.

In LQ 2 most of the revised passage is absent, and the text reads simply: 'in the land of Hildórien in the midmost parts of Middle-earth; for measured time had come upon Earth ...' If this is significant, it must depend on a verbal direction from my father. On the other hand, the revision was written on the manuscript in two parts: 'in the midmost parts' in the margin and the remainder on another part of the page, where it would be possible to miss it; and I think this much the likeliest explanation.

§83 The opening of the footnote (V.245) was changed from 'The Eldar called them Hildi' to '*Atani* they were called in Valinor, but the Eldar called them also Hildi'; and 'the birth of the Hildi' was changed to 'the arising of the Hildi'. For *Atani* see GA §57 and commentary. As frequently before, the typist of LQ 1 placed the footnote in the body of the text, where my father left it to stand; but it reappears as a footnote to LQ 2 – a first indication that the typescript was taken from the QS manuscript.

After 'those fathers of Men' (in which the *f* should not have been capitalised) was added 'the *Atanatardi*'. Here LQ 1 has *Atanatarni*, which was not corrected; while LQ 2 – based not on LQ 1 but on the manuscript – has *Atanatardi*. But the form *Atanatarni* occurs in the *Narn* text given in Note 2 to Part One: there Fingon before the beginning of the Battle of Unnumbered Tears cries *Aiya Eldalië ar Atanatarni* (p. 166). In GA §87, in a different passage, the form is

Atanatári (which was adopted in *The Silmarillion*); cf. also *Atanatárion*, X.373.

§85 The sentence 'Only in the realm of Doriath, whose queen Melian was of divine race, did the Ilkorins come near to match the Elves of Kôr' was changed to: 'whose queen Melian was of the kindred of the [gods >] Valar, did the [Ekelli >] Sindar come near to match the [Elves of Túna >] Kalaquendi of the Blessed Realm.' On the term *Ekelli* 'the Forsaken' and its replacement by *Sindar* see X.169–70.

Eruman > *Araman* (cf. X.123, 194).

'the ancient wisdom of their race' > '... of their folk'.

§86 'What befell their spirits after death' > 'What may befall...'

'beside the Western Sea' > 'beside the Outer Sea' (see V.248, §86).

§87 'vanished from the earth' > 'vanished from the Middle-earth'.

To one or other copies of the LQ 2 typescript my father made a few changes. The chapter, typed without a number, was now numbered 'XI'. 'Gnomes' was changed to 'Noldor' at each occurrence, and in the first sentence of §85 'Dark-elves' to 'Sindar'. Against §82 he wrote: 'This depends upon an old version in which the Sun was first made after the death of the Trees (described in a chapter omitted).' I have already noticed this in X.299–300, and explained why he numbered the present chapter 'XI'. He also bracketed in pencil three passages in the account of the mortality of the Elves in §85: 'Yet their bodies were of the stuff of earth ... consumeth them from within in the courses of time'; 'days or years, even a thousand'; 'and their deserts'.

10 OF THE SIEGE OF ANGBAND

This chapter was numbered 8 in the QS manuscript, and the text is given in V.248–55, §§88–104. As in the preceding chapter, all post-*Lord of the Rings* revision was carried out on the QS manuscript: that is to say, no further revisions were made to the typescript LQ 1; and here again the late typescript LQ 2 was derived from the manuscript, not from LQ 1. In this chapter, on the other hand, by no means all the revisions made to the manuscript are found in LQ 1; and in the account that follows I notice all such cases. I do not notice the changes *Eruman* > *Araman*; *Tûn* > *Túna*; *Gnomes* > *Noldor*; *Thorndor* > *Thorondor*; *Bladorion* > *Ard-galen* (see p. 113, §44).

§88 The opening passage of the chapter in QS was rewritten on a slip attached to the manuscript – this slip being the reverse of a letter to my father dated 14 November 1951: but it was not incorporated into LQ 1. The introduction of this rider led the typist of LQ 2 to ignore the fact that a new chapter begins at this point, and to type *Of the Siege of Angband* as all of a piece with *Of Men*; subsequently my father inserted a new heading *Of the Siege of Angband* with the number 'XII' (on which see p. 175). The new opening reads:

> As was before told Fëanor and his sons came first of the Exiles to Middle-earth, and they landed in the waste of Lammoth upon the outer shores of the Firth of Drengist. Now that region was so named, for it lay between the Sea and the walls of the echoing mountains of the Eryd Lómin. And even as the Noldor set foot upon the strand their cries were taken up into the hills and multiplied, so that a great clamour as of countless mighty voices filled all the coasts of the North; and it is said that the noise of the burning of the ships at Losgar went down the winds of the Sea as a tumult of great wrath, and far away all that heard that sound were filled with wonder.
>
> Under the cold stars before the rising of the Moon Fëanor and his folk marched eastward, and they passed the Eryd Lómin, and came into the great land of Hithlum, and crossing the country of Dor-lómin they came at length to the long lake of Mithrim, and upon its north-shore they made their first camp in that region which was called by the like name.
>
> There a host of the Orcs, aroused by the tumult of Lammoth, and the light of the burning at Losgar, came down upon them; and beside the waters of Mithrim was fought the first battle upon Middle-earth...

This is the story of Lammoth told (at about this same time) in the later *Tale of Tuor* (*Unfinished Tales* p. 23):

> Tuor was now come to the Echoing Mountains of Lammoth about the Firth of Drengist. There once long ago Fëanor had landed from the sea, and the voices of his host were swelled to a mighty clamour upon the coasts of the North ere the rising of the Moon.

On the much later and apparently distinct story that Lammoth was so called because the echoes of Morgoth's cry were awakened by 'any who cried aloud in that land' see X.296, §17 and commentary, and *Unfinished Tales* p. 52. Both 'traditions' were incorporated in the published *Silmarillion*, pp. 80–1, 106.

At the end of this paragraph my father pencilled on the manuscript: 'He [Fëanor] gives the green stone to Maidros', but then noted that this was not in fact to be inserted; see under §97 below.

§90 'and they were unwilling to depart, whatever he might do' > '... whatever he might do, being held by their oath.' This addition is not present in LQ 1; while the typist of LQ 2, unable to read the first word, put 'They held by their oath', and this was allowed to stand. Cf. GA §50.

§91 'the Sun rose flaming in the West' > 'the Sun rose flaming above the shadows' (not in LQ 1).
'and good was made of evil, as happens still' removed.
§93 'the bright airs of those earliest of mornings' > 'the bright airs in the first mornings of the world.'
§94 A subheading was pencilled in the margin at the beginning of this paragraph: *Of Fingon and Maeðros* (apparently first written *Maidros*: see p. 115, §61). Not found in LQ 1, this was incorporated in LQ 2.

In the second sentence 'most renowned' > 'most honoured' (not in LQ 1).

To the words 'for the thought of his torment troubled his heart' was added (not in LQ 1): 'and long before, in the bliss of Valinor, ere Melkor was unchained, or lies came between them, he had been close in friendship with Maedros.' Cf. GA §61 and commentary (p. 115).
§95 'for the banished Gnomes!' > 'for the Noldor in their need!'
§97 A new page in the QS manuscript begins with the opening of this paragraph, and at the top of the page my father pencilled: 'The Green Stone of Fëanor given by Maidros to Fingon.' This can hardly be other than a reference to the *Elessar* that came in the end to Aragorn; cf. the note given under §88 above referring to Fëanor's gift at his death of the Green Stone to Maidros. It is clear, I think, that my father was at this time pondering the previous history of the *Elessar*, which had emerged in *The Lord of the Rings*; for his later ideas on its origin see *Unfinished Tales* pp. 248–52.
§98 '(Therefore the house of Fëanor were called the Dispossessed,) because of the doom of the Gods which gave the kingdom of Tûn [*later* > Túna] to Fingolfin, and because of the loss of the Silmarils' was changed (but the change is not present in LQ 1) to: '... (as Mandos foretold) because the overlordship passed from it, the elder, to the house of Fingolfin, both in Elendë and in Beleriand, and because also of the loss of the Silmarils.'

With the words 'as Mandos foretold' cf. AAm §153 (X.117); and on the content of the paragraph see p. 115, commentary on GA §§65–71.
§99 At the end of the paragraph, after 'he [Thingol] trusted not that the restraint of Morgoth would last for ever', was added: 'neither would he ever wholly forget the deeds at Alqualondë, because of his ancient kinship with [Elwë >] Olwë lord of the Teleri.' On the change of *Elwë* to *Olwë* see X.169–70.
§100 'in unexplored country' > 'in untrodden lands'.
§101 This passage on the finding of Nargothrond and Gondolin was expanded in three stages. The first alteration to QS replaced the sentence 'But Turgon went alone into hidden places' thus:

Yet Galadriel his sister went never to Nargothrond, for she remained long in Doriath and received the love of Melian, and abode with her and there learned great lore and wisdom. But the heart of Turgon remembered rather the white city of Tirion upon its hill, and its tower and tree, and he journeyed alone into hidden places...

Subsequently the whole of QS §101 was struck through and replaced by the following rider on a separate sheet. This was taken up into the first typescript LQ 1, but in a somewhat different form from the rider to the manuscript, which was followed in LQ 2 and is given here.

> And it came to pass that Inglor and Galaðriel were on a time the guests of Thingol and Melian; for there was friendship between the lord of Doriath and the House of Finrod that were his kin, and the princes of that house alone were suffered to pass the girdle of Melian. Then Inglor was filled with wonder at the strength and majesty of Menegroth, with its treasuries and armouries and its many-pillared halls of stone; and it came into his heart that he would build wide halls behind everguarded gates in some deep and secret place beneath the hills. And he opened his heart to Thingol, and when he departed Thingol gave him guides, and they led him westward over Sirion. Thus it was that Inglor found the deep gorge of the River Narog, and the caves in its steep further shore; and he delved there a stronghold and armouries after the fashion of the mansions of Menegroth. And he called that place Nargothrond, and made there his home with many of his folk; and the Gnomes of the North, at first in jest, called him on this account Felagund, or 'lord of caverns', and that name he bore thereafter until his end. Yet Galaðriel his sister dwelt never in Nargothrond, but remained in Doriath and received the love of Melian, and abode with her, and there learned great lore and wisdom concerning Middle-earth.

The statement that 'Galaðriel dwelt never in Nargothrond' is at variance with what is said in GA §108 (p. 44), that in the year 102, when Nargothrond was completed, 'Galadriel came from Doriath and dwelt there a while'. — To this point the two forms of the rider differ only in a few details of wording, but here they diverge. The second form, in LQ 2, continues:

> Now Turgon remembered rather the City set upon a Hill, Tirion the fair with its Tower and Tree, and he found not what he sought, and returned to Nivrost, and sat at peace in Vinyamar by the shore. There after three years Ulmo himself appeared to him, and bade him go forth again alone to the Vale of Sirion; and Turgon went forth and by the guidance of Ulmo

he discovered the hidden vale of Tumladen in the encircling mountains, in the midst of which there was a hill of stone. Of this he spoke to none as yet, but returned to Nivrost, and there began in his secret counsels to devise the plan of a fair city [*struck out:* a memorial of Tirion upon Túna for which his heart still yearned in exile, and though he pondered much in thought he]

For this concluding passage LQ 1 returns to the first rewriting given at the beginning of this discussion of QS §101, 'But the heart of Turgon remembered rather the white city of Tirion upon its hill ...' The explanation of the differences in the two versions must be that a first form of the rider (which has not survived) was taken up into LQ 1, and that subsequently a second version was inserted into the QS manuscript in its place, and so used in LQ 2.

This replacement text for QS §101 is closely related to GA §§75–6 (p. 35); and since on its reverse side is a rejected draft for the replacement annal for the year 116 in GA (§§111–13, pp. 44–5), also concerned with Gondolin, it is clear that my father was working on the story of the origins of Nargothrond and Gondolin in both the *Silmarillion* and the *Annals* at the same time. See further pp. 198 ff.

§102 At the beginning of this paragraph a sub-heading *Of Dagor Aglareb* was pencilled on the manuscript, but this was not taken up in either typescript.

'the Blue Mountains' > 'Eredluin, the blue mountains'
'the second great battle' > 'the third great battle': see p. 116, §77.

A few corrections were made to one or the other, or to both, of the copies of LQ 2. In addition to those listed below, *Inglor* was changed to *Finrod*, and *Finrod* to *Finarphin* or *Finarfin*, throughout.

§92 *Túna > Tirion*
§98 '(the feud) was healed' > 'was assuaged'
§99 'Dark-elves of Telerian race' > 'Dark-elves, the Sindar of Telerian race'.
§100 At the beginning of this paragraph my father inserted a new chapter number and title: XIII *The Founding of Nargothrond and Gondolin*; and the next chapter, *Of Beleriand and its Realms*, was given in LQ 2 the number XIV.

Nivrost > Nevrast (and subsequently); the first appearance of the later form of the name (its appearance in the later *Tale of Tuor* was by editorial change).

§101 Against the name *Felagund* my father wrote this note: 'This was in fact a Dwarfish name; for Nargothrond was first made by Dwarves as is later recounted.' An important constituent text among the *Narn* papers is a 'plot-outline' that begins with Túrin's flight from Doriath and moves towards pure narrative in a long account of Túrin's relations with Finduilas and Gwindor in Nargothrond (which with some editorial development was given in *Unfinished Tales*, pp. 155–9). In this text the following is said of Mîm the Petty-dwarf:

> Mîm gets a certain curious liking for Túrin, increased when he learns that Túrin has had trouble with Elves, whom he detests. He says Elves have caused the end of his race, and taken all their mansions, especially Nargothrond (*Nulukhizidûn*).

Above this Dwarvish name my father wrote *Nulukkhizdīn* (this name was used, misspelt, in *The Silmarillion*, p. 230).

§104 *Glómund* > *Glaurung*. At the head of the page in QS my father wrote '*Glaurung* for *Glómund*', but the LQ typescript, as typed, has *Glómund* – whereas *Glaurung* appears already in the *Grey Annals* as written.

11 OF BELERIAND AND ITS REALMS

In Volume V (p. 407) I wrote as follows about the second *Silmarillion* map:

> The second map of Middle-earth west of the Blue Mountains in the Elder Days was also the last. My father never made another; and over many years this one became covered all over with alterations and additions of names and features, not a few of them so hastily or faintly pencilled as to be more or less obscure. ...
>
> The original element in the map can however be readily perceived from the fine and çareful pen (all subsequent change was roughly done); and I give here on four successive pages a reproduction of the map *as it was originally drawn and lettered*. ...
>
> The map is on four sheets, originally pasted together but now separate, in which the map-squares do not entirely coincide with the sheets. In my reproductions I have followed the squares rather than the original sheets. I have numbered the squares horizontally right across the map from 1 to 15, and lettered them vertically from A to M, so that each square has a different combination of letter and figure for subsequent reference. I hope later to give an account of all changes made to the map afterwards, using these redrawings as a basis.

This I will now do, before turning to the changes made to the chapter *Of Beleriand and its Realms*. On the following pages are reproduced the same four redrawings as were given in V.408–11, but with the subsequent alterations and additions introduced (those cases where I cannot interpret at all faint pencillings are simply ignored). Corrections to names (as *Nan Tathrin* > *Nan Tathren*, *Nan Dungorthin* > *Nan Dungortheb*, *Rathlorion* > *Rathloriel*) are replaced, not shown as corrections. It is to be remembered that, as I have said, all later changes were roughly done, some of them mere scribbled indications, and also that they were made at many different times, in pencil, coloured pencil, blue, black and red ink, and red, green and blue ball-point pen; so that the appearance of the actual map is very different from these redrawings. I have however retained the placing of the new lettering in almost all cases as accurately as possible.

There follows here a list, square by square, of features and names where some explanation or reference seems desirable; but this is by no means an exhaustive inventory of all later alterations and additions, many of which require no comment.

1 North-western section (p. 182)

(1) A 4–5 The mountain-chain is a mere zigzag line pencilled in a single movement, as also are the mountains on A 7 (extending east to the peaks encircling Thangorodrim on section 2, A 8).

(2) B 4 to C 4 The name *Dor-Lómen* was almost illegibly scribbled in; it seems to imply an extension of Dor-Lómen northwards.

(3) B 7 to C 7 The name beginning *Fen* is continued on Section 2, B 8 *of Rivil*, changed to *of Serech* (see p. 113, commentary on GA §44). An arrow, not inserted on the redrawing, points to three dots above the inflowing of Rivil as marking the Fen.

(4) C 1 I can cast no light on the name *Ened* of the island in the ocean.

(5) C 3 It seems probable that the name *Falasquil* referred to the small round bay, blacked in, on the southern shore of the great bay leading into the Firth of Drengist. On the remarkable reappearance of this ancient name see p. 344.

(6) C 4 The clearly-marked gap in the stream flowing into the Firth of Drengist represents its passage underground; with the name *Annon Gelyð* cf. *Annon-in-Gelydh* (the Gate of the Noldor) in the later *Tale of Tuor, Unfinished Tales* p. 18. The ravine of *Cirith Ninniach* is described in the same work (*ibid.* p. 23). The upper course of the stream is very faintly pencilled and uncertain, but it seems clear that it rises in the Mountains of Mithrim (*ibid.* p. 20).

(7) C 6 For the peak shaded in and marked *Amon Darthir*, with *Morwen* beside it, see *Unfinished Tales*, where it is told (p. 68) that the stream Nen Lalaith 'came down from a spring under the shadow of Amon Darthir', and (p. 58) that it 'came singing out of the hills past the walls of [Húrin's] house'.

(8) C 6 to D 7 For the river *Lithir* see p. 261.

(9) C 7 For the stream (Rivil) that flows into Sirion see Section 2, C 8.

(10) D 2–4 Both *Nevrast* and the *Marshes of Nevrast* were first

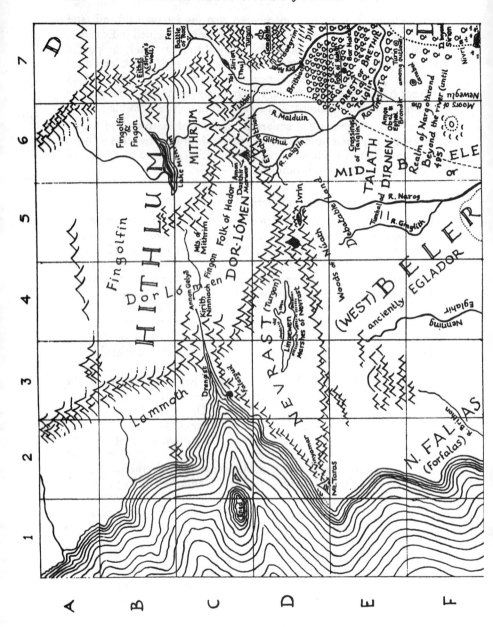

Sheet 1 North-west

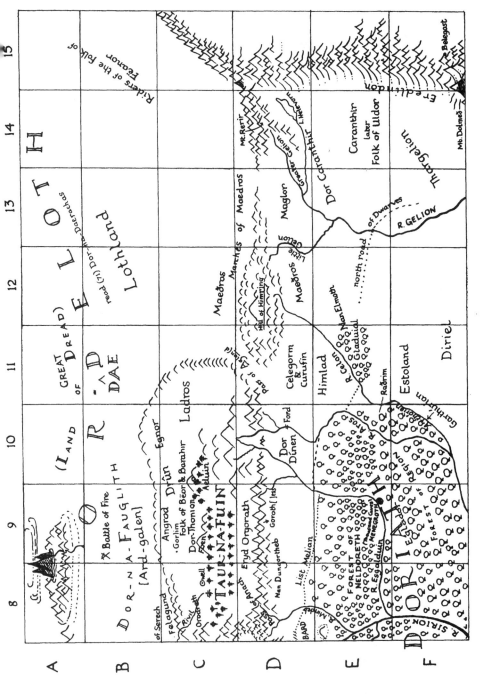

Sheet 2 North-east

184 THE WAR OF THE JEWELS

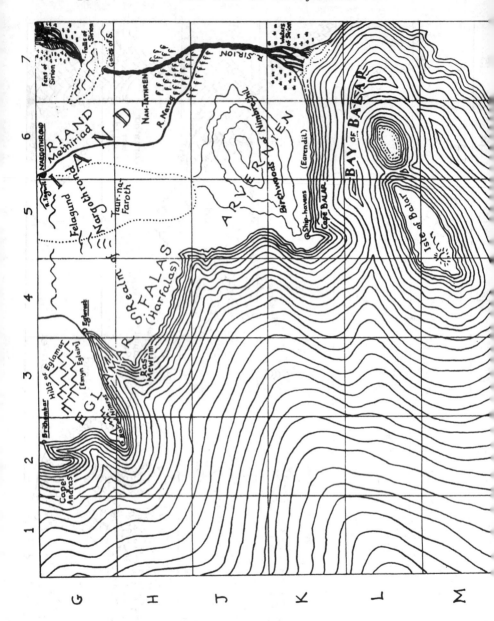

Sheet 3 South-west

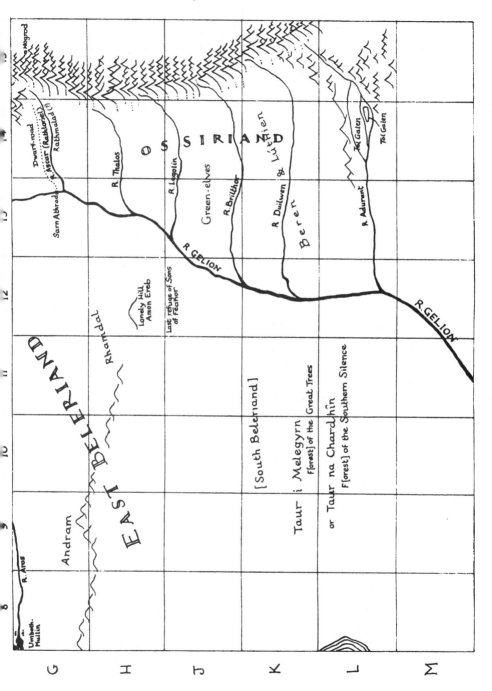

Sheet 4   South-east

written *Nivrost* (see p. 179, §100). On Lake Linaewen and the marshes see p. 192 and *Unfinished Tales* p. 25.

(11) D 6 For the river *Glithui* see *Unfinished Tales* p. 38 and note 16, and p. 68. In the first of these passages (the later *Tale of Tuor*) the name is *Glithui* as on the map, but in the second (the *Narn*) it is equally clearly *Gilthui*. For *Malduin* see *Unfinished Tales* p. 38 and *The Silmarillion* p. 205.

(12) D 7 The line of dots extending east from the Brithiach was struck out as shown; see Section 2, §38. For the ford of Brithiach see p. 228, §28.

(13) D 7 *Dim* is the first part of the name *Dimbard*: see Section 2, D 8.

(14) E 4 to F 4 *anciently Eglador*: *Eglador* was the original name of Doriath, 'land of the Elves' (see the *Etymologies*, V.356, stem ELED), and is so entered on the map (Section 2, F 9). For its later sense, 'land of the *Eglain*, the Forsaken People, the Sindar' see p. 189, §57; and here *Eglador* is used with a much wider reference: the western parts of Beleriand (see pp. 379–80). This is perhaps to be related to the statement in *The Tale of Years* (pp. 343–4), 'The foremost of the Eldar reach the coastlands of Middle-earth and that country which was after named Eglador' – to which however is added the puzzling phrase 'Thereof Beleriand was the larger part'.

(15) E 4 to D 5 *Woods of Núath*: see the later *Tale of Tuor* in *Unfinished Tales*, p. 36 and note 14.

(16) E 5 The name *Tumhalad* appears to be written twice, above and below the two short parallel lines shown. See pp. 139–40, commentary on GA §275.

(17) E 5–6 *Talath Dirnen* was first written *Dalath Dirnen*; see p. 228, §28.

(18) E 6 to F 6 South of the Crossings of Taiglin it is difficult to be sure, among various incomplete dotted lines, what was the course of the road to Nargothrond, but my father seems subsequently to have entered it as a straight line of short dashes as shown.

(19) E 6–7 From Ephel Brandir various lines, which I cannot certainly interpret and have not marked on the map, run west towards the Crossings of Taiglin. Possibly one line marks the road to the Crossings and another the course of Celebros. – *Tavrobel* on the map as originally lettered was struck out and replaced by *Bar Haleth* (also struck out), but no precise site is indicated. For *Bar Haleth* see p. 157, commentary on GA §324.

(20) E 7 *Folk of Haleth* clearly belongs to the first making of the map and should have been entered on the redrawing (V.408).

(21) F 2 The name *Forfalas* ('North Falas') seems not to occur

elsewhere; similarly with *Harfalas* ('South Falas'), Section 3, H 4.

(22) F 4   The original name *R.Eglor* was struck out and replaced by *Eglahir*. Later the name *Nenning* was written in, but *Eglahir* was not struck out. See p. 117, commentary on GA §85.

(23) F 5   For the dotted line on this square see §59 below.

(24) F 6   The word 'or' refers to the name *Methiriad*, Section 3, G 6.

(25) F 6   For the change of date from 195 to 495 see V.139, 407.

(26) F 6–7   *Moors of the Neweglu*: among the *Narn* papers there are many texts concerned with the story of Mîm, and in these are found an extraordinary array of names for the Petty-dwarves: *Neweg, Neweglîn; Niwennog; Naug-neben, Neben-naug; Nebinnog, Nibennog, Nibinnogrim, Nibin-noeg; Nognith.* The name on the map, *Neweglu*, does not occur in the *Narn* papers.

(27) F 7   The name of an isolated hill *Carabel* stands at the point where *Amon Rûdh* (the abode of Mîm) is shown on my map accompanying *The Silmarillion*. The name of the hill was changed many times: *Amon Garabel* > *Carabel*; *Amon Carab* (translated 'Hill of the Hat'); *Amon Narðol* and *Nardol* (cf. the beacon-hill *Nardol* in Anórien); *Amon Rhûg* 'the Bald Hill'; and *Amon Rûdh* of the same meaning.

(28) F 7   For *Nivrim* see QS §110 (V.261).

2 North-eastern section (p. 183)

(29) B 8   *(Fen) of Serech*: see Section 1, §3.

(30) B 12 to A 13   'read (71) *Dor-na-Daerachas*': the number 71 oddly but certainly refers to the year 1971; the addition is very late, since it does not appear on the photocopy of the map used by my father c.1970 (see p. 330 and note 1, also p. 191, after §74).

(31) B 12–13   *Lothland*: see p. 128, commentary on GA §§173–4.

(32) C 9   The mountain named *Foen*: in a philological fragment of uncertain date it is stated that Dorthonion 'was called also *Taur-na-Foen*, the Forest of the Foen, for that was the name (which signifies "Long Sight") of the high mountain in the midst of that region.'

(33) C 9–10   *Drûn*: cf. the later form of the *Lay of Leithian*, III.344, line 520: 'ambush in Ladros, fire in Drûn' (see commentary, III. 350).

(34) C 10–11   For mentions of *Ladros* see p. 224 and §33 above; also *Unfinished Tales* p. 70, where Túrin is named 'heir of Dor-lómin and Ladros'.

(35) C 11   On the left side of the square my father wrote *Orodreth*, subsequently striking it out. This placing of Orodreth's

territory goes back to the old story that of the sons of Finrod (Finarfin) on Dorthonion 'easternmost dwelt Orodreth, nighest to his friends the sons of Fëanor' (AB 1, IV.330).

(36) C 12 Maeðros was corrected from Maiðros, so also on D 12; in the original Marches of Maidros the name was corrected to Maedros.

(37) D 8 bard is the second element of Dimbard (see Section 1, D 7). The name is certainly written thus, with final -d, but elsewhere the form is always Dimbar.

(38) D 8–9, E 9–10 The line of dots marked List Melian was struck out for some distance east of the Brithiach, as shown (see Section 1, D 7), and its discontinuous extension between Esgalduin and Aros was put in later and more roughly. On the significance of these dotted lines see p. 333, and for the name List Melian (the Girdle of Melian) see pp. 223, 228.

(39) D 9 Eryd Orgorath seems to be written so, and above it apparently Gorgorath, but the forms are very hard to make out.

(40) D 9 Goroth[ ]ess: the illegible letter in this otherwise totally unknown name (which was struck through) might be r.

(41) D 9 For the bridge of Esgalduin marked on the published map (and named Iant Iaur) in the position equivalent to the S.E. corner of D 9 see pp. 332–3.

(42) D 10 For Dor Dínen see pp. 194, 333.

(43) D 10 The Ford over Aros can be shown to be a very late addition to the map: see p. 338, note 6.

(44) D 11 Pass of Aglon(d: for the forms Aglon and Aglond see p. 338, note 3.

(45) D 14 Mt. Rerir: in QS §114 (V.263) it is said that Greater Gelion came from Mount Rerir (the first occurrence of the name); about it were 'many lesser heights' (§118), and on its western slopes was built a Noldorin fortress (§142). The map was made before the emergence of Mount Rerir, and my father contented himself with writing the name against the not specially conspicuous mountain near the end of the line marking Greater Gelion.

(46) E 8 to D 8 The name R. Mindeb was written on the map at its making but was inadvertently omitted from my redrawing (V.409).

(47) E 11 Himlad: on the meaning of the name, and the reason for it, see p. 332 and note 4.

(48) E 11 Gladuial: I have not found this name anywhere else.

(49) E 11 Raðrim: the line directing the name to the wooded land between Aros and Celon is faintly pencilled on the map. Raðrim does not occur in any narrative text, but is found in

the *Etymologies* (V.382–3, stems RAD and RĪ): '*Radhrim* Eastmarch (part of Doriath)'.

(50) E 12–13, F 13   The words 'north road of Dwarves' are very faint and blurred, but this seems to be the only possible interpretation. On the extremely puzzling question of the Dwarf-roads in East Beleriand see pp. 334–6.

(51) E 12   A word faintly pencilled across the upper part of this square could be interpreted as 'Marshes'.

(52) F 9   *Eglador* pencilled under *Doriath*: see §14 above.

(53) F 10   *Arthórien*: see pp. 112–13, commentary on GA §38; and the next entry.

(54) F 10   *Garthúrian* (which could also be read as *Garthúrien*): in the text cited at §32 above it is said that 'the Noldor often used the name *Arthúrien* for Doriath, though this is but an alteration of the Sindarin *Garthúrian* "hidden realm".'

(55) F 11   *Estoland*: the form is clear, but at all other occurrences of the name it is *Estolad*.

3   South-western section (p. 184)

(56) G 2   *Cape Andras* is referred to in *Quendi and Eldar*, p. 379. Cf. *Andrast* 'Long Cape' in the extreme west of Gondor (Index to *Unfinished Tales*).

(57) G 3 to H 3   The names *Eglamar* (as applied here) and *Emyn Eglain* (or *Hills of Eglamar*) are not found in any narrative text. *Eglamar* is one of the oldest names in my father's *legendarium*: together with *Eldamar* of the same meaning, 'Elf-home', it referred to the land of the Elves in Valinor, *Egla* being 'the Gnome name of the Eldar who dwelt in Kôr' (see I.251, II.338; also the *Etymologies*, V.356, stem ELED). The old names *Eglamar*, *Eglador*, *Eglorest* (> *Eglarest*), not abandoned, were afterwards related to the name by which the Sindar called themselves, *Eglath* 'the Forsaken People' (see X.85, 164). In *Quendi and Eldar* (p. 365) the etymology of *Eglain*, *Egladhrim* is given – though it is not the only one that my father advanced; and later in that essay (pp. 379–80) it is explained why these names were found in the Falas among the people of Círdan. (I cannot account for the application of the name *Eglamar* to Arthórien, the small land in the S.E. of Doriath between Aros and Celon, in the note cited on p. 112, commentary on GA §38.)

(58) G 4   The name *Eglorest* of the map as originally made was not emended to the later form *Eglarest*.

(59) G 5–6, H 5–6   The extent of the *Taur-na-Faroth* (or *High Faroth*) is marked out by the dotted line (extending somewhat north of Nargothrond on Section 1, F 5) as a very large region,

somewhat in the shape of a footprint: cf. the representation of the Hills of the Hunters on the first *Silmarillion* map (Vol.IV, between pp. 220 and 221). The dots outlining the more southerly part were cancelled, and rough lines (not represented in the redrawing) across G 5 (from left-centre to bottom-right) suggest a reduction in the extent of the highlands. See further §65 below.

(60) G 5 The name *Ingwil* was not corrected to the later form *Ringwil* (see p. 197, §112).

(61) G 6 I have not found the name *Methiriad* of 'Mid-Beleriand' elsewhere.

(62) H 2 *Barad Nimras* replaced *Tower of Tindabel* (jumping the intervening name *Ingildon*): see p. 197, §120.

(63) H 3 The coastline south-west of Eglarest was extended into a small cape named *Ras Mewrim*, a name not found elsewhere; in *Quendi and Eldar* (pp. 379–80) it is named *Bar-in-Mŷl* 'Home of the Gulls'.

(64) H 4 *Harfalas*: see §21 above.

(65) J 5–7, K 5–6 I have mentioned under §59 above that the dotted line marking the extent of the Taur-na-Faroth was later cancelled in its southern part; but the high country of *Arvernien* (clearly added to the map after the dotted line) is shown extending by a narrow neck to join the southern extremity of the Taur-na-Faroth as originally indicated: i.e., there is a great range of hills extending from near the southern coast, through this 'neck', to a little north of Nargothrond.

(66) K 5–6 The name *Earendil* on K 6, though separated, very probably belongs with *Ship-havens* on K 5. Cf. the beginning of Bilbo's song at Rivendell:

> Eärendil was a mariner
> that tarried in Arvernien;
> he built a boat of timber felled
> in Nimbrethil to journey in ...

4 *South-eastern section (p. 185)*

(67) G 8–9, H 8–11 The *Andram* is marked only as a faint pencilled line of small curves, more vague and unclear than in my redrawing.

(68) G 11–13 A vaguely marked line of dashes (not represented on the redrawing) runs westward from just above *Sarn Athrad* on G 13: this perhaps indicates the course of the Dwarf-road after the passage of Gelion. This line bends gently north-west across G 12 and leaves G 11 at the top left corner, possibly reappearing on Section 2, F 10, where (if this is correct) it reached Aros just below the inflow of Celon. See p. 334.

(69) G 14 The correction of *Rathlorion* to *Rathloriel* was an early

THE LATER *QUENTA SILMARILLION* 191

change (V.407). A name beneath, hastily pencilled, is very probably *Rathmalad* (cf. the name *Rathmallen* of this river in *The Tale of Years*, p. 353).

(70) H 11–12 *Rhamdal*: this spelling is found in QS §142 (beside *Ramdal* in §113, adopted in *The Silmarillion*) and in the *Etymologies*, V.390, stem TAL; cf. ibid. V.382, stem RAMBĀ, 'Noldorin *rhamb, rham*'.

(71) K 10–11 The scribbled named *South Beleriand* was struck out.

(72) K 9–11, L 9–11 For the name *Taur-im-Duinath* of the great forested region between Gelion and Sirion in the published *Silmarillion* and map see p. 193, §108.

(73) L 14–15 *Tol Galen*: the divided course of the river Adurant (whence its name, according to the *Etymologies*, V.349, stem AT(AT)) enclosing the isle of Tol Galen is shown in two forms. The less extensive division was drawn in ink (it seems that the oblong shape itself represents the island, in which case the area between it and the two streams is perhaps to be taken as very low-lying land or marsh); the much larger division, in which the northern stream leaves the other much further to the east and rejoins it much further to the west, was entered in pencil, together with the name. The name *Tol Galen* was written a third time (again in pencil) across the upper part of square M 14.

(74) L 14–15 The mountains on these squares, extending northward onto K 15, were pencilled in very rapidly, and those to the north of Tol Galen were possibly cancelled.

On line M at the foot of the map are these pencilled notes (again with the number 71, see p. 187, §30): 'These river-names need revision to etymologizable words. *Celon* should go. *Gelion* should be *Duin Dhaer*.' On these changes see pp. 336–7 and note 10.

I turn now to the development of the chapter *Of Beleriand and its Realms*. The great majority of the changes made to the text of QS (Chapter 9, V.258–66, §§105–21) are found in the early typescript LQ 1, but some are not, and appear only in LQ 2: these cases are noticed in the account that follows. I do not record the changes *Melko* > *Melkor*, *Helkaraksë* > *Helkaraxë*, *Bladorion* > *Ard-galen*, *Eglorest* > *Eglarest*.

§105 After the words 'in the ancient days' at the end of the first sentence the following footnote was added to QS. As usual, the typist of LQ 1 took up the footnote into the text, but it appears as a footnote in LQ 2, whose typist was again working directly from the manuscript.

> These matters, which are not in the *Pennas* of Pengolod, I have added and taken from the *Dorgannas Iaur* (the account of the shapes of the lands of old that Torhir Ifant made and is kept in Eressëa), that those who will may understand more clearly, maybe, what is later said of their princes and their wars: quoth Ælfwine.

On the *Pennas* of Pengolod see V.201-4.

'These Melko built in the elder days' > 'These Melkor had built in ages past'

§106 *Hísilóme* was written in the margin of the manuscript against *Hithlum* in the text (the latter not struck out). This is not in LQ 1, but LQ 2 has 'Hithlum (Hísilómë)' in the text.

Eredlómin > *the Eryd Lammad*. This form (not in LQ 1) has not occurred before, and is not (I believe) found elsewhere: in §105 *Eredlómin* was left unchanged.

'And Nivrost was a pleasant land watered by the wet winds from the sea, and sheltered from the North, whereas the rest of Hithlum was open to the cold winds' was struck out and replaced by the following (which does not appear in LQ 1):

> And Nivrost was by some held to belong rather to Beleriand than to Hithlum, for it was a milder land, watered by the wet winds from the Sea and sheltered from the North and East, whereas Hithlum was open to cold north-winds. But it was a hollow land, surrounded by mountains and great coast-cliffs higher than the plains behind, and no river flowed thence. Wherefore there was a great mere amidmost, and it had no certain shores, being encircled by wide marshes. Linaewen was the name of that mere, because of the multitude of birds that dwelt there, of such as love tall reeds and shallow pools. Now at the coming of the Noldor many of the Grey-elves (akin to those of the Falas) lived still in Nivrost, nigh to the coasts, and especially about Mount Taras in the south-west; for to that place Ulmo and Ossë had been wont to come in days of old. All that folk took Turgon for their lord, and so it came to pass that in Nivrost the mingling of Noldor and Sindar began sooner than elsewhere; and Turgon dwelt long in those halls that he named Vinyamar, under Mount Taras beside the Sea. There it was that Ulmo afterwards appeared to him.

This passage introduced a number of new elements: the topography of Nivrost (the high coast-cliffs are represented on the second map as originally drawn, p. 182), and Lake Linaewen (which appears also in the later *Tale of Tuor*, *Unfinished Tales* p. 25, with the same description of Nivrost as a 'hollow land'); the coming of Ulmo and Ossë to Mount Taras in the ancient days; and the conception that Sindarin Elves dwelt in Nivrost near the coast and especially about Mount Taras, and that they took Turgon to be their lord at the coming of the Noldor to Middle-earth. The later story that there were many Grey-elves among Turgon's people appears in the rewritten annal for the year 116 in GA (see §§107, 113 and the commentary on those passages).

The footnote in the QS manuscript 'Ilkorin name' to the sentence 'the great highland that the Gnomes first named Dorthonion' was struck out, and in the text 'Gnomes' was changed to 'Dark-elves'.

The extent of Dorthonion from west to east was changed from 'a hundred leagues' to 'sixty leagues'; on this change, made to bring the distance into harmony with the second map, see V.272.

§107 The length of Sirion from the Pass to the Delta was changed from 'one hundred and twenty-one leagues' to 'one hundred and thirty-one leagues'. The former measurement (see V.272) was the length of Sirion in a straight line from the northern opening of the Pass to the Delta; the new measurement is from Eithel Sirion to the Delta.

§108 A footnote was added to the first occurrence of *Eredlindon*:

Which signifieth the Mountains of Ossiriand; for the Gnomes [LQ 2 Noldor] called that land Lindon, the region of music, and they first saw these mountains from Ossiriand. But their right name was Eredluin the Blue Mountains, or Luindirien the Blue Towers.

This note, which may go back to a time near to the writing of QS, has been given and discussed in V.267, §108. The last five words were struck out on the manuscript and do not appear in LQ 1, the typist of which put the footnote into the body of the text and garbled the whole passage, which however remained uncorrected. The words 'quoth Ælfwine' were added to the manuscript at the end of the footnote, but appear only in LQ 2.

'a tangled forest' > 'Taur-im-Duinath, a tangled forest' (of the land between Sirion and Gelion south of the Andram; see under §113 below). On the second map this region is named *Taur i Melegyrn* or *Taur na Chardhîn* (see p. 185).

'while that land lasted' > 'while their realm lasted'

§109 The extent of West Beleriand between Sirion and the Sea was changed from 'seventy leagues' to 'ninety-nine leagues', another change harmonising the distance with the second map (see V.272).

In 'the realm of Nargothrond, between Sirion and Narog' 'Sirion' was changed to 'Taiglin'.

§110 From the words 'first the empty lands' at the beginning of the paragraph all that followed in QS as far as 'Next southward lay the kingdom of Doriath' was struck out and replaced by the following on an attached rider:

first between Sirion and Mindeb the empty land of Dimbar under the peaks of the Crissaegrim, abode of eagles, south of Gondolin (though that was for long unknown); then between Mindeb and the upper waters of Esgalduin the no-land of Nan Dungorthin. And that region was filled with fear, for upon its one side the power of Melian fenced the north-march of Doriath, but upon the other side the sheer precipices of Ered Orgoroth [> Orgorath], mountains of terror, fell down from high Dorthonion. Thither Ungoliantë had fled from the whips of the Balrogs, and had dwelt there a while, filling the hideous ravines with her deadly gloom, and there still, when she had passed away, her foul broods lurked and wove their evil nets; and the thin waters that spilled from Ered Orgoroth [> Orgorath] were all defiled, and perilous to drink, for the hearts of those that tasted them were filled with shadows of madness and despair. All living things shunned that land, and the Noldor would pass through Nan Dungorthin only at great need, by paths nigh to the borders of Doriath, and furthest from the haunted hills.

But if one fared that way he came eastward across Esgalduin and Aros (and Dor Dínen the silent land between) to the North Marches of Beleriand, where the sons of Fëanor dwelt. But southward lay the kingdom of Doriath...

On the name *Crissaegrim* (which occurs, in the spelling *Crisaegrim*, in GA §161) see V.290, §147. In this passage is the first appearance of *Dor Dínen* 'the Silent Land' (added to the map p. 183, square D 10). The story that Ungoliantë dwelt in Nan Dungorthin when she fled from the Balrogs appears in the *Annals of Aman* (X.109, 123; cf. also X.297, §20).

'where he turned westward' (with reference to the river Esgalduin) > 'where it turned westward'.

§111 The marginal note to the name Thargelion 'or Radhrost' was changed to 'Radhrost in the tongue of Doriath.'

'This region the Elves of Doriath named Umboth Muilin, the Twilight Meres, for there were many mists' > 'This region the Noldor named Aelinuial and the Dark-elves Umboth Muilin, the Twilight Meres, for they were wrapped in mists', and the footnote giving the Gnomish names Hithliniath and Aelin-uial was struck out (thus LQ 1). Later emendation removed the words 'and the Dark-elves Umboth Muilin' (thus LQ 2).

§112 The opening word 'For' was changed to 'Now'; and in the following sentence 'Umboth Muilin' was changed to 'Aelin-uial'.

The passage beginning 'Yet all the lower plain of Sirion' was changed to read thus: 'Yet all the lower fields of Sirion were divided from the upper fields by this sudden fall, which to one looking from the south northward appeared as an endless chain of hills'. In the following sentence 'Narog came south through a deep gorge' > 'Narog came through these hills in a deep gorge'. (There is an error in the text of this sentence as printed (V.262): 'on its west bank rose' should read 'on its west bank the land rose'.)

§113 The last sentence of the paragraph (and the beginning of §114) was rewritten to read:

> But until that time all the wide woods south of the Andram and between Sirion and Gelion were little known. Taur-im-Duinath, the forest between the two rivers, the Gnomes [LQ 2 Noldor] called that region, but few ever ventured in that wild land; and east of it lay the far green country of Ossiriand ...

On *Taur-im-Duinath* see under §108 above.

§114 At the name *Adurant* there is a footnote to the text in QS, which like that in §108 may belong to a relatively early time (see my remarks in the commentary, V.268):

> And at a point nearly midway in its course the stream of Adurant divided and joined again, enclosing a fair island; and this was called Tolgalen, the Green Isle. There Beren and Lúthien dwelt after their return.

§115 The opening sentence of the paragraph was rewritten thus: 'There dwelt the Nandor, the Elves of the Host of Dân, who in the beginning were of Telerian race, but forsook their lord Thingol upon the march from Cuiviénen ...' On the first appearance of the name *Nandor*, a people originally from the host of the Noldor, see X.169, §28.

'Of old the lord of Ossiriand was Denethor': 'son of Dân' added after 'Denethor'. In the same sentence 'Melko' > 'Morgoth'.

It is notable that the phrase 'in the days when the Orcs were first made' was never altered.

At the end of the paragraph was added: 'For which reason the Noldor named that land Lindon', with a footnote '[The Country of Music >] The Land of Song' (see under §108 above); and '(Here endeth the matter taken from the *Dorgannas*)', on which see under §105 above.

§116 The whole of the latter part of this paragraph, from after the words 'But Turgon the wise, second son of Fingolfin, held Nivrost', was struck out and the following substituted (which does not appear in LQ 1):

> (But Turgon the wise ... held Nivrost), and there he ruled a numerous folk, both Noldor and Sindar, for one hundred years and sixteen, until he departed in secret to a hidden kingdom, as afterwards is told.'

This passage belongs with the long replacement in §106 given above, which likewise does not appear in LQ 1.

§117 'But Angrod and Egnor watched Bladorion' > 'His younger brethren Angrod and Egnor watched the fields of Ard-galen'

§120 *Tindobel* (see V.270, commentary on QS §§119–20) > *Ingildon* (cf. GA §90 and commentary, p. 118).

★

These are all the changes (save for a very few of no significance) made to the QS manuscript. A number of further changes were made to the top copy of the late typescript LQ 2 (the carbon copy was not touched).

The chapter-number 'XIV' was inserted (see p. 179, §100); and at the head of the first page my father wrote: 'This is a geographical and political insertion and may be omitted. It requires a map, of which I have not had time to make a copy.' This sounds as if he were preparing the LQ 2 typescript for someone to see it (cf. his words against §82 in the chapter 'Of Men' in LQ 2: 'This depends upon an old version in which the Sun was first made after the death of the Trees (described in a chapter omitted)', p. 175); in which case the words here 'and may be omitted' were much more probably advice to the presumed reader than a statement of intention about the inclusion of the chapter in *The Silmarillion*.

§105 *Ered-engrin* > *Eryd Engrin*

'(Utumno) ... at the western end' > 'at the midmost'. This shift of Utumno eastwards is implied in the hasty note pencilled on the LQ 2 text of Chapter 2, *Of Valinor and the Two Trees*, in which the story entered that Angband also was built in the ancient days, 'not far from the northwestern shores of the Sea' (see X.156, §12, and the addition made to this paragraph, given below).

Eredwethion > *Erydwethrin* (and subsequently).

Eredlómin > *Erydlómin*. In LQ 2 §106 the name of the Echoing Mountains is *Eryd Lammad*, following the change made to the QS manuscript there (p. 192) but not here; and *Eryd Lammad* was allowed to stand.

The passage 'Behind their walls Melkor coming back into Middle-earth made the endless dungeons of Angband, the hells of iron, where of old Utumno had been. But he made a great tunnel under them ...' was emended on LQ 2 to read:

> Behind their walls Melkor had made also a fortress (after called Angband) as a defence against the West, if any assault should come from Valinor. This was in the command of Sauron. It was captured by the Valar, and Sauron fled into hiding; but being in haste to overthrow Melkor in his great citadel of Utumno, the Valar did not wholly destroy Angband nor search out all its deep places; and thither Sauron returned and many other creatures of Melkor, and there they waited in hope for the return of their Master. Therefore when he came back into Middle-earth Melkor took up his abode in the endless dungeons of Angband, the hells of iron; and he made a great tunnel under them ...

§106 *Nivrost* > *Nevrast* (and subsequently; see p. 179, §100). The footnote to the first occurrence of *Nivrost* 'Which is West Vale in the tongue of Doriath' was struck out and replaced by the following:

> Which is 'Hither Shore' in the Sindarin tongue, and was given at first to all the coast-lands south of Drengist, but was later limited to the land whose shores lay between Drengist and Mount Taras.

§108 To the name *Taur-im-Duinath* (a later addition to QS, p. 193) a footnote was added: 'Forest between the Rivers (sc. Sirion and Gelion)'. This interpretation occurs in fact in a rewriting of the QS text at a later point: p. 195, §113.

§110 At the two occurrences of *Nan Dungorthin* in the long replacement passage in this paragraph given on p. 193-4 the later form *Nan Dungortheb* was substituted.

§111 *Damrod and Díriel* > *Amrod and Amras*, and in §118; cf. X.177.

The revised footnote against the name *Thargelion*, 'Radhrost in the tongue of Doriath' (p. 194), was struck out and not replaced (see under §118 below).

Cranthir > *Caranthir*, and in §118; cf. X.177, 181.

§112 *Taur-na-Faroth* > *Taur-en-Faroth* at both occurrences.

Ingwil (the torrent joining Narog at Nargothrond) > *Ringwil*.

Inglor > *Finrod* (and subsequently).

§117 *Finrod* > *Finarfin*

§118 At the end of the paragraph *Dor Granthir* > *Dor Caranthir*; in the footnote the same change was made, and *Radhrost* was replaced by *Talath Rhúnen*, the translation 'the East Vale' remaining. See under §111 above.

§119 'But Inglor was king of Nargothrond and overlord of the Dark-elves of the western havens; and with his aid Brithombar and Eglorest were rebuilt' was rewritten thus:

> But Finrod was king of Nargothrond and over-lord of all the Dark-elves of Beleriand between Sirion and the Sea, save only in the Falas. There dwelt still those of the Sindar who still loved ships and the Sea, and they had great havens at Brithombar and Eglarest. Their lord was Círdan the Shipbuilder. There was friendship and alliance between Finrod and Círdan, and with the aid of the Noldor Brithombar and Eglarest were rebuilt...

Finrod (Inglor) now loses the overlordship of the Elves of the Falas, with the emergence of Círdan, but my father failed to correct the earlier passage in QS (§109) telling that 'the Dark-elves of the havens ... took Felagund, lord of Nargothrond, to be their king.' The statement here in §119 agrees with what is said in GA §85 (see also the commentary, p. 117).

§120 In the opening sentence of this paragraph the old name *Tindobel* had been changed to *Ingildon* (p. 196); it was now changed to *Nimras* (cf. *Barad Nimras*, the replacement of *Tower of Tindabel* on the second map, p. 190, §62).

Some of the changes made to LQ 2 were made also to the much earlier typescript LQ 1: *Ringwil* (§112), *Talath Rhúnen* (§118), *Nimras* (§120). In addition, *Dor Granthir* was corrected to *Dor Cranthir* (§118), and the passage concerning the lordship of the Falas (§119) was inserted, but still with the name *Inglor*: thus these changes were not made at the same time as those in LQ 2, which has *Dor Caranthir* and *Finrod*.

12 OF TURGON AND THE BUILDING OF GONDOLIN

This short chapter on three manuscript pages, with this title but without chapter-number, was inserted into the QS manuscript following *Of Beleriand and its Realms*.

At an earlier point in the manuscript (§101 in the chapter *Of the Siege of Angband*) a long rider was introduced on the subject of the foundation of Nargothrond by Inglor and the discovery of Gondolin by Turgon: see pp. 177–9. As I have explained there, this rider is extant in two partially distinct forms, the first in the early LQ 1 typescript series, and the second on a sheet inserted into the QS manuscript (whence it appears in the late typescript LQ 2). Without question the new chapter (which does not appear in the LQ 1 series) was written at the same time as the revised form of this rider to §101, and it is to this that the opening words of the new chapter ('It hath been told how by the guidance of Ulmo ...') refer. (I have also noticed, p. 179, that on the reverse of this rider is a rejected draft for the replacement text of the year 116 in the *Grey Annals*, §§111–13; on this see below, at the end of the third paragraph of the text.)

There is no need to give *Of Turgon and the Building of Gondolin* in full, because, as will be seen shortly, a substantial part of it has been given already.

Of Turgon and the Building of Gondolin

It hath been told how by the guidance of Ulmo Turgon of Nivrost discovered the hidden vale of Tum-laden; and that (as was after known) lay east of the upper waters of Sirion, in a ring of mountains tall and sheer, and no living thing came there save the eagles of Thorondor. But there was a deep way under the mountains delved in the darkness of the world by waters that flowed out to join the stream of Sirion; and this Turgon found and so came to the green plain amid the mountains, and saw the island-hill that stood there of hard smooth stone; for the vale had been a great lake in ancient days. Then Turgon knew that he had found the place of his desire, and resolved there to build a fair city, a memorial of Tirion upon Túna, for which his heart still yearned in exile. But he returned to Nivrost, and remained there in peace, though he pondered ever in his thought how he should accomplish his design.

> The conclusion of this paragraph had already been used, but abandoned before it was completed, at the end of the rider to QS §101, p. 179.

Therefore, after the Dagor Aglareb, the unquiet that Ulmo set in his heart returned to him, and he summoned many of the hardiest and most skilled of his people and led them secretly to the hidden vale, and there they began the building of the city that Turgon had devised in his heart; and they set a watch all about it that none might come upon their work from without, and the power of Ulmo that ran in Sirion protected them.

> In this second paragraph my father was following and all but simply copying the revised annal for the year 64 in GA (§89); 'the hidden vale' was substituted for 'Gondolin' of GA because Turgon was now not to name his city until it was completed.

Now Turgon dwelt still for the most part in Nivrost, but it came to pass that at last the City was full-wrought, after two and fifty years of labour; and Turgon appointed its name, and it was called Gondolin [*in margin:* the Hidden Rock]. Then Turgon prepared to depart from Nivrost and leave his fair halls beside the Sea; and there Ulmo came to him once again and spake with him.

> From this point the new *Silmarillion* chapter follows almost word for word the replacement text of the annal for 116 in GA (§§111–13): the words of Ulmo to Turgon, and the departure from Vinyamar to Gondolin. The reason for this is simple: as I have noticed in the commentary on GA §113 (p. 120), my father wrote against the revised annal for 116: 'Set this rather in the *Silmarillion* and substitute a short notice' (the proposed 'short notice' is given *ibid.*).
>
> The text of the new chapter leaves that in the *Grey Annals* at the words 'passed the gates in the mountains and they were shut behind him'; the concluding words of GA §113 ('But Nivrost was empty of folk and so remained until the ruin of Beleriand') were not repeated here, but were brought in subsequently.

And through many long years none passed inward thereafter (save Húrin and Handir only sent by Ulmo); and the host of

Turgon came never forth again until the Year of Lamentation [*struck out, probably at the time of writing:* and the ruin of the Noldor], after three hundred and fifty years and more. But behind the circle of the mountains the folk of Turgon grew and throve, and they put forth their skill in labour unceasing, so that Gondolin upon Amon Gwareth became fair indeed and meet to compare even with Elven Tirion beyond the Sea. High and white were its walls, and smooth were its stairs, and tall and strong was the Tower of the King. There shining fountains played, and in the courts of Turgon stood images of the Trees of old, which Turgon himself wrought with elven-craft; and the Tree which he made of gold was named Glingal, and the Tree whose flowers he made of silver was named Belthil, and the light which sprang from them filled all the ways of the city. But fairer than all the wonders of Gondolin was Idril Turgon's daughter, she that was called Celebrindal the Silver-foot for the whiteness of her unshod feet, but her hair was as the gold of Laurelin ere the coming of Melkor. Thus Turgon lived long in bliss greater than any that hath been east of the Sea; but Nivrost was desolate, and remained empty of living folk until the ruin of Beleriand; and elsewhere the shadow of Morgoth stretched out its fingers from the North.

The opening sentence of this concluding section, with the reference to the entry of Húrin and Handir of Brethil into Gondolin, shows that it belongs with the original form of that story in the *Grey Annals* (§§149–50, and see the commentary, pp. 124–5); the later story that it was Húrin and his brother Huor appears in the long rider GA §§161–6.

This is the only account, brief as it is, of the actual city of Gondolin that my father wrote after that in Q (IV.139–40) – although there are also the notes that follow the abandoned text of the later *Tale of Tuor* (*Unfinished Tales* p. 56, note 31). That the Trees of Gondolin were images made by Turgon was stated in a footnote to Chapter 2 *Of Valinor and the Two Trees* in QS (see V.210–11; X.155), and this is repeated here – but with the addition that 'the light which sprang from them filled all the ways of the city'.

There is only one other text of the new chapter, the LQ 2 typescript, in which it is numbered 'XV' (see p. 196). To this my father made some corrections: *Nivrost* > *Nevrast* as in the preceding chapters; *Eryd Wethion* > *Eryd Wethrin*; *Handir* > *Huor* (see above); and *Amon Gwareth* > *Amon Gwared*. The marginal note rendering *Gondolin* as 'the Hidden Rock' was placed in a footnote in LQ 2, which my father then extended as follows:

Or so its name was afterwards known and interpreted; but its ancient form and meaning are in doubt. It is said that the name was given first in Quenya (for that language was spoken in Turgon's house), and was *Ondolindë*, the Rock of the Music of Water, for there were fountains upon the hill. But the people (who spoke only the Sindarin tongue) altered this name to *Gondolin* and interpreted [it] to mean Hidden Rock: *Gond dolen* in their own speech.

With the interpretation of Quenya *Ondolindë* as 'Rock of the Music of Water' cf. the early translation of *Gondolin* as 'Stone of Song' in the name-list to the tale of *The Fall of Gondolin* (II.216); and with the interpretation 'Hidden Rock' cf. the *Etymologies* in Vol.V, p. 355, stem DUL, where *Gondolin(n)* is said to contain three elements: 'heart of hidden rock'.

---

13 CONCERNING THE DWARVES

The reason for this title will be seen at the end of the chapter (pp. 213–14). To the original Chapter 10 *Of Men and Dwarfs* in the QS manuscript (V.272–6, §§122–31) only a few changes were made before a radical revision overtook it.

§122 'whom the Dark-elves named Naug-rim' > 'whom they named the Naug-rim', i.e. this became a Noldorin name for the Dwarves given to them by Cranthir's people.

§123 The marginal note 'quoth Pengolod' against the bracketed passage concerning the origin and nature of the Dwarves was struck out (see V.277–8, §123).

§124 'Nogrod, the Dwarfmine': above 'Dwarfmine' is pencilled 'Dwarrowdelf', and in the margin again 'Dwarrowdelf Nogrod was afar off in the East in the Mountains of Mist; and Belegost was in Eredlindon south of Beleriand.' At the head of the page, with a direction for insertion in the text after 'Belegost, the Great Fortress' the following is written very rapidly:

> Greatest of these was Khazaddûm that was after called in the days of its darkness Moria, and it was far off in the east in the Mountains of Mist; but Gabilgathol was on [the] east side of Eredlindon and within reach of the Elves.

In the text of QS as written *Nogrod* (which goes back to the old *Tale of the Nauglafring*) is a translation of *Khazaddûm*, and the meaning is 'Dwarfmine'; both Nogrod and Belegost (Gabilgathol) are specifically stated (QS §122) to have been 'in the mountains east of Thargelion', and were so placed in additions to the second map. In *The Lord of the Rings* Khazad-dûm is Moria, and Nogrod and Belegost are 'ancient cities in the Blue Mountains' (Appendix A, III). The notes in the margin of QS just given must represent an idea that was not adopted, whereby Belegost remained in Eredlindon, but *Nogrod / Khazad-dûm was removed to the Misty Mountains, and Nogrod became the ancient Elvish name of Moria.*

The statement in the first of these notes that 'Belegost was in Eredlindon *south of Beleriand*' is surprising: it seems to represent a reversion to the older conception of the place of the Dwarf-cities: see the Eastward Extension of the first *Silmarillion* map, IV.231, where the dwarf-road after crossing the Blue Mountains below Mount Dolmed turns south and goes off the map in the south-east corner, with the direction 'Southward in East feet of Blue Mountains are Belegost and Nogrod.'

§126 Against the words in the first sentence of the paragraph 'when some four hundred years were gone since the Gnomes came to Beleriand' my father noted: 'This must be removed to 300', changed to '310'. See p. 226, §1.

§127 'They were the first of Men that wandering west' > 'They were the first of Men that after many lives of wandering westward'
Gumlin > *Galion* (see p. 123, §127).

§128 The footnote was changed to read:

It is recorded that this name was *Vidri* in the ancient speech of these Men, which is now forgotten; for afterwards in Beleriand they forsook their own speech for the tongue of the Gnomes. Quoth Pengolod.

In the sentence following the place of the footnote 'whom we call the Gnomes' was changed to '(whom we here call the Gnomes)'.

§129 'the lordship of Gumlin was in Hithlum' > 'the lordship of Galion was in Dorlómen'

Throughout the text the form *Dwarfs* (see V.277, §122) was changed to *Dwarves*.

★

The next step was the striking out of the entire text of Chapter 10 from the beginning as far as 'Hador the Goldenhaired' at the end of §125, and the substitution of a new and much enlarged form, carefully written and inserted into the QS manuscript. This has a few subsequent emendations (almost all made at the same time in red ink), and these are shown in the text that now follows. One of these emendations concerns the title itself. As the revised version was first written the title was *Of Dwarves and Men*, with a subtitle *Concerning the Dwarves* (but no subtitle where the section on Men begins). The title was struck out, and replaced by *Of the Naugrim and the Edain*; the subtitle *Concerning the Dwarves* was retained; and a new subtitle *Of the Edain* was inserted at the appropriate place.

In order not to interrupt the numbering of the QS text in Vol.V, for reference in the commentary that follows the text I number the paragraphs of the revised version from §1. – It will be seen that the opening paragraph repeats almost exactly that of QS (§122), but loses the original concluding sentence: 'For though the Dwarfs did not serve Morgoth, yet they were in some things more like to his people than to the Elves.'

Of the Naugrim and the Edain

Concerning the Dwarves

§1 Now in time the building of Nargothrond was completed, and Gondolin had been raised in secret; but in the days of the Siege of Angband the Gnomes had yet small need of hiding-places, and they ranged far and wide between the Western Sea and the Blue Mountains. And it is said that they climbed Eredlindon and looked eastward in wonder, for the lands of Middle-earth seemed wild and wide; but few ever passed over the mountains while Angband lasted. In those days the folk of Cranthir first came upon the Dwarves, whom they [> the Dark-elves] named the Naugrim; for the chief dwellings of that race were then in the mountains east of Thargelion, the land of Cranthir, and were digged deep in the eastern slopes of Eredlindon. Thence they journeyed often into Beleriand, and were admitted even into Doriath. There was at that time no enmity between Elves and Dwarves, but nonetheless no great love.

Here are the words of Pengolod concerning the Naugrim*

§2 The Naugrim are not of Elf-kind, nor of Man-kind, nor yet of Melkor's breeding; and the Noldor in Middle-earth knew not whence they came, holding that they were alien to the Children, albeit in many ways like unto them. But in Valinor the wise have learned that the Dwarves were made in secret by Aulë, while Earth was yet dark; for he desired the coming of the Children of Ilúvatar, that he might have learners to whom he could teach his crafts and lore, and he was unwilling to await the fulfilment of the designs of Ilúvatar. Wherefore, though the Dwarves are like the Orcs in this: that they came of the wilfulness of one of the Valar, they are not evil; for they were not made out of malice in mockery of the Children, but came of the desire of Aulë's heart to make things of his own after the

---

* All that follows in the section 'Concerning the Dwarves' is written in a much smaller script than that of the opening paragraph.

pattern of the designs of Ilúvatar. And since they came in the days of the power of Melkor, Aulë made them strong to endure. Therefore they are stone-hard, stubborn, fast in friendship and in enmity, and they suffer toil and hunger and hurt of body more hardily than all other speaking-folk. And they live long, far beyond the span of Men, and yet not for ever. Aforetime the Noldor held that dying they returned unto the earth and the stone of which they were made; yet that is not their own belief. For they say that Aulë cares for them and gathers them in Mandos in halls set apart for them, and there they wait, not in idleness but in the practice of crafts and the learning of yet deeper lore. And Aulë, they say, declared to their Fathers of old that Ilúvatar had accepted from him the work of his desire, and that Ilúvatar will hallow them and give them a place among the Children in the End. Then their part shall be to serve Aulë and to aid him in the re-making of Arda after the Last Battle.

§3 Now these Fathers, they say, were seven in number, and they alone return (in the manner of the Quendi) to live again in their own kin and to bear once more their ancient names. Of these Durin was the most renowned in after ages, father of that Dwarf-kin most friendly to the Elves whose mansions were at Khazad-dûm.

§4 In the darkness of Arda already the Naugrim wrought great works, for they had, even from the first days of their Fathers, marvellous skill with metals and with stone, though their works had little beauty until they had met the Noldor and learned somewhat of their arts. And they gave their friendship more readily to the Noldor than to any others of Elves or Men, because of their love and reverence for Aulë; and the gems of the Gnomes they praised above all other wealth. But in that ancient time the Dwarves still wrought iron and copper rather than silver and gold; and the making of weapons and gear of war was their chief smith-craft. They it was that first devised mail of linked rings, and in the making of byrnies and of hauberks none among Elves or Men have proved their equals. Thus they aided the Eldar greatly in their war with the Orcs of Morgoth; though the Noldor believed that some of that folk would not have been loath to smithy also for Morgoth, had he been in need of their work or open to their trade. For buying and selling and exchange were their delight, and the winning of wealth thereby; and this they gathered rather to hoard than to use, save in further trading.

§5 The Naugrim were ever, as they still remain, short and squat in stature; they were deep-breasted, strong in the arm, and stout in the leg, and their beards were long. Indeed this strangeness they have that no Man nor Elf has ever seen a beardless Dwarf – unless he were shaven in mockery, and would then be more like to die of shame than of many other hurts that to us would seem more deadly. For the Naugrim have beards from the beginning of their lives, male and female alike; nor indeed can their womenkind be discerned by those of other race, be it in feature or in gait or in voice, nor in any wise save this: that they go not to war, and seldom save at direst need issue from their deep bowers and halls. It is said, also, that their womenkind are few, and that save their kings and chieftains few Dwarves ever wed; wherefore their race multiplied slowly, and now is dwindling.

§6 The father-tongue of the Dwarves Aulë himself devised for them, and their languages have thus no kinship with those of the Quendi. The Dwarves do not gladly teach their tongue to those of alien race; and in use they have made it harsh and intricate, so that of those few whom they have received in full friendship fewer still have learned it well. But they themselves learn swiftly other tongues, and in converse they use as they may the speech of Elves and Men with whom they deal. Yet in secret they use their own speech only, and that (it is said) is slow to change; so that even their realms and houses that have been long and far sundered may to this day well understand one another. In ancient days the Naugrim dwelt in many mountains of Middle-earth, and there they met mortal Men (they say) long ere the Eldar knew them; whence it comes that of the tongues of the Easterlings many show kinship with Dwarf-speech rather than with the speeches of the Elves.*

§7 In their own tongue the Dwarves name themselves Khuzûd [> Khazâd]; and the Dark-elves called them / the Naugrim [> Naug], the stunted. Which name the exiled Noldor also used [> likewise took for them], but called them also the Nyrn [*struck out*: of like meaning], and the Gonnhirrim masters of stone; and those who dwelt in Belegost they called the Ennfeng or Longbeards, for their beards swept the floor before their feet. The chief cities of the Khuzûd [> Khazâd] in the west of Middle-earth in those days were at Khazaddûm, and at

---

* [Marginal note] Thus the *Lammas*.

Gabilgathol and Tumunzahar, which are interpreted in the Gnomish tongue Nornhabar the Dwarrowdelf, and Belegost Mickleburg, and Nogrod the Hollowbold. Greatest of all the mansions of the Naugrim was Khazaddûm, that was after called in the days of its darkness Moria, but it was far off in the Mountains of Mist beyond the wide leagues of Eriador; whereas Belegost and Nogrod were upon the east side of Eredlindon and nigh to the lands of the Eldar. Yet few of the Elves, save Meglin of Gondolin, went ever thither; and the Dwarves trafficked into Beleriand, and made a great road that passed under the shoulders of Mount Dolmed and followed thence the course of Ascar, crossing Gelion at Sarn-athrad. There battle later befell; but as yet the Dwarves troubled the Elves little, while the power of the Gnomes lasted.

§8 *Here end the words that Pengolod spoke to me concerning the Dwarves*, which are not part of the *Pennas* as it was written, but come from other books of lore, from the *Lammas*, the *Dorgannas*, and the *Quentalë Ardanómion*: quoth Ælfwine.

Of the Edain

§9 It is reckoned that the first meeting of the Noldor and the Naugrim befell in the land of Cranthir Fëanor's son about that time when Fingolfin destroyed the Orcs at Drengist, one hundred and fifty-five years after the crossing of the Ice, and one hundred and five before the first coming of Glómund the dragon. After his defeat there was long peace, and it lasted for wellnigh two hundred years of the sun. During this time the fathers of the Houses of the Men of the West, the Atani [> Edain], the Elf-friends of old, were born in the land of Eriador east of the mountains: Bëor the Vassal, Haleth the Hunter, and Hador the Goldenhaired.

Here the revised part of QS Chapter 10 ends. It will be seen that while it was composed with the original QS text before him and with the actual retention of some of it, my father now introduced many new conceptions concerning the Dwarves. The long-enduring 'hostile' view has at last virtually vanished, with the loss of the sentence at the end of the first paragraph (see p. 203) – although in the original QS text the likeness of Orcs and Dwarves was subsequently (§123) spoken of only in terms of the analogous origin of the two races, each deriving from one of the Valar acting independently, and this remains in the revision. We learn now that:

– the Dwarves live far longer than Men (§2);

- they themselves believe that Aulë gathers them after their death into halls in Mandos set apart, and that after the Last Battle they will aid Aulë in the remaking of Arda (§2);
- there were Seven Fathers of the Dwarves, who are reincarnated in their own kin (after the manner of the Elves), bearing their ancient names (§3);
- Durin was the father of the Dwarf-kindred of Khazad-dûm, most friendly to the Elves (§3);
- the Dwarves were better disposed to the Noldor than to any others among Elves or Men on account of their reverence of Aulë (§4);
- the Dwarves are bearded from birth, both male and female (§5);
- Dwarf-women cannot be distinguished from the men by those of other race (§5);
- Dwarf-women are very few, and never go to war, nor leave their deep homes save at the greatest need (§5);
- few Dwarves ever wed (§5);
- the Dwarf-speech changes only very slowly, so that sundering of houses and realms does not greatly impair understanding between them (§6);
- Dwarves met Men in Middle-earth long before the Eldar met them, and hence there is kinship between Dwarf-speech and the languages of the Easterling Men (§6).

This revised version was of course a part of the 1951 revision. There are notable likenesses to what is said in the Appendices to *The Lord of the Rings* concerning the Dwarves: thus in Appendix A, III *(Durin's Folk)* there are references to the fewness of Dwarf-women, who remain hidden in their dwellings, to the indistinguishability of Dwarf-women from Dwarf-men to people of other races, and to the rarity of marriage (III.360); and in Appendix F (III.410) the slow changing of their tongue is described.

There follows now a commentary on particular points.

§1 The change made to the original QS text (p. 201, §122) of 'whom the Dark-elves named Naug-rim' to 'whom they [the Noldor] named the Naug-rim' was now reversed, by a subsequent emendation (later, in §7, the attribution of the name to the Dark-elves appears in the text as written).

§2 'And since they came in the days of the power of Melkor': i.e., before the awakening of the Elves, the Battle of the Gods, and the captivity of Melkor in Mandos.

§3 It is here that Durin of Khazad-dûm, 'most renowned' of the Seven Fathers of the Dwarves, enters *The Silmarillion*. It is not said here that Durin's people were the Longbeards; but his association with the Longbeards goes back in fact to *The Hobbit*, where at the end of the chapter *A Short Rest* Thorin says (in the text as originally published): 'He was the father of the fathers of *one of the two races of dwarves, the Longbeards*, and my grandfather's ancestor.' In the

Tale of the Nauglafring there were the two peoples, the Dwarves of Nogrod and the Dwarves of Belegost, and the latter were the Indrafangs or Longbeards; in the *Quenta* the same was true (or at least, no other peoples were mentioned), although the Longbeards had become the Dwarves of Nogrod (IV.104), and this remained the case in QS (§124).

In the present text two things are said on the subject. Durin was 'the father of that Dwarf-kin ... whose mansions were at Khazad-dûm' (§3); but (reverting to the *Tale of the Nauglafring*) the Longbeards were the Dwarves of Belegost (§7) – and this is said also both in the *Annals of Aman* and in the *Grey Annals* (see p. 108, §22). I am not altogether certain how to interpret this; but the simplest solution is to suppose that when my father wrote these texts he had forgotten Thorin's mention of Durin as the ancestor of the Longbeards in *The Hobbit* (or, less probably, that he consciously disregarded it), and the following considerations support it.

At the beginning of the section *Durin's Folk* in Appendix A (III) to *The Lord of the Rings* the reading of the First Edition was: 'Durin is the name that the Dwarves use for the eldest of the Seven Fathers of all their race', without mention of the Longbeards. Years later, on his copy of the second edition of *The Hobbit*, my father noted: 'Not so in *Silmarillion* nor see [sic] LR III p. 352' – this being a reference to the passage just cited from Appendix A in the First Edition: what was 'not so' was Thorin's reference to 'one of the two races of dwarves', become obsolete since the emergence of the conception of the Seven Fathers. At the same time he wrote on this copy many tentative phrases to replace Thorin's original words, such as 'the eldest of the Seven Fathers of the Dwarves', 'the father of the fathers of the eldest line of the Dwarf-kings, the Longbeards', before arriving at the final form as subsequently published, 'He was the father of the fathers of the eldest race of Dwarves, the Longbeards, and my first ancestor: I am his heir.' It was obviously consideration of Thorin's words in *The Hobbit* and the need for their correction that led him to alter the text of Appendix A, which in the Second Edition (1966) reads: 'Durin is the name that the Dwarves used for the eldest of the Seven Fathers of their race, *and the ancestor of all the kings of the Longbeards*', with the addition of a footnote reference to the passage in *The Hobbit*, now published in its corrected form.

Thus, circuitously, the Longbeards finally entered *The Lord of the Rings*, as the Dwarves of Khazad-dûm; but the texts of *The Silmarillion* and the *Annals* were never changed, and the Longbeards remained the Dwarves of Belegost.

§6 The marginal note 'Thus the *Lammas*' apparently refers specifically to the statement in the text concerning the kinship of languages of the Easterlings with Dwarf-speech. Cf. V.179 (*Lham-*

THE LATER *QUENTA SILMARILLION* 209

mas §9): 'the languages of Men are derived in part from them' (the tongues of the Dwarves); this was repeated in the footnote to QS §123, from which the present paragraph was developed, and which also has a marginal note 'So, the *Lhammas*'.

§7 The names and places of the Dwarf-cities now achieve almost their final form, and I recapitulate here the complex development:

QS original form, §124 (V.274)
  Khazad-dûm = Nogrod = Dwarfmine (in the Blue Mountains)
  Gabilgathol = Belegost = Great Fortress

QS original form emended, p. 201
  Khazad-dûm = Nogrod = Dwarrowdelf, later *Moria*
  Gabilgathol = Belegost = Great Fortress

QS revised version, §7
  Tumunzahar = Nogrod = Hollowbold (in the Blue Mountains)
  Gabilgathol = Belegost = Mickleburg
  Khazad-dûm = Nornhabar = Dwarrowdelf, later *Moria*

The Dwarvish name *Tumunzahar* of Nogrod appears in GA §19, but this is the first occurrence of the Elvish name *Nornhabar*.

Of the names of the Dwarves themselves, there first occur here *Gonnhirrim* masters of stone, and *Nyrn* (cf. *Nornwaith* in AAm, X.93, *Norn-folk* in GA §19, and the name *Nornhabar* of Khazad-dûm). *Naugrim* is now said to mean 'stunted', and *Nyrn* is 'of like meaning', though this statement was struck out; in the original text (§124) *Neweg* = 'stunted'. In addition, *Khuzûd* was subsequently changed to *Khazâd*, and *Naugrim* to *Naug*. I give here a summary of the development of these confusing names and forms:

Tale of the Nauglafring	Nauglath
Q	Nauglir
AB 1 (IV.311)	Nauglar (also in the List of Names, V.405: Dark-elvish name, adopted by the Gnomes)
QS (original form)	Naugrim (Dark-elvish name > (p. 201) Gnomish name)
	Neweg 'stunted' (Gnomish name)
QS (revised version)	Naugrim (> Naug) 'stunted' (Gnomish name > Dark-elvish name, adopted by the Gnomes)
	Nyrn (Gnomish name, 'stunted' – but this meaning rejected)
AAm	Nauglath > Naugrim
	Nornwaith (later rejected, X.106, §84)
GA	Naugrim
	Norn-folk (§19)

An important element in this revised section remains to be mentioned: at this stage the myth of the creation of the Dwarves lacked the element of the Fathers being laid to sleep, by the command of Ilúvatar, after their first arising. This is apparent from the text as it stands; and the entry of this element will be seen in a moment.

The next text was the typescript of the LQ 1 series, which followed the manuscript text exactly (but the changes of *Khuzûd* > *Khazâd* and *Naugrim* > *Naug* in §7 do not appear, nor in LQ 2), and after the first paragraph of the section *Of the Edain* (§9), where the revised version ends, followed the original text of QS, with the very few alterations that were made to it and which have been given on pp. 201–2.

The opening of 'the words of Pengolod [> Pengoloð] concerning the Naugrim' (§2) were struck out, long afterwards, on LQ 1, as far as 'the desire of Aulë's heart to make things of his own after the pattern of the designs of Ilúvatar.' Associated with the QS manuscript at this point are two pages headed 'Of Aulë and the Dwarves', enclosed in a paper wrapper bearing the words 'Amended Legend of Origin of Dwarves'; this begins as a good manuscript but breaks up into confusion and variant forms. A new text was written out fair in a late script of my father's, without title, and attached to LQ 1 as a replacement for the passage struck out; it begins thus, differing little from the rejected form:

> The Naugrim are not of the Elf-kind, nor of Man-kind, nor yet of Melkor's breeding; and the Noldor, when they met them in Middle-earth, knew not whence they came, holding that they were alien to the Children, although in many ways they resembled them. But here in Valinor we have learned that in their beginning the Dwarves were made by Aulë, while Earth was still dark; for Aulë desired the coming of the Children so greatly, to have learners to whom he could teach his lore and his crafts, that he was unwilling to await the fulfilment of the designs of Ilúvatar.

The remainder of the text will be found in the published *Silmarillion*, Chapter 2 *Of Aulë and Yavanna*, pp. 43–4, to its end at 'Then Aulë took the Seven Fathers of the Dwarves, and laid them to rest in far-sundered places; and he returned to Valinor, and waited while the long years lengthened.' There are a number of insignificant editorial alterations in the published text, and among them one point should be mentioned: my father was uncertain whether to use 'thou' or 'you' in the converse of Aulë with Ilúvatar (in one case he changed 'you may' to 'thou mayst' and then reverted to 'you may'). In the end he decided on 'you', whereas the published text has 'thou' throughout.

At the end of the insertion the chapter continues with 'Since they came in the days of the power of Melkor ...' (p. 204), but concomitantly with the introduction of the new form of the legend, in which the Fathers of the Dwarves were laid to sleep until after the awakening of the Elves and the imprisonment of Melkor, this was changed on LQ 1 to 'Since they were to come ...' The only other significant alteration made to LQ 1 was in the opening sentence of §3, which was changed to read: 'Now these Seven Fathers, they say, return to live again and to bear once more their ancient names.' It might be expected that my father would have made some change to the opening sentence of §4 after the entry of the new form of the legend, but he was evidently content with an internal shift of meaning: 'even from the first days of their Fathers' is to be understood as 'even from the first days of their Fathers when they awoke from their sleep'.

The earlier of the two texts of the inserted passage shows my father much exercised about the details of the making of the first Dwarves. Thus there are the following tentative and roughly-written passages:

(a) But it is said that to each Dwarf Ilúvatar added a mate of female kind, yet because he would not amend the work of Aulë, and Aulë had yet made only things of male form, therefore the women of the Dwarves resemble their men more than all other [?speaking] races.

(b) He wrought in secret in a hall under the mountains in Middle-earth. There he made first one Dwarf, the eldest of all, and after he made six others, the fathers of their race; and then he began to make others again, like to them but of female kind to be their mates. But he wearied, and when he [had] made six more he rested, and he returned to the seven fathers and he looked at them, and they looked at him, and whatever motion was in his thought that motion they performed. And Aulë was not pleased, but he began to teach them the language that he had designed for them, hoping thus to instruct them.

But Ilúvatar knew all that was done, and in the very hour that the Eldest Dwarf first spoke with tongue, Ilúvatar spoke to Aulë; and Aulë

(c) Aulë made one, and then six, and he began to make mates for them of female form, and he made six, and then he wearied. Thus he buried six pairs, but one (Durin) the eldest he laid alone.

(d) And Aulë took the Seven Dwarves and laid them to rest under stone in far-sundered places, and beside each [of] them he laid a mate as the Voice bade him, and then he returned to Valinor.

(e) Then Aulë took the Seven Dwarves and laid them to rest under stone in far-sundered places, and beside each he laid his mate, save only beside the Eldest, and he lay alone. And Aulë returned to Valinor and waited long as best he might. But it is

> not known when Durin or his brethren first awoke, though some think that it was at the time of the departure of the Eldar over sea.

With passage *(b)* cf. the essay on Orcs in Vol.X, p. 417:

> But if [Melkor] had indeed attempted to make creatures of his own in imitation or mockery of the Incarnates, he would, like Aulë, only have succeeded in producing puppets: his creatures would have acted only while the attention of his will was upon them, and they would have shown no reluctance to execute any command of his, even if it were to destroy themselves.

In the final text, as printed in *The Silmarillion*, my father evidently abandoned the question of the origin of the female Dwarves, finding it intractable and the solutions unsatisfactory. Moreover in the finished form the element of the Eldest (Durin) being distinct from the others, and without mate, finds no place.

There is another version of the legend in the draft continuation (not sent) of a letter to Miss Rhona Beare dated 14 October 1958 (*The Letters of J. R. R. Tolkien* no.212); and here appears the idea of the one and the six, and the six mates of the six, making thirteen in all. I reprint the passage here, since it may not be readily available.

> Aulë, for instance, one of the Great, in a sense 'fell'; for he so desired to see the Children, that he became impatient and tried to anticipate the will of the Creator. Being the greatest of all craftsmen he tried to *make* children according to his imperfect knowledge of their kind. When he had made thirteen,* God spoke to him in anger, but not without pity: for Aulë had done this thing *not* out of evil desire to have slaves and subjects of his own, but out of impatient love, desiring children to talk to and teach, sharing with them the praise of Ilúvatar and his great love of the *materials* of which the world is made.
>
> The One rebuked Aulë, saying that he had tried to usurp the Creator's power; but he could not give independent *life* to his makings. He had only one life, his own derived from the One, and could at most only distribute it. 'Behold' said the One: 'these creatures of thine have only thy will, and thy movement. Though you have devised a language for them, they can only report to thee thine own thought. This is a mockery of me.'
>
> Then Aulë in grief and repentance humbled himself and asked for pardon. And he said: 'I will destroy these images of my presumption, and wait upon thy will.' And he took a great hammer, raising it to smite the eldest of his images; but it flinched and cowered from him. And as he withheld his stroke, astonished, he heard the laughter of Ilúvatar.

---

* One, the eldest, alone, and six more with six mates.

THE LATER *QUENTA SILMARILLION*   213

'Do you wonder at this?' he said. 'Behold! thy creatures now live, free from thy will! For I have seen thy humility, and taken pity on your impatience. Thy making I have taken up into my design.'

This is the Elvish legend of the making of the Dwarves; but the Elves report that Ilúvatar said thus also: 'Nonetheless I will not suffer my design to be forestalled: thy children shall not awake before mine own.' And he commanded Aulë to lay the fathers of the Dwarves severally in deep places, each with his mate, save Dúrin the eldest who had none. There they should sleep long, until Ilúvatar bade them awake. Nonetheless there has been for the most part little love between the Dwarves and the children of Ilúvatar. And of the fate that Ilúvatar has set upon the children of Aulë beyond the Circles of the world Elves and men know nothing, and if Dwarves know they do not speak of it.

It seems to me virtually certain that all this work on the later legend of Aulë and the Dwarves derives from the same time, and it is obvious that this letter belongs with the first or draft text from which extracts are given on pp. 211–12, preceding the final text attached to LQ 1 and printed in *The Silmarillion*. That text was incorporated in LQ 2 as typed, and for that typescript I have proposed (on wholly distinct grounds) 1958 as the approximate date (see X.141–2, 300). This, I think, fits well enough with the date of the letter (October 1958). It seems likely that my father revised the existing *Silmarillion* materials *pari passu* with the making of the typescript LQ 2, carried out under his guidance.

As already noticed (see p. 210), the original QS text (lightly emended) in the second part of the chapter, that concerned with the Edain, was followed in the early typescript LQ 1. At a later time the whole of the section on the Edain was struck through both on the QS manuscript (with the direction 'Substitute new form') and on LQ 1 (with the direction 'Cancel'). This new form was a typescript, made by my father himself, with the title *Of the Coming of Men into the West and the Meeting of the Edain and the Eldar*. In the LQ 2 series the section on the Dwarves, now much altered and expanded from its original form, was made into a separate chapter, on which my father inserted the number 'XVI' (following 'XV' *Of Turgon and the Building of Gondolin*, p. 200), retaining as title the original subtitle *Concerning the Dwarves* (p. 202). The new text of the second part, *Of the Coming of Men into the West*, then followed in LQ 2 as a further chapter and was given the number 'XVII'. I have followed this arrangement.

The complex textual evolution of the original chapter in QS can be displayed thus (the dates have been made definite except in one case).

QS ch.10 *Of Men and Dwarfs*
(1937)
↓
QS ch.10 New title *Of the Naugrim and the Edain*: section on the Dwarves rewritten; section on the Edain retained (1951)
↓
Typescript LQ 1 (1951)
↓

Insertion of new legend of Aulë and the Dwarves (1958)

Typescript LQ 2 (1958): ch.XVI *Concerning the Dwarves* (no section on the Edain)

———

Wholly new text on the Edain: *Of the Coming of Men into the West* (date uncertain: 1958?)

Typescript LQ 2 (1958): ch.XVII

★

It remains only to notice the changes made to LQ 2 *Concerning the Dwarves*. The chief of these is a further revision of the names of the Dwarves (see the table on p. 209). In §1 (p. 203) 'whom the Dark-elves named the Naugrim' was struck out, and at every occurrence the name *Naugrim* was replaced by *Dwarves* (except in the heading to §2, where it was no doubt retained inadvertently). In §7 the opening passage now read, both in LQ 1 and in LQ 2:

> In their own tongue the Dwarves name themselves Khuzûd; but the Dark-elves called them Naugrim, the stunted. Which name the exiled Noldor likewise took for them, but called them also the Nyrn...

(The changes of *Khuzûd* to *Khazâd* and *Naugrim* to *Naug* made on the manuscript did not appear in the typescripts as typed, see pp. 205, 210.) The passage was rewritten on LQ 2 thus:

> In their own tongue the Dwarves name themselves Khazâd; but the Grey-elves called them the Nyrn, the hard. This name the exiled Noldor likewise took for them, but called them also the Naugrim, the stunted folk...

Other changes were: in §1, in the sentence 'few ever passed over the mountains', 'few' > 'none'; also *Cranthir* > *Caranthir*. In §7, in the sentence concerning Nornhabar, Belegost, and Nogrod, which were said to be interpretations 'in the Gnomish tongue' of the Dwarvish names, 'Gnomish' > 'Elvish'.

14 OF THE COMING OF MEN INTO THE WEST

The introduction of what very soon became an entirely new chapter – a massive extension of and departure from the 'traditional' history of the Edain – has been briefly described on p. 213. It emerges in a typescript (with carbon copy) made by my father: of antecedent draft material there is now no trace, but it seems to me very improbable that the text reached this form *ab initio*. It has in fact two titles: that typed as heading to the text is *Of the Coming of Men into the West and the Meeting of the Edain and the Eldar*, but on a separate title-page in manuscript it is called *Of the Coming of the Edain & their Houses and Lordships in Beleriand*.

The text was emended in ink on both copies almost identically; these changes were made, I feel sure, at much the same time as the original typing, and in the text that follows I adopt the emendations, but notice some of the original readings in the commentary. The separate title-page with the different title may belong with these, but I use here the other, in a shortened form *Of the Coming of Men into the West*, as was done in the published *Silmarillion*. The chapter (as emended) was incorporated in the typescript series LQ 2, as already mentioned, and subsequently given the number 'XVII'; perhaps (as with the new legend of Aulë and the Dwarves, see p. 213) it belongs to the period when the LQ typescript was being made (see p. 227, §13, and p. 229).

The text is found in the published *Silmarillion*, Chapter 17, but I have thought it best in this case to give the original in full. To show the editorial alterations and insertions in the published text takes much space, and it is difficult to make them clear, while the chapter is an essential companion to *The Wanderings of Húrin* in Part Three.

Of the Coming of Men into the West and the Meeting of the Edain and the Eldar

§1 Now it came to pass, when three hundred years and ten were gone since the Noldor came to Beleriand, in the days of the Long Peace, that Felagund journeyed east of Sirion and went hunting with Maglor and Maedros, sons of Fëanor. But he wearied of the chase and passed on alone towards the Mountains of Ered-lindon that he saw shining afar; and taking the

Dwarf-road he crossed Gelion at the ford of Sarn-athrad, and turning south over the upper streams of Ascar, he came into the north of Ossiriand.

§2   In a valley among the foothills of the Mountains, below the springs of Thalos, he saw lights in the evening, and far off he heard the sound of song. At this he wondered much, for the Green-elves of that land lit no fires, and they did not sing by night. At first he feared that a raid of Orcs had passed the leaguer of the North, but as he drew near he perceived that this was not so. For the singers used a tongue that he had not heard before, neither that of Dwarves nor of Orcs, and their voices were fair, though untutored in music.

§3   Then Felagund, standing silent in the night-shadow of the trees, looked down into the camp, and there he beheld a strange folk. They were tall, and strong, and comely, though rude and scantily clad; but their camp was well-ordered, and they had tents and lodges of boughs about the great fire in the midst; and there were fair women and children among them.

§4   Now these were a part of the kindred and following of Bëor the Old, as he was afterwards called, a chieftain among Men. After many lives of wandering out of the East he had led them at last over the Mountains, the first of the race of Men to enter Beleriand; and they sang because they were glad, and believed that they had escaped from all perils and had come to a land without fear.

§5   Long Felagund watched them, and love for them stirred in his heart; but he remained hidden in the trees until they had all fallen asleep. Then he went among the sleeping people, and sat beside their dying fire where none kept watch; and he took up a rude harp which Bëor had laid aside, and he played music upon it such as the ears of Men had not heard; for they had as yet no teachers in the art, save only the Dark-elves in the wild lands.

§6   Now men awoke and listened to Felagund as he harped and sang, and each thought that he was in some fair dream, until he saw that his fellows were awake also beside him; but they did not speak or stir while Felegund still played, because of the beauty of the music and the wonder of the song. Wisdom was in the words of the Elven-king, and the hearts grew wiser that hearkened to him; for the things of which he sang, of the making of Arda, and the bliss of Aman beyond the shadows of the Sea, came as clear visions before their eyes, and his Elvish speech was interpreted in each mind according to its measure.

§7 Thus it was that Men called King Felagund, whom they first met of all the Eldar, Wisdom, and after him they named his people The Wise.* Indeed they believed at first that Felagund was one of the gods, of whom they had heard rumour that they dwelt far in the West; and this was (some say) the chief cause of their journey. But Felagund dwelt among them and taught them true lore; and they loved him and took him for their lord, and were ever after loyal to the House of Finrod.**

§8 Now the Eldar were beyond all other peoples skilled in tongues; and Felagund discovered also that he could read in the minds of Men such thoughts as they wished to reveal in speech, so that their words were easily interpreted.† It was not long therefore before he could converse with Bëor; and while he dwelt with him they spoke much together. But when Felagund questioned Bëor concerning the arising of Men and their journeys, Bëor would say little; and indeed he knew little, for the fathers of his people had told few tales of their past and a silence had fallen upon their memory.

§9 'A darkness lies behind us,' Bëor said; 'and we have turned our backs on it, and we do not desire to return thither even in thought. Westwards our hearts have been turned, and we believe that there we shall find Light.'

§10 But Felagund learned from Bëor that there were many other Men of like mind who were also journeying westward. 'Others of my own kin have crossed the Mountains,' he said, 'and they are wandering not far away; and the Haladin, a people that speak the same tongue as we, are still in the valleys on the eastern slopes, awaiting tidings before they venture

---

* *Nóm* and [*Nómil* >] *Nómin* in the ancient language of this people (which afterwards was forgotten); for Bëor and his folk later learned the language of the Eldar and forsook their own, though they retained many names that came down to them [out of the past >] from their fathers.

** Thus Bëor got his name; for it signified Vassal in their tongue, and each of their chieftains after him bore this name as a title until the time of Bregolas and Barahir.

† It is said also that these Men had long had dealings with the Dark-elves of Middle-earth, and from them had learned much of their speech; and since all the languages of the Quendi were of one origin, the language of Bëor and his folk resembled the Elven-tongues in many words and devices.

further. There are also Men of a different speech, with whom we have had dealings at times. They were before us in the westward march, but we passed them; for they are a numerous people, and yet keep together and move slowly, being all ruled by one chieftain whom they call Marach.'

§11 Now the Nandor, the Green-elves of Ossiriand, were troubled by the coming of Men, and when they heard that a lord of the Eldar from over the Sea was among them they sent messengers to Felagund. 'Lord,' they said, 'if you have power over these new-comers, bid them to return by the ways that they came, or else to go forward. For we desire no strangers in this land to break the peace in which we live. And these folk are hewers of trees and hunters of beasts; therefore we are their unfriends, and if they will not depart we shall afflict them in all ways that we can.'

§12 Then by the advice of Felagund Bëor gathered all the wandering families and kindreds of his folk, and they removed over Gelion and took up their abode in the lands of Diriol, upon the east-banks of the Celon near to the borders of Doriath. But when after a year had passed Felagund wished to return to his own country, Bëor begged leave to come with him; and he remained in the service of the king while his life lasted. In this way he got his name Bëor, whereas his name before had been Balan; for Bëor signified Servant in the ancient tongue of his people. The rule of his folk he committed to his elder son Baran, and he did not return again to Estolad.*

Of the Kindreds and Houses of the Edain

§13 Soon after the departure of Felagund the other Men of whom Bëor had spoken came also into Beleriand. First came the Haladin; but meeting the unfriendship of the Nandor they turned north and dwelt in Radhrost, in the country of Caranthir son of Fëanor; and there for a time they had peace, though the people of Caranthir paid little heed to them. The next year, however, Marach led his people over the Mountains; and they were a tall and warlike folk, and they marched in ordered companies; and the Green-elves hid themselves and did not waylay them. And Marach hearing that the people of Bëor were dwelling in a green and fertile land, came down the Dwarf-road

---

* The Encampment. This was the name ever after of the land east of Celon and south of Nan Elmoth.

and settled his people in the country to the south and east of the dwellings of Baran son of Bëor. There was great friendship between the peoples, though they were sundered in speech, until they both learned the Sindarin tongue.

§14 Felagund himself often returned to visit Men; and many other Elves out of the westlands, both Noldor and Sindar, journeyed to Estolad, being eager to see the Edain, whose coming had long been foretold.* And Fingolfin, King of all the Noldor, sent messengers of welcome to them. Then many young and eager men of the Edain went away and took service with the kings and lords of the Eldar. Among these was Malach son of Marach, and he dwelt in Hithlum for fourteen years; and he learned the Elven-tongue and was given the name of Aradan.

§15 The Edain did not long dwell content in Estolad, for many still desired to go westwards; but they did not know the way: before them lay the fences of Doriath, and southward lay Sirion and its impassable fens. Therefore the kings of the three houses of the Noldor, seeing hope of strength in the sons of Men, sent word that any of the Edain that wished might remove and come to dwell among their people. In this way the migration of the Edain began: at first little by little, but later in families and kindreds, they arose and left Estolad, until after some fifty years many thousands had entered the lands of the kings.

§16 Most of these took the long road northwards, under the guidance of the Elves, until the ways became well known to them. The people of Bëor came to Dorthonion and dwelt in lands ruled by the House of Finrod. The people of Aradan (for Marach remained in Estolad until his death) for the most part went on westwards; and some came to Hithlum, but Magor son of Aradan and the greater number of his folk passed down Sirion into Beleriand and dwelt in the vales on the southern slopes of the Ered-wethion. A few only of either people went to Maedros and the lands about the Hill of Himring.

* *Atani* was the name given to Men in Valinor, in the lore that told of their coming; according to the Eldar it signified 'Second', for the kindred of Men was the second of the Children of Ilúvatar. *Edain* was the form of the name in Beleriand, and there it was used only of the three kindreds of the first Elf-friends. Men of other kind were called *Hravani* (or *Rhevain*), the 'Wild'. But all Men the Elves called *Hildi* [> *Hildor*], the Followers, or *Firyar*, the Mortals (in Sindarin *Echil* and *Firiath*).

§17   Many, however, remained in Estolad; and there was still a mingled people of Men living there long years after, until in the ruin of Beleriand they were overwhelmed or fled back into the East. For beside the old who deemed that their wandering days were over there were not a few who desired to go their own ways and feared the Eldar and the light of their eyes; and dissensions awoke among the Edain, in which the shadow of Morgoth may be discerned, for it cannot be doubted that he knew of the coming of Men and of their growing friendship with the Elves.

§18   The leaders of discontent were Bereg of the House of Bëor and Amlach one of the grandsons of Marach; and they said openly: 'We took long roads, desiring to escape the perils of Middle-earth and the dark things that dwell there; for we heard that there was Light in the West. But now we learn that the Light is beyond the Sea. Thither we cannot come where the gods dwell in bliss. Save one. For the Lord of the Dark is here before us, and the Eldar, wise but fell, who make endless war upon him. In the North he dwells, they say; and there is the pain and death from which we fled. We will not go that way.'

§19   Then a council and assembly of Men was called, and great numbers came together. And the Elf-friends answered Bereg, saying: 'Truly from the Dark King come all the evils from which we fled; but he seeks dominion over all Middle-earth, and whither now shall we turn and he will not pursue us? Unless he be vanquished here, or at least held in leaguer. Only by the valour of the Eldar is he restrained, and maybe it was for this purpose, to aid them at need, that we were brought into this land.'

§20   To this Bereg answered: 'Let the Eldar look to it! Our lives are short enough.' But there arose one who seemed to all to be Amlach son of Imlach, speaking fell words that shook the hearts of all that heard him: 'All this is but Elvish lore, tales to beguile new-comers that are unwary. The Sea has no shore. There is no Light in the West. You have followed a fool-fire of the Elves to the end of the world! Which of you has seen the least of the gods? Who has beheld the Dark King in the North? Those who seek the dominion of Middle-earth are the Eldar. Greedy for wealth they have delved in the Earth for its secrets and have stirred to wrath the things that dwell beneath it, as they ever have done and ever shall. Let the Orcs have the realm that is theirs, and we will have ours. There is room in the world, if the Eldar will let us be!'

§21 Then those that listened sat for a while astounded, and a shadow of fear fell on their hearts; and they resolved to depart far from the lands of the Eldar. But later Amlach returned among them and denied that he had been present at their debate or had spoken such words as they reported; and there was doubt and bewilderment among Men. Then the Elf-friends said: 'You will now believe this at least: there is indeed a dark Lord and his spies and emissaries are among us; for he fears us and the strength that we may give to his foes.'

§22 But some still answered: 'He hates us, rather, and ever the more the longer we dwell here, meddling in his quarrel with the kings of the Eldar, to no gain of ours.' Many therefore of those that yet remained in Estolad made ready to depart; and Bereg led a thousand of the people of Bëor away southwards and they passed out of the songs of those days. But Amlach repented, saying: 'I now have a quarrel of my own with this Master of Lies which will last to my life's end'; and he went away north and entered the service of Maedros. But those of his people who were of like mind with Bereg chose a new leader and went back over the Mountains into Eriador and are forgotten.

§23 During this time the Haladin remained in Radhrost and were content. But Morgoth, seeing that by lies and deceits he could not yet wholly estrange Elves and Men, was filled with wrath and endeavoured to do Men what hurt he could. Therefore he sent out an orc-raid and passing east it escaped the leaguer and came in stealth back over the Mountains by the passes of the Dwarf-road and fell upon the Haladin in the southern woods of the land of Caranthir.

§24 Now the Haladin did not live under the rule of lords or many together, but each homestead was set apart and governed its own affairs, and they were slow to unite. But there was among them a man named Haldad who was masterful and fearless; and he gathered all the brave men that he could find, and retreated to the angle of land between Ascar and Gelion, and in the utmost corner he built a stockade across from water to water; and behind it they led all the women and children that they could save. There they were besieged, until they were short of food.

§25 Now Haldad had twin children: Haleth his daughter and Haldar his son; and both were valiant in the defence, for

Haleth was a woman of great heart and strength. But at last Haldad was slain in a sortie against the Orcs; and Haldar, who rushed out to save his father's body from their butchery, was hewn down beside him. Then Haleth held the folk together, though they were without hope; and some cast themselves in the rivers and were drowned. Seven days later, as the Orcs made their last assault and had already broken through the stockade, there came suddenly a music of trumpets, and Caranthir with his host came down from the north and drove the Orcs into the rivers.

§26 Then Caranthir looked kindly upon Men and did Haleth great honour, and he offered her recompense for her father and brother. And seeing, over late, what valour there was in the Edain, he said to her: 'If you will remove and dwell further north, there you shall have the friendship and protection of the Eldar and free lands of your own.'

§27 But Haleth was proud, and unwilling to be guided or ruled, and most of the Haladin were of like mood. Therefore she thanked Caranthir, but answered: 'My mind is now set, lord, to leave the shadow of the Mountains and go west whither others of our kin have gone.' When therefore the Haladin had gathered all that they could find alive of their folk who had fled wild into the woods before the Orcs, and had gleaned what remained of their goods in their burned homesteads, they took Haleth for their chief; and she led them at last to Estolad, and there they dwelt for a time.

§28 But they remained a people apart, and were ever after known to Elves and Men as the People of Haleth. Haleth remained their chief while her days lasted, but she did not wed, and the headship afterwards passed to Hardan son of Haldar her brother. Soon, however, Haleth desired to move westward again; and though most of her people were against this counsel, she led them forth once more; and they went without help or guidance of the Eldar, and passing over Celon and Aros they journeyed in the perilous land between the Mountains of Terror and the Girdle of Melian. That land was not yet so evil as it after became, but it was no road for mortal Men to take without aid, and Haleth only brought her folk through it with hardship and loss, constraining them to go forward by the strength of her will. At last they crossed over the Brithiach, and many bitterly repented their journey; but there was now no returning. Therefore in new lands they went back to their old life as best they could; and they dwelt in free homesteads in the woods of the Dalath Dirnen beyond Teiglin, and some wandered far into the realm of Nargothrond. But there were many who loved the Lady Haleth and wished to go whither she would and dwell under her rule; and these she led into the Forest of Brethil. Thither in the evil days that followed many of her scattered folk returned.

§29 Now Brethil was claimed as part of his realm by King Thingol, though it was not within the List Melian, and he would have denied it to Haleth; but Felagund, who had the friendship of Thingol, when he heard of all that had befallen the people of Haleth, obtained this grace for her: that she should dwell free in Brethil upon condition only that her folk should guard the Crossings of Teiglin against all enemies of the Eldar, and allow no Orcs to enter their woods. To which Haleth answered: 'Where are Haldad my father, and Haldar my brother? If the king fears a friendship between Haleth and those who devoured her kin, then the thoughts of the Eldar are strange to Men.' And Haleth dwelt in Brethil until she died; and her people raised a green mound over her in the heights of the Forest: Tûr Daretha, the Ladybarrow, Haudh-en-Arwen in the Sindarin tongue.

§30 In this way it came to pass that the Edain dwelt in the lands of the Eldar, some here, some there, some wandering, some settled in kindreds or small peoples. Nearly all learned soon the Grey-elven tongue, both as a common speech among themselves and because many were eager to learn the lore of the Elves. But after a time the Elf-kings, seeing that it was not good for Elves and Men to dwell mingled together without order, and that Men needed lords of their own kind, set regions apart where Men could lead their own lives, and appointed chieftains to hold these lands freely. No conditions were laid upon them, save to hold Morgoth as their foe and to have no dealings with him or his. They were the allies of the Eldar in war, but marched under their own leaders. Yet many of the Edain had delight in the friendship of the Elves and dwelt among them for so long as they had leave; and their young men often took service for a time in the hosts of the Kings.

§31 Now Hador Glorindol, son of Hathol, son of Magor, son of Malach Aradan entered the household of Fingolfin in youth, and was loved by the king. Fingolfin therefore gave to him the lordship of Dor-lómin, and into that land he gathered most of the people of his kin and became the mightiest of the chieftains of the Edain. In his house only the elven-tongue was spoken, though their own speech was not forgotten by his people.* But in Dorthonion the lordship of the people of Bëor and the country of Ladros was given to Boromir, son of Boron who was the grandson of Bëor the Old.

§32 The sons of Hador were Galdor and Gundor; and the sons of Galdor were Húrin and Huor; and the son of Húrin was Túrin the bane of Glaurung; and the son of Huor was Tuor, father of Eärendil the Blessed. And the son of Boromir was Bregor, whose sons were Bregolas and Barahir; and the daughters of the sons of Bregolas were Morwen the mother of Túrin, and Rían the mother of Tuor; but the son of Barahir was Beren One-hand who won the love of Lúthien Thingol's daughter and returned from the Dead; from them came Elwing the wife of Eärendil and all the Kings of Númenor after.

§33 All these were caught in the net of the Doom of the Noldor; and they did great deeds which the Eldar remember still among the histories of the Kings of old. And in those days the strength of Men was added to the power of the Noldor, and hope was renewed; and the people of the three houses of Men throve and multiplied. Greatest was the House of Hador Golden-head, peer of Elven-lords. Many of his people were like him, golden-haired and blue-eyed; they were tall and strong, quick to wrath and laughter, fierce in battle, generous to friend and to foe, swift in resolve, fast in loyalty, joyous in heart, the children of Ilúvatar in the youth of Mankind. But the people of the House of Bëor were dark or brown of hair; their eyes were grey and keen and their faces fair and shapely. Lithe and lean in body they were long-enduring in hardship. Of all Men they were most like the Noldor and most loved by them; for they were eager of mind, cunning-handed, swift in understanding, long in memory; and they were moved sooner to pity than to mirth, for the sorrow of Middle-earth was in their hearts. Like to them were the woodland folk of Haleth; but they were shorter and broader, sterner and less swift. They were less eager for lore, and used few words; for they did not love great concourse of men, and many among them delighted in solitude, wandering free in the greenwoods while the wonder of the

---

* From this speech came the common tongue of Númenor.

world was new upon them. But in the lands of the West their time was brief and their days unhappy.

§34 The years of the Edain were lengthened, according to the reckoning of Men, after their coming to Beleriand; but at last Bëor the Old died, when he had lived three and ninety years, for four and forty of which he had served King Felagund. And when he lay dead, of no wound or sickness, but stricken by age, the Eldar saw for the first time the death of weariness which they knew not in themselves, and they grieved for the swift loss of their friends. But Bëor at the last had relinquished his life willingly and passed in peace; and the Eldar wondered much at the strange fate of Men, for in all their lore there was no account of it and its end was hidden from them. Nonetheless the Edain of old, being of races eager and young, learned swiftly of the Eldar all such art and knowledge as they could receive, and their sons increased in wisdom and skill, until they far surpassed all others of Mankind, who dwelt still east of the Mountains and had not seen the Eldar and the faces that had beheld the Light.

★

I record here the few changes that were made to the LQ 2 typescript of the new chapter.

§1 *Felagund* > *Finrod Felagund*
§4 'had come to a land' > 'had come at last to a land'
§7 The second footnote was struck out (as it was also on the original typescript).
§12 *Diriol* > *Diriel* > *Amras*
§13 *Radhrost* > *Thargelion*, and again in §23.
§28 *Dalath Dirnen* > *Talath Dirnen*
§29 *List Melian*: 'Girdle of' written over the word *List* (which was not struck out).
§31 *Glorindol* > *Glórindol*
§33 'the wonder of the world' > 'the wonder of the lands of the Eldar'
    'But in the lands of the West' > 'But in the realms of the West'

In addition, certain changes were made in pencil to the carbon copy only of the original typescript, and these were not taken up into LQ 2, nor were they added to it. They are as follows:

§16 'Magor son of Aradan' > 'Hador son of Aradan'
§29 *List Melian* > *Lest Melian*
    Tûr Daretha > *Tûr Haretha*
§31 'Now Hador Glorindol, son of Hathol, son of Magor, son of

Malach Aradan' was emended to read thus (the emendation was incorrectly made, but my father's intention is plain): 'Now Magor Dagorlind, son of Hathol, son of Hador Glorindal, son of Malach Aradan'

§32 'The sons of Hador' > 'The sons of Magor'

On the reversal of the places of Magor and Hador in the genealogy see p. 235.

Commentary

§1 'three hundred years and ten': the words 'and ten' were an addition. The original chapter in QS had 'four hundred', against which my father noted (p. 202, §126): 'This must be removed to 300', altering the date to '310'. This radical shift, putting back by ninety years the date of Felagund's meeting with Bëor (and so extending the lines of the rulers of the Edain in Beleriand by several generations), has been encountered in the opening of the *Athrabeth Finrod ah Andreth* (X.307 and third footnote).

§4 'Bëor the Old': the words 'the Old' were an addition, and 'as he was afterwards called' refer to 'Bëor' simply (see the second footnote to §7). – With 'After many lives of wandering out of the East' cf. the change made to the original QS chapter, p. 202, §127.

§7 The opening sentence of this paragraph as typed read:

Thus it was that Men called King Felagund, whom they first met of all the Eldar, *Sômar* that is Wisdom, and after him they named his people *Samûri* (that is the Wise).

As typed, the footnote was added to the word 'Wisdom', and read:

In the ancient language of the Edain (from which afterwards came the Númenórean tongue); but Bëor and his House later learned the language of the Eldar and forsook their own.

See V.275 (footnote) and p. 202, §128. – In 'the House of Finrod' *Finrod* = *Finarfin*. The footnote at this point in the text as typed read:

Thus Bëor got his name; for it signifies Vassal in the tongue of the Edain. But after Bëor all the children of his House bore Elvish names.

The revised footnote as given in the text printed was later struck out in pencil. See §12 in the text.

§9 The paragraph beginning 'But it was said afterwards ...' in the published *Silmarillion* between §9 and §10 of the original text was derived from the *Grey Annals*, §§79–80 (pp. 36–7).

§10 The reversal in the published *Silmarillion* of what is said in the original text (and cf. X.305) concerning the affinities of the languages of the Edain (so that the Haladin become 'sundered in speech' from the People of Bëor, and the tongue of the People of Marach becomes 'more like to ours') is based on late and very express statements of my father's. – In the present passage are the first occurrences of the names *Haladin* and *Marach*.

§12 The form *Diriol* seems not to occur elsewhere (see p. 225, §12).
– Above the word 'Servant' my father pencilled 'Vassal', but then struck it through. – The region of *Estolad* was entered on the second map, but in the form *Estoland* (p. 189, §55).

§13 The heading *Of the Kindreds and Houses of the Edain* was an addition to the manuscript. Against the opening words 'Soon after the departure of Felagund' the date 311 was typed; 312 against the coming of the Haladin; and 313 against the coming of Marach and his people.

Radhrost: Dark-elvish name of Thargelion. See p. 225, §13.

Caranthir: the name as typed (twice) was *Cranthir*, emended to *Caranthir*, but later in the text (§23 and subsequently) *Caranthir* was the form as typed. This is an indication that the emendation of the text followed soon after its typing (p. 215), and may give support to the suggestion *(ibid.)* that *Of the Coming of Men into the West* belongs to the period when the LQ 2 typescript series was being made, since the change of *Cranthir > Caranthir* occurs as an emendation in *Of Beleriand and its Realms* in the LQ 2 series (p. 197, §111).

On the statement that the peoples of Bëor and Marach were 'sundered in speech', omitted in the published text, see under §10 above.

§14 After the words 'dwelt in Hithlum' there followed in the typescript 'in the household of Fingolfin', which was struck out.

§15 Against the words 'some fifty years' the date 330–380 is typed in the margin.

§16 'the House of Finrod': see under §7 above. – The paragraph beginning 'It is said that in all these matters ...' in the published *Silmarillion* was derived from the *Grey Annals*, §§130–1 (pp. 49–50).

§18 With the speech of Bereg and Amlach compare the words of Andreth to Felagund in the *Athrabeth*, X.309–10.

§19 Against the first sentence of the paragraph the date 369 was added.

§20 After 'new-comers that are unwary' the text as typed read before emendation:

Which of you has seen the Light or the least of the gods? Who has beheld the Dark King in the North? The Sea has no shore. There is no Light in the West, for we stand now in the West of the world.

§23 The form *Caranthir* appears here in the typescript as typed: see under §13 above. In the carbon copy a stroke was drawn through the *n* of *Caranthir*, sc. *Carathir*, and the same was done at the first occurrence of the name (§13) in the top copy.

§24 The siege of the Haladin behind their stockade is dated 375, typed in the margin.

§25 It is here that the Lady Haleth enters the history; Haleth the Hunter, Father of Men, who first appeared long before in the

Quenta as the son of Hador (when the 'Hadorian' and 'Halethian' houses were one and the same, see IV.104, 175), has now disappeared.

§27 Against the last sentence, referring to the sojourn of the Haladin in Estolad, the date 376–390 is typed in the margin.

§28 *Hardan* son of *Haldar*: the substitution of *Haldan* for *Hardan* in the published text was derived from a late change to a genealogical table of the Haladin (see p. 238).

Brithiach: the Ford of Brithiach over Sirion north of the Forest of Brethil had first appeared in the later *Tale of Tuor* (*Unfinished Tales* p. 41), and again in GA §161; see the map on p. 182, square D 7. – Against the sentence 'At last they crossed over the Brithiach' is the date 391.

Dalath Dirnen: the Guarded Plain east of Narog. The name first appears in the tale of Beren and Lúthien in QS (V.299), and was marked in on the second map, where it was subsequently changed to *Talath Dirnen* (p. 186, §17), as also on the LQ 2 typescript of the present text (p. 225, §28).

Teiglin: this was the form of the name adopted in the published *Silmarillion*; see pp. 309–10, at end of note 55.

§29 In the *Grey Annals* §132 (p. 50) the story had entered (under the year 422) that 'at the prayer of Inglor [Felagund] Thingol granted to Haleth's people to live in Brethil; for they were in good friendship with the woodland Elves' (Haleth here is of course Haleth the Hunter, who had entered Beleriand two years before).

List Melian, the Girdle of Melian: this name was entered on the second map (p. 183, D 8–9), and changed to *Lest Melian* on the carbon copy of the original typescript of the chapter (p. 225, §29).

Tûr Daretha: for the form *Tûr Haretha* in the published text see p. 225, §29. – The date of the death of the Lady Haleth is given in the margin: 420.

§31 In the newly devised history, Marach having displaced Hador Goldenhead as the leader of the people in the journey out of Eriador, Hador now appears as the descendant of Marach in the fourth generation; but the House of Hador retained its name (see IV.175). This is the first occurrence of the name *Glorindol*; but the later form *Lorindol* (adopted in the published *Silmarillion*) has been met with in the *Athrabeth* (X.305), and see pp. 233–5.

Marginal dates give Hador's years in Fingolfin's household as 405–415, and the granting to him of the lordship of Dor-lómin as 416.

The concluding sentence of the paragraph as typed read:
But in Dorthonion the lordship of the people of Bëor was given to Bregor son of Boromir ...
The date of this gift, as typed in the margin, was 410. – 'The country

of Ladros', in the emended version, was marked on the second map in the north-east of Dorthonion: p. 187, §34.

§32 For the remainder of its length *Of the Coming of Men into the West* returns to follow, with much rewriting and expansion, the form of the original chapter in QS. – *Galdor* first occurs here (otherwise than in later corrections), replacing *Galion* which itself replaced *Gumlin* (p. 123, §127).

The new genealogies of the Edain

My father's decision that the coming of the Edain over the Blue Mountains into Beleriand took place nearly a century earlier than he had supposed led to a massive overhauling of the chronology and the genealogies.

(i) The House of Bëor

From the new chapter it is seen that in the case of the Bëorians the original 'Father', Bëor the Old, remained, but four new generations were introduced between him and Bregolas and Barahir, who until now had been his sons. These generations are represented by Baran, Boron, Boromir, and Bregor (who becomes the father of Bregolas and Barahir), descendants in the direct line of Bëor the Old – though it is not actually stated that Boron was Baran's son, only that he was Bëor's grandson (§31). In the *Grey Annals* (§121) Bëor was born in the year 370, his encounter with Felagund took place in 400, the year in which his elder son Bregolas was born (§124), and he died in 450. In the new history he met Felagund in 310, departed with him in 311 (commentary on §13), and remained in his service for forty-four years until his death at the age of 93 (§34); from which his dates can be seen to be 262–355. His true name was *Balan* (§12); and it is stated in the second footnote to §7 that each of the chieftains of this people bore the name *Bëor* ('Vassal') as a title until the time of Bregolas and Barahir – though this note was afterwards struck out (commentary on §7). Boromir his great-grandson received the lordship of Dorthonion and Ladros in 410 (§31 and commentary).

There are two genealogical tables of the House of Bëor that relate closely to the new chapter and almost certainly belong to the same period (this is strongly suggested by the fact that a group of Elvish genealogies, closely resembling in form those of the Edain, is accompanied by notes dated December 1959). The two tables were obviously made at the same time. The first ('Bëor table I') was written neatly and clearly; it differs from the second in many of the dates and in its presentation of the descendants of Boron (grandson of Bëor the Old), thus:

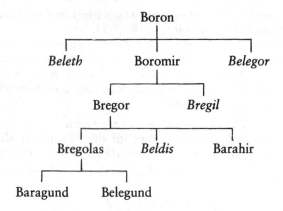

Names in italics show members of the House of Bëor who have not appeared before; of these Beleth, Bregil, and Beldis are marked on the table as daughters. Subsequent alterations, carried out in complex stages, brought the genealogy to the fuller form that it has in 'Bëor table II'; of these changes the most notable is the replacement of Boromir's daughter Bregil (who is moved down a generation) by *Andreth*, the first appearance of the name. The only other point to notice in table I is that Morwen was named *Eledhwen* (with *Eðelwen*, as in table II, added above).

Bëor table II took up all the changes made to I, and I have redrawn it on p. 231 in the form in which it was first made. The numerals added to certain of the names indicate the rulers of the House in their order.

It is seen from this genealogy that Boron was indeed the son of Baran ('Bëor the Young'); and that Bereg the dissident (§18), in the text said only to be 'of the House of Bëor', was the son of Baranor son of Baran, and thus a great-grandson of Bëor the Old. It is seen also that the further extension of the House of Bëor that appears in the *Athrabeth Finrod ah Andreth* (X.305–6) was now present, with Andreth the sister of Bregor, and Belen the second son of Bëor the Old, father of Beldir (not previously named), father of Belemir the husband of Adanel. (Adanel is here said to be the daughter of Malach Aradan, son of Marach, whereas in the *Athrabeth* she is the sister of Hador Lorindol: on this see p. 235.)

A few changes were made subsequently, at different times, to Bëor table II, as follows:
- *(Bar Bëora)* added after 'The House of Bëor';
- Boron's dates changed to 315–408, and Boromir's birth to 338;
- the name *Saelin* pencilled beside *Andreth*, and also 'A[ndreth] the Wise';
- a remote descent from Beleth, sister of Baragund and Belegund, indicated, leading to *Erendis of Númenor*;

THE LATER *QUENTA SILMARILLION* 231

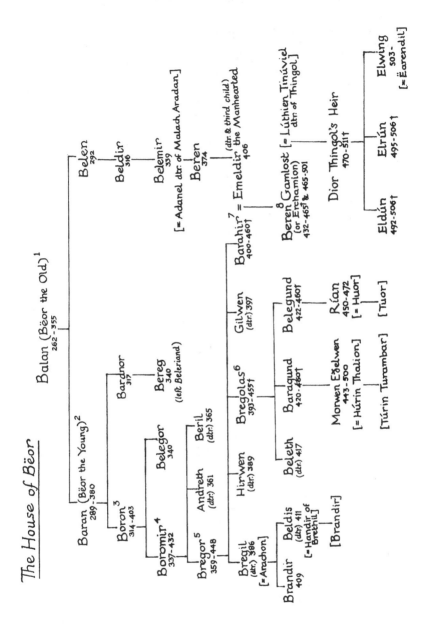

– a daughter *Hiril*, sister of Beren One-hand, given to Barahir and Emeldir.

On the name *Saelin* beside *Andreth* see p. 233. With the descent of Erendis of Númenor from Beleth daughter of Bregolas cf. *Aldarion and Erendis* in *Unfinished Tales*, p. 177, where it is said of Beregar the father of Erendis that he 'came of the House of Bëor': in my note on this (p. 214, note 10) I referred to her descent as given in the present genealogical table, but gave her ancestor's name wrongly as 'Bereth'.

Some of the later dates in the table differ from those in other sources. The first death of Beren is placed under 466 in the texts of *The Tale of Years*: 465 is a reversion to the date in AB 2 (see p. 131, §203). The second death of Beren, in the table dated 501, was placed in AB 2 in 503, while in *The Tale of Years* it is given as 505, then reverting to 503 (pp. 346, 348). In GA Bregolas was born in 400, Barahir in 402, Baragund in 424, and Belegund in 428 (these were the original dates going back to the earliest *Annals of Beleriand*, allowing for the extension by one and then by two centuries in subsequent versions; see the genealogical table in IV.315).

On the much changed date of the Second Kinslaying (here given as 511), in which Dior Thingol's heir was slain in fighting with the Fëanorians and his young sons Eldún and Elrún were taken and abandoned to starve in the forest, see *The Tale of Years*, pp. 345 ff.; it is plainly a mere inadvertence that in the same table the date of their death is given as 506, five years before that of Dior. In (later) sources Eldún and Elrún are twin brothers, born in the year 500 (see p. 257 and note 16 on p. 300; p. 349).

(ii) The House of Hador

In the old history of the Edain, now rejected, Hador the Goldenhaired, third of 'the Fathers of the Men of the West', was born in Eriador in 390, and came over the Blue Mountains into Beleriand in 420. Unlike the development in the House of Bëor, however, Hador (Glorindol, §31) retained his chronological place in the history (as will be seen shortly, his original birth-date remained the same), and his sons Galdor (< Galion < Gumlin) and Gundor; but with the much earlier date of 'the Coming of Men into the West' he was moved downwards in the genealogy, to become the ruler of the people in the fourth generation from Marach, under whose leadership they had entered Beleriand in 313 (commentary on §13). His father was Hathol, son of Magor, son of Malach, son of Marach (§31).

As with the House of Bëor, there are here also two genealogical tables closely related to the new conception. The earlier of these ('Hador table I') was made on my father's old typewriter using his 'midget type' (VIII.233). It was a good deal altered by revision of dates, and by additions, but these latter chiefly concern the extension of the genealogy to include the descendants of Húrin and Huor, with whom the table ended in the form as typed: the structure of the descent from the ancestor was far less changed than in the case of Bëor table I, and indeed the only addition here was the incorporation of Amlach, one of the leaders of discontent in Estolad, who is said in the text of the chapter (§18) to have been 'one of the grandsons of Marach'. Changes were also made to the names of the Haladin who appear in the genealogy.

A fair copy in manuscript ('Hador table II'), identical in appearance to the tables of the House of Bëor, followed, no doubt immediately, and this I have redrawn on p. 234, in the form in which it was made (i.e. omitting subsequent alterations). I notice here some points arising from these tables.

The date of Marach's entry into Beleriand differs by one year (314 for 313) from that given in the chapter (commentary on §13); table I had 315 altered to 314. In table I Marach's son Imlach, father of Amlach, is named *Imrach*.

In agreement with the genealogical tables of the House of Bëor, Adanel wife of Belemir is the daughter of Malach Aradan; in Hador table I it was said that Adanel 'wedded Belemir of the House of Bëor, and he joined the people of Aradan', the last words being struck out. It is also said in table I that Beren (I) was the fifth child of Adanel and Belemir; and that Emeldir was the third child of Beren.

In Hador table I there is the statement that 'the other children of Aradan' (i.e. beside Adanel and Magor) 'are not named in the Chronicles'. In table II a third child of Malach Aradan was named, however: 'Sael..th the Wise 344', together with the mention of 'others not concerned in these Chronicles'; *Sael..th* was first changed to *Saelon*, and then the name and the birth-date were struck out, so that the middle letters of the first name cannot be read. This was probably done at the time of the making of the table. *Saelon* appears in draft material for the *Athrabeth* (X.351–2) as the name of Andreth, replaced in the finished text (X.305) by *Saelind* ('the Eldar called her *Saelind*, "Wise-heart"'). In this sister of Magor and Adanel is seen, very probably, the first hint of the *Athrabeth*; subsequently, when my father perceived that the wise-women came of different houses of the Edain, with different 'lore and traditions' (X.305), he wrote *Saelin* and *Andreth the Wise* against the name *Andreth* in Bëor table II (p. 230). It seems a possibility that Adanel and Andreth were already present in the genealogies before their significance as 'wise-women' emerged.

In Hador table I Hador was named *Glorindol*, as in the text of the chapter (§31), emended to *Lorindol*, the form in table II. – I do not know why Gundor's death should be dated (in both I and II) a year later (456) than that of his father Hador. All the sources state that they both died at Eithel Sirion.

The 'double marriage' of Hador's daughter and elder son, named Glorwendil and Galion, to the son (Hundor) and daughter (unnamed)

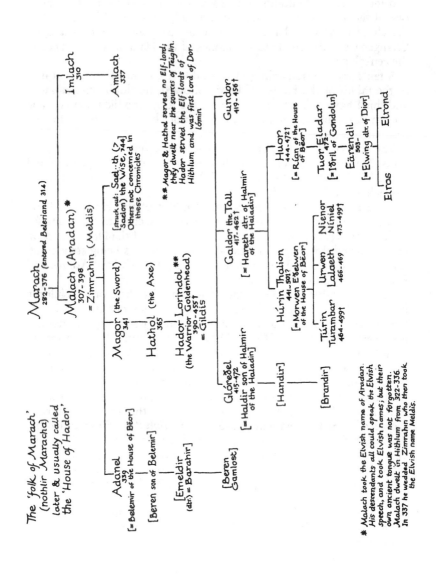

of Haleth the Hunter had already emerged in the *Grey Annals* (see the commentary on §§161, 171, pp. 126, 128). Now named Glóreðel and Galdor, the double marriage remains, but with the entire reconstitution of the People of Haleth the chronological place of Haleth the Hunter had been taken by *Halmir*: it is now his son *Haldir* and his daughter *Hareth* who marry Glóreðel and Galdor.*

The date of Húrin's death is given as '500?' in table I ('501?' in table II).

Tuor's name *Eladar* is translated 'Starfather' in table I, and in addition he is named *Ulmondil*; the form *Irildë* was added after *Idril* (so spelt): see II.343 and V.366–7 (stem KYELEP); and to Eärendil was added 'whose name was foretold by Ulmo'.

For *Urwen Lalaeth* see *Unfinished Tales* pp. 57–9.

In hasty pencillings on Hador table II the note saying that Magor and Hathol served no Elf-lord but dwelt near the sources of Teiglin, and that Hador was the first lord of Dor-lómin, was struck out; while at the same time *Hador Lorindol first lord of Dorlómin* was written above *Magor (the Sword)*, and *Magor Dagorlind the Sword singer in battle* above *Hador Lorindol*. This reversal has been seen already in emendations made to the carbon copy only of the text of the chapter (pp. 225–6, §§16, 31–2 – where my father changed *Glorindol*, not to *Lorindol*, but to *Glorindal*). That this was not an ephemeral change is seen from the *Athrabeth*, where Adanel is the sister of Hador Lorindol, not of Magor.

I do not know of any statement elsewhere that bears on this change, but the words 'first lord of Dorlómin' that (so to speak) accompanied Hador's movement back by half a century are evidently significant, suggesting that my father had in mind to place Fingolfin's gift of the lordship of Dorlómin much earlier: he had said both in the text of the chapter and in the genealogical table that Malach (whose son was now Hador Lorindol) passed fourteen years in Hithlum. This change would not of itself entail the reversal of the names Magor and Hador; but the House of Hador was a name so embedded in the tradition that my father would not lose it even when Hador was no longer the first ruler in Beleriand, while on the other hand the importance and illustriousness of that house was closely associated with the lordship of Dorlómin – in other words, the name must accompany the first lordship. But it seems that he never wrote anything further on the matter, nor made any other alterations to the existing texts in the light of it.

The only other change made to Hador table II (it was made also to table I) was the writing of the name *Ardamir* above Eärendil.

* In table I the son of Halmir was still *Hundor*, and his daughter was *Hiriel*. *Hiriel* was changed to *Hareth*; and *Hundor* was changed to *Hundar* before reaching *Haldir*. See pp. 236–7.

(iii) The Haladin

This house of the Edain underwent the greatest change, since in this case the original 'Father' Haleth the Hunter disappeared, and of the Haladin (a name that first occurs in this new chapter, §10) it is said (§24) that they 'did not live under the rule of lords or many together'. The name *Haleth* now becomes that of the formidable Lady Haleth, daughter of Haldad, who had become the leader when the Haladin were attacked by Orcs in Thargelion. In the genealogical table of the House of Hador *Halmir* occupies the place in the history formerly taken by Haleth the Hunter, and it was his son and daughter who married the son and daughter of Hador Goldenhead.

A genealogical table of the Haladin exists in a single copy (preceded by rough workings in which the names were moved about in a bewildering fashion), this table being a companion, obviously made at the same time, to those of the Houses of Bëor and Hador. I give it on p. 237 as it was first made. As in the table of the Bëorians, the numerals against certain of the names refer to the leaders of the Haladin in sequence.

A particularly confusing element in the transformation of 'the People of Haleth' (who are confusing enough in any event) lies in the offspring of Halmir.

(1) In GA §212 (p. 70) it was told, in the annal for 468, that at the time of the Union of Maidros Haleth the Hunter 'gathered his folk in Brethil, and they whetted their axes; but he died of age ere the war came, and Hundor his son ruled his people' (in *The Silmarillion*, Chapter 20, p. 189, I retained this, substituting Halmir for Haleth the Hunter and Haldir for Hundor).

(2) I have noticed (p. 235, footnote) that in 'Hador table I' Halmir's son was still *Hundor*; and that this was changed to *Hundar* (found also in one of the constituent texts of the *Narn* as the name of the son) before reaching the final form *Haldir*.

(3) In the *Narn* version of the story of the Battle of Unnumbered Tears the leader of the men of Brethil is *Hundar* (pp. 166, 168).

(4) In a late alteration to the GA version of the story (see p. 133, commentary on §221) the sentence 'many of the woodmen came also with Hundor of Brethil' was changed to 'came also with Haldir and Hundar'.

(6) In the genealogical table of the Haladin both *Haldir*, son of Halmir and leader of the Haladin after his father's death, and his brother *Hundar*, are shown as having been slain in the Nirnaeth in the year 472.

It is seen therefore that when *Hundar* son of Halmir became *Haldir*, the name *Hundar* was not lost but was given to a brother of Haldir; and both went to the battle and both were slain. This is expressly stated in *The Wanderings of Húrin* (p. 281 and note 37); and indeed the line of Hundar is of great importance in that tale.

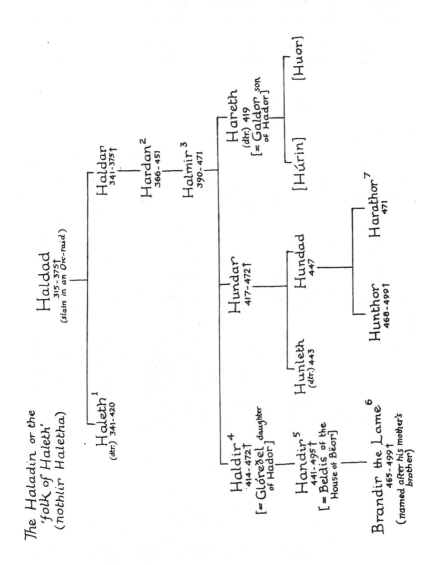

Handir, son of Haldir, retained his name from far back; but the original story of his death in the battle of Tumhalad in 495 had been changed: he was slain in Brethil earlier in that year by 'Orcs that invaded his land' (GA §275). On his marriage with Beldis of the House of Bëor see p. 268.

Hunthor was Túrin's companion in the attack on Glaurung, killed by a falling stone (*Unfinished Tales*, p. 134); called *Torbarth* in GA (see p. 156).

Most of the later changes made to this table relate closely to the story of *The Wanderings of Húrin*, and these I neglect here. Of other alterations, one has been mentioned already (commentary on §28, p. 228): *Hardan* son of Haldar (twin brother of the Lady Haleth) was changed to *Haldan*, and this name was adopted in the published *Silmarillion*; but also pencilled against *Hardan* (either before or after the change to *Haldan*) is the name *Harathor* (the name repeated in his descendant, the seventh leader of the Haladin, four generations later). – The birth-dates of Hundar and Hareth were changed to 418 and 420; and Hundar's daughter *Hunleth* was an addition, though probably of the time of the making of the table.

Pencilled on a corner of the page is: '*Hal-* in old language of this people = head, chief. *bar* = man. *Halbar* = chieftain'; at the same time my father wrote '*b*' against the name *Haldar* (Haleth's brother) and perhaps very faintly struck out the '*d*' of this name: sc. *Halbar*. On this see p. 309.

15   OF THE RUIN OF BELERIAND AND THE
FALL OF FINGOLFIN

We come now to Chapter 11 in QS, given in V.279–89. The text was not much emended on the manuscript, and I give such changes as were made in the form of notes referenced to the numbered paragraphs in Vol.V.

§134   *Bladorion* > *Ard-galen* and subsequently.

 'fires of many colours, and the fume stank upon the air' > 'fires of many poisonous hues, and the fume thereof stank upon the air'

 Dor-na-Fauglith > *Dor-no-Fauglith*

 Dagor Vreged-úr > *Dagor Bragollach*

 'the Battle of Sudden Fire' > 'the Battle of Sudden Flame' (and subsequently)

§137   'In that battle King Inglor Felagund was cut off from his folk and surrounded by the Orcs, and he would have been slain ...' > 'surrounded by the Orcs in the Fen of Serech betwixt Mithrim and Dorthonion, and there he would have been slain'. The *Fen of Rivil*, changed to *Fen of Serech*, was added to the second map (p. 181, §3), and the latter name occurs several times in GA.

§138 'fled now from Dorthonion' > 'fled away from Dorthonion'
'it was after called by the Gnomes Taur-na-Fuin, which is Mirkwood, and Delduwath, Deadly Nightshade' > 'it was after called by the Dark-elves Taur-na-Fuin, which is Mirkwood, but by the Gnomes Delduwath, Deadly Nightshade'

§141 'Celegorn and Curufin ... sought harbour with their friend Orodreth' > '... sought harbour with Inglor and Orodreth'. See V.289, §141.

§142 'or the wild of South Beleriand' > 'nor to Taur-im-Duinath and the wilds of the south'. On *Taur-im-Duinath* see p. 193, §108, and p. 195, §113.

§143 'Sauron was the chief servant of the evil Vala, whom he had suborned to his service in Valinor from among the people of the gods. He was become a wizard of dreadful power, master of necromancy, foul in wisdom' > 'Now Sauron, whom the Noldor call Gorthú, was the chief servant of Morgoth. In Valinor he had dwelt among the people of the gods, but there Morgoth had drawn him to evil and to his service. He was become now a sorcerer of dreadful power, master of shadows and of ghosts, foul in wisdom'. On this passage, and the name *Gorthú*, see V.333, 338, and the commentary on QS §143 (V.290).

In the footnote to this paragraph *Tol-na-Gaurhoth* > *Tol-in-Gaurhoth* (cf. GA §154 and commentary, pp. 54, 125).

§144 In 'for though his might is greatest of all things in this world, alone of the Valar he knows fear' the words 'is' and 'knows' were changed to 'was' and 'knew'.

§147 'for sorrow; but the tale of it is remembered, for Thorondor, king of eagles, brought the tidings to Gondolin, and to Hithlum. For Morgoth' > 'for their sorrow is too deep. Yet the tale of it is remembered still, for Thorondor, king of eagles, brought the tidings to Gondolin, and to Hithlum afar off. Lo! Morgoth'

Gochressiel > *Crisaegrim* (see V.290, §147).

§149 'And most the Gnomes feared' > 'And ever the Gnomes feared most'

§151 'Dwarfs' > 'Dwarves'

All these changes were taken up into the early typescript LQ 1 (in which the footnotes to §§143, 156 were as usual incorporated in the text, and so remained). LQ 1 received no emendation from my father, not even the correction of misspelt names and other errors. These errors reappear in the late typescript of the LQ 2 series, showing that in this case the typist did not work from the manuscript. To the text in LQ 2 my father gave the chapter-number 'XVIII' (see p. 215), and made the following emendations.

§134 *Dor-no-Fauglith* (changed from *Dor-na-Fauglith* on the manuscript, as noted above) > *Dor-nu-Fauglith*; a translation of the name added in a footnote 'That is Land under Choking Ash'; and 'in the Noldorin tongue' (where LQ 1 had 'in the Gnomish tongue') > 'in the Sindarin tongue'.

Eredwethion > *Eredwethrin* (and subsequently)

§135   *Glómund* > *Glaurung* (and subsequently). See p. 180, §104.

§137   *Finrod* > *Finarfin* (this change was missed in §144).

'Bregolas, son of Bëor [the typescript has *Breor*, a mere error going back to LQ 1], who was lord of that house of men after his father's death' > 'Bregolas, son of Bregor ... after Boromir his father's death'. This accommodates the text to the new genealogy that came in with the new chapter *Of the Coming of Men into the West*. That was extant in the LQ 2 series, but for the present chapter my father gave the typist the old LQ 1 text to copy.

Inglor > *Finrod* (and subsequently)

'Barahir son of Bëor' > 'Barahir son of Bregor'

§138   *Taur-na-Fuin* > *Taur-nu-Fuin* (cf. GA §158 and commentary, pp. 56, 126).

§139   The name *Arthod* of one of the companions of Barahir had been misspelt *Arthrod* by the typist of LQ 1, and this error surviving into LQ 2 was not observed by my father. In GA (§159, p. 56) the name is *Arthad*, which was adopted in the published *Silmarillion*.

§140   *Gumlin* > *Galdor* and subsequently (see p. 229, §32); the intervening name *Galion*, appearing in GA (§127), was here jumped.

§141   'sought harbour with Inglor and Orodreth' (see p. 239, §141) > 'sought harbour with Finrod and Orodreth'

§142   *Cranthir* > *Caranthir*
       Damrod and Díriel > *Amrod and Amras*

§143   'Now Sauron, whom the Noldor call Gorthú' (see p. 239, §143) > 'Now Sauron, whom the Sindar call Gorthaur'
       'In Valinor he had dwelt among the people of the Valar, but there Morgoth had drawn him to evil and to his service' (see p. 239, §143; LQ 1 has 'gods'): this was struck out.

§147   In 'Morgoth goes ever halt of one foot since that day, and the pain of his wounds cannot be healed; and in his face is the scar that Thorondor made' the words 'goes', 'since', 'cannot', and 'is' were changed to 'went', 'after', 'could not', and 'was'. Cf. p. 239, §144.

§151   *Borlas and Boromir and Borthandos* > *Borlad and Borlach and Borthand*. In GA, in a passage extant in two versions, appear both *Borthandos* and *Borthand* (pp. 61, 64), the other names remaining as in QS. Here *Borlad* replaces *Borlas* and *Borlach* replaces *Boromir*, which latter had become the name of the fourth ruler of the People of Bëor.

§152   'Yet Haleth and his men' > 'Yet the People of Haleth'
       Haleth > *Halmir* (and subsequently); at the first occurrence >

'Halmir Lord of the Haladin'. For *Halmir* see p. 236 and the genealogical table of the Haladin on p. 237.

§153 Since no alteration to this passage in QS had ever been made, at this late date the LQ 2 typescript still retained the old story that it was Haleth the Hunter and his fosterson Húrin who, hunting in the vale of Sirion in the autumn of the year of the Battle of Sudden Flame (455), came upon the entrance into Gondolin. That story had already been altered in the *Grey Annals* (§149), in that Húrin's companion had become Haleth's grandson Handir, and in a long rider inserted into the *Annals* (§§161–6, and see the commentary, pp. 126–7) it had been much further changed: Húrin's companion was now his brother Huor, and it was their presence (as fostersons of Haleth) among the Men of Brethil in the battle against the Orcs three years later (458) that led to their coming to Gondolin. The only alterations that my father made to the passage in LQ 2, however, were the replacement of *Gumlin* by *Galdor* and *Haleth* by *Halmir* – thus retaining the long since rejected story while substituting the new names that had entered with the chapter *Of the Coming of Men into the West*. This was obviously not his intention (probably he altered the names rapidly throughout the chapter without considering the content in this paragraph), and indeed he marked the passage in the margin with an X and noted against it 'This is incorrect story. See Annals and tale of Túrin'. This treatment may have been due to haste, or disinclination to deal with the text at that time; but it possibly implies uncertainty as to how he should relate the content of the *Quenta Silmarillion* at this point to the same material appearing in closely similar form both in the *Grey Annals* and in the *Narn*: see pp. 165 ff. In the published work the old text of QS §153 was replaced by that of GA §§161–6 (with a different ending: see p. 169).

Two alterations made hastily to the QS manuscript are not found in the typescripts. The first of these concerns the opening of §133: 'But when the sons of the sons of the Fathers of Men were but newly come to manhood'; this referred to the second generation after Bëor, Hador, and Haleth according to the old genealogies, i.e. Baragund, Belegund, Beren; Húrin, Huor; Handir of Brethil. When correcting the LQ 2 text my father had not observed the need to correct this in the light of the revised history of the Edain in Beleriand, and when he did recognise it he made the change only on the QS manuscript, thus:

But when the fifth generation of Men after Bëor and Marach were not yet come to full manhood

Even so, the change is not quite as is to be expected; for in the fifth generation after Bëor and Marach were Bregolas, Barahir; Gundor, Galdor. There is of course no question that the men referred to are not these, but their sons – and even so the new reading 'not yet come to full manhood' is hardly suitable to Baragund and Belegund, who according to the changed dates in the genealogical table (pp. 231-2) were at this time 35 and 33 years old. At any rate it seems clear that 'fifth' was an error for 'sixth'.

The other alteration made to QS only, and obviously made much earlier than that just given, was an addition to the end of §137, after the words 'he [Felagund] gave to Barahir his ring'.

> But fearing now that all strong places were doomed to fall at last before the might of Morgoth, he sent away his wife Meril to her own folk in Eglorest, and with her went their son, yet an elvenchild, and *Gilgalad* Starlight he was called for the brightness of his eye.

Felagund's wife Meril has not been named before, nor any child of his; and this is the first appearance of Gil-galad from *The Lord of the Rings*. Another note on the subject is found in the QS manuscript near the opening of the 'short' (i.e. condensed) version of the tale of Beren and Lúthien (see V.293), pencilled rapidly at the foot of a page but clearly referring to the statement in the text that Felagund gave the crown of Nargothrond to Orodreth before his departure with Beren (*The Silmarillion* p. 170):

> But foreseeing evil he commanded Orodreth to send away his son Gilgalad, and wife.

This was struck out; and somewhat further on in the tale of Beren and Lúthien in the same version is a third hasty note, without direction for insertion but evidently referring to the passage in which Orodreth expelled Celegorn and Curufin from Nargothrond (*The Silmarillion* p. 176):

> But the Lady   wife of Inglor forsook the folk of Nargothrond and went with her son Gilgalad to the Havens of the Falas.

A blank space is here left for the name of Felagund's wife. In each of these mentions, taking them in sequence, her departure is displaced to a later point; but of course they need not have been written in that sequence (although the third presumably replaced the second, which was struck out). On the other hand it seems very unlikely that the three additions do not belong together, though there seems to be no way of discovering with certainty when they were written. – It may also be noticed that a later correction to the old AB 2 manuscript changed the sentence in the concluding annal (V.144) 'But Elrond the Half-elfin remained, and ruled in the West of the world' to 'But Elrond the Half-elven remained with Gilgalad son of Inglor Felagund who ruled in the West of the world.'

In this connection must be mentioned the passage in the *Grey Annals* §§108-9 (p. 44), where it is expressly stated that 'King Inglor Felagund had no wife', and that when Galadriel came to Nargothrond for the feast celebrating its completion in the year 102 she asked him why:

> ... but foresight came upon Felagund as she spoke, and he said:

'An oath I too shall swear and must be free to fulfill it and go into darkness. Nor shall anything of all my realm endure that a son should inherit.'

But it is said that not until that hour had such cold thoughts ruled him; for indeed she whom he had loved was Amárië of the Vanyar, and she was not permitted to go with him into exile.

Amárië appears again in GA, in both versions of the retelling of the story of Beren and Lúthien (§§180, 199), where it is said that Felagund dwells in Valinor with Amárië.

Later evidence makes it certain that the notes on the QS manuscript represent a rejected idea for the incorporation of Gil-galad into the traditions of the Elder Days; and the passage just cited from the *Grey Annals* is to be taken as showing that it had been abandoned. That Gil-galad was the son of Fingon (*The Silmarillion* p. 154) derives from the late note pencilled on the manuscript of GA (§157), stating that when Fingon became King of the Noldor on the death of Fingolfin 'his young son (?Findor) [*sic*] Gilgalad he sent to the Havens.' But this, adopted after much hesitation, was not in fact by any means the last of my father's speculations on this question.

THE LAST CHAPTERS OF THE QUENTA SILMARILLION

Of the next chapters in QS (12–15), the tale of Beren and Lúthien, there is almost nothing to add to my account in V.292 ff. A typescript in the LQ 1 series was made, but my father only glanced through it cursorily, correcting a few errors in the typing and missing a major one; from this it was copied in the LQ 2 series, which again he looked at in a cursory and uncomparative fashion: such old names as *Inglor* and *Finrod* were not changed to *Finrod* and *Finarfin*. The only change that he made to the LQ 2 text was at the very beginning (V.296), where against 'Noldor' he wrote in the margin 'Númenor', i.e. 'which is the longest save one of the songs of [the Noldor >] Númenor concerning the world of old.' With this cf. X.373.

The textual history of the following chapters (16 and 17) of the *Quenta Silmarillion* has been fully described in Vol.V (see especially pp. 293–4), and need not be repeated here. To Chapter 16, the story of the Battle of Unnumbered Tears, no further changes to the text as given in V.306–13 had been made (apart from those mentioned in V.313, §1) when the LQ 1 typescript was taken from it, and this my father did not correct or change at any point. Years later, the LQ 2 typescript was simply a copy of LQ 1, perpetuating its errors, and similarly neglected. Thus the confused account of Turgon's emergence from Gondolin, discussed in V.314–15, which had been resolved in the story as told in the *Grey Annals* (see p. 133, §221), remained in this text without so much as a comment in the margin.

With Chapter 17, the beginning of the story of Túrin (V.316–21), my father abandoned, in December 1937, the writing of the continuous *Quenta Silmarillion*. He had made no changes to the chapter when the last typescript of the LQ 1 series was taken from it, and this text he never touched. In this case he did indeed return later to the manuscript, making many additions and corrections (and rejecting the whole of the latter part of the chapter, V.319–21, §§34–40); but this is best regarded as an aspect of the vast, unfinished work on the 'Saga of Túrin' that engaged him during the 1950s, from which no brief retelling suitable in scale to the *Quenta Silmarillion* ever emerged. LQ 2 was again a simple copy of LQ 1, by that time altogether obsolete.

Chapter 17 ended with Túrin's flight from Menegroth after the slaying of Orgof and his gathering of a band of outlaws beyond the borders of Doriath: 'their hands were turned against all who came in their path, Elves, Men, or Orcs' (V.321). The antecedent of this passage is found in Q *(Quenta Noldorinwa)*, IV.123; and from this point, in terms of the *Silmarillion* narrative strictly or narrowly defined, there is nothing later than Q (written, or the greater part of it, in 1930) for the rest of the tale of Túrin, and for all the story of the return of Húrin, the Nauglamír, the death of Thingol, the destruction of Doriath, the fall of Gondolin, and the attack on Sirion's Haven, until we come to the rewriting of the conclusion of Q which my father carried out in 1937.

This is not to suggest for a moment, of course, that he had lost interest in the later tales: 'Túrin' is the most obvious contradiction to that, while the later *Tale of Tuor* was undoubtedly intended to lead to a richly detailed account of the Fall of Gondolin, and *The Wanderings of Húrin* was not to end with his departure from Brethil, but to lead into the tale of the Necklace of the Dwarves. But the *Quenta Silmarillion* was at an end. I have said of the *Quenta Noldorinwa* (Q) in IV.76:

> The title ['This is the brief History of the Noldoli or Gnomes, drawn from the Book of Lost Tales'] makes it very plain that while Q was written in a finished manner, my father saw it as a compendium, a 'brief history' that was 'drawn from' a much longer work; and this aspect remained an important element in his conception of 'The Silmarillion' properly so called. I do not know whether this idea did indeed arise from the fact that the starting point of the second phase of the mythological narrative was a condensed synopsis (S) [the *Sketch of the Mythology*]; but it seems likely enough, from the step by step continuity that leads from S through Q to the version that was interrupted towards its end in 1937.

In these versions my father was drawing on (while also of course continually developing and extending) long works that already existed in prose and verse, and in the *Quenta Silmarillion* he perfected that characteristic tone, melodious, grave, elegiac, burdened with a sense of loss and distance in time, which resides partly, as I believe, in the literary fact that he was drawing down into a brief compendious history what he could also see in far more detailed, immediate, and dramatic form. With the completion of the great 'intrusion' and departure of *The Lord of the Rings*, it seems that he returned to the Elder Days with a desire to take up again the far more ample scale with which he had begun long before, in *The Book of Lost Tales*. The completion of the *Quenta Silmarillion* remained an aim; but the 'great tales', vastly developed from their original forms, from which its later chapters should be derived were never achieved.

It remains only to record the later history of the final element in QS, the rewritten conclusion of the *Quenta Noldorinwa*, which was given in V.323 ff. with such emendations as I judged to have been made very early and before the abandonment of work on QS at the end of 1937.

It is curious to find that a final typescript in the LQ 2 series of 1958(?) was made, in which the text of Q was copied from the words 'Húrin gathered therefore a few outlaws of the woods unto him, and they came to Nargothrond' (IV.132) to the end. It has no title, and apart from some corrections made to it by my father has no independent value: its interest lies only in the fact of its existence. The reason why it begins at this place in the narrative is, I think, clear (though not why it begins at precisely this point). At the time when my father decided to 'get copies made of all copyable material' (December 1957, see X.141–2) he provided the typist not only with the *Quenta Silmarillion* papers but also with (among other manuscripts) the *Grey Annals*. Thus the story of Túrin, in that form, was (or would be) secure in two typescript copies. But from the death of Túrin, if anything of the concluding parts of *The Silmarillion* was to be copied in this way, it had to be the text of Q: for there was nothing later (except the rewritten version of the conclusion). Yet in this text we are of course in quite early writing: for a single example among many, Q has (IV.139) 'For Turgon deemed, when first they came into that vale after the dreadful battle ...' – an explicit reference to the now long-discarded story of the foundation of Gondolin after the Battle of Unnumbered Tears; and so this appears in the late typescript. That was of course a mere *pis-aller*, an insurance against the possibility of a catastrophe, but its existence underlines, and must have underlined for my father, the essential and far-reaching work that still awaited him, but which he would never achieve.

The typist of LQ 2 was given the manuscript (see V.323) of the 1937 rewriting of the conclusion of Q, beginning 'And they looked upon the

246   THE WAR OF THE JEWELS

Lonely Isle and there they tarried not'. Some of the later, roughly made emendations (see V.324) had already been made to the manuscript, but others had not. Up to the point where the rewritten text begins my father understandably paid no attention at all to the typescript, but the concluding portion he corrected cursorily – it is clear that he did not have the actual manuscript by him to refer to. These corrections are mostly no more than regular changes of name, but he made one or two independent alterations as well, and these are recorded in the notes that follow.

The corrections to the manuscript, carried out as it appears in two stages (before and after the making of the typescript), are mostly fairly minor, and a few so slight as not to be worth recording. I refer to the numbered paragraphs in V.324–34.

Changes of name or forms of name were: *Airandir* > *Aerandir* (§1); *Tûn* > *Tirion* (§3 and subsequently); *Kôr* > *Túna* (§4); *Lindar* > *Vanyar* (§§6, 26); *Vingelot* > *Vingilot* (§11, but not at the other occurrences); *Gumlin* > *Galion* (§16); *Gorthû* > *Gorthaur* (§30, see p. 240, §143); *Palúrien* > *Kementári* (§32); *Eriol* > *Ereol* (§33).

Fionwë was changed to *Eönwë* throughout, and 'son of Manwë' to 'herald of Manwë' in §5 (but in §6 'Fionwë son of Manwë' > 'Eönwë to whom Manwë gave his sword'); 'the sons of the Valar' became 'the host of the Valar' in §6, but 'the Children of the Valar' in §18, 'the sons of the Gods' in §20, and 'the sons of the Valar' in §§29, 32, were not corrected (see also under §15 below).

Other changes were:

§6 'Ingwiel son of Ingwë was their chief': observing the apparent error, in that Ingwiel appears to be named the leader of the Noldor (see V.334, §6), my father changed this to 'Finarphin son of Finwë': see IV.196, second footnote. In the typescript he let the passage stand, but changed *Ingwiel* to *Ingwion* (and also 'Light-elves' to 'Fair-elves', see X.168, 180).
§9 'Manwë' > 'Manwë the Elder King'
§12 'she let build for her' > 'there was built for her'
§13 'they took it for a sign of hope' > 'they took it for a sign, and they called it Gil-Orrain, the Star of high hope', with *Gil-Orrain* subsequently changed to *Gil-Amdir* (see X.320). The typescript had the revised reading, with *Gil-Orrain*, which my father emended to *Gil-Estel*; on the carbon copy he wrote *Orestel* above *Orrain*.
§15 'the Light-elves of Valinor' > 'the Light-elves in Valinor'
    'the sons of the Gods were young and fair and terrible' > 'the host of the Gods were arrayed in forms of Valinor'
§16 'the most part of the sons of Men' > 'a great part of the sons of Men'
§17 'was like a great roar of thunder, and a tempest of fire' > 'was with a great thunder, and lightning, and a tempest of fire'
§18 'and in his fall the towers of Thangorodrim were thrown down'

> 'and he fell upon the towers of Thangorodrim and they were broken and thrown down'

'the chain Angainor, which long had been prepared' > 'the chain Angainor, which he had worn aforetime'

§20 'But Maidros would not harken, and he prepared ... to attempt in despair the fulfilment of his oath' > 'But Maidros and Maglor would not harken ...', with change of 'he' to 'they' and 'his' to 'their'.

§26 'and especially upon the great isles' > 'and upon the great isles'

§30 'and bears dark fruit even to these latest days' > 'and will bear dark fruit even unto the latest days'

'Sauron ... who served Morgoth even in Valinor and came with him' > '... who served Morgoth long ago and came with him into the world' (cf. the removal of the passage on this subject from the chapter *Of the Ruin of Beleriand*, p. 240, §143).

§31 'Túrin Turambar ... coming from the halls of Mandos' > 'Túrin Turambar ... returning from the Doom of Men at the ending of the world'. In the margin of the manuscript my father wrote 'and Beren Camlost' without direction for its insertion.

§32 'and she will break them [the Silmarils] and with their fire rekindle the Two Trees': this was emended on the carbon copy of the typescript only to: 'and he [Fëanor] will break them and with their fire Yavanna will rekindle the Two Trees'

Approximately against the last two sentences of the paragraph (from 'In that light the Gods will grow young again ...') my father put a large X in the margin of the manuscript.

Among these later changes were also the subheadings (*Of the Great Battle and the War of Wrath* at §15, *Of the Last End of the Oath of Fëanor and his Sons* at §20, and *Of the Passing of the Elves* at §26) which were noticed in the commentary on this text, V.336; I neglected however to mention there the introduction of a further subheading, *The Second Prophecy of Mandos*, at §31.

I said of this text in V.324: 'The very fact that the end of "The Silmarillion" still took this form when *The Lord of the Rings* was begun is sufficiently remarkable'. It seems much more remarkable, and not easy to interpret, that my father was treating it as a text requiring only minor and particular revision at this much later time. But his mode of emendation could sometimes be decidedly perfunctory, suggesting not a close, comparative consideration of an earlier text so much as a series of descents on particular points that struck his attention; and it may be that such later emendations as he made in this case are to be regarded rather in that light than as implying any sort of final approval of the content. But this text was peculiar in its inception, jumping forward from the beginning of the story of Túrin to the middle of a sentence much further on in the *Quenta*, and its later history does not diminish its somewhat mysterious nature.

PART THREE

THE WANDERINGS OF HÚRIN

AND OTHER WRITINGS
NOT FORMING PART OF THE *QUENTA SILMARILLION*

I
THE WANDERINGS OF HÚRIN

In *The Wanderings of Húrin* ('WH') it is not convenient to use the device of numbered paragraphs, and commentary (pp. 298 ff.) is here related to numbered notes in the text.

The earliest account of Húrin after his release by Morgoth is found in the *Tale of Turambar* (II.112–15, 135–6), leading to that in the *Sketch of the Mythology* (IV.32) and in Q (IV.132); see also AB 1 and AB 2 (IV.306, V.141). It is not necessary to say anything about these here, since in none of them is there any suggestion that Húrin returned to Hithlum (or went to Brethil) before he came to Nargothrond.

I have described (p. 103) how the manuscript of the *Grey Annals* (GA) ends with strange abruptness at the foot of a page, and said that 'it always seemed to me strange that my father should have abandoned the *Grey Annals* where he did, without at least writing the inscription that was carved on the stone'. At some later time (see *ibid.*) he entered roughly on the manuscript the inscription on the stone, and the words of conclusion to the tale, derived from the last part of the *Narn* (NE).

The explanation of this was simple, when I discovered, misplaced among miscellaneous papers, manuscript pages that are very obviously the continuation of the *Grey Annals* (the first of these pages is indeed numbered continuously with the last page of the main manuscript); this continuation, it is plain, was already lost in my father's lifetime. The original conclusion was in fact exactly as in the addition made to GA when he presumed the original ending lost, except that the title of the work was then *Glaer nia Chîn Húrin*, as in NE (p. 160, §349). Subsequently my father had added the words 'and was made by Men', as in the conclusion added to GA (p. 103), and later again he changed the title to *Narn i Chîn Húrin*, as he did also in NE.

In the scarcely changing script of the main manuscript this 'lost' text stopped here, but was then continued on the same page in a different ink and script, with the date 500 twice written against this further entry and each time struck out.

It is said by some that Morwen on a time came in her witless wandering to that stone and read it, and died afterwards, though haply she did not understand the tale that it told, and in that was less tormented than Húrin. For all that Morgoth knew of the working of his curse Húrin knew also; but lies and malice were mingled with the truth, and he that sees through the eyes of Morgoth, willing or unwilling, sees all things crooked. [*Written in the margin later:* Some fate of Morwen must be devised. Did Morwen and Húrin meet again?]¹

At this point the ink and to a slight degree the style of the script change again. The following narrative is the first account of Húrin's release since the *Quenta* of 1930.

500

Especially Morgoth endeavoured to cast an evil light upon all that Thingol and Melian had done (for he hated and feared them most); and when at last he deemed the time ripe, in the year after the death of his children, he released Húrin from bondage and let him go whither he would. He feigned that in this he was moved by generosity to a defeated enemy, but in truth his purpose was that Húrin should further his malice. And little though Húrin trusted aught that Morgoth said or did, he went forth in grief, embittered by the lies of the Dark Lord.

Twenty-eight years Húrin was captive in Angband, and at his release was in his sixtieth year,² but great strength was in him still, in spite of the weight of his grief, for it suited the purpose of Morgoth that this should be so. He was sent under guard as far as the east-marches of Hithlum, and there he was let go free.

None that had known him [in] youth could mistake him still, though he had grown grim to look on: his hair and beard were white and long, but there was a fell light in his eyes. He walked unbowed, and yet carried a great black staff; but he was girt with his sword. Great wonder and dread fell on the land when it was noised in Hithlum that the Lord Húrin had returned. The Easterlings were dismayed, fearing that their Master would prove faithless again and give back the land to the Westrons, and that they would be enslaved in their turn. For watchmen had reported that Húrin came out of Angband.

'There was a great riding,' they said, 'of the black soldiers of Thangorodrim over the Anfauglith, and with them came this man, as one that was held in honour.'

Therefore the chieftains of the Easterlings dared not lay hands on Húrin, and let him walk at will. In which they were wise; for the remnant of his own people shunned him, because of his coming from Angband, as one in league and honour with Morgoth; and indeed all escaped captives were held in suspicion of spying and treachery in those days, as has been told. Thus freedom only increased the bitterness of Húrin's heart; for even had he so wished, he could not have roused any rebellion against the new lords of the land. All the following that he gathered was a small company of the homeless men and outlaws that lurked in the hills; but they had done no great deed against the Incomers since the passing of Túrin, some five years before.

Of Túrin's deeds in Brodda's hall Húrin now learned from the outlaws the true tale; and he looked on Asgon[3] and his men, and he said: 'Men are changed here. In thraldom they have found thrall hearts. I desire no longer any lordship among them, nor elsewhere in Middle-earth. I will leave this land and wander alone, unless any of you will go with me, to meet what we may. For I have no purpose now, unless I find chance to avenge the wrongs of my son.'

Asgorn[4] and six other desperate men were willing to go with him; and Húrin led them to the halls of Lorgan, who still called himself the Lord of Hithlum. Lorgan heard of their coming and was afraid, and he gathered other chieftains and their men in his house for defence. But Húrin coming to the gates looked on the Eastrons[5] in scorn.

'Fear not!' he said. 'I should have needed no companions, if I had come to fight with you. I am come only to take leave of the lord of the land. I have no liking for it any more, since you have defiled it. Hold it while you may, until your Master recalls you to the slave-tasks that fit you better.'

Then Lorgan was not ill-pleased to think that he would so soon and easily be rid of the fear of Húrin, without crossing the will of Angband; and he came forward.

'As you will, friend,' he said. 'I have done you no ill, and have let you be, and of this I hope you will bring a true tale, if you come again to the Master.'

Húrin eyed him in wrath. 'Friend me not, thrall and churl!' he said. 'And believe not the lies that I have heard: that I have ever entered into the service of the Enemy. Of the Edain am I and so remain, and there shall be no friendship between mine and yours for ever.'

Then hearing that Húrin had not after all the favour of Morgoth, or forswore it, many of Lorgan's men drew their swords to put an end to him. But Lorgan restrained them; for he was wary, and more cunning and wicked than the others, and quicker therefore to guess at the purposes of the Master.

'Go then, greybeard, to evil fortune,' he said. 'For that is your doom. Folly and violence and self-hurt are all the deeds of your kin. Fare you ill!'

'*Tôl acharn!*' said Húrin. 'Vengeance comes. I am not the last of the Edain, whether I fare ill or well.' And with that he departed, and left the land of Hithlum.

501

Of the wanderings of Húrin there is no tale told, until he came at last late in this year to Nargothrond. It is said that he had then gathered to him other fugitives and masterless men in the wild, and came south with a following of a hundred or more. But why it was that he went to Nargothrond is uncertain, save that so his doom and the fate of the Jewels led him. Some have said that

At this point the 'lost continuation' of the *Grey Annals* stops, at the foot of a page; but a further page is found, written in a wholly different script (a rapid italic that my father used quite frequently in the period after the publication of *The Lord of the Rings*), that clearly joins to the abandoned sentence 'Some have said that'. Together with the first extension of the Annals, that concerning Morwen (pp. 251-2), and then the narrative recounting Húrin's return to Hithlum, this page is a further and final link in the series of additions that were made at intervals whose length cannot be determined.

[Some have said that] maybe he knew not that Glaurung was dead, and hoped in his heart distraught to take vengeance on this evil thing – for Morgoth would conceal the death of Glaurung, if he could, both because the loss was a grief to him and a hurt to his pride, and because (from Húrin especially) he would conceal all that was most valiant or successful of Túrin's deeds. Yet this can scarce be so,[6] since the death of Glaurung was so bound up with the death of his children and revelation of their evil case; while the rumour of the assault of Glaurung upon Brethil went far and wide. Certainly Morgoth fenced men in Hithlum, as he was able, and little news came to them of events in other lands; but so soon as Húrin passed southward or met any wanderers in the wild he would hear tidings of the battle in the ravine of Taiglin.

More likely is it that he was drawn thither to discover news of Túrin; to Brethil he would not yet come, nor to Doriath.

He went first seeking a way into Gondolin, and the friendship of Turgon (which indeed would have been great); but he found it not. His doom was unwilling (for Morgoth's curse was ever upon him still); and moreover since the Nírnaeth Turgon had expended every art upon the hiding of his realm. It was then that Húrin finding

Here the text stops abruptly; but on the same page and clearly at the same time my father wrote the following:

Húrin goes to seek Gondolin. Fails. Passes by Brethil, and his anguish is increased. They will not admit him – saying that the Halethrim do not wish any more to become enmeshed in the shadow of his kin. But ∧ [?new] Lord[7] gives the dragon-helm to Húrin. His heart is hot against Thingol. He passes it [Doriath] by and goes on to Nargothrond. Why? To seek news, plunder, – he had been an admirer of Felagund.

News of the fall of Nargothrond came to sons of Fëanor, and dismayed Maeðros, but did not all displease Celeg[orn] and Curufin. But when the news of the dragon's fall was heard, then many wondered concerning its hoard and who was the master? Some Orc-lord, men thought. But the Dwarves of [sic]   How did Mîm find it? He must come of a different race.[8]

These two pieces, especially the latter, are plainly a record of emerging ideas. In the first there is what is probably the earliest reference to the story that Húrin sought but failed to find the entrance to Gondolin. In the second appears a new articulation in the unwritten history of the Dragon-helm, together with other new detail (Húrin's admiration of Felagund, and the effect of the news of the fall of Nargothrond on the sons of Fëanor); and there is seen the first adumbration of a story of Húrin's adventures in Brethil before he went to Nargothrond.

Before coming to the fully achieved story of Húrin in Brethil there remains one further text to consider. When my father was engaged on his later work on the *Narn i Chîn Húrin* he made several plot-synopses arranged in annalistic form. Much of that material is not relevant here, since it is primarily concerned with the evolving story of Túrin; but one of them, which begins with the birth of Túrin, continues beyond his death and gives some account, though very brief, of Húrin after his release by Morgoth.

I give here the conclusion of this text (certainly somewhat later than any of the writings given thus far in Part Three), taking it up a little before the death of Túrin, since there are many interesting details in the annals for 490–9 bearing on the accounts given in NE and GA. The text was written legibly but very rapidly.

490-5

Túrin becomes a great captain in Nargothrond under the name of *Iarwaeth*, and is called *Mormegil* 'Black Sword'. [*Altered later to read:* Túrin becomes a great captain in Nargothrond. He only tells that he was lord of Cúarthol, and gives out his name as *Thuringud* the Hidden Foe; but is called *Mormegil* 'Black Sword'.

Gwindor reveals his true name to Finduilas, and Túrin is angry.[9]

494

Morgoth stirs up the Eastrons to greater hatred of Elves and Edain, and sends Orcs to aid them and impel them. Lorgan hearing of Niënor's beauty is eager to take her by force. Morwen and Niënor flee the land and come to Doriath. They seek news of Túrin.[10]

495

Tuor escapes from Hithlum by Cirith Ninniach and comes to Nivrost. He meets Gelmir and Arminas. Ulmo visits him on the shores by Mount Taras, and sends Voronwë to him. Tuor and Voronwë go to seek Gondolin which they reach in winter. Winter of 495-6 is the Fell Winter with ice and snow from November to March (5 months).

Gelmir and Arminas come to Nargothrond and bring warning of forces mustering in Narrow Land and under Erydwethian [sic]. They are rejected by Túrin.

Handir of Brethil slain in battle with the Orcs at the Crossings of Taeglin [sic]. His son Brandir the lame is chosen Chieftain, though many would have preferred his cousins Hunthor or Hardang.

Túrin and Orodreth defeated in Battle of Tum-halad by the dread of Glaurung. Gwindor also slain. Glaurung ravages Nargothrond, and cozens Túrin.

Túrin breaks his word to Gwindor to endeavour to save Finduilas, who is carried off. Instead under the spell of Glaurung he goes to Dorlómin to seek Morwen and Niënor.

Finduilas is slain by the Orcs near Crossings of Taeglin and buried by Men of Brethil in Haudh-en-Elleth.

Tuor sees Túrin near ravaged place of Eithil Ivrin but does not know who he is.

Glaurung takes possession of Nargothrond.[11]

496

Early in year Túrin comes to Dorlómin. He slays Brodda in his hall. Death of Sador. Túrin flies with Asgon and other outlawed Edain to the Mountains, and then leaves Dorlómin by himself. He comes at last to Brethil and learns of the fate of Finduilas.

Morwen and Niënor come to Nargothrond, but their escort (under Mablung) is scattered, and Morwen is lost in the wild, but Niënor is bewitched by Glaurung, and loses her memory, and runs into the wild.

Niënor comes to Brethil, and is called *Níniel*.[12]

496–

Under the name of *Turambar* Túrin becomes chief warrior of Brethil, and men give no heed to Brandir. Brandir falls in love with Níniel, but she loves Turambar.

497

Dior Halfelven weds Lindis of Ossiriand.[13]

498

Túrin weds Níniel (autumn).[14]

499

Glaurung assails Brethil. Túrin goes against him with Hunthor and Dorlas. Dorlas' heart fails and he leaves them. Hunthor is slain by a falling stone. Túrin slays Glaurung. Glaurung ere death reveals to Túrin and Niënor who they are. Túrin slays Brandir. Niënor casts herself into Taeglin. [*The following are separate additions to the text:*] Túrin slays Brandir and takes his own life. / Men of Brethil erect the *Talbor* or St[anding] Stone to their memory. / Mîm comes to Nargothrond and takes possession of the treasure.[15]

500

Elrún and Eldún twin sons of Dior are born.
Morgoth releases Húrin. Húrin goes to Hithlum.[16]

501

Húrin leaves Hithlum and with Asgon and six men goes down into the Narrow Land.

Húrin leaves his companions and seeks in vain an entrance to

Gondolin, but Morgoth's spies thus learn in what region it stands.

Húrin comes to the Stone and there finds Morwen, who dies. Húrin is put in prison by Hardang Chief of Brethil, but is aided by Manthor his kinsman (cousin of Hardang). In uprising Hardang and Manthor are slain and Obel Halad is burned. Húrin finds Asgon again and gathers other men and goes towards Nargothrond.[17]

502

Tuor weds Idril daughter of Turgon.

Húrin comes to Nargothrond and slays Mîm the petty-dwarf. He and his men carry off the treasure of Glaurung and bring it to Doriath. Húrin is admitted in pity.[18]

Here this plot-synopsis ends, at the foot of a manuscript page. I come now to the substantial complex of writing leading to a final text which my father ultimately entitled *The Wanderings of Húrin* (earlier *Of the Fate of Húrin and Morwen*). The final title seems not to be entirely apposite to the content of the work, which is wholly concerned with the story of Húrin in Brethil; it may have been intended to have a larger scope, to include the further story of Húrin told on the same scale, which was never written (see p. 310, note 57, and also the other title given below).

There is, first, a draft manuscript and associated rough workings (often of an extreme roughness). Many pages of the draft material are the backs of University documents dated 1954, others are documents from 1957. Secondly, there is a typescript made by my father on his later typewriter (see X.300), much emended in manuscript and with some substantial passages rejected and replaced by new material in typescript; and lastly an amanuensis typescript of virtually no independent value. The work can be placed with fair certainty towards the end of the 1950s.

My father's typescript, as typed, bore no title, but he wrote in ink on the top copy:

Of the Fate of Húrin and Morwen
Link to the Necklace of the Dwarves, 'Sigil Elu-naeth'
Necklace of the Woe of Thingol

The text opens thus:

So ended the tale of Túrin the hapless; and it has ever been held one of the worst of the deeds of Morgoth among Men in the ancient world. It is said by some that on a time Morwen came in her witless wandering to the graven stone, and knowing that her children were dead, though she understood not in what way their tale had ended, she sat beside the stone awaiting death; and there Húrin found her at last, as is after told.

Less happy than hers was the lot of Húrin.

This passage derives, in its first sentence, from Q (IV.131), and then from the first continuation of the *Grey Annals* (pp. 251–2), with the addition that Húrin found Morwen beside the stone (cf. p. 258, annal 501). The passage was struck from the typescript and replaced by the following, written on a document dating from 1957:

So ended the tale of Túrin the Hapless, the worst of the works of Morgoth among Men in the ancient world. But Morgoth did not sleep nor rest from evil, and this was not the end of his dealings with the House of Hador, against which his malice was unsated, though Húrin was under his Eye, and Morwen wandered distraught in the wild.

Unhappy was the lot of Húrin.

At the head of this my father subsequently wrote *The Wanderings of Húrin*, and the final amanuensis typescript was given this title also (see p. 258). The typescript continues, from 'Less happy than hers was the lot of Húrin':

For all that Morgoth knew of the working of his malice Húrin knew also; but lies were mingled with the truth, and aught that was good was hidden or distorted. He that sees through the eyes of Morgoth, willing or unwilling, sees all things crooked.

It was Morgoth's special endeavour to cast an evil light upon all that Thingol and Melian had done, for he feared and hated them most; and when, therefore, he deemed the time ripe, in the year after the death of Túrin he released Húrin from bondage, bidding him go whither he would.

He feigned that in this he was moved by pity for an enemy utterly defeated, marvelling at his endurance. 'Such steadfastness,' he said, 'should have been shown in a better cause, and would have been otherwise rewarded. But I have no longer any use for you, Húrin, in the waning of your little life.' And he lied, for his purpose was that Húrin should still further his malice against Elves and Men, ere he died.

Then little though Húrin trusted aught that Morgoth said or did, knowing that he was without pity, he took his freedom and went forth in grief, embittered by the deceits of the Dark Lord. Twenty-eight years Húrin was captive in Angband...

In this passage my father was following, with some expansion, the continuation of the *Grey Annals* (p. 252); from this point he followed it almost without alteration as far as 'And with that he departed, and left the land of Hithlum' (p. 254).[19] There are thus two closely similar, and for most of their length all but identical, texts of this short narrative, which may be called 'Húrin in Hithlum'; but the first of them is the continuation of the *Annals*, and the second is the opening of a wholly new story of Húrin in Brethil – causing a postponement of the story of 'Húrin in Nargothrond', which in the event was never reached. Seeing then that the second text of 'Húrin in Hithlum' has an entirely distinct function, there is clearly no question of regarding the story of Húrin in Brethil as a further extension of the *Annals*. As will be seen, my father was very evidently no longer writing annals of Beleriand: that work was now abandoned – or possibly, in his intention, left in abeyance, until the new story had been completed on the scale that he found congenial.

I now give the further text of *The Wanderings of Húrin* (following from the words 'And with that he departed, and left the land of Hithlum'). The work is of peculiar complexity in this, that when my father was well advanced in the story he came to a clearer understanding (as he might have said) of the situation in Brethil at the time of Húrin's advent; and these new conceptions overtook it before it was completed in a primary form. In other words, the story grew and changed as he wrote, but in this case he did not abandon it and start again at the beginning: he returned to earlier parts of the story and reconstructed them. For the most part the text as actually typed could stand, but required continual emendation in respect of names and other details. It is not easy to find a perfectly satisfactory and readily comprehensible way of presenting this, but after much experimentation I concluded that the best method is to give as the text the final form achieved in the typescript, but to interrupt it (pp. 265 ff.) at the point where the new conceptions first appear and give an account of the development. Two passages are concerned: the revised form of the first is marked by single asterisks on pp. 262–3, and of the second by double asterisks on pp. 264–5.

It is said that the hunters of Lorgan dogged his footsteps and did not leave his trail until he and his companions went up into the mountains. When Húrin stood again in the high places he descried far away amid the clouds the peaks of the Crisaegrim, and he remembered Turgon; and his heart desired to come again to the Hidden Realm, if he could, for there at least he would be remembered with honour. He had heard naught of the things that had come to pass in Gondolin, and knew not that Turgon now hardened his heart against wisdom and pity, and allowed no one either to enter or to go forth for any cause whatsoever.[20] Therefore, unaware that all ways were shut beyond hope, he resolved to turn his steps towards the Crisaegrim; but he said nothing of his purpose to his companions, for he was still bound by his oath to reveal to no one that he knew even in what region Turgon abode.

Nonetheless he had need of help; for he had never lived in the wild, whereas the outlaws were long inured to the hard life of hunters and gatherers, and they brought with them such food as they could, though the Fell Winter had much diminished their store. Therefore Húrin said to them: 'We must leave this land now; for Lorgan will leave me in peace no longer. Let us go down into the vales of Sirion, where Spring has come at last!'

Then Asgon[21] guided them to one of the ancient passes that led east out of Mithrim, and they went down from the sources of the Lithir, until they came to the falls where it raced into Sirion at the southern end of the Narrow Land.[22] Now they went with great wariness; for Húrin put little trust in the 'freedom' that Morgoth had granted him. And rightly: for Morgoth had news of all his movements, and though for a while he was hidden in the mountains, his coming down was soon espied. Thereafter he was followed and watched, yet with such cunning that he seldom got wind of it. All the creatures of Morgoth avoided his sight, and he was never waylaid or molested.[23]

They journeyed southward on the west side of Sirion, and Húrin debated with himself how to part from his companions, at least for so long that he could seek for an entrance to Gondolin without betraying his word. At length they came to the Brithiach; and there Asgon said to Húrin: 'Whither shall we go now, lord? Beyond this ford the ways east are too perilous for mortal men, if tales be true.'

'Then let us go to Brethil, which is nigh at hand,' said Húrin. 'I have an errand there. In that land my son died.'

So that night they took shelter in a grove of trees, first outliers of the Forest of Brethil on its northern border only a short way south of the Brithiach. Húrin lay a little apart from the others; and next day before it was light he arose while they slumbered deep in weariness, and he left them and crossed the ford and came into Dimbar.

When the men awoke he was already gone far, and there was a thick morning mist about the river. As time passed and he did not return nor answer any call they began to fear that he had been taken by some beast or prowling enemy. 'We have become heedless of late,' said Asgon. 'The land is quiet, too quiet, but there are eyes under leaves and ears behind stones.'

They followed his trail when the mist lifted; but it led to the ford and there failed, and they were at a loss. 'If he has left us, let us return to our own land,' said Ragnir.[24] He was the youngest of the company, and remembered little of the days before the Nirnaeth. 'The old man's wits are wild. He speaks with strange voices to shadows in his sleep.'

'Little wonder if it were so,' said Asgon. 'But who else could stand as straight as he, after such woe? Nay, he is our right lord, do as he may, and I have sworn to follow him.'

'Even east over the ford?' said the others.

'Nay, there is small hope in that way,' said Asgon, 'and I do not think that Húrin will go far upon it. All we know of his purpose was to go soon to Brethil, and that he has an errand there. We are on the very border. Let us seek him there.'

'By whose leave?' said Ragnir. 'Men there do not love strangers.'

'Good men dwell there,' said Asgon, 'and the [Master >] Lord of Brethil is kin to our old lords.'[25] Nonetheless the others were doubtful, for no tidings had come out of Brethil for some years. 'It may be ruled by Orcs for all we know,' they said.

'We shall soon find what way things go,' said Asgon. 'Orcs are little worse than Eastrons, I guess. If outlaws we must remain, I would rather lurk in the fair woods than in the cold hills.'

Asgon, therefore, turned and went back towards Brethil; and the others followed him, for he had a stout heart and men said that he was born with good luck. Before that day ended they had come deep into the forest, and their coming was marked; for the Haladin were more wary than ever and kept close watch on their borders. In the [middle of the night >] grey of the morning, as all but one of the incomers were asleep, their camp was surrounded, and their watchman was held and gagged as soon as he cried out.

Then Asgon leapt up, and called to his men that they should draw no weapon. 'See now,' he cried, 'we come in peace! Edain we are out of [Mithrim > Hithlum >] Dorlómin.'

*'That may be so,' said the march-wardens. 'But the morn is dim. Our captain will judge you better when light is more.'

Then being many times outnumbered Asgon and his men were made prisoners, and their weapons were taken and their hands bound. Thus they were brought to Ebor their captain; and he asked their names and whence they came.

'So you are Edain of the North,' he said. 'Your speech bears you out, and your gear. You look for friendship, maybe. But alas! evil things have befallen us here, and we live in fear. Manthor my lord, Master of the North-march, is not here, and I must therefore obey the commands of the Halad, the Chieftain of Brethil. To him you must be sent at once without further question. There may you speed well!'

So Ebor spoke in courtesy, but he did not hope over much. For the new Chieftain was now Hardang son of Hundad. At the death of Brandir childless he had been made Halad, being of the Haladin, the kin of Haleth, from which all chieftains were chosen. He had not loved Túrin, and he had no love now at all for the House of Hador, in whose blood he had no part. Neither had he much friendship with Manthor, who was also of the Haladin.

To Hardang Asgon and his men were led by devious ways, and they were blindfolded. Thus at length they came to the hall of the Chieftains in Obel Halad;[26] and their eyes were uncovered, and the guards led them in. Hardang sat in his great chair, and he looked unkindly upon them.

'From Dorlómin you come, I am told,' he said. 'But why you come I know not.* Little good has come to Brethil out of that land; and I look for none now: it is a fief of Angband. Cold welcome you will find here, creeping in thus to spy out our ways!'

Asgon restrained his anger, but answered stoutly: 'We did not come in stealth, lord. We have as great craft in woods as your folk, and we should not so easily have been taken, if we had known any cause for fear. We are Edain, and we do not serve Angband but hold to the House of Hador. We believed that the Men of Brethil were of like sort and friendly to all faithful men.'

'To those of proved faith,' said Hardang. 'To be Edain is not enough alone. And as for the House of Hador it is held in little love here. Why should the folk of that House come here now?'

To that Asgon made no answer; for from the unfriendship of the [Master >] Chieftain he thought it best not to speak yet of Húrin.

'I see that you will not speak of all that you know,' said Hardang. 'So be it. I must judge as I see; but I will be just. This is my judgement. Here Túrin son of Húrin dwelt for a time, and he delivered the land from the Serpent of Angband. For this I give you your lives. **But he scorned Brandir, right Chieftain of Brethil, and he slew him without justice or pity. Therefore I will not harbour you here. You shall be thrust forth, whence you entered. Go now, and if you return it will be to death!'

'Then shall we not receive our weapons again?' said Asgon. 'Will you cast us back into the wild without bow or steel to perish among the beasts?'

'No man of Hithlum shall ever again bear weapon in Brethil,' said Hardang. 'Not by my leave. Lead them hence.'

But as they were haled from the hall Asgon cried: 'This is the justice of Eastrons not of Edain! We were not here with Túrin, either in good deed or evil. Húrin we serve. He lives still. Lurking in your wood do you not remember the Nirnaeth? Will you then dishonour him also in your spite, if he comes?'

'If Húrin comes, do you say?' said Hardang. 'When Morgoth sleeps, maybe!'

'Nay,' said Asgon. 'He has returned. With him we came to your borders. He has an errand here, he said. He will come!'

'Then I shall be here to meet him,' said Hardang. 'But you will not. Now go!' He spoke as in scorn, but his face whitened in sudden fear that some strange thing had happened boding yet worse to come. Then a great dread of the shadow of the House of Hador fell upon him, so that his heart grew dark. For he was not a man of great spirit, such as were Hunthor and Manthor, descendants of Hiril.

Asgon and his company were blindfolded again, lest they should espy out the pathways of Brethil, and they were led back to the North-march. Ebor was ill pleased when he heard of what had passed in Obel Halad, and he spoke to them more courteously.

'Alas!' he said, 'you must needs go forth again. But see! I return to you your gear and weapons. For so would my lord Manthor do, at the least. I would he were here! But he is the doughtiest man now among us; and by Hardang's command is Captain of the guards at the Crossings of Taiglin. There we have most fear of assault, and most fighting. Well, this much I will do in his stead; but I beg you, do not enter Brethil again, for if you do, we may feel constrained to obey the word of Hardang that has now gone out to all the marches: to slay you at sight.'

Then Asgon thanked him, and Ebor led them to the eaves of Brethil, and there wished them good speed.

'Well, thy luck has held,' said Ragnir, 'for at least we are not slain, though we came nigh it. Now what shall we do?'

'I desire still to find my lord Húrin,' said Asgon, 'and my heart tells me that he will come to Brethil yet.'

'Whither we cannot return,' said Ragnir, 'unless we seek a death swifter than hunger.'

'If he comes, he will come, I guess, by the north-march, between Sirion and [Taiglin >] Taeglin,' said Asgon. 'Let us go down towards the Crossings of [Taiglin >] Taeglin. There it is more likely that we may hear news.'

'Or bow-strings,' said Ragnir. Nonetheless they took Asgon's counsel, and went away westward, keeping such watch as they could from afar upon the dark eaves of Brethil.

But Ebor was troubled, and sent swiftly to Manthor reporting the coming of Asgon and his strange words concerning Húrin. But of this matter rumour now ran through all Brethil. And Hardang sat in Obel Halad in doubt, and took counsel with his friends.**

In the foregoing text two passages are replacements in the typescript of shorter passages that were rejected. The first of these, marked by asterisks at its beginning and end, runs from '"That may be so," said the march-wardens' on p. 262 to '"But why you come I know not"' on p. 263. The rejected passage read as follows:

'Maybe,' answered the captain of the guards; 'but the morn is dim. Others shall judge you in a better light.'

Then, being many times outnumbered, Asgorn and his men were made prisoners, and their weapons were taken and their hands bound; and in this way they were brought at last before the new Master of the Haladin.

He was Harathor, brother of that Hunthor who perished in the ravine of Taeglin. By the childless death of Brandir he had inherited the lordship descending from Haldad. He had no love for the house of Hador, and no part in their blood; and he said to Asgorn, when the captives stood before him: 'From [Hithlum >] Dorlómin you come, I am told, and your speech bears it out. But why you come I know not.

For reference in the following pages I shall call this passage A 1 and its replacement A 2.

The second replacement passage, marked by two asterisks at

beginning and end, runs from 'But he scorned Brandir' on p. 264 to 'And Hardang sat in Obel Halad in doubt, and took counsel with his friends' on p. 265. Here the rejected passage read:

> '... But he scorned Brandir, right Master of Brethil, and he slew him without justice or pity. For this I will take your freedom. You shall be held in bonds; and I shall not relent until good reason is shown me.'
>
> Then he ordered them to be taken and shut in a cave and there to be guarded day and night. But as they were led away Asgorn cried: 'This is the justice of Eastrons not of Edain! We were not here with Túrin, either in good deed or evil. Húrin we serve, who still lives. Maybe lurking in your little wood you do not remember the Nirnaeth or his great deeds. Will you slay him to ease your griefs, if he comes?'
>
> 'If Húrin comes, do you say?' said Harathor. 'When Morgoth sleeps, maybe.'
>
> 'Nay,' said Asgorn. 'He has returned, and we came with him to your borders. He has an errand here, he said. He will come!'
>
> 'Then we will await him. And you shall too,' said Harathor, smiling grimly. But afterwards his heart misgave him, fearing that Asgorn spoke the truth and that some strange thing had happened, boding worse to follow. For he dreaded the shadow of the House of Hador, lest it should overwhelm his lesser folk, and he was not a man of great heart such as Hunthor his brother [*later* > such as the descendants of Haldir and Hiril his sister].

The rejected text then moved straight on to 'Now Húrin, coming into Dimbar' on p. 271. The passage just given I will call B 1 and its replacement B 2.

Among the draft manuscript papers is found the following text, which I will call 'C': in this my father reflected on the development of the story. Written very rapidly and roughly, with many abbreviations which I have expanded, it *preceded*, and was the basis for, the two replacement passages A 2 and B 2.

> The Wanderings of Húrin.
> ? Where is to come in the revelation that Asgorn and company are in jail. They do not seem to fit, yet their coming to Brethil is needed to 'cast the shadow' by arousing fear and hatred in the heart of Harathor.
>
> I suggest that the two jailings [i.e. that of Asgorn and his men and that of Húrin, told later] are too repetitive; and also Harathor is too fierce all at once. His doom is that because of the killing of Glaurung their lives are spared; but because of the killing of Brandir they are to be *thrust out*: he will have none of the House of Hador.
>
> Asgorn says this is cruel treatment. He demands return of their

weapons, 'or how else are they to live in the wild?' But Harathor says no man of Dorlómin shall bear a weapon in Brethil. Asgorn as they are led off asks if he will treat Húrin in like orkish manner. 'We will wait and see,' said Harathor.

[*This paragraph was struck out as soon as written:* [Manthor, captain >] The captain / of the Taiglin-guard returns their weapons, and bids them a fairly courteous farewell; but warns them that 'state of war' has been declared (which gives the Master / Warden right to issue orders to all under duty-rota) and that if they cross again into Brethil he or any other captain or watchman will shoot them. They go off but lurk in watch of the crossings, but miss Húrin, who entered out of Dimbar. Húrin should *not* enter by Taiglin-crossing, *nor* be found by Hauð-en-Elleth. (This has no significance in his case, and overworks the Hauð.)]

Asgorn and company are blindfolded as they are brought to Obel Halad and are put out *by the same way* as they entered (so as to learn no more of the ways of Brethil). They therefore lurk near the eaves in that region, and so miss Húrin who crossed the Brithiach and went to the Crossings of Taiglin.

The region nigh Brithiach and along Sirion for some way was the land of Manthor (brother of Hunthor who fell in the ravine). But Manthor, as one of the chief warriors and of the kin of the Haladin, was in command of the chief forces kept near the Crossings of Taiglin. (Manthor was not liked by Harathor, for many had wished to elect him Warden – it being ... law to do so. And maybe Manthor too desired the Wardenship.) The captain of the guards near Brithiach was Enthor [> was therefore a chief henchman, called Ebor, of Manthor's (appointed by him)] younger brother of Hunthor and Manthor. So Manthor heard soon of what had happened: for all this family had been supporters and admirers of Túrin, and were proud of their *kinship* with the House of Hador. So Enthor [> Ebor] sent messengers to Manthor to tell him that Húrin might come, escaping from Angband.

In the last part of the *Narn* (NE) the emergence of Hunthor (< Torbarth) can be followed, from his origin in Albarth, at first simply one of those who volunteered to accompany Túrin to the attack on Glaurung and named only because he fell and was drowned at Cabed-en-Aras. In the first of these rejected passages (A 1, p. 265) the new lord of Brethil after the death of Brandir is Harathor, 'brother of that Hunthor who perished in the ravine of Taeglin'; and it is expressly said of him that 'he had no love for the house of Hador *and no part in their blood*'. These words, repeated in the revision A 2 (p. 263), are of great importance in the story.

An essential element in the older history of the People of Haleth was the intermingling of the line of their lords with that of the House of

Hador which came about through the 'double marriage' of Hador's son Galion with the daughter (unnamed) of Haleth the Hunter, and of his daughter Glorwendil with Haleth's son Hundor (GA §171 and commentary). This double marriage was preserved in the later transformed history of the Edain, when the genealogical place of Haleth the Hunter had been taken by Halmir (p. 236); the resulting relationships can be displayed thus:

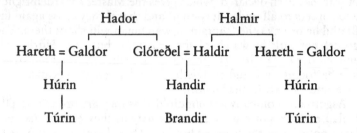

But the complexity was further increased by the introduction of another connection with the House of Bëor in the marriage of Beldis to Handir of Brethil (see the tables on pp. 231, 237):

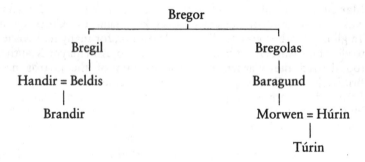

Thus Túrin was the second cousin of Brandir on the 'Hadorian' side, and he was also his second cousin on the Haladin side; while in the 'Bëorian' line he was Brandir's second cousin once removed – a genealogical situation to delight the heart of Hamfast Gamgee. Pointing out these relationships in an isolated note of this time, my father observed that 'Túrin would be more readily accepted by the Haladin when his true name and lineage were known or guessed', since he was akin to their lords in these ways. Harathor, on the other hand, 'had no love for the house of Hador and no part in their blood' (although he also was Túrin's second cousin, his great-aunt Hareth being Túrin's grandmother).

The genealogical table of the Haladin (p. 237) belongs to this stage: Harathor is shown as the seventh lord of the Haladin, succeeding

Brandir, and as the brother of Hunthor: they are the sons of Hundad, son of Hundar who died in the Nírnaeth.

The hostility of the new lord to the House of Hador was an essential idea in the story of Húrin in Brethil from the beginning; but in the last paragraph of the discussion C (p. 267) we see the emergence of a family within the larger clan who, on the contrary, took pride in their kinship with the House of Hador, and were thus divided in spirit from the new lord.

In C the significance of Hunthor is moved a stage further: he becomes the dead brother of Manthor (and must therefore, as will be seen in a moment, cease to be the brother of Harathor). Manthor had indeed already entered the story in the original drafting of WH, but he did not make his appearance until the discovery of Húrin beside the Hauð-en-Elleth (p. 275 in the final version), as captain of the guard in those parts; now in C he becomes a kinsman of Húrin, and an upholder of the values and virtues of the Edain. How his kinship with the House of Hador was introduced is seen from the correction made to the ending of the rejected passage B 1 (p. 266): '[Harathor] was not a man of great heart such as Hunthor his brother' > '... such as the descendants of Haldir and Hiril his sister'.* *Hiril* here enters the line of the People of Haleth, and the family tree is extended by a fourth child of Halmir: Haldir, Hundar, Hareth, and Hiril. In the replacement B 2 (p. 264) the phrase becomes 'he was not a man of great spirit, such as were Hunthor and Manthor, descendants of Hiril'. (That Manthor's mother was the daughter of Hiril is stated later in the text of WH, p. 289.)

In C Harathor was still so named, but he must have been on the point of receiving a new name, and must have already received a new lineage, separating him from those with 'Hadorian' sympathies, Hunthor and Manthor. The new name, *Hardang*, appears in the replacement text A 2 (p. 263) – and the occurrence of this name in the plot-sequence from the *Narn* papers shows incidentally that that text was written when my father's work on *The Wanderings of Húrin* was far advanced, if not completed. It is said there (p. 256) that when Brandir the Lame was chosen to be the Chieftain of Brethil 'many would have preferred his cousins Hunthor or Hardang', and (p. 258) that Manthor was a kinsman of Húrin and a cousin of Hardang.

This new 'family within the larger clan' was entered in roughly made alterations to the table of the Haladin (p. 237), of which I give the essentials in compressed form:

---

* Before Hiril was introduced as a second daughter of Halmir, his daughter Hareth was first named *Hiriel* (p. 235, footnote).

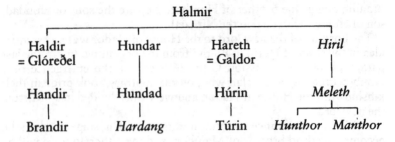

Hardang's birthdate is given as 470, Hunthor's as 467, and Manthor's as 469.

It also appears from C (p. 267) that a new conception of the social organisation of the Men of Brethil had entered, and with it a new meaning of the name *Haladin*: Manthor is said to be 'one of the chief warriors and of the kin of the Haladin', and that 'many had wished to elect him Warden'. In this connection, an isolated note (written on the reverse of that on the relationships of Túrin referred to on p. 268) states:

> The title of the chieftains of Brethil should be not *lord* nor *Master*. They were elected from the family of Haldad – called the *Haladin*, that is 'wardens'. For *hal(a)* = in the old tongue of Bëor's house and Haldad's 'watch, guard'. *Halad* was a warden. (*Haldad* = watchdog.)

These new conceptions appear in the revision A 2 (p. 263), where Hardang is said to have been made *Halad*, 'being of the Haladin, the kin of Haleth, from which all chieftains were chosen'. It is also said, following the discussion in C, that Hardang was no friend to Manthor, 'who was also of the Haladin'. In contrast, in the first form of the passage (p. 265) Harathor is called 'the new Master of the Haladin', where *Haladin* clearly still means the whole people.

In the last paragraph of C (p. 267) a younger brother of Hunthor and Manthor appears, Enthor, 'captain of the guards near Brithiach' (in the additions made to the genealogical table of the Haladin this name *Enthor* was given to Hiril's husband, not otherwise named; and Meleth's husband is apparently named *Agathor*). The removal of the name Enthor in this sentence and substitution of 'a chief henchman, called Ebor, of Manthor's (appointed by him)' suggests that my father intended to cut out the words 'younger brother of Hunthor and Manthor', but omitted to do so; this is supported by the fact that Ebor, when he appears in the revision A 2 (p. 263), refers to 'Manthor my lord, Master of the North-march', who was not there. Manthor was not there because, as stated in C, he was 'in command of the chief forces kept near the Crossings of Taiglin'; Asgon and his companions entered Brethil from the north, near the Brithiach, and they left by the same way, meeting Ebor again and retrieving their weapons.

The only obscure point concerns the failure of Asgon's party to encounter Húrin on his return. My father was in two minds about this. The rejected fourth paragraph in C (p. 267) shows him (having decided that Asgorn and his men were not imprisoned) taking the view that they were ejected from Brethil near the Crossings: it is 'the captain of the Taiglin-guard' who restores their weapons; and they remain lurking in that neighbourhood. Thus they missed Húrin, 'who entered out of Dimbar' (i.e. came into Brethil from the north after crossing the Brithiach, as Asgorn had done). Húrin, he wrote, must *not* enter Brethil at the Crossings and be found lying beside the Hauð-en-Elleth (as the story was already in the draft manuscript).

But he at once, and understandably, thought better of this, and (in the fifth paragraph) retained the existing story that Húrin was found by the guards near the Crossings; he said now that Asgorn and his men were put out of Brethil in the same region as they entered, and that they lurked 'near the eaves in that region' – hence their failure to meet with Húrin. But in the replacement passage B 2 (p. 265) he has them decide not to stay near the north eaves of the forest, and they go down towards the Crossings.

I return now to the text, left at the end of the second passage of rewriting (B 2) on p. 265. It must be borne in mind that the typescript from this point belongs to the stage *before* the important alterations in the narrative entered in the two replacement passages discussed above. Thus for a long way 'the Master of Brethil' remains Harathor; the term *Halad* was not yet devised, and his dwelling was not yet named *Obel Halad*. Rather than rewrite the existing text after the new conceptions had arisen, my father found it sufficient to correct it. These corrections are very numerous but for the most part repetitive and systematic (as 'Master' to 'Halad' or 'Chieftain'), and to record each case in the text would make it unreadable. I have therefore ignored the rejected names and titles (this applies also to the short passage on pp. 263–4 between the two rewritten sections: here *Hardang* is in fact a correction on the typescript of *Harathor*).

Now Húrin, coming into Dimbar, summoned his strength and went on alone towards the dark feet of the Echoriad.[27] All the land was cold and desolate; and when at last it rose steeply before him and he could see no way to go further, he halted and looked about him in little hope. He stood now at the foot of a great fall of stones beneath a sheer rock-wall, and he did not know that this was all that was now left to see of the old Way of Escape: the Dry River was blocked and the arched gate was buried.[28]

Then Húrin looked up to the grey sky, thinking that by fortune he might once more descry the Eagles, as he had done long ago in his youth.[29] But he saw only the shadows blown from the East, and clouds swirling about the inaccessible peaks; and wind hissed over the stones. But the watch of the Great Eagles was now redoubled, and they marked Húrin well, far below, forlorn in the failing light. And straightaway Sorontar himself, since the tidings seemed great, brought word to Turgon.

But Turgon said: 'Nay! This is past belief! Unless Morgoth sleeps. Ye were mistaken.'

'Nay, not so,' answered Sorontar. 'If the Eagles of Manwë were wont to err thus, Lord, your hiding would have been in vain.'

'Then your words bode ill,' said Turgon; 'for they can mean only that even Húrin Thalion hath surrendered to the will of Morgoth. My heart is shut.' But when he had dismissed Sorontar, Turgon sat long in thought, and he was troubled, remembering the deeds of Húrin. And he opened his heart, and he sent to the Eagles to seek for Húrin, and to bring him, if they could, to Gondolin. But it was too late, and they saw him never again in light or in shadow.

For Húrin stood at last in despair before the stern silence of the Echoriad, and the westering sun, piercing the clouds, stained his white hair with red. Then he cried aloud in the wilderness, heedless of any ears, and he cursed the pitiless land: 'hard as the hearts of Elves and Men'. And he stood at last upon a great stone, and spreading wide his arms, looking towards Gondolin, he called in a great voice: 'Turgon, Turgon! Remember the Fen of Serech!' And again: 'Turgon! Húrin calls you. O Turgon, will you not hear in your hidden halls?'

But there was no answer, and all that he heard was wind in the dry grasses. 'Even so they hissed in Serech at the sunset,' he said. And as he spoke the sun went behind the Mountains of Shadow, and a darkness fell about him, and the wind ceased, and there was silence in the waste.

Yet there were ears that had heard the words that Húrin spoke, and eyes that marked well his gestures; and report of all came soon to the Dark Throne in the North. Then Morgoth smiled, and knew now clearly in what region Turgon dwelt, though because of the Eagles no spy of his could yet come within sight of the land behind the encircling mountains. This was the first evil that the freedom of Húrin achieved.[30]

As darkness fell Húrin stumbled from the stone, and fell, as one aswoon, into a deep sleep of grief. But in his sleep he heard the voice of Morwen lamenting, and often she spoke his name; and it seemed to him that her voice came out of Brethil. Therefore, when he awoke with the coming of day, he arose and returned; and he came back to the ford, and as one led by an unseen hand [he passed along the river Taeglin, until ere evening of the third day he reached the place >] he went along the eaves of Brethil, until he came in four days' journey to the Taeglin, and all his scanty food was then spent, and he was famished. But he went on like the shadow of a man driven by a dark wind, and he came to the Crossings by night, and there he passed over into Brethil.

The night-sentinels saw him, but they were filled with dread, so that they did not dare to move or cry out; for they thought that they saw a ghost out of some old battle-mound that walked with darkness about it. And for many days after men feared to be near the Crossings at night, save in great company and with fire kindled.

But Húrin passed on, and at evening of the sixth day he came at last to the place / of the burning of Glaurung, and saw the tall stone standing near the brink of Cabed Naeramarth.

But Húrin did not look at the stone, for he knew what was written there, and his eyes had seen that he was not alone. Sitting in the shadow of the stone there was a figure bent over its knees. Some homeless wanderer broken with age it seemed, too wayworn to heed his coming; but its rags were the remnants of a woman's garb. At length as Húrin stood there silent she cast back her tattered hood and lifted up her face slowly, haggard and hungry as a long-hunted wolf. Grey she was, sharp-nosed with broken teeth, and with a lean hand she clawed at the cloak upon her breast. But suddenly her eyes looked into his, and then Húrin knew her; for though they were wild now and full of fear, a light still gleamed in them hard to endure: the elven-light that long ago had earned her her name, Eðelwen, proudest of mortal women in the days of old.

'Eðelwen! Eðelwen!' Húrin cried; and she rose and stumbled forward, and he caught her in his arms.

'You come at last,' she said. 'I have waited too long.'

'It was a dark road. I have come as I could,' he answered.

'But you are late,' she said, 'too late. They are lost.'

'I know,' he said. 'But thou art not.'

'Almost,' she said. 'I am spent utterly. I shall go with the sun. They are lost.' She clutched at his cloak. 'Little time is left,' she said. 'If you know, tell me! How did she find him?'

But Húrin did not answer, and he sat beside the stone with Morwen in his arms; and they did not speak again. The sun went down, and Morwen sighed and clasped his hand and was still; and Húrin knew that she had died.

So passed Morwen the proud and fair; and Húrin looked down at her in the twilight, and it seemed that the lines of grief and cruel hardship were smoothed away. Cold and pale and stern was her face. 'She was not conquered,' he said; and he closed her eyes, and sat on unmoving beside her as night drew down. The waters of Cabed Naeramarth roared on, but he heard no sound and saw nothing, and he felt nothing, for his heart was stone within him, and he thought that he would sit there until he too died.

Then there came a chill wind and drove sharp rain in his face; and suddenly he was roused, and out of a black deep anger rose in him like a smoke, mastering reason, so that all his desire was to seek vengeance for his wrongs, and for the wrongs of his kin, accusing in his anguish all those who ever had had dealings with them.

He arose and lifted Morwen up; and suddenly he knew that it was beyond his strength to bear her. He was hungry and old, and weary as winter. Slowly he laid her down again beside the standing stone. 'Lie there a little longer, Eðelwen,' he said, 'until I return. Not even a wolf would do you more hurt. But the folk of this hard land shall rue the day that you died here!'

Then Húrin stumbled away, and he came back towards the ford of Taeglin; and there he fell beside the Hauð-en-Elleth, and a darkness overcame him, and he lay as one drowned in sleep. In the morning, before the light had recalled him to full waking, he was found by the guards that Hardang had commanded to keep special watch in that place.

It was a man named Sagroth who first saw him, and he looked at him in wonder and was afraid, for he thought he knew who this old man was. 'Come!' he cried to others that followed. 'Look here! It must be Húrin. The incomers spoke truly. He has come!'

'Trust you to find trouble, as ever, Sagroth!' said Forhend.

'The Halad will not be pleased with such findings. What is to be done? Maybe Hardang would be better pleased to hear that we had stopped the trouble at his borders and thrust it out.'

'Thrust it out?' said Avranc. He was Dorlas' son,[31] a young man short and dark, but strong, well-liked by Hardang, as his father had been. 'Thrust it out? Of what good would that be? It would come again! It can walk – all the way from Angband, if it is what you guess. See! He looks grim and has a sword, but he sleeps deep. Need he wake to more woe? [*Added:*] If you would please the Chieftain, Forhend, he would end here.'

Such was the shadow that now fell upon the hearts of men, as the power of Morgoth spread, and fear walked far and wide; but not all hearts were yet darkened. 'Shame upon you!' cried Manthor the captain, who coming behind had heard what they said. 'And upon you most, Avranc, young though you are! At least you have heard of the deeds of Húrin of Hithlum, or did you hold them only fireside fables? What is to be done, indeed! So, slay him in his sleep is your counsel. Out of hell comes the thought!'

'And so does he,' answered Avranc. 'If indeed he is Húrin. Who knows?'

'It can soon be known,' said Manthor; and coming to Húrin as he lay he knelt and raised his hand and kissed it. 'Awake!' he cried. 'Help is near. And if you are Húrin, there is no help that I would think enough.'

'And no help that he will not repay with evil,' said Avranc. 'He comes from Angband, I say.'

'What he may do is unknown,' said Manthor. 'What he has done we know, and our debt is unpaid.' Then he called again in a loud voice: 'Hail Húrin Thalion! Hail, Captain of Men!'

Thereupon Húrin opened his eyes, remembering evil words that he had heard in the drowse before waking, and he saw men about him with weapons in hand. He stood up stiffly, fumbling at his sword; and he glared upon them in anger and scorn. 'Curs!' he cried. 'Would you slay an old man sleeping? You look like Men, but you are Orcs under the skin, I guess. Come then! Slay me awake, if you dare. But it will not please your black Master, I think. I am Húrin Galdor's son, a name that Orcs at least will remember.'

'Nay, nay,' said Manthor. 'Dream not. We are Men. But these are evil days of doubt, and we are hard pressed. It is perilous here. Will you not come with us? At least we can find you food and rest.'

'Rest?' said Húrin. 'You cannot find me that. But food I will take in my need.'

Then Manthor gave him a little bread and meat and water; but they seemed to choke him, and he spat them forth. 'How far is it to the house of your lord?' he asked. 'Until I have seen him the food that you denied to my beloved will not go down my throat.'

'He raves and he scorns us,' muttered Avranc. 'What did I say?' But Manthor looked on him with pity, though he did not understand his words. 'It is a long road for the weary, lord,' he said; 'and the house of Hardang Halad is hidden from strangers.'

'Then lead me thither!' said Húrin. 'I will go as I can. I have an errand to that house.'

Soon they set forth. Of his strong company Manthor left most to their duty; but he himself went with Húrin, and with him he took Forhend. Húrin walked as he could, but after a time he began to stumble and fall; and yet he always rose again and struggled on, and he would not allow them to support him. In this way at last with many halts they came to the hall of Hardang in Obel Halad deep in the forest; and he knew of their coming, for Avranc, unbidden, had run ahead and brought the tidings before them; and he did not fail to report the wild words of Húrin at his waking and his spitting forth of their food.

So it was that they found the hall well guarded, with many men in the [fenced courtyard >] outer garth, and men at the doors. At the gate of the [court >] garth the captain of the guards stayed them. 'Deliver the prisoner to me!' he said.

'Prisoner!' said Manthor. 'I have no prisoner, but a man you should honour.'

'The Halad's words, not mine,' said the captain. 'But you may come too. He has words for you also.'

Then they led Húrin before the Chieftain; and Hardang did not greet him, but sat in his great chair and eyed Húrin up and down. But Húrin returned his gaze, and held himself as stiffly as he could, though he leaned on his staff. So he stood a while in silence, until at last he sank to the ground. 'Lo!' he said. 'I see that there are so few chairs in Brethil that a guest must sit on the floor.'

'Guest?' said Hardang. 'Not one bidden by me. But bring the old carl a stool. If he will not disdain it, though he spits on our food.'

Manthor was grieved at the discourtesy; and hearing one laugh in the shadow behind the great chair he looked and saw that it was Avranc, and his face darkened in wrath.

'Your pardon, lord,' he said to Húrin. 'There is misunderstanding here.' Then turning to Hardang he drew himself up. 'Has my company a new captain then, my Halad?' he said. 'For otherwise I do not understand how one who has left his duty and broken my command should stand here unrebuked. He has brought news before me, I see; but it seems he forgot the name of the guest, or Húrin Thalion would not have been left to stand.'

'The name was told to me,' answered Hardang, 'and his fell words also which bear it out. Such are the House of Hador. But it is the part of a stranger to name himself first in my house, and I waited to hear him. Also to hear his errand hither – since he says that he has one. But as for your duty, such matters are not dealt with before strangers.'

Then he turned towards Húrin, who sat meanwhile bent on the low stool; his eyes were closed, and he seemed to take no heed of what was said. 'Well, Húrin of Hithlum,' said Hardang, 'what of your errand? Is it a matter of haste? Or will you not perhaps take thought and rest and speak of it later more at your ease? Meanwhile we may find you some food less distasteful.' Hardang's tone was now more gentle, and he rose as he spoke; for he was a wary man, and [*struck out:* in his heart not over sure of his seat in the Master's chair; and] he had marked the displeasure on the faces of others beside Manthor.

Then suddenly Húrin rose to his feet. 'Well, Master Reed of the Bog,' he said. 'So you bend with each breath, do you? Beware lest mine blow you flat. Go take thought to stiffen you, ere I call on you again! Scorner of grey hairs, food-niggard, starver of wanderers. This stool fits you better.' With that he cast the stool at Hardang, so that it smote him on the forehead; and then he turned to walk from the hall.

Some of the men gave way, whether in pity or in fear of his wrath; but Avranc ran before him. 'Not so swift, carl Húrin!' he cried. 'At least I no longer doubt your name. You bring your manners from Angband. But we do not love orc-deeds in hall. You have assaulted the Chieftain in his chair, and a prisoner you now shall be, whatever your name.'

'I thank you, Captain Avranc,' said Hardang, who sat still in his chair, while some staunched the blood that flowed from his brow. 'Now let the old madman be put in bonds and kept close. I will judge him later.'

Then they put thongs about Húrin's arms, and a halter about his neck, and led him away; and he made no more resistance, for the wrath had run off him, and he walked as one in a dream with eyes closed. But Manthor, though Avranc scowled at him, put his arm about the old man's shoulder and steered him so that he should not stumble.

But when Húrin was shut in a cave [*struck out:* nigh to the one in which Asgorn and his men were still imprisoned] and Manthor could do no more to help him, he returned to the hall. There he found Avranc in speech with Hardang, and though they fell silent at his coming, he caught the last words that Avranc spoke, and it seemed to him that Avranc urged that Húrin should be put to death straightway.

'So, Captain Avranc,' he said, 'things go well for you today! I have seen you at like sports before: goading an old badger and having him killed when he bites. Not so swift, Captain Avranc! Nor you, Hardang Halad. This is no matter for lordly dealing out of hand. The coming of Húrin, and his welcome here, concerns all the folk, and they shall hear all that is said, before any judgement is given.'

'You have leave to go,' said Hardang. 'Return to your duty on the marches, until Captain Avranc comes to take command.'

'Nay, lord,' said Manthor, 'I have no duty. I am out of your service from today. I left Sagroth[32] in charge, a woodsman somewhat older and wiser than one you name. In due time I will return to my own marches.*[33] But now I will summon the folk.'

As he went to the door Avranc seized his bow to shoot Manthor down, but Hardang restrained him. 'Not yet,' he said. But Manthor was unaware of this (though some in the hall had marked it), and he went out, and sent all he could find that were

---

* For Manthor was a descendant of Haldad, and he had a little land of his own on the east march of Brethil beside Sirion where it runs through Dimbar. But all the folk of Brethil were freemen, holding their homesteads and more or less land about them of their right. Their Master was chosen from the descendants of Haldad, out of reverence for the deeds of Haleth and Haldar; and though as yet the mastership had been given, as if it were a lordship or kingdom, to the eldest of the eldest line, the folk had the right to set anyone aside or to remove him, for grave cause. And some knew well enough that Harathor had tried to have Brandir the Lame passed over in his own favour.

willing to go as messengers to bring together all the masters of homesteads and any others that could be spared. [*Struck out:* It was the custom of the Haladin[34] that in all matters other than war the wives were also summoned to counsel and had equal voices with the husbands.]

Now rumour ran wild through the woods, and the tales grew in the telling; and some said this, and some that, and the most spoke in praise of the Halad and set forth Húrin in the likeness of some fell Orc-chieftain; for Avranc was also busy with messengers. Soon there was a great concourse of folk, and the small town [35] about the Hall of the Chieftains was swelled with tents and booths.[36] But all the men bore arms, for fear lest a sudden alarm should come from the marches.

When he had sent out his messengers Manthor went to Húrin's prison, and the guards would not let him enter. 'Come!' said Manthor. 'You know well that it is our good custom that any prisoner should have a friend that may come to him and see how he fares and give him counsel.'

'The friend is chosen by the prisoner,' the guards answered; 'but this wild man has no friends.'

'He has one,' said Manthor, 'and I ask leave to offer myself to his choice.'

'The Halad forbids us to admit any save the guards,' they said. But Manthor who was wise in the laws and customs of his people replied: 'No doubt. But in this he has no right. Why is the incomer in bondage? We do not bind old men and wanderers because they speak ill words when distraught. This one is imprisoned because of his assault upon Hardang, and Hardang cannot judge his own cause, but must bring his grievance to the judgement of the Folk [*struck out:* and some other must sit in the chair at the hearing]. Meanwhile he cannot deny to the prisoner all counsel and help. If he were wise he would see that he does not in this way advance his own cause. But maybe another mouth spoke for him?'

'True,' they said. 'Avranc brought the order.'

'Then forget it,' said Manthor. 'For Avranc was under other orders, to remain on his duty on the marches. Choose then between a young runagate, and the laws of the Folk.'

Then the guards let him in to the cave; for Manthor was well esteemed in Brethil, and men did not like the [masters >] chieftains who tried to overrule the folk. Manthor found Húrin sitting on a bench. There were fetters on his ankles, but his hands were unbound; and there was some food before him untasted. He did not look up.

'Hail, lord!' said Manthor. 'Things have not gone as they should, nor as I would have ordered them. But now you have need of a friend.'

'I have no friend, and wish for none in this land,' said Húrin.

'One stands before you,' answered Manthor. 'Do not scorn me. For now, alas! the matter between you and Hardang Halad must be brought to the judgement of the Folk, and it would be well, as our law allows, to have a friend to counsel you and plead your case.'

'I will not plead, and I need no counsel,' said Húrin.

'You need this counsel at least,' said Manthor. 'Master your wrath for the time, and take some food, so that you may have strength before your enemies. I do not know what is your errand here, but it will speed better, if you are not starved. Do not slay yourself while there is hope!'

'Slay myself?' cried Húrin, and he staggered up and leant against the wall, and his eyes were red. 'Shall I be dragged before a rabble of wood-men with fetters upon me to hear what death they will give me? I will slay myself first, if my hands are left free.' Then suddenly, swift as an old trapped beast, he sprang forward, and before Manthor could avoid him he snatched a knife from his belt. Then he sank down on the bench.

'You could have had the knife as a gift,' said Manthor, 'though we do not deem self-slaughter a noble deed in those who have not lost their reason. Hide the knife and keep it for some better use! But have a care, for it is a fell blade, from a forge of the Dwarves. Now, lord, will you not take me for your friend? Say no word; but if you will now eat with me, I will take that for yea.'

Then Húrin looked at him and the wrath left his eyes; and together they drank and ate in silence. And when all was finished, Húrin said: 'By your voice you have overcome me. Never since the Day of Dread have I heard any man's voice so fair. Alas! alas! it calls to my mind the voices in my father's house, long ago when the shadow seemed far away.'

'That may well be,' said Manthor. 'Hiril my foremother was sister of thy mother, Hareth.'

'Then thou art both kin and friend,' said Húrin.

'But not I alone,' said Manthor. 'We are few and have little wealth, but we too are Edain, and bound by many ties to your people. Your name has long been held in honour here; but no news of your deeds would have reached us, if Haldir and Hundar had not marched to the Nirnaeth. There they fell, but [seven >] three of their company returned, for they were succoured by Mablung of Doriath and healed of their wounds.[37] The days have gone dark since then, and many hearts are overshadowed, but not all.'

'Yet the voice of your Chieftain comes from the shadows,' said Húrin, 'and your Folk obey him, even in deeds of dishonour and cruelty.'

'Grief darkens your eyes, lord, dare I say it. But lest this should prove true, let us take counsel together. For I see peril of evil ahead, both to thee and to my folk, though maybe wisdom may avert it. Of one thing I must warn thee, though it may not please thee. Hardang is a lesser man than his fathers, but I saw no evil in him till he heard of thy coming. Thou bringest a shadow with thee, Húrin Thalion, in which lesser shadows grow darker.'

'Dark words from a friend!' said Húrin. 'Long I lived in the Shadow, but I endured it and did not yield. If there is any darkness upon me, it is only that grief beyond grief has robbed me of light. But in the Shadow I have no part.'

'Nevertheless, I say to thee,' said Manthor, 'that it follows behind thee. I know not how thou hast won freedom; but the thought of Morgoth has not forgotten thee. Beware.'

'Do not dote, dotard, you would say,' answered Húrin. 'I will take this much from you, for your fair voice and our kinship, but no more! Let us speak of other things, or cease.'

Then Manthor was patient, and stayed long with Húrin, until the evening brought darkness into the cave; and they ate once more together. Then Manthor commanded that a light should be brought to Húrin; and he took his leave until the morrow, and went to his booth with a heavy heart.

The next day it was proclaimed that the Folkmoot for Judgement should be held on the morning following, for already five hundred of the headmen had come in, and that was by custom deemed the least number which might count as a full meeting of the Folk. Manthor went early to find Húrin; but the guards had been changed. Three men of Hardang's own household now stood at the door, and they were unfriendly.

'The prisoner is asleep,' their leader said. 'And that is well; it may settle his wits.'

'But I am his appointed friend, as was declared yesterday,' said Manthor.

'A friend would leave him in peace, while he may have it. To what good would you wake him?'

'Why should my coming wake him, more easily than the feet of a jailer?' said Manthor. 'I wish to see how he sleeps.'

'Do you think all men lie but yourself?'

'Nay, nay; but I think that some would fain forget our laws when they do not suit their purpose,' answered Manthor. Nonetheless it seemed to him that he would do little good to Húrin's case if he debated further, and he went away. So it was that many things remained unspoken between them until too late. For when he returned day was waning. No hindrance was now offered to his entry, and he found Húrin lying on a pallet; [*added:*] and he noted with anger that he now had fetters also upon his wrists with a short chain between them.

'A friend delayed is hope denied,' said Húrin. 'I have waited long for thee, but now I am heavy with sleep and my eyes are dimmed.'

'I came at mid-morning,' said Manthor, 'but they said that thou wert sleeping then.'

'Drowsing, drowsing in wanhope,' said Húrin; 'but thy voice might have recalled me. I have been so since I broke my fast. That counsel of thine at least I have taken, my friend; but food doth me ill rather than good. Now I must sleep. But come in the morning!'

Manthor wondered darkly at this. He could not see Húrin's face, for there was little light left, but bending down he listened to his breathing. Then with a grim face he stood up and took up under his cloak such food as remained, and went out.

'Well, how did you find the wild man?' said the chief guard.

'Bemused with sleep,' answered Manthor. 'He must be wakeful tomorrow. Rouse him early. Bring food for two, for I will come and break fast with him.'[38]

The next day, long before the set time at mid-morn, the Moot began to assemble. Almost a thousand had now come, for the most part the older men [*struck out:* and women],[39] since the watch on the marches must still be maintained. Soon all the Moot-ring was filled. This was shaped as a great crescent, with seven tiers of turf-banks rising up from a smooth floor delved back into the hillside. A high fence was set all about it, and the only entry was by a heavy gate in the stockade that closed the open end of the crescent. In the middle of the lowest tier of seats was set [*added:*] the Angbor or Doom-rock, / a great flat stone upon which the Halad[40] would sit. Those who were brought to judgement stood before the stone and faced the assembly.

There was a great babel of voices; but at a horn-call silence fell, and the Halad entered, and he had many men of his household with him. The gate was closed behind him, and he paced slowly to the Stone. Then he stood facing the assembly and hallowed the Moot according to custom. First he named Manwë and Mandos, after the manner which the Edain had learned from the Eldar, and then, speaking the old tongue of the Folk which was now out of daily use, he declared that the Moot was duly set, being the three hundred and first Moot of Brethil, called to give judgement in a grave matter.

When as custom was all the assembly cried in the same tongue 'We are ready', he took his seat upon the [stone >] Angbor, and called in the speech of Beleriand[41] to men that stood by: 'Sound the horn! Let the prisoner be brought before us!'[42]

The horn sounded twice, but for some time no one entered, and the sound of angry voices could be heard outside the fence. At length the gate was thrust open, and six men came in bearing Húrin between them.

'I am brought by violence and misuse,' he cried. 'I will not walk slave-fettered to any Moot upon earth, not though Elven-kings should sit there. And while I am bound thus I deny all authority and justice to your dooms.' But the men set him on the ground before the Stone and held him there by force.

Now it was the custom of the Moot that, when any man was brought before it, the Halad should be the accuser, and should first in brief recite the misdeed with which he was charged. Whereupon it was his right, by himself or by the mouth of his friend, to deny the charge, or to offer a defence for what he had done. And when these things had been said, if any point was in doubt or was denied by either side, then witnesses were summoned.

Hardang,[43] therefore, now stood up and turning to the assembly he began to recite the charge. 'This prisoner,' he said, 'whom you see before you, names himself Húrin Galdor's son, once of Dorlómin, but long in Angband whence he came hither. Be that as it may.'[44]

But hereupon Manthor arose and came before the Stone. 'By your leave, my lord Halad and Folk!' he cried. 'As friend to the prisoner I claim the right to ask: Is the charge against him any matter that touches the Halad in person? Or has the Halad any grievance against him?'

'Grievance?' cried Hardang, and anger clouded his wits so that he did not see Manthor's trend. 'Grievance indeed! This is not a new fashion in headgear for the Moot. I come here with wounds new-dressed.'

'Alas!' said Manthor. 'But if that is so, I claim that the matter cannot be dealt with in this way. In our law no man may recite an offence against himself; nor may he sit in the seat of judgement while that charge is heard. Is not this the law?'

'It is the law,' the assembly answered.

'Then,' said Manthor, 'before this charge is heard some other than Hardang son of Hundad must be appointed to the Stone.'

Thereupon many names were cried, but most voices and the loudest called upon Manthor. 'Nay,' said he, 'I am engaged to one part and cannot be judge. Moreover it is the Halad's right in such a case to name the one who should take his place, as doubtless he knows well.'

'I thank you,' said Hardang, 'though I need no self-chosen lawman to teach me.' Then he looked about him, as if considering whom he should name. But he was in a black anger and all wisdom failed him. If he had named any of the headmen there present, things might have gone otherwise. But in an evil moment he chose, and to all men's wonder he cried: 'Avranc Dorlas' son! It seems that the Halad needs a friend also today, when lawmen are so pert. I summon you to the Stone.'

Silence fell. But when Hardang stepped down and Avranc came to the Stone there was a loud murmuring like the rumour of a coming storm. Avranc was a young man, not long wedded, and his youth was taken ill by all the elder headmen that sat there. [For he was not loved for himself. >] And he was not loved for himself; for though he was bold, he was scornful, as was Dorlas his father before him. / And dark tales were [*struck out:* still] whispered concerning Dorlas [*struck out:* his father, who had been Hardang's close friend];[45] for though naught was known for certain, he was found slain far from the battle with

Glaurung, and the reddened sword that lay by him had been the sword of Brandir.[46]

But Avranc took no heed of the murmur, and bore himself airily, as if it were a light matter soon to be dealt with.

'Well,' he said, 'if that is settled, let us waste no more time! The matter is clear enough.' Then standing up he continued the recital. 'This prisoner, this wild man,' he said, 'comes from Angband, as you have heard. He was found within our borders. Not by chance, for as he himself declared, he has an errand here. What that may be he has not revealed, but it cannot be one of good will. He hates this folk. As soon as he saw us he reviled us. We gave him food and he spat on it. I have seen Orcs do so, if any were fools enough to show them mercy. From Angband he comes, it is clear, whatever his name be. But worse followed after. By his own asking he was brought before the Halad of Brethil – by this man who now calls himself his friend; but when he came into hall he would not name himself. And when the Halad asked him what was his errand and bade him rest first and speak of it later, if it pleased him, he began to rave, reviling the Halad, and suddenly he cast a stool in his face and did him great hurt. It is well for all that he had nothing more deadly to hand, or the Halad would have been slain. As was plainly the prisoner's intent, and it lessens his guilt very little that the worst did not happen, for which the penalty is death. But even so, the Halad sat in the great chair in his hall: to revile him there was an evil deed, and to assault him an outrage.

'This then is the charge against the prisoner: that he came here with evil intent against us, and against the Halad of Brethil in special (at the bidding of Angband one may guess); that gaining the presence of the Halad he reviled him, and then sought to slay him in his chair. The penalty is under the doom of the Moot, but it could justly be death.'

Then it seemed to some that Avranc spoke justly, and to all that he had spoken with skill. For a while no one raised a voice upon either side. Then Avranc, not hiding his smile, rose again and said: 'The prisoner may now answer the charge if he will, but let him be brief and not rave!'

But Húrin did not speak, though he strained against those that held him. 'Prisoner, will you not speak?' said Avranc, and still Húrin gave no answer. 'So be it,' said Avranc. 'If he will not speak, not even to deny the charge, then there is no more to do.

The charge is made good, and the one that is appointed to the Stone must propound to the Moot a penalty that seems just.'

But now Manthor stood up and said: 'First he should at least be asked why he will not speak. And to that question reply may be made by his friend.'

'The question is put,' said Avranc with a shrug. 'If you know the answer give it.'

'Because he is fettered [*added:* hand and foot],'[47] said Manthor. 'Never before have we dragged to the Moot in fetters a man yet uncondemned. Still less one of the Edain whose name deserves honour, whatsoever may have happened since. Yes, "uncondemned" I say; for the accuser has left much unsaid that this Moot must hear before judgement is given.'

'But this is foolishness,' said Avranc. 'Adan or no, and whatever his name, the prisoner is ungovernable and malicious. The bonds are a needed precaution. Those who come near him must be protected from his violence.'

'If you wish to beget violence,' answered Manthor, 'what surer way than openly to dishonour a proud man, old in years of great grief. And here is one now weakened by hunger and long journeying, unarmed among a host. I would ask the folk here assembled: do you deem such caution worthy of the free men of Brethil, or would you rather that we used the courtesy of old?'

'The fetters were put on the prisoner by the order of the Halad,' said Avranc. 'In this he used his right for the restraint of violence in his hall. Therefore this order cannot be gainsaid save by the full assembly.'

Then there went up a great shout 'Release him, release him! Húrin Thalion! Release Húrin Thalion!' Not all joined in this cry, yet there were no voices heard on the other side.

'Nay, nay!' said Avranc. 'Shouting will not avail. In such a case there must be a vote in due form.'

Now by custom in matters grave or doubtful the votes of the Moot were cast with pebbles, and all who entered bore with them each two pebbles, a black and a white for *nay* and for *yea*. But the gathering and counting would take much time, and meanwhile Manthor saw that with each moment the mood of Húrin grew worse.

'There is another way more simple,' he said. 'There is no danger here to justify the bonds, and so think all who have used their voice. The Halad is in the Moot-ring, and he can remit his own order, if he will.'

'He will,' said Hardang, for it seemed to him that the mood of the assembly was restive, and he hoped by this stroke to regain its favour. 'Let the prisoner be released, and stand up before you!'

Then the fetters were struck off Húrin's hands and feet. Straightway he stood up, and turning away from Avranc he faced the assembly. 'I am here,' he said. 'I will answer my name. I am Húrin Thalion son of Galdor Orchal,[48] Lord of Dorlómin and once a high-captain in the host of Fingon King of the North-realm. Let no man dare to deny it! That should be enough. I will not plead before you. Do as you will! Neither will I bandy words with the upstart whom you permit to sit in the high seat. Let him lie as he will! [*Struck out:* But if my friend wishes to speak and to set forth the truth of what has chanced, let him do so. Listen who will!]

'In the name of the Lords of the West, what manner of folk are you, or to what have you become? While the ruin of Darkness is all about you will you sit here in patience and hear this runagate guard ask for a doom of death upon me – because I broke the head of an insolent young man, whether in a chair or out of it? He should have learned how to treat his elders before you made him your Chieftain forsooth.

'Death? 'Fore Manwë, if I had not endured torment for twenty years and eight, if I were as at the Nirnaeth, you would not dare to sit here to face me. But I am not dangerous any longer, I hear. So you are brave. I can stand up unbound to be baited. I am broken in war and made tame. Tame! Be not too sure!' He lifted up his arms and knotted his hands.

But here Manthor laid a restraining hand on his shoulder, and spoke earnestly in his ear. 'My lord, you mistake them. Most are your friends, or would be. But there are proud freemen here too. Let me now speak to them!'

Hardang and Avranc said naught, but smiled one to another, for Húrin's speech, they thought, did his part no good. But Manthor cried: 'Let the Lord Húrin be given a seat while I speak. His wrath you will understand better, and maybe forgive, when you have heard me.

'Hear me now, Folk of Brethil. My friend does not deny the main charge, but he claims that he was misused and provoked beyond bearing. My masters [*struck out:* and good wives],[49] I was captain of the march-wardens that found this man asleep by the Hauð-en-Elleth. Or asleep he seemed, but he lay rather in weariness on the brink of awaking, and as he lay he heard, as I fear, words that were spoken.

'There was a man called Avranc Dorlas' son, I remember, as one of my company, and he should be there still, for such were my orders. As I came behind I heard this Avranc give counsel to the man who had first found Húrin and guessed at his name. Folk of Brethil, I heard him speak thus. "It would be better to slay the old man asleep and prevent further trouble. And so the Halad would be pleased," said he.

'Now maybe you will wonder less that when I called him to full waking and he found men with weapons all about him, he spoke bitter words to us. One at least of us deserved them. Yet as for despising our food: he took it from my hands, and he did not spit upon it. He spat it forth, for it choked him. Have you never, my masters, seen a man half-starved who could not swallow food in haste though he needed it? And this man was in great grief also and full of anger.

'Nay, he did not disdain our food. Though well he might, if he had known the devices to which some who dwell here have fallen! Hear me now and believe me, if you may, for witness can be brought. In his prison the Lord Húrin ate with me, for I used him with courtesy. That was two days ago. But yesterday he was drowsed and could not speak clearly, nor take counsel with me against the trial today.'

'Little wonder in that!' cried Hardang.

Manthor paused and looked at Hardang. 'Little wonder indeed, my lord Halad,' he said; 'for his food had been drugged.'

Then Hardang in wrath cried out: 'Must the drowsy dreams of this dotard be recited to our weariness?'

'I speak of no dreams,' answered Manthor. 'Witness will follow. But since against custom I am challenged while I speak, I will answer now. I took away from the prison food of which Húrin had eaten some. Before witnesses I gave it to a hound, and he lies still asleep as if dead. Maybe the Halad of Brethil did not contrive this himself, but one who is eager to please him. But with what lawful purpose? To restrain him from violence, forsooth, when he was already fettered and in prison? There is malice abroad among us, Folk of Brethil, and I look to the assembly to amend it!'

At this there was great stir and murmur in the Moot-ring; and when Avranc stood up calling for silence, the clamour grew greater. At last when the assembly had quieted a little Manthor said: 'May I now continue, for there is more to be said?'

'Proceed!' said Avranc. 'But let your wind be shortened. And I must warn you all, my masters, to hear this man warily. His good faith cannot be trusted. The prisoner and he are close akin.'

These words were unwise, for Manthor answered at once: 'It is so indeed. The mother of Húrin was Hareth daughter of Halmir, once Halad of Brethil, and Hiril her sister was the mother of my mother. But this lineage does not prove me a liar. More, if Húrin of Dorlómin be akin to me, he is kinsman of all the House of Haleth. Yea, and of all this Folk. Yet he is treated as an outlaw, a robber, a wild man without honour!

'Let us proceed then to the chief charge, which the accuser has said may bear the penalty of death. You see before you the broken head, though it seems to sit firm on its shoulders and can use its tongue. It was hurt by the cast of a small wooden stool. A wicked deed, you will say. And far worse when done to the Halad of Brethil in his great chair.

'But my masters, ill deeds may be provoked. Let any one of you in thought set himself in the place of Hardang son of Hundad. Well, here comes Húrin, Lord of Dorlómin, your kinsman, before you: head of a great House, a man whose deeds are sung by Elves and Men. But he is now grown old, dispossessed, grief-laden, travel-worn. He asks to see you. There you sit at ease in your chair. You do not rise. You do not speak to him. But you eye him up and down as he stands, until he sinks to the floor. Then of your pity and courtesy you cry: "Bring the old carl a stool!"

'O shame and wonder! He flings it at your head. O shame and wonder rather I say that you so dishonour your chair, that you so dishonour your hall, that you so dishonour the Folk of Brethil!

'My masters, I freely admit that it would have been better, if the Lord Húrin had shown patience, marvellous patience. Why did he not wait to see what further slights he must endure? Yet as I stood in hall and saw all this I wondered, and I still wonder and I ask you to tell me: How do you like such manners in this man that we have made Halad of Brethil?'

Great uproar arose at this question, until Manthor held up his hand, and suddenly all was still again. But under cover of the noise Hardang had drawn near to Avranc to speak with him, and surprised by the silence they spoke too loud, so that Manthor and others also heard Hardang say: 'I would I had not hindered thy shooting!'[50] And Avranc answered: 'I will seek a time yet.'

But Manthor proceeded. 'I am answered. Such manners do not please you, I see. Then what would you have done with the caster of the stool? Bound him, put a halter on his neck, shut him in a cave, fettered him, drugged his food, and at last dragged him hither and called for his death? Or would you set him free? Or would you, maybe, ask pardon, or command this Halad to do so?'

Thereupon there was even greater uproar, and men stood up on the turfbanks, clashing their arms, and crying: 'Free! Free! Set him free!' And many voices were heard also shouting: 'Away with this Halad! Put him in the caves!'

Many of the older men who sat in the lowest tier ran forward and knelt before Húrin to ask his pardon; and one offered him a staff, and another gave him a fair cloak and a great belt of silver. And when Húrin was so clad, and had a staff in hand, he went to the [*added:* Angbor] Stone and stood up on it, in no wise as a suppliant, but in mien as a king; and facing the assembly he cried in a great voice: 'I thank you, Masters of Brethil here present, who have released me from dishonour. There is then justice still in your land, though it has slept and been slow to awake. But now I have a charge to bring in my turn.

'What is my errand here, it is asked? What think you? Did not Túrin my son, and Nienor my daughter, die in this land? Alas! from afar I have learned much of the griefs that have here come to pass. Is it then a wonder that a father should seek the graves of his children? More wonder it is, meseems, that none here have yet ever spoken their names to me.

'Are ye ashamed that ye let Túrin my son die for you? That two only dared go with him to face the terror of the Worm? That none dared go down to succour him when the battle was over, though the worst evils might thus have been stayed?

'Ashamed ye may be. But this is not my charge. I do not ask that any in this land should match the son of Húrin in valour. But if I forgive those griefs, shall I forgive this? Hear me, Men of Brethil! There lies by the Standing Stone that you raised an old beggar-woman. Long she sat in your land, without fire, without food, without pity. Now she is dead. Dead. She was Morwen my wife. Morwen Eðelwen, the lady elven-fair who bore Túrin the slayer of Glaurung. She is dead.

'If ye, who have some ruth, cry to me that you are guiltless, then I ask who bears the guilt? By whose command was she thrust out to starve at your doors like an outcast dog?

'Did your Chieftain contrive this? So I believe. For would he not have dealt with me in like manner, if he could? Such are his gifts: dishonour, starvation, poison. Have you no part in this? Will you not work all his will? Then how long, Masters of Brethil, will you endure him? How long will you suffer this man called Hardang to sit in your chair?'

Now Hardang was aghast at this turn, and his face went white with fear and amazement. But before he could speak, Húrin pointed a long hand at him. 'See!' he cried. 'There he stands with a sneer on his mouth! Does he deem himself safe? For I am robbed of my sword; and I am old and weary, he thinks. Nay, too often has he called me a wild man. He shall see one! Only hands, hands, are needed to wring his throat full of lies.'

With that Húrin left the Stone and strode towards Hardang; but he gave back before him, calling his household-men about him; and they drew off towards the gate. Thus it appeared to many that Hardang admitted his guilt, and they drew their weapons, and came down from the banks, crying out upon him.[51]

Now there was peril of battle within the hallowed Ring. For others joined themselves to Hardang, some without love for him or his deeds, who nonetheless held to their loyalty and would at least defend him from violence, until he could answer before the Moot.

Manthor stood between the two parties and cried to them to hold their hands and shed no blood in the Moot-ring; but the spark that he had himself kindled now burst to flame beyond his quenching, and a press of men thrust him aside. 'Away with this Halad!' they shouted. 'Away with Hardang, take him to the caves! Down with Hardang! Up Manthor! We will have Manthor!' And they fell upon the men that barred the way to the gate, so that Hardang might have time to escape.

But Manthor went back to Húrin, who now stood alone by

the Stone. 'Alas, lord,' he said, 'I feared that this day held great peril for us all. There is little I can do, but still I must try to avert the worst evil. They will soon break out, and I must follow. Will you come with me?'

Many fell at the gate on either side ere it was taken. There Avranc fought bravely, and was the last to retreat. Then as he turned to flee suddenly he drew his bow and shot at Manthor as he stood by the Stone. But the arrow missed in his haste and hit on the Stone, striking fire beside Manthor as it broke. 'Next time nearer!' cried Avranc as he fled after Hardang.

Then the rebels burst out of the Ring and hotly pursued Hardang's men to the Obel Halad, some half mile away. But before they could come there Hardang had gained the hall and shut it against them; and there he was now besieged. The Hall of the Chieftains stood in a garth with a round earthwall all about it rising from a dry outer dyke. In the wall there was only one gate, from which a stone-path led to the great doors. The assailants drove through the gate and swiftly surrounded all the hall; and all was quiet for a while.

But Manthor and Húrin came to the gate; and Manthor would have a parley, but men said: 'Of what use are words? Rats will not come out while dogs are abroad.' And some cried: 'Our kin have been slain, and we will avenge them!'

'Well then,' said Manthor, 'allow me at least to do what I can!'

'Do so!' they said. 'But go not too near, or you may receive a sharp answer.'

Therefore Manthor stood by the gate and lifted up his great voice, crying out to both sides that they should cease from this kin-slaying. And to those within he promised that all should go free who came forth without weapons, even Hardang, if he would give his word to stand before the Moot the next day. 'And no man shall bring any weapon thither,' he said.

But while he spoke there came a shot from a window, and an arrow went by the ear of Manthor and stood deep in the gate-post. Then the voice of Avranc was heard crying: 'Third time shall thrive best!'

Now the anger of those without burst forth again, and many rushed to the great doors and tried to break them down; but there was a sortie, and many were slain or hurt, and others also in the garth were wounded by shots from the windows. So the assailants being now in mad wrath brought kindlings and great store of wood and set it by the gate; and they shouted to those within: 'See! the sun is setting. We give you till nightfall. If you do not come forth ere then, we will burn the hall and you in it!' Then they all withdrew from the garth out of bowshot, but they made a ring of men all round the outer dyke.

The sun set, and none came from the hall. And when it was dark the assailants came back into the garth bearing the wood, and they piled it against the walls of the hall. Then some bearing flaming pine-torches ran across the garth to put fire in the faggots. One was shot to his death, but others reached the piles and soon they began to blaze.

Manthor stood aghast at the ruin of the hall and the wicked deed of the burning of men. 'Out of the dark days of our past it comes,' he said, 'before we turned our faces west. A shadow is upon us.' And he felt one lay a hand on his shoulder, and he turned and saw Húrin who stood behind him, with a grim face watching the kindling of the fires; and Húrin laughed.

'A strange folk are ye,' he said. 'Now cold, now hot. First wrath, then ruth. Under your chieftain's feet or at his throat. Down with Hardang! Up with Manthor! Wilt thou go up?'

'The Folk must choose,' said Manthor. 'And Hardang still lives.'

'Not for long, I hope,' said Húrin.

Now the fires grew hot and soon the Hall of the Haladin was aflame in many places. The men within threw out upon the faggots earth and water, such as they had, and great smoke went up. Then some sought to escape under its cover, but few got through the ring of men; most were taken, or slain if they fought.

There was a small door at the rear of the hall with a jutting porch that came nearer to the garth-wall than the great doors in front; and the wall at the back was lower, because the hall was built on a slope of the hillside. At last when the roof-beams were on fire, Hardang and Avranc crept out of the rear-door, and they reached the top of the wall and stole down into the dyke, and they were not marked until they tried to climb out. But then with shouts men ran upon them, though they did not know who they were. Avranc flung himself at the feet of one that would seize him, so that he was thrown to the ground, and Avranc sprang up and away and escaped in the mirk. But another cast a spear at Hardang's back as he ran, and he fell with a great wound.

When it was seen who he was, men lifted him up and laid him before Manthor. 'Set him not before me,' said Manthor, 'but before the one he misused. I have no grudge against him.'

'Have you not?' said Hardang. 'Then you must be sure of my death. I think that you have always begrudged that the Folk chose me to the chair and not you.'

'Think what you will!' said Manthor and he turned away. Then Hardang was aware of Húrin who was behind. And Húrin stood looking down on Hardang, a dark form in the gloom, but the light of the fire was on his face, and there Hardang saw no pity.

'You are a mightier man than I, Húrin of Hithlum,' he said. 'I had such fear of your shadow that all wisdom and largesse forsook me. But now I do not think that any wisdom or mercy would have saved me from you, for you have none. You came to destroy me, and you at least have not denied it. But your last lie against me I cast back upon you ere I die. Never' — but with that blood gushed from his mouth, and he fell back, and said no more.

Then Manthor said: 'Alas! He should not have died thus. Such evil as he wrought did not merit this end.'

'Why not?' said Húrin. 'He spoke hate from a foul mouth to the last. What lie have I spoken against him?'

Manthor sighed. 'No lie wittingly maybe,' he said. 'But the last charge that you brought was false, I deem; and he had no chance to deny it. I would that you had spoken to me of it before the Moot!'

Húrin clenched his hands. 'It is not false!' he cried. 'She lies where I said. Morwen! She is dead!'

'Alas! lord, where she died I do not doubt. But of this I judge that Hardang knew no more than I till you spoke. Tell me, lord: did she ever walk further in this land?'

'I know not. I found her as I said. She is dead.'

'But, lord, if she came no further, but finding the Stone there sat in grief and despair by the grave of her son, as I can believe, then ...'

'What then?' said Húrin.

'Then, Húrin Hadorion, out of the darkness of your woe know this! My lord, so great a grief, and so great a horror of the things that there came to pass is upon us that no man and no woman since the setting up of the Stone has ever again gone nigh to that place. Nay! the Lord Oromë himself might sit by that stone with all his hunt about him, and we should not know. Not unless he blew his great horn, and even that summons we should refuse!'

'But if Mandos the Just spake, would you not hear him?' said Húrin. 'Now some shall go thither, if you have any ruth! Or would you let her lie there till her bones are white? Will that cleanse your land?'

'Nay, nay!' said Manthor. 'I will find some men of great heart and some women of mercy, and you shall lead us thither, and we will do as you bid. But it is a long road to wend, and this day is now old in evil. A new day is needed.'

The next day, when the news that Hardang was dead went abroad, a great throng of people sought for Manthor, crying that he must be Chieftain. But he said: 'Nay, this must be laid before the full Moot. That cannot be yet; for the Ring is unhallowed, and there are other things more pressing to do. First I have an errand. I must go to the Field of the Worm and the Stone of the Hapless, where Morwen their mother lies untended. Will any come with me?'

Then ruth smote the hearts of those that heard him; and though some drew back in fear, many were willing to go, but among these there were more women than men.

Therefore at length they set off in silence on the path that led down along the falling torrent of Celebros. Wellnigh eight leagues was that road, and darkness fell ere they came to Nen Girith,[52] and there they passed the night as they could. And the next morning they went on down the steep way to the Field of Burning, and they found the body of Morwen at the foot of the Standing Stone. Then they looked upon her in pity and wonder; for it seemed to them that they beheld a great queen whose dignity neither age nor beggary nor all the woe of the world had taken from her.

Then they desired to do her honour in death; and some said: 'This is a dark place. Let us lift her up, and bring the Lady Morwen to the Garth of the Graves and lay her among the House of Haleth with whom she had kinship.'

But Húrin said: 'Nay, Niënor is not here, but it is fitter that she should lie here near her son than with any strangers. So she would have chosen.' Therefore they made a grave for Morwen above Cabed Naeramarth on the west side of the Stone; and when the earth was laid upon her they carved on the Stone: *Here lies also Morwen Eðelwen*, while some sang in the old tongue the laments that long ago had been made for those of their people who had fallen on the March far beyond the Mountains.

And while they sang there came a grey rain and all that desolate place was heavy with grief, and the roaring of the river was like the mourning of many voices. And when all was ended they turned away, and Húrin went bowed on his staff. But it is said that after that day fear left that place, though sorrow remained, and it was ever leafless and bare. But until the end of Beleriand women of Brethil would come with flowers in spring and berries in autumn and sing there a while of the Grey Lady who sought in vain for her son. And a seer and harp-player of Brethil, Glirhuin, made a song saying the Stone of the Hapless should not be defiled by Morgoth nor ever thrown down, not though the Sea should drown all the land. As after indeed befell, and still the Tol Morwen stands alone in the water beyond the new coasts that were made in the days of the wrath of the Valar. But Húrin does not lie there, for his doom drove him on, and the Shadow still followed him.

Now when the company had come back to Nen Girith they halted; and Húrin looked back, out across Taeglin towards the westering sun that came through the clouds; and he was loth to return into the Forest. But Manthor looked eastward and was troubled, for there was a red glow in the sky there also.[53]

'Lord,' he said, 'tarry here if you will, and any others who are weary. But I am the last of the Haladin and I fear that the fire which we kindled is not yet quenched. I must go back swiftly, lest the madness of men bring all Brethil to ruin.'

But even as he said this an arrow came from the trees, and he stumbled and sank to the ground. Then men ran to seek for the bowman; and they saw a man running like a deer up the path towards the Obel, and they could not overtake him; but they saw that it was Avranc.

Now Manthor sat gasping with his back to a tree. 'It is a poor archer that will miss his mark at the third aim,' he said.

Húrin leaned on his staff and looked down at Manthor. 'But thou hast missed thy mark, kinsman,' he said. 'Thou hast been a valiant friend, and yet I think thou wert so hot in the cause for thyself also. Manthor would have sat more worthily in the chair of the Chieftains.'

'Thou hast a hard eye, Húrin, to pierce all hearts but thine own,' said Manthor. 'Yea, thy darkness touched me also. Now alas! the Haladin are ended; for this wound is to the death. Was not this your true errand, Man of the North: to bring ruin upon us to weigh against thine own? The House of Hador has conquered us, and four now have fallen under its shadow: Brandir, and Hunthor, and Hardang, and Manthor. Is that not enough? Wilt thou not go and leave this land ere it dies?'

'I will,' said Húrin. 'But if the well of my tears were not utterly dried up, I would weep for thee, Manthor; for thou hast saved me from dishonour, and thou hadst love for my son.'

'Then, lord, use in peace the little more life that I have won for thee,' said Manthor. 'Do not bring your shadow upon others!'

'Why, must I not still walk in the world?' said Húrin. 'I will go on till the shadow overtakes me. Farewell!'

Thus Húrin parted from Manthor. When men came to tend his wound they found that it was grave, for the arrow had gone deep into his side; and they wished to bear Manthor back as swiftly as they could to the Obel to have the care of skilled leeches. 'Too late,' said Manthor, and he plucked out the arrow, and gave a great cry, and was still. Thus ended the House of Haleth, and lesser men ruled in Brethil in the time that was left.

But Húrin stood silent, and when the company departed, bearing away the body of Manthor, he did not turn. He looked ever west till the sun fell into dark cloud and the light failed; and then he went down alone towards the Hauð-en-Elleth.

Both my father's typescript and the amanuensis typescript end here, and this is clearly the designed conclusion of 'Húrin in Brethil'; but in draft manuscript material there are some suggestions (very slight) as to the course of the narrative immediately beyond this point.[54] There are also a few other brief writings and notes of interest.[55]

My father never returned to follow the further wanderings of Húrin.[56] We come here to the furthest point in the narrative of the Elder Days that he reached in his work on *The Silmarillion* (in the widest sense) after the Second War and the completion of *The Lord of the Rings*. There are bits of information about the succeeding parts – not much – but no further new or revised narrative; and the promise held out in his words (p. 258) 'Link to the Necklace of the Dwarves, *Sigil Elu-naeth*, Necklace of the Woe of Thingol' was never fulfilled. It is as if we come to the brink of a great cliff, and look down from highlands raised in some later age onto an ancient plain far below. For the story of the Nauglamîr and the destruction of Doriath, the fall of Gondolin, the attack on the Havens, we must return through more than a quarter of a century to the *Quenta Noldorinwa* (Q), or beyond. The huge abruptness of the divide is still more emphasised by the nature of this last story of the Elder Days, the Shadow that fell upon Brethil.[57] In its portrayal of the life of Brethil into which Húrin came for its ruin, the intricacies of law and lineage, the history of ambition and conflicting sentiment within the ruling clan, it stands apart. In the published *Silmarillion* I excluded it, apart from using Húrin's vain attempt to reach Gondolin and his finding of Morwen dying beside the Standing Stone. Morwen's grave is made by Húrin alone; and having made it, 'he passed southwards down the ancient road that led to Nargothrond'.

To have included it, as it seemed to me, would have entailed a huge reduction, indeed an entire re-telling of a kind that I did not wish to undertake; and since the story is intricate I was afraid that this would produce a dense tangle of narrative statement with all the subtlety gone, and above all that it would diminish the fearful figure of the old man, the great hero, Thalion the Steadfast, furthering still the purposes of Morgoth, as he was doomed to do. But it seems to me now, many years later, to have been an excessive tampering with my father's actual thought and intention: thus raising the question, whether the attempt to make a 'unified' *Silmarillion* should have been embarked on.

NOTES

1 With the beginning of this passage cf. Q (IV.131): 'Some have said that Morwen, wandering woefully from Thingol's halls, when she found Nienor not there on her return, came on a time to that stone and read it, and there died.' – For the abandoned idea that it was Túrin who met Morwen in her wandering see pp. 161–2.

2 Húrin was born in 441 (GA §141). – At this point the first side of the 'lost manuscript' ends. The text on the reverse was struck through and replaced by a new text on a new sheet, all but identical in content but finely written – suggestive of confidence in this further extension of the *Grey Annals*.

3 Asgon reappears here, without introduction, from NE (*Unfinished Tales* p. 109), one of the men who fled with Túrin from Brodda's hall; in the condensed account in GA (§297) he was not named.

4 The spellings *Asgorn* here, but *Asgon* in the preceding paragraph (see note 3), are clear. See note 21.

5 The term *Eastron* has not been used before.

6 'Yet this can scarce be so': i.e., ignorance of Glaurung's death can scarcely be the reason for Húrin's going to Nargothrond.
7 The space marked by a caret evidently awaited the name of the new Lord of Brethil.
8 'He must come of a different race': is this the first reference to the Petty-dwarves?
9 *(Annal 490–5)* The name *Iarwaeth* has appeared in GA §268 (see also p. 142, commentary on §277, at end), but *Thuringud* 'the Hidden Foe' is found nowhere else: cf. Finduilas' name for Túrin, *Thurin* 'the Secret', *Unfinished Tales* pp. 157, 159).
10 *(Annal 494)* The statements that Morgoth stirred up the Eastrons (see note 5) to greater hatred of the Elves and Edain, and that Lorgan sought to take Niënor by force, are entirely new. In GA (§274) it is clear that Morwen and Niënor left Dor-lómin because the lands had become more safe.
11 *(Annal 495) Cirith Ninniach*, the final name of the Rainbow Cleft, is found in the later *Tale of Tuor* (*Unfinished Tales* p. 23), where also the meeting of Tuor with Gelmir and Arminas is recounted (pp. 21–2); the name was added to the map (p. 182, square C 4). On the story of their coming to Nargothrond and its relation to the *Grey Annals* see pp. 141–2, commentary on §277. It may be mentioned here that in another 'plot-synopsis' concerning Túrin my father referred to the two Elves by the names Faramir and Arminas, adding in a note: 'Faramir and Arminas were later Eärendil's companions on voyage'.

The 'Narrow Land' is the Pass of Sirion. The form *Erydwethian* occurs in the typescript text of 'Gelmir and Arminas' (p. 142).

'[Handir's] son Brandir the lame is chosen Chieftain, though many would have preferred his cousins Hunthor or Hardang': there has been no previous suggestion of a disagreement over the succession to Brandir; judging by the outspokenness of the people of Brethil as recorded in NE, they would surely have used it against Brandir if they had known of it. – The name *Hunthor* replaced *Torbarth* as that of the 'kinsman of Brandir', who died at Cabed-en-Aras, in NE (this change was not made in GA: see p. 156). He appears in the genealogical table of the Haladin (p. 237), but his descent had by this time been changed: for this, and for Hardang, another cousin, see pp. 268–70.

The defeat of Tum-halad has not previously been attributed to 'the dread of Glaurung', nor has it been said that Túrin gave his word to Gwindor that he would endeavour to save Finduilas.

On the form *Haudh-en-Elleth* see p. 148, §301.

The story that Tuor and Voronwë saw Túrin journeying northward at Eithil Ivrin has appeared in an inserted annal entry in GA (§299), but no more was said there than that 'they saw

Túrin pass, but spoke not with him'. For the fullest account see the later *Tale of Tuor, Unfinished Tales* pp. 37–8.

12 *(Annal 496)* The death of Sador in the fighting in Brodda's hall is told in NE *(Unfinished Tales* p. 108), where also Asgon of Dor-lómin first appears (p. 109).

13 *(Annal 497)* Lindis of Ossiriand: no mention has been made before of the wife of Dior Thingol's heir. See further *The Tale of Years*, pp. 349–51.

14 *(Annal 498)* In GA (§319) Túrin and Níniel were married 'at the mid-summer' of 498, and she conceived in the spring of 499.

15 *(Annal 499)* Of course Glaurung did not reveal to Túrin 'who he was': he did not need to. But this is without significance: it was a short-hand when writing very fast (in the same annal my father wrote 'Nargothrond' for 'Brethil' and 'Tuor' for 'Túrin'), and means that it was through the words of Glaurung that Túrin and Nienor came to know that they were brother and sister.

The name *Talbor* of the memorial stone raised at Cabed-en-Aras has not been given before.

For previous mentions of Mîm and the treasure of Nargothrond, and his death at the hand of Húrin, see the *Tale of Turambar*, II.113–14; the *Sketch of the Mythology*, IV.32; the *Annals of Beleriand* (AB 1 and AB 2), IV.306 and V.141; and Q, IV.132 and commentary IV.187–8.

16 *(Annal 500)* The names *Elrún* and *Eldún* of the sons of Dior appear in emendations made to Q (IV.135) and AB 2 (V.142 and note 42), replacing *Elboron* and *Elbereth*. It has not been said that they were twin brothers (in the *Genealogies* associated with AB 1, of which some extracts were given in V.403, their birthdates were three years apart, 192 and 195, – later 492, 495: these latter are found in the genealogical table of the House of Bëor, p. 231).

In AB 2 (following AB 1) Húrin was released by Morgoth in the year 499 (IV.306, V.141), and 'he departed and sought for Morwen'; in the continuation of GA (p. 252) the year was 500, as here.

17 *(Annal 501)* In AB 2 (following AB 1) Húrin and his companions (described simply as 'men'; in Q, IV.132, as 'a few outlaws of the woods') came to Nargothrond in 500 (see note 16), whereas in this text, after his visit to Brethil, he sets out for Nargothrond in 501 and comes there in 502. The earlier sources do not say that he found Morwen (cf. the note written against the first continuation of GA, p. 252: 'Some fate of Morwen must be devised. Did Morwen and Húrin meet again?'), nor do they know of his attempting to return to Gondolin (see the end of the continuation of GA, pp. 254–5, where this is first referred to, though without mention of the discovery by Morgoth's spies of the region where Gondolin lay).

The story of Húrin in Brethil was now in existence and probably in its final form (see p. 269). – A first mention of Obel Halad, replacing Ephel Brandir, is found in a note pencilled on the typescript of NE (p. 148, §302).

18 *(Annal 502)* In AB 2 Tuor wedded Idril in 499 (V.141); the date in *The Tale of Years* is (with some hesitation) 502 (pp. 346 ff.). On the bringing of the treasure of Nargothrond to Doriath see IV.188.

19 Only the following points in the WH version need be noted. After the words (p. 252) 'it suited the purpose of Morgoth that this should be so' my father added to the typescript later: 'and the needs of his body had been well served to this end'; and 'unless I find chance to avenge the wrongs of my children' (where GA has 'the wrongs of my son', p. 253) was changed to 'unless I find chance to hear more news of my kin, or to avenge their wrongs, if I may.' Where the GA continuation has *Asgon* and then *Asgorn* (note 4), WH has *Asgorn*, corrected to *Asgon*, and further on in the narrative *Asgon* as typed (see note 21). *Eastrons* of GA is here *Easterlings*. On the amanuensis typescript Húrin's words *Tôl acharn* were corrected to *Tûl acharn*.

20 The passage recounting Húrin's ignorance of what had happened in Gondolin to his crossing the Brithiach into Dimbar was a good deal changed at the time of typing, though for the most part this was a matter of rearrangement. Here the text as first typed read:

He knew not the things that had come to pass there, since Tuor brought thither the message of Ulmo, as is yet to be told; and now Turgon, refusing the counsel of the Lord of Waters, allowed none to enter or to go forth for any cause whatsoever, hardening his heart against pity and wisdom.

Tuor had reached Gondolin in 495 (GA §299).

21 *Asgon* was an emendation of the name as typed, *Asgorn*. This was a regular change, until the form *Asgon* appears in the text as typed: I print *Asgon* throughout, except in passages that were rejected before the name was changed.

22 Here the text as first typed read:

Húrin came down from the sources of the Lithir, which fell tumbling into Sirion and was held to be the south bounds of the Narrow Land. There Sirion was already too wide and deep to cross, and too perilous for any but the young and hardiest to swim; so Húrin and his men journeyed on, seeking the fords of the Brithiach.

The name *Lithir* was written against a river already shown on the original form of the second map: p. 182, squares C 6 to D 7.

23 At this point there followed in the draft manuscript and in the typescript as first typed: 'and though this seemed to him to bode evil rather than good, after a time he grew less heedful.'

24 The name *Ragnir* is found also as that of a blind servant of Morwen's in Dor-lómin (*Unfinished Tales* p. 71). In a rejected phrase in the draft manuscript this companion of Asgon's is called 'Ragnir the tracker'.

25 Asgon supposed that the Lord of Brethil was still Brandir the Lame. Cf. what is said of Brandir's successor Hardang a little further on: 'he had no love now at all for the House of Hador, in whose blood he had no part.'

26 On *Obel Halad* see note 17.

27 *Echoriad*: the Encircling Mountains about Gondolin. The form *Echoriath* in the published *Silmarillion* derives from the later *Tale of Tuor*; but *Echoriad* here is much later.

28 The old story in the tale of *The Fall of Gondolin* (II.189) that those of the fugitives from the sack of Gondolin who fled to the Way of Escape were destroyed by a dragon lying in wait at its outer issue, a story that survived into Q (IV.144), had been abandoned, and was excluded from *The Silmarillion* on the basis of the present passage: see II.213, second footnote, and IV.194.

29 Cf. GA §161 (p. 57), of the escape of Húrin and Huor into Dimbar forty-three years before this time: they 'wandered in the hills beneath the sheer walls of the Crisaegrim. There Thorondor espied them, and sent two Eagles that took them and bore them up...'

30 At this point in the draft manuscript my father wrote:

Later when captured and Maeglin wished to buy his release with treachery, Morgoth must answer laughing, saying: Stale news will buy nothing. I know this already, I am not easily blinded! So Maeglin was obliged to offer more – to undermine resistance in Gondolin.

Almost exactly the same note is found on the slip giving information about the new meaning of the name *Haladin* (p. 270); but here, after the words 'undermine resistance in Gondolin', my father continued: 'and to compass the death of Tuor and Eärendel if he could. If he did he would be allowed to retain Idril (said Morgoth).'

Thus the story in Q was changed (IV.143):

[Meglin] purchased his life and freedom by revealing unto Morgoth the place of Gondolin and the ways whereby it might be found and assailed. Great indeed was the joy of Morgoth...

Both the present passage in WH (telling that Morgoth learned from Húrin's wandering 'in what region Turgon dwelt') and that from Q were used in the published *Silmarillion* (pp. 228, 242), 'the *very* place of Gondolin' for 'the place of Gondolin' being an editorial addition.

31 There was a series of alterations to the names of the men of Manthor's company near the Crossings of Taeglin (and some

speeches were reassigned among the speakers). In the draft manuscript the names were *Sagroth*; *Forhend* son of Dorlas; and his friend *Farang*. In the typescript as typed they were *Sagroth*; *Forhend*; and his friend *Farang* son of Dorlas. The son of Dorlas is the one who plays an important part in the story. By emendation to the typescript the statement that Farang was the friend of Forhend was removed, and – further on in the narrative – the name *Farang* became *Faranc*; then, near the end of WH, it became *Avranc*, and this name was substituted throughout the text from his first appearance. I print throughout the final formulation only.

32 *Sagroth* was here emended to *Galhir*, but later *Sagroth* was reinstated. Galhir was perhaps intended to be another member of Manthor's company, rather than a replacement of the name *Sagroth*.

33 The footnote at this point was typed at the same time as the text. The statement concerning Manthor's domain in the east of Brethil preceded that in the text C (p. 267): 'The region nigh Brithiach and along Sirion for some way was the land of Manthor'. Haldar was the son of Haldad, founder of the line, and twin brother of the Lady Haleth (p. 221, §25). With the last sentence cf. the plot-synopsis, p. 256: 'Brandir the lame is chosen Chieftain, though many would have preferred his cousins Hunthor or Hardang.' The whole footnote was struck through (before the emendation of *Harathor* to *Hardang*).

34 The term *Haladin* is used here, in a sentence that was rejected rather than corrected, in the original sense of the whole 'People of Haleth'.

35 With the use of the word *town* cf. p. 148, §302.

36 The word *booth* is used in the old sense of 'a temporary dwelling covered with boughs of trees or other slight materials' (O.E.D.). My father may well have had in mind the Norse word *búð*, used in the Sagas especially of the temporary dwellings at the Icelandic parliament, and regularly rendered 'booth' in translations.

37 It is said also in the *Narn* plot-synopsis, of which a part is given on pp. 256–8, but at an earlier point (the year 472), that Haldir and Hundar were slain in the Nírnaeth, and that 'three only of their men were left alive, but Mablung of Doriath healed their wounds and brought them back.' See further pp. 236–7.

38 The draft manuscript has here:
'He must be wakeful tomorrow. It may be that better food is needed. Take care, or maybe the guards will have to stand before the Folk also.'
'What do you mean by that?' said the leader.
'Unriddle it as you will,' said Manthor.

39 'and women' derives from the draft manuscript. Cf. the passage

struck out on p. 279, concerning the summoning of wives to counsel according to the customs of Brethil.

40 Here and often subsequently *Halad* is an emendation of *Warden*; see the statement cited on p. 270, where *Halad*, plural *Haladin*, is translated 'warden(s)'. I give *Halad* in all these cases and do not record the changes.

41 There seems not to have been any specific reference previously to the passing out of common use of the old speech of the People of Haleth (where the draft manuscript has 'the old tongue of the Haladin', and also 'Moot of the Haladin'), and its replacement by 'the speech of Beleriand'.

42 The draft manuscript has here a passage depending on the story, still in being, of the captivity of Asgorn (Asgon) and his men (cf. the rejected sentence in the typescript, p. 278: Húrin was shut in a cave 'nigh to the one in which Asgorn and his men were still imprisoned'):

'Let the first prisoners be brought before us!' Then Asgorn and his companions were led in, with their hands bound behind them.

At that there was much murmuring; and [an old man >] Manthor stood up. 'By your leave, Master and Folk,' he said. 'I would ask: why are these men in bonds?'

There is then a note: 'Harathor should conceal the fact that Asgorn &c. are still in durance, and Manthor should reveal why.' Here the text stops, and begins on a new page with a draft for the changed story as found in the typescript text.

43 At this point the name *Hardang*, for *Harathor*, appears in the text as typed.

44 The draft manuscript has 'Be that as it may —', i.e. Hardang's sentence was interrupted by Manthor.

45 An addition to the draft manuscript says: 'He [Dorlas] had also been Harathor's friend, and a scorner of Brandir while Harathor desired to oust him.' That Dorlas had been a friend of Hardang (Harathor) has been mentioned earlier, at the first appearance of Dorlas' son Avranc (p. 275): 'well-liked by Hardang, as his father had been.'

46 In the story of Dorlas' death in the last part of the *Narn* (NE) as told in the manuscript, Brandir retained his sword. It is said subsequently in that text that 'Brandir, seeing his death in Túrin's face, drew his small sword and stood in defence'; and Túrin 'lifted up Gurthang and struck down Brandir's sword, and smote him to death.' By changes made to the much later amanuensis typescript of NE the story was altered to that given in *Unfinished Tales*: Brandir cast down his sword after the slaying of Dorlas (p. 139), facing Túrin 'he stood still and did not quail, though he had no weapon but his crutch', and the words 'struck down

Brandir's sword' were removed (p. 143). It seems to me unlikely that my father would have made these changes, whereby Túrin's murder of Brandir becomes even worse, in order to make Dorlas' reputation seem more murky in the rumours current in Brethil: I believe that he made them precisely because he wished so to represent Túrin in his encounter with Brandir – in which case, of course, the changes to the NE typescript had already been made when the present passage was written. Subsequently it was bracketed, from 'And dark tales were whispered concerning Dorlas', presumably implying doubt about its inclusion; and the matter is not referred to again.

47 'hand and foot': an addition had been made earlier (p. 282) concerning the further fettering of Húrin on his wrists.

48 *Galdor Orchal*: 'Galdor the Tall'. The 'title' has not previously appeared in Elvish form.

49 With the rejected words 'and good wives' cf. note 39.

50 'I would I had not hindered thy shooting': see p. 278.

51 The story of the events in the Moot-ring was told in the draft manuscript (written in ink over a pencilled text) in fairly close accord with the final form to the point where Húrin cries out on Harathor (as is still the name): 'Only hands, hands, are needed to wring such a throat full of lies'. Then follows:

With that, in a fury, Húrin sprang off the Stone and made for Harathor. But Harathor fled before him, calling on his household men to gather round him; and at the gate he turned, crying: 'It is a lie that he speaks, Men of Brethil. He raves as ever. I knew naught of this till now!' In this he spoke the truth; but too late. In their wrath few of the assembly believed him.

(In the original pencilled text Harathor said more in his defence, using the argument given in the final form to Manthor (pp. 294–5): 'None of the Folk go ever to that stone, for the place is accursed. Not till now have I or any man or woman of the Folk heard tale of her coming to the stone.') At this point in the superimposed text in ink my father stopped, and wrote: 'Do not allow Harathor to defend himself. He flies in fear – and so seems to most of the Folk to acknowledge his guilt.'

From here onwards the draft manuscript becomes chaotic. The pencilled text, in part illegible, continues, interspersed here and there with later passages written in ink, to the end of the story, but the 'layers' are so confused that a coherent development can scarcely be deduced. It seems, however, that at this stage the story of the siege and burning of the Hall of the Chieftains had not entered. The rout of Harathor and his supporters from the Moot-ring seems to have been followed at once by Manthor's reproaches to Húrin – a defence of the conduct of the Men of Brethil towards Túrin, and a denial that Harathor could have known anything of the coming of Morwen, which in turn leads at once to the expedition to Cabed Naeramarth and the burial of Morwen. In his words to Húrin Manthor declares himself to be now 'the last of the Haladin', but there seems to be no indication of the fate of Harathor. See further note 53.

A new draft text, very roughly written but coherent, takes up at the opening of Húrin's speech to the assembly (p. 290): this was the text from which the final form was closely derived.

52 In NE (*Unfinished Tales* p. 136) it was 'five leagues at the least' from Ephel Brandir to Nen Girith; in an earlier draft of that passage it was seven leagues (commentary on GA §§329–32, p. 158).

53 The end of the original draft manuscript (see note 51) is partly illegible, but after the burial of Morwen 'they return and see red fire. The Obel is burning as the rebels assault the ... But as they make their way an arrow comes out of the wood and Manthor falls.' This suggests that the burning of the Hall of the Chieftains originally followed the burial of Morwen, and that when that burning became a central event in the story the red glow in the sky seen from Nen Girith was retained as the sign of a further eruption of rioting on the following day. This is supported by the conclusion of the second draft manuscript, given in note 54 (at end); but the matter is very uncertain.

54 The end of the original draft manuscript (see notes 51, 53) after the death of Manthor, pencilled over by my father to make it clearer but with a gap where there is a word, or words, that he could not interpret, reads thus:

> A few men fearing the end of Brethil and desiring to flee further from Morgoth – having no homes or lands of their own – are willing to go with Húrin. They depart – and fall in [*sic*] But now Húrin seems to pick up strength and youth – vengeance seems to have heartened him, and he [   ] and walks now strongly. They pass into the woods and gather the last fugitives of the wood-men (the kin of the folk of Brethil).
>
> Asgorn they choose for captain, but he treats Húrin as lord, and does as he will[s]. Whither shall we go? They must [?know] a place of refuge. They go towards Nargothrond.

Another, isolated page gives this version of the end:

> For a while he stood there grim and silent. But Manthor looked back and saw red light far away. 'I must return,' he said. The party begins to go back wearily towards Obel Halad.
>
> An arrow slays Manthor. – The voice of Faranc [*see note 31*] cries: 'Third time thriven. At least you shall not sit in the Chair you coveted.' They give chase but he escapes in the dark.

The Moot Ring has been 'unhallowed'. The confederation breaks up. Men go each to their own homesteads. Húrin must depart. He gathers a few men who despair now of defending Brethil from the growing strength of Morgoth [and] wish to fly south. At the Taiglin crossing they fall in with Asgon, who has heard rumour of the wild deeds in Brethil, and of Húrin's coming, and are now venturing back into the land to seek him. Asgon greets him – and is glad that Harathor has been punished. Angered that no one had told Húrin of their coming.

They go on and gather fugitive 'wood-men'. They elect Asgon captain but he ever defers to Húrin. Whither to go? Húrin elects to go to Nargothrond. Why?

The references to 'wood-men' ('kin of the folk of Brethil') in these passages are no doubt to the men who dwelt in the woodland south of the Taeglin, described in the *Narn* (*Unfinished Tales* p. 85, and thereafter called 'the Woodmen'):

There before the Nirnaeth many Men had dwelt in scattered homesteads; they were of Haleth's folk for the most part, but owned no lord, and they lived both by hunting and by husbandry, keeping swine in the mast-lands, and tilling clearings in the forest which were fenced from the wild. But most were now destroyed, or had fled into Brethil, and all that region lay under the fear of Orcs, and of outlaws.

These hasty sketches of Húrin's immediate movements after leaving Brethil agree with what is said in the plot-synopsis (p. 258): 'Húrin finds Asgon again and gathers other men and goes towards Nargothrond'. The question 'Why?' of his decision to go there reappears from the final addition to the end of the *Grey Annals* (p. 255), which probably did not long precede the writing of *The Wanderings of Húrin*.

The second draft manuscript (see note 51, at end) continues on from the point where the typescript text ends, though with a line drawn across the page beneath the words 'he went down alone towards the Hauð-en-Elleth'. I give this partly illegible conclusion from the death of Manthor.

... and plucked out the arrow, and gave a great cry, and lay still.

Then they wept, and they took him up, and prepared to bear him back, and they took no more heed of Húrin. But he stood silent, and turned soon away; the sun was gone down into cloud and the light failed, and he went down alone towards the Hauð-en-Elleth.

[Thus befell the ruin of Brethil. For >] Now it is said that / those who ... with Hardang were not all caught, and others came in hearing the news, and there was fighting in the Obel, and a great burning, until all was well nigh destroyed [*see note 53*]. But when the madness [*written above:* wrath] of men had cooled they made peace, and some said: 'What hath bewitched us? Surely Húrin begot all this evil, and Hardang and Avranc were more wise. They would have kept him out if they could.' So they chose Avranc to be their chief, since none of the House of Haleth were left, but [?? he wielded no] such authority and reverence as the Chieftains before, and the Folk of Brethil fell back again to be more like their kinsmen in the [?open] woods – each minding his own houselands and little ... and their ... was loosened.

But some misliked this and would not serve under Avranc and made ready to depart, and they joined Húrin.

55 The following brief writing on the subject of Manthor is another 'discussion' like the text 'C' (pp. 266–7) and no doubt belongs to much the same time. Here as there the name is *Harathor*, but I suggested (p. 269) that he must have been on the point of receiving a new name, and on the same page as the present passage appear the workings leading to the name *Hardang*.

The page begins with a draft for the last words of Húrin and Manthor at Nen Girith, closely similar to the ending both in the second draft manuscript (on which see note 51, at end) and in the final typescript (pp. 296–7). I believe that the present form was the first, and that my father set it down experimentally, as it were, and then proceeded to explain and justify it, as follows (the many contractions of words and names are expanded):

I think it would be good to make Manthor a less merely 'good' character. For so his extremely zealous and cunning espousal of Húrin's cause would better be explained. Certainly he has a great natural concern for 'courtesy' – sc. civilized behaviour *and* mercy, and he would have been angry at the treatment of Húrin whoever he was. But (a) he was *proud* of his kinship with the House of Hador; (b) he had desired the Wardenship – and many had wanted to elect him. He was of the senior line, but by a daughter (Hiril). But though so far descent had been by eldest son, it had been laid down by Haleth (and Haldar her brother) that daughters and their descendants were to be eligible for election. The descendants of Hundar: Hundad, Harathor had not been men of mark or gallantry.

So plainly Manthor was also using the coming of Húrin to further his ambition – or rather, the shadow of Húrin fell on him, and awoke the ambition (dormant). Note: Manthor never raises the matter of Húrin's *errand*, or (as was fairly plain) that Húrin came with ill-will, especially towards the rulers of Brethil and the 'anti-Túrin' party.

Mention should be made in the tale of Túrin (dwelling in Brethil and death) – à propos of Hunthor? – of Manthor and the friendship of his branch for Túrin and reverence for the House of Hador.

There was some ill-feeling between the branches: on the one side akin to the House of Hador (via Glóreðel and via Hareth and Hiril) and [on the other] the line of Hundar.

This enlarges and defines some of the things said in the last paragraph of the discussion in the text 'C' (p. 267), where the friendship for Túrin among the descendants of Hiril, and pride in their kinship with the House of Hador, were referred to, and the idea that Manthor 'desired the Wardenship' referred to as a possibility.

An isolated slip, headed *Names*, has the following notes:

The *Haladin* name of people directly descended from Haldar Haleth's brother (by male or female line), a family or *'nothlir'* from which the Chieftains or *Halbars* of Brethil were chosen by the Folk.

For *halad* sg. 'chieftain' ..... *halbar*.

The Chieftain after Brandir was *Hardang*.

His evil-counsellor friend to be *Daruin*.

Dorlas > Darlas

Dar = mastery, lordship

bor = stone. The Stone in the Ring was the *halabor*. The Standing Stone was the *Talbor*.

The word *halbar* 'chieftain', to be substituted for *halad*, appears in a note pencilled on the genealogical table of the Haladin, where also the name *Haldar* was apparently altered to *Halbar*: see p. 238. The name *Talbor* of the Standing Stone appears also in an addition to the *Narn* plot-synopsis (p. 257), but the stone in the Moot-ring is named *Angbor* 'Doom-rock' in additions to the typescript text of WH (see p. 283). These new names, and *Darlas* for *Dorlas*, *Daruin* for *Avranc*, must represent a further group of substitutions subsequent to the final text of WH, although it is odd in that case that *Hardang* should be included.

Following these notes on the same slip of paper are notes on the name *Taeglin*; these were struck out, but virtually the same notes in more finished form are found on another slip:

Taeglin(d) better *Taeglind*

*taika (√*taya* mark, line, limit > *tayak*) *mære*, boundary, limit, boundary line.

linde 'singer / singing', name (or element in names) of many rivers of quick course that make a rippling sound.

mære is an Old English word of the same meaning. – It seems that the form chosen for the published *Silmarillion* should have been *Taeglin* rather than *Teiglin* (see p. 228, §28).

56 Some interesting remarks of my father's concerning *The Wanderings of Húrin* are found on the back of one of the slips on which Professor Clyde Kilby wrote comments and criticisms of the work:

> The criticisms seem to me largely mistaken – no doubt because this is a fragment of a great saga, e.g. Thingol and Melian are mentioned as objects of Morgoth's malice, because Húrin's next exploit will be to bring ruin to Doriath. The outlaws are not a 'device', but already accounted for – and play a part in the story of Túrin when he came to Dor Lómin. Húrin does pick them up again and they are the nucleus of the force with which he goes to Nargothrond and slays Mîm and seizes the gold of the dragon.
>
> As for 'too little action,' 'too much speech', I have re-read this quite impersonally after many years when I had practically forgotten it – the speeches are bitter and pungent and in themselves exciting. I thought the whole business from the entry of Húrin not only moving but very exciting.

The reference to Thingol and Melian arose from Professor Kilby's taking exception to their only being mentioned in one place (p. 259). The response that his remarks (written, I believe, in 1966) elicited is particularly interesting in that they show that the story of Húrin's seizing the treasure of Nargothrond was still fully in being, although my father never even approached it again. Very striking is his phrase, 'Húrin's next exploit will be to bring ruin to Doriath'.

57 On the amanuensis typescript my father pencilled, beneath *The Wanderings of Húrin*: 'I   *The Shadow Falls on Brethil*'. At the beginning of his discussion of the story in text C (p. 266) he said of Asgorn and his men that 'their coming to Brethil is needed to "cast the shadow" by arousing fear and hatred in the heart of Harathor.' It may be therefore that the subheading *The Shadow Falls on Brethil* was intended to refer only to the first part of the story of Húrin in Brethil. On the other hand, he introduced no other sub-headings into the body of the text, and it seems equally possible that he meant this as the title of the whole story, 'II' to be the next stage of Húrin's 'wanderings', *Húrin in Nargothrond*.

II
ÆLFWINE AND DÍRHAVAL

In *Unfinished Tales* (p. 146) I referred to the existence of an 'introductory note' to the *Narn i Chîn Húrin*, found in different forms, and I gave a very condensed and selective account of the content. The two versions are in fact more distinct than this suggests, and here I print them both in full. One of them is a clear manuscript written with almost no hesitations or alterations (whether at the time or later): this, which I will call '**A**', clearly preceded the other, and I give it first. The numbered notes will be found on p. 315.

Túrin Turumarth[1]

Here begins that tale which Ælfwine made from the *Húrinien*: which is the longest of all the lays of Beleriand now held in memory in Eressëa. But it is said there that, though made in Elvish speech and using much Elvish lore (especially of Doriath), this lay was the work of a Mannish poet, Dírhavel, who lived at the Havens in the days of Eärendel and there gathered all the tidings and lore that he could of the House of Hador, whether among Men or Elves, remnants and fugitives of Dorlómin, of Nargothrond, or of Doriath. From Mablung he learned much; and by fortune also he found a man named Andvír, and he was very old, but was the son of that Andróg who was in the outlaw-band of Túrin, and alone survived the battle on the summit of Amon Rûdh.[2] Otherwise all that time between the flight of Túrin from Doriath and his coming to Nargothrond, and Túrin's deeds in those days, would have remained hidden, save the little that was remembered among the people of Nargothrond concerning such matters as Gwindor or Túrin ever revealed. In this way also the matter of Mîm and his later dealings with Húrin were made clear. This lay was all that Dírhavel ever made, but it was prized by the Elves and remembered by them. Dírhavel they say perished in the last raid of the sons of Fëanor upon the Havens. His lay was composed in that mode of verse which was called *Minlamad thent / estent*.[3] Though this verse was not wholly unlike the verse known to Ælfwine, he translated the lay into prose (including in it, or adding in the margins as seemed fit to him, matter from the Elvish commentaries that he had heard or seen); for he was not himself skilled in the making of verse, and the transference of this long tale from Elvish into English was difficult enough. Indeed even as it was made, with the help of the Elves as it would seem from his notes and additions, in places his account is obscure.

This version into 'modern' English, that is forms of English intelligible to living users of the English tongue (who have some knowledge of letters, and are not limited to the language of daily use from mouth to mouth) does not attempt to imitate the idiom of Ælfwine, nor that of the Elvish which often shows through especially in the dialogue. But since it is even to Elves now 'a tale of long ago', and depicts high and ancient persons and their speech (such as Thingol and Melian), there is in Ælfwine's version, and clearly was in Dírhavel's day, much archaic language, of words and usage, and the older and nobler Elves do not speak in the same style as Men, or in quite the same language as that of the main narrative; there are therefore here retained similar elements. It is for this reason that, for example, Thingol's speech is not that of our present day: for indeed the speech of Doriath, whether of the king or others, was even in the days of Túrin more antique than that used elsewhere. One thing (as Mîm observed) of which Túrin never rid himself, despite his grievance against Doriath, was the speech he had acquired during his fostering. Though a Man, he spoke like an Elf of the Hidden Kingdom,[4] which is as though a Man should now appear, whose speech and schooling until manhood had been that of some secluded country where the English had remained nearer that of the court of Elizabeth I than of Elizabeth II.

The second text ('**B**') is very much briefer, and was composed on the typewriter which my father used for several of the *Narn* texts, and other writings such as the chapter *Of the Coming of Men into the West*.

Many songs are yet sung and many tales are yet told by the Elves in the Lonely Isle of the Nirnaeth Arnoediad, the Battle of Unnumbered Tears, in which Fingon fell and the flower of the Eldar withered. But here I will tell as I may a Tale of Men that Dírhaval[5] of the Havens made in the days of Eärendel long ago.

Narn i Chîn Húrin he called it, the Tale* of the Children of Húrin, which is the longest of all the lays that are now remembered in Eressëa, though it was made by a man.

For such was Dírhaval. He came of the House of Hador, it is said, and the glory and sorrow of that House was nearest to his heart. Dwelling at the Havens of Sirion, he gathered there all the tidings and lore that he could; for in the last days of Beleriand there came thither remnants out of all the countries, both Men and Elves: from Hithlum and Dor-lómin, from Nargothrond and Doriath, from Gondolin and the realms of the Sons of Fëanor in the east.

This lay was all that Dírhaval ever made, but it was prized by the Eldar, for Dírhaval used the Grey-elven tongue, in which he had great skill. He used that mode of Elvish verse which is called [*long space left in typescript*] which was of old proper to the *narn*; but though this verse mode is not unlike the verse of the English, I have rendered it in prose, judging my skill too small to be at once *scop* and *walhstod*.[6] Even so my task has been hard enough, and without the help of the Elves could not have been completed. I have not added to Dírhaval's tale, nor omitted from it anything that he told; neither have I changed the order of his history. But on matters that seemed of interest, or that were become dark with the passing of the years, I have made notes, whether within the tale or upon its margins, according to such lore as I found in Eressëa.

That A preceded B, at whatever interval (but I do not think that it was long), is seen, among other considerations, from the use of the old name 'the *Húrinien*' in the opening sentence of A (whereas in B it is called *Narn i Chîn Húrin*). This name had appeared years before in QS Chapter 17, *Of Túrin Turamarth or Túrin the Hapless*: 'that lay which is called *iChúrinien*, the Children of Húrin, and is the longest of all the lays that speak of those days' (V.317). (For *Húrinien* beside *iChúrinien*, and my reason for substituting *Hîn* for *Chîn* in *Unfinished Tales*, see V.322.)

It is possible to state with certainty at what period these pieces were written. I said in *Unfinished Tales* (p. 150): 'From the point in the story where Túrin and his men established themselves in the ancient dwelling of the Petty-dwarves on Amon Rûdh there is no completed narrative on the same detailed plan [as in the preceding parts], until the *Narn* takes up again with Túrin's journey northwards after the fall

---

* [*footnote to the text*] *narn* among the Elves signifies a tale that is told in verse to be spoken and not sung.

of Nargothrond': from the existing materials I formed a brief narrative in *The Silmarillion*, Chapter 21, and gave some further citations from the texts in *Unfinished Tales*, pp. 150–4. Now the story of Túrin and Beleg in Mîm's hidden dwelling on Amon Rûdh and the short-lived 'Land of Bow and Helm', Dor-Cúarthol, belongs (like all the rest of the huge extension of this part of the 'Túrins Saga') to the period after the publication of *The Lord of the Rings*; and the mention in text A of the man Andvír, 'the son of that Andróg who was in the outlaw-band of Túrin, and alone survived the battle on the summit of Amon Rûdh' (see note 2) shows that this story was fully in being (so far as it ever went) when A was written – indeed it seems likely enough that A belongs to the time when my father was working on it.

It is therefore very notable that at this relatively late date he was propounding such a view of the 'transmission' of the *Narn i Chîn Húrin* (in contrast to the statement cited in X.373, that 'the three Great Tales must be Númenórean, and derived from matter preserved in Gondor': the second of the 'Great Tales' being the *Narn i Chîn Húrin*). Striking also is the information (in both texts) that the verse-form of Dírhaval's lay bore some likeness to the verse known to Ælfwine (meaning of course the Anglo-Saxon alliterative verse), but that because Ælfwine was no *scop* (see note 6) he translated it into (Anglo-Saxon) prose. I do not know of any other statement bearing on this. It is tempting to suspect some sort of oblique reference here to my father's abandoned alliterative *Lay of the Children of Húrin* of the 1920s, but this may be delusory.

The second version B, in which the introductory note becomes a preface by Ælfwine himself, rather than an 'editorial' recounting of what Ælfwine did, was clipped to and clearly belonged with a twelve-page typescript composed *ab initio* by my father and bearing the title 'Here begins the tale of the Children of Húrin, *Narn i Chîn Húrin*, which Dírhaval wrought.' This text provides the opening of the *Narn* in *Unfinished Tales* (pp. 57–8), and continues into the story of Húrin and Huor in Gondolin (omitted in *Unfinished Tales*) which was based very closely indeed on the version in the *Grey Annals* and is described on pp. 169–70 (then follows the story of Túrin's sister Lalaeth and of his friendship with Sador Labadal, ending with the riding away of Húrin to the Battle of Unnumbered Tears, which is given in *Unfinished Tales* pp. 58–65). It is very difficult to interpret, in the story of the visit to Gondolin, the close similarity or (often) actual identity of wording in Dírhaval's lay with that of the version in the *Grey Annals*. The same question arises, despite a central difference in the narrative, in the case of the *Narn* version of the Battle of Unnumbered Tears and that in the *Annals* (see pp. 165 ff.). The *Narn* text is not linked, as is the Gondolin story, to the name of Dírhaval; but it is a curious fact that it begins (p. 165) 'Many songs are yet sung, and many tales are yet told by the

Elves of the Nirnaeth Arnoediad, the Battle of Unnumbered Tears, in which Fingon fell and the flower of the Eldar withered' – for this is identical to the opening of Ælfwine's preface (text B, p. 312), except that the latter has 'are yet told by the Elves *in the Lonely Isle*'.

NOTES

1. In the old *Tale of Turambar* the Gnomish form of *Turambar* was *Turumart*, and in Q *Turumarth*, where however it was changed to *Turamarth*, as it was also in QS (V.321). *Turumarth* here must represent a reversion to the original form.
2. Andvír son of Andróg appears nowhere else. It is expressly stated in a plot-outline of this part of the *Narn* that Andróg died in the battle on the summit of Amon Rûdh (see *Unfinished Tales* p. 154). The wording here is plain, and can hardly be taken to mean that it was Andvír (also a member of the outlaw-band) who alone survived.
3. The name of the verse is clearly *Minlamad thent / estent*: *Minlamed* in *Unfinished Tales* p. 146 is erroneous.
4. Cf. the 'linguistic excursus' in the *Grey Annals*, p. 26, where there is a reference to the speech of the Grey-elves becoming the common tongue of Beleriand and being affected by words and devices drawn from Noldorin – 'save in Doriath where the language remained purer and less changed by time'.
5. The name is perfectly clearly *Dírhavel* in A, but is typed *Dírhaval* in B, which being the later should have been adopted in *Unfinished Tales*.
6. Against *scop* my father noted: 'O.English = poet', and against *walhstod* 'O.English = interpreter' (on the carbon copy 'interpreter / translator').

III
MAEGLIN

The tale of Isfin and Eöl and their son Meglin (in the earliest form of his name) had long roots, and I have set out its earlier history in concise form on pp. 121–2, §§117–20. As the text of the *Grey Annals* was first written the form of the story in AB 2 was repeated: Isfin left Gondolin in the year before the Battle of Unnumbered Tears, and twenty-one years later Meglin was sent alone to Gondolin (GA original annals 471 and 492, pp. 47, 84). It was at that stage that a full tale of Meglin and how he came to Gondolin was first written.

This was a clear manuscript of 12 sides, fairly heavily emended both at the time of writing and later; it belongs in style very evidently with the *Annals of Aman*, the *Grey Annals*, the later *Tale of Tuor*, and the text which I have called the *End of the Narn* ('NE', see p. 145), and can be firmly dated to the same time (1951). It was on the basis of this work that revised annals concerning the story were introduced into GA (years 316, 320, and 400, pp. 47–8), as noticed earlier (p. 123); these were written on a page from an engagement calendar for November 1951 (p. 47).

An amanuensis typescript with carbon copy was made many years later, as appears from the fact that it was typed on my father's last typewriter. This typescript took up almost all of the emendations made to the manuscript. For the present purpose I shall call the manuscript of 1951 'A' and the late typescript 'B', distinguishing where necessary the top copy as 'B(i)' and the carbon as 'B(ii)'.

The B text was corrected and annotated in ball-point pen, and so also was the carbon copy – but not in the same ways; the original manuscript A also received some late emendations, which do not appear in B as typed. Moreover, a great deal of late writing in manuscript from the same time was inserted into B(i), with other similar material, overlapping in content, found elsewhere; for this my father used scrap paper supplied to him by Allen and Unwin, and two of these sheets are publication notes issued on 19 January 1970 – thus this material is very late indeed, and it is of outstanding difficulty.

Although the typescript B was also very late, as evidenced by the typewriter used, details of names show that the manuscript A had actually reached many years earlier the form from which it was typed; it seems very probable that my father had it typed in order to provide a copy on which substantial further change and annotation could be carried out c.1970. Only those few changes to A made in ball-point

MAEGLIN

pen and not taken up into B belong to the final period of work on the story.

To set out in detail the evolution of all this material would take a very great deal of space, and for much of its length involve the simple repetition of Chapter 16 *Of Maeglin* in the published *Silmarillion*. In this case, therefore, I shall use that chapter as the text for reference, and concentrate chiefly on the very late work, which has many notable features that of their nature could have no place in the published book. I shall refer in this account to the paragraphs in *The Silmarillion*, numbering them for convenience of internal reference, and giving the opening words of each for ease of identification. It should be noted here that the *Silmarillion* text takes up emendations from both the top copy (B(i)) and carbon (B(ii)) of the typescript, and that in cases (which are numerous) where they differ in the rewriting of original passages the published text is often an amalgam of both.

The Title

The manuscript A as written had no title; later my father pencilled on it *Of Meglin*, changing this to *Of Isfin and Glindûr*. The typescript B has the title (as typed) *Of Maeglin*, with the subtitle *Sister-son of Turgon, King of Gondolin*. At the head of the first page of B(i) my father wrote that the text is 'An enlarged version of the coming of Maeglin to Gondolin, to be inserted in FG in its place', and noted also that 'FG = Fall of Gondolin'. This can only be a reference to the abandoned *Tale of Tuor* (entitled *Of Tuor and the Fall of Gondolin*, but retitled *Of Tuor and his Coming to Gondolin* for inclusion in *Unfinished Tales*), which belongs to the same period as the manuscript A. Thus at this very late date my father was still holding to the hope of an entirely rewritten story of the Fall of Gondolin, of which so little had actually been done (and those parts some twenty years before). The only evidence that he at any time considered the story of Maeglin as a possible component in the *Quenta Silmarillion* is the word *Silmarillion* with a query pencilled against the opening paragraphs of the manuscript; and this was struck out.

§1   *Aredhel Ar-Feiniel, the White Lady of the Noldor...*

Here, and throughout B(i), *Isfin* was changed to *Areðel*; and in the margin against the first occurrence my father wrote:

This name is derived from the oldest (1916) version of FG. It is now quite unacceptable in form, unsuitable to the position and character of Turgon's sister, and also meaningless.

Presumably he meant that since no etymology of *Isfin* was feasible it was on that account unsuitable to be the name of Turgon's sister (cf. II.344, where the original explanation of the name as 'snow-locks' or 'exceeding-cunning' is given, and the present note is referred to). Also written in the margin is '? *Rodwen* = High Virgin Noble' and

'*Rodwen Los* in Golodh..' (last letters illegible; the word 'Virgin' is also not perfectly clear).

At the top of the first page of the carbon B(ii) the notes on the name are different. Here my father wrote: 'Name *Isfin* must be changed throughout to *Feiniel* (= White Lady)'. Against this he wrote an X, and 'Change *Isfin* to *Aredhel* (Noble-elf)'. Whereas in B(i), as I have noted, *Isfin* was changed to *Areðel* throughout, in B(ii) *Isfin* was merely circled, except in two cases where it was replaced by *Feiniel*, and in one case where it was replaced by *Ar-Feiniel*. My father was correcting the top copy and the carbon independently but at (more or less) the same time, very probably because he had the one in one place and the other in another. In the published *Silmarillion* I combined them as *Aredhel Ar-Feiniel*, although there is no warrant for this; they were evidently competing names, and the notes at the head of the carbon copy cited above suggest that *Areðel (Aredhel)* was his final choice.

The name *Nivrost* was changed on both copies of B to *Nevrost* (not *Nevrast*, the usual later form).

In the manuscript A it was said of Isfin that she longed to 'hunt' in the forests, emended to 'walk' and thus appearing in B. With this cf. the rider inserted into the passage in QS concerning the princes of the Noldor, where it is told that in Valinor Isfin 'loved much to ride on horse and to hunt in the forests, and there was often in the company of her kinsmen, the sons of Fëanor'. Subsequently *Isfin* in this passage was changed to *Íríth* (see X.177, 182); this name is found in *Quendi and Eldar* (see p. 409 and note 34).

The published text uses 'you' forms throughout. In A 'thou' forms were used throughout, but in the passage (§5) in which the marchwardens of Doriath address Isfin the 'thou' forms were altered to the 'polite' plural. *Noldor* was changed to *Ñoldor* throughout B(i).

In A, the text begins with the date 316.

§4 *And Turgon appointed three lords of his household...*
On B(i) only, my father pencilled with reference to these opening words the names *Glorfindel, Egalmoth*, and *Ecthelion*, and also 'On etymologies of *Egalmoth* and *Ecthelion* see note'. This note is written on the same typescript page and its reverse, but is very hard to read:

These names are also derived from primitive FG, but are well-sounding and have been in print. They are late popular forms of archaic *Ægamloth, Ægthelion*. Note *amloth* is said (where?) to be probably not S[indarin]. Q **ambalotse* 'uprising-flower' – referring to the flower or floreate device used as a crest fixed to point of a tall ... helmet. Name therefore = pointed helm-crest.

Ecthelion must be similarly from *Aegthelion*. Latter element is a derivative of √*stel* 'remain firm'. The form with prefix *'sundóma'*, *estel*, was used in Q and S for 'hope' – sc. a temper of mind, steady, fixed in purpose, and difficult to dissuade and unlikely to fall into despair or abandon its purpose. The unprefixed *stel-* gave [? S verb] *thel* 'intend, mean, purpose, resolve, will'. So Q ? *þelma* 'a fixed idea, ..., will.'

The illegible word in 'a tall ... helmet' might possibly be 'archaic'. The word *sundóma* is an important term in the analysis of Quendian phonological structure. Very briefly indeed, the Quendian consonantal 'base' or *sundo* was characterised by a 'determinant vowel' or *sundóma*: thus the *sundo* KAT has a medial *sundóma* 'A', and TALAT has the *sundóma* repeated. In derivative forms the *sundóma* might be placed before the first consonant, e.g. ATALAT; thus *estel* beside *stel* in this note.

On the words 'These names ... have been in print' (referring to the Ruling Stewards of Gondor named Egalmoth and Ecthelion) see II.211–12 and footnote, where the present note is referred to; for my remark there that my father 'subsequently decided against naming Aredhel's escort' see p. 328.

§5 *But when she came to the Ford of Brithiach...*

'his kinsfolk of the house of Finarfin': B still has *Finrod* here, and the change to *Finarfin* was made on B(ii) only.

In A and B the march-wardens said to Isfin: 'The speediest way is by the East Road from Brithiach through eastern Brethil, and so along the north-march of this Kingdom, until you pass Esgalduin and Aros, and so come to the woods behind the Hill of Himring.' In B(ii) only, 'Esgalduin and Aros' was changed to 'the Bridge of Esgalduin and the Ford of Aros'.

In the published text 'the lands that lie behind the Hill of Himring' seems to be a mere error for 'the woods ...' which was not observed.

§6 *Then Aredhel turned back...*

A and B have 'the Eryd Gorgoroth', but on B(ii), and also on A at the same time, this was changed to 'the haunted valleys of the Gorgorath'; similarly A and B 'Dungorthin' > 'Nan Dungortheb' on A and B(ii).

The original form of this paragraph was not changed on B(i), but was rewritten on B(ii). This rewriting did not significantly change the sense, but added that the companions of 'Feiniel' (see under §1 above) 'had no choice but to follow her, for they were not permitted to restrain her by force', and that when they returned to Gondolin 'Turgon said to them: "At least I should be glad that three whom I trust and love were not led to death by the wilfulness of one."' These additions were not included in the published text.

§7 *But Aredhel, having sought in vain for her companions...*

Where the published text has 'she held on her way' the original text, preserved in B(i), has 'she held to the East Road'; in B(ii) this was emended to 'At last she found the East Road again'. In B(ii) the name

Celon was at both occurrences in the paragraph circled for correction, and at the second the name *Limhir* was written above (see p. 337).

Of Isfin's coming to the land of Himlad (a name which first occurs in this story) the original text of A and B read:

> ... at that time they [Celegorm and Curufin] were from home, riding with Cranthir, east in Thargelion. But the folk of Celegorm welcomed her, and did all that she asked; and for a while she had great joy in the freedom of the woods. And ever she would ride further abroad, often alone, save it were for hounds that she led, seeking for new paths ...

This was rewritten on B(i) to the form it has in the published text. In a first stage of the rewriting the phrase 'save it were for hounds that she led' was bracketed with the note: 'Omit unless the presence of dogs is afterwards of importance'; in the second stage it was omitted. Against the *o* of *Thargelion* my father wrote *a* (sc. *Thargelian*), with a query. In B(ii) the rewriting was different, retaining more of the original text, including the reference to hounds; *Thargelion* was changed here also to *Thargelian*, without a query (on the latter form see pp. 336–7).

§8 *In that wood in ages past ...*

On B(i) my father wrote the following note in the margin of the typescript against the first occurrence in the story of the name Eöl, which he bracketed:

> Another name from prim[itive] FG – meaningless then and now. But it was not intended to have any meaning in Q[uenya] or S[indarin]. For Eöl was said to be a 'Dark Elf', a term then applied to any Elves who had not been willing to leave Middle-earth – and were then (before the history and geography had been organized) imagined as wandering about, and often ill-disposed towards the 'Light-Elves'. But it was also sometimes applied to Elves captured by Morgoth and enslaved and then released to do mischief among the Elves. I think this latter idea should be taken up. It would explain much about Eöl and his smithcraft. (I think the name might stay. It isn't really absolutely necessary that names should be significant.)

In the old tale of *The Fall of Gondolin* Eöl was not in fact called 'the Dark Elf', although in the soon abandoned *Lay of the Fall of Gondolin* (III.146) he is called 'dark Eöl', and it is said that 'the Dark Elves were his kindred that wander without home'. In the *Sketch of the Mythology* (IV.34) he was called 'the Dark Elf Eöl', and so also in the *Quenta* (IV.136); in AB 1 (IV.301) he is 'Eöl a Dark-elf', and in AB 2 (V.136) 'Eöl the Dark-elf' – so also in all the entries in GA. I do not think that 'Dark-elves' had ever been used in the sense referred to in this note, that of 'darkened Elves', Elves ensnared and corrupted by Morgoth. The words 'I think this latter idea should be taken up. It would explain much about Eöl and his smithcraft' were the basis for an abandoned sketch of Eöl's history given below.

The original text had 'Of old he was of the kin of Thingol, but he loved him not, and when the Girdle of Melian was set about the Forest of Region he fled thence to Nan Elmoth.' In a passage of the 'Túrins Saga' which was excluded in *Unfinished Tales* (p. 96 and note 12) because it had been used in *The Silmarillion* (pp. 201-2), it is told that Eöl gave the sword Anglachel which he had made 'to Thingol as fee, which he begrudged, for leave to dwell in Nan Elmoth'.

Against the words 'but he loved him not' my father wrote in the margin of the carbon copy, B(ii): 'Because Thingol was friendly with the Noldor before they left Middle-earth' (cf. X.172). On B(i) he emended the words 'he loved him not' to 'he was ill at ease in Doriath', and on an inserted page he roughed out a new story about Eöl. This is in two versions, which are however largely identical. The first reads:

but he was restless and ill at ease in Doriath, and when the Girdle of Melian was set about the Forest of Region where he dwelt he departed. It is thought (though no clear tale was known) that he was captured by orks and taken to Thangorodrim, and there became enslaved; but owing to his skills (which in that place were turned much to smithcraft and metalwork) he received some favour, and was freer than most slaves to move about, and so eventually he escaped and sought hiding in Nan Elmoth (maybe not without the knowledge of Morgoth, who used such 'escaped' slaves to work mischief among the Elves).

The second version begins:

and when he heard that Melian would put a Girdle about Doriath that none could pass ..... without the leave of the king or of Melian herself, he left the Forest of Region where he had dwelt and sought for a place to dwell. But since he did not love the Noldor he found it hard to find a place where he would be unmolested. It was believed afterwards (though no certain tale was known) that in his wandering he was captured [*&c. as in the first version*]

This is possibly compatible with the story that Eöl gave Anglachel to Thingol as fee to dwell in Nan Elmoth. It would be interesting to know why my father wished thus to change Eöl's history – or rather, why he wished to attribute Eöl's skill in metals to a time of slavery in Angband; but in any event he thought better of it, for in a scribbled note beside the two versions of the story he said that this would not do, being too repetitive of the later history of Maeglin, and that Eöl's skill was derived from the Dwarves.

§9 *Now the traffic of the Dwarves*...

The opening of this paragraph read as follows in A:

Now the traffic of the Dwarves followed two roads, the northern of which, going towards Himring, passed nigh Nan Elmoth, and there Eöl would meet the Enfeng and hold converse with them. And, as their friendship grew, he would at times go and dwell as a guest in the deep mansions of Belegost.

The only emendation to A was the replacement of the old term *Enfeng* (Longbeards, the Dwarves of Belegost, see pp. 108, 207–8) by *Anfangrim*, here first appearing. In B(ii) 'the deep mansions of Belegost' was changed to '... of Nogrod or Belegost'; adopting this in the published text I altered in consequence *Anfangrim* 'Longbeards' to the general term *Naugrim*.

In the following passage A had originally:
> There he learned much of metalwork, and came to great skill therein; and he devised a metal hard and thin and yet pliable, and it was black and shining like jet. *Rodeöl*, the metal of Eöl, he named it, and he was clad therein, and so escaped many wounds.

The name of the metal was changed many times. First *Rodeöl* was altered to *Glindûr*, then to *Targlîn* and *Morlîn*; then (apparently) back to *Glindûr*, and finally to *Maeglin*, the form in B.

The idea that the name of Eöl's son was derived from that of the metal is found in the revised annal for 320 in GA (p. 48): 'Ëol named him Glindûr, for that was the name of the metal of Ëol'; subsequently *Glindûr* was changed to *Maeglin* both as the name of the metal and as the name of the son (as also in A: see under §10 below).

The passage was left as it stood in B(i), but at the head of the first page of B(ii) my father wrote: 'The metal must *not* have same name as Maeglin'; and he emended the text to the form that it has in the published *Silmarillion*, with the name of the metal *galvorn*. (Following 'whenever he went abroad' the words 'and so escaped many wounds' were omitted in *The Silmarillion*, apparently through inadvertence.)

To the passage 'But Eöl ... was no Dwarf, but a tall Elf of a high kin of the Teleri' my father wrote on the manuscript A (only) a note beginning with the words 'Not in revision' – which probably means that what follows is not in the corrections made to the copies of the typescript ('the revision'). In this note my father was copying a very faint and illegible form of it on the same page, and trying to interpret his own writing; I give it exactly as it stands:
> Eöl should not be one of Thingol's kin, but one of the Teleri who refused to cross the Hithaeglir. But [later] he and a few others of like mood, averse to concourse of people, ... [had] crossed the [Mts] long ago and come to Beleriand.

Against this note he wrote 'but the relationship to Thingol would have point', and the date 1971.

Aredhel Ar-Feiniel: B(ii) has here *Ar-Feiniel* (emended from *Isfin*); see p. 318.

§10 *It is not said that Aredhel was wholly unwilling...*

In the margin of the manuscript at the mention of the birth of Eöl's son my father wrote later the date 320 (cf. p. 48, §119). The sentence in A as originally written read:
> After some years Isfin bore to Eöl a son in the shadows of Nan

Elmoth, and he was named Meglin by his father, for he was dark and supple, as the metal of Eöl.

The fact that the metal was originally named *Rodeöl* in A (see under §9 above) but the son *Meglin* (the original name) seems to suggest that the idea that the son was named from the metal only arose after the initial writing of the manuscript, despite the words 'for he was dark and supple, as the metal of Eöl'. The changing forms of the son's name in A were *Meglin* > *Targlîn* > *Morlîn* > *Glindûr* and finally *Maeglin*.

The sentence in this form (with the name *Maeglin*, as of the metal also) was preserved in B(i); but in B(ii), the text on which my father declared that the same name must not be used both of Eöl's son and Eöl's metal and changed that of the latter to *galvorn*, he altered it to the form in the published text, in which Aredhel secretly gave her son the Noldorin name *Lómion* 'Child of the Twilight', and Eöl named him *Maeglin* (interpreted 'Sharp Glance', see p. 337) when he was twelve years old.

§12 *Yet it is said that Maeglin loved his mother better...*

'Turgon... had no heir; for Elenwë his wife perished in the crossing of the Helcaraxë': here A has 'Turgon ... had no heir: for his wife, Alairë, was of the Vanyar and would not forsake Valinor'. On the page of jottings that concludes the abandoned later *Tale of Tuor* (see *Unfinished Tales* p. 56) a note which I did not include says that 'Alairë remained in Aman'. That this was the case because she was a Vanya is reminiscent of the story of Amárië, beloved of Felagund, who was a Vanya, 'and was not permitted to go with him into exile' (p. 44, §109). The typescript B as typed has *Alairë*, but on both A and B(ii), not on B(i), my father corrected (presumptively in 1970) the name to *Anairë*. The substitution of *Elenwë* in *The Silmarillion* was based on the Elvish genealogies of 1959 (see pp. 229, 350), where *Anairë* (defined as a Vanya 'who remained in Túna') was later corrected to '*Elenwë* who perished in the Ice'; on the same table at the same time *Anairë* was entered as the wife of Fingolfin, with the note that she 'remained in Aman'.

In a note added to the typescript of the *Annals of Aman* (X.128, §163) my father said that in the crossing of the Helkaraxë 'Turgon's wife was lost and he had then only one daughter and no other heir. Turgon was nearly lost himself in attempts to rescue his wife – and he had less love for the Sons of Fëanor than any other'; but Turgon's wife is not named.

§13 *In the telling of these tales...*

Golodhrim: A had *Noldor*, changed immediately to *Goloðrim* (*Golodhrim* B).

In this paragraph, and in §14, the name of Eöl's son (see under §§9, 10 above) passed through these forms in A: *Morleg* (which has not occurred before) > *Morlîn* > *Glindûr* > *Maeglin*.

§§14 ff.   *It came to pass that at the midsummer* ...

Against the opening sentence in A my father later wrote the date 400 (cf. p. 48, §120). The original text, preserved unchanged in both copies of B, read here:

> And it came to pass that the Dwarves bade Eöl to a feast in Nogrod, and he rode away. Then Maeglin went to his mother and said: 'Lady, let us depart while there is time! What hope is there in the wood for thee or for me? Here we are held in bondage, and no profit more shall I find in this place. For I have learned all that my father or the [Nornwaith >] Naugrim have to teach, or will reveal to me; and I would not for ever dwell in the dark woods with few servants, and those skilled only in smith-craft. Shall we not go to Gondolin? Be thou my guide, and I will be thy guard.'
>
> Then Isfin was glad, and looked with pride upon her son. 'That indeed I will do, and swiftly,' she said; 'and no fear shall I have upon the road with a guard so valiant.'
>
> Therefore they arose and departed in haste, as secretly as they might. But Eöl returned, ere his time, and found them gone; and so great was his wrath that he followed after them, even by the light of day.

(For *Nornwaith*, replaced by *Naugrim*, see p. 209.) At this point there are two earlier versions of the text in A, both struck through. The first reads:

> But Morleg had also mistrusted his father, and he took cunning counsel, and so he went not at once by the East Road, but rode first to Celegorm and found him in the hills south of Himring. And of Celegorm he got horses surpassing swift, and the promise of other aid. Then Morleg and Isfin passed over Aros and Esgalduin far to the north where they spilled from the highlands of Dorthonion, and turned then southward, and came to the East Road far to the west. But Celegorm and Curufin waylaid the East Road and its ford over Aros, and denied it to Eöl, and though he escaped from them in the darkness he was long delayed.

The next version reads:

> For his servants reported to him that they had fled to the fords of the East Road over Aros and Esgalduin. But they were two days ahead, and had taken the swiftest of his horses, and hard though he pursued them, he came never in sight of them, until they passed over the Brithiach and abandoned their horses. But there by ill fate he saw them even as they took the secret path, which lay in the course of the Dry River; and he followed them with great stealth, step by step, and came upon them even in the darkness of the great vault where the Guards of the Way kept watch unceasing. Thus he was taken, even as they, by the Guards

It is interesting to see the intervention of Celegorm and Curufin in the story here, removed at once but reappearing many years later.

On the page carrying these rejected passages there follow very rapidly pencilled notes outlining the further course of the story:

After they entered he entered. Taken by guards. Claims to be Isfin's husband. Words to Turgon. Isfin acknowledges it. Turgon treats Eöl with honour. Eöl draws a bow and shoots at Morleg in the King's hall, saying that his own son shall not be filched. But Isfin sets herself in way and is wounded. While Eöl is in prison Isfin dies of venom. Eöl condemned to death. Taken to the precipice of Caragdur. Morleg stands by coldly. They hurl him over the precipice and all save Idril approve.

After the rejection of the passages given above my father wrote a final version, beginning again at 'even by the light of day' on p. 324:

even by the light of day; for his servants reported to him that they had ridden to the East Road and the ford over Aros. But they were two days ahead, and hard though he pursued them, and had the swiftest steed, he came never in sight of them, until they [came under the shadows of the Crisaegrim, and sought for the secret path >] reached the Brithiach, and abandoned their horses.

The text then continues as in *The Silmarillion* §23 (paragraph beginning *Then Eöl rode off in haste*...).

The final text of A was preserved in the typescript B, and in neither the top copy nor the carbon did my father change it (except for 'a feast' > 'a midsummer feast' in the latter). From here onwards, in fact, there were no further emendations or annotations made to the carbon copy B(ii), and this text no longer concerns us. But in B(i) my father inserted into the typescript a long text on separate pages; and this appears to be the last piece of substantial *narrative* that he wrote on the Matter of the Elder Days – it cannot be earlier than 1970 (see p. 316). It begins at the words 'It came to pass that at the midsummer', and continues through the flight of Maeglin and Aredhel, Eöl's pursuit, and the intervention of Curufin: *The Silmarillion* pp. 134–6, §§14–23, where it joins the original A text at 'until they reached the Brithiach, and abandoned their horses'.

As has been seen (p. 317) this story of Maeglin was not written to stand as an element in the *Quenta Silmarillion*; and the detail of the narrative in this very late interpolation was somewhat reduced in the published text, chiefly by the removal of all the precise timing and numbering of days and a return to the manner of the original simpler and more remote narrative. The chief omissions and consequent alterations are as follows.

§14 *and he rode away*. Original text: 'and he rode away, though he thought it likely that in his absence Maeglin might seek to visit the sons of Fëanor in spite of his counsels, and he secretly ordered his servants to keep close watch on his wife and son.'

Therefore he said to Aredhel: 'Therefore when Eöl had been gone some days Maeglin went to his mother and said:'

§§15–16 *and telling the servants of Eöl that they went to seek the sons of Fëanor* ...: 'Therefore that night as secretly as they could they made provision for a journey, and they rode away at daybreak to the north-eaves of Nan Elmoth. There as they crossed the slender stream of Celon they spied a watchman, and Maeglin cried to him: "Tell your master that we go to visit our kin in Aglon." Then they rode on over the Himlad to the Fords of Aros, and then westward along the Fences of Doriath. But they had tarried overlong. For on the first night of the three days feast, as he slept, a dark shadow of ill foreboding visited Eöl, and in the morning he forsook Nogrod without ceremony and rode homeward with all speed. Thus he returned some days earlier than Maeglin had expected, coming to Nan Elmoth at nightfall of the day after their flight. There he learned from his watchman that they had ridden north less than two days before and had passed into the Himlad, on their way to Aglon.

'Then so great was Eöl's anger that he resolved to follow them at once; so staying only to take a fresh horse, the swiftest that he had, he rode away that night. But as he entered the Himlad he mastered his wrath...'

Against *Celon* is written *? Limhir* (see under §7 above).

§16 *Curufin moreover was of perilous mood; but the scouts of Aglon had marked the riding of Maeglin and Aredhel*...: 'Curufin was a man of perilous mood. So far they had left him [Eöl] free to go his ways, but could if they wished confine him within the bounds of Nan Elmoth and cut him off from his friendship with Dwarves, of which Curufin was jealous. Things proved little better than he feared; for the scouts of Aglon...'

And before Eöl had ridden far...: 'So ere Eöl had ridden half the way over Himlad he was waylaid by well-armed horsemen, who forced him to go with them to their lord Curufin. They reached his camp about noon; and he greeted Eöl with little courtesy.'

§19 *It is not two days since they passed over the Arossiach*...: 'Nearly two days ago they were seen to pass the Fords of Aros, and to ride swiftly westward.' For the name *Arossiach* introduced into the published text see p. 338, note 2.

§22 *to find a kinsman thus kindly at need*: 'to find one's nephew so kindly at need.' On this alteration see §23 below.

By the laws of the Eldar I may not slay you at this time: here there is a footnote in the original: 'Because the Eldar (which included the Sindar) were forbidden to slay one another in revenge for any grievance however great. Also at this time Eöl had ridden towards Aglon with no ill intent, and it was not unjust that he should seek news of Areðel and Maeglin.'

§23 *for he perceived now that Maeglin and Aredhel were fleeing to Gondolin*: 'For he saw now that he had been cheated, and that his wife and son were fleeing to Gondolin, and he had been delayed, so that it was now more than two days since they crossed the Fords.'

This narrative is followed by various notes. One of these is a genealogical table:

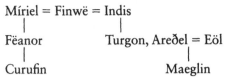

To this is added: 'So Curufin was half-nephew of Turgon and Areðel. Eöl was uncle by marriage of Curufin, but that was denied as a "forced marriage".' This genealogy is the basis for Eöl's words cited under §22 above, 'to find one's nephew so kindly at need'; but it is of course entirely wrong. The correct genealogy is:

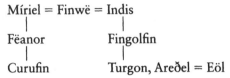

Curufin was not Eöl's nephew (through Areðel), but his cousin (by marriage). It is a strange error, one might say unprecedented, since it is not a mere casual slip.

On another page is the following long, rapidly written, and remarkably elaborate discussion of the motives of Celegorm and Curufin.

> The meeting between Eöl and Curufin (if not too long an interruption) is good, since it shows (as is desirable) Curufin, too often the villain (especially in the Tale of Tinúviel), in a better and more honourable light – though still one of dangerous mood and contemptuous speech. Curufin of course knew well of Eöl's hatred of the Noldor, and especially of Fëanor and his sons, as 'usurpers' (though in this case unjust, since the lands occupied by the 5 sons had not been peopled before by the Sindar). Also he knew of Eöl's friendship with the Dwarves of Nogrod (indeed Eöl could not have journeyed alone across E. Beleriand to Nogrod unless allowed by the 5 sons), among whom he had tried with some success to stir up unfriendliness to the Noldor. Which was a grievance to the 5 sons, who had, before Eöl's coming to Nan Elmoth, had much profit from the help of the Dwarves. Curufin also knew that Eöl's wife was of the Noldor, indeed he had long known who she was, and now shrewdly guessed that she was [?seeking] to escape from her husband at last. Curufin could have slain Eöl (as he greatly wished!) and no one beyond the few men with him at his camp (who would never have betrayed him) would ever have heard of it – or much mourned it. In Elmoth it would simply be learned that Eöl had ridden in pursuit of Areðel and never come back, and there were

perils enough upon the road to account for that. But this would have been in Eldarin law and sentiment *murder*; Eöl came alone, on no errand of mischief at that time, but in distress. Also [he] had answered Curufin's contempt and insults soberly or indeed with courtesy (whether it were ironic or not). Also and more cogently he was one of the Eldar, and not so far as was known under any shadow of Morgoth – unless that vague one which afflicted many others of the Sindar (? due to whispers inspired by Morgoth) – jealousy of the Noldor. Which was dangerous (whatever the faults of their rebellion) since if Morgoth had not been followed by the Exiles, it seems clear that all the Sindar would soon have been destroyed or enslaved.

An important point not made clear is Curufin and Celegorm's earlier action in the matter of Areðel. She had actually stayed with them, and made no secret of who she was – indeed they knew her well from of old. Why did they not send word to Gondolin? Her escort though valiant chiefs would seem to have been so bewildered and daunted by the horrors of the valleys west of Esgalduin that they had never reached the Bridge of Esgalduin or come near to Aglond. This makes it necessary, I think, *not* to name the most eminent and bravest chieftains (Glorfindel, Egalmoth, and Ecthelion) as her escort. The answer then to the above question is this: the perils of Dungorthin etc. were universally dreaded by the Eldar, and not least by the sons of Fëanor, to him [*read* whom] refuge southward into Doriath was utterly closed. It had, of course, been expressly forbidden by Turgon that Areðel should go that way. Only her wilfulness had done this. Her escort plainly endured to the utmost of their strength the perils in their search, and so doubtless in fact aided her escape, by drawing to themselves the chief attention of the evil creatures. Now there had [been] since Gondolin was 'closed' no communication at all between the sons of Fëanor and Turgon. It was known of course that any of these sons (or any fully accredited messengers) bearing tidings of Areðel would at once have been admitted. But Areðel had evidently told Curufin (and later Celegorm of whom she was most fond) enough of herself, to understand that she had escaped from Gondolin by her own will and was glad to dwell [with] them and be free. Now they could only get word to Gondolin by facing evil perils, which only her rescue from misery would have seemed to them sufficient reason. Moreover while she was happy and at ease they delayed – believing that even if Turgon was informed he would only have demanded her return (since his permission to her to depart was void after her disobedience). But before they had made up their minds she was again lost, and it was a long time before they knew or even guessed what had become of her. This they did eventually when Areðel again began to visit the borders of Nan Elmoth, or stray beyond them. For they held a constant watch on Nan Elmoth, mistrusting the doings and goings of Eöl, and their scouts espied her at times riding in the sunlight by the wood-eaves. But now it seemed too late [to] them; and they all [? *read* they thought that all] they would get for any peril would be the rebuke or wrath of Turgon. And this [they] wished in no way to receive. For they were now under a shadow of fear, and beginning to prepare for war again ere the strength of Thangorodrim became insuperable.

In this piece there are major difficulties, and also some minor points to mention. (1) It is said that Curufin 'knew of Eöl's friendship with the Dwarves of Nogrod': in the narrative Eöl's visits were to Belegost, changed on B(ii) to 'Nogrod or Belegost' (see under §9 above), but already in A the feast to which he had gone at the time of the flight of his wife and son was held at Nogrod (§14). Elsewhere among these late 'Maeglin' writings it is said of Eöl: 'Lately he had visited Nogrod often; he had become very friendly with the Dwarves of Nogrod, since those of Belegost to the north had become friends of Caranthir son of Fëanor.' (2) The pass is here named *Aglond*, though in the interpolated narrative itself it is named *Aglon*; see p. 338, note 3. (3) For the naming of Aredhel's escort, here rejected, see under §4 above. (4) The reference to *Dungorthin* rather than *Dungortheb* is a casual reversion to the old and long-enduring name.

(5) The *five* sons of Fëanor are three times mentioned, but I cannot explain this. It does not seem credible that the Seven Sons of Fëanor, so deeply rooted and so constantly recurring in the tradition, should become five by a mere slip of forgetfulness, as in the omission of Fingolfin from the genealogy (p. 327). By this time the story had entered that one of the twin brothers Damrod and Díriel, later Amrod and Amras, the youngest of Fëanor's sons, died in the burning of the ships of the Teleri at Losgar, because he 'had returned to sleep in his ship': this was stated in a pencilled note on the typescript of the *Annals of Aman* (X.128, §162), although no consequential alteration to any text was ever made. Possibly my father had come to believe that both Amrod and Amras died in the burning ship.

(6) Lastly, the concluding sentence of the discussion, concerning the preparation for war by Celegorm and Curufin, is surprising. The Siege of Angband ended very suddenly at midwinter of the year 455. Between the rout of Glaurung in 260 and the Battle of Sudden Flame there was (in the words of the *Grey Annals*, p. 46) 'the long peace of wellnigh two hundred years. In that time there was naught but affrays on the north-marches ...' It is true that in 402 (p. 49) there was 'fighting on the north-marches, more bitter than there had been since the routing of Glaurung; for the Orcs attempted to pierce the pass of Aglon'; while in 422 (p. 50) Fingolfin 'began to ponder an assault upon Angband', which came to nothing, because 'most of the Eldar

were content with matters as they were and slow to begin an assault in which many must surely perish'. But Maeglin and Aredhel fled to Gondolin from Nan Elmoth in 400. There has nowhere been any indication that the sons of Fëanor were beginning to prepare for war 55 years before the Dagor Bragollach, with which the Siege of Angband ended.

For the remainder of the narrative there are very few alterations to the top copy B(i) of the typescript, and I notice only the following:
§35 *It was appointed that Eöl should be brought* ...: at the end of the paragraph my father added:
For the Eldar never used any poison, not even against their most cruel enemies, beast, ork, or man; and they were filled with shame and horror that Eöl should have meditated this evil deed.
From this point also the published text follows the original very closely, and the small amount of editorial alteration in no way affects the narrative.

I have mentioned (p. 316) that in addition to the very late emendations and annotations, recorded above, made to the text of *Maeglin* there is also much further material from the same time. These writings are primarily concerned with the geography, times, and distances of the journeys on horseback, but they are complicated and confused, often repeating themselves with slight differences of calculation, and in part virtually illegible. They contain however many curious details about the geography and the ways taken by travellers in those regions.

To set out this material in ordered form, treating it page by page and attempting to trace the development in sequence, is not possible, and if it were possible unnecessary. My father himself noted: 'These calculations of times in Eöl's journeys though interesting (and sufficient to establish their possibility) are not really necessary in the narrative – which seems credible as it stands even when faced by a map.' What follows is a discussion with some citation of what can be learned (and still more, of what can not be learned) of the roads in East Beleriand. The numbered notes are found on pp. 338–9.

Associated with this material are rather pale photocopies of the North-east and South-east sections of the map. These photocopies were taken when the map had received almost all the alterations that were ever made to it;[1] and my father used the copies, not the original, to indicate features arising from his reconsideration and development of the story of Maeglin c.1970. Since the tracks are far more readily understood visually than by description, the redrawing of the North-east section (p. 183) is reproduced again on p. 331 with the alterations shown; the markings on the South-east section are few and easily understood from a description, and for these reference is made to the redrawing on p. 185.

My father had stated in a note on the back of the original 'second

MAEGLIN 331

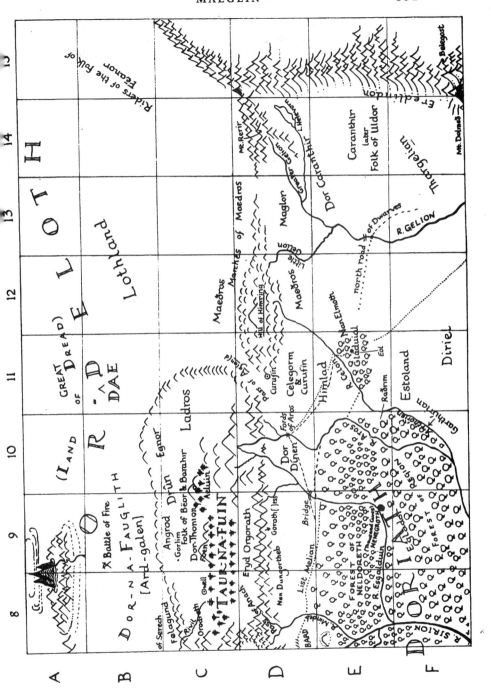

Sheet 2 North-east (with additions)

map' (see V.272) that the scale is 50 miles to 3·2 cm, which is the length of the sides of the squares. On the back of one of these photocopies, however, he wrote: 'The centimetre reckoning on the original map is unnecessary, clumsy, and inaccurate. Actually 2 squares of 1·25 [inches] each = 100 miles. ... The scale is therefore 40 miles to an inch. 50 miles to 1·25 inches = one square.' Although he did not precisely say so here, it looks to me as if he made the original grid on the basis of inches, but subsequently interpreted it as if it were in centimetres.

The East Road. In the original text of *Maeglin* (p. 319, §5) the march-wardens of Doriath said to Isfin that 'the speediest way is by the East Road from Brithiach through eastern Brethil, and so along the north-march of this Kingdom, until you pass Esgalduin and Aros, and so come to the woods behind the Hill of Himring', which was not altered when the corrections were made to the text long afterwards, except by changing 'Esgalduin and Aros' to 'the Bridge of Esgalduin and the Ford of Aros' on one copy. In §6, she 'sought' the 'road' between the Mountains of Terror and the north fences of Doriath, and in §7 'she held to the East Road, and crossed Esgalduin and Aros', changed on one copy to 'At last she found the East Road again ...' In one of the rejected passages in the manuscript A given under §§14 ff on p. 324 it is said that 'Morleg [Maeglin] went not at once by the East Road, but rode first to Celegorm', while in the second rejected passage *(ibid.)* '[Eöl's] servants reported to him that they had fled to the fords of the East Road over Aros and Esgalduin'; in the third form (p. 325) 'his servants reported to him that they had ridden to the East Road and the ford over Aros.'

From all these passages it is clear that when he wrote the original text of *Maeglin* in 1951 my father conceived of an East–West road running from the ford of Brithiach between the Mountains of Terror and the northern borders of Doriath, and across the rivers Esgalduin and Aros; and the fact that the first of these passages was allowed to stand in both typescripts seems to show that he still retained this conception in 1970. The only difference seems to be the introduction of a bridge, rather than a ford, over Esgalduin. That this was certainly the case is seen from the following passage:

Eöl's house (in the middle of Elmoth) was about 15 miles from the northmost point of the wood beside Celon. From that point it was about 65 miles N.W. to the Ford of Aros.[2] At that time Curufin was dwelling at the S.E. corner of the Pass of Aglond[3] about 45 miles N.E. from the Ford of Aros. The Himlad (cool-plain) behind Aglond and Himring, between the northern courses of the Rivers Aros and Celon, he claimed as his land.[4] He and his people naturally kept watch on the Ford of Aros; but they did not prevent the few hardy travellers (Elves or Dwarves) that used the road West – East past the north fences of Doriath. (Beyond the Ford was an entirely uninhabited region between the mountains north [? *read* in the north,] Esgalduin and Aros and Doriath: not even birds came there. It was thus called *Dor Dhínen* the 'Silent Land'.)[5]

Beyond the Aros (some 25 miles) lay the more formidable obstacle of the Esgalduin in which no fordable point was to be found. In the 'peaceful days' before the return of Morgoth and Ungoliant, when Doriath's north borders were the mountains of Fuin (not yet evil), the West – East road passed over the Esgalduin by a bridge outside the later fence of Melian. This stone-bridge, the *Esgaliant* or *Iant Iaur* (old bridge) was still in existence, and watched by the wardens of Doriath, but its use by Eldar was not hindered. It was necessary therefore to fugitives crossing Aros to turn S.W. to the bridge. From there they would keep as close as they could to the Fences of Doriath (if Thingol and Melian were not hostile to them). At the time of this story, though many evils lurked in the Mountains the chief peril lay in passing Nan Dungortheb from which clouds and darkness would creep down almost to the Fences.

Turning to the photocopy of the map, Eöl's house was marked in Nan Elmoth as shown in my redrawing (p. 331). A line in green ballpoint pen connects his house to a point on the northern border of the wood beside the river; and from here a green dotted line (represented as a line of dashes in the redrawing) runs across the Himlad to the 'Fords of Aros', marked in red ball-point pen.[6] The green dots then run S.W. to the bridge over Esgalduin, this being labelled 'Bridge' simply (*Esgaliant* or *Iant Iaur* in the text just cited).[7] Beyond the Iant Iaur the green dots continue S.W. for a short way and then stop: they are not shown in relation to the *List Melian* (the Girdle of Melian).

It is stated in a note on the photocopy map that this green line marks the 'track of Maeglin and his mother, fleeing to Gondolin'. In the light of the text just cited, it is also the line of the East–West road from the Ford of Aros to the Iant Iaur; but otherwise the course of the road is not represented. The dotted line along the edge of Neldoreth is named on the map *List Melian*, and does not mark a road. Westward this line was indeed extended beyond Mindeb to the Brithiach, but these dots were struck out (p. 188, §38); eastwards it was extended between Esgalduin and Aros, and then between Aros and Celon, and this seems to represent the continuation of the *List Melian*.

On account of these obscurities I excluded from the text of the chapter *Of Maeglin* in *The Silmarillion* the references to the 'East Road' and rephrased the passages; but on the map accompanying the book I marked in its course. This seems now to have been the wrong thing to do in both cases: for there certainly was an East Road, but its course is unclear and its destination unknown. Beyond Aros going east there is no indication of where it went: it is said in the passage cited above that it and the bridge by which it passed over Esgalduin were ancient works deriving from the 'peaceful days' before the return of Morgoth: it was not a road made by the Noldor for communication between the western realms and the Fëanorians. There is also no justification for marking it as turning S.E. after the Fords of Aros. Beyond Esgalduin going west it is said in this passage that travellers 'would keep as close as they could to the Fences of Doriath', which does not sound like the following of a beaten road.

The Dwarf-roads. Equally obscure is the question of the Dwarf-roads in Eastern Beleriand. In the earliest *Annals of Beleriand* (AB 1, IV.332) it was said that 'the Dwarves had of old a road into the West that came up along Eredlindon to the East and passed westward in the passes south of Mount Dolm and down the course of the River Ascar and over Gelion at the ford Sarn Athrad and so to Aros.' This agrees exactly with the (revised) course of the road on the 'Eastward Extension' of the first *Silmarillion* map (see IV.231, 336). It is seen from the central (original) part of the first map that it crossed Celon and Aros west of Nan Elmoth (which of course did not at that time yet exist) and so ran in a W.S.W. direction to the Thousand Caves (between pp. 220 and 221 in Vol.IV). But the course of the ancient route of the Dwarves after the passage of Sarn Athrad was never marked in on the second map – unless the vague line described in the notes on the map, p. 190, §68, is correctly interpreted as the Dwarf-road. If that is so, then its course had been changed to cross Aros much further to the south, and then to run northwards through the Forest of Region to Menegroth. But better evidence is provided in the late *Quenta Silmarillion* chapter *Of the Coming of Men into the West,* pp. 218–19, where it is said that 'Marach ... came down the Dwarf-road and settled his people in the country to the south and east of the dwellings of Baran son of Bëor': this was Estolad, 'the name ever after of the land east of Celon and south of Nan Elmoth'. On the disuse of the old Dwarf-road(s) into Beleriand after the coming of the Noldor see p. 121, commentary on GA §114.

It was said already in the original text of *Maeglin* (p. 321, §9) that 'the traffic of the Dwarves followed two roads, the northern of which, going towards Himring, passed nigh Nan Elmoth'. This was not altered in the late work on *Maeglin*; and on the primary map (already present when the photocopy was made) a line of faintly pencilled dots marked 'north road of Dwarves' (see p. 189, §50) runs E.S.E. from near Nan Elmoth, crosses Gelion some way south of the confluence of its arms, and then turns southward, running more or less parallel to the river. There is no trace of its course west or north of Nan Elmoth, and it is impossible to be sure whether any further continuation southwards or eastwards is marked beyond the point where it ends in my redrawing (p. 183).

The *Maeglin* papers do not resolve the course of this 'north road of the Dwarves', because (although all obviously belong to the same time) they evidently represent different conceptions.

(i) Writing of Eöl's journey to Nogrod, my father said:

From Elmoth to Gelion the land was, north of the Andram and the Falls below the last Ford over Gelion[8] (just above the inflow of the River Ascar from the Mountains), mostly rolling plain, with large regions of big trees without thickets. There were several beaten tracks made originally by Dwarves from Belegost and Nogrod, the best (most used and widest) being from the Little Ford past the north of Elmoth and to the Ford of Aros, it crossed the Bridge of Esgalduin but went no further for, if the Dwarves wished to visit Menegroth

This text then becomes altogether illegible. At the mention of 'the last Ford over Gelion' he added a note that the name *Sarn Athrad* of this ford must be changed to *Harathrad* 'South Ford', 'in contrast to the much used northern ford where the river was not yet very swift or deep, nearly due east of Eöl's house (72 miles distant)'; and against *Harathrad* here he wrote *Athrad Daer* ('the Great Ford').[9]

The implication seems to be that Eöl crossed Gelion at the northern ford, but this is not actually stated. There are two alterations to the photocopies of the map that relate to what is said here. One is the marking of a crossing over Gelion on square E 13 (p. 331), just above the point where the dotted line 'north road of Dwarves' crosses the river on the primary map, but without any track leading to this crossing. The other is at the ford of Sarn Athrad on the South-east section (p. 185), where on the photocopy my father wrote the name anew over the existing name, circled it, and wrote beside it *Harathrad*.

Beyond this nothing can be said of the north road of the Dwarves, and there is no indication in map or text of where, or indeed whether, it joined the 'south road'. It is indeed very puzzling that this northerly road, which in the text of *Maeglin* is said to have gone 'towards Himring' (as is to be expected: leading to territories of the Sons of Fëanor), is in the citation (i) just given said to pass the Ford of Aros and the Bridge of Esgalduin: for these crossings were on the East Road to the Brithiach (pp. 332–3). And apart from this, why should this road turn westward, and why should it go no further than the Bridge of Esgalduin?

(ii) On another page my father said that the journey from Eöl's house to Nan Elmoth in the direction of Nogrod was

through wilds (but not generally in difficult country for horses) without any made roads, but along a beaten track made by Dwarvish traders to the Sarn Athrad (the last point where the River

Gelion could be crossed) meeting the Dwarf-road up to and through the high pass in the mountains leading to Nogrod.

Here there is no mention of the northern ford, or indeed of the northern road; and it seems to be implied that Eöl would necessarily cross at Sarn Athrad (still so called, not Harathrad); moreover it is said that Eöl riding from Nan Elmoth to Nogrod took 'a beaten track made by Dwarvish traders' to Sarn Athrad that *met* the Dwarf-road up to the high pass.

In addition to the green dotted line entered on the photocopy of the map and stated to be the track of Maeglin and Aredhel fleeing from Nan Elmoth (p. 333), lines of red dots (represented on my redrawing as lines of closely-spaced dots) run from Nan Elmoth to the Ford of Aros, and also south-east from Nan Elmoth (p. 331). On the Southeast section in the photocopy (see the redrawing of the primary map on p. 185) this red dotted line continues straight on across square G 13 to Sarn Athrad, and then coincides with the Dwarf-road up into the mountains, already present on the primary map. There is no note on the photocopy to explain what these lines represent, but there can be no doubt that they mark the journeys of Eöl (even though the dots continue all the way to the Ford of Aros, whereas he was arrested in his pursuit of Maeglin and Aredhel by the riders of Curufin 'ere he had ridden half the way over Himlad', p. 326, §16). Thus the line running from Nan Elmoth to Sarn Athrad clearly corresponds to what is said in citation (ii).

The absence of any really clear and full statement – indeed the suggestion that my father's ideas on the subject had not reached any stability, and the extreme doubtfulness of some of the markings on the map, led me to omit the course of the Dwarf-roads on the published map.

Apart from the matter of roads, there are some notes on names in these papers that show my father's dissatisfaction with old names already seen in the cases of *Isfin* and *Eöl* (pp. 317, 320): here those in question are *Gelion* and *Celon* (cf. his note on the primary map, p. 191, where he said that 'these river-names need revision to etymologizable words').[10] In notes in different places he proposed (in sequence) *Gelduin, Gevilon, Gevelon,* and also *Duin Daer* (cf. *Duin Dhaer* in the note on the primary map just referred to); *Gevelon* is derived from Dwarvish *Gabilān* 'great river'. On the back of one of the photocopies of the map he wrote:

> The land east of it [the river] is Thorewilan [the *a* is underlined]. The Dwarvish name was also often translated *Duin Daer*. The name *Gabilān* was by the Dwarves given only to the River south of the Falls where (after the junction of the River with the Asgar coming from the Mountains) it became swift and was steadily increased in volume by the inflow of five more tributaries.

The name *Thargelion* on the primary map was changed to *Thargelian* (with the *a* underlined: p. 331): the latter form has appeared in emendations to the typescripts of *Maeglin* (p. 320). The form *Asgar* appeared in the 1930s (beside *Ascar*), see IV.209; cf. the *Etymologies*, V.386, stem SKAR: 'N[oldorin] *asgar, ascar* violent, rushing, impetuous'.

The substitution of the name *Limhir* for *Celon* has appeared as a proposal in one of the typescripts of *Maeglin* (p. 320), and among the 'geographical' papers is the following note:

> *Celon* is too hackneyed a river-name. *Limhîr* (the clear / sparkling river) – repeated in L.R. as were not unnaturally other names from Beleriand – is more suitable for the river, a tributary of the Aros and a clear *slender* stream coming down from the Hill of Himring.

The name *Limhîr* does not occur in *The Lord of the Rings*, unless my father was referring to the Limlight, of which he said in *Guide to the Names in The Lord of the Rings* (*A Tolkien Compass*, ed. Lobdell, p. 188): 'The spelling *-light* indicates that this is a Common Speech name; but leave the obscured element *lim-* unchanged and translate *-light*: the adjective *light* here means "bright, clear".'

Lastly, it remains to mention the etymology of *Maeglin* found among these papers.

> *mik* pierce: *$mikr\bar{a}$ sharp-pointed (Q *mixa*, S *$megr$): 'strong adjective' *maikā* sharp, penetrating, going deep in – often in transferred sense (as Q *hendumaika* sharp-eye, S *maegheneb* > *maecheneb*).
>
> *glim* gleam, glint (usually of fine slender but bright shafts of light). Particularly applied to light of eyes; not Q. S *glintha-* glance (at), *glinn*.
>
> From these two is derived the name *Maeglin*, since Maeglin had, even more than his father, very bright eyes, and was both physically very keen-sighted and mentally very penetrant, and quick to interpret the looks and gestures of people, and perceive their thoughts and purposes. The name was only given to him in boyhood, when these characteristics were recognized. His father till then was contented to call him *Iôn*, son. (His mother secretly gave him a N. Quenya name *Lómion* 'son of twilight'; and taught Maeglin the Quenya tongue, though Eöl had forbidden it.)

This development of the story of Maeglin from the form in which he had written it twenty years before seems to have been the last concentrated work that my father did on the actual narratives of the Elder Days. Why he should have turned to this legend in particular I do not know; but one sees, in his minute consideration of the possibilities of the story, from the motives of the actors to the detail of terrain, of roads, of the speed and endurance of riders, how the focus of his vision of the old tales had changed.

NOTES

1 The words 'read (71) *Dor-na-Daerachas*' were added to the primary map later: see p. 187, §30, and note 6 below.
2 In another passage among these papers the Ford(s) of Aros are called *Arossiach*; this name was adopted on the map accompanying *The Silmarillion* and introduced into the text.
3 The text has 'at the S.W. corner', but this was a slip of the pen. It is stated elsewhere in these papers that the dwelling of Curufin and Celegorm was on a low hill at the S.E. corner of the Pass of Aglond, and on the photocopy map *Curufin* is marked with a circle on the most westerly of the lower heights about the Hill of Himring (p. 331, square D 11). – The form *Aglond* occurs in the discussion of the motives of Celegorm and Curufin (p. 328), beside *Aglon* in the interpolated narrative of Eöl's encounter with Curufin. On the map the name is written *Aglon(d*, which I retained on my redrawing (V.409) of the map as first made and lettered, in the belief that the variant *lond* was an original element. Although it looks to be so, it may be that the *(d* was added much later.
4 My father noted here: 'In spite of what Eöl said, it had in fact not been inhabited by Sindar before the coming of the Noldor'; and also that the name 'cool-plain' derived from the fact that 'it was higher in its middle part and felt often the chill northern airs through Aglon. It had no trees except in its southern part near the rivers.' In another place it is said that 'Himlad rose to a swelling highland at its centre (some 300 feet high at its flat top)'.
5 For the first mention of Dor Dínen (so spelt, as also on the map, not Dor Dhínen) see p. 194.
6 The primary map had no crossing marked on the Aros when the photocopy was made. The word *Ford* was put in after, or at the same time as, *Fords of Aros* was entered on the photocopy.
7 The name *Iant Iaur* was adopted from this text in *The Silmarillion*, both on the map and in a mention of 'the stone bridge of Iant Iaur' in Chapter 14, *Of Beleriand and its Realms*, p. 121 (for the original passage see p. 194).
8 The falls in Gelion below Sarn Athrad have not been referred to before, and indeed in QS Chapter 9 *Of Beleriand and its Realms* (V.262–3, §113; *The Silmarillion* p. 122) their existence is denied: 'Gelion had neither fall nor rapids throughout his course'.
9 On another page the following names are proposed as replacements for *Sarn Athrad*: '*Athrad i-Nogoth* [> *Negyth*] or *Athrad Dhaer*, "Ford of the Dwarves" or "Great Ford"'.
10 The fact that the note on the primary map (p. 191) saying that the names *Celon* and *Gelion* need to be changed bears (like the

addition of *Dor-na-Daerachas*, p. 187, §30) the number '71', clearly meaning the year 1971, suggests that all the late work on *Maeglin* belongs to that year. My father died two years later.

IV
OF THE ENTS AND THE EAGLES

This brief text belongs to the late, or last, period of my father's work, and must be dated at the earliest to 1958-9, but may well be later than that. The original draft is extant, a manuscript on two sides of a single sheet, written at great speed with very little correction in a script that is just legible. It is titled *Anaxartamel*.

This was followed by a text made on my father's later typewriter (see X.300) that expanded the first draft, but from which scarcely anything of any significance in that draft was excluded. It bears no title. In the published *Silmarillion* it was used to form the second part of Chapter 2 *Of Aulë and Yavanna*, pp. 44-6, beginning at the words 'Now when Aulë laboured in the making of the Dwarves ...' This was of course a purely editorial combination.

The published text followed the typescript with very little deviation, except in the matter of 'thou' and 'you' forms, about which my father was initially uncertain, as he was also in the text concerning Aulë and the Dwarves which forms the first part of the chapter in the published *Silmarillion* (see p. 210). In the manuscript draft he used 'you' throughout; in the typescript he used both 'you' and 'thy, hast' in the opening paragraphs, but then 'you, your' exclusively, subsequently correcting the inconsistencies. As in the first part of the chapter 'thou, thee, thy' forms were adopted in the published work.

There are two amanuensis typescripts, independent of each other, taken from the typescript after all corrections had been made. They have no textual value, except that on one of them my father pencilled the title *Of the Ents and the Eagles*, and on the other the title *Anaxartaron Onyalië*.

NOTES

In these notes, which are largely confined to differences of reading, the original draft is called A, the typescript B, and the published text S.

When Yavanna went to Manwë (p. 45) 'she did not betray the counsel of Aulë': the meaning of this is that Yavanna did not reveal anything to Manwë of the making of the Dwarves; in the first part of the chapter (p. 43) 'fearing that the other Valar might blame his work, he wrought in secret', and the intervention of Ilúvatar (who 'knew what was done') was directly to Aulë. The word *betray* in S is an editorial alteration of *bewray* in A and B.

'But the *kelvar* can flee or defend themselves, whereas the *olvar* that grow cannot' (p. 45): in B there is a marginal note against *kelvar*, 'animals, all living things that move', which was omitted in S. In A these words were not used, but a blank space was left where *kelvar* stands in B. Immediately following this, A has: 'Long in the growing, swift in the felling, and unless they pay toll with fruit upon the bough little mourned at the ending, as even among the Valar I have seen'; in B the last phrase became 'as I have seen even among the Maiar in Middle-earth', but this was at once rejected. The final text of the passage is as in S.

In Yavanna's following words beginning 'I lifted up the branches of great trees...' B has 'and some sang to Eru amid the wind and the rain and the glitter of the Sun'; the last words were omitted in S on account of the implication that the Sun existed from the beginning of Arda.

In the passage describing Manwë's experience of the renewal of the Vision of the Ainur (p. 46; entirely lacking in A) the text of B as typed read: 'but it was not now remote, for he was himself in the midst, and yet he saw that all was upheld by the hand of Eru and that too was within', subsequently changed to the reading of S (in which *Eru* > *Ilúvatar*).

In the words of Eru recounted by Manwë to Yavanna on Ezellohar the sentence 'For a time: while the Firstborn are in their power, and while the Secondborn are young' was bracketed for exclusion in B, but was retained in S.

In Manwë's last speech, 'In the mountains the Eagles shall house, and hear the voices of those who call upon us' was first written in B: '... and hear the voices of those who call upon me, and of those who gainsay me.'

At the end of a draft letter dated September 1963, of which a passage is cited on p. 353, my father added in a very rough note (given in *Letters* p. 335):

No one knew whence they (Ents) came or first appeared. The High Elves said that the Valar did not mention them in the 'Music'. But some (Galadriel) were [of the] opinion that when Yavanna discovered the mercy of Eru to Aulë in the matter of the Dwarves, she besought Eru (through Manwë) asking him to give life to things made of living things not stone, and that the Ents were either souls sent to inhabit trees, or else that slowly took the likeness of trees owing to their inborn love of trees.

With the words 'the Ents were either souls sent to inhabit trees' cf. the words of Eru in the text (p. 46): 'When the Children awake, then the thought of Yavanna will awake also, and it will summon spirits from afar, and they will go among the *kelvar* and the *olvar*, and some will dwell therein ...' It seems likely enough that the note on the draft letter and the writing of *Anaxartaron Onyalië* belong to much the same time.

V
THE TALE OF YEARS

The Tale of Years was an evolving work that accompanied successive stages in the development of the *Annals*. I have given it no place hitherto in *The History of Middle-earth* (but see X.49), because its value to the narrative of the Elder Days is very small until towards the end of the later (post-*Lord of the Rings*) version, when it becomes a document of importance; but here some very brief account of it must be given.

The earliest form is a manuscript with this title that sets out in very concise form the major events of the Elder Days. The dates throughout are in all but perfect accord with those given in the pre-*Lord of the Rings* texts 'The Later Annals of Valinor' and 'The Later Annals of Beleriand' (AV 2 and AB 2). Since this *Tale of Years* was obviously written as an accompaniment to and at the same time as those versions of the *Annals*, adding nothing to them, I did not include it in Volume V.

Much later a new version of *The Tale of Years* was made, and this alone will concern us here. It very clearly belongs with the major work on the *Annals* carried out in 1951(–2), issuing in the last versions, the *Annals of Aman* and the *Grey Annals*. My father subsequently made a typescript text of it, but this obviously belongs to the same period.

The manuscript of this version as originally written was a very good clear text, but it was heavily corrected, interpolated, and rewritten in many stages; and since it was my father's working chronology during that period the dates, more especially in the first or Valinórean part, were changed so often, with bewildering movements back and forth, as to make the evolution of the chronology extremely difficult to understand. The important point, so far as the Valinórean part is concerned, is that the dates in the manuscript of *The Tale of Years* as originally written were essentially the same as those in the *Annals of Aman* as originally written; while modification to that chronology went together step by step in the two texts. In the case of AAm I noted (X.47–8) that with so many alterations to the dates it was impracticable to do more than give the final chronology, and in the case of *The Tale of Years* the evolution is even more complex. In the result, the latter work is of very little independent value in this part; there are however a small number of matters that should be recorded.

In the manuscript as it was originally written the Elder Days began with the Awakening of the Elves: 'Here begin the Elder Days, or the First Age of the Children of Ilúvatar'; but 'the Elder Days' was struck out and does not appear in the typescript. Further on in *The Tale of Years* there is recorded a difference in application of the term 'Elder Days' in respect of their ending (a difference not, to my knowledge, found elsewhere): after the entry for V.Y.1500 'Fingolfin and Inglor cross the Straits of Ice' (this being the date in the *Grey Annals*, p. 29) it is said in the manuscript:

> Here end the Elder Days with the new reckoning of time, according to some. But most lore-masters give that name also to the years of the war with Morgoth until his overthrow and casting forth.
> So far did Quennar Onótimo compile this count and compute the years.
> Here follows the continuation which Pengoloð made in Eressëa.

In the typescript text this was retained, but with this difference: 'Here end the Elder Days, with the new reckoning of Time, according to the Lore-masters of Valinor. But the Lore-masters of the Noldor give that name also to the years of the war with Morgoth ...'

Quennar Onótimo appears in the *Annals of Aman* (see X.49), where he is cited as the source for the passage on the reckoning of time. This passage was marked for transference to *The Tale of Years*, and appears in manuscript pages (one of which is reproduced as the frontispiece to Vol.X, *Morgoth's Ring*) of a new opening of the work written in forms so splendid that it is not surprising that it did not proceed very far.

The authorship of the *Annals* underwent many changes. In the earliest *Annals of Valinor* (AV 1, IV.263) Pengolod is named as the author, and also of the *Annals of Beleriand* (AB 1), but the conception soon entered that Rúmil was the author of the first part of AV and that the work was only completed by Pengolod: in AV 2 Rúmil's part ends with the return to Valinor of those Noldor, led by Finrod (Finarfin), who did not continue the northward journey after the Doom of Mandos (see V.116, 123). In the first form of the opening of the *Annals of Aman* (X.48) it is said that they 'were written by Quennar i Onótimo, who learned much, and borrowed much also, from Rúmil; but they were enlarged by Pengoloð'. In the second version of the opening, however, Rúmil alone is named: 'Here begin the Annals of Aman, which Rúmil made'. In the fine manuscript pages of the opening of *The Tale of Years* referred to above there is no ascription of authorship (apart from the naming of Quennar Onótimo as the author of the passage on the reckoning of time).

A few points of content in this part remain to be mentioned. In the entry for 1125 (cf. X.83) the manuscript reads: 'The foremost of the Eldar reach Beleriand. They are filled with a great fear of the Sea and for long refuse to go further. Oromë departs to Valinor to seek counsel.' This was not emended, but in the typescript this entry appears in its place: 'The foremost of the Eldar reach the coastlands of Middle-earth and that country which was after named Eglador.

Thereof Beleriand was the larger part.' This is apparently to be related to one of the entries *Eglador* added to the map: see p. 186, §14; but the concluding phrase is mysterious.

In this connection, the entry for the year 1150 reads thus in the manuscript: 'The Teleri of Olwë's host at length also depart over Sea. The friends of Elwë remain behind: these are the Eglath, the Forsaken, or the Sindar (the Grey-elves).' The form *Eglath* is found in the annal for this year in AAm (X.85); but on the manuscript of *The Tale of Years* it was emended subsequently to *Eglim*, while in the typescript the form is *Eglir*: it seems that neither of these occur elsewhere (see pp. 365, 379).

Lastly, the entry for 1497 begins with the words 'Morgoth from a new stronghold at Angband assails the Grey-elves of Beleriand.' At this stage the story was still that Angband was built on the ruins of Utumno (see GA §35 and commentary, pp. 15, 111). My father pencilled on the typescript (referring to the interval since Morgoth's return from Valinor in 1495): 'Too small a time for Morgoth to build Angband', and also 'Time too small, should be 10 at least or 20 Valian Years'. This would have required substantial modification of the chronology; and it seems conceivable that this consideration was a factor in the emergence of the later story that Utumno and Angband were distinct fortresses in different regions, both built by Morgoth in ancient days (X.156, §12).

Of the latter or Beleriandic part of *The Tale of Years* there is little to say until the last entries are reached. The chronology agrees closely with that of the *Grey Annals*, including the revised stories of the origins of Gondolin and of Eöl, and the brief entries (agreeing with GA in such names as *Galion* for *Galdor* and *Glindûr* for *Maeglin*) add nothing to the major text. There is in fact only one point that need be noticed: in the entry for 495 my father added to the manuscript 'Tuor leaves Dorlómin, dwells a year at Falasquil.' The last five words were subsequently struck out. *Falasquil* was the name of the cove in the sea-coast where Tuor dwelt for a while in the tale of *The Fall of Gondolin* (II.152); and it was written also onto the map (see p. 181, §5). It seems quite likely that both these additions were made at the time when my father was writing the later *Tale of Tuor*, and had been rereading the old tale (as he clearly did, II.203); but *Falasquil* does not appear in the later *Tuor*.

Subsequent very cursory emendation of the typescript brought in the radically changed legend of the Coming of the Edain, revision of names to later forms, and additions to the story of Túrin.

But from the point where the *Grey Annals* were abandoned *The Tale of Years* becomes a major source for the end of the Elder Days, and indeed in almost all respects the only source deriving from the time following the completion of *The Lord of the Rings*, woefully inadequate as it is. As the manuscript was originally made (in which condition I will distinguish it as 'A') the entries from 500 to the end, very brief, followed the first (pre-*Lord of the Rings*) version of *The Tale of Years* (see p. 342) closely: my father clearly had that in front of him, and did no more than make a fair copy with fuller entries, introducing virtually no new matter or dates not found in AB 2 (V.141–4). It will make things clearer, however, to give the text of the entries for those years as they were first written.

500 Birth of Eärendil in Gondolin.
501 Making of the Naugla-mír. Thingol quarrels with the Dwarves.
502 The Dwarves invade Doriath. Thingol is slain and his realm ended. Melian returns to Valinor. Beren destroys the Dwarf-host at Rath-lóriel.
506 The Second Kin-slaying.
507 The Fall of Gondolin. Death of King Turgon.
508 The gathering of the remnants of the Elves at the Mouths of Sirion is begun.
524 Tuor and Idril depart over Sea.
525 The voyages of Eärendil begun.
529 The Third and Last Kin-slaying.
533 Eärendil comes to Valinor.
540 The last free Elves and remnants of the Fathers of Men are driven out of Beleriand and take refuge in the Isle of Balar.
547 The host of the Valar comes up out of the West. Fionwë son of Manwë lands in Beleriand with great power.
550–597 The last war of the Elder Days, and the Great Battle, is begun. In this war Beleriand is broken and destroyed. Morgoth is at last utterly overcome, and Angband is unroofed and unmade. Morgoth is bound, and the last two Silmarils are regained.
597 Maidros and Maglor, last surviving sons of Fëanor, seize the Silmarils. Maidros perishes. The Silmarils are lost in fire and sea.
600 The Elves and the Fathers of Men depart from Middle-earth and pass over Sea.
Here ends the First Age of the Children of Ilúvatar.

The only points of any significance in which this differs from what was said in AB 2 or the original version of *The Tale of Years* that accompanied it are the additions in the entry 540 of the statement that when 'the last free Elves' took refuge in the Isle of Balar they were accompanied by 'remnants of the Fathers of Men', and in the entry 600 that the Fathers of Men departed from Middle-earth with the Elves and passed over the Sea.

In the next stage, which I will call 'B', many corrections and interpolations and alterations of date were made to A; I give here the text in this form, so far as is necessary.

501 Return of Húrin.
502 After seven years' service Tuor weds Idril of Gondolin.
     Making of the Naugla-mír. Thingol quarrels with the Dwarves.
503 Birth of Eärendil in Gondolin.
     The Dwarves invade Doriath. Thingol is slain and his realm ended. Melian takes Nauglamír to Beren and Lúthien and then returns to Valinor. Celegorm and Curufin destroy the Dwarf-host at Sarn-athrad in Rath-lóriel; and are wroth to find the Silmaril not there. Dior goes to Doriath.
505 (Spring) Second death of Beren, and Lúthien dies also. Dior Thingol's heir wears Silmaril [*struck out*: and returns to Doriath].
509 (Spring) Second Kinslaying. Last warning of Ulmo to Gondolin.
510 The fall of Gondolin at Midsummer. Death of King Turgon.
511 The gathering of the remnants of the Elves at the Mouths of Sirion is begun.

In the remaining entries some of the dates were altered but very few changes were made to the content; the text of A need not therefore be repeated.

533 The date of Eärendil's coming to Valinor was changed several times, apparently > 536 > 540 > 542.
547 The coming of the host of the Valar was moved to 545.
550–597 The dates of 'the last war of the Elder Days' were changed to 545–587, and after the last words of the original entry the following was added: 'Ancalagon is cast down by Eärendil and all save two of the Dragons are destroyed.'
597 This entry was changed to 587.
600 This final entry was changed to 590, and the following was added to it: 'Morgoth is thrust from Arda into the Outer Dark.'

'Here ends the First Age of the Children of Ilúvatar' was changed to: 'Here end the Elder Days with the passing of Melkor, according to the reckoning of most lore-masters; here ends also the First Age ...'

The hastily made alterations and additions to the entry 503 (502 in A) introduced major new turns into the story as it had been told in all the versions: the tale of *The Nauglafring* (II.238), the *Sketch of the Mythology* (IV.33), the *Quenta* (IV.134), and AB 2 (V.141). There it was Beren, after his return from the dead, who with his host of Elves ambushed the Dwarves at Sarn-athrad, and took from them the Nauglamír in which was set the Silmaril; now it becomes Celegorm and Curufin who fought the battle at Sarn-athrad – but the Silmaril was not there, because Melian had taken it from Menegroth to Beren and Lúthien in Ossiriand. In the old tale, Gwendelin (Melian), coming to the Land of the Dead that Live after the battle, was wrathful when she saw Lúthien wearing the Necklace of the Dwarves, since it was made of accursed gold, and the Silmaril itself was unhallowed from its having been set in Morgoth's crown; while in the *Sketch* (probably) and in the *Quenta* (explicitly) it was Melian who told Beren of the approach of the Dwarves coming from Doriath and enabled the ambush to be prepared (her warning afterwards, when the Necklace of the Dwarves had been recovered, against the Silmaril being retained).

The entrance of Celegorm and Curufin into the story seems to have arisen in the act of emending the text; for my father first added to the original entry ('Beren destroys the Dwarf-host at Rath-lóriel') the words 'and is wounded in battle', referring to Beren (cf. the *Tale*, II.237: 'Beren got many hurts'). He then at once changed 'Beren destroys' to 'Celegorm and Curufin destroy' and 'is wounded in battle' to 'are wroth to find the Silmaril not there'.

In the original entry in A '*at* Rath-lóriel' was just a slip for 'in'; but the replacement 'at Sarn-athrad in Rath-lóriel' is strange, for Sarn-athrad was not a ford over that river (Ascar) but over Gelion, and so remained in the latest writing, though the name was changed (see p. 335).

In 505, the striking out of Dior's return to Doriath preceded its inclusion under 503. There has never been any mention of a further warning of Ulmo (509) since the coming of Tuor to Gondolin. On the addition in 545–587 concerning Ancalagon see V.329, §18; and with the reference to the end of the Elder Days 'according to the reckoning of most lore-masters' cf. p. 343.

The third stage was the striking out of the whole manuscript from the year 400 almost to the end, and its replacement by a new version ('C'), which I give here for the same period, from the return of Húrin from Angband: this is a clear text with some later changes to the dates (changes which largely return the dates to those in B).

501 Return of Húrin from captivity. He goes to Nargothrond and seizes the treasure of Glaurung.

502 Making of the Nauglamír. Thingol quarrels with the Dwarves.

503 The Dwarves of Belegost and Nogrod invade Doriath. Thingol is slain, and his realm ended. The Dwarves carry off the Dragon-gold, but Melian escaped and carried off the Nauglamír and the Silmaril, and brought it to Beren and Lúthien. Then she returned to Valinor; but Lúthien wore the

Silmaril. Now Curufin and Celegorm hearing of the sack of Menegroth ambushed the Dwarves at the fords of Ascar and defeated them; but the Dwarves cast the gold into the river, which was after named Rathlóriel. Great was the chagrin of the Sons of Fëanor to discover that the Silmaril was not with the Dwarves; but they dared not assail Lúthien.

Dior goes to Doriath and endeavours to reestablish the realm.

504 [> 502] Tuor wedded Idril Celebrindal Turgon's daughter of Gondolin.

505 [> 503] Birth of Earendil Half-elven in Gondolin (Spring). Here a messenger brought the Silmaril by night to Dior in Doriath, and he wore it; and by its power Doriath revived for a while. But it is believed that in this year Lúthien and Beren passed away, for they were never heard of again on earth: mayhap the Silmaril hastened their end, for the flame of the beauty of Lúthien as she wore it was too bright for mortal lands.

511 [> 509] The Second Kinslaying. The Sons of Fëanor assail[ed] Dior, and he was slain; slain also were Celegorm and Curufin and Cranthir. Eldún and Elrún sons of Dior were left in the woods to starve. Elwing escaped and came with the Silmaril to the Mouths of Sirion. Ulmo sends a last warning to Gondolin, which now alone is left; but Turgon will have no alliance with any after the kinslaying of Doriath. Maeglin Eöl's son, sister-son of Turgon, was taken in the hills, and betrayed Gondolin to Morgoth.

512 [> 510] The Fall of Gondolin. Death of King Turgon.

513 [> 511] Tuor and Idril bring Earendil and the remnant of Gondolin to the Mouths of Sirion.

527 [> 530] Earendil weds Elwing. Unquiet of Ulmo comes upon Tuor. Tuor and Idril depart over Sea, and are heard of no more on earth.

528 [> 530 > 534] Voyages of Earendil begin.

[*Added entry:*] 528 [> 532] Elros and Elrond twin sons of Earendil born.

532 [> 534 > 538] The Third and Last Kinslaying. The Havens of Sirion destroyed and Elros and Elrond sons of Earendel taken captive, but are fostered with care by Maidros. Elwing carries away the Silmaril, and comes to Earendel [> Earendil] in the likeness of a bird.

536 [> 540 > 542] Earendil comes to Valinor.

Here the replacement text C comes to an end. In the entries 400–499 in C (not given here) this text is so close in every date and detail of narrative to the *Grey Annals* as to be scarcely an independent document; and *The Tale of Years* was beginning to turn in on itself, so to speak, and to become 'Annals' again. In the entries given above, where we reach narrative not treated in GA and where AB 2 is otherwise the latest source, it is much to be regretted that my father did not allow this tendency even fuller scope, and did not extend into a more substantial narrative of Celegorm and Curufin at Sarn Athrad, the revival of Doriath, and the Second Kinslaying.

I add a few notes on particular points.

503 The ford at which the Dwarves were ambushed, not now itself named, is still over Ascar, not Gelion (see p. 347). The statement that the Dwarves 'cast the gold into the river' is at variance with the story told in the *Sketch* and the *Quenta* (where this was done by Beren and the Green-elves), and was perhaps a conscious return to the tale of *The Nauglafring* (II.237), in which the gold fell into the river with the bodies of the Dwarves who bore it, or else was cast into the water by Dwarves seeking to reach the banks.

505 With the changed dating of this entry the whole narrative of the invasion of Doriath, the battle at the ford, the coming of Dior to Doriath, the deaths of Beren and Lúthien, and the bringing of the Silmaril to Dior, is comprised within the single year 503. – The brief revival of Doriath under Dior has not before been associated with the Silmaril; cf. what is said of its presence at the Havens of Sirion (pp. 351, 354). On the probable association of the Silmaril with the deaths of Beren and Lúthien (though of an entirely different nature from that suggested here) see IV.63, 190.

511 On the fate of Dior's sons cf. AB 2 (V.142), where it is told that they 'were taken captive by the evil men of Maidros' following, and they were left to starve in the woods; but Maidros lamented the cruel deed, and sought unavailingly for them.' – It seems possible that 'Turgon will have no alliance with any' was intended to be 'no alliance with any son of Fëanor'; cf. the *Quenta* (IV.140): 'Tidings Turgon heard of Thorndor concerning the slaying of Dior, Thingol's heir, and thereafter he shut his ear to word of the woes without; and he vowed to march never at the side of any son of Fëanor.'

528 (added entry) On the statement that Elros and Elrond were twins see V.152. It is stated in *The Line of Elros* (*Unfinished Tales* p. 218) that Elros was born 58 years before the Second Age began: this agrees with the changed date here (532) and the end of the First Age in 590 (p. 346).

Finally, we come to stage 'D', the typescript of *The Tale of Years*; but before turning to the entries beginning with the return of Húrin there are two pencilled entries on the typescript at a slightly earlier point which must be noticed:

497 Dior weds   of the Green-elves > Dior weds Nimloth.
500 Birth of the twin sons of Dior, Elrún and Eldún.

In connection with the first of these, there is an isolated note (it was written in fact on the back of the single page concerning the Dragon-helm of Dorlómin referred to on pp. 140, 143):

> Dior born (in Tol Galen?) c.470. He appears in Doriath after its ruin, and is welcomed by Melian with his wife Elulin of Ossiriand.

On this note see p. 353, year 504. The fourth letter of *Elulin* is not perfectly certain. – In addition, the name of Dior's wife is also given as *Lindis*: see pp. 351, 353.

The name *Nimloth* was adopted in the published *Silmarillion* (see p. 234, where she is said to be 'kinswoman of Celeborn') on account of its appearance in the series of Elvish genealogies which can be dated to December 1959 (p. 229). This table gives the descendants of Elwë (Thingol) and of his younger brother Elmo, of whom it is said that he was 'beloved of Elwë with whom he remained.' On one side of the table (descent from Elwë) the wife of Dior Eluchil (Thingol's heir) is Nimloth 'sister of Celeborn'. Similarly on the other side, Elmo's son is Galaðon, and Galaðon has two sons, Galathil and Celeborn 'prince of Doriath', and a daughter Nimloth, wife of Dior Eluchil. But on the same table Nimloth wife of Dior also appears as the daughter of Galathil (thus in the first case she was the second cousin of Dior, and in the latter the third cousin of Elwing). It is clear from rough pencillings on this page that my father was uncertain about this, and it looks as if Nimloth as niece of Celeborn was his second thought. I referred to this genealogy in *Unfinished Tales*, p. 233, but did not mention the alternative placing of Nimloth as Celeborn's sister.

On the second of these late additions to the typescript, the birth of Eldún and Elrún in the year 500, see pp. 257 and 300, note 16.

I give now the text of the typescript of *The Tale of Years* in its concluding entries. At the end the typescript becomes manuscript, and it is convenient to distinguish the two parts as 'D 1' and 'D 2'.

501   Húrin is released from captivity. He goes to Nargothrond and seizes the treasure of Glaurung. He takes the treasure to Menegroth and casts it at the feet of Thingol.

502   The Nauglamír is wrought of the treasure of Glaurung, and the Silmaril is hung thereon. Thingol quarrels with the Dwarves who had wrought for him the Necklace.

503   The Dwarves of Belegost and Nogrod invade Doriath. King Elu Thingol is slain and his realm ended. Melian escapes and carries away the Nauglamír and the Silmaril, and brings them to Beren and Lúthien. She then forsook Middle-earth and returned to Valinor.

   Curufin and Celegorm, hearing of the sack of Menegroth, ambushed the Dwarves at the Fords of Ascar as they sought to carry off the Dragon-gold to the mountains. The Dwarves were defeated with great loss, but they cast the gold into the river, which was therefore after named Rathlóriel. Great was the anger of the sons of Fëanor to discover that the Silmaril was not with the Dwarves; but they dared not to assail Lúthien. Dior goes to Doriath and endeavours to recover the realm of Thingol.

In this year, or according to others in the year before, Tuor wedded Idril Celebrindal Turgon's daughter of Gondolin; and in the spring of the year after was born in Gondolin Eärendil Halfelven. [*This paragraph was struck out later with the words* Must be placed in 502.]

In the autumn of this year a messenger brought by night the Silmaril to Dior in Doriath.

Here the typewritten text D 1 ends abruptly near the head of a page, but is continued in very rough manuscript for some distance (D 2), though not so far as the end of version C (which itself did not go by any means so far as B).

503 Elwing the White daughter of Dior born in Ossiriand.
504 Dior returns to Doriath, and with the power of the Silmaril restores it; but Melian departed to Valinor. Dior now publicly wore the Nauglamír and the Jewel.
505 The sons of Fëanor hearing news of the Silmaril that it is in Doriath hold council. Maidros restrains his brethren, but a message is sent to Dior demanding the Jewel. Dior returns no answer.
506 Celegorn inflames the brethren, and they prepare an assault on Doriath. They come up at unawares in winter.
506–507 At Yule Dior fought the sons of Fëanor on the east marches of Doriath, and was slain. There fell also Celegorn (by Dior's hand) and Curufin and Cranthir. The cruel servants of Celegorn seize Dior's sons (Elrún and Eldún) and leave them to starve in the forest. (Nothing certain is known of their fate, but some say that the birds succoured them, and led them to Ossir.) [*In margin:* Maidros repenting seeks unavailingly for the children of Dior.] The Lady Lindis escaped with Elwing, and came hardly to Ossir, with the Necklace and the Jewel. Thence hearing the rumour she fled to the Havens of Sirion.
509 Maeglin captured by spies of Melkor (Sauron?).
510 Midsummer. Assault and sack of Gondolin, owing to treachery of Maeglin who revealed where it lay.
511 Exiles of Gondolin (Tuor, Idril and Eärendil &c.) reach Sirion, which now prospers in the power of the Silmaril.
512 Sons of Fëanor learn of the uprising of the New Havens, and that the Silmaril is there, but Maidros forswears his oath.

525 The Unquiet of Ulmo came upon Tuor and he built a ship *Eärámë*, and departed into the West with Idril (and Voronwë?) and is heard of in no tale since. Eärendil wedded Elwing and became Lord of the men of the Havens.

527 Torment fell upon Maidros and his brethren (Maglor, Damrod and Diriel) because of their unfulfilled oath.

Here the text ends, halfway down the last page. A commentary on it follows.

501 In the original story of Húrin's coming to Menegroth in the *Tale of Turambar* (II.114–15) he with his 'band' or 'host' of 'wild Elves' brought the treasure of Nargothrond in a huge assemblage of sacks and boxes, and they 'cast down that treasury at the king's feet.' So also in the *Sketch of the Mythology* (IV.32) 'Húrin casts the gold at Thingol's feet', without however any indication of how the gold was brought to Doriath; but in the *Quenta* (IV.132) 'Húrin went unto Thingol and sought his aid, and the folk of Thingol bore the treasure to the Thousand Caves' (on the unsatisfactory nature of this version see IV.188). In AB 2 (V.141) 'Húrin brought the gold to Thingol.' See further p. 258.

503 Against 'The Dwarves of Belegost and Nogrod invade Doriath' my father pencilled an X and the single word 'cannot': i.e., the Dwarves *could not* pass the Girdle of Melian. In the old sources the protective magic was defeated by the device of a treacherous Elf (in the *Tale*) or Elves (in the *Sketch* and the *Quenta*); but since the *Quenta* the question had never again come to the surface. In this connection there is a page of rough notes, such as my father often made when meditating on a story at large, concerned with the 'Túrins Saga' (such as 'An account of Beleg and his bow must be put in at the point where Túrin first meets him', and 'Túrin must be *faithless* to Gwindor – for his character is throughout that of a man of good will, kind and loyal, who is carried away by emotion, especially wrath ...'); and among these and written at the same time, though entirely unconnected, is the following:

> Doriath cannot be entered by a hostile army! Somehow it must be contrived that Thingol is lured outside or induced to go to war beyond his borders and is there slain by the Dwarves. Then Melian departs, and the girdle being removed Doriath is ravaged by the Dwarves.

The word 'cannot' may well have been written against the entry for 503 in *The Tale of Years* at the same time as this.

The story that it was Celegorm and Curufin who ambushed the Dwarves at 'the Fords of Ascar' is repeated without change from the previous version C (p. 348). There is a passing reference to a similar story (for in this case it was Caranthir, not Celegorm and Curufin) in the post-*Lord of the Rings* text *Concerning Galadriel and Celeborn*. This was published in *Unfinished Tales* in a 'retold', somewhat selective form for the purposes of that section of the book; and in the passage (p. 235) saying that Celeborn had no love for any Dwarves, and never forgave them for their part in the destruction of Doriath ('passing over Morgoth's part in this (by angering of Húrin), and Thingol's own faults'), my father proposed rather than stated that only the Dwarves of Nogrod took part in the assault, and that they were 'almost entirely destroyed by Caranthir'.

This was not, however, his final view, as it appears. In a letter of 1963 (*Letters* no.247, p. 334) he wrote that he could 'foresee' one event in the Elder Days in which the Ents took a part:

> It was in Ossiriand ... that Beren and Lúthien dwelt for a while after Beren's return from the Dead. Beren did not show himself among mortals again, except once. He intercepted a dwarf-army that had descended from the mountains, sacked the realm of Doriath and slain King Thingol, Lúthien's father, carrying off a great booty, including Thingol's necklace upon which hung the Silmaril. There was a battle about a ford across one of the Seven Rivers of Ossir, and the Silmaril was recovered ... It seems clear that Beren, who had no army, received the aid of the Ents – and that would not make for love between Ents and Dwarves.

In this it is also notable that the old story that the Dwarves took the Nauglamír from Menegroth reappears (see pp. 346–7).

Beneath the *-lóriel* of *Rathlóriel* my father wrote in pencil: *lórion* (*Rathlórion* was the original form of this river-name), but he struck this out and then wrote *mallen*, sc. *Rathmallen* (cf. *Rathmalad* (?) on the map, p. 191, §69).

504 Dior's return to Doriath has been given already under 503 in D 1, the typescript part of the text. – In the B and C versions (pp. 346–7) Melian brought the Silmaril to Beren and Lúthien in Ossiriand and then departed to Valinor, and this is said also in D 1 (p. 350). The present entry in D 2, a year later, repeats that Melian went to Valinor, and the suggestion is that she was in Doriath when Dior came; cf. the note cited on p. 350: 'Dior ... appears in Doriath after its ruin, and is welcomed by Melian'. This seems clearly to have been the story in AB 1 (IV.307) and AB 2 (V.141–2). But it is impossible to be certain of anything with such compressed entries.

506–507 *Ossir*: Ossiriand. – On Maidros' unavailing search for Elrún and Eldún see p. 349, year 511.

The Lady Lindis: Lindis appears elsewhere as the name of Dior's wife (see p. 257). The sentence 'Thence hearing the rumour she fled to the Havens of Sirion' presumably means that Lindis heard the rumour that the survivors of Gondolin had reached the Havens (an event recorded in this text under the year 511).

510 The story that the site of Gondolin was revealed to Morgoth by Maeglin was later changed: see pp. 272–3 and note 30.

511 Cf. the *Quenta* (IV.152): 'for them seemed that in that jewel lay the gift of bliss and healing that had come upon their houses and their ships'; also AB 2 (V.143).

512 That Maidros 'forswore his oath' was stated in AB 2 (V.142); in this and the following entries my father was following that text very closely (indeed D 2 is based upon it throughout).

525 The suggestion that Voronwë was the companion of Tuor and Idril on their voyage into the West is notable. He (Bronweg / Voronwë) was originally Eärendil's fellow-mariner (IV.38, 150). Cf. Tuor's words to him in the later *Tale of Tuor* (*Unfinished Tales* p. 33): 'far from the Shadow your long road shall lead you, and your hope shall return to the Sea.'

It would be interesting to know when this manuscript conclusion D 2 was written. It looks as if it belongs with some of the alterations and additions made to the typescript in earlier entries, particularly those pertaining to the story of Túrin, and in these there are suggestions that they derive from the period of my father's work on the *Narn*. But this is very uncertain; and if it is so, it is the more remarkable that he should have based these entries so closely on the old pre-*Lord of the Rings* annals.

★

*A note on Chapter 22 Of the Ruin of Doriath
in the published Silmarillion*

Apart from a few matters of detail in texts and notes that have not been published, all that my father ever wrote on the subject of the ruin of Doriath has now been set out: from the original story told in the *Tale of Turambar* (II.113–15) and the *Tale of the Nauglafring* (II.221 ff.), through the *Sketch of the Mythology* (IV.32–3, with commentary 61–3) and the *Quenta* (IV.132–4, with commentary 187–91), together with what little can be gleaned from *The Tale of Years* and a very few later references (see especially pp. 352–3). If these materials are compared with the story told in *The Silmarillion* it is seen at once that this latter is fundamentally changed, to a form for which in certain essential features there is no authority whatever in my father's own writings.

There were very evident problems with the old story. Had he ever turned to it again, my father would undoubtedly have found some solution other than that in the *Quenta* to the question, How was the treasure of Nargothrond brought to Doriath? There, the curse that Mîm laid upon the gold at his death 'came upon the possessors in this wise. Each one of Húrin's company died or was slain in quarrels upon the road; but Húrin went unto Thingol and sought his aid, and the

THE TALE OF YEARS

folk of Thingol bore the treasure to the Thousand Caves.' As I said in IV.188, 'it ruins the gesture, if Húrin must get the king himself to send for the gold with which he is *then* to be humiliated'. It seems to me most likely (but this is mere speculation) that my father would have reintroduced the outlaws from the old *Tales* (II.113–15, 222–3) as the bearers of the treasure (though not the fierce battle between them and the Elves of the Thousand Caves): in the scrappy writings at the end of *The Wanderings of Húrin* Asgon and his companions reappear after the disaster in Brethil and go with Húrin to Nargothrond (pp. 306–7).

How he would have treated Thingol's behaviour towards the Dwarves is impossible to say. That story was only once told fully, in the *Tale of the Nauglafring*, in which the conduct of Tinwelint (precursor of Thingol) was wholly at variance with the later conception of the king (see II.245–6). In the *Sketch* no more is said of the matter than that the Dwarves were 'driven away without payment', while in the *Quenta* 'Thingol ... scanted his promised reward for their labour; and bitter words grew between them, and there was battle in Thingol's halls'. There seems to be no clue or hint in later writing (in *The Tale of Years* the same bare phrase is used in all the versions: 'Thingol quarrels with the Dwarves'), unless one is seen in the words quoted from *Concerning Galadriel and Celeborn* on p. 353: Celeborn in his view of the destruction of Doriath ignored Morgoth's part in it 'and Thingol's own faults'.

In *The Tale of Years* my father seems not to have considered the problem of the passage of the Dwarvish host into Doriath despite the Girdle of Melian, but in writing the word 'cannot' against the D version (p. 352) he showed that he regarded the story he had outlined as impossible, for that reason. In another place he sketched a possible solution *(ibid.)*: 'Somehow it must be contrived that Thingol is lured outside or induced to go to war beyond his borders and is there slain by the Dwarves. Then Melian departs, and the girdle being removed Doriath is ravaged by the Dwarves.'

In the story that appears in *The Silmarillion* the outlaws who went with Húrin to Nargothrond were removed, as also was the curse of Mîm; and the only treasure that Húrin took from Nargothrond was the Nauglamír – which was here supposed to have been made by Dwarves for Finrod Felagund, and to have been the most prized by him of all the hoard of Nargothrond. Húrin was represented as being at last freed from the delusions inspired by Morgoth in his encounter with Melian in Menegroth. The Dwarves who set the Silmaril in the Nauglamír were already in Menegroth engaged on other works, and it was they who slew Thingol; at that time Melian's power was withdrawn from Neldoreth and Region, and she vanished out of Middle-earth, leaving Doriath unprotected. The ambush and destruction of the Dwarves at Sarn Athrad was given again to Beren and the Green

Elves (following my father's letter of 1963 quoted on p. 353, where however he said that 'Beren had no army'), and from the same source the Ents, 'Shepherds of the Trees', were introduced.

This story was not lightly or easily conceived, but was the outcome of long experimentation among alternative conceptions. In this work Guy Kay took a major part, and the chapter that I finally wrote owes much to my discussions with him. It is, and was, obvious that a step was being taken of a different order from any other 'manipulation' of my father's own writing in the course of the book: even in the case of the story of The Fall of Gondolin, to which my father had never returned, something could be contrived without introducing radical changes in the narrative. It seemed at that time that there were elements inherent in the story of the Ruin of Doriath as it stood that were radically incompatible with 'The Silmarillion' as projected, and that there was here an inescapable choice: either to abandon that conception, or else to alter the story. I think now that this was a mistaken view, and that the undoubted difficulties could have been, and should have been, surmounted without so far overstepping the bounds of the editorial function.

PART FOUR

QUENDI
AND
ELDAR

QUENDI AND ELDAR

The title *Quendi and Eldar* clearly belongs properly to the long essay that is printed here, though my father used it also to include two other much briefer works, obviously written at much the same time; one of these, on the origin of the Orcs, was published in *Morgoth's Ring* (see X.415, where a more detailed account is given). *Quendi and Eldar* is extant in a typescript with carbon copy that can be fairly certainly dated to the years 1959–60 *(ibid.)*; and both copies are preceded by a manuscript page that in addition to the following preamble gives a parallel title *Essekenta Eldarinwa*.

> Enquiry into the origins of the Elvish names for Elves and their varieties clans and divisions: with Appendices on their names for the other Incarnates: Men, Dwarves, and Orcs; and on their analysis of their own language, Quenya: with a note on the 'Language of the Valar'.

My father corrected the two copies carefully and in precisely the same ways (except for a few later pencilled alterations). The text printed here follows the original very closely, apart from very minor changes made for consistency or clarity, the omission of a passage of extremely complex phonology, and a reorganisation of the text in respect of the notes. As often elsewhere in his later writings, my father interrupted his main text with notes, some of them long; and these I have numbered and collected at the end, distinguishing them from my own numbered notes by referring to them in the body of the text as *Note 1*, *Note 2*, &c., with a reference to the page on which they are found. Also, and more drastically, I have omitted one substantial section from Appendix D (see p. 396). This was done primarily for reasons of space, but the passage in question is a somewhat abstract account of the phonological theories of earlier linguistic Loremasters and the contributions of Fëanor, relying rather allusively on phonological data that are taken for granted: it stands apart from the content of the work at large (and entered, I suspect, from the movement of my father's train of thought rather than as a planned element in the whole).

Also for reasons of space my commentary is kept to a severe minimum. Abbreviations used are PQ (Primitive Quendian), CE (Common Eldarin), CT (Common Telerin), Q (Quenya), T (Telerin), Ñ (Ñoldorin), S (Sindarin), V (Valarin).

QUENDI AND ELDAR

Origin and Meanings of the Elvish words referring to *Elves* and their varieties. With Appendices on their names for other Incarnates.

    A. The principal linguistic elements concerned.

1. *KWENE
   (a) PQ *kwene 'person' (m. or f.). CE *kwēn (-kwen), pl. *kwenī, 'person' (m. or f.), 'one', '(some)body'; pl. 'persons', '(some) people'.
   (b) PQ and CE *kwende, pl. *kwendī. This form was made from *kwene by primitive fortification of the median n > nd. It was probably at first only used in the plural, in the sense 'people, the people as a whole', sc. embracing all the three original clans.
   (c) *kwendjā adj. 'belonging to the *kwendī, to the people as a whole'.
2. *ELE According to Elvish legend this was a primitive exclamation, 'lo!' 'behold!' made by the Elves when they first saw the stars. Hence:
   (a) CE *el, *ele, *el-ā, 'lo!' 'look!' 'see!'
   (b) CE *ēl, pl. *eli, ēli, 'star'.
   (c) CE *elen, pl. *elenī, 'star', with 'extended base'.
   (d) CE *eldā, an adjectival formation 'connected or concerned with the stars', used as a description of the *kwendī. According to legend this name, and the next, were due to the Vala Oromë. They were thus probably at first only used in the plural, meaning 'star-folk'.
   (e) CE *elenā, an adjectival form made from the extended stem *elen, of the same meaning and use as *eldā.
3. *DELE
   (a) A verbal base *dele, also with suffix *del-ja, 'walk, go, proceed, travel'.
   (b) *edelō, an agental formation of primitive pattern: 'one who goes, traveller, migrant'. A name made at the time of the Separation for those who decided to follow Oromë.
   (c) *awa-delo, *awā-delo, ?*wā-delō. Old compounds with the element *awa 'away' (see below). A name made in Beleriand for those who finally departed from Middle-earth.

4. *HEKE Probably not in origin a verbal base, but an adverbial element 'aside, apart, separate'.

(a) PQ **heke* 'apart, not including'.

(b) PQ and CE verbal derivative, transitive: **hek-tā* 'set aside, cast out, forsake'.

(c) PQ **hekla* 'any thing (or person) put aside from, or left out from, its normal company'. Also in personal form **heklō* 'a waif or outcast'; adjectival forms **heklā* and **hekelā*.

The element *AWA, appearing in 3(c) above, referred to movement away, viewed from the point of view of the thing, person, or place left. As a prefix it had probably already developed in CE the form *au-. The form *awā was originally an independent adverbial form, but appears to have been also used as a prefix (as an intensive form of *awa-, *au-). The form *wā- was probably originally used as a verbal stem, and possibly also in composition with verbal stems.

In the Eldarin languages this stem made contact in form with other elements, distinct in origin and in sense. *ABA 'refuse', 'say nay (in refusal or denial)': this is the source of the CE *abar, pl. *abarī 'a refuser', one who declined to follow Oromë. *WO in forms *wō and *wo- (the latter only as a prefix): this was a dual adverb 'together', referring to the junction of two things, or groups, in a pair or whole. The plural equivalent was *jō, *jōm, and as a prefix *jo, *jom. *HO in forms *hō and *ho: this was an adverb 'from, coming from', the point of view being outside the thing referred to.

The principal derivatives in form (their use is discussed below) of the CE words given above were as follows:

*KWEN

QUENYA 1(a) *quēn*, pl. *queni*; unstressed, as a pronoun or final element in a compound, *quen*.

1(b) *Quendi*. The sg. *quende* (not much used) was made in Quenya from *Quendi*, on the model of other nouns in *-e*, the majority of which formed their plurals in *-i*. There were also two old compounds: *Kalaquendi* 'Light-elves' and *Moriquendi* 'Dark-elves'.

1(c) *Quendya*, which remained in the Vanyarin dialect, but in Ñoldorin became *Quenya*. This was only used with reference to language.

TELERIN 1(a) *pen* as a pronoun, and *-pen* in a few old compounds.

1(b) *Pendi*, plural only. Also in the compounds *Calapendi* and *Moripendi*.

1(c) Not found.

SINDARIN 1(a) *pen*, usually mutated *ben*, as a pronoun. Also *-ben*, *-phen* in a few old compounds.

1(b) Not found. The compounds *Calben* (pl. *Celbin*) and *Morben* (pl. *Moerbin, Morbin*) must certainly have descended from the same source as those mentioned above, but their final element was evidently altered to agree with the compounds of *kwen. The unaltered derivatives would have been *Calbend, *Moerbend; but though final *-nd* eventually became *-n* in Sindarin, this change had not occurred in the early records, and no cases of *-bend* are found. In addition, the form *Morben* (without affection[1] of the *o*) shows either an alteration to **mora-* for *mori-*, after **kala-*, or more probably substitution of S *morn-* from *mornā, the usual S adjectival form.

1(c) Not found.

*EL

QUENYA 2(a) *ela!* imperative exclamation, directing sight to an actually visible object.

2(b) *ēl*, pl. *ēli*, 'star' (poetic word).

2(c) *elen*, pl. *eleni* (occasionally in verse *eldi*), 'star'. The normal word for a star of the actual firmament. The pl. form *eleni*, without syncope, is re-formed after the singular.

2(d) *Elda* only used as a noun, chiefly in the pl. *Eldar*. See also (Quenya) 3(b) below.

2(e) *Elda* as above. As an adjective referring to stars the form used was *elenya*.

TELERIN 2(a) *ela!* as in Quenya.

2(b) *ēl*, pl. *ēli*. The ordinary word for 'star'.

2(c) *elen*, pl. *elni*. An archaic or poetic variant of the preceding.

2(d) *Ella*. An occasional variant of *Ello*, which was the normal form of the word. This shows contact with the products of *edelō: see further under (Telerin) 3.

2(e) Not found. The form would have been *Elna.

SINDARIN 2(a) *elo!* An exclamation of wonder, admiration, delight.

2(b) Not found.

2(c) *êl*, pl. *elin*, class-plural *elenath*. An archaic word for 'star', little used except in verse, apart from the form *elenath* 'all the host of the stars of heaven'.

2(d) *Ell-*, only used in the m. and f. forms *Ellon*, *Elleth*, elf-man, elf-woman; the class-plural *El(d)rim*; and final *-el*, pl. *-il*, in some old compounds: see (Sindarin) 3(b).

2(e) *Elen*, pl. *Elin*, with class-plural *Eledhrim*, Elf, Elves. *dh* is < *n-r* in secondary contact. On usage see further below.

*DEL

QUENYA 3(a) *lelya-* 'go, proceed (in any direction), travel'; past tense *lende*. This form is due to the early change in Q of initial $d > l$. The change was regular in both Vanyarin and Ñoldorin dialects of Quenya. It occurs occasionally also in Telerin languages, though this may be due rather to *d/l* variation in PQ, for which there is some evidence. A notable example being *de/le* as pronominal elements in the 2nd person.

In Q **del-* seems to have become *led, by dissimilation. The past form clearly shows *led, while *lelya* may also be derived from *ledja, since *dj* became *ly* medially in Quenya.

3(b) *Eldo*. An archaic variant of *Elda*, with which it coalesced in form and sense. *Eldo* cannot however be directly descended from *edelō. Its form is probably due to a change *edelo > *eledo*, following the change in the verb. The change of initial $d > l$ was early and may have preceded syncope, and the loss of feeling for the etymological connexions of the word, which finally resulted in the blending of the products of 2 and 3. Unchanged *edelō would by syncope have given *eðlo > *ello (which is not found). See, however, under Sindarin for reasons for supposing that there may have been a variant form *edlō (with loss of *sundóma*):[2] this could have produced a Quenya form *eldo, since transposition of *dl* in primary contact to the favoured sequence *ld* not infrequently occurred in the pre-record period of Quenya.

3(c) *Aurel* < **aw(a)delo*. *Oärel* < *awādelo. In the Vanyarin dialect *Auzel* and *Oäzel*. *Oärel* (*Oäzel*) were the forms commonly used in Q. The plurals took the forms *-eldi*. This shows that the ending *-el* was associated with the noun *Elda*. This was facilitated by a normal development in Q morphology: a word of such a form independently as *eldā, when used as the final element in a compound of early date, was shortened to *elda, pl. *eldī > *eld, *eldī > historic Q -el, -eldi. In addition öar was in actual use in Q as an adverbial form derived from *AWA (see below): a fact which also accounts for the selection of öarel, öazel.

TELERIN 3(a) delia 'go, proceed'. Past tense delle.

3(b) Ello. The usual form, preferred to Ella, from which, however, it did not differ in sense. Both *edelō and *edlō regularly became ello in Telerin.

3(c) Audel, pl. Audelli. This shows the same association with -el, the shortened form in composition of ella, ello, as that seen in Q.

SINDARIN 3(a) Not found.

3(b) Edhel, pl. Edhil. The most used word in Sindarin; but only normally used in these forms. As noted above under (Sindarin) 2(d) the m. and f. forms were Ellon, Elleth; and there was also a class-plural Eldrim, Elrim (ll-r in secondary contact > ldr, later again simplified). As suggested under (Quenya) 3(b), there may have been a variant *edlō, which would regularly give ell- in Sindarin. Since this shorter form would be most likely to appear in compounds and extended forms, it would account for the limitation of Sindarin ell- to such forms as Ellon, Elleth, Eldrim. It would also account for the blending of the products of stems 2 El and 3 Del in Sindarin, as well as in Quenya. The form -el, pl. -il also occurs in some old compounds (especially personal names), where it may be due also to a blending of *elda and *edlo. In later compounds -edhel is used.

3(c) Ódhel, pl. Ódhil; beside later more usual Gódhel, Gódhil. Also a class-plural Ódhellim, Gódhellim. Ódhel is from *aw(a)delo, and the exact equivalent of Q Aurel, T Audel. Gódhel could be derived from *wādelo: S initial *wā- > gwǭ > go. But since it appears later than Ódhel, and after this term had become specially applied to the Exiled Ñoldor, it seems most probable that it took g- from the old clan-name Golodh, pl. Goelydh, which it practically replaced. Golodh was the S equivalent of Q Ñoldo, both from PQ *ñgolodō.

*HEK

QUENYA 4(a) heka! imperative exclamation 'be gone! stand aside!'. Normally only addressed to persons. It often appears in the forms hekat sg. and hekal pl. with reduced pronominal affixes of the 2nd person. Also hequa (? from *hek-wā) adverb and preposition 'leaving aside, not counting, excluding, except'.

4(b) *hehta-*, past tense *hehtane*, 'put aside, leave out, exclude, abandon, forsake'.

4(c) *hekil* and *hekilo* m., *hekile* f.: 'one lost or forsaken by friends, waif, outcast, outlaw'. Also *Hekel*, pl. *Hekeldi*, re-formed to match *Oärel*, especially applied to the Eldar left in Beleriand. Hence *Hekelmar* and *Hekeldamar*, the name in the language of the loremasters of Aman for Beleriand. It was thought of as a long shoreland beside the Sea (cf. *Eglamar* under Sindarin below).

TELERIN 4(a) *heca!* For Q *hequa* the T form is *heco* (? < **hek + au*).

4(b) *hecta-* 'reject, abandon'.

4(c) *hecul, heculo*. Also with special reference to those left in Beleriand, *Hecello*; *Heculbar* or *Hecellubar*, Beleriand.

SINDARIN PQ *h-* only survived in the dialects of Aman. It disappeared without trace in Sindarin. **hek* therefore appears as **ek*, identical in form with PQ **eke* 'sharp point'.

4(a) *ego!* 'be off!' This is from **hek(e) ā:* *ā* the imperative particle, being originally independent and variable in place, survived in S as *ō > o*, though this now always followed the verb stem and had become an inflexion.

4(b) *eitha-*. This is in the main a derivative of PQ **ek-tā*, and means 'prick with a sharp point', 'stab'; but the sense 'treat with scorn, insult' (often with reference to rejection or dismissal) may show the effect of blending with PQ **hek-ta*. To say to anyone *ego!* was indeed the gravest *eithad*.

4(c) *Eglan*, mostly used in the plural *Eglain, Egladhrim*. The name that the Sindar gave to themselves ('the Forsaken') as distinguished from the Elves who left Middle-earth. *Eglan* is < an extended adjectival form **heklanā*. The older shorter form (**hekla* or **heklā*) survives in a few place-names, such as *Eglamar* (cf. *Hekelmar*, etc.), *Eglarest*. These are shown to be old from their formation, with the genitival element preceding: **ekla-mbar, *ekla-rista*.

*AWA

QUENYA *au-* as a verbal prefix: < either **au* or **awa*; as in *au-kiri-* 'cut off'. The point of view was in origin 'away from the speaker or the place of his thought', and this distinction is usually preserved in Q. Thus *aukiri* meant 'cut off, so that a portion is lost or no longer available', but *hókiri* (see below) meant 'cut off a required portion, so as to have it or use it'.

öa, öar. Adverbs: < **awā*; the form *öar* shows addition of the ending *-d* (prehistoric *-da*) indicating motion to or towards a point. The form *awā* appears originally to have been used either of rest or motion, and *öa* can still be so used in Q. This adverbial *öa, öar* was occasionally used as a prefix in compounds of later formation. Though, as has been shown, in *Oäreldi*, the most commonly used, the *r* is in fact of different origin.

The verb *auta-* 'go away, leave (the point of the speaker's thought)' had an old 'strong' past tense *anwe*, only found in archaic language. The most frequently used past and perfect were *väne, avānie*, made from the stem **wā*; together with a past participle form *vanwa*. This last was an old formation (which is also found in Sindarin), and was the most frequently used part of the verb. It developed the meanings 'gone, lost, no longer to be had, vanished, departed, dead, past and over'. With it the forms *väne* and *avānie* were specially associated in use and meaning. In the more purely physical sense 'went away (to another place)' the regular forms (for a *-ta* verb of this class) *öante, öantie* were used. The form perfect *avānie* is regularly developed from **a-wāniiē*, made in the prehistoric period from the older perfect form of this type **awāwiiē*, with intrusion of *n* from the past (the forms of past and perfect became progressively more closely associated in Quenya). The accent remained on the *wā*, since the augment or reduplication in verbal forms was never accented even in the retraction period of Quenya (hence no form **öanie* developed: contrast *öante* < **áwa-n-tē*). The form *vānie* appearing in verse has no augment: probably a phonetic development after a preceding vowel; but such forms are not uncommon in verse.

SINDARIN The only normal derivative is the preposition *o*, the usual word for 'from, of'. None of the forms of the element **awa* are found as a prefix in S, probably because they became like or the same as the products of **wō, *wo* (see next). The form *Ódhel* is isolated (see above, Sindarin 3(c)). As the mutations following the preposition *o* show, it must prehistorically have ended in *-t* or *-d*. Possibly, therefore, it comes from **aud*, with *d* of the same origin as that seen in Q *öar* (see above). Some have thought that it received the addition -*t* (at a period when *au had already become *ǭ* > *o*) by association with *et 'out, out of'. The latter retains its consonant in the form *ed* before vowels, but loses it before consonants, though *es*, *ef*, *eth* are often found before *s*, *f*, *th*. *o*, however, is normally *o* in all positions, though *od* appears occasionally before vowels, especially before *o-*. The influence of *et > *ed* is therefore probably only a late one, and does not account for the mutations.

TELERIN The Telerin forms are closely similar to those of Quenya in form and meaning, though the development *áua > *öa* does not occur, and *v* remains *w* in sound. Thus we have prefix *au-*, adverb *au* or *avad*; verb *auta-* with past participle *vanua*, and associated past and perfect *váne* and *avánie*; and in physical senses *vante*, *avantie*.

*WO

QUENYA This does not remain in Q as an independent word. It is however a frequent prefix in the form *ó-* (usually reduced to *o-* when unstressed), used in words describing the meeting, junction, or union of two things or persons, or of two groups thought of as units. Thus: *o-mentie* (meeting or junction of the directions of two people) as in the familiar greeting between two people, or two companies each going on a path that crosses that of the other: *Elen síla lúmenna omentielvo!*[3] 'A star shines upon the hour of the meeting of our ways.' *(Note 1, p. 407)*

This prefix was normally unstressed in verbs or derivatives of verbs; or generally when the next following syllable was long. When stressed it had the form *ó-*, as in *ónoni* 'twins', beside the adj. *onóna* 'twin-born', also used as a noun 'one of a pair of twins'.

TELERIN use does not materially differ; but in form the *w-* (lost in Quenya before *ō*) is retained: prefix *vō*, *vo-*. *(Note 1, p. 407)*

SINDARIN In the prefix *gwa-*, *go-* 'together, co-, com-'. The dual limitation was no longer made; and *go-* had the senses both of *wo and *jo. *jo, **jom-* disappeared as a living prefix. *gwa-* occurred only in a few S dissyllables, where it was stressed, or in their recognizable derivatives: e.g. *gwanūn* 'a pair of twins', *gwanunig* one of such a pair. These were mostly of ancient formation, and so retained their dual significance. *gwa-* is regularly developed from *wo > *wa >

gwa, when stressed in prehistoric Sindarin. *go-* is from **wo* > *gwo* > *go*, when primitively unstressed; and also from *gwa-* > *go-*, when it became again unstressed. Since PQ **wā* (one of the forms of *AWA) would also have produced *gō-*, *go-*, or *gwa-* if primitively shortened (e.g. before two consonants), while **au* would have produced *o-*, the same as the frequent initially mutated form of *go-* 'together', the prefixal forms of *AWA were lost in Sindarin.

*HO

QUENYA This was evidently an ancient adverbial element, occurring principally as a proclitic or enclitic: proclitic, as a prefix to verb stems; and enclitic, as attached to noun stems (the usual place for the simpler 'prepositional' elements in PQ). Hence Quenya *hō-* (usually so, even when it had become unstressed), as a verb prefix. It meant 'away, from, from among', but the point of view was outside the thing, place, or group in thought, whereas in the derivatives of *AWA the point in thought was the place or thing left. Thus Q *hókiri-* 'cut off', so as to have or use a required portion; whereas *aukiri-* meant 'cut off' and get rid of or lose a portion. *hótuli-* 'come away', so as to leave a place or group and join another in the thought or place of the speaker; whereas *au* could not be used with the stem *tul-* 'come'.

As a noun enclitic *-*hō* became *-ō*, since medial *h* was very early lost without trace in CE. This was the source of the most used 'genitive' inflexion of Quenya. Properly it was used partitively, or to describe the source or origin, not as a 'possessive', or adjectivally to describe qualities; but naturally this 'derivative genitive' (as English *of*) could be used in many circumstances that might have possessive or adjectival implications, though 'possession' was indicated by the adjectival suffix *-va*, or (especially in general descriptions) by a 'loose compound'. Thus 'Orome's horn' was *róma Oroméva* (if it remained in his possession); *Orome róma* would mean 'an Orome horn', sc. one of Orome's horns (if he had more than one); but *róma Oromëo* meant 'a horn coming from Orome', e.g. as a gift, in circumstances where the recipient, showing the gift with pride, might say 'this is Orome's horn'. If he said 'this *was* Orome's horn', he would say *Oroméva*. Similarly *lambe Eldaron* would not be used for 'the language of the Eldar' (unless conceivably in a case where the whole language was adopted by another people), which is expressed either by *Elda-lambe* or *lambe Eldaiva*. *(Note 2, p. 407)*

There remained naturally many cases where either possessive-adjectival or partitive-derivative genitives might be used, and the tendency to prefer the latter, or to use them in place of the former, increased. Thus *alkar Oromëo* or *alkar Oroméva* could be used for 'the splendour of Oromë', though the latter was proper in a description of Oromë as he permanently was, and the former of his splendour as seen at the moment (proceeding from him) or at some point in a narrative. 'The Kings of the Eldar' might be either *i arani Eldaron* or *i arani Eldaive*, though the former would mean if accurately used 'those among the Eldar who were kings' and the latter 'those (kings) in a particular assembly who were Elvish'. In such expressions as 'Elwe, King of the Sindar (people), or Doriath (country)' the derivative form was usual: *Elwe, Aran Sindaron*, or *Aran Lestanóreo*.

TELERIN   The Telerin use of the prefix *ho-* was as in Quenya. The inflexion was *-o*, as in Quenya, but it did not receive *-n* addition in the plural. It was more widely used than in pure Quenya, sc. in most cases where English would employ the inflexion *-s*, or *of*; though the possessive, especially when it concerned a single person or possessor, was expressed without inflexion: either with the possessor placed first (the older usage), or (possibly under the influence of the genitival or adjectival expressions which were placed second) following the possessed. In the latter case, the appropriate possessive suffix ('his, hers, its, their') was usually appended to the noun. So *Olue cava*; or *cava Olue*, usually *cavaria Olue* (sc. 'the house of him, Olwe'); = 'Olwe's house'. The last form was also used in Quenya with proper names, as *köarya Olwe*. Both languages also used the adjectival possessive suffixes in a curious way, attaching them to adjectives attributed to proper names (or names of personal functions, like 'king'): as *Varda Aratarya*, 'Varda the Lofty, Varda in her sublimity'. This was most usual in the vocative: as in *Meletyalda*, or fuller *Aran Meletyalda* (literally 'your mighty' or 'king your mighty'), more or less equivalents of 'Your Majesty'. Cf. Aragorn's farewell: *Arwen vanimalda, namárie!*[4]

SINDARIN   Since initial *h-* disappeared in Sindarin **hō* would have become *ū* and so, clashing with the negative *ū*, naturally did not survive. *ho as a proclitic might have given o; but it does not occur as a verbal prefix, although it possibly contributed to the Sindarin preposition o (see under *Awa, Sindarin) which is used in either 'direction', from or to the point of view of the speaker. Since all final vowels disappeared in Sindarin, it cannot be determined whether or not this language had in the primitive period developed inflexional -ō. Its presence in Telerin of Aman makes its former presence in Sindarin probable. The placing of the genitive noun second in normal Sindarin is also probably derived from inflexional forms. Compounds of which the first element was 'genitival' were evidently in the older period still normal, as is seen in many place- and personal names (such as *Egla-mar*), and was still in more limited use later, especially where the first element was or was regarded as an adjective (as *Mordor* 'Land of Darkness' or 'Dark Land'). But genitival sequences with the possessor or qualifier second in the later period also became fixed compounds: as *Dóriath*, for *Dôr Iâth* 'Land of the Fence'.

*ABA

Though this became a verbal stem, it is probably derived from a primitive negative element, or exclamation, such as *BA 'no!' It did not, however, deny facts, but always expressed concern or will; that is, it expressed *refusal* to do what others might wish or urge, or *prohibition* of some action by others. As a verbal stem it developed the form *aba-* (with connecting vowel *a* in the aorist); as a particle or prefix the forms *aba, *bā, and *abā.

QUENYA In Quenya the verb *ava-* was little used in ordinary language, and revealed that it was not in origin a 'strong' or basic verbal stem by having the 'weak' past form *avane*. In ordinary use it was replaced by the compound *vá-quet* (*váquetin, váquenten*) 'to say no', sc. 'to say I will not', or 'do not', 'to refuse' or 'to forbid'.

As a prefix the form used was usually *ava-*, the force of which can be observed in *avaquétima* 'not to be said, that must not be said', *avanyárima* 'not to be told or related', as contrasted with *úquétima* 'unspeakable', that is, 'impossible to say, put into words, or unpronounceable', *únyárima* 'impossible to recount', sc. because all the facts are not known, or the tale is too long. Compare also *Avamanyar* 'those who did not go to Aman, because they would not' (an equivalent of *Avari*) with *Úamanyar* 'those who did not in the event reach Aman' (an equivalent of *Hekeldi*).

As a particle (the form of this stem most used in ordinary language) the Quenya form was usually *vá!* This was an exclamation or particle expressing the will or wish of the speaker, meaning according to context 'I will not' or 'Do not!' Note that it was not used, even in the first person, in a statement about the speaker's future action, depending on foresight, or a judgement of the force of circumstances. It could sometimes, as seen in *váquet-* (above), be used as a verbal prefix.

A longer form *áva* or *avá* (stressed on the last syllable), which shows combination with the imperative particle **ā*, was commonly used as a negative imperative 'Don't!', either used alone or with an uninflected verbal stem, as *áva kare!* 'Don't do it!' Both *vá* and *áva* sometimes received verbal pronominal affixes of the first singular and first plural exclusive: as *ávan, ván, ványe* 'I won't', *avamme, vamme* 'we won't'.

An old derivative of **aba-* as a quasi-verbal stem was **abaro* > CE **abar*. This was an old agental formation, as seen also in *Teler*, pl. *Teleri*, made with the suffix *-rŏ*, added to *ómataina*.[5] (Other forms of this suffix were *-rō* added to stem, with or without *n*-infixion; and *-rdŏ* > *rd*.) **abar* thus meant 'recusant, one who refuses to act as advised or commanded'. It was specially applied to (or first made to describe?) the section of the Elves who refused to join in the Westward March: Q *Avar*, pl. *Avari*.

TELERIN The Telerin use was closely similar to that of Quenya. The forms were the same, except that Telerin preserved CE *b* distinct from *v* or *w*: hence the prefix was *aba-* (*abapétima* 'not to be said'); the particle *bá*; the exclamation *abá*. The verbal form, however, was in normal use: *aban* 'I refuse, I will not'. In a negative command only the uninflected *abá* was used: *abá care* 'don't do it!'

SINDARIN In Sindarin the following forms are found. *baw!* imperious negative: 'No, no! Don't!' *avo* negative adverb with verbs, as *avo garo!* 'don't do it'; sometimes used as a prefix: *avgaro* (< **aba-kar ā*). This could be personalized in the form *avon* 'I won't', *avam* 'we won't': these were of course not in fact derived from *avo*, which contained the imperative -*o* < **ā*, but from the verb stem **aba*, with inflexions assimilated to the tense stems in -*ā*; but no other parts of the verb survived in use, except the noun *avad* 'refusal, reluctance'. Derived direct from *baw! (*bā)* was the verb *boda-* 'ban, prohibit' *(*bā-ta)*.

(With the uses of this stem, primary meaning 'refuse, be unwilling', to form negative imperatives, cf. Latin *nōlī, nōlīte.*)

B. Meanings and use of the various terms applied to the Elves and their varieties in Quenya, Telerin, and Sindarin.

Quenya

1. *quén*, pl. *queni*, person, individual, man or woman. Chiefly used in the unstressed form *quen*. Mostly found in the singular: 'one, somebody'; in the pl. 'people, they'. Also combined with other elements, as in *aiquen* 'if anybody, whoever', *ilquen* 'everybody'. In a number of old compounds -*quen*, pl. *queni* was combined with noun or adjective stems to denote habitual occupations or functions, or to describe those having some notable (permanent) quality: as -*man* in English (but without distinction of sex) in *horseman, seaman, workman, nobleman*, etc. Q *roquen* 'horseman, rider'; *(Note 3, p. 407) kiryaquen* 'shipman, sailor'; *arquen* 'a noble'. These words belong to everyday speech, and have no special reference to Elves. They were freely applied to other Incarnates, such as Men or Dwarves, when the Eldar became acquainted with them.

2. *Quendi* Elves, of any kind, including the Avari. The sg. *Quende* was naturally less frequently used. As has been seen, the word was made when the Elves as yet knew of no other 'people' than themselves. The sense 'the Elvish people, as a whole', or in the sg. 'an Elf and not some other similar creature', developed first in Aman, where the Elves lived among or in contact with the Valar and Maiar. During the Exile when the Ñoldor became re-associated with their Elvish kin, the Sindar, but met other non-Elvish people, such as Orcs, Dwarves, and Men, it became an even more useful term. But in fact it had ceased in Aman to be a word of everyday use, and remained thereafter mainly used in the special language of 'Lore': histories or tales of old days, or learned writings on peoples and

languages. In ordinary language the Elves of Aman called themselves *Eldar* (or in Telerin *Elloi*): see below.

There also existed two old compounds containing **kwendī*: **kala-kwendī* and **mori-kwendī*, the Light-folk and the Dark-folk. These terms appear to go back to the period before the Separation, or rather to the time of the debate among the Quendi concerning the invitation of the Valar. They were evidently made by the party favourable to Oromë, and referred originally to those who desired the Light of Valinor (where the ambassadors of the Elves reported that there was no darkness), and those who did not wish for a place in which there was no night. But already before the final separation **mori-kwendī* may have referred to the glooms and the clouds dimming the sun and the stars during the War of the Valar and Melkor,[6] so that the term from the beginning had a tinge of scorn, implying that such folk were not averse to the shadows of Melkor upon Middle-earth.

The lineal descendants of these terms survived only in the languages of Aman. The Quenya forms were *Kalaquendi* and *Moriquendi*. The *Kalaquendi* in Quenya applied only to the Elves who actually lived or had lived in Aman; and the *Moriquendi* was applied to all others, whether they had come on the March or not. The latter were regarded as greatly inferior to the *Kalaquendi*, who had experienced the Light of Valinor, and had also acquired far greater knowledge and powers by their association with the Valar and Maiar.

In the period of Exile the Ñoldor modified their use of these terms, which was offensive to the Sindar. *Kalaquendi* went out of use, except in written Ñoldorin lore. *Moriquendi* was now applied to all other Elves, except the Ñoldor and Sindar, that is to Avari or to any kind of Elves that at the time of the coming of the Ñoldor had not long dwelt in Beleriand and were not subjects of Elwë. It was never applied, however, to any but Elvish peoples. The old distinction, when made, was represented by the new terms *Amanyar* 'those of Aman', and *Úamanyar* or *Úmanyar* 'those not of Aman', beside the longer forms *Amaneldi* and *Úmaneldi*.

3. *Quendya*, in the Ñoldorin dialect *Quenya*. This word remained in ordinary use, but it was only used as a noun 'the Quendian language'. *(Note 4, p. 407)* This use of *Quendya* must have arisen in Aman, while *Quendi* still remained in general use. Historically, and in the more accurate use of the

linguistic Loremasters, *Quenya* included the dialect of the Teleri, which though divergent (in some points from days before settlement in Aman, such as **kw > p*), remained generally intelligible to the Vanyar and Ñoldor. But in ordinary use it was applied only to the dialects of the Vanyar and Ñoldor, the differences between which only appeared later, and remained, up to the period just before the Exile, of minor importance.

In the use of the Exiles *Quenya* naturally came to mean the language of the Ñoldor, developed in Aman, as distinct from other tongues, whether Elvish or not. But the Ñoldor did not forget its connexion with the old word *Quendi*, and still regarded the name as implying 'Elvish', that is the chief Elvish tongue, the noblest, and the one most nearly preserving the ancient character of Elvish speech. For a note on the Elvish words for 'language', especially among the Ñoldorin Loremasters, see Appendix D (p. 391).

4. *Elda* and *Eldo*. The original distinction between these forms as meaning 'one of the Star-folk, or Elves in general', and one of the 'Marchers', became obscured by the close approach of the forms. The form *Eldo* went out of use, and *Elda* remained the chief word for 'Elf' in Quenya. But it was not in accurate use held to include the Avari (when they were remembered or considered); i.e. it took on the sense of *Eldo*. It may, however, have been partly due to its older sense that in popular use it was the word ordinarily employed for any Elf, that is, as an equivalent of the *Quende* of the Loremasters. When one of the Elves of Aman spoke of the *Eldalie*, 'the Elven-folk', he meant vaguely all the race of Elves, though he was probably not thinking of the Avari.

For, of course, the special kinship of the *Amanyar* with those left in Beleriand (or *Hekeldamar*) was remembered, especially by the Teleri. When it was necessary to distinguish these two branches of the *Eldar* (or properly *Eldor*), those who had come to Aman were called the *Oäzeldi*, Ñ *Oäreldi*, for which another form (less used) was *Auzeldi*, Ñ *Aureldi*; those who had remained behind were the *Hekeldi*. These terms naturally belonged rather to history than everyday speech, and in the period of the Exile they fell out of use, being unsuitable to the situation in Beleriand. The Exiles still claimed to be *Amanyar*, but in practice this term usually now meant those Elves remaining in Aman, while the Exiles called themselves *Etyañgoldi* 'Exiled Ñoldor', or simply (since the great majority of their clan had come into exile) Ñoldor. All the subjects of Elwë they called *Sindar* or 'Grey-elves'.

Telerin

1. The derivatives of *KWEN were more sparingly represented in the Telerin dialects, of Aman or Beleriand. This was in part due to the Common Telerin change of *kw* > *p*, *(Note 5, p. 407)* which caused **pen* < **kwen* to clash with the PQ stem *PEN 'lack, be without', and also with some of the derivatives of *PED 'slope, slant down' (e.g. **pendā* 'sloping'). Also the Teleri felt themselves to be a separate people, as compared with the Vanyar and Ñoldor, whom taken together they outnumbered. This sentiment began before the Separation, and increased on the March and in Beleriand. In consequence they did not feel strongly the need for a general word embracing all Elves, until they came in contact with other non-Elvish Incarnates.

As a pronoun enclitic (e.g. in *aipen*, Q *aiquen*; *ilpen*, Q *ilquen*) **kwen* survived in Telerin; but few of the compounds with *pen* 'man' remained in ordinary use, except *arpen* 'noble (man)', and the derived adjective *arpenia*.

Pendi, the dialectal equivalent of Q *Quendi*, survived only as a learned word of the historians, used with reference to ancient days before the Separation; the adjective **Pendia* (the equivalent of *Quendya*) had fallen out of use. *(Note 6, p. 408)* The Teleri had little interest in linguistic lore, which they left to the Ñoldor. They did not regard their language as a 'dialect' of Quenya, but called it *Lindārin* or *Lindalambe*. Quenya they called *Goldōrin* or *Goldolambe*; for they had few contacts with the Vanyar.

The old compounds in Telerin form *Calapendi* and *Moripendi* survived in historical use; but since the Teleri in Aman remained more conscious of their kinship with the Elves left in Beleriand, while *Calapendi* was used, as *Kalaquendi* in Quenya, to refer only to the Elves of Aman, *Moripendi* was not applied to the Elves of Telerin origin who had not reached Aman.

2. *Ello* and *Ella*. The history of the meanings of these words was almost identical with that of the corresponding *Elda* and *Eldo* in Quenya. In Telerin the -*o* form became preferred, so that generally T *Ello* was the equivalent of Q *Elda*. But *Ella* remained in use in quasi-adjectival function (e.g. as the first element in loose or genitival compounds): thus the equivalent of Q *Eldalie* was in T *Ellālie*.

In contrast to the *Elloi* left in Beleriand those in Aman were in histories called *Audel*, pl. *Audelli*. Those in Beleriand were the *Hecelloi* of *Heculbar* (or *Hecellubar*).

Sindarin

1. Derivatives of *KWEN were limited to the sense: pronominal 'one, somebody, anybody', and to a few old compounds that survived. PQ *kwende, *kwendī disappeared altogether. The reasons for this were partly the linguistic changes already cited; and partly the circumstances in which the Sindar lived, until the return of the Ñoldor, and the coming of Men. The linguistic changes made the words unsuitable for survival; the circumstances removed all practical need for the term. The old unity of the Elves had been broken at the Separation. The Elves of Beleriand were isolated, without contact with any other people, Elvish or of other kind; and they were all of one clan and language: Telerin (or Lindarin). Their own language was the only one that they ever heard; and they needed no word to distinguish it, nor to distinguish themselves.

As a pronoun, usually enclitic, the form *pen*, mutated *ben*, survived. A few compounds survived, such as *rochben* 'rider' (m. or f.), *orodben* 'a mountaineer' or 'one living in the mountains', *arphen* 'a noble'. Their plurals were made by *i*-affection, originally carried through the word: as *roechbin*, *oerydbin*, *erphin*, but the normal form of the first element was often restored when the nature of the composition remained evident: as *rochbin*, but always *erphin*. These words had no special association with Elves.

Associated with these compounds were the two old words *Calben (Celbin)* and *Morben (Moerbin)*. On the formal relation of these to Quenya *Kalaquendi* and *Moriquendi* see p. 362. They had no reference to Elves, except by accident of circumstance. *Celbin* retained what was, as has been said, probably its original meaning: all Elves other than the Avari; and it included the Sindar. It was in fact the equivalent (when one was needed) of the Quenya *Eldar*, Telerin *Elloi*. But it referred to Elves only because no other people qualified for the title. *Moerbin* was similarly an equivalent for Avari; but that it did not mean only 'Dark-*elves*' is seen by its ready application to other Incarnates, when they later became known. By the Sindar anyone dwelling outside Beleriand, or entering their realm from outside, was called a *Morben*. The first people of this kind to be met were the *Nandor*, who entered East Beleriand over the passes of the Mountains before the return of Morgoth; soon after his return came the first invasions of his Orcs from the North.[7] Somewhat later the Sindar became aware of Avari, who had crept in small and secret groups into Beleriand from the South. Later came the Men of the Three Houses, who were friendly; and later still Men of other kinds. All these were at first acquaintance called *Moerbin*. *(Note 7, p. 408)* But when the Nandor were recognized as kinsfolk of Lindarin origin and speech (as was still recognizable), they were received into the class of *Celbin*. The Men of the Three Houses were also soon removed from the class of *Moerbin*. *(Note 8, p. 408)* They were given their own name, *Edain*, and were seldom actually called *Celbin*, but they were recognized as belonging to this class, which became practically equivalent to 'peoples in alliance in the War against Morgoth'. The Avari thus remained the chief examples of *Moerbin*. Any individual Avar who joined with or was admitted among the Sindar (it rarely happened) became a *Calben*; but the Avari in general remained secretive, hostile to the Eldar, and untrustworthy; and they dwelt in hidden places in the deeper woods, or in caves. *(Note 9, p. 408)* *Moerbin* as applied to them is usually translated 'Dark-elves', partly because *Moriquendi* in the Quenya of the Exiled Ñoldor usually referred to them. But that no special reference to Elves was intended by the Sindarin word is shown by the fact that *Moerbin* was at once applied to the new bands of Men (Easterlings) that appeared before the Battle of the Nírnaeth. *(Note 9, p. 408)* If in Sindarin an Avar, as distinct from other kinds of *Morben*, was intended, he was called *Mornedhel*.

2. *Edhel*, pl. *Edhil*. In spite of its ultimate derivation (see p. 360) this was the general word for 'Elf, Elves'. In the earlier days it naturally referred only to the Eldarin Sindar, for no other kind was ever seen; but later it was freely applied to Elves of any kind that entered Beleriand. It was however only used in these two forms.

The masculine and feminine forms were *Ellon* m. and *Elleth* f. and the class-plural was *Eldrim*, later *Elrim*, when this was not replaced by the more commonly used *Eledhrim* (see below). The form without the m. and f. suffixes was not in use, and survived only in some old compounds, especially personal names, in the form *el*, pl. *il*, as a final element.

The form *Elen*, pl. *Elin* was only used in histories or the works of the Loremasters, as a word to include all Elves (Eldar and Avari). But the class-plural *Eledhrim* was the usual word for 'all the Elvish race', whenever such an expression was needed.

All these words and forms, whatever their etymologies (see above), were applicable to any kind of Elf. In fact *Edhel* was properly applied only to Eldar; *Ell-* may have a mixed origin; and *Elen* was an ancient general word. *(Note 10, p. 410)*

3. The Sindar had no general name for themselves as distinct from other varieties of Elf, until other kinds entered Beleriand. The descendant of the old clan name **Lindāi* (Q *Lindar*) had fallen out of normal use, being no longer needed in a situation were all the *Edhil* were of the same kind, and people were more aware of the growing differences in speech and other matters between those sections of the Elves that lived in widely sundered parts of a large and mostly pathless land. They were thus in ordinary speech all *Edhil*, but some belonged to one region and some to another: they were *Falathrim* from the sea-board of West Beleriand, or *Iathrim* from Doriath (the land of the Fence, or *iath*), or *Mithrim* who had gone north from Beleriand and inhabited the regions about the great lake that afterwards bore their name. *(Note 11, p. 410)*

The old clan-name **Lindāi* survived in the compound *Glinnel*, pl. *Glinnil*, a word only known in historical lore, and the equivalent of Quenya *Teleri* or *Lindar*; see the Notes on the Clan-names below. All the Sindarin subjects of King Elu-Thingol, as distinguished from the incoming Ñoldor, were sometimes later called the *Eluwaith*. *Dúnedhil* 'West-elves' (the reference being to the West of Middle-earth) was a term made to match *Dúnedain* 'West-men' (applied only to the Men of the Three Houses). But with the growing amalgamation, outside Doriath, of the Ñoldor and Sindar into one people using the Sindarin tongue as their daily speech, this soon became applied to both Ñoldor and Sindar.

While the Ñoldor were still distinct, and whenever it was desired to recall their difference of origin, they were usually called *Ódhil* (sg. *Ódhel*). This as has been seen was originally a name for all the Elves that left Beleriand for Aman. These were also called by the Sindar *Gwanwen*, pl. *Gwenwin* (or *Gwanwel*, *Gwenwil*) 'the departed': cf. Q *vanwa*. This term, which could not suitably be applied to those who had come back, remained the usual Sindarin name for the Elves that remained in Aman.

Ódhil thus became specially the name of the Exiled Ñoldor.

In this sense the form *Gódhel*, pl. *Gódhil* soon replaced the older form. It seems to have been due to the influence of the clan-name *Golodh*, pl. *Goelydh*; or rather to a deliberate blending of the two words. The old clan-name had not fallen out of memory (for the Ñoldor and the Sindar owing to the great friendship of Finwe and Elwe were closely associated during their sojourn in Beleriand before the Departure) and it had in consequence a genuine Sindarin form (< CE **ñgolodō*). But the form *Golodh* seems to have been phonetically unpleasing to the Ñoldor. The name was, moreover, chiefly used by those who wished to mark the difference between the Ñoldor and the Sindar, and to ignore the dwelling of the Ñoldor in Aman which might give them a claim to superiority. This was especially the case in Doriath, where King Thingol was hostile to the Ñoldorin chieftains, Fëanor and his sons, and Fingolfin, because of their assault upon the Teleri in Aman, the people of his brother Olwe. The Ñoldor, therefore, when using Sindarin, never applied this name *(Golodh)* to themselves, and it fell out of use among those friendly to them.

4. *Eglan*, pl. *Eglain, Egladrim*. This name, 'the Forsaken', was, as has been said, given by the Sindar to themselves. But it was not in Beleriand a name for all the Elves who remained there, as were the related names, *Hekeldi, Hecelloi*, in Aman. It applied only to those who wished to depart, and waited long in vain for the return of Ulmo, taking up their abode on or near the coasts. There they became skilled in the building and management of ships. Círdan was their lord.

Círdan's folk were made up both of numbers of the following of Olwe, who straying or lingering came to the shores too late, and also of many of the following of Elwe, who abandoned the search for him and did not wish to be separated for ever from their kin and friends. This folk remained in the desire of Aman for long years, and they were among the most friendly to the Exiles.

They continued to call themselves the *Eglain*, and the regions where they dwelt *Eglamar* and *Eglador*. The latter name fell out of general use. It had originally been applied to all western Beleriand between Mount Taras and the Bay of Balar, its eastern boundary being roughly along the River Narog. *Eglamar*, however, remained the name of the 'Home of the Eglain': the sea-board from Cape Andras to the headland of Bar-in-Mŷl

('Home of the Gulls'),[8] which included the ship-havens of Círdan at Brithonbar[9] and at the head of the firth of Eglarest.

The *Eglain* became a people somewhat apart from the inland Elves, and at the time of the coming of the Exiles their language was in many ways different. *(Note 12, p. 411)* But they acknowledged the high-kingship of Thingol, and Círdan never took the title of king.[10]

*Abarī

This name, evidently made by the Eldar at the time of the Separation, is found in histories in the Quenya form *Avari*, and the Telerin form *Abari*. It was still used by the historians of the Exiled Ñoldor, though it hardly differed from *Moriquendi*, which (see above) was no longer used by the Exiles to include Elves of Eldarin origin. The plural *Evair* was known to Sindarin loremasters, but was no longer in use. Such Avari as came into Beleriand were, as has been said, called *Morben*, or *Mornedhel*.

C. The Clan-names,
with notes on other names for divisions of the Eldar.

In Quenya form the names of the three great Clans were *Vanyar*, *Ñoldor*, and *Lindar*. The oldest of these names was *Lindar*, which certainly goes back to days before the Separation. The other two probably arose in the same period, if somewhat later: their original forms may thus be given in PQ as *wanjā, *ñgolodō, and *lindā / glindā*. *(Note 13, p. 411)*

According to the legend, preserved in almost identical form among both the Elves of Aman and the Sindar, the Three Clans were in the beginning derived from the three Elf-fathers: *Imin*, *Tata*, and *Enel* (sc. One, Two, Three), and those whom each chose to join his following. So they had at first simply the names *Minyar* 'Firsts', *Tatyar* 'Seconds', and *Nelyar* 'Thirds'. These numbered, out of the original 144 Elves that first awoke, 14, 56, and 74; and these proportions were approximately maintained until the Separation.[11]

It is said that of the small clan of the *Minyar* none became Avari. The *Tatyar* were evenly divided. The *Nelyar* were most reluctant to leave their lakeside homes; but they were very cohesive, and very conscious of the separate unity of their Clan (as they continued to be), so that when it became clear that their chieftains Elwe and Olwe were resolved to depart and would have a large following, many of those among them who had at first joined the Avari went over to the Eldar rather than be separated from their kin. The Ñoldor indeed asserted that most of the *'Teleri'* were at heart *Avari*, and that only the *Eglain* really regretted being left in Beleriand.

According to the Ñoldorin historians the proportions, out of 144, that when the March began became Avari or Eldar were approximately so:

Minyar 14: Avari 0   Eldar 14
Tatyar 56: Avari 28   Eldar 28
Nelyar 74: Avari 28   Eldar 46 > Amanyar Teleri 20;
  Sindar and Nandor 26

In the result the Ñoldor were the largest clan of Elves in Aman; while the Elves that remained in Middle-earth (the *Moriquendi* in the Quenya of Aman) outnumbered the Amanyar in the proportion of 82 to 62.[12]

How far the descriptive Clan-names, *wanjā, *ñgolodō, and *lindā were preserved among the Avari is not now known; but the existence of the old clans was remembered, and a special kinship between those of the same original clan, whether they had gone away or remained, was still recognized. The first Avari that the Eldar met again in Beleriand seem to have claimed to be Tatyar, who acknowledged their kinship with the Exiles, though there is no record of their using the name *Ñoldo* in any recognizable Avarin form. They were actually unfriendly to the Ñoldor, and jealous of their more exalted kin, whom they accused of arrogance.

This ill-feeling descended in part from the bitterness of the Debate before the March of the Eldar began, and was no doubt later increased by the machinations of Morgoth; but it also throws some light upon the temperament of the Ñoldor in general, and of Fëanor in particular. Indeed the Teleri on their side asserted that most of the Ñoldor in Aman itself were in heart Avari, and returned to Middle-earth when they discovered their mistake; they needed room to quarrel in. For in contrast the Lindarin elements in the western Avari were friendly to the Eldar, and willing to learn from them; and so close was the feeling of kinship between the remnants of the Sindar, the Nandor, and the Lindarin Avari, that later in Eriador and the Vale of Anduin they often became merged together.

Lindar (Teleri)[13]

These were, as has been seen, much the largest of the ancient clans. The name, later appearing in Quenya form as *Lindar* (Telerin *Lindai*), is already referred to in the legend of 'The Awakening of the Quendi', which says of the Nelyar that 'they sang before they could speak with words'. The name **Lindā* is therefore clearly a derivative of the primitive stem **LIN* (showing reinforcement of the medial N and adjectival *-ā*). This stem was possibly one of the contributions of the Nelyar to Primitive Quendian, for it reflects their predilections and associations, and produces more derivatives in Lindarin tongues than in others. Its primary reference was to melodious or pleasing sound, but it also refers (especially in Lindarin) to water, the motions of which were always by the Lindar associated with vocal (Elvish) sound. The reinforcements, either medial *lind-* or initial *glin-*, *glind-*, were however almost solely used of musical, especially vocal, sounds produced with intent to please. It is thus to the love of the Nelyar for song, for vocal music with or without the use of articulate words, that the name *Lindar* originally referred; though they also loved water, and before the Separation never moved far from the lake and waterfall[14] of Cuiviénen, and those that moved into the West became enamoured of the Sea. *(Note 14, p. 411)*

In Quenya, that is, in the language of the Vanyar and Ñoldor, those of this clan that joined in the March were called the *Teleri*. This name was applied in particular to those that came at last and latest to Aman; but it was also later applied to the Sindar. The name *Lindar* was not forgotten, but in Ñoldorin lore it was chiefly used to describe the whole clan, including the Avari among them. *Teleri* meant 'those at the end of the line, the hindmost', and was evidently a nickname arising during the March, when the Teleri, the least eager to depart, often lagged far behind. *(Note 15, p. 411)*

Vanyar

This name was probably given to the First Clan by the Ñoldor. They accepted it, but continued to call themselves most often by their old numerical name *Minyar* (since the whole of this clan had joined the Eldar and reached Aman). The name referred to the hair of the Minyar, which was in nearly all members of the clan yellow or deep golden. This was regarded as a beautiful feature by the Ñoldor (who loved gold), though they were themselves mostly dark-haired. Owing to intermarriage the golden hair of the Vanyar sometimes later appeared among the Ñoldor: notably in the case of Finarfin, and in his children Finrod and Galadriel, in whom it came from King Finwë's second wife, Indis of the Vanyar.

Vanyar thus comes from an adjectival derivative **wanjā* from the stem *WAN. Its primary sense seems to have been very similar to English (modern) use of 'fair' with reference to hair and complexion; though its actual development was the reverse of the English: it meant 'pale, light-coloured, not brown or dark', and its implication of beauty was secondary. In English the meaning 'beautiful' is primary. From the same stem was derived the name given in Quenya to the Valie *Vána* wife of Orome.

Since the Lindar had little contact with the Vanyar either on the March or later in Aman, this name was not much used by them for the First Clan. The Amanyar Teleri had the form *Vaniai* (no doubt taken from the Ñoldor), but the name appears to have been forgotten in Beleriand, where the First Clan (in lore and history only) were called *Miniel*, pl. *Mínil*.

Ñoldor

This name was probably older than *Vanyar*, and may have been made before the March. It was given to the Second Clan by the others. It was accepted, and was used as their regular and proper name by all the Eldarin members of the clan throughout their later history.

The name meant 'the Wise', that is those who have great knowledge and understanding. The Ñoldor indeed early showed the greatest talents of all the Elves both for intellectual pursuits and for technical skills.

The variant forms of the name: Q *Ñoldo*, T *Goldo*, S *Golodh (Ngolodh)*, indicate a PQ original **ñgolodō*. This is a derivative of the stem *NGOL 'knowledge, wisdom, lore'. This is seen in Q *ñóle* 'long study (of any subject)', *iñgole* 'lore', *ingolmo* 'loremaster'. In T *góle*, *engole* had the same senses as in Q but were used most often of the special 'lore' possessed by the Ñoldor. In S the word *gûl* (equivalent of Q *ñóle*) had less laudatory associations, being used mostly of secret knowledge, especially such as possessed by artificers who made wonderful things; and the word became further darkened by its frequent use in the compound *morgul* 'black arts', applied to the delusory or perilous arts and knowledge derived from Morgoth. Those indeed among the Sindar who were unfriendly to the

Ñoldor attributed their supremacy in the arts and lore to their learning from Melkor-Morgoth. This was a falsehood, coming itself ultimately from Morgoth; though it was not without any foundation (as the lies of Morgoth seldom were). But the great gifts of the Ñoldor did not come from the teaching of Melkor. Fëanor the greatest of them all never had any dealings with Melkor in Aman, and was his greatest foe.

Sindar

Less commonly the form *Sindel*, pl. *Sindeldi*, is also met in Exilic Quenya. This was the name given by the Exiled Ñoldor (see Note 11) to the second largest of the divisions of the Eldar. *(Note 16, p. 412)* It was applied to all the Elves of Telerin origin that the Ñoldor found in Beleriand, though it later excluded the Nandor, except those who were the direct subjects of Elwe, or had become merged with his people. The name meant 'the Grey', or 'the Grey-elves', and was derived from *THIN, PQ *thindi* 'grey, pale or silvery grey', Q *pinde*, Ñ dialect *sinde*.

On the origin of this name see Note 11. The Loremasters also supposed that reference was made to the hair of the Sindar. Elwe himself had indeed long and beautiful hair of silver hue, but this does not seem to have been a common feature of the Sindar, though it was found among them occasionally, especially in the nearer or remoter kin of Elwe (as in the case of Círdan).[15] In general the Sindar appear to have very closely resembled the Exiles, being dark-haired, strong and tall, but lithe. Indeed they could hardly be told apart except by their eyes; for the eyes of all the Elves that had dwelt in Aman impressed those of Middle-earth by their piercing brightness. For which reason the Sindar often called them *Lachend*, pl. *Lechind* 'flame-eyed'.

Nandor

This name must have been made at the time, in the latter days of the March, when certain groups of the Teleri gave up the March; and it was especially applied to the large following of Lenwe, *(Note 17, p. 412)* who refused to cross the Hithaeglir.[16] The name was often interpreted as 'Those who go back'; but in fact none of the Nandor appear to have returned, or to have rejoined the Avari. Many remained and settled in lands that they had reached, especially beside the River Anduin; some turned aside and wandered southwards. *(Note 18, p. 412)* There was, however, as was later seen, a slow drift westward of the Moriquendi during the captivity of Melkor, and eventually groups of the Nandor, coming through the Gap between the Hithaeglir and Eryd Nimrais, spread widely in Eriador. Some of these finally entered Beleriand, not long before the return of Morgoth.[17] These were under the leadership of Denethor, son of Denweg (see Note 17), who became an ally of Elwe in the first battles with the creatures of Morgoth. The old name *Nandor* was however only remembered by the Ñoldorin historians in Aman; and they knew nothing of the later history of this folk, recalling only that the leader of the defection before the crossing of the dread Hithaeglir was named Lenwe (i.e. Denweg). The Sindarin loremasters remembered the Nandor as *Danwaith*, or by confusion with the name of their leader *Denwaith*.

This name they at first applied to the Nandor that came into Eastern Beleriand; but this people still called themselves by the old clan-name *Lindai, which had at that time taken the form *Lindi* in their tongue. The country in which most of them eventually settled, as a small independent folk, they called *Lindon* (< *Lindānā): this was the country at the western feet of the Blue Mountains (Eryd Luin), watered by the tributaries of the great River Gelion, and previously named by the Sindar *Ossiriand*, the Land of Seven Rivers. The Sindar quickly recognized the *Lindi* as kinsfolk of Lindarin origin (S *Glinnil*), using a tongue that in spite of great differences was still perceived to be akin to their own; and they adopted the names *Lindi* and *Lindon*, giving them the forms *Lindil* (sg. *Lindel*) or *Lindedhil*, and *Lindon* or *Dor Lindon*. In Exilic Quenya the forms used (derived from the Sindar or direct from the Nandor) were *Lindi* and *Lindon* (or *Lindóne*). The Exiled Ñoldor also usually referred to the Eryd Luin as *Eryd Lindon*, since the highest parts of that range made the eastern borders of the country of Lindon.

These names were however later replaced among the Sindar by the name 'Green-elves', at least as far as the inhabitants of Ossiriand were concerned; for they withdrew themselves and took as little part in the strife with Morgoth as they could. This name, S *Laegel*, pl. *Laegil*, class-plural *Laegrim* or *Laegel(d)-rim*, was given both because of the greenness of the land of Lindon, and because the *Laegrim* clothed themselves in green as an aid to secrecy. This term the Ñoldor translated into Quenya *Laiquendi*; but it was not much used.

Appendix A. Elvish names for Men.

The first Elves that Men met in the world were Avari, some of whom were friendly to them, but the most avoided them or were hostile (according to the tales of Men). What names Men and Elves gave to one another in those remote days, of which little was remembered when the Loremasters in Beleriand made the acquaintance of the After-born, there is now no record. By the Dúnedain the Elves were called *Nimîr* (the Beautiful).[18]

The Eldar did not meet Men of any kind or race until the Ñoldor had long returned to Beleriand and were at war with Morgoth. The Sindar did not even know of their existence, until the coming of the Nandor; and these brought only rumour of a strange people (whom they had not themselves seen) wandering in the lands of the East beyond the Hithaeglir. From these uncertain tales the Sindar concluded that the 'strange people' were either some diminished race of the Avari, or else related to Orcs, creatures of Melkor, bred in mockery of the true Quendi. But the Ñoldor had already heard of Men in Aman. Their knowledge came in the first place from Melkor and was perverted by his malice, but before the Exile those who would listen had learned more of the truth from the Valar, and they knew that the newcomers were akin to themselves, being also Children of Ilúvatar, though differing in gifts and fate. Therefore the Ñoldor made names for the Second Race of the Children, calling them the *Atani* 'the Second Folk'. Other names that they devised were *Apanónar* 'the After-born', and *Hildor* 'the Followers'.

In Beleriand *Atan*, pl. *Atani*, was the name most used at first. But since for a long time the only Men known to the Ñoldor and Sindar were those of the Three Houses of the Elf-friends, this name became specially associated with them, so that it was seldom in ordinary speech applied to other kinds of Men that came later to Beleriand, or that were reported to be dwelling beyond the Mountains. The Elf-friends *(Note 19, p. 412)* were sometimes called by the Loremasters *Núnatani* (S *Dúnedain*), 'Western Men', a term made to match *Dúnedhil*, which was a name for all the Elves of Beleriand, allied in the War (see p. 378). The original reference was to the West of Middle-earth, but the name *Núnatani, Dúnedain* was later applied solely to the Númenóreans, descendants of the *Atani*, who removed to the far western isle of *Númenóre*.

Apanónar 'the After-born' was a word of lore, not used in daily speech. A general term for Men of all kinds and races, as distinct from Elves, was only devised after their mortality and brief life-span became known to the Elves by experience. They were then called *Firyar* 'Mortals', or *Fírimar* of similar sense (literally 'those apt to die'). *(Note 20, p. 412)* These words were derived from the stem *PHIRI 'exhale, expire, breathe out', which had no original connexion with death.[19] Of death, as suffered by Men, the Elves knew nothing until they came into close association with the *Atani*; but there were cases in which an Elf, overcome by a great sorrow or weariness, had resigned life in the body. The chief of these, the departure of Míriel wife of King Finwë, was a matter of deep concern to all the Ñoldor, and it was told of her that her last act, as she gave up her life in the body and went to the keeping of Mandos, was a deep sigh of weariness.

These Quenya names were later adapted to the forms of Sindarin speech: *Atan > Adan*, pl. *Edain*; *Firya > Feir*, pl. *Fîr* (with *Firion* m.sg., *Firieth* f.sg.), class-plural *Firiath*; *Fírima > Fíreb*, pl. *Fírib*, class-plural *Firebrim*. These forms, which cannot for historical reasons have been inherited from CE, but are those which the words if inherited would have taken, show that they were adapted by people with considerable knowledge of both tongues and understanding of their relations to one another; that is, they were probably first made by the Ñoldor for use in Sindarin, when they had adopted this language for daily use in Beleriand. *Fíreb* as compared with *Fírima* shows the use of a different suffix, *(Note 21, p. 412)* since the S equivalent of Q *-ima* (*-ef*) was not current. *Apanónar* was rendered by *Abonnen*, pl. *Eboennin*, using a different participial formation from the stem *ONO 'beget, give birth to'. *Hildor*, since the stem *KHILI 'follow' was not current in Sindarin, was rendered by *Aphadon*, pl. *Ephedyn*, class-plural *Aphadrim*, from S *aphad-* 'follow' < *ap-pata* 'walk behind, on a track or path'.

Appendix B. Elvish names for the Dwarves.

The Sindar had long known the Dwarves, and had entered into peaceful relations with them, though of trade and exchange of skills rather than of true friendship, before the coming of the Exiles. The name (in the plural) that the Dwarves gave to themselves was *Khazâd*, and this the Sindar rendered as they might in the terms of their own speech, giving it the form *chaðǭd > *chaðaud > Hadhod. (Note 22, p. 412) Hadhod, Hadhodrim was the name which they continued to use in actual intercourse with the Dwarves; but among themselves they referred to the Dwarves usually as the Naugrim 'the Stunted Folk'. The adjective naug 'dwarf(ed), stunted', however, was not used by itself for one of the Khazâd. The word used was Nogoth, pl. Noegyth, class-plural Nogothrim (as an occasional equivalent of Naugrim). (Note 23, p. 413) They also often referred to the Dwarves as a race by the name Dornhoth 'the Thrawn Folk', because of their stubborn mood as well as bodily toughness.

The Exiles heard of the Dwarves first from the Sindar, and when using the Sindarin tongue naturally adopted the already established names. But later in Eastern Beleriand the Ñoldor came into independent relations with the Dwarves of Eryd Lindon, and they adapted the name Khazâd anew for use in Quenya, giving it the form Kasar, pl. Kasari or Kasári. (Note 24, p. 413) This was the word most commonly used in Quenya for the Dwarves, the partitive plural being Kasalli, and the race-name Kasallie. But the Sindarin names were also adapted or imitated, a Dwarf being called Nauko or Norno (the whole people Naukalie or Nornalie). Norno was the more friendly term. (Note 25, p. 413)

The Petty-dwarves. See also Note 7. The Eldar did not at first recognize these as Incarnates, for they seldom caught sight of them in clear light. They only became aware of their existence indeed when they attacked the Eldar by stealth at night, or if they caught them alone in wild places. The Eldar therefore thought that they were a kind of cunning two-legged animals living in caves, and they called them Levain tad-dail, or simply Tad-dail, and they hunted them. But after the Eldar had made the acquaintance of the Naugrim, the Tad-dail were recognized as a variety of Dwarves and were left alone. There were then few of them surviving, and they were very wary, and too fearful to attack any Elf, unless their hiding-places were approached too nearly. The Sindar gave them the names Nogotheg 'Dwarf-let', or Nogoth niben 'Petty Dwarf'.[20]

The great Dwarves despised the Petty-dwarves, who were (it is said) the descendants of Dwarves who had left or been driven out from the Communities, being deformed or undersized, or slothful and rebellious. But they still acknowledged their kinship and resented any injuries done to them. Indeed it was one of their grievances against the Eldar that they had hunted and slain their lesser kin, who had settled in Beleriand before the Elves came there. This grievance was set aside, when treaties were made between the Dwarves and the Sindar, in consideration of the plea that the Petty-dwarves had never declared themselves to the Eldar, nor presented any claims to land or habitations, but had at once attacked the newcomers in darkness and ambush. But the grievance still smouldered, as was later seen in the case of Mîm, the only Petty-dwarf who played a memorable part in the Annals of Beleriand.

The Ñoldor, for use in Quenya, translated these Sindarin names for the Petty-dwarves by *Attalyar* 'Bipeds', and *Pikinaukor* or *Pitya-naukor*.

The chief dwellings of the Dwarves that became known to the Sindar (though few ever visited them) were upon the east side of the Eryd Luin. They were called in the Dwarf-tongue *Gabilgathol* and *Tumunzahar*. The greatest of all the mansions of the Dwarves, *Khazad-dûm*, beneath the Hithaeglir far to the east, was known to the Eldar only by name and rumour derived from the western Dwarves.

These names the Sindar did not attempt to adapt, but translated according to their sense, as *Belegost* 'Mickleburg'; *Novrod*, later *Nogrod*, meaning originally 'Hollowbold'; and *Hadhodrond* 'Dwarrowvault'.[21] *(Note 26, p. 414)* These names the Ñoldor naturally used in speaking or writing Sindarin, but for use in Quenya they translated the names anew as *Túrosto*, *Návarot*, and *Casarrondo*.

Appendix C. Elvish names for the Orcs.

The opening paragraphs of this Appendix have been given in *Morgoth's Ring* p. 416 and are not repeated here. The words that now follow, 'these shapes and the terror that they inspired', refer to the 'dreadful shapes' that haunted the dwellings of the Elves in the land of their awakening.

For these shapes and the terror that they inspired the element chiefly used in the ancient tongue of the Elves appears to have been *RUKU. In all the Eldarin tongues (and, it is said, in the Avarin also) there are many derivatives of this stem, having such ancient forms as: *ruk-, rauk-, uruk-, urk(u), runk-, rukut/s*, besides the strengthened stem *gruk-*, and the elaborated *guruk-*, *ñguruk.* *(Note 27, p. 415)* Already in PQ that word must have been formed which had in CE the form **rauku* or **raukō*. This was applied to the larger and more terrible of the enemy shapes. But ancient were also the forms *uruk, urku/ō*, and the adjectival *urkā* 'horrible'. *(Note 28, p. 415)*

In Quenya we meet the noun *urko*, pl. *urqui*, deriving as the plural form shows from **urku* or **uruku*. In Sindarin is found the corresponding *urug*; but there is in frequent use the form *orch*, which must be derived from **urkō* or the adjectival **urkā*.

In the lore of the Blessed Realm the Q *urko* naturally seldom occurs, except in tales of the ancient days and the March, and then is vague in meaning, referring to anything that caused fear to the Elves, any dubious shape or shadow, or prowling creature. In Sindarin *urug* has a similar use. It might indeed be translated 'bogey'. But the form *orch* seems at once to have been applied to the Orcs, as soon as they appeared; and *Orch*, pl. *Yrch*, class-plural *Orchoth* remained the regular name for these creatures in Sindarin afterwards. The kinship, though not precise equivalence, of S *orch* to Q *urko, urqui* was recognized, and in Exilic Quenya *urko* was commonly used to translate S *orch*, though a form showing the influence of Sindarin, *orko*, pl. *orkor* and *orqui*, is also often found.

These names, derived by various routes from the Elvish tongues, from Quenya, Sindarin, Nandorin, and no doubt Avarin dialects, went far and wide, and seem to have been the source of the names for the Orcs in most of the languages of the Elder Days and the early ages of which there is any record. The form in Adunaic *urku, urkhu* may be direct from Quenya or Sindarin; and this form underlies the words for Orc in the languages of Men of the North-West in the Second and Third Ages. The Orcs themselves adopted it, for the fact that it referred to terror and detestation delighted them. The word *uruk* that occurs in the Black Speech, devised (it is said) by Sauron to serve as a lingua franca for his subjects, was probably borrowed by him from the Elvish tongues of earlier times. It referred, however, specially to the trained and disciplined Orcs of the regiments of Mordor. Lesser breeds seem to have been called *snaga*.[22]

The Dwarves claimed to have met and fought the Orcs long before the Eldar in Beleriand were aware of them. It was indeed their obvious detestation of the Orcs, and their willingness to assist in any war against them, that convinced the Eldar that the Dwarves were no creatures of Morgoth. Nonetheless the Dwarvish name for Orcs, *Rukhs*, pl. *Rakhās*, seems to show affinity to the Elvish names, and was possibly ultimately derived from Avarin.

The Eldar had many other names for the Orcs, but most of these were 'kennings', descriptive terms of occasional use. One was, however, in frequent use in Sindarin: more often than *Orchoth* the general name for Orcs as a race that appears in the Annals was *Glamhoth*. *Glam* meant 'din, uproar, the confused yelling and bellowing of beasts', so that *Glamhoth* in origin meant more or less 'the Yelling-horde', with reference to the horrible clamour of the Orcs in battle or when in pursuit – they could be stealthy enough at need. But *Glamhoth* became so firmly associated with Orcs that *Glam* alone could be used of any body of Orcs, and a singular form was made from it, *glamog*. (Compare the name of the sword *Glamdring*.)

Note. The word used in translation of Q *urko*, S *orch*, is Orc. But that is because of the similarity of the ancient English word *orc*, 'evil spirit or bogey', to the Elvish words. There is possibly no connexion between them. The English word is now generally supposed to be derived from Latin *Orcus*.

The word for Orc in the now forgotten tongue of the Drúedain in the realm of Gondor is recorded as being (? in the plural) *gorgûn*. This is possibly derived ultimately from the Elvish words.

Appendix D.
*Kwen, Quenya, and the Elvish (especially Ñoldorin) words for 'Language'.

The Ñoldorin Loremasters state often that the meaning of *Quendi* was 'speakers', 'those who form words with voices' – *i karir quettar ómainen*. Since they were in possession of traditions coming down from ancient days before the Separation, this statement cannot be disregarded; though the development of sense set out above may also stand as correct.

It might be objected that in fact no stem *KWEN clearly referring to speech or vocal sound is found in any known Elvish tongue. The nearest in form is the stem *KWET 'speak, utter words, say'. But in dealing with this ancient word we must go back to the beginnings of Elvish speech, before the later organisation of its basic structure, with its preference (especially in stems of verbal significance) for the pattern X-X(-), with a fixed medial consonant, as e.g. in stems already exemplified above, such as *Dele, *Heke, *Tele, *Kala, *Kiri, *Nuku, *Ruku, etc. A large number of monosyllabic stems (with only an initial consonant or consonant group) still appear in the Eldarin tongues; and many of the dissyllabic stems must have been made by elaboration of these, just as, at a later stage again, the so-called *kalat- stems were extended from the disyllabic forms: *kala > *kalat(a).

If we assume, then, that the oldest form of this stem referring to vocal speech was *KWE, of which *KWENE and *KWETE were elaborations, we shall find a striking parallel in the forms of *KWA. This stem evidently referred to 'completion'. As such it survives as an element in many of the Eldarin words for 'whole, total, all', etc. But it also appears in the form *KWAN, and cannot well be separated from the verb stem *KWATA, Q *quat-* 'fill'. The assumption also helps to explain a curious and evidently archaic form that survives only in the languages of Aman: *ekwē, Q *eque*, T *epe*. It has no tense forms and usually receives no pronominal affixes, *(Note 29, p. 415)* being mostly used only before either a proper name (sg. or pl.) or a full independent pronoun, in the senses *say / says* or *said*. A quotation then follows, either direct, or less usually indirect after a 'that'-conjunction.

In this *ekwē we have plainly a last survivor of the primitive *KWE. It is again paralleled by a similar formation (though of different function) from *KWA: *akwā. This survives in Quenya only as *aqua* 'fully, completely, altogether, wholly'. *(Note 30, p. 415)* Compare the use of *-kwā* in the formation of adjectives from nouns, such as *-ful* in English, except that the sense has been less weakened, and remains closer to the original meaning of the stem: 'completely'. *(Note 31, p. 415)*

In Quenya the form *eques*, originally meaning 'said he, said someone' (see Note 29) was also used as a noun *eques*, with the analogical plural *equessi*, 'a saying, dictum, a quotation from someone's uttered words', hence also 'a saying, a current or proverbial dictum'.

We may therefore accept the etymology of *kwene, *kwēn that would make its original meaning 'speaking, speaker, one using vocal language'. It would indeed be natural for the Elves, requiring a word for one of their own kind as distinguished from other creatures then known, to select the use of speech as a chief characteristic. But once formed the word must have taken the meaning 'person', without specific reference to this talent of the Incarnates. Thus *nere, *nēr 'a male person, a man' was derived from *NERE referring to physical strength and valour, but it was possible to speak of a weak or cowardly nēr; or indeed to speak of a dumb or silent kwēn.

It might therefore still be doubted that in the derivative *kwendī the notion of speaking was any longer effectively present. The statement of the Loremasters cannot, however, be dismissed; while it must be remembered that the Elves were always more deeply concerned with language than were other races. Up to the time at least of the Separation, then, *Kwendī must still have implied 'we, the speaking people'; it may indeed have primarily applied to concourses for discussion, or for listening to speeches and recitations. But when the Elves came to know of other creatures of similar forms, and other Incarnates who used vocal language, and the name *Kwendī, Quendi was used to distinguish themselves from these other kinds, the linguistic sense must have been no longer present in ordinary language.

With regard to the word *Quenya*: an account is given above of the way in which this word became used first in Aman for Elvish speech, *(Note 32, p. 416)* and then for the dialects of the Eldar in Aman, and later for the language of the Vanyar and Ñoldor, and finally in Middle-earth for the ancient tongue of the Ñoldor preserved as a language of ritual and lore. This is historically correct, whatever may be the ultimate etymology of *Quenya* before the Eldar came to Aman. The view taken above (p. 360) is that it is derived from an adjective *kwendjā formed upon the stem *kwende (of which *kwendi was the plural), meaning 'belonging to the Quendi or Elves'.

Pengolodh the Loremaster of Eressëa says, in his *Lammas* or Account of Tongues, that *Quenya* meant properly 'language, speech', and was the oldest word for this meaning. This is not a statement based on tradition, but an opinion of Pengolodh; and he appears to mean only that *Quendya, Quenya* is actually never recorded except as the name of a language, and that language was the only one known to exist when this word was first made.

In any case it is clear that *Quenya* was always in fact

particular in its reference; for when the Ñoldorin Loremasters came to consider linguistic matters, and required words for speech or vocal language in general, as a mode of expression or communication, and for different aspects of speech, they made no use of the element *kwen*, *quen* or its derivatives.

The usual word, in non-technical use, for 'language' was *lambē*, Q and T *lambe*, S *lam*. This was undoubtedly related to the word for the physical tongue: *lambā*, Q and T *lamba*, S *lam*. It meant 'tongue-movement, (way of) using the tongue'. *(Note 33, p. 416)* This use of a word indicating the tongue and its movements for articulate language no doubt arose, even in a period when all known speakers spoke substantially the same language, from elementary observation of the important part played by the tongue in articulate speaking, and from noticing the peculiarities of individuals, and the soon-developing minor differences in the language of groups and clans.

Lambe thus meant primarily 'a way of talking', within a common generally intelligible system, and was nearer to our 'dialect' than to 'language'; but later when the Eldar became aware of other tongues, not intelligible without study, *lambe* naturally became applied to the separate languages of any people or region. The Loremasters, therefore, did not use *lambe* as a term for language or speech in general. Their terms were derived from the stem *TEÑ 'indicate, signify', from which was formed the already well-known word *tenwe* > Q *tengwe* 'indication, sign, token'. From this they made the word *tengwesta* 'a system or code of signs'. Every 'language' was one such system. A *lambe* was a *tengwesta* built of sounds *(hloni)*. For the sense Language, as a whole, the peculiar art of the Incarnates of which each *tengwesta* was a particular product, they used the abstract formation *tengwestie*.

Now *TEÑ had no special reference to sound. Ultimately it meant 'to point at', and so to indicate a thing, or convey a thought, by some gesture, or by any sign that would be understood. This was appreciated by the Loremasters, who wished for a word free from any limitations with regard to the kind of signs or *tengwi* used. They could thus include under *tengwesta* any group of signs, including visible gestures, used and recognized by a community.

They knew of such systems of gesture. The Eldar possessed a fairly elaborate system, *(Note 34, p. 416)* containing a large number of conventional gesture-signs, some of which were as 'arbitrary' as those of phonetic systems. That is, they had no more obvious connexion with self-explanatory gestures (such as pointing in a desired direction) than had the majority of vocal elements or combinations with 'echoic' or imitative words (such as *māmā, Q máma 'sheep', or *k(a)wāk, Q quáko 'crow').

The Dwarves indeed, as later became known, had a far more elaborate and organized system. They possessed in fact a secondary *tengwesta* of gestures, concurrent with their spoken language, which they began to learn almost as soon as they began learning to speak. It should be said rather that they possessed a number of such gesture-codes; for unlike their spoken language, which remained astonishingly uniform and unchanged both in time and in locality, their gesture-codes varied greatly from community to community. And they were differently employed. Not for communication at a distance, for the Dwarves were short-sighted, but for secrecy and the exclusion of strangers.

The component sign-elements of any such code were often so slight and so swift that they could hardly be detected, still less interpreted by uninitiated onlookers. As the Eldar eventually discovered in their dealings with the Naugrim, they could speak with their voices but at the same time by 'gesture' convey to their own folk modifications of what was being said. Or they could stand silent considering some proposition, and yet confer among themselves meanwhile.

This 'gesture-language', or as they called it *iglishmêk*, the Dwarves were no more eager to teach than their own tongue. But they understood and respected the disinterested desire for knowledge, and some of the later Ñoldorin loremasters were allowed to learn enough of both their *lambe (aglâb)* and their *iglishmêk* to understand their systems.

Though a *lambe* was thus theoretically simply a *tengwesta* that happened to employ phonetic signs, *hlonîti tengwi*, the early loremasters held that it was the superior form, capable of producing a system incalculably more subtle, precise and extensive than any *hwerme* or gesture-code. When unqualified, therefore, *tengwesta* meant a spoken language. But in technical use it meant more than *lambe*. The study of a language included not only *lambe*, the way of speaking (that is what we should call its phonetics and phonology), but also its morphology, grammar, and vocabulary.

The section omitted from Appendix D (see p. 359) begins here. The remainder of the text, which now follows, was all included in this Appendix.

Before he turned to other matters Fëanor completed his alphabetic system, and here also he introduced a change in terms that was afterwards followed. He called the written representation of a spoken *tengwe* (according to his definition)[23] a *tengwa*. A 'letter' or any individual significant mark had previously been called a *sarat*, from *SAR 'score, incise' > 'write'.[24] The Fëanorian letters were always called *tengwar* in Quenya, though *sarati* remained the name for the Rúmilian letters. Since, however, in the mode of spelling commonly used the full signs were consonantal, in ordinary non-technical use *tengwar* became equivalent to 'consonants', and the vowel-signs were called *ómatehtar*. When the Fëanorian letters were brought to Beleriand and applied (first by the Ñoldor) to Sindarin, *tengwa* was rendered by its recognized Sindarin equivalent *têw*, pl. *tîw*. The letters of the native S alphabet were called *certh*, pl. *cirth*. The word in Exilic Quenya *certa*, pl. *certar* was an accommodated loan from Sindarin; there was no such word in older Quenya. The Sindarin *certh* is probably from *kirtē 'cutting', a verbal derivative of a type not used in Quenya, the form of which would in any case have been *kirte, if inherited.

Though Fëanor after the days of his first youth took no more active part in linguistic lore and enquiry, he is credited by tradition with the foundation of a school of *Lambengolmor* or 'Loremasters of Tongues' to carry on this work. This continued in existence among the Ñoldor, even through the rigours and disasters of the Flight from Aman and the Wars in Beleriand, and it survived indeed to return to Eressëa.

Of the School the most eminent member after the founder was, or still is, Pengolodh,[25] an Elf of mixed Sindarin and Ñoldorin ancestry, born in Nevrast, who lived in Gondolin from its foundation. He wrote both in Sindarin and in Quenya. He was one of the survivors of the destruction of Gondolin, from which he rescued a few ancient writings, and some of his own copies, compilations, and commentaries. It is due to this, and to his prodigious memory, that much of the knowledge of the Elder Days was preserved.

All that has here been said concerning the Elvish names and their origins, and concerning the views of the older loremasters, is derived directly or indirectly from Pengolodh. For before the overthrow of Morgoth and the ruin of Beleriand, he collected much material among the survivors of the wars at Sirion's Mouth concerning languages and gesture-systems with which, owing to the isolation of Gondolin, he had not before had any direct acquaintance. Pengolodh is said to have remained in Middle-earth until far on into the Second Age for the furtherance of his enquiries, and for a while to have dwelt among the Dwarves of Casarrondo (Khazad-dûm). But when the shadow of Sauron fell upon Eriador, he left Middle-earth, the last of the *Lambengolmor*, and sailed to Eressëa, where maybe he still abides.

Note on the 'Language of the Valar'

Little is said in Ñoldorin lore, such as has been preserved, concerning the 'language of the Valar and Maiar'; though it has been supposed above that the application of *Quenya* to the speech of the Elves in Aman was due to the contrast between the tongue of the Valar and the tongue of the Elves, which they had before supposed to be the only language in the world. Considering the interest of the Ñoldor in all matters concerning speech this is strange. Pengolodh indeed comments upon it and offers explanations. What he says in the beginning of his *Lammas* is here summarized; for his comment contains all that is now known of the matter.

'Even if we had no knowledge of it,' he says, 'we could not reasonably doubt that the Valar had a *lambe* of their own. We know that all members of their order were incarnated by their own desire, and that most of them chose to take forms like those of the Children of Eru, as they name us. In such forms they would take on all the characters of the Incarnates that were due to the co-operation of *hröa* with indwelling *fëa*, for otherwise the assumption of these forms would have been needless, and they arrayed themselves in this manner long before they had any cause to appear before us visibly. Since, then, the making of a *lambe* is the chief character of an Incarnate, the Valar, having arrayed them in this manner, would inevitably during their long sojourn in Arda have made a *lambe* for themselves.

'But without argument we know that they did so; for there are references to the *Lambe Valarinwa* in old lore and histories, though these are few and scattered. Most of these references appear to be derived, by tradition of mouth, from "the Sayings of Rúmil" *(I Equessi Rúmilo),* the ancient sage of Tirion, concerning the early days of the Eldar in Aman and their first dealings with the Valar. Only part of these *Equessi*[26] were preserved in the memory of the *Lambengolmor* during the dark years of the Flight and the Exile. All that I can find or remember I have here put together.'

The information that Pengolodh then gives is here set out more briefly. His preliminary points are these. Few of the Eldar ever learned to speak Valarin, even haltingly; among the people as a whole only a small number of words or names became widely known. Fëanor indeed, before the growth of his discontent, is said to have learned more of this tongue than any others before his time, and his knowledge must at any rate have far surpassed the little that is now recorded; but what he knew he kept to himself, and he refused to transmit it even to the *Lambengolmor* because of his quarrel with the Valar.

Our knowledge *(Note 35, p. 416)* is therefore now limited (1) to statements of the 'ancients' that certain words in Quenya were actually derived from Valarin; (2) to the occasional citation of words and names purporting to be Valarin (neither adopted in Quenya nor adapted to it), though undoubtedly recorded with only approximate accuracy, since no signs or letters not already known in the Elvish alphabets are employed; (3) to statements that certain names (especially those of the Valar or of places in Valinor) were translations of the Valarin forms. In cases (1) and (3) the actual Valarin words are not always indicated.

With regard to group (1) Pengolodh cites a 'Saying' of Rúmil: 'The Eldar took few words from the Valar, for they were rich in words and ready in invention at need. But though the honour which they gave to the Valar might have caused them to take words from their speech, whether needed or not, few words of Valarin could be fitted to Elvish speech without great change or diminution. For the tongues and voices of the Valar are great and stern, and yet also swift and subtle in movement, making sounds that we find hard to counterfeit; and their words are mostly long and rapid, like the glitter of swords, like the rush of leaves in a great wind or the fall of stones in the mountains.'

Pengolodh comments: 'Plainly the effect of Valarin upon Elvish ears was not pleasing.' It was, he adds, as may be seen or guessed from what survives, filled with many consonants unfamiliar to the Eldar and alien to the system of their speech.[27]

The examples that Pengolodh gives are as follows.

(1) (a) words

Ainu 'one of the "order" of the Valar and Maiar, made before Eä'. Valarin *ayanūz*. It was from this *ainu* that in Quenya was made the adjective *aina* 'holy', since according to Quenya derivation *ainu* appeared to be a personal form of such an adjective.

aman 'blessed, free from evil'. Chiefly used as the name of the land in which the Valar dwelt. V form not given; said to mean 'at peace, in accord (with Eru)'. See *Manwe*.

apar, Ñ *asar* 'fixed time, festival'. V *apāra* 'appointed'.

axan 'law, rule, commandment'. V *akašān*, said to mean 'He says', referring to Eru.

indil 'a lily, or other large single flower'. V *iniðil*.

mahalma 'throne'. V *maχallām* (adapted to Quenya), properly one of the seats of the Valar in the *Máhanaxar* or 'Doom Ring'. The element *māχan*, said to mean 'authority, authoritative decision', was also used in the form *Máhan*, one of the eight chiefs of the Valar, usually translated as *Aratar*.

miruvóre, miruvor 'a special wine or cordial'. V *mirubhōzē-*; said to be the beginning of a longer word, containing the element *mirub-* 'wine'.[28]

telluma 'dome', especially the 'Dome of Varda' over Valinor; but also applied to the domes of the mansion of Manwe and Varda upon Taniquetil. V *delgūmā*, altered by association with Q *telume*. See Note 15.

Pengolodh also cites the colour-words, which he says may be found in ancient verse, though they are used only by the Vanyar, 'who, as Rúmil reports, adopted many more words than did the Ñoldor':

ezel, ezella 'green'. See *Ezellohar*.
nasar 'red'; *ulban* 'blue'. V forms not given.
tulka 'yellow'. See *Tulkas*.

(b) names

Aule V *Aʒūlēz* (meaning not given).

Manwe Reduction and alteration to fit Quenya, in which words of this shape, ending in *-we*, were frequent in personal names. V *Mānawenūz* 'Blessed One, One (closest) in accord with Eru'. Oldest Q forms *Mánwen, Mánwe*.

Tulkas V *Tulukhastāz*; said to contain V elements *tulukha(n)* 'yellow', and *(a)šata-* 'hair of head': 'the golden-haired'.

Osse, Orome On these two names, the only ones that became known to the Eldar before they reached Aman, see note below.

Ulmo Like *Manwe*, a reduction and alteration to fit Quenya, in which the ending *-mo* often appeared in names or titles, sometimes with an agental significance: *Ulmo* was interpreted as 'the Pourer' < *UL 'pour out'. The V form is given as *Ul(l)ubōz*, containing the element *ul(l)u* 'water'.

Osse and Orome. Orome was the first of the Valar that any of the Eldar saw. Osse they met in Beleriand, and he remained long upon the coasts, and became well known to the Sindar (especially to the Eglain). Both these names therefore have Sindarin forms. To *Osse* corresponds S *Yssion* or *Gaerys*; to *Orome* the S *Araw*. The V forms are given as *Oš(o)šai* (said to mean 'spuming, foaming'); and *Arǭmēz*.

The first name was evidently adopted in the form *Ossai*, which became naturally Q *Osse*. In S *Ossai* would become *ossī* > *ussi* > *yssi* to which the ending (of male names) -*on* was added; or else the adjective **gairā* 'awful, fearful' was prefixed, producing *Gaerys*. The latter was more often used by the inland Teleri. **gairā* is from **gay-* 'astound, make aghast', which was also used in the oldest Eldarin word for the Sea: **gayār*, Q *ëar*, S *gaear*.

Arǭmēz evidently, as was pointed out by Fëanor, contained the open *a*-like *ǭ* (which did as a matter of later observation occur frequently in Valarin). This was treated as was the Eldarin *ǭ*, so that the Sindarin development was > **arāmē* > *arǭmæ* > *araum(a)* > *arauṁ*, *arauv* > *araw*. (In North Sindarin or Mithrim, where the diphthongization of *ō* and the opening of intervocalic *m* did not occur, the form produced was *Arum*; cf. the North Sindarin transformation of the Exilic Ñoldorin name *Hísilóme* > *Hithlum*.) The Quenya form with *Orome* for **Arome* < **Arōmē*, may show assimilation of the initial *o* to the following *ō* before the retraction of the normal Q accent to the first syllable; but Pengolodh says that it was due to the association of the name with the native Q **rom*, used of the sound of trumps or horns, seen in the Q name for the great horn of Orome, the *Vala-róma* (also in Q *romba* 'horn, trumpet', S *rom*).

'The Eldar,' he says, 'now take the name to signify "horn-blowing" or "horn-blower"; but to the Valar it had no such meaning. Now the names that we have for the Valar or the

Maiar, whether adapted from the Valarin or translated, are not right names but titles, referring to some function or character of the person; for though the Valar have right names, they do not reveal them. Save only in the case of Orome. For it is said in the histories of the most ancient days of the Quendi that, when Orome appeared among them, and at length some dared to approach him, they asked him his name, and he answered: *Orome*. Then they asked him what that signified, and again he answered: *Orome. To me only is it given; for I am Orome.* Yet the titles that he bore were many and glorious; but he withheld them at that time, that the Quendi should not be afraid.'

Nahar, the name of Orome's horse. 'Otherwise it was,' says Pengolodh, 'with the steed upon which the Lord Orome rode. When the Quendi asked his name, and if that bore any meaning, Orome answered: "*Nahar*, and he is called from the sound of his voice, when he is eager to run".' But the V form that is recorded by Rúmil was *næχærra*.

Ezellohar (also translated as *Koron Oiolaire, Korollaire*), the Green Mound upon which grew the Two Trees. V *Ezellōχār*.

Máhanaxar, the 'Doom-ring' in which were set the thrones of the Valar whereon they sat in council (see *mahalma* above, p. 399). Reduced and altered from V *māχananaškād*. Also translated as *Rithil-Anamo*.

(2) Valarin words and names, recorded but not adopted.
   (a) words
uruš, rušur 'fire'.
ithīr 'light'.
ul(l)u 'water'.
šebeth 'air'.

   (b) names
Arda: V *Apāraphelūn* (said to mean 'appointed dwelling'). Arda Unmarred: *Apāraphelūn Amanaišāl;* Arda Marred: *Apāraphelūn Dušamanūðān*.
Telperion: V *Ibrīniðilpathānezel*.
Laurelin: V *Tulukhedelgorūs*.
Ithil 'moon': V *Phanaikelūth*. Said to mean 'bright mirror'.
Anar 'Sun': V *Apāraigas*. Said to mean 'appointed heat'.

At the end of this short list Pengolodh cites another *eques* of Rúmil, which might seem contrary to that already quoted above: 'Let none be surprised who endeavour to learn somewhat of the tongue of the Lords of the West, as have I, if they find therein many words or parts of words that resemble our own words for the same or similar meanings. For even as they took our form for love of us, so in that form their voices would be likely to light upon similar *tengwi*.'

Upon this Pengolodh comments: 'He knew not of Men or of Dwarves. But we who have dwelt among Men know that (strange though that seems to some) the Valar love them no less. And for my part I perceive a likeness no less, or indeed greater, between the Valarin and the tongues of Men, notably the language of the Dúnedain and of the Children of Marach (sc. Adunaic). Also in general manner it resembles the tongues of the Kasāri; though this is not to be wondered at, if the tradition that they have is true that Aule devised for them their tongue in its beginning, and therefore it changes little, whereas the *iglishmēk* which they made for themselves is changeable.'

(3) [Cf. p. 398: 'statements that certain names (especially those of the Valar or of places in Valinor) were translations of the Valarin forms']

Arda Q *arda* (< **gardā*, S *gardh*) meant any more or less bounded or defined place, a region. Its use as a proper name for the World was due to V *Apāraphelūn*.

Aratar 'the Supreme', was a version of the V *māχanāz*, pl. *māχanumāz* 'Authorities', also adapted as *Máhan*, pl. *Máhani*.

Eä 'All Creation', meaning 'it is', or 'let it be'. Valarin not recorded.

Ambar 'the Earth', meaning 'habitation'. Though the Eldar often used *Arda* in much the same sense, the proper meaning of *Ambar* was the Earth only, as the place where the Aratar had taken up their dwelling, and the Incarnate were destined to appear.[29]

Eru 'the One'. *Ilúvatar* was, however, a name made by the Eldar (when they had learned of Eru from the Valar), which they used more often than *Eru*, reserved for the most solemn occasions. It was made from *ilúve* 'allness, the all', an equivalent of *Eä*, and *atar* 'father'.

Varda 'the Sublime'. V form not given.

Melkor 'He who arises in Might', oldest Q form **mbelekōro*. V form not given.

Námo 'Judge'; usually called by the Eldar *Mandos*, the place of his dwelling.

Irmo 'Desirer'; usually called by the name of his dwelling *Lórien*.

Este 'Repose'. (*SED: CE **esdē* > **ezdē*, Q *Este*, T *Ēde* (as names only); S *îdh* 'rest, repose'.)

Vala 'has power' (sc. over the matter of Eä), 'a Power'; pl. *Valar*, 'they have power, the Powers'. Since these words are from the point of Q structure verbal in origin, they were probably versions of V words of verbal meaning. Cf. *axan* (p. 399), *Eä*; and also Q *eques*.

Atan, pl. *Atani* 'Men', meaning 'the Second, those coming next'. The Valar called them in full 'the Second Children of Eru', but the Quendi were 'the first Children of Eru'. From these terms the Q *Minnónar* 'First-born' and *Apanónar* 'After-born' were imitated; but Q *Eruhin*, pl. *Eruhíni* 'Children of Eru', or 'Elves and Men', is a translation of the Valarin expression 'Children of Eru' (of which the actual Valarin form is not recorded, probably because the V equivalent of *Eru* is nowhere revealed). Besides the form *-hin*, *-híni* only used in composition after a parental name, Q has *hína* 'child', and *hina* only used in the vocative addressing a (young) child, especially in *hinya* (< *hinanya*) 'my child'. S has *hên*, pl. *hîn*, mostly used as a prefix in patronymics or metronymics: as *Hîn Húrin* 'The Children of Húrin'. These words are derivatives of stem **khin*: *khīnā* (in composition *khīna* > Q *-hin*), and *khīnā*.

Kalakiryan 'the Cleft of Light', the pass in the Pelóri not far from the north side of Taniquetil through which the Light of the Trees in Valinor flowed out to the shores of Aman.

Taniquetil, the highest of the mountains of the Pelóri, upon which were the mansions of Manwë and Varda. The name was properly only that of the topmost peak, meaning High-Snow-Peak. The whole mountain was most often called by the Eldar *(Oron) Oiolossë*, '(Mount) Everwhite' or 'Eversnow'. There were many names for this mountain in Quenya. A variant or close equivalent of *Taniquetil* was *Arfanyaras(se)*. The Sindarin forms of the names were made by the Ñoldor, for the Sindar knew nothing of the land of Aman except by report of the Exiles: e.g. *Amon-Uilos* and *Ras-Arphain*.

Pelóri 'the fencing, or defensive Heights'. The mountains of Aman, ranging in a crescent from North to South, close to the western shores.

On this list Pengolodh comments: 'These are all that I can find in old lore or remember to have read or heard. But the list is plainly incomplete. Many of the names once known and used, whether they be now found in the surviving histories or passed over, must have belonged to the first or the last group. Among those that are still remembered I note *Avathar*, the name of the dim and narrow land between the southern Pelóri and the Sea in which Ungoliante housed. This is not Elvish. There are also the names *Nessa*, the spouse of Tulkas, and *Uinen* the spouse of Osse. These too are not Elvish, so far as cán now be seen; and since the names *Tulkas* and *Osse* come from Valarin, the names of their spouses may also represent titles in the Valarin tongue, or such part of them as the Eldar could adapt. I say "so far as can now be seen", for there is no certainty in this matter without record. It is clear that some, or indeed many, of these adoptions and translations were made in very early days, when the language of the Eldar was otherwise than it became before the Exile. In the long years, owing to the restlessness and inventiveness of the Eldar (and of the Ñoldor in particular), words have been set aside and new words made; but the names of the enduring have endured, as memorials of the speech of the past. There is also this to consider. When words of Elvish tongue had been used to make the names of things and persons high and admirable, they seem to have been felt no longer suitable to apply to lesser things, and so passed from the daily speech.

'Thus we see that *vala* is no longer used of any power or authority less than that of the Valar themselves. One may say *Ā vala Manwe!* "may Manwe order it!"; or *Valar valuvar* "the will of the Valar will be done"; but we do not say this of any lesser name. In like manner *Este* or *Ēde* is the name only of the spouse of Lórien, whereas the form that that word has in Sindarin *(îdh)* means "rest", such as even a tired hound may find before a fire.' *(Note 36, p. 416)*

The reasons that Pengolodh gives or surmises for the scanty knowledge of Valarin preserved in Ñoldorin lore are here summarized. Some have already been alluded to.

Though Valarin had many more sounds than Eldarin, some alien to the Eldarin style and system, this only imposed any real difficulty upon the borrowing of words and their adaptation to Eldarin. To learn Valarin was probably not beyond the powers of the Eldar, if they had felt the need or desire to do so;

references to the difficulty of Valarin are mainly due to the fact that for most of the Eldar learning it was an ungrateful and profitless task.

For the Eldar had no need to learn the language of Valinor for the purposes of communication; and they had no desire either to abandon or to alter their own tongue, which they loved and of which they were proud. Only those among them, therefore, who had special linguistic curiosity desired to learn Valarin for its own sake. Such 'loremasters' did not always record their knowledge, and many of the records that were made have been lost. Fëanor, who probably knew more of the matter than any of the younger generations born in Aman, deliberately withheld his knowledge.

It was probably only in the very early days that the Eldar heard Valarin much spoken, or had opportunity for learning it, unless by special individual effort. The Teleri had little immediate contact with the Valar and Maiar after their settlement on the shores. The Ñoldor became more and more engrossed with their own pursuits. Only the Vanyar remained in constant association with the Valar. And in any case the Valar appear quickly to have adopted Quenya.

All the orders of Eru's creatures have each some special talent, which higher orders may admire. It was the special talent of the Incarnate, who lived by *necessary* union of *hröa* and *fëa*, to make language. The Quendi, first and chief of the Incarnate, had (or so they held) the greatest talent for the making of *lambe*. The Valar and Maiar admired and took delight in the Eldarin *lambe*, as they did in many other of the skilled and delicate works of the Eldar.

The Valar, therefore, learned Quenya by their own choice, for pleasure as well as for communication; and it seems clear that they preferred that the Eldar should make new words of their own style, or should translate the meanings of names into fair Eldarin forms, rather than [that] they should retain the Valarin words or adapt them to Quenya (a process that in most cases did justice to neither tongue).

Soon after the coming of the Vanyar and Noldor the Valar ceased to speak in their own tongue in the presence of the Eldar, save rarely: as for instance in the great Councils, at which the Eldar were sometimes present. Indeed, it is said that often the Valar and Maiar might be heard speaking Quenya among themselves.

In any case, to speak of the early days of the settlement at Tirion, it was far easier and swifter for the Valar to learn Quenya than to teach the Eldar Valarin. For in a sense no *lambe* was 'alien' to the Self-incarnate. Even when using bodily forms they had less need of any *tengwesta* than had the Incarnate; and they had made a *lambe* for the pleasure of exercising the powers and skills of the bodily form, and (more remotely) for the better understanding of the minds of the Incarnate when they should appear, rather than for any need that they felt among themselves. For the Valar and Maiar could transmit and receive thought directly (by the will of both parties) according to their right nature;[30] and though the use of bodily form (albeit assumed and not imposed) in a measure made this mode of communication less swift and precise, they retained this faculty in a degree far surpassing that seen among any of the Incarnate.

At this point Pengolodh does not further discuss this matter of the transmission and reception of thought, and its limitations in any order of creatures. But he cites, as an example of the speed with which by its aid a *tengwesta* may be learned by a higher order, the story of the Finding of the Edain. According to this the Ñoldorin king, Finrod, quickly learned the tongue of the folk of Bëor whom he discovered in Ossiriand, for he understood in large measure what they meant while they spoke. 'Now Finrod,' he says, 'was renowned among the Eldar for this power which he had, because of the warmth of his heart and his desire to understand others; yet his power was no greater than that of the least of the Maiar.'[31]

Pengolodh concludes as follows. 'In the histories the Valar are always presented as speaking Quenya in all circumstances. *(Note 37, p. 417)* But this cannot proceed from translation by the Eldar, few of whose historians knew Valarin. The translation must have been made by the Valar or Maiar themselves. Indeed those histories or legends that deal with times before the awaking of the Quendi, or with the uttermost past, or with things that the Eldar could not have known, must have been presented from the first in Quenya by the Valar or the Maiar when they instructed the Eldar. Moreover this translation must have concerned more than the mere words of language. If we consider the First History, which is called the *Ainulindalë*: this must have come from the Aratar themselves (for the most part indeed from Manwe, it is believed). Though it was plainly put into its present form by Eldar, and was already in that form when it was recorded by Rúmil, it must nonetheless have been from the first presented to us not only in the words of Quenya, but also according to our modes of thought and our imagination of the visible world, in symbols that were intelligible to us. And these things the Valar understood because they had learned our tongue.'

Author's Notes to Quendi and Eldar

Note 1 (p. 367; referred to in two passages)
Distinguish *yomenie* 'meeting, gathering' (of three or more coming from different directions). The Telerin form was: *ël sīla lūmena vomentienguo.*

Note 2 (p. 369)
It was a later development in Quenya, after the elements *-ō* and *-vā* had become inflexions, applicable to all nouns, to pluralize *-o* by the addition of the plural sign *-n*, when added to a plural stem (as by natural function it could be): as *lasseo* 'of a leaf', *lassio* > *lassion* 'of leaves'. Similarly with *-va*; but this was and remained an adjective, and had the plural form *-ve* in plural attribution (archaic Q *-vai*); it could not, however, indicate plurality of source, originally, and the Q distinction *Eldava* 'Elf's' and *Eldaiva* 'Elves'' was a Q innovation.

Note 3 (p. 372)
roquen is < **roko-kwēn* with Quenya syncope, **roko* being an older simpler form of the stem, found in some compounds and compound names, though the normal form of the independent word 'horse' had the fortified form *rokko*. These compounds being old were accented as unitary words and the main stress came on the syllable preceding *-quen*: *kirya:quen*, *kirya:queni*.

Note 4 (p. 373)
That is, elliptically for *Quenya lambe*, as *English* for *English language*. When historians needed a general adjective 'Quendian, belonging to the Elves as a whole', they made the new adjective *Quenderin* (on the model of *Eldarin*, *Ñoldorin*, etc.); but this remained a learned word.

Note 5 (p. 375)
This change took place far back in Elvish linguistic history; possibly before the Separation. It is in any case common to the Telerin of Aman, Sindarin, and Nandorin.

Note 6 (p. 375)
The Ñoldorin Loremasters record that *Pendi* was used by the Teleri only of the earliest days, because they felt that it meant 'the lacking, the poor' (*PEN), with reference to the indigence and ignorance of the primitive Elves.

Note 7 (p. 377)
The Dwarves were in a special position. They claimed to have known Beleriand before even the Eldar first came there; and there do appear to have been small groups dwelling furtively in the highlands west of Sirion from a very early date: they attacked and waylaid the Elves by stealth, and the Elves did not at first recognize them as Incarnates, but thought them to be some kind of cunning animal, and hunted them. By their own account they were fugitives, driven into the wilderness by their own kin further east, and later they were called the *Noegyth Nibin*[32] or Petty-dwarves, for they had become smaller than the norm of their kind, and filled with hate for all other creatures. When the Elves met the powerful Dwarves of Nogrod and Belegost, in the eastern side of the Mountains, they recognized them as Incarnates, for they had skill in many crafts, and learned the Elvish speech readily for purposes of traffic. At first the Elves were in doubt concerning them, believing them to be related to Orcs and creatures of Morgoth; but when they found that, though proud and unfriendly, they could be trusted to keep any treaties that they made, and did not molest those who left them in peace, they traded with them and let them come and go as they would. They no longer classed them as *Moerbin*, but neither did they ever reckon them as *Celbin*, calling them the *Dornhoth* ('the thrawn folk') or the *Naugrim* ('the stunted people'). [See further on the Petty-dwarves pp. 388–9.]

Note 8 (p. 377)
Though *Morben* might still be applied to them by any who remained hostile to Men (as were the people of Doriath for the most part); but this was intended to be insulting.

Note 9 (p. 377; referred to in two passages)
The implication that as opposed to *Celbin* the *Moerbin* were allies of Morgoth, or at least of dubious loyalty, was, however, untrue with regard to the Avari. No Elf of any kind ever sided with Morgoth of free will, though under torture or the stress of great fear, or deluded by lies, they might obey his commands: but this applied also to *Celbin*. The 'Dark-elves', however, often

were hostile, and even treacherous, in their dealings with the Sindar and Ñoldor; and if they fought, as they did when themselves assailed by the Orcs, they never took any open part in the War on the side of the *Celbin*. They were, it seems, filled with an inherited bitterness against the Eldar, whom they regarded as deserters of their kin, and in Beleriand this feeling was increased by envy (especially of the *Amanyar*), and by resentment of their lordliness. The belief of the *Celbin* that, at the least, they were weaker in resistance to the pressures or lies of Morgoth, if this grievance was concerned, may have been justified; but the only case recorded in the histories is that of Maeglin, the son of Eöl. Eöl was a *Mornedhel*, and is said to have belonged to the Second Clan (whose representatives among the Eldar were the Ñoldor).[33] He dwelt in East Beleriand not far from the borders of Doriath. He had great smith-craft, especially in the making of swords, in which work he surpassed even the Ñoldor of Aman; and many therefore believed that he used the *morgul*, the black arts taught by Morgoth. The Ñoldor themselves had indeed learned much from Morgoth in the days of his captivity in Valinor; but it is more likely that Eöl was acquainted with the Dwarves, for in many places the Avari became closer in friendship with that people than the Amanyar or the Sindar. Eöl found Írith,[34] the sister of King Turgon, astray in the wild near his dwelling, and he took her to wife by force: a very wicked deed in the eyes of the Eldar. His son Maeglin was later admitted to Gondolin, and given honour as the king's sisterson; but in the end he betrayed Gondolin to Morgoth. Maeglin was indeed an Elf of evil temper and dark mind, and he had a lust and grudge of his own to satisfy; but even so he did what he did only after torment and under a cloud of fear. Some of the Nandor, who were allowed to be *Celbin*, were not any better. Saeros, a counsellor of King Thingol, who belonged to a small clan of Nandor living in eastern Doriath, was chiefly responsible for the driving into outlawry of Túrin son of Húrin. Túrin's mother was named *Morwen* 'dark maiden', because of her dark hair, and it was one of Saeros' worst insults to call her *Morben*. For that Túrin smote him in the king's hall.[35]

This resentment on the part of the Avari is illustrated by the history of PQ **kwendī*. This word, as has been shown, did not survive in the Telerin languages of Middle-earth, and was almost forgotten even in the Telerin of Aman. But the Loremasters of later days, when more friendly relations had been established with Avari of various kinds in Eriador and the Vale of Anduin, record that it was frequently to be found in Avarin dialects. These were numerous, and often as widely sundered from one another as they were from the Eldarin forms of Elvish speech; but wherever the descendants of *kwendī were found, they meant not 'Elves in general', but were the names that the Avari gave to themselves. They had evidently continued to call themselves *kwendī, 'the People', regarding those who went away as deserters – though according to Eldarin tradition the numbers of the Eldar at the time of the Separation were in the approximate proportion of 3:2, as compared with the Avari (see p. 381). The Avarin forms cited by the Loremasters were: *kindi, cuind, hwenti, windan, kinn-lai, penni*. The last is interesting as showing the change $kw > p$. This might be independent of the Common Telerin change; but it suggests that it had already occurred among the Lindar before the Separation. The form *penni* is cited as coming from the 'Wood-elven' speech of the Vale of Anduin, and these Elves were among the most friendly to the fugitives from Beleriand, and held themselves akin to the remnants of the Sindar.

Note 10 (p. 378)
It is not surprising that the Edain, when they learned Sindarin, and to a certain extent Quenya also, found it difficult to discern whether words and names containing the element *el* referred to the stars or to the Elves. This is seen in the name *Elendil*, which became a favourite name among the Edain, but was meant to bear the sense 'Elf-friend'. Properly in Quenya it meant 'a lover or student of the stars', and was applied to those devoted to astronomical lore. 'Elf-friend' would have been more correctly represented by *Quen(den)dil* or *Eldandil*.

Note 11 (p. 378)
Lake Mithrim, meaning originally 'Lake of the Mithrim'. *Mithrim* was a name given to them by the southern-dwellers, because of the cooler climate and greyer skies, and the mists of the North. It was probably because the Ñoldor first came into contact with this northerly branch that they gave in Quenya the name *Sindar* or *Sindeldi* 'Grey-elves' to all the Telerin inhabitants of the Westlands who spoke the Sindarin language.[36] Though this name was also later held to refer to Elwe's name *Thingol (Sindikollo)* 'Grey-cloak', since he was acknowledged as high-king of all the land and its peoples. It is said also that the

folk of the North were clad much in grey, especially after the return of Morgoth when secrecy became needed; and the Mithrim had an art of weaving a grey cloth that made its wearers almost invisible in shadowy places or in a stony land. This art was later used even in the southern lands as the dangers of the War increased.

Note 12 (p. 380)
The language of Mithrim was also a marked dialect; but none of the dialects of Sindarin differed widely enough to interfere with intercourse. Their divergences were no greater than those that had arisen between the Quenya as spoken by the Vanyar, and as spoken by the Ñoldor at the time of the Exile.

Note 13 (p. 380)
For the late PQ *gl-* as an initial variation of *l-* see General Phonology.[37] Though this Clan-name has **glind-* in Sindarin, the *g-* does not appear in Amanya Telerin, nor in Nandorin, so that in this case it may be an addition in Sindarin, which favoured and much increased initial groups of this kind.

Note 14 (p. 382)
For this reason the most frequently used of the 'titles' or secondary names of the Lindar was *Nendili* 'Water-lovers'.

Note 15 (p. 382)
A simple agental formation (like **abaro* > **abar* from *ABA) from the stem *TELE, the primary sense of which appears to have been 'close, end, come at the end': hence in Q *telda* 'last, final'; *tele-* intransitive verb 'finish, end', or 'be the last thing or person in a series or sequence of events'; *telya* transitive verb 'finish, wind up, conclude'; *telma* 'a conclusion, anything used to finish off a work or affair'. This was possibly distinct from **tel-u* 'roof in, put the crown on a building', seen in Q *telume* 'roof, canopy'. (This was probably one of the earliest Quendian words for the heavens, the firmament, before the increase of their knowledge, and the invention of the Eldarin word *Menel*. Cf. *Telumehtar* 'warrior of the sky', an older name for *Menelmakil*, Orion.) The word *telluma* 'dome, cupola' is an alteration of *telume* under the influence of Valarin *delgūmā*: see p. 399. But **telu* may be simply a differentiated form of *TELE, since the roof was the final work of a building; cf. *telma*, which was often applied to the last item in a structure, such as a coping-stone, or a topmost pinnacle.

Note 16 (p. 384)
See above, p. 381. The proportion, per 144, of the Eldar remaining in Middle-earth was reckoned at 26, of which about 8 were Nandor.

Note 17 (p. 384)
Lenwe is the form in which his name was remembered in Ñoldorin histories. His name was probably *Denwego, Nandorin Denweg. His son was the Nandorin chieftain Denethor. These names probably meant 'lithe-and-active' and 'lithe-and-lank', from *dene- 'thin and strong, pliant, lithe', and *thara- 'tall (or long) and slender'.

Note 18 (p. 384)
The name Nandor was a derivative of the element *dan, *ndan- indicating the reversal of an action, so as to undo or nullify its effect, as in 'undo, go back (the same way), unsay, give back (the same gift: not another in return)'. The original word *ndandō, therefore, probably only implied 'one who goes back on his word or decision'.

Note 19 (p. 386)
In Q Eldameldor, S Elvellyn. That is, 'Elf-lovers'. The words Quendili, Eldandili (see Note 10), though not excluding affection and personal loyalties, would have implied also deep concern with all lore relative to the Elves, which was not necessarily included in the words meldor, mellyn 'lovers, friends'.

Note 20 (p. 387)
That is, to die by nature, of age or weariness, and inevitably, not only (as the Elves) of some grievous hurt or sorrow.

Note 21 (p. 387)
S -eb is from *ikwā, CT *-ipā, probably related to the Q -inqua. Cf. S aglareb 'glorious', Q alkarinqua. Both are probably related to the element *kwa, *kwa-ta seen in Eldarin words for 'full'.

Note 22 (p. 388)
S ch was only an approximation; the Dwarvish kh was in fact a strong aspirate, not a spirant. Similarly at the time of the borrowing Sindarin did not possess either the sound z or long ā. This does not mean that the Elves could not imitate or acquire sounds alien to their native speech. All the Elves had great skill in language, and far surpassed Men in this matter. The Ñoldor

were the chief linguists of the Elves, but their superiority was shown not so much in the acquisition of new tongues as in their love of language, their inventiveness, and their concern with the lore of language, and the history and relations of different tongues. In adopting a word for use in their own tongue (which they loved) Elves fitted it to their own style for aesthetic reasons.

Note 23 (p. 388)
These words are derived from the stem *NUKU 'dwarf, stunted, not reaching full growth or achievement, failing of some mark or standard', seen in *nuktā-, Q *nuhta-* 'stunt, prevent from coming to completion, stop short, not allow to continue', S *nuitha-* of similar senses. An adjectival formation was *naukā, from which were derived S *naug*, Q *nauka*, especially applied to things that though in themselves full-grown were smaller or shorter than their kind, and were hard, twisted or ill-shapen. *Nogoth* is probably from some such form as *nukotto/a 'a stunted or ill-shapen thing (or person)'.

Note 24 (p. 388)
The Q *h* had become too weak to represent aspirate *kh* which was therefore rendered by *k*. Final *d* had become *r*, and this change was recognized in the adaptation. Medial *z* < *s* had become *r* in the Ñoldorin dialect of Q except when an adjacent syllable, or (as here) the same syllable, already contained an *r*.

Note 25 (p. 388)
Norno is a personalized form of the adjective *norna* 'stiff, tough', the Q equivalent of S *dorn*. Both are from the stem *DORO 'dried up, hard, unyielding'. With the frequent initial enrichment *d* > *nd* this appears in PQ *ndorē 'the hard, dry land as opposed to water or bog > land in general as opposed to sea; a land (a particular region with more or less defined bounds)'. Hence S *dôr* (*-ndor* > *-nor, -nnor*) 'land'. In Q this word became confused or blended with the distinct *nōrē from the stem *ONO (see p. 387), 'family, tribe or group having a common ancestry, the land or region in which they dwelt'. Thus Q *nóre* was generally used for 'land' associated with a particular people, and the old *ndorē survived only in name-compounds: as *Valinóre* < *Valinōrē 'the people and land of the Valar', beside *Valinor, Valandor*. A particular land or region was in Q *arda*; 'land' as opposed to water or sea was *nór* (< *ndōro) as opposed to *eär*. The Q forms *norna, Norno* may also contain *nd-*, though S *dorn* does not; but this is probably

one of the cases in which Q initial *d* became *n*-, not *l*-, by assimilation to an *n* occurring later in the word.

Note 26 (p. 389)
Novrod was the oldest form, and appears in the earlier annals, beside the variant *Grodnof*. These contain the CE elements **nābā* 'hollow', and *(g)rotā* 'excavation, underground dwelling'. *Novrod* retains the older Eldarin (and the Dwarvish) order with the adjectival element first. At the time of its making **nāba-grota* had no doubt already reached its archaic S form **nǭv-ʒrot* > *novrod*. *Grodnof* has the same elements in the later more usual Sindarin order. The form *Nogrod* which later became usual is due to the substitution of *Nog-*, taken as a form of *Naug* 'dwarf' (with the usual change of *au* > *o*), after the element *Nov-* had become obscure. The adjective **nābā* > *nǭv*, *nǫf* only remained current in the Northern dialect, where the name *Novrod* originated. In the other dialects *nǭv*, as a stressed independent word, proceeded to *nauv* > *naw* (with the usual loss of final *v* after *au, u*), and this word ceased to be used in current speech. *Novrod* in earlier annals is sometimes found glossed *Bar-goll* 'hollow dwelling', using the more current adjective *coll* < **kuldā*.

Hadhodrond uses the adapted form *Hadhod* = *Khazād*. The element *rond* is not related to *grod, -rod*. The latter is from **groto* 'dig, excavate, tunnel'. S *rond*, Q *rondo* are from **rono* 'arch over, roof in'. This could be applied both to natural and to artificial structures, but its view was always from below and from the inside. (Contrast the derivatives of **tel, *telu* mentioned in Note 15.) CE **rondō* meant 'a vaulted or arched roof, as seen from below (and usually not visible from outside)', or 'a (large) hall or chamber so roofed'. It was still often applied pictorially to the heavens after the Elves had obtained much greater knowledge of 'Star-lore'. Cf. the name *Elrond* 'Star-dome' (*Elros* meant 'Star-glitter'). Cf. also S *othrond* applied to an underground stronghold, made or enlarged by excavation, containing one or more of such great vaulted halls. *othrond* is < S *ost+rond*. CE **ostō*, Q *osto*, S *ost*, is derived from **soto* 'shelter, protect, defend', and was applied to any fortress or stronghold made or strengthened by art. The most famous example, after the great dwelling of Elwe at Menegroth, was *Nargothrond* < *Narog-ost-rond* ('the great underground burg and halls upon the River Narog'), which was made by Finrod, or completed and enlarged by him from the more primitive dwellings made by the Petty-dwarves.

Though distinct in origin the derivatives of *groto and *rono naturally came into contact, since they were not dissimilar in shape, and a *rondō was usually made by excavation. Thus S *groth* < *grottā (an intensified form of *grod* < *grotā) 'a large excavation' might well apply to a *rond*. *Menegroth* means 'the Thousand Caves or Delvings', but it contained one great *rond* and many minor ones.

Note 27 (p. 390)
*(ñ)guruk is due to a combination of *(g)ruk with *NGUR 'horror', seen in S *gorth, gorthob* 'horror, horrible', and (reduplicated) *gorgor* 'extreme horror'.

Note 28 (p. 390)
Some other derivatives are in Quenya: *rukin* 'I feel fear or horror' (constructed with 'from' of the object feared); *ruhta-* 'terrify'; *rúkima* 'terrible'; *rauko* and *arauko* < *grauk-) 'a powerful, hostile, and terrible creature', especially in the compound *Valarauko* 'Demon of Might', applied later to the more powerful and terrible of the Maia servants of Morgoth. In Sindarin appear, for instance, *raug* and *graug*, and the compound *Balrog* (equivalents of Q *rauko*, etc.); *groga-* 'feel terror'; *gruitha* 'terrify'; *gorog* (< *guruk) 'horror'.

Note 29 (p. 392)
Affixes appear in *equen* 'said I', *eques* 'said he / she', used in reporting a dialogue.

Note 30 (p. 392)
*ekwē was probably a primitive past tense, marked as such by the 'augment' or reduplicated base-vowel, and the long stem-vowel. Past tenses of this form were usual in Sindarin 'strong' or primary verbs: as *akāra 'made, did' > S *agor*. *akwā, however, was probably not verbal, but an extension or intensification of *kwā, used adverbially.

Note 31 (p. 392)
In Eldarin languages this is usually found in the forms -*ikwā* or -*ukwā*, or with nasal infixion -*iñkwā*, -*uñkwā*. The vowels *i, u* were probably derived from the terminations of nouns or other stems to which *kwā* was added, but the dissyllabic suffixal forms had become quite independent of this origin. The forms using *u* were mainly applied to things heavy, clumsy, ugly or bad.

Note 32 (p. 393)
Little is said in Ñoldorin lore concerning the language of the Valar and Maiar; but on this point a note is added at the end of this Appendix (pp. 397 ff.).

Note 33 (p. 394)
lamba is derived from *LABA 'move the tongue, lick', and may be referred to *lab-mā (with a suffix frequent in the names of implements): the group bm > mb in CE and possibly earlier. *lambe* is probably from *lab-mē, denoting the action of *LABA, or the use of the *lambā. (Cf. *JULU 'drink', *julmā, Q *yulma*, S *ylf* 'drinking-vessel'; *julmē, Q *yulme*, 'drinking, carousal'.) These words have no original connexion with *LAMA which refers to sounds, especially to vocal sounds, but was applied only to those that were confused or inarticulate. It was generally used to describe the various cries of beasts. Hence the word *laman(a), *lamān, Q *laman*, pl. *lamni* or *lamani*; S *lavan*, pl. *levain*, 'animal', usually only applied to four-footed beasts, and never to reptiles or birds. (This may be compared with *kwene 'user of articulate speech'.) The Sindarin *glam* < *glamb* / *glamm* (p. 391) is an elaboration of *LAM.

Note 34 (p. 394)
In genuine independent use mainly employed between persons out of earshot: the Elves had astonishingly acute eyesight at a distance. These 'signals' were really distinct from the gestures (especially those of the hands) made as concomitants to speech and additions to tone-changes for the conveyance of feeling, though some of the gestures in both systems were similar. The Elves made considerable use of the concomitant gestures, especially in oration or recitation.

Note 35 (p. 398)
By which Pengolodh meant the knowledge available in Middle-earth. The *Lammas* was composed in Eriador.

Note 36 (p. 404)
Other later Loremasters conjectured that *Nessa* was in fact Elvish in form (though archaic, on Pengolodh's own principle), being < *neresā, a feminine adjectival formation from *NER, meaning 'she that has manlike valour or strength'. They also would remove *Taniquetil* from the group of 'translations'. *Arfanyarasse*, they say, is the translation: 'high (i.e. noble, revered) – shining white – peak', but *Taniquetil* is an adaptation, though one that has probably greatly altered the original

in the attempt to give the name some kind of Eldarin significance: ? high white point. As they say, *ta-* does not mean 'lofty' in Eldarin, though it may remind one of *tára* 'tall, high' (*TAR); *nique* does not refer to snow, but to cold; and Q *tilde*, *-til* is not a mountain peak, but a fine sharp point (mostly used of small and slender things). For *nique* cf. Q *niku-* 'be chill, cold (of weather)'; *nique* 'it is cold, it freezes'; *ninque* 'chill, pallid', *nixe* 'frost', *niquis, niquesse* 'frost-patterns' (the latter by association with *quesse* 'feather').

Most significant, they cite from an ancient legend of the Flight the tale that as the mists of Araman wrapped the distant mountains of Valinor from the sight of the Ñoldor, Fëanor raised his hands in token of rejection and cried: 'I go. Neither in light or shadow will I look upon you again, *Dahanigwishtilgūn*.' So it was recorded, though the writers of the histories no longer knew what he meant. For which reason the strange word may have been ill transmitted. But even so it still bears some likeness to *Taniquetil*, though it can no longer be analysed. (In a few versions, say the Loremasters, it is written *dāhanigwiš-telgūn*.) They also cite *Fionwe* [read *Eönwe*?] (the herald of Manwe) as another name for which no Elvish etymology is known.

Note 37 (p. 406)
Usually in a formal and elevated style. Often, when there were differences, rather according to the Vanyarin manner than the Ñoldorin, for the Vanyar were most in their company; though the Ñoldorin writers have sometimes substituted their own forms.

Editorial Notes

1 'affection': mutation (of the vowel *o* caused by the following *i* in *Mori(quendi)*).
2 *sundóma*: see p. 319.
3 *omentielvo*: this was typed *omentielmo*, subsequently changed to *omentielvo*. The same change was made in the Second Edition of *The Fellowship of the Ring* (p. 90).
4 *The Fellowship of the Ring* p. 367 (at the end of the chapter *Lothlórien*); First Edition *vanimalda*, Second Edition *vanimelda*.
5 The term *ómataina* or 'vocalic extension' is used of the addition to the 'base' of a final vowel identical to the *sundóma* (p. 319).
6 'The glooms and the clouds dimming the sun and the stars': an explicit reference, it seems, to some form of the changed astronomical myth adumbrated in Text II of the section 'Myths

Transformed' in *Morgoth's Ring*. In that text my father raised the question 'how can the Eldar be called the "Star-folk"?' if the Sun is 'coeval with the Earth' (X.375); and proposed a complex story (X.377–8) in which the darkening of the world by Melkor, who brought up vast glooms to shut out all vision of the heavens, is a chief element. See further pp. 423–4.

7 'The first people of this kind to be met were the Nandor': this strangely contradicts the history recorded in the *Annals* (GA §19, p. 9; also AAm §84, X.93), according to which the Dwarves first entered Beleriand in Valian Year 1250, and the building of Menegroth was achieved before the coming of Denethor, leader of the Nandor, in 1350 (pp. 11–13). The following statement here that the first invasions of the Orcs followed Morgoth's return is an equally striking contradiction of the *Annals*: according to GA §27 Orcs entered Beleriand in 1330 (cf. also X.106, §85): 'Whence they came, or what they were, the Elves knew not then, deeming them to be Avari, maybe, that had become evil and savage in the wild.'

8 'from Cape Andras to the headland of Bar-in-Mŷl': *Cape Andras* was entered on the map (p. 184, square G 2), but the headland to the south (itself an extension of the coastline as originally drawn) is there called *Ras Mewrim* (p. 190, §63). The name in the present text was typed *Bar-in-Gwael*; the translation 'Home of the Gulls' was added at the same time as the change to *Bar-in-Mŷl* (by a later pencilled change on one copy -*in*- > -*i*-).

9 *Brithonbar*, not *Brithombar*, is the form typed, and not corrected.

10 With this passage on the subject of the Eglain cf. p. 189, §57, and pp. 343–4. The concluding sentence 'But they acknowledged the high-kingship of Thingol, and Círdan never took the title of king' differs from the *Annals*, where Círdan either acknowledged Felagund of Nargothrond as overlord, or else was (as it seems) an independent Lord of the Falas 'yet ever close in friendship with Nargothrond' (GA §85, and commentary p. 117).

11 For the legend of *Imin*, *Tata*, and *Enel* see pp. 420 ff.

12 The story found in the *Annals of Aman* of the kindreds of Morwë and Nurwë, who refused the summons of the Valar and became the Avari (X.81–2, 88, 168), had been abandoned.

13 The name *Lindar* 'Singers' of the Teleri has appeared in the 'Glossary' to the *Athrabeth Finrod ah Andreth* (X.349); it was for long the name of the First Kindred, the later Vanyar.

14 On the waterfall of Cuiviénen see p. 424.

15 In other late writing Círdan is said to have been of the kin of Elwë, but I have not found any statement of the nature of the kinship.

16 *Lenwë* has replaced the long-standing name *Dân* of Denethor's

17 The statement that the Nandor entered Beleriand 'not long before the return of Morgoth' is another remarkable contradiction of the *Annals* (cf. note 7 above). Earlier (p. 377) it is said that they came 'before the return of Morgoth', which no doubt implies the same. But in GA §31 there is a marvellous evocation of 'the long years of peace that followed after the coming of Denethor', and they were indeed long: from 1350 to 1495, 145 Valian Years, or 1389 Years of the Sun. I am at a loss to explain these profound changes in the embedded history.

18 On the Adunaic word *Nimir* 'Elf' see *The Drowning of Anadûnê* (Vol.IX, Index II, p. 473).

19 *Fírimar*: the old form was *Fírimor* (QS §83, V.245, footnote). An account of the development of meaning in the verb *fírë* is given in connection with *Fíriel*, the later name of Míriel, in X.250.

20 The name *Nogoth niben* was adopted in *The Silmarillion* (in the plural, *Noegyth nibin*: see Note 7 to the present text, p. 408); the word *nogoth* of the Dwarves has not occurred before (see note 32 below). For other names and name-forms of the Petty-dwarves see p. 187, §26.

21 In the revision of the QS chapter on the Dwarves the Sindarin name of Khazad-dûm was *Nornhabar*, translated 'Dwarrowdelf' (p. 206). 'Dwarrowdelf' is found also in *The Fellowship of the Ring*; in the present text the Sindarin name was typed *Hadhodrûd* and translated 'Dwarrowmine', but the change to *Hadhodrond* 'Dwarrowvault' was made immediately. *Hadhodrond* was adopted in *The Silmarillion*.

22 Cf. Appendix F to *The Lord of the Rings*, p. 409: 'The lesser kinds were called, especially by the Uruk-hai, *snaga* "slave".'

23 Fëanor held that, in spite of the usual mode of spelling, vowels were each independent *tengwi* or word-building elements.

24 On one copy only a later pencilled correction changed *SAR to *SYAR.

25 At the head of the page is a pencilled note on one copy only: 'Change *Pengolodh* to *Thingódhel*'.

26 For the word *equessi* see p. 392. Both in that passage and in the present one the word was typed *Equeri* and then corrected.

27 For the old conception in the *Lhammas* of the 1930s, according to which the origin of all Elvish speech was in the language of the Valar (communicated to the Elves by Oromë), see V.168, 192–3.

28 In *The Road Goes Ever On*, p. 61, the name *miruvórë* (occurring in *Namárië*) is said to be of Valarin origin.

29 Cf. Note 2 on the Commentary on the *Athrabeth Finrod ah Andreth* (X.337), where it is said that 'Physically Arda was what we should call the Solar System', and that in Elvish traditions 'the principal part of Arda was the Earth (*Imbar* "the Habitation") ...

420   THE WAR OF THE JEWELS

so that loosely used Arda often seems to mean the Earth'. For *Ambar* see the references given in X.359, note 12.

30   Cf. AAm §164 (X.129): 'without voices in silence [the gods] may hold council one with another', and the passage cited from *The Return of the King* in my note on that passage (X.135).

31   Cf. the late QS chapter *Of the Coming of Men into the West*, p. 217: 'Felagund discovered ... that he could read in the minds of Men such thoughts as they wished to reveal in speech, so that their words were easily interpreted.'

32   *Noegyth Nibin* was a correction of the name typed, *Nibinn..g*, probably *Nibinnoeg* (see p. 187, §26). The notes being interspersed in the text, this note was written before the passage on p. 388 was reached.

33   It is curious that – as in the original text of *Maeglin*, where he was 'of the kin of Thingol' – in my father's very late work on the story Eöl becomes again 'one of the Eldar' (p. 328), though consumed with hatred of the Noldor; whereas here he is a *Mornedhel* (one of the Avari), and moreover of the aboriginal Second Clan.

34   The name *Írith* is found as a correction (made after the publication of *The Lord of the Rings*) of the old name *Isfin* in QS §42 (X.177). When my father worked on the *Maeglin* story c.1970 he appears to have forgotten *Írith*, for his notes at that time express dissatisfaction with the 'meaningless' name *Isfin* as if it had never been replaced (pp. 317–18).

35   Saeros' insulting of Túrin by calling his mother Morwen *Morben* was a development in the story (see QS §39, V.321, and *Unfinished Tales* p. 80) that could only arise, of course, with the emergence of the words *Calben* and *Morben*.

36   Neither the interpretation of *Mithrim* as the name of a people (for the old etymology see V.383–4, stem RINGI) nor this explanation of the name *Sindar* have been met before.

37   'General Phonology': my father was not here referring to any specific, completed work.

APPENDIX

The legend of the Awaking of the Quendi
(Cuivienyarna)

It is said in *Quendi and Eldar*, p. 380:

According to the legend, preserved in almost identical form among both the Elves of Aman and the Sindar, the Three Clans were in the beginning derived from the three Elf-fathers: *Imin*, *Tata*, and *Enel* (sc. One, Two, Three), and those whom each chose to join his following. So they had at first simply the names *Minyar* 'Firsts', *Tatyar* 'Seconds', and *Nelyar* 'Thirds'. These numbered, out of the original 144 Elves that first awoke, 14, 56, and 74; and these proportions were approximately maintained until the Separation.

A form of this legend is found in a single typescript with carbon copy. On one copy my father wrote (and similarly but more briefly on the other): 'Actually written (in style and simple notions) to be a surviving Elvish "fairytale" or child's tale, mingled with counting-lore'. Corrections to either copy are taken up in the text that follows.

While their first bodies were being made from the 'flesh of Arda' the Quendi slept 'in the womb of the Earth', beneath the green sward, and awoke when they were full-grown. But the First Elves (also called the Unbegotten, or the Eru-begotten) did not all wake together. Eru had so ordained that each should lie beside his or her 'destined spouse'. But three Elves awoke first of all, and they were elf-men, for elf-men are more strong in body and more eager and adventurous in strange places. These three Elf-fathers are named in the ancient tales *Imin*, *Tata*, and *Enel*. They awoke in that order, but with little time between each; and from them, say the Eldar, the words for one, two, and three were made: the oldest of all numerals.*

Imin, Tata and Enel awoke before their spouses, and the first thing that they saw was the stars, for they woke in the early twilight before dawn. And the next thing they saw was their destined spouses lying asleep on the green sward beside them. Then they were so enamoured of their beauty that their desire for speech was immediately quickened and they began to 'think of words' to speak and sing in. And being impatient they could not wait but woke up their spouses. Thus, the Eldar say, the first thing that each elf-woman saw was her spouse, and her love for him was her first love; and her love and reverence for the wonders of Arda came later.

Now after a time, when they had dwelt together a little, and had devised many words, Imin and Iminyë, Tata and Tatië, Enel and Enelyë walked together, and left the green dell of their waking, and they came soon to another larger dell and found there six pairs of Quendi, and the stars were again shining in the morrow-dim and the elf-men were just waking.

Then Imin claimed to be the eldest and to have the right of

---

* [footnote to the text] The Eldarin words referred to are *Min*, *Atta* (or *Tata*), *Nel*. The reverse is probably historical. The Three had no names until they had developed language, and were given (or took) names after they had devised numerals (or at least the first twelve).

first choice; and he said: 'I choose these twelve to be my companions.' And the elf-men woke their spouses, and when the eighteen Elves had dwelt together a little and had learned many words and devised more, they walked on together, and soon in another even deeper and wider hollow they found nine pairs of Quendi, and the elf-men had just waked in the starlight.

Then Tata claimed the right of second choice, and he said: 'I choose these eighteen to be my companions.' Then again the elf-men woke their spouses, and they dwelt and spoke together, and devised many new sounds and longer words; and then the thirty-six walked abroad together, until they came to a grove of birches by a stream, and there they found twelve pairs of Quendi, and the elf-men likewise were just standing up, and looking at the stars through the birch boughs.

Then Enel claimed the right of third choice, and he said: 'I choose these twenty-four to be my companions.' Again the elf-men woke their spouses; and for many days the sixty Elves dwelt by the stream, and soon they began to make verse and song to the music of the water.

At length they all set out together again. But Imin noticed that each time they had found more Quendi than before, and he thought to himself: 'I have only twelve companions (although I am the eldest); I will take a later choice.' Soon they came to a sweet-smelling firwood on a hill-side, and there they found eighteen pairs of Quendi, and all were still sleeping. It was still night and clouds were in the sky. But before dawn a wind came, and roused the elf-men, and they woke and were amazed at the stars; for all the clouds were blown away and the stars were bright from east to west. And for a long time the eighteen new Quendi took no heed of the others, but looked at the lights of Menel. But when at last they turned their eyes back to earth they beheld their spouses and woke them to look at the stars, crying to them *elen, elen!* And so the stars got their name.

Now Imin said: 'I will not choose again yet'; and Tata, therefore, chose these thirty-six to be his companions; and they were tall and dark-haired and strong like fir-trees, and from them most of the Ñoldor later were sprung.

And the ninety-six Quendi now spoke together, and the newly-waked devised many new and beautiful words, and many cunning artifices of speech; and they laughed, and danced upon the hill-side, until at last they desired to find more companions. Then they all set out again together, until they came to a lake dark in the twilight; and there was a great cliff about it upon the east-side, and a waterfall came down from the height, and the stars glittered on the foam. But the elf-men were already bathing in the waterfall, and they had waked their spouses. There were twenty-four pairs; but as yet they had no formed speech, though they sang sweetly and their voices echoed in the stone, mingling with the rush of the falls.

But again Imin withheld his choice, thinking 'next time it will be a great company'. Therefore Enel said: 'I have the choice, and I choose these forty-eight to be my companions.' And the hundred and forty-four Quendi dwelt long together by the lake, until they all became of one mind and speech, and were glad.

At length Imin said: 'It is time now that we should go on and seek more companions.' But most of the others were content. So Imin and Iminyë and their twelve companions set out, and they walked long by day and by twilight in the country about the lake, near which all the Quendi had awakened – for which reason it is called Cuiviénen. But they never found any more companions, for the tale of the First Elves was complete.

And so it was that the Quendi ever after reckoned in twelves, and that 144 was for long their highest number, so that in none of their later tongues was there any common name for a greater number. And so also it came about that the 'Companions of Imin' or the Eldest Company (of whom came the Vanyar) were nonetheless only fourteen in all, and the smallest company; and the 'Companions of Tata' (of whom came the Ñoldor) were fifty-six in all; but the 'Companions of Enel' although the Youngest Company were the largest; from them came the Teleri (or Lindar), and they were in the beginning seventy-four in all.

Now the Quendi loved all of Arda that they had yet seen, and green things that grew and the sun of summer were their delight; but nonetheless they were ever moved most in heart by the Stars, and the hours of twilight in clear weather, at 'morrow-dim' and at 'even-dim', were the times of their greatest joy. For in those hours in the spring of the year they had first awakened to life in Arda. But the Lindar, above all the other Quendi, from their beginning were most in love with water, and sang before they could speak.

It seems that my father had resolved (at least for the purpose of this 'fairy-tale') the problem of the name 'Star-folk' of the Elves (see p. 417, note 6) in a beautifully simple way: the first Elves awoke in the late night under skies of unclouded stars, and the stars were their earliest memory.

In *Quendi and Eldar* (p. 382) my father wrote of 'the lake and waterfall of Cuiviénen', and this is explained in the *Cuivienyarna*: 'they came to a lake dark in the twilight; and there was a great cliff about it upon the east-side, and a waterfall came down from the height, and the stars glittered on the foam.' Through so many years he was returning to Gilfanon's Tale in *The Book of Lost Tales* (I.232):

> Now the places about Koivië-néni the Waters of Awakening are rugged and full of mighty rocks, and the stream that feeds that water falls therein down a deep cleft ... a pale and slender thread, but the issue of the dark lake was beneath the earth into many endless caverns falling ever more deeply into the bosom of the world.

INDEX

Elements in this book have greatly taxed my limited powers as an index-maker: notably, the reconstitution of the genealogy of the ruling house of the people of Brethil, introducing extremely complex movements of closely similar names, but also in such matters as the Dwarf-cities or the terms in different languages for 'Eldar', 'Elves'. I have found it often impossible within a short space to give an adequate indication of the bearings and relations of names, and my brief explanatory identifications cannot in such cases be pressed.

Whereas in the texts themselves I have very largely followed my father's very variable usage in respect of capitalisation, hyphenation, separation of elements, or placing of a diaeresis (*Ëarendil, Eärendil*), in the index I employ constant forms (and such devices as the combination of *Eryd-* and *Ered-* in the names of mountain-ranges in a single entry). For 'voiced *th*' I use '*dh*' (*Aredhel*) rather than 'ð' (*Areðel*).

Names appearing in the genealogical tables of the houses of the Edain are included, as also are those on the maps (pp. 182–5), these latter being indicated by asterisks; but names on the map repeated on p. 331 are not, unless additional or altered.

In the entries relating to Part Four (*Quendi and Eldar*) names of languages, as *Quenya*, *Sindarin*, or *Common Eldarin*, include the many instances where abbreviations are used in the text. No Valarin names are recorded in the index, and only exceptionally the 'deduced' or 'unrecorded' name-forms marked in the text by asterisks.

Names occurring in the titles or sub-titles of chapters, etc. are only exceptionally included.

Abari   See *Avari*.
Abonnen   See *Apanónar*.
Adan   See *Edain*.
Adanel   'Wise-woman' of the People of Marach. 230–1, 233–5
Adûnaic   390, 402, 419
Adurant, River   In Ossiriand. 13, *185, 191, 195
Ælfwine   192–3, 206, 311–12, 314–15
Aelin-uial   194. See *Hithliniath, Umboth Muilin, Twilight Meres*.
Aeluin   See *Tarn-aeluin*.
Aerandir   Companion of Eärendil on his voyages; earlier form *Airandir*. 246

Aerin Wife of Brodda. 145; earlier form *Airin*. 88, 90, 145–6
After-born, The Men. 386–7. See *Apanónar*.
Agarwaen 'Blood-stained', name taken by Túrin in Nargothrond. 138, 142. See *Iarwaeth*.
Agathor Father of Manthor of Brethil. 270
Aglon, Pass of 38, 49, 53, 77 *(Gorge of)*, 188, 326, 329, 338; Aglond 188, 328–9, 332, 338; Aglon(d *183, 188. On the two forms see 338.
Ainulindalë 3, 406; *the First History* 406
Ainur Vision of the Ainur 341; singular *Ainu* 399; *the Music* 341
Alairë Vanyarin Elf, wife of Turgon. 323. See *Anairë, Elenwë*.
Albarth Precursor of Hunthor of Brethil. 153, 155–6, 164, 267; Albard 153. See *Torbarth, Gwerin*.
Aldarion and Erendis 232
Alqualondë 19, 26, 43, 177
Aman 5–8, 16–17, 21, 24–6, 35–6, 40–2, 105–7, 121, 216, 323, 365, 370–6, 378–86, 392–3, 396–400, 403, 405, 407, 409, 420. The Chronicle(s) of Aman 5, 30, 105; Mountains of Aman 403 (see *Pelóri, Valinor*).
Amaneldi =*Amanyar*. 373
Amanyar '(Elves) of Aman'. 373–4, 381, 409; adjectivally *Amanya(r)* 381, 383, 411
Amárië Vanyarin Elf, beloved of Felagund. 44, 62, 67, 129–30, 243, 323
Ambar ('Habitation'), the Earth. 402, 420. See *Imbar*.
Ambarkanta 104–5, 109, 174
Amlach Grandson of Marach, a leader of dissension in Estolad. 220–1, 227, 233–4
Amon Carab See *Carabel*.
Amon Darthir Mountain above Húrin's house in Dor-lómin. 181, *182
Amon Ereb 'The Lonely Hill' in East Beleriand. 16, 112, *185
Amon Ethir 'The Hill of Spies' east of Nargothrond. 93–4, 149–50
Amon Garabel See *Carabel*.
Amon Gwareth The hill of Gondolin. 200; *Amon Gwared* 200
Amon Obel Hill in the Forest of Brethil. 89, 92, 145, 151, 159, *182
Amon Rûdh 'The Bald Hill', abode of Mîm. 138, 187, 311, 313–15. Discarded names *Carabel, Amon Carab,* ~ *Garabel,* ~ *Nardol,* ~ *Rhûg* 187
Amon Uilos Sindarin name of Oiolossë. 403. See *Ras-Arphain*.
Amras Later name of Díriel son of Fëanor. 197, 225, 240, 329
Amrod Later name of Damrod son of Fëanor. 197, 240, 329
Anach, Pass of *183
Anairë (1) Vanyarin Elf, wife of Turgon. 323 (see *Alairë, Elenwë*). (2) Wife of Fingolfin. 323
Anar The Sun. 401

Anaxartaron Onyalië, Anaxartamel Titles of *Of the Ents and the Eagles*. 340–1
Ancalagon The Black Dragon. 346–7
Andram 'The Long Wall' across Beleriand. 15, *185, 190, 193, 195, 335
Andras, Cape The 'long cape' west of Brithombar. *184, 189, 379, 418
Andrast The 'long cape' in the west of Gondor. 189
Andreth 'Wise-woman' of the House of Bëor. 227, 230–3. See *Saelin*.
Andróg Member of Túrin's outlaw-band. 311, 314–15
Androth, caves of In the hills of Mithrim. 91
Anduin 105–6, 110, 384; *Vale of Anduin* 110, 381, 410; *Mouths of Anduin* 13. See *Great River*.
Andvír Son of Andróg. 311, 314–15
Anfangrim 'Longbeards', the Dwarves of Belegost. 322. See *Enfeng*.
Anfauglith 'The Gasping Dust', name of Ardgalen after its desolation. 52, 55, 60, 63, 68, 70–3, 79, 85, 124–5, 131, 141, 167–8, 252. See *Dor-na-Fauglith*.
Angainor The chain with which Melkor was bound. 247
Angband 15–18, 30–1, 35–7, 46, 50, 54–6, 60, 63, 68, 71–5, 77, 79, 82–4, 86, 97, 111, 113, 116, 118, 121, 124–5, 128, 131–2, 134, 137–8, 166–8, 196, 203, 252–3, 259, 263–4, 267, 275, 277, 284–5, 321, 329–30, 344–5, 347; *the Iron Prison* 15, *the hells of iron* 196; called *hell* 46. Later story of the origin of Angband 196, 344. *The Siege of Angband, the leaguer* 36, 38–9, 46, 52, 54, 116, 203, 216, 221, 329
Angbor The 'Doom-rock' in the Moot-ring in Brethil. 283, 290, 309; called *Halabor* 309; *the Stone* 283–4, 286, 290–2, 305, 309
Anglachel Beleg's sword (made by Eöl) that was reforged for Túrin. 321. See *Gurthang*.
Anglo-Saxon 141 *(Chronicle)*, 314 (verse). See *English*.
Angrod Son of Finarfin (= Finrod (1)). 32–3, 38, 43, 52, 115, 119, 136, *183, 195
Annael Elf of Mithrim, fosterfather of Tuor. 79, 136–7.
Annon(-in-)Gelydh 'The Gate of the Noldor' in Dor-lómin. 181, *182
Anórien 187
Apanónar 'The After-born', Men. 386–7, 403; Sindarin *Abonnen*, plural *Eboennin* 387
Aphadon, plurals *Ephedyn, Aphadrim* 387. Sindarin rendering of *Hildor*. See *Echil*.
Arachon Father of Beldis the mother of Brandir the Lame. 231
Aradan See *Malach*.
Aragorn 130, 177, 369
Araman Wasteland between the Pelóri and the Sea, north of Taniquetil. 175, 417. See *Eruman*.

Aranel Name of Dior Thingol's Heir. 71, 133
Aratar The Chiefs of the Valar. 399, 402 *('the Supreme')*, 406. See *Máhani, Varda.*
Araw (Sindarin) Oromë. 400; *Arum* in Mithrim 400
Arda 10–11, 18, 24, 41, 69, 78, 204, 207, 216, 341, 346, 397, 401–2, (413), 419–21, 423; *Arda Marred,* ~ *Unmarred* 401; *Spring of Arda* 106, *Second* ~ 20, 27, 30
Ardamir Name of Eärendil. 235
Ardgalen The great northern plain. 17, 36, 38, 46, 52, (111), 113–14, 175, *183, 191, 195, 238. See *Bladorion.*
Aredhel 'Noble-elf' (318), sister of Turgon, wife of Eöl. 317–19, 322–3, 325–30, (333), 336; *the White Lady of the Noldor* 317. See *Isfin, Írith, Feiniel.*
Arfanyarassë Taniquetil. 403, 416. See *Ras-Arphain.*
Ar-Feiniel See *Feiniel.*
Arminas Noldorin Elf who with Gelmir (2), also called Faramir, came to Nargothrond with warning of its peril. 141–2, 256, 299
Aros, River 15, 112, *183, *185, 188–90, 194, 222, 319, 324, 332–4, 337–8. *Ford(s) of Aros* *183, 188, 319, 324–6, (327), *331, 332–6, 338
Arossiach The Fords of Aros. 326, 338
Arthad Companion of Barahir. 56, 126, 240; earlier *Arthod* 126, 240; erroneous *Arthrod* 240
Arthórien Doriath between Aros and Celon. 112–13, *183, 189; *Arthúrien,* name of Doriath, 189 (see *Garthúrian*).
Arvernien High country west of Sirion's mouths. *184, 190
Arwen 71, 132, 369
Ascar, River In Ossiriand. 13, *185, 206, 216, 221, 334–5, 337, 347–9; *Ford(s) of Ascar* 347–50, 352(–3); *Asgar* 336–7. See *Rathlóriel.*
Asgon (also earlier *Asgorn,* see 301) Companion of Húrin after his release. 146, 253, 257–8, 261–7, 270–1, 278, 298, 300–1, 304, 306–7, 310, 355
Atanatári 'Fathers of Men'. 39, 175; *Atanatardi* 174; *Atanatarni* 166, 174. *Atanatárion,* 'Legendarium of the Fathers of Men', 175
Atani 'The Second', Men. 31, 114, 174, 206, 219, 386–7, 403; *Atan* singular 386–7, 403. See *Edain.*
Athrabeth Finrod ah Andreth 226–8, 230, 233, 235, 418–19
Athrad Daer 'The Great Ford', Sarn Athrad. 335; ~ *Dhaer* 338. See *Harathrad, Sarn Athrad,* and next entry; also *Northern Ford.*
Athrad i-Nogoth, ~ *i-Negyth* 'Ford of the Dwarves', Sarn Athrad. 338
Attalyar (Quenya) Petty-dwarves. 389
Aulë 10, 108, 203–5, 207, 210–15, 340–1, 399, 402; called *the Maker* 10. *Children of Aulë,* the Dwarves, 213. See *Mahal.*
Aureldi, Auzeldi Elves who left Middle-earth for Aman; singular

Aurel, Auzel. 363–4, 374; Telerin *Audel, Audelli* 364, 376. See *Oäreldi.*
Avamanyar Elves who would not go to Aman (Avari). 370
Avari Elves who refused the Great March. 12, 112, 173–4, 371–4, 376–8, 380–2, 384, 386, 408–10, 418, 420; singular *Avar* 371, 377; Telerin *Abari* 380. See *Avarin, Evair.*
Avarin (languages) 381, 389–91, 410; Avarin forms cited 410
Avathar 'The Shadows', wasteland between the Pelóri and the Sea, south of Taniquetil. 404
Avranc Son of Dorlas of Brethil, enemy of Húrin and slayer of Manthor. 275–9, 284–90, 292–3, 296, 303–4, 308–9; rejected names *Farang, Faranc* 303, 306; late change to *Daruin* 309
Awakening of the Elves 105, 108, 207, 211, 342, 389; ~ *of the Quendi* 37, 117, 406; legend of the Awakening *(Cuivienyarna)* 380, 382, 420–3
Axe-elves The Sindar. 109, 126
Azaghâl Lord of Belegost. 75, 143

Balan True name of Bëor. 218, 229, 231
Balar Name of Ossë. 5, 104; origin of the name *Beleriand* 5, 104; *Bay of Balar* 6–7, 104, *184, 379; *Cape Balar* 104, 107, *184; *Isle of Balar* 5, 7–8, 11, 54, 80, 104, 107, 125, 136, *184, 345
Balrog(s) 18, 74–5, 110, 113–14, 134, 194, 415; number of 74, 134; etymology 415
Ban Father of Blodren. 82
Barad Eithel Fortress of the Noldor at Eithel Sirion. 168
Barad Nimras Tower on the cape west of Eglarest. *184, 190, 198; *Nimras* 198. (Replaced *Ingildon.*)
Baragund Father of Morwen. 51, 56, 61, (79), 162, (224), 230–2, 241–2, 268; his wife 126
Barahir Father of Beren; originally son of Bëor, later son of Bregor. 49, 51–2, 56, 59, 61, 64(–5), 71, 126, *183, 217, 224, 229–32, 234, 240–2
Baran Elder son of Bëor the Old. 218–19, 229–31, 334; called *Bëor the Young* 230–1
Baranor Son of Baran. 230–1
Bar Bëora The House of Bëor. 230
Bar-goll 'Hollow dwelling', translation of *Novrod* (Nogrod). 414
Bar Haleth Transient name replacing *Ephel Brandir.* 157, *182, 186
Bar-in-Mŷl 'Home of the Gulls', cape south-west of Eglarest (replacing *Bar-in-Gwael* 418). 190, 379–80, 418. See *Ras Mewrim.*
Battle of Sudden Flame The Fourth Battle of Beleriand (formerly the third). 52, 127, 134, 238, 241, 329; *the Sudden Flame* 53; earlier ~ *of Sudden Fire* 124, 126, 238, ~ *of Fire* *183. See *Dagor Bragollach.*
Battle of the Gods (when Melkor was chained) 207

Battle of Unnumbered Tears   The Fifth Battle of Beleriand (formerly the fourth). 28, 71, 121–2, 136–7, 165, 168–9, 174, *182, 236, 243, 245, 312, 314–16. See *Nírnaeth Arnoediad*.

Battle-under-Stars   The Second Battle of Beleriand (formerly the first). 17, 111, 113–14. See *Dagor-nuin-Giliath*.

Bauglir   Name of Morgoth. 84

Beldir   Son of Belen son of Bëor the Old. 230–1

Beldis   Wife of Handir of Brethil, mother of Brandir the Lame. 231, 237–8, 268; earlier the daughter of Bregor 230

Beleg   'The Bowman', of Doriath. 56, 63, 81–3, 102, 126, 133, 138, 140, 160, 314, 352

Belegor   Son of Boron. 230–1

Belegost   'Great Fortress', city of the Dwarves in the Blue Mountains. 10, 45, 75, 108–9, 134, 143, 167, *183, 201–2, 205–6, 208–9, 215, 321, 329, 335, 347, 350, 352, 389, 408. See *Gabilgathol*; *Turosto*; *Great Fortress*, *Mickleburg*.

Belegund   Father of Rían the mother of Tuor. 51–2, 56, 71, (224), 230–2, 241–2; his wife 126

Belemir   The husband of Adanel. 230–1, 233–4

Belen   Second son of Bëor the Old. 230–1

Beleriand   5–9, 12–15, 19–33, 36–9, 42, 44–7, 49, 52, 54, 59–61, 64, 70, 77–80, 103–12, 116, 118–19, 121–4, 127–8, 132, 135–6, 160, 177, 186, 192, 197, 199–203, 206, 215–16, 218–20, 225–6, 228–9, 231–5, 241, 260, 283, 296, 304, 311, 313, 315, 322, 334, 337, 343–5, 360, 365, 373–81, 383–7, 389–90, 396–7, 400, 408–10, 418–19; *Belerian* 5, 104

   East(ern) Beleriand 7, 49, 53, 59, 127–8, *185, 189, 327, 330, 334, 377, 385, 388, 409; *West(ern)* ~ *182/184, 193, 378–9; *Mid-Beleriand* *182/184, 190 (see *Methiriad*); *South* ~ *185, 191, 239; *Northern* ~ 7, *North Marches of* ~ 194.

   Origin and reference of the name 5, 104. *Lays of Beleriand* 103, 160, 311

Beleriandic   (of language) 22–4, 110; (with other reference) 107, 344

Beleth   Daughter of Bregolas. 230–2; earlier the daughter of Boron 230

Belthil   Image of Telperion in Gondolin. 200

Bëor (the Old)   48–9, 51–2, 123, 206, 216–19, 224–6, 229–31, 240–1, 334; name signified 'Vassal' 206, 217, 226–7, 229, 'Servant' 218, 227; used as title of Bëor's successors 217, 229; see *Balan*.

   House, People, Folk, Men of Bëor 50–2, 61, 64, 77–8, 123–4, 126, 128, 161, *183, 217–21, 224, 226–34, 236–8, 240, 268, 270, 300, 406; *Bëorian(s)* 229, 236, 268; see *Bar Bëora*. Ancient tongue of 202, 217, 226–7, 270, 406; genealogical table 231

Bëor the Young   See *Baran*.

INDEX

Bereg Son of Baranor, a leader of dissension in Estolad. 220–1, 227, 230–1
Beregar Father of Erendis of Númenor. 232
Beren (1) Grandfather of Beren One-hand. 231, 233–4
Beren (2) 'One-hand'. 22, (50), 51, 56, 59, 61–71, 79, 83, 126, 129–32, *185, 195, 224, 228, 231–2, 234, 241–3, 247, 345–50, 353, 355–6. Called *the blessed* 65; and see *Camlost, Erchamion*.
Beril Daughter of Boromir (2). 231
Bilbo 190
Black Speech 390
Black Sword, The Túrin. 83, 90, 97, 99, 101, 152, 158, 162, 256; *the Blacksword of the South* 90. See *Mormegil*.
Bladorion Earlier name of Ardgalen. 113–14, 175, 191, 195, 238
Blessed Realm, The 6, 8, 106, 130, 175, 390; ~ *Realms* 39
Blodren Easterling who betrayed Túrin's lair in Dimbar. 82; earlier *Blodrin*, a Noldorin elf, 137
Blue Mountains 5, 9, 45, 104, 108–9, 121, 123, 128, 179–80, 193, 201–3, 209, 229, 232, 385; *the mountains* 9, 12–14, 20, 45, 48, 59–60, 107, 109, 121, 127, 203, 206, 215–18, 221–2, 225, 296, 335–6, 350, 353, 377, 386, 408. See *Eryd Lindon, Eryd Luin*.
Book of Lost Tales, The 121, 244–5, 424; *the Lost Tales* 130. *Gilfanon's Tale* 424; *Turambar and the Foalókë* 121, 141, 144, 152, 154–5, 160, 251, 300, 315, 352, 354–5; *The Fall of Gondolin* 120–1, 201, 302, 317–18, 320, 344; *The Nauglafring* 108, 201, 208–9, 346–7, 349, 352, 354–5
Bór A chieftain of the Easterlings, faithful to the Eldar. 61, 64, 70, 74, 128–9; his sons (unnamed) 74, 135
Borlach Son of Bór. 240. See *Boromir* (1).
Borlad Son of Bór. 240; earlier *Borlas* 61, 64, 128, 240
Boromir (1) Son of Bór (replaced by *Borlach*). 61, 64, 128, 240.
Boromir (2) Son of Boron; fourth ruler of the House of Bëor. 224, 228–31, 240
Boron Third ruler of the House of Bëor. 224, 229–31
Borthand Son of Bór. 61, 240; earlier *Borthandos* 61, 64, 128, 240
Bragollach, The See *Dagor Bragollach*.
Brandir (1) Uncle of Brandir (2). 231, (237). (2) Brandir the Lame, son of Handir of Brethil. 89, 92, 96–7, 99–102, 148, 151–2, 155–61, 163–4, 231, 234, 237, 256–7, 263–70, 278, 285, 297, 299, 302–5, 309. See *Tamar*.
Bregil Daughter of Bregor, grandmother of Brandir the Lame. 230–1, 268; earlier the daughter of Boromir 230
Bregolas Brother of Barahir; originally son of Bëor, later son of Bregor. 49, 51–2, 56, 217, 224, 229–32, 240–1, 268
Bregor Fifth ruler of the House of Bëor. 224, 228–31, 240, 268
Brethil, (Forest of) 47, 49–50, 56–8, 70, 72, 79, 84–5, 89, 92, 95–7,

101, 122–4, 126, 132, 139, 141, 144–5, 147, 157–8, (161)–2, 166, *182, 200, 223, 228, 231, 236, 238, 241, 244, 251, 254–8, 260–71, 273, 276, 278–9, 283, 285, 288–91, 296–310, 332, 355
    Men of Brethil 74, 92, 97, 102, 127, 141, 147, 163, 168, 236, 241, 256–7, 263, 270, 286, 290, 305, and see Woodmen. Folk of Brethil 278, 287–9, 306–8; the Folk 278–81, 283–4, 286, 289, 293–4, 303–5, 309. Folk-moot 281, the Moot 282–6, 291–2, 294–5, 304; Moot-ring 282, 287, 289, 291, 305, 307, 309, the Ring 291–2, 295, 309; the Stone in the Moot-ring, see Angbor. The Garth of the Graves 295
    Titles of the Chieftains of Brethil: Lord 262, 270, 299, 302; Master 262–3, 265–7, 270–1, 277–9, 304; Warden (see Halad) 267, 270, 304, 308–9; Chieftain (the final term) 148, 256, 263–4, 269, 271, 275–7, 279, 281, 287, 291, 293, 295, 297, 299, 303, 308–9, Chief 258. Hall of the Chieftains 263, 279, 292, 305–6, Hall of the Haladin 293; and see Obel Halad.
Brilthor, River   In Ossiriand. 13, *185
Brithiach   Ford over Sirion at the northern edge of Brethil. 57, 127, *182, 186, 188, 222, 228, 261(–2), 267, 270–1, (273), 301, 303, 319, 324–5, 332–3, 335
Brithombar   The northern Haven of the Falas. 8, 40, 80, 111, 117, *184, 197, 418; Brithonbar 380, 418
Brithon, River   80, *182
Brodda   Easterling in Hithlum, slain by Túrin. 88, 90, 145–6, 253, 257, 298, 300; the Incomer 90
Bronwë   Companion of Tuor. 90–1, 137, 146; Bronweg 137, 354. See Voronwë.

Cabad Amarth   'Leap of Doom'. 160. See Cabed Naeramarth.
Cabed-en-Aras   (also earlier Cabad ~) 'The Deer's Leap' (157), deep gorge in the Taiglin. 98, 100, 102, 156–7, 159–60, 267, 299–300. Original name Mengas Dûr 156
Cabed Naeramarth   (also earlier Cabad ~) 'Leap of Dreadful Doom', name of Cabed-en-Aras after Nienor's death. 100, 102, 160, 273–4, 296, 306
Calapendi   See Kalaquendi.
Calben, plural Celbin   Sindarin name derived from Kalaquendi (for the meaning see 376–7, 409). 362, 376–7, 408–9, 420
Camlost   'Empty-handed', name of Beren. 51, 69, 247; Gamlost 231, 234
Carabel   Also Amon Carab 'Hill of the Hat', Amon Garabel; names of Amon Rûdh. *182, 187
Caragdar   Precipice of Amon Gwareth from which Eöl was cast. 325. (Later form Caragdûr.)
Caranthir   Son of Fëanor. 115–16, 119, *183, 197, 215, 218, 221–2,

INDEX 433

227, 240, 329, 352–3; *Carathir* 227; earlier form *Cranthir* 33, 43, 45–6, 53, 61, 64, 115, 119–21, 134, 197, 201, 203, 206, 215, 227, 240, 320, 348, 351

Carcharoth 63, 68–9, 131

Casarrondo (Quenya) Khazad-dûm. 389, 397. Cf. *Kasari*.

Celbin See *Calben*.

Celeborn 350, 353, 355

Celebros (1) The Falls. 96, 151, 153; *the Falls of Silver-bowl* 151. See *Dimrost, Nen Girith*. (2) The name of the torrent (tributary of Taiglin). 151, 164, 186, 295

Celegorm Son of Fëanor. 47, 62, 122, 130–1, *183, 320, 324, 327–9, 332, 338, 346–50, 352; *Celegorn* 17, 53–4, 62–3, 65–7, 69, 113, 125, 130–2, 239, 242, 255, 351

Celon, River 6, 15, 53, 112, *183, 188–91, 218, 222, 320, 326, 332–4, 336–8. See *Limhir*.

Children of Aulë See *Aulë*.

Children of Eru 51, 63, 397, 403; see *Eruhíni*. *Children of Ilúvatar* 9, 30, 203, 213, 219, 224, 342, 345–6, 386. *The Children* 203–4, 210, 212, 341; *Elder* ~ 63, 83, *First* ~ 403; *Younger* ~ 30, 63, 83, *Second (race of the)* ~ 386, 403

Children of Húrin See *Húrin*.

Children of the Valar See *Valar*.

Chronology (of composition) 3–4, 47, 57, 105–6, 117, 122, 127, 140–2, 144, 175, 187, 191, 207, 213–15, 229, 244, 258–9, 316, 322, 325, 338–42, 354, 359

Circles of the World 213

Círdan (also *Cirdan*) 'The Shipwright'. 8–9, 11, 15–17, 21, 34, 39, 42, 60, 77, 80, 107, 116–18, 128, 135–6, 189, 197, 379–80, 384, 418

Cirith Ninniach 'Rainbow Cleft', at the head of the Firth of Drengist. 181, 256, 299; *Kirith* ~ *182

Cirth 14, 110, 396; singular *Certh* 396; Quenya *certa(r)* 396. See *Runes*.

Common Speech 337

Cranthir See *Caranthir*.

Creator, The 212

Crisaegrim Mountains south of Gondolin. 57, *182, 194, 239, 260–1, 302, 325; *Crissaegrim* 193–4

Crossings of Taiglin See *Taiglin*.

Cúarthol See *Dor-Cúarthol*.

Cuiviénen The Waters of Awakening. 195, 382, 418, 423–4; *Kuiviénen* 5, 105, 117, 174; the waterfall of ~ 382, 418, 423–4. See *Koivië-néni*.

Cuivienyarna Legend of the Awakening of the Quendi. 420, 424

Curufin Son of Fëanor. 53–4, 62–3, 65–9, 115, 125, 131–2, *183, 239, 242, 255, 320, 324–9, *331, 332, 336, 338, 346–52

Dagnir   Companion of Barahir. 56
Dagnir Glaurunga   Title of Túrin. 103, 156; cf. *Túrin the bane (slayer) of Glaurung* 224, 291
Dagor Aglareb   21, 25–6, 28, 36, 38, 116, 118, 199. See *Glorious Battle*.
Dagor Arnediad   22, 28. See *Nírnaeth Arnoediad*.
Dagor Bragollach   52, 121, 124, 127, 136, 238, 330; *the Bragollach* 59, 70, 73; old names *Dragor Húr-Breged* 124, *Dagor Vreged-úr* 124, 238. See *Battle of Sudden Flame*.
Dagor-nuin-Giliath   17, 36, 113; ~ *nui-Ngiliath* 113. See *Battle-under-Stars*.
Dairon   13–14, 20, 26, 28, 34, 65–6, 69, 110, 116, 129; *Alphabet of Dairon* 110; later form *Daeron* 110. See *Runes*.
Dairuin   Companion of Barahir. 56
Dalath Dirnen   See *Talath Dirnen*.
Damrod   Son of Fëanor, twin-brother of Díriel. 39, 53, 197, 240, 329, 352. See *Amrod*.
Dân   First leader of the Danas; father of Denethor. 13, 111 *(Dan)*, 195, 418; *Host of Dân* 195. (Replaced by *Lenwë*.)
Danas   The people of Dân, the Nandor. 118; *Danian Elves* 110
Danwaith   The Nandor. 385; *Denwaith* 385
Dark-elves   12, 39, 79, 107, 117–18, 136, 175, 179, 193–4, 197, 201, 203, 205, 207, 214, 216–17, 239, 320, 361, 376–7, 408; *Elves of the Dark* 8; *Dark-elf* (applied to Thingol) 33, 115, (to Eöl) 47–8, 320. *Dark-elven* 121, *Dark-elvish* 118, 209. See *Moriquendi*.
Dark Foe   Morgoth. 14; *Dark King* 220, 227; *Dark Lord* 15, 221, 252, 259, *Lord of the Dark* 220; *Dark Power* 39; *Dark Throne* 272
Darlas   See *Dorlas*. *Daruin*, see *Avranc*.
Day of Dread   The end of the Battle of Unnumbered Tears. 280
Debatable Land   South of Ivrin. *182
Deldúwath   'Deadly Nightshade', Taur-na-Fuin. 239
Denethor   Leader of the Nandor into Beleriand. 4, 13, 15–16, 109–12, 195, 385, 412, 418–19; etymology 412; earlier *Denithor* 111
Denweg   Nandorin form of Lenwë. 385, 412. See *Lenwë*; *Dân*.
Dimbar   Land between Sirion and Mindeb. 57, 81–2, 137–8, 188, 193, 261, 266–7, 271, 278, 301–2; *Dimbard* *182–3, 186, 188
Dimrost   'The Rainy Stair', the falls in the stream Celebros. 151. See *Nen Girith*.
Dior   (often called *Dior Thingol's Heir*) 22, 71, 133, 231–2, 234, 257, 300, 346–51, 353; called *Half-elven* 257, and see *Aranel*, *Eluchil*.
Dírhaval   Man of Dor-lómin, author of the *Narn i Chîn Húrin*. 312–15; *Dírhavel* 311–12, 315

Díriel (also *Diriel*) Son of Fëanor, twin-brother of Damrod. 39, 53, *183, 197, 225, 240, 329, 352; *Diriol* 218, 225, 227. See *Amras*.
Dispossessed, The The House of Fëanor. 33, 177
Distances 15, 89, 111, 145, 149, 158, 193, 295, 306, 332-3, 335
Dolmed, Mount In the Blue Mountains. 10, 16, 75, 112, 134, 202, 206; *Mount Dolmeð* *183; earlier *Mount Dolm* 334
Doom of the Noldor 224 (see *Mandos*). *Doom of Men* 247
Doom-ring (of the Valar) 399, 401. See *Máhanaxar*.
Dor Caranthir Thargelion. *183, 197-8; *Dor Cranthir* 198, *Dor Granthir* 197-8
Dor-Cúarthol 'The Land of Bow and Helm', defended by Túrin and Beleg from Amon Rûdh. 144, 314; *Cúarthol* 256
Dor-Daedeloth 'Land of Great Dread', the land of Morgoth. 18, 30-2, *183. See *Dor-na-Daerachas*.
Dor Dínen 'The Silent Land' between the upper waters of Esgalduin and Aros. *183, 188, 194, 338; *Dor Dhínen* 333, 338
Dorgannas Iaur 'Account of the shapes of the lands of old'. 192; *Dorgannas* 195, 206. See *Torhir Ifant*.
Doriath 5, 14, 16, 19, 21-7, 32-5, 39, 44, 50, 53, 56, 59, 62-70, 72, 77, 79-81, 83, 85, 88-90, 93-4, 101-3, 107-8, 110-13, 116, 119, 121, 123, 127, 129, 132, 135-6, 138, 150-1, 175, 178, 180, 186, 189, 193-4, 197, 203, 218-19, 244, 254-6, 258, 281, 298, 301, 303, 310-13, 315, 318(-19), 321, 326, 328, 332-4, 345-56, 369-70, 378-9, 408-9; *Land of the Girdle* 16; *Dôr Iâth* 'Land of the Fence' 370, 378; *Guarded Kingdom*, ~ *Realm* 16, 21; *Hidden Kingdom* 89, 102, 158, 161-2, 312; *Annals of Doriath* 4, 12, 104. See *Arthórien, Garthúrian, Eglador; Nivrim, Radhrim*.
Doriathrin (language) 22
Dorlas Man of Brethil. 92, 96-8, 100, 147-8, 152-6, 163, 257, 275, 284, 288, 303-5, 309; his wife 101, 163; late change to *Darlas* 309
Dor Lindon See *Lindon*.
Dor-lómin 49, 51, 56, 58, 61, 64, 78, 81-2, 85, 87-92, 102, 123-4, 126, 138, 145-6, 150, 166, 169, 176, 187, 223, 228, 234-5, 256-7, 262-3, 265, 267, 284, 287, 289, 299-300, 302, 310-11, 313, 344, 350; *Dor-Lómen* 181, *182, 202; *Lómínórë* 145
Dor-na-Daerachas Late substitution for *Dor-Daedeloth*. *183, 187, 338-9
Dor-na-Fauglith Earlier name of Anfauglith. 124, *183, 238-9; *Dor-no-* ~ 238-9, *Dor-nu-* ~ 239, translated 'Land under Choking Ash' 240; *Fauglith* 128, 134
Dornhoth 'The Thrawn Folk', the Dwarves. 388, 408
Dorthonion 6, 15, 17, 32, 38, 46, 49-52, 56, 58-9, 61, 64, 70, 104, 113, 132, 167-8, *183, 187-8, 193-4, 219, 224, 228-9, 238-9, 324

Dragon-helm *(of Galion, of Hador, of Dor-lómin)* 81–2, 85–7, 93, 135, 137–8, 140, 142–4, 255, 350
Dragon(s) (not including references to Glaurung) 46, 74, 302, 346; *dragon-gold* 347, 350; *fire-drakes* 46 (see *Urulókë*).
Draugluin The werewolf. 67–8, 131
Drengist, (Firth of) 5–6, 8, 16–17, 38, 46, 60, 89, 107, 176, 181, *182, 197, 206
Druedain 391
Drûn Region north of Tarn-aeluin. *183, 187
Dry River The entrance to Gondolin. *182, 271, 324
Duilwen, River In Ossiriand. 13, *185
Duin Daer The river Gelion. 336; *Duin Dhaer* 191, 336
Dúnedain 378, 386, 402. See *Núnatani*.
Dúnedhil 'West-elves' (of Middle-earth). 378, 386
Durin 204, 207–8, 211–13; called *the Eldest* (of the Seven Fathers of the Dwarves) 208, 211–13
Dwarfmine Nogrod. 108, 201, 209
Dwarf-road(s) 121, *185, 189–90, 202, 206, 216, 218, 221, 321, 334–6; North road of the Dwarves *183, 189, 321, 334–6
Dwarrowdelf Khazad-dûm (Moria). 201, 206, 209, 419 (also *Dwarrowmine, Dwarrowvault* 389, 419). See *Dwarfmine*.
Dwarves (including many compounds as *Dwarf-kings, -knife, -mines, -speech, -women,* etc.) 9–12, 45, 59–60, 68, 71, 107–9, 113, 118, 120–1, 128, 132, 134, 138, 143, 167, 179, 189, 201–16, 239, 255, 280, 321–2, 324, 326–7, 329, 332, 334–6, 340–1, 345–53, 355, 359, 372, 387–91, 395, 397, 402, 408–9, 418–19; *Dwarfs* 202–3, 239
  Origin of the Dwarves 10, 108, 203, 210–13; Elvish names for 209, 214, 387–8; language (*aglâb* 395) 10, 108, 205, 207–9, 211–12, 395, 402, gesture-language (*iglishmêk*) 395, 402; Dwarf-cities and their names 108, 201–2, 205–6, 209, 389, 419; nature of the Dwarves 109, 203–7, 395. See *Fathers of, Necklace of, the Dwarves*.
Dwarvish (of language, names) 108, 179 (*Dwarfish*), 180, 336, 391, 412, 414; (with other reference) 335–6, 355

Eä 399, 402–3
Eagles 55, 57–8, 63, 126–7, 170, 193, 198, 239, 272, 302, 341, *the Great Eagles* 272, *the Eagles of Manwë* 272; and see *Gwaihir, Lhandroval, Sorontar, Thorondor*.
Eärámë Tuor's ship. 352
Eärendil 135, *184, 190, 224, 231, 234–5, 299, 345–6, 348, 351–2, 354; *Eärendel* 22, 302, 311–12, 348; called *the Blessed* 224, *Half-elven* 348, 351, *a new star* 76. See *Ardamir*.
Earth, (The) 9, 39, 106, 174–5, 203, 210, 220, 348 ('on earth'), 402, 418–21. See *Ambar, Imbar; Arda*.

INDEX

Eärwen Olwë's daughter, wife of Finarfin (= Finrod (1)). 32(–3), 43, 115
East, The 9, 37, 39, 47, 60, 70, 116, 118, 146, 173, 216, 220, 226, 272, 386; *the Eastlands* 39
Easterling(s) 74, 79, 81–2, 88, 90–1, 128, 137, 167, 205, 207–8, 252, 301, 377. See *Eastrons, Swarthy Men.*
Eastern Sea 173–4
East Road See *Roads.*
Eastrons Easterlings. 253, 256, 262, 264, 266, 298–9, 301
Ebor Man of Brethil, liege of Manthor. 263–5, 267, 270–1
Echil Sindarin name = *Hildor* 'the Followers', Men. 219. (The existence of *Echil* denied, 387; see *Aphadon.*)
Echoing Mountains 176, 196; *Echoing Hills* 17. See *Eryd Lómin.*
Echoriad The mountains about Gondolin. 271–2, 302; earlier *Echoriath* 302. See *Encircling Mountains, Gochressiel.*
Ecthelion (1) A lord of Gondolin. 18, 318, 328; etymology 319. (2) Name borne by two Stewards of Gondor. 319
Edain 112, 168, 206, 213–15, 219–20, 222–6, 229, 232–3, 236, 241, 253–4, 256–7, 262–4, 266, 268–9, 281, 283, 286, 299, 344, 377, 387, 406, 410; singular *Adan* 286, 387. Ancient tongue of 226, and see *Bëor, Haladin* (1), *Marach*; genealogical tables 229–38. See *Atani, Three Houses.*
Ēdë See *Estë.*
Edhel, plural *Edhil* The general Sindarin word for 'Elf, Elves'. 364, 377–8. See *Mornedhel.*
Edhelwen Name of Morwen. 142, 230–1, 234, 273–4, 291, 296. Earlier form *Eledhwen* 51, 56, 142, 230, translated *Elfsheen* 51, 61, 64, 79
Edrahil Elf of Nargothrond. 66
Egalmoth (1) A lord of Gondolin. 318, 328; etymology 319. (2) Name borne by a Steward of Gondor. 319
Egla (Originally) Gnomish name = *Elda.* 189
Egladhrim 'The Forsaken' (the Sindar, but applied especially to the Elves of the Falas). 189, 365, 379; also *Eglain* (singular *Eglan*) 186, 189, 365, 379–81, 400, 418. See *Emyn Eglain*; *Eglath.*
Eglador (1) ('Land of the Elves'), Doriath. 16, 113, *183, 186, 189. (2) The land of the *Eglain*, western Beleriand. *182, 186, 343–4, 379 (cf. *Eglamar* (3)).
Eglahir, River 117, *182, 187. (Replaced *Eglor*, replaced by *Nenning*.)
Eglain See *Egladhrim.*
Eglamar (1) 'Elf-home' in Valinor (= *Eldamar*). 189. (2) = *Arthórien* (Doriath beyond Aros). 112–13, 189. (3) The Land of the *Eglain*, the region of the Falas. *184, 189, 365, 370, 379; *Hills of Eglamar (Emyn Eglain)* *184, 189
Eglarest The southern Haven of the Falas. 8, 15, 18, 39–40, 80, 111,

189–91, 197, 365; *Firth of Eglarest* 380; earlier *Eglorest* 111, 117, *184, 189, 191, 197, 242
Eglath 'The Forsaken', the Sindar. 8–9, 57, 126, 189, 344; other forms *Eglim, Eglir* 344. See *Egladhrim*.
Eglor, River 117, 187. See *Eglahir*.
Egnor Son of Finarfin (= Finrod (1)). 38, 52, *183, 195. (Later form *Aegnor*.)
Eilinel Wife of Gorlim the Unhappy. 59
Eithel Sirion Sirion's Well, often with reference to the fortress (see *Barad Eithel*). 17–18, 38, 52–3, 60, 114, 165, 168, 193, 233; *Eithel* *182; *Sirion's Well* *182
Eithil Ivrin Sources of the Narog. 85, 139, 256, 299; earlier *Ivrineithel* 139. See *Ivrin*.
Ekelli 'The Forsaken' (the Sindar). 175
Eladar Name of Tuor, 'Starfather' (i.e. father of Eärendil). 234–5
Elboron and Elbereth Sons of Dior. 300. (Replaced by *Eldún and Elrún*.)
Eldalië The Elvenfolk. 44, 70, 166, 174, 374–5; Telerin *Ellalië* 375
Eldamar 'Elf-home' (= *Eglamar* (1)). 189
Eldameldor 'Elf-friends'. 412; Sindarin *Elvellyn* 412
Eldandil(i) 'Elf-friend(s)'. 410, 412
Eldar (and singular *Elda*) 6–7, 10, 12–13, 15, 17, 20–1, 23–5, 28, 30–1, 36–8, 41, 49–50, 52–3, 58–60, 69–71, 74–5, 77, 105, 118, 121, 127–8, 132, 165–6, 173–4, 186, 189, 204–7, 212, 217–26, 233, 283, 312–13, 315, 326, 328–30, 333, 343, 362–3, 365, 368–9, 372–8, 380–2, 384, 386, 388–91, 393–5, 398, 400, 402–10, 412, 418, 420–1; for the forms *Eldo*, plural *Eldor*, see 363, 374–5. Telerin *Ello (Ella)*, plural *Elloi*, 362, 364, 373, 375–6. See *Star-folk*.
Eldarin (of language) 361, 389, 392, 400, 404–5, 407, 410–12, 414–15, 417, 421; *Common Eldarin* (abbreviated CE) 359–61, 368, 371, 379, 387, 390, 403, 414, 416; (with other reference) 328, 377, 380, 383, 410
Elder Children See *Children of Eru*.
Elder Days 3–5, 23, 27, 51, 105, 110, 116–17, 142, 180, 243, 245, 297, 325, 337, 342–7, 353, 390, 396; see especially 342–3
Elder King Manwë. 246
Eldún and Elrún Sons of Dior. 231–2, 257, 300, 348–51
Eledhwen Name of Morwen. See *Edhelwen*.
Elen, plurals *Elin, Eledhrim* (Sindarin) Elf, Elves. 363, 377–8
Elendë Land of the Eldar in Aman. 177
Elendil Meaning of the name, 410
Elenwë Wife of Turgon. 323. See *Alairë, Anairë*.
Elessar The Elfstone. 177; the Green Stone of Fëanor 176–7
Elf-fathers 380, 420–1
Elf-friends 37, 39, 48, 60, 70, 80, 118, 206, 219–21, 386, (412); as

INDEX 439

translation of *Elendil* 410. See *Eldameldor, Eldandil(i), Quendil.*
Elf-kind 203, 210; *-kings* 223; *-lord(s)* 50, 234–5; *-maid* 67 (Lúthien); *-man, -men* 363, 421–3; *-riders* 150; *-woman* 87 (Finduilas), 363, 421
Elf-Latin Quenya. 22–3
Elizabeth I, Queen 312; Elizabeth II 312
Ello, Elloi See *Eldar.*
Ellon, Elleth (Sindarin) 'Elf' (m. and f.), plural *El(d)rim.* 363–4, 377
Elmo Younger brother of Elwë (Thingol). 350
Elmoth See *Nan Elmoth.*
Elrond 71, 132, 234, 242, 348–9; meaning of the name 414
Elros 234, 348–9; meaning of the name 414. *The Line of Elros* 349
Elrún See *Eldún and Elrún.*
Eluchil 'Thingol's Heir', name of Dior. 350
Elulin Wife of Dior. 350. See *Lindis, Nimloth.*
Elu Thingol See *Elwë.*
Eluwaith Subjects of King Thingol. 378
Elvellyn See *Eldameldor.*
Elven 200 (Tirion); *-child* 242 (Gilgalad); *-craft* 200; *-fair* 291 (Morwen); *-folk* 374; *-host* 17; *-king(s)* 52, 55, 66, 131, 283; *-kirtle* 151; *-light* 273; *-lords* 39, 224; *-sight* 166; *-speech* 21; *-tongue(s)* 10, 49, 217, 219, 224
Elves (and *Elf*) 9–12, 14–16, 22–3, 27–8, 30, 37–9, 45–6, 50, 55–6, 60–1, 64, 71–7, 79, 81–2, 87, 95, 102–4, 107, 109–12, 121–2, 124, 126–8, 131–2, 136, 139, 141, 147–50, 164–7, 174–5, 180, 186, 189, 192, 194–5, 197, 201, 203–7, 211, 213, 219–23, 228, 244, 256, 259, 272, 289, 299, 311–13, 315, 320–2, 332, 345–6, 352, 355, 359–60, 365, 371–81, 383–4, 386–90, 392–3, 396–7, 403, 407–10, 412–14, 416, 418–23
Elvish (of language) 149, 202, 209, 215–16, 226, 234, 305, 311-12, 359–60, 374, 382, 386–7, 389–91, 393, 396, 398, 404, 407–8, 410, 416–17; (with other reference) 148, 213, 220, 229, 311–13, 323, 350, 360, 369, 372–3, 375–6, 378, 419, 421
Elwë (1) Original name of Olwë. 177. (2) Thingol of Doriath, called *Singollo* 'Greymantle'. 6–9, 107, 177, 344, 350, 369, 373, 375, 379–80, 384–5, 410, 414, 418; Sindarin *Elu Thingol* 9, 21, 350, 378. See *Greymantle, Singollo, Thingol.*
Elwing 22, 224, 231, 234, 348, 350–1; called *the White* 351
Emeldir Mother of Beren One-hand; called *the Manhearted.* 51, 56, 124, 126, 231–4
Emyn Eglain The Hills of Eglamar. *184, 189. See *Egladhrim, Eglamar* (3).
Encircling Mountains (about Gondolin) 35, 179, (198, 200), 272, 302. See *Echoriad, Gochressiel.*
End, The 204; *World's end, end of the World* 66, 70
Endar Middle-earth. 30, 114; *Endor* 114

Ened Island in the Ocean west of Drengist. 181, *182
Enel 'Three', the third of the Fathers of the Elves. 380, 418, 420–3; Companions of Enel 423. See *Nelyar.*
Enelyë Spouse of Enel. 421
Enemy, The 17, 29, 31, 50, 55, 59, 118, 166, 253
Enfeng 'Longbeards', Dwarves of Belegost. 10–13, 75, 108, 134, 321–2, *Ennfeng* 205, *Enfengs* 112; of Nogrod 75, 108, 134. See *Anfangrim, Indrafangs, Longbeards.*
English 312, 368–9, 372, 383, 392, 407; *(Old) English* 309, 312–15, 391–2. See *Anglo-Saxon.*
Enthor Younger brother of Hunthor and Manthor. See 267, 270.
Ents 341, 353, 356; *Shepherds of the Trees* 356
Eöl 47–8, 71, 84, 121–3, 127, 139, 316, 320–30, *331, 332–3, 335–8, 344, 348, 409, 420. See *Dark-elves.*
Eönwë Herald of Manwë. 246, 417. (Replaced *Fionwë*, son of Manwë.)
Ephel Brandir Dwellings of the Men of Brethil on Amon Obel. 89, 92, 96–7, 145, 148, 151–2, 157–8, 164, *182, 186, 301, 306; *the Ephel* 97. See *Bar Haleth, Obel Halad.*
Erchamion 'One-handed', name of Beren. 51, 231
Ered- (in names of mountain-ranges) See *Eryd-.*
Erendis of Númenor 230, 232
Ereol, Eriol 246
Eressëa See *Tol Eressëa.*
Eriador 13, 39, 48–9, 60–1, 64, 109–10, 123, 128–9, 206, 221, 228, 232, 381, 385, 397, 410, 416
Eru 130, 341, 399, 402–3, 405, 421; *Eru-begotten* (the first Elves) 421; *the One* 212, 402. See *Children of Eru.*
Eruhíni Children of Eru (singular *Eruhin*). 403
Eruman Earlier name of Araman. 115, 175
Eryd (Ered) Engrin 6, 104, 196. See *Iron Mountains.*
Eryd (Ered) Gorgoroth 319, ~ *Gorgorath* 129, 188, *the Gorgorath* 319; ~ *Orgoroth* 15, 129, 194, ~ *Orgorath* 61, 64, 129, *183, 188, 194. See *Mountains of Terror.*
Eryd Lammad See *Eryd Lómin.*
Eryd (Ered) Lindon 49, 105, *183, 193, 201–3, 206, 215, 334, 385, 388. See *Blue Mountains, Eryd Luin, Ossiriand.*
Eryd (Ered) Lómin 17, 38, 117, 176, 192, 196; *Eryd Lammad* 192, 196. See *Echoing Mountains.*
Eryd (Ered) Luin 5, 7, 10, 13, 32, 38–9, 60, 104, 108, 117, 179, 193, 385, 389. See *Blue Mountains, Eryd Lindon, Luindirien.*
Eryd (Ered) Nimrais 110, 385. See *White Mountains.*
Eryd (Ered) Orgoroth See *Eryd Gorgoroth.*
Eryd (Ered) Wethrin 17–18, 38, 40, 46, 60, 74, 85, 113–14, 117, 196, 200, 240; earlier ~ *Wethion* 45, 74, 89, 91, 113, 120, 134,

166, *182, 196, 200, 219, 240; *Eryd Wethian* 142, 256, 299. See *Mountains of Shadow.*

Esgalduin, River 11, 94, 150, *183, 188, 194, 319, 324, 328, 332–4; the Bridge over Esgalduin 188, 319, 328, *331, 332–5, and see *Esgaliant, Iant Iaur;* (earlier) the Ford of Esgalduin 324, 332

Esgaliant The Bridge of Esgladuin. 333. See *Esgalduin, Iant Iaur.*
Essekenta Eldarinwa Title of *Quendi and Eldar.* 359
Estë 'Repose'; the wife of Lórien. 403–4; Telerin *Ëdë* 403–4
Estolad Dwelling of the peoples of Bëor and Marach south of Nan Elmoth. 112, 189, 218–22, 227–8, 233, 334; *Estoland* *183, 189, 227; translated *the Encampment* 218
Etyañgoldi 'Exiled Noldor'. 374
Etymologies, The In Vol. V, *The Lost Road.* 104, 116, 128, 137, 186, 189, 191, 201, 235, 337
Evair (Sindarin) Avari. 380
Exiles, The The Noldor in Middle-earth. 21, 23, 25–6, 32–3, 44, 176, 328, 374, 379–81, 384, 387–8, 403; *Exiled Noldor* 364, 374, 377, 379–80, 384–5 (see *Etyañgoldi, Gódhel, Ódhel*); *the Exile* 19, 21, 372–4, 386, 398, 404, 411; *Exilic (Quenya)* 384–5, 390, 396, 400
Ezellohar The Green Mound of the Trees (Valarin name). 341, 399, 401. See *Korollairë.*

Fair-elves The Vanyar. 246
Falas The coasts of Beleriand. 8, 12, 15–16, 72, 80, 84, 89, 107, 117, 166, 189, 192, 197–8, 242, 418. See *Forfalas, Harfalas.*
Falasquil Bay in the Firth of Drengist. 181, *182, 344
Falathrim Elves of the Falas. 378
Falls of Gelion See *Gelion.*
Faramir = Gelmir (2), companion of Arminas. 299
Farang, Faranc See *Avranc.*
Father(s) of Men 39, 52, 75, 166, 174, 227, 229, 236, 241, 345; ~ *of (the) Men of the West* 48, 206, 232. See *Atanatári.*
Fathers of the Dwarves 204, 207–8, 210–11, 213
Fauglith See *Dor-na-Fauglith.*
Fëanor (including references to his house, people, host, etc.) 14, 16–22, 24–5, 27, 31–3, 38, 41–3, 45, 47, 54, 65–6, 69–70, 77, 108, 113–15, 119, 176–7, *183, 206, 215, 218, 247, 327, 329, 359, 379, 381, 384, 396, 398, 400, 405, 417, 419; his alphabetic system 396, Fëanorian letters 396. See *Sons of Fëanor.*
Fëanorians 19, 115, 132, 134, 137, 232, 334. Oath of the Fëanorians 18–19, 29, 34, 41, 62, 65–6, 69, 176, 351–2, 354
Feast of Reuniting 34, 114. See *Mereth Aderthad.*

Feiniel 'White Lady' (318), Turgon's sister, wife of Eöl. 318-19; *Ar-Feiniel* 317-18, 322. See *Isfin, Írith, Aredhel.*
Feir, plurals *Fîr, Firiath* Sindarin, = Quenya *Firya(r)* 'Mortal(s)'. 219, 387
Felagund King of Nargothrond; name used alone or with *Inglor, Finrod* (2). 35, 38, 44, 48-9, 52, 59, 62-3, 65-7, 88, 94, 116-17, 120, 123-4, 129-31, 135, 147, 149, 178-9, *183-4, 197, 215-19, 223, 225-9, 238, 242-3, 255, 323, 355, 418, 420; said to be a Dwarvish name 179; as father of Gilgalad, see *Gilgalad*; his wife 44, 242; his ring 52, 59, 65, 242; *the Doors of Felagund* 84, 86, 143, 149. *Lord of Caves* 35, ~ *Caverns* 178
Fell Winter, The The winter of the year 495, after the fall of Nargothrond. 88, 93, 256, 261
Fell Year, The The year (455) of the Battle of Sudden Flame. 52, 125
Fen of Rivil, Fen of Serech See *Rivil, Serech.*
Field of the Worm, Field of Burning At Cabed Naeramarth. 295
Fifth Battle of Beleriand 71, 133. See *Battle of Unnumbered Tears* (formerly the Fourth Battle).
Finarfin Later name of Finrod (1), son of Finwë. 115, 130, 142, 179, 188, 197, 226, 240, 243, 319, 343, 383; *Finarphin* 179, 246
Findor See *Gilgalad.*
Finduilas Daughter of Orodreth King of Nargothrond. 83-5, 87-9, 91-2, 95, 101, 138-43, 147-8, 160, 180, 256-7, 299
Fingolfin (including references to his house and people) 17, 21, 23, 25-6, 29-34, 36, 38, 40, 43, 45-6, 49-50, 52, 54-6, 72-3, 75, 77, 114-15, 117, 121, 124-6, 134, 136, 177, *182, 195, 206, 219, 223, 227-8, 235, 243, 323, 327, 329, 343, 379; his wife *Anairë* 323
Fingon 31, 38, 46-7, 52, 56, 59-60, 70-7, 115, 117, 122, 124, 128, 133-4, 165-8, 174, 177, *182, 243, 287, 312, 315; as father of Gilgalad, see *Gilgalad.*
Finrod (1) Earlier name of Finarfin. (Most references are to his children or his house.) 22, 31-4, 38, 40, 42-4, 49, 52, 54, 67, 83, 115, 119, 130, 142, 178-9, 188, 197, 217, 219, 226-7, 240, 243, 319, 343. *Finrodian* (language) 22
Finrod (2) Later name of Inglor (see 65, 130); references include *Finrod Felagund.* 65, 130, 179, 197-8, 225, 240, 243, 355, 383, 406, 414; *Finrod Inglor* 130. See *Felagund.*
Finwë 6-8, 21, 33-4, 41, 62, 67, 246, 327, 379, 383, 387
Fionwë Son of Manwë. 6, 105, 246, 345; Herald of Manwë 417. See *Eönwë.*
Fíreb, plurals *Fírib, Firebrim* Sindarin, = Quenya *Fírima(r)* 'Mortal(s)'. 387
Firiath 'Mortals', see *Feir.*
Fíriel Name given to Míriel wife of Finwë. 419
Fírima(r) 'Mortal(s)'. 387, 419; *Fírimor* 419. See *Fíreb.*
First Age 342, 345-6, 349

First Battle of Beleriand 15, 111–12. (Formerly the Battle-under-Stars.)
Firstborn, The Elves. 65, 341
First Clan The Vanyar. 382–3; *First Kindred* 418. See *Minyar*.
First Elves, The 421, 423
Firya(r) 'Mortal(s)'. 219, 387. See *Feir*.
Flight, The (of the Noldor) 396, 398, 417
Flinding Earlier name of Gwindor of Nargothrond. 138, 140
Foen Mountain in Dorthonion. *183, 187; *Taur-na-Foen* 'Forest of the Foen' 187
Followers Men. 31, 219, 386. See *Aphadon, Echil, Hildor*.
Ford(s) of Aros See *Aros*.
Forfalas *182, 186; *North Falas* *182, 186
Forhend Man of Brethil. 274–6, 303
Fourth Battle of Beleriand 121. See *Battle of Sudden Flame* (formerly the Third Battle).
Fuin, Mountains of 333. See *Taur-nu-Fuin*.

Gabilān Dwarvish name, 'Great River' (see *Gevelon*). 336
Gabilgathol Dwarvish name translated as *Belegost*. 10, 108, 201, 206, 209, 389
Gaerys Sindarin name of Ossë. 400. See *Yssion*.
Galadhon Son of Elmo and father of Celeborn. 350
Galadriel, Galaðriel (for the spellings see 116, 119) 35, 40–2, 44, 50, 64–5, 116, 119, 123, 129–30, 178, 242, 341, 383; *Concerning Galadriel and Celeborn* 352, 355
Galathil Brother of Galadhon. 350
Galdor Son of Hador and father of Húrin and Huor; called *the Tall* (234), *Galdor Orchal* (287, 305). 123, 146, 170, 224, 229, 232, 234–5, 237, 240–1, 268, 270, 275, (280), 283, 287, 305, 344. (Replaced *Galion*.)
Galhir Man of Brethil. 303
Galion Earlier name of Galdor Húrin's father. 49, 51, 53, 56–8, 60–1, 71, 81, 86, 123, 126, 128, 137, 146, 170, 202, 229, 232–3, 240, 246, 268, 344. (Replaced *Gumlin*.)
Galvorn The metal of Eöl. 322–3. For rejected names see *Rodëol, Morlîn, Targlîn, Glindûr, Maeglin*.
Gamlost See *Camlost*.
Gap (of Rohan) 385
Garthúrian Doriath ('hidden realm'). *183, 189
Gelduin Proposed name replacing *Gelion*. 336
Gelion, River 5, 7, 13, 15, 45, 53, 105, *183, *185, 190–1, 193, 195, 197, 206, 216, 218, 221, 334–6, 338, 347, 349, 385; *Greater Gelion* *183, 188; *Little Gelion* *183; *the Falls of Gelion* 335–6, 338. See *Duin Daer, Gelduin, Gevelon*.
Gelmir (1) Brother of Gwindor of Nargothrond. 73, 134, 168

Gelmir (2)   Companion of Arminas. 141–2, 256, 299. See *Faramir*.
Gevelon, Gevilon   Proposed name replacing *Gelion*, derived from Dwarvish *Gabilān*. 336
Gildis   Wife of Hador Goldenhead. 234
Gildor   Companion of Barahir. 56
Gil-Estel   'Star of high hope' (Eärendil's star); other names *Gil-Amdir*, ~ *Orestel*, ~ *Orrain*. 246
Gilgalad   ('Starlight', 242). As son of Fingon 56, 126, 243; as son of Felagund 120, 242–3; named *Findor* 56, 243
Gilwen   Sister of Barahir. 231
Ginglith, River   139, *182
Girdle of Melian   16, 32, 50, 61, 81, 90, 151, 178, 188, 222, 225, 228, 321, 333, 352, 355; other references, as *Girdle of Doriath*, *Fence of Melian* 64, 114, 333. See *List Melian*; *Doriath*.
Gladuial   Name of Nan Elmoth (?). *183, 188
Glamdring   Gandalf's sword. 391
Glamhoth   ('Yelling-horde'), Orcs; also *Glam*, singular *Glamog*. 391
Glaurung   (including references to *the Dragon*, *the (Great) Worm* 46, 49, 52, 74–5, 85–8, 90, 93–4, 96–102, 121, 139–43, 148–50, 152–64, 167, 180, 224, 238, 240, 254–8, 266–7, 273, 285, 290–1, 299–300, 310, 329, 347, 350; *Father of Dragons* 52, 74, *the Serpent of Angband* 264, and see *Urulókë*; his speed and power of sight 149. (Replaced *Glómund*.)
Glindûr   Earlier name of Maeglin. 48, 58, 76, 91, 122–3, 127, 135, 146, 322–3, 344; as name also of the metal of Eöl 48, 122, 322. See *Maeglin, Galvorn*.
Glingal   Image of Laurelin in Gondolin. 200
Glinnel, plural *Glinnil*   Sindarin, = *Lindar* (Teleri). 378, 385
Glirhuin   Seer and harper of Brethil. 296
Glithui, River   *182, 186; *Gilthui* 186
Glómund   Earlier name of Glaurung. 121, 154, 180, 206, 240. (Replaced *Glórund*.)
Glóredhel   Daughter of Hador, wife of Haldir of Brethil. 234–5, 237, 268, 270, 309. (Replaced *Glorwendil*.)
Glorfindel   A lord of Gondolin. 318, 328
Glorindol   Name of Hador, 'Goldenhead'. 223, 225, 228, 232–3, 235; *Glórindol* 225; *Glorindal* 226, 235. See *Lorindol*.
Glorious Battle   The Third Battle of Beleriand (formerly the second). 28, 36, 116. See *Dagor Aglareb*.
Glórund   Original name of Glaurung, replaced by *Glómund*. 154(–5)
Glorwendil   Daughter of Hador, wife of Hundor of Brethil. 51, 79, 126, 128, 136, 233, 268. (Replaced by Glóredhel wife of Haldir.)
Gnome(s)   108, 113, 125, 131, 137, 175, 177–8, 189, 193, 195, 202–4, 206, 209, 239, 244
Gnomish   (of language) 194, 206, 209, 215, 240, 315

INDEX

Gochressiel The Encircling Mountains about Gondolin. 239. See *Echoriad*.
God 212
Gódhel, plurals *Gódhil, Gódhellim* (Sindarin) The Exiled Noldor. 364, 379. See *Ódhel*.
Gods 42, 55, 65, 175, 177, 217, 220, 227, 240, 246–7, 420; *Battle of the Gods* 207, *People* ~ 239, *Sons* ~ 246
Goldo (Telerin) = *Noldo*. 383. *Goldorin, Goldolambë*, Telerin names of Quenya. 375
Golodh, plurals *Goelydh, Golodhrim* Sindarin form of *Noldo*. 323, 364, 379 383
Gondolin 5, 18, 22–3, 25–8, 35, 40, 44–5, 47–8, 53, 55, 57(–8), 68, 70, 72–6, 84, 91, 110, 116, 118–23, 125–7, 133, 135–6, 139, 146, 166, 169, 177, 179, *182, 193, 198–201, 203, 206, 234, 239, 241, 243–5, 254–6, 258, 260–1, 272, 298, 300–2, 313–14, 316–17, 319, 324, 326, 328, 330, 333, 344–8, 351, 353, 356, 396–7, 409; translated *the Hidden Rock* 199–201; *the Guarded City,* ~ *Realm* 53, 57, *the Hidden City,* ~ *Kingdom,* ~ *Realm* 56–7, 91, 195, 260. *Lay of the Fall of Gondolin* 121, 320; the tongue of Gondolin 22–3, 25–8, and its population 25–8, 40, 44–5, 55–6, 119, 126; etymology 201. See *Ondolindë*.
Gondor 189, 314, 319, 391
Gonnhirrim 'Masters of stone', the Dwarves. 205, 209
Gorgûn Name of the Orcs in the language of the Drúedain. 391
Gorlim the Unhappy Companion and betrayer of Barahir. 56, 59, *183
Gorothress(?) See *183, 188
Gorsodh Name of Sauron 'in Beleriand'. 54
Gorthaur Sindarin name of Sauron. 240, 246; replacing *Gorthú* (Noldorin name) 239–40, 246
Gothmog 18 ('Lord of the Balrogs'), 168 ('High-captain of Angband'), 169
Great, The 212. See *Aratar*.
Great Battle (at the end of the Elder Days) 345. See *Last Battle*.
Great Fortress 108, 201, 209. See *Belegost, Mickleburg*.
Great Gulf 6, 104–5, 109
Great March (of the Eldar) 122; *the March* 13, 20–1, 23, 106, 195, 373, 375, 381–4, 390; *the Westward March* 371; *Marchers* 374; *Great Journey* 174
Great River 13, 109, 173–4; *Vale of the* ~ 13. See *Anduin*.
Great Sea 6, 8, 91, 104–7, 111. See *(The) Sea, Western Sea*.
Great Tales 314
Green-elves 13, 16, 21, 28, 39, 111–12, 118, *185, 216, 218, 349, 355–6, 385. See *Danas, Laegel, Nandor*.
Green Mound (of the Two Trees) 401. See *Ezellohar, Korollairë*.
Green Stone See *Elessar*.

Grey-elves 5, 9, 18–19, 26, 28, 33–5, 39, 72, 79, 101, 104, 114, 117, 136, 192–3, 214, 315, 344, 375, 384, 410 (origin of the name). *Grey-elven* (tongue) 223, 313. See *Sindar*.

Greymantle Translation of *Sindikollo*, *Singollo*, Thingol (Elwë). 7, 9; *Greycloak* 410

Grinding Ice 29, 43; *the Ice* 6, 31, 206, 323; *the Straits of Ice* 343. See *Helkaraxë*.

Grodnof Variant of *Novrod* (Nogrod). 414

Grond 'The hammer of Angband'. 55

Guarded City See *Gondolin*; ~ *Kingdom*, see *Doriath*; ~ *Realm*, see both *Doriath* and *Gondolin*.

Guarded Plain North of Nargothrond. 85, 139–40, 149, 228. See *Talath Dirnen*.

Guest-elves Nandorin Elves in Doriath. 112

Guilin Father of Gelmir (1) and Gwindor. 73, 82

Gumlin Original name of Húrin's father (see *Galion, Galdor*). 123, 202, 229, 232, 240–1, 246

Gundor Son of Hador. 49, 53, 123, 224, 232–4, 241

Gurthang 'Iron of Death', Túrin's sword. 83, 86, 92, 98–9, 101–3, 138, (160), 304. Earlier names *Gurtholfin*, *Gurtholf* 138, 160. See *Anglachel*.

Gwaihir The eagle, vassal of Thorondor. 68, 131

Gwanwen, plural *Gwenwin* 'The departed', Sindarin name of the Elves who went to Aman; also *Gwanwel*, plural *Gwenwil*. 378

Gwendelin Old name of Melian. 347

Gwerin Another name for Brandir's kinsman Hunthor (Torbarth). 97, 156, 163–5; his wife 163

Gwerth-i-guinar The Land of the Dead that Live. 71; earlier forms *Gwerth-i-cuina*, *Gyrth-i-Guinar* 132

Gwindor Elf of Nargothrond. 73, 82–6, 134, 138–42, 168, 180, 256, 299, 311, 352. See *Flinding*.

Hadhod, Hadhodrim Sindarin name of the Dwarves (derived from *Khazâd*). 388, 414

Hadhodrond 'Dwarrowvault', city of the Dwarves in the Misty Mountains (replaced *Nornhabar*). 389, 414 (etymology), 419; rejected form *Hadhodrûd* 419. See *Khazad-dûm*; *Casarrondo*; *Nornhabar*; *Dwarrowdelf*.

Hador Lord of Dor-lómin; called 'the Goldenhaired', and later 'Goldenhead' (see *Glorindol, Lorindol*). 48–9, 51–2, 56, 79, 123–4, 126, 128, 142, 202, 206, 223–6, 228, 230, 232–7, 241, 268; *House of Hador* 48–9, 53, 57, 60–1, 64, 77–8, 135, 165, 224, 228, 232, 234–6, 259, 263–9, 277, 289, 297, 302, 308–9, 311, 313; *People, Folk, Men of Hador* 49–51, 75–7, 79, 90, 123, 128, *182. For the changed genealogy of the House of Hador see 232–5.

INDEX 447

Halabor See *Angbor.*
Halad 'Warden', title of the Chieftain of Brethil (see 263, 270, and *Haladin* (2)). 263, 270–1, 275–80, 283–91, 304, 309. See *Brethil; Obel Halad; Halbar.*
Haladin (1) The People of (the Lady) Haleth. 217–18, 221–2, 226–8, 233–4, 236–7, 240–1, 265, 268–70, 279, 299, 303–4, 309; ancient tongue of 217, 226, 238, 270, 283, 296, 304; genealogical table 237. See next entry.
Haladin (2) (Later sense) The kindred of the Lady Haleth, descendants of Haldad; 'wardens' (see 263, 270, 278, and *Halad*). 262–3, 267, 270, 293, 296–7, 302, 304, 306, 309
Halbar Proposed replacement of the term *Halad*, and of the name *Haldar*. 238, 309
Haldad Father of the Lady Haleth, slain by Orcs in Thargelion. 221–3, 236–7, 265, 270, 278, 303 (name translated 'watchdog' 270).
Haldan Proposed replacement of *Hardan*. 228, 238
Haldar Son of Haldad, slain with him in Thargelion; brother of the Lady Haleth. 221–3, 228, 237–8, 278, 303, 308–9. See *Halbar.*
Haldir (1), *of Nargothrond* Son of Orodreth. 82, 137. See *Halmir* (1).
Haldir (2), *of Brethil* Son of Halmir and husband of Glóredhel; fourth chieftain of the Haladin, slain in the Nírnaeth. 133, 234–7, 266, 268–70, 281, 303. See *Hundor.*
Haleth (1), *the Hunter* 48–9, 51, 53, 56–7, 60, 70, 74, 97, 123, 125–6, 128, 133, 136, 157, 168, 206, 227–8, 235–6, 240–1, 268; *House, Kin, People, Folk of Haleth* 50–1, 53, 56, 77, 89, 92, 98, 124, 127–8, 132, 147, 157, *182, 186, 228, 267; and see *Halethrim.*
Haleth (2), *the Lady* 221–3, 227–8, 236–8, 263, 270, 278, 303, 308–9; *People, Folk of Haleth* 133, 222–4, 235–7, 240, 269, 303–4, 307; *House of Haleth* 289, 295, 297, 308; *Nothlir Haletha* 237, (309); and see *Haladin* (1).
Halethrim The People of Haleth. 164, 255
Half-elven 71, 242, 257, 348, 351; *Half-elfin* 242
Halmir (1), *of Nargothrond* Earlier name of Haldir son of Orodreth. 137
Halmir (2), *of Brethil* Third chieftain of the Haladin, father of Haldir and grandfather of Húrin. 168, 234–7, 240–1, 268–70, 289
Hamfast Gamgee 268
Handir (Old genealogy) Son of Hundor, son of Haleth the Hunter. 51, 53, 84–5, 89, 92, 125–6, 139, 141, 145, 147, 152, 157, 199–200, 241. (Later genealogy) Son of Haldir son of Halmir; fifth chieftain of the Haladin. 231, 234, 237–8, 256, 268, 270, 299

Harathor (1) Proposed replacement of *Hardan*. 238. (2) Chieftain of the Haladin when Húrin came to Brethil (replaced by *Hardang*). 237–8, 265–71, 278, 303–5, 307–8, 310

Harathrad The 'South Ford', Sarn Athrad. 335–6. See *Athrad Daer, Sarn Athrad; Northern Ford.*

Hardan Son of Haldar and father of Halmir; second chieftain of the Haladin. 222, 228, 237–8. See *Haldan, Harathor* (1).

Hardang Chieftain *(Halad)* of the Haladin when Húrin came to Brethil (replaced *Harathor* (2)). 256, 258, 263–6, 269–71, 274–81, 283–4, 287–95, 297, 299, 302–4, 307–9

Hareth Daughter of Halmir, wife of Galdor, and mother of Húrin. 234–5, 237–8, 268–70, 280, 289, 309. See *Hiriel.*

Harfalas *184, 187, 190; *South Falas* *184, 187

Hathaldir Companion of Barahir. 56

Hathol Father of Hador in the revised genealogy. 223, 225, 232, 234 ('the Axe'), 235; later, son of Hador 226, (235)

Haudh-en-Arwen The burial-mound of the Lady Haleth. 223. See *Tûr Haretha.*

Haudh-en-Elleth The burial-mound of Finduilas. 95, 148, 256, 267, 269, 271, 274, 288, 297, 299, 307; earlier *Haudh-en-Ellas* 92–3, 95, 99, 101, 148; *Mound of the Elf-maid* 148

Haudh-en-Ndengin The Mound of the Slain in Anfauglith. 169; *Haudh-na-Dengin* 72, 79, 133; other variants 79; *Haudh-en-Nirnaeth* 169 . See *Hill of Slain.*

Havens (1) Of the Falas (see *Brithombar, Eglarest*). 5, 8, 16, 34, 56, 77, 80, 89, 104, 107, 111, 117, 135, 197, 242–3. (2) The *Ship-havens* at Cape Balar. *184, 190. (3) Of Sirion: see *Sirion.*

Hecelloi; Heculbar See *Hekeldi; Hekelmar.*

Hekeldi Quenya name of the Eldar who remained in Beleriand. 365, 371, 374, 379; singular *Hekel* 365. Telerin *Hecello,* plural *Hecelloi,* 365, 376, 379

Hekelmar Quenya name of Beleriand. 365; also *Hekeldamar* 365, 374. Telerin *Heculbar* and *Hecellubar* 365, 376

Helevorn Lake in Thargelion. 34, 45, 121, *183

Helkar The Inland Sea. 174

Helkaraxë 6, 29, 191, 323; *Helkaraksë* 191. See *Grinding Ice.*

Hidden City, Hidden Realm See *Gondolin; Hidden Kingdom,* see *Gondolin* and *Doriath; Hidden Way* (into Gondolin) 48

High Elves 341

High Faroth 35, 116, 189. See *Taur-en-Faroth, Hills of the Hunters,*

High Speech (of the West) 21, 26–7, 44; *High Tongue (of Valinor)* 25

Hildor 'The Followers', Men. 219, 386–7; earlier form *Hildi* 31, 174, 219. See *Aphadon, Echil.*

Hildórien The region where Men awoke. 30, 114, (site of) 173–4

Hill of Slain 133, 135; *Mound of the Slain* 169. See *Haudh-en-Ndengin.*
Hill of Spies 149–50; *the Spyhill* 149; origin of 149. See *Amon Ethir.*
Hills of the Hunters 116, 190; *Hunters' Wold* 116. See *High Faroth, Taur-en-Faroth.*
Himlad 'Cool-plain', land between the upper waters of Celon and Aros. *183, 188, 320, 326, 332–3, 336, 338; for the name see 338.
Himring, Hill of 34, 53, 59, 67, 70, 77, *183, 219, 319, 321, 324, 326, 332, 334–5, 337–8; earlier form *Himling* 127
Hiriel Earlier name of Hareth. 235, 269
Hiril (1) Daughter of Barahir. 232. (2) Daughter of Halmir of Brethil, sister of Hareth. 264, 266, 269–70, 280, 289, 308–9
Hirwen Sister of Barahir. 231
Hísilómë Exilic Noldorin name = North Sindarin *Hithlum*. 192, 400
Hithaeglir The Misty Mountains. 322, 384–6, 389
Hither Lands Middle-earth. 22
Hithliniath 'Pools of Mist'. 194. See *Aelin-uial, Umboth Muilin.*
Hithlum 5–6, 17, 29, 31–2, 38, 46, 49–52, 54, 56, 59–60, 70–2, 76–81, 85, 104, 120, 123, 125–8, 134–7, 139, 162, 166, 168, 176, 192, 202, 219, 227, 234–5, 239, 251–4, 256–7, 260, 262, 264–5, 275, 277, 294, 313, 400; *the North-realm* 287. See *Hísilómë.*
Hobbit, The 207–8
Hollowbold Nogrod. 206, 209, 389; translation of the original form *Novrod*, see 389, 414.
Hravani Men other than the Edain, 'the Wild'. 219; Sindarin *Rhevain* 219
Húan The Hound of Valinor. 62–3, 66–8, 129, 131
Hundad Son of Hundar and father of Hardang. 237, 263, 269–70, 284, 289, 308
Hundar (1) Name intermediate between *Hundor* and *Haldir* (of Brethil). 166, 168, 235–6. (2) Brother of Haldir of Brethil, slain with him in the Nírnaeth; grandfather of Hardang. 133, 236–8, 269–70, 281, 303, 308–9
Hundor (Old genealogy) Son of Haleth the Hunter. 49, 51, 70, 72, 74, 126, 128, 133, 136, 157, 168, 233, 236, 268. (Later genealogy) Name retained as son of Halmir, 235–6; replaced by *Hundar* (1), and finally by *Haldir*, q.v.
Hunleth Daughter of Hundar (2). 237–8
Hunthor Companion of Túrin in the attack on Glaurung. 152, 156, 164, 237–8, 256–7, 264–7, 269–70, 297, 299, 303, 309. See *Albarth, Gwerin, Torbarth,* and for the development of his story and genealogy see 155–6, 267, 269–70.
Huor 51, 57(–8), 71, 75–6, 79, 81–2, 89–91, 126–7, 133, 135, 166,

169–70, 200, 224, 231–2, 234, 237, 241, 302, 314

Húrin (including *Húrin Thalion*, 'the Steadfast') 51, 53, 57–8, 60–1, 63–4, 71–2, 74–80, 83–90, 92–3, 96, 99–101, 125–9, 134–5, 137–8, 143, 145–6, 148, 152, 162–3, 165–70, 181, 199–200, 224, 231–2, 234–5, 237, 241, 244–5, 251–5, 257–308, 310–11, 314, 346–7, 349–50, 352–5, 409; *Húrin Hadorion* 294. See *Thalion*.

The children of Húrin (not as title) 102–3, 164–5, 252, 254, (258, 274), 290, 301, 403; *Hîn Húrin* 403. See *Lay of the Children of Húrin, Narn i Chîn Húrin*.

Húrinien, iChúrinien 'The Children of Húrin' (title). 311, 313. See *Narn i Chîn Húrin*.

Iant Iaur 'The Old Bridge'. 188, 333, 338. See *Esgalduin, Esgaliant*.
Iarwaeth Name taken by Túrin in Nargothrond. 83–4, 138, 142, 256, 299. (Replaced by *Agarwaen*.)
Iathrim Elves of Doriath *(Dôr Iâth)*. 378
Ice, The See *Grinding Ice*.
Icelandic 303
Idril (Celebrindal) Daughter of Turgon, mother of Eärendil. 200, 234 *(Iðril)*, 235, 258, 301–2, (323), 325, 345–6, 348, 351–2, 354; *Irildë* 235
Ilkorins Old name of the Sindar and Nandor. 22, 107, 175; *Ilkorindi* 22. *Ilkorin* (language) 23, 193
Ilúvatar 203–4, 210–13, 340–1, 402. See *Children of Eru*.
Imbar The Earth. 419. See *Ambar*.
Imin 'One', the eldest of the Fathers of the Elves. 380, 418, 420–3; *Companions of Imin* 423. See *Minyar*.
Iminyë Spouse of Imin. 421, 423
Imlach Son of Marach. 220, 233–4; earlier form *Imrach* 233
Incarnate(s) 212, 359–60, 372, 375–6, 388, 393–4, 397, 402, 405–6, 408; *Self-incarnate* (the Valar) 406
Incomers Easterlings in Hithlum. 253 (and see *Brodda*). Used of Asgorn and his companions in Brethil 262, 274; of Húrin 279
Indis Second wife of Finwë. 327, 383
Indrafangs Old name of the Longbeard Dwarves. 108, 208. See *Anfangrim, Enfeng*.
Ingildon Tower on the cape west of Eglarest. 40, 80, 118, 190, 196–7. (Replaced *Tindobel*; replaced by *Barad Nimras*.)
Inglor Earlier name of Finrod (2); references include *Inglor Felagund*. 31–2, 34–5, 38, 42–4, 48–50, 52, 54, 62, 65, 67, 116–18, 130, 178–9, 197–8, 228, 238–40, 242–3, 343. See *Felagund*.
Ingwë King of the Vanyar. 6, 246
Ingwil Tributary stream of Narog. *184, 190, 197. (Replaced by *Ringwil*.)
Ingwion Son of Ingwë. 246; *Ingwiel* 246

Inland Sea See *Helkar, Rhûn.*
Inner Sea See 173–4.
Iôn Eöl's first name for Maeglin ('Son'). 337
Irildë See *Idril.*
Írith Turgon's sister. 318, 409, 420. See *Isfin , Aredhel, Feiniel.*
Irmo 'Desirer', true name of the Vala Lórien. 403
Iron Crown 38, 63, 68; other references to Morgoth's crown 62, 65, 69, 347
Iron Mountains 6, 15, 31, 36, 60, 104, 112, 128. See *Eryd Engrin.*
Iron Prison See *Angband.*
Isfin Called *the White*; original name of Turgon's sister. 47–8, 71, 84, 121–3, 127, 139, 316–20, 322, 324–5, 332, 336, 420. On the name see 317–18; and see *Írith, Aredhel, Feiniel, Rodwen.*
Ithil The Moon. 401
Ivrin 91, 139–40, 145–6; *the Pools of Ivrin* 34, 83, 88–9. See *Eithil Ivrin.*
Ivrineithel See *Eithil Ivrin.*

Jewel(s), The The Silmaril(s). 63, 65, 68–9, 254, 351, 354

Kalakiryan 'The Cleft of Light'. 119, 403
Kalaquendi 'Light-elves', Elves of Aman. 19, 175, 361, 373, 375–6; Telerin *Calapendi* 362, 375. See *Calben.*
Kasari Quenya name of the Dwarves (derived from *Khazâd*); singular *Kasar.* 388, 402; *Kasallië* 388. Cf. *Casarrondo.*
Kay, Guy G. 356
kelvar Animals, living things that move. 340–1. See *olvar.*
Kementári Name of Yavanna. 246. (Replaced *Palúrien.*)
Khazâd The Dwarves. 205, 209–10, 214, 387–8, 414; earlier form *Khuzûd* 205, 209–10, 214. See *Hadhod, Kasari.*
Khazad-dûm 201–2, 204–9, 389, 397, 419; originally name of Nogrod 108, 201, 209. See *Casarrondo, Hadhodrond, Nornhabar; Dwarrowdelf.*
Kilby, Clyde S. 310
Kinslayings, The The first (at Alqualondë) 19, 26, 37, 41; the second (the attack on Dior) 232, 345–6, 348–9; the third (the attack on the Havens of Sirion) 345, 348
Kirith Ninniach See *Cirith Ninniach.*
Koivië-néni Original form of *Kuiviénen.* 424
Kôr Original name of the city of the Elves in Valinor. 23, 175, 189, 246. See *Tûn, Túna, Tirion.*
Koreldar The Elves of Kôr. 107
Kornoldorin, Korolambë The ancient Noldorin tongue of Kôr. 22–3
Korollairë, Koron Oiolairë The Green Mound of the Trees. 401. See *Ezellohar.*
Kuiviénen See *Cuiviénen.*

Lachend, plural *Lechind* 'Flame-eyed', a Sindarin name of the Noldor. 384
Ladros Land in the east of Dorthonion. *183, 187, 224, 229
Laegel, plurals *Laegil, Laegrim, Laegel(d)rim* (Sindarin) The Green-elves; whence Quenya *Laiquendi*. 385
Laiquendi See *Laegel*.
Lalaeth See *Urwen*.
Lambengolmor 'Loremasters of Tongues'. 396–8
Lambë Valarinwa Valarin. 397
Lammas The 'Account of Tongues' by Pengolodh. 205–6, 208, 393, 397, 416; older form *Lhammas* (the work as published in *The Lost Road*) 3, 22–3, 108–9, 118, 208–9, 419; *Lammasethen* 22
Lammoth Region north of the Firth of Drengist. 176, *182
Lamps, The 106
Land of Bow and Helm 144, 314. See *Dor-Cúarthol*.
Land of Seven Rivers 13, 385. See *Ossir, Ossiriand*.
Land of the Dead that Live 71, 132, 347. See *Gwerth-i-guinar*.
Last Battle At the end of the Elder Days. 27, 117; *last war of the Elder Days* 345–6; *the Great Battle* 345. The final battle of Arda 204, 207
Latin 372, 391. See *Elf-Latin*.
Laurelin 20, 401
Lay of Leithian 59, 62, 65, 69, 108, 125, 129–31, 187
Lay of the Children of Húrin (in *The Lays of Beleriand*: alliterative verse) 109, 137–8, 314
Lay of the Fall of Gondolin 121, 320
Legolin, River In Ossiriand. 13, *185
Lembi Dark-elves. 118
Lenwë First leader of the Nandor (replaced *Dân*). 384–5, 412, 418. See *Denweg*.
Letters of J. R. R. Tolkien, The 118, 212, 341, 353, 356
Levain tad-dail 'Two-legged animals' (see 416), original Sindarin name of the Petty-dwarves. 388; *Tad-dail* 388
Lhammas See *Lammas*.
Lhandroval The eagle, vassal of Thorondor. 68, 131
Light, (The) (and ~ *of Aman, of the Trees, in the West*, etc.) 6–9, 17, 39, 41, 217, 220, 225, 227, 373, 403
Light-elves (1) The Lindar (Vanyar). 246. (2) Elves of Aman. 320, 361. See *Kalaquendi*.
Limhir, River Late replacement of *Celon*. 320, 326, 337.
Limlight, River 337
Linaewen, Lake In Nivrost (Nevrast). *182, 186, 192
Lindai See *Lindar*.
Lindalambë The language of the Lindar (Teleri). 375. See *Lindarin*.
Lindar The 'Third Clan' (formerly the name of the 'First Clan', the Vanyar, 246, 418). 378, 380–3, 410–11, 418, 423; meaning of the

INDEX

name 382. Original and Telerin form *Lindai* 378, 382, 385; Nandorin *Lindi* 385; Sindarin *Lindil, Lindedhil* 385. See *Glinnel, Nendili; Teleri.*

Lindarin (1) The language of the Lindar = Vanyar. 22. (2) The language of the Lindar = Teleri. 375-6, 382; as adjective to *Lindar* 376-7, 381-2, 385

Lindis of Ossiriand Wife of Dior. 257, 300, 350-1, 353. See *Elulin, Nimloth.*

Lindon Ossiriand. 193, 195, 385; *Dor Lindon* 385; *Lindónë* 385

List Melian *183, 188, 223, 225, 228, 333; *Lest Melian* 225, 228. Cf. *Aran Lestanórëo* 'King of Doriath' 369; and see *Girdle of Melian.*

Lithir, River Tributary of Sirion north of Brethil. 181, *182, 261, 301

Little Ford (over Gelion) See *Northern Ford.*

Lóminórë 145. See *Dor-lómin.*

Lómion 'Child (Son) of Twilight', name given to Maeglin by his mother. 323, 337

Lonely Isle 246, 312, 315. See *Tol Eressëa.*

Longbeards The Dwarves of Belegost. 10, 108, 205, 207-8, 322; of Nogrod 108, 208. See *Anfangrim, Enfeng, Indrafangs.*

Long Peace, The 46, 58, 206, 215, 329

Lord of the Rings, The (title) 3, 107, 110-11, 129-30, 142, 144, 173-5, 177, 201, 207-8, 242, 245, 247, 254, 297, 314, 337, 342, 344-5, 352, 354, 419-20; *The Fellowship of the Ring* 417, 419; *The Return of the King* 420

Lords of the West 287, 402

Loremaster(s) 10, 25, 343, 346-7, 359, 365, 374, 378, 380, 383-6, 391, 393-6, 405, 408-10, 416-17; with reference to Dairon 13, 20, 110

Lorgan Chief of the Easterlings of Hithlum. 82, 91, 137, 146, 253(-4), 256, 260-1, 299

Lórien (also *Lorien*) The abode of the Vala Irmo, but used also as his name. 11, 108, 403-4. See *Irmo.*

Lorindol Name of Hador, 'Goldenhead'. 228, 230, 233-5. See *Glorindol.*

Losgar The place of the burning of the ships of the Teleri. 16, 31, 38, 43, 115, 117, 119, 176, 329

Lost Tales See *(The) Book of Lost Tales.*

Lothlann Great plain east of Dorthonion. 60, 128; *Lhothlann* 128; *Lothland* 128, *183, 187

Lothlórien 110

Luindirien 'The Blue Towers'. 193. See *Blue Mountains.*

Lúthien 9, 14, 61-71, 129-33, *185, 195, 224, 228, 231, 242-3, 346-51, 353. See *Tinúviel.*

Mablung Elf of Doriath, chief captain of Thingol. 34, 63, 72, 93–5, 101–2, 116, 133, 148, 150, 161–2, 164, 257, 281, 303, 311
Maedros, Maedhros See *Maidros*.
Maeglin 48, 58, 76, 122–3, 127, 139, 146, 169, 302, 317, 321–7, 330, 332–3, 336–7, 344, 348, 351, 353, 409; as name also of the metal of Eöl 48, 122, 322–3; later translated 'Sharp-glance' 323 (etymology 337). See *Iôn, Lómion*. For names of the metal of Eöl see *Galvorn*; for rejected names of Maeglin see *Meglin, Morleg, Morlîn, Targlîn, Glindûr*.
Maglor Son of Fëanor. 34, 47, 49, 53, 64, 74, 116, 131, 134, *183, 215, 247, 345, 352
Magor Son of Malach Aradan, son of Marach; 'the Sword' (234–5). 219, 223, 225–6, 232–5; called *Dagorlind* 'Singer in battle' 226, 235. For the changed place of Magor in the genealogy see 225–6, 235.
Mahal Dwarvish name of Aulë. 10, 108
Máhanaxar The Doom-ring of the Valar. 399, 401. See *Rithil-Anamo*.
Máhani The chiefs of the Valar, the Aratar; singular *Máhan*. 399, 402
Maiar (and singular *Maia*) 5–7, 9–10, 16, 71, 113, 341, 372–3, 399, 401, 405–6; *Maia* as adjective 415; *language of the Valar and Maiar* 397, 416
Maidros Son of Fëanor. 18, 29–30, 32–4, 36, 38, 46, 49, 53, 59–61, 64, 69–72, 74, 114–17, 121, 128, 131–2, 134, 167–8, 176–7, 247, 345, 348–9, 351–4; later forms *Maiðros* 32, 115, 188, *Maedhros, Maeðros* 115, *183, 188, 255, *Maedros* 115, 165–8, 177, *183, 188, 215, 219, 221. See *March of Maidros, Union of Maidros*.
Malach (also with Elvish name *Aradan* conjoined, or *Aradan* alone, see 219, 234) Son of Marach. 219, 223, 225–6, 230–5; *the people of Aradan* 233
Malduin, River *182, 186
Mandos The abode of the Vala Námo, but used also as his name. 18, 33, 43, 67, 69, 119, 130, 177, 204, 207, 247, 283, 295, 387, 402; *the Curse, Doom of Mandos* 19, (31), 37, 43, 45, 343, *the shadow of* ~ 43; called *the Just* 295. See *Námo*.
Mannish 311
Manthor A lord of the Haladin, brother of Hunthor; 'Master of the Northmarch' of Brethil (263). 258, 263–5, 267, 269–70, 275–82, 284, 286–97, 302–9
Manwë 41, 70, 246, 272, 280, 287, 340–1, 345, 399–400, 403–4, 406, 417; *son of, herald of, Manwë* 246; *Mánwë, Mánwen*, and origin of the name 399. See *Elder King*.
Maps (1) The first *Silmarillion* map. 149, 190, 202, 334. (2) The second map. 111–13, 117, 139–40, 145, 149, 157, 159, 180–94,

198, 201, 227–9, 238, 299, 301, 330–8, 344, 353, 418; scale of this map 111, 332; photocopy used in connection with *Maeglin* 330–8. (3) Map accompanying the published *Silmarillion*. 112, 159, 187–8, 191, 333, 336, 338

Marach   218–20, 226–8, 230, 232–4, 241, 334. The People, Folk, of Marach 218, 226–7, 234; the Children of Marach 402; Nothlir Maracha 234; ancient tongue of 49, 123, 218–19, 224, 226–7, 234, 402; genealogical table 234

March, The   (1) Of the Eldar. See *Great March*. (2) Of the Edain. 218, 296

March of Maidros   34, 38–9, 53, 77, 128; Marches ~ *183, 188; the March 34, 61

Meglin   Original name of Maeglin. 84, 91, 121–2, 139, 146, 206, 302, 316, 323. See *Maeglin*.

Meldis   Elvish name of Zimrahin wife of Malach Aradan. 234

Meleth   Daughter of Hiril (2) and mother of Manthor. 270, (289)

Melian   5–7, 9–11, 14–16, 21, 25, 35, 40–3, 50, 59, 61, 64–5, 70–1, 82, 90, 93, 95, 105–8, 110–11, 113–14, 119, 123, 129–30, 132, 175, 178, 194, 252, 259, 310, 312, 321, 333, 345–7, 350–3, 355. See *Girdle of Melian; Gwendelin*.

Melkor   5, 9–10, 12, 14, 17, 36, 44, 78, 104–5, 109, 117, 134, 150, 177, 191–2, 196, 200, 203–4, 207, 210–12, 346, 351, 373, 384, 386, 402, 418; 'He who arises in Might' 402; the Chaining of Melkor 9–10. Earlier form *Melko* 111, 121, 191–2, 195. War of the Valar and Melkor 373

Men   Selected references. Awakening, coming of Men 30, 37, 49–50, 217; their fate, doom 52, 225, 247, 387; languages 39, 60, 118, 128, 205, 208–9, 402 (and see *Bëor, Haladin* (1), *Marach*); in relation to Elves 39, 49–50, 77, 124, 128, 219–21, 224, 386–7; Elvish names for Men 219, 386–7; corruption by Morgoth and rebellion 37, 39, 118, 217; Men of Eriador 61, 64

Menegroth   10–12, 14–16, 18, 20–1, 23, 32, 35, 43, 63–5, 67, 69–70, 81–2, 95, 108, 110–12, 132, 135, 138, 140, 149, 178, *183, 244, 334–5, 347–8, 350, 352–3, 355, 414–15, 418; Menegroth described 11, 415; etymology 414. See *Thousand Caves*.

Menel   The heavens. 411, 422

Menelmakil   Orion. 411. See *Telumehtar*.

Mengas Dûr   See *Cabed-en-Aras*.

Mereth Aderthad   34, 114, 116. See *Feast of Reuniting*.

Meril   Wife of Felagund. 242. See *Felagund*.

Methiriad   Mid-Beleriand. *184, 187, 190

Mickleburg   Belegost. 206, 209, 389. See *Great Fortress*.

Middle-earth   5–6, 8–10, 13–14, 16, 18, 20–4, 26, 30, 33, 37, 39, 42, 45, 50, 62, 67, 69, 85, 104–7, 109, 114, 116, 118, 130, 161–3, 173–6, 178, 180, 186, 193, 196, 203, 205, 207, 210–11, 217,

220, 224, 253, 320–1, 341, 343, 345, 350, 355, 360, 365, 373, 378, 381, 384, 386, 393, 397, 409, 412, 416. See *Endar*.
Mîm 180, 187, 255, 257–8, 300, 310–12, 314, 354–5, 389
Mindeb, River 81, *183, 188, 193–4, 333
Miniel, plural *Minil* Sindarin name of the Vanyar. 383
Minnas-tirith The fortress on Tol Sirion. 38, 54, 125
Minnónar 'The First-born', Elves. 403
Minyar Elves of the First Clan (Vanyar). 380–2, 420. See *Imin*.
Míriel First wife of Finwë, mother of Fëanor. 327, 387, 419
Mirkwood 110; translation of *Taur-na-Fuin* 239
miruvórë The cordial of the Valar. 399, 419
Misty Mountains 202; *Mountains of Mist* 13, 201, 206. See *Hithaeglir*.
Mithrim The Elves of Mithrim (primary meaning of the name). 378, 410–11, 420; name of their dialect of Sindarin 400. Lake Mithrim (originally = 'Lake of the Mithrim', 410) 17, 31, 81, 176, *182, 378, 410; the land of Mithrim 17–18, 31, 33–4, 79–82, 89, 91, 113–14, 128, 136–7, 146, 176, *182, 238, 261–2, 411 (language); *the Mountains of Mithrim* 17, 181, *182
Moon, The 17, 20, 30, 114, 176. See *Ithil*.
Moors of the Neweglu (Petty-dwarves) *182, 187. See *Neweg*.
Moot (of Brethil) See *Brethil*.
Morben, plural *Moerbin (Morbin)* Sindarin name derived from *Moriquendi* (for the meaning see 376–7, 409). 362, 376–7, 380, 408–9, 420
Mordor 370, 390
Morgoth 14–19, 22, 29–33, 35–42, 45–6, 50, 52–6, 58–9, 61–6, 68–80, 82–5, 89, 91, 99, 105, 109–11, 113–21, 127–8, 134–7, 141–2, 146, 149–50, 159, 166–70, 176–7, 195, 200, 203–4, 220–1, 223, 239–40, 242, 247, 251–9, 261, 264, 266, 272, 275, 281, 296, 298–302, 306–7, 310, 320–1, 328, 333–4, 343–8, 353, 355, 376, 381, 383–6, 391, 397, 408–9, 411, 415, 418–19; the Eye of Morgoth 259. See *Bauglir, Dark Foe*.
Moria 201–2, 206, 209
Moriquendi 'Dark-elves', 'Elves of the Dark' (8). 8–9, 19, 361, 373, 376–7, 380–1, 384, 417; Telerin *Moripendi* 362, 375. See *Morben*.
Morleg Rejected name of Maeglin. 323–5, 332. See *Maeglin*.
Morlîn Rejected name of (1) Maeglin, 323; (2) the metal of Eöl, 322 (see *Galvorn*).
Mormegil Name of Túrin in Nargothrond. 83–5, 89, 92–3, 138, 147–8, 256; *Mormael, Mormaglir* 138. See *(The) Black Sword*.
Mornedhel 'Dark-elf'. 377, 380, 409, 420
Morwë Leader of a kindred of the Avari. 418
Morwen 51, 56, 61, 64, 78–9, 81, 85, 87–8, 90, 93–5, 102, 124, 126, 129, 137, (142)–3, 145, 148–50, 161–4, 181, *182, 224,

230–1, 234, 251–2, 254, 256–9, 268, 273–4, 291, 294–6, 298–300, 302, 306, 409, 420; *the Grey Lady* 296. See *Edhelwen*; *Tol Morwen*.
Mound of the Slain   See *Hill of Slain*.
Mountains of Aman, ~ of Valinor   See *Aman, Valinor, Pelóri*; ~ of Mist, see *Misty Mountains*; ~ of Mithrim, see *Mithrim*; ~ of Ossiriand, see *Ossiriand*.
Mountains of Shadow   272; Shadowy Mountains 128, 146; *the mountains* 18, 31, 34, 52, 73, 77, 79, 91, 257, 260–1. See *Eryd Wethrin*.
Mountains of Terror   15, 111, 194, 222, 332(–3). See *Eryd Gorgoroth*.
Music (of the Ainur), The   341

Nahar   Oromë's horse. 14, 401 (etymology).
Namárië   419
Námo   'Judge', true name of the Vala Mandos. 402
Nandor   The people of Lenwë (Dân) who abandoned the Great March; the Green-elves of Ossiriand. 13, 34, 109–10, 112, 126, 195, 218, 377, 381, 384–6, 409, 412, 418–19; origin of the name 109, 412. See *Danwaith*.
Nandorin   (of language) 390, 407, 411–12; (with other reference) 412
Nan Dungortheb   110, 180, *183, 197, 319, 333, *Dungortheb* 329; earlier *Nan Dungorthin* 47, 61, 64, 110, 122, 180, 194, 197, *Dungorthin* 319, 328–9
Nan Elmoth   6–7, 9, 21, 47–8, 106, 122, *183, 218, 321–3, 326–30, 333–6; *Elmoth* 327, 332, 335. See *Gladuial*.
Nan Tathren   The Land of Willows. 80, 116, 180, *184; earlier *Nan Tathrin* 90, 180
Nardol   (1) Beacon-hill in Anórien. 187. (2) *Nardol* and *Amon Nardol*, see *Amon Rûdh*.
Nargothrond   5, 35, 38–9, 44, 52, 54, 62–3, 65–7, 70, 72–3, 77, 82–6, 89, 92–4, 97, 99, 101, 116–17, 120, 125, 129–31, 133–4, 137–47, 149–50, 152, 157, 162, 166, 168, 177–80, *184, 186, 189–90, 197–8, 203, 223, 242, 245, 251, 254–8, 260, 298–301, 306–7, 310–11, 313–14, 347, 350, 352, 354–5, 414 (etymology), 418; Realm of Nargothrond 85, *182, *184, 193. See *Nulukkhizdîn*.
Narn i Chîn Húrin   103, 160, 251, 255, 311, 313–14; *Glaer nia* ~ 160, 251; (the Tale of) the Children of Húrin 144, 160, 165, 313–14; the *Narn* (excluding detailed references to the last section 'NE', see 144–5) 112, 139–45, 148, 156, 164–5, 167–9, 174, 180, 186–7, 236, 241, 251, 267, 269, 303–4, 307, 309, 312–16, 354; the name and the verse-form 311, 313–15. See *Húrinien* and *'Turins Saga'* in entry *Túrin*.

Narog, River 15, 34–5, 38, 84–6, 88, 93, 116, 139–40, 150, 178, *182, *184, 193–4, 197, 228, 379, 414; *Caverns of Narog* 35, 116

Narrow Land The Pass of Sirion. 256–7, 261, 299, 301. See *Sirion*.

Nauglamîr 244, 298, 345–7, 350–1, 353, 355. See *Necklace of the Dwarves*.

Nauglath, Nauglar, Nauglir See *Naugrim*.

Naugrim 'The Stunted Folk', the Dwarves. 9–14, 16, 20, 45, 60, 70, 75, 107–9, 126, 134, 167, 201, 203–7, 209–10, 214, 322, 324, 388, 395, 408; earlier *Nauglath* 28, 107–8, 209, *Nauglar, Nauglir* 209; *Naug* 205, 209–10, 214, 388, 413–14; *Naug-neben* (Petty-dwarf), see *Nibinnoeg*.

Nauko (Quenya) Dwarf; *Naukalië*, the people of the Dwarves. 388. See *Naugrim*.

Návarot (Quenya) Nogrod. 389

Neben-naug, Nebinnog See *Nibinnoeg*.

Necklace of the Dwarves 244, 258, 297, 347; *the Necklace, Thingol's necklace* 350–1, 353; *Sigil Elu-naeth* 'Necklace of the Woe of Thingol' 258, 297. See *Nauglamîr*.

Neldoreth The northern forest of Doriath. 7, 9, 11, 15–16, 61, 64, 106, 111, *183, 333, 355

Nelyar Elves of the Third Clan (Lindar). 380–2, 420. See *Enel*.

Nendili 'Water-lovers', the Lindar. 411

Nen Girith 'Shuddering Water', name given to the falls in the stream Celebros. 96–100, 151, 156–9, 163, 295–6, 306–7. See *Dimrost*.

Nen Lalaith The stream that flowed past Húrin's house in Dor-lómin. 181

Nenning, River 39, 80, 84, 117–18, *182, 187. See *Eglor, Eglahir*.

Nessa Wife of the Vala Tulkas. 404, 416 (etymology).

Nevrast The region south of Drengist. 107, 179, 181, *182, 197, 200, 318, 396; *Nevrost* 318; translated 'Hither Shore' 197. Earlier form *Nivrost* 28, 35, 38, 40, 44–5, 80, 91, 104, 107, 120, 146, 178–9, 181, 192 (described), 195, 197–200, 256, 318; translated 'West Vale' 197. *The Marches of Nevrast (Nivrost)* 181, *182, 186

Neweg The Dwarves. 187, 209; *Neweglîn*, Petty-dwarves, 187, *Neweglu* *182, 187

Nibin-noeg Petty-dwarves. 187, 420; *Nibennog, Nibinnogrim, Nebinnog, Neben-naug, Naug-neben, Niwennog* 187. See *Nogoth*.

Nienor 79, 81, 85, 87–8, 90, 93–5, 100–3, 137, 143, 148–50, 162–4, 234, 256–7, 290, 295, 298–300. See *Níniel*.

Nimbrethil Birchwoods in Arvernien. *184, 190

Nimîr The Elves (Adunaic). 386; singular *Nimir* 419

Nimloth Wife of Dior. 349–50. See *Elulin, Lindis*. (*Nimloth* was a name of Telperion, and the name of the White Tree of Númenor.)

Nimphelos   A great pearl given by Thingol to the Lord of Belegost. 10, 108
Nimras   See *Barad Nimras*.
Níniel   'Tear-maiden', name of Nienor. 96–101, 103, 151–2, 156–61, 163–4, 234, 257, 300
niphredil   A white flower in Doriath. 9, 107
Nírnaeth Arnoediad (including references to *the Nírnaeth* used alone, and spellings *Nírnaith* and *Arnediad*; the element *Nír-* often without accent) 28, 71, 73, 77, 128, 133, 136, 165, 167, ·236, 255, 262, 264, 266, 269, 281, 287, 303, 307, 312, 315, 377; *Dagor Arnediad* 22, 28; and cf. *Haudh-en-Nirnaeth* 169. See *Battle of Unnumbered Tears*.
Nivrim   151, *182, 187; the West-march of Doriath 56, 150–1; Doriath beyond Sirion *182. Cf. *Radhrim*.
Nivrost   See *Nevrast*.
Niwennog   Petty-dwarves. See *Nibin-noeg*.
Noad, Charles   157, 159
Nognith   Petty-dwarves. 187
Nogoth, plurals *Noegyth*, *Nogothrim* 'Stunted'; Dwarf, Dwarves. 388, 412, 419. *Nogoth niben*, Petty-dwarf, 388, plural *Noegyth nibin* 408, 419–20; *Nogotheg* 388. See *Athrad i-Nogoth*.
Nogrod   'Hollowbold', city of the Dwarves in the Blue Mountains (for the different applications and relations of the name see 201–2, 209). 10, 12, 45, 75, 108–9, 134, *185, 201–2, 206, 208–9, 215, 322, 324, 326–7, 329, 335–6, 347, 350, 352–3, 389, 408, 414 (etymology). See *Tumunzahar*; *Návarot*; *Novrod*, *Grodnof*, *Bar-goll*; *Hollowbold*.
Noldoli   See *Noldor*.
Noldor (and singular *Noldo*) 5–9, 12, 15–29, 31–48, 50, 52, 54–6, 59–60, 62, 70, 72–7, 79, 83, 90, 106–7, 113–16, 119, 121–2, 124–6, 136, 165–6, 168, 175–7, 181, 189, 192–5, 197, 200, 203–7, 210, 214–15, 219, 224, 239–40, 243, 246, 317–18, 321, 323, 327–8, 333–4, 338, 343, 364, 372–89, 393, 396–7, 399, 403–5, 409–12, 417, 420, 422–3; meaning of the name 383; earliest form *Noldoli* 244. See *Gódhel*, *Golodh*, *Goldo*; *Nómin*, *Samûri*; *Exiles*; *Second Clan*.
Noldorin (of language) 20–8, 116, 120, 191, 201, 240, 315, 323, 337, 359, 361, 363, 373–4, 384, 391, 399–400, 407, 413, 417; (with other reference) 4, 26–8, 119, 136, 141, 188, 373, 379, 381–2, 385, 391, 394–7, 404, 406, 408, 412, 416–17
Nóm   'Wisdom', name given to Felagund in the language of Bëor's people. 217. See *Sômar, Vidri*.
Nómin   'The Wise', name given to the Noldor in the language of Bëor's people (rejected form *Nómil*). 217. See *Samûri*.
Norn-folk   The Dwarves. 9, 107, 209. See *Norno, Nornwaith*.
Nornhabar   'Dwarrowdelf', city of the Dwarves in the Misty Moun-

tains (replaced by *Hadhodrond*). 206, 209, 215, 419. See *Khazad-dûm*; *Casarrondo*; *Hadhodrond*; *Dwarrowdelf*.
Norno (Quenya) Dwarf; *Nornalië*, the people of the Dwarves. 388, 413. See *Norn-folk*, *Nornwaith*, *Nyrn*.
Nornwaith The Dwarves. 107, 209, 324. See *Norno*, *Norn-folk*.
Norse 303
North, The 6, 12–15, 30–2, 34, 36, 46, 50, 57, 60, 79, 88, 90, 92, 109, 111–12, 117, 121, 124, 128, 176, 178, 200, 216, 220, 227, 263, 272, 297, 377, 410–11; *the northlands* 31, 33, 56; *the North-realm* (Hithlum) 287
Northern Ford (over Gelion) 335–6; *Little Ford* 335
Novrod 'Hollowbold', the original name later transformed to *Nogrod*: see 389, 414. See *Bar-goll*, *Grodnof*.
Núath, The Woods of Forest to the west of Ivrin. *182, 186
Nulukkhizdīn Dwarvish name of Nargothrond; also *Nulukhizidûn*. 180
Númenor 224, 230, 232, 243; *Númenórë* 386; *Drowning of Númenor* 105; *Númenóreans* 386; *Númenórean* (tongue, tales) 226, 314
Núnatani (Quenya) The Dúnedain. 386
Nurwë Leader of a kindred of the Avari. 418
Nyrn 'The hard', the Dwarves. 205, 209, 214. See *Norno*, *Norn-folk*.

Oäreldi, Oäzeldi Elves who left Middle-earth for Aman (= *Aureldi*, *Auzeldi*); singular *Oärel*, *Oäzel*. 363–6, 374
Obel Halad The fortified place in which stood the Hall of the Chieftains of Brethil. 148, 258, 263–7, 271, 276, 292, 301–2, 306; *the Obel* 296–7, 306, 308. See *Brethil*, *Halad*.
Ódhel, plurals Ódhil, Ódhellim The Exiled Noldor (= *Gódhel*). 364, 366, 378–9
Oiolossë (Oron Oiolossë) '(Mount) Everwhite', 'Eversnow'. 403. See *Amon Uilos*.
Old English See *English*; *Anglo-Saxon*.
olvar Living things that grow in the earth. 340–1. See *kelvar*.
Olwë Brother of Elwë (Thingol), lord of Alqualondë. 7–8, 13, 19, (32), 41, 115, 177, 344, 369, 379–80. See *Elwë* (1).
Ondolindë 'Rock of the Music of Water', Quenya name of Gondolin. 201
One, The See *Eru*.
Orchal Name of Galdor. 287, 305
Orc(s) (including many compounds as *Orc-camp*, *-host*, *-legion*, etc.) 15–18, 33, 36–7, 46, 49, 52–3, 56–60, 66, 70, 72–7, 79–82, 84–9, 92–7, 105, 109, 111–13, 118, 121, 125, 127–8, 132, 138–44, 147, 150, 162, 169, 176, 195, 203–4, 206, 212, 216, 220–3, 236–8, 241, 244, 255–6, 262, 275, 277, 279, 285, 307,

329, 359, 372, 377, 386, 389–91, 408–9, 418; *Ork(s)* 321, 330; *orkish* 267. Origin of the Orcs 12, 109, 195
  Sindarin *Orch*, plurals *Yrch*, *Orchoth* 390–1. Quenya *Orko*, plural *Orqui* 390, also *Orkor* 12, 36–7, 390; and see *Urko*. Etymology 389–91
Orgof Earlier name of Saeros. 81, 135, 138, 244; *Orgoph*, *Orgol* 112
Orion 411. See *Menelmakil*, *Telumehtar*.
Ornil Elf of Nargothrond. 86
Orodreth Son of Finarfin (= Finrod (1)); second king of Nargothrond. 38, 54, 63, 66–7, 73, 82–5, 92, 125, 131, 133–4, 137–9, 141–2, 149, *183, 187–8, 239–40, 242, 256
Oromë 5–6, 11, 14, 55, 105–6, 109–10, 295, 343, 360–1, 368, 373, 383, 400–1, 419. See *Araw*.
Ossë 5, 7–8, 80, 104, 107, 112, 192, 400, 404. See *Balar*; *Gaerys*, *Yssion*.
Ossir Ossiriand. 351, 353; *the Seven Rivers of Ossir* 353
Ossiriand 13, 15–16, 22, 24, 28, 34, 39, 48, 71, 80, 110–12, 193, 195, 216, 218, 257, 300, 347, 350–1, 353, 385, 406; *the Mountains of Ossiriand* 193. See *Land of Seven Rivers*, *Lindon*.
Outer Dark 346
Outer Sea 175

Palúrien Name of Yavanna. 246. (Replaced by *Kementári*.)
Pelóri The Mountains of Aman. 30, 403–4
Pendi (Telerin) = *Quendi*. 362, 375, 408
Pengolodh 107, 109, 210, 343, 393, 396–404, 406, 416, 419; called the *Loremaster of Eressëa* 393; his origin and history 396–7. Earlier form *Pengolod* 110 ('the Wise, of Gondolin'), 192, 201–3, 206, 210, 343. See *Thingódhel*.
Pennas The *Quenta Silmarillion*. 192, 206
Petty-dwarves 187, 299, 313, 388–9, 408, 415, 419; *Petty-dwarf* (referring to Mîm) 180, 258, 389. For Elvish names see *Neweg*, *Nibin-noeg*, *Nogoth*; *Attalyar*, *Levain tad-dail*, *Pikinaukor*.
Pikinaukor, *Pitya-naukor* (Quenya) Petty-dwarves. 389
Powers, The 6, 39, 403; *Powers of Light*, 39; *War of the Powers* 6, 106; *the (Dark) Power* 39, 43

Quenderin 'Of the Quendi'. 407
Quendi Elves (see 372). 5–6, 28, 37, 105, 117, 204–5, 217, 361, 372–5, 382, 386, 391, 393, 401, 403, 405–6, 409–10, 421–3; singular *Quende* 361, 372, 374. See *Awakening of the Elves*; *Pendi*.
Quendian 'Of the Quendi'. 407; with reference to language 20, 319,

373, 411; *Primitive Quendian* (abbreviated PQ) 359–61, 363–5, 368, 375–6, 380, 382–4, 390, 409, 411, 413
Quendil, Quendendil 'Elf-friend'. 410; plural *Quendili* 412
Quennar (i) Onótimo Eldarin loremaster. 343
Quentalë Ardanómion Unknown work of learning referred to by Ælfwine. 206
Quenta (Noldorinwa) The *Quenta Silmarillion* (references in the texts only). 27–8, 32, 38, 48, 59, 117, 120
Quenya (= *Quenya lambë* 407) 22–3, 145, 201, 318–20, 337, 359, 361–78, 380–5, 387–400, 402–3, 405–7, 410–17; original and Vanyarin form *Quendya* 361, 373, 375, 393

Radhrim 'East-march', Doriath beyond Aros. *183, 188–9. Cf. *Nivrim*.
Radhrost 'East Vale', Thargelion. 194, 197, 218, 221, 225, 227. Cf. *Nivrost* 'West Vale' (entry *Nevrast*), and see *Talath Rhúnen*.
Radhruin Companion of Barahir. 56, 126. Earlier name *Radros* 126
Ragnir (1) Servant of Morwen. 302. (2) Companion of Asgon. 262, 265, 302
Ragnor Companion of Barahir. 56
Ramdal See *Rhamdal*.
Ras-Arphain Sindarin name of Taniquetil. 403. See *Arfanyarassë; Amon Uilos*.
Ras Mewrim Cape south-west of Eglarest. *184, 190, 418. See *Bar-in-Mŷl*.
Rathlóriel, River (also *Rathloriel*) Name given to the Ascar: 'Bed of Gold'. 180, *185, 190, 345–8, 351, 353; earlier name *Rathlorion* 180, 190, 353; late names *Rathmalad, Rathmallen* *185, 191, 353
Region The southern forest of Doriath 7, 11, 15–16, 106, 112, *183, 321, 334, 355; *Region over Aros* 112
Rerir, Mount Source of Greater Gelion. 34, *183, 188
Rhamdal 'Wall's End' in East Beleriand. *185, 191; *Ramdal* 191. See *Andram*.
Rhevain See *Hravani*.
Rhûn, Sea of 174
Rían Mother of Tuor. 52, 56, 71, 79, 126, 133, 135, 224, 231, 234
Ringil Fingolfin's sword. 55
Ringwil, River Tributary stream of Narog. 190, 197–8. (Replaced *Ingwil*.)
Rithil-Anamo The Doom-ring of the Valar. 401. See *Máhanaxar*.
Rivendell 190
Rivil Tributary stream of Sirion. 72, 113, 181, *183; *Rivil's Well* 59, 113, *183; *Fen of Rivil* 113, 181, 238 (see *Serech*).
Road Goes Ever On, The 419
Roads In Brethil 157, 186; to Nargothrond 157, 186, 398. *The East*

INDEX 463

Road (East-West Road) 319, 324–5, 332–5. See *Dwarf-road(s)*.
Rochallor Fingolin's horse. 55–6, 125
Rodëol The metal of Eöl. 322–3. See *Galvorn*.
Rodwen Proposed name to replace *Isfin*. 317–18
Rohan, Rochan(d) 104; and see *Gap (of Rohan)*.
Rúkhs, plural *Rakhās* Dwarvish name for Orcs. 391
Rúmil 'The ancient sage of Tirion' (398). 343, 398–9, 401, 407; *I Equessi Rúmilo* 'the Sayings of Rúmil' 397–8, 401; *Rúmilian letters* 396
Runes (all references are to the Runes of Dairon or 'of Doriath') 14, 20, 26, 28, 103, 110. See *Cirth*.

Sador Labadal Servant of Húrin. (90), 145–6, 257, 300, 314
Saelin Name of Andreth. 230, 232–3; *Saelind* 233; *Saelon* 233–4
Saeros Nandorin Elf of Doriath, enemy of Túrin. 112, 409, 420. See *Orgof*.
Sagroth Man of Brethil. 274, 278, 303
Samûri 'The Wise' (the Noldor), name replaced by *Nómin*. 226
Sarn Athrad The Stony Ford over Gelion. *185, 190, 206, 216, 334–6, 338, 346–7, 349, 355. See *Athrad Daer, Harathrad*.
Sauron 37, 54, 56, 59, 62, 66–7, 82, 125, 131, 135, 196, 239–40, 247, 351, 390, 397; *Sauron's Isle* (Tol-in-Gaurhoth) 62, 67, 131. See *Gorsodh, Gorthaur*.
Sea, The 6–8, 11–13, 16–17, 20, 22, 24, 38–41, 44–6, 80, 91, 106, 109–10, 112, 118, 164, 176, 192–3, 196–7, 200, 212, 216, 218, 220, 227, 296, 343–5, 348, 354, 365, 382, 400, 404. See *Great Sea, Western Sea*.
Second Age 61, 64, 128, 349, 390, 397
Second Battle of Beleriand 17, 111. See *Battle-under-Stars* (formerly the First Battle).
Secondborn, The Men. 341. See *After-born, Apanónar, Atani*.
Second Clan The Noldor (and Avari of this clan, see 381). 383, 409, 420. See *Tatyar*.
Separation, The Between the Eldar and the Avari. 360, 373, 375–6, 380, 382, 391, 393, 407, 410, 421
Serech, Fen of 17, 52, 59, 76, 113, 168, 181, *182–3, 187, 238, 272. See *Rivil*.
Seven Rivers See *Land of Seven Rivers, Ossir*.
Shadow, The Of Morgoth. 34, 200, 220, 275, 280–1, 296–7, 354; of Húrin, or of the House of Hador 255, 264, 266, 281, 294, 297–8, 308, 310; of Túrin 90; of Sauron 397; of Mandos 43; a shadow over Aman 40; *the shadows* 281
Shadowy Mountains See *Mountains of Shadow*.
Siege of Angband See *Angband*.
Silmarillion, The (1) = *Quenta Silmarillion*. 120, 129, 179, 196, 199, 207–8, 213, 244–5, 247, 297–8, 317. (2) 'The Silmarillion

tradition' 106, 113, 132–3. (3) The published *Silmarillion*. 4, 115–16, 123, 126, 129–32, 135–6, 138, 140, 144, 148–9, 151, 156, 165, 168–70, 175–6, 180, 186, 191, 210, 212–13, 215, 226–8, 236, 238, 240–3, 298, 302, 310, 314, 317–19, 321–3, 325, 333, 338, 340–1, 350, 354–6, 419; and see *Maps* (3).

Silmaril(s) 36, 38, 41, 62–6, 68–9, 130–2, 177, 247, 345–51, 353, 355. See *(The) Jewel(s)*.

Silver-bowl See *Celebros*.

Sindar 5, 9, 12–14, 19–21, 23–8, 35–6, 38, 40, 42–7, 104, 107, 109, 113, 116, 120, 126, 175, 179, 186, 189, 192, 195, 197, 219, 240, 326–8, 338, 344, 365, 369, 372–3, 375–89, 400, 403, 409–10, 420; origin of the name 9, 384, 410–11. See *Eglath*, *Grey-elves*, *Sindel*.

Sindarin (of language) 20–8, 44, 104, 116, 189, 197, 201, 219, 223, 240, 318–20, 337, 359, 362–72, 376–9, 383, 385, 387–91, 394, 396, 400, 402–4, 407, 410–16, 419; North Sindarin 400 (see *Mithrim*); (with other reference) 4, 25, 28, 104, 126, 192, 378, 380, 385, 396

Sindel, plural *Sindeldi* (Quenya) Sindar. 384, 410

Sindikollo 'Greycloak', Thingol. 410. See *Greymantle*, *Singollo*.

Singollo 'Greymantle', Thingol. 7, 9. See *Elwë*.

Sirion, River 5–6, 15, 38, 49, 53, 56–7, 72–3, 76, 81, 84–5, 90–1, 104–6, 113, 127, 150, 178, 181, *183–4, 191, 193–5, 197–9, 215, 219, 228, 261, 265, 267, 278, 301, 303, 408; length of the river 193; its source, see *Eithel Sirion*.

Pass of Sirion 38, 59, 76–7, 89, 125, 133–4, 157, 193, 299; west(ward) pass 54, 125; Passes of Sirion 52, 71–2, 75, 85, 92, 141; see *Narrow Land*. Vale of Sirion 6, 36, 44, 49, 53, 90, 113, 127, 178, 241; Vales of Sirion 17, 54, 261, north vales 85, 142. Falls, Fens, Gates of Sirion *184

Mouths of Sirion 5, 7, 23, 38, 54, 80, 89–90, 136–7, 146, 345–6, 348, Sirion's Mouth 397; Waters of Sirion *184. Delta of Sirion 193

Havens (of Sirion) 298, 311–13, 348–9, 351–3; Sirion's Haven 244; the New Havens 351; Sirion 351

Snaga Name of lesser kinds of Orc. 390, 419

Solar System 419

Sômar 'Wisdom' (Felagund), name replaced by *Nóm*. 226. See *Samûri*; *Vidri*.

Sons of Fëanor, The 18–19, 26, 29, 31, 33–4, 39, 41–3, 53, 62, (66), 70, 72, 74–5, 77, 113–15, 122, 165, 167, 176, *185, 188, 194, 255, 311, 313, 318, 323, 325–30, 335, 345, 348–9, 351, 379; Five Sons of Fëanor 327, 329. See *Fëanorians*.

Sons of the Gods, of the Valar See *Gods*, *Valar*.

Sorontar King of Eagles. 272. See *Thorondor*.

South, The 12, 15, 29, 53, 90, 95, 109–11, 239, 377

Star-folk   Elves (for the original linguistic elements and the development of meaning see 360, 362–3, 374). 360, 374, 418, 423

Stars, The   (including references to *starlight*) 6–7, 9, 14, 30, 47, 105–6, 108, 110–11, 113, 176, 360, 373, 410, 417, 421–4; *the great stars* 5; Elvish words for 'star' 360, 362–3; *'Star-lore'* 414

Stone of the Hapless, Standing Stone   See *Talbor.*

Sun, The   20–1, 24, 26, 30–1, 47, 110, 113–14, 175, 177, 196, 341, 373, 417–18, 423; *the Daystar* 30; *Years of the Sun* (8, 16), 20, 22, 24, 27, 30, 206, 419. See *Anar.*

Swarthy Men   60 (described), 61, 64, 74, 127. See *Easterlings, Eastrons.*

Tad-dail   Petty-dwarves. See *Levain tad-dail.*

Taiglin, River   49, 57, 66, 88–9, 92, 97–8, 100, 103, 139, 147, 151, 153, 156–8, (159), 160, 164, *182, 193, 254, 265, 267, 271. Later forms *Teiglin* 147, 223, 228, 234–5, 310; *Taeglin* 257, 265, 267, 273, 296, 307, 309, *Taeglind* (and etymology) 309. On the forms of the name see 309–10.

Crossings of Taiglin (Teiglin, Taeglin), also *the Crossings*, 92–3, 95, 99, 101, 141, 147–8, 157, 159, 161, *182, 186, 223, 256, 264–5, 267, 270–1, 273, 302, 307; *Ford of Taeglin* 274

Talath Dirnen   85, 140, *182, 186, 225, 228; earlier form *Dalath Dirnen* 140, 186, 223, 225, 228. See *Guarded Plain.*

Talath Rhúnen   Name replacing *Radhrost* (Thargelion). 197–8

Talbor   The stone of Túrin and Niënor at Cabed Naeramarth. 257, 300, 309. *The Standing Stone* 257, 274, 290, 295, 298, 309; *Stone of the Hapless* 295–6; other references to the Stone 103, 251, 258–9, 273–4, 294–6, 298. See *Tol Morwen.*

Tamar   Precursor of Brandir in the *Tale of Turambar.* 160

Taniquetil   'High-Snow-Peak', properly the highest peak of the mountain Oiolossë. 399, 403, 416–17 (origin of the name). See *Arfanyarassë, Ras-Arphain.*

Taras, Mount   44, *182, 192, 197, 256, 379

Targlîn   Rejected name of (1) Maeglin, 323; (2) the metal of Eöl, 322 (see *Galvorn*).

Tata   'Two', the second of the Fathers of the Elves. 380, 418, 420–2; *Companions of Tata* 423. See *Tatyar.*

Tatië   Spouse of Tata. 421

Tatyar   Elves of the Second Clan. 380–1, 420

Taur-en-Faroth   The highlands west of Narog. 197; earlier form *Taur-na-Faroth* 116, *184, 189–90, 197. See *High Faroth, Hills of the Hunters.*

Taur-im-Duinath   'Forest between the Rivers' (Sirion and Gelion). 191, 193, 195, 197, 239. See next entries.

Taur-i-Melegyrn   'Forest of the Great Trees', a name of *Taur-im-Duinath.* *185, 193

Taur-na-Chardhîn 'Forest of the Southern Silence', a name of *Taur-im-Duinath*. *185, 193
Taur-na-Foen See *Foen*.
Taur-nu-Fuin (also earlier *Taur-na-Fuin*) 'The Forest under Nightshade' (56), 'Mirkwood' (239), later name of Dorthonion. 56, 67–8, 82, 121–2, 126, 133, 140, 143, *183, 239–40. See *Fuin (Mountains of)*.
Tavrobel In the Forest of Brethil. 148, 157, 186
Teiglin, River See *Taiglin*.
Telchar Dwarf smith of Nogrod (formerly of Belegost). 12, 109
Teleri 6–8, 13, 16, 20, 25, 28, 104, 109, 112, 177, 322, 329, 344, 371, 374–5, 378–84, 400, 405, 408, 418, 423; singular *Teler* 371; origin of the name 382, 411. See *Lindar*.
Telerian 19, 22–3, 179, 195
Telerin (of language) 21, 359, 362–5, 367, 369–73, 375–6, 380, 382–3, 392, 394, 403, 407, 409, 411; *Common Telerin* 375, 410, 412; (with other reference) 115, 375–6, 384, 410
Telperion 401
Telumehtar 'Warrior of the Sky', Orion. 411. See *Menelmakil*, and also I.268.
Thalion Name of Húrin, 'Steadfast'. 231, 234, 272, 275, 277, 281, 286–7, 298
Thalos, River In Ossiriand. 13, *185, 216
Thangorodrim 15, 18, 29–30, 52, 68, 73, 78, 111–14, 135, 166, 168, 181, 246–7, 252, 321, 329; *the Tyrannous Towers, Mountains of Oppression* 111
Thargelion The country beyond Gelion's upper waters. 121, *183, 194, 197, 201, 203, 225, 227, 236, 320, 337; *Thargelian* 320, *331, 337. See *Thorewilan*.
Thingódhel Late proposed substitution for *Pengolodh*. 417
Thingol 4, 9–16, 19, 21–3, 25–7, 32–5, 39, 41–4, 49–50, 57, 59, 61–7, 69–72, 79–82, 85, 89, 93, 95, 108–12, 114–16, 119, 123, 126–7, 129–30, 132–3, 136, 138, 148–9, (158), 162–3, 177, 195, 223–4, 228, 231, 244, 252, 255, 258–9, 297–8, 310, 312, 321–2, 333, 345–7, 350–5, 379–80, 409–10, 418, 420; his high-kingship, overlordship 19, 21, 23, 25–6, 115, 380, 410, 418; his ban on Noldorin 23, 25–7, 43. For *Elu Thingol* see *Elwë*, and see *Greymantle, Sindikollo, Singollo; Tinwelint; Dior*.
Third Age 390
Third Battle of Beleriand 21, 25–6, 36–7, 179. See *Glorious Battle* (formerly the Second Battle).
Third House of the Noldor The House of Finarfin (= Finrod (1)). 115
Thorewilan = Thargelion; see 336.
Thorin (Oakenshield) 207–8
Thorondor King of Eagles. 32, 53, 55, 57–8, 63, 68, 123, 175, 198,

239–40, 302; earlier *Thorndor* 175, 349. See *Sorontar.*
Thousand Caves   11, 108, 111, 138, *183, 334, 352, 355, 415. See *Menegroth.*
Three Clans   (of the Elves) 360, 380, 420
Three Houses   (of Men)   50, 77, 128, 224, 377–8, 386; *Three Kindreds* 219
Thû   *182. See *Gorthaur.*
Thurin   'The Secret', Finduilas' name for Túrin. 299
Thuringud   'The Hidden Foe', Túrin's name for himself in Nargothrond. 256, 299
Thuringwethil   The bat-messenger of Sauron. 68, 131
Tilion   'Guardian of the Moon'. 30, 114
Time, Reckoning of   16, 20, 24, 174, 343
Tindobel, Tower of   Of the cape west of Eglarest. 118, 196–7; *Tindabel* 118, 190, 198. See *Ingildon, Barad Nimras.*
Tinúviel   'Nightingale' (Lúthien). 62, 65, 69, 231, 327
Tinwelint   Precursor of Thingol in *The Book of Lost Tales.* 355
Tirion   35, 41, 178–9, 199–200, 246, 398, 406; *the Tree of Tirion* 178. See *Kôr, Tûn, Túna.*
Tol Eressëa and Eressëa   21–3, 36, 106–7, 117, 192, 311, 313, 343, 393, 396–7
Tol Galen   'The Green Isle' in the River Adurant. *185, 191, 195, 350
Tol-in-Gaurhoth   'Isle of Werewolves'. 54, 62, 66, 68, 125, 131, 239; earlier *Tol-na-Gaurhoth* 125, 239. See *Sauron's Isle* in entry *Sauron.*
Tol Morwen   Island in the sea after the drowning of Beleriand on which stood the Stone of the Hapless. 296
Tol Sirion   (38), 54, 66–7, 77, 125, 131, 135, *182
Torbarth   Companion of Túrin in the attack on Glaurung (replaced by *Hunthor*). 97–8, 152, 156–7, 164, 238, 267, 299
Torhir Ifant   Maker of the work *Dorgannas Iaur.* 192
Trees, The   6, 8–9, 14, 16, 20, 22, 24, 30, 40, 175, 196, 200, 247, 401, 403; *Years of the Trees* 30. The Trees of Gondolin 200
Tulkas   77, 399 (origin of the name), 404
Tumhalad   The site (see 139–40) of the battle before the fall of Nargothrond. 85, 89, 139–40, 142, 144, 147, 149, *182, 186, 238, 256, 299
Tumladen   The vale of Gondolin. 57, 118, 179, 198; *Tumladin* 53
Tumunzahar   Dwarvish name translated as *Nogrod (Novrod)*. 10, 108, 206, 209, 389
Tûn   Name replacing *Kôr.* 22, 116, 175, 177, 246. See *Túna.*
Túna   Name replacing *Tûn.* 175, 177, 179; subsequently the hill on which the city (Tirion) was built, 35, 179, 199, 246, but still used also of the city, 323
Tuor   (45), 52, 79, 81–2, 88–91, (120), 124, 135–7, 146–7, 176,

224, 231, 234–5, 256, 258, 299–302, 344–8, 351–2, 354; called *the Blessed* 52, 124; and see *Eladar, Ulmondil*.

The later *Tale of Tuor* 176, 179, 181, 186, 192, 200, 228, 244, 299–300, 302, 316–17, 323, 344, 354

Turambar 'Master of Doom' (154), name of Túrin in Brethil. 92, 95–103, 148, 150–7, 160, 163–4, 231, 234, 247, 257, 315. See *Turumarth*.

Turgon 26, 28, 35, 38, 40, 44–5, 47–8, 53–4, 57–8, 70, 72–6, 77–8, 80, 84, 91, 116, 118, 120–2, 125–7, 133–7, 146, 166–70, 177–9, *182, 192–3, 195, 198–201, 243, 245, 254–5, 258, 260–1, 272, 301, 317–19, 323, 325, 327–9, 345–6, 348–9, 351, 409; his wife 323

Tûr Haretha The burial-mound of the Lady Haleth. 225, 228; earlier *Tûr Daretha* 223, 225, 228; *the Ladybarrow* 223. See *Haudh-en-Arwen*.

Túrin 4, 51, (60)–1, 63–4, (78), 79–93, 96, 99–103, 124, 129–31, 135–48, 152, 156, 160–4, 180, *182, 187, 224, 231, 234, 238, 241, 244–5, 247, 253–9, (261), 263–4, 266–8, 270, 290–1, (294–7), 298–300, (301), 304–5, 308–14, 344, 352, 354, 409, 420; *'Túrins Saga', 'Saga of Túrin'* 244, 314, 321, 352. See *Turambar, Turumarth; Agarwaen, Iarwaeth, Mormegil, Thurin, Thuringud, Wildman of the Woods*.

Turosto (Quenya) Belegost. 389

Turumarth Sindarin form of *Turambar*. 311, 315; *Turamarth* 135, 315; original form *Turumart* 315

Twilight Meres 35, 194; *Twilit Meres* 149. See *Aelin-uial, Umboth Muilin*.

Two Kindreds Elves and Men. 50, 63, 130, (219)

Uinen 7, 404

Uldor the Accursed Son of Ulfang. 61, 64, 72, 74–5, 82, 133–4, 167–8; *Folk of Uldor* *183

Ulfang Easterling; called 'the Swart'. 61, 64, 70, 74, 127

Ulfast Son of Ulfang. 61, 64, 74

Ulmo 7–8, 35, 40–1, 44–5, 53, 57, 77, 80, 89–91, 120, 135, 141, 146, 178, 192, 198–9, 235, 256, 301, 346–8, 352, 379, 400 (etymology); *Lord of Waters* 53, 301

Ulmondil Name of Tuor. 235

Ulwarth Son of Ulfang. 61, 64, 74

Úmaneldi = Úmanyar. 373

Úmanyar (Eldar) not of Aman. 373; *Úamanyar* 371, 373

Umboth Muilin *185, 194. See *Aelin-uial, Twilight Meres*.

Unfinished Tales 103–4, 110, 112, 116, 137, 140–5, 148–9, 151, 157, 159–60, 165, 169, 176–7, 180–1, 186–7, 189, 192, 200, 228, 232, 235, 238, 298–300, 302, 304–5, 307, 311, 313–15, 317, 321, 323, 349–50, 352, 354, 420

Ungoliantë 14–15, 110–11, 194, 404; *Ungoliant* 333
Union of Maidros 69, 236
Urko, plural *Urqui* (Quenya) Orc(s). 390–1. For Quenya *Orko* see *Orcs*.
Urthel Companion of Barahir. 56
Uruk (Black Speech) Orc. 390; *Uruk-hai* 419
Urulókë 'Fire-serpent', dragon. 85, 141 (referring to Glaurung); plural *Urulóki* 46, 121
Urwen Túrin's sister who died in childhood, called also *Lalaeth*. *Urwen Lalaeth* 234–5, *Lalaeth* 314. See *Nen Lalaith*.
Utumno 105, 111, 196, 344; *the War of Utumno* 104

Valar (and singular *Vala*) 5–7, 11–12, 14, 18–19, 30, 36–7, 41–2, 54–5, 104–6, 111, 119, 173, 175, 196, 203, 206, 239–40, 246, 296, 340–1, 345–6, 360, 372–3, 386, 397–407, 413, 418; etymology 403; *language of the Valar* 118, 359, 397, 419, ~ *and Maiar* 397, 416, and see *Valarin*.
 Years of the Valar, Valian Years 6, 8, 16, 20, 24, 28, 105, 108–9, 344, 419; *War of the Valar and Melkor* 373; *Children of the Valar* 246, *Sons* ~ 14, 246, *host* ~ 246, 345–6. See *Gods*.
Valarauko 'Demon of Might' (Balrog). 415
Valarin 359, 398–406, 411, 419, and see *Valar*; *lambë Valarinwa* 397; Valarin words and names 399–402, 411, 417; the language described 398, 402
Valaróma The horn of Oromë. 14, 400
Valier The Queens of the Valar; singular *Valië* 383
Valinor 5–11, 14, 16, 19–25, 29–30, 32, 38, 40, 47, 54, 62–3, 66–7, 77, 105, 108–9, 116–17, 119, 122, 130, 135, 174, 177, 189, 196, 203, 210–11, 219, 239–40, 243, 246–7, 318, 323, 343–8, 350–1, 353, 373, 398–9, 402–3, 409, 413; *Valinórë, Valandor* 413; *Mountains of Valinor* 417 (see *Aman, Pelóri*); *Valinórean* 342
Vána 383
Vanyar (and singular *Vanya*) 6–7, 28, 44, 106, 130, 243, 246, 323, 374–5, 380, 382–3, 393, 399, 405, 411, 417–18, 423; meaning of the name 382–3. Telerin *Vaniai* 383. See *Lindar*; *First Clan*.
Vanyarin (of language) 361, 363, 417
Varda 5, 105, 369, 399, 402–3; *Varda Aratarya* 369; 'the Sublime' 402; *the Dome of Varda* 399
Vidri 'Wisdom' (Felagund), name replaced by *Sômar* (itself replacing the original word *Widris*, V.275). 202
Vingelot, Vingilot Eärendil's ship. 246
Vinyamar Turgon's dwelling in Nevrast. 44, 120, 146, 178, *182, 192, 199
Voice, The (of Ilúvatar) 211
Voronwë Companion of Tuor. 80, 91, 136, 146, 256, 299, 352, 354. See *Bronwë*.

War(s), The   Also *the Wars of Beleriand*. 14–15, 17, 22, 24, 27, 36–7, 112, 116, 133, 343, 377, 386, 396–7, 409, 411

Waters of Awakening   See *Cuiviénen*.

Way of Escape   The tunnel beneath the mountains encircling Gondolin. 271, 302

Weathertop   130

Werewolves   17, 54, 62, 66–7. Cf. *Tol-in-Gaurhoth*.

West, The   (across the Great Sea) 5–6, (8), 17, 19, 21–2, 27, 32, 39–41, 44, 54, 80, 146, 196, 217, 227, 345, 352, 354, and see *Lords of the West*; (the West of Middle-earth) 48, 72–3, 76, 118, 206, 220, 225, 227, 232, 242, (293), 334, 378, 382, 386, *the Westlands* 13, 219, 410

Western Sea   64, 175, 203; *Western Ocean* 136

Westrons   Men of the West. 252

White Mountains   13, 110. See *Eryd Nimrais*.

Wildman of the Woods   Name taken by Túrin in Brethil. 92, 148

Wisdom   Name of Felagund among Bëor's people. 217, 226. See *Nóm, Sómar, Vidri*.

Wise, The   (in Valinor) 108, 203; name of the Noldor 217, 226

Wise-women   (of the Edain) 233

Wood-elven   (speech) 410

Woodmen   (of Brethil) 51, 72, 92, 95–7, 147–8, 150–2, (166), 236, 280, *Wood-folk* 97, and see *Brethil*; (of the woods south of Taiglin) 306–8

World, The   10, 15, 22, 30–1, 41, 50, 63, 70, 111, 173, 177, 198, 212, 220, 224–5, 227, 242–3, 247, 297, 397, 402 (= *Arda*), 424; *the ancient world* 258–9; *the Change of the World* (at the end of the Elder Days) 105; *the World made Round* 105; and see *Circles of the World, (The) End*.

Yavanna   106, 247, 340–1; *the Sleep of Yavanna* 6, 9, 20, 24, 28, 30, 105–7

Year of Lamentation   The year of the Battle of Unnumbered Tears. 71, 200

Younger Children   See *Children of Eru*.

Yrch   See *Orcs*.

Yssion   Sindarin name of Ossë. 400. See *Gaerys*.

Yule   351

Zimrahin   Wife of Malach Aradan. 234. See *Meldis*.

Dangweth Pengolod

the
Answer
of
Pengolod
*to Aelfwine who asked him how came
it that the tongues of the Elves changed
and were sundered*

Now you question me, Ælfwine, concerning the tongues of the Elves, saying that you wonder much to discover that they are many, akin indeed and yet unalike; for seeing that they die not and their memories reach back into ages long past, you understand not why all the race of the Quendi have not maintained the language that they had of old in common still one and the same in all their kindreds. But behold! Ælfwine, within Eä all things change even the Valar; for in Eä we perceive the unfolding of a History in the unfolding: as a man may read a great book, and when it is full-read it is rounded and complete in his mind, according to his measure. Then at last he perceives that some fair thing that long endured: as some mountain or river of renown, some realm, or some great city; or else some mighty being, as a king or maker, or a woman of beauty and majesty, or even one maybe of the Lords of the West: that each of these is, if at all, all that is said of them from the beginning even to the end. From the spring in the mountains to the mouths of the sea, all is Sirion; and from its first upwelling even to its passing away when the land was broken in the great battle, that also is Sirion, and nothing less. Though we, who are set to behold the great History, reading line by line, may speak of the river changing as it flows and grows broad, or dying as it is spilled or devoured by the sea. Yea, even from his first coming into Eä from the side of Ilúvatar, and from the young lord of

THE PEOPLES OF MIDDLE-EARTH

J. R. R. TOLKIEN

The Peoples of Middle-earth

Christopher Tolkien

To Baillie Tolkien

CONTENTS

Foreword *page* vii

PART ONE

THE PROLOGUE AND APPENDICES TO THE LORD OF THE RINGS

I	The Prologue	3
II	The Appendix on Languages	19
III	The Family Trees	85
IV	The Calendars	119
V	The History of the Akallabêth	140
VI	The Tale of Years of the Second Age	166
VII	The Heirs of Elendil	188
VIII	The Tale of Years of the Third Age	225
IX	The Making of Appendix A	
	(i) The Realms in Exile	253
	(ii) The Tale of Aragorn and Arwen	262
	(iii) The House of Eorl	270
	(iv) Durin's Folk	274

PART TWO

LATE WRITINGS

X	Of Dwarves and Men	295
XI	The Shibboleth of Fëanor	331
XII	The Problem of *Ros*	367
XIII	Last Writings	377

PART THREE

TEACHINGS OF PENGOLOÐ

XIV Dangweth Pengoloð	395
XV Of Lembas	403

PART FOUR

UNFINISHED TALES

XVI The New Shadow	409
XVII Tal-Elmar	422

Index	439

FOREWORD

In my Foreword to *Sauron Defeated* I wrote that I would not attempt a study of the Appendices to *The Lord of the Rings* 'at this time'. That was an ambiguous remark, for I rather doubted that I would ever make the attempt; but I justified its postponement, at least, on the ground that 'my father soon turned again, when *The Lord of the Rings* was finished, to the myths and legends of the Elder Days', and so devoted the following volumes to the later history of 'The Silmarillion'. My intentions for the twelfth book were uncertain; but after the publication of *The War of the Jewels* I came to think that since (contrary to my original conception) I had included in *The History of Middle-earth* a lengthy account of the writing of *The Lord of the Rings* it would be a strange omission to say nothing whatever of the Appendices, in which the historical structure of the Second and Third Ages, based on a firm chronology, actually emerged.

Thus I embarked on the study of the history of these works, of which I had little precise knowledge. As with the narrative texts of *The Lord of the Rings*, those of the Appendices (and of the Prologue) became divided, in some cases in a bewildering fashion, at the time of the sale of the papers to Marquette University; but I received most generous help, prompt and meticulous, from Charles Elston, the Archivist of the Memorial Library at Marquette, which enabled me to determine the textual relations. It was only now that I came to understand that texts of supplementary essays to *The Lord of the Rings* had reached a remarkably finished form, though in many respects far different from the published Appendices, at a much earlier date than I had supposed: in the period (as I judge) immediately following my father's writing of the last chapter of *The Lord of the Rings* in 1948. There is indeed a total absence in these texts of indications of external date; but it can be seen from many points that when they were written the narrative was not yet in final form, and equally clearly that they in fact preceded my father's return to the First Age at the beginning of the 1950s, as described in the Foreword to *The War of the Jewels*. A major upheaval in the historical-linguistic structure was still to come:

the abandonment of their own tongue by the Noldor returning out of the West and their adoption of the Sindarin of Middle-earth.

In my account I have of course concentrated on these early forms, which belong so evidently, in manner and air, with the narrative itself. I have little doubt that my father had long contemplated such a supplement and accompaniment to *The Lord of the Rings*, regarding it as an essential element in the whole; and I have found it impossible to show in any satisfactory way how he conceived it at that time without setting out the early texts in full, although this naturally entails the recital, especially in the case of the history of Arnor and Gondor, of much that is known from its survival in the published versions of the Appendices. I have excluded the Appendix E ('Writing and Spelling'), but I have included the Prologue; and I have introduced into this part of the book an account of the origin and development of the *Akallabêth*, since the evolution of the chronological structure of the Second Age was closely related to my father's original formalised computation of the dates of the Númenórean kings.

Following this part I have given three essays written during his last years; and also some brief writings that appear to derive from the last years of his life, primarily concerned with or arising from the question whether Glorfindel of Rivendell and Glorfindel of Gondolin were one and the same. These late writings are notable for the many wholly new elements that entered the 'legendarium'; and also for the number of departures from earlier work on the Matter of the Elder Days. It may be suggested that whereas my father set great store by consistency at all points with *The Lord of the Rings* and the Appendices, so little concerning the First Age had appeared in print that he was under far less constraint. I am inclined to think, however, that the primary explanation of these differences lies rather in his writing largely from memory. The histories of the First Age would always remain in a somewhat fluid state so long as they were not fixed in published work; and he certainly did not have all the relevant manuscripts clearly arranged and set out before him. But it remains in any case an open question, whether (to give a single example) in the essay *Of Dwarves and Men* he had definitively rejected the greatly elaborated account of the houses of the Edain that had entered the *Quenta Silmarillion* in about 1958, or whether it had passed from his mind.

The book concludes with two pieces further illustrating the instruction that Ælfwine of England received from Pengoloð the Wise in Tol Eressëa, and the abandoned beginnings of two remarkable stories, *The New Shadow* and *Tal-elmar*.

With the picture of such clarity in the tale of Tal-elmar of the great ships of the Númenóreans drawing into the coast, and the fear among men of Middle-earth of the terrible 'Go-hilleg', this 'History' ends. It is a long time since I began the work of ordering and elucidating the vast collection of papers in which my father's conception of Arda, Aman, and Middle-earth was contained, making, not long after his death, some first transcriptions from *The Book of Lost Tales*, of which I knew virtually nothing, as a step towards the understanding of the origins of 'The Silmarillion'. I had little notion then of what lay before me, of all the unknown works crammed in disorder in that formidable array of battered box-files. Nearly a quarter of a century later the story, as I have been able to tell it, is at last concluded.

This is not to say that I have given an account of everything that my father wrote, even leaving aside the great body of his work on the languages of the Elves. My father's very late writings have been selectively presented, and much further detail, especially concerning names and the etymology of names, can be found in texts such as those that I excerpted in *Unfinished Tales*, notably in the part of that book entitled 'The History of Galadriel and Celeborn'. Other omissions have arisen almost one might say from inadvertence as the work and its publication proceeded.

It began indeed as an entirely 'private' study, without thought or purpose of publication: an exhaustive investigation and analysis of all the materials concerned with what came to be called the Elder Days, from the earliest beginnings, omitting no detail of name-form or textual variation. From that original work derives the respect for the precise wording of the texts, and the insistence that no stone (especially stones bearing names) be left unturned, that characterises, perhaps excessively, *The History of Middle-earth*. *Unfinished Tales*, on the other hand, was conceived entirely independently and in an essentially different mode, at a time when I had no notion of the publication of a massive and continuous history; and this constitutes an evident weakness in my presentation of the whole corpus, which could not be remedied. When Rayner Unwin, to whom I am greatly indebted, undertook the uncertain venture of publishing my work on the history of 'The Silmarillion' (in form necessarily much altered) I had no intention of entering into the history of the Later Ages: the inclusion of *The Lost Road*, *The Drowning of Anadûnê*, *The Notion Club Papers*, and above all the history of the writing of *The Lord of the Rings*, extending the work far beyond my original design, was entirely unforeseen.

Thus it came about that the later volumes were written and published under much greater pressure of time and with less idea of the overall structure than the earlier. Attempting to make each book an independent entity in some degree, within the constraints of length, I was often uncertain of what it would or could contain until it was done; and this lack of prevision led to some misjudgements of 'scale' – the degree of fulness or conciseness that would ultimately prove appropriate to the whole. Thus, for example, I should have returned at the end of my account of the writing of *The Lord of the Rings* to give some description, at least, of the later developments in the chapters *The Shadow of the Past* and *The Council of Elrond*, and the evolution in relation to these of the work *Of the Rings of Power and the Third Age*. However, all the stories and all the histories have now been told, and the 'legendarium' of the Elder Days has been very fully mined.

Since the ceaseless 'making' of his world extended from my father's youth into his old age, *The History of Middle-earth* is in some sense also a record of his life, a form of biography, if of a very unusual kind. He had travelled a long road. He bequeathed to me a massive legacy of writings that made possible the tracing of that road, in as I hope its true sequence, and the unearthing of the deep foundations that led ultimately to the true end of his great history, when the white ship departed from the Grey Havens.

> In the twilight of autumn it sailed out of Mithlond, until the seas of the Bent World fell away beneath it, and the winds of the round sky troubled it no more, and borne upon the high airs above the mists of the world it passed into the ancient West, and an end was come for the Eldar of story and of song.

It has been an absorbing and inspiring task, from the splendours of the *Ainulindalë* or the tragedy of the Children of Húrin down to the smallest detail of changing expression and shifting names. It has also of its nature been very laborious, and with times of doubt, when confidence faltered; and I owe a great deal to all those who have supported the work with generous encouragement in letters and reviews. Most of all do I owe to my wife Baillie, to whom I dedicate this last volume: but the dedication may stand for the whole. Without her understanding and encouragement over the years, making mutual the weight of such a long and demanding work, it would never have been achieved.

Note on the text

As a general rule I have preserved my father's often varying usage in the spelling of names (as e.g. *Baraddur* beside *Barad-dûr*), but in certain cases I have given a standard form (as *Adûnaic* where *Adunaic* is sometimes written, and *Gil-galad* rather than *Gilgalad*). In his late texts he seldom used the diaeresis (as in *Finwë*), but (in intention at least) always employed Ñ to represent initial *ng* sounded as in English *sing* (thus *Ñoldor*); in this book I have extended the diaeresis throughout (other than in Old English names, as *Ælfwine*), but restricted Ñ to the texts in which it occurs.

References to *The History of Middle-earth* are given as in previous volumes in Roman numerals (thus VI.314). For the necessarily abundant references to the published Appendices I have used the letters RK (*The Return of the King*), the page-numbers being those of the three-volume hardback edition; and occasionally FR and TT for *The Fellowship of the Ring* and *The Two Towers*.

To the removal of error (especially in the citation of texts) from *The Peoples of Middle-earth*, which was completed under great pressure of time, Mr Charles Noad has contributed more perhaps than to any of the previous volumes which he has read independently in proof; and with the conclusion of the work I must express again my gratitude to him for his meticulous, informed, and extraordinarily generous labour. I wish also to record my appreciation of the great skill and care which Mr Norman Tilley of Nene Phototypesetters has again brought to this particularly demanding text – including the 'invisible mending' of errors in my manuscript tables.

Mr Noad has also made a number of suggestions for the improvement of the text by clarification and additional reference which where possible I have adopted. There remain some points which would have required too much rewriting, or too much movement of text, to introduce, and two of these may be mentioned here.

One concerns the translation of the curse of the Orc from the Dark Tower given on p. 83. When writing this passage I had forgotten that Mr Carl Hostetter, editor of the periodical *Vinyar Tengwar*, had pointed out in the issue (no. 26) for November 1992 that there is a translation of the words in a note to one of the typescripts of Appendix E (he being unaware of the existence of the certainly earlier version that I have printed); and I had also overlooked the fact that a third version is found among notes on words and phrases 'in alien speech' in *The Lord of the Rings*. All three differ significantly (*bagronk*, for example, being rendered both as 'cesspool' and as 'torture (chamber)'); from which it seems clear that my father was at this time devising interpretations of the words, whatever he may have intended them to mean when he first wrote them.

I should also have noticed that the statement in the early texts of Appendix D (The Calendars), pp. 124, 131, that the Red Book 'ends before the Lithe of 1436' refers to the Epilogue to *The Lord of the Rings*, in which Samwise, after reading aloud from the Book over many months, finally reached its end on an evening late in March of that year (IX.120-1).

Lastly, after the proofs of this book had been revised I received a letter from Mr Christopher Gilson in which he referred to a brief but remarkable text associated with Appendix A that he had seen at Marquette. This was a curious chance, for he had no knowledge of the book beyond the fact that it contained some account of the Appendices; while although I had received a copy of the text from Marquette I had passed it over without observing its significance. Preserved with other difficult and disjointed notes, it is very roughly written on a slip of paper torn from a rejected manuscript. That manuscript can be identified as the close predecessor of the Appendix A text concerning the choice of the Half-elven which I have given on pp. 256-7. The writing on the verso reads:

> and his father gave him the name Aragorn, a name used in the House of the Chieftains. But Ivorwen at his naming stood by, and said 'Kingly Valour' (for so that name is interpreted): 'that he shall have, but I see on his breast a green stone, and from that his true name shall come and his chief renown: for he shall be a healer and a renewer.'

Above this is written: 'and they did not know what she meant, for there was no green stone to be seen by other eyes' (followed by illegible words); and beneath it: 'for the green Elfstone was given to him by Galadriel'. A large X is also written, but it is not clear whether this relates to the whole page or only to a part of it.

Mr Gilson observes that this text, clearly to be associated with work on the Tale of Aragorn and Arwen (see p. 263), seems to be the only place where the name *Aragorn* is translated; and he mentions my father's letter of 17 December 1972 to Mr Richard Jeffery (*Letters* no. 347), who had asked whether *Aragorn* could mean 'tree-king'. In his reply my father said that it 'cannot contain a "tree" word', and that '"Tree-King" would have no special fitness for him'. He continued:

The names in the line of Arthedain are peculiar in several ways; and several, though Sindarin in form, are not readily interpretable. But it would need more historical records and linguistic records of Sindarin than exist (sc. than I have found time or need to invent!) to explain them.

PART ONE

THE PROLOGUE AND APPENDICES TO THE LORD OF THE RINGS

I
THE PROLOGUE

It is remarkable that this celebrated account of Hobbits goes so far back in the history of the writing of *The Lord of the Rings*: its earliest form, entitled *Foreword: Concerning Hobbits*, dates from the period 1938–9, and it was printed in *The Return of the Shadow* (VI.310–14). This was a good 'fair copy' manuscript, for which there is no preparatory work extant; but I noticed in my very brief account of it that my father took up a passage concerning Hobbit architecture from the chapter *A Short Cut to Mushrooms* (see VI.92, 294–5).

Comparison with the published *Prologue* to *The Lord of the Rings* will show that while much of that original version survived, there was a great deal still to come: the entire account of the history of the Hobbits (FR pp. 11–15) in section 1 of the *Prologue*, the whole of section 2, *Concerning Pipe-weed*, and the whole of section 3, *Of the Ordering of the Shire*, apart from the opening paragraph; while corresponding to section 4, *Of the Finding of the Ring*, there was no more than a brief reference to the story of Bilbo and Gollum (VI.314).

In order to avoid confusion with another and wholly distinct 'Foreword', given in the next chapter, I shall use the letter P in reference to the texts that ultimately led to the published *Prologue*, although the title *Foreword: Concerning Hobbits* was used in the earlier versions. The original text given in *The Return of the Shadow* I shall call therefore **P 1**.

My father made a typescript of this, **P 2**, and judging from the typewriter used I think it probable that it belonged to much the same time as P 1 – at any rate, to a fairly early period in the writing of *The Lord of the Rings*. In my text of P 1 in *The Return of the Shadow* I ignored the changes made to the manuscript unless they seemed certainly to belong to the time of writing (VI.310), but all such changes were taken up into P 2, so that it was probably not necessary to make the distinction. The changes were not numerous and mostly minor,[1] but the whole of the conclusion of P 1, following the words 'his most mysterious treasure: a magic ring' (VI.314), was struck out and replaced by a much longer passage, in which my father recounted the actual story of Bilbo and Gollum, and slightly altered the final paragraph. This new conclusion I give here. A part of the story as told here survived into the published *Prologue*, but at this stage there was no suggestion of any other version than that in *The Hobbit*, until the chapter *Riddles in the Dark* was altered in the edition of 1951. With all these changes incorporated, the typescript P 2 was a precise copy of the original version (see note 7).

This ring was brought back by Bilbo from his memorable journey. He found it by what seemed like luck. He was lost for a while in the tunnels of the goblins under the Misty Mountains, and there he put his hand on it in the dark.

Trying to find his way out, he went on down to the roots of the mountains and came to a full stop. At the bottom of the tunnel was a cold lake far from the light. On an island of rock in the water lived Gollum. He was a loathsome little creature: he paddled a small boat with his large flat feet, and peered with pale luminous eyes, catching blind fish with his long fingers and eating them raw. He ate any living thing, even goblin, if he could catch and strangle it without a fight; and he would have eaten Bilbo, if Bilbo had not had in his hand an elvish knife to serve him as a sword. Gollum challenged the hobbit to a Riddle-game: if he asked a riddle that Bilbo could not guess, then he would eat him; but if Bilbo floored him, then he promised to give him a splendid gift. Since he was lost in the dark, and could not go on or back, Bilbo was obliged to accept the challenge; and in the end he won the game (as much by luck as by wits). It then turned out that Gollum had intended to give Bilbo a magic ring that made the wearer invisible. He said he had got it as a birthday present long ago; but when he looked for it in his hiding-place on the island, the ring had disappeared. Not even Gollum (a mean and malevolent creature) dared cheat at the Riddle-game, after a fair challenge, so in recompense for the missing ring he reluctantly agreed to Bilbo's demand that he should show him the way out of the labyrinth of tunnels. In this way the hobbit escaped and rejoined his companions: thirteen dwarves and the wizard Gandalf. Of course he had quickly guessed that Gollum's ring had somehow been dropped in the tunnels and that he himself had found it; but he had the sense to say nothing to Gollum. He used the ring several times later in his adventures, but nearly always to help other people. The ring had other powers besides that of making its wearer invisible. But these were not discovered, or even suspected, until long after Bilbo had returned home and settled down again. Consequently they are not spoken of in the story of his journey. This tale is chiefly concerned with the ring, its powers and history.

Bilbo, it is told, following his own account and the ending he himself devised for his memoirs (before he had written most of them), 'remained very happy to the end of his days, and those were extraordinarily long.' They were. How long, and why so long, will here be discovered. Bilbo returned to his home at Bag-End on June 22nd in his fifty-second year, having been away since April 30th[2] in the year before, and nothing very notable occurred in the Shire for another sixty years, when Mr. Baggins began to make preparations for the celebration of his hundred and eleventh birthday. At which point the tale of the Ring begins.

Years later my father took up the typescript P 2 again. He made a number of minor alterations in wording, replaced the opening paragraph, and rewrote a part of the story of Bilbo and Gollum (improving the presentation of the events, and elaborating a little Bilbo's escape from the tunnels); these need not be recorded. But he also introduced a lengthy new passage, following the words (VI.313) 'but that was not so true of other families, like the Bagginses or the Boffins' (FR p. 18). This begins 'The Hobbits of the Shire had hardly any "government" ...', and is the origin of most of section 3 (*Of the Ordering of the Shire*) in the published *Prologue*, extending as far as 'the first sign that everything was not quite as it should be, and always used to be' (cf. FR p. 19).

Much of the new passage survived into the final form, but there are some interesting differences. In the third paragraph of the section (as it stands in FR) the new text in P 2 reads:

There was, of course, the ancient tradition in their part of the world that there had once been a King at Fornost away north of the Shire (Northworthy the hobbits called it),[3] who had marked out the boundaries of the Shire and given it to the Hobbits; and they in turn had acknowledged his lordship. But there had been no King for many ages, and even the ruins of Northworthy were covered with grass ...

The name *Northworthy* (for later *Norbury*) is not found in the *Lord of the Rings* papers, where the earlier 'vernacular' names are the *Northburg, Northbury*. See p. 225, annal c.1600.

The fourth paragraph of the section reads thus in the P 2 text:

It is true that the Took family had once a certain eminence, quite apart from the fact that they were (and remained) numerous, wealthy, peculiar, and of great social importance. The head of the family had formerly borne the title of The Shirking. But that title was no longer in use in Bilbo's time: it had been killed by the endless and inevitable jokes that had been made about it, in defiance of its obvious etymology. The habit went on, however, of referring to the head of the family as The Took, and of adding (if required) a number: as Isengrim the First.

Shirking is of course a reduction of *Shire-king* with shortening (and in this case subsequent alteration) of the vowel, in the same way as *Shirriff* is derived from *Shire-reeve*; but this was a joke that my father decided to remove – perhaps because the choice of the word 'king' by the Hobbits seemed improbable (cf. p. 232 and note 25, and Appendix A (I, iii), RK p. 323).[4]

The new passage in P 2 does not give the time of the year of the Free Fair on the White Downs ('at the Lithe, that is at Midsummer', FR p. 19), and nothing is said of the letter-writing proclivities of Hobbits. To the mention of the name 'Bounders' my father added '(as they were called unofficially)'; the word 'unofficially' he subsequently removed, thus in this case retaining the joke but not drawing attention to it.

It seems to me all but certain that this new element in the text is to be associated with the emergence of the Shirriffs in the chapter *The Scouring of the Shire* – where the office is shown to have been long established 'before any of this began', as the Shirriff Robin Smallburrow said to Sam (RK p. 281). The fact that the term 'Thain' had not yet emerged does not contradict this, for that came in very late (see IX.99, 101, 103). I have concluded (IX.12–13) that Book Six of *The Lord of the Rings* was written in 1948.

At the end of this passage on the ordering of the Shire, which as already noted (p. 5) ends with the words 'the first sign that everything was not quite as it should be, and always used to be', the addition to P 2 continues (with a later pencilled heading 'Tobacco'):[5]

> There is one thing more about these hobbits of old that must be mentioned: they smoked tobacco through pipes of clay or wood. A great deal of mystery surrounds the origin of this peculiar custom ...

From this point the remainder of section 2 in the final form of the *Prologue* was achieved in P 2 with only a very few minor differences: 'Old Toby' of Longbottom was Tobias (not Tobold) Hornblower (on which see p. 69), and the date of his first growing of the pipe-weed was 1050 (not 1070), in the time of Isengrim the First (not the Second); the third of the Longbottom varieties was 'Hornpipe Twist' (not 'Southern Star'); and it is not said of *sweet galenas* that the Men of Gondor 'esteem it only for the fragrance of its flowers'. There is also a footnote to the words 'about the year 1050 in Shire-reckoning':

> That is about 400 years before the events recorded in this book. Dates in the Shire were all reckoned from the legendary crossing of the Brandywine River by the brothers Marco and Cavallo.

Later changed to Marcho and Blanco, these names do not appear in the narrative of *The Lord of the Rings*: they are found only in the further long extension to the *Prologue* concerning Hobbit-history (FR p. 13) and in the introductory note to Appendix C, *Family Trees* (RK p. 379).

For the history of the passage on pipe-weed, which began as a lecture on the subject delivered by Merry to Théoden at the ruined gates of Isengard, see VIII.36–9. After much development my father marked it 'Put into Foreword' (VIII.38 and note 36).[6] – On Isengrim Took the First and the date 1050 see VIII.45, note 37. When this addition to P 2 was written the old genealogical tree of the Tooks (given and discussed in VI.316–18), found on the back of a page from the 'Third Phase' manuscript of *A Long-expected Party*, was still in being.[7]

As has been seen (p. 4), in P 2 as revised the story of Bilbo and Gollum was still that of the original edition of *The Hobbit*, in which Gollum fully intended to give Bilbo the Ring if he lost the riddle-contest (see VI.86). The curious story of how the rewritten narrative in the chapter *Riddles in the Dark* came to be published in the edition of 1951 is sufficiently indicated in *Letters* nos.111, 128–9. In September 1947 my father sent to Sir Stanley Unwin what he called a 'specimen' of such a rewriting, not intending it for publication, but seeking only Sir Stanley's comments on the idea. Believing that it had been rejected, he was greatly shocked and surprised when nearly three years later, in July 1950, he received the proofs of a new edition with the rewriting incorporated. But he accepted the *fait accompli*. Beyond remarking that the full correspondence makes it very clear how, and how naturally, the misunderstandings on both sides that led to this result arose, there is no need to say any more about it here: for the present purpose its significance lies in the conclusion that the revision of P 2 cannot have been carried out after July 1950. In fact, I believe it to belong to 1948 (see pp. 14–15).

From the revised and extended text P 2, now in need of a successor, my father made a new typescript (P 3). This was again an uncharacteristically exact copy. It received a good deal of correction, in the earlier part only, but these corrections were restricted to minor alterations of wording and a few other details, such as the change of 'Northworthy' to 'Norbury' and of the date of Bilbo's departure with Gandalf and the Dwarves to April 28th (note 2). From this in turn an amanuensis typescript was made (P 4), but this my father barely touched. These texts both bore the original title, *Foreword, Concerning Hobbits*.

The next stage was a very rough manuscript, P 5, without title (but with *Concerning Hobbits* added later), and without either the section on pipe-weed or that on the story of Bilbo and Gollum, which while constantly moving the detail of expression further towards the final form held still to the original structure, and retained such features as the Shirking.[8] To convey the way in which the text was developed (with minute attention to tone, precision of meaning, and the fall of sentences) in successive stages I give this single brief example.

P 1 (VI.311)

And yet plainly they must be relatives of ours: nearer to us than elves are, or even dwarves. For one thing, they spoke a very similar language (or languages), and liked or disliked much the same things as we used to. What exactly the relationship is would be difficult to say. To answer that question one would have to re-discover a great deal of the now wholly lost history and legends of the Earliest Days; and that is not likely to happen, for only the Elves preserve any traditions about the Earliest Days, and their traditions are mostly about themselves – not unnaturally: the Elves were much the most important people of those times.

P 2 (as revised)

And yet plainly they must be relatives of ours: nearer to us than Elves are, or even Dwarves. For one thing, they spoke a very similar language (or languages), and liked and disliked much the same things as we used to. What exactly the relationship is would be difficult to say. To answer that question one would have to re-discover much that is now lost and forgotten for ever. Only the Elves now preserve traditions of the Elder Days, and even their traditions are incomplete, being concerned chiefly with Elves.

P 5

Yet plainly they are relatives of ours: far nearer to us than are Elves, or even Dwarves. They spoke the languages of Men, and they liked and disliked much the same things as we once did. What exactly our relationship was in the beginning can, however, no longer be told. The answer to that question lies in the Elder Days that are now lost and forgotten for ever. Only the Elves preserve still any traditions of that vanished time, but these are concerned mostly with their own affairs.

To the manuscript P 5, however, my father added, at the time of writing, much new material. One of these passages was that concerning the martial qualities of the Hobbits, or lack of them, the existence of arms in the Shire (and here the word *mathom* first appears in the texts of the *Prologue*), and the 'curious toughness' of Hobbit character. This was already fairly close to the published form (FR pp. 14–15), and its most notable omission is the absence of the reference to the Battle of Greenfields; the text reads here:

The Hobbits were not warlike, though at times they had been obliged to fight to maintain themselves in a hard and wild world. But at this period there was no living memory of any serious assault on the borders of the Shire. Even the weathers were milder ...

The original text of the chapter *The Scouring of the Shire* had no reference to the Battle of Greenfields: 'So ended the fierce battle of Bywater, the only battle ever fought in the Shire' (IX.93). In the second text (IX.101) my father repeated this, but altered it as he wrote to 'the last battle fought in the Shire, and the only battle since the Greenfields, 1137, away up in the North Farthing'. It seems a good guess that (as with the passage concerning the Shirriffs, p. 6) the appearance of the Battle of Greenfields in the *Prologue* soon after this (see below) is to be associated with the writing of *The Scouring of the Shire*.

It is convenient here, before turning to the rest of the new material that came in with the manuscript P 5, to notice a text written on two small slips and attached to the amanuensis typescript P 4. This is the origin of the passage concerning the founding of the Shire in the published *Prologue* (FR pp. 13–14), but it is worth giving in full.

In the Year 1 (according to the reckoning of Shire-folk) and in the month of Luyde[9] (as they used to say) the brothers Marco and Cavallo, having obtained formal permission from the king Argeleb II in the waning city of Fornost, crossed the wide brown river Baranduin. They crossed by the great stone bridge that had been built in the days of the power of the realm of Arthedain; for they had no boats. After their own manner and language they later changed the name to Brandywine. All that was demanded of the 'Little People' was (1) to keep the laws of Arthedain; (2) to keep the Bridge (and all other bridges) in repair; (3) to allow the king to hunt still in the woods and moors thrice a year. For the country had once been a royal park and hunting ground.

After the crossing the L[ittle] P[eople] settled down and almost disappeared from history. They took some part as allies of the king in the wars of Angmar (sending bowmen to battle), but after the disappearance of the realm and of Angmar they lived mostly at peace. Their last battle was against Orcs (Greenfields S.R. 1347?). For the land into which they had come, though now long deserted, had been richly tilled in days of yore, and there the kings had once had many farms, cornlands, vineyards, and woods. This land they called the Shire [*struck out:* (as distinct from the Old Home at Bree)], which in their language meant an ordered district of government and business – the business of growing food and eating it and living in comparative peace and content. This name Shire served to distinguish it from the wilder lands eastward, which became more and more desolate, all the way back to the dreadful Mountains over which (according to their own tales) their people had long ago wandered westward; also from the smaller country, the Oldhome at Bree, where they first settled – but not by themselves: for Bree they shared with the Bree-men. Now these folk (of whom the brothers Marco and Cavallo were in their day the largest and boldest) were of a kind concerning which the records of ancient days have little to say – except of course their own records and legends. They called themselves *Hobbits*. Most other peoples called them *Halflings* (or words of similar meaning in various languages), when they knew of them or heard rumour of them. For they existed now only in the Shire, Bree, and [?lonely] here and there were a few wild Hobbits in Eriador. And it is said that there were still a few 'wild hobbits' in the eaves of Mirkwood west and east of the Forest. *Hobbit* appears to be a 'corruption' or shortening of older *holbytla* 'hole dweller'.[10] This was the name by which they were known (to legend) in Rohan, whose people still spoke a tongue very like the most ancient form of the Hobbit language. Both peoples originally came from the lands of the upper Anduin.[11]

The date '1347?' of the Battle of Greenfields[12] suggests that it was here that that event re-entered from *The Hobbit* (see IX.119); later my father changed it here to 1147, while in *The Scouring of the Shire* it was first given as 1137 (IX.101 and note 31).

Returning briefly to the manuscript P 5, I have not yet mentioned that in this text, as originally written, the old passage in P 1 concerning the Hobbits of the Marish ('the hobbit-breed was not quite pure', 'no pure-bred hobbit had a beard', VI.312), still preserved in the revision of P 2, was now altered:

The Hobbits of that quarter, the Eastfarthing, were rather large and heavy-legged; and they wore dwarf-boots in muddy weather. But they were Stoors in the most of their blood, as was shown by the down that some grew on their chins. However, the matter of these breeds and the Shire-lore about them we must leave aside for the moment.

In the published *Prologue* this passage (apart of course from the last sentence) comes after the account of the 'three breeds' (FR p. 12), in which the Stoors had been introduced. But a further new passage was added on a separate page of the P 5 manuscript, corresponding to that in FR pp. 11–13 from 'Of their original home the Hobbits in Bilbo's time preserved no knowledge' to '... such as the Tooks and the Masters of Buckland'; and the account here of the Harfoots, Stoors and Fallohides was derived with little change from the earliest version of Appendix F, in which (p. 55, note 10) the idea of the 'three breeds' is seen in its actual emergence. The text in P 5 is all but identical to that in the final form, lacking only the statement that many of the Stoors 'long dwelt between Tharbad and the borders of Dunland before they moved north again', and still placing the Stoors before the Harfoots (see *ibid.*).

The word *smial(s)* first occurs, in the texts of the *Prologue*, in P 5. Its first occurrence in the texts of *The Lord of the Rings* is in *The Scouring of the Shire*: see IX.87 and note 16 (where I omitted to mention that in Pippin's reference to 'the Great Place of the Tooks away back in the Smials at Tuckborough' in the chapter *Treebeard* (TT p. 64) the words 'the Smials at' were a late addition to the typescript of the chapter).

A further manuscript, P 6, brought the *Prologue* very close to the form that it had in the First Edition of *The Lord of the Rings*.[13] This was a clear and fluently written text bearing the title *Prologue: Concerning Hobbits*; and here entered the last 'missing passage', FR pp. 13–14, from 'In the westlands of Eriador ...' to 'They were, in fact, sheltered, but they had ceased to remember it.'

The text of P 6 differed still from the published form in a number of ways, mostly very minor (see note 14). The text was not yet divided into four numbered sections, though the final ordering and succession of the parts was now reached; and the concluding section, on the finding of the Ring, was still the original story (see p. 7): this was derived, with some rewriting, from the text of P 2, but with a notable addition. After the reference to Gollum's saying that he had got the Ring as a birthday present long ago there follows:

Bilbo might indeed have wondered how that could be, and still more why Gollum should be willing to give such a treasure away, if his case had been less desperate, and if in fact Gollum had ever given him the present. He did not, for when he returned to his island to fetch it the Ring was not to be found.

This part then concludes much as in P 2, with the addition of a passage about Bilbo's secrecy concerning the Ring, and his disposal of Sting and the coat of mail; ending 'And the years passed, while he wrote in his leisurely fashion the story of his journey.'

In P 6 the 'Shirking' had disappeared, and in its place stood at first the title 'Elder', though this was replaced by 'Thane' before the manuscript was completed, and the spelling 'Thain' was substituted later (see p. 6). In this text the Battle of Greenfields, with the date S.R. 1147, appears.[14]

The manuscript ends with a passage, subsequently struck out, that was preserved with little material change as the conclusion of the Foreword to the First Edition of 1954. This begins with the remarks about the map of the Shire (now with the addition 'besides other maps of wider and more distant countries') and the 'abridged family-trees' that go back to P 1 (VI.313–14), but then continues:

12   THE PEOPLES OF MIDDLE-EARTH

There is also an index of names [*struck out:* with explanations] and strange words; and a table of days and dates. For those who are curious and like such lore some account is given in an appendix of the languages, the alphabets, and the calendars that were used in the Westlands in the Third Age of Middle-earth. But such lore is not necessary, and those who do not need it, or desire it, may neglect it, and even the names they may pronounce as they will. Some care has been given to the translation of their spelling from the original alphabets, and some notes on the sounds that are intended are offered. But not all are interested in such matters, and many who are not may still find the account of these great and valiant deeds worth the reading. It was in that hope that this long labour was undertaken; for it has required several years to translate, select, and arrange the matter of the Red Book of Westmarch in the form in which it is now presented to Men of a later Age, one no less darkling and ominous than were the great years 1418 and 1419 of the Shire long ago.[15]

This text was followed by a typescript copy (P 7). To this my father made the corrections and additions that brought the *Prologue* to its final form (many being made to its exemplar P 6 as well); and it was on this typescript that he rejected the original tale of Bilbo's encounter with Gollum and introduced the 'true tale' (FR pp. 20–2). The story is told here on appended pages in exactly its form in the published *Prologue*, ending with Gollum's cry '*Thief, thief! Baggins! We hates it for ever!*'

From this point, however, there are two texts. In one of these the original story, now become Bilbo's untrue version, is not mentioned at all, and the text moves at once from Gollum's cry of hatred to 'Of Bilbo's later adventures little more need be said here'. But my father was in doubt, whether or not to say anything in the *Prologue* about Bilbo's doctored accounts of the events; for at the point where the actual story ends ('*We hates it for ever!*') he subsequently added in this text a direction to a 'Note' on a separate sheet, which was apparently written quite independently. In this 'Note' (which was the origin of the passage concerning the two versions in FR p. 22) the satisfying explanation of the difference in the story as told in the two editions of *The Hobbit* is probably seen at its emergence. He began: 'This is not the story as Bilbo first told it to his companions and to Gandalf, or indeed as he *first* set it down in his book' (my italics), but struck out the words following 'Gandalf'; he then went on to say that though Bilbo set down the false story in his memoirs, and 'so it probably appeared in the original Red Book', nonetheless 'many copies contain the true account (alone or as an alternative), derived, no doubt, from notes made by Frodo or Samwise, both of whom knew the truth.'

On this page he noted (later): 'Alternative, if the only reference to this is made in Chapter II (second fair copy).' This is a reference to the final typescript of the chapter *The Shadow of the Past*, that went to the printers. The explanation of this apparently very obscure comment is as follows. On the text preceding the one to which he referred, that is to say the penultimate typescript, he had introduced a long rider[16] after Gandalf's words (FR p. 66) 'I put the fear of fire on him, and wrung the true story out of him, bit by bit, with much snivelling and snarling.' In this rider Gandalf continued:

'... I already suspected much of it. Indeed I already suspected something that I am sure has never occurred to you: Bilbo's story was not true.'

'What do you mean?' cried Frodo. 'I can't believe it.'

'Well, this is Gollum's account. Bilbo's reward for winning was merely to be shown a way out of the tunnels. There was no question of a present, least of all of giving away his "precious". Gollum confesses that he went back to his island to get it, simply so as to kill Bilbo in safety, for he was hungry and angry. But as Bilbo had already picked up the ring, he escaped, and the last Gollum knew of him was when he crept up behind and jumped over him in the dark. That is much more like Gollum!'

'But it is quite unlike Bilbo, not to tell the true tale,' said Frodo. 'And what was the point of it?'

'Unlike Bilbo, yes. But unlike Bilbo with the ring? No, I am afraid not. You see, half-unknown to himself he was trying to strengthen his claim to be its rightful owner: it was a present, a prize he had won. Much like Gollum and his "birthday-present". The two were more alike than you will admit. And both their tales were improbable and hobbitlike. My dear Frodo, Elven-rings are never given away as presents, or prizes: *never*. You are a hobbit yourself or you would have doubted the tale, as I did at once.

'But as I have told you, I found it impossible to question Bilbo on the point without making him very angry. So I let it be, for our friendship's sake. His touchiness was proof enough for me. I guessed then that the ring had an unwholesome power over its keeper that set to work quickly. Yes, even on Bilbo the desire for ownership had gripped at once, and went on growing. But fortunately it stayed at that, and he took little other harm. For he got the ring blamelessly. He did not steal it; he found it, and it was quite impossible to give it back: Gollum would have killed him at once. He paid for it, you might say, with mercy, and gave

Gollum his life at great risk. And so in the end he got rid of the thing, just in time.

'But as for Gollum: he will never again be free of the desire for it, I fear. When I last saw him, he was still filled with it, whining that he was tricked and ill-used. [But when he had at last told me his history ...

In the following (final) typescript of the chapter the rider is not present; but my father added a note at this point 'Take in rider' – and then struck it out. It was clearly at this time that he wrote the note referred to above, 'Alternative, if the only reference to this is made in Chapter II': he meant, if no more was to be said of the matter in Chapter II than Gandalf's words 'I put the fear of fire on him, and wrung the true story out of him, bit by bit, with much snivelling and snarling' – i.e., *without* the rider just given. If that rider was to be rejected, then a passage on the subject must be given in the *Prologue*. This was ultimately his decision; and the second of the two texts appended to P 6 is exactly as it stands in the published *Prologue*, p. 22: 'Now it is a curious fact that this is not the story as Bilbo first told it to his companions ...'[17]

The *Note on the Shire Records* entered in the Second Edition. In one of his copies of the First Edition my father noted: 'Here should be inserted Note on the Shire Records'; but he wrote against this later: 'I have decided against this. It belongs to Preface to *The Silmarillion*.' With this compare my remarks in the Foreword to *The Book of Lost Tales Part One*, pp. 5–6.

I have given this rather long account of the history of the *Prologue*, because it is one of the best-known of my father's writings, the primary source for knowledge of the Hobbits, on which he expended much thought and care; and also because it seems of special interest to see how it evolved in relation to the narrative of *The Lord of the Rings*. I will here briefly recapitulate some elements that seem to me to emerge from this history.

While it is not strictly demonstrable, I think it extremely likely that my father returned after many years to the original form of the *Prologue* (or *Foreword* as he still called it) about the time, or soon after it, when he was writing the long first draft that went from *Many Partings* through *Homeward Bound* and *The Scouring of the Shire* to *The Grey Havens*, that is to say in the summer of 1948 (IX.12–13, 108). I have pointed to a number of indications that this was so. On the one hand, we see the appearance, at successive stages in the writing of the *Prologue*, of the Shirriffs in the revision of the old P 2 text (p. 6); of the word *smial* in P 5 (p. 11); of the Battle of Greenfields in P 6 (see pp. 9–11); of the title of Thane (Thain) in the same text (p. 11). On the other hand, all these first appear in *The Scouring of the*

Shire – and in two cases, the Battle of Greenfields and the title of Thain, they were absent from the original draft of that chapter. I believe that my father's return to the Shire at the end of *The Lord of the Rings* provided the impulse for his renewed work on the *Prologue* and its subsequent extension by stages. Moreover it is seen from the history of this text how much of the account of Hobbits and their origins actually emerged *after* the narrative of *The Lord of the Rings* was completed – most notably, perhaps, the idea of their division into Harfoots, Stoors, and Fallohides, which entered from the earliest version of the appendix on languages (p. 10). Some of these new elements were then introduced into the existing narrative, such as *smials* into the chapter *Treebeard* (p. 11), or Stoors into the chapter *The Shadow of the Past* (p. 66, §20).

Successive stages in the development of the *Prologue* were accompanied, of course, by development in the Appendices, as is seen from references to the languages and to dates, and from such points as the naming of Argeleb II as the king who granted possession of the Shire to the Hobbits (p. 9, and see p. 209). But the latest stage of the *Prologue* discussed here, the manuscript P 6 and its typescript copy P 7, which in all other respects closely approached the final form, still had the old story of the finding of the Ring, and can therefore be dated, at the latest, to before July 1950.

NOTES

1 *The Hobbit* was now said to have been 'based on [Bilbo's] own much longer memoirs'; 'Earliest Days' was changed to 'Elder Days', and 'Folco Took' (by way of 'Faramond Took' and 'Peregrin Boffin', see VII.31–2) to 'Peregrin Took'; 'the one really populous town of their Shire, Michel-Delving' became 'the only town of their Shire, the county-town, Michel-Delving'; and the boots of the hobbits of the Marish became 'dwarf-boots'. The Hobbits' antipathy to vessels and water, and to swimming in it, was the only actual addition.

   In a letter to Sir Stanley Unwin of 21 September 1947 (*Letters* no.111) my father said that he was sending 'the preliminary chapter or Foreword to the whole: "Concerning Hobbits", which acts as a link to the earlier book and at the same time answers questions that have been asked.' From the date, this must have been a copy of the original version, as corrected.

2 The date April 30th was corrected to April 28th on the text P 3 (p. 7).

3 *Northworthy*: the Old English *worð*, *worðig* were common elements in place-names, with the same general meaning as *tūn* (*-ton*), an enclosed dwelling-place.

4 The fiction of 'translation' from the 'true' Hobbit language (the

16   THE PEOPLES OF MIDDLE-EARTH

Common Speech) was inimical to puns in any case, good though this one was.

5 The extension to P 2 on the ordering of the Shire was a typescript, but that on pipe-weed was a manuscript written on slips. My father inserted them into P 2 as a unit, but they clearly originated separately: see note 6.

6 In his letter to me of 6 May 1944 (cited in VIII.45, note 36) my father said that 'if [Faramir] goes on much more a lot of him will have to be removed to the appendices – where already some fascinating material on the hobbit Tobacco industry and the Languages of the West have gone.' I remarked (VIII.162) that Faramir's exposition of linguistic history 'survived into subsequent typescripts, and was only removed at a later time; thus the excluded material on "the Languages of the West" was not the account given by Faramir.' It is indeed difficult to say what it was. On the other hand, the 'pipe-weed' passage was removed from the chapter *The Road to Isengard* before the first completed manuscript was written (VIII.39). It is in fact quite possible that the account of 'pipe-weed' in the long addition to P 2 does go back so early, seeing that it was certainly written quite independently of the first part of the addition, on the ordering of the Shire (see note 5).

7 Similarly the statement in P 1 (VI.311) that Bandobras Took, the Bullroarer, was the son of Isengrim the First was retained in P 2 as revised: in the published genealogical tree he became the grandson of Isengrim II. – A curious exception to my statement (p. 4) that P 2 as typed was a precise copy of the original version is found in the name *Bandobras*, which in P 2 became *Barnabas*; but this was probably a mere slip. It was corrected back to *Bandobras* in the revision.

8 In P 5 the name *Lithe* entered as my father wrote, changing 'at Midsummer' to 'at the Lithe (that is Midsummer)'.

9 The name *Luyde* for the month of March is found once elsewhere, a comparative calendar of Hobbit and modern dates written on the back of a page of the earliest text of the Appendix on Calendars (see p. 136, note 3). Above *Luyde* here my father wrote a name beginning *Re* which is certainly not as it stands *Rethe*, the later Hobbit name of March, but must be taken as an ill-written form of that name.

10 On *holbytla* translated 'hole dweller' see p. 49, §48 and commentary (p. 69).

11 This is to be associated with the early version of Appendix F, §§22-3 (p. 38): '... before their crossing of the Mountains the Hobbits spoke the same language as Men in the higher vales of the Anduin ... Now that language was nearly the same as the language of the ancestors of the Rohirrim'.

12 The second figure of the date 1347 is slightly uncertain, but it looks much more like a '3' than a '1'.

13 The significant changes made in the Second Edition (1966) were few. On FR p. 14, where the later text has 'There for a thousand years they were little troubled by wars ...' to '... the Hobbits had again become accustomed to plenty', the First Edition had simply 'And thenceforward for a thousand years they lived in almost unbroken peace' (thus without the mention of the Dark Plague, the Long Winter, and the Days of Dearth). At the beginning of the next paragraph the reading of the Second Edition, 'Forty leagues it stretched from the Far Downs to the Brandywine Bridge, and fifty from the northern moors to the marshes in the south', was substituted for 'Fifty leagues it stretched from the Westmarch under the Tower Hills to the Brandywine Bridge, and nearly fifty from the northern moors ...'. My father noted that the word 'nearly' was (wrongly) omitted in the text of the Second Edition, 'so this must be accepted'.

On FR p. 16, in 'Three Elf-towers of immemorial age were still to be seen on the Tower Hills', the words 'on the Tower Hills' were an addition, and in a following sentence 'upon a green mound' was changed from 'upon a green hill'. At the end of this first section of the *Prologue* (FR p. 17) the sentence 'Hobbits delighted in such things ...' was in the First Edition put in the present tense throughout.

Lastly, in the first paragraph of the third section, FR p. 18, the sentence 'Outside the Farthings were the East and West Marches: the Buckland; and the Westmarch added to the Shire in S.R. 1462' was an addition.

14 A few further differences in P 6 from the published text may be recorded. In the paragraph concerning the script and language of the Hobbits (FR p. 13) P 6 had: 'And if ever Hobbits had a language of their own (which is debated) then in those days they forgot it and spoke ever after the Common Speech, the Westron as it was named', this being changed to the reading of FR, 'And in those days also they forgot whatever languages they had used before, and spoke ever after the Common Speech ...' And at the end of the paragraph the sentence 'Yet they kept a few words of their own, as well as their own names of months and days, and a great store of personal names out of the past' is lacking. Cf. the original version of Appendix F, pp. 37–8, §§21–3.

The founders of the Shire were still Marco and Cavallo (pp. 6, 9; later changed to Marcho and Blanco); and the second of the conditions imposed on the Hobbits of the Shire (cf. the text given on p. 9) was 'to foster the land' (changed later to 'speed the king's messengers'). The first grower of pipe-weed in the Shire was still Tobias Hornblower, and still in the time of Isengrim the First

(p. 6); the date was apparently first written 1050 as before, but changed to 1020. Later Isengrim the Second and the date 1070 were substituted, but Tobias remained. The footnote to this passage (p. 6) was retained, but 'about 400 years' was later altered to 'nearly 350'. The third of the Longbottom brands now became 'Hornpipe Cake', but was changed back to 'Hornpipe Twist'.

15   In the Foreword as published this concluding paragraph began:

> Much information, necessary and unnecessary, will be found in the Prologue. To complete it some maps are given, including one of the Shire that has been approved as reasonably correct by those Hobbits that still concern themselves with ancient history. At the end of the third volume will be found also some abridged family-trees ...

When P 6 was written, of course, the idea that *The Lord of the Rings* should be issued as a work in three volumes was not remotely envisaged. The published Foreword retained the reference to 'an index of names and strange words with some explanations', although in the event it was not provided.

16   I did not carry my account of the history of *The Shadow of the Past* so far as this: see VII.28–9.

17   In this connection it is interesting to see what my father said in his letter to Sir Stanley Unwin of 10 September 1950 (*Letters* no.129):

> I have now on my hands two printed versions of a crucial incident. Either the first must be regarded as washed out, a mere miswriting that ought never to have seen the light; or the story as a whole must take into account the existence of two versions and use it. The former was my original simpleminded intention, though it is a bit awkward (since the Hobbit is fairly widely known in its older form) if the literary pretence of historicity and dependence on record is to be maintained. The second can be done convincingly (I think), but not briefly explained in a note.

The last words refer to the note required for the new edition of *The Hobbit* explaining the difference in the narrative in *Riddles in the Dark*. Four days later he wrote again (*Letters* no.130):

> I have decided to accept the existence of both versions of Chapter Five, so far as the sequel goes – though I have no time at the moment to rewrite that at the required points.

II
THE APPENDIX ON LANGUAGES

Beside the *Foreword: Concerning Hobbits*, whose development, clear and coherent, into the *Prologue* has been described in the last chapter, there is another text of a prefatory or introductory nature; and it is not easy to see how my father designed it to relate to the *Foreword: Concerning Hobbits*. Indeed, except in one point, they have nothing in common; for this further text (which has no title) is scarcely concerned with Hobbits at all. For a reason that will soon be apparent I give it here in full.

It was typed on small scrap paper, and very obviously set down by my father very rapidly *ab initio* without any previous drafting, following his thoughts as they came: sentences were abandoned before complete and replaced by new phrasing, and so on. He corrected it here and there in pencil, either then or later, these corrections being very largely minor improvements or necessary 'editorial' clarifications of the very rough text; in most cases I have incorporated these (not all are legible). I have added paragraph numbers for subsequent reference. Notes to this section will be found on page 26.

§1   This tale is drawn from the memoirs of Bilbo and Frodo Baggins, preserved for the most part in the Great Red Book of Samwise. It has been written during many years for those who were interested in the account of the great Adventure of Bilbo, and especially for my friends, the Inklings (in whose veins, I suspect, a good deal of hobbit blood still runs), and for my sons and daughter.

§2   But since my children and others of their age, who first heard of the finding of the Ring, have grown older with the years, this tale speaks more clearly of those darker things which lurked only on the borders of the other tale, but which have troubled the world in all its history.

§3   To the Inklings I dedicate this book, since they have already endured it with patience – my only reason for supposing that they have a hobbit-strain in their venerable ancestry: otherwise it would be hard to account for their interest in the history and geography of those long-past days, between the end of the Dominion of the Elves and the beginning of the

Dominion of Men, when for a brief time the Hobbits played a supreme part in the movements of the world.

§4 For the Inklings I add this note, since they are men of lore, and curious in such matters. It is said that Hobbits spoke a language, or languages, very similar to ours. But that must not be misunderstood. Their language was like ours in manner and spirit; but if the face of the world has changed greatly since those days, so also has every detail of speech, and even the letters and scripts then used have long been forgotten, and new ones invented.[1]

§5 No doubt for the historians and philologists it would have been desirable to preserve the original tongues; and certainly something of the idiom and the humour of the hobbits is lost in translation, even into a language as similar in mood as is our own. But the study of the languages of those days requires time and labour, which no one but myself would, I think, be prepared to give to it. So I have except for a few phrases and inscriptions transferred the whole linguistic setting into the tongues of our own time.

§6 The Common Speech of the West in those days I have represented by English. This noble tongue had spread in the course of time from the kingdoms of Fornost and Gondor, and the hobbits preserved no memory of any other speech; but they used it in their own manner, in their daily affairs very much as we use English; though they had always at command a richer and more formal language when occasion required, or when they had dealings with other people. This more formal and archaic style was still the normal use in the realm of Gondor (as they discovered) and among the great in the world outside the Shire.

§7 But there were other languages in the lands. There were the tongues of the Elves. Three are here met with. The most ancient of all, the High-Elven, which they used in secret as their own common speech and as the language of lore and song. The Noldorin, which may be called Gnomish, the language of the Exiles from Elvenhome in the Far West, to which tongue belong most of the names in this history that have been preserved without translation. And the language of the woodland Elves, the Elves of Middle-earth. All these tongues were related, but those spoken in Middle-earth, whether by Exiles or by Elves that had remained here from the beginning, were much changed.[2] Only in Gondor was the Elvish speech known commonly to Men.

§8 There were also the languages of Men, when they did not speak the Common Tongue. Now those languages of Men that are here met with were related to the Common Speech; for the Men of the North and West were akin in the beginning to the Men of Westernesse that came back over the Sea; and the Common Speech was indeed made by the blending of the speech of Men of Middle-earth with the tongues of the kings from over the Sea.[3] But in the North old forms survived. The speech of the Men of Dale, therefore, to show its relationship has been cast in a Northern form related distantly to the English which has been taken to represent the Common Speech. While the speech of the Men of Rohan, who came out of the North, and still among themselves used their ancestral language (though all their greater folk spoke also the Common Speech after the manner of their allies in Gondor), I have represented by ancient English, such as it was a thousand years ago, or as far back from us about as was the day of Eorl the Young from Théoden of Rohan.[4]

§9 The orcs and goblins had languages of their own, as hideous as all things that they made or used; and since some remnant of good will, and true thought and perception, is required to keep even a base language alive and useful even for base purposes, their tongues were endlessly diversified in form, as they were deadly monotonous in purport, fluent only in the expression of abuse, of hatred and fear. For which reason they and their kind used (and still use) the languages of nobler creatures in such intercourse as they must have between tribe and tribe.[5]

§10 The dwarves are a different case. They are a hard thrawn folk for the most part, secretive, acquisitive, laborious, retentive of the memory of injuries (and of benefits), lovers of stone, of metals, of gems, of things that grow and take shape under the hands of craft rather than of things that live by their own life. But they are not and were not ever among the workers of wilful evil in the world nor servants of the Enemy, whatever the tales of Men may later have said of them; for Men have lusted after the works of their hands, and there has been enmity between the races. But it is according to the nature of the Dwarves that travelling, and labouring, and trading about the world they should use ever openly the languages of the Men among whom they dwell; and yet in secret (a secret which unlike the Elves they are unwilling to unlock even to those whom they know are friends and desire learning not power) they use a strange slow-changing tongue.[6] Little is known about it. So it is that here such Dwarves as appear have names of the same Northern kind as the Men of Dale that dwelt round about, and speak the Common Speech, now in this manner now in that; and only in a few names do we get any glimpse of their hidden tongue.

§11 And as for the scripts, something must be said of them, since in this history there are both inscriptions and old books, such as the torn remnants of the Book of Mazarbul,[7] that must be read. Enough of them will appear in this book to allow, maybe, the skilled in such matters to decipher both runes and running hands. But others may wish for a clearer key. For them the Elvish Script (in its more formal shape, as it was used in Gondor for the Common Speech) is set out in full; though its various modifications used in writing other tongues, especially the High-Elven or the Noldorin, must here be passed over. Another script plays a part both in the previous account and the present one: the Runes. These also, as most other things of the kind, were also an Elvish invention. But whereas the flowing scripts (of two kinds, the alphabet of Rúmil and the alphabet of Fëanor, only the later of which concerns this tale) were developed in Elvenhome far from Middle-earth, the Runes, or *cirth*, were devised by the Elves of the woods; and from that origin derive their peculiar character, similar to the Runes of the North in our days, though their detail is different and it is very doubtful if there is any lineal connexion between the two alphabets. The Elvish *cirth* are in any case more elaborate and numerous and systematic. The Dwarves devised no letters and though they used such writing as they found current for necessary purposes, they wrote few books, except brief chronicles (which they kept secret). In the North in those regions from which the Dwarves of this tale came they used the *cirth*, or Runes. Following the general lines of translation, to which these records have been submitted, as the names of the North have been given the forms of Northern tongues in our own time, so the Runes were represented by the runes of ancient England. But since the scripts and runes of that account interested many of its readers, older and younger, and many enquiries concerning them have been made, in this book it has been thought better to give any runic inscriptions or writings that occur in their truer form, and to add at the end a table of the *cirth*, with their names, according to the usage of Dale, among both Dwarves and Men. A list of the names that occur is also given, and where they are taken from the ancient records the language to which they belong is stated and their meaning, or the meaning of their component parts, is added.

§12 The word Gnomish is used above; and it would be an apt name, since whatever Paracelsus may have thought (if indeed he invented the word), to the learned it suggests knowledge. And their own true name in High-Elven is Noldor, Those that Know; for of the Three Kindreds of the Elves in the beginning, ever the Noldor were distinguished both by their knowledge of things that are and were in this world, and by the desire to know yet more. Yet they were not in fact in any way like to the gnomes of our learned theory, and still less to the gnomes of popular fancy in which they have been confused with dwarves and goblins, and other small creatures of the earth. They belonged to a race high and beautiful, the Elder Children of the World, who now are gone. Tall they were, fairskinned and grey-eyed, though their locks were dark, and their voices knew more melodies than any mortal speech that now is heard. Valiant they were and their history was lamentable, and though a little of it was woven with the fates of the Fathers of Men in the Elder Days, their fate is not our fate, and their lives and the lives of Men cross seldom.[8]

§13 It will be noted also that in this book, as before, Dwarves are spoken of, although dictionaries tell us that the plural of *dwarf* is *dwarfs*. It should, of course, be *dwarrows*; meaning that, if each, singular and plural, had gone its own natural way down the years, unaffected by forgetfulness, as *Man* and *Men* have, then *dwarf* and *dwarrows* we should have said as surely as we say *goose* and *geese*. But we do not talk about *dwarf* as often as we talk of *man*, or even *goose*, and memories are not good enough among men to keep hold of a special plural for a race now relegated (such is their fate and the fall of their great pride) to folktales, where at least some shadow of the truth is preserved, or at last to nonsense tales where they have become mere figures of fun who do not wash their hands. But here something of their old character and power (if already diminished) is still glimpsed; these are the Nauglir[9] of old, in whose hearts still smouldered the ancient fires and the embers of their grudge against the Elves; and to mark this *dwarves* is used, in defiance of correctness and the dictionaries – although actually it is derived from no more learned source than childhood habit. I always had a love of the plurals that did not go according to the simplest rule: *loaves*, and *elves*, and *wolves*, and *leaves*; and *wreaths* and *houses* (which I should have liked better spelt *wreathes* and *houzes*); and I persist in *hooves* and *rooves* according to ancient authority. I said therefore *dwarves* however I might see it spelt, feeling that the good folk were a little dignified so; for I never believed the sillier things about them that were presented to my notice. I wish I had known of *dwarrows* in those days. I should have liked it better still. I have enshrined it now at any rate in my translation of the name of Moria in the Common Speech, which meant The Dwarf-delving, and that I have rendered by The Dwarrow-delf. But Moria itself is an Elvish name of Gnomish kind, and given without love, for the true Gnomes, though they might here and there in the bitter wars against the Enemy and his orc-servants make great fortresses beneath the Earth, were not dwellers in caves or tunnels of choice, but lovers of the green earth and of the lights of heaven; and Moria in their tongue means the Black Chasm. But the Dwarves themselves, and this name at any rate was never secret, called it simply *Khazad-dûm*, the Mansion of the Khazad, for such is their own name for their own race, and has been so, since their birth in the deeps of time.[10]

The opening remarks of this text certainly suggest that the narrative of *The Lord of the Rings* had been completed; and this in turn suggests that it was not far removed in time from the renewed work on the *Foreword: Concerning Hobbits* (i.e. the *Prologue*). Though it is not much more than a guess, I incline to think that when my father began it he intended it as a personal and dedicatory 'preface', entirely distinct in nature from the account of the Hobbits, which was a prologue expressly relating to the narrative; but that involuntarily he was soon swept into writing about those matters of languages and scripts that he felt needed some introduction and explanation at least as much as did the Hobbits. The result was, clearly, a combination wholly unsuitable to his purpose, and he put it aside. I would also guess that it was the writing of this text that gave rise to the idea of a special Appendix on languages and scripts (ultimately divided into two); and this is why I place it at the beginning of this account of the evolution of what came to be 'Appendix F', *The Languages and Peoples of the Third Age*. Since I shall number the texts of this Appendix from 'F 1', it is convenient to call this anomalous 'Foreword' F*.

My father did not lose sight of this text, however, and later used elements from it, both in Appendix F[11] and in the *Foreword* that accompanied the First Edition of *The Fellowship of the Ring*, published in 1954. Since copies of the First Edition may not be easy to come by, I print the greater part of it again here (for the concluding section see p. 12 with note 15).

This tale, which has grown to be almost a history of the great War of the Ring, is drawn for the most part from the memoirs of the renowned Hobbits, Bilbo and Frodo, as they are preserved in the Red Book of Westmarch. This chief monument of Hobbit-lore is so called because it was compiled, repeatedly copied, and enlarged and handed down in the family of the Fairbairns of Westmarch, descended from that Master Samwise of whom this tale has much to say.

I have supplemented the account of the Red Book, in places, with information derived from the surviving records of Gondor, notably the Book of the Kings; but in general, though I have omitted much, I have in this tale adhered more closely to the actual words and narrative of my original than in the previous selection from the Red Book, *The Hobbit*. That was drawn from the early chapters, composed originally by Bilbo himself. If 'composed' is a just word. Bilbo was not assiduous, nor an orderly narrator, and his account is involved and discursive, and sometimes confused: faults that still appear in the Red Book, since the copiers were pious and careful, and altered very little.

The tale has been put into its present form in response to the many requests that I have received for further information about the history of the Third Age, and about Hobbits in particular. But since my children and others of their age, who first heard of the finding of the Ring, have grown older with the years, this book speaks more plainly of those darker things which lurked only on the borders of the earlier tale, but which have troubled Middle-earth in all its history. It is, in fact, not a book written for children at all; though many children will, of course, be interested in it, or parts of it, as they still are in the histories and legends of other times (especially in those not specially written for them).

I dedicate the book to all admirers of Bilbo, but especially to my sons and my daughter, and to my friends the Inklings. To the Inklings, because they have already listened to it with a patience, and indeed with an interest, that almost leads me to suspect that they have hobbit-blood in their venerable ancestry. To my sons and my daughter for the same reason, and also because they have all helped me in the labours of composition. If 'composition' is a just word, and these pages do not deserve all that I have said about Bilbo's work.

For if the labour has been long (more than fourteen years), it has been neither orderly nor continuous. But I have not had Bilbo's leisure. Indeed much of that time has contained for me no leisure at all, and more than once for a whole year the dust has gathered on my unfinished pages. I only say this to explain to those who have waited for this book why they have had to wait so long. I have no reason to complain. I am surprised and delighted to find from numerous letters that so many people, both in England and across the Water, share my interest in this almost forgotten history; but it is not yet universally recognized as an important branch of study. It has indeed no obvious practical use, and those who go in for it can hardly expect to be assisted.

Much information, necessary and unnecessary, will be found in the Prologue. ...

In the Second Edition of 1966 this Foreword was rejected in its entirety. On one of his copies of the First Edition my father wrote beside it: 'This Foreword I should wish very much in any case to cancel. Confusing (as it does) real personal matters with the "machinery" of the Tale is a serious mistake.'[12]

NOTES

1. On this passage see note 11.
2. On my father's conception at this time of the use in Middle-earth in the Third Age of Noldorin on the one hand, and of 'the language of the woodland Elves' on the other, see p. 36, §18, and commentary (pp. 65–6).
3. On this passage concerning the origin of the Common Speech see p. 63, §9.
4. In Appendix A (RK pp. 349–50) the length of time between the birth-dates of Eorl the Young and Théoden was 463 years.
5. My father was asserting, I think, that a language so base and narrow in thought and expression cannot remain a common tongue of widespread use; for from its very inadequacy it cannot resist change of form, and must become a mass of closed jargons, incomprehensible even to others of the same kind.
6. This passage concerning the Dwarves, absent in the original version of Appendix F, reappeared subsequently (p. 75), and was retained, a good deal altered, in the final form of that Appendix (RK p. 410).
7. My father deeply regretted that in the event his 'facsimiles' of the torn and burned pages from the Book of Mazarbul were not reproduced in *The Lord of the Rings* (see *Letters* nos.137, 139–40; but also pp. 298–9 in this book). They were finally published in *Pictures by J. R. R. Tolkien*, 1979.
8. This is where the passage that concludes Appendix F in the published form first arose. See further pp. 76–7.
9. *Nauglir*: curiously, my father here returned to the form found in

the *Quenta* of 1930, rather than using *Naugrim*, found in the *Quenta Silmarillion* and later (see V.273, 277; XI.209). As with those referred to in notes 6 and 8, this passage, absent in the original version of Appendix F, was reinstated and appears with little change in the published form (where the name is *Naugrim*).

10 Years later my father called this text a 'fragment' (see note 12). It ends at the foot of a page, the last words typed being 'since their birth', with 'in the deeps of time' added in pencil.

11 For passages from F* that reappeared in the course of the development see notes 6, 8 and 9. In this connection there is a curious and puzzling point arising from F*. In this text my father showed his intention to say something in the published work about the fiction of translation: that he had converted the 'true' languages of Men (and Hobbits) in the Third Age of Middle-earth, wholly alien to us, into an analogical structure composed of English in modern and ancestral form, and Norse (§§5–6, 8). Introducing this subject, he wrote (§4): 'It is said that Hobbits spoke a language, or languages, very similar to ours. But that must not be misunderstood. Their language was like ours in manner and spirit; but if the face of the world has changed greatly since those days, so also has every detail of speech ...'

One might wonder for a moment who said this of Hobbits, and why my father should introduce it only to warn against taking it literally; but it was of course he himself who said it, in the original version P 1 of the *Foreword: Concerning Hobbits* (VI.311, cited on p. 8): 'And yet plainly they must be relatives of ours ... For one thing, they spoke a very similar language (or languages), and liked or disliked much the same things as we used to.' This was repeated years later in the revision of the second text P 2 (see the comparative passages given on p. 8), but here the qualifying statement, warning against misunderstanding, is not present.

I cannot explain why my father should have made this cross-reference to the *Foreword: Concerning Hobbits*, in order to point out that it is misleading, nor why he should have retained it – without this caveat – in his revision of P 2. What makes it still odder is that, whereas in the first versions of Appendix F (in which the 'theory and practice' of the translation of the true languages was greatly elaborated) the remark is absent, it reappears in the third version (F 3, p. 73), and here in a form almost identical to that in F*: it is given as a citation, 'It has been said that "the Hobbits spoke a language, or languages, very similar to ours"', and this is followed by the same qualification: 'But this must not be misunderstood. Their language was like ours in manner and tone ...' As a final curiosity, by the time the third version of Appendix F was written the remark had been removed from the *Prologue* (see the citation from the text P 5 on p. 8), and replaced by 'They spoke the languages of Men, and they liked and disliked much the same things as we once did', though still, as in the published *Prologue*, in the context of this being a sign of the close original relationship of Hobbits and Men.

12 Many years after the writing of F* my father noted on the typescript: 'Fragment of an original Foreword afterwards divided into Foreword and Prologue'. This was misleading, because F* played no part in the *Prologue*, but did contribute to the Foreword of the First Edition and to Appendix F.

The history of Appendix F, whose final title was *The Languages and Peoples of the Third Age* (while the discussion of alphabets and scripts, originally joined to that of the languages, became Appendix E, *Writing and Spelling*), undoubtedly began with the abortive but not unproductive text F*, but the first version of that Appendix is best taken to be constituted by two closely related manuscripts, since these were written as elaborate essays to stand independently of any 'Foreword'.

Long afterwards my father wrote (p. 299) that 'the actual Common Speech was sketched in structure and phonetic elements, and a number of words invented'; and in this work he is seen developing the true forms in the Westron tongue to underlie the translated (or substituted) names, especially of Hobbits. A great deal of this material was subsequently lost from the Appendix. This original version is also of great interest in documenting his conception of the languages of Middle-earth and their interrelations at the time when the narrative of *The Lord of the Rings* had recently been completed; and also in showing how substantially that conception was still to be developed before the publication of *The Lord of the Rings* in 1954–5.

To date this version precisely seems scarcely possible, but at least it can certainly be placed before the summer of 1950, and I think that it may well be earlier than that.[1]

The earlier of the two texts, which I will refer to as F 1, is a fairly rough and much emended, but entirely legible, manuscript entitled *Notes on the Languages at the end of the Third Age*. A second manuscript, F 2, succeeded it, as I think, very soon if not immediately, with the title *The Languages at the end of the Third Age*. Writing with great care and clarity, my father followed F 1 pretty closely: very often changing the expression or making additions, but for the most part in minor ways, and seldom departing from the previous text even in the succession of the sentences. The two texts are far too close to justify giving them both, and I print therefore F 2, recording in the primarily textual notes on pp. 54 ff. the relatively few cases where different readings in F 1 seem of some significance or interest (but in the section on

THE APPENDIX ON LANGUAGES 29

Hobbit names, where there was much development in F 2, all differences between the two texts are detailed).

F 2 was substantially corrected and added to (more especially in the earlier part of the essay), and some pages were rewritten. These alterations are not all of a kind, some being made with care and others more roughly, and I have found it extremely difficult to determine, in relative terms, when certain of them were made: the more especially since the development after F 2 was not a steady progression, my father evidently feeling that a different treatment of the subject was required. Some corrections undoubtedly belong to a time when the text as a whole had been supplanted. I have therefore included in the text that follows all alterations made to the manuscript, and in most cases I have shown them as such, though in order to reduce the clutter I have in some cases introduced them silently, when they do no more than improve the text (largely to increase its clarity) without in any way altering its purport.

In general I treat F 2 as the representative text of the original version, and only distinguish F 1 when necessary. The paragraph-numbers are of course added editorially. A commentary follows the notes on pp. 61 ff.

The Languages at the end of the Third Age

§1 I have written this note on the languages concerned in this book not only because this part of the lore of those days is of special interest to myself, but because I find that many would welcome some information of this kind. I have had many enquiries concerning such matters from readers of the earlier selections from the Red Book.*

§2 We have in these histories to deal with both Elvish and Mannish[2] tongues. The long history of Elvish speech I will not treat; but since three [> two] varieties of it are glimpsed in this book a little may be said about it.

§3 According to Elvish historians the Elven-folk, by themselves called the *Quendi*, and Elven-speech were originally one. The primary division was into *Eldar* and *Avari*. The Avari were those Elves who remained content with Middle-earth [*struck out:*] and refused the summons of the Powers; but they and their

---

* *The Hobbit*, drawn from the earlier chapters of the Red Book, those mainly composed by Bilbo and dealing only with the discovery of the Ring.

many secret tongues do not concern this book. The Eldar were those who set out and marched to the western shores of the Old World. Most of them then passed over the Sea and came to that land in the Ancient West which they called Valinor, a name that means the Land of the Powers or Rulers of the World. But some of the Eldar [*added:* of the kindred of the Teleri] remained behind in the north-west of Middle-earth, and these were called the *Lembi* or 'Lingerers'. It is with Eldarin tongues, Valinórean or Lemberin [> Telerian] that these tales are concerned.

§4 In Valinor, from the language of that Elvish kindred known as the Lindar, was made a High-Elven speech that, after the Elves had devised letters, was used not only for lore and formal writing, but also for high converse and for intercourse among Elves of different kindreds. This, which is indeed an 'Elven-latin' as it were, unchanging in time and place, the Elves themselves called *Quenya*: that is simply 'Elvish'.

§5 Now after long ages of peace it came to pass, as is related in the *Quenta Noldorion*, that the Noldor, who were of all the kindreds of the Eldar the most skilled in crafts and lore, departed as exiles from Valinor and returned to Middle-earth, seeking the Great Jewels, the *Silmarilli*, which Fëanor chief of all their craftsmen had made. Their language, Noldorin, that at first differed little from the Lindarin or Quenya, became on their return to Middle-earth subject to the change which even things devised by the Elves here suffer, and in the passing of time it grew wholly unlike to the Quenya of Valinor, which tongue the exiles nonetheless retained always in memory as a language of lore and song and courtesy.*

§6 According to the Elves Men shared, though in a lesser degree, many of the powers of the Elves, and they were capable of devising languages of a sort for themselves, as indeed they have done, it seems, in many remote lands. But in fact Men did not in all regions go through the slow and painful process of invention. In the North and West of the Old World they learned language direct and fully made from Elves who befriended them in their infancy and early wanderings; and the tongues of Men

---

* On the other hand the Noldorin and Lemberin tongues, that had long been sundered, being now spoken by peoples dwelling side by side, drew closer together; and though they remained wholly distinct they became similar in sound and style.

which are, however remotely, of this origin the Quendi have at all times found the more pleasant to their own ears. Yet soon even these western tongues of Men became estranged from the speech of Elves, being changed by process of time, or by Men's own inventions and additions, or by other influences, notably that of the Dwarves from whom long ago some Men learned much, especially of delving, building, and smithying.

§7 Now the Men who first came westward out of the heart of Middle-earth to lands near the shores of the Sea were called by the Elves Atani,[3] *[added:* or in Noldorin the Edain,] the Fathers of Men, and there was great friendship between the two races. For when the Fathers of Men came over the mountains they met for the first time the Eldar, or High-elves; and the Eldar were at that time engaged in a ceaseless war with the Dark Lord of that Age, one greater far than Sauron, who was but one of his minions. In that war three houses of the Fathers of Men aided the Elves, especially the Noldor, and lived among them and fought beside them; and the people [> lords] of these houses learned the Noldorin speech [*struck out:*] and forsook their own tongue.[4]

§8 When at last that war was ended, most of the exiled Noldor returned over the Sea to Valinor or to the land of Eressëa that lies / within sight of it [> near]. Then the people of the Three Houses of Men were permitted as a reward to pass also over the Sea, if they would, and to dwell in an isle set apart for them. The name of that great isle was Númenor, which in Quenya signifies Westernesse. Most of the Fathers of Men departed and dwelt in Númenor and there became great and powerful; and they were fair of face and tall, and masters of craft and lore only less than the Eldar, and the span of their lives was thrice that of men in Middle-earth, though they remained mortal nonetheless, and were not permitted to set foot upon the shores of the deathless land of Valinor. They were called Kings of Men, the Númenóreans, or in Noldorin the Dúnedein [> Dúnedain].[5]

§9 The language of the Dúnedain was thus the Elvish Noldorin, though their high lords and men of wisdom knew also the Quenya, [> Thus in Númenor two languages were used: the Númenórean (or Adûnaic), and the Elvish Noldorin, which all the lords of that people knew and spoke, for they had many dealings with the Elves in the days ere their fall. But their men of wisdom learned also the Quenya, and could read the books of Elven lore;] and in that high tongue they gave names to many places of fame or reverence, and to men of royalty and great renown.* After the Downfall of Númenor (which was contrived by Sauron) Elendil and the fugitives from the West fled eastwards. But in the west-lands of Middle-earth, where they established their exiled realms, they found a common tongue in use along the coast-lands from the Mouths of Anduin to the icy Bay of Forochel in the North. This tongue was in Noldorin called *Falathren* or 'Shore-language', but by its users was called *Yandūnë* [> *Andúnar* > *Adúnar*] (that is Westron) or *Sōval Phārë* (that is Common Speech).⁶

§10 This Common Speech was [*struck out:*] in the beginning / a Mannish language, and was indeed only a later form of the native tongue of the Fathers of Men themselves before those of the Three Houses passed over the Sea. It was thus closely akin to other languages of Men that [> Other languages of Men, derived also from the tongues of the Edain or closely akin to them] were still spoken further inland, especially in the northern regions of the west-lands or about the upper waters of the Anduin. Its spread [> The spread of the Westron] had been at first due largely to the Dúnedain themselves; for in the Dark Years they had often visited again the shores of Middle-earth, and in the days of their great voyages before the Downfall they had made many fortresses and havens for the help of their ships. One of the greatest of these had been at Pelargir above the Mouths of Anduin, and it is said that it was the language of that region (which was afterwards called Gondor) that was the foundation of the Common Speech. But Sauron, who could turn all things devised by Elves or Men to his own evil purposes, had also favoured the spread of this Common Speech, for it was useful to him in the governing of his vast lordship in the Dark Years.

§11 Beside the Common or Westron Speech, and other kindred tongues of Men, there remained also in the days of Elendil the languages of the Eldar. Strange though it may seem,

---

* Of Quenya form, for instance, are the names *Elendil*, *Anárion*, *Isildur*, and all the royal names of Gondor, including *Elessar*; also the names of the kings of the Northern Line as far as the tenth, *Eärendil*. [*Added:* The names of other lords of the Dúnedain such as *Arathorn*, *Aragorn*, *Boromir*, *Denethor* are for the most part Noldorin; but *Imrahil* and *Adrahil* are Númenórean (Adûnaic) names.]

seeing that the Dúnedain had dwelt for long years apart in Númenor, the people of Elendil could still readily converse with the Eldar that spoke Noldorin. The reasons for this are various. First, the Númenóreans had never become wholly sundered from the Noldor; for while those who had returned into the West often came to Númenor in friendship, the Númenóreans, as has been said, often visited Middle-earth and had at times aided the Elves that remained there in their strife with Sauron.[7] Again, the change and decay of things, though not wholly removed, was yet much delayed in the land of the Dúnedain in the days of its blessedness; and the like may be said of the Eldar.[8]

[*This paragraph was rewritten thus:* Beside the Common or Westron Speech, and other kindred tongues of Men, there remained also in the days of Elendil the languages of the Eldar; for many still dwelt in Eriador. With those that spoke Noldorin the people of Elendil could still readily converse. For friendship had long endured between the Númenóreans and the Noldor, and the folk of Eressëa had often visited Númenor, while the Númenóreans had sailed often to Middle-earth and had at times aided the Elves in their strife with Sauron.]

§12 Moreover, those were the days of the Three Rings. Now, as is elsewhere told, these rings were hidden, and the Eldar did not use them for the making of any new thing while Sauron still reigned and wore the Ruling Ring; yet their chief virtue was ever secretly at work, and that virtue was to defend the Eldar who abode in Middle-earth [*added:* and all things pertaining to them] from change and withering and weariness. So it was that in all the long time from the forging of the Rings to their ending, when the Third Age was over, the Eldar even upon Middle-earth changed no more in a thousand years than do Men in ten; and their language likewise.

§13 Now the people of Elendil were not many, for only a few great ships had escaped the Downfall or survived the tumult of the Seas. They found, it is true, many dwellers upon the west-shores who came of their own blood, wholly or in part, being descended from mariners and from wardens of forts and havens that had been set there in days gone by; yet all told the Dúnedain were now only a small folk in the midst of strangers. They used, therefore, the Westron speech in all their dealings with other men, and in the governing of the realms of which they had become the rulers; and this Common Speech became now enlarged, and much enriched with words drawn from the language of the Dúnedain, which was, as has been said, a form of the Elvish Noldorin [> and much enriched with words drawn from the Adûnaic language of the Dúnedain, and from the Noldorin]. But among themselves the kings and high lords, and indeed all those of Númenórean blood in any degree, for long used the Noldorin speech; and in that tongue they gave names to men and to places throughout the realms of the heirs of Elendil.

§14 In this way it had come about that at the time when the events recorded in this book began it might be said that nearly all speaking-folk of any race west of the east-eaves of Mirkwood spoke after some fashion this Common Speech; while Men who dwelt in Eriador, the wide land between the Misty Mountains and Ered Lindon, or in the coast-lands south of the White Mountains, used the Westron only and had long forgotten their own tongues. So it was with the folk of Gondor (other than the lords) and of the Anfalas and beyond; and with the Bree-folk / and the Dunlendings [> in the North]. East of the Misty Mountains, even far to the north, the Common Speech was known; though there, as in Esgaroth [> as beside the Long Lake] or in Dale, or among the Beornings and the Woodmen of the west-eaves of Mirkwood, Men also retained their own tongues in daily use. The Eorlings, or the Rohirrim as they were called in Gondor, still used their own northern tongue, yet all but their humbler folk spoke also the Common Speech after the manner of Gondor; for the Riders of Rohan had come out of Éothéod near the sources of Anduin only some five hundred years before the days here spoken of.

[*The conclusion of this paragraph was rewritten thus:* The Eorlings, or the Rohirrim as they were called in Gondor, still used their own northern tongue; for the Riders of Rohan had come out of Éothéod near the sources of Anduin only some five hundred years before the days here spoken of. Yet all but their humbler folk spoke also the Common Speech after the manner of Gondor. In the Dunland also the Dunlendings, a dwindling people, remnant of those who had dwelt in western Rohan before the coming of the Rohirrim, still clung to their own speech. This was wholly unlike the Westron, and was descended, as it seems, from some other Mannish tongue, not akin to that of the Atani, Fathers of Men. A similar and kindred language was probably once spoken in Bree: see (the footnote to §25).]

§15 More remarkable it may be thought that the Common Speech had also been learned by other races, Dwarves, Orcs, and even Trolls. The case of the Dwarves can, however, be easily understood. At this time they had no longer in the west-lands any great cities or delvings where many lived together. For the most part they were scattered, living in small groups among other folk, often wandering, seldom staying long in any place, until, as is told in the beginning of the Red Book, their old halls under the Lonely Mountain were regained and the Dragon was slain. They had therefore of necessity long used the Common Speech in their dealings with other folk, even with Elves.* Not that Dwarves were ever eager to teach their own tongue to others. They were a secretive people, and they kept their own speech to themselves, using it only when no strangers were near. Indeed they even gave themselves 'outer' names, either in the Westron or in the languages of Men among whom they dwelt, but had also 'inner' and secret names in their own tongue which they did not reveal. So it was that the northern Dwarves, the people of Thorin and Dáin, had names drawn from the northern language of the Men of Dale, and their secret names are not known to us. For that reason little is known of Dwarf-speech at this period, save for a few names of mines and meres and mountains.

§16 The Orcs had a language of their own, devised for them by the Dark Lord of old, but it was so full of harsh and hideous sounds and vile words that other mouths found it difficult to compass, and few indeed were willing to make the attempt. And these creatures, being filled with all malice and hatred, so that they did not love even their own kind, had soon diversified their barbarous and unwritten speech into as many jargons as there were groups or settlements of Orcs. Thus they were driven to use the language of their enemies even in conversing with other Orcs of different breed or distant dwellings. In the Misty Mountains, and in other lingering Orc-holds in the far North-west, they had indeed abandoned their native tongue and used the Common Speech, though in such a fashion as to make it scarcely less unlovely than the Orkish.

§17 Trolls, in their beginning creatures of lumpish and brutal nature, had nothing that could be called true language

---

* For there was an ancient enmity between Dwarf and Elf and neither would learn the other's tongue.

of their own; but the evil Power had at various times made use of them, teaching them what little they could learn, and even crossing their breed with that of the larger Orcs. Trolls thus took such language as they could from the Orcs, and in the west-lands the Trolls of the hills and mountains spoke a debased form of the Common Westron speech.

§18 Elves, it may be thought, had no need of other languages than their own. They did not, indeed, like the Dwarves hide their own language, and they were willing to teach the Elven-tongues to any who desired or were able to learn them. But these were few, apart from the lords of Númenórean descent. The Elves, therefore, who remained in the west-lands used the Common Speech in their dealings with Men or other speaking-folk; but they used it in an older and more gracious form, that of the lords of the Dúnedain rather than that of the Shire. Among themselves they spoke and sang in Elven-tongues, and throughout Eriador from Lindon to Imladrist [> Imladris] they used the Noldorin speech; for in those lands, especially in Rivendell and at the Grey Havens, but also elsewhere in other secret places, there were still many of the exiled Noldor abiding or wandering in the wild. Beyond the Misty Mountains there were still Eldar who used the Lemberin [> Telerian] tongue. Such were the people of the elf-kingdom in Northern Mirkwood, whence came Legolas. Lemberin [> Telerian] was the native tongue also of Celeborn and the Elves of the hidden land of Lórien. There the Common Speech was known only to a few, for that people strayed seldom from their borders.*

§19 The Elvish names that appear in this book are mainly of Noldorin form; but some are Lemberin [> Telerian], of which the chief are [*added:* Thranduil,] *Legolas, Lórien, Caras Galadon, Nimrodel, Amroth*; and also the names of the House of Dol Amroth: *Finduilas,* [*added:* Adrahil,] and *Imrahil*. The exiled Eldar still preserved in memory, as has been said, the High-elven Quenya; and it was from Noldorin visitors to the Shire that Bilbo (and from him Frodo) learned a little of that ancient speech. In Quenya is the polite greeting that Frodo addressed to Gildor (in Chapter III). The farewell song of Galadriel in Lórien (in Chapter) [*sic*] is also in Quenya. Tree-

---

* But the lady of that land, Galadriel, was of Noldorin race, and in her household that language was also spoken.

beard knew this tongue as the noblest of the 'hasty' languages, and frequently used it. His address to Galadriel and Celeborn is in Quenya; so are most of the words and names that he uses which are not in the Common Speech.[9]

§20 To speak last of Hobbits. According to accounts compiled in the Shire, the Hobbits, though in origin one race, became divided in remote antiquity into three somewhat different breeds: Stoors, Harfoots, and Fallohides, which have already been described. [*Struck out:*] No tradition, however, remains of any difference of speech between these three kinds.[10]

§21 Since Hobbits were a people more nearly akin to Men than any other of the speaking-folk of the ancient world, it might be supposed that they would possess a language of their own, different from the languages of Men but not unlike them. Yet of this there is no evidence in any record or tradition. Admittedly none of the legends of the Hobbits refer to times earlier than some centuries after the beginning of the Third Age, while their actual records did not begin until after the western Hobbits had settled down, somewhere about Third Age 1300; but it remains remarkable that all such traditions assume that the only language spoken by Hobbits of any kind was the Westron or Common Speech. They had, of course, many words and usages peculiar to themselves, but the same could be said of any other folk that used the Common Speech as a native tongue.

[*The latter part of this paragraph, following* any record or tradition, *was rewritten thus:* They had, of course, many words and usages peculiar to themselves, but the same could be said of any other folk that used the Westron as a native tongue. It is true that none of the legends of Hobbits refer to times earlier than some centuries after the beginning of the Third Age, while their actual records did not begin until after the western Hobbits had settled down, somewhere about Third Age 1300, and had then long adopted the Common Speech. Yet it remains remarkable that in all such traditions, if any tongue other than the Common Speech is mentioned, it is assumed that Hobbits spoke the language of Men among whom, or near whom, they dwelt.]

§22 Among Hobbits [*added:* now] there are two opinions. Some hold that originally they had a language peculiar to themselves. Others assert that from the beginning they spoke a Mannish tongue [> Mannish tongues], being in fact a branch of the race of Men. But in any case it is agreed that after migration to Eriador they soon adopted the Westron under the influence of the Dúnedain of the North-kingdom. The first opinion is now favoured by Hobbits [> is favoured by many Hobbits], because of their growing distaste for Men;* but there is in fact no trace to be discovered of any special Hobbit-language in antiquity. The second opinion is clearly the right one, and is held by those of most linguistic learning. Investigation not only of surviving Hobbit-lore but of the far more considerable records of Gondor supports it. All such enquiries show that before their crossing of the Mountains the Hobbits spoke the same language as Men in the higher vales of the Anduin, roughly between the Carrock and the Gladden Fields.†[11]

§23 Now that language was nearly the same as the language of the ancestors of the Rohirrim; and it was also allied, as has been said above, both to the languages of Men further north and east (as in Dale and Esgaroth), and to those further south from which the Westron itself was derived. It is thus possible to understand the rapidity with which evidently the Hobbits adopted the Common Speech as soon as they crossed into Eriador, where it had long been current. In this way, too, is explained the occurrence among the western and settled Hobbits of many peculiar words not found in the Common Speech but found in the tongues of Rohan and of Dale.‡[12]

* Supported, as it appears to them to be, by the fact that among themselves they speak now a private language, though this is probably only a descendant, the last to survive, of the old Common Speech.

† [*The following footnote was added:* Though the Stoors, especially the southern branch that long dwelt in the valley of the Loudwater, by Tharbad and on the borders of Dunland, appear to have acquired a language akin to Dunlandish, before they came north and adopted in their turn the Common Speech.]

‡ In Gandalf's view the people of 'Gollum' or Smeagol were of hobbit-kind. If so, their habits and dwelling-places mark them as Stoors. Yet it is plain that they spoke [> as Stoors; though they appear to have used] the Common Speech. Most probably they were a family or small clan that, owing to some quarrel or some sudden 'homesickness', turned back east and came down into Wilderland again beside the River Gladden. There are many references in Hobbit legend to families or small groups going off on their own 'into the wild', or returning 'home'. For eastern Eriador was less friendly and fertile than Wilderland and many of the tales speak of the hard times endured by the early emigrants. It may be noted, however, that the names *Deagol* and *Smeagol* [> *Déagol* and *Sméagol*] are both words belonging to the Mannish languages of the upper Anduin.

§24 An example of this is provided by the name *Stoor* itself. It seems originally to have meant 'big', and though no such word is found in the Common Speech, it is usual in the language of Dale. The curious Hobbit-word *mathom*, which has been mentioned, is clearly the same as the word *máthum* used in Rohan for a 'treasure' or a 'rich gift'. The horn given at parting to Meriadoc by the Lady Éowyn was precisely a *máthum*. Again, *smile* or *smial*, in Hobbit-language the word for an inhabited hole, especially one deep-dug and with a long, narrow, and often hidden entrance, seems related to the word *smygel* in Rohan meaning 'a burrow', and more remotely to the name *Smeagol* [> *Sméagol*] (cited [in the footnote to §23]), and to *Smaug* the name in [> among men of] the North for the Dragon of the Lonely Mountain.[13] But most remarkable of all are the Hobbit month-names, concerning which see the note on Calendar and Dates.[14]

§25 The Hobbits in the west-lands of Eriador became much mingled together, and eventually they began to settle down. Some of their lesser and earlier settlements had long disappeared and been forgotten in Bilbo's time; but one of the earliest to become important still endured, if much reduced in size. This was at Bree, and in the country round about. Long before the settlement at Bree Hobbits had adopted the Common Speech, and all the names of places that they gave were in that language; while the older names, of Elvish or forgotten Mannish origin,* they often translated (as *Fornost* to *Norbury*), or twisted into a familiar shape (as Elvish *Baranduin* 'brown river' to *Brandywine*).

[*The end of this paragraph was rewritten thus:* ... (as *Fornost* to *Norbury*). The Elvish names of hills and rivers often endured changed only to fit better into Hobbit speech. But the Brandywine is an exception. Its older name was the *Malvern*, derived from its Noldorin name *Malevarn*, but the new name appears in the earliest records. Both names refer to the river's colour, often in flood a golden brown, which is indeed the meaning of the

---

* The Men of Bree, who claimed, no doubt justly, to have dwelt in those regions from time out of mind, long before the coming of Elendil, had of course also adopted the Common Speech, but there were names in those parts that pointed to an older Mannish tongue, / only remotely connected if at all [> unconnected] with the language of the Fathers of Men, or Westron. *Bree* is said in that tongue to have signified 'hill', and *Chet* (as in *Chetwood*, *Archet*) 'forest'.

Elvish name. *This was further changed to read:* ... Of this the Brandywine is an example. Its Elvish name was the *Baranduin* 'brown river'. Both names refer to the river's colour, often in flood a golden brown, but the Hobbit name is historically only a picturesque alteration of the Noldorin name.]

§26 As soon as they had settled down the Hobbits took to letters. These they learned, with many other matters, from the Dúnedain; for the North-kingdom had not yet come to an end in Eriador at that time. The letters used by the Dúnedain, and learned and adopted by the Hobbits, were those of the Noldorin or Fëanorian alphabet (see below).[15] It was soon after their learning of letters, about Third Age 1300, that Hobbits began to set down and collect the considerable store of tales and legends and oral annals and genealogies that they already possessed. The lore-loving Fallohides played a chief part in this. The original documents had, of course, in Bilbo's time long been worn out or lost, but many of them had been much copied. When the Shire was colonized, about Third Age 1600, it is said that the leading families among the migrants took with them most of the writings then in existence.

§27 In the Shire, which proved a rich and comfortable country, the old lore was largely neglected; but there were always some Hobbits who studied it and kept it in memory; and copying and compilation, and even fictitious elaboration, still went on. In Bilbo's time there were in the book-hoards many manuscripts of lore more than 500 years old. The oldest known book, The Great Writ of Tuckborough, popularly called Yellowskin, was supposed to be nearly a thousand years old. It dealt in annalistic form with the deeds of Took notables from the foundation of the Shire, though its earliest hand belonged to a period at least four centuries later.

§28 In this way it came about that the Hobbits of the Shire, especially in the great families, such as Took, Oldbuck (later Brandybuck), and Bolger, developed the habit, strange and yet not unparallelled in our times, of giving names to their children derived not from their daily language nor from fresh invention, but from books and legends. These to the Hobbits high-sounding names were often in somewhat comic contrast with the more homely family names. Hobbits were, of course, fully aware of this contrast and amused by it.

[*The following passage was an addition:* The sections that follow are written mainly for those of linguistic curiosity.

Others may neglect them. For these histories are intelligible, if it is assumed that the Common Speech of the time was English, and that if any language of Men appears which is related to the Common Speech, though not the same, it will be represented by languages of our world that are related to English: as for example the archaic language of Rohan is represented by ancient English, or the related tongues of the far North (as in Dale) by names of a Norse character.

But this was not, of course, historically the case. None of the languages of the period were related discernibly to any now known or spoken. The substitution of English (or forms of speech related to modern English) for the Common Speech (and kindred tongues) of the day has involved a process of translation, not only of narrative and dialogue but also of nomenclature, which is described below, for the benefit of those interested in such matters.]

On Translation[16]

§29 The linguistic situation sketched above, simple* though it is compared with that observable in many European countries in our times, presents several problems to a translator who wishes to present a picture of Hobbit life and lore in those distant days; especially if he is more concerned to represent, as closely as he can, in terms now intelligible the actual feeling and associations of words and names than to preserve a mere phonetic accuracy.

§30 The Elven-tongues I have left untouched. I have in my selection and arrangement of matter from the once famous and much copied Red Book reduced the citations of these languages, apart from the unavoidable names of places and persons, to a minimum, keeping only enough to give some indication of their sound and style. That has not been altogether easy, since I have been obliged to transliterate the words and names from the rich and elegant Fëanorian alphabet, specially devised for them, into our own less adequate letters, and yet present forms that while reasonably close to the phonetic intentions of the originals are

---

* We are in fact in this book only primarily concerned with the Elvish Noldorin and the Mannish 'Common Speech' (with some local variations), while the Quenya or 'Elf-latin' and the archaic tongue of the Rohirrim and the Elvish Lemberin make an occasional appearance.

not (I hope) too strange or uncouth to modern eyes.*[17]

§31 My treatment of the Common Speech (and of languages connected with it) has, however, been quite different. It has been drastic, but I hope defensible. I have turned the Common Speech and all related things into the nearest English equivalents. First of all, the narrative and dialogue I have naturally been obliged to translate as closely as possible. The differences between the use of this speech in different places and by persons of higher and lower degree, e.g. by Frodo and by Sam, in the Shire and in Gondor, or among the Elves, I have tried to represent by variations in English of approximately the same kind. In the result these differences have, I fear, been somewhat obscured. The divergence of the vocabulary, idiom, and pronunciation in the free and easy talk of the Shire from the daily language of Gondor was really greater than is here represented, or could be represented without using a phonetic spelling for the Shire and an archaic diction for Gondor that would have puzzled or infuriated modern readers. The speech of Orcs was actually more filthy and degraded than I have shown it. If I had tried to use an 'English' more near to the reality it would have been intolerably disgusting and to many readers hardly intelligible.

§32 It will be observed that Hobbits such as Frodo, and other persons such as Aragorn and Gandalf, do not always use quite the same style throughout. This is intentional. Hobbits of birth and reading often knew much of higher and older forms of the Common Tongue than those of their colloquial Shire-usage, and they were in any case quick to observe and adopt a more archaic mode when conversing with Elves, or Men of high lineage. It was natural for much-travelled persons, especially for those who like Aragorn were often at pains to conceal their origin and business, to speak more or less according to the manner of the people among whom they found themselves.

Note

§33 I will here draw attention to a feature of the languages dealt with that has presented some difficulty. All these languages, Mannish and Elvish, had, or originally had, no distinction between the singular and plural of the second

---

* A note on my spelling and its intended values will be found below.

person pronouns; but they had a marked distinction between the *familiar* forms and the *courteous*.

§34 This distinction was fully maintained in all Elvish tongues, and also in the older and more elevated forms of the Common Speech, notably in the daily usage of Gondor. In Gondor the courteous forms were used by men to all women, irrespective of rank, other than their lovers, wives, sisters, and children. To their parents children used the courteous forms throughout their lives, as soon as they had learned to speak correctly. Among grown men the courteous form was used more sparingly, chiefly to those of superior rank and office, and then mainly on official or formal occasions, unless the superior was also of greater age. Old people were often addressed with the courteous form by much younger men or women, irrespective of all other considerations.

§35 It was one of the most notable features of Shire-speech that the courteous form had in Bilbo's time disappeared from the daily use, though its forms were not wholly forgotten: a reversal of the case of *thou* and *you* in English. It lingered still among the more rustic Hobbits, but then, curiously enough, only as an endearment. It was thus used both by and to parents and between dear friends.

§36 Most of these points cannot be represented in English; but it may be remembered by readers that this is one of the features referred to when people of Gondor speak of the strangeness of hobbit-language. Pippin, for instance, used the familiar form throughout his first interview with the Lord Denethor. This may have amused the aged Steward, but it must have astonished the servants that overheard him. No doubt this free use of the familiar form was one of the things that helped to spread the popular rumour in the City that Pippin was a person of very high rank in his own country.

§37 Only in a few places where it seemed specially important have I attempted to represent such distinctions in translation, though this cannot be done systematically. Thus *thou* and *thee* and *thy* have occasionally been used (as unusual and archaic in English) to represent a ceremonious use of the courteous form, as in the formal words spoken at the coronation of Aragorn. On the other hand the sudden use of *thou, thee* in the dialogue of Faramir and Éowyn is meant to represent (there being no other means of doing this in English) a significant change from the courteous to the familiar. The *thee* used by Sam

Gamgee to Rose at the end of the book is intentional, but corresponds there to his actual use of the old-fashioned courteous form as a sign of affection.

§38 Passing from the translation of narrative and dialogue to *names* I found yet greater difficulties. For it seemed to me that to preserve all names, Elvish and Westron alike, in their original forms would obscure an essential feature of the times, as observed by the ears and eyes of Hobbits, through whom for the most part we are ourselves observing them: the contrast between a wide-spread language, as ordinary and diurnal to the people of that day as is English now to English-speakers, and the remains of far older more reverend and more secret tongues. All names, if merely transliterated, would seem to modern readers equally strange and remote.

§39 For instance, if I had left unaltered not only the Elvish name *Imladrist* [> *Imladris*] but also the Westron name *Carbandur*, both would have appeared alien. But the contrast between *Imladrist* [> *Imladris*] and *Rivendell*, a translation of *Carbandur*[18] and like it having a plain meaning in everyday language, represents far more truly the actual feeling of the day, especially among Hobbits. To refer to Rivendell as *Imladrist* [> *Imladris*] was to Men and Hobbits as if one now was to speak of Winchester as Camelot. Save that the identity was certain, while in Rivendell there still dwelt a lord of renown older than Arthur would be, were he still living in Winchester today.

§40 To translate the names in the Common Speech into English in this way has the advantage also that it often, as in the case of Rivendell, provides the key to the meaning of the Elvish name as well; for the one was frequently a direct translation of the other. This is not, however, always so. Some place-names have no meaning now discernible and derive, no doubt, from still older and forgotten days. In some cases the names had different meanings in different tongues. Thus the C.S. *Dwarrowdelf**[19] was a translation of the Dwarvish name *Khazad-dûm*,

---

* That is 'Dwarves' mine'. I have translated the actual C.S. *Phūru-nargian* as *Dwarrowdelf*, since in Bilbo's time the word *phūru* (related to *phur-* 'to delve') was obsolete in ordinary speech, and *nargian* contained a derivative form of *narac* 'dwarf' that had long disappeared from use. *Dwarrow* is what the ancient English genitive plural *dwerga* 'of dwarves' would have become had it survived in use or in a place-name.

whereas the Elvish name *Moria* (older *Mornyā*) meant 'black pit'.

§41 The nomenclature of the Hobbits themselves and of the places in which they lived has, nonetheless, presented some obstacles to the satisfactory carrying out of this process of translation. Their place-names, being (in the Shire especially) almost all originally of C.S. form, have proved least difficult. I have converted them into as nearly similar English terms as I could find, using the elements found in English place-names that seemed suitable both in sense and in period: that is in being still current (like *hill*), or slightly altered or reduced from current words (like *ton* beside *town*), or no longer found outside place-names (like *wich*, *bold*, *bottle*). The Shire seems to me very adequately to translate the Hobbit *Sūza-t*, since this word was now only used by them with reference to their country, though originally it had meant 'a sphere of occupation (as of the land claimed by a family or clan), of office, or business'. In Gondor the word *sūza* was still applied to the divisions of the realm, such as Anórien, Ithilien, Lebennin, for which in Noldorin the word *lhann* was used. Similarly *farthing* has been used for the four divisions of the Shire, because the Hobbit word *tharni* was an old word for 'quarter' seldom used in ordinary language, where the word for 'quarter' was *tharantīn* 'fourth part'. In Gondor *tharni* was used for a silver coin, the fourth part of the *castar* (in Noldorin the *canath* or fourth part of the *mirian*).[20]

§42 The personal names of the Hobbits were, however, much more awkward to manage on this system. Rightly or wrongly, I have attempted to translate these also into English terms, or to substitute equivalents, wherever possible. Many of the family names have more or less obvious meanings in the Common Speech: such as *Goodenough*, *Bracegirdle*, *Proudfoot*, *Burrows*, and the like, and these can fairly be treated in the same way as the place-names.* In these cases translation will not, I think, be quarrelled with, and may even be allowed to be necessary. For if his name clearly meant to contemporaries 'horn-blower', it is truer to the facts to call a character Hornblower than *Raspūta*,[21] which though the actual Hobbit

---

* Some family-names, but fewer than in England, for the use of such names outside a few 'great families' was of more recent development, were actually place-names or derived from them. *Gamgee* is one (see below).

sound-form is now meaningless. But, of course, if a large part of the names are thus anglicized the rest must be made to fit; for a mixture of English and alien names would give a wholly false impression. It is thus with the less clearly interpretable names that difficulties arise. Some are border-line cases, such as *Baggins* itself, which because of its importance I have dealt with below more fully. Some defy translation, since they were to the Hobbits themselves just 'names', of forgotten origin and meaning. *Tūc*,[22] for instance, the name of the most eminent of the 'great families' of the Shire. According to their own tradition *tūca* was an old word meaning 'daring',[23] but this appears to be a wholly unfounded guess; and I have in this case been content with anglicization of the form to *Took*.

§43 More debatable, perhaps, has been my procedure with the many curious names that Shire-hobbits, as observed above, gave to their children. Here I long hesitated between leaving them alone, and finding equivalents for them. I have in the end compromised. I have left some unaltered. These are the not uncommon names which even to Hobbits had no 'meaning' or derivation or connexion with books or legends: names such as *Bilbo, Bungo, Bingo, Polo, Porro, Ponto*. Hobbits readily coined such names, and I do not think that the impression made by them in their day differed much from their effect today.*[24] But it would have given a very false impression of Hobbitry to the modern reader, if these personal names had in general been simply transliterated. All would then have today sounded equally outlandish, whereas to Hobbits personal names had many gradations of association and suggestion. Some derived from early history and ancient Hobbit-legend; some from stories about Elves and Men and even about dwarves and giants. Some were rare, others familiar; some comic in tone, others romantic or elevated; some were of high and some of lower social standing.

§44 It seemed to me that, once embarked on translation, even of dialogue, names of this sort would be best represented by drawing on the similar wealth of names that we find or could find in our own traditions, in Celtic, Frankish, Latin and Greek and other sources.

§45 This method entails, of course, far-reaching alteration

---

* In fact they ended as a rule in *a (Bunga)* not *o*, since an ending *a* was as a rule masculine. I have changed the *a* to *o*.

of the actual phonetic forms of such given-names; but I do not feel it more illegitimate than altering *Raspūta* to *Hornblower*, or indeed than translating the dialogue of the Red Book into English, whereby naturally its true sound is changed and many of its verbal points are obscured. I have, in any case, done the 'translation' with some care. The fondness of families for runs of similar names, or of fathers for giving to their sons names that either alliterated with their own or had a similar ending, has been duly represented.* The choice of equivalents has been directed partly by meaning (where this is discernible in the original names), partly by general tone, and partly by length and phonetic style. The heroic and romantic names, of Fallohide legend according to the Hobbits, specially but not solely affected by Tooks, have been represented by names of a Germanic or Frankish cast. 'Classical' names or ones of similar form on the other hand represent usually names derived by Hobbits from tales of ancient times and far kingdoms of Men.†[25]

§46 Hobbits very frequently gave their daughters flower-names. But even these are not so simple to deal with as might be expected. Where the flower is certainly to be identified I have naturally translated the name into English (or botanical Latin). But not all the wild flowers of the Shire, and certainly not all the flowers cultivated in its gardens can be identified with flowers that are now familiar. In cases of doubt I have done the best that I could. For instance: I have translated *Hamanullas*[26] by *Lobelia*, because although I do not know precisely what flower is intended, *hamanullas* appears to have been usually small and blue and cultivated in gardens, and the word seems to have been a gardener's rather than a popular name.

§47 For the benefit of the curious in such matters I add here a few notes in supplement of what has been said above to illustrate my procedure.

---

* The curious alternation between initial H and initial I in the names of the Old Took's many children represents an actual alternation between S and E.

† Thus the perhaps to us rather ridiculous subnames or titles of the Brandybucks adopted by the heads of the family, *Astyanax*, *Aureus*, *Magnificus*, were originally half-jesting and were in fact drawn from traditions about the Kings at Norbury. [This note was later struck out.]

Family names

Took   Hobbit *Tūc*, as noted above.[27]

Baggins   H. *Labingi*. It is by no means certain that this name is really connected with C.S. *labin* 'a bag'; but it was believed to be so, and one may compare *Labin-nec* 'Bag End' as the name of the residence of Bungo Baggins *(Bunga Labingi)*. I have accordingly rendered the name *Labingi* by *Baggins*, which gives, I think, a very close equivalent in readily appreciable modern terms.

Brandybuck   Earlier *Oldbuck*. These are direct translations of H. *Assargamba* [> *Brandugamba*] and *Zaragamba*.[28] [Added: *Zaragamba* is translated by sense, but since *Zaragamba* (Old-buck) was altered to *Brandugamba* by adoption of the first half of the river-name *(Branduhim)* I have used for it *Brandybuck*. For the treatment of the river-name *Branduhim* see (the note at the end of the text, §58).]

Bolger   Merely an anglicized form of H. *Bolgra*. By chance in C.S. *bolg-* has much the same significance as our 'bulge', so that if *Bolger* suggests to a modern reader a certain fatness and rotundity, so did *Bolgra* in its own time and place.

Boffin   Anglicized from H. *Bophan*. This was said (by members of the family) to mean 'one who laughs loud'. I thought at first, therefore, of rendering it by *Loffin*; but since, as in the case of *Took*, the family tradition is a mere guess, while in C.S. *Bophan* had in fact no suggestion of laughter, I have remained content with a slight anglicization.[29]

Gamgee   H. *Galbassi*. A difficult name. According to family tradition (in this case reliable) duly set out by Sam Gamgee at the end of the Red Book, this name was really derived from a place-name: *Galb(b)as*. That name I have closely rendered by Gamwich (to be pronounced *Gammidge*), comparing *galb-* = *Gam* with C.S. *galap, galab-* = 'game'; and the ending *bas* in place-names with our *-wick, -wich*. *Galbassi* may thus be fairly represented by *Gammidgee*. In adopting the spelling *Gamgee* I have been led astray by Sam Gamgee's connexion with the family of Cotton into a jest which though Hobbit-like enough does not really reside in the suggestions of the names *Galbassi* and *Lothran* to people of the Shire.[30]

Cotton   H. *Lothran*. A not uncommon village name in the Shire, corresponding closely to our *Cotton (cot-tūn)*, being derived from C.S. *hlotho* 'a two-roomed dwelling', and *rān* 'a village, a small group of dwellings on a hill-side'. But in this case the name may be an alteration of *hloth-ram(a)*, 'cotman, cottager'. *Lothram*, which I have rendered *Cotman*, was the name of Farmer Cotton's grandfather. It is notable that, though the resemblance is not so complete as between our *Cotton* and the noun *cotton*, in C.S. the words *luthur*, *luthran* meant 'down, fluff'. But unfortunately no such suggestions are associated with *Galbas*, and the village of that name was known only locally for rope-making, and no tissues were produced there of any fibre softer than hemp.

§48 *Hobbit*

Hobbit This, I confess, is my own invention; but not one devised at random. This is its origin. It is, for one thing, not wholly unlike the actual word in the Shire, which was *cūbuc* (plural *cūbugin*).* But this *cūbuc* was not a word of general use in the Common Speech and required an equivalent that though natural enough in an English context did not actually occur in standard English. Some Hobbit-historians have held that *cūbuc* was an ancient native word, perhaps the last survivor of their own forgotten language. I believe, however, that this is not the case. The word is, I think, a local reduction of an early C.S. name given to Hobbits, or adopted by them in self-description, when they came into contact with Men. It appears to be derived from an obsolete *cūbug* 'hole-dweller', which elsewhere fell out of use. In support of this I would point to the fact that Meriadoc himself actually records that the King of Rohan used the word *cūgbagu* 'hole-dweller' for *cūbuc* or 'Hobbit'. Now the Rohirrim spoke a language that was in effect an archaic form of the Common Speech.† The

---

*For another, I must admit that its faint suggestion of *rabbit* appealed to me. Not that hobbits at all resembled rabbits, unless it be in burrowing. Still, a jest is a jest as all *cūbugin* will allow, and after all it does so happen that the coney (well-known in the Shire if not in ancient England) was called *tapuc*, a name recalling *cūbuc*, if not so clearly as *hobbit* recalls *rabbit*. [This note was later struck out.]

†More accurately: the tongue of the Mark of Rohan was derived from a northern speech which, belonging at first to the Middle Anduin, had later moved north to the upper waters of that river,
continued on page 50

primitive form represented by Rohan *cūg-bagu* would in the later C.S. have acquired the form *cūbug(u)*, and so Hobbit *cūbuc*.[31] Since, as is explained below, I have represented C.S. by modern English and have therefore turned the language of Rohan into archaic English terms also, I have converted the archaic *cūgbagu* of Rohan into an ancient English *hol-bytla* 'hole-dweller'. Of this *hol-bytla* (with the common loss of *l* in English between *a*, *o*, *u*, and *b*, *m*, *v*) my fictitious *hobbit* would be a not impossible local 'corruption'.

§49 Personal names

Bilbo   The actual H. name was *Bilba*, as explained above.[32]

Frodo   On the other hand the H. name was *Maura*.[33] This was not a common name in the Shire, but I think it probably once had a meaning, even if that had long been forgotten. No word *maur-* can be found in the contemporary C.S., but again recourse to comparison with the language of Rohan is enlightening. In that language there was an adjective *maur-*, no longer current at this time, but familiar in verse or higher styles of speech; it meant 'wise, experienced'. I have, therefore, rendered *Maura* by *Frodo*, an old Germanic name, that appears to contain the word *frōd* which in ancient English corresponded closely in meaning to Rohan *maur*.

Meriadoc (Merry)   The real name was *Chilimanzar* [> *Cilimanzar*], a high-sounding and legendary name. I have chosen Meriadoc for the following reasons. Buckland in many ways occupied a position with regard to the Shire such as Wales does to England; and it is not wholly inappropriate, therefore, to represent its many very peculiar names by names of a Celtic or specifically Welsh character. Among such names I chose *Meriadoc*, mainly because it gives naturally a shortening 'Merry'; for the abbreviation of *Chilimanzar* [> *Cilimanzar*] by which this character was usually known was *Chilic* [> *Cilic*], a C.S. word meaning exactly 'gay or merry'.[34]

---

before coming south in the days of Eorl. It was thus nearly akin to the language of the lower Anduin, the basis of the C.S., but isolated in the North it had changed far less and had remained little mingled with alien words.

Peregrin (Pippin) The H. name was *Razanul* [> *Razanur*]. This was the name of a legendary traveller, and probably contains the C.S. elements *raza* 'stranger', *razan* 'foreign'. I therefore chose *Peregrin* to represent it, though it does not fit quite so well. Of *Peregrin*, *Pippin* is I suppose a not impossible 'pet-form'; but it is not so close to its original, as is *Razal* [> *Razar*] (a kind of small red apple) by which abbreviation *Razanul Tūca* [> *Razanur Tūc*] was almost inevitably known to his contemporaries.[35]

Sam His real name was *Ban*, short for *Banzīr*. In C.S. *ba-*, *ban-* occurred in many words with the meaning 'half-, almost', while *zīr(a)* meant 'wise'. I have therefore translated his name by ancient English *samwīs* of similar sense. This was convenient, since *Samwise* will yield an abbreviation *Sam*. Now *Ban* was a common short name in the Shire, but was usually then derived from the more elevated name *Bannātha*, as *Sam* is with us usually shortened from *Samuel*.[36]

The following passage (§§50–1) is a note (a part of the manuscript as originally written) to the name *Samuel*, but in appearance is a part of the main text, and is most conveniently given so.

§50 It will be observed that I have not [> rarely] used Scriptural names or names of Hebraic origin to represent Hobbit-names. There is nothing in Hobbit lore or history that corresponds [*added:* closely] to this element in our names. *Bildad*, a name occurring among the Bolgers, is an accidental resemblance; it is a genuine Hobbit name which I have left unaltered. Other abbreviations like *Tom* and *Mat* I have also often left unchanged. Many such monosyllables were current in the Shire, but were the shortenings of genuine Hobbit names. For instance *Tom* of *Tomacca*, *Tomburān*; *Mat* of *Mattalic*; *Bill (Bil)* of *Bildad (Bildat)*, *Bilcuzal*, or any of the numerous names ending in *-bil*, *-mil*, as *Arambil*. Farmer Cotton's full name was in fact *Tomacca Lothran*.[37] [*Added:* *Tobias* (Hornblower) is an exception. I have used this name because the resemblance of the real Hobbit-name *Tōbi* was so close, and it seemed inevitable to translate *Zāra-tōbi* by 'Old Toby'; no other name could be found to fit so well. *This was changed to:* *Tobias* (Hornblower) is not an exception. *Tobias* was his real name, though accented *Tóbias*. I have retained this name because the resemblance of the real Hobbit-name was so close, &c.]

§51 *Barnabas* is [*added:* not] an exception. *Barnabas*

Butterbur was a Man of Bree, not a hobbit. I gave him this name for various reasons. First of all a personal one. On an old grey stone in a quiet churchyard in southern England I once saw in large letters the name *Barnabas Butter*. That was long ago and before I had seen the Red Book, but the name came back to me when the character of the stout innkeeper of Bree was presented to me in Frodo's record. The more so because his name, in agreement with the generally botanical type of name favoured in Bree, was actually *Butterburr*, or in the C.S. *Zilbarāpha* [> *Zilbirāpha*]. *Barnabas* has unfortunately only a very slight phonetic similarity to the real first-name of the innkeeper: *Barabatta* (or *Batti*). This was the nickname of the landlord of 'The Pony' which he had borne so long that if he ever had another given-name it had been forgotten: it means 'quick-talker or babbler'. Still, in converting *Batti Zilbarāpha* [> *Zilbirāpha*] into *Barney Butterbur* I do not think I have been unjust.[38]

§52 A final consequence of the conversion of the Common Speech, and of all names formed in that language, into English terms has already been referred to above. It entailed translation of the related languages of Rohan and the North into terms that would correspond linguistically, as closely as possible, to the ancient situation.

§53 In the records of the Red Book there are in several places allusions to the fact that Hobbits hearing the tongue of the Riders of Rohan felt that it was akin to their own, and recognized some of the words used, though they could not understand the language as a whole. Since I had, necessarily, converted the C.S. of the Hobbits into English, it seemed to me that it would be absurd then to leave the related language of Rohan in its wholly alien form. Now the tongue of the Rohirrim was not only related to the C.S., but it had remained in a much more archaic state, and it was, even in its newer southern home, much less mingled with alien (Noldorin and Quenya) words; I therefore substituted for it a form of language resembling Old English, since this tongue, that was removed from its ancestral home to another, closely corresponds in its relation to modern English (especially in its freedom from accretions of French and Latin origin) with the relations of the tongues of the Shire and the Mark.

§54 This translation was not difficult, since the Rohirrim in fact used a very similar type of nomenclature to that of our own ancestors. I have usually considered the sense of their names rather than the form; except that I have chosen names in Old English of the same length, where possible, and have only used compound names, such as *Fréawine*, *Éomer*, *Éowyn*, *Hasufel*, *Halifirien*, when the originals were also compounded. The element *éo-*, which so often appears (not unnaturally, being an old word meaning 'horse', among a people devoted to horses), represents an element *loho-*, *lō-* of the same sense. Thus *Éothéod*, 'Horse-folk' or 'Horse-land', translates *Lohtūr*. *Théoden*, as are many of the other royal names, is an old word for 'king', corresponding to Rohan *tūrac-*.[39]

§55 Note. In a few cases I have, not quite consistently, modified the words and names of the Mark, making them more like modern English, especially in spelling. Examples of this process in varying degrees are: *Dunharrow* (= *Dūn-harug* 'hill-sanctuary'), *Starkhorn*, *Entwash*, *Helm's Deep*, *Combe* (= *Cumb*); *Halifirien* (= *Hálig-firgen* 'holy-mountain'); *Fenmarch* for *Fenmerce*; *Shadowfax* for *Scadufax*. In a similar way in 'The Hobbit' *Oakenshield* was anglicized from *Eikinskialdi*. The name *Rohan* itself is of Noldorin origin, a translation of the native *Lōgrad* (sc. *Éo-marc* 'the Horse-mark' or 'Borderland of the Horsemen'). Its strictly correct form was *Rochann*, but the form *Rohan* represents the actual pronunciation of Gondor, in which medial *ch* was colloquially weakened to *h*.

§56 This translation had a disadvantage which I did not foresee. The 'linguistic notes' on the origin of peculiar Hobbit words had also to be 'translated'. I have already alluded to the translation of the actual relation of Rohan *cūgbagu* and Shire *cūbuc* into an imagined one of *holbytla* and *hobbit*. Other examples are these (cf. [§24]): *Stoor* in relation to a Northern word meaning 'big' (cf. Scandinavian *stór-* 'big') is a translation of actual Hobbit *tung*[40] in relation to a similar word in Dale. Supposed Hobbit *mathom* in relation to Rohan (that is Old English) *māthum* is a translation of actual Hobbit *cast* (older *castu*) compared with Rohan *castu*.

§57 Similarly, Rohan *smygel*, actually an Old English word for a burrow, related to a Northern stem *smug* / *sméag* (*smaug*),[41] here represents the genuine Rohan *trahan* related to Hobbit *trān*. From *smygel* I have derived an imaginary modern *smile* (or *smial*) having a similar relation to the older form. *Sméagol* and *Déagol* are thus Old English equivalents for actual

Trahand and *Nahand* 'apt to creep into a hole' and 'apt to hide, secretive' respectively. (*Smaug*, the Dragon's name, is a representation in similar terms, in this case of a more Scandinavian character, of the Dale name *Trāgu*, which was probably related to the *trah-* stem in the Mark and Shire.)

§58 *Note*. In cases where 'folk-etymology' has operated to alter older (Elvish) names into the appearance of names in the C.S. special difficulty may be met, since it is unlikely that suitable words will be found in modern English that will at once translate the C.S. name and yet also have some similarity in sound to the Elvish name. The chief example is that of the River *Baranduin*, the ancient boundary eastward of the Shire. This is an Elvish name composed of *baran* 'golden-brown' and *duin* '(large) river'. But it was by the Hobbits picturesquely perverted into *Branduhim*, signifying in their tongue 'foaming beer' (*brand(u)* 'foam'; *hīm(a)* 'beer'). I have imitated this by calling the river the *Brandywine*, similar in sound and a very possible 'corruption' of *Baranduin*, although the sense is not very closely similar. (There is, in fact, no evidence for the distillation of brandy in the Shire.)

§59 For the same reasons the Northern, or rather North-easterly, 'outer' names of the Dwarves taken from the Mannish languages of that region have been all given a Scandinavian style: they are indeed all genuine Norse dwarf-names.[42]

NOTES

1 The idea of the three kinds of Hobbit, Harfoots, Stoors, and Fallohides, arose in the first of the two texts (F 1), and was then transferred (before the second text F 2 was written) to the *Prologue* (see note 10 below, and p. 10). But the text of the latter (P 5) in which it appeared gave only the old story of Bilbo and Gollum, and thus must have been earlier than July 1950: see p. 7.

2 F 1 as written had 'Human', subsequently changed to 'Mannish'; this term occurs later in F 1 as first written. See the commentary on §2.

3 *Atani*: in F 1 as written no Elvish name appears here, but *Atanatári* was added in the margin, then changed to *Atanni* (so spelt).

4 As originally written, F 1 had: 'In that war the Fathers of Men aided the Elves, and lived with them and fought beside them; and their chieftains learned the Noldorin speech, and some indeed forsook their own tongue, even in the daily use of their own

houses.' This was changed to: 'In that war three houses of the Fathers of Men aided the Elves, and lived with them and fought beside them; and the people of these houses learned the Noldorin speech, and forsook their own tongue.' On this see the commentary on §7.

The final reading in F 2, 'the lords of these houses learned the Noldorin speech', belongs with the changes made in §9 and §13 introducing Adûnaic, which were made after the third version of the text had been written, or was at any rate in progress (see pp. 74–5).

5   Throughout F 2 the name was written *Dúnedein*, subsequently corrected at all occurrences to *Dúnedain* (the spelling in F 1). This is not further indicated in the text printed, where I have spelt the name in the usual form.

6   At first F 1 read here: 'This tongue was in Noldorin called *Falathren* "Shore-language", but by its speakers Westnish or the Common Speech.' The name *Westnish* was used throughout F 1, changed everywhere to *Westron* (see the commentary on §9). The present sentence was altered to read: '... but by its speakers *Undūna* (that is Westron) or *Sōval Phārë* the Common Speech.'

7   F 1 has: 'First: the Númenóreans had not been wholly sundered from the Eldar that remained in Middle-earth, and there had been much coming and going between Númenor and the westlands.'

8   After 'in the days of its blessedness' F 1 has: 'and there the language of the Kings of Men had changed little and slowly. And the like may be said of the Eldar.'

9   For the passage in F 2 concerning Treebeard F 1 has: 'As was natural in one so ancient Treebeard also knew this tongue, and such words and names as he is here recorded to have used, other than those in the Common Speech, are Quenya.'

10 F 1 is here altogether different. Following the words 'To speak last of Hobbits' it continues:

> These were a people who, as has been said, were more nearly akin to Men than any other of the speaking-peoples of the ancient world. Their language must then be supposed to have been of similar kind and origin to the language of Men. But, owing to the absence of all records among the Hobbits before their settlement in the West, the remoter history of Hobbit-language is difficult and obscure. [*This passage was struck out.*]
>
> Among the Hobbits of the Shire, though a love of learning was far from general (unless it be of genealogical lore), there were always some few, especially in the greater families, who were lore-masters, and gathered information concerning older times and distant lands, either from their own traditions, or from Elves and Men and Dwarves. According to the accounts thus compiled in the Shire, Hobbits, though originally one

race, became divided in remote antiquity into three somewhat different kinds: Stoors, Harfoots, and Fallohides.

Here there follows in F 1 an account of the three kinds that is already very close to that in the *Prologue* (FR pp. 12–13); and it is clear that it was here that the conception of the three Hobbit-kinds first entered (see the commentary on §20). It is notable that while the actual wording of F 1 was little changed subsequently, the Stoors were at first placed before the Harfoots, and a part of the description of the Harfoots was at first applied to the Stoors and vice versa.

> The Stoors were broader, heavier in build, and had less hair on their feet and more on their chins, and preferred flat lands and riversides. [*Added:* Their feet and hands were large.] The Harfoots were browner of skin, smaller and shorter, and they were beardless and bootless; they preferred highlands and hillsides. [*Added:* Their hands and feet were neat and nimble.] The Fallohides were fairer of skin and often of hair, and were taller than the others; they were lovers of trees and woodlands. [*Added:* All Hobbits were 'good shots' with stone, sling or bow, but the Fallohides were the surest on the mark.]
>
> The Stoors [> Harfoots] had much to do with Dwarves in ancient times, and long lived in the foothills of the Misty Mountains. They moved westward early, and crossed the Mountains and roamed over the land of Eriador beyond, as far as Weathertop or further, while the others were still in Wilderland. [*Struck out:* The Harfoots lingered long by the Great River, and were friendly with Men. They came westward after the Stoors.] They were probably the most normal and representative variety of Hobbits and were certainly the most numerous. They were the most inclined to settle, and the most addicted to living in holes and tunnels. [*Added:* The Stoors lingered by the banks of the Great River, and were friendly with Men. They came westward after the Harfoots, owing to the great increase of Men in Anduin Vale according to the[ir] tales, and followed the course of the Bruinen (or Loudwater) southwards.] The Fallohides were the least numerous, a northerly branch. ...

The text F 1 then proceeds in almost the same words as in the *Prologue*, as far as 'they were often found as leaders or chieftains among clans of Stoors or Harfoots' (FR p. 13). At this point there is a footnote:

> Thus it is said to have been clans of a still markedly Stoorish strain that first moved on west again from Bree and colonized the Shire, attracted originally to the riverbanks of the Baranduin. In Bilbo's time the inhabitants of the Marish in the East

THE APPENDIX ON LANGUAGES 57

Farthing, and also of Buckland, still showed Stoorish characteristics. Yet even there the chief families, notably the Brandybucks, had a strong Fallohidish strain in their make-up.

(On this see the commentary on §20.)

Before F 2 was written the account of the Harfoots, Stoors, and Fallohides was removed to stand in the *Prologue*, where at its first appearance it had almost word for word its form in the published work (see p. 10).

From this point F 1 continues as the basis for the F 2 version from §§21 ff.

11 For this paragraph F 1 reads as follows:

> More recent enquiries have failed, it is true, to find any trace of a special Hobbit language, but they do suggest that Westnish [> Westron] was not in fact the oldest language spoken by this people. The very earliest glimpses of Hobbits to be caught, either in their own legends or those of their neighbours, show them rather to have at that time spoken the language of Men in the higher vale of Anduin, roughly between the Carrock and the Gladden Fields.

The footnote here in F 1 corresponds in subject to that in F 2 at the end of §23, and reads:

> If Gandalf's theory is correct the people of Gollum must have been a late-lingering group of Stoors in the neighbourhood of the Gladden. And it may be that the memories of Smeagol provide one of the earliest glimpses of Hobbitry that we have. It may be noted therefore that *Deagol* and *Smeagol* are both words in the languages of Anduin-vale.

12 The footnote here in F 1 (see note 11) reads:

> Of course, since the Common Speech was itself derived from a related speech, it may sometimes have happened that the Hobbits preserved in use a word that had once been more widely current in Westnish [> Westron].

13 F 1 has here: 'and to the name of the Dragon *Smaug* (if that is a name given to him by the northern men of Dale, as seems likely).'

14 F 1 does not have the reference to the Hobbit month-names, but introduces a paragraph that was not taken up here in F 2 (cf. §28, which appears also in F 1).

> Hobbits therefore appear from their linguistic history to have had in early times a special aptitude for adopting language from their neighbours, and in no other point is this better illustrated than in their giving of names. They had of course many names of their own invention – usually short and often comic in sound (to us and to Hobbits) – but from very

early times they had also in traditional use a wealth of other names drawn not from the language of daily use but from their legends and histories and fictitious tales which dealt by no means solely with their own heroes and adventures, but with Elves and Men and Dwarves and even giants.

15 This is a reference to the conclusion of the text, which is omitted in this book (see note 42).
16 The heading *On Translation* is absent in F 1.
17 For the reference of the footnote at this point see note 15. In F 1 the footnote reads: 'A note on the spelling and intended pronunciation of the Elvish words and names will be found at the beginning of the Index.'
18 In a draft of this passage in F 1 the Westron name of Imladris was *Karbandul*.
19 The footnote to the name *Dwarrowdelf* differs somewhat in F 1. The Common Speech name of Moria was *Kubalnarga* (changed to *Kubalnargia*), translated as *Dwarrowdelf* 'since in Bilbo's time the word *kubal* (related to *kubu* "delve") was obsolete in ordinary speech, and *narga* [> *nargia*] contained a plural [> derivative] form of *narag* "dwarf" that had long disappeared from use. *Dwarrows* is what our older *dwergas* would have become if the singular *dwarf* from older *dwerh* had not replaced it, long ago.' Subsequently the C.S. name was changed in F 1 to *Satun-nargia*, and finally to *Phurun-nargia* (with corresponding changes of *kubal, kubu* to *phurūn, phur-*).
20 The whole of the discussion in §41 of the name *Sūza* of the Shire and the reason for the use of 'Farthing' is lacking in F 1; but after the reference to English *wich, bold, bottle* there is a footnote which was not taken up in F 2:

> In one case I have coined a word: *smial* (or *smile* if you prefer it so). The Hobbits used a peculiar word of their own, *gluva* [*written later nearby:* Rohan *glōba*], for 'an inhabited hole'. I would have left it unchanged but it would have looked outlandish in an English context. Accordingly I have used *smial*, since the ancient English *smygel* 'a hole to creep in' would, had it survived or been adopted by latterday Hobbits, have now had some such form.

21 In F 1 the Hobbit name for 'Hornblower' was *Rhaspûtal*, changed to *Raspûta* as in F 2.
22 In F 1 my father first wrote *Tûk* but emended it to *Tûca*; in F 2 he wrote *Tûca*, but then erased the final *-a*.
23 In F 1 the adjective *tûca* was described as 'a Fallohide word meaning "great"', corrected to the reading of F 2.
24 The footnote at this point concerning the masculine ending *-a* is absent in F 1.

25 The footnote concerning the 'to us rather ridiculous subnames or titles' of the heads of the Brandybuck clan is absent in F 1. See the commentary on §45.
26 *Hamanullas*: in F 1 the name was *Amanullith*, subsequently changed to *Hamanulli*.
27 In F 1 the name was *Tûk*, later corrected to *Tūca*, as previously (see note 22).
28 The names in F 1 were *Shûran-kaphir* and *Zarkaphir*, changed to *Assargamba* and *Zaragamba* as in F 2.
29 F 1 has the same note, but in addition it is said that *Bophan* was 'of Harfoot origin', and also that 'to Hobbits in general *Bophan* was as devoid of meaning as *Boffin* today.'
30 In F 1 the account of *Gamgee* was the same, but the underlying names were different: the Hobbit name was *Charbushi*, derived from the place-name *Charb(b)ash*; the Common Speech word meaning 'game' was *charab*; and the place-name ending was *-bash, -bas*. These forms were then corrected to those in F 2. *Charbash* appears again in the note on *Cotton* in F 1.
31 In F 1 the Shire word for 'Hobbit' was *kubud* and the obsolete Common Speech word from which it was derived was *kubud(u)r* 'hole-dweller'; Théoden's word was *kugbadru*. These forms were then changed: the Shire word became *cubut* (plural *cubudil*), derived from obsolete C.S. *cubadul*, and Théoden's word *cugbadul*.

In F 2 *cūbuc* and the associated words and forms were all first written *cu-*, changed to *cū-*. The Common Speech and Rohan forms were a good deal altered in the text and I have given only those finally adopted: thus the plural of *cūbuc* was first *cūbuga* and then *cūbugen*, the obsolete C.S. word was *cūbugl(a)*, and the Rohan word was *cūgbagul* (again in §56).
32 In F 1 it is said that '*Bilbo* is the actual Hobbit name': see note 24.
33 In F 1 the name was written *Maurō* before being changed to *Maura*.
34 The note in F 1 on the true name of Meriadoc is the same, but with the spellings *Khilimanzar, Khilik*.
35 The note on *Peregrin (Pippin)* read in F 1, before emendation:

The Hobbit name is *Rabanul*. This is not a name of C.S. form; it is said to be [Fallohide >] a Harfoot name; but since it is also said to mean 'traveller', and was in any case the name of a legendary rover and wanderer, I have chosen *Peregrin* to represent it. Of *Peregrin, Pippin* is I suppose a not impossible pet-form, though it is not so close to *Peregrin* as *Rubul* is to *Rubanul*. But *rubul* is in C.S. the name of a kind of small apple.

36 The original discussion of the name *Sam* in F 2 was rejected and

replaced. I give the second form, since it scarcely differs from the first except in clarity. In F 1 the same statement was made, but the linguistic elements were different. His real name was *Bolnōth*; the common Shire-name (*Ban* in F 2) was *Bol*, held to be an abbreviation of *Bolagar*; the prefix meaning 'half-, almost' was *bol-*; and the word in the Common Speech meaning 'wise' (*zīr(a)* in F 2) was *nōth*. These were changed to the forms in F 2, but with *Bannātho* for *Bannātha* (see note 24).

37 For *Tomacca* F 1 has *Tōmak* (and *k* for *c* in other names in this passage, as throughout), and for *Arambil* has *Shambil*; Farmer Cotton's full name is *Tomakli Lothron*, changed subsequently to *Tomacci*.

38 In F 1 Butterbur's real name was *Barabush Zilibraph*, the first name meaning (like *Barabatta* in F 2) 'quick-talker, babbler', shortened to *Barabli*, and the second a compound of *zilib* 'butter' and *raph(a)* a 'burr'. This latter was changed to *Zilbarāpha*, the form first written in F 2. At the end of the note F 1 has: 'the nickname which the landlord of "The Pony" had so long borne that Frodo had never heard his true given-name'.

With the discussion of *Butterbur* the text F 1 ends, but my father added the following in pencil later:

> A final note on the other languages. Now since the language of Rohann and of Dale were akin, that of Rohann closely akin in origin to the Common Speech, it seemed plain that having converted all C.S. into English the more northerly (archaic and less blended) tongues must be represented in the same way. The language of Men in Dale has thus been given (so far as its *names* show) a Norse cast; and since as has been said the Dwarves adapt their names and speech to those of Men among whom they live, all the Dwarves of the North have names of this Northern type (in fact the actual names of Dwarves in Norse). The Rohirrim are therefore appropriately represented by speaking a tongue resembling ancient English. It will thus be noted that for the archaic Rohan *cugbadul* in relation to Hobbit *cubut* [see note 31] I have ..... [?ancient] English *holbytla* in relation to *hobbit*.

From here to the end of the text (so far as it is given here, see note 42) F 2 exists in two forms, both consisting of two sides of a single manuscript page: the second form is a fair copy of the first, and follows it very closely, with for the most part only very minor alterations of wording. I give here the second version, with a couple of differences of form recorded in the following notes.

39 In the first form of the F 2 text the real word in Rohan corresponding to Théoden is *tūran*, where the second form has *tūrac-*.

40 The first form had *tunga* where the second has *tung*.
41 These are forms of the same prehistoric stem, with differing vowels (*sméag* being the ancient English form, *smaug* the Scandinavian, while *smygel* is an English development of the stem *smug*).
42 The remaining eight pages of the F 2 manuscript are taken up with an account of pronunciation, with sections on consonants, vowels, and accent, which was subsequently removed to become (in much developed form) the first part of Appendix E. I give here only the brief preface to this account.

> In transliterating words and names from the ancient languages that appear in the Red Book I have attempted to use modern letters in a way as agreeable to modern English eyes as could be combined with reasonable accuracy. Also I have used them as far as possible with the same value in all the languages concerned. Fortunately the languages of the Westlands of the period were fairly euphonious (by European standards) and simple in phonetic structure, and no very rare or difficult sounds appear to have occurred in them.
>
> Hobbit names, as has been explained, have all been converted into English forms and equivalents and can be pronounced accordingly. Thus *Celador Bolger* has *c* as in *cellar*, and *g* as in *bulge*. But in the alien languages the following points may be observed by those who are interested in such matters.

Noldorin appears, of course, for *Sindarin* throughout (see the commentary on §§5, 18). For Celador Bolger, who does not appear in *The Lord of the Rings*, see pp. 94, 96.

COMMENTARY

§2 So far as I have been able to discover, my father never used the adjective 'Mannish', whether of language or tradition, before its occurrence in this work. The change of 'Human' to 'Mannish' in F 1 (see note 2 above) therefore marks the entry of this term.

§3 The use of the term *Lembi* 'Lingerers', for those of the Eldar who 'remained behind in the north-west of Middle-earth', is a clear indication of date, substantiating the conclusion already reached that this earliest version of Appendix F was at any rate written before the middle of 1950 (see p. 28 and note 1). In the long and extremely complex history of the classification of the divisions of the Elvish peoples and their names, this represents the stage reached in the *Quenta Silmarillion* §29 (V.215), where by a change that can be dated to November 1937 the old term *Lembi* 'Lingerers' became the name for those of the Eldar who were 'lost upon the long road' and never crossed the Great Sea (V.215, 219). Thus while this earliest version of Appendix F certainly belongs to the time when the end of the actual narrative of *The Lord of the Rings* had been reached, it equally clearly preceded the new work on the legends of the First Age which included (as well as the *Annals of Aman*, the *Grey Annals*, and many other works) the revision of the *Quenta Silmarillion*: for in that revision the term *Lembi* was first changed to *Lemberi* and then removed, and the name *Sindar* emerged (for a detailed account see X.163–4, 169–71). As noted in X.91, the name *Sindar* does not occur in *The Lord of the Rings* apart from the Appendices.

§4 The name *Lindar* had been replaced by *Vanyar* when the *Annals of Aman* and the *Grey Annals* were written.

The statement here concerning Quenya, the 'Elven-latin' originally deriving from the language of the Lindar, echoes that in the *Lhammas* or 'Account of Tongues' of the 1930s (see V.172; 193, 195). It may be noted that the expression 'Elven-latin' survived in the published form of Appendix F (RK p. 406): '[Quenya] was no longer a birth-tongue, but had become, as it were, an "Elven-latin" ...'.

§5 The name *Quenta Noldorion*, for *Quenta Silmarillion*, seems to be unique in this place (where it occurs in both texts). – Nothing is said in this work of the adoption of Sindarin (or as it is called here, Lemberin) by the Exiled Noldor: this fundamental development (which first appears in the earliest version of the 'linguistic excursus' in the *Grey Annals*, XI.20–1) had not yet emerged (see further under §18 below). But the idea found in the earlier forms of that 'excursus' (XI.21, 25, 27) that the two languages, Noldorin and Sindarin, changed in similar ways and 'drew together' appears in the footnote to §5.

§7 In the list of *Alterations in last revision 1951* (see X.7), often referred to, occurs '*Atani* N[oldorin] *Edain* = Western Men or Fathers of Men'. It is possible that the form in F 1, *Atanni*, replacing *Atanatári* (note 3 above), was the earliest occurrence of the name.

In the sentence 'In that war three houses of the Fathers of Men aided the Elves ...' the word 'the' is not casually absent before 'three houses': cf. §10, 'the native tongue of the Fathers of Men themselves before those of the Three Houses passed over the Sea.'

The statement concerning the loss of the original language of the Atani shows a curious uncertainty (see note 4 above): from the original version in F 1, 'their chieftains learned the Noldorin speech, and some indeed forsook their own tongue', revised to the form in F 2 'the people of these houses learned the Noldorin speech, and forsook their own tongue', which was then altered to 'the lords of these houses learned the Noldorin speech'. That my father should have entertained at all at this time the idea that the original language of the Atani (of the Three Houses) was wholly lost is remarkable. In this connection it is interesting to compare what he wrote in drafting for the chapter *Faramir* (later *The Window on the West*), which can be dated precisely to May 1944 (VIII.144). Here, in a passage concerning the Common Speech which was only removed from the chapter at a late stage (see VIII.162), Faramir had said: 'Some there are of Gondor who have dealings with the Elves ... One great advantage we have: we speak an elvish speech, or one so near akin that we can in part understand them and they us.' At this Sam exclaimed: 'But you speak the ordinary language! Same as us, though a bit old-fashioned like, if you'll pardon my saying it.' Then Faramir replied (VIII.159–60):

> 'Of course we do. For that is our own tongue which we perhaps preserve better than you do far in the North. The Common Tongue, as some call it, is derived from the Númenóreans, being but a form changed by time of that speech which the Fathers of the Three Houses [*struck out*: Hador and Haleth and Beor] spoke of old. This language it is that has spread through the western world amongst all folk and creatures that use words, to some only a second tongue for use in intercourse with strangers, to some the only tongue they know. But this is not an Elvish speech in my meaning. All speech of men in this world is Elvish in descent; but only if one go back to the beginnings. What I meant was so: [the lords >] many men of the Three Houses long ago gave up man-speech and spoke the tongue of their friends the Noldor or Gnomes: a high-elvish tongue [*struck out*: akin to but changed from the Ancient Elvish of Elvenhome]. And always the lords of Númenor knew that tongue and used it among themselves. And so still do we among ourselves ...

See further under §9 below.

§9 It is an extraordinary feature of this account that there is no suggestion that the Númenóreans retained their own Mannish language, and it is indeed expressly stated here that 'The language of the Dúnedain was thus the Elvish Noldorin'. This is the explanation of the statement discussed under §7 that the Men of the Three Houses learned Noldorin and abandoned their ancestral tongue (as has been mentioned already in note 4 above, the emendation to F 2, whereby it was reduced to 'the *lords* of these houses learned the Noldorin speech', was made at the same time as the rough alterations of the text here and in §13 whereby Adûnaic was introduced as the language of Númenor).

I am altogether at a loss to account for this, in view of Faramir's disquisition to Sam cited under §7. Moreover, in the anomalous 'Foreword' that I have called F* my father had said (p. 21, §8): 'Now those languages of Men that are here met with were related to the Common Speech; for the Men of the North and West were akin in the beginning to the Men of Westernesse that came back over the Sea; and the Common Speech was indeed made by the blending of the speech of Men of Middle-earth with the tongues of the kings from over the Sea.' This is not very clearly expressed, but the implication seems clear that the Númenórean language that entered into the Common Speech was a Mannish and not an Elvish tongue. One seems to be driven to the explanation that my father when writing the present account had actually shifted away from his view that the Mannish language of the Three Houses was the common speech of Númenor; yet what does that imply of all his work on Adûnaic and *The Drowning of Anadûnê* in 1946?

In the footnote to §9 the tenth king of the Northern Line is named *Eärendil*, not as in Appendix A (RK pp. 318, 320) *Eärendur*; see p. 189.

It was undoubtedly here that the name *Westron* arose (apparently devised by my father on the analogy of the old form *southron*, itself an alteration of *southern*); the F 1 text as originally written had *Westnish* throughout (note 6 above). *Westron* occurs only once in the actual narrative of *The Lord of the Rings*, in the chapter *Lothlórien*, where Legolas says 'this is how it runs in the Westron Speech' (FR p. 353), and this was a late change from 'the Common Speech', made to the typescript following the fair copy manuscript: see VII.223 and 235 with note 48.

§10 In Faramir's account (see under §7) the Common Speech was expressly said to be 'derived from the Númenóreans': changed by time, it was nonetheless directly descended from 'that speech which the Fathers of the Three Houses spoke of old'. In fact, in corrections made to the completed manuscript of that chapter, the conception was changed to the extent that Faramir now says: 'The Common Tongue, as some call it, is derived from the Númenóreans; for the Númenóreans coming to the shores of these lands took the rude tongue of the men that they here found and whom they ruled, and they enriched it, and it spread hence through the Western world'; and he also says that 'in intercourse with other folk we use the Common Speech which we made for that purpose' (VIII.162). Of this I said (*ibid.*): 'Here the idea that the Common Speech was derived from "that speech which the Fathers of the Three Houses spoke of old" is denied'; but by 'the rude tongue of the men that they here found' Faramir may have meant language that in the course of millennia had become greatly altered and impoverished, not that it bore no ancestral kinship to that of the Númenóreans.

In Appendix F as published the section *Of Men* (RK p. 406) begins: 'The *Westron* was a Mannish speech, though enriched and softened under Elvish influence. It was in origin the language of those whom the Eldar called the *Atani* or *Edain*, "Fathers of

Men" ...' And further on in this section my father wrote of the great Númenórean haven of Pelargir: 'There Adûnaic was spoken, and mingled with many words of the languages of lesser men it became a Common Speech that spread thence along the coasts ...'

All these conceptions differ somewhat among themselves, but as is often the case when comparing varying texts of my father's one may feel unsure whether the differences do not lie more in differing emphasis than in real contradiction. In the present text, however, it is perfectly clear that the Common Speech was in origin one form of the skein of Mannish speech that extended from the North (Dale, Esgaroth, and the old lands of the Rohirrim) southward down the vales of Anduin (see §23); that this particular form was centred on the Númenórean haven of Pelargir (§10); and that it was for this reason much influenced by the Númenórean language – *but that language was the Elvish Noldorin* as it had evolved in Númenor.

§14 The statement (before revision) that the Dunlendings had forgotten their own tongue and used only the Westron conflicts with the passage in the chapter *Helm's Deep*, where the Men of Dunland cried out against the Rohirrim in their ancient speech, interpreted to Aragorn and Éomer by Gamling the Old (see VIII.21). In the revised form of the paragraph the Dunland tongue is said to have been 'wholly unlike the Westron, and was descended, as it seems, from some other Mannish tongue, not akin to that of the Atani, Fathers of Men'; cf. Appendix F (RK p. 407): 'Wholly alien was the speech of the Wild Men of Drúadan Forest. Alien, too, or only remotely akin, was the language of the Dunlendings.' In an earlier form of Faramir's exposition cited under §7 he said that there was a 'remote kinship' between the Common Speech and 'the tongues of Rohan and of Dale and of Westfold and Dunland and other places', VIII.159.

§16 'The Orcs had a language of their own, devised for them by the Dark Lord of old': in view of what is said in §7, 'the Eldar were at that time engaged in a ceaseless war with the Dark Lord of that Age, one greater far than Sauron', this may seem to refer to Morgoth; but cf. Appendix F (RK p. 409), 'It is said that the Black Speech was devised by Sauron in the Dark Years'.

§18 The entire conception of the relations of the Elvish languages in Middle-earth at the end of the Third Age as presented here was of course fundamentally altered by the emergence of the idea that the Exiled Noldor of the First Age adopted Sindarin, the (Telerian) language of the Eldar who remained in Middle-earth. Thus the language of the Elves dwelling west of the Misty Mountains is here Noldorin (see under §5 above), while the Lemberin (i.e. Sindarin) of Middle-earth is found among the Elves of Northern Mirkwood and Lórien. At the beginning of §19 names such as *Lórien, Caras Galadon, Amroth, Nimrodel* are cited as examples of Lemberin;

whereas in Appendix F (RK p. 405, footnote) they are cited as 'probably of Silvan origin', in contrast to Sindarin, the language spoken in Lórien at the end of the Third Age. – With the present passage cf. that in the text F*, p. 20, §7.

§20 It has been seen (note 10 above) that it was in the text F 1 that the threefold division of the Hobbits into Harfoots, Stoors, and Fallohides entered, whence it was removed, before F 2 was written, to stand in the *Prologue*. In the actual narrative of *The Lord of the Rings* there is no reference to Harfoots or Fallohides, but the Stoors are named once, in the chapter *The Shadow of the Past*, where Gandalf spoke of Gollum's family. The introduction of the name was made at a very late stage in the evolution of the chapter, when the passage read (cf. the oldest version of the text, VI.78): 'I guess they were of hobbit-kind; or akin to the fathers of the fathers of the hobbits, though they loved the River, and often swam in it, or made little boats of reeds'; this was altered to the final text (FR p. 62) by omitting the word 'or' in 'or akin', and by changing 'hobbits' to 'Stoors' and 'though they loved' to 'for they loved'.

§22 My father was writing of Hobbits as if they were still to be found, as he did in the published *Prologue* ('Hobbits are an unobtrusive but very ancient people, more numerous formerly than they are today', &c., though altering present tense to past tense in one passage in the Second Edition, p. 17, note 13). Here indeed he attributed at least to some of them a lively interest in linguistic history.

§§22–3 In the footnotes to these paragraphs the more complex history of the Stoors can be seen evolving. In the footnote in F 1 (note 11 above) corresponding to that to §23 in F 2, concerning Gandalf's opinion about Gollum's origin, it is said that his people 'must have been a late-lingering group of Stoors in the neighbourhood of the Gladden' (i.e. after the Stoors as a whole had crossed the Misty Mountains into Eriador). In the footnote in F 2 (belonging with the writing of the manuscript) my father suggested rather that they were 'a family or small clan' of Stoors who had gone back east over the Mountains, a return to Wilderland that (he said) was evidenced in Hobbit legends, on account of the hard life and hard lands that they found in eastern Eriador.

Later, there entered the story that many Stoors remained in the lands between Tharbad and the borders of Dunland: this was an addition to the *Prologue* (FR p. 12) made when the text was close to its final form (cf. p. 11), and no doubt the footnote to §22 was added at the same time.

In Appendix A (RK p. 321) the return to Wilderland by some of the Stoors is directly associated with the invasion of Arnor by Angmar in Third Age 1409:

It was at this time that the Stoors that had dwelt in the Angle (between Hoarwell and Loudwater) fled west and south, because of the wars, and the dread of Angmar, and because the land and clime of Eriador, especially in the east, worsened and became unfriendly. Some returned to Wilderland, and dwelt beside the Gladden, becoming a riverside people of fishers.

These Stoors of the Angle who returned to Wilderland are distinguished from those who dwelt further south and acquired a speech similar to that of the people of Dunland: see the section *Of Hobbits* in Appendix F, RK p. 408 and footnote.

§25 The name Brandywine emerged very early in the writing of *The Lord of the Rings* (VI.29–30 and note 5), but the Elvish name first appeared in the narrative in work on the chapter *Flight to the Ford* (VII.61; FR p. 222), where Glorfindel, in a rejected draft, spoke of 'the Branduin (which you have turned into Brandywine)' (the word 'have' was erroneously omitted in the text printed). In F 1, and again at first in F 2, my father repeated this: 'older names, of Elvish or forgotten Mannish origin, they often translated ... or twisted into a familiar shape (as Elvish *Baranduin* "brown river" to *Brandywine*).' But in revision to F 2 he rejected this explanation, saying that the Elvish name of the river was in fact *Malevarn* ('golden-brown'), transformed in the Hobbits' speech to *Malvern*, but that this was then replaced by *Brandywine* – this being exceptional, since it bore no relation in form to the Elvish name. This idea he also rejected, and in the final form of §25 went back to the original explanation of *Brandywine*, that it was a characteristic Hobbit alteration of Elvish *Baranduin*.

In the passage of *Flight to the Ford* referred to above the name of the river appears in the manuscript as *Branduin*, changed to *Baranduin*, and then to *Malevarn* (VII.66, note 36). It is surprising at first sight to see that *Malevarn* survived into the final typescript of the chapter, that sent to the printer, where my father corrected it to *Baranduin*; but the explanation is evidently that this typescript had been made a long time before. Glorfindel's use of *Baranduin* or *Malevarn* is in fact the only occurrence of the Elvish name of the river in the narrative of *The Lord of the Rings*.

§27 In Appendix D (RK p. 389) Yellowskin is called 'the Yearbook of Tuckborough'.

§37 It is often impossible to be sure of my father's intention in the usage of 'thou, thee' and 'you' forms of address: when writing rapidly he was very inconsistent, and in more careful manuscripts he often wavered in his decision on this insoluble question (if the distinction is to be represented at all). In the case of the chapter *The Steward and the King*, referred to here, the first manuscript (see IX.54) is a very rapidly written draft from which no conclusion can be drawn; while in the second manuscript, a good clear text, he decided while in the course of writing the dialogue between Faramir and Éowyn against showing the distinction at all. The 'sudden change' to which he referred here (but in F 1 he wrote only of 'the intrusion of *thou, thee* into the dialogue') is possibly to be seen in their first meeting in the garden of the Houses of Healing, where Faramir says (RK p. 238): 'Then, Éowyn of Rohan, I say to you that you are beautiful', but at the end of his speech changes to the 'familiar' form, 'But thou and I have both passed under the wings of the Shadow' (whereas Éowyn continues to use 'you'). In the following meetings, in this text, Faramir uses the 'familiar' forms, but Éowyn does not do so until the last ('Dost thou not know?', RK p. 242); and soon after this point my father went back over what he had written and changed every 'thou' and 'thee' to 'you'. In the third manuscript (preceding the final typescript) there is no trace of the 'familiar' form.

I record these details because they are significant of the (relative) date of the present text, showing very clearly that when he wrote this earliest form of what would become Appendix F he had not yet completed the second manuscript of this chapter.

'The *thee* used by Sam Gamgee to Rose at the end of the book' refers to the end of the *Epilogue* (IX.118): 'I did not think I should ever see thee again'. At this stage only the first version of the *Epilogue* was in being (though these words are used in both versions): see IX.129, 132.

On a loose page associated with my father's later work on this Appendix my father wrote very rapidly:

Where *thou, thee, thy* appears it is used mainly to mark a use of the familiar form where that was not usual. For instance its use by Denethor in his last madness to Gandalf, and by the Messenger of Sauron, was in both cases intended to be contemptuous. But elsewhere it is occasionally used to indicate a deliberate change to a form of affection or endearment.

The passages referred to are RK pp. 128–30 and p. 165; in Denethor's speeches to Gandalf there are some occurrences of 'you' that were not corrected.

§39 For Westron *Carbandur* (F 1 at first *Karbandul*, note 18) Appendix F has *Karningul* (RK p. 412).

§41 With the Noldorin word *lhann*, said here to be the equivalent of Westron *sūza* as used in Gondor for the divisions of the realm, cf. the *Etymologies*, V.367, stem LAD, where Noldorin *lhand, lhann* 'wide' is cited, and also the region *Lhothland, Lhothlann*, east of Dorthonion (see XI.60, 128).

§42 The Westron name *Raspūta* 'Hornblower' is only recorded here (F 1 *Rhaspûtal*, note 21 above). Since it is said (§13) that the Common Speech was 'much enriched with words drawn from the language of the Dúnedain, which was ... a form of the Elvish Noldorin', it is perhaps worth noting that the stem RAS in the

Etymologies (V.383) yields Quenya *rassë*, Noldorin *rhaes* 'horn', with citation of *Caradras*. – In Appendix F (RK p. 413) the name *Tûk* is said to be an old name 'of forgotten meaning'.

§43 For the name *Porro*, not found in *The Lord of the Rings*, see pp. 87–8, 92.

§45 The 'classical' titles of the heads of the Brandybuck family given in the second footnote to this paragraph do not appear in *The Lord of the Rings*, but see pp. 102–3. Cf. Appendix F (RK p. 413): 'Names of classical origin have rarely been used; for the nearest equivalents to Latin and Greek in Shire-lore were the Elvish tongues, and these the Hobbits seldom used in nomenclature. Few of them at any time knew the "languages of the kings", as they called them.'

§46 Apart from the opening sentence nothing of this paragraph remained in Appendix F, and Lobelia Sackville-Baggins' true name *Hamanullas* was lost.

§47 Much information is given here on Hobbit family-names that was subsequently lost, notably the true Westron name of *Baggins* and its supposed etymology; other names (*Brandybuck, Cotton, Gamgee*), discussed in the notes that conclude Appendix F, differ in details of the forms. On the name *Gamgee* see the references in the index to *Letters*, and especially the letter to Naomi Mitchison of 25 April 1954 (no.144, near the end), which is closely related to what is said here and in Appendix F.

§48 In the note at the end of Appendix F it is said that the word for 'Hobbit' in use in the Shire was *kuduk*, and that Théoden used the form *kûd-dûkan* 'hole-dweller' when he met Merry and Pippin at Isengard, which in the narrative (TT p. 163) is 'translated' by *Holbytla(n)*, though no rendering of this given. In the present passage, both in F 1 (see note 31) and in F 2, the meaning 'hole-dweller' is given for *holbytla* and for the real Westron and Rohan words (cf. also p. 10). In view of the etymology of *bytla (bylta)*, for which see VII.424, VIII.44, one would expect 'hole-builder', but this only occurs in fact at an earlier point in Appendix F (RK p. 408): the word *hobbit* seems to be 'a worn-down form of a word preserved more fully in Rohan: *holbytla* "hole-builder"' (see further p. 83, note 7).

My father's remarks in the footnote to this paragraph on his association of the words 'hobbit' and 'rabbit' are notable.

§49 In Appendix F (RK p. 414) Meriadoc's true name was *Kalimac*, shortened *Kali*; but nothing is said of the true names of Frodo or Peregrin.

§50 In the chapter *The Road to Isengard* the originator of pipe-weed in the Shire was first named Elias Tobiasson, and then Tobias Smygrave, before Tobias Hornblower emerged (VIII.36–7). Tobias remained to a late stage in the development of the chapter before he was renamed Tobold, though it is seen from the present text that my father for a time retained Tobias while asserting that the name (pronounced *Tóbias*) was not in fact a 'translation' of Hebraic origin at all.

Bildad (Bolger) is not found in *The Lord of the Rings* (but see pp. 94, 96); while the abbreviated names *Tom* and *Mat* are differently explained in Appendix F.

§51 As with Tobias Hornblower, my father retained Barnabas Butterbur, despite what he had written in §50, but accounted for it on the grounds that Butterbur was not a Hobbit but a Man of Bree. In Appendix F all discussion of the name of the landlord of *The Prancing Pony* was lost. The change of *Barnabas* to *Barliman* was made in very late revisions to the text of *The Lord of the Rings* (cf. IX.78).

§58 These remarks on the history of the Hobbits' name of the *Baranduin* (see also §§25, 47) were further altered in the final note at the end of Appendix F.

This is the most detailed account that my father wrote of his elaborate and distinctive fiction of translation, of transposition and substitution. One may wonder when or by what stages it emerged; but I think that this is probably unknowable: the evidences are very slight, and in such matters he left none of those discussions, records of internal debate, that sometimes greatly assisted in the understanding of the development of the narrative. It seems to me in any case most probable that the idea evolved gradually, as the history, linguistic and other, was consolidated and became increasingly coherent.

Central to the 'fiction of authenticity' is of course the Common Speech. I concluded that this was first named in the *Lord of the Rings* papers in the chapter *Lothlórien* (dating from the beginning of the 1940s): see VII.223, 239. In the second of these passages my father wrote that the speech of the wood-elves of Lórien was 'not that of the western elves which was in those days used as a common speech among many folk'. In a note of the same period (VII.277) he said that 'Since Aragorn is a *man* and the common speech (especially of mortals) is represented by English, then he must not have an Elvish name'; and in another note (VII.424), one of a collection of jottings on a page that bears the date 9 February 1942 (at which time he was working on the opening chapters of what became *The Two Towers*) he wrote:

Language of Shire = modern English
Language of Dale = Norse (used by Dwarves of that region)
Language of Rohan = Old English
'Modern English' is *lingua franca* spoken by all people (except a few secluded folk like Lórien) – but little and ill by orcs.

In this, 'Language of Dale = Norse (used by Dwarves of that region)' shows plainly that a major obstacle, perhaps the chief obstacle, to a coherent 'authentication' had by this time been resolved. When my father wrote *The Hobbit* he had of course no notion that the Old Norse names of the Dwarves required any explanation, within the terms of the story: those were their names, and that was all there was to it. As he said in a letter of December 1937, cited in the Foreword to *The Return of the Shadow* (p. 7): 'I don't much approve of *The Hobbit* myself, preferring my own mythology (which is just touched on) with its consistent nomenclature ... and organized history, to this rabble of Eddaic-named dwarves out of Völuspá ...' But now this inescapable Norse element had to be accounted for; and from that 'rabble of Eddaic-named dwarves out of Völuspá' the conception emerged that the Dwarves had 'outer names' derived from the tongues of Men with whom they had dealings, concealing their true names which they kept altogether secret. And this was very evidently an important component in the theory of the 'transposition of languages': for the Dwarves had *Norse* names because they lived among Men who *were represented* in *The Lord of the Rings* as speaking Norse. It may not be too far-fetched, I think, to suppose that (together with the idea of the Common Speech) those Dwarf-names in *The Hobbit* provided the starting-point for the whole structure of the Mannish languages in Middle-earth, as expounded in the present text.

My father asserted (§53) that he had represented the tongue of the Rohirrim as Old English because their real language stood in a relation to the Common Speech somewhat analogous to that of Old English and Modern English. This is perhaps difficult to accept: one may feel that the impulse that produced the Riders of Rohan and the Golden Hall was more profound, and that my father's statement should be viewed as an aspect of 'the fiction of authenticity'; for the idea of 'translation' had a further fictional dimension in its presentation as a conception established from the outset – which in the case of the Dwarf-names (and the Hobbit-names) it was most assuredly not.

On the other hand, he knew very soon that the Rohirrim were originally Men of the North: in a note made at the time when his work on the chapter *The Riders of Rohan* was scarcely begun (VII.390) he wrote:

> Rohiroth are relations of Woodmen and Beornings, old Men of the North. But they speak Gnomish – tongue of Númenor and Ondor, as well as [?common] tongue.

Taken with 'Language of Rohan = Old English' among the equations in the note cited above, from about the same time, it may be better not to force the distinction, but to say rather that the emergent 'transpositional' idea (Modern English – Old English – Old Norse) may well have played a part in my father's vision of Rohan.

In the present text it can be seen that as he penetrated more deeply into the logic of the theory he came up against complexities that were difficult to manage. For example, it seems clear that when he wrote in

§25 that the Hobbits had 'twisted into a familiar shape' the Elvish name *Baranduin*, making out of it *Brandywine*, he had not taken into account the fact that the Hobbits would have had no such word as 'Brandywine' (whether or not they knew of brandy, §58). This realisation led to his avowal in §56: 'This translation had a disadvantage which I did not foresee. The "linguistic notes" on the origin of peculiar Hobbit words had also to be "translated" '; and in §58 he is seen ingeniously introducing the necessary 'third term' into the history of *Brandywine*: the 'picturesque perversion' of the river-name *Baranduin* by the Hobbits was to their real word *Branduhim*, which meant in their Westron 'foaming beer'. He could still say that *Brandywine* was 'a very possible "corruption" of *Baranduin*', because *Baranduin* being an Elvish name was not translated; thus *Brandywine* must both 'imitate' the Hobbit word *Branduhim*, and at the same time stand in Modern English as a corruption of *Baranduin*.

It will be seen shortly that in the text of this Appendix next following my father moved sharply away from F 2, and removed almost all exemplification of true Westron names. It may be that at that stage he had come to think that the subtleties demanded by so close an examination of the 'theory' were unsuitable to the purpose; on the other hand it seems possible that mere considerations of length were the cause.

Note on an unpublished letter

A long letter of my father's was sent for sale at auction on 4 May 1995 at Sotheby's in London. This letter he wrote on 3 August 1943, during the long pause in the writing of *The Lord of the Rings* (between the end of Book Three and the beginning of Book Four) that lasted from about the end of 1942 to the beginning of April 1944 (VIII.77–8). It was addressed to two girls named Leila Keene and Pat Kirke, and was largely concerned to answer their questions about the runes in *The Hobbit*; but in the present connection it contains an interesting passage on the Common Speech. My father made some brief remarks on the problem of the representation of the languages actually spoken in those days, and continued:

> In some ways it was not too difficult. In Bilbo's time there *was* a language very widely used all over the West (the Western parts of the Great Lands of those days). It was a sort of lingua-franca, made up of all sorts of languages, but the Elvish language (of the North West) for the most part. It was called the Western language or Common Speech; and in Bilbo's time had already passed eastward over the Misty Mountains and reached Lake Town, and Beorn, and even Smaug (dragons were ready linguists in all ages). ...
>
> If hobbits ever had any special language of their own, they had given it up. They spoke the Common Speech only and every

day (unless they learned other languages, which was very seldom). The most notable point in this is the description of the composition of the Common Speech: 'a sort of lingua-franca, made up of all sorts of languages, but the Elvish language (of the North West) for the most part.' Allowance should perhaps be made for the nature of the letter (my father was not, obviously, writing a precise statement); but it certainly seems that as late as 1943, when half of *The Lord of the Rings* had been written, he had as yet no conception of the origin of the Common Speech in a form of Mannish language of the west of Middle-earth, and that Faramir's account of the matter (see p. 63), written nine months later, had not emerged. It may be that what he said in this letter ('the Elvish language (of the North West) for the most part') is to be associated with what he had written in the chapter *Lothlórien*, where he said (VII.239) that the language of 'the western elves' 'was in those days used as a common speech among many folk.'

He also referred in this letter to the adoption by the Dwarves of the Lonely Mountain of the language of the Men of Dale, in which they gave themselves names, keeping their true names in their own tongue entirely secret (see p. 71).

For the notes to this concluding section of the chapter see pp. 82 ff.

The third text ('F 3') was a typescript with the title *The Languages of the Third Age*, above which my father wrote 'Appendix I'. No other of the many texts that followed has any mention of its being an 'Appendix'.

This text F 3 represents in some degree a new departure. The first part of the work (that preceding the discussion of 'Translation') was reduced to not much more than a third of its length in F 2, and while my father had F 2 in front of him he turned also to the curious 'Foreword' F* that I have given on pp. 19 ff., and made a good deal of use of it, as has been mentioned already.

At this stage he had not changed his view that the Exiled Noldor retained their own language in Beleriand (see p. 62, §5), and the 'Telerian' speech (which in F 2 was originally called 'Lemberin') is confined to a few names. Thus the conception in F 2, §18, was in essentials preserved, although there entered here the more complex account of the Elvish peoples of Mirkwood and Lórien:

There were also Elves of other kind. The East-elves that being content with Middle-earth remained there, and remain even now; and the Teleri, kinsfolk of the High Elves who never went westward, but lingered on the shores of Middle-earth until the return of the Noldor.[1] In the Third Age few of the Teleri were left, and they for the most part dwelt as lords among the East-elves in woodland realms far from the Sea, which nonetheless they longed for in their hearts. Of this kind were the Elves of Mirkwood, and of Lórien; but Galadriel was a lady of the Noldor. In this book there are several names of Telerian form,[2] but little else appears of their language.

The extremely puzzling feature of the original version, that the language of the Númenóreans was Noldorin (for the Edain in Beleriand learned that tongue and abandoned their own) was at first retained in F 3; and thus the account of the Common Speech remained unchanged, becoming if anything more explicit (cf. F 2, §§9–10, 13):

The language of the Dúnedain in Númenor was thus the Elvish, or Gnomish speech ... After the Downfall of Númenor, which was brought about by Sauron, and the ending of the Second Age, Elendil and the survivors of Westernesse fled back eastward to Middle-earth. On the western shores in the days of their power the Númenóreans had maintained many forts and havens for the help of their ships in their great voyages; and the chief of these had been at Pelargir at the mouths of the Anduin in the land that was after called Gondor. *There the language of the Edain that had not passed over Sea was spoken*, and thence it spread along the coastlands, as a common speech of all who had dealings with Westernesse and opposed the power of Sauron. Now the people of Elendil were not many, for only a few great ships had escaped the Downfall. There were, it is true, many dwellers upon the west-shores who came in part of the blood of Westernesse, being descended from mariners and wardens of forts set there in the Dark Years; yet all told the Dúnedain were only a small people in the midst of lesser Men. They used therefore this Common Speech in all their dealings with other folk and in the government of the wide realms of which they became the rulers, and it was enriched with many words drawn from the tongues of the Elves and the Númenórean lords. Thus it was that the Common Speech spread far and wide in the days of the Kings, even among their enemies, and it became used more and more by the Númenóreans themselves; so that at the time of this history the Elvish speech was spoken by only a [*added:* small] part of the people of Minas Tirith, the city of Gondor, and outside that city only by the lords and princes of fiefs.

The account of the origin and spread of the Common Speech as it appears in Appendix F (RK p. 407) had, in point of actual wording, been quite largely attained – and yet still with the fundamental difference, that the Númenóreans themselves spoke an Elvish tongue, and Adûnaic does not exist.

Probably while this text was still in the making, my father retyped a portion of it, and it was only now that Adûnaic entered, or re-entered, the linguistic history. Making similar changes at the same time to the previous text F 2 (see p. 54, note 4), he wrote now that it was the lords of the Edain who learned the Noldorin tongue, and that 'in Númenor two speeches were used: the Númenórean (or Adûnaic); and the Elvish or Gnomish tongue of the Noldor, which all the lords of that people knew and spoke'. In the passage just given he altered the words that I italicised to: 'There [at Pelargir] the Adûnaic, the Mannish language of the Edain, was spoken, and thence it spread along the coastlands...', the remainder of the passage being left unchanged. No further light is cast on this matter in the texts of 'Appendix F', and it remains to me inexplicable.

There is not a great deal more that need be said about the part of the text F 3 that deals with the languages. For the language of Orcs and Trolls my father followed F 2, §§16–17, but for that of the Dwarves he turned to F* (p. 21, §10), and repeated closely what he had said there. But at that point, still following this text (§11), he turned now to the subject of alphabets ('Of the alphabets of the Third Age something also must be said, since in this history there are both inscriptions and old writings ...'), and repeated what he had said in F* as far as 'the Runes, or *cirth*, were devised by the Elves of the woods'. Here he left the earlier text and continued as follows (the forerunner of the passage in Appendix E, RK pp. 395, 397):

... the Runes, or *Cirth* as they were called, were first devised by the Danians (far kin of the Noldor) in the woods of Beleriand, and were in the beginning used mainly for incising names and brief memorials upon wood, stone, or metal. From that beginning they derive their peculiar character, closely similar in many of their signs to the Runes of the North in our own times. But their detail, arrangement, and uses were different, and there is, it seems, no connexion of descent between the Runes and the Cirth. Many things were forgotten and found again in the ages of Middle-earth, and so it will be, doubtless, hereafter.

The Cirth in their older and simpler form spread far and wide, even into the East, and they became known to many races of Men, and developed many varieties and uses. One form of the old Cirth was used among Men of whom we have already spoken, the Rohirrim and their more northerly kindred in the vale of Anduin and in Dale. But the richest and most well-ordered alphabet of Cirth was called the Alphabet of Dairon, since in Elvish tradition it was said to have been arranged and enlarged from the older Cirth by Dairon, the minstrel of King Thingol in Doriath. This was preserved in use in Hollin and Moria, and there mostly by the Dwarves. For after the coming of the Noldor the Fëanorian script replaced the Cirth among the Elves and the Edain.

In this book we meet only the Short Cirth of Dale and the Mark; and the Long Cirth of Moria, as they were called at this time; for though the Dwarves, as with their speech, used in their dealings with other folk such scripts as were current among them, among themselves and in their secret memorials they still used the ancient Alphabet of Dairon. A table is given setting out the Short Cirth of Dale and the Mark; and the Long Cirth of Moria in the form and arrangement applied to the Common Speech. [*The following was subsequently struck out*: A list is also given of all the strange words and the names of persons and places that appear in the tale, in which it is shown from what language they are derived, and what is their meaning (where that is known);] and also the English Runes in the forms that were used for the translation of the Cirth in *The Hobbit*.

The first devising of the Runes by 'the Danians (far kin of the Noldor) in the woods of Beleriand' (where F* has 'the Elves of the woods') is found also in the two texts given in VII.453–5, where the origin is attributed to 'the Danian elves of Ossiriand (who were ultimately of Noldorin race)'. The old view that the Danas or Danians (Nandor) came from the host of the Noldor on the Great March was changed in the course of the revision of the *Quenta Silmarillion*, when they became Teleri from the host of Olwë (X.169–70; cf. the use of the old term *Lembi* in F 2, p. 61, §3).

The final section of F 3, *On Translation*, presents a very greatly reduced form of that in the original version, and loses virtually all of the exemplification and discussion of the 'true' names from which the 'translation' was made: the sole Westron names that survived were *Carbandur* (Rivendell) and *Phuru-nargian* (Moria). The new text had indeed the structure and much of the actual wording of Appendix F, but it was a good deal briefer; and the published text represents a re-expansion, in which some of the old material had been reinstated, if in altered form.[3] But since no new material was introduced in F 3, there is no need to give more account of this part of it.

The text ends with a return to the conclusion of F*, pp. 23–4, §§12–13:

In conclusion I will add a note on two important modern words used in translation. The name *Gnomes* is sometimes used for the Noldor, and *Gnomish* for Noldorin. This has been done, because whatever Paracelsus may have thought (if indeed he invented the name), to some *Gnome* will still suggest Knowledge. Now the High-elven name of this folk, Noldor, signifies Those who Know; for of the Three Kindreds of the Elves from their beginning the Noldor were ever distinguished both by their knowledge of things that are and were in this world and by their desire to know more. Yet they were not in any way like to the gnomes of learned theory, or of literary and popular fancy. They belonged to a race high and beautiful, the Elder Children of the world, who now are gone. Tall they were, fair-skinned and grey-eyed, though their locks were dark, save in the golden house of Finrod; and their voices knew more melodies than any mortal speech that now is heard. Valiant they were, but their history was grievous; and though it was in far-off days woven a little with the fates of the Fathers, their fate is not that of Men. Their dominion passed long ago, and they dwell now beyond the circles of the world, and do not return.

The naming of 'the golden house of Finrod' (later Finarfin) seems to have been the first mention of this character that marked out the third son of Finwë, and his children.

In a later (in fact the penultimate) text of the section *On Translation* my father still retained this passage, even though by that time he had decided against using *Gnome*, *Gnomish* at all in *The Lord of the Rings* (as being 'too misleading'), and introduced it with the words 'I have sometimes (not in this book) used Gnomes for *Noldor*, and Gnomish for *Noldorin*'. Perhaps because the passage now seemed otiose, in the final text he still retained a part of it but changed its application: the word to be justified was now *Elves*, used to translate *Quendi* and *Eldar*. In my discussion of this in I.43–4 I pointed out that the words 'They were tall, fair of skin and grey-eyed, though their locks were dark, save in the golden house of Finrod [Finarfin]' were originally written of the Noldor only, and not of all the Eldar, and I objected that 'the Vanyar had golden hair, and it was from Finarfin's Vanyarin mother Indis that he, and Finrod Felagund and Galadriel his children, had their golden hair', finding in the final use of this passage an 'extraordinary perversion of meaning'. But my father carefully remodelled the passage in order to apply it to the Eldar as a whole, and it does indeed seem 'extraordinary' that he should have failed to observe this point. It seems possible that when he re-used the passage in this way the conception of the golden hair of the Vanyar had not yet arisen.[4]

Despite the great contraction in F 3 of the original version, my father repeated the long last paragraph of F* concerning *dwarves* and *dwarrows* (pp. 23–4, §13) almost in its entirety, omitting only his remarks on his liking for irregular plurals, and introducing the

Westron name *Phurunargian* of Moria. With the words 'and has been so since their birth in the deeps of time' this text ends.

The next typescript, F 4, still called *The Languages of the Third Age* but changed to *The Languages and Peoples of the Third Age*, followed the major revision of 1951. My father's long experimentation with the structure and expression of this Appendix now issued in his most lucid account of the Elvish languages, in which the terms *Sindar* and *Sindarin* at last appeared, and the acquisition of the Grey-elven tongue by the exiled Noldor.

Besides this Common Speech there were, however, many other tongues still spoken in the West-lands. Noblest of these were the languages of the Western Elves (Eldar) of which two are met: the High-elven (Quenya) and the Grey-elven (Sindarin).

The Quenya was no longer a daily speech but a learned tongue, descended from ages past, though it was still used in courtesies, or for high matters of lore and song, by the High Elves, the Noldor whose language it had been in Eldamar beyond the Sea. But when the Noldor were exiled and returned to Middle-earth, seeking the Great Jewels which the Dark Power of the North had seized, they took for daily use the language of the lands in which they dwelt. Those were in the North-west, in the country of Beleriand, where Thingol Greycloak was king of the Sindar or Grey-elves.

The Sindar were also in origin Eldar, and kindred of the Noldor, yet they had never passed the Sea, but had lingered on the shores of Middle-earth. There their speech had changed much with the changefulness of mortal lands in the long Twilight, and it had become far estranged from the high and ancient Quenya. But it was a fair tongue still, well fitted to the forests, the hills, and the shores where it had taken shape.

In the fall of the Dark Power and the end of the First Age most of Beleriand was overwhelmed by the waters, or burned with fire. Then a great part of its folk went west over Sea, never to return. Yet many still lingered in Middle-earth, and the Greyelven tongue in those days spread eastward; for some of the elven-peoples of Beleriand crossed the mountains of Lune (Ered Luin), and wherever they came they were received as kings and lords, because of their greater wisdom and majesty. These were for the most part Sindar; for the Exiles (such few as remained), highest and fairest of all speaking-peoples, held still to Lindon, the remnant of Beleriand west of the Ered Luin. There Gil-galad was their lord, until the Second Age drew to its end.

THE APPENDIX ON LANGUAGES 79

Nonetheless to Rivendell (Imladris) there went with Master Elrond many Noldorin lords; and in Hollin (Eregion) others of the Noldor established a realm near to the West-gate of Moria, and there forged the Rings of Power. Galadriel, too, was of the royal house of Finrod of the Noldor; though Celeborn, her spouse of Lórien, was a Grey-elf, and most of their people were of a woodland race.

For there were other Elves of various kind in the world; and many were Eastern Elves that had hearkened to no summons to the Sea, but being content with Middle-earth remained there, and remained long after, fading in fastnesses of the woods and hills, as Men usurped the lands. Of that kind were the Elves of Greenwood the Great; yet among them also were many lords of Sindarin race. Such were Thranduil and Legolas his son. In his realm and in Lórien both the Sindarin and the woodland tongues were heard; but of the latter nothing appears in this book, and of the many Elvish names of persons or of places that are used most are of Grey-elven form.

From the assured and perspicuous writing alone one might think that this belonged to the time of the *Grey Annals* and the *Annals of Aman*. But it was by no means the last in the series of texts that finally issued in the published form of Appendix F.

Of F 4 there are only a few other points to mention. The origin of the Common Speech is here formulated in these words:

There [at Pelargir] Adûnaic was spoken, to which language the tongues of Men that dwelt round about were closely akin, so that already a common speech had grown up in that region and had spread thence along the coasts among all those that had dealings with Westernesse.

After typing the text my father added this sentence:

Of the speech of Men of the East and allies of Sauron all that appears is *múmak*, a name of the great elephant of the Harad.

A carbon copy of F 4 is extant, and here my father in a similar addition named beside *múmak* also *Variag* and *Khand* (RK pp. 121, 123, 329).

Lastly, it was in F 4 that there entered the passage concerning the new race of Trolls that appeared at the end of the Third Age. Here the name was first *Horg-hai*, but changed as my father typed the text to *Olg-hai* (*Olog-hai* in RK, p. 410). The account of them did not differ from the final form except in the statement of their origin:

That Sauron bred them none doubted, though from what stock was not known. Some held that they were a cross-breed between trolls and the larger Orcs; others that they were indeed not trolls at all but giant Orcs. Yet there was no kinship from the beginning between the stone-trolls and the Orcs that they might breed together;[5] while the Olg-hai were in fashion of mind and body quite unlike even the largest of Orc-kind ...

With this text and its successors the section *On Translation* was typed and preserved separately, and it is not possible to relate these precisely to the texts of the first section. Of these latter there are four after F 4, textually complex and not all complete, and for the purposes of this account it is not necessary to describe them.[6] Even if my father had not said so very plainly himself in his letters, it would be very evident from these drafts that the writing of an account that would satisfy him was exceedingly tasking and frustrating, largely (I believe) because he found the constraint of space profoundly uncongenial. In March 1955 (*Letters* no.160) he wrote to Rayner Unwin: 'I now wish that no appendices had been promised! For I think their appearance in truncated and compressed form will satisfy nobody'; and in the same letter he said:

> In any case the 'background' matter is very intricate, useless unless exact, and compression within the limits available leaves it unsatisfactory. It needs great concentration (and leisure), and being completely interlocked cannot be dealt with piecemeal. I have found that out, since I let part of it go.

Even the final typescript of Appendix F was not a fair copy, but carried many emendations.

Two texts of the second section of Appendix F, *On Translation*, are extant, following the reduced version in F 3 (p. 76) and preceding the final typescript. They were evidently made at a late stage in the evolution of this appendix; and it was in the first of these, which may conveniently be called 'A', that my father reinstated a part of the detailed discussion of names in the original version that had been discarded in F 3. At this stage he very largely retained the name-forms found in F 2, in his discussion of *Baggins*, *Gamgee*, *Cotton*, *Brandywine*, *Brandybuck*; the word *hobbit*; the origin of Hobbit-names such as *Tom*, *Bill*, *Mat*; *Meriadoc*, *Samwise*. There are however some differences and additions,[7] notably in his account of the curious names found in Buckland (cf. RK pp. 413-14):

> These I have often left unaltered, for if queer now, they were queer in their own day. Some I have given a Celtic cast, notably *Meriadoc* and *Gorhendad*. There is some reason for this. Many of the actual Buckland (and Bree) names had something of that style: such as *Marroc*, *Madoc*, *Seredic*; and they often ended in

ac, ic, oc. Also the relation of, say, Welsh or British to English was somewhat similar to that of the older language of the Stoors and Bree-men to the Westron.

Thus Bree, Combe, Archet, and Chetwood are modelled on British relics in English place-names, chosen by sense: *bree* 'hill', *chet* 'wood'. Similarly *Gorhendad* represents a name *Ogforgad* which according to Stoor-tradition had once meant 'great-grandfather or ancestor'. While *Meriadoc* was chosen to fit the fact that this character's shortened name meant 'jolly, gay' in Westron *kili*, though it was actually an abbreviation of *Kilimanac* [> *kali, Kalamanac*].

The text A lacks the discussion (RK pp. 414–15) of the words *mathom* and *smial* and the names *Sméagol* and *Déagol*, and ends, at the bottom of a page, with this passage:

> The yet more northerly tongue of Dale is here seen only in the names of the Dwarves that came from that region, and so used the language of Men there, and took their 'outer' names in that language. The Dwarvish names in this book and in *The Hobbit* are in fact all genuine Norse dwarf-names; though the title *Oakenshield* is a translation.

Thus the concluding passage in F 3 (see pp. 76–7) concerning the use of the word *Gnomes* and of the plural *Dwarves* is absent, but whether because my father had rejected it, or because the end of the A typescript is lost, is impossible to say.

In the second of these texts *On Translation*, which I will call 'B', he retained all this reinstated material from A, changing some of the name-forms,[8] and even extended it, going back to the original version F 2 again for a passage exemplifying his treatment of the true names in the language of the Mark. Here reappears material derived from F 2 §§54–5 concerning the real native name of Rohan *Lôgrad*, the translation of *Lohtûr* by *Éothéod* and of *tûrak* 'king' by Théoden; and this is followed by the discussion of *mathom, smial, Sméagol* and *Déagol* – the only portion of this passage retained in the final form of Appendix F.

In B my father followed the passage given above from A ('The yet more northerly language of Dale ...') with a statement on the different treatment of the 'true' Runes in *The Hobbit* and *The Lord of the Rings* that derives from that in F* (p. 22, §11):

> In keeping with the general method of translation here outlined, as applied to the Common Speech and other languages akin to it, in *The Hobbit* the *Cirth* were turned into Runes, into forms and values, that is, practically the same as those once used in

England. But since the *Cirth* were actually of Elvish origin, and little used for writing the Common Speech (save by Dwarves), while many readers of *The Hobbit* found the matter of scripts of interest, in this larger history it seemed better to present the *Cirth* as well as the Fëanorian letters in their proper shapes and use. Though naturally an adaptation by the translator of these alphabets to fit modern English has had to replace their actual application to the Westron tongue, which was very different from ours.

This is followed by the conclusion concerning *Gnomes* and *Dwarves* which is lacking in A.

In the final typescript, that sent to the printer, many changes entered that were not, as was almost invariably my father's practice when proceeding from one draft to the next, anticipated by corrections made to the preceding text: they seem in fact to have entered as he typed.[9] There is no suggestion in text B, for instance, of the footnote to RK p. 414 warning against an assumption, based on the linguistic transposition, 'that the Rohirrim closely resembled the ancient English otherwise'; nor of the removal from the body of the text of the detailed discussion of the word *hobbit* and the names *Gamgee* and *Brandywine* to a note at its end;[10] nor yet of the alteration of the passage (discussed on p. 77) concerning the word *Gnomes* so that it should apply to the word *Elves*, and the placing of it at the end of the text instead of preceding the discussion of *Dwarves*. Nothing could show more clearly the extreme pressure my father was under when, after so much labour, he at last sent Appendix F to the publishers. It seems to me more than likely that had circumstances been otherwise the form of that appendix would have been markedly different.

NOTES

1 The apparent implication here that *Teleri* was the name exclusively of those of the Eldar who remained in Middle-earth was certainly unintentional.
2 A footnote at this point reads: 'Such as *Thranduil* and *Legolas* from Mirkwood; *Lórien, Galadriel, Caras Galadon, Nimrodel, Amroth* and others from Loth-lórien.'
3 For an account of this reinstatement of material from F 2 see pp. 80–1, with notes 7 and 8.
4 It must be admitted, however, that the statement in the chapter *Of Maeglin* in *The Silmarillion* (p. 136) that Idril Celebrindal 'was golden as the Vanyar, her mother's kindred' appears already in the original text (1951; see XI.316); and of course even if the re-use of the passage did precede the appearance of the idea of the 'golden Vanyar', it needed correction subsequently.

5   With this cf. the passage in F 2 concerning Trolls (p. 36, §17): 'the evil Power had at various times made use of them, teaching them what little they could learn, and even crossing their breed with that of the larger Orcs.'

6   There is scarcely anything in the last texts that calls for special notice, but it should be recorded that in the penultimate draft my father revealed the meaning of the sentence in the Black Speech uttered by one of the Orcs who was guarding Pippin in the chapter *The Uruk-hai* (TT p. 48): *Uglúk u bagronk sha pushdug Saruman-glob búbhosh skai*. At the end of the section *Orcs and the Black Speech* (RK p. 410) this text reads:

> ... while the curse of the Mordor-orc in Chapter 3 of Book Three is in the more debased form used by the soldiers of the Dark Tower, of whom Grishnákh was the captain. *Uglúk to the cesspool, sha! the dungfilth; the great Saruman-fool, skai!*

7   Where F 2 in the discussion of *Baggins* (p. 48) had Westron *labin* 'bag', and *Labin-nec* 'Bag End', the text A has *laban, Laban-nec*. For the origin of 'hobbit' my father retained the form *cubuc* and Théoden's archaic *cûgbagu* (p. 49), noting that it meant ' "hole-dweller" (or "hole-builder") ': see p. 69. He also gave here for the first time the Westron name for 'hobbits', *nathramin*, though later in the text the form *banathin* appears; and he provided the true name of Hamfast Gamgee:

> The Gaffer's name on the other hand was *Ranadab*, meaning 'settled, living in a fixed abode or group of hobbit-holes', and hence often 'stay-at-home', the opposite of 'wanderer'. Since this closely corresponds with ancient English *hamfæst*, I have translated it as *Hamfast*. The shortenings [*Sam* and *Ham*] at any rate rhyme, as did *Ban* and *Ran* in the Shire. Moreover neither *Banzîra* nor *Ranadab* were any longer current in the Shire as ordinary words and survived only as names, originally given no doubt as (not entirely complimentary) nicknames, but used traditionally in certain families without much more recognition than is the case today with, say, Roy or Francis.

8   For *Laban-nec* 'Bag End' in A the second text B has *Laban-neg*. The 'hobbit' word became *kubug*, and the Rohan form *kûgbagul*, changed on the typescript to *cuduc* and *kûddûka*. The true name of Gorhendad Oldbuck became *Ogmandab*, and that of Meriadoc *Kalimanac*, altered to *Kalimanoc* (*Kalimac* in RK); that of Hamfast Gamgee became *Ranagad* (*Ranugad* in RK), and of Sam *Banzîra*. The Westron word for 'hobbit' became *banakil*, as in RK; but *Branduhîm* 'foaming beer' as the Hobbits' perversion of *Baranduin* remained (see note 10), as did *Carbandur* for Imladris (with *Karningul*, as in RK, pencilled against it).

9 It is clear that there was no intermediate text.
10 The introduction of the Hobbits' original name for the river, *Branda-nîn* 'border-water' or 'Marchbourn', transformed into *Bralda-hîm* 'heady ale', was only made in this last typescript.

III
THE FAMILY TREES

This chapter is an account of the evolution of the genealogical tables given in Appendix C to *The Lord of the Rings*; and since such a development can obviously be followed far more easily and rapidly by successive stages of the tables themselves than by any account in words, I present it here largely by redrawings of the original family trees. My father followed his usual course of emending each one (most of them being carefully, even beautifully, made) more or less roughly in preparation for its successor; I have therefore in my redrawings excluded subsequent alterations, when the distinction can be clearly made.

Baggins of Hobbiton

The first four genealogical tables of the Baggins family, to which I give the references **BA 1** to **BA 4**, are found on pp. 89–92.

BA 1 (p. 89)

This is the earliest tree of the family of Baggins of Hobbiton (by which I mean the earliest fully formed and carefully presented table, excluding such hasty genealogies as that referred to in VI.222). It was very carefully made, but was much used and corrected later, and is now a very battered document. The number of members of the Baggins family shown is still far fewer than in the published table; and the presence of *Folco Took* (with *Faramond* pencilled beside it) suggests that it belongs to the period that I have called 'the Third Phase' in the writing of the earlier chapters of *The Fellowship of the Ring*, before the emergence of Peregrin Took (see VII.31–2). It may be related therefore to the original text of the *Prologue* (see p. 3 and note 1), and to the original tree of the Took family given in VI.317. As in that table, the ages of those present at the Farewell Party are given, but not extended as a system of relative dating for all members of the family including those long dead; and dates are also given according to the Shire Reckoning (which appeared quite early, in the autumn of 1939, see VII.9).

It will be seen that virtually all the dates in BA 1 differ from those for the corresponding persons in the published form, though seldom by much.

A good deal of this genealogy was present already in the first stages of the writing of *The Lord of the Rings*, but I will not return here to the early history of the Baggins family tree, since it has been fully recounted in *The Return of the Shadow* and all the names indexed. It may be noted, however, that the maiden name of Miranda Burrows, who was described (VI.283) as the 'overshadowed wife' of Cosimo Sackville-Baggins, was never given in the narrative texts before she disappeared (VI.324); and that Flambard Took, son of the Old Took, and his wife Rosa Baggins had appeared in the original Took family tree given in VI.317.

BA 2 (p. 90)

This table was a rough working version, taking up changes marked on BA 1, and with further alterations and additions entering in the course of its making. It was immediately followed by an even hastier version without dates, hardly differing from BA 2, but introducing one or two further changes that appear in BA 3 (and changing Miranda Burrows to Miranda Noakes and then to Miranda Sandyman). I have given no number to this text, regarding it simply as an extension of BA 2.

As my father first made this table Bingo Baggins was moved down to become the youngest of the three sons of Mungo, but remained the husband of Maxima Proudfoot. While it was in progress, however, a daughter Linda Baggins was introduced above him, and she took over the Proudfoot connection, becoming the wife of Marco Proudfoot and the mother of Odo Proudfoot; while Bingo, now the youngest of a family of five, as he remained, became the husband of Fatima Chubb.

Olo Proudfoot was first named Rollo; and Rosa Baggins' husband Flambard Took becomes Hildigrim Took (the final name: see the Took genealogy T 3 on p. 110). The names Ponto, Largo, Longo, Fosco, Dora, replacing Longo, Tango, Largo, Togo, Semolina respectively, remained into the final form of the genealogy. It may also be noted that Drogo's birth-date was changed to make him a year younger than his sister Dora, though his place in the tree was not altered; it will be seen that in BA 3 he is again made older than her by a year.

BA 3 (p. 91)

The third Baggins family tree is one of a series of carefully made tables, and being the first carries an explanatory head-note, as follows:

> The dates in these Trees are given according to the 'Shire-reckoning', in the traditional Hobbit manner, calculated from the crossing of the Baranduin (Brandywine River), Year 1, by the brothers Marco and Cavallo. The persons mentioned in these tables are only a selection from many names. All are either concerned with the events recounted in the memoirs of Bilbo and Frodo; or are mentioned in them; or are persons present at the Farewell Party, or the direct ancestors of the guests on that occasion. The names of these guests (such of the 144 as room has been found for) are marked *.

Bilbo Baggins, born 1290, went on his famous journey 1341–2. At the age of 111 he gave his Farewell Party in 1401. Frodo Baggins sold Bag End in 1418 and returned at the end of 1419. He left the Shire in 1421. Meriadoc Brandybuck succeeded to Brandy Hall and the headship of the family in 1432. Peregrin became The Took (and Seventeenth Shirking) in 1434. The memoirs (and additions by Samwise Gamgee) close in 1436.

The mention here of Peregrin becoming the seventeenth Shirking relates this table at once to the texts of the *Prologue* (see pp. 5–7, 11) composed after the narrative of *The Lord of the Rings* had been completed, and suggests that the family trees followed something of the same succession as is found in the Prologue texts. – I have not included in my redrawing the stars indicating presence at the Farewell Party, for my father only put them in later and incompletely.

On the family name Gaukroger (subsequently lost), appearing in Togo Baggins' wife Selina Gaukroger, see VI.236 and note 10; and on Belisarius Bolger see note 3.

BA 4 (p. 92)

The fourth tree is the first text of another set of genealogies, and seems to belong to much the same time as BA 3. This also is finely written, with an introductory note that is virtually the same as that in the published form (RK p. 379), apart from the preservation of the names Marco and Cavallo, but then continues with the second paragraph (giving dates) of that to BA 3, and includes the reference to Peregrin's becoming the 'Seventeenth Shirking'.

This version retains the dates of BA 3 (not repeated in the redrawing), and differs from it chiefly in the addition of descendants from Bingo and Ponto Baggins; also by the loss of Togo Baggins and his wife Selina Gaukroger and their replacement by a second daughter of Inigo and Belinda, Laura, and her husband Togo Gaukroger.

The new names Polo, Porro are referred to in both texts of the original version of the Appendix on Languages (see p. 46, §43), showing that that work followed or accompanied this stage in the development of the family trees.

The starred names, indicating presence at the Farewell Party, are as in the published table, with the omission of Cosimo Sackville-Baggins and Dora Baggins: this was perhaps inadvertent, but neither name is starred in BA 3.

Sweeping changes to the existing names were entered subsequently on BA 4. In the introductory note Marco and Cavallo were changed to Marcho and Blanco (see pp. 6, 17), and 'Seventeenth Shirking' to 'Twentieth Thane' (see under BA 3). In the family tree the following changes were made, listed by generations:

Inigo Baggins > Balbo Baggins

Belinda Boffin > Berylla Boffin
Regina Grubb > Laura Grubb
Ansegar Bolger > Fastolph Bolger
Maxima Bunce > Mimosa Bunce
Cornelia Hornblower > Tanta Hornblower
Laura Baggins > Lily Baggins
Togo Gaukroger > Togo Goodbody

Bertha Baggins > Belba Baggins
Rudigor Bolger > Rudigar Bolger
Magnus Proudfoot > Bodo Proudfoot
Fatima Chubb > Chica Chubb
Robinia Bolger > Ruby Bolger

Conrad Bolger > Wilibald Bolger

Cosimo Sackville-Baggins > Lotho Sackville-Baggins
Gerda Chubb-Baggins > Poppy Chubb-Baggins
Arnor Bolger > Filibert Bolger
Porro Baggins > Porto Baggins
Crassus Burrows > Milo Burrows
Duenna Baggins > Daisy Baggins
Guido Boffin > Griffo Boffin

Flavus, Crispus, Rhoda, Fulvus Burrows > Mosco, Moro, Myrtle, Minto Burrows

In addition, the wife of Posco Baggins was introduced, named (as in the final form) Gilly Brownlock; and Ponto Baggins' daughter Angelica appeared.

On the removal of the Latin names of Peony Baggins' husband and their offspring see p. 47, §45, and commentary (p. 69).

The nomenclature and structure of the Baggins genealogy as published was now present, except in this respect. In the final form Frodo's aunt Dora again becomes older than her brother Drogo (see under BA 2 above), and her husband Wilibald Bolger (see the list just given) is removed; while Posco Baggins has a sister Prisca, born in 1306, and she gains Wilibald as her husband.

In subsequent manuscripts (of which there were five, making nine all told, not including incomplete drafts) these changes entered, and in one of them the word 'spinster' was written against Dora Baggins.

Bolger of Budgeford

It is a curious fact that the genealogical tables of the families of Bolger of Budgeford and Boffin of the Yale were already in print when they were rejected from Appendix C, but I have not been able to find any evidence bearing on the reason for their rejection. In a letter from the publishers of 20 May 1955 my father was told: 'We have dropped Bolger and Boffin from Appendix C', and on 24 May Rayner Unwin

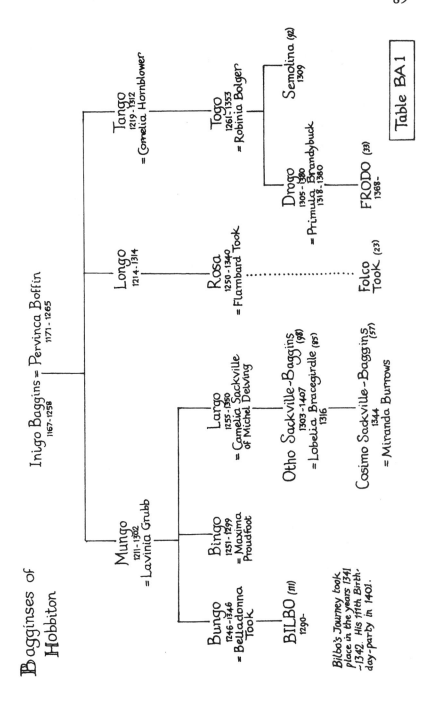

Table BA1

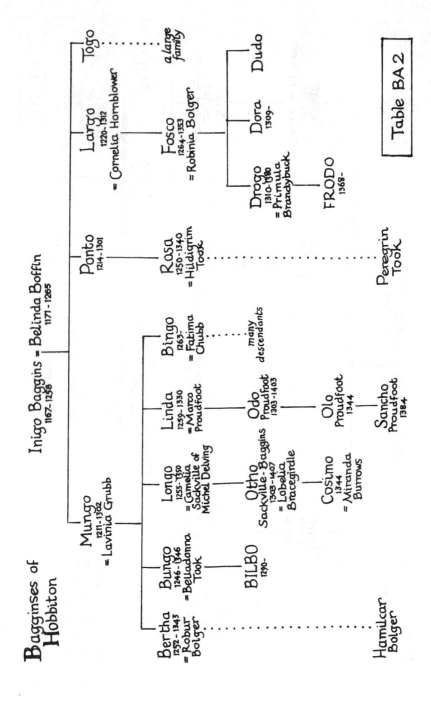

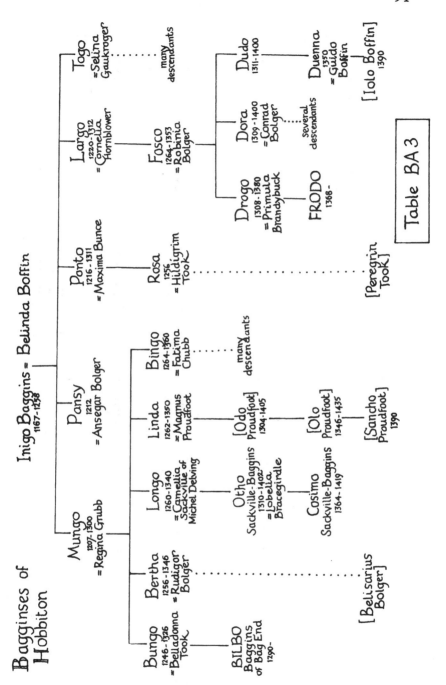

91

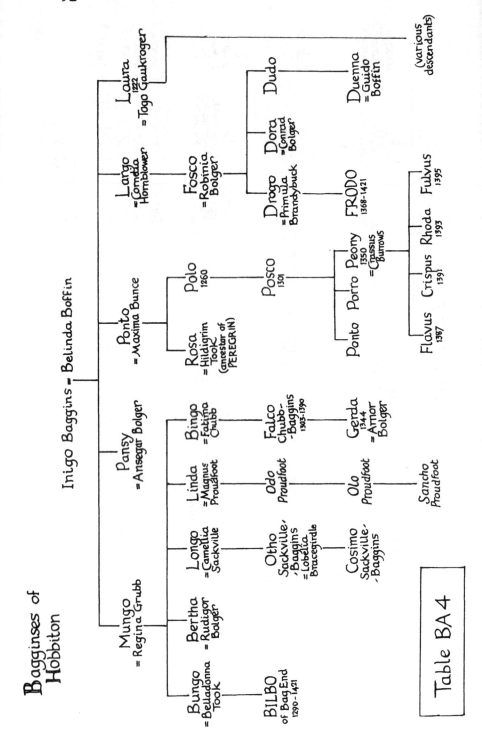

THE FAMILY TREES

wrote: 'I have deleted the two family trees and the redundant note that introduced them' (no copy of either tree has any note specifically relating to them). These remarks might suggest that it was my father who proposed their omission, though no trace can now be found of any such request; but it is hard to see why he should have done so. That he was pressed for space, and greatly oppressed by that necessity, is certain, but it seems strange (if this is the explanation) that he should have been so limited as to abandon these genealogies in order to obtain a couple of pages elsewhere in the Appendices.

I refer to the versions of the Bolger genealogy by the letters **BG**, and the three that I have redrawn, BG 1, BG 2, and BG 4, will be found on pp. 95–7.

BG 1 (p. 95)

This earliest form of the Bolger family tree is entitled *Bolgers of Woodhall*. On my father's original map of the Shire, reproduced as frontispiece to *The Return of the Shadow*, the Bolger territory is marked as lying north of the Woody End and south of the East Road (i.e. west of the Brandywine Bridge).

The very brief table is found, together with genealogies of the Tooks and Brandybucks, on the page that carries the original Baggins family tree BA 1, and was very plainly made at the same time, at an early stage in the writing of *The Lord of the Rings* (see pp. 85, 89); but these early Bolgers, Scudamor, Cedivar, Savanna, Sagramor, are not found in those texts. Robinia Bolger in the fourth generation appears also in BA 1 as the wife of Togo Baggins; but her brother Robur is seen to have existed independently before he was introduced into the Baggins family in BA 2 (p. 90) as the husband of Bertha Baggins, Bilbo's aunt, who first emerged in that version. Rollo Bolger is that friend of Bilbo's to whom he bequeathed his feather-bed (VI.247). Olo and Odo appear in the Took genealogy given in VI.317; for my attempt to expound briefly the history of 'Odo Bolger' see VII.31–2.

BG 2 (p. 96)

The second version of the Bolger genealogy[1] is one of the group of which the Baggins table BA 3 (p. 91) is the first, carrying the explanatory head-note. The title is now changed to *Bolgers of Budgeford*. In the chapter *A Conspiracy Unmasked* (FR p. 118) Fredegar's family is said to come 'from Budgeford in Bridgefields' (the only occurrence of these names in the narrative of *The Lord of the Rings*).[2]

Apart from Odovacar, Rudigor (later Rudigar), and Fredegar (applied to a different person), none of the actual names of members of the Bolger family in this genealogy appear in the family-trees in RK, but some recur in other tables made at the same time: thus in the Baggins table BA 3 are found Ansegar (husband of Pansy Baggins),

Robinia (wife of Fosco Baggins), Conrad (husband of Dora Baggins), and Belisarius (replacing Hamilcar).[3]

Two of the names subsequently rejected are mentioned in the text F 2 of the Appendix on Languages: Celador Bolger (p. 61, note 42), and Bildad Bolger. Bildad is mentioned in F 2 (p. 51, §50) in the context of my father's not using scriptural names to 'translate' Hobbit names: it was 'a genuine Hobbit name', he explained, that bore a merely accidental resemblance to the Biblical Bildad (one of the friends of Job).

The name *Miranda* (Gaukroger) reappears after the disappearance of Miranda Burrows, wife of Cosimo Sackville-Baggins (p. 86). Robur Bolger (see under BG 1) has been replaced, as in BA 3, by Rudigor, but Robur remains as the name of Rudigor's younger brother.

BG 3

This table corresponds to BA 4 of the Baggins clan, but it repeats BG 2 exactly except in the addition of Robur's descendants, and in the change of the name *Gundobad* to *Gundahad*. I have not redrawn it, therefore, but give here the added element:

Robur = Amelia Hornblower
|
Omar = Alma Boffin
|
Arnor = Gerda Chubb-Baggins

Arnor and his wife Gerda Chubb-Baggins appear in BA 4. – The birth-dates of these Bolgers are the same as those of their replacements in BG 4: Robur (Rudibert) 1260, Omar (Adalbert) 1301, Arnor (Filibert) 1342.

BG 4 (p. 97)

On the Baggins table BA 4 my father made many changes to the existing names, and in so doing brought the Baggins genealogy close to its final form. On the accompanying Bolger table BG 3 he did the same, but even more extensively, so that of the existing names none were left save Gundahad, Rudigar (altered from Rudigor), Odovacar (see VII.20), and Fredegar (who becomes the former Fredegar's grandson), and the Bolger clan have uniformly 'translated' names of Germanic origin. At the same time three children of Wilibald Bolger (formerly Conrad) were added; and the Hobbit family names Diggle and Lightfoot (not found in *The Lord of the Rings*) appear.[4]

Of those who do not appear in the published genealogies the following are marked as guests at the Farewell Party: Wilimar, Heribald, and Nora, and also their mother Prisca Baggins (see p. 88), who is not so marked in the Baggins tree. She was 95; but Frodo's still more ancient aunt Dora was present at the age of ninety-nine.

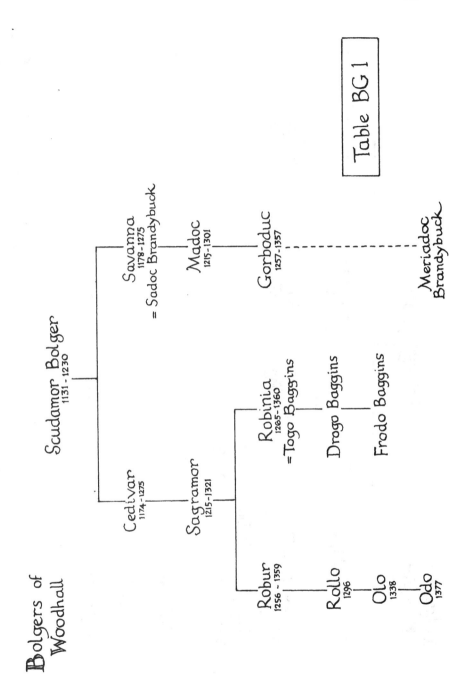

Table BG 1

96

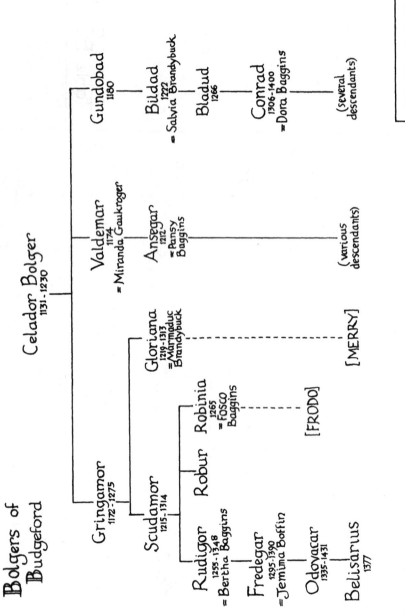

Table BG 2

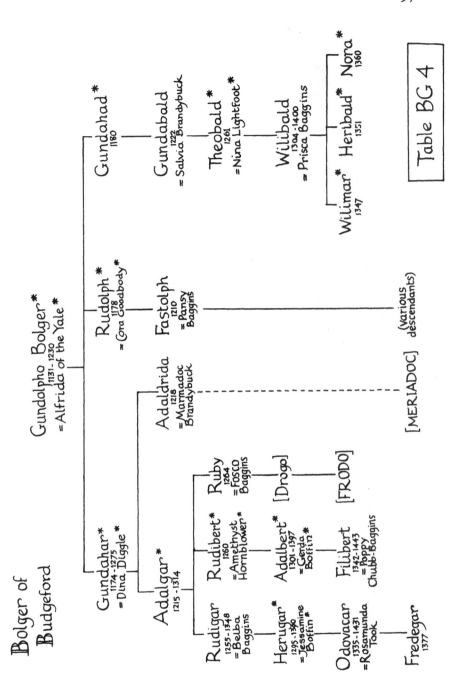

In this case, since there is no family tree of the Bolgers in *The Lord of the Rings*, I have redrawn the last of the manuscript tables, in which the alterations made to BG 3 were set out fair; and it was in this form that the genealogy was printed.[5] In this redrawing the names with asterisks are those that do not appear in the genealogies of other families in *The Lord of the Rings*.

Boffin of the Yale

In *The Lord of the Rings* no 'homeland' of the Boffins is named, and in the First Edition there was no mention of the Yale; but on the original map of the Shire (frontispiece to Vol.VI) the name *Boffins* is written to the north of Hobbiton Hill,[6] and Boffins are clearly associated in early texts with the village of Northope in that region, 'only a mile or two behind the Hill' (VI.319, 385). Northope was subsequently renamed Overhill, and 'Mr. Boffin at Overhill' remained into FR (p. 53).

But on the first Shire-map the name Northope was corrected, not to Overhill but to The Yale, although that name does not appear in the texts; and this must be the reference in the genealogical trees, which retained 'Boffin of the Yale' into the printed form. Much later the name was added to the Shire map in the Second Edition in a different place, south of Whitfurrows and west of Stock, and a reference was inserted into the text (FR p. 86), 'the lowlands of the Yale' (see VI.387, note 10); but the Boffin genealogy had been abandoned before the publication of the First Edition (p. 88).

I refer to the Boffin family trees by the letters **BF**, and those that I have redrawn, BF 2 and BF 4, are found on pp. 100–1.

BF 1

There is no Boffin genealogy accompanying the very early tables of the Baggins and Bolger families. The earliest form consists of two closely similar, extremely rough drafts on the same pages as the two versions of BA 2 (see p. 86): so rough and so much corrected that I have not attempted to redraw either of them. They were in any case very largely repeated in the following version.

BF 2 (p. 100)

This genealogy is extant in two forms, differing only in that the first of them sets out the earliest generations separately, and begins the main table with Otto the Fat, whereas in the second form the elements are combined: for these purposes they can be treated as one. This table belongs with BA 3 (p. 91) and BG 2 (p. 96).

Hugo Boffin, whose wife was Donnamira Took, and their son Jago go back to the Took genealogy given in VI.317; Guido and his wife Duenna Baggins, with their son Iolo, are found in the Baggins table BA 3; and Jemima Boffin wife of Fredegar Bolger in the Bolger table

BG 2. Hugo Bracegirdle, who does not appear in the published genealogies, is named in FR (p. 46) as the recipient of a book-case belonging to Bilbo.

Lobelia Sackville-Baggins' dates make her 92 at her death: at the beginning of the chapter *The Grey Havens* (RK p. 301) the text had 'she was after all quite ninety years old', changed on the late typescripts to 'more than a hundred'; and on the following version of the Boffin genealogy her dates were altered to 1318–1420.

The subsequent development of the Boffin genealogy exactly parallels that of the Bolgers, and I treat them in the same way.

BF 3

This is written on the same page as BG 3, and as in that table the previous version was followed exactly, but with the corresponding addition (see p. 94) introducing Alma Boffin, the wife of Omar Bolger. This table is not redrawn. As in the case of BG 3 (and also of the accompanying Baggins table BA 4) a great many of the names were changed on the manuscript of BF 3, and new Boffins were introduced in the second generation.

BF 4 (p. 101)

As with the Bolger genealogy, I give here the final manuscript of the Boffin table (written on the same page as BG 4), the form from which it was printed, in which the changed names and additions made on BF 3 appear in a fair copy; and here also the starred names indicate those that are not found in the genealogies of other families in *The Lord of the Rings*. Folco Boffin, who is not present in any of these, was a friend of Frodo's (FR pp. 51, 76–7, and see VII.30–2); for Hugo Bracegirdle see under BF 2 above.

Of those who do not appear in the published genealogies the following are marked as being present at the Farewell Party: Vigo, Folco, Tosto, Bruno Bracegirdle, Hugo Bracegirdle, and the 'various descendants' of Rollo Boffin and Druda Burrows.

Brandybuck of Buckland

The Brandybuck genealogies are referred to by the letters **BR**; for the redrawn versions BR 1 and BR 4 see pp. 104–5.

BR 1 (p. 104)

This earliest version of the Brandybuck family tree is written below the earliest of the Baggins clan (BA 1), with those of the Bolgers (BG 1) and the Tooks (not the earliest) on the reverse.

Many of the names found here are found also in the Took genealogy given in VI.317: Gorboduc Brandybuck and his wife Mirabella Took, and their six children (see VI.318) Roderic, Alaric, Bellissima, Theodoric, Athanaric, and Primula; also Caradoc, Merry's father, and

100

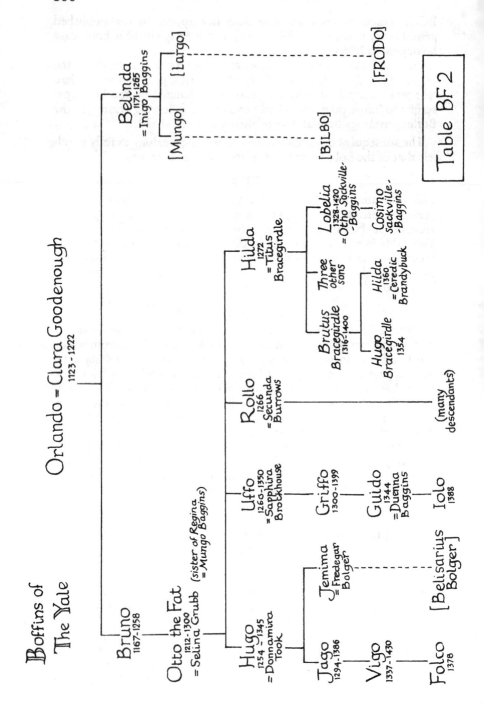

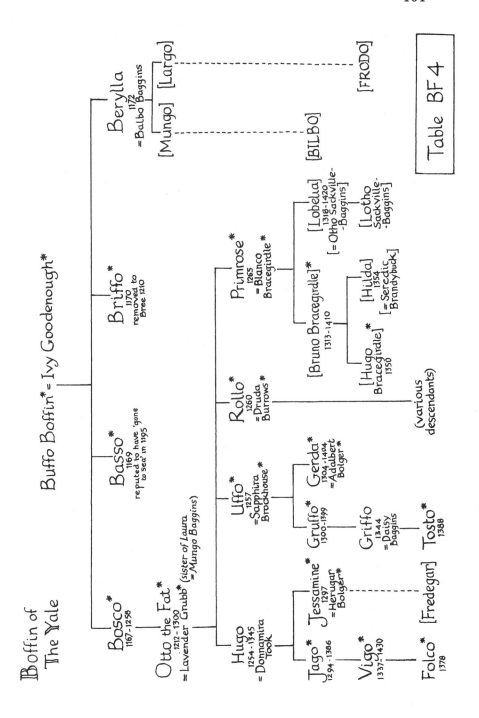

Table BF 4

his wife Yolanda Took (cf. VI.100, 251). Merry's cousin Lamorac appears in early texts of *The Lord of the Rings*,[7] where the name replaced Bercilak (VI.273) who in the genealogy is his father. Of Madoc (Gorboduc's father) and the descendants of his second son Habaccuc there is no trace in those texts, except for Melissa (afterwards replaced by Melilot, see pp. 105–6, who made herself conspicuous at the Farewell Party, VI.38, 101).

BR 2

This is an extremely rough table, written in ink over pencil on the reverse of the page carrying the rough Baggins and Bolger tables BA 2 and BF 1: here my father is seen devising a much changed genealogy of the Brandybucks. I have not redrawn it, since its names and structure largely survived into the fair copy BR 4, and it needs only to be recorded that it was here that Gorhendad Brandybuck the 'founder' first appeared, but with the dates 1134–1236, and not yet as the remote ancestor Gorhendad Oldbuck of four centuries before; while his son is Marmaduc, not as subsequently his grandson, and Madoc, Sadoc, and Marroc are the sons of Marmaduc. 'Old Rory' is called Cadwalader; and all the Latin titles (see BR 4) were already present.

BR 3

This was another rough draft, scarcely differing from BR 2 except in the reversal of Madoc and Marmaduc and in the addition of their wives: Madoc's wife is Savanna Hogpen, and Marmaduc's Sultana Bolger. In the original Bolger table (BG 1, p. 95) Savanna Bolger was the wife of Sadoc Brandybuck, while in BG 2 the wife of Marmaduc was Gloriana Bolger. Corrections to the text altered the name of 'Old Rory' from Cadwalader to Sagramor (taken over from Sagramor Bolger in BG 1), and of his wife from Matilda Drinkwater to Matilda Goold.

BR 4 (p. 105)

This carefully made version is one of the series that includes (Baggins) BA 3 (p. 91), (Bolger) BG 2 (p. 96), and (Boffin) BF 2 (p. 100). Additions were made subsequently to BR 4, but in this case it is convenient to treat them as part of the table as first written (see below).

In this new version of the Brandybuck tree, comprised in BR 2–4, my father's enjoyment of the incongruity of Hobbit customs of namegiving culminated in such marriages as that of Madoc Superbus with Savanna Hogpen, and in the grandiose epithets of the heads of the clan, with Meriadoc taking his title Porphyrogenitus from imperial Byzantium, 'born in the purple (chamber)'. In the text F 2 of the Appendix on Languages my father wrote (p. 47, §45): ' "Classical" names ... represent usually names derived by Hobbits from tales of ancient times and far kingdoms of Men', and added in a footnote:

'Thus the perhaps to us rather ridiculous subnames or titles of the Brandybucks adopted by the heads of the family, *Astyanax, Aureus, Magnificus*, were originally half-jesting and were in fact drawn from traditions about the Kings at Norbury.' Afterwards he struck out this note and rejected classical names (see p. 69, §45).

The following additions, included in the redrawing, were made to the table after it had been completed. Sadoc Brandybuck, at first said to have had 'many descendants', is given 'Two sons' and a daughter Salvia, the wife of Bildad Bolger (see BG 2, p. 96); Basilissa Brandybuck becomes the wife of Fulvus Burrows; their son Crassus Burrows is added, who on account of his marriage to Peony Baggins has appeared in BA 4 (p. 92), together with their four children; and Hilda Bracegirdle enters as the wife of Ceredic Brandybuck, with their three children. As the table was made Marmaduc's wife was still Sultana Bolger, but she was changed to Gloriana as in BG 2.

BR 5

Following the general pattern, BR 5 was recopied from BR 4 almost as it stood: the only change made was that Gorhendad was now actually named Gorhendad Oldbuck, retaining the note 'Built Brandy Hall and changed the family name to Brandybuck' (retaining also the dates 1134–1236); and then subsequently a great many of the names were altered on the manuscript.

Gorhendad Oldbuck was replaced by Gormadoc 'Deepdelver', and his wife Malva Headstrong was introduced. 'Gorhendad Oldbuck of the Marish', however, is Gormadoc's father, and his dates are 1090–1191. At this time all the Latin or Greek titles of the heads of the Brandybuck clan were replaced by English names, as in the final genealogy. Other changes were (following the generations):

Savanna Hogpen > Hanna Goldworthy

Marmaduc > Marmadoc
Gloriana Bolger > Adaldrida Bolger (see BG 4)
Bildad Bolger > Gundabald Bolger (see BG 4)

Gorboduc > Gormanac > Gorbadoc
Orgulus > Orgulas

Sagramor > Rorimac
Matilda Goold > Menegilda Goold
Bellissima > Amaranth
Carados > Saradas
Basilissa > Asphodel
Fulvus Burrows > Rufus Burrows
Priamus > Dinodas
Columbus > Gorgulas > Gorbulas

Caradoc > Saradoc

104

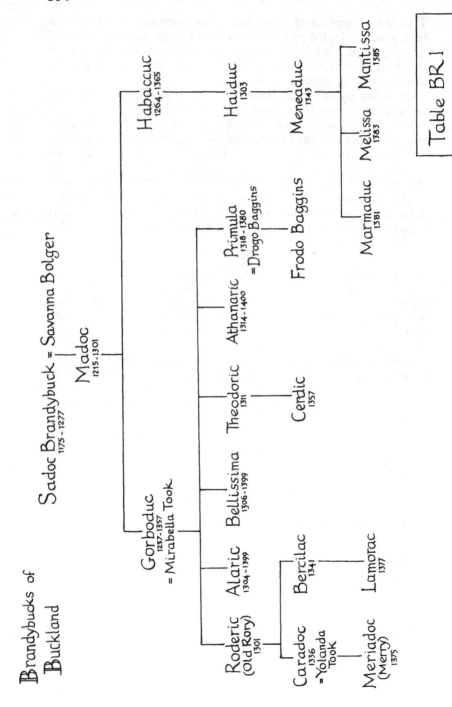

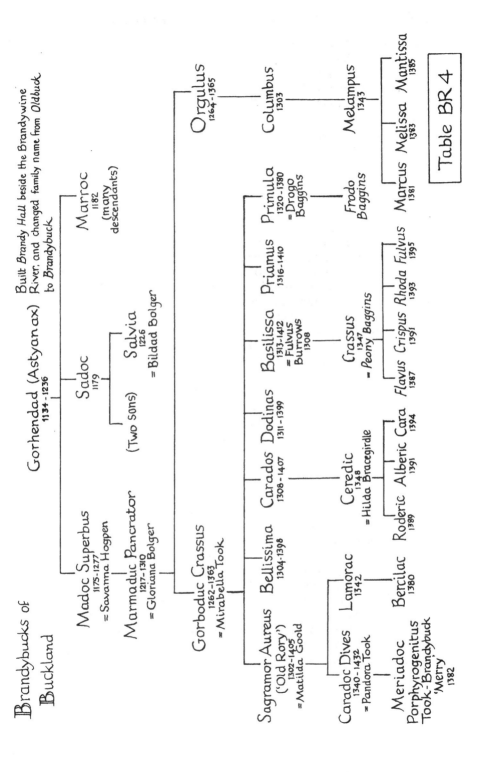

106   THE PEOPLES OF MIDDLE-EARTH

Pandora Took > Esmeralda Took
Lamorac > Merimac
Ceredic > Seredic
Crassus Burrows > Milo Burrows (see p. 88)
Melampus > Marmadas

Bercilac > Berilac
Roderic > Doderic
Alberic > Ilberic
Cara > Celandine
Marcus > Merimas
Melissa > Mentha
Mantissa > Melilot

The names of the children of Milo Burrows and Peony Baggins, Flavus, Crispus, Rhoda, and Fulvus, were struck out but not replaced, since they appear in the Baggins genealogy (see p. 88 and RK p. 380).

Only in these respects does BR 5 as corrected differ from the final form (RK p. 382): Gorhendad Oldbuck is the father, not the remote ancestor of Gormadoc Brandybuck; and Merry is still named Meriadoc Took-Brandybuck. Subsequently my father altered the note on Gorhendad to begin 'c.740 began the building of *Brandy Hall*', but left in his dates as 1090–1191, which survived into the proof, as did Meriadoc Took-Brandybuck, when they were deleted.

Took of Great Smials

The final genealogy of the Tooks was achieved without the great upheaval of names that took place in those of the Baggins, Bolger, Boffin and Brandybuck families. I give the letter T to the versions, T 1 being the very early form printed in VI.317; the redrawn versions T 2, T 3, and T 4 appear on pp. 109–11.

T 2 (p. 109)

This version is found on the page that carries also the first genealogies of the Baggins, Bolger, and Brandybuck families, BA 1, BG 1, and BR 1. It is very closely related to T 1, and indeed differs from it chiefly in giving the dates according to the years of the Shire Reckoning, rather than the ages of the persons relative to the Farewell Party. If the age of each person given in T 1 is subtracted from the year of the Farewell Party, the birth-dates in T 2 agree in nearly every case.[8] The only other changes are the reversal of the order of Isambard and Flambard, sons of the Old Took;[9] the addition of Vigo's son Uffo, and of Uffo's son Prospero (see VI.38); and the change of Odo Took-Bolger to Odo Bolger.

T 3 (p. 110)

The development of this version is best understood by comparison with T 2; but it may be noted that Isembard (for earlier Isambard) has been restored to the second place among the sons of the Old Took, while Flambard, husband of Rosa Baggins, is renamed Hildigrim (a change seen also in the Baggins tables BA 1 and 2). Fosco becomes Sigismond, and rather oddly both Hildigrim and Sigismond have a son named Hildibrand (formerly Faramond and Vigo): the Hildibrand son of Hildigrim was replaced subsequently on the manuscript by Adalgrim, as he remained. Among the many changes in the third and fourth generations from the Old Took may be noted the arrival of Peregrin son of Paladin (see VII.35), while Odo Bolger becomes Hamilcar; the replacement of Merry's mother Yolanda by Pandora (cf. the Brandybuck tables BR 1 and 4); and the appearance of Odovacar Bolger (cf. BG 2).[10]

T 4 (p. 111)

At this stage (corresponding to BA 3, BG 2, BF 2, and BR 4) my father made a series of four tables all closely similar – differing scarcely at all, in fact, except in the names of the children of the Old Took, who were increased in number without thereby altering the subsequent generations as they now existed. I have redrawn the fourth of these, calling it T 4, but note below the differences in the three preceding versions.

In all four copies the first ancestor recorded in the tree is now Isengrim II, with the title 'Seventh Shirking' (in the first copy 'Shireking or Shirking'), on which see p. 87. Isengrim eldest son of the Old Took, now Isengrim III, retained through three copies the dates given to him in T 3, 1232–1282, remarkably short-lived among all the centenarians, with the note added 'no children'. In all the copies the holders of the title Shirking are underlined, as the Thains are starred in the final form (RK p. 381).

A daughter named Gloriana, following Isengrim III, was introduced in the first copy, but was changed at once to Hildigunda (see below), either because Gloriana Bolger (BG 2, BR 4) already existed or because the name Gloriana was at once transferred to her. Hildigunda had a brief life, her dates on the first copy being 1235–1255; on subsequent copies no dates were given, but she is said to have 'died young'. On the third copy her name was changed to Hildigard, as it remained.

Between Hildigunda / Hildigard and Hildigrim, a son of the Old Took named Isumbras IV (the remote ancestor being now Isumbras III) was introduced, himself the father and grandfather of subsequent Shirkings. Since Isengrim III had no descendants, on the death of the unmarried Ferumbras III the headship of the family passed to the descendants of the third son of the Old Took, Hildigrim, and thus Pippin's father Paladin became the Shirking. It seems probable that the alterations to this part of the genealogy were made in order to achieve this.[11]

After Hildigrim there enters Isembold, with no descendants indicated; and after Isembold there was in the first copy Hildigunda, changed to Hildifuns when Hildigunda replaced Gloriana (see above). On the third copy Hildifuns became Hildifons: he lived to the ripe age of 102 (see below), again with no descendants shown.

Isembard was moved down to become the seventh child of the Old Took; while Sigismond (the fourth child in T 3) changes place with his son Hildibrand. Finally, a twelfth child entered on the third copy: Isengar, about whom nothing is said.

Pippin's son Faramir I and his wife Goldilocks, daughter of Samwise, entered on the fourth copy (T 4).

The version T 4 received a number of changes of name, though far fewer than in the preceding families, and some added notes; the title was changed to 'Tooks of Great Smials'.

Isengrim II (seventh Shirking) > Isengrim II (tenth Thain of the Took line)
Bandobras: (many descendants) > (many descendants, including the Northtooks of Long Cleeve)
Isembold: [added:] (many descendants)
Hildifons 1244–1346 > Hildifons 1244– (went off and never returned)
Gorboduc Brandybuck > Gormanac Brandybuck (see below)
Isengar: [added:] said to have 'gone to sea' in his youth
Paladin II > Pharamond II (see below)
Pandora > Esmeralda (see p. 101)
Caradoc Brandybuck > Saradoc Brandybuck (see p. 103)
Diamanda > Rosamunda (see BG 4)
Prima > Pearl
Pamphila > Pimpernel
Belisarius Bolger > Fredegar Bolger
Faramond > Ferdibrand

In addition, Pippin's mother Eglantine Banks was introduced, and his wife Diamond of Long Cleeve; and 'several [> three] daughters' were given to Adelard Took.

In subsequent manuscript versions the points in which the genealogy still differed from the final form were corrected: thus Pippin's father reverted from Pharamond II to Paladin II; Gormanac Brandybuck became Gorbadoc, as also in the Brandybuck genealogy (p. 103); and Folco Boffin was omitted, perhaps because of the difficulty of fitting him in (he appeared in any case in the Boffin genealogy).

The Longfather-tree of Master Samwise

There is no very early genealogy of the Gamgees and Cottons, and the first version to appear belongs with the group beginning with the Baggins table BA 3: it is indeed written on the same page as BG 2 of

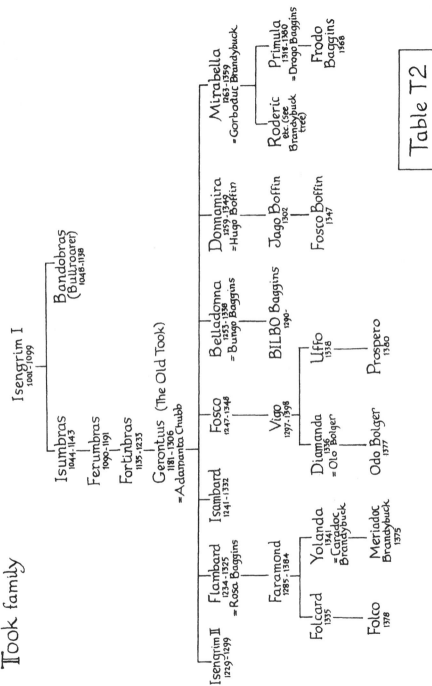

Table T2

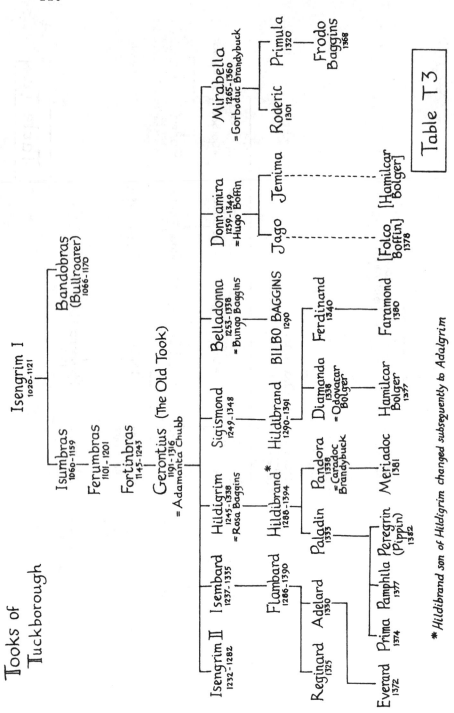

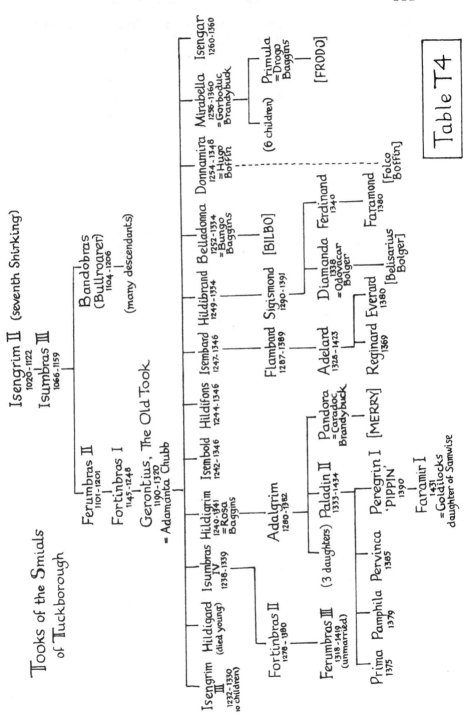

112   THE PEOPLES OF MIDDLE-EARTH

the Bolgers. The tables have different titles, and I letter them S, those that I have redrawn being found on pp. 114–16.

S 1 (p. 114)

This consists of two brief tables set out side by side without interconnection: the only link between the two families being the marriage of Sam Gamgee with Rose Cotton. It is notable that their children are only eight in number, ending with Daisy born in 1436. In the first version of the *Epilogue* to *The Lord of the Rings*, which takes place in that year, Daisy was the youngest, in her cradle (IX.114). In the second version (IX.122) this was repeated, but corrected to say that it was Primrose, the ninth child, who was in the cradle.

S 2 (p. 115)

I include under this reference two closely related tables both with the same title (the first form, not redrawn, differs from the second only in these points: Wiseman Gamwich is absent, and Hamfast of Gamwich, who 'moved to Tighfield', is the father of Hob Gammidge the Roper; Ham Gamgee's sister May is absent; and neither the husband of Elanor nor the husband of Goldilocks is shown). The second form, like S 1, is part of the series beginning with the Baggins table BA 3.

In these texts the Cotton family is again written out separately from the Gamgees, but Sam's sister Marigold is now the wife of Rose Cotton's brother Tom ('Young Tom', RK p. 286). It will be seen that at this stage the third family, beginning with Holman 'the greenhanded' of Hobbiton (as he is named in the final form), had not yet entered the genealogy; and that Sam and Rose had fourteen children, not as later thirteen, the youngest being Lily (born when her parents were very advanced in years, according to the dates given!). Lily survived into the first proof, when she was deleted.

Later correction to S 2 replaced Goodwill Whitfoot (Elanor's husband) by Fastred Fairbairn (in the final form Fastred of Greenholm), and rejected the Whitfoots of the White Downs, adding this hasty note: 'They removed to a new country beyond the Far Downs, the Westmarch between Far Downs and Tower Hills. From them are come the Fairbairns of the Towers, Wardens of Westmarch.' The sentence in the *Prologue* (FR p. 18) 'Outside the Farthings were the East and West Marches: the Buckland; and the Westmarch added to the Shire in S.R.1462' was added in the Second Edition (see p. 17).

S 3 (p. 116)

This version, untitled, was written on the reverse of the 'Note' concerning the two versions of Bilbo's story about his meeting with Gollum (see p. 12).

Here the 'greenhanded' strain entered the genealogy, but the generations, in relation to the Gamgees and the Cottons, would subsequently be displaced 'upwards': see under S 4. This version has no note on the Fairbairns.

S 4

In this finely made tree, entitled 'Genealogy of Master Samwise, showing the rise of the family of Gardner of the Hill', the final form was reached in all but a few points. The moving up of the 'Greenhands' by a generation now entered: Hending 'greenhand' of Hobbiton remained, but was now born in 1210; his children likewise have birthdates earlier by some forty years; and Hending's daughters Rowan and Rose now marry, not Hobson Gamgee and Wilcome Cotton, but their fathers, Hob Gammidge and Cotman.

At first sight my father's alteration of names in the family trees, as here, with its baffling movement of Holmans and Halfreds, may seem incomprehensibly finicky, but in some cases the reasons can be clearly seen, and this is in fact a good example. In S 3 Ham Gamgee is said to have 'taken up as a gardener with his uncle Holman': this is Holman Greenhand the gardener, brother of his mother Rowan – and he is 'old Holman' who looked after the garden at Bag End before Ham Gamgee took on the job (FR p. 30). But with the displacement of the 'Greenhand' generations that entered in S 4 Holman Greenhand would become Ham Gamgee's great-uncle (brother of his grandmother Rowan), and so too old. It was for this reason that my father changed Holman Greenhand of S 3, born in 1292, to Halfred Greenhand (born in 1251), and gave him a son named Holman, born in 1292, described in the final genealogy as Ham Gamgee's 'Cousin Holman': he was Ham Gamgee's first cousin once removed.

In S 4 Hending's third son (Grossman in S 3) is Holman: the names of father and son were subsequently reversed. Ham Gamgee's brother Holman of Overhill remained (later Halfred of Overhill); and Wilcome Cotton becomes Holman Cotton, as in the final form, but his nickname is 'Long Holm', not 'Long Hom'. This name *Holman* is to be taken, I think, in the sense 'hole-dweller'.

Elanor's husband remains in S 4 Fastred Fairbairn, and Frodo's son, Samwise Gardner in S 3, reverts to Samlad Gardner as in S 2: this was corrected to the final name, Holfast. The dates of birth of the children of Sam Gamgee and Rose Cotton remain as they were in S 3; thus Primrose, the ninth child, was born in 1439 (see under S 1 above).

In all other respects S 4 was as the final genealogy, including the note on the Fairbairns; and it was on this manuscript that the last corrections were made (the birth-date of Sam and Rose's last child, Lily, becoming 1444).

S 4 was followed by a beautifully drawn tree, from which the genealogy in *The Lord of the Rings* was printed, and here the final title entered. As already noticed, it was on the first proof that Lily was removed.

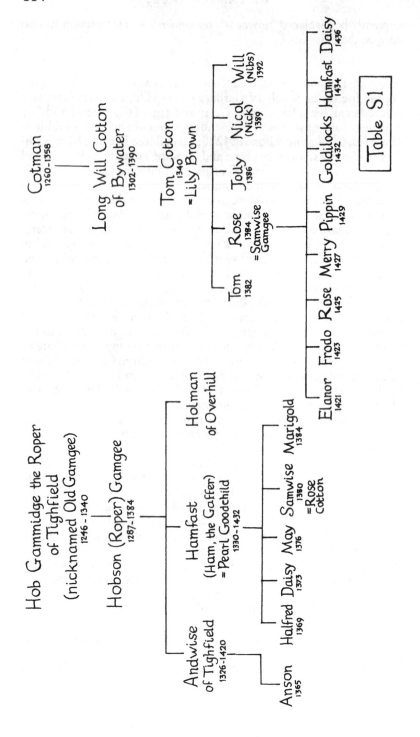

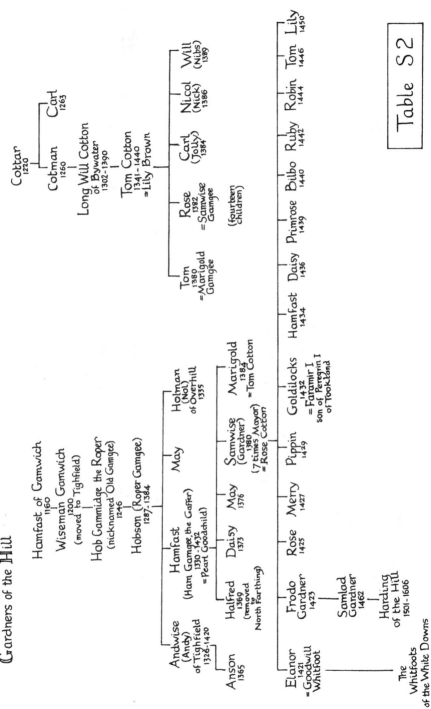

Table S2

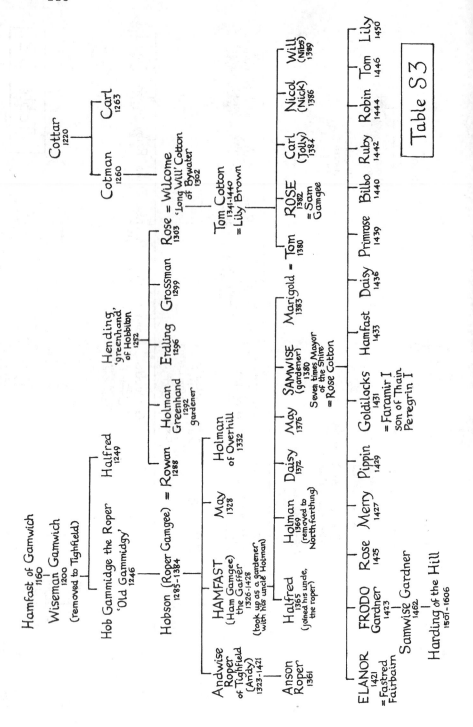

Table S3

NOTES

1 This manuscript of the Bolger family was the latest that remained in my father's possession, and he had of course no copies of the texts that went to Marquette. Years later he wrote on BG 2: 'Doesn't fit genealogies published. Fredegar should be born about 1385–8. Put in Estella 1387'. On one of his copies of the First Edition he added to the genealogy of the Tooks (Fredegar's mother being Rosamunda Took) 'Estella' as the sister of Fredegar and her birth-date 1385; and to the Brandybuck genealogy he added to Meriadoc '= Estella Bolger 1385', noting beside this that he had told a correspondent in 1965 that 'I believe he married a sister of Fredegar Bolger of the Bolgers of Budgeford'. These corrections, for a reason unknown to me, were not incorporated in the Allen and Unwin Second Edition, but they did occur in a later impression of the Ballantine edition of 1966, and hence Estella Bolger and her marriage to Merry Brandybuck are entered in *The Complete Guide to Middle-earth* by Robert Foster.

These additions to the family trees were made at the instance of Douglas A. Anderson in the Houghton Mifflin edition of 1987, to which he contributed a note on the history of the text. Estella Bolger and her marriage to Meriadoc have finally entered the British 'tradition' in the re-set edition published by HarperCollins in 1994 (see Douglas Anderson's 'Note on the Text' in this edition, p. xii).

2 My statement in VII.39, note 19, that Bridgefields does not appear on the original map of the Shire is erroneous: it is pencilled on that map (and can be seen in the reproduction, frontispiece to Vol.VI) beside the name Bolger, a region just south-west of the Brandywine Bridge. As noted in VII.39, on my large map of the Shire made in 1943 my father pencilled in the name Budgeford, this being the crossing of the Water by the road (entered on the map at the same time) from Whitfurrows on the East Road to Scary. At the same time he wrote in Bridgefields in a new position, north-west of the Brandywine Bridge and north of the East Road, as it appears on the published map of the Shire.

3 In late typescripts of the chapters in which Fredegar Bolger appears in *The Lord of the Rings* the name *Belisarius* (with the nickname *Belly*, which no doubt accounts for the choice) replaced the earlier *Hamilcar*, and was then itself replaced by *Fredegar*.

4 Jemima Boffin of BG 2 was first renamed *Jasmine*, which was replaced by the form *Jessamine*; and so also in the Boffin genealogy.

5 On one of the proofs my father corrected Fredegar's birth-date from 1377 to 1380, but the genealogy was omitted from the book

before this was introduced; in the Took table, however, the date was changed. See note 1.

6 This was in fact an alteration (VI.298 and note 1): originally my father marked the Boffins north-west of the Woody End, and the Bolgers north of Hobbiton, subsequently changing them about; cf. VI.298, 'as far west as Woodhall (which was reckoned to be in the Boffin-country)'.

7 In VI.273, 275 I printed the name as *Lanorac*, which was a misreading of the difficult manuscript.

8 In VI.316 I noted that some of the figures in T 1 were changed on the manuscript, and gave a list of them; but I said that these were 'the earlier ones', whereas they are in fact the corrected figures. See note 9.

9 In T 1 the birth-dates of Isambard and Flambard were 170 and 165 years before the Farewell Party, but these were changed (see note 8) to 160 and 167 (in T 2 1241 and 1234); hence the reversal of the positions of the brothers in T 2.

10 On T 2 Uffo Took and his son Prospero were corrected to Adelard and Everard (see VI.247, 315), Uffo becoming a Boffin name (see BF 2). It will thus be seen that they have been removed from the descent of the fourth son (Fosco > Sigismond) and given to that of the second son Isembard (formerly without any descendants named), whose son Flambard takes over the former name of Hildigrim.

11 Farmer Cotton's reference to Pippin's father as the Thain ('You see, your dad, Mr. Peregrin, he's never had no truck with this Lotho, not from the beginning: said that if anyone was going to play the chief at this time of day, it would be the right Thain of the Shire and no upstart ...') was a late addition to the text of the chapter *The Scouring of the Shire* (RK p. 289); for the original form of the passage see IX.99.

IV
THE CALENDARS

The earliest text of what became Appendix D to *The Lord of the Rings* is a brief, rough manuscript without title, which I will call **D 1**. In style and appearance it suggests association with the first of the two closely related manuscripts of the Appendix on Languages, F 1 (see p. 28), and that this is the case is shown by a reference in the text to 'the note on Languages p. 11'. This in fact refers to the second version, F 2, which was thus already in existence (see p. 136, note 2). D 1 was followed, clearly at no long interval, by a fair copy, D 2, exactly parallel to the manuscripts F 1 and F 2 of the Appendix on Languages; and thus the order of composition was F 1, F 2; D 1, D 2. I have no doubt at all that all four texts belong to the same time, which was certainly before the summer of 1950 (see p. 28 and note 1), and probably earlier: in fact, an envelope associated with D 1 is postmarked August 1949.

In this case, since the texts are far briefer than F 1 and F 2, and since the second manuscript D 2 was substantially altered from its predecessor, I give them both. These earliest versions of the Appendix on Calendars show, as do those of the Appendix on Languages, how far the conception still was, when *The Lord of the Rings* had been completed, from the published form. There follows here the text of the manuscript D 1.

In the Shire the Calendar was not arranged as ours is; though the year seems to have been of the same length, for long ago as those times are now, reckoned in years and men's lives, they were not (I suppose) far back in the age of Middle-earth. According to the Hobbits themselves they had no 'week' when they were a wandering people, and though they had months, reckoned by the moon, their keeping of dates and time was not particularly accurate. In Eriador (or the West-lands) when they settled down they adopted the reckoning of the Dúnedain, which was of Elvish origin. But the Hobbits of the Shire after a while altered things to suit their own convenience better. 'Shire-reckoning' was eventually adopted also in Bree.

It is difficult to discover from old records precise details about those things which everybody knows and takes for granted, nor am I skilled in such abstruse matters. But in that part of Middle-earth at that time it seems that the Eldar (who had, as Sam said, more time at their disposal) reckoned in centuries. Now they had observed – I do not know how, but the Eldar have many powers, and had observed many centuries – that a century contains, as near as no matter for practical purposes, 36524 days. They therefore divided it into 100 years (or sun-rounds) of 366 days, and dealt with the inaccuracy, not as we do by inserting at intervals an additional day to make up for the deficit, but by ejecting a few days at stated times to reduce the surplus. Every *four* years they would have used *three* days too many, if they had done nothing to correct it.

Normally they divided their year of 366 days into twelve months, six of 31 and six of 30 days. They alternated from January to June 31, 30; from July to December 30, 31. It will be observed that their months thus had the same lengths as ours, except for February, 30, and July, 30. Every *eighth* year they got rid of their excess of 6 days by reducing all months to 30 days; and these years were called ['Equal-month Years' or 'Thirty-day Years' >] 'Sixty-week Years' or 'Short Years'.

The Elvish week had only *six* days; so normal years had 61 weeks, and every eighth year had 60 weeks. The first day of the year always began on the first day of the week. In the Short (eighth) Years every month began on the first day of the week. In the normal years they progressed thus: 1, 2, 2, 3, 3, 4, 4, 4, 5, 5, 6, 6.[1]

The Eldar still at the end of a century would have had 36525 days, not 35624; so once a century they left out the last day of the last month (reducing December to 30 days). The week-day went with it: there was no sixth day of the week in the last week of the century.

The Dúnedain altered these arrangements. They favoured the number 7, and also found a seven-day week more convenient. They also preferred a system by which all the months had the same lengths and did not vary at intervals. [*Struck out later:* They had 12 months (not 13) so that the year could be divided into two exact halves.]

In Gondor, therefore, and in most regions where the Common Speech was used, the year had 365 days; there were 12 months of 30 days each; and 52 weeks of 7 days each. But the method of dealing with the extra 5 days differed in different countries.

In Gondor, between June 30 and July 1 they placed a kind of short month of 5 days, which were called *The Summer Days*, and were a time of holiday. The middle day of the Summer Days (the third) was called Midyear's Day and was a festival. Every fourth year there were 6 Summer Days, and the Midyear festival was two days long (celebrated on the third and fourth days). In the last or hundredth year of a century the additional Summer Day was omitted, bringing the total to 36524.

In the Shire (and eventually in Bree where Shire-reckoning was finally adopted) there were 3 Summer Days, called in the Shire *The Lithe* or *The Lithedays*; and 2 *Yule Days*, the last of the Old Year and the first of the New.* Every fourth year there were 4 Lithedays [*added:* except in the last year of a century]. The Lithedays and the Yuledays were the chief holidays and times of feasting. The additional Litheday, called *Overlithe*, was a day of special feasting and merrymaking. *Yule* was in full the last week of the old year and the first of the new, or in Shire-reckoning (since December had only 30 days) December 24 to January 7 inclusive; but the two middle days of the period, *Old Year's Day* or *Yearsend* (December 30) and *New Year's Day* or *Yearsday* (January 1), were the great Yuledays, or Yule proper.

The Hobbits introduced one notable innovation (the Shire-reform). They found the shifting of the weekday name in relation to dates from year to year untidy and inconvenient. So in the time of Isengrim II they arranged that the odd day, which put the succession out, should have no weekday name. So Midyear's Day (the second and middle day of the Lithe) had no weekday name, and neither had Overlithe (which followed it in every fourth year). After this reform the year always began on the first day of the week and ended on the last day of the week; and the same date in one year always had the same weekday name in all other years. In consequence of which Hobbits never troubled to put weekdays on their letters. They found this very

---

* The reckoning of the year's beginning had varied much in various times and places. The beginning after Yule (originally intended to be at the Winter Solstice) was used in the North Kingdom and eventually adopted by Hobbits. The wild Hobbits were said to have begun their year with the New Moon nearest to the beginning of Spring. The settled Hobbits for a time began their year after Harvest, roughly October 1st. This habit long endured in Bree. In Gondor after the downfall of Baraddur a new era was begun with that day reckoned as the first day of its first year.

convenient in the Shire, but of course, if they travelled further than Bree, where the reform was adopted, they found it rather confusing.

It will be observed if one glances at a Hobbit (perpetual) Calendar that the only day on which no month began was a -Friday. It was thus a jesting idiom in the Shire to speak of 'on Friday the first' when referring to a day that did not exist, or to a day on which impossible events like the flying of pigs or (in the Shire) the walking of trees might be expected to occur. In full the expression was 'Friday the first of Summerfilth', for there was no such month.

In the above notes I have used our modern month and weekday names, though of course neither the Eldar nor the Dúnedain nor the Hobbits actually did so. But dates are both important and easily confused, so that I thought a translation into our familiar names essential. These may very properly be allowed to represent the usual names in Gondor and in the Common Speech. But in fact, the Hobbits of the Shire and of Bree adhered to old-fashioned month-names, which they seem to have picked up in antiquity from the Men of the Anduin-vale; at any rate very similar names were found in Dale and in Rohan (see the note on Languages p. 11).[2] The original meanings of these had been as a rule long forgotten and they had become in consequence worn down in form, -*math* for instance at the end of four of them is a reduction of *month*. There was some variation in the names. Several of the Bree-names differed from those of the Shire, and in one or two cases the East-farthingers agreed with Bree.

	Shire	*Bree*
January	Afteryule	Frery (also East Farthing)
February	Solmath[a]	Solmath[a]
March	Rethe[3]	Rethe
April	Astron	Chithing (also East Farthing)
May	Thrimilch[b]	Thrimidge
June	Forelithe	Lithe
	The Lithe or Lithedays	The Summer Days
July	Afterlithe	Mede
August	Wedmath	Wedmath
September	Halimath	Harvest(math) (also East Farthing)
October	Winterfilth	[Wintermath >] Wintring

| November | Blotmath[c] | Blooting |
| December | Foreyule | Yulemath |

(a) Pronounced *So'math*. (b) Pronounced *Thrimidge* and also written *Thrimich*, *Thrimidge*, the latter being already most usual in Bilbo's time. (c) Often pronounced *Blommath*. There were often jests in Bree about 'Winterfilth in the Shire', after the Breefolk had altered their name to *Wintring*; but the name had probably meant 'filling, completion' and may have derived from the time when the year ended and began in October after Harvest. Winter was indeed (as still with us) often used for 'year' in reckoning age.[4]

The Hobbit week was taken from the Dúnedain and the names were translations of the names given by the Dúnedain following the Eldar. The six-day week of the Eldar had days dedicated to the Stars, Sun, Moon, the Two Trees of Valinor, the Sky, and the Valar or Rulers, in that order, the last day being the chief or high day.

The Dúnedain kept the dedications and order, but altered the fourth day to Tree-day with reference to the Eldest Tree of which a descendant grew in Númenor, and desiring a seven day week and being great mariners they inserted a Sea-day after the Sky-day.

The Hobbits took over this arrangement, but the meanings of the days were soon forgotten and the names reduced in form. The 'translation' was made more than a thousand years before Bilbo's time. In the oldest known records of the Shire, in the earlier parts of the Great Writ of Tuckborough,[5] the names appeared in the following archaic forms.

1. *Sterrendei*   that is   Stars' day
2. *Sunnendei*   Sun's day
3. *Monendei*   Moon's day
4. *Treowesdei*   Tree's day
5. *Heovenesdei*   Heaven's (Sky's) day
6. *Meresdei*   Sea's day
7. *Hihdei*   High day

But in the language of the date of the Red Book these names had become written: *Sterday* (or *Stirday*), *Sunday*, *Munday*, *Trewsday*, *Hevensday*, *Mersday*, *Hiday*; and *Hevensday* was universally pronounced *Hensdy* and often written *He'nsday*. The spelling *Stirday* (usual in the Red Book) was due to the fact that, the old meaning being forgotten, *Stirday*, which began the week again, after the holiday of *Hiday*, was popularly supposed to be connected with *Stirring*.

Since the Hobbit-names are accidentally somewhat like our own, and two are identical (in spoken form)[6] I thought it would be inconvenient to translate them according to their *order*. I have therefore translated them according to their *sound*. But it must be remembered that the associations in the Shire were different. Translated the week runs: Saturday, Sunday, Monday, Tuesday, Wednesday, Thursday, Friday. But Saturday was the first day of the week, and Friday the last. In associations Saturday was more like our Monday and Friday like our Sunday.

The month names I have, as explained above, translated. But for fear of getting into confusion I have left Bilbo's and Frodo's *dates* unchanged: that is, I have kept the Hobbit lengths of month. This only closely concerns this book at the turn of the years 1418–19. It must then be remembered by those who wish to follow the various movements of the characters that while December 1418 and January 1419 have (because of the addition of a Yule-day to each) the same length as ours, February has 30, so that e.g. March 25 would be March 27 in our reckoning.

The Leapday or Overlithe does not concern the Red Book, as it did not occur in any of the important years for the story of the Ring. It occurred in the year before Bilbo went to the Lonely Mountain, 1340; it had been missed in 1400 being the end of a century (just before Bilbo's Farewell Party in 1401), and so had not occurred from 1396 until 1404. The only years dealt with in the Red Book in which it occurred were 1420, the famous Harvest, and 1436. But though no doubt the feasting at Overlithe in 1420 was tremendous it is not mentioned specially.[7] The Book ends before the Lithe of 1436.

It will be seen that the account of the Eldarin calendar in Middle-earth given in D1 bears no relation to that in the published text. Moreover, while the Shire Calendar as described in D 1 was preserved without change, it is much more closely based on the Númenórean system than in Appendix D. In D 1 both calendars had a year of 12 months of 30 days each, and the only difference in that of the Shire was the distribution of the five Summer Days of Gondor into two Yuledays and three Summer Days or Lithedays (the leap-year day of Overlithe or fourth Litheday corresponding to the sixth Summer Day in Gondor). In Appendix D, on the other hand, the Númenórean calendar had ten months of 30 days and two of 31 (making 362), with the three 'extra days' being *yestarë* (the beginning of the year), *löendë* (the mid-day), and *mettarë* (the ending of the year).

In writing of the names of the months and days of the week my father used the word 'translation'. He was referring, of course, to the substitution of e.g. *Thursday* for *Mersday* or *March* for *Rethe*. But it is to be remembered that *Mersday, Rethe*, etc. were themselves feigned to be 'translations' of the true Hobbit names. We do not know what the 'real' translation of the Númenórean name *Oraearon* (RK p. 388) was; the theory is that my father devised a translation of the Hobbit name, which he knew, in archaic English form, *Meresdei* later *Mersday*, and then substituted *Thursday* in the narrative. The rhyming of 'Trewsday, Hensday, Mersday, Hiday' with our 'Tuesday, Wednesday (Wensday), Thursday, Friday' he naturally called an accidental likeness; but it was an astonishing coincidence! I am much inclined to think that the Hobbit calendar was the original conception, and that the names of the days were in fact devised precisely in order to provide this 'accidental likeness'. If this is so, then of course the earlier history of the names of the week (going back to the six-day week of the Eldar) was a further evolution in this extraordinarily ingenious and attractive conception. It is notable, I think, that the Elvish names do not appear until the text D 2 (where the Sindarin names are called, as is to be expected, Noldorin).

This second text now follows (with certain omissions, which are noted). It is a very carefully written manuscript, bearing the title *The Calendar*. I believe it to have been written soon after D 1.

The Calendar

The Calendar in the Shire differed in several features from ours. The year seems to have been of the same length, for long ago as those times are now, reckoned in years and lives of men, they were not, I suppose, very remote according to the memory of the Earth. It is recorded by the Hobbits that they had no 'week' when they were still a wandering people, and though they had 'months', governed more or less by the Moon, their keeping of dates and calculations of time were vague and inaccurate. In the west-lands of Eriador, when they had begun to settle down, they adopted the reckoning of the Dúnedain of the North-kingdom, which was ultimately of Elvish origin; but the Hobbits of the Shire introduced several minor alterations. This calendar, or 'Shire-reckoning' as it was called, was eventually adopted also in Bree, except for the Shire-usage of counting as Year 1 the year of the foundation or colonization of the Shire.

It is often difficult to discover from old tales and traditions precise information about those things which people knew well and took for granted in their own day, like the names of letters, or of the days of the week, or the names and lengths of months. I have done as well as I could, and have looked into some of the surviving works on chronology. Owing to their general interest in genealogy, and to the [*added:* later] interest of the learned among them in ancient history, the Shire-hobbits seem to have concerned themselves a good deal with dates; and they even drew up complicated tables showing the relations of their own system with others. I am not learned or skilled in these abstruse matters, and may have made many mistakes; but at any rate the chronology of the crucial years (Shire-reckoning 1418, 1419) is so carefully set out in the Red Book that there cannot be much doubt about days and times at this point.

It seems clear that the Eldar, who had, as Samwise remarks, more time at their disposal, reckoned in centuries, and the Quenya word *yén*, often translated 'year', really means a hundred of our years, sometimes called *quantiën* or 'full year'. Now they observed – I do not know how or when: but the Eldar have many powers, and they had observed many centuries – that the century or *quantiën* contained, exactly or exactly enough for practical purposes, 36524 days. They therefore divided it into 100 *coranári** (sun-rounds or years) of 366 days. This would have given them 36600 days, or 76 too many; and they dealt with the inaccuracy, not as we do by inserting at intervals an additional day to make up for a deficit, but by ejecting a few days at stated times to reduce the surplus. Every *four* years they would have had (very nearly) *three* days too many, if they had done nothing to correct this. Their method of correction may seem complicated to us, but they favoured the numbers six and twelve, and they were chiefly concerned to make things work out properly at the end of their 'full year' or century.

Normally they divided their *coranar* of 366 days into twelve months, six of 31 days and six of 30 days. The lengths alternated from January† to June 31, 30; and from July to December 30, 31. It will be observed that their months thus had the same lengths as ours, except for February, 30 (usual in all the calendars of this period), and July, 30. Every *eighth* year they

---

* Also called in less astronomical contexts *loa* 'time of growth', sc. of plants, etc.

† The month-names are here translated to avoid confusion.

got rid of the excess of 6 days by reducing all the months to 30 days and thus having a year (or *coranar*) of only 360 days. These years they called 'Short Years' or 'Sixty-week Years'.

The Eldarin week had only *six* days, so normal years had 61 weeks, and every eighth year had 60 weeks. The first day of the *coranar* always began on the first day of the week. In the Short Years every month also began with the first day.

These eight-year cycles ran on regularly until the end of the 96th year of the *quantiën* or century. There then remained four more years to deal with, and 1460 days were required to complete the full tale of 36524. Four years of 365 days would have done this, but that would not have fitted the Elves' six-day week. Their actual arrangement, rounding off the *quantiën* neatly, was this: at the end of the century they had a half-cycle of *three* long years of 366 days (total 1098), and *one* short year (the last of the century) of 360: making 1458 and exactly completing the weeks. The two more days still required[8] were added at the end and the beginning of the *quantiën*; they had no weekday name nor month, but only their names: *Quantarië* Day of Completion, Oldyear's Day, and *Vinyarië* Newyear's Day; they were times of festival. Thus the year 1 of the Eldarin century had 367 days; Years 8, 16, 24, 32, 40, 48, 56, 64, 72, 80, 88, 96 had 360 days; Year 100 had 361; and the remainder had 366. It is thus impossible to translate an Eldarin date into our terms without a possible error of some days, unless one knows at what point in an Eldarin century a given year stands, and whether that century did in fact begin on what we should call January 1.*

* I believe that the Elves observe the Sun and stars closely, and make occasional corrections. Their *quantiéni* are arranged, I am told, to begin as nearly as possible with the first sunset after the Winter Solstice. The Eldarin 'day' or *arë* was reckoned not from midnight, but from the moment of the disappearance of the sun below the horizon as observed from the shores of the sea. Among other peoples the reckoning of the year's beginning had varied much at different times, though it was usually at mid-winter, or at a date taken as the beginning of Spring, and occasionally after Harvest. The beginning after Yule (taken as at or near the Winter Solstice) was used by the Dúnedain in the North-kingdom, and eventually was adopted by the Hobbits. The Wild Hobbits were said to have begun their year with the New Moon nearest the beginning of Spring. The settled Hobbits for some time began their year after Harvest, or after the introduction of regular fixed months on October the first. A trace of this was left in the keeping of October 1 as a minor festival in the Shire and Bree.

The Dúnedain altered these arrangements. Being mortal if long-lived the actual 'sunround' or year was their natural unit. They required therefore a system in which months had the same length from year to year. Also they much favoured the number seven. The following was the system used in Númenor, and after the Downfall in the North-kingdom, and also in Gondor until the end of the line of Kings: it is called, therefore, King's Reckoning.

The year had 365 days; there were 12 months, normally of 30 days each; but the months on either side of the mid-year and the year's-end had 31 (in our terms January, June, July, December). The 183rd day or Midyear Day belonged to no month. Every *fourth* year, except in the last year of a century, there were two Midyear Days. From this system the Shire-reckoning, described below, was derived.

But in Gondor later, in the time of the Stewards, the length of the months was equalized. Each month had 30 days, but between June 30 and July 1 were inserted 5 days, called the Summer Days. These were usually a time of holiday. The middle or third of these days, the 183rd of the year, was called Midyear Day and was a festival. As before, it was doubled in every *fourth* year (except the hundredth year of a century). This was called the Steward's Reckoning, and was usual in nearly all countries where the Common Speech was used (except among Elves, who used it only in their dealings with Men).

The Hobbits, however, remained conservative, and continued to use a form of King's Reckoning adapted to fit their own customs. Their months were all equal and had 30 days, but they had *three* Summer Days, called in the Shire the Lithe or the Lithedays between June and July; and *two* Yuledays, the last of the old year and the first of the new year. So that in effect January, June, July, December still had 31 days, but the Lithedays and Yuledays were not counted in the month (January 1st was the second and not the first day of the year). Every *fourth* year, except in the last year of the century,* there were *four* Lithedays. The Lithedays and the Yuledays were the chief holi-

---

* Earlier it had been the *first year* of the century, for it so happened that Hobbits adopted King's Reckoning in the last year of a Dúnedain century, probably Third Age 1300, which became the first year of their reckoning. But as Shire Reckoning 1 was found to correspond to King's Reckoning 1601 things were later adjusted to fit in with King's Reckoning.

days and times of feasting. The additional Litheday added after Midyear Day (and so the 184th day of the longer years) was called Overlithe and was a day of special merrymaking. In full 'Yuletide' was fourteen days long, the last week of the old and the first of the new year (from December 25 to January 6 inclusive), but the two middle days of the period, *Yearsend* or Oldyear's Day, and *Yearsday* or Newyear's Day were the great Yuledays.

The Hobbits introduced one small but notable innovation, the 'Shire-reform'. ...

> The text continues without significant change from that of D 1 (p. 121), with the same page-reference to the text F 2 of the Appendix on Languages (see note 2), and without the Quenya names of the months which are given in Appendix D (RK p. 388). In the list of Hobbit month-names *Yulemath* (as well as *Harvest(math)*) is now included as being current in the East Farthing as well as in Bree, and the Shire-name of May becomes *Thrimidge*, as in Bree, with the note 'formerly written *Thrimich* and archaically *Thrimilch*'. The explanation of the name *Winterfilth* is altered, 'the name had probably originally meant the *filling* or *completion* of winter, or rather of the year leading up to the entry of winter', the precise meaning of which is obscure to me (see note 4).
>
> Following the list of month-names and the notes on them the text D 2 continues:

I have not ventured to use these actual unfamiliar names in the course of the narrative; but it must be understood that the reference is always to the Shire Calendar, even where 'Shire-reckoning' is not specified, as it sometimes is. Thus the points essential to the turn of the years S.R.1418, 1419 are that October 1418 has only 30 days; while January 1st is the second day of 1419, and February 1419 has 30 days. In consequence Bilbo's birthday September 22nd being the 99th and not the 100th day from the year-end corresponds to our September 23rd; February 1st corresponds to our February 1st, but 29, 30 to our March 1, 2; and the date of the downfall of Baraddur and Sauron, S.R. March 25, corresponds to our March 27th.

The Hobbit week was taken from the Dúnedain, and the names were translations of the names given to the week-days in the old North-kingdom, those in turn deriving from the Eldar. These names were at that time almost universal among users of the Common Speech, though there were some local variations.

The six-day week of the Eldar had days dedicated to, or

named after, the Stars, the Sun, the Moon, the Two Trees,* the Heavens, and the Valar or Powers, in this order, the last day being the chief or high day of the week. Their Quenya names were: *Elenya, Anarya, Isilya, Aldarya, Menelya, Valarya* (or *Tárinar*). The Noldorin names were [*Argiliath* >] *Argilion, Aranor, Arithil,* [*Argelaid* >] *Argaladath, Arvenel* (*-fenel, -mhenel*), *Arvelain* (or *Ardórin*).⁹

The Dúnedain kept the dedications and order, but altered the fourth day to *Argalad* 'Tree-day' with reference to the Elder Tree only, of which the White Tree that grew in the King's Court in Númenor was a descendant. Also, desiring a seventh day, and being the greatest of mariners, they inserted a 'sea-day' *Aroeren* (Quenya *Eärenya*) after the Heavens' day.

The Hobbits took over this arrangement ...

The text then follows that of D 1 (p. 123) almost exactly in the account of the names of the days of the week in the Hobbit calendar, but the Red Book spellings of *Sterrendei* and *Hihdei* are given as *Starday* and *Hiday (or Highday)*. *Starday* was then changed to *Sterday*, with the note: 'The spelling *Stirday*, sometimes found in the Red Book, was due to the forgetting of the meaning of the name. *Sterday*, which began the week, was popularly supposed to be connected with "stirring" after the holiday of *Highday*.'

D 2 then concludes thus:

I have translated these names also into our familiar names, and in deciding which name to equate with which modern name I have observed not the Hobbit order (beginning with *Sterday*), but the meanings. Thus since *Sunday* and *Munday* are practically identical with our *Sunday* and *Monday* and have the same 'dedications' in the same order, I have equated these and taken the rest in the same order as they stand in the Shire list: thus Hobbit 1, 2, 3, 4, 5, 6, 7 have been translated by our 7, 1, 2, 3, 4, 5, 6. It must be remembered, however, that the associations of the weekday names will thus be different: Saturday, for instance, will correspond closely in Hobbit-custom with our Monday, while Friday will correspond as closely as anything in the Shire did with Sunday.

The Overlithe or Leapday does not concern the Red Book since it did not occur in any of the important years in the story

---

*The Two Trees of Valinor, Silpion of silver (the Elder), and Laurelin of gold (the Younger), which gave light to the Blessed Realm.

of the Great Ring. It occurred in the year before Bilbo went to the Lonely Mountain, namely in 1340; it had been missed out in 1400,* the year before his Farewell Party (1401), and so had not occurred from 1396 to 1404. The only years dealt with in the Red Book in which it occurred were 1420, the famous Harvest, and 1436. No doubt the merrymaking of Overlithe in 1420 was as marvellous as everything else in that marvellous year, but it is not mentioned specially by Master Samwise. He had many other things to think about, and his brief account of them has not been enlarged upon. The book ends before the Lithe of 1436.

On the assumption, which I feel sure is correct, that D 2 belongs to very much the same time as D 1, my father quickly became dissatisfied with his first account of the antecedents of the Hobbit calendar (which itself remained virtually unchanged throughout). In the Eldarin calendar he now introduced the words *yén* and *quantiën*, both meaning a hundred of our years (*coranári* 'sun-rounds'), but retained the essential structure described in D 1 of 366 days to the year, divided into six months alternating between 30 and 31 days, with a reduction of all months to 30 days in every eighth year, these being called 'Short Years'. On the other hand, he altered the Eldarin treatment of the last four years of the century: whereas in D 1 (p. 120) a day was simply rejected at the very end of the century, in D 2 two were added, one at the beginning and one at the end of the century (see note 8).

The Númenórean calendar was more radically changed. In D 1 there were 12 months of 30 days each in a year of 365 days, with a period of 5 days (standing outside the months) called 'the Summer Days' between June 30 and July 1, the third of these being called 'Midyear's Day'. Every fourth year was a leap-year with six 'Summer Days' including two 'Midyear's Days'. From this calendar that of the Hobbits was derived, with the 5 'extra' days dispersed into 3 'Summer Days' ('Lithedays') and 2 'Yuledays', the leap-year day being 'Overlithe'.

In D 2, on the other hand, the Númenórean calendar had 8 months of 30 days and 4 months of 31 (January, June, July, December), requiring only one 'extra' day, Midyear Day, standing outside the months, this (as in D 1) being doubled every fourth year. This was called 'King's

---

* The determination of the centuries was ultimately taken from the reckoning of the Dúnedain. For though 'Shire-reckoning' only began with the settlement of the Shire, it was found that this had occurred in year 1601 of the Third Age according to King's Reckoning. To convert S.R. years into T.A. years one therefore adds 1600. Bree-years began 300 years earlier than Shire-years.

Reckoning'. Despite this alteration of the Númenórean calendar the Hobbit calendar (unchanged from D 1) is still, rather curiously, derived from it: for my father explained (p. 128) that they did 'in effect' retain the four 31-day months in the two Yuledays (January, December) and two Lithedays (June, July, on either side of Midyear's Day), although these in the Hobbit calendar were not counted in the months.

A further innovation in D 2 is the later revision of the calendar in Gondor, 'in the time of the Stewards', when the months were all reduced to 30 days, with 5 inserted 'Summer Days'. This was called 'Steward's Reckoning', and was widely adopted – but not by the Hobbits. 'Steward's Reckoning' is of course a reversion to the original Númenórean calendar in D 1 – which was the source of that of the Hobbits.

In Appendix D the conservative nature of the Hobbit calendar was retained, being a form of the King's Reckoning rather than of the reformed Steward's Reckoning, but these were again altered. The precise relations can best be understood from the actual texts, but the following is an attempt to summarise the essential differences.

D 1   *Númenórean*: all months of 30 days, 5 'Summer Days' outside the months. Hobbit calendar derived from this, with 2 Yuledays and 3 Lithedays outside the months.

D 2   *Númenórean 'King's Reckoning'*: 4 months of 31 days, Midyear Day outside the months. Hobbit calendar derived from this.
      Númenórean 'Steward's Reckoning': all months of 30 days, 5 'Summer Days' outside the months. Not adopted by Hobbits.

Appendix D   *Númenórean 'Kings' Reckoning'*: 2 months of 31 days, with 3 days outside the months (*yestarë, loëndë, mettarë* at the beginning, middle, and end of the year). Hobbit calendar (still as in D 1, D 2) derived from this.
      Númenórean 'Stewards' Reckoning': introduced by Mardil: all months of 30 days, with 2 further days outside the months (*tuilérë, yávië́rë*, at end of March and September) added. Not adopted by Hobbits.

In D 2 there is no reference to the introduction of a new calendar in Third Age 3019 (S.R.1419), the year of the fall of Barad-dûr and the coronation of King Elessar, beginning on March 25 (RK p. 390); but in D 1 there is such a reference (p. 121, footnote) to a new reckoning, the year beginning, however, in the autumn: 'The settled Hobbits for a time began their year after Harvest, roughly October 1st. ... In Gondor after the downfall of Baraddur a new era was begun with that day reckoned as the first day of its first year.'

My father wrote two statements at this time on the subject of the new reckoning, differently arranged but virtually identical in content: I give the second version, which is somewhat clearer.

New Era

Gondor Calendar of the Fourth Age. After the downfall of Sauron and the return of the King, a new calendar was devised in Gondor and adopted throughout the realm and in all the westlands. This was calculated to begin on the day of the fall of Barad-dûr. That took place in Third Age 3019 (Shire-reckoning 1419), on March 25th according to Shire-reckoning, King's reckoning, and the Elvish calendars (March 27th in our calendar, and March 26th in Steward's reckoning).[10]

In honour of the Halflings (Hobbits) their week-day Sunday (for 25 March) was taken for the first week-day of the first year of the New Era, and so became also the first day of every week. Also the 'Shire-reform' was adopted, by which Midyear's Day had no weekday name, so that weekday names remained fixed in relation to dates, and each year began on a Sunday *(Anarya)* and ended on a Saturday *(Elenya)*.

The calendar of months and seasons was also entirely reformed. The year now began with *Spring* (25 March old style). It was divided into *five* seasons: two long (three months), and three short (two months): *Spring* (April, May); *Summer* (June, July, August); *Autumn* or *Harvest* (September, October); *Winter* (November, December, January); *Stirring* (February, March).*

Each month was 30 days long. There were thus 5 days (or in Leap-years 6) outside the months. These were: 2 'Spring-days' before April 1st, which began the new year, and were festivals.† 'Midyear's Day' fell between September and October and became now a harvest festival. In Leap-years this Day was doubled. The year ended with 2 'Stirring-days' after March 30: these days were days of preparation for the New Year and of commemoration of the dead and fallen.

Dates were usually given in official documents by the Seasons, but the old month-names (Common-speech, Noldorin or Quenya) remained in private and popular use, though their

---

* When the year was divided into two halves, Winter was held to run from October to Year's end, and Summer from Year's beginning to the end of September.

† The first Spring-Day and the first day of the Year was especially the commemoration of the fall of Sauron, since it corresponded to 25 March in earlier reckoning.

New Era

							Shire Reckoning	Steward's Reckoning
								March
Entarë	Year's beginning: Tuilëar Springdays	1		1			25	26
		2		2			26	27
Víressë	First Spring (April)	1	Tuilë Spring	3	Úrien: Summer		27	28
								April
Lótessë	Second Spring (May)	1		33			27	28
								May
		30		62	Lairë or		26	27
Nárië	First Summer (June)	1		1			27	28
								June
Cermië	Second Summer (July)	1	Lairë Summer	31			27	28
								July
Úrimë	Third Summer (August)	1		61			24	23
								Aug.
		30		90			23	22
Yavannië	First Autumn (Sept.)	1		1			24	23
								Sept.
Arendiën	Midyear's Day	1	Quellë Autumn	31			24	23
Narquelië	Second Autumn (Oct.)	1		32			25	24
								Oct.
		30		61			24	23
Hísimë	First Winter (November)	1		1			25	24
								Nov.
Ringarë	Second Winter (December)	1	Hrívë Winter	31	Fúrien: Winter		25	24
								Dec
Narvinyë	Third Winter (January)	1		61			25	24
								Jan.
		30		90	Hrívë or		22	23
Nendessë	First Stirring (Feb.)	1		1			23	24
								Feb.
Súlimë	Second Stirring (March)	1	Coirë Stirring	31			23	24
								March
		30		60			22	23
	Coirëar Stirringdays	1		61			23	24
Mettarë	Year's-end	2		62			24	25

Every fourth year save the last in the
Quantiën or Century there were two Arendiéni.

incidence was somewhat altered: they began and ended earlier in the year than in older calendars.

On the reverse of the page carrying the first of these accounts of the calendar of the New Era is a table made at the same time; this was struck out and replaced by another, identical in all essentials, and this latter I have redrawn (p. 134). In this table the first column of figures refers to actual dates (with the five days standing outside the months numbered 1 and 1, 2); thus the five figures given for *Tuilë* (Spring), 1, 2, 1, 1, 30, refer respectively to the two *Tuilëar* (Springdays), 1 (*Entarë*) and 2; the first day of *Víressë* (April 1); the first day of *Lótessë* (May 1); and the last day of *Lótessë* (May 30). The second column of figures is the *cumulative* total of days in each season corresponding to those in the first column: thus 1 *Lótessë* is the 33rd day of the year (2 *Tuilëar*, *Víressë* 30 days, *Lótessë* 1, = 33).

In Appendix D this elegantly balanced structure had been abandoned and replaced by a different system, somewhat obscurely recounted. But it seems extremely probable that it was here, in this original account of the calendar of the New Era, that the Quenya names of the months first entered. It will be seen that the names given in Appendix D are all present except that of February, *Nénimë*, which is here *Nendessë*; while the opening day of the year is *Entarë* (on the first form of the table written *Entalë* and then changed) for later *Yestarë*, and Midyear's Day is *Arendiën* for later *Loëndë*. The changed names were written onto the table later, probably much later.

On the back of the second table, and clearly intended to be continuous with it, is the following.

Alternative names.[11]
Autumn: *Endien* (Midyear).
April: *Ertuilë*   October: *Lasselanta (Nóquellë)*
May: *Nótuilë*   November: *Errívë*
June: *Ellairë*   December: *Norrívë*
July: *Nólairë*   January: *Meterrívë*
August: *Metelairë*   February: *Ercoirë*
September: *Erquellë*   March: *Nócoirë*

The Noldorin month names and seasons corresponding were:
Spring: *Ethuil*: April *Gwirith*. May *Lothron*.
Summer: *Loer*: June *Nórui*. July *Cerfeth*. August *Úrui*
Autumn: *Firith*: September *Ifonneth*. October *Narbeleth*.
Winter: *Rhíw*: November *Hithui*. December *Girithron*.
   January *Nerwinien*.
Stirring: *Echuir*: February *Nenneth*. March *Gwaeron*.
Occasional variants: Autumn: [*Dant*, *Dantilais* >] *Dannas*,

136   THE PEOPLES OF MIDDLE-EARTH

Lasbelin. June: *Ebloer.* July: *Cadloer.* December: *Ephriw.* January: *Cathriw.*

The old *Year beginning* corresponded to N[ew] E[ra] January 8, the 68th day of Winter, and 281st day of the year.
The old *Midyear* corresponded to N.E. July 6, the 36th day of Summer, and 98th day of the year.
The old *Year's-end* corresponded to N.E. January 7, the 67th day of Winter, and 280th day of the year.
The Shire *Lithedays* = N.E. July 5, 6, 7
The old Gondor *Summerdays* = N.E. July 4–8 inclusive.

Here the Noldorin (Sindarin) names first appear, and are the same as those given in Appendix D, with two exceptions: *Nerwinien* for *Narwain* (January) and *Nenneth* for *Nínui* (February). *Narwain* and *Nínui* were written in much later, together with the following changes: *Metelairë, Meterrívë > Mettelairë, Metterrívë; Cerfeth > Cerveth; Ifonneth > Ivanneth; Loer > Laer, Ebloer > Eblaer, Cadloer > Cadlaer.*

Together with many other tables of comparative reckoning, some beautifully made, this effectively completes all the calendar material that I can certainly identify as belonging to this primary phase of my father's work on the subject. It is remarkable that (amid abundant but very rough and difficult notes) there is no further text until the typescript (itself rough and a good deal emended) from which the text of Appendix D was printed.[12] It seems very unlikely that any intervening text should have been lost, and I am inclined to think that my father was still developing and refining his theory of the Calendars when the need to submit his text to the publishers became imperative and urgent. Of the final form I believe that what I said of Appendix F, that 'had circumstances been otherwise the form of that appendix would have been markedly different' (p. 82), can be repeated of Appendix D with greater force.[13]

NOTES

1 I have added the final 6, absent in the manuscript.
2 As noted on p. 119 this is a reference to the manuscript F 2 of the Appendix on Languages, pp. 38–9, §§23–4. The sentence at the end of §24, 'But most remarkable of all are the Hobbit month-names, concerning which see the note on Calendar and Dates', was an addition, but one made with care near to the time of writing of F 2 – no doubt when my father reached this point in D 1.
3 *Rethe* was not the original name. On the back of this page of the manuscript is a comparative table, struck through, of Hobbit

dates and modern dates by month and day; and the third month is here *Luyde*, not *Rethe*. *Luyde* occurs also in one of the *Prologue* texts (see p. 9), but I have not found it anywhere else; nor have I found any other names preceding those in the list given here, which survived without change.

4   *Winterfylleth* was the Old English name of October. Its meaning was discussed by Bede (died 735), who explained the name by reference to the ancient English division of the year into two parts of six months each, Summer and Winter: *Winterfylleth* was so called because it was the first month of Winter, but *fylleth*, Bede supposed, referred to the full moon of October, marking the beginning of that period of the year. My father's interpretation of the name in D 1, 'the filling (completion) of the year', 'winter' being used in the sense 'year', is at variance both with Bede and apparently with that in the published text (RK p. 388, footnote), 'the filling or completion of the year *before Winter*'. In either case it must be supposed that the 'true' words underlying translated 'filth' and 'Winterfilth' could make the same pun!

On the former beginning of the Hobbit year after Harvest see p. 121, footnote.

5   The Great Writ of Tuckborough (later the Yearbook of Tuckborough) is mentioned also in the Appendix on Languages, p. 40, §27.

6   The words '(in spoken form)' refer to the spelling *Munday*. In the published text the sentence reads: 'In the language of the time of the War of the Ring these had become *Sterday, Sunday, Monday* ...', instead of 'had become written', thus avoiding the question of *Munday, Monday*: the latter being a mere peculiarity of English spelling, as in many other words with the vowel of *but*, as *monk, son*, etc. *Sunday* was once often spelt *Sonday*. – So also *Hiday* of D 1 is given the modern spelling *Highday* in the published text. But in the list of archaic (Old English) forms it should not be *Highdei* but *Hihdei*, as in D 1.

7   Contrast Appendix D (RK p. 384): 'the merrymaking in that year [1420] is said to have been the greatest in memory or record.'

8   The different computation in D 1 (p. 120), whereby the Eldarin calendar would have 36525 days in a century (leading to the removal of the last day of a century) was reached thus: the last four years of a century were computed as half of an eight-year cycle, that is 2922 (seven long years and one short year) divided by two, 1461. Added to the total (35064) of the days in 96 years this made 36525. In D 2 the last four years are not half of an eight-year cycle but three full years and one short year, that is 35064 + 1458 in a century, total 36522 (leading to the addition of the two extra days outside the structure of weeks and months, *Quantárië* and *Vinyárië*).

9   I have found no further list of the Elvish names of the days of the week, nor any mention of individual names, before the third (and final) text, from which Appendix D was printed (see p. 136). There, the Quenya names of the fourth and sixth days, *Aldarya* and *Valarya*, were still in that form (but *Tárion* had replaced *Tárinar*); my father emended them very clearly, on both copies of the typescript, to *Aldauya* and *Valanya*. On the proof of the first of these was printed *Aldanya*, and he emended this to *Aldúya*, as it appears in Appendix D.

On the use of 'Noldorin' for 'Sindarin' see the Appendix on Languages, especially p. 36, §18, and commentary, pp. 65–6. These month-names next reappear in the final typescript, already changed to *Orgilion, Oranor, Orithil, Orgaladhad, Ormenel, Orebelain* (or *Rodyn*); and similarly with the name of the 'Sea-day' added by the Númenóreans, changed from *Aroeren* to *Oraearon*.

10 In the Eldarin calendar (p. 126), in the long (normal) years, January had 31 days and February 30; thus March 25th was the 86th day of the year. In the Gondorian King's Reckoning (p. 131) the same was true. In the Shire Reckoning Yuleday preceded January 1, but both January and February had 30 days, so that March 25 was again the 86th day of the year.

In the Gondorian Steward's Reckoning (p. 132), on the other hand, the count is simply 30 days in January and 30 days in February, so that March 25 is the 85th day of the year; while in our calendar 31 + 28 + 25 makes March 25 the 84th day.

11 Some of these alternative names are included in the first form of the table, with the difference that *Errívë* and *Norívë* (so spelt) are alternatives respectively for *Ringarë* (December) and *Narvinyë* (January).

12 It is a curious point that this typescript begins with the *printed* 'Shire Calendar for use in all years' exactly as it appears in Appendix D (RK p. 384): my father's typescript begins below it ('Every year began on the first day of the week ...'), and the same is true of the carbon copy. Presumably this calendar was printed first and separately and copies were sent to my father, who used them in this way.

The manuscript calendar from which this was printed is extant, and it is interesting to see that on the left-hand side there is a column headed 'Weekday' with the names of the days of the week set out against each of the three transverse groups of months, thus for example in the second month *Solmath*:

Stirday	–	5	12	19	26
Sunday	–	6	13	20	27
Munday	–	7	14	21	28
Trewsday	1	8	15	22	29

and so on. This column of the days of the week would have made the calendar easier to understand; but on the manuscript it is struck through, by whom is not clear. I can see no reason for this but that of space on the page, which one would think could have been quite easily accommodated. – This manuscript table undoubtedly goes back to the original phase of my father's work on the calendars, described in this chapter.

13 Among various alterations made by my father on the proof, it may be noted that the text of Appendix D as first printed ended thus: 'Some said that it was old Sam Gardner's birthday, some that it was the day on which the Golden Tree first flowered in 1420, and some that it was the Elves' New Year. The last was (more or less) true, so all may have been.'

V
THE HISTORY OF THE AKALLABÊTH

The development of Appendix B, *The Tale of Years*, was naturally associated with and dependent on that of Appendix A, which as published bears the title *Annals of the Kings and Rulers*. But more unexpectedly, the Tale of Years of the Second Age was closely associated with the evolution of the history of Númenor and of the *Akallabêth*. In the presentation of the early forms of these Appendices I have found after trial and error that the best course is to divide the Tale of Years into two parts, the Second and the Third Ages, and to treat them separately; and also, to introduce at this point an account of the *Akallabêth*, followed by the Tale of Years of the Second Age in Chapter VI.

In the *History of Middle-earth* I have given no indication of how this work, a primary narrative of the Second Age, developed to the form given in the published *Silmarillion*, or when it first came into being. The early history of the legend, closely related to the abandoned story *The Lost Road*, was studied in Volume V, where the two original narratives of *The Fall of Númenor*, which I called FN I and FN II, were printed (V.13 ff.). In *Sauron Defeated* (IX.331 ff.) I gave a third version, FN III, which I have ascribed to a fairly early stage in the writing of *The Lord of the Rings*. The massive development of the legend in the work called *The Drowning of Anadûnê*, closely associated with *The Notion Club Papers* and the emergence of the Adûnaic language, was studied in *Sauron Defeated*, where I ascribed it to the first half of 1946 (IX.147, 389–90): this dating was subsequently confirmed by the observation of John Rateliff that W. H. Lewis recorded in his diary that my father read the work to the Inklings in August 1946 (Foreword to *Morgoth's Ring*, X.x).

In my commentary on *The Drowning of Anadûnê* I indicated and discussed at many points its relationship to the *Akallabêth*, but for the text of the latter I made use only of the final form, as printed in *The Silmarillion*, pp. 259 ff. Since the writing of the *Akallabêth* evidently post-dated the writing of *The Lord of the Rings* I postponed discussion of its history, but I found no room for it in the very long books *Morgoth's Ring* and *The War of the Jewels*.

I did, however, in *Sauron Defeated* make an extraordinary misstatement on the subject of the *Akallabêth*, which must be repaired.

THE HISTORY OF THE AKALLABÊTH

When discussing (IX.406) my father's late note on *The Drowning of Anadûnê*, in which he referred it to 'Mannish tradition', I said:

> The handwriting and the use of a ball-point pen suggest a relatively late date, and were there no other evidence I would guess it to be some time in the 1960s. But it is certain that what appears to have been the final phase of my father's work on Númenor (*A Description of Númenor, Aldarion and Erendis*) dates from the mid-1960s (*Unfinished Tales* pp. 7–8);[1] and it may be that the *Akallabêth* derives from that period also.

This last remark is patent nonsense. The great extension of the line of the Númenórean kings, which entered in the course of the development of the *Akallabêth*, was present in Appendix A (and a mere glance through the texts of the work is sufficient to show, simply from their appearance, that they could not conceivably date from so late a time). How I came to write this I do not know, nor how it escaped all subsequent checking and revision. I perhaps meant to say that my father's note on *The Drowning of Anadûnê* may have derived from the same period as *Aldarion and Erendis*.

When I wrote *Sauron Defeated* I was nonetheless not at all clear about the time of the original writing of the *Akallabêth*, and I assumed without sufficient study of the texts that it was later than it proves to be.

The textual history is relatively brief and simple in itself. The earliest text, which I will call **A**, is a clear manuscript of 23 pages; a good deal of this text is extant also in pages that were rejected and written out again, but virtually nothing of any significance entered in the rewriting, and the two layers of this manuscript need not be given different letters.

My father then corrected A, fairly extensively in the earlier part, very little in the story of the Downfall, and made a second text, a typescript, which I will call **B**. He followed the corrected manuscript with an uncharacteristic fidelity, introducing only a very few changes as he typed. It cannot be demonstrated, but I think it virtually certain, that the series A, A corrected, B, belong to the same time; and there is usually no need to distinguish the stages of this 'first phase', which can be conveniently referred to as **AB**.

After some considerable interval, as I judge, he returned to the typescript B and emended it. This left the greater part of the text untouched, but introduced a vast extension into Númenórean history: primarily by the insertion of a long rider in manuscript, but also by transpositions of text, alteration of names, and the rewriting of certain passages.

The third and final text (C) was an amanuensis typescript (in top copy and carbon) taken from B when all alterations had been made to it. It seems to me very probable that this was made at the same time

142   THE PEOPLES OF MIDDLE-EARTH

(?1958) as the typescripts of the *Annals of Aman*, the *Grey Annals*, and the text LQ 2 of the *Quenta Silmarillion* (see X.300, XI.4). To this typescript my father made only a very few and as it were casual corrections.

The alterations (including the long inserted rider) made to B constitute a 'second phase'; and this is the final form of the *Akallabêth* (apart from the few corrections to C just mentioned). There are thus only two original texts, the manuscript A and the typescript B, but the corrections and extensions made to B represent a significantly different 'layer' in the history of the work. To make this plain I will call the typescript B *as subsequently altered* B 2.

While the development of the *Akallabêth* is of much interest in particular features, a very great deal of the text never underwent any significant change; and as I noted in IX.376, something like three-fifths of the precise wording of the second text of *The Drowning of Anadûnê* (which was printed in full in that book) survived in the *Akallabêth*. Moreover the final form of the *Akallabêth*, if with some editorial alteration, is available in *The Silmarillion*. In order to avoid an enormous amount of simple repetition, therefore, I use the *Silmarillion* text, which I will refer to as SA ('Silmarillion-Akallabêth'), as the basis from which to work back, so to speak, rather than working forward from A. To do this I have numbered the paragraphs in SA throughout, and refer to them by these numbers, together with the opening words to aid in their identification.

The *Silmarillion* text was of course that of B 2 (with the corrections made in C), but as I have said a number of editorial changes were made, for various reasons, but mostly in the quest (somewhat excessively pursued, as I now think) for coherence and consistency with other writings. Unless these changes were trivial they are noticed in the account that follows.

I do not here go into the relations of the *Akallabêth* to its sources (*The Drowning of Anadûnê*, and to a more minor degree the third version of *The Fall of Númenor*, FN III), since these are fully available in *Sauron Defeated*, where also the most crucial developments were extensively discussed.

The original title in the manuscript A was *The Fall of Númenor*, which was corrected to *The Downfall of Númenor* and so remained: none of the texts bears the title *Akallabêth*, but my father referred to the work by that name (cf. p. 255).

§§1–2 The original opening of A was almost a simple copy of the opening of FN III (IX.331–2): 'In the Great Battle when Fionwë son of Manwë overthrew Morgoth', etc.; but this was at once rejected, though appearing in revised form in SA §3, and a new opening substituted, which constitutes, with some editorial changes, that in SA (§§1–2). The authentic text begins: 'Of Men, Ælfwine, it is said by the Eldar that they came into the world in the time of the Shadow of Morgoth ...', and in SA I removed the address to Ælfwine.[2] The *Akallabêth* was conceived as a tale told by Pengoloð the Wise (as it must be supposed, though he is not named) in Tol Eressëa to Ælfwine of England, as becomes again very explicit (in the original) at the end; and no change was made in this respect in the 'second phase' B 2, nor on the final amanuensis typescript C.[3]

In §1 I also altered the sentence 'and the Noldor named them the Edain' to 'The Edain these were named in the Sindarin tongue'; on this change see under §9 below.

In §2, Eärendil's ship was named *Vingilot* in AB, but this was changed to the otherwise unrecorded *Eälótë* in B 2; in SA I reverted to *Vingilot*. The name *Rothinzil* is derived from *The Drowning of Anadûnê*.[4]

§3 *In the Great Battle ...* The opening of this paragraph in AB read:

> In the Great Battle when at last Fionwë son of Manwë overthrew Morgoth and Thangorodrim was broken, the Edain fought for the Valar, whereas other kindreds of Men fought for Morgoth.

This was changed in B 2 to read:

> In the Great Battle when at last Eönwë herald of Manwë overthrew Morgoth and Thangorodrim was broken, the Edain alone of the kindreds of Men fought for the Valar, whereas many others fought for Morgoth.

In SA the reference to Eönwë was removed; and similarly later in the paragraph 'refusing alike the summons of [Fionwë >] Eönwë and of Morgoth' was changed to 'refusing alike the summons of the Valar and of Morgoth'. The reason for this lay in the treatment of the last chapter of the *Quenta Silmarillion* in the published work. The only narrative of the Great Battle at the end of the First Age (V.326 ff.) derived from the time when the Children of the Valar were an important conception, and Fionwë son of Manwë was the leader and commanding authority in the final war against Morgoth and his overthrow; but the abandonment of that conception, and the change in the 'status' of Fionwë / Eönwë to that of Manwë's herald led to doubt whether my father, had he ever returned to a real retelling of the story of the end of the Elder Days (see XI.245–7), would have retained Eönwë in so mighty and elemental a rôle. His part was in consequence somewhat diminished by omissions and ambiguous wording (as may be seen by comparing the text in Vol.V with that of the published *Silmarillion*; cf. also the editorial addition made to the *Valaquenta*, X.203). There is however no evidence for this supposition, and I now believe it to have been a mistaken treatment of the original text, and so also here in the *Akallabêth*.[5]

§4 *But Manwë put forth Morgoth* ... In this paragraph my father was still closely following FN III (IX.332), but at the end, after 'Andor, the Land of Gift' he turned to *The Drowning of Anadûnê*, which was thereafter the primary source, though with some interweaving of passages from FN III. In FN III the passage concerning Morgoth, originally written in the present tense, was corrected to the past tense, and this was followed in A; but it is curious that in B my father reverted in one of the phrases to the present: 'and he *cannot* himself return again into the World, present and visible, while the Lords of the West *are* still enthroned.' This was retained in SA.

After the words 'life more enduring than any others of mortal race have possessed' I omitted in SA the following sentence in the original: 'Thrice that of Men of Middle-earth was the span of their years, and to the descendants of [Húrin the Steadfast >] Hador the Fair even longer years were granted, as later is told.' This omission, scarcely necessary, was made on account of divergent statements on the subject (see *Unfinished Tales* p. 224, note 1). The erroneous reference to Húrin, surviving from FN III (see IX.332 and note 1), was only corrected in B 2.

In the original manuscript A the words of FN III concerning Eressëa were retained: 'and that land was named anew Avallon; for it is hard by Valinor and within sight of the shores of the Blessed Realm.' This was corrected to the text that appears in SA ('and there is in that land a haven that is named Avallónë ...'). On this see further under §12 below.

§5 *Then the Edain set sail* ... The original opening of this paragraph, not subsequently changed, was:

> Then the Edain gathered all the ships, great and small, that they had built with the help of the Elves, and those that were willing to depart took their wives and their children and all such wealth as they possessed, and they set sail upon the deep waters, following the Star.

I cannot now say with certainty why this passage (derived from *The Drowning of Anadûnê*, IX.360, §12) was omitted from SA: possibly on account of a passage in the 'Description of Númenor', not included in the extracts given in *Unfinished Tales*, in which the ships of the migration are described as Elvish:

> The legends of the foundation of Númenor often speak as if all the Edain that accepted the Gift set sail at one time and in one fleet. But this is only due to the brevity of the narrative. In more detailed histories it is related (as might be deduced from the events and the numbers concerned) that after the first expedition, led by Elros, many other ships, alone or in small fleets, came west bearing others of the Edain, either those who were at first reluc-

tant to dare the Great Sea but could not endure to be parted from those who had gone, or some who were far scattered and could not be assembled to go with the first sailing.

Since the boats that were used were of Elvish model, fleet but small, and each steered by one of the Eldar deputed by Círdan, it would have taken a great navy to transport all the people and goods that were eventually brought from Middle-earth to Númenor. The legends make no guess at the numbers, and the histories say little. The fleet of Elros is said to have contained many ships (according to some a hundred and fifty vessels, to others two or three hundred) and to have brought 'thousands' of the men, women, and children of the Edain: probably between five thousand or at the most ten thousand. But the whole process of migration appears in fact to have occupied at least fifty years, possibly longer, and finally ended only when Círdan (no doubt instructed by the Valar) would provide no more ships or guides.

In this paragraph is the first appearance of the name *Elenna* ('Star-wards') of Númenor.

§6 *This was the beginning of that people* ...   In the first sentence the words 'that people that in the Grey-elven speech are called the Dúnedain' were an editorial alteration from 'that people that the Noldor call the Dúnedain'.[6] Cf. the similar change made in §1, and see under §9.

§7 *Of old the chief city and haven* ...   Following the words 'it was called Andúnië because it faced the sunset' A had originally the following passage:

But the high place of the King was at Númenos in the heart of the land, and there was the tower and citadel that was built by Elros son of Eärendil, whom the Valar appointed to be the first king of the Dúnedain.

Númenos survived from FN III (IX.333) and earlier (see V.25, §2). This was replaced in B by the passage in SA: 'But in the midst of the land was a mountain tall and steep, and it was named the Meneltarma,' etc. The name of the city was given here, however, as *Arminalêth* (the name in *The Drowning of Anadûnê*), with a note: 'This is the Númenórean name, for by that name it was chiefly known, *Tar Kalimos* in the Eldarin tongue.' In B 2 the name was changed here (and at the subsequent occurrences) from *Arminalêth* to *Armenelos*, and the note changed to read: '*Arminalêth* was the form of the name in the Númenórean tongue; but it was called by its Eldarin name *Armenelos* until the coming of the Shadow.' Thus the statement in Index II to *Sauron Defeated* (IX.460) that *Arminalêth* was 'replaced by *Armenelos*' is incorrect: *Armenelos* was a *substitution* in the *Akallabêth* because my father was now asserting that this was the name by which the city was known through long ages, but its Adûnaic form remained *Arminalêth*. It was *Tar Kalimos* that was replaced by *Armenelos*. – This note was omitted in SA.

§8 *Now Elros and Elrond his brother* ... The words in SA 'were descended from the Three Houses of the Edain' were an editorial change from 'were descended from the lines of both Hador and Bëor'. – Near the end of the paragraph, the span of years granted to Elros was said (in all texts) to have been 'seven times that of the Men of Middle-earth', but on one copy of C my father changed 'seven' to 'three' and placed an X against the statement that Elros lived for five hundred years. The reading 'many times' in SA was an editorial substitution.

§9 *Thus the years passed* ... In the sentence 'For though this people used still their own speech, their kings and lords knew and spoke also the Elven tongue, which they had learned in the days of their alliance' AB had 'the Noldorin tongue'. Similarly in §§1, 6 it was said that *Edain*, *Dúnedain* were Noldorin names, but only in the present case did my father change (in B 2) 'Noldorin' to 'Elven'. Thus the old conception that the Noldor in Beleriand retained their own tongue was still present, as it was also in the original forms of the Appendices on Languages and Calendars (see p. 138, note 9). This at once shows a relatively early date for the *Akallabêth*; and as noted earlier the adoption of Sindarin by the Exiled Noldor had already emerged in the *Grey Annals* (p. 62, §5).

The continuation of the same sentence originally read 'and they remained in great friendship with the Eldar, whether of Avallon or of the westlands of Middle-earth', but this was changed to the text in SA, 'and thus they held converse still with the Eldar, whether of Eressëa', etc. The same removal of the word 'friendship' of the relations between the Eldar and the Númenóreans is found also in §§12, 29.

§§10, 11 *For the Dúnedain became mighty* ..., *But the Lords of Valinor* ... There were no editorial alterations made to these paragraphs, which go back with no change of any significance to the earliest text.

§12 *For in those days Valinor still remained* ... In A the name of the Mountain of Númenor was *Menelmindon*; in FN III it was *Menelmin* (IX.335), and *Menelmindo*, *Menelminda* occur in *The Notion Club Papers*. But *Meneltarma* is found already in A at a later point in the narrative.

In A as originally written the name *Avallon* was still the new name of the isle of Eressëa, but in the rewriting of that passage (see under §4) it was corrected to *Avallónë*, now the name of the haven of the Eldar in Eressëa. In the present paragraph A had: 'But the wise among them knew that this distant land was not indeed Valinor, the Blessed Realm, but was Avallónë, the Isle of the Eldar, easternmost of the Undying Lands'; *Avallónë* was here the form first written, and thus my father moved from *Avallon* to *Avallónë* while writing the manuscript, without however changing the significance of the name (but see under §75). The text was then altered, to embody the new conception, but only by changing 'Isle' to 'Haven', to which in SA I added 'upon Eressëa' to make the meaning clear. (Much of the present passage derives fairly closely from *The Drowning of Anadûnê*, IX.361, §16: on the extremely difficult question of the meaning of *Avallóni* in that work see IX.379–80, 385–6.)

In the passage describing the coming of the Eldar to Númenor AB had:

> And thence at times the Firstborn still would come to Númenor in oarless boats, or as birds flying, for the friendship that was between the peoples.

The text of SA here is that of B 2, and here again (see §9 above) the 'friendship' of the Eldar and the Númenóreans was removed.

The conclusion of the paragraph provides further clear evidence of the early date of the *Akallabêth*. This passage began as an addition to A (following the words 'for the friendship that was between the peoples' cited above) as follows, with the changes made to it shown:

> And they brought to Númenor many gifts: birds of song, and flowers of sweet fragrance and herbs of great virtue. And a seedling they brought of the White Tree [Nimloth the Fair >] Galathilion that grew in the [courts of Avallónë >] midst of Eressëa, and was in his turn a seedling of the Eldest Tree, [Galathilion the light of Valinor >] Telperion of many names, the light of Valinor. And the tree grew and blossomed in the courts of the King in [Númenos >] Ar-minalêth; Nimloth the fair it was named, and the night-shadows departed when Nimloth was in flower.

The history of the names of the White Trees is complex, for several reasons: the names were applied to the Two Trees of Valinor and re-used as names for the later trees; the later trees (of Tirion (Túna), Eressëa, Númenor) entered at different times; and there was shifting in their applications. It is simplest to consider first the statements deriving from the major period of work on the Elder Days between the completion and the publication of *The Lord of the Rings*.

In the *Annals of Aman* (X.85, §69) Yavanna gave to the Noldor of Túna (Tirion) 'Galathilion, image of the Tree Telperion'. In the revision of the *Quenta Silmarillion* from the same period (X.176, §39) it is said of this tree that 'Yavanna made for them a tree in all things like a lesser image of Telperion, save that it did not give light of its own being'; its name is not given. It is also said in the same version of the *Quenta Silmarillion* (X.155) that *Galathilion*, a name of Telperion, was given also to the White Tree of Túna, which was known as 'Galathilion the Less'; and that 'his seedling was named *Celeborn* in Eressëa, and *Nimloth* in Númenor, the gift of the Eldar.'

As my father first wrote this addition to A he named the Tree of Eressëa *Nimloth*, saying that it was 'a seedling of the Eldest Tree, Galathilion the light of Valinor'; he thus omitted the Tree of Túna (Galathilion the Less). He immediately changed the name of the Tree of Eressëa to *Galathilion*, a seedling of Telperion, and gave the name *Nimloth* to the Tree of Númenor. (This shows incidentally that the addition preceded the writing of the account of the fate of the Tree of Númenor later in A, for there the name was *Nimloth* from the first.)

The passage as emended reappears without any further change in the second text, the typescript B. But on this text my father struck it out and rewrote it thus (B 2):

> And a seedling they brought of the White Tree that grew in the midst of Eressëa, and was in its turn a seedling of the Tree of Túna, Galathilion, that Yavanna gave to the Eldar in the Land of the Gods to be a memorial of Telperion, Light of Valinor. And the tree grew and blossomed in the courts of the King in Ar-Minalêth [> Ar-Menelos]; Nimloth the Fair it was named, and flowered in the evening and the shadows of night it filled with its fragrance.

Here, in this 'second phase' of the *Akallabêth*, with the introduction of the Tree of Túna (Galathilion), the gift of Yavanna, the same succession is found as in the *Annals of Aman* and the contemporary revision of the *Quenta Silmarillion*: Telperion of Valinor; Galathilion of Túna; [Celeborn] of Eressëa; Nimloth of Númenor. The conclusion is thus inescapable that the first phase (AB) of the *Alkallabêth* was earlier than those works (the *Annals of Aman*, etc.) that can be dated with sufficient accuracy to 1951.

In SA the passage was slightly rewritten, introducing the name *Celeborn* of the Tree of Eressëa (X.155) and (unnecessarily) the word 'image' of the Tree of Túna from the *Annals of Aman* (X.85).

In this connection it is interesting to compare the passage in *The Return of the King* (p. 250, at the end of the chapter *The Steward and the King*) where the finding of the sapling tree on Mount Mindolluin is recounted. Gandalf's words are:

> Verily this is a sapling of the line of Nimloth the fair; and that was a seedling of Galathilion, and that a fruit of Telperion of many names, Eldest of Trees.

It will be seen that this agrees with the emended form of the passage in the first phase (AB) of the *Akallabêth*: for Galathilion (as the parent of Nimloth) is here the Tree of Eressëa, there is no mention of the Tree of Túna, and Galathilion is a 'fruit' of Telperion (not an 'image', or a 'memorial'). The conclusion must be that this passage was not revised when the Tree of Túna entered the history.[7]

§13 *Thus it was that because of the Ban of the Valar ...* The development of the opening passage concerning the great voyage is curious. In *The Drowning of Anadûnê* (IX.362, §17) it was said that the mariners of Númenor sailed 'from the darkness of the North to the heats of the South, and beyond the South to the Nether Darkness. And the Eruhîn [Númenóreans] came often to the shores of the Great Lands, and they took pity on the forsaken world of Middle-earth.' In the *Akallabêth*, after the words 'to the Nether Darkness', my father introduced a passage from FN III (IX.334):

> They ranged from Eressëa in the West to the shores of Middle-earth, and came even into the inner seas; and they sailed about the North and the South and glimpsed from their high prows the Gates of Morning in the East.

This goes back to the earliest texts of *The Fall of Númenor* (V.14, 20, 25). But when incorporating it into the *Akallabêth* he changed this to 'and they came even into the inner seas, and sailed about Middle-earth and glimpsed from their high prows the Gates of Morning in the East' – returning to *The Drowning of Anadûnê* with 'And the Dunedain came often to the shores of the Great Lands' (with 'often' > 'at times' in B 2).

This is the text in SA. It seems altogether impossible to say what geographical conception of the East of the World lies behind this passage.

In SA, after the words 'the Númenóreans taught them many things', the following passage (likewise derived from *The Drowning of Anadûnê, ibid.*) was omitted:

> Language they taught them, for the tongues of the Men of Middle-earth, save in the old lands of the Edain, were fallen into brutishness, and they cried like harsh birds, or snarled like savage beasts.

§14 *Then the Men of Middle-earth were comforted ...* to §17 *And some there were who said ...* (SA pp. 263–4). No changes entered the text in B 2, but two editorial changes were made in §17: for 'the bliss of the Great' and 'the people of Earth' I substituted 'the bliss of the Powers' and 'the people of Arda'.

§18 *The Eldar reported these words ...* A has: 'and he sent messengers to the Dúnedain, who spoke earnestly to the King, Tar-Atanamir'. My father was closely following *The Drowning of Anadûnê* in this paragraph (IX.364, §23), but in that work the king was Ar-Pharazôn: Tar Atanamir here first appears.[8] See further under §§24–5.

§19 *'The Doom of the World,' they said ...* to §23 *Then the Messengers said ...* Scarcely any changes, and none that need be recorded, entered the text in B 2 in this part of the *Akallabêth*; there were however some minor editorial alterations made in SA. In §21 there is in the original a complex interchange between 'thou' and 'you' in the reply of the Messengers, according as they are addressing the King or referring to the people as a whole, for example: 'thou and thy people are not of the Firstborn, but are mortal Men as Ilúvatar made you', or 'And you, thou sayest, are punished for the rebellion of Men'. In SA 'you' was employed throughout. In §23 'within the girdle of the Earth' was changed to 'within the Circles of the World', and 'The love of this Earth' to 'The love of Arda'.

§§24, 25 *These things took place ..., Then Tar-Ancalimon ...* These two paragraphs have to be considered together. AB §24 opened:

> These things took place in the days of Tar-Atanamir, and he was the seventh of those kings that succeeded Elros upon the throne of Númenor; and that realm had then endured for more than two thousand years ...

And AB §25 opened:

> Then [Kiryatan > Ar-Kiryatan >] Tar-Kiryatan the Shipbuilder, son of Atanamir, became King, and he was of like mind ...

It would be clear in any case from these new names that a development had taken place, or was taking place, in the history of the royal house of Númenor from that in *The Drowning of Anadûnê*; but in fact there is an extremely interesting isolated page in which my father set forth the new conception, and it is most convenient to give this page here.

Second Age

Elros	died	S.A. 460	
King 1	„	c. 682	
2	„	c. 903	
3	„	c. 1125	
4	„	c. 1347	
5	„	c. 1568	
6	„	c. 1790	[*added:*] In his day the Númenóreans aided Gil-glad in the defeat of Sauron
7	„	c. 2061	

In his time the Shadow first fell on Númenor. His name was *Tar-Atanamir*. To him came messages from the Valar, which he rejected. [*Added:*] He clung to life for an extra 50 years.

        8   died   S.A. c. 2233

In his time first began the division of the folk between the

King's folk and the *Nimruzîrim*[9] *(Elendilli)* or Elf-friends. The King's folk and Royal House cease to learn or use Elvish speech and are more usually known by their Númenórean names. This king was *Tar-Kiryatan* (Shipwright) or in Númenórean *Ar-Balkumagān*. Settlements of *dominion* in Middle-earth begin.

    9   died   S.A. c. 2454

Estrangement of Elf-friends and King's Men deepens. The King makes the Elf-friends dwell in East, and their chief place becomes Rómenna. Many depart to settle on shores of N.W. of Middle-earth. The King's folk as a rule go further south.

    10   died   S.A. c. 2676
    11   „   c. 2897
    12   „   c. 3118

Power but not bliss of Númenor reaches zenith.

    13 and last *Tarkalion* or *Arpharazôn*. Challenges Sauron and lands at Umbar 3125

    Downfall of Númenor   3319

General aspects of this text are discussed later (pp.171–2 and note 4). There can be no doubt that it is a scheme that my father had beside him when writing the original manuscript A of the *Akallabêth*. For the moment, it can be observed that, as in A, Atanamir (to whom the Messengers came) was the father of Kiryatan; and that when my father wrote in A that Atanamir 'was the seventh of those kings that succeeded Elros' he meant this precisely: for in the 'Scheme' (as I will refer to it) he is numbered 7, and Kiryatan is numbered 8, while Elros has no number.

In B 2 the openings of these two paragraphs, §§24–5, were changed to the text given in SA: 'These things took place in the days of Tar-Kiryatan the Shipbuilder, and of Tar-Atanamir his son …', and 'Then Tar-Ankalimon, son of Atanamir, became King …' In this 'second phase' not only was the order of Atanamir and Kiryatan reversed, but (although it was still to him that the Messengers came) Atanamir becomes the thirteenth king (the original words in A, 'of those kings *that succeeded Elros*' being now removed: in *The Line of Elros* in *Unfinished Tales* (p. 221) Kiryatan was the twelfth and Atanamir the thirteenth, with Elros counted as the first). The second phase (B 2) of the *Akallabêth* thus represents, or rather rests on, a further large development of the Númenórean history from that seen in the first phase, or AB.

At the end of §25 there is a paragraph in AB which was omitted in its entirety in B 2 (i.e. it was struck out on the B typescript):

    The Elendili dwelt mostly near the west coasts of the land; but as the shadow deepened in men's hearts, the estrangement between the two parties grew greater, and the king commanded them to remove and dwell in the east of the island, far from the haven of Andúnië, to which the Eldar had been wont to come; and thereafter the Eldar visited them only seldom and in secret. The chief dwelling of the Elf-friends in the later days was thus about the harbour of Rómenna; and thence many set sail and returned to Middle-earth, where they might speak with the Elves in the Kingdom of Gil-galad. For they still taught to their children the Eldarin tongues, whereas among the King's Men these tongues fell into disuse, and even the heirs of Eärendil became known to their people by names in the Númenórean tongue. And the kings desired to put an end to all friendship between their people and the Eldar (whom they called now the Spies of the Valar), hoping to keep their deeds and their counsels hidden from the Lords of the West. But all was known to Manwë that they did, and the Valar were wroth with the Kings of Númenor and gave them counsel no more.

For the explanation of this omission see p. 155. B 2 now continues with SA §26.

§26 *Thus the bliss of Westernesse became diminished ...* At the end of this paragraph AB has 'after the days of [Ar-Kiryatan >] Tar-Kiryatan' (Kiryatan being then the son of Atanamir); in B 2 this became 'after the days of Tar-Ankalimon' (who has already appeared in §25 as the son of Atanamir).

There is extant some original drafting for the passage concerning the mounting obsession with death among the Númenóreans, including the following passage that was not taken up in A:

And some taught that there was a land of shades filled with the wraiths of the things that they had known and loved upon the mortal earth, and that in shadow the dead should come there bearing with them the shadows of their possessions.

§27 *Thus it came to pass ...* This paragraph in SA goes back without change to the earliest text.

§28 *In all this the Elf-friends had small part ...* The end of this paragraph, from 'lending them aid against Sauron', was altered in SA; the authentic text reads:

But the King's Men sailed far away to the south, and though the kingdoms and strongholds they made have left many rumours in the legends of Men, the Eldar know naught of them. Only Pelargir they remember, for there was the haven of the Elf-friends above the mouths of Anduin the Great.

Pengoloð implied, no doubt, that after the great division arose among the Númenóreans the Elves of Eressëa were cut off from any knowledge of the imperial enterprises of the King's Men in the further south of Middle-earth. But with the removal of Pengoloð and Ælfwine from the published text, the *Akallabêth* lost its anchorage in expressly Eldarin lore; and this led me (with as I now think an excess of vigilance) to alter the end of the paragraph. – This was the first appearance of Pelargir in the narratives of Númenor.

§29 *In this Age, as is elsewhere told* ...   In AB the second sentence of this paragraph ran: 'It was indeed in the days of Atanamir in Númenor that in Mordor the Tower of Barad-dûr was full-wrought, and thereafter Sauron began to strive for the dominion of Middle-earth ...' In B 2 this was altered to the text of SA, 'Already in the days of Tar-Minastir, the eleventh King of Númenor, he had fortified the land of Mordor and had built there the Tower of Barad-dûr ...' The appearance here of Tar-Minastir the eleventh king is of course a further element in the enlarged history already encountered in §§24–6. So also in this paragraph the text of AB 'nor did he forget the aid that they [the Númenóreans] had rendered to Gil-galad of old' was changed in B 2 to 'the aid that Tar-Minastir had rendered ...'

In the sentence 'And Sauron hated the Númenóreans, because of the deeds of their fathers and their ancient alliance with the Elves' the word 'alliance' was an early change from the original word 'friendship'; see under §9 above.

The words in SA 'in that time when the One Ring was forged and there was war between Sauron and the Elves in Eriador' were an editorial addition.

§30 *Yet Sauron was ever guileful* ...   This paragraph goes back to A unaltered, except for the early change of 'great lords of Númenor' to 'great lords of Númenórean race'. – The name *Úlairi* of the Ringwraiths seems to mark a period in my father's work: it is found also in a text of the Tale of Years (p. 175); in *The Heirs of Elendil* (Chapter VII); and in *Of the Rings of Power and the Third Age* (published in *The Silmarillion*).

At the end of the paragraph my father wrote on the typescript C, to follow 'he began to assail the strong places of the Númenóreans upon the shores of the sea': 'but Umbar he could not yet take'. See §41 below.

After SA §30 there is a second passage in AB (see p. 151) that was excluded in B 2:

In those days there arose and took the throne of the Sea-kings the great Tar-Calion, whom men called Ar-Pharazôn the Golden, the mightiest and the proudest of all his line. And twelve kings had ruled the Númenóreans between Elros and Ar-Pharazôn, and slept now in their deep tombs under the mount of the Meneltarma, lying upon beds of gold. Great and glorious was Ar-Pharazôn, sitting upon his carven throne in the city of

Ar-minalêth in the noon-tide of his realm; and to him came the masters of ships and men returning out of the East, and they spoke of Sauron, how he named himself the Great, and purposed to become master of all Middle-earth, and to destroy even Númenor, if that might be.

Then great was the anger of Ar-Pharazôn hearing these tidings, and he sat long in thought, and his mood darkened. And he determined without the counsel of the Valar, or the aid of any wisdom but his own, that he would demand the allegiance and homage of this lord; for in his pride he deemed that no king should ever arise so mighty as to vie with the Heir of Eärendil.

Ar-Pharazôn is here named the fourteenth king, since 'twelve kings had ruled the Númenóreans *between* Elros and Ar-Pharazôn'; and this agrees with *The Drowning of Anadûnê*[10] and also with the Scheme on p. 151, where Ar-Pharazôn is numbered 13 and Elros is not counted.

At this point (i.e. following the conclusion of SA §30) there is a direction on the typescript B to take in a rider, this being a finely-written manuscript of four sides.

§31 *In those days the Shadow grew deeper ...* to §40 *Great was the anger ...* This passage in SA (pp. 267–70) follows almost exactly the text of the rider just referred to. Here there entered the narrative of Númenor the story of the reigns of Ar-Adûnakhôr and Ar-Gimilzôr; of the Lords of Andúnië, who were of the Line of Elros; of the sons of Ar-Gimilzôr, Inziladûn and Gimilkhâd, and their conflict; of the unhappy reign of Inziladûn (Tar-Palantir); and of the forced marriage of his daughter Míriel (Ar-Zimraphel), the rightful Queen, to Pharazôn son of Gimilkhâd, who seized the sceptre for himself.

The few significant points in which the text of the rider was changed in SA are as follows.

In §31 I altered 'the twentieth king' (Ar-Adûnakhôr) and 'the twenty-third king' (Ar-Gimilzôr) to 'nineteenth' and 'twenty-second', and in §38 I altered 'four and twenty Kings and Queens had ruled the Númenóreans' before Ar-Pharazôn to 'three and twenty'. My reason for making these (incorrect) changes (an omission in the list of the rulers of Númenor given in Appendix A (I, i)) has been fully explained in *Unfinished Tales* p. 226, note 11.

In §33 I omitted two notes (belonging to the same time as the manuscript and forming part of it) concerning the Lords of Andúnië. The first of these refers to the words 'for they were of the line of Elros' and reads: 'And they took names in Quenya, as did no other house save the kings'; the second refers to the following words, 'being descended from Silmarien, daughter of Tar-Elendil the fourth king':

And in their line the sceptre would indeed have descended had the law been in his day as it was later made. For when Tar-Ankalimë became the first ruling Queen, being the only child of Tar-Aldarion the Sixth King, the law was made that the oldest child of the King whether man or woman should receive the sceptre and the kingly authority; but Silmarien was older than her brother Meneldur who succeeded Tar-Elendil.

On this see *Unfinished Tales* p. 208, where the different formulations of the new law brought in by Tar-Aldarion are discussed. The law is stated here in the same words as in Appendix A (I, i), i.e. simple primogeniture irrespective of sex (rather than inheritance of the throne by a daughter only if the Ruler had no son).[11]

In §37 the Adûnaic name of Tar-Míriel is not *Ar-Zimraphel* in the long rider, but *Ar-Zimrahil*, and this is the form in all the sources: in *The Drowning of Anadûnê* (IX.373, §48), in *Akallabêth* AB (see §78 below), in *The Line of Elros* (*Unfinished Tales* p. 224), and in *Aldarion and Erendis* (*ibid.* p. 190). *Ar-Zimraphel* actually occurs in one place only, a change made by my father in the present paragraph on the amanuensis typescript C. This I adopted in SA, and the change to *Ar-Zimraphel* was also made silently to the passages in *The Line of Elros* and *Aldarion and Erendis*.

Under §§24–5 and 30 above I have given two passages in AB that were struck out when the long rider was introduced. The first of these, following SA §25 and beginning 'The Elendili dwelt mostly near the west coasts ...' (p. 151) was largely re-used in the rider (SA §32, *Now the Elendili dwelt mostly in the western regions* ...), but the forced removal of the Elf-friends to the east of Númenor was now carried out by Ar-Gimilzôr, whereas in AB the king who commanded it is not named. The second omitted passage, following SA §30 and beginning 'In those days there arose and took the throne of the Sea-kings the great Tar-Calion' (p. 153), was postponed to the end of the rider, where it reappears in revised form (SA §§38–40, p. 270). At the words in §40 'so mighty as to vie with the Heir of Eärendil' the rider ends, and the AB or 'first phase' text takes up again with 'Therefore he began in that time to smithy great hoard of weapons ...'.[12]

Several pages were placed with the rider, written on the same paper, in which my father is seen devising a different story of the marriage of Pharazôn and Míriel. For this see pp. 159 ff.

§41 *And men saw his sails coming up out of the sunset ...* In the first sentence the words 'gleaming with red and gold' (of the sails of the ships of Ar-Pharazôn) should read 'gleaming with red gold' (a phrase that goes back to *The Drowning of Anadûnê*, IX.389, §28).

In the second sentence I altered the original text 'Umbar, where there was a mighty haven that no hand had wrought' to 'Umbar, where was the mighty haven of the Númenóreans that no hand had wrought', in view of Appendix B, Second Age 2280: 'Umbar is made into a great fortress of Númenór' (nearly a thousand years before the coming of Ar-Pharazôn). For the same reason I changed the original text in the following sentence, from 'Empty and silent under the sickle moon was the land when the King of the Sea set foot upon the shore' to 'Empty and silent were all the lands about when the King of the Sea marched upon Middle-earth'. (It is probable that when my father wrote this he did not yet suppose that Umbar was a Númenórean fortress and harbour at the time of Ar-Pharazôn's landing.)

§§42 ff. In the remainder of the *Akallabêth* the text of the original manuscript A underwent very little change indeed at any subsequent stage; there is thus no further need to comment on the text paragraph by paragraph. Only occasional editorial alteration was made in SA, and in the rest of this account it can be understood that except as stated the published work follows the original exactly, or at most with very slight modification not worth recording.[13]

§44 *Yet such was the cunning of his mind* ... (p. 271). The text of AB reads 'all the councillors, save Valandil only, began to fawn upon him'. In B 2 my father changed *Valandil* to *Amandil* here and at all subsequent occurrences. Since Amandil had not been mentioned in the text previously I added the words 'lord of Andúnië' in SA. – It is curious that the naming of Elendil's father *Valandil* was a reversion to *The Lost Road* (V.60, 69). In the course of the writing of *The Lord of the Rings* the name was variously and fleetingly applied to a brother of Elendil, to a son of Elendil, and to Elendil himself (VI.169, 175; VII.121, 123–4).

§53 *Nonetheless for long it seemed to the Númenóreans* ... (p. 274). In the last sentence 'the kindly kings of the ancient days' is an editorial change from 'the kindly kings of the Elder Days'.

§57 *'The days are dark, and there is no hope for Men* ... (p. 275). The text has 'there is no hope in Men', and the reading in SA appears to be a mere error, since there is no reason for the change. In the speeches of Amandil and Elendil that follow my father evidently intended a distinction between 'thou' from father to son and 'you' from son to father, but his usage was not consistent. In SA I substituted 'you' throughout.

§73 *Then Ar-Pharazôn hardened his heart* ... (p. 278). The name of the great ship of Ar-Pharazôn is *Aglarrâma* in AB (as in *The Drowning of Anadûnê*, IX.372, §44), changed in B 2 to *Alkarondas*.

§75 *But the fleets of Ar-Pharazôn* ... (p. 278). In the original text (at all stages) this paragraph begins:

> But who among Men, Ælfwine, can tell the tale of their fate? For neither ship nor man of all that host returned ever to the lands of the living; and the world was changed in that time, and in Middle-

earth the memory of all that went before is dim and unsure. But among the Eldar word has been preserved of the deeds and things that were; and the wisest in lore among them tell this tale, Ælfwine, that I tell now to thee. And they say that the fleets of Ar-Pharazôn came up out of the deeps of the Sea and encompassed Avallónë and all the Isle of Eressëa ...

Since this last phrase is found already in A it is clear that the changed meaning of *Avallónë* (signifying the eastern haven in Eressëa, not the Isle itself) had entered during the writing of A (see under §12 above).

In SA 'Taniquetil' is an editorial change from 'the Mountain of Aman', and 'the light of Ilúvatar' from 'the light of God'.

§76 *Then Manwë upon the Mountain* ... In the first sentence 'their government of Arda' was a change in SA from 'their government of the Earth'.

§77 *But the land of Aman* ... Two changes were made here in SA. The original text has 'were taken away and removed from the circles of the world beyond the reach of Men for ever', and 'there is not now within the circles of the world any place abiding ...'.

§78 *In an hour unlooked for by Men* ... AB has 'Ar-Zimrahil', changed in B 2 to 'Tar-Míriel'; see note 12.

§80 *Nine ships there were* ... All the texts have 'Twelve ships there were: six for Elendil, and for Isildur four, and for Anárion two', but on the amanuensis typescript C my father changed the numbers to 'nine: four, three, two', noting in the margin: 'Nine, unless the rhyme in LR is altered to *Four times three.*' The reference is to the song that Gandalf sang as he rode on Shadowfax with Pippin across Rohan on their way to Minas Tirith (*The Two Towers* p. 202):

> Tall ships and tall kings
>   Three times three,
> What brought they from the foundered land
>   Over the flowing sea?

§81 *Elendil and his sons* ... The opening of this paragraph was altered in SA to remove a reference to Ælfwine: 'And here ends the tale, Ælfwine, to speak of Elendil and his sons, who later founded kingdoms in Middle-earth ...'.

§83 *But these things come not into the tale* ... B had 'the Drowning of Anadûnê', corrected to 'the Drowning of Númenor' (a reversion to the reading of A). At the end of the paragraph AB had 'spoke of Akallabêth that was whelmed in the waves, the Downfallen, Atalantë in the Eldarin tongue', with *Akallabêth* changed to *Mar-nu-Falmar* in B 2. The removal of *Akallabêth* (restored in SA) belongs with the general replacement of Adûnaic by Elvish names: see under §78 above, and note 12. – On one of the copies of the typescript C my father wrote this note on the name *Atalantë*:

The Adûnaic or Númenórean name of the same meaning was *Akallabêth*, √KALAB. By a curious coincidence (not consciously prepared) before this tale was written a base √TALAT 'collapse, fall in ruin' had already been invented, and from that base *atalantë* 'it has fallen down' was a correct formation according to grammatical rules devised before Númenor had been thought of. The resemblance to *Atlantis* is thus by chance (as we say).

Against this note is written '71', which must mean '1971' (see XI.187, 191). With this statement on the subject cf. Lowdham's remarks in *The Notion Club Papers*, IX.249; my father's letter of July 1964 cited in V.8 (footnote); and the *Etymologies*, V.390, stem TALÁT.

§§84–6 The concluding section of the *Akallabêth*, beginning in SA *Among the Exiles many believed ...*' (pp. 281–2), was headed in A *Epilogue*; this was omitted in B. There is a full discussion of this section in relation to *The Drowning of Anadûnê* in IX.391–6.

§84 *Among the Exiles many believed ...* The original text, not changed from A, reads:

But if thou wouldst know, Ælfwine, ere thou goest, why it is that men of the seed of Eärendil, or any such as thou to whom some part, however small, of their blood is descended, should still venture upon the Sea, seeking for that which cannot be found, this much I will say to thee.

The summit of the Meneltarma, the Pillar of Heaven, in the midst of the land, had been a hallowed place, and even in the days of Sauron none had defiled it. Therefore among the Exiles many believed that it was not drowned for ever, but rose again above the waves, a lonely island lost in the great waters, unless haply a mariner should come upon it. And some there were that after sought for it, because it was said among lore-masters that the far-sighted men of old could see from the Meneltarma a glimmer of the Deathless Land.

§86 *Thus in after days ...* The sentence 'until it came to Tol Eressëa, the Lonely Isle' was a change in SA from the original 'until it came to Eressëa where are the Eldar immortal'. Immediately following, 'where the Valar still dwell and watch the unfolding of the story of the world' was an early change from the reading of A, 'where the Valar still dwell but watch only and meddle no longer in the world abandoned to Men'.

In the last sentence 'and so had come to the lamplit quays of Avallónë' was an editorial change from 'and so had come to Avallónë and to Eressëa' ('to Eressëa and to Avallónë' A). For the 'lamplit quays of Avallónë' see V.334.

After the conclusion of the *Akallabêth* in SA the following lines were omitted:

And whether all these tales be feigned, or whether some at least be true, and by them the Valar still keep alight among Men a memory beyond the darkness of Middle-earth, thou knowest now, Ælfwine, in thyself. Yet haply none shall believe thee.

Note on the marriage of Míriel and Pharazôn

My father did much work on this story, but it is not easy to see how it is to be related to the paragraph (SA §37, *And it came to pass that Tar-Palantir grew weary* ...) in the long rider inserted into the typescript B, which is exactly repeated in SA except for the change of Ar-Zimrahil to Ar-Zimraphel (p. 155). It will in any case be clearer if the genealogy is set out (cf. *The Line of Elros* in *Unfinished Tales*, p. 223).

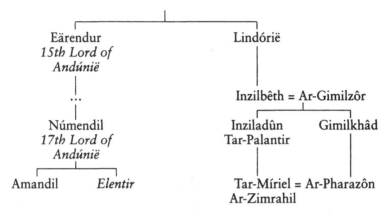

The significance of Amandil's brother Elentir will be seen in the texts given here: so far as I am aware he appears nowhere else. These texts were written on the same paper as the long rider and were inserted with it into the typescript B.

(a)

This is a very rough manuscript written in such haste that it has proved extraordinarily difficult to decipher. The text that follows is uncertain in many points, but these do not affect the narrative and I have largely dispensed with brackets and queries; it does not convey at all the appearance of the original.

He [Ar-Pharazôn] was a man of great beauty and strength/stature after the image of the first kings, and indeed in his youth was not unlike the Edain of old in mind also, though he had strength of will rather than of wisdom as after appeared, when he was corrupted by the counsels of his father and the acclaim of the people. In his earlier days he had a close friendship with Amandil who was afterwards Lord of Andunië,[14] and he had loved the people of the House of

Valandil with whom he had kinship (through Inzilbêth his father's mother). With them he was often a guest, and there came Zimrahil his cousin, daughter of Inziladûn who was later King Tar-Palantir. Elentir the brother of Amandil loved her, but when first she saw Pharazôn her eyes and her heart were turned to him, for his beauty, and for his wealth also.

But he went away[15] and she remained unwed. And now it came to pass that her father Tar-Palantir grew weary of grief and died, and as he had no son the sceptre came to her, in the name of Tar-Míriel, by right and the laws of the Númenóreans. But Pharazôn [?arose] and came to her, and she was glad, and forsook the allegiance of her father for the time, being enamoured of Pharazôn. And in this they broke the laws of Númenor that forbade marriage even in the royal house between those more nearly akin than cousins in the second degree. But they were too powerful for any to gainsay them. And when they were wedded she yielded the sceptre to Pharazôn, and he sat upon the throne of Elros in the name of Ar-Pharazôn the Golden, but she retained also her title as hers by right, and was called Ar-Zimrahil.[16]

The Elendili alone were not subservient to him, or dared to speak against his wishes, and it became well-known to all in that time that Amandil the Lord of Andúnië was head of their party though not openly declared. Therefore Ar-Pharazôn persecuted the Faithful, stripping them of any wealth that they had, and he deprived the heirs of Valandil of their lordship. Andúnië he took then and made it a chief haven for the king's ship-building, and Amandil who was now the Lord he commanded to move and dwell also in Rómenna. Yet he did not otherwise molest him [?at this time], nor dismiss him from the Council of the Sceptre, because he remembered still in his heart their friendship of old; and Amandil was well beloved also by many who were not of the Elendili.

And now when he deemed himself [?firm] upon the throne and beyond all gainsaying he sat in A[rmenelos] in the glory of his power, and he found it too little to appease his [?lust], and amid all his splendour he brooded darkly upon war.

There are a number of phrases in this text that are identical or almost so to those found in the long rider ('Tar-Palantir grew weary of grief and died', 'by right and the laws of the Númenóreans', 'those more nearly akin than cousins in the second degree', 'he brooded darkly upon war', SA §§37, 39). It would be natural to suppose that these phrases made their first appearance in this text, which was dashed down on the page, and that they were repeated in the rider, which was a manuscript written with great care; and in that case it would have to be concluded that my father discarded this story of the love of Amandil's brother Elentir for Zimrahil, and of her turning away from him and from the Elf-friends and glad acceptance of Pharazôn, before writing the final version. But I doubt that this was the case.

(b)

A second page is in handwriting even more obscure, and I have not been able to make out the whole of it after repeated attempts.

In his boyhood he had a close friendship with Amandil son of Númendil Lord of Andúnië, who being one of the chief councillors of the Sceptre dwelt often in Armenelos.

Cut out friendship. Ar-Pharazôn's policy to Amandil was due to his wife?

Now Zimrahil, whom her father called Míriel, only daughter of Tar-Palantir, was a woman of great beauty, smaller [?in ... stature] than were most women of that land, with bright eyes, and she had great skill in ... She was older than Ar-Pharazôn by one year,[17] but seemed younger, and his eyes and heart were turned to her; but the laws of Númenor lay between, beside the displeasure of her father whom Gimilkhâd opposed in all ways that he could. For in Númenor cousins in the first degree did not marry even in the royal house. And moreover Zimrahil was betrothed to Elentir Amandil's [?older] brother and heir of Númendil.[18]

From a distance,[19] for Gimilkhâd and his son were not welcome in the house of the king.

In the remainder of the text there are a number of whole sentences, clearly essential to the briefly sketched narrative, in which I can decipher virtually nothing.

Now it came into his heart that he would .... Pharazôn was not disposed to admit hindrance to his desires, and he asked leave therefore of Amandil to be a guest in his house, learning ..... Zimrahil was at the time in Andúnië. Gimilkhâd was little pleased with this, for the Lords of Andúnië were his chief opponents. But Pharazôn [?laughed] saying he would do as he would, and ....

And Amandil and Pharazôn rode in Andúnië and Elentir and Zimrahil saw them afar as they [?stood] ..... for Elentir loved his brother. But when Zimrahil saw Pharazôn in the splendour of his young manhood come riding [?in] .... Suddenly Zimrahil's heart turned towards him. And when Pharazôn was greeted upon the steps of the house their eyes met .... and were abashed.

I take this to be a further movement in the story struggling to emerge, in which my father was considering a different treatment of Pharazôn's intrusion into the relationship of Míriel and Elentir (who are now said to be betrothed); but the sketch is so rapid, and so much is indecipherable, that the actual course of the story is obscure.

(c)

A brief, clearly written text is the third of these papers associated with the rider inserted into the text of the *Akallabêth*.

> For Pharazôn son of Gimilkhâd had become even more restless and eager for wealth and power than his father. He was a man of great beauty and stature, in the likeness of the first kings of men; and indeed in his youth he was not unlike the Edain of old in mind also, though he had courage and strength of will rather than of wisdom, as after appeared, when he was corrupted by the counsels of his father, and the acclaim of the people. In his earlier days he had a close friendship with Amandil son of Númendil, Lord of Andúnië, and he loved the people of that House, with whom he himself had kinship (through Inzilbêth his father's mother). With them he was often a guest, and there also his cousin, daughter of Inziladûn, was often to be found. For Elentir Amandil's brother loved her, and she had turned her heart to him, and it was known that soon they would be betrothed.

In this my father was closely following the opening of text *(a)*, but the last sentence of the text, before it was abandoned, turns away, with the mention of the approaching betrothal of Elentir and Zimrahil, and was perhaps about to take a different course.

(d)

Finally, my father wrote the following passage in the margin of the inserted rider against §37, though without indication of its placing: most probably at the end of the paragraph ('... and the name of his queen he changed to Ar-Zimrahil').

> And he persecuted the Faithful, and deprived the Lords of Andúnië of their lordship, since they had aided Tar-Palantir and supported his daughter. Andúnië he took then and made it the chief harbour of the king's ships, and Amandil the Lord he commanded to dwell in Rómenna. Yet he did not otherwise molest him, nor dismiss him yet from his Council. For in the days of his youth (ere his father corrupted him) Amandil had been his dear friend.

This is very closely related to the end of text *(a)*, p. 160, 'Therefore Ar-Pharazôn persecuted the Faithful ...'; on the other hand, it seems clear from the words 'and supported his daughter' that the story of Zimrahil's love for Pharazôn is not present.

It is not perfectly clear to me how the textual puzzle presented by these writings is to be resolved, but I am inclined to think that, contrary to appearance, the texts *(a)*, *(b)*, and *(c)* in fact followed the writing of the long rider to the *Akallabêth*, and that they represent the emergence of a doubt in my father's mind whether the marriage of Pharazôn and Zimrahil was indeed 'against her will', and the sketching of a new story on the subject. The close agreement of phrases in *(a)* with those in the rider (see pp. 160–1) must then be interpreted as simple repetition of what was already present there, rather than as drafting for it. Finally, on this view, he abandoned the new story, and returned to that already present in §37. Amandil's brother Elentir was lost, at any rate in the recorded tradition.

It may be noted that the youthful friendship of Pharazôn and Amandil is referred to in SA §47 (*Then Ar-Pharazôn the King turned back* ..., p. 272), and this indeed goes back to the original manuscript of the *Akallabêth*: 'In the days of their youth together Valandil [> Amandil] had been dear to Ar-Pharazôn, and though he was of the Elf-friends he remained in his council until the coming of Sauron.'

NOTES

1   I think now that such slight evidence as there is points rather to about 1960 as the date of these works.
2   In §1 I altered the original 'yet they came at last to the lands that look upon the Sea. These are indeed that folk *of whom thou hast heard* that came into Beleriand in the days of the war of the Noldor and Morgoth' in order to remove the italicised words (the alteration of the last sentence to 'entered Beleriand in the days of the War of the Jewels' was a very late change, one of the very few that my father made to the typescript C). In §2, similarly, I changed 'and *thou hast heard* how at the last' to 'and in the *Lay of Eärendil* it is told how at the last'.
3   *The Line of Elros* ends with the words (*Unfinished Tales* p. 224): 'Of the deeds of Ar-Pharazôn, of his glory and his folly, more is told in the tale of the Downfall of Númenor, *which Elendil wrote*, and which was preserved in Gondor.'
4   In A my father added a footnote here, omitted in B: '*Rothinzil* is a name in the Númenórean tongue, and it has the same meaning as *Vingilot*, which is Foamflower.'
5   It is true that in the opening sentence of the Tale of Years my father substituted in the final typescript 'The *First Age* ended with the Great Battle, in which the Host of Valinor broke Thangorodrim and overthrew Morgoth', replacing a reference to 'Fionwë and the sons of the Valar' of preceding versions (see pp. 172–3); but he may not have removed the name Fionwë (Eönwë) for the same reason as I did in the *Akallabêth*.
6   The manuscript A had 'called', which became 'call' in B.
7   Cf. Elrond's words in *The Council of Elrond* (FR p. 257): 'There in the courts of the King [in Minas Anor] grew a white tree, from the seed of that tree which Isildur brought over the deep waters, and the seed of that tree before came from Eressëa, and before

that out of the Uttermost West in the Day before days when the world was young.'

8   'Tar-Atanamir' was struck out in A and does not appear in B, but this seems to have been due only to my father's wish to postpone the naming of the king to §24.

9   *Nimruzîrim*: *Nimruzîr* is the name of Elendil in *The Drowning of Anadûnê*.

10 In *The Drowning of Anadûnê* (IX.363, §20) 'seven kings had ruled ... between Indilzar [Elros] and Ar-Pharazôn', but 'seven' was changed to 'twelve' (IX.381).

11 Other footnotes (on the inscription of the Quenya name *Herunúmen* of Ar-Adûnakhôr in the Scroll of Kings, §31, and on the explanation of the name Tar-Palantir, §35, with which cf. *The Line of Elros* in *Unfinished Tales* p. 223) were incorporated into the body of the text in SA. At the end of §35 I extended the words of the original text 'the ancient tower of King Minastir upon Oromet' to '... upon the hill of Oromet nigh to Andúnië', this being taken from *The Line of Elros*, p. 220; and in §37 after 'Míriel' I added the words 'in the Elven-tongue'.

12 Before the second of these passages was struck out (and so before the insertion of the rider) my father went through it and all the remainder of the typescript B and replaced *Ar-Pharazôn* by *Tar-Kalion* (in the rejected passage, p. 153, he cut out the words 'whom men called Ar-Pharazôn', thus leaving 'Tar-Calion the Golden'). His intention, presumably, was to use Elvish names exclusively; nonetheless, in the inserted rider he named the king *Ar-Pharazôn*. The typist of C therefore moved from one name to the other; and seeing this my father began on C to change *Tar-Kalion* back to *Ar-Pharazôn*, but soon wearied of it. In SA I adopted *Ar-Pharazôn*.

13 Throughout this concluding part of the *Akallabêth* I substituted the name Ar-Pharazôn for Tar-Kalion, as explained in note 12. *Arminalêth* was changed to *Armenelos* on B, and this was taken up in SA.

14 The following is written in the margin here: '3rd in line from Eärendur and 18th from Valandil the First Lord of Andúnië'.

15 Above 'he went away' is written '[?Pharazôn] went to the wars'; cf. SA §36 (*Now Gimilkhâd died* ...): 'He [Pharazôn] had fared often abroad, as a leader in the wars that the Númenóreans made then in the coastlands of Middle-earth'.

16 At this point in the manuscript stands the following: 'And his love therefore of the Lords of Andúnië turned to hate, since they alone were powerful or wise enough to restrain him and give counsel against his desires.' A second version following this was struck out, and no doubt my father intended the rejection of the first also.

17 In *The Line of Elros* Ar-Pharazôn was born in 3118, and Tar-Míriel in 3117 (*Unfinished Tales* p. 224).
18 The word I have given as 'older' is scarcely interpretable at all as it stands, but 'older' or 'elder' seems inevitable, since Elentir is called the heir of Númendil, Lord of Andúnië, apparently displacing Amandil.
19 'From a distance' presumably refers back to the words 'his eyes and heart were turned to her'.

VI
THE TALE OF YEARS OF THE SECOND AGE

The chronology of the Second Age can be traced back to its origin in two small half-sheets of paper. That these are not only the first written record of such a chronology, but represent the actual moment of its establishment, seems certain from the obviously experimental nature of the calculations. I will refer to the various texts of the Tale of Years by the letter T, and call the first of these pages, given below, T(a) to indicate its primary nature. The rejected figures, being overwritten, are in some cases hard to make out, but I believe this to be a substantially correct representation of the text as it was first written; following it, I give the subsequent changes.

Time Scheme
'Ages' last *about* 3000 years.
The 'Black Years' or the age between the Great Battle and defeat of Morgoth, and the Fall of Númenor and the overthrow of Sauron lasted about 3500.
Thus:
Great Battle
Judgement of Fionwë and establishment of Númenor	10
Reign of Elros	410
11 other kings averaging 240 each	2640
Last 13th king	220
	3280

Elendil (very long-lived) was [*many rejected figures*] 200 years old at Fall of Númenor, and Isildur 100. The new realms lasted 100 years before Sauron opened war. 100
The gathering of Alliance 3 years, the Siege 7   10
  3390

The Third Age was 'drawing to its end' in Frodo's time. So that *Loss of Ring* was about 3000 years ago. For 500 years Sauron remained quiet and then began slowly to grow in Mirkwood – that stirred events and wakened the Ring to come back.
So Smeagol and Deagol's finding occurred about 600 years after

THE TALE OF YEARS OF THE SECOND AGE 167

Isildur's death. Gollum therefore had the Ring near[ly] 2400 years.

Average life of a Númenórean   210 years (3 × 70)
Average life of royal house   350 years (5 × 70)
A King of Númenor usually acceded when about 100–120 and ruled about 250 years.

These dates seem to have been changed in this order. First, the duration of the new realms before Sauron assailed them was changed from 100 to 110 years, giving a total of 3400 (and at the beginning of the text the figure of 'about 3500' for the length of the Black Years, i.e. the Second Age, was changed to 'about 3400', and not subsequently altered). Then the establishment of Númenor was changed from 10 to 50, giving the date 3320 for the Fall of Númenor, and a total of 3440 years in the Second Age.

Sauron's 'remaining quiet' (in the Third Age) was changed from 500 to 1000 years, the finding of the Ring in the Anduin from 600 to 1100 years after Isildur's death, and Gollum's possession of it from 2400 to 1900 years.

A pencilled note, very probably of the same time, on this page reads: 'In character Aragorn was a hardened man of say 45. He was actually 90, and would live at least another 50 (probably 70) years. Aragorn was a Númenórean of pure blood but the span had dwindled to double life.'

The second of these two primary pages, unquestionably written at the same time as the first (as is shown by the paper used), is headed 'The Second Age and the Black Years', and gives dates from 'B.Y.' 0 (the end of the Great Battle) to the loss of the One Ring and the end of the Second Age, the date of which (3440 in T(a)) now becomes 3441, which was never changed. This page, being the earliest version of an actual 'Tale of Years', I will call T 1. In its earlier part T 1 was so much corrected and reworked as my father proceeded that it is scarcely possible to analyse the successive stages of its endlessly changed chronology; but in a subsequent text he followed the final form of T 1 so closely that it can be given in its place. The chief point to notice in it is the entry 'Foundation of Tarkilion', which was changed (probably at once) to 'Foundation of Artheden (Dunhirion) and Gondor'. The name *Dunhirion* is also found, but not so far as I know elsewhere, in a late text of the chapter *The Council of Elrond*, where it was corrected to *Annúminas*; while *Tarkilion* is found in the original manuscript of *Of the Rings of Power and the Third Age*, likewise corrected to *Annúminas*, and likewise apparently not found elsewhere. *Artheden* is clearly the first appearance of Arthedain, though not with its later significance.

The page T 1 (in its final form) was followed so closely by the next text that it seems probable that no long interval had elapsed. This is a clearly written manuscript on two sides of a single sheet; I will refer to it as T 2. A few changes were made to it in red ink, but they were made after the subsequent version had been written (since the same changes were made to that, also in red ink), and I do not notice them here.

Of the Tale of Years
in the latter ages

The 'First Age'[1] ended with the Great Battle and the departure of the Elves and Fathers of Men, and the foundation of Númenor.

The 'Second Age' ended with the overthrow of Sauron, and the Loss of the One Ring.

The 'Third Age' is drawing to its end in the tales of the Shire and of the Hobbits.

Each 'Age' last[ed] somewhat more or less than 3000 years; so that the Loss of the Ring was about 3000 years before Frodo's time. Deagol finds it about 1100 years after Isildur's death. 'Gollum' therefore had the Ring for about 1900 years.

The Second Age or the Black Years
reckoned from the overthrow of Morgoth

End of the Great Battle.
- 10 Foundation of the Havens, and the kingdom of Lindon.
- 50 Foundation of Númenor.
- 460 Death of Elros, Ëarendel's son, first king of Númenor.
- 500 Reawakening[2] of Sauron in Middle-earth.
- 700 First ships of the Númenóreans return to Middle-earth. Others come at times, but seldom, and they do not stay.
- 750 Foundation of Imladrist[3] (Rivendell) and Eregion (Hollin).
- 900– Sauron begins in secret to build the fortress of Barad-dûr in Mordor, and makes the forges of Orodruin.
- 1200–1500 The Rings of Power are made in Eregion.
- 1550 War of the Elves and Sauron. The 'Days of Flight' begin, or the Black Years properly so called.
- 1600 Gil-galad defends Lindon; and Imladris is besieged but holds out. Eregion is laid waste.
- 1700 The great voyages of the Númenóreans begin. They come in many ships to Lindon, and they aid Gil-galad and Elrond.
- 1900 Barad-dûr is completed.

THE TALE OF YEARS OF THE SECOND AGE 169

2000–3000 Sauron's dominion slowly extends over all Middle-earth, but it is withheld from the North-West, and all along the West-shores, even far southwards, the Númenóreans have fortresses and outposts.

3118 Tar-kalion the young king, the thirteenth of his line, ascends the throne of Númenor. He resolves to challenge Sauron the Great, and begins an armament (3120).

3125 Tar-kalion sets sail to Middle-earth. Sauron is obliged to yield and is taken to Númenor.

3319 Downfall of Númenor. Elendil, Anárion and Isildur fly to Middle-earth. Foundation of Arthedain (with the city Annúminas) in the North; and of Gondor (with the city Osgiliath) in the South.

3320 Sauron returns to Mordor.

3430–3 Sauron at last being ready makes war in Gondor. The Last Alliance is formed.

3433 [> 3434] Battle of Dagorlad. Siege of Barad-dûr begun.

3441 Sauron overthrown. Ring taken and lost. End of the Second Age.

The following are the only differences in the chronology of T 2 from its forerunner. In T 1 Sauron's departure to Númenor is given a separate entry under the year 3128; and (while T 1 already has the final date 3319 for the Downfall, where T(a) had 3320) the flight of Elendil and his sons is placed, most strangely, a year later, in 3320.

It will be seen that the dates of events in the Second Age are for the most part at variance with those in Appendix B, in many cases very widely so (thus Imladris was founded at the same time as Eregion, in 750, but in Appendix B not until 1697, in the War of the Elves and Sauron, when Eregion was laid waste). The most extreme of these differences refers in fact to the Third Age, in the headnote to the text, where the statement in T(a) that Déagol found the Ring in about Third Age 1100 and therefore Gollum possessed it for some 1900 years (p. 167) is repeated: in Appendix B Déagol finds the Ring in T.A.2463, by which reckoning Gollum had it for 478 years, until Bilbo found it in 2941.

There are a number of points of agreement between T 2 (under which I include here the closely similar T 1) and the 'Scheme' of the Númenórean kings accompanying the original manuscript A of the *Akallabêth*, given on pp. 150–1. In both, the death of Elros is placed in the year 460 (not as later in 442); in T 2 the coming of the Númenóreans to the aid of Gil-galad in Lindon is dated 1700, while in the 'Scheme' this is said to have occurred in the days of the unnamed sixth king (after Elros), who died in 1790; in T 2 the accession of Tar-kalion is placed in 3118, and in the 'Scheme' his father, the unnamed twelfth king (after Elros) died in that year; and in both the date of Tar-kalion's landing in Middle-earth is 3125. A further point of agreement between both, and also with the manuscript A of the *Akallabêth*, concerns the completion of Barad-dûr: in T 2 this is dated 1900; in *Akallabêth* A (see p. 153, §29) it is said to have occurred in the days of Atanamir; and in the 'Scheme' Atanamir is said to have died in 2061, his father having died in 1790.

Two other points in this earliest version (or strictly versions) of the Tale of Years of the Second Age remain to be mentioned. The loss of the One Ring is expressly placed in the last year of the Second Age, 3441; whereas in Appendix B the headnote states that that Age 'ended with the first overthrow of Sauron ... and the *taking* of the One Ring' (cf. also the last words of section I (i) of Appendix A, RK p. 318), while the planting of the White Tree in Minas Anor, the handing over of the South Kingdom to Meneldil, and the death of Isildur are placed in the year 2 of the Third Age. Secondly, in the entry for 3319 Anárion is placed before Isildur, and it will be seen shortly that this does indeed mean that Anárion was the elder of Elendil's sons (cf. the text FN III in IX.335: 'his sons Anárion and Isildur'). In *Akallabêth* A and subsequently Isildur had four ships and Anárion two (p. 157, §80), from which it seems clear that the reversal of this had already taken place. On the other hand, in an early version of the chapter *The Council of Elrond* Isildur was expressly stated to be the elder (VII.126).

Found with T 2 and to all appearance belonging to the same time is another page in which my father restated in the same or closely similar terms a part of his notes on Númenor and the aftermath of the Downfall in T(a), pp. 166–7. This page I will call T(b). Corrections to it were made at the same time as those to T 2, and are not noticed here.

Average life of a Númenórean before the fall was about 210 years (3 × 70). Average life of the royal house of the line of Eärendel was about 350 years (5 × 70). A king of Númenor usually came to the throne when about 120 years old and reigned 200 years or more.

50	Númenor founded
410	years Elros reigned
2640	11 other kings (averaging 240 each)
220	Last king (Tarkalion)
3320	

Elendil was very long-lived (being of Eärendel's line). He was about 200 years old at the time of the Fall of Númenor and Anárion 110, Isildur 100. The new realms of Arnor and Gondor lasted about 110 years before Sauron made his first attacks on them. The gathering of the Last Alliance, the march, battle

THE TALE OF YEARS OF THE SECOND AGE 171

and siege, lasted about 11 years. (121)
3320 + 121, 3441.

The remainder of this page and its verso are taken up with the earliest version of the Tale of Years of the Third Age, obviously written continuously from T(b) just given; for this see p. 225.

These initial computations of the chronology of the Second Age are remarkable in themselves and perplexing in the detail of their interrelations.

The text T(a), self-evidently the starting-point, made 3320 the date of the Downfall. After a lapse of 110 years Sauron opened war on the new kingdoms (3430), and a further ten passed before his overthrow in 3440, the last year of the Second Age.

In T 1, written at the same time as, but after, T(a), the Downfall is placed in 3319 (no reason for the change being evident), but the flight of Elendil and his sons is incomprehensibly placed in the following year, 3320 (p. 169). Again after 110 years Sauron attacked Gondor (3430), but now *eleven* years passed before his overthrow in 3441.

In T 2, which is little more than a fair copy of T 1, the founding of the kingdoms in Middle-earth is placed in the year of the Downfall, which is now 111 years before Sauron's attack in 3430; as in T 1, eleven years passed before the overthrow of Sauron in 3441.

Finally, the extremely puzzling text T(b) goes back to T(a) in placing the Downfall in 3320, and 110 years passed before the war began in 3430; but the total of 3441 is reached as in T 1 and T 2 by the lapse of eleven years before the overthrow. T(b) is apparently a companion page to T 2, and must be later than the other texts, since the Northern Kingdom is here called Arnor, not Arthedain, and this change only entered after a further text of the Tale of Years had been written.

If we now turn to the *Akallabêth* 'Scheme' (pp. 150-1) it will be seen that the date 3319 of the Downfall is reached by an entirely different route. In the 'Scheme' the intervals between the death-dates of the kings are in every case either 221 or 222 years, except for those between the unnamed sixth king and Atanamir, the seventh, which was 50 years longer (271 years), and between Atanamir and his son Kiryatan which was 50 years shorter (172 years). If all these intervals are added together they reach a total of 2658 years; and if to this is added the year of the death of Elros (460) and the length of the reign of Tar-kalion (201 years) we reach 3319, the date of the Downfall.[4] In the 'Scheme' Tar-kalion is numbered '13', but he is expressly the thirteenth king *excluding* Elros, as he is also in *Akallabêth* A and *The Drowning of Anadûnê* as revised (see p. 154 and note 10), so that there were fourteen kings of Númenor in all.

In the texts T(a) and T(b), on the other hand, 'eleven other kings' ruled between Elros and Tar-kalion, making thirteen in all; and the average length of their reigns being here 240 years, the total is 2640.

172   THE PEOPLES OF MIDDLE-EARTH

When to this is added 460 and Tar-kalion's reign of 220 years the total is 3320.

A final element is the fact that in T 1, the companion page to T(a), Tar-kalion ascended the throne in 3118 and reigned for 201 years, just as in the 'Scheme'.

Every explanation of this extraordinary textual puzzle seems to founder. It is not in itself perhaps a matter of great significance, though one certainly gets the impression that there is more to the date 3319 (and possibly also to 3441) than the evidence reveals. It is clear, at any rate, that all these texts, the original manuscript of the *Akallabêth* and its associated 'Scheme', the computations in the texts T(a) and T(b), and the initial version of the Tale of Years, arose at the same time, before the narrative of *The Lord of the Rings* was in final form; while the evidence suggests that it was these computations of the Númenórean kings, formulaic as they were, that provided the chronological 'vehicle' of the Second Age, established at that time. It can be seen from the text T 1 that the Númenórean history provided the fixed element, while the dating of events in Middle-earth before the Downfall were at first of an extreme fluidity (the making of the Rings of Power, for instance, was moved from 1000–1200 to 1200–1500, and the War of the Elves and Sauron from 1200 to 1550).

The third text of the Tale of Years, which I will call T 3, is (so far as the Second Age is concerned) little more than a copy of T 2, with a number of entries somewhat expanded, and one sole additional entry: '3440 Anárion is slain'; no dates were altered. Anárion and Isildur still appear in that order, and the North Kingdom is still named Arthedain, though both were subsequently corrected. The statement in the opening passage of T 2 concerning the length of the Ages and the finding of the Ring by Déagol was omitted, and in its place the following was introduced:

The *Fourth Age* ushered in the Dominion of Men and the decline of all the other 'speaking-folk' of the Westlands.

Following the usual pattern, a number of additions, some of them substantial, were made to the manuscript T 3, but virtually all of them were taken up into the following version, the greatly expanded T 4, whose entries for the Second Age are given here. This is a good clear manuscript with few subsequent alterations in this part of the text; those which were made before the following text was taken from it are noticed if significant.

The Tale of Years
in the
Latter Ages

The *First Age* was the longest. It ended with the Great Battle in which Fionwë and the sons of the Valar broke Thangorodrim and overthrew Morgoth.[5] Then most of the exiled Elves returned into the West and dwelt in Eressëa that was afterwards named Avallon, being within sight of Valinor.[6] The Atani or Edain, Fathers of Men, sailed also over Sea and founded the realm of Númenor or Westernesse, on a great isle, westmost of all mortal lands.

The *Second Age* ended with the first overthrow of Sauron and the loss of the One Ring.

The *Third Age* came to its end in the War of the Ring, and the destruction of the Dark Tower of Sauron, who was finally defeated.

The *Fourth Age* ushered in the Dominion of Men and the decline of all other 'speaking folk' of the Westlands.

[*Added*: The first three ages are now by some called *The Elder Days*, but of old and ere the Third Age was ended that name was given only to the First Age and the world before the casting forth of Morgoth.][7]

The Second Age

These were the *Dark Years* of Middle-earth, but the high tide of Númenor. Of events in Middle-earth scant record is preserved even among the Elves, and their dates here given are only approximate.

10   Foundation of the Grey Havens, and the Kingdom of Lindon. This was ruled by Gil-galad son of Felagund,[8] chief of all the Noldor who did not yet depart to Avallon.

50   Foundation of Númenor. [*Added*: About the same time the works of Moria were begun by Durin the Dwarf and his folk from the ruins of the ancient dwarf-cities in the Blue Mountains. *This was struck out and replaced by*: About this time many dwarves fleeing from the ruins of the dwarf-cities in the Blue Mountains came to Moria, and its power and the splendour of its works were greatly increased.][9]

460 Death of Elros Eärendil's son, first King of Númenor.

500 Sauron, servant of Morgoth, begins to stir again in Middle-earth.

700 First ships of the Númenóreans return to Middle-earth. At first they came only seldom, and the Númenóreans did not stay long in any place.

750 Foundation of Imladris (or Rivendell) and of Eregion (or Hollin) as dwellings of the Noldor or High Elves. Remnants of the Telerian Elves (of Doriath in ancient Beleriand) establish realms in the woodlands far eastward, but most of these peoples are Avari or East-elves. The chief of these were Thranduil who ruled in the north of Greenwood the Great beyond Anduin, but Lórien was fairer and had the greater power; for Celeborn had to wife the Lady Galadriel of the Noldor, sister of Gil-galad [> sister of Felagund Gil-galad's sire].[10]

900 Sauron in secret begins the building of the fortress, Barad-dûr, in Mordor, and makes there the forges of Orodruin, the Mountain of Fire. But he professes great friendship with the Eldar, and especially with those of Eregion, who were great in smith-craft.

1200–1500 The Rings of Power are forged in Eregion; but the Ruling Ring is forged by Sauron in Orodruin.

1550 War of the Elves and Sauron begins. The 'Days of Flight' begin, or the 'Dark Years' properly so called, being the time of the dominion of Sauron. Eregion is laid waste. The Naugrim (or Dwarves) close the gates of Moria. Many of the remaining Noldor depart west over Sea.

1700 The great voyages of the Númenóreans begin. Gil-galad defends Lindon and the Grey Havens. Imladris is besieged but holds out under the command of Elrond Eärendil's son. The Númenóreans come with many ships to Lindon and they aid Gil-galad and Elrond. Sauron retreats from Eriador (west of the Misty Mountains).

1900 Barad-dûr is completed with the power of the Ruling Ring.

c.2000 The Shadow falls on Númenor. The Númenóreans begin to murmur against the Valar, who will not permit them to sail west from their land; and they become jealous of the immortality of the Eldar. [*Added:* (c.2250).] A division appears among the Númenóreans between the Elf-friends, the smaller party, and the King's Folk. The latter become slowly estranged from the Valar and the Eldar, and abandon the use of the Elven tongues; the kings take names of Númenórean form. The Elf-friends, dwelling most in the east of Númenor,[11] remain loyal to the kings except in the matter of rebellion against the decrees of the Valar.

2000–3000 The Númenóreans now make permanent dwellings on the shores of Middle-earth, seeking wealth and dominion; they build many havens and fortresses. The Elf-friends go chiefly to the North-west, but their strongest place is at Pelargir above the Mouths of Anduin. The King's Folk establish lordships in Umbar[12] and Harad and in many other places on the coasts of the Great Lands.

During the same time Sauron extends his dominion slowly over the great part of Middle-earth; but his power reaches out eastward, since he is withheld from the coasts by the Númenóreans. He nurses his hatred for them, but cannot yet challenge them openly. Towards the end of this time the *Úlairi*, the Ringwraiths, servants of Sauron and slaves of the Nine Rings first appear.

3118 Tar-kalion, calling himself Ar-Pharazôn the Golden, thirteenth king of the line of Eärendil, ascends the throne of Númenor. He resolves to challenge Sauron the Great, and builds an armament.

3125 Ar-Pharazôn sets sail for Middle-earth. The might and splendour of the Númenóreans fills the servants of Sauron with fear. Ar-Pharazôn lands at Umbar, and in pursuance of his own secret design Sauron humbles himself and submits. Sauron is taken as a hostage to Númenor.

3140–3310 Sauron slowly gains the confidence of Ar-Pharazôn, until he dominates his counsels. He urges Ar-Pharazôn to make war on the Lords of the West to gain everlasting life.

Most of the Númenóreans fall under the sway of Sauron, and they persecute the Elf-friends; and they become tyrants over men in Middle-earth.

3310 Ar-Pharazôn feeling the approach of death at last takes the counsel of Sauron and prepares a vast fleet for an assault upon Avallon and Valinor. Valandil [> Amandil][13] the faithful breaks the ban of the Valar and sails west, hoping to repeat the embassy of Eärendil, and obtain the help of the Lords of the West. He is never heard of again. His son Elendil, as his father had bidden, makes ready ships on the east coast of Númenor, preparing for flight with all the faithful that he can gather.

3319 The great fleet of Ar-Pharazôn sails into the West and encompassing Avallon assails the shores of Valinor. Númenor is destroyed, and swallowed up by the sea. The world is broken and Valinor separated from the lands of the living.

Elendil and his sons Isildur and Anárion escape and fly east with nine great ships[14] to Middle-earth. They bring with them the Seven Stones or *Palantíri*, gifts of the Eldar of Avallon, and Isildur brings also a seedling of the White Tree of Avallon.

3320 Foundation of the realm of Arnor in the north of the Westlands, with the city Annúminas; and of Gondor about the waters of Anduin in the south, with the city Osgiliath. The Stones are divided: Elendil retains three in the North-kingdom, at Annúminas, and on Amon Súl, and in the tower of Emyn Beraid (the Tower Hills).[15] His sons take four, and set them at Minas Ithil, at Minas Anor, at Osgiliath, and at Orthanc.

In the same year Sauron returns to Middle-earth, and being at first filled with fear by the power and wrath of the Lords of the West he hides himself in Mordor and is quiet.

3430–3 [> 3429–30] Sauron, being at last ready again, makes war upon Gondor. Orodruin bursts into smoke and flame, and Men of Gondor seeing the sign re-name it Amon Amarth, Mount Doom.[16] Sauron comes forth and assails Minas Ithil, and destroys the White Tree that Isildur planted there. Isildur takes a seedling of the Tree and escapes by ship down Anduin with his wife and sons. He sails to Elendil in the North. The Last Alliance is formed between Gil-galad Elven-king and Elendil and his sons. They march east to Imladris summoning all folk to their aid.

3434 The Host of the Alliance crosses the Misty Mountains and marches south. They encounter the host of Sauron upon Dagorlad north of the gates of Mordor, and they are victorious. Sauron takes refuge in Barad-dûr.

3434– Siege of Barad-dûr begins and lasts seven years.

3440 Anárion is slain in Gorgoroth.

3441 Sauron comes forth, and wrestles with Elendil and Gil-galad. They overthrow him but are themselves slain.

THE TALE OF YEARS OF THE SECOND AGE 177

The One Ring is taken from the hand of Sauron by Isildur as the weregild of his father, and he will not permit it to be destroyed. He plants the seedling of the White Tree in Minas Anor in memory of his brother Anárion, but he will not himself [*added:* long] dwell there. He delivers the South-kingdom to Meneldil son of Anárion and marches north up the vale of Anduin, purposing to take up the realm of Elendil. He is slain by Orcs near the Gladden fields and the Ring is lost in the River.[17] The Ringwraiths fall into darkness and silence. The Second Age ends.[18]

In this fourth text of the Tale of Years the pattern of dating seen in T 1, T 2, with its great differences from the final form in Appendix B, is preserved. Thus Rivendell was still founded far earlier, in 750; Barad-dûr was begun in 900 and its building still took a thousand years; the making of the Rings of Power in Eregion, and the War of the Elves and Sauron, are dated as they were, extending over far greater periods of time. The work was becoming a condensed history rather than a list of dates; but scarcely any new dates were introduced.

In new material in the entry for c.2000 the sentence 'The Shadow falls on Númenor' is clearly related to the *Akallabêth* 'Scheme' (p. 150), where it is noted of the reign of Tar-Atanamir (c.1790–c.2061) that 'In his time the Shadow first fell on Númenor'. The fullness of the entries concerning the reign of Ar-Pharazôn reinforces the view that my father made these early versions of the Tale of Years when he was writing the *Akallabêth*, as do a number of particular features, such as the sentence concerning the Great Battle in the headnote to T 4 (see note 5) and the occurrence of the name *Úlairi* of the Ringwraiths in the entry for 2000–3000 (see p. 153, §30). The fact that *Avallon* was still the name of Eressëa (and not that of the haven) shows beyond doubt that the *Akallabêth* was still at the stage of the earliest manuscript (see note 6).

I think it extremely probable that this text T 4 (of which the part pertaining to the Third Age is very much longer) belongs in time with the texts F 2 and D 2 of the Appendices on Languages and on Calendars, and with the third text of *The Heirs of Elendil*, given in the next chapter. But external evidence of date seems to be entirely lacking.

From T 4 an amanuensis typescript T 5 was made, carefully following the original. At some stage my father subjected one of the copies to very heavy correction, but his chief (though not the only) purpose in doing so seems to have been to abbreviate it by the omission of phrases. By this time the 'second phase' of the *Akallabêth* (see p. 154, §31) had entered, and the last years of Númenor were altered on the typescript (cf. p. 175):

3118   Birth of Ar-Pharazôn.
3255   Ar-Pharazôn the Golden, twenty-fifth king of the line of Elros, seizes the sceptre of Númenor. He resolves to challenge Sauron the Great, and builds an armament.
3261   Ar-Pharazôn sets sail for Middle-earth. The might of the Númenóreans fills the servants of Sauron with fear. Ar-Pharazôn lands at Umbar, and Sauron humbles himself and submits. Sauron is taken as a hostage to Númenor.
3262–3310   Sauron slowly gains the confidence of Ar-Pharazôn ...

The opening dates of the Second Age were also changed: Year 1, Foundation of the Grey Havens; 32 Foundation of Númenor; 442 Death of Elros; 600 First ships of the Númenóreans return to Middle-earth. Other changes were the replacement of *Úlairi* by *Nazgûl* in the entry for 2000–3000 (changed to 2200–3000), and the removal of *Avallon* at all occurrences, either by altering it to *Eressëa* or by the omission of any name.

The evident reason for the revision of the typescript (in respect of the abbreviation of the text) is discussed later (see p. 246). The next stage in the development was an attempt to reduce the Tale of Years much more drastically. This is represented by a confused collection of typescript pages (from which a good deal of the Third Age is missing) made very evidently under stress: the deadline for the publication of *The Return of the King* was fast approaching, and the situation was indeed afflicting. Not only must the record of events be further pruned and curtailed, but fundamental features of the chronology of the Second Age were not yet established; and this work must be done against time.

I give in illustration a portion of the first version of the Second Age chronology comprised in this material. My father was typing very rapidly, faster than he could manage, and there are very many errors, which I have of course corrected; I have also introduced divisions to indicate successive shifts in the dating, though there is no suggestion of these in the typescript, where the rejected passages are not even struck through. Thus the text that follows has a very much more ordered appearance than does the original.

900   Sauron secretly begins the building of Barad-dûr. He makes the forges of the Mountain of Fire.
1200   Sauron seeks the friendship of the Elves, especially those of Eregion, who are great in smith-craft.
1200–1500   The Rings of Power are forged in Eregion; but the Ruling Ring is forged by Sauron in Mordor.
1550   The war of Sauron and the Elves begins. The 'Dark Years' follow, the time of the dominion of Sauron. Many of the remaining Eldar depart west over Sea. The great voyages of the Númenóreans begin.

THE TALE OF YEARS OF THE SECOND AGE 179

1600 Eregion is laid waste. The gates of Moria are shut. The forces of Sauron overrun Eriador. Imladris is besieged, but holds out under the command of Elrond Eärendil's son, sent from Lindon. The forces of Sauron overrun Eriador. Gil-galad defends Lindon and the Grey Havens.

1603 A Númenórean navy comes to the Grey Havens. The Númenóreans aid Gil-galad, and Sauron's forces are driven out of Eriador and Sauron retreats from Eriador. The Westlands have peace for some while.

From the time of the defeat in Eriador Sauron does not molest the Westlands for many years, but plots in secret. He slowly extends his dominion eastward, since he is withheld from the coasts by the Númenóreans. He nurses his hatred for them, but cannot yet challenge them openly.

1700 Barad-dûr is completed with the power of the Ruling Ring.

1200 Sauron seeks the friendship of the Elves (in hope to subject them). He is still fair to look on, and the Elves become enamoured of the knowledge he can impart.

1300 The Elves begin the forging of the Rings of Power. It is said that this took many long years. S[auron] secretly makes the forges [*sic*]

1500 The Three Great Rings are made by Celebrimbor of the Silver Grasp (*celebrin* 'silver', *paur* 'the fist or closed hand'). The Ruling Ring is made secretly by Sauron in Mordor.

1000 Sauron begins the building of Barad-dûr in Mordor.

1200 Sauron courts the friendship of the Elves, hoping to get them, the chief obstacle to his dominion, into his power. Gil-galad refuses to treat with him. But Sauron is still fair to look on and the Elves of Eregion are won over by their desire of skill and knowledge.

1500 The Elves of Eregion under the guidance of Sauron begin the forging of the Rings of Power. This takes many long years. Sauron secretly forges the One Ring in Orodruin.

1690 The Three Rings are completed. Celebrimbor becomes aware of the designs of Sauron. Barad-dûr is completed with the power of [*sic*]

1695 The War of the Elves and Sauron begins. Many of the remaining Eldar depart west over Sea.

1696 Elrond Eärendil's son is sent to Eregion by Gil-galad.

1697 Eregion is laid waste. The gates of Moria are shut. Elrond retreats with the remnant of the Eldar to Imladris.

1600 The great voyages of the Númenóreans begin. The ships are welcomed by Gil-galad and Círdan.

1699 Imladris is besieged but holds out under the command of Elrond. Sauron overruns Eriador. Gil-galad defends Lindon and the Grey Havens.

1700 A great navy of the Númenóreans comes to the Grey Havens.

Here this text seems to have been abandoned and replaced by another and more coherent version, with entries further reduced and dates following the latest formulations in the text just given. These dates from 1500 to 1700 were then corrected on the typescript, being reduced (advanced) by a hundred years, and so moving them away from those in Appendix B, as seen in the following table (in which I give only brief indications of the actual entries).

		Appendix B
1500 [> 1400]	(Forging of the Three Rings begun)	c.1500
1600 [> 1500]	(Forging of the One Ring)	c.1600
1690 [> 1590]	(Three Rings completed)	c.1590
1690 [> 1590]	(Barad-dûr completed)	c.1600
1695 [> 1595]	(War of Elves and Sauron begins)	1693
1697 [> 1597]	(Eregion laid waste)	1697
1699 [> 1599]	(Sauron overruns Eriador)	1699
1700 [> 1600]	(Coming of Númenórean navy)	1700

At this stage Imladris was still founded in the year 750. The correction of all the entries from 1500 to 1700 was subsequently abandoned; the dates before correction were now those of the final chronology or very close to them, with the exception of the completion of Barad-dûr and the completion of the Three Rings. In this text, by either dating, the Three Rings were not achieved for a further ninety years after the forging of the One Ring, whereas in the final chronology (by adopting in this one case the revised date, 1590) the One Ring was made ten years after the Three.

This second text then continues:

1869 Tar-Ciryatan, twelfth king of Númenor, receives the sceptre. The first shadow falls on Númenor. The Kings become greedy of wealth and power.

2060–2251 Reign of Tar-Atanamir the Great, thirteenth King of Númenor.[19] The shadow deepens. The King's ships exact heavy tribute from Men on the coasts of Middle-earth. The Númenóreans become jealous of the immortality of the Eldar; and the King speaks openly against [the] command of the Valar that they should not sail west from their land.

2250–3000 During this time the power and splendour of the Númenóreans continues to increase; and they build many fortresses on the west shores of Middle-earth. Sauron extends his power eastward, being withheld from the coasts, and nurses his hatred of Númenor. But the Númenóreans become divided against

Here the entry breaks off, and is immediately followed by a long account (more than 2000 words) of the Númenóreans, of their origin, their division, the coming of Sauron, and the Downfall.

I believe that this strange development can be explained in this way. At that time, as things stood, *The Lord of the Rings* would be published without any account, however brief, of the story of Númenor. In the manuscript T 4 my father had written (pp. 174–6) what I have called 'a condensed history rather than a list of dates'; for it is to be remembered that in the narrative of *The Lord of the Rings*, despite all the many mentions of the names Númenor and Westernesse, he had told nothing of its history, and of the Downfall no more than Faramir's words in Minas Tirith, when he told Éowyn that he was thinking 'of the land of Westernesse that foundered, and of the great dark wave climbing over the green lands and above the hills'. He must now attempt to contract even what he had written in T 4, and as a comparison of the last entries in the present text just given with those in T 4 (pp. 174–5) shows, he was not succeeding. The reduction into a mere chronological scheme of a large history that could not be understood by a recital of events was a task profoundly uncongenial to him. He despaired of it, and broke off in mid-sentence.

It may well have been at that point, having typed the words 'But the Númenóreans become divided against', that he decided that *The Lord of the Rings* must contain some account of the story of Westernesse, separate from the Tale of Years, and set it down there and then, beginning with the words 'As a reward for their sufferings in the cause against Morgoth, the Valar, the Guardians of the World, granted to the Edain a land to dwell in, removed from the dangers of Middle-earth.' Removed from the Tale of Years, it found a place in Appendix A, *Annals of the Kings and Rulers*, RK pp. 315–18.[20]

There are in fact two typescripts of this text, both composed *ab initio* on the typewriter; the second of these my father described in a pencilled note as a 'variant' of the first, and it was this that he used, with many minor alterations of wording and some omissions, in Appendix A. Neither version has the list of the Kings and Queens of Númenor (RK p. 315), and both have a more detailed account of the rebellion against Tar-Palantir and the marriage of Míriel his daughter to Pharazôn (said in both texts to have been 'by force'), which was omitted in Appendix A. Both versions, also, have an account of Sauron's policy in his attack on the coastal fortresses and harbours of the Númenóreans which was likewise omitted, and is not found in the *Akallabêth*. I cite here two passages from the first version of the text.

> Proudest of all the Kings was Ar-Pharazôn the Golden, and no less than the kingship of all the world was his desire. But still he retained enough wisdom to fear the Lords of the West, and turned therefore his thoughts to Middle-earth. Now Sauron knowing of the dissension in Númenor thought how he might

use it to achieve his revenge. He began therefore to assail the havens and forts of the Númenóreans, and invaded the coastlands under their dominion. As he foresaw this aroused the great wrath of the King, who resolved to challenge Sauron the Great for the lordship of Middle-earth. For five years Ar-Pharazôn prepared, and at last he himself set sail with a great navy and armament, the greatest that had yet appeared in the world.

If Sauron had thought thus to decoy the King to Middle-earth and there destroy him, his hope deceived him. And Ar-Pharazôn landed at Umbar, and so great was the splendour and might of the Númenóreans at the noon of their glory that at the rumour of them alone all men flocked to their summons and did obeisance; and Sauron's own servants fled away. The land of Mordor he had indeed fortified and made so strong that he need fear no assault upon it; but he was in doubt now, and even the Barad-dûr seemed no longer secure.

Sauron therefore changed his design, and had recourse to guile. He humbled himself, and came himself on foot before Ar-Pharazôn, and did him homage and craved pardon for his offences. And Ar-Pharazôn spared his life; but took from him all his titles, and made him prisoner, and carried him at length back to Númenor to be hostage for the submission and faith of all who had before owed him allegiance.

'This is a hard doom,' said Sauron, 'but great kings must have their will', and he submitted as one under compulsion, concealing his delight; for things had fallen out according to his design.

Now Sauron had great wisdom and knowledge, and could find words of seeming reason for the persuasion of all but the most wary; and he could still assume a fair countenance when he wished. He was brought as a prisoner to Númenor in 3261, but he had not been there five years before he had the King's ear and was deep in his counsel.

'Great kings must have their will': this was the burden of all his advice; and whatever the King desired he said was his right, and devised plans whereby he might gain it.

Then darkness came upon the minds of the Númenóreans, and they held the Guardians in hatred, and openly denied the One who is above all; and they turned to the worship of the Dark, and of Morgoth the Lord of the Darkness. They made a great temple in the land and there did evil; for they tormented the remnant of the faithful, and there slew them or burned them. And the like they did in Middle-earth, and filled the west coasts with tales of dread, so that men cried 'Has then Sauron become King of Númenor?'

So great was his power over the hearts of the most of that people that maybe had he wished he could have taken the sceptre; but all that he wished was to bring Númenor to ruin. Therefore he said to the King: 'One thing only now you lack to make you the greatest King in the world, the undying life that is withheld from you in fear and jealousy by the lying Powers in the West. But great kings take what is their right.' And Ar-Pharazôn pondered these words, but for long fear held him back.

But at last even Ar-Pharazôn the Golden, King of kings, having lived one hundred and ninety-two years,[21] felt the waning of his life and feared the approach of death and the going out into the darkness that he had worshipped. Therefore he began to prepare a vast armament for the assault upon Valinor, that should surpass the one with which he had come to Umbar even as a great galleon of Númenor surpassed a fisherman's boat.

There follows a brief account of the expulsion of those of doubtful loyalty from the western coasts of Númenor, the voyage of Amandil into the West,[22] the sailing of the Great Armament, and the cataclysm of the Downfall. At the end of this, following the words 'But Elendil and his sons escaped with nine ships, and were borne on the wings of a great storm and cast up on the shores of Middle-earth', is a notable statement of the destruction caused by the drowning of Númenor:

These were much changed in the tumult of the winds and seas that followed the Downfall; for in some places the sea rode in upon the land, and in others it piled up new coasts. Thus while Lindon suffered great loss, the Bay of Belfalas was much filled at the east and south, so that Pelargir which had been only a few miles from the sea was left far inland, and Anduin carved a new path by many mouths to the Bay. But the Isle of Tolfalas was almost destroyed, and was left at last like a barren and lonely mountain in the water not far from the issue of the River.

No such statement is found elsewhere.[23] In the *Akallabêth* (*The Silmarillion* p. 280), in a passage taken virtually without change from *The Drowning of Anadûnê* (IX.374, §52), there is no reference to any named region or river.[24]

There is no further text of the Tale of Years extant before the typescript from which Appendix B was printed. Of this it may be noted that in the preamble to the entries for the Second Age the reference to *mithril* reads:

> This they did because they learned that *mithril* had been discovered in Moria. It had been believed before that this could only be got in the Ered Luin; but no more could now be found there in the old dwarf-mines.

My father struck out the second sentence on the proof.

NOTES

1 Against this opening statement concerning the Three Ages my father later scribbled 'These Ages are called the Elder Days'. On this see p. 173 and note 7.
2 T 1 has the more natural 'Arising of Sauron'.
3 *Imladrist* was corrected at once to *Imladris*. In T 1 the form is *Imladris*, as also in T 2 in the entry for 1600, so that this was a mere casual reversion to the earlier form.
4 It is plain that in the 'Scheme' the death-date of one king indicates also the accession of the next, and thus the interval between two death-dates is the length of the reign of the king: for example, the fourth king died in 1347, and the fifth in 1568, and thus the fifth king reigned for 221 years.

It certainly seems most natural to suppose that the 'Scheme' was precisely that, and that the representation of the reigns as all of the same length (differing only by one year) was a mere formula of convenience for working out the chronology as a whole. But Atanamir reigned for 50 years longer than any other, and his son for 50 years less; and this obviously relates to the passage in the *Akallabêth* (SA §24, going back to the original manuscript):

> And Atanamir lived to a great age, clinging to his life beyond the end of all joy; and he was the first of the Númenóreans to do this, refusing to depart until he was witless and unmanned, and denying to his son the kingship at the height of his days.

The much greater age of Atanamir must imply that all the other kings died by act of their own will long before the end of their physical span, and thus allowed their sons a period of rule equivalent to their own. It would be mistaken to press this early and experimental text too closely on the matter, but it certainly suggests a difference from the developed conception in *The Line of Elros*, where it is said (*Unfinished Tales* p. 218) that it was the custom 'until the days of Tar-Atanamir that the King should yield the sceptre to his successor before he died'; there were thus a number of years (recorded in the entries of *The Line of Elros*)

THE TALE OF YEARS OF THE SECOND AGE 185

between the king's surrender of the sceptre and his death.
5   With this sentence cf. the original version of the *Akallabêth*, p. 143, §3.
6   It is notable that here and subsequently *Avallon* is still the name of the whole Isle of Eressëa, as it was in the original manuscript A of the *Akallabêth*, although the later form *Avallónë* and the later meaning (the Haven) entered before that manuscript was completed (see p. 146, §12).
7   Cf. the preamble to the Tale of Years in Appendix B: 'In the Fourth Age the earlier ages were often called the *Elder Days*; but that name was properly given only to the days before the casting out of Morgoth.' In the *Akallabêth* 'the Elder Days' was apparently used of the earlier part of the Second Age (p. 156, §53).
8   For other references to the abandoned idea that Gil-galad was the son of Felagund see XI.242–3, and pp. 349–50.
9   It looks as if the added passage concerning the Dwarves was rejected and replaced immediately. It is strange that my father should have written first that Durin founded Moria at the beginning of the Second Age, with 'his folk' coming from the ruins of Nogrod and Belegost.
10 With this entry compare the headnote to the Second Age in Appendix B. – The words 'the Lady Galadriel of the Noldor, sister of Gil-galad' were not, as might be thought, a slip, but record a stage in her entry into the legends of the First Age. In one of the earliest texts of the work *Of the Rings of Power and the Third Age* my father wrote of Galadriel: 'A Queen she was and lady of the woodland elves, yet she was herself of the Noldor and had come from Beleriand in the days of the Exile.' To this he added subsequently: 'For it is said by some that she was a handmaid of Melian the Immortal in the realm of Doriath'; but striking this out at once he substituted: 'For it is said by some that she was a daughter of Felagund the Fair and escaped from Nargothrond in the day of its destruction.' In the following text this was changed to read: 'And some have said that she was the daughter of Felagund the Fair and fled from Nargothrond before its fall, and passed over the Mountains into Eriador ere the coming of Fionwë'; this in turn was altered to: 'For she was the daughter of Felagund the Fair and the elder sister of Gil-galad, though seldom had they met, for ere Nargothrond was made or Felagund was driven from Dorthonion, she passed east over the mountains and forsook Beleriand, and first of all the Noldor came to the inner lands; and too late she heard the summons of Fionwë.' – In the *Annals of Aman* and the *Grey Annals* she had become, as she remained, the sister of Felagund.
11 In the *Akallabêth* the Elendili dwelt mostly in the west of Númenor, and were forced to remove into the east (p. 152); but

the statement here that they dwelt mainly in the east may be due simply to compression.

12 This is the first reference to the establishment of a Númenórean settlement at Umbar before the landing of Ar-Pharazôn (see p. 156, §41).

13 On the name *Valandil* for *Amandil* (as in the first version of the *Akallabêth*) see p. 156, §44.

14 It is curious that all the texts of the *Akallabêth* have twelve ships, and only on the late amanuensis typescript did my father change the number to nine (see p. 157, §80); whereas in the present text T 4, certainly no later than the earliest text of the *Akallabêth*, the number is nine as first written.

15 The statement in this entry concerning the division of the *palantíri* appeared first in additions to the preceding text T 3; and there they are called *Gwahaedir*, while the Tower Hills are called *Emyn Gwahaedir*, replaced by *Emyn Hen Dúnadan*, and then again by *Emyn Beraid*. This last name does not appear in the actual narrative of *The Lord of the Rings*.

16 This was probably the first appearance of *Amon Amarth*, which only occurs in Appendix A (I, i, at end, RK p. 317).

17 All the material in these last entries first appears as rough and complex marginal additions to the manuscript T 3, but at this point there is an addition in T 3 which my father did not take up, perhaps because he missed it:

> The shards of the Sword of Elendil are brought to Valandil Isildur's heir at Imladris. He becomes king of the North Kingdom of Arnor, and dwells at Fornost.

The name Valandil of Isildur's heir thus does not appear in T 4; but the entry for 3310 was not added to T 3, and thus Valandil as the name of Elendil's father does not appear in that text.

18 On the ending of the Second Age with the death of Isildur and the loss of the One Ring in the Anduin see p. 170.

19 In Appendix B the entry for S.A.2251 begins 'Tar-Atanamir takes the sceptre. Rebellion and division of the Númenóreans begins.' In *Unfinished Tales* (p. 226, note 10) I discussed this, concluding that the entry was certainly an error, although at that time I was apparently unaware of the present text, or at any rate did not consult it; I suggested that the correct reading should be: '2251 Death of Tar-Atanamir. Tar-Ancalimon takes the sceptre. Rebellion and division of the Númenóreans begins.' No further text is extant before the final typescript from which Appendix B was printed, and it cannot be said how the error arose, moving from '2060–2251 Reign of Tar-Atanamir' to '2251 Tar-Atanamir takes the sceptre'.

20 I have found nothing in the correspondence of that time touching

on Appendix A, and I cannot answer the question how it was possible, if the Tale of Years had to be so contracted for reasons of space, to include a further long section in that Appendix at that stage.

21 'having lived one hundred and ninety-two years': from 3118 to 3310. In the text T 4 3118 was the year of his accession, corrected in the later revision of the typescript T 5 (p. 178) to the year of his birth.

22 The date of Amandil's voyage is given in this text, 3316; it was added also in the revision of the typescript T 5, entry 3310.

23 This appears to be the sole reference in any text to Tolfalas, apart from a mention of its capture by Men of the South in an outline made in the course of the writing of *The Two Towers* (VII.435). The isle and its name appeared already on the First Map of Middle-earth (VII.298, 308), but on all maps its extent appears much greater than in the description of it here.

24 On the extremely difficult question of the relation between the destruction caused in Middle-earth in the Great Battle at the end of the First Age, and that caused by the Drowning of Númenor, see V.22–3, 32–3, 153–4.

VII
THE HEIRS OF ELENDIL

While the development of the Appendices as a whole, and the *Prologue*, was to some degree an interconnected work, the Tale of Years was of its nature (since chronology became a paramount concern of my father's) closely interwoven with the evolution of the history of Númenor and the Númenórean kingdoms in Middle-earth, as has been seen already in the relation of the Tale of Years of the Second Age to the development of the *Akallabêth*. For the history and chronology of the Realms in Exile the primary document is a substantial work entitled *The Heirs of Elendil*.

The textual history of this is not easy to fathom. It is divided into two parts, the Northern Line (the Kings and the Chieftains) and the Southern Line (the Kings and the Stewards). The oldest manuscript, which I will call A, is headed *The Heirs of Elendil   The Southern Line of Gondor*; it is clearly if rapidly written for the most part, but in the concluding section recounting the names and dates of the Stewards of Gondor becomes very rough and is obviously in the first stage of composition.

The second manuscript, B, has both the Northern and the Southern Lines, in that order; but though my father fastened the two sections together, they are distinct in appearance. I believe that the second part began as a fair copy of A, but quickly developed and expanded into a much fuller (and increasingly rough) text. To this he added the Northern Line. This section in B seems to be in the first stage of composition (a rejected page shows the names of the later kings and chieftains in the process of emergence) – and there is no trace of any earlier work on the Northern Line, a companion text to A. On the other hand there are clear indications that the Northern Line and its history did already exist when A was set down.

Heavily emended, the composite text B paved the way for a fine manuscript, C; this in turn was much emended in the Northern Line, less so in the remainder, and an amanuensis typescript D was made (much later) from the corrected text (see p. 190).

There is as usual no hint or trace of external dating for any of this work on *The Heirs of Elendil*, and the most that can be done is to try to relate it to other texts. The relative date of B is shown by the fact that the North Kingdom was still called *Arthedain* and that Anárion was still the elder son of Elendil, for this was also the case in the third text of the Tale of Years, T 3 (p. 172). The name of the tenth king of the Northern Line is in B *Eärendil*, which is found in the early texts F 1, F 2 of the Appendix on Languages as that of the tenth king (p. 32, footnote to §9). In the fourth text T 4 of the Tale of Years the name of the realm is *Arnor*, Isildur is the elder son, and King Eärendur enters.

There can be no doubt therefore that all the fundamental structure and chronology of the Realms in Exile reached written form in the first phase of the work on what would become the Appendices (cf. p. 177). That the final text C, and many at least of the corrections and additions made to it, belongs to the same time is equally clear. One might suppose this to be the case on general grounds: from the care and calm that are evident in the fine manuscript as it was originally made, in contrast to the latter ragged and chaotic work on the Appendices, and from the fact that corrections to the preceding text B were made (according to my father's constant practice) in preparation for this further version. But the occurrence on the first page of C of the names *Valandil* of Elendil's father and of *Avallon* for *Eressëa* (the latter remaining uncorrected) shows that it belongs to the time when the original text of the *Akallabêth* still stood and T 4 of the Tale of Years had not yet been revised, for both of these have *Valandil* (pp. 156, 175) and *Avallon* (p. 173 and note 6). To this may be added the use of 'Noldorin' for 'Sindarin'.

Work on *The Heirs of Elendil* gave rise to alterations in the text of *The Lord of the Rings*. A good example of this is found in the passage of the chapter *A Knife in the Dark* (FR p. 197) where Strider speaks of the history of Weathertop. As this passage stood at the end of work on the chapter (scarcely differing from the original text, VI.169) he said:

> There is no barrow on Weathertop, nor on any of these hills. The Men of the West did not live here. I do not know who made this path, nor how long ago, but it was made to provide a road that could be defended, from the north to the foot of Weathertop; some say that Gil-galad and Elendil made a fort and a strong place here in the ancient days, when they marched into the East.

This was altered and expanded, in a late typescript, to the passage in FR, where Strider's account of the great tower of Amon Sûl that was burned and broken derives from the addition made to the entry for Arveleg I (eighteenth king of the Northern Line) in *Heirs of Elendil* B, reappearing in the final text C (see pp. 194, 209). But the addition made to C in the entry for Argeleb I, seventeenth king, 'Argeleb fortifies the Weather Hills', belongs with the alteration of Strider's words about the path, which now became:

> The Men of the West did not live here; though in their latter days they defended the hills for a while against the evil that came out of Angmar. This path was made to serve the forts along the walls.

The date of the making of the typescript D, however, is very much later. It is a good text, in top copy and carbon, made by an experienced typist, which fact alone would strongly suggest that it comes from the time after the publication of *The Lord of the Rings*; but in addition it was made on the same machine as that used for the *Annals of Aman*, the *Grey Annals*, the text LQ 2 of the *Quenta Silmarillion*, and the *Akallabêth*, about 1958 (see pp. 141–2). It is remarkable (seeing that all the essential material of C had been taken up into Appendix A, if presented there in a totally different form) that my father should have selected this text as one of those to be copied 'as a necessary preliminary to "remoulding" [of *The Silmarillion*]', as he said in his letter to Rayner Unwin of December 1957 (X.141). He did indeed make use of it later still, writing on the folded newspaper that contains the texts of *The Heirs of Elendil* 'Partly revised August 1965' – i.e. in preparation for the Second Edition of *The Lord of the Rings* published in 1966: from this time comes a long insertion in typescript greatly expanding the account of the events leading to the Kin-strife in Gondor, which in somewhat contracted form was introduced into Appendix A in the Second Edition (see further p. 259).

It has been difficult to find a satisfactory way of presenting this complex material, especially in view of the lack of correspondence in the texts of the Northern and Southern Lines (B–C; A–B–C). As with the two texts F 1 and F 2 of the Appendix on Languages, it has seemed best to give first the full text of C, with the corrections and expansions noted as such (though without any attempt to distinguish the relative times of their making), and to indicate significant differences in B in the Commentary following the text. In addition, I give an account of the brief manuscript A of the Southern Line at the beginning of the Commentary on that part of the work (p. 211).

As I have already mentioned, there is no writing extant before the manuscript A. It will be seen, however, that the names of the southern kings and their dates were already very largely fixed in A as first written down, and that (although the historical notes are very scanty and brief by comparison with the final form) such matters as the Kin-strife and the claim of Arvedui (last king in the North) to the southern crown were fully if not very substantially present; it may be supposed therefore that initial notes and lists have not survived (see also p. 216, under *Ondohir*). It is generally impossible to say how much of the matter that entered at each successive stage had newly arisen, and how much was present but at first, when the scope of the work was not yet fully realised, held in abeyance. But there is reason to think (see p. 213) that a firm if undeveloped structure of the history of the Realms in Exile had arisen a good while before the first texts of *The Heirs of Elendil* were composed. There are cases in text B where the actual working out of the history can be clearly seen, but always within that structure.

The Heirs of Elendil

Summary of the Annals in the 'Book of the Kings' and the 'Roll of Stewards of Gondor'. The dates are corrected to the reckoning of the Ages according to the Eldar, as also used in Arnor. In Gondor the dates were reckoned from the foundation of Osgiliath, Second Age 3320. Twenty-one years thus have to be added to the year-numbers here given to find the dates of the first Gondor era.

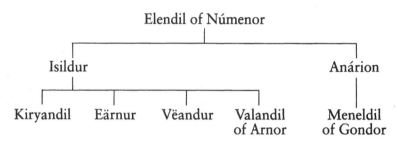

Year
Second Age
3119   Elendil born in Númenor. His father was Valandil [> Amandil] chief of the party of the Elf-friends.
3209   Isildur, elder son of Elendil, born in Númenor.
3219   Anárion, second son of Elendil, born in Númenor.
3299   Kiryandil, son of Isildur, born in Númenor.
3318   Meneldil, son of Anárion, born. He was the last man to be born in Númenor.
3319   Downfall of Númenor.
3320   Establishment of the Númenórean 'realms in exile' in the west of Middle-earth: Arnor in the north of the westlands (with chief city at Annúminas) by Elendil; Gondor in the south (with chief city at Osgiliath) by his sons. Isildur planted a seedling of the White Tree of Avallon, gift of the Eldar, in Minas Ithil. The *Palantíri*, or Seven Stones of Sight, were divided, and set up in towers: three in Arnor, at Annúminas, and at Amon Sûl, and upon the Emyn Beraid looking towards the Sea; four in the realm of Gondor, at Osgiliath, at Minas Ithil, at Minas Anor, and at Orthanc in Angrenost (Isengard).
3339   Eärnur, second son of Isildur, born in Gondor.
3379   Veändur, third son of Isildur, born in Minas Ithil.
3429   Sauron attacks Gondor from the neighbouring land of Mordor. He destroys Minas Ithil and burns the White

Tree. Isildur escapes by ship down Anduin, and sails north from Anduin's Mouths to Elendil in Arnor, with his wife and sons; he bears with him a seedling of the White Tree, grown from its first fruit in Middle-earth. Anárion holds out in Osgiliath.

3430 The last Alliance is begun. Elendil and Isildur obtain the help of Gil-galad and Elrond and gather great forces. They march east to Imladris. Valandil son of Isildur born in Imladris.

3434 The Battle of Dagorlad. Gil-galad and Elendil are victorious. The Siege of Barad-dûr is begun.

3440 Anárion is slain before Barad-dûr.

3441 Fall of Barad-dûr and overthrow of Sauron. Elendil and Gil-galad are slain. Isildur delivers Gondor to Meneldil son of Anárion. He plants the White Tree again in Minas Anor in memory of his brother, and marches up Anduin, intending to return to Arnor.

Isildur and his three elder sons are slain by Orcs in the Gladden Fields. His fourth son Valandil succeeds to Arnor, but being a child remains for a time with Elrond at Imladris.

The Second Age ends and the Third Age begins

Here follows the roll of the Kings of the Northern Line, and after the ending of the kings the names of the chieftains of the Dúnedain of the North who maintained throughout this Age the line of Valandil son of Isildur unbroken.

In the tenth year of the Third Age Valandil being come to manhood took up the kingship of Arnor and dwelt at Annúminas by Lake Nenuial.

The Heirs of Elendil
The Northern Line of Arnor: the Isildurioni

1	Elendil	born S.A.3119	lived 322 years	†slain 3441 or T.A.1
2	Isildur	3209	232	†slain 3441 or T.A.1
3	Valandil	3430	260	died T.A.249
4	Eldakar	T.A. 87	252	339
5	Arantar	185	250	435
6	Tarkil	280	235	515
7	Tarondor	372	230	602

8	Valandur	462	190	†slain	652
9	Elendur	552	225	died	777
10	Eärendur	640	221		861

After Eärendur the Northern Kingdom of Arnor was broken up. The sons of the king established smaller independent kingdoms. The direct line of the eldest son ruled the realm of Arthedain in the north-west; their city was Fornost. Annúminas became deserted owing to the dwindling of the people. The chief of the lesser realms were [Cardolan east of the Baranduin; and Rhudaur north of the Bruinen. Arthedain still claimed the overlordship, but this was disputed. >] Cardolan south of the Great Road and east of the Baranduin; and Rhudaur north of the Great Road between the Weather Hills and the Bruinen. There was often strife between the kingdoms; the chief matter of debate was the possession of the Weather Hills and the land westward thence towards Bree. For both Rhudaur and Cardolan desired to control Amon Sûl (which stood upon their borders), because of the Tower built there by Elendil, in which was kept the chief *palantír* of the North. / From this time on the official names of the kings were no longer given, after the manner of Númenor, in High-elven or 'Quenya' form; but the kings of Arthedain used Elvish names of Noldorin form and still maintained their friendship with the Eldar of Lindon and Imladris.

11	Amlaith of Fornost	born 726	lived 220 years	died 946
12	Beleg	811	218	1029
13	Mallor	895	215	1110

In his time an evil shadow fell upon Greenwood the Great, and it became known as Mirkwood. The Sorcerer of Dol Guldur (later known to be Sauron returned) begins to work evil. The Periannath cross the Mountains and come into Arnor.

14	Celepharn	born 979	lived 212 years	died 1191
15	Celebrindol [> Celebrindor]	1062	210	1272
16	Malvegil	1144	205	1349

In the days of Malvegil Orcs again became a menace, and invaded the lands of Arnor. The Úlairi or Ringwraiths began to stir again. The chief of the Úlairi comes north and establishes himself as a king of evil men in Angmar in the far north regions. The Witch-king makes war on the realms of the Dúnedain, which are disunited. The lesser realms resist the claim of the King at Fornost to be overlord of all the former lands of Arnor. In token of this claim all the kings of Arthedain, and the chieftains after them, take names with the prefix *aran, ar(a)* signifying 'high king'. [*Added:* The purpose of the Witch-king is to destroy

Arnor, for there is more hope of success in the North (where the realm is disunited) than in the South while Gondor remains strong. At this time no descendants of Isildur remain in Rhudaur or Cardolan; therefore the kings of Arthedain again claim overlordship in all Arnor. The claim is rejected by Rhudaur, in which power has been seized by men in secret league with Angmar.]
[*Struck out:* The kings of Arthedain also claim to be guardians of the *palantir* of Amon Sûl, though this is outside their territory, standing on the borders of Cardolan and Rhudaur between whom also it is a matter of bitter dispute.]

17   Argeleb I   born 1226   lived 130 years   †slain 1356
[He was slain in battle with Cardolan in the strife of the *palantir* of Amon Sûl. >] Argeleb fortifies the Weather Hills. He was slain in battle with Rhudaur (with secret aid of Angmar); the enemy tries to seize the *palantir* of Amon Sûl.

18   Arveleg I   born 1309   lived 100 years   †slain 1409
The Witch-king of Angmar taking advantage of war among [the Númenóreans or Dúnedain >] the Dúnedain comes down out of the North. He overruns Cardolan and Rhudaur. [Cardolan is ravaged and destroyed and becomes desolate. The Tower of Amon Sûl is razed and the *palantir* is broken. Evil spirits come and take up their abode in the mounds of the hills of Cardolan. In Rhudaur an evil folk, workers of sorcery, subjects of Angmar, slay the remnants of the Dúnedain and build dark forts in the hills. But the Dúnedain of Fornost, in spite of the death of their king, hold out, and repel the forces of Angmar with the help of Cirdan of Lindon. >] Cardolan is ravaged; the Tower of Amon Sûl is razed and the *palantir* is removed to Fornost. In Rhudaur an evil folk ... [*as above*] build dark forts in the hills, while the remaining Dúnedain of Cardolan hold out in the Barrow Downs and the Forest; the Dúnedain of Arthedain repel the forces of Angmar from Fornost with the help of Cirdan of Lindon.

19   Araphor   born 1391   lived 198 years   died 1589
20   Argeleb II   1473   197   1670
In his day the people of the old lands of Arnor become further diminished by the coming of the plague out of the south and east, which also devastated Gondor. [The plague does not pass beyond the Baranduin. >] The plague lessens in deadliness as it goes north; but Cardolan becomes desolate. Evil spirits come out of Angmar and take up their abode in the mounds of Tyrn Goerthaid. / It was Argeleb II who granted the land west of the Baranduin to the Periannath; they crossed the river and entered the land in 1601.

21   Arvegil   born 1553   lived 190 years   died 1743
22   Arveleg II   1633   180   1813

23 Araval   1711   180   1891
With the help of Lindon and Imladris he won a victory over Angmar in 1851, and sought to reoccupy Cardolan, but the evil wights terrify all who seek to dwell near.

24 Araphant   born 1789   lived 175 years   died 1964
Angmar recovers and makes war on the Dúnedain. Araphant seeks to renew ancient alliance and kinship with Gondor. In 1940 his heir Arvedui wedded Fíriel daughter of King Ondohir [> Ondonir] of Gondor. But Gondor is engaged in the long Wars of the Wainriders, and sends little help. Ondohir [> Ondonir] and his sons fell in battle in 1944, and Arvedui claimed the crown of Gondor, on behalf of Fíriel and himself as representing 'the elder line of Isildur', since no close male claimant to the throne in Gondor could at first be found. The claim was rejected by Gondor, but Arvedui and his descendants continued to consider themselves as the true heirs of Anárion as well as of Isildur.

25 Arvedui
      born 1864   lived 110 years   †drowned 1974 [> 1975]
He was the last king at Fornost. In [*added:* the winter of] 1974 the Witch-king destroyed Fornost, laid Arthedain waste, and scattered the remnants of the Dúnedain. Arvedui escaped from Fornost and fled north, taking the *palantíri* of Annúminas and Emyn Beraid. He attempted to go by ship from Forochel to Gondor but was wrecked and the Stones were lost. The sons of Arvedui took refuge with Cirdan of Lune. The following year Elrond and Cirdan, with some belated help from Gondor, sent by sea, defeated the forces of Angmar. The Witch-king was overthrown by Elrond, and his realm brought to an end. The northern lands though desolate were now made somewhat more wholesome again. But it was found later that the Witch-king had fled away secretly southwards, and had entered Minas Ithil (now called Minas Morgul) and become Lord of the Ringwraiths.

The remnants of the Dúnedain of the North become rangers and errants, living largely in hiding, but waging ceaseless war on all evil things that still are abroad in the land. The sons of their chieftains are usually fostered in Imladris by Elrond, to whose keeping are given the chief remaining heirlooms of their house, especially the shards of Elendil's sword, Narsil.

End of the North Kingdom

Here follows the roll of the Chieftains of the Dúnedain
of Eriador, heirs of Isildur
Little is preserved of the tale of their wanderings and deeds,
until the end of the Third Age.

The Chieftains of the Dúnedain

26 (and 24th heir of Isildur)
    1   Aranarth   born 1938   lived 168 years   died 2106
27 2   Arahail   2012   165   2177
28 3   Aranuir   2084   163   2247
29 4   Aravir   2156   163   2319
30 5   Aragorn I   2227   100   †slain 2327
     Aragorn was slain by wolves which infested eastern Eriador.
31 6   Araglas   born 2296   lived 159 years   died 2455
32 7   Arahad I   2365   158   2523
33 8   Aragost   2431   157   2588
• 34 9   Aravorn   2497   157   2654
35 10 Arahad II   2563   156   2719
36 11 Arassuil   2628   156   2784
     In his time there was much war with Orcs that infesting the Misty Mountains harried Eriador. The chief battles were in 2745–8. In 2747 the Periannath (Halflings) defeated a westerly ranging force of the invaders that came down from the north into their land west of Baranduin.
37 12 Arathorn I born 2693   lived 155 years   died 2848
38 13 Argonui   2757   155   2912
39 14 Arador   2820   110   †slain 2930
     He was slain by trolls in the mountains north of Imladris.
40 15 Arathorn II born 2873 lived 60 years †slain 2933
     He wedded Gilrain daughter of Dirhael, a descendant also, but by a younger branch, of Arathorn I. He was slain by an orc-arrow when hunting Orcs in the company of Elladan and Elrohir, the sons of Elrond. He wedded in 2929. His infant son (aged 2 at his father's death) was fostered and brought up at Imladris.
41 16 Aragorn II born 2931   lived 190 years   died 3121
                                                                 or the Fourth Age 100
     Aragorn became King of Arnor and Gondor in the name of *Elessar*. He played a great part in the War of the Ring in which at last Sauron and the power of Mordor was destroyed. He wedded Arwen Undómiel daughter of Elrond and restored the majesty and blood of the Númenóreans. The Third Age ended with the departure of Elrond in 3022 [> 3021]; and the descendants of Elessar through Arwen became also heirs of the elf-realms of the westlands.

The Heirs of Elendil
The Southern Line of Gondor: the Anárioni

1 Elendil
      born S.A.3119   lived 322 years   †slain 3441 = T.A.1
2 Anárion   3219   221   †slain 3440
3 Meneldil   3318   280   died T.A.158
     [*added:* 4th child]
4 Kemendur   3399   279   238
5 Eärendil T.A. 48   276   324
6 Anardil   136   275   411
7 Ostohir [> Ostonir]
                   222   270   492
   He rebuilt and enlarged Minas Anor, where afterwards the kings dwelt always in summer rather than at Osgiliath.
8 Rómendakil I   born 310   lived [231] years   †slain 541
   His original name was *Tarostar*. In his father's time wild men out of the East first assailed Gondor. Tarostar defeated them and drove them out, and took the name *Rómendakil*, East-slayer. He was, however, later slain in battle with fresh hordes of Easterlings.
9 Turambar   born 397   lived 270 years   died 667
   He avenged his father, and conquered much territory eastwards.
10 Atanatar I   born 480   lived 268 years   died 748
11 Siriondil   570   260   830
12 Falastur   654   259   913
   He was first called *Tarannon*. He took the name *Falastur*, on coming to the throne, to commemorate his victories that had extended the sway of Gondor far along the shore-lands on either side of the Mouths of Anduin. He was the first childless king. He was succeeded by the son of his brother Tarkiryan.
13 Eärnil I   born 736   lived 200 years
                                              †drowned 936
   He began the building of a great navy, and repaired the ancient havens of Pelargir [*added:* and seized and fortified Umbar, 933]. He was lost with many ships and men in a great storm off Umbar.
14 Kiryandil   born 820   lived 195 years   †slain 1015
   He continued to increase the fleets of Gondor; but he fell in a battle with the Men of Harad [who contested the designs of Gondor to occupy Umbar and there make a great fort and haven. >] They contested the designs of Gondor to occupy the coast-lands beyond R. Harnen; they therefore tried to take Umbar, where Gondor maintained a great fort and haven.
15 Hyarmendakil I
                  born 899   lived 250 years   died 1149

At first called *Kiryahir*, he avenged his father, defeated the kings of Harad, and made them acknowledge the overlordship of Gondor, 1050. Gondor occupied all the land south of the Mouths of Anduin up to [Umbar and the borders of Near Harad; >] the River (Poros >) Harnen and the borders of Near Harad; and also all the coast-lands as far as Umbar. / Umbar became a great fortress and haven of fleets. After his victory Kiryahir took the name of Hyarmendakil 'South-slayer'. He reigned 134 years, the longest of all save Tarondor (twenty-seventh king).

16 Atanatar II   born 977   lived 249 years   died 1226
Surnamed *Alkarin*, the Glorious. In his time, owing to the vigour of the 'Ship-kings', the line from Falastur onwards, Gondor reached the height of its power. This extended in direct rule as far north as Celebrant and the south-eaves of Mirkwood, east to the Sea of [Rúnaer >] Rhúnaer, and south to Umbar, and westward to the River Gwathlo or Greyflood. In addition many other regions were tributary: the Men of Anduin Vale as far as its sources, and the folk of Harad in the South. But Atanatar in fact did nothing to increase this power, and lived mostly in splendour and ease. The waning of Gondor began before he died, and the watch on the borders was neglected.

17 Narmakil I   born 1049   lived 245 years   died 1294
The second childless king. He was succeeded by his younger brother.

18 Kalmakil   born 1058   lived 246 years   died 1304
19 Rómendakil II   1126   240   1366
20 Valakar   1194   238   1432
In his time there broke out the disastrous civil war called the Kin-strife. After the death of Atanatar the Glorious the Northmen of Mirkwood and the Upper Anduin, who had increased much in the peace brought by the power of Gondor, became powerful. Though these people were ultimately related in speech and blood to the Atani (and so to the Númenóreans), and were usually friendly, they now became restless. Rómendakil was forced to withdraw his northern border east of Anduin to the Emyn Muil. He there built the Gates of Argonath with images of Isildur and Anárion beyond which no stranger was allowed to come south without leave. But Rómendakil being at this time much troubled by assaults of Easterlings sought to attach the Northmen more closely to his allegiance. He took many into his service and gave them high rank. His son Valakar dwelt long among them in the house of [*added*: Vidugavia] the King of Rhovannion. Rómendakil permitted him to wed the king's daughter. The marriage of the heir to a woman of an alien people

THE HEIRS OF ELENDIL

and without any Númenórean blood had never occurred before, and caused great displeasure. Before Valakar died there was already open rebellion in the southern fiefs. Various claimants to the crown appeared, descendants of Atanatar II. The most favoured especially by the fleet, and ship-folk of the southern shores, was the Captain of the Ships, Kastamir [great-grandson >] grandson of Kalmakil's second son Kalimehtar.

21(a) Eldakar   born 1255   deposed 1437
When Valakar died his son, who had the alien name of *Vinitharya*, took the name *Eldakar*, and succeeded. At first he held Osgiliath, and Minas Anor, but he was driven out and deposed by Kastamir, and fled to the north. In this war Osgiliath suffered much damage, and the tower of the *palantir* was destroyed and the *palantir* lost.

22   Kastamir   born 1259   seized throne 1437   †slain 1447
After ten years Eldakar defeated Kastamir with the help of his mother's kin. Kastamir was slain [*added:* by Eldakar in battle in Lebennin, at Ethraid Erui], but his sons and many of his kin and party fled to Umbar, and long held it as an independent realm at war with Gondor.

21(b) Eldakar
regained the kingdom 1447   lived 235 years   died 1490
After Eldakar's return the blood of the kingly house and kindred became more mixed, for many Northmen settled in Gondor, and became great in the land, and high officers in its armies. But the friendship with the Northmen, which continued as part of the policy of the kings, proved of great service in later wars.

23   Aldamir   born 1330   lived 210 years   †slain 1540
He was the second son and third child of Eldakar. His elder brother Ornendil was slain in the wars of the Kin-strife (1446). Aldamir fell in battle with the rebelling kings of Harad allied with the rebels of Umbar.

24   Vinyarion   born 1391   lived 230 years   died 1621
He later (1551) took the name *Hyarmendakil II*, after a great victory over Harad in vengeance for his father.

25   Minardil   born 1454   lived 180 years   †slain 1634
The rebels of Umbar had never ceased to make war on Gondor since the death of Kastamir, attacking its ships and raiding its coast at every opportunity. They had however become much mixed in blood through admission of Men of Harad, and only their chieftains, descendants of Kastamir, were of Númenórean race. Learning through spies that Minardil was at Pelargir, suspecting no peril since the crushing of Harad and Umbar by his father, Angomaitë and Sangahyanda, leaders of the Corsairs of Umbar, great-grandsons of Kastamir, made a raid up Anduin,

slew the king, ravaged Pelargir and the coasts, and escaped with great booty.

26 Telemnar   born 1516   lived 120 years   died 1636
Telemnar immediately began to fit out a fleet for the reduction of Umbar. But a deadly plague or sickness, coming with dark winds out of the East, fell on the land. Great numbers of the folk of Gondor, especially those that dwelt in Osgiliath, and other cities and towns, took sick and died. The White Tree of Minas Anor withered and died. Telemnar and all his children perished. The crown was taken by his nephew.

27 Tarondor   born 1577   lived 221 years   died 1798
He was the eldest son of Minastan, second son of Minardil. He removed the king's house permanently to Minas Anor, and there replanted a seedling of the White Tree in the citadel. During the plague in Osgiliath those folk that survived fled from the city to the western dales or into the woods of Ithilien, and few were willing to return. Osgiliath became largely deserted and partly ruinous. Tarondor had the longest reign of all the Kings of Gondor (162 years), but was unable to do more than attempt to re-establish life and order within his borders. Owing to the fewness of his people the watch on Mordor was neglected and the fortresses guarding the passes became emptied.

28 Telumehtar   born 1632   lived 218 years   died 1850
He took the title *Umbardakil* after the storming and destruction of the haven and stronghold of the Corsairs of Umbar (1810). But this was later reoccupied and rebuilt in the troublous times that later befell Gondor.

29 Narmakil II   born 1684   lived 172 years   †slain 1856
In his time it is said that the Úlairi or Ringwraiths re-entered Mordor, owing to the ceasing of the vigilance, and there they secretly prepared in the darkness for the return of their Dark Lord. Men out of the East appeared of a new sort, stronger, better armed, journeying in huge wains, and fighting in chariots. Stirred up maybe by Sauron they made a great assault on Gondor, and continued to be a great peril for very many years. Narmakil was slain in battle with their host beyond Anduin, north-east of the Morannon.

30 Kalimehtar   born 1736   lived 200 years   died 1936
He continued the War of the Wainriders, and in 1899 won a great victory over them on Dagorlad, which checked their attacks for some time. He built the White Tower in Minas Anor to house the *palantir*.

31 Ondohir
    [> Ondonir]   born 1787   lived 157 years   †slain 1944

War continued with the Wainriders. In 1940 Ondohir [> Ondonir] gave the hand of his daughter Fíriel (born 1896), his third child, to Arvedui heir of Araphant, King of the North-kingdom; but he was unable to send any help to the north against the evil realm of Angmar, because of his own peril. In 1944 Ondohir [> Ondonir] and both his sons Faramir and Artamir fell in battle against an alliance of the Wainriders and the Haradrim. The king and his sons fell in battle in the north and the enemy poured into Ithilien. But in the meantime Eärnil Captain of the southern army won a victory in South Ithilien, destroyed the army of Harad, and hastening north succoured the retreating remnants of the northern army, and drove the Wainriders off. In the great rout that followed most of the enemy were driven into the Dead Marshes.

On the death of Ondohir [> Ondonir] and his sons Arvedui of the North claimed the crown of Gondor as the 'direct descendant of Elendil', and as husband of Fíriel. The claim was rejected by Gondor. At length Eärnil the victorious Captain received the crown (in 1945), since he was of the royal house.

32 Eärnil II   born 1883   lived 160 years   died 2043

He was son of Siriondil, son of Kalimmakil, son of Narmakil II. In his time the North-kingdom came to an end with the overthrow and death of Arvedui, claimant to both crowns. He sent [some help north by sea >] his son Eärnur north with a fleet, and so aided in the destruction of the realm of Angmar. But, though not revealed until later, the Witch-king fled south and joined the other Ringwraiths in Mordor, becoming their Lord. When they were ready the Úlairi suddenly issued from Mordor over the pass of Kirith Ungol. They took Minas Ithil, and were never again expelled from it during that Age. It became a place of great fear, and was renamed Minas Morgul. Few people were willing any longer to dwell in Ithilien, but this was still held and garrisoned by Gondor. At this time probably the *palantir* of Minas Ithil was captured and so came to the hands of Sauron.

33 and last of the Third Age

Eärnur   born 1928   lived 122 years   †slain 2050

He renamed Minas Anor Minas Tirith, as the city on guard against the evil of Minas Morgul. On the death of his father the Lord of the Ringwraiths challenged Eärnur to single combat to make good his claim to the throne. Mardil the Steward restrained him.

The challenge was repeated with taunts in 2050, seven years later, and against the counsel of Mardil Eärnur accepted. He rode with a small escort of knights to Minas Morgul, but neither he nor his company were ever heard of again. It was thought that the faithless enemy had merely decoyed him to the gates and then trapped him and either slain him or kept him in torment as a prisoner.

Since his death was not certain Mardil the Good Steward ruled Gondor in his name for many years. In any case no male descendants of the royal line, among those whose blood was little mixed, could be found.

For a long time before Mardil's day the Stewardship had usually been held by a member of his family (the *Hurinionath*, descended from Húrin, Steward to King Minardil). It now became hereditary like a kingship; but each new Steward took office with the formula: 'to hold rule and rod in the King's name and until the King's return'. Though this soon became a mere formality and the Stewards exercised all the power of kings, it was believed by many in Gondor that a king would return, and the Stewards never sat on the ancient throne nor used the royal standard and emblems. The banner of the Stewards was plain white. The royal standard was sable with a silver tree in blossom beneath seven stars.

34 Elessar   born 2931   lived 190 years   died 3121
                                                    or the Fourth Age 100

After a lapse of 969 years Aragorn, son of Arathorn, 16th chieftain of the Dúnedain of the North, and 41st heir of Elendil in the direct line through Isildur, being also in the direct line a descendant of Fíriel daughter of Ondohir [> Ondonir] of Gondor, claimed the crown of Gondor and of Arnor, after the defeat of Sauron, the destruction of Mordor, and the dissolution of the Ringwraiths. He was crowned in the name of *Elessar* at Minas Tirith in 3019. A new era and calendar was then begun, beginning with 25 March (old reckoning) as the first day. He restored Gondor and repeopled it, but retained Minas Tirith as the chief city. He wedded Arwen Undómiel, daughter of Elrond, brother of Elros first King of Númenor, and so restored the majesty and high lineage of the royal house, but their life-span was not restored and continued to wane until it became as that of other men.

The Third Age ended according to the reckoning of the Eldar in 3021 and the same year Elrond departed. In 3022 the Fourth Age started and the Elder Days and their Twilight were over.

The son of Elessar and Arwen was Eldarion, first king of the Fourth Age, whose realm was great and long-enduring, but this roll does not contain the names of the Fourth Age.

Here follows the roll of the Stewards of Gondor
that ruled the realm and city between the going of Eärnur

and the coming of Elessar

The Ruling Stewards of Gondor

The names of these rulers are here added; for though the *Hurinionath* were not in the direct line of descent from Elendil, they were ultimately of royal origin, and had in any case kept their blood more pure than most other families in the later ages.

They were descended, father to son, from Húrin, Steward to King Minardil, who had laboured greatly for the ordering of the realm in the disastrous days of the plague, when King Telemnar died within two years of the slaying of King Minardil by the Corsairs. From that time on the kings usually chose their steward from this family, though a son did not necessarily succeed a father. But in fact it had descended from father to son since Pelendur, Steward to King Ondohir, and after the ending of the kings it became hereditary, though if a Steward left no son, the office might pass in the female line, that is to his sister-son, or to his father's sister-son.

The choice was made according to their worth among the near kin by the Council of Gondor. But the Council had no power of choice if there was a son living.

The Stewards belonged to a family of the ancient Elf-friends who used (beside the Common Speech) the Noldorin tongue after the fashion of Gondor.* Their official names (after Mardil) were in that tongue and drawn mostly from the ancient legends of the Noldor and their dealings with the Edain.

All the time of the Stewards was one of slow dwindling and waning both of the power and numbers of the Men of Gondor, and of the lore and skill of Númenor among them. Also the life-span of those even of the purer blood steadily decreased. They were never free from war or the threat of war with the evil that dwelt in Minas Morgul and watched them. They counted it glory and success to hold that threat at bay. Osgiliath became a ruin, a city of shadows, often taken and re-taken in petty battles. For a while, during the 300 years peace, after the

---

* Since this had long ceased to be a 'cradle-tongue' in Gondor, but was learned in early youth (by those claiming Númenórean descent) from loremasters, and used by them as a mark of rank, it had changed very little since the Downfall; and though the Men of Gondor altered a little some of the sounds, they could still understand the Eldar and be understood by them. In the later days, however, they saw them seldom.

formation of the White Council, Ithilien was reoccupied and a hardy folk dwelt there, tending its fair woods and fields, but after the days of Denethor I (2435–77) most of them fled west again. But it is true that but for Minas Tirith the power of Mordor would much sooner have grown great and would have spread over Anduin into the westlands. After the days of Eärnur the White Tree waned and seldom flowered. It slowly aged and withered and bore no fruit, so far as men knew.

    Pelendur   born 1879   lived 119 years   died 1998
He was steward to King Ondohir and advised the rejection of the claim of Arvedui, and supported the claim of Eärnil who became king in 1945. He remained steward under Eärnil, and was succeeded by his son.
    Vorondil   born 1919   lived 110 years   died 2029
He was succeeded by his son. [*Added:* Vorondil was a great hunter and he made a great horn out of the horn of the wild oxen of Araw, which then still roamed near the Sea of Rhûn.]

1   Mardil Voronwë ('steadfast')
                    born 1960   lived 120 years   died 2080
He became steward to King Eärnil in his later days, and then to King Eärnur. After the disappearance of Eärnur he ruled the realm for thirty years from 2050, and is reckoned the first of the line of *Ruling Stewards* of Gondor.

2   Eradan   born 1999   lived 117 years   died 2116
3   Herion   2037   111   2148
4   Belegorn   2074   130   2204
5   Húrin I   2124   120   2244
6   Túrin I   2165   113   2278
He was the third child of Húrin. He was wedded twice and had several children (a thing already rare and remarkable among the nobles of Gondor); but only the last, a child born in his old age, was a son.

7   Hador   born 2245   lived 150 years   died 2395
The last recorded Man of Gondor to reach such an age. After this time the life-span of those of Númenórean blood waned more rapidly.

8   Barahir   born 2290   lived 122 years   died 2412
9   Dior   2328   107   2435
He was childless and was succeeded by the son of his sister Rían.
10 Denethor I   born 2375   lived 102 years   died 2477
Great troubles arose in his day. The Morgul-lords having bred in secret a fell race of black Orcs in Mordor assail Ithilien and overrun it. They capture Osgiliath and destroy its renowned bridge.

Boromir son of Denethor in 2475 defeated the host of Morgul and recovered Ithilien for a while.

11 Boromir
  born 2410   lived [89 >] 79 years   died [2499 >] 2489
  He was third child of Denethor. His life was shortened by the poisoned wounds he received in the Morgul-war.

12 Cirion   born 2449   lived 118 years   died 2567
  In his time there came a great assault from the North-east. Wild men out of the East crossed Anduin north of the Emyn Muil and joining with Orcs out of the Misty Mountains overran the realm (now sparsely populated) north of the White Mountains, pouring into the wold and plain of Calenardon. Eorl the Young out of Éothéod brings great help of horsemen and the great victory of the Field of Celebrant (2510) is won. Eorl's people settle in Calenardon, which is after called Rohan, a free folk but in perpetual alliance with the Stewards of Gondor. (According to some Eorl was a descendant of the Northmen that were allied with the royal house in the days of Eldakar.) [*Added:* Eorl was slain in battle in the 'Wold of Rohan' (as it was later called), 2545.]

13 Hallas   born 2480   lived 125 years   died 2605
14 Húrin II   2515   113   2628
15 Belecthor I   2545   110   2655
16 Orodreth   2576   109   2685
17 Ecthelion I   2600   98   2698
  He repaired and rebuilt the White Tower in Minas Tirith, which was afterwards often called Ecthelion's Tower. He had no children and was followed by Egalmoth, grandson of Morwen sister of Orodreth.

18 Egalmoth   born 2626   lived 117 years   died 2743
  In this time there was renewed war with the Orcs.

19 Beren   born 2655   lived 108 years   died 2763
  In his time [there was a renewed attack on Gondor by the pirates of Umbar. >] there was a great attack on Gondor (2758) by three fleets of the pirates of Umbar. All the coasts were invaded. / Gondor received no help from Rohan, and could send no help thither. Rohan was invaded from the North-east, and also from the West (by rebelling Dunlendings). The Long Winter 2758–9. Rohan lies for five months under snow. [*Added:* Saruman comes to Orthanc.]

20 Beregond   born 2700   lived 111 years   died 2811
  In his time the War of the Dwarves and Orcs in the Misty Mountains occurred [(2766–9) >] (2793–9). Many Orcs flying south are slain and they are prevented from establishing themselves in the White Mountains.

21 Belecthor II   born 2752   lived 120 years   died 2872

Only child, late-born, of Beregond. The last of his line to pass the age of 100 years. At his death the White Tree finally dies in the citadel, but is left standing 'until the King come'. No seedling can be found.

22   Thorondir   born 2782   lived 100 years   died 2882
23   Túrin II   2815   99   2914

In his time [folk finally fled >] many more folk removed west over Anduin from Ithilien, which became wild and infested by Mordor-orcs. But Gondor makes and keeps up secret strongholds there, especially in North Ithilien. The ancient refuge of Henneth Annûn is rebuilt and hidden. The isle of Cair Andros in Anduin is fortified. The Men of Harad are stirred up by the servants of Sauron to attack Gondor. In 2885 Túrin fought a battle with the Haradrim in South Ithilien and defeated them with aid from Rohan; but the sons of King Folcwine of Rohan, Folcred and Fastred, fell in this battle. Túrin paid Folcwine a rich weregild of gold.

24   Turgon   born 2855   lived 98 years   died 2953

In the last year of his rule Sauron declared himself again, and re-entered Mordor, long prepared for him. Barad-dûr rose again. Mount Doom long dormant bursts into smoke and flame. [*Added*: Saruman takes possession of Orthanc, and fortifies it.]

25   Ecthelion II   born 2886   lived 98 years   died 2984

He is visited by Mithrandir (Gandalf) to whom he is friendly. Aragorn of the North serves as a soldier in his forces. He strengthens Pelargir again, and refortifies Cair Andros.

26   Denethor II
                       born 2930   lived 89 years   †slew himself 3019

He was first son and third child of Ecthelion and more learned in lore than any Steward for many generations. He was very tall and in appearance looked like an ancient Númenórean. He wedded late (for his time) in 2976 Finduilas daughter of Prince Adrahil of Dol Amroth, a noble house of southern Gondor of Númenórean blood, reputed also to have Elven-blood from ancient days: the Elven-folk of Amroth of Lórien dwelt in the region of Dol Amroth before they sailed over sea. His elder son Boromir (2978) was slain by orcs near Rauros in 3019. His younger son Faramir (2983) became the last Ruling Steward. His wife Finduilas died untimely in 2987.

In his time the peril of Gondor steadily grew, and he awaited always the great assault of Sauron that he knew was preparing. It is said that he dared to use the *palantír* of the White Tower, which none since the kings had looked in, and so saw much of the mind of Sauron (who had the Stone of Ithil), but was aged prematurely by this combat, and fell into despair.

The attack began in the summer of 3018. The Ringwraiths issued once more from Minas Morgul in visible form. The sons of Denethor resisted them but were defeated by the Black Captain, and retreated over Anduin; but they still held West Osgiliath.

Boromir departed to Imladris soon after on a mission to seek the counsel of Elrond. He was slain as he returned. Minas Tirith was besieged in March 3019, and Denethor burned himself on a pyre in the Tomb of the Stewards.

27   Faramir   born 2983   lived 120 years   died 3103
= Fourth Age 82

He succeeded by right on the death of his father, but in the same year surrendered rod and rule to the King Elessar, and so was the last Ruling Steward. He retained the title of Steward, and became Prince of the restored land of Ithilien, dwelling in the Hills of Emyn Arnen beside Anduin. He wedded in 3020 Éowyn sister of King Éomer of Rohan.

So ends the tale of
the Ruling
Stewards of Gondor

The manuscript C of *The Heirs of Elendil* ends here, but clipped to it is a genealogy of the line of Dol Amroth: for this see p. 220.

Commentary

As I have explained (p. 188), the manuscript B is for the Northern Line the earliest text, and the commentary to this part is largely a record of significant differences from the text printed (C). Corrections to B are not as a rule noticed if they merely bring it to the form in C (in substance: usually not in the precise expression), nor are additions to B as first written necessarily noticed as such.

References to the historical accounts following the names and dates of the kings and rulers are made simply by the name, with the page-reference to the C text. A notable feature of *The Heirs of Elendil* is the record of the birthdates of the rulers, which were excluded from Appendix A; other dates are in all cases the same as those in Appendix A unless the contrary is noted.

The preamble concerning dates in C (p. 191) is absent from B, which begins with the genealogy. This differs from that in C in showing Anárion as the elder son of Elendil, and in naming 'Valandil of Arthedain': thus B belongs with the early texts of the Tale of Years, as already noted (pp. 188–9).

Only Isildur's youngest son, Valandil, is named in *The Lord of the Rings*. In the very late work *The Disaster of the Gladden Fields* the three elder are named Elendur, Aratan, and Ciryon (*Unfinished Tales* p. 271 and note 11); on one of the copies of the typescript D (p. 190) my father pencilled a note remarking on this, and saying that the names found in 'Gladdenfields' were to be accepted.

In the chronological outline that follows in B as in C, the birth-date of Anárion is 3209 and of Isildur 3219; Meneldil was born in 3299, and it was Kiryandil son of Isildur who was the last man to be born in Númenor (3318). Arthedain appears for Arnor in 3320; the birthdates of Eärnur and Vëandur are 3349 and 3389; and Valandil was born in Annúminas, not Imladris.

In both texts Isildur died in 3441 (which in the list of the Northern kings that follows is made equivalent to Third Age 1), the same year as the overthrow of Sauron (see pp. 170, 177).

Following the words 'The Second Age ends and the Third Begins' B continues at once with the naming of the kings of the Northern Line (without the name *Isildurioni*). The list of these kings up to the disintegration of the North Kingdom was the same in B as in C with the sole difference (apart from the different date of Isildur's birth, 3219) that the tenth king Eärendur is named Eärendil in B: on this see p. 189.

Valandil (p. 192)   In B there was a note here: 'Removed to Fornost and Annúminas was deserted'; this was struck out, and 'Annúminas became deserted' added to the note following King Eärendil.

Eärendur (p. 193)   The note in B begins 'After Eärendil the Northern Kingdom of Arthedain disintegrated', and the north-western kingdom ruled by Amlaith is referred to by the name of the city of its kings: 'Fornost still claimed the overlordship, but this was disputed.' The other realms are thus described in B: 'Cardolan (where later were Bree and the Barrowdowns) and Rhudaur north of the R. Bruinen (where later were the Trollshaws).'

Mallor (p. 193)   In B the corresponding note follows Beleg the twelfth king: 'In his reign Sauron took shape again in Mirkwood and evil things began again to multiply.'

Celebrindor (p. 193)   The name of the fifteenth king in B as first written was *Celem...gil*, perhaps *Celemenegil*; this was struck out and replaced by *Celebrindol*, as in C before correction to *Celebrindor*.

Malvegil (p. 193)   The note in B is, as generally, briefer but has all the essentials of that in C; here it is said that 'Fornost is at war with the lesser kingdoms, the chief dispute being about the *palantír* of Amon Sûl'. The conclusion of the note in C, concerning this, was rejected when the disputed claim to Amon Sûl was introduced much earlier, at the disintegration of Arnor after the death of Eärendur. – On the name *Úlairi* see p. 153.

The kings from Argeleb I to Arvedui (pp. 194–5)   An earlier form of the page in B that begins with the last sentence of the note following

Malvegil, the taking of the prefix *aran, ar(a)* by the kings at Fornost, is extant, and here the names of these kings are seen evolving. The original names were as follows (it is curious that despite the words at the head of the page the first three kings do not have the prefix *Ar*):

17 Celebrindol (> Argeleb I)
18 Beleg II (> Arveleg I)
19 Malvegil II (> Araphor)
20 Arveleg (> Argeleb II)
21 Arvegil
22 Argeleb (> Arveleg II)
23 Arvallen (> Araval)
24 Araphant
25 Arvedui

But the dates of these kings underwent no change. The original name of the seventeenth king, Celebrindol, was given to the fifteenth, originally Celemenegil (?), as noted above.

Argeleb I (p. 194)   On the rejected page of B the note following this king states only: 'slain in battle 1356. Angmar is repulsed but turns upon the lesser kingdoms.' The replacement page has: 'Slain in battle with subkingdoms of Cardolan and Rhudaur'. Neither text refers to the *palantir* of Amon Sûl. On the mention in the altered text in C of Argeleb's fortifying of the Weather Hills see p. 189.

Arveleg I (p. 194)   The rejected page of B has no note here; in the replacement page it reads:

Angmar taking advantage of war among the Númenóreans comes down and overruns Cardolan and Rhudaur. These realms become subject to the Sorcerer-king and full of evil things, especially Cardolan. But Fornost in spite of death of King Arveleg holds out with aid from Lindon and Imladrist.

An addition concerning the *palantir* of Amon Sûl was made to this:

The tower of the *palantir* on Amon Sûl is destroyed, but no one knows what became of the Stone. Maybe it was taken by the Witch-king.

This addition was probably made in revision of the original statement in C that the *palantir* was broken.

Argeleb II (p. 194)   In B there was no note here and so no mention of the plague, but the following was added in: 'He gave "the Shire" to the Hobbits.' This is stated in an addition to an early text of the *Prologue* (p. 9): 'In the Year 1 ... the brothers Marco and Cavallo, having obtained formal permission from the king Argeleb II in the waning city of Fornost, crossed the wide brown river Baranduin.'

Araval (p. 195)   The statement in B reads: 'With help of Lindon and Imladrist Araval wins great victory over Angmar, and drives the evil wights north. He reoccupies Cardolan.' In the rejected page of B this victory is ascribed to the next king, Araphant, who 'drives back the

Sorcerer-king and in 1900 destroys Cardolan.' There is no reference to the victory of Araval in the history of the North Kingdom in Appendix A.

Araphant (p. 195)   More briefly, B has here:
Angmar recovers, and makes war again. Araphant seeks alliance with Gondor and weds his son Arvedui to daughter of King Ondohir of Gondor; so that his descendants come also from the southern line of Anárion. But Gondor is waning and fallen on evil days, and sends little help.

The original note to Araphant has been given under Araval, but an addition to this mentions the marriage of Araphant's son Arvedui to Ondohir's daughter, and here she is named: *Ilmarë* (see further pp. 215–16, *Ondohir*). The change of *Ondohir* to *Ondonir* in C was made also at all occurrences of the name in the Southern Line, and also that of the seventh king of Gondor, *Ostohir*, was altered to *Ostonir*. These changed names appear in the late typescript D, where my father let them stand; but *Ostohir, Ondohir* reappear in Appendix A. In the Second Edition he changed them to *Ostoher, Ondoher* (and also the original name of Hyarmendacil I, *Ciryahir* (*Kiryahir*), which was altered to *Ciryaher*). In an isolated note on these changes he said that *Ondohir* was a hybrid name: in pure Quenya it should be *Ondoher* (Q. *heru, hēr-* 'lord'), and *-hir* seems to be due to the influence of Sindarin *hīr* 'lord', and also that of other names ending in *-ir*, especially *-mir, -vir.*

Arvedui (p. 195)   The statement in B here lacks very little that is told in C, although as my father first wrote it there was no mention of Arvedui's fate: his death is given as 'slain 1974'. In a subsequent addition the same is said of his flight by ship and drowning as in C, and the loss of the *palantíri* in the shipwreck is mentioned, but they are not identified: they are called simply 'the two that remain'. In this text that of Amon Sûl was lost when the tower was destroyed ('Maybe it was taken by the Witch-king', p. 209, *Arveleg I*). So also in C the *palantíri* taken by Arvedui are those of Annúminas and Emyn Beraid, for in that text the Stone of Amon Sûl was said to have been broken (p. 194, *Arveleg I*). C was emended to say that it was saved and removed to Fornost (*ibid.*): this was the final version of the history, with the Stones lost in the sea becoming those of Annúminas and Amon Sûl, while that of Emyn Beraid, which had a special character, remained in the North (see RK p. 322, footnote, and *Unfinished Tales* p. 413, note 16). But the C text was not emended in the present passage.

Of the tale told in Appendix A of Arvedui's sojourn among the Lossoth, the Snowmen of Forochel, there is here no trace.

The Chieftains of the Dúnedain (p. 195)   The rejected page of B carries the names of the Chieftains, and some of these as first written were corrected on the manuscript, thus:

27 Araha[n]til (sixth letter illegible) > Arahail
28 Aranuil > Aranuir
31 Arallas > Araglas
33 Arandost > Aragost
35 Arangar > Arahad II
36 Arasuil > Arassuil
39 Arv[or]eg (fifth and sixth letters uncertain) > Arador

The dates were also different from the final chronology, save for those of Aranarth and Aragorn II, in both versions of B; they were corrected on the replacement page of B to those of C. The original dates were:

Arahail	2011–2176	Aravorn	2490–2647
Aranuir	2083–2246	Arahad II	2555–2711
Aravir	2154–2316	Arassuil	2619–2775
Aragorn I	2224–2324	Arathorn I	2683–2838
Araglas	2292–2451	Argonui	2746–2901
Arahad I	2359–2517	Arador	2808–2912
Aragost	2425–2583	Arathorn II	2870–2933

These changes of date were carefully made, in several cases in more than one stage; in the result the length of the lives of the Chieftains remained the same, except in the cases of Aravir, Aragost, Arador, and Arathorn II.

Aragorn I (p. 196) In the rejected page of B he was 'lost in wilderness while hunting'; in the replacement page he was 'lost in the wilderness; probably slain by orcs [> wolves].'

Arassuil (p. 196) The victory of the Hobbits in 2747 was the Battle of Greenfields.

Arador (p. 196) Arador's death is referred to at the beginning of the tale of Aragorn and Arwen in Appendix A, as also is that of Arathorn II (RK pp. 337–8).

Aragorn II (p. 196) B has here: 'Became King Elessar of Gondor and Arthedain, aided in the overthrow of Sauron with which Third Age ended in 3019. He wedded Arwen Undómiel, daughter of Elrond. His descendants became thus heirs of the Númenórean realms, and of Lúthien and the Elf-kingdoms of the West.' The statement in C that 'The Third Age ended with the departure of Elrond in 3022' was presumably a mere slip, since the date of Aragorn's death is given immediately above as 3121 = Fourth Age 100, which assumes the beginning of that Age in 3022. Later in C, when Aragorn appears at the end of the roll of the kings of the Southern Line (p. 202), the departure of Elrond is given as 3021, the Fourth Age is said to have begun in 3022, and 3121 is again equated with Fourth Age 100.

The Southern Line of Gondor

The earliest extant list of the rulers of Gondor is the manuscript A briefly described on p. 188. This has precisely the same form as the two later texts of *The Heirs of Elendil*, with the dates of birth and death (and the manner of death) of each king, and the length of his life. There is only one difference of name in A, that of the fourteenth king (p. 197), who was first called *Kiryahir* but subsequently renamed *Kiryandil* (at the same time *Kiryahir* entered as the original name of Hyamendakil I). There are only two differences in the succession, the first being in that following the sixteenth king Atanatar II (p. 198), which in A as first written went:

16 Atanatar II 977–1226
17 Alkarin 1049–1294
18 Narmakil I

It was evidently at this point that my father stopped, moved 'Alkarin' to stand beside Atanatar II with the words 'also named', and changed Narmakil I from 18 to 17, entering as his dates those previously given to 'Alkarin'. The next king, Kalmakil, was then entered as 18. I have no doubt whatever that this was a mere slip, *Alkarin* being an honorific name; and this is significant, for it shows that my father was copying from an existing text, or existing notes. There is no trace now of anything of the sort, and it must be concluded that the written origin of the history of the rulers of Gondor is lost.

The other difference in the succession occurs after the thirtieth king Kalimehtar (p. 200), where A has:

31 Ostohir II 1787–1985, lived 198 years
32 Ondohir 1837–1944 (slain), lived 107 years

Eärnil II and Eärnur the last king are numbered 33 and 34. The death of Ostohir II is thus placed 41 years *after* that of his successor Ondohir. How this peculiar anomaly arose can only be surmised: the likeliest explanation is that there were variant and contradictory conceptions in the text that my father was using, and that he failed to observe it. It was not corrected in A, and indeed the same succession survived into B, with Eärnur numbered the thirty-fourth king. When he did observe it he resolved it by simply striking out Ostohir II and giving his birth-date of 1787 to Ondohir, so that he lived for 157 and not 107 years.

A also differed from the final chronology in the dates of the kings from Anárion to Anardil (see p. 197), which were:

Anárion S.A.3209–3440
Meneldil S.A.3299–T.A.139
Kemendur S.A.3389–T.A.228
Eärendil T.A.40–316
Anardil T.A.132–407

The dates of these five kings remained in B as they were in A, but were then corrected to those found in C; after correction the life-span of each king remained the same as before, with the exception of Anárion, since he became the younger son of Elendil while the date of his death was fixed. All other dates in A were retained into the final chronology.

The notes in A were brief and scanty until Valakar the twentieth king (and those to Rómendakil I and Hyarmendakil I were subsequent additions):

7   Ostohir I   Rebuilt and enlarged Minas Anor.
8   Rómendakil I   At this time Easterlings assailed kingdom.
13 Eärnil I   Began rebuilding the neglected navy. Lost at sea in a storm.
15 Hyarmendakil I   Defeated Harad and made them subject.
16 Atanatar II   In his day Gondor reached its widest extent owing to the vigour of the 'line of Eärnil'. But he loved life of ease and began to neglect the guards in the East. Waning of Gondor began.

There are also some notes on the nature of the succession: Falastur had no son, and his successor Eärnil I was the son of Falastur's brother Tarkiryan; Narmakil I had no children, and his successor Kalmakil was his brother.

It seems plain that a firm structure at least in outline had already arisen: that my father had in his mind a clear picture of the chronology, the major events, the triumphs and vicissitudes of the history of Gondor, whether or not it was committed to writing now lost.

From Valakar the notes in the A text as written become more frequent and some of them much fuller, a pattern still reflected in the entries in the greatly expanded C text. Some of these entries are given in the commentary on the Southern Line in C that now follows.

Ostohir (p. 197)   In all three texts Ostohir is the first of that name, but the figure I was struck out in C: see p. 212. On the change of the name to *Ostonir* see p. 210, *Araphant*.

Rómendakil I (p. 197)   In Appendix A *Rómendakil* is translated 'East-victor', but in texts B and C 'East-slayer'; so also in the case of *Hyarmendakil*, translated 'South-slayer' in B and C.

Falastur (p. 197)   This king's former name *Tarannon* first appears in C, though the reason for *Falastur* is recorded in B.

Kiryandil (p. 197)   B has only 'Continued to increase fleets, but fell in a sea-battle against the Kings of Harad'. The alterations to C under Eärnil I and Kiryandil bring the history to its form in Appendix A, where it was Eärnil who captured Umbar.

Valakar (p. 198)   As the first extant account of the Kin-strife in Gondor I give here the entry in A, where the whole history of the civil war is placed in the note following Valakar:

In 1432 broke out the Kin-strife. Valakar had wedded as wife a daughter of the King of Rhovannion, not of Dúnedain blood. The succession of his son Eldakar was contested by other descendants of Kalmakil and Rómendakil II. In the end Eldakar was driven into exile and Kastamir, great-grandson of Kalmakil's second son

Kalimehtar, became king. But Eldakar drove him out again, and after that time the blood of the kingly house became more mixed, for Eldakar had the assistance of the Northmen of the Upper Anduin his mother's kin, and they were favoured by the kingly house afterwards, and many of them served in the armies of Gondor and became great in the land.

Thus nothing was told of the political and military circumstances that led to the marriage of Valakar to the daughter of the (as yet unnamed) King of Rhovannion. In B something is said of this:

> Since the days of Atanatar II the Northmen of Mirkwood and upper Anduin had been increasing greatly in numbers and power, and in Rómendakil's time hardly acknowledged the overlordship of Gondor. Rómendakil having enough to do with Easterlings sought to attach the Northmen more closely to their allegiance, and arranged that his son Valakar should wed the daughter of the King of Róvannion (Wilderland).

B then follows A in placing the whole history of the Kin-strife in the note following Valakar, and makes only the additional statements that such a marriage was unheard of, and that Valakar's son bore before his accession the alien name *Vinthanarya*. In both texts it is said that Kastamir was slain by Eldakar in 1447, but there is no mention in either of the flight to Umbar by his defeated adherents and the arising there of an independent pirate realm (see below under *Minardil*).

Aldamir (p. 199)   In A it is said that 'his elder son Ornendil was slain with him in battle with rebels of Harad'; B is the same as C, making Ornendil the brother of Aldamir who had been slain in the Kin-strife, but without the reference to 'the rebels of Umbar' (see under *Minardil*).

Vinyarion (p. 199)   The victory of Vinyarion in Harad in vengeance for his father, mentioned in almost the same words in all three texts, is not referred to in the account in Appendix A, and thus the reason for his taking the name Hyarmendakil II is not given; but the event is recorded in the Tale of Years, Third Age 1551.

Minardil (p. 199)   In A the story of the founding of the hostile lordship of the Corsairs of Umbar by the followers of Kastamir does not appear and had probably not yet arisen: this is suggested by the fact that in B it first enters long after the event in the note on Minardil:

> The sons of Kastamir and others of his kin, having fled from Gondor in 1447, set up a small kingdom in Umbar, and there made a fortified haven. They never ceased to make war upon Gondor, attacking its ships and coasts when they had opportunity. But they married women of the Harad and had in three generations lost most of their Númenórean blood; but they did not forget their feud with the house of Eldakar.

The entry in B then continues with the account (much fuller than that in Appendix A) of the slaying of Minardil at Pelargir, which was repeated almost exactly in C.

The names *Angomaitë* and *Sangahyanda* were changed to *Angamaitë* and *Sangahyando* in the Second Edition.

Telemnar, Tarondor, Telumehtar (p. 200) In B the text of these entries closely approached those in C; but most of the entry concerning Tarondor, including the account of the desertion of Osgiliath and the removal of the king's house to Minas Anor, was a later addition.

Narmakil II (p. 200) The note in A read: 'Battle with the Ringwraiths who seized Mordor. Osgiliath ceases to be the chief seat of the kings'. In B this was somewhat developed:

At this time the Úlairi (or Ringwraiths) who had seized Mordor long before began to assail Ithilien. Narmakil was slain by the Sorcerer-king. Osgiliath ceased to be the seat of the kings.

This was roughly rewritten to read:

In his time it is said that the Úlairi (or Ringwraiths) arose again and re-entered Mordor secretly. There they prepared in the darkness for the return of their Dark Lord. Men out of the East, a fierce people riding in great wains, came against Gondor, doubtless stirred up by Sauron and Úlairi. Narmakil slain in battle.

This was the first appearance of the Wainriders.

Kalimehtar (p. 200) The note in A recorded only that Kalimehtar 'built the White Tower of Minas Anor and removed his court thither'. B repeated this, and continued: 'Minas Anor becomes called Minas Tirith, since Minas Ithil is lost and becomes a stronghold of the Úlairi, and is called Minas Morgul.' This was struck out immediately, and the fall of Minas Ithil postponed to the time of King Ondohir; subsequently the entry was replaced by the following:

Built the White Tower of Minas Anor. Continued war against the Wainriders, and defeated them before the Morannon.

The building of the White Tower by Kalimehtar is not referred to in Appendix A, but is recorded in the Tale of Years, Third Age 1900. – For Ostohir II who followed Kalimehtar in A and (before correction) in B see p. 212.

Ondohir (pp. 200–1) A has here a more substantial entry, though very largely concerned with the claim of Arvedui:

His sons Faramir and Artamir were both slain in the war with Mordor. Minas Ithil fell and became Minas Morgul. In 1940 his daughter (third child), born 1896, wedded Arvedui (son of Araphant) last king of the North. Arvedui in 1944 claimed the Southern crown, but this was refused. There was a time without a king and the steward Pelendur governed. The claim of Arvedui lapsed with his death in battle in 1974, but though too weak ever to press their claim the descendants of Arvedui and Fíriel daughter of Ondohir, chieftains of the Dúnedain of the North, continued to claim the Southern crown; though in fact it passed after an interregnum to Eärnil II, a descendant (great-grandson) of Narmakil II's second son Kalimmakil.

The omission in the note of the death of Ondohir was a mere oversight in rapid writing: he is marked as 'slain' in 1944. Ondohir's daughter is here named *Fíriel*, as in B and C; the name *Ilmarë* in the rejected page of B in the section on the Northern Line (p. 210, *Araphant*) can then only be explained as a passing change of name. The fact that the Northern kings Araphant and Arvedui are named in A (and the date of Arvedui's death given) shows that work on the history of the Northern Line existed before the writing of B, the earliest extant text for that part (see p. 188).

In B the entry for Ondohir, as first written, began thus:

War continued with the Úlairi. Minas Ithil fell and became a stronghold of the enemy, and was renamed Minas Morgul. Minas Anor became Minas Tirith.

This followed the original entry in B under Narmakil II, in which the assault of the Úlairi on Ithilien was recorded (before the entry into the history of the Wainriders). The fall of Minas Ithil and the renaming of the two cities was now moved on from its placing in the reign of Kalimehtar (and thus returns to the text of A, given above).

The opening of B was subsequently struck out, apart from the first sentence, which was corrected to 'War continued with the Wainriders', as in C. The rest of the original entry in B records the fall of Ondohir and his sons 'in battle in Ithilien' (which as written referred to battle with the Ringwraiths, but which was subsequently extended to read 'in battle in Ithilien against an alliance of the Wainriders and the Harad that assailed eastern Gondor from north and south'), and then recounts the claim of Arvedui, closely following A. The statements in A that 'there was a time without a king' when the Steward Pelendur governed, and that the crown passed to Eärnil after an 'interregnum', were retained but then struck out (see below under *Eärnil II*). There is thus no mention in B of the great victory of Eärnil in South Ithilien followed by his rout of the Wainriders, which led to his accession as king.

On the correction of *Ondohir* to *Ondonir* see p. 210, *Araphant*.

Eärnil II (p. 201) In A it is said only that he was 'son of Kiryandil son of Siriondil son of Kalimmakil son of Narmakil II', and that he came to the throne in 1960 (thus after an interregnum of sixteen years). This was repeated without change in B, and allowed to stand, although my father had rejected the references to an interregnum, when Pelendur governed, in the entry for Ondohir. Kiryandil was later removed, and Siriondil became the father of Eärnil. In all three texts Kalimmakil was the son of Narmakil II, but in Appendix A (RK p. 330) the son of Arciryas the brother of Narmakil.

Nothing further is said of Eärnil in B as originally written, but in an addition the flight of the Sorcerer-king out of the North is recorded

THE HEIRS OF ELENDIL 217

(though without any mention of the great fleet from Gondor under Eärnil's son Eärnur which in large part brought about the destruction of Angmar), and the fall of Minas Ithil moves to its final place in the history:

In his time the Sorcerer-king of Angmar, chief of the Úlairi, fled from the North and came to Mordor, and built up a new power. Under his leadership the Úlairi took Minas Ithil, and made it their city and stronghold, from which they were never expelled. S. Ithilien abandoned by Gondor, but a garrison holds the bridges of Osgiliath. Minas Ithil becomes called Minas Morgul, and Minas Anor is renamed Minas Tirith.

In C, as in Appendix A (RK p. 332), the renaming of Minas Anor took place in the time of Eärnur. – A further, later addition in B notes: 'The Nazgûl seize the Ithil-stone'.

Eärnur (p. 201)   This final note in A reads:

The last king. He went to war with Minas Ithil and Mordor and never returned; nor was his body ever recovered. Some said he was carried off alive by the evil king. He left no children. No male descendants of clear title (or nearly pure blood) of Elendil could be discovered. Mardil the Steward, grandson of Pelendur, governed nominally 'until the King's return', and this became an habitual formula. There had been a tendency (but no rule) for the Stewardship to be hereditary or at least chosen from one family. It now became hereditary like a kingship.

Here the A text of the Southern Line ends. In B this note was repeated without change of substance, but continues after the words 'hereditary like a kingship':

But the Stewards no longer took official names of Quenya form, and their names were all of Noldorin origin, that tongue still being used by the noble houses of Gondor.

After the time of Eärnur the White Tree never [> seldom] again bore fruit, and ever its blossom grew less as it slowly died [> aged].

It is clear that the story of the challenge to Eärnur by the Lord of the Ringwraiths had not emerged. Later, the opening of the passage in B was rejected and the following substituted:

He accepted the challenge [*added:* to fight for the *palantír* of Ithil?] of the Lord of the Úlairi and rode over the bridge of Osgiliath [> to the gates of Morgul] to meet him in single combat, but was betrayed and taken, and was never again seen by men.

The two challenges to Eärnur, and the restraint on the king exercised by Mardil the Steward, did not appear until the text C.

Elessar (p. 202)   The text in B is very close to its form in C, but lacks the reference to the continued waning of the life-span of the royal house. After the words 'and so restored the majesty and high blood of the royal house' B concludes:

Here ends the Red Book. But it was foretold that Eldarion the son of Elessar should rule a great realm, and it should endure for a hundred generations of men; and from him should come the kings of many realms in after days.

I have said (p. 190) that 'it is generally impossible to say how much of the matter that entered at each successive stage had newly arisen, and how much was present but at first ... held in abeyance.' Nonetheless, from this (inevitably complex) account of the development of the history of the kings of Gondor recorded in increasing detail through the texts, new elements can be seen emerging and becoming established, as the founding of the corsair-kingdom of Umbar, the invasions of the Wainriders, or the sending of the fleet from Gondor to assail Angmar.

The Stewards of Gondor

The earliest text recording the names and dates of the Stewards of Gondor is constituted by two pages attached to the manuscript A of the Southern Line. These pages were obviously written on continuously from the preceding section, but the text becomes very rapid and rough in its latter part and ends in a scrawl of confused dates.

For the C-text of the Stewards see pp. 202 ff. The B-text is headed: 'Appendix. The Stewards of Gondor', with a brief preamble:

These may be added, for though not in the direct line, the *Hurinionath*, the family to which Pelendur and Mardil belonged, were of Númenórean blood hardly less pure than that of the kings, and undoubtedly had some share in the actual blood of Elendil and Anárion.

To this was added later:

During all the days of the Stewards there was unceasing war between Minas Morgul and Minas Anor. Osgiliath was often taken and retaken. In North Ithilien a hardy folk still dwelt as borderers and defenders, but slowly they dwindled and departed west over the River.

The notes in B as originally written were few, and those mostly concerned (as in A) with individual Stewards as their lives and life-spans affected the nature of the succession. References to other events were in nearly all cases subsequent additions.

Pelendur B has here, almost exactly following A: 'Became Steward 1940; ruled the realm during the interregnum 1944–1960, when he surrendered authority to Eärnil II.' On this see *Eärnil II*, p. 216. That Pelendur did become briefly the ruler of Gondor is not stated in C (as it is in Appendix A, RK p. 319), but that there was an interregnum for a year is implied by the revised dating (Ondohir slain in 1944, Eärnil's accession in 1945).

Vorondil There is no note on Vorondil in A and B. With the addition in C cf. the chapter *Minas Tirith*, RK p. 27, where it is not said (though no doubt implied) that Vorondil was the actual maker of the horn last borne by Boromir: 'since Vorondil father of Mardil hunted the wild kine of Araw in the far fields of Rhûn' (on this passage see VIII.281 and note 14).

Mardil Voronwë   A has a note here, which was not repeated in B, 'After his time the names are usually Noldorin not Quenya. Few are left who know Quenya.' Cf. Appendix A (RK p. 319): 'His successors ceased to use High-elven names.'

Belegorn   In A the name of the fourth Ruling Steward was *Bardhan*, later changed to *Belgorn*; *Belegorn* in B.

Túrin I   The same note is present in all three texts.

Hador   In A the name of the seventh Ruling Steward was *Cirion*, and *Hador* that of the twelfth; this was retained in B, but the names were later reversed. A has simply 'lived to great age 150'; B is as C, but the note ends 'the life-span of the nobles is waning steadily.'

Dior   In A and B the same is said as in C, but Dior's sister (Rían in C) is not named.

Denethor I   The note in A reads: 'Great troubles arose. Enemy destroyed Osgiliath. Boromir son (third child) of the Steward defeats them, and for a time recovers Ithilien.' B repeated this, but the text was altered to read: 'Enemy overran all Ithilien and destroyed the bridges of Osgiliath.'

Boromir   A has: 'Death hastened by wounds got in the war'; B: 'His life was shortened by wounds received from the poisoned weapons of Morgul.'

Cirion   In neither A nor B was there a note following Cirion (first written *Hador*), but the following was added in B: 'War with Orcs and Easterlings. Battle of Celebrant' (with the date 2510 put in subsequently), and also:

   Sauron stirs up mischief, and there is a great attack on Gondor. Orcs pour out of the Mountains and of Mirkwood and join with Easterlings. Hador [> Cirion] gets help from the North. Eorl the Young wins the victory of the Field of Celebrant and is given Calenardon or Rohan.

Since the mentions of the Field of Celebrant in the narrative of *The Lord of the Rings* were all late additions (see e.g. IX.72, note 16) it may be that the story was evolving at the time of the writing of *The Heirs of Elendil*.

Ecthelion I   A's note here makes Egalmoth, successor of the childless Ecthelion, the grandson of Morwen sister of Belecthor I. This introduces a generation too many, and was obviously due to the mention of Egalmoth under his predecessor Ecthelion – a testimony to the rapidity with which my father sketched out the dates and relations of the later Stewards in this earliest text. In B Morwen becomes the sister of Orodreth, Ecthelion's father.

Egalmoth In B a note was added (repeated in C): 'Orc-wars break out'. This is referred to in the Tale of Years in Appendix B: '2740 Orcs renew their invasions of Eriador.' A later pencilled note in B says 'Dwarf and Orc war in Misty Mountains' (see under *Beregond* below).

Beren There was no note in B, but these were added: 'Long winter 2758', and 'In his reign there is an attack on Gondor by [Pirates >] Corsairs of Umbar [2758 >] 2757'.

Beregond In A and B his name was *Baragond*, with the note that he was the third child of Beren. A pencilled note in B repeats the notice of the War of the Dwarves and the Orcs from the entry under Egalmoth, with the date '2766–'.

The Stewards from Belecthor II to Ecthelion II By this point A has become no more than a working-out of dates; and the brief notes in B can be collected together. That to Belecthor II is the same as in C but without mention of the death of the White Tree; that to Túrin II is 'Bilbo was born in the Shire during his rule'; and that to Turgon is 'Aragorn born in Eriador during his rule'. Very rough and hasty additions were made later in preparation for the much fuller notes in C.

The statement in C under Ecthelion II that 'Aragorn of the North serves as a soldier in his forces' is the first mention of Aragorn's years of service in disguise in Rohan and Gondor.

Denethor II B has only a statement of dates and relationships, including that of Denethor's marriage to Finduilas daughter of Adrahil of Dol Amroth: this is seen in A (where the father of Finduilas is named *Agrahil*) at the moment of its emergence.

Faramir The note in B is the same in substance as that in C, but adds that as the Prince of Ithilien he 'dwelt in a fair new house in the Hills of Emyn Arnen, whose gardens devised by the Elf Legolas were renowned.'

The Line of Dol Amroth

Arising from the reference to Denethor's marriage to Finduilas, at the foot of the last page of the B manuscript my father began working out the genealogy of the descendants of Adrahil of Dol Amroth; and a carefully made table beginning with Angelimir the twentieth prince was attached by my father to the manuscript C of *The Heirs of Elendil*. This I have redrawn on p. 221 (the Princes are marked with crosses as in the original). Beneath the table is a note on the origins of the house of Dol Amroth, telling that Galador the first lord was the son of Imrazôr the Númenórean, who dwelt in Belfalas, and Mith-

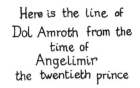

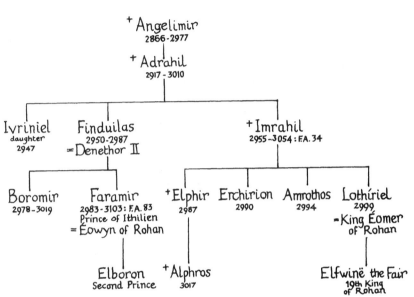

In the tradition of his house *Angelimir* was the twentieth in unbroken descent from *Galador* first Lord of Dol Amroth (c. T.A. 2004-2129). According to the same traditions *Galador* was the son of *Imrazôr* the Númenórean who dwelt in *Belfalas*, and the Elven-lady *Mithrellas*. She was one of the companions of *Nimrodel*, among many of the Elves of *Lórien* that fled to the coast about T.A. 1980, when evil arose in *Moria*; and *Nimrodel* and her maidens strayed in the wooded hills, and were lost. But in this tale it is said that *Imrazôr* harboured *Mithrellas*, and took her to wife. But when she had borne him a son, *Galador*, and a daughter, *Gilmith*, she slipped away by night, and he saw her no more. But though *Mithrellas* was of the lesser silvan race (and not of the High Elves or the Grey) it was ever held that the house and kin of the Lords of Dol Amroth were noble by blood, as they were fair in face and mind.

rellas one of the companions of Nimrodel. This note is printed in *Unfinished Tales*, p. 248, with the unaccountable error of *Angelimar* for *Angelimir* (an editorial mistake, since it occurs twice in the text and again in the index).

The page obviously belongs with the writing of C to which it is attached, since on the reverse are the first entries for the Southern Line in exactly the same form as they appear in the text, but abandoned, as it appears, simply because of an error in the writing out of the dates in what was designed to be a fine manuscript.

Another briefer account of the origin of the Line of Dol Amroth is found on a page attached by my father to the (as I believe, contemporary) manuscript T 4 of the Tale of Years, followed by a list of the dates of the Princes, those from the second to the eighteenth without names. This, however, is much later; for there is another form of the same list written on the back of a college document from the earlier part of 1954, and this is plainly the earlier of the two (see p. 223).

The House of Dol Amroth

Amroth brother of Celeborn flies from northern Lórien when the Balrog drives out the Dwarves about 1980 T.A.

Mithrellas, one of the companions of Nimrodel, is lost in the woods of Belfalas, and is harboured by Imrazôr the Númenórean [*added in margin:* Imrazôr 1950–2076], who takes her to wife (according to the legends and traditions of Dol Amroth); though after a few years she vanishes, whether to wander in the woods or seek the havens. The son of the union of Mithrellas and Imrazôr received the elven-name of Galador; from him the lords of Dol Amroth traced their descent. After the ending of the kings they became virtually independent princes, ruling over Belfalas, but they were at all times loyal to the Steward as representing the ancient crown.

1	Galador	2004–2129	(125)
2	...	2060–2203	(143)
3	...	2120–2254	(134)
4	...	2172–2299	(127)
5	...	2225–2348	(123)
6	...	2274–2400	(126)
7	...	2324–2458	(134)
8	...	2373–2498	(125)
9	...	2418–2540	(122)
10	...	2463–2582	(119)
11	...	2505–2623	(118)
12	...	2546–2660	(114)
13	...	2588–2701	(113)
14	...	2627–2733	(106)
15	...	2671–†2746	(75) slain by Corsairs of Umbar

THE HEIRS OF ELENDIL

16	...	2709–†2799	([90]) slain in battle
17	...	2746–2859	(113)
18	...	2785–2899	(114)
19	Aglahad	2827–2932	(105)
20	Angelimir	2866–2977	(111)
21	Adrahil	2917–3010	(93)
22	Imrahil	2955–3054	(99)
23	Elphir	2987–(3087 =) F.A.57	(100)
24	Alphros	3017–(3115 =) F.A.95	(98)

In contrast to this carefully written page, the other form of this list (that written on the back of the document of 1954) has a scrawled note at its head, the same as that in the text just given but extending only to the words 'harboured by Imrazôr the Númenórean, who weds her'; and the dates are written in pencil, with some corrections. Imrazôr is numbered 1, so that Angelimir is the twenty-first prince; but this was corrected. The life-span of the sixteenth prince was given as 91 years instead of 90, and my father followed this in the second text; and where the second text has 'slain in battle' the first has 'Battle with Orcs'.

The statement here that Amroth was the brother of Celeborn appears to be unique (for other accounts of him see *The History of Galadriel and Celeborn* in *Unfinished Tales*: but all the material concerning Amroth collected there comes from after, much of it long after, the publication of *The Lord of the Rings*). On both forms of the present text the words were struck out, and on the second my father pencilled 'was a Sinda from Beleriand'. With the time of Amroth's flight from Lórien cf. the entry for 1981 in Appendix B: 'The Dwarves flee from Moria. Many of the Silvan Elves of Lórien flee south. Amroth and Nimrodel are lost'; also *Unfinished Tales* pp. 240, 245.

No events are recorded elsewhere in the years 2746 and 2799 that cast light on the deaths in battle of the fifteenth and sixteenth Princes of Dol Amroth.

The dates of the deaths of Prince Imrahil and of Faramir Prince of Ithilien in the genealogy redrawn on p. 221 (3054 = Fourth Age 34, and 3103 = F.A.83) place the beginning of the Fourth Age in 3021; similarly in the list of the princes given above the dates of the deaths of Elphir and Alphros, 3087 and 3115, and equated with F.A.67 and 95. In text C of *The Heirs of Elendil* the Fourth Age began in 3022, and in text B the Third Age ended in 3019 (see pp. 196, 211).

The Princes Aglahad, Angelimir, Elphir, and Alphros are only recorded in these texts, as also are other members of the line of Dol Amroth in the genealogical table, Ivriniel, Erchirion, and Amrothos. Faramir's son Elboron likewise only appears in this genealogy. In him an old name reappears: Elboron and Elbereth were the original names of the young sons of Dior Thingol's Heir who were murdered by the followers of Maidros (IV.307, V.142). Later the sons of Elrond were named Elboron and Elbereth, before they became Elladan and Elrohir (VIII.297, 301, 370).

The further development of Appendix A is postponed to Chapter IX.

VIII
THE TALE OF YEARS OF THE THIRD AGE

The earliest text of the Tale of Years of the Third Age is a brief manuscript apparently closely associated with the very early form of that of the Second Age which I have called T 2 (see pp. 168–70); and although they are separate texts and not continuous it is convenient to refer to this likewise as T 2.

Though subsequently covered with somewhat haphazard accretions, for the most part obviously associated with work on the chronology of the Realms in Exile, it is possible to extricate with fair certainty the text of T 2 as originally set down, and I give it in this form here.

> Of the History of the Third Age
> little is known

0   If we reckon from the death of Isildur.
Years of Third Age
1000–   Sauron wakes again, and enters Mirkwood. Establishes a stronghold at Dol Dûgul[1] and slowly grows.
c.1100   Deagol finds the One Ring and is slain by Smeagol.[2] Smeagol becomes Gollum.
c.1105   Gollum enters eaves of Misty Mountains.
c.1300   The people of Smeagol grow and begin to multiply. They cross the Misty Mountains and journey westward. They become Hobbits.[3] Orcs begin to reappear.
c.1500   Hobbits settle at Bree.
c.1600   (S.R.1)[4] Marco and Cavallo cross the Baranduin (Brandywine) and are given 'the Shire' to live in by the king at Northworthy[5] (Fornost). 'Shire-reckoning' begins.
c.1900   Last 'king at Northworthy'. The Dúnedain or Rangers (last of the Númenóreans in the North) wander in the wild; but the heirs of the kings live at Imladris (Rivendell) with Elrond.
c.2000   The line of the Kings of Gondor becomes extinct with death of Eärnur.[6] The Line of the Stewards begins with Mardil the Good Steward.

c.2500 Elrond who had never before been wed, wedded Celebrían daughter of Galadriel of Lórien.[7] His children were Elrohir and Elladan and a daughter Finduilas[8] in whom the likeness of Lúthien reappeared. These children are of men's stature but Elven-blood.[9]
c.2600 Celebrían is slain by Orcs on the road over the Mountains to visit Galadriel.
c.2620 Isengrim Took the First establishes the Took family in the Shire.
c.2890 Bilbo born.
2910 Aragorn son of Arathorn heir of Isildur born.
2940 Bilbo goes on his adventures.
2950 Sauron re-enters Mordor.
3001 Bilbo's Farewell Party.
3018 Frodo sets out.

Whatever may have been the reasons for the selection of these particular events, it is striking that there are no entries referring to the history of Arnor and Gondor except those to the last king in the North and to the last king in the South (Eärnur), with the beginning of the line of Stewards; and the dates of these entries show that this text preceded the earliest extant forms of *The Heirs of Elendil*.

The next version was the manuscript T 3 (see p. 172), which in the part of it treating the Second Age, as I have said, was 'little more than a copy of T 2, with a number of entries expanded'. This is not at all the case, however, with the Third Age. It was here that my father introduced a comprehensive and coherent chronology of the Age, and set his course, in this work that he called 'the Tale of Years', in a direction remarkably unlike its ultimate appearance in Appendix B to *The Lord of the Rings*. That it was closely associated with *The Heirs of Elendil* is very plain. The manuscript was covered with alterations, expansions and additions, and became a working draft for the major text T 4 which I have no doubt soon followed it.

As will be seen subsequently, T 4 was and remained for a long time the form of the Tale of Years that my father thought appropriate, and was indeed proposed to the publishers in 1954. I shall here pass over the text T 3, though with some reference to it in the notes at the end of the chapter, and give that of T 4 in its entirety.

This is a very clear manuscript with a notable lack of hesitation or second thoughts. That it was intended to be a final and publishable text is shown also by the fact that, when my father came to the conclusion that the establishment of the White Council was placed four hundred years too early, he rejected two pages and wrote two new ones in such a way that they fitted precisely into the original text. I give it here as it was written, say in the years 1949–50 (as I believe), but with the text of the substituted pages, since it seems probable that they were written before the manuscript was completed, or at any rate soon after. It was a good deal altered later, chiefly with respect to certain matters: the migrations of the Stoors; the machinations of Saruman; and the movements of Gollum. I have not included any revisions in the text, but give an account of them at the end of the chapter (p. 250).

The opening statement concerning the Four Ages, and the entries for the Second Age, have been given on pp. 172–7.

The Third Age

These were the Fading Years. Of this Age in its beginnings little is now known, save for the traditions of the realm of Gondor. For a thousand years and more the Eldar in Middle-earth, protected by the Three Rings, were content and at peace, while Sauron slept; but they attempted no great deeds, and made no new things of wonder, living mostly in memory of the past. In all this time the things of old were slowly fading, and new things were stirring, though few observed the signs.

The Dwarves became ever more secretive, and hid themselves in deep places, guarding their hoards from their chief enemies, the dragons and the Orcs. One by one their ancient treasuries were plundered, and they became a wandering and dwindling people. In Moria the Dwarves of the race of Durin long held out, but this people once numerous steadily waned, until their vast mansions became dark and empty.

The might and lore and the life-span of the Númenóreans (or Dúnedain as they were called by the Elves) also waned as the years passed and their blood became mingled with that of lesser Men.[10] More swift was the waning in the North-kingdom, for the lands of Eriador, as that region was now called, became colder and less friendly to Men in that time. There the Dúnedain became ever less. After the days of Eärendur[11] of Arnor the North-kingdom became divided into petty realms, and the Heirs of Isildur of the direct line ruled only over Arthedain in the far North-west. In Gondor the power of the kings of Anárion's line endured longer, and their sway extended over many lands of Men; but there was little coming and going between the realms except in times of need.

> 1 Ohtar Isildur's esquire escapes with two other men only from the slaughter of the Gladden Fields.[12] He brings the shards of Elendil's sword, Narsil, which Isildur had saved, and delivers it to Valandil Isildur's son

in Imladris. Valandil was a child, fourth son of Isildur. His brothers perished with their father.

10   Valandil Isildur's son becomes King of Arnor and dwells at Annúminas.

420–30   Ostohir King of Gondor rebuilds and enlarges Minas Anor.

490   First invasion of Gondor by Easterlings.

500   Tarostar defeats the Easterlings and takes the name of Rómendakil, East-slayer.

541   Rómendakil slain in battle with a second invasion of Easterlings, who are driven out by his son Turambar.

861   Death of Eärendur last and tenth king of Arnor. The North-kingdom becomes divided among Eärendur's sons. The direct line of the eldest son, Amlaith of Fornost, rules the realm of Arthedain. Annúminas is deserted. The other realms were Cardolan (where later was Bree and the Barrowdowns) and Rhudaur, north of the River Baranduin. From this time the official names of the kings at Fornost were no longer given in High-elven form, but in Noldorin. Amlaith and his descendants maintained friendship with the Eldar, especially with Cirdan at the Havens.[13]

c.1000   About this time the *Istari*, that is the Wise Men or wizards, appeared in the westlands of Middle-earth. It was not known whence they came (unless to Cirdan and Elrond). But afterwards, when it was revealed that the shadow of Sauron had first begun to take new shape at this same time, it was said by many that they came out of the Far West, and were messengers sent to contest the power of Sauron, if he should arise again, and to move all good folk and kindly creatures to resist him.

The Wizards appeared nonetheless in the likeness of Men, and resembled Men in most things, save that they were never young and aged but slowly, and had many powers of mind and hand. For long they journeyed far and wide among Elves and Men and all speaking-folk, and held converse also with beasts and birds. They did not reveal their true names, but used those that the peoples of Middle-earth gave to them, and they were many. The chief of this order were the two whom the Eldar called Mithrandir and Curunír, but Men in the North named Gandalf and Saruman. Of them Mithrandir was closest in counsel with the Eldar and with Elrond; he wandered far in the North and West and never made for himself any lasting abode. But Curunír journeyed often far into the East, and when he returned he dwelt at Orthanc in the Ring of Isengard.[14]

About this time also the *Periannath*, of whom there are no earlier accounts among Elves or Men, are first mentioned in ancient tales. These were a strange small people, called by Men[15] Halflings, but by themselves (later in the west of Eriador) Hobbits. They are thought to have long dwelt in Greenwood the Great or near its western eaves, and in the vale of the upper Anduin. But at this time they began to move westward over the Misty Mountains into Eriador. It is said that they moved from their earlier dwellings because Men increased much at that time; and because a shadow fell on Greenwood, and it became darkened, and was called Mirkwood, for an evil spirit stirred there.[16] The Harfoots were the first clan of Hobbits to enter Eriador.[17]

c.1100 It becomes known to the Wise (being the chieftains of the Eldar and the Istari) that an evil power had arisen in Mirkwood and had established a stronghold on the hill of Dol Guldur in the southern forest. But it was still some time before they knew for certain that this was the shadow of Sauron himself and that he was awake again.

c.1150 The Fallohides, a clan of the Periannath, crossed into Eriador and came down from the North along the River Hoarwell. About the same time the Stoors, another clan, came over the Redhorn Pass and moved south towards Dunland.[18]

c.1200 Under Atanatar the Glorious Gondor reaches the height of its power, and its sway extends from the Greyflood in the West to the Sea of Rhúnaer in the East, and from the south-eaves of Mirkwood in the North to the land of the Haradrim in the South. The Haradrim acknowledge the overlordship of Gondor for many years.

c.1300 The western Periannath, now for the most part mingled together, move westward from the region of Amon Sûl (Weathertop), and begin to make small settlements among the remnants of the peoples of the old North-kingdom. Their chief settlement was on and about the Hill of Bree.

c.1350 Evil things begin to multiply again. Orcs increase rapidly and delve in the Misty Mountains, and attack the Dwarves. The Ringwraiths stir once more. The chief of these, the wielders of the Nine Rings, becomes the Witch-king of the realm of Angmar in the North beyond Arnor, and makes war on the remnants of the Dúnedain.

1356 Argeleb king at Fornost is slain in battle with the realms of Cardolan and Rhudaur, which resist his claim to overlordship.

c.1400 About this time, owing to dissensions and to the unfriendliness of the lands and clime of eastern Eriador, some of the Stoors return to Wilderland and dwell beside the R. Gladden that flows into Anduin. They become a riverside people, fishers and users of small boats. Others of the Stoors move north and west and join with the Harfoots and Fallohides.

1409 The Witch-king of Angmar taking advantage of the civil war among the Dúnedain comes out of the North and overwhelms the petty realms of Cardolan and Rhudaur and destroys the remnants of the Númenóreans that dwelt there. Cardolan is forsaken. The deserted mounds of Cardolan become filled with deadly spirits; but in Rhudaur for long there dwelt an evil people out of the North, much given to sorcery. The Men of Bree and the Periannath of the same region maintain their independence.

In this year 1409 King Arveleg I of Fornost was slain in battle by the Witch-king, but the Heirs of Isildur still hold out at Fornost with aid from Lindon. Arveleg is succeeded by Araphor.

In this war the Palantir of Amon Sûl was destroyed. Help did not come from the South-kingdom for their peace also was troubled by dissensions. King Valakar took to wife the daughter of an alien king of the Northmen of Anduin, with whom Gondor had sought alliance and aid in their war with the Easterlings. No king or heir to the throne of Gondor had before done such a thing.

1432 War of the Kin-strife breaks out in Gondor. Valakar dies and the succession of his son, half of alien blood, is contested by other descendants of Atanatar the Glorious. The war lasts till 1447. Kastamir who had driven out Valakar's son Eldakar was ejected by Eldakar and slain. The sons of Kastamir flee from Gondor and set up a pirate fortress at Umbar, and remain at war with the king.

1601 (S.R.1)[19] A host of Periannath migrates from Bree westward, and crosses the R. Baranduin (Brandywine). The land beyond, between the Baranduin and Emyn Beraid, had been a demesne of the Kings of Arnor, where they had both chases and rich farms; but they were now untended and falling into wilderness. The king Argeleb II therefore allowed the Periannath to settle there, for they were good husbandmen.[20] They became his subjects in name but were virtually independent and ruled by their own chieftains. Their numbers were swelled by Stoors that came up from southern Eriador and entered the land from the south and dwelt mostly near to the Baranduin. This land the Periannath or Halflings called 'The Shire'. Shire-reckoning begins with the crossing of the Baranduin in this year.

1634 The Corsairs of Umbar slew King Minardil and ravaged Pelargir. They were led by Angomaitë and Sangahyanda grandsons of Kastamir.[21]

1636 A great plague comes out of the East, and devastates Gondor. King Telemnar and all his children died. The White Tree of Isildur in Minas Anor withered and died. The power of Gondor dwindles.

1640 King Tarondor removed the king's house to Minas Anor. He planted there again a seedling of the White Tree. Osgiliath becomes deserted owing to the fewness of the people, and begins to fall into ruin. The watch on Mordor is relaxed, and the fortresses at the passes become empty.

The plague spreads north and west, and wide regions of Eriador become desolate. But the virulence of the plague decreases as it passes west and the Periannath in the Shire suffer little loss.[22]

c.1700 Mordor being now left unguarded evil things enter in again and take up their abode there secretly. Communication between the North and South kingdoms ceases for a long while.

1850 Assault of the Wainriders out of the East upon Gondor. War lasts for many years.
1900 Kalimehtar of Gondor builds the White Tower in Minas Anor.
1940 Messengers pass between the two kingdoms, since both are in peril: the South from the Wainriders of the East, and the North from renewed attacks of Angmar. Arvedui heir of Araphant of Arthedain weds Fíriel, the daughter of King Ondohir of Gondor.
1944 Ondohir with both his sons, Faramir and Artamir, slain in battle against a great alliance of the Wainriders and the Men of Harad. Arvedui of the North claims the southern crown, both on his wife's behalf and on his own as representing 'the elder line of Isildur'. The claim is refused by Gondor and lapses with the death of Arvedui; but all his descendants, though too weak to press their claim, continue to maintain that they are also by rights kings of Gondor, being descended both from Isildur and Anárion (through Fíriel).
1960 Pelendur the king's steward for a time ruled Gondor, but after a while Eärnil, descendant of a previous king, receives the crown.[23]
1974 End of the North-kingdom. The Witch-king destroys Fornost, lays the land waste, and scatters the remnants of the Dúnedain. Arvedui flies north taking the Palantíri (the two that remain). He attempts to escape by ship to Gondor from Forochel, but is lost at sea, and the Stones disappear. His sons take refuge with Cirdan.[24]
1975 Cirdan of Lune and Elrond, with belated help sent by sea from King Eärnil, defeat Angmar. The Witch-king is overthrown and his realm destroyed. He flies south and comes at last to Mordor.
1976 Aranarth son of Arvedui takes refuge with Elrond at Imladris. He abandons the title of 'king', since he now has no people, but the chieftains of the Dúnedain descended from him continue to bear names with the royal prefix *Ar, Ara*. The Periannath sent archers to the Battle of Fornost, but after the end of the kingdom they claim the Shire as their own. They elect a Thain to take the place of the king.[25] According to their tradition the first independent Shire-thain was one Bucca of the Marish, from whom later the Oldbuck family claimed

descent. The beginning of his office dated from S.R.379.

1980–2000 The Witch-king gathers the other eight Ringwraiths to him and they issue from Mordor, and folk flee from Ithilien in terror. The Úlairi captured Minas Ithil and made it their stronghold, from which they were not again expelled while the Third Age lasted. The Palantir of Minas Ithil is captured. Minas Ithil is re-named Minas Morgul (Tower of Sorcery), and Minas Anor is called Minas Tirith (the Tower of Guard).

About this time also other evil things were roused. A terror of the Elder Days, a Balrog of Thangorodrim, appeared in Moria. Some say that the Dwarves delving too deep in their search for *mithril* or true-silver disturbed this evil creature from its sleep far under the world. The remnants of Durin's folk are slain by the Balrog or driven out of Moria. Many of them wandered into the far North, as far as the Grey Mountains or the Iron Hills.

c.2000 Curunír (Saruman), returning out of the East, takes up his abode in the Tower of Orthanc in the Ring of Isengard.[26] This had been an ancient stronghold of Gondor, guarding their north-west frontier, but the northern parts of the realm were now largely empty and King Eärnil was glad to have the aid of Curunír against the Ringwraiths, and gave Isengard to him for his own.

About this time it is thought that Déagol the Stoor found the Ring in Anduin near the Gladden Fields where Isildur was slain as he swam. Déagol was murdered by his friend Sméagol, who took the Ring.

c.2010? Sméagol, now called Gollum, is cast out by his own people, and hides in the Misty Mountains. He vanishes out of all knowledge taking the Ring with him.[27]

2043 Death of King Eärnil. His son Eärnur (the Last King of Gondor in that Age) comes to the throne. The Lord of the Ringwraiths challenged him to battle.

2050 Against the counsel of Mardil his Steward King Eärnur accepts the renewed challenge of the Lord of Morgul to single combat. He rides to the gates of Minas Morgul, but he was betrayed and taken and never again seen by mortal men. Eärnur left no children. No male descendants (of clear title or nearly pure blood) of Anárion could be discovered. Mardil the good Steward governed the realm, nominally 'until the King's return'. For a long time previously the stewardship had usually been held by a member of the same family (one of nearly pure Númenórean descent). It now became hereditary in that family like a kingship. But each Steward took office with the formula 'to hold the rule and rod until the King's return'; and they did not take official names of Quenya or High-elven form. Their names were mostly of Noldorin kind, that tongue being still used by those descended from the Elf-friends of Númenor.

After the disappearance of Eärnur and the ending of the kings the White Tree seldom again bore fruit, and each year its blossom grew less as it slowly aged.

2060 The fear of the Ringwraiths, or Úlairi, spreads far and wide. The Elves deem that the Power in Dol Guldur is one of these; but in the hearts of Elrond and Gandalf the fear grows that the darkness in Mirkwood should prove to be the shadow of Sauron himself awakening.[28]

2063 Gandalf goes alone to Dol Guldur in secret, to discover the truth concerning the Sorcerer. But the Sorcerer is aware of him; and being not yet grown to great power, he fears the eyes of Gandalf, and the strength of the Wise, and he deserts Dol Guldur and hides in the East again for a while.

Here begins a time that is called the Watchful Peace. For there was a long quiet, but no certainty. During that time the Ringwraiths never again appeared in visible shape beyond the walls of Minas Morgul; but the Wise were in doubt what should yet come to pass, and Gandalf made great journeys to discover the plans and devices of their enemies.

2300 Elrond, who had remained unwed through all his long years, now took to wife Celebrían, daughter of Galadriel and Celeborn of Lórien. His children were the twin brethren, Elladan and Elrohir, and Arwen Undómiel, the fairest of all the maidens of the Third Age, in whom the likeness of Lúthien her foremother returned to Middle-earth. These children were three parts of Elven-race, but the doom spoken at their birth was that they should live even as the Elves so long as their father remained in Middle-earth; but if he departed they should have then the choice either to pass over the

THE TALE OF YEARS OF THE THIRD AGE

Sea with him, or to become mortal, if they remained behind.

2340 Isumbras I, head of the Took family in the Shire, becomes thirteenth Thain, the first of the Took line.[29] After his day the office became hereditary in the family of the Tooks of the Great Smials. About this time the Oldbucks occupied the Buckland, east of the River Brandywine and on the edge of the Old Forest.

2349 Birth of Elladan and Elrohir, sons of Elrond, in Imladris.[30]

2349 Birth of Arwen Undómiel.

2460 After a space of nearly four hundred years the Watchful Peace ends, and the powers of evil move again. The Sorcerer returns to Dol Guldur with increased strength, and gathers all evil things under his rule.

2463 The White Council is formed to unite and direct the forces of the West, in resistance to the shadow. Curunír (or Saruman the White) is chosen to be the head of the Council, since he has studied all the arts and ways of Sauron and his servants most deeply. Galadriel of Lórien wishes Gandalf to be made chief, but he refuses. Saruman begins his study of the Rings of Power and their uses and history.

2475 The attack upon Gondor is begun again with new vigour, in the days of Denethor I, son of Dior,[31] the tenth Steward. His son Boromir defeats the enemy before East Osgiliath, but Osgiliath is finally ruined in this war, and the ancient and marvellous stone-bridge is broken. The Men of Gondor still maintain their hold upon Ithilien, but little by little its people desert it and pass west over Anduin to the valleys of the White Mountains.

2480 onwards Orcs again multiply in secret and occupy many deep places (especially those anciently made by the Dwarves) in the Misty Mountains. They do this so stealthily that none are aware of it, until they have great forces hidden and are ready to bar all the passes from Eriador into Anduin's vales, according to the plan of their master in Dol Guldur. Orcs and Trolls occupy parts of the now empty Mines of Moria.

2509 Celebrían, wife of Elrond, journeys to Lórien to visit Galadriel, her mother; but she is taken by Orcs in the passes of the mountains. She is rescued by Elrond and his sons, but after fear and torment she is no longer willing to remain in Middle-earth, and she departs to the Grey Havens and sails over Sea.[32]

2510 A great host of Orcs, with Easterlings as allies, assail the northern borders of Gondor, and occupy a great part of Calenardon. Gondor sends for help. Eorl the Young leads his people, the Éothéod or Rohirrim, out of the North from the sources of Anduin, and rides to the help of Cirion, Steward of Gondor. With his aid the great victory of the Field of Celebrant is won. Elladan and Elrohir rode also in that battle. From that time forth the brethren never cease from war with the Orcs because of Celebrían. Eorl and his people are given the plains of Calenardon to dwell in, and that land is now called *Rochann* (Rohan). There the Rohirrim live as free men under their own kings, but in perpetual alliance with Minas Tirith.

2569 The Golden Hall of Meduseld is built by Brego son of Eorl.

2570 Baldor son of Brego takes a rash vow to enter the Forbidden Door in Dunharrow, and is never seen again.

2590 Thrór the Dwarf (of Dúrin's race) founds the realm of Erebor (the Lonely Mountain), and becomes 'King under the Mountain'.[33] He lives in friendship with the Men of Dale, who are nearly akin to the Rohirrim.

2620 Isengrim II, tenth Thain of the Took-line, born in the Shire.

2698 Ecthelion I, Steward of Gondor, repairs and rebuilds the White Tower of Minas Tirith, afterwards often called the Tower of Ecthelion.[34]

2740– Wars with the Orcs break out again.

2747 Orcs passing far to the north raid down into Eriador. A large force invades the Shire. Bandobras Took, second son of Isumbras III, defeats them at the Battle of the Greenfields in the Northfarthing and slays the Orc-chief Golfimbul. This was the last battle in which Hobbits (Periannath) were engaged until the end of the Third Age.

2757 Rohan is overrun by Orcs and Easterlings. At the same time Gondor is attacked by the Corsairs of Umbar.

2758–9 The Long Winter. Helm of Rohan takes refuge from his enemies in Helm's Deep in the White Mountains.

THE TALE OF YEARS OF THE THIRD AGE

2763   New line of kings in Rohan is begun with Fréaláf Hildeson (sister-son of Helm). The second row of King's Mounds is begun.

2765   Smaug the Dragon descends on Erebor and destroys the realm of Thrór the Dwarf, and lays waste the town and lordship of Dale. Thrór and his son Thráin escape with a few only of their people.

2766   Thrór the Dwarf, descendant of Durin, being now homeless and robbed of his treasure, ventures into Moria, but is slain by an Orc in the dark. Thráin and Thorin escape. In vengeance for Thrór and in hope of re-establishing a kingdom the scattered Dwarves of Durin's race gather together out of the North and make war on the Orcs of the Misty Mountains. The War of the Dwarves and Orcs was long and terrible and fought largely in the dark in deep places.

2769   The War of Orcs and Dwarves comes to an end in a great battle before the East-gate of Moria: the Battle of the Dimrill Dale (Nanduhirion). The Orcs were almost annihilated, and Moria is once more emptied, but the Dwarves also lost very heavily and were too few at the end to reoccupy Moria or face the hidden terror. Dáin returns to the Iron Hills; but Thráin and Thorin become wanderers.[35]

2790   Birth of Gerontius Took: later the fourteenth Thain,[36] and known as 'the Old Took' because of his great age (he lived to be 130 years old).

2850   Gandalf visits Dol Guldur again to discover the purposes of the Sorcerer. He finds there Thráin the Dwarf son of Thrór and receives from him the secret key of Erebor. Thráin had come thither seeking for one of the Seven Rings; but he dies in Dol Guldur.[37] Gandalf discovers beyond doubt that the Sorcerer is none other than Sauron himself, and that he is gathering again all the Rings of Power, and seeking to learn the fate of the One, and the dwelling of Isildur's Heirs.

2851   Gandalf urges the White Council to assail Dol Guldur, but he is overruled by Saruman. For Saruman has begun to lust for power and desires himself to discover the One Ring. He thinks that it will come to light again, seeking its Master, if Sauron is let be for a while. He does not reveal his thought to the Council, but feigns that his studies have led him to believe that the Ring has been rolled down Anduin and into the deeps of the Sea. But Saruman himself keeps a watch upon Anduin and the Gladden Fields and he fortifies Isengard.

2872 Belecthor II, twenty-first Steward of Gondor, dies.[38] The White Tree dies in the court of Minas Tirith. No seedling can be found. The dead tree is left standing in the court under the White Tower.

c.2880 Ithilien becomes desolate and untilled and the remnant of its people remove west over Anduin to Lossarnach and Lebennin. But the Men of Minas Tirith still hold Ithilien as a border country and patrol it; they keep forces in the ruins of Osgiliath and in secret places in Ithilien.[39]

2885 In the days of Túrin II, twenty-third Steward, the Haradrim attack Gondor and ravage South Ithilien. The Rohirrim send help. Folcred and Fastred sons of King Folcwine of Rohan fall in battle in the service of Gondor.

2891 Bilbo born in the Shire (his mother was a daughter of the Old Took).

2911 The Fell Winter. White Wolves invade the Shire over the frozen Brandywine River. About this time Saruman discovers that Sauron's servants are also searching the Great River near the Gladden Fields. He knows then that Sauron has learned the manner of Isildur's end (maybe from Orcs), and he is afraid. He withdraws to Isengard and fortifies it, but he says nothing to the Council.

2920 Death of Gerontius Took at age of 130.

2929 Arathorn, son of Arador chieftain of the Dúnedain, weds Gilrain daughter of Dirhoel [> Dirhael].

2930 Arador slain by Trolls.

2931 Aragorn son of Arathorn born.

2933 Arathorn II chief of the Dúnedain slain by Orcs when riding with Elladan and Elrohir. His infant son Aragorn is fostered by Elrond. Elrond keeps the heirlooms of his father, but his ancestry is kept secret, since the Wise know that Sauron is seeking for the Heir of Isildur.

2940 Thorin Oakenshield the Dwarf, son of Thráin, son of Thrór of Erebor visits Bilbo in the Shire in the company of Gandalf. Bilbo sets out for Dale with Gandalf and the

Dwarves. Bilbo meets Sméagol-Gollum and becomes possessed of the Ring; but it is not guessed what Ring this is.

Meeting of the White Council. Saruman, since he now wishes to prevent the Sorcerer from searching the River, agrees to an attack on Dol Guldur. The Sorcerer is driven out of Mirkwood. The Forest for a time becomes wholesome again. But the Sorcerer flies east, and returns in secret.

Battle of the Five Armies fought in Dale. Thranduil of Mirkwood, the Men of Esgaroth, and the Dwarves, with the help of the Eagles of the Misty Mountains, defeat a great host of Orcs. Bard of Esgaroth slays Smaug the Dragon. Thorin Oakenshield dies of wounds. Dáin of the Iron Hills re-enters Erebor and becomes 'King under the Mountain'.

2941 Bilbo returns to the Shire with a share of the treasure of Smaug, and the Ring.

2948 Théoden son of Thengel king of the Rohirrim is born in Rohan.

2953 Aragorn returns from errantry in the company of Elladan and Elrohir. Elrond reveals to him his ancestry and destiny and delivers to him the Shards of Narsil, the Sword of Elendil. Elrond foretells that in his time either the last remnant of Númenor shall pass away, or the kingdoms of Arnor and Gondor shall be united and renewed. He bids Aragorn prepare for a hard life of war and wandering.

Arwen Undómiel had now long dwelt with Galadriel in Lórien, but she desired to see her father again, and her brethren, Elladan and Elrohir, brought her to Imladris. On the day in which his ancestry was revealed to him Aragorn met her at unawares walking under the trees in Rivendell, and so began to love her. Elrond is grieved, for he foresees the choice that will lie before her; and says that at least Aragorn must wait until he has fulfilled his task. He reveals that as one of the pure blood of Númenor, born to a high purpose, Aragorn will have a long life-span. Aragorn says farewell to Rivendell and goes out into the world.

At this time Sauron, having gathered fresh power, declares himself and his true name again, and he re-enters Mordor which the Ringwraiths have prepared for him, and rebuilds Barad-dûr. This had never been wholly destroyed, and its foundations were unmoved; for they were made by the Power of the One Ring. But Mithrandir (Gandalf) journeys far and wide to counter the plans of Sauron and prepare Elves and Men for war against the Lord of Barad-dûr.

2954 Orodruin (Mount Doom), long dormant, bursts into smoke and flame again, and fear falls on Minas Tirith.

2956 Aragorn meets Gandalf, and their great friendship begins. Aragorn undertakes great journeys, even far into the East and deep into the South, exploring the purposes of Sauron and all his movements. As an unknown warrior he fights in the service of Gondor and of Rohan. Because of his high race, the noblest among mortal men, his fostering by Elrond, and his learning from Mithrandir, and his many deeds and journeys he becomes the most hardy of Men, both Elven-wise and skilled in craft and lore.

2980 Aragorn returning on a time to Rivendell from perils on the borders of Mordor passes through Lórien, and there again meets Arwen Undómiel. He is now a mighty man and she returns his love. They plight their troth on the hill of Cerin Amroth in Lórien. Théoden becomes King of Rohan.

2984 Denethor II becomes the twenty-sixth Steward of Gondor on the death of his father Ecthelion II. He married (late) Finduilas daughter of Adrahil, Prince of Dol Amroth. His elder son Boromir was born in 2978. His younger son Faramir was born in 2983. His wife Finduilas died untimely in 2987.

2989 In the spring of this year Balin the Dwarf with Óin and Ori and other folk of Erebor went south and entered Moria.

2993 Éomer Éomundsson born in Rohan. His mother was Théodwyn youngest sister of Théoden.

2996 Éowyn sister of Éomer born.

c.3000 onwards The Shadow of Mordor creeps over the lands, and the hearts of all the folk in the Westlands are darkened. About this time it is thought that Saruman dared to use the Palantir of Orthanc, but was ensnared thus by Sauron who had possession of the Stone of

THE TALE OF YEARS OF THE THIRD AGE

Minas Ithil (captured long before by the Úlairi). Saruman becomes a full traitor to the Council and his friends; but still schemes to acquire power for himself, and searches all the more eagerly for the One Ring. His thought turns towards Bilbo and the Shire, and he spies on that land.

3001 Bilbo gives a farewell feast and banquet in Hobbiton and vanishes from the Shire. He goes, after some journeying and a visit to Erebor, back in secret to Rivendell, and there is given a home by Elrond. Gandalf at last also suspects the nature of the Ring of Gollum, which Bilbo has handed on to his kinsman and heir, Frodo.

3002 Gandalf begins to explore the history of Bilbo's Ring, and with the aid of Aragorn searches for news of Gollum.

3004 Gandalf visits the Shire again, and continues to do so at intervals, to observe Frodo, for some years.

3009 Last visit of Gandalf to Frodo before the end. The hunt for Gollum begins. Aragorn goes to the confines of Mordor.

3016 Elrond sends for Arwen and she returns to Rivendell; for the Misty Mountains and all lands east of them are becoming full of peril and threat of war.

3018 Gandalf visits Frodo and reveals the true nature of the Ring that he possesses. Frodo decides to fly from the Shire to Rivendell, but will wait till the autumn, or until Gandalf returns. Saruman the traitor decoys Gandalf and takes him prisoner in Isengard (shortly after midsummer). The Ringwraiths appear again. At midsummer Sauron makes war on Gondor. The Witch-king appears again in person as the Black Captain of the hosts of Mordor. The sons of Denethor hold off the attack. Words in a dream bid Denethor to seek for counsel in Imladris where Isildur's Bane shall be revealed and strength greater than that of Morgul shall be found. Boromir sets out for Imladris from Minas Tirith.

Gandalf is aware of the coming of the Ringwraiths, but being imprisoned in Orthanc cannot send warning or help to Frodo.

Frodo leaves the Shire in autumn, but barely escapes the Ringwraiths that in the shape of Black Riders have come north to hunt for the Ring. Assisted by Aragorn he and his companions reach Rivendell at the end of October. At the same time Boromir arrives there, and also messengers from Erebor (Glóin and his son Gimli) and from Thranduil of Mirkwood (his son Legolas). Gandalf escapes from Isengard and reaches Rivendell.

A great council is held in the House of Elrond. It is resolved to attempt the destruction of the Ring by sending it to the fire of Orodruin in Sauron's despite. Frodo the Halfling accepts the perilous office of Ringbearer.

At the end of the year the Company of the Ring ('The Nine Walkers') leave Rivendell.

3019 The War of the Ring begins, between Sauron and his creatures, and their allies in the East and South (among all Men that hate the name of Gondor), and the peoples of the Westlands. Saruman plays a treacherous part and attacks Rohan. Théodred son of Théoden is slain in war with Saruman. Boromir son of Denethor is slain by Orcs near the Falls of Rauros. Minas Tirith is besieged by great forces led by the Black Captain, and is partly burnt. Denethor slays himself in despair. The Rohirrim by a great ride break the siege, but Théoden is slain by the Witch-king. The Battle of the Pelennor Fields followed, of which the full tale is told elsewhere. The greatest deed of that day was the deed of Éowyn Éomund's daughter. She for love of the King rode in disguise with the Rohirrim and was with him when he fell. By her hand the Black Captain, the Lord of the Ringwraiths, the Witch-king of Angmar, was destroyed.

Even so the battle would have been lost but for the coming of Aragorn. In the hour of need he sailed up Anduin from the south, in the fleet which he captured from the Corsairs of Umbar, bringing new strength; and he unfurled the banner of the kings.

After taking counsel the Host of the West marches to the Black Gate of Mordor. There it is trapped and surrounded by the forces of Sauron. But in that hour Frodo the Halfling with his faithful servant reached Mount Doom through perils beyond hope and cast the Ring into the Fire. Then Sauron was unmade and his power passed away like a cloud and the Dark Tower fell in utter ruin. This is that Frodo who was long remembered in the songs of Men as Frodo of the Nine Fingers, and

THE TALE OF YEARS OF THE THIRD AGE 243

renowned as one of the greatest heroes of Gondor; but though often later this was forgotten he was not a Man of Gondor but a Halfling of the Shire.

The Host of the West enters Mordor and destroys all the Orc-holds. All Men that had allied themselves with Sauron were slain or subjugated.

In the early summer Aragorn was crowned King of Gondor in Minas Tirith taking the name of Elessar (the Elfstone). He became thus King both of Arnor and Gondor, and overlord of the ancient allies of Mordor to whom he now granted mercy and peace. He found a seedling of the White Tree and planted it.

At midsummer Arwen came with Elrond and Galadriel and her brethren, and she was wedded with Aragorn Elessar, and made the choice of Lúthien.

In Gondor a new era and a new calendar was made, to begin with the day of the fall of Barad-dûr, March 25, 3019. But the Third Age is not held to have ended on that day, but with the going of the Three Rings. For after the destruction of the Ruling Ring the Three Rings of the Eldar lost their virtue. Then Elrond prepared at last to depart from Middle-earth and follow Celebrían.

3021 In the autumn of this year Elrond, Galadriel, and Mithrandir, the guardians of the Three Rings, rode westward through the Shire to the Grey Havens. With them went, it is said, the Halflings Bilbo and Frodo, the Ringbearers. Círdan had made ready a ship for them, and they set sail at evening and passed into the uttermost West. With their passing ended the Third Age, the twilight between the Elder Days and the Afterworld which then began.

Here ends the main matter of the Red Book. But more is to be learned both from notes and additions in later hands in the Red Book (less trustworthy than the earlier parts which are said to have been derived from the Halflings that were actual witnesses of the deeds); and from the Annals of the House of Elessar, of which parts of a Halfling translation (made it is said by the Tooks) are preserved.

So much may here be noted. The reign of King Aragorn was long and glorious. In his time Minas Tirith was rebuilt and made stronger and fairer than before; for the king had the assistance of the stone-wrights of Erebor. Gimli Glóin's son of Erebor had been his companion and had fought in all the battles of the War of the Ring, and when peace was made he brought part of the dwarf-folk and they dwelt in the White Mountains and wrought great and wonderful works in Gondor. And the Dwarves also forged anew great gates of *mithril* and steel to replace those broken in the siege. Legolas Thranduil's son had also been one of the king's companions and he brought Elves out of Greenwood (to which name Mirkwood now returned) and they dwelt in Ithilien, and it became the fairest region in all the Westlands. But after King Elessar died Legolas followed at last the yearning of his heart and sailed over Sea. It is said in the Red Book that he took Gimli Glóin's son with him because of their great friendship, such as had never else been seen between Elf and Dwarf. But this is scarcely to be believed: that a dwarf should be willing to leave Middle-earth for any love, or that the Elves should admit him to Avallon if he would go, or that the Lords of the West should permit it. In the Red Book it is said that he went also out of desire to see again the Lady Galadriel whose beauty he revered; and that she being mighty among the Eldar obtained this grace for him. More cannot be said of this strange matter.

It is said also that in 3020 Éowyn Éomund's daughter wedded Faramir, last Steward of Gondor and first Prince of Ithilien, in the king's house of Rohan. Éomer her brother received the kingship upon the field of battle from Théoden ere he died. In 3022 (or Fourth Age 1) he wedded Lothíriel daughter of Imrahil of Dol Amroth, and his reign over Rohan was long and blessed, and he was known as Éomer Éadig.

King Elessar and Queen Arwen reigned long and in great blessedness; but at the last the weariness came upon the King, and then, while still in vigour of mind and body, he laid himself down after the manner of the ancient kings of Númenor, and died, in the hundred and second year of his reign and the hundred and ninetieth year of his life.

Then Arwen departed and dwelt alone and widowed in the fading woods of Loth-lórien; and it came to pass for her as Elrond foretold that she would not leave the world until she had lost all for which she made her choice. But at last she laid herself to rest on the hill of Cerin Amroth, and there was her green grave until the shape of the world was changed.

Of Eldarion son of Elessar it was foretold that he should rule a great realm, and that it should endure for a hundred generations of Men after him, that is until a new age brought in again new things; and from him should come the kings of many realms in long days after. But if this foretelling spoke truly, none now can say, for Gondor and Arnor are no more; and even the chronicles of the House of Elessar and all their deeds and glory are lost.

The account of the history of the Realms in Exile in *The Heirs of Elendil*, where it is set out in the framework of the succession of the kings and rulers, necessarily overlaps with that in the Tale of Years, where it forms part of a general chronology of the Westlands. It would therefore be interesting to know whether my father wrote the latter before or after the final (unrevised) manuscript C of *The Heirs of Elendil*; but the evidence on this question is strangely conflicting. On the one hand, the entry in T 4 for the year 1960 seems to establish that it preceded C, where the interregnum after the death of King Ondohir was only of one year and Eärnil II came to the throne in 1945, and the correction to the text (see note 23) was plainly made after the manuscript was completed. There are other pointers to the same conclusion; thus the passage under 2050 concerning the Stewards was taken straight from the B text of *The Heirs of Elendil* (see p. 217). On the other hand, there are a number of features in T 4 that seem to show that my father had C in front of him: as for example the statement under 1409 that the *palantír* of Amon Sûl was destroyed, where C (before correction) had 'the *palantír* is broken', but B (in an addition) had 'no one knows what became of the Stone' (pp. 194, 209); or again the two challenges made by the Lord of the Ringwraiths to Eärnur, in 2043 and 2050, which very clearly first entered *The Heirs of Elendil* in C (pp. 201, 217). Close similarities of wording are found between entries in T 4 and both B and C.

One might suppose that the writing of T 4 and the writing of C proceeded together; but the two manuscripts are at once very distinct in style, and very homogeneous throughout their length. Each gives the impression that it was written from start to finish connectedly. On the other hand, there can be little doubt that T 3 and T 4 belong to very much the same time as *The Heirs of Elendil*.

My father may not have precisely intended such near-repetition between the two works as occurs, but it is possible to regard it as the necessary consequence of his design at that time. This long Tale of Years, ample in expression, seems to me to show that he wished, having at long last brought the story to its end, to provide for the reader a clear and accessible (still in the manner of the story) 'conspectus' of all the diverse threads and histories that came together in the War of the Ring: of the Hobbits, the Wizards, the Dúnedain of the North, the rulers of Gondor, the Rohirrim, the Ringwraiths, the Dark

Lord; the High-elves of Rivendell and Lindon also, the Dwarves of Erebor and Moria, and further back the lost world of Númenor. This account (a chronology, but with a narrative view and tone) was to be read at the end of the book, a Tale of Years in which the story of the Fellowship and the quest of the Ringbearer could be seen, when all was over, as the culmination of a great and many-rooted historical process – for which chronology was a prime necessity. And so also, at the end of this Tale of Years, he moved 'outside the frame' of the story, and looked further on to the later lives of Gimli and Legolas, of Faramir and Éowyn and Éomer, the reign and the deaths of Elessar and Arwen, and the realm of their son Eldarion in 'the Afterworld'.

I have mentioned when discussing the Tale of Years of the Second Age (p. 177) that an amanuensis typescript in two copies (T 5) – very intelligently and professionally done – was made from the manuscript T 4; and that one of them was emended in a most radical fashion by my father, chiefly if by no means exclusively in order to abbreviate the text by the omission of phrases that could be regarded as not strictly necessary. This cutting out of phrases ceases altogether towards the end, at the beginning of the entry for 3019.

There is no certain evidence to show when the typescript was made, but I think that it was a long while after the writing of the manuscript. The question is in any case not of much importance, for what is certain is that the typescript was sent to the publishers in 1954; in a letter of 22 October in that year Rayner Unwin said:

> The Tale of Years which I am returning herewith was interesting, but as you, I think, agree, probably too long for the appendices as it stands. I suggest that considerable reduction be made in the accounts of events already told in The Lord of the Rings, and a somewhat more staccato style be adopted (make less of a narrative of the events of the Third Age).

It was of course the typescript in its unrevised form that he had sent: the revision (in so far as it entailed abbreviation) was obviously undertaken in response to Rayner Unwin's criticism.

If my interpretation of my father's intention for the Tale of Years is at all near the truth, it may be supposed that he carried out this work of shortening with reluctance; certainly, in the result, the amount lost from the original text was not proportionately very great, the long concluding passage was not touched, and the rounded, 'narrative' manner was little diminished. But after this time there is no external evidence that I know of to indicate whether there was further discussion of the matter – whether, for instance, my father was given a more express limitation with regard to length. There is indeed nothing actually to show that the subsequent far more drastic compression was not his own idea. But there is also nothing to bridge the gap before the next text, a typescript (from which the entries before 1900 are

THE TALE OF YEARS OF THE THIRD AGE 247

missing, and which breaks off in the middle of that for 2941) already in full 'staccato' mode, and approaching (after a good deal of correction) closely the text in Appendix B. After this the only further extant text is the typescript from which Appendix B was printed.

NOTES

1 On the name *Dol Dûgul* for later *Dol Guldur* see VIII.122. In the manuscripts of *The Lord of the Rings* it is always spelt *Dol Dúghul* (replacing original *Dol Dúgol*).
2 On the date of Déagol's finding the One Ring see pp. 166–7.
3 'They become Hobbits': cf. the passage in *The Shadow of the Past*, later revised, cited on p. 66, §20.
4 From this point all the dates are given also in the years of the Shire Reckoning, but I do not include these in the text. Here 1600 is made S.R.1, but in all the following annals the final figure of the year corresponds in both reckonings, as '2940 (S.R.1340)', as if S.R.1 = 1601. The correction to 1601 was not made until the third text, T 4.
5 On *Northworthy* see p. 5 and note 3.
6 King Eärnur is named in the text of *The Lord of the Rings*, in the chapter *The Window on the West* (TT p. 278), where it was a late change from *Elessar* (VIII.153).
7 In Appendix B Elrond wedded Celebrían 2400 years before, in Third Age 100 (changed to 109 in the Second Edition).
8 Finduilas, earlier name of Arwen: see VIII.370, etc.
9 This was changed later to 'three parts Elven-blood'.
10 To this point the text was retained in abbreviated form in the preamble to the annals of the Third Age in Appendix B.
11 Eärendur: T 3 has here Eärendil (see p. 189).
12 In this text Isildur's death had been recorded under Second Age 3441 (p. 177).
13 In T 3 there are no entries at all before the coming of the Istari c.1000, but my father noted on that manuscript that more should be said here of Gondor and Arnor.
14 This entry concerning the Istari was preserved with some alteration in the preamble to the annals of the Third Age in Appendix B.
15 T 3 had here '(of whose kindred they were maybe a branch)', which was struck out.
16 With this passage concerning the region in which the Hobbits anciently dwelt and the reasons for their westward migration cf. the *Prologue*, FR p. 12.
17 T 3 has here: 'The families of the Harfoots, the most numerous of the Periannath (though this people were ever small in number),

crossed the Misty Mountains and came into eastern Eriador. The Fallowhides, another and smaller clan, moved north along the eaves of the Forest, for the shadow was deeper in its southern parts. The Stoors tarried still beside the River.'

18   In T 3 the same is said concerning the 'Fallowhides', but the Stoors 'came over the Redhorn Pass into the desolate land of Hollin'.

19   On the date 1601 see note 4. Subsequent entries for some distance are given also in Shire-reckoning, but I have not included these dates in the text printed.

20   With this passage cf. the *Prologue* text given on p. 9. The entry in T 3 here begins: 'Owing to an increase in their numbers, which became too great for the small Bree-land, many of the Periannath crossed the R. Baranduin'; the text is then as in T 4, but without the reference to the Stoors.

21   In both the B and C texts of *The Heirs of Elendil* Angomaitë and Sangahyanda were the great-grandsons of Kastamir (so also in Appendix A, RK p. 328).

22   T 3 ends the entry for 1640 'The Periannath were little harmed, for they mingled little with other folk.'

23   This entry belongs to the stage in the history of Gondor when there was an interregnum of sixteen years before Eärnil II came to the throne, during which time Pelendur the Steward ruled the realm (see p. 216). It was later corrected to read: '1945   Eärnil, descendant of a previous king, receives the crown of Gondor.'

24   In T 3 it is said that Arvedui was slain by the Witch-king; this apparently agrees with the original form of the B text of *The Heirs of Elendil* (p. 210).

25   T 3 has here: 'but after the end of the kingdom they claim "The Shire" as their own land, and elect a "Shire-king" from among their own chieftains.' On the name *Shireking* or *Shirking* see pp. 5–6, 87, 107. It seems to have been in this entry in T 3 that Bucca of the Marish first emerged.

26   This record of Saruman's coming to Orthanc is far earlier than in the additions made to text C of *The Heirs of Elendil*, where (pp. 205–6) 'Saruman comes to Orthanc' during the rule of the Steward Beren (2743–63), and in that of the Steward Turgon (2914–53) 'Saruman takes possession of Orthanc, and fortifies it'. In Appendix B 'Saruman takes up his abode in Isengard' in 2759.

27   These two entries concerning the finding of the Ring and Gollum's disappearance in the Misty Mountains are nine hundred years later than in the earliest text (p. 225).

28   With the entry for 2060 the substituted pages (see pp. 226–7) begin. The original entry for this year began:

The White Council is formed to unite and direct the resistance

THE TALE OF YEARS OF THE THIRD AGE 249

to the growing forces of evil, which the Wise perceive are all being governed and guided in a plan of hatred for the Eldar and the remnants of Númenor. The Council believe that Sauron has returned. Curunír, or Saruman the White, is chosen to be head of the White Council ...

The original text was then the same as that in the entry that replaced it under the year 2463.

29 The opening of this entry in T 3 seems to have been written first: 'Isumbras I, head of the rising Took family, becomes first Shire-king (Shirking) of the Took-line', then changed immediately to 'becomes seventeenth [> thirteenth] Shire-king and first of the Took-line.'

30 The dates of the births of Elladan and Elrohir, and of Arwen, are given thus as two separate entries for the same year 2349 in the replacement text, with Arwen's birth subsequently changed to 2359. In the rejected version her birth was placed in 2400. Concomitantly with the far earlier date introduced much later for the wedding of Elrond and Celebrían (see note 7), in Appendix B Elladan and Elrohir were born in 139 (changed to 130 in the Second Edition) and Arwen in 241.

31 In *The Heirs of Elendil* Denethor I was the son not of Dior the ninth Steward but of Dior's sister (called in the C text Rían): pp. 204, 219. – The rejected text having placed the forming of the White Council four hundred years earlier, under 2060 (note 28), at this point it moved directly from the end of the Watchful Peace and the return of Sauron to Dol Guldur in 2460 to the attack on Gondor in the days of Denethor I. The postponement of the establishment of the White Council was the primary reason for the rejection and replacement of the two pages in the original manuscript, and the entries following 2463 were copied with little change into the new text to the point where it rejoins the old, near the end of the entry for 2510.

32 As in the earliest text (p. 226), T 3 states that Celebrían was slain by the Orcs.

33 'Thrór ... founds the realm of Erebor': the history of Thrór's ancestors had not yet emerged.

34 The year 2698 was the date of the death of Ecthelion I in the texts of *The Heirs of Elendil*.

35 The War of the Dwarves and Orcs entered the history at this time. In very difficult scribbled notes at the end of T 3 my father asked himself: 'When were the Dwarf and Goblin wars? When did Moria become finally desolate?' He noted that since the wars were referred to by Thorin in *The Hobbit* they 'must have been recent', and suggested that there was 'an attempt to enter Moria in Thráin's time', perhaps 'an expedition from Erebor to Moria'. 'But the appearance of the Balrog and the desolation of Moria

must be more ancient, possibly as far back as c.1980–2000'. He then wrote:

> 'After fall of Erebor Thrór tried to visit Moria and was killed by a goblin. The dwarves assembled a force and fought Orcs on east side of Moria and did great slaughter, but could not enter Moria because of "the terror". Dáin returns to the Iron Hills, but Thorin and Thráin wander about.'

Entries were then added to the text of T 3 which were taken up into T 4. At this time the story was that Thráin and Thorin accompanied Thrór, but made their escape. – Much later the dates of the war were changed from 2766–9 to 2793–9.

36 'the fourteenth Thain': that is, of the Took line.

37 The statement here that Thráin had come to Dol Guldur seeking for one of the Seven Rings is strange, for the story that he received Thrór's ring and that it was taken from him in the dungeons of Sauron goes back to the earliest text of *The Council of Elrond* (VI.398, 403). It seems to be a lapse without more significance; see further p. 252.

38 The date of the death of the Steward Belecthor II in all three texts of *The Heirs of Elendil* is 2872. The date 2852 in the later typescripts of the Tale of Years and in Appendix B is evidently a casual error.

39 In text C of *The Heirs of Elendil* (p. 206) the final desolation of Ithilien, where however Gondor keeps hidden strongholds, is placed in the time of the Steward Túrin II (2882–2914). In Appendix B the corresponding entry is given under 2901.

*Note on changes made to the manuscript T 4
of the Tale of Years*

(i) The Stoors

c.1150 The original entry was covered by a pasted slip that cannot be removed, but the underlying text as printed (p. 229) can be read with fair certainty. The replacement differs only in the statement concerning the Stoors: after coming into Eriador by the Redhorn Pass 'some then moved south towards Dunland; others dwelt for a long time in the angle between the Loudwater and the Hoarwell.'

c.1400 This entry was struck out and replaced by another under the year 1600, but the date was then changed to 1550. This was almost the same as the rejected form, but for 'some of the Stoors return to Wilderland' has 'the northern Stoors leave the Angle and return to Wilderland'.

On the evolution of the early history of the Stoors see pp. 66–7, §§22–3.

THE TALE OF YEARS OF THE THIRD AGE 251

(ii) Saruman

c.2000   The far earlier coming of Saruman to Isengard (see note 26) was allowed to stand, but the reference to his becoming the head of the White Council in 2060 (note 28) was removed with the displacement of its forming to four hundred years later (2463). See p. 262, note 5.

2851   Saruman next appears in this entry, which was changed to read:

> He does not reveal his thought to the Council, but sets a watch upon Anduin and the Gladden Fields, where he himself secretly searches for the One Ring.

The words of the original text 'and he fortifies Isengard' were presumably struck out while the manuscript was in progress, since they reappear under 2911 (where they were again removed).

2911   The last sentence in the original text was altered to 'He redoubles the search for the Ring, but he says nothing to the Council.'

2940   This entry was not changed.

2953   The conclusion of this long entry, after the words 'the Power of the One Ring', was expanded thus:

> The White Council meets and debates concerning the Rings, fearing especially that Sauron may find the One. Saruman feigns that he has discovered that it passed down Anduin to the Sea. He then withdraws to Isengard and fortifies it, and consorts no more with members of the Council. But Mithrandir (Gandalf) journeys far and wide ...

The new text then returns to the original. (Saruman's pretence that he knew that the Ring had gone down Anduin to the Sea had been cut out of the entry for 2851, and the reference to his fortifying Isengard from that for 2911.)

c.3000   The last sentence of the original text was replaced thus:

> His spies bring him rumours of Sméagol-Gollum and his ring, and of Bilbo of the Shire. He is angry that Gandalf should have concealed this matter from him; and he spies upon Gandalf, and upon the Shire.

(iii) Gollum

c.2000 and c.2010   These entries concerning the finding of the Ring and Gollum's disappearance were struck out and replaced by additions under 2463 and 2470 (the dates in Appendix B). Many other additions were made concerning Gollum, but these are closely similar to those in Appendix B. There is no mention of his 'becoming acquainted with Shelob' under 2980, but an addition to the original entry for 3001 says 'About this time Gollum was captured and taken to Mordor and there held in prison.'

(iv) The return of Sauron to Mordor

In the original text of T 4 it was said in the entry for 2953 that Sauron declared himself and his true name, re-entered Mordor prepared for him by the Ringwraiths, and rebuilt Barad-dûr. In the revision, an addition was made to 2941: 'The Sorcerer returns in secret to Mordor which the Ringwraiths have prepared for him'; and at the same time the entry for 2953 was altered to read: 'At this time Sauron, having gathered fresh power, openly declares himself and his true name again, and claims Lordship over the West. He rebuilds Barad-dûr ...'

The corresponding dates in Appendix B are 2942 and 2951.

(v) The Dwarves

The statement under 2850 that Thráin went to Dol Guldur seeking one of the Seven Rings (see note 37) was replaced thus: 'Thráin was the possessor of the last of the Seven Rings of Power to survive destruction or recapture; but the ring was taken from him in Dol Guldur with torment, and he died there.' At the same time a new entry was added for the year 2840: 'Thráin the Dwarf goes wandering and is captured by the Sorcerer (about 2845?)'.

The entry for 2590 recording the founding of the realm of Erebor was changed to read: 'In the Far North dragons multiply again. Thrór ... comes south and re-establishes the realm of Erebor ...' At the same time, at the end of the entry, this addition was made: 'He was the great-great-grandson of Thráin I Náin's son' (which does not agree with the genealogical table in Appendix A, RK p. 361: see pp. 276–7).

For the correction of the entry for 1960 (the accession of Eärnil II to the throne of Gondor after a long interregnum) see note 23.

All the revisions of T 4 given above were taken up into the typescript T 5 as it was first made.

IX
THE MAKING OF APPENDIX A

(I) THE REALMS IN EXILE

As with the major manuscript T 4 of the Tale of Years given in the last chapter, I believe that years passed after the making of the manuscript C of *The Heirs of Elendil* (pp. 191 ff.) before my father took up the matter again, with a view to its radical alteration, when *The Lord of the Rings* was assured of publication. His later work on this, almost entirely in typescript, is extremely difficult to explain.

The earliest text, which I will call I, of the later period is a very rough typescript which begins thus:

The Heirs of Elendil

There is no space here to set out the lines of the kings and lords of Arnor and Gondor, even in such brief form as they appear in the Red Book. For the compiling of these annals the Hobbits must have drawn both on the books of lore in Rivendell, and on records made available to them by King Elessar, such as the 'Book of the Kings' of Gondor, and the 'House of the Stewards'; for until the days of the War of the Ring they had known little of such matters, and afterwards were chiefly interested in them in so far as they concerned Elessar, or helped in the correction of the dating of their own annals.

The line of Arnor, the Heirs of Isildur. After Elendil and Isildur there were eight high kings in Arnor, ending with Eärendur. The realm of Arnor then became divided, and the kings ceased to take names in High-elven form. But the line was maintained by Amlaith son of Eärendur, who ruled at Fornost.

After Amlaith there were thirteen kings[1] at Fornost, of whom the last was Arvedui, the twenty-fifth of the line. When he was lost at sea, the kingship came to an end in the North, and Fornost was deserted; but the line was continued by the Lords of the Dúnedain, who were fostered by Elrond.

Of these the first was Aranarth son of Arvedui, and after him there followed fifteen chieftains, ending with Aragorn II, who became king again both of Arnor and Gondor.

It was the token and the marvel of the Northern line that, though their power departed and their people dwindled to few, through all the many generations the succession was unbroken from father to son. Also, though the length of the lives of the Dúnedain grew ever less in Middle-earth, and their waning was swifter in the North, while the kings lasted in Gondor, afterwards it was otherwise; and many of the chieftains of the North lived still to twice the age of the oldest of other Men. Aragorn indeed lived to be one hundred and ninety years of age, longer than any of his line since Arvegil son of King Argeleb II; but in Aragorn the dignity of the kings of old was renewed, and he received in some measure their former gifts.

In his opening words 'There is no space here to set out the lines of the kings and lords of Arnor and Gondor' my father was surely thinking of *The Heirs of Elendil* in the elaborate form it had reached in the manuscript C. Merely to set out the names and dates of the rulers would take little enough space, yet that would serve little purpose in itself. It seems plain that he either knew or feared that he would be under severe constraint in the telling of the history of the Realms in Exile; but it seems extraordinary that he should have felt impelled to reduce the history of Arnor and the later petty realms almost to vanishing point.

After the passage given above, however, he continued with *The line of Gondor, the Heirs of Anárion*, and here he adopted another course: to give 'excerpts' from the history of Gondor. He began with a passage that remained with little change as the opening paragraph of the section *Gondor and the Heirs of Anárion* in Appendix A (I, iv); but then passed at once to 'the first great evil' that came upon Gondor, the civil war of the Kin-strife, thus omitting the first fourteen centuries of its history. This was quite briefly told, and was followed by a short account of 'the second and greatest evil', the plague that came in the reign of Telemnar; and that by 'the third evil', the invasion of the Wainriders. He had recounted the marriage of Arvedui, last king in the North, to the daughter of King Ondohir, and the great victory of Eärnil in 1944, when he abandoned the text.

One might suppose that he perceived that, in so short a space as he had determined was necessary, this would not work. The 'excerpts' could not stand in isolation without further explanation. At the end of this text he had written that the northern kingdom could send no aid to Gondor 'for Angmar renewed its attack upon Arthedain': yet neither Angmar nor Arthedain had been mentioned. What was required (one might think) was a brief précis of the whole history of the two kingdoms; but as will be seen in a moment, this was not at all what he had in mind.

It is notable that at this stage he said very little about the sources for the history; and it seems probable that his conception of them was still very undeveloped.

In a second text, II, still with the same title, he substantially expanded the opening passage:

Until the War of the Ring the people of the Shire had little knowledge of the history of the Westlands beyond the traditions of their own wanderings; but afterwards all that concerned the King Elessar became of deep interest to them, while in the Buckland the tales of Rohan were no less esteemed. Thus the Red Book from its beginning contained many annals, genealogies, and traditions of the realms of the South, drawn through Bilbo from the books of lore in Rivendell, or through Frodo and Peregrin from the King himself, and from the records of Gondor that he opened to them: such as 'The Book of the Kings and Stewards' (now lost), and the *Akallabêth*, that is 'The Downfall of Númenor'.[2] To this matter other notes and tales were added at a later date by other hands, after the passing of Elessar.

There is no space here to set out this matter, even in the brief forms in which it usually appears in the Book; but some excerpts are given that may serve to illustrate the story of the War of the Ring, or to fill up some of the gaps in the account.

My father now expressly referred to 'excerpts' from the Red Book. He retained from text I the very brief statement concerning the Northern Line; and in the section on the Southern Line he did as he had done in I, omitting all the history of Gondor before the Kin-strife. But when he came to the story of the civil war he expanded it to ten times its length in I. One may wonder what his intention now was in respect of the shape and length of this Appendix; but I doubt whether he was thinking of such questions when he wrote it. The historian of Gondor reasserted himself, and he told the story as he wished to tell it.

The remarkable thing is that this text was the immediate forerunner of the story of the Kin-strife as it was published in Appendix A (in the First Edition: in the Second Edition the events leading to it were altered and expanded, see p. 258).[3] And at the words 'Eldakar ... was king for fifty-eight years, of which ten were spent in exile' (RK p. 328) text II was abandoned in its turn.[4]

In a third text, III, my father retained the actual first page of II, carrying the opening remarks on the sources and the scanty statement on the Northern Line. For the Southern Line he entered, as before, immediately into the history of the Kin-strife, and brought the text virtually word for word to its form in Appendix A in the First Edition. Then, having recounted the plague and the invasion of the Wainriders without much enlarging what was said in text I, he wrote a very full account of the claim of Arvedui on the southern crown: and this was for most of its length word for word the text in Appendix A, beginning 'On the death of Ondohir and his sons ...' (RK p. 329), with the record of the exchanges between Arvedui and the Council of Gondor, and the appearance of Malbeth the Seer who named him Arvedui at his birth. The only difference is the absence of the reference to the Steward Pelendur, who in the Appendix A text is said to have 'played the chief part' in the rejection of the claim.

He then went on, in a passage that was again retained in Appendix A (RK pp. 330–1), to describe the message of Eärnil to Arvedui, the fleet sent into the North under Eärnur, and the destruction of Arthedain by Angmar. The story of the defeat of the Witch-king (RK pp. 331–2) had not yet been written; and with a brief reference to the overthrow of Angmar my father continued with 'It was thus in the reign of King Eärnil, as later became clear, that the Witch-king escaping from the North came to Mordor ...' With the account of the character of Eärnur (RK p. 332) text III ends.[5]

By now it can be seen how the long account of the Realms in Exile in Appendix A came into being. Strange as it seems, the evidence of the texts described above can lead only to this conclusion: that what began as an attempt (for whatever reason) to reduce the rich material of *The Heirs of Elendil* in a more than drastic fashion developed by steps into a long and finely written historical essay taking up some twenty printed pages. What considerations made this acceptable in relation to the requirements of brevity, in the absence of any evidence external to the texts themselves I am entirely unable to explain.

There are three versions of a brief text, which I will call IV for it certainly followed III, in which the opening section of Appendix A (I *The Númenórean Kings*. (i) *Númenor*), RK pp. 313 ff., is seen emerging. The opening paragraph 'Fëanor was the greatest of the Eldar in arts and lore ...', very briefly recounting the history of the Silmarils, the rebellion of Fëanor, and the war against Morgoth, was not present in the First Edition, where, as here in IV, the section opened with the words 'There were only three unions of the High Elves and Men ...'; but at this stage my father had not yet introduced the brief history of Númenor (RK pp. 315 ff., beginning 'As a reward for their sufferings in the cause against Morgoth ...'), which arose from his attempt to curtail and compress the Tale of Years of the Second Age (see pp. 180–1), and the passage concerning the Choice of Elros and Elrond, here called *i·Pheredhil*, differed from that published.

At the end of the First Age an irrevocable choice was given to the Half-elven, to which kindred they would belong. Elros chose to be of Mankind, and was granted a great life-span; and he became the first King of Númenor. His descendants were long-lived but mortal. Later when they became powerful they begrudged the choice of their forefather, desiring the immortality within the life of the world that was the fate of the Elves. In this way began their rebellion which, under the evil teaching of Sauron, brought about the Downfall of Númenor and the ruin of the ancient world.

Elrond chose to be of Elvenkind, and became a master of wisdom. To him therefore was granted the same grace as to those of the High Elves that still lingered in Middle-earth: that when weary at last of the mortal lands they could take ship from the Grey Havens and pass into the Uttermost West, notwithstanding the change of the world. But to the children of Elrond a choice was also appointed: to pass with him from the circles of the world; or if they wedded with one of Mankind, to become mortal and die in Middle-earth. For Elrond, therefore, all chances of the War of the Ring were fraught with sorrow.

Elros was the first king of Númenor, and was afterwards known by the royal name of Tar-Minyatur.

The fourth king of Númenor was Tar-Elendil. From his daughter Silmarien came the line of the Lords of Andúnië, of whom Amandil the Faithful was the last.

Elendil the Tall was the son of Amandil. He was the leader of the remnant of the Faithful who escaped from the Downfall with the Nine Ships, and established realms in exile in the North-west of Middle-earth. His sons were Isildur and Anárion.

Then follows in IV the lists of the kings, chieftains, and stewards of the Realms in Exile much as they are given in Appendix A (RK pp. 318–19). The references to Númenor in the passage just given were of course removed when the much longer account was introduced.

The Choice of the Children of Elrond as stated here differs notably from that in the final form, in the express statement that they would choose mortality if they chose to wed a mortal. In the text T 4 of the Tale of Years (p. 234, entry for the year 2300), as also in T 3, the choice is (as here in Appendix A): 'if [Elrond] departed they should have then the choice either to pass over the Sea with him, or to become mortal, if they remained behind.'[6]

After the abandoned text III, in which the account of the Northern Line was still confined to half a page, there is scarcely any rejected, preliminary material before the final typescript from which section I (iii) of Appendix A was printed, *Eriador, Arnor, and the Heirs of Isildur*. On the evidence of the extant texts this final typescript was the very one in which my father first set down the history of the North Kingdom in continuous narrative form. The story of Arvedui and the Lossoth, the Snowmen of Forochel, RK pp. 321–2, 'wrote itself' in precisely the form in which it was printed. But this is scarcely credible (see p. 279).

At the end of the story of the Lossoth, however, my father is seen in rejected pages taking a course that he decided against. At the end of the penultimate paragraph of this section (concerning the journeys of King Elessar to Annúminas and the Brandywine Bridge, RK p. 324) he continued: 'Arador was the grandfather of the king', and typed out part of a new text of the story of Aragorn and Arwen, which after some distance was abandoned. On this matter see the next section of this chapter, pp. 268 ff.

The next section of Appendix A, I (iv), *Gondor and the Heirs of Anárion*, is a fearful complex of typescript pages. Though it is possible to unravel the textual history up to a point,[7] it defies presentation, which is in any case unnecessary. The whole complex clearly belongs to one time. It was now that new elements entered the history, notably the story of the overthrow of the Witch-king of Angmar (RK pp. 331–2), and the account of the service of Aragorn under the name Thorongil with the Steward Ecthelion II (only referred to in a brief sentence in *The Heirs of Elendil*, p. 206), and of his relations with Denethor (RK pp. 335–6).

Note on the expansion of the tale of the Kin-strife in the Second Edition

In the First Edition of *The Lord of the Rings* the account of the Kin-strife (or more accurately of the events leading to it) was much briefer than that in the Second Edition, and read as follows (RK pp. 325–6 in both editions):[8]

Nonetheless it was not until the days of Rómendacil II that the first great evil came upon Gondor: the civil war of the Kin-strife, in which great loss and ruin was caused and never fully repaired.

'The Northmen increased greatly in the peace brought by the power of Gondor. The kings showed them favour, since they were the nearest in kin of lesser Men to the Dúnedain (being for the most part descendants of those peoples from whom the Edain of old had come); and they gave them wide lands beyond Anduin south of Greenwood the Great, to be a defence against men of the East. For in the past the attacks of the Easterlings had come mostly over the plain between the Inland Sea and the Ash Mountains.

'In the days of Rómendacil II their attacks began again, though at first with little force; but it was learned by the King that the Northmen did not always remain true to Gondor, and some would join forces with the Easterlings, either out of greed for spoil, or in the furtherance of feuds among their princes.

'Rómendacil therefore fortified the west shore of Anduin as far as the inflow of the Limlight, and forbade any stranger to pass down the River beyond the Emyn Muil. He it was that built the pillars of the Argonath at the entrance to Nen Hithoel. But since he needed men, and desired to strengthen the bond between Gondor and the Northmen, he took many of them into his service and gave to some high rank in his armies.

'In return he sent his son Valacar to dwell for a while with Vidugavia, who called himself the King of Rhovanion, and was indeed the most powerful of their princes, though his own realm lay between Greenwood and the River Running. There Valacar was wedded to Vidugavia's daughter, and so caused later the evil war of the Kin-strife.

'For the high men of Gondor already looked askance at the Northmen among them ...

From here the text of the Second Edition returns to that of the First, but there was a further alteration in the next paragraph, where the First Edition had: 'To the lineage of his father he added the fearless spirit of the Northmen. When the confederates led by descendants of the kings rose against him ...', inserting the sentence 'He was handsome and valiant, and showed no sign of ageing more swiftly than his father.'

As I have mentioned earlier (p. 190), in 1965, the year before the publication of the Second Edition, my father wrote a new version of this account; this he inserted into the late typescript copy D of *The Heirs of Elendil*. It is remarkable that though this new text was incorporated, in more concise form, into Appendix A, he actually wrote it as an addition to the text of *The Heirs of Elendil*, to be placed beneath the nineteenth king Rómendakil II, whose entry (see p. 198) he emended, on the typescript D, thus (the dates refer to birth, lifespan, and death):

19   Rómendakil II   1126   240   1366
     (Minalkar)   (Lieutenant of the King 1240, King 1304)

In the text of the First Edition there was no reference to the name Rómendacil as having been taken by Calmacil's son after his victory over the Easterlings in 1248, and indeed there was no mention of the victory. In the Second Edition, in the list of the Kings of Gondor (RK p. 318), the original text 'Calmacil 1304, Rómendacil II 1366, Valacar' was altered to 'Calmacil 1304, Minalcar (regent 1240–1304), crowned as Rómendacil II 1304, died 1366, Valacar'.

There is no need to give the whole of the new version, since the substance of it was largely retained in the revised text of Appendix A, but there are some portions of it that may be recorded. As originally composed, it opened:

Narmakil[9] and Kalmakil were like their father Atanatar lovers of ease; but Minalkar elder son of Kalmakil was a man of great force after the manner of his great-grandsire Hyarmendakil, whom he revered. Already at the end of Atanatar's reign his voice was listened to in the councils of the realm; and in 1240 Narmakil, wishing to be relieved of cares of state, gave him the new office and title of *Karma-kundo* 'Helm-guardian', that is in terms of Gondor Crown-lieutenant or Regent. Thereafter he was virtually king, though he acted in the names of Narmakil and Kalmakil, save in matters of war and defence over which he had complete authority. His reign is thus usually dated from 1240, though he was not crowned in the name of Rómendakil until 1304 after the death of his father. The Northmen increased greatly in the peace brought by the power of Gondor. ...

In the long version there is a footnote to the name *Vinitharya*: 'This, it is said, bore much the same meaning as *Rómendakil*.' After the birth of Vinitharya this version continues:

Rómendakil gave his consent to the marriage. He could not forbid it or refuse to recognize it without earning the enmity of Vidugavia. Indeed all the Northmen would have been angered, and those in his service would have been no longer to be trusted. He therefore waited in patience until 1260, and then he recalled Valakar, saying that it was now time that he took part in the councils of the realm and the command of its armies. Valakar returned to Gondor with his wife and children; and with them came a household of noble men and women of the North. They were welcomed, and at that time all seemed well. Nonetheless in this marriage lay the seeds of the first great evil that befell Gondor: the civil war of the Kin-strife, which brought loss and ruin upon the realm that was never fully repaired.

Valakar gave to his son the name Eldakar, for public use in Gondor; and his wife bore herself wisely and endeared herself to all those who knew her. She learned well the speech and manners of Gondor, and was willing to be called by the name Galadwen, a rendering of her Northern name into the Sindarin tongue. She was a fair and noble lady of high courage, which she imparted to her children; but though she lived to a great age, as such was reckoned among her people, she died in 1344 [*in one copy* > 1332]. Then the heart of Rómendakil grew heavy, foreboding the troubles that were to come. He had now long been crowned king, and the end of his reign and life were drawing nearer. Already men were looking forward to the accession of Valakar when Eldakar would become heir to the crown. The high men of Gondor had long looked askance at the Northmen among them, who had borne themselves more proudly since the coming of Vidumavi. Already among the Dúnedain murmurs were heard that it was a thing unheard of before that the heir to the crown, or any son of the King should wed one of lesser race, and short-lived; it was to be feared that her descendants would prove the same and fall from the majesty of the Kings of Men.

20 Valakar   1194   238   crowned 1366 1432

Valakar was a vigorous king, and his son Eldakar was a man of great stature, handsome and valiant, and showed no sign of ageing more swiftly than his father. Nonetheless the disaffection steadily grew during his reign; and when he grew old there was already open rebellion in the southern provinces. There were gathered many of those who declared that they would never accept as king a man half of foreign race, born in an alien country. 'Vinitharya is his right name,' they said. 'Let him go back to the land where it belongs!'

NOTES

1 'thirteen kings' is an error for 'fourteen kings'.
2 This was almost exactly retained as the opening to Appendix A in the First Edition, as far as the reference to the *Akallabêth*, but *The Book of the Kings and Stewards* was separated into two works, which were not said to be lost. (The old opening to Appendix A was replaced in the Second Edition by an entirely new text, and the *Note on the Shire Records* was added at the end of the Prologue.) The published text then continued:

> From Gimli no doubt is derived the information concerning the Dwarves of Moria, for he remained much attached to both Peregrin and Meriadoc. But through Meriadoc alone, it seems, were derived the tales of the House of Eorl; for he went back to Rohan many times, and learned the language of the Mark, it is said. For this matter the authority of Holdwine is often cited, but that appears to have been the name which Meriadoc himself was given in Rohan. Some of the notes and tales, however, were plainly added by other hands at later dates, after the passing of King Elessar.
>
> Much of this lore appears as notes to the main narrative, in which case it has usually been included in it; but the additional material is very extensive, even though it is often set out in brief and annalistic form. Only a selection from it is here presented, again greatly reduced, but with the same object as the original compilers appear to have had: to illustrate the story of the War of the Ring and its origins and fill up some of the gaps in the main account.

The absence in the present text of the references to Gimli and Meriadoc as sources possibly suggests that my father had not yet decided to include sections on Rohan and the Dwarves in this

Appendix (although brief texts entitled *The House of Eorl* and *Of Durin's Race* were in existence).

3 This version lacked the account (RK pp. 327–8) of the great white pillar above the haven of Umbar set up in memorial of the landing of Ar-Pharazôn in the Second Age. The name of the King of Rhovanion was Vinitharya; this was corrected on the typescript to Vidugavia, and the name Vinitharya made that of Eldakar in his youth.

4 At the top of the page on which this account begins my father wrote, then or later, 'Hobbit-annal of the Kin-strife'.

5 After the words 'Many of the people that still remained in Ithilien deserted it' text III continues 'It was at this time that King Eärnil gave Isengard to Saruman.' This agrees with the statement in the text T 4 of the Tale of Years in the entry c.2000: see p. 233 and note 26, and p. 251.

6 In the two earlier versions of text IV the conclusion of the passage was extended, that of the first reading:

> Therefore to Elrond all chances of the War of the Ring would bring grief: to fly with his kin from ruin and the conquering Shadow, or to be separated from Arwen for ever. For either Aragorn would perish (and he loved him no less than his sons); or he would wed Arwen his daughter when he had regained his inheritance, according to the condition that Elrond himself had made when first their love was revealed. (See III.252, 256).

7 My father's almost exclusive use of a typewriter at this time greatly increases the difficulty of elucidating the textual history. His natural method of composition in manuscript was inhibited; and he constantly retyped portions of pages without numbering them.

8 The quotation marks indicated 'actual extracts from the longer annals and tales that are found in the Red Book'.

9 My father reverted to the use of *k* instead of *c* in this text.

(II) THE TALE OF ARAGORN AND ARWEN

Of the texts of *Aragorn and Arwen* the earliest in succession is also very plainly the first actual setting down of the tale. It was not 'a part of the tale', as it came to be called in Appendix A, and was indeed quite differently conceived. It is a rough, much corrected manuscript, which I will call 'A', and a portion of it is in typescript (not separate, but taking up from manuscript and returning to it on the same pages). Unless this peculiarity itself suggests that it belongs with the late work on the Appendices, there seems to be no clear and certain evidence of its relative date; but its peculiar subsequent history may indicate that it had been in existence for some time when my father was working on the narrative of the Realms in Exile described in the preceding section.

The manuscript, which bears the title *Of Aragorn and Arwen Undómiel*, begins thus.

In the latter days of the last age [> Ere the Elder Days were ended],[1] before the War of the Ring, there was a man named Dírhael [> Dírhoel], and his wife was Evorwen [> Ivorwen] daughter of Gilbarad, and they dwelt in a hidden fastness in the wilds of Eriador; for they were of the ancient people of the Dúnedain, that of old were kings of men, but were now fallen on darkened days. Dírhael [> Dírhoel] and his wife were of high lineage, being of the blood of Isildur though not of the right line of the Heirs. They were both foresighted in many things. Their daughter was Gilrain, a fair maid, fearless and strong as were all the women of that kin. She was sought in marriage by Arathorn, the son of Arador who was the Chieftain of the Dúnedain of the North.

Arathorn was a stern man of full years; for the Heirs of Isildur, being men of long life (even to eight score years and more) who journeyed much and went often into great perils, were not accustomed to wed until they had laboured long in the world. But Gilrain was younger than the age at which women of the Dúnedain were wont at that time to take husbands; and she did not yet desire to be a wife, and sought the counsel of her parents. Then Dírhael said: 'Arathorn is a mighty man, and he will be Lord of the Dúnedain sooner than men look for, yet soon again he will be lord no longer; for I forebode that he will be short-lived.' But Evorwen said: 'That may well be, yet if these two wed, their child shall be great among the great in this age of the world, and he shall bring the Dúnedain out of the shadows.'

Therefore Gilrain consented and was wedded to Arathorn; and it came to pass that after one year Arador was taken by trolls and slain in the Coldfells, and Arathorn became Lord of the Dúnedain; and again after one year his wife bore a son and he was named Aragorn. And Aragorn being now the son of the Heir of Isildur went with his mother and dwelt in the House of Elrond in Imladris, for such was the custom in that day, and Elrond had in his keeping the heirlooms of the Dúnedain, chief of which were the shards of the sword of Elendil who came to Middle-earth out of Númenor at its downfall. In his boyhood Arathorn also had been fostered in that house, and he was a friend of Elladan and Elrohir, the sons of Elrond, and often he went a-hunting with them. Now the sons of Elrond did not hunt wild beasts, but they pursued the Orcs wherever they might find them; and this they did because of Celebrían their mother, daughter of Galadriel.

On a time long ago, as she passed over the Mountains to visit her mother in the Land of Lórien, Orcs waylaid the road, and she was taken captive by them and tormented; and though she was rescued by Elrond and his sons, and brought home and tended, and her hurts of body were healed, she lay under a great cloud of fear and she loved Middle-earth no longer; so that at the last Elrond granted her prayer, and she passed to the Grey Havens and went into the West, never to return.

Thus it befell that when Aragorn was only two years of age Arathorn went riding with the sons of Elrond and fought with Orcs that had made an inroad into Eriador, and he was slain, for an orc-arrow pierced his eye; and so he proved indeed short-lived for one of his race, being no more than sixty winters when he fell.

But the child Aragorn became thus untimely Chieftain of the Dúnedain, and he was nurtured in the House of Elrond, and there he was loved by all, and Elrond was a father to him. Straight and tall he grew with grey eyes both keen and grave, and he was hardy and valiant and strong of wit, and eager to learn all lore of Elves and Men.

And when he was still but a youth, yet strong withal, he went abroad with Elladan and Elrohir and learned much of hunting and of war, and many secrets of the wild. But he knew naught of his own ancestry, for his mother did not speak to him of these things, nor any else in that House; and it was at the bidding of Elrond that these matters were kept secret. For there was at that time a Shadow in the East that crept over many lands, and filled the Wise with foreboding, since they had discovered that this was indeed the shadow of Sauron, the Dark Lord that had returned to Middle-earth again, and that he desired to find the One Ring that Isildur took, and sought to learn if any heir of Isildur yet lived upon earth; and the spies of Sauron were many.

But at length, when Aragorn was twenty years of age, it chanced that he returned to Imladris ...

I leave the original manuscript here, for this is sufficient to show the nature of its relation to the published text: the latter being marked by a general reduction, compression of what was retained and omission of allusive passages, notably the story of Celebrían.² But as will be seen, the reason for this was not, or was not primarily, the result of a critical view taken by my father of the telling of the tale, but of the use to which he later thought of putting it.

From this point the final version offers no contradiction to the original text, and in fact remains closer to it than in the part that I have cited,³ until the plighting of troth by Aragorn and Arwen on the hill of Kerin Amroth (RK p. 341); soon after this, however, it diverges altogether.

And there upon that hill they looked east to the shadow and west to the twilight, and they plighted their troth and were glad. Yet many years still lay between them.⁴

For when Elrond learned the choice of his daughter he did not forbid it; but he said to Aragorn: 'Not until you are come to your full stature shall you wed with Arwen Undómiel, and she shall not be the bride of any less than a king of both Gondor and Arnor.'

But the days darkened in Middle-earth, as the power of Sauron grew, and in Mordor the Dark Tower of Barad-dûr rose ever taller and stronger. And though Aragorn and Arwen at times met briefly again their days were sundered. For the time drew on now to the War of the Ring at the end of that age of the world ...

There follows now a long passage (more than 500 words, with a part of it rejected and replaced by a new version) in which the history of the war is given in summary: telling of Mithrandir and the Halflings, the doubts of the Wise, the Ringwraiths, the Company of the Ring, and the quest of the Ringbearer; and then more expressly of Aragorn, of the Paths of the Dead, the Pelennor Fields, the battle before the Morannon, and his crowning at the gates of Minas Tirith. At the end of this the tale moves quickly to its conclusion.

And when all this was done Elrond came forth from Imladris and Galadriel from Lórien, and they brought with them Arwen Undómiel Evenstar of her people. And she made the choice of Lúthien, to become mortal and abide in Middle-earth, and she was wedded to Aragorn Arathornsson, King of Gondor and Arnor, and she was Queen and Lady of Elves and Men.

Thus ended the Third Age. Yet it is said that bitterest of all the sorrows of that age was the parting of Arwen and Elrond. For they were sundered by the Sea and by a doom beyond the end of the world. For when the Great Ring was unmade the Three Rings of the Elves failed also, and Elrond was weary of Middle-earth at last and departed seeking Celebrían, and returned never again. But Arwen became a mortal woman, and yet even so it was not her lot to die until she had lost all that she gained. For though she lived with Aragorn for five score years after and great was their glory together, yet at the last he said farewell and laid him down and died ere old age unmanned him. But she went from the city and from her children, and passed away to the land of Lothlórien, and dwelt there alone under the fading trees: for Galadriel also was gone and Lórien was withering. And then at last, it is said, she laid herself to rest upon Kerin Amroth; and there was her green grave, until all the world was changed, and all the days of her life utterly forgotten by men that came after, and elanor and nifredil bloomed no more east of the Sea.[5]

This earliest manuscript was followed by a fair copy of it in typescript ('B'), in which only a few and minor changes were introduced.[6] But the whole of the latter part of it, from the beginning of the account of the War of the Ring and its origins, was struck out, and my father clipped to the typescript new pages, in which he extended that account to nearly twice its original length. Most of this new version was then again rewritten, at even greater length, and attached as a rider to the typescript. It was now much less of a résumé than it was at first, and its purpose in the work as a whole is clearly seen. 'It was the part of Aragorn,' my father wrote, 'as Elrond foresaw, to be the chief Captain of the West, and by his wisdom yet more than his valour to redress the past and the folly of his forefather Isildur.' I cite a part of it from this final form.

Thus the War of the Ring began; and the shards of the sword of Elendil were forged anew, and Aragorn Arathorn's son arose and fulfilled his part, and his valour and wisdom were revealed to Men. Songs were made after in Gondor and Arnor concerning his deeds in that time which long were remembered, but are not here full-told. It was not his task to bear the burden of the Ring, but to be a leader in those battles by which the Eye of Sauron was turned far from his own land and from the secret peril which crept upon him in the dark. Indeed, it is said that Sauron believed that the Lord Aragorn, heir of Isildur, had found the Ring and had taken it to himself, even as his forefather had done, and arose now to challenge the tyrant of Mordor and set himself in his place.

But it was not so, and in this most did Aragorn reveal his strength; for though the Ring came indeed within his grasp, he took it not, and refused to wield its evil power, but surrendered it to the judgement of Elrond and to the Bearer whom he appointed. For it was the hard counsel of Elrond that though their need might seem desperate and the time overlate, nonetheless the Ring should even now be taken in secret, if it might be, to the land of their Enemy and there cast into the fire of Mount Doom in Mordor where it was made. Aragorn guided the Ringbearer on the long and perilous journey from Imladris in the North, until he was lost in the wild hills and passed beyond the help of his friends. Then Aragorn turned to war and the defence of the City of Gondor, Minas Tirith upon Anduin, the last bulwark of the westlands against the armies of Sauron.

In all this time, while the world darkened and Aragorn was abroad in labour and danger, Arwen abode in Imladris; and there from afar she watched over him in thought, and in hope under the Shadow she wrought for him a great and royal standard, such as only one might display who claimed the lordship of the Númenóreans and the inheritance of Elendil and Isildur. And this she sent to him by the hands of his kinsfolk, the last of the Dúnedain of the North; and they came upon Aragorn on the plain of Rohan, after the battles in which Saruman the traitor was overcome and Isengard destroyed, and they delivered to Aragorn the standard of Arwen and her message; for she bade him look to the peril from the sea, and to take the Paths of the Dead. Now this was a way beneath the White Mountains of Gondor that no man dared to tread, because of the fell wraiths of the Forgotten Men that guarded it. But Aragorn dared to take that way with the Grey Company of the North, and he passed through, and so came about by the shores of the sea, unlooked-for by foe or by friend. Thus he captured the ships of the Enemy, and came up out of the deep by the waters of Anduin to the succour of Gondor in the hour of its despair; for the city of Minas Tirith was encircled by the armies of Mordor and was perishing in flame. Then was fought and won beyond hope the great battle of the Fields of Pelennor, and the Lord of the Black Riders was destroyed; but Aragorn unfurled the standard of Arwen, and in that day men first hailed Aragorn as king.

At the end of this account of Aragorn's commanding significance in the War of the Ring, the revised ending of the story in the typescript B concludes with his farewell to Arwen at his death almost exactly as it stands in Appendix A.[7] The original manuscript pages in which my father first set down this inspired passage are preserved. He wrote them so fast that without the later text scarcely a word would be interpretable.

The revised text in B ends with the words 'Here endeth the tale of the Elder Days'. My father altered this in manuscript to 'Here endeth the Tale, and with the passing of the Evenstar all is said of the Elder Days.'

Briefly to recapitulate, the typescript B as originally made had been scarcely more than a clear text of the original rough manuscript A. The latter part of it was rewritten and expanded (Aragorn's part in the War of the Ring, his dying words with Arwen) and incorporated into the typescript. My father then made a further typescript ('C'), which was a fair copy of the text as it now stood in B, much of it indeed scarcely necessary. At this stage, therefore, none of the compression and small stylistic changes that distinguish the original manuscript from the final form in Appendix A had yet entered. It still began 'Ere the Elder Days were ended', still included the story of Celebrían, and of course the major element of Aragorn's part in the War of the Ring; in relation to the final version all it lacked was Aragorn's parting from his mother Gilrain (RK p. 342).

It is hard to say how my father saw *Aragorn and Arwen* at that time, when he clearly felt that it was in finished form, or where it should stand. He took great pains with the story of Aragorn which was afterwards lost. He ended it with great finality: 'Here endeth the Tale, and with the passing of the Evenstar all is said of the Elder Days.' Can it have been his intention that it should stand as the final element of *The Lord of the Rings*?

The subsequent history is very curious. I have mentioned (p. 258) that when writing the narrative of the North Kingdom he experimented with the introduction of the story of Aragorn and Arwen. This was to follow the account of how, when King Elessar came to the North, Hobbits from the Shire would visit him in his house in Annúminas (RK p. 324); and it enters on the typescript page with extraordinary abruptness (even allowing for the device of supposed extracts from written sources to account for such transitions):

> ... and some ride away with him and dwell in his house as long as they have a mind. Master Samwise the Mayor and Thain Peregrin have been there many times.
> Arador was the grandfather of the King. ...

It may seem that my father did not know what to do with the story, or perhaps rather, did not know what it might be possible to do with it. But it was here, strangely enough, that the abbreviation and compression and stylistic 'reduction' that distinguishes the final form of *Aragorn and Arwen* from the original version first entered. The text in these abandoned pages of 'The Realms in Exile' is (if not quite at all points) that of the story in Appendix A.[8] It extended only to the words 'She shall not be the bride of any Man less than the King of both Gondor and Arnor' (RK p. 342); but in manuscript notes accompanying it my father sketched out a reduction of the story of Aragorn's part in the War of the Ring to a few lines: for this element in the original story was obviously wholly incompatible with such a placing of it – which would seem in any case unsuitable and unsatisfactory. He obviously thought so too. But it is interesting to see that in the final typescript from which the story as it stands in Appendix A was printed the page on which it begins still carries at the top the words 'Master Samwise the Mayor and Thain Peregrin have been there many times', struck out and replaced by 'Here follows a part of the Tale of Aragorn and Arwen'. 'A part', presumably, because so much had gone.

A few changes were made to this last typescript of the tale, among them the substitution of *Estel* for *Amin* (see note 8) at all occurrences, and the introduction of the departure of Gilraen from Rivendell (RK p. 342) and her parting with Aragorn, with the words *Onen i-Estel Edain, ú-chebin estel anim*.

Thus the original design of the tale of Aragorn and Arwen had been lost; but the actual reason for this was the abandoned experiment of inserting it into the history of the North Kingdom. I can say no more of this strange matter.

NOTES

1 So also Aragorn declared to Arwen on his deathbed that he was 'the latest King of the Elder Days' (RK p. 343), and at the end of text B of the primary version 'with the passing of the Evenstar all is said of the Elder Days' (p. 268). See p. 173 and note 7.

2 On the other hand, while the concealment of Aragorn's ancestry from him in his youth was present in the original form of the tale, the giving to him of another name (*Estel* in the final version, see note 8) was not.

3 The distinction between 'thou' and 'you' was clearly made in the original manuscript, though sometimes blurred inadvertently, and it was retained and made precise in the text that followed it: thus Aragorn uses 'you' to Elrond, and to Arwen at their first meeting, whereas Elrond and Arwen address him with 'thou, thee'.

4 Thus their words together on Kerin Amroth, concerning the Shadow and the Twilight, were not yet present; see note 6.

5 The last sentences are put in the present tense in the published text. But when my father wrote *Aragorn and Arwen* he did not conceive it as a citation from an ancient source, and did not place it all within quotation marks.

6 To this text were added in a rider the words of Aragorn and Arwen on Kerin Amroth (see note 4); but after Arwen's words the passage

ended: 'For very great was her love for her father; but not yet did Aragorn understand the fullness of her words.'

7 There were a few differences from the final form. When Arwen spoke of 'the gift of Eru Ilúvatar' which is bitter to receive, Aragorn answered: 'Bitter in truth. But let us not be overthrown at the final test, who fought the Shadow of old. In sorrow we must go, for sorrow is appointed to us; and indeed by sorrow we do but say that that which is ended is good. But let us not go in despair.' He named himself 'the latest King of the Elder Days' (see note 1), but when he was dead 'long there he lay, an image of the splendour of the Kings of Men in glory undimmed, before the passing of the Elder Days and the change of the world': this was altered on the typescript to 'before the breaking of the world'. And at the moment of his death Arwen did not cry 'Estel, Estel!', for the name given to him in his youth had not yet arisen (see notes 2 and 8).

8 It was in this text that Aragorn's name in Rivendell entered, but here it was *Amin*, not *Estel*, though likewise translated 'Hope'. Here Aragorn's mother's name became *Gilraen* for earlier *Gilrain*, and Ivorwen's father Gilbarad disappeared.

(III) THE HOUSE OF EORL

The history of Appendix A II, *The House of Eorl*, has no perplexities. From the early period of my father's work on the Appendices there are three brief texts, which I will refer to as I, II, and III, probably written in close succession, and with the third he had evidently achieved a satisfactory formulation of all that he wished to say of the rulers of the Mark. As I judge, he then put it aside for a long time.

It seems that the names of the Kings of the Mark were first set down on paper in the course of the writing of the chapter *The Last Debate*: when Gimli in his story of the Paths of the Dead (at that time placed at this point in the narrative) spoke of the mailclad skeleton by the closed door and Aragorn's words 'Here lies Baldor son of Brego', my father interrupted the story with the list of names, to which he added dates in the Shire-reckoning (see VIII.408). I concluded that it was only the dates of Fengel, Thengel, and Théoden that belong with the writing of the manuscript; but it is a striking fact that already at that time the dates of those kings were not greatly different from those in Appendix A (RK p. 350). Particularly noteworthy is that of the birth of Théoden, S.R.1328 = 2928. In text I it remains 2928 (in both I and II the dates were all still given in Shire-reckoning, but it is more convenient to convert them); so also in II, but corrected to 2948 (the final date). In the draft manuscript T 3 of the Tale of Years it was 2928, but in T 4 (p. 239) it was 2948. This is sufficient to show that these early texts of *The House of Eorl* were contemporary with those texts of the Tale of Years.

In the first two texts my father was chiefly concerned with the elaboration of the chronology in detail, and they consist only of the names of the kings and their dates,[1] with notes added to a few of them. In I, which was written very rapidly on a small sheet, under Eorl the Field of Celebrant and the gift of Rohan are mentioned, and it is said that he began the building of Meduseld and died in battle against Easterlings in the Wold in 2545; of Brego that he drove them out in 2546, completed Meduseld, and died of grief for his son Baldor in 2570; of Aldor the Old that 'he first established Dunharrow as a refuge-fort'. In the note on Helm, however, is seen the first appearance of the tale told in Appendix A, very hastily written and still undeveloped:

> In his day there was an invasion from west of Dunlanders and of S. Gondor by pirates and by Easterlings and Orcs. In 2758 in the Long Winter they took refuge in Helm's Deep.[2] Both his sons Háma and Haeleth were killed (lost in snow). At his death there was in the kingdom an upstart king Wulf not of Eorl's line [who] with help of Dunlanders tried to seize throne. Eventually Fréalaf son of Hild his sister and nearest heir was victorious and became king. A new line of mounds was started to symbolize break in direct line.

There are no notes on the Kings of the Second Line save Fengel, of whom it is recorded that he was the youngest son of Folcwine, for his elder brothers, named here Folcwalda and Folcred, were 'killed in battle in service of Gondor against Harad'. The final note in I states that Éomer was the son of Théoden's sister Théodwyn (who does not appear in the narrative), and that 'he wedded Morwen daughter of Húrin of Gondor'. This is Húrin of the Keys, who was in command of Minas Tirith when the host of the West rode to the Black Gate (RK p. 237); I do not think that there is any other reference to the marriage of Éomer with his daughter, who was corrected on the text to Lothíriel daughter of Prince Imrahil.

The second text II was a fair copy of I, with scarcely any change in content other than in detail of dates. Where in I it was said only that Eorl was 'born in the North', in II he was 'born in Irenland in the North'. This name was struck out and replaced by *Éothéod*, and this is very probably where that name first appeared (it is found also in both texts of the original 'Appendix on Languages', p. 34, §14). It was now further said of Éomer that he 'became a great king and extended his realm west of the Gap of Rohan to the regions between Isen and Greyflood, including Dunland.'[3]

The last text (III) of this period was a finely written manuscript which begins with a brief account of the origin of the Rohirrim in the Men of Éothéod and their southward migration.

The House of Eorl

Eorl the Young was lord of the Men of Éothéod. This land lay near the sources of the Anduin, between the upper ranges of the Misty Mountains and the northernmost parts of Mirkwood. Thither the Éothéod had removed some hundreds of years before from lands further south in the vale of Anduin. They were originally close kin of the Beornings and the men of the west-eaves of the forest; but they loved best the plains and wide fields, and they delighted in horses and in all feats of horsemanship. In the days of Garman father of Eorl they had grown to a numerous people somewhat straitened in the land of their home.

In the two thousand five hundred and tenth year of the Third Age a great peril threatened the land of Gondor in the South and wild men out of the East assailed its northern borders, allying themselves with Orcs of the mountains. The invaders overran and occupied Calenardon, the great plains in the north of the realm. The Steward of Gondor sent north for help, for there had ever been friendship between the men of Anduin's vale and the people of Gondor. Hearing of the need of Gondor from afar Eorl set out with a great host of riders; and it was chiefly by his valour and the valour of the horsemen of Éothéod that victory was obtained. In the great battle of the Field of Celebrant the Easterlings and Orcs were utterly defeated and the horsemen of Eorl pursued them over the plains of Calenardon until not one remained.

Cirion Steward of Gondor in reward gave Calenardon to Eorl and his people, and they sent north for their wives and their children and their goods, and they settled in that land. They named it anew the Mark of the Riders, and themselves they called the Eorlingas; but in Gondor the land was called Rohan, and the people the Rohirrim (that is the Horse-lords). Thus Eorl became the first King of the Mark, and he chose for his dwelling a green hill before the feet of the White Mountains that fenced in that land at the south.

This is the origin of the opening, greatly expanded, of *The House of Eorl* in Appendix A (RK pp. 344–5). In the remainder of the text, the line of the Kings of the Mark, there was very little further development: the story of Helm Hammerhand remained in substance exactly as it was, and nothing further was said of any of the kings except Thengel, Théoden, and Éomer. Of Thengel it is recorded that he married late, and had three daughters and one son, but his long sojourn in Gondor (and the character of his father Fengel that led to it) had not emerged. The death of Éomund chief Marshal of the Mark in an Orc-raid in 3002 is recorded, with the note that 'Orcs at this time began often to raid eastern Rohan and steal horses', and the fostering of his children Éomer and Éowyn in the house of Théoden. The note on Théoden that entered in III was retained almost unchanged in Appendix A.[4]

A long note was now appended to Éomer, with the same passage as is found in Appendix A (RK p. 351, footnote) concerning Éowyn, 'Lady of the Shieldarm', and the reference to Meriadoc's name Holdwine given to him by Éomer; and the statement of the extent of his realm appearing in II (p. 271) was rewritten: 'In Éomer's time the realm was extended west beyond the Gap of Rohan as far as the Greyflood and the sea-shores between that river and the Isen, and north to the borders of Lórien, and his men and horses multiplied exceedingly.'

There is no other writing extant before the final typescript of *The House of Eorl* from which the text in Appendix A was printed, save for a single typescript page. This is the first page of the text, beginning 'Eorl was the lord of the Men of Éothéod', and my father wrote it with the old version III, given above, before him; but he expanded it almost to the form that it has in Appendix A.[5] It includes, however, the following passage (struck out on the typescript) after the words 'the Riders hunted them over the plains of Calenardhon':

> In the forefront of the charge they saw two great horsemen, clad in grey, unlike all the others, and the Orcs fled before them; but when the battle was won they could not be found, and none knew whence they came or whither they went. But in Rivendell it was recorded that these were the sons of Elrond, Elladan and Elrohir.[6]

There is also the curious point that where in Appendix A it is said that 'Cirion ... gave Calenardhon between Anduin and Isen to Eorl and his people' this text had (before correction) 'Cirion ... gave Calenardhon, and Dor Haeron between Entwash and Isen, to Eorl and his people'. I do not know of any other occurrence of this name, or of any other suggestion that the name Calenardhon applied only to the region east of the Entwash.

The father of Eorl was still named Garman, as in the old version III (p. 272), and that name appeared in the final text, where it was emended to Léod.

It is, once again, possible and indeed probable that this page survived for some reason from a complete or more complete draft, which has been lost; for if no text has been lost it would have to be concluded that my father composed *ab initio* on the typewriter the whole narrative of *The House of Eorl*, with the stories of Léod and the horse Felaróf, and of Helm Hammerhand, exactly as it stands in Appendix A.

NOTES

1 As far as Folcwine the fourteenth king the dates were already in I almost the same as those in Appendix A, though in many cases differing by a year; it was only with the last kings that there was much movement in the dates.
2 Cf. the entry in the text T 4 of the Tale of Years, entry 2758–9 (p. 236): 'Helm of Rohan takes refuge from his enemies in Helm's Deep in the White Mountains'; and also the note to the Steward Beren in *The Heirs of Elendil*, p. 205.
3 In text II Helm's son Haeleth became Haleth; and the eleventh king Léof was replaced probably at the time of writing by Brytta (on this see IX.68 and note 11). The sons of Folcwine (Folcwalda and Folcred in I) were not named in II, but my father changed Fengel to Fastred; he then added in the names of Folcwine's sons as Folcred and Fastred and changed that of the king to Felanath, before finally reverting to Fengel. In the manuscript T 4 of the Tale of Years (p. 238, year 2885) the death of Folcwine's sons 'in the service of Gondor' is recorded, and there their names are Folcred and Fastred.
4 The note on Théoden in III ends with the statement that his only child and son was Théodred 'whose mother Elfhild of Eastfold died in childbirth', and a record of Théodred's death in battle against Saruman. Théoden's name *Ednew* ('Renewed') is here given in the Old English form *Edníwe*; and Minas Tirith is called *Mundberg* (although text II has *Mundburg*: on which see VII.449, note 7, and VIII.356, note 9).
5 In the First Edition there were no notes, in the list of the Kings of the Mark, to the eleventh, twelfth, and thirteenth kings, Brytta, Walda, and Folca.
6 Cf. p. 236, annal 2510.

(IV) DURIN'S FOLK

My father's original text of what would become the section *Durin's Folk* in Appendix A is extant: a brief, clear manuscript written on scrap paper entitled *Of Durin's Line*, accompanied by a genealogy forming a part of the text. It was corrected in a few points, and one substantial passage was added; these changes were made, I think, at or soon after the writing of the manuscript. I give this text in full, with the changes shown where they are of any significance.

Durin was the name of one of the fathers of all the race of the Dwarves. In the deeps of time and the beginning of that people he came to Azanulbizar, the Dimrill Dale, and in the caves above Kibil-nâla [> Kheled-zâram],[1] the Mirrormere, in the east of the Misty Mountains, he made his dwelling, where after were the Mines of Moria renowned in song. There long he dwelt: so long that he was known far and wide as Durin the Deathless. Yet he died indeed at the last ere the Elder Days were ended, and his tomb was in Moria; but his line never failed, from father to son, and ever and anon [> thrice][2] there was born an heir to that house so like unto his Forefather that he received the name of Durin, being held indeed by the Dwarves to be the Deathless that returned. It was after the end of the First Age that the great power and wealth of Moria began, for it was enriched by many folk and much lore and craft, when the ancient cities of Nogrod and Belegost were ruined in the change of the western world and the breaking of Morgoth. And it came to pass that / at the height of the glory of Moria [> in the midst of the Third Age, while the wealth of Moria was still undiminished] Durin was the name of its king, being the second since the Forefather that had borne that title. And the Dwarves delved deep in his days, seeking ever for *mithril*, the metal beyond price that was found in those mines alone, beneath Barazinbar, the mighty Redhorn Mountain. But they roused thus from sleep a thing of terror that had lain hidden at the foundations of the world, and that was a Balrog of Morgoth. And Durin was slain by the Balrog, and after him Náin his son was slain, and the glory of Moria passed, and its people were destroyed or fled far away. For the most part they passed into the North; but Thráin Náin's son, the king by inheritance, came to Erebor, the Lonely Mountain, nigh to the eastern eaves of Mirkwood, and established his realm for a while.

But Glóin his grandson [> Thorin his son] removed and abandoned Erebor, and passed into the far North where the most of his kin now dwelt. But it came to pass that dragons arose and multiplied in the North, and made war upon the Dwarves, and plundered their works and wealth; and many of the Dwarves fled again southward and eastward. Then Thrór Dáin's son, the great-great-grandson of Thráin, returned to Erebor and became King-under-the-Mountain, and prospered exceedingly, having the friendship of all that dwelt near, whether Elves or Men or the birds and beasts of the land.

But Smaug the Golden heard rumour of his treasure and came upon him at unawares, and he descended upon the Mountain in flame, and destroyed all that region, and he entered the deep halls of the Dwarves and lay there long upon a bed of gold. / And it is elsewhere told how the Dwarves were avenged, [> From the sack and the burning Thrór escaped, and being now homeless he returned to Moria, but there was slain in the dark by an Orc. Thráin his son and Thorin his grandson gathered then the scattered folk of Durin's race and made war on the Orcs of the Misty Mountains in revenge for Thrór. They were victorious but their people were so diminished that they could not and dared not re-enter Moria. Dáin their kinsman went away to the Iron Hills, but Thráin and Thorin became wanderers. Thráin, it is said, was the possessor of the last of the Seven Rings of the Dwarf-lords of old, but he was captured by the Sorcerer and taken to Dol Guldur, and there perished in torment. Elsewhere is told of the wanderings of Thorin Oakenshield, last of the direct line of Durin,[3] in search of revenge and the restoration of his fortune; and how by the help of Gandalf the Grey he was indeed avenged at last,][4] and Smaug was slain, and after the Battle of Five Armies the kingship under the Mountain was restored. Yet Thorin Oakenshield, grandson of Thrór, was slain in that battle, and the right line was broken, and the crown passed to Dáin, a kinsman of Thorin. And the line of Dáin and the wealth and renown of the kingship endured in Erebor until the world grew old, and the days of the Dwarves were ended.

In this text and its accompanying genealogical table (which I have here redrawn) it is seen that an important advance had been made from the text T 4 of the Tale of Years, where it was told under the year 2590 that Thrór 'founded the realm of Erebor' (p. 236): as I said in a note on that entry, 'the history of Thrór's ancestors had not yet emerged'.[5] Here that history is present, but not yet precisely in the final form; for the names of 'the kings of Durin's folk' in the genealogical table here run Thorin I : Glóin : Dáin I, whereas in that in Appendix A they are Thorin I : Glóin : Óin : Náin II : Dáin I; thus in the present text Thrór is called 'the great-great-grandson of Thráin [I]'. While the history was at this stage the corrections and additions were made to T 4: see p. 252, *The Dwarves*.

Various names found in the later genealogy are absent here, Thrór's brother Frór and Thorin Oakenshield's brother Frerin; most notably, the brother of Dáin I is not Borin but Nár (and of his descendants only Óin and Glóin are shown). Nár was the name of the sole companion

277

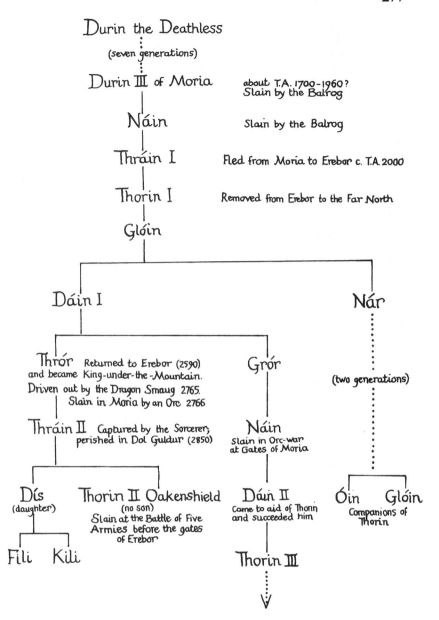

of Thrór on his ill-fated journey to Moria (RK pp. 354–5), who brought to Thráin the news of his father's slaying by Azog; he is called 'old', but there is no suggestion that he was Thrór's uncle. Since *Nár* is an Old Norse dwarf-name (occurring in the Völuspá), and since there is no evidence that the story of Thrór's death (apart of course from the fact of his having been killed in Moria by an Orc) had yet emerged, it seems unlikely that there was any connection between the two. – It will also be seen that while Thorin III appears, Durin the Last does not.

This text was followed by a second version, a well-written and scarcely corrected manuscript with the title *Of Durin's Race*, very similar in appearance to text III of *The House of Eorl* (p. 272) and probably contemporary with it. So closely did my father preserve the original text (as emended and expanded) that I think that it must have followed at once, or at any rate after no long interval.

The passage added to the first version was slightly filled out and improved, but the only difference worth noticing here lies in the sentences following the words 'made war on the Orcs of the Misty Mountains in revenge for Thrór', which now read: 'Long and deadly was that war, and it was fought for the most part in dark places beneath the earth; and at the last the Dwarves had the victory, and in the Battle before the Gate of Moria ten thousand Orcs were slain. But the Dwarves suffered also grievous loss and his folk were now so diminished that Thráin dared not to enter Moria, and his people were dispersed again.' The only really significant difference from the first version, however, lies in the final sentence, which became:

> And the line of Dáin prospered, and the wealth and renown of the kingship was renewed, until there arose again for the last time an heir of that House that bore the name of Durin, and he returned to Moria; and there was light again in deep places, and the ringing of hammers and the harping of harps, until the world grew old and the Dwarves failed and the days of Durin's race were ended.

Thus it was here that 'Durin the Last' emerged, and it is said of him that he returned from Erebor to Moria and re-established it (as is said in the accompanying genealogical table). To this my father never referred again; as Robert Foster noted in *The Complete Guide to Middle-earth*, 'There is no mention of a recolonization of Khazad-dûm in the Fourth Age, despite the death of the Balrog.' It is impossible to discover whether my father did in fact reject this idea, or whether it simply became 'lost' in the haste with which the Appendices were finally prepared for publication. The fact that he made no reference to 'Durin VII and Last', though he appears in the genealogy in Appendix A, is possibly a pointer to the latter supposition.

There are two copies of the genealogical table accompanying the second version, but they are essentially the same: my father made the second one simply because he had not left enough space in the first and the names on the right-hand side had to be cramped (as with the other 'finished' manuscripts of that time he clearly intended this to be in publishable form as it stood, or at any rate to be in a form from which a perfectly accurate typescript could be made). In these tables he did little more than copy the preceding version (p. 277), but there are certain differences. He retained 'seven generations' between Durin the Deathless and Durin III of Moria, but carefully erased 'seven' and replaced it by 'twelve' (later pencilling 'many'). The name Nár of the brother of Dáin I was replaced by Borin, and where the original table only marks 'two generations' between Nár and Óin and Glóin this is now filled out as in the final table, with Fundin the father of Balin and Dwalin and Gróin the father of Óin and Glóin; but a space is left blank for Borin's son Farin. The notes and dates in the original table remain the same, with no additions that need be recorded, save 'Balin returned to Moria and there perished (2994)', and the same note concerning Ori, Nori, Dori, Bifur, Bofur, and Bombur as appears in the final genealogy. Thorin III is now called 'Stonehelm', and 'Durin the Last' is shown as his son, 'who re-established the Realm of Moria'; beneath his name is a dotted arrow (as beneath Thorin III in the original table) indicating unnamed descendants.

There is no other writing on this subject from the early period of work on the Appendices. But unlike the textual situation in the case of the Northern Line of the Realms in Exile and of *The House of Eorl*, in which the final typescripts have virtually no antecedents (see pp. 257–8, 273–4), a substantial part of *Durin's Folk* is extant in a draft typescript leading directly to that sent to the printer. My father did indeed achieve in that draft a form that required little further work, but it was achieved through much rewriting as he typed.[6] This underlines, I think, the extreme improbability that those other texts came into being at once in a form that required scarcely any further change; and therefore supports the conclusion that a good deal of the late drafting in typescript has been lost.

But in this case, at any rate, the loss of the draft typescript would have done little more than distort the textual development in some details; it would have deprived this history only of the Dwarvish name *Zigilnâd* of the Silverlode (cf. *Zirak-zigil* 'Silvertine', VII.174–5, note 22) – in itself surprising, in view of *Kibil-nâla* in *The Lord of the Rings* (see note 1).

The draft typescript, however, became rough manuscript, though still closely approaching the final form (RK pp. 356–7), with the story of the great burning of the dead at the end of the Battle of Azanulbizar, and the departure of Thráin and Thorin Oakenshield to Dunland and afterwards to a new home in exile in the Blue Mountains, where they prospered, though forced to work with iron. This section ends, as in the published text, 'But, as Thrór had said, the Ring needed gold to breed gold, and of that or any other precious metal they had little or none.' My father drew a line here, as if the text were completed; but the mention of the Ring of Thráin led him to say something further about it. From this point the manuscript becomes rougher, and as it proceeded he wrote so fast that it is only barely legible and with much difficulty; and from this point also the published text soon departs from it altogether.

This Ring was the last of the Seven. It may well be that this was known to Sauron, and that the singular misfortunes of his House were due to that. For the days were passed when it would bring profit, but demanded payment rather, and its possession brought only the hate of Sauron. For the Dwarves had proved hard to tame. They were too tough, being made of a purpose to resist such onslaughts of evil will and power, and though they could be slain or broken they could not be made into shadows or slaves of any other will; and for like reason their lives were little affected, to live either longer or shorter because of the Ring.[7] The more did Sauron hate them. Nonetheless each possessor kept his ring as a secret unless he surrendered it; and though those about him doubtless guessed it, none knew for certain that Thráin had the Ring.

Partly by the very power of the Ring therefore Thráin after some years became restless and discontented. He could not put the thought of gold and gems out of his mind. Therefore at last when he could bear it no longer his heart turned again to Erebor and he resolved to return. He said little to Thorin of what was in his heart. But with Balin and Dwalin and a few others he arose and said farewell and departed (2841).

Little indeed is known of what happened to him afterwards. It would seem (from afterknowledge) that no sooner was he abroad with few companions (and certainly after he came at length back into Rhovanion) he was hunted by the emissaries of Sauron. Wolves pursued him, orcs waylaid him, evil birds shadowed his path, and the more he tried to go north the more he was driven back. One dark night, south of Gladden and the eaves of Mirkwood, he vanished out of their camp, and after long search in vain his companions gave up hope (and returned to Thorin). Only long after was it known that he had been taken alive and brought to the pits of Dol Guldur (2845). There he was tormented and the Ring taken from him; and there at last (2850) he died.[8]

So it would seem that Moria had ended and the line of Durin. After the sack of Erebor Thorin Oakenshield was but 24 (and not yet war-worthy according to Dwarf-custom); but he was 53 at Nanduhirion, and there fought in the van of the assault. But as has been told the first assault was thrown back, and Thráin and Thorin were driven for refuge in a thicket that grew in the valley not far from Kheledzâram before the great burning. There Frerin Thráin's son fell and Fundin his cousin and many others, and both Thráin and Thorin were wounded. Thorin's shield was cloven and he cast it away, and hewing with an axe a branch of an oak tree he held it in his left hand to ward off the strokes of his foes or to wield as a club. Thus he got his name, or also because in memory of this he bore ever after at his back a shield made of oak wood without colour or device, and vowed to do so until he was hailed again as king.[9]

When Thráin went away Thorin was 95, a great dwarf of proud bearing and full manhood. Maybe because rid of the Ring, Thorin long remained in Ered Luin, labouring and journeying and gathering such wealth as he could, until his people had fair houses in the hills, and were not [? ill content], though in their songs they spoke ever of the Lonely Mountain and the wealth and bliss of the Great Hall and the light of the Arkenstone. But the years lengthened, and the embers of his heart began to grow hot as Thorin brooded on the wrongs of his house and people. Remembering too that Thrór had lain upon him the vengeance due to Smaug.

But Erebor was far away and his people only few; and he had little hope that Dáin Ironfoot would help in any attempt upon the dragon. For Thorin thought ever after the manner of his kingly forefathers, counting forces and weapons and the chances of war, as his hammer fell on the red iron in his forge.

It was at this point that Mithrandir entered the story of the House of Durin. He had before troubled himself little with Dwarves. He was a friend to those of good will, and liked well the exiles of Durin's Folk that dwelt in the west. But on a time it happened that Mithrandir was passing west through Eriador (journeying to see Cirdan, maybe, or to visit the Shire which he had not entered for some years) when he fell in with Thorin Oakenshield going the same way, and they spoke much together on the road, and at Bree where they rested.

In the morning Mithrandir said to Thorin: 'I have thought much in the night. Now if that seems good to you I will come home with you for a while and we will talk further in greater privacy.' From this meeting there came many events of great moment in the matter of the War of the Ring. Indeed it led to the finding of the Ring and to the involvement of the Shire-folk and the means whereby the Ring was at last destroyed. Wherefore many have supposed that all this Mithrandir purposed and foresaw. But we believe that is not so. For Frodo wrote this passage in the first copy of the Red Book, which because of its length was not included in the tale of the War: *Those were glad days when after the crowning we dwelt in the fair house in Minas Tirith with Gandalf ...*

I have given the text thus far in order to make clearer than I did, or indeed was able to do, in the section *The Quest of Erebor* in *Unfinished Tales* how my father originally introduced the story of Gandalf and Thorin, and the taking of Bilbo on the journey to the Lonely Mountain, into the appendix on *Durin's Folk*. At that time I was unaware of this text, and have only recently put it together from its dismembered parts, not having realised what they were. I assumed that the manuscript which I called A in *Unfinished Tales* was the original text; but the story that follows from the point where I have left it above was my father's first expression of the idea, and A was a (moderately) fair copy, much rewritten if not essentially changed.[10]

He did a great deal of work on this story before 'it had to go', as he said years later (*Unfinished Tales* p. 11). From the manuscript A he developed the typescript B (of which long extracts were given in *Unfinished Tales*), and B was clearly designed to fit into the text of *Durin's Folk* as it existed by then (see *Unfinished Tales* pp. 327–8).[11] I shall not follow here the evolution in expression and structure through the texts, but I give two notes that belong with the original manuscript, the first of which shows my father's initial thoughts on the story before he wrote it.

From 2842 onwards Thorin lives in exile, but a good many of Durin's Folk gather to him in Ered Luin. They are reduced to poverty (since mines are poor) and travel about as metal-workers. Thorin begins to think of vengeance on Smaug and recovery of his wealth, but he can only envisage this in terms of war – a gathering of all his people and an attempt to slay Smaug. But it is difficult to do. The Iron Hills are a long way away and elsewhere Durin's Folk are widely scattered.

Gandalf now takes a hand. (Since his action led ultimately to the finding of the Ring, and the successful part played by the Hobbits in its destruction, many suppose that all this was in his conscious purpose. Probably not. He himself would say he was 'directed', or that he was 'meant' to take this course, or was 'chosen'.[12] Gandalf was incarnate, in [?real] flesh, and therefore his vision was obscured: he had for the most part (at any rate before his 'death') to act as ordinary people on reason, and principles of right and wrong.) His immediate conscious purposes were probably various. Largely strategic. He knows it is Sauron in Dol Guldur.[13] Knowing the situation in Gondor he may very well have feared the reoccupation of Mordor (but not yet). At present he is concerned with Lórien and Rivendell – Sauron will certainly proceed to war. The presence of Smaug and the depression of Men in the North makes an attack that way toward Angmar and against Rivendell likely. Also he knew and approved of Durin's Folk. Also he was very fond of the Shire-folk and appreciated ..... Bilbo. He wished the Shire-folk to be 'educated'[14] before evil days came, and chose Bilbo (unattached) as an instrument.

In the second passage he was revolving questions arising from Gandalf's finding of Thráin dying in Dol Guldur.

'Your plan is grandiose and belongs to an earlier day. If you wish to regain your wealth or any part of it, you will have to go yourself – with a small band of your most faithful kinsfolk and following.' [*Struck out*: He then reveals to Thorin that] Why did he not then (or much earlier) reveal to Thorin that he had met Thráin in Dol Guldur? Two answers. He had not met him [Thorin] and did not even know where he was. From 2850 on his chief concern had been with Dol Guldur (Saruman) and the Council. He had not been west for a long time (*Hobbit* pp. 13–14. The Old Took died in 2920, so Gandalf had not in 2942 been in the Shire for 22 years and then probably only briefly).[15] He was probably unaware who the Dwarf was in Dol Guldur, since the 7th Ring would be no clue (Dwarves kept the possession of Rings very secret), and Thráin did not know his own name (*Hobbit* p. 35). It was probably only from Thorin's conversation that he guessed – and produced the evidence characteristically at a suitable chance.

In the earliest version of the story (and also in the second text A) Gandalf made no mention of his finding Thráin in Dol Guldur until the very end of the text, in response to a question from Merry about the map and the key; and my father clearly introduced it when the problem discussed in this note presented itself.

'But about that map and key,' said Merry. 'They proved useful, but you never said anything to Thorin about this beforehand. Why, you must have kept them by your own account 100 years without a word!'

'I did,' said Gandalf, 'very nearly. 91 to be exact. But I assure you I could have done little else. Thráin did not know his own name when I found him; and I certainly did not know his. By what toughness of resistance he had kept the key and map hidden in his torments I don't know. Maybe having got the Ring Sauron troubled no further, but left him to rave and die. But of course the map told me the key had something to do with Erebor. But it was far from my concerns at the time. And for long after I was concerned with other matters, with Saruman and his strange reluctance to disturb Sauron in Dol Goldur. It was not until my meeting with Thorin and conversation that I suddenly guessed who the dying Dwarf must have been. Well, well, after that I kept the things back to the last moment. They just turned the scale, and began to make Thorin accept the idea.'[16]

Among other material for *Durin's Folk* are many versions of the genealogical table, beginning with one associated with the draft typescript in which the original form (see pp. 276–8) was still retained, with only five generations between Durin VI (formerly Durin III) and Thrór. The addition of (the first) Óin and Náin II arose when my father formulated a specific pattern of aging and life-span on a page headed 'Notes on Chronology of Durin's Line', from which I cite some extracts, very slightly edited for clarity.

Dwarves of different 'breeds' vary in their longevity. Durin's race were originally long-lived (especially those named Durin), but like most other peoples they had become less so during the Third Age. Their average age (unless they met a violent death) was about 250 years, which they seldom fell far short of, but could occasionally far exceed (up to 300).[17] A Dwarf of 300 was about as rare and aged as a Man of 100.

Dwarves remained young – e.g. regarded as too tender for really hard work or for fighting – until they were 30 or nearly that (Dáin II was very young in 2799 (32) and his slaying of Azog was a great feat). After that they hardened and took on the appearance of age (by human standards) very quickly. By forty all Dwarves looked much alike in age, until they reached what they regarded as old age, about 240. They then began to age and wrinkle and go white quickly (baldness being unknown among them), unless they were going to be long-lived, in which case the process was delayed. Almost the only physical disorder they suffered from (they were singularly immune from diseases such as affected Men, and Halflings) was corpulence. If in prosperous circumstances, many grew very fat at or before 200, and could not do much (save eat) afterwards. Otherwise 'old age' lasted not much more than ten years, and from say 40 or a little before to near 240 (two hundred years) the capacity for toil (and for fighting) of most Dwarves was equally great.

This is followed by the information attributed to Gimli concerning the Dwarf-women, which was preserved in Appendix A (RK p. 360). There is no difference in substance in the present text, except for the statements that they are never forced to wed against their will (which 'would of course be impossible'), and that they have beards. This latter is said also in the 1951 revision of the *Quenta Silmarillion* (XI.205, §5).

It is then said that Dwarves marry late, seldom before they are ninety or more,[18] that they have few children (so many as four being rare), and continues:

To these they are devoted, often rather fiercely: that is, they may treat them with apparent harshness (especially in the desire to ensure that they shall grow up tough, hardy, unyielding), but they defend them with all their power, and resent injuries to them even more than to themselves. The same is true of the attitude of children to parents. For an injury to a father a Dwarf may spend a life-time in achieving revenge. Since the 'kings' or heads of lines are regarded as 'parents' of the whole group, it will be understood how it was that the whole of Durin's Race gathered and marshalled itself to avenge Thrór.

Finally, there is a note on the absence of record concerning the women of the Dwarves:

They are seldom named in genealogies. They join their husbands' families. But if a son is seen to be 110 or so years younger than his father, this usually indicates an elder daughter. Thorin's sister Dís is named simply because of the gallant death of her sons Fili and Kili in defence of Thorin II. The sentiment of affection for sister's children was strong among all peoples of the Third Age, but less so among Dwarves than Men or Elves among whom it was strongest.

The concluding passage in Appendix A, concerning Gimli and Legolas, was derived from the old text of the Tale of Years (p. 244), which had now of course been abandoned.

NOTES

1 Since *Kheled-zâram* and *Kibil-nâla* as the Dwarvish names of Mirrormere and Silverlode entered early in the history of the writing of *The Lord of the Rings* (see VII.167, 174), it seems clear that the naming of Mirrormere *Kibil-nâla* here was a slip without significance, and is unlikely to have any connection with the curious appearance of the name *Zigilnâd* for Silverlode in the draft typescript of *Durin's Folk* (p. 279).
2 'thrice': the Durin who was slain by the Balrog in Moria is named in the accompanying genealogical table 'Durin III'.
3 Thorin Oakenshield was not the 'last of the direct line of Durin'; no doubt my father meant that he was the last in the unbroken descent of the kings from father to son (cf. 'the right line was broken' a few lines below).
4 This addition was roughly written in the margins, with a number of corrections, and the passage from 'They were victorious ...' to 'Dáin their kinsman went away to the Iron Hills' is put in the present tense.
5 The extension of the line beyond Thrór appears to have had its starting-point in my father's explanation of the words on Thrór's Map in *The Hobbit* ('Here of old was Thrain King under the Mountain') as referring not to Thráin son of Thrór but to a remote ancestor also named Thráin: see VII.160.
6 My father's method of composition at this time was to continue typing, without rejecting anything, as the sentences developed. A characteristic if extreme case is seen in Dáin's words to Thráin at the end of the Battle of Azanulbizar:

> Only I have passed seen looked through the Shadow of the Gate. Beyond the Shadow it waits for you still. The world must change and some other power than ours must come,   Durin's Bane   before   Some other power must come than ours must come, before Khazad-dûm   Durin's folk walk again in

By crossing out unwanted words and putting directions on the typescript he produced the passage that stands in Appendix A (RK p. 356).

7 In a draft for this passage my father wrote at this point the following, which was not repeated: 'The Ring-wearer became rich especially in gold: that is his dealings brought him wealth according to what he traded in: if in lead, lead, if in silver, silver, if in gems, then gems more abundant and of greater size and worth.'

THE MAKING OF APPENDIX A

8 This is where the story of how Thráin came to Dol Guldur was first told.

9 The deaths of Frerin and Fundin, and the retreat to the wood where Thorin cut the oak-bough from which he got his name (RK p. 355 and footnote), had not been mentioned in the draft typescript in the account of the Battle of Azanulbizar. The story that Thorin carried an unpainted shield of oak wood disappeared.

10 The tone and total effect of the original version, as my father dashed it down, is rather different from that of the subsequent texts, where the expression becomes a little more reserved. To give a single example, when Thorin (later Glóin) sneered at 'those absurd little rustics down in the Shire' (cf. *Unfinished Tales* p. 333), Gandalf riposted: 'You don't know much about those folk, Thorin. If you think them all that simple because they pay you whatever you ask for your bits of iron and don't bargain hard like some Men, you're mistaken. Now I know one that I think is just the fellow for you. Honest, sensible, and very far from rash – and brave.'

11 A begins with the words 'In the morning Thorin said to Mithrandir ...', and continues as in the third version B (*Unfinished Tales* p. 328): here it was Thorin who invited Gandalf to his home in the Blue Mountains, whereas in the earliest text (p. 282) it was Gandalf who proposed it. I do not know why A should have begun at this point.

12 There is here a direction to 'see LR I 65/71' (read '70'), which was thus already in print.

13 From this was derived a passage in the earliest version of the story:

> 'Well then, I was I suppose "chosen". But as far as I was aware, I had my reasons for what I did. Don't be abashed if I say that the chief in my mind was unconcerned with you: it was, well "strategic". When I met Thorin at Bree I had long known that Sauron was arisen again in Dol Guldur, and every day I expected him to declare himself.'

14 'Educated' is the word that Gandalf used in the original version of the passage given from the text B in *Unfinished Tales* p. 331.

> 'In 2941 I already saw that the Westlands were in for another very bad time sooner or later. Of quite a different sort. And I would like the Shire-folk to survive it, if possible. But to do that I thought they would want something a bit more than they had had before. What shall I say – the clannish sort of stocky, sturdy family feeling was not quite enough. They were become a bit parochial, forgetting their own stories, forgetting their own beginnings, forgetting what little they had known about the greatness and peril of the world – or of the allies they had

in it. It was not buried deep, but it was getting buried: memory of the high and noble and beautiful. In short, they needed education! I daresay he was "chosen", and I was chosen to choose him, but I picked on Bilbo as an instrument. You can't educate a whole people at once!'

15 The reference is to Gandalf's first appearance in *The Hobbit*: 'He had not been down that way under The Hill for ages and ages, not since his friend the Old Took died, in fact, and the hobbits had almost forgotten what he looked like.' – On the date of 'The Quest of Erebor' given here, 2942, see the Note below.

16 It was not until text B of *The Quest of Erebor* that Gandalf's account of his finding Thráin in Dol Guldur was moved back in the story (see *Unfinished Tales* p. 324), though still in that version Gandalf returned to it again at the end (*ibid.* p. 336).

17 It will be found in the genealogical table that the life-span of all the 'kings of Durin's Folk' from Thráin I to Náin II varied only between 247 and 256 years, and no Dwarf in the table exceeded that, save Borin (261) and Dwalin, who lived to the vast age of 340 (the date of his death appears in all the later texts of the table, although the first to give dates seems – it is hard to make out the figures – to make him 251 years old at his death).

18 In the genealogical table all the 'kings of Durin's Folk' from Náin I to Thorin Oakenshield were born either 101 or 102 (in one case 100) years after their fathers.

Note on the date of the Quest of Erebor

Among the papers associated with the original manuscript of the story my father set down some notes headed 'Dates already fixed in *printed* narrative are these:'

Bilbo born 2891 (1291). He was visited in 2942 by Thorin II, since that autumn he was 51 (*Lord of the Rings* Chapter I): therefore Battle of Five Armies was in same year, and Thorin II died then.

Thráin must have 'gone off' (to seek Erebor) in 2842 ('a hundred years ago', *Hobbit* p. 35). (It is thus assumed that after wandering he was caught in 2845 and died in dungeons 2850.)

Dáin II is said (LR I p. 241) 'to have passed his 250th year' in 3018. He was then, say, 251, therefore he was born in 2767 [the date given in the genealogy, RK p. 361].

My father had given the date of Bilbo's birth in 2891 in the Tale of Years (p. 238), and he here referred to it as a date 'fixed in printed narrative' (*The Fellowship of the Ring* was published in July 1954, and *The Two Towers* in November). But without Volume III the date is fixed in the following way: Frodo left Bag End in September 3018 (Gandalf's letter that he finally received at Bree was dated 'Midyear's Day, Shire Year, 1418'), and he left on his fiftieth birthday (FR p. 74), which was seventeen years after Bilbo's farewell party (when Frodo was 33); the date of the party was therefore 3001. But that was Bilbo's 111th birthday; and therefore he was born in — 2890. It seems only possible to explain this as a simple miscalculation on my father's part which he never checked, – or rather never checked until now, for in another note among these papers he went through the evidence and arrived at the date 2890 for Bilbo's birth, and therefore 2941 for Thorin's visit to him at Bag End. This new date had been reached by the time that the earliest version of *The Quest of Erebor* was written.

PART TWO

LATE WRITINGS

LATE WRITINGS

It is a great convenience in this so largely dateless history that my father received from Allen and Unwin a quantity of their waste paper whose blank sides he used for much of his late writing; for this paper consisted of publication notes, and many of the pages bear dates: some from 1967, the great majority from 1968, and some from 1970. These dates provide, of course, only a *terminus a quo*: in the case, for instance, of a long essay on the names of the rivers and beacon-hills of Gondor (extensively drawn on in *Unfinished Tales*) pages dated 1967 were used, but the work can be shown on other and entirely certain grounds to have been written after June 1969. This was the period of *The Disaster of the Gladden Fields, Cirion and Eorl,* and *The Battles of the Fords of Isen,* which I published in *Unfinished Tales*.

It was also a time when my father was moved to write extensively, in a more generalised view, of the languages and peoples of the Third Age and their interrelations, closely interwoven with discussion of the etymology of names. Of this material I made a good deal of use in the section *The History of Galadriel and Celeborn* (and elsewhere) in *Unfinished Tales*; but I had, of course, to relate it to the structure and content of that book, and the only way to do so, in view of the extremely diffuse and digressive nature of my father's writing, was by the extraction of relevant passages. In this book I give two of the most substantial of these 'essays', from neither of which did I take much in *Unfinished Tales*.

The first of these, *Of Men and Dwarves*, arose, as my father said, 'from consideration of the Book of Mazarbul' (that is, of his representations of the burnt and damaged leaves, which were not in fact published until after his death) and the inscription on the tomb of Balin in Moria, but led far beyond its original point of departure. From this essay I have excluded the two passages that were used in *Unfinished Tales,* the account of the Drúedain, and that of the meeting of the Númenórean mariners with the Men of Eriador in the year 600 of the Second Age (see pp. 309, 314). The second, which I have called *The Shibboleth of Fëanor,* is of a very different nature, as will be seen, and from this only a passage on Galadriel was used in *Unfinished Tales*; I have included also a long excursus on the names of the descendants of Finwë, King of the Ñoldor, which was my father's final, or at any rate last, statement on many of the great names of

Elvish legend, and which I used in the published *Silmarillion*. I have also given a third text, which I have called *The Problem of Ros*; and following these are some of his last writings, probably in the last year of his life (p. 377).

A word must be said of these 'historical-philological' essays. Apart from the very last, just referred to, they were composed on a typewriter. These texts are, very clearly, entirely *ab initio*; they are not developments and refinements of earlier versions, and they were not themselves subsequently developed and refined. The ideas, the new narrative departures, historical formulations, and etymological constructions, here first appear in written form (which is not to say, of course, that they were not long in the preparing), and in that form, essentially, they remain. The texts are never obviously concluded, and often end in chaotic and illegible or unintelligible notes and jottings. Some of the writing was decidedly experimental: a notable example is the text that I have called *The Problem of Ros*, on which my father wrote 'Most of this fails', on account of a statement which had appeared in print, but which he had overlooked (see p. 371). As in that case, almost all of this work was etymological in its inspiration, which to a large extent accounts for its extremely discursive nature; for in no study does one thing lead to another more rapidly than in etymology, which also of its nature leads out of itself in the attempt to find explanations beyond the purely linguistic evolution of forms. In the essay on the river-names of Gondor that of the Gwathló led to an account of the vast destruction of the great forests of Minhiriath and Enedwaith by the Númenórean naval builders in the Second Age, and its consequences (*Unfinished Tales* pp. 261–3); from the name *Gilrain* in the same essay arose the recounting of the legend of Amroth and Nimrodel (*ibid*. pp. 240–3).

In the three texts given here will be found many things that are wholly 'new', such as the long sojourn of the People of Bëor and the People of Hador on opposite sides of the great inland Sea of Rhûn in the course of their long migration into the West, or the sombre legend of the twin sons of Fëanor. There will also be found many things that run counter to what had been said in earlier writings. I have not attempted in my notes to make an analysis of every real or apparent departure of this kind, or to adduce a mass of reference from earlier phases of the History; but I have drawn attention to the clearest and most striking of the discrepancies. At this time my father continued and intensified his practice of interposing notes into the body of the text as they arose, and they are abundant and often substantial. In the texts that follow they are numbered in the same series as the editorial notes and are collected at the end of each, the editorial notes being distinguished by placing them in square brackets.

X
OF DWARVES AND MEN

This long essay has no title, but on a covering page my father wrote:
> An extensive commentary and history of the interrelation of the languages in *The Silmarillion* and *The Lord of the Rings*, arising from consideration of the Book of Mazarbul, but attempting to clarify and where necessary to correct or explain the references to such matters scattered in *The Lord of the Rings*, especially in Appendix F and in Faramir's talk in LR II.

'Faramir's talk' is a reference to the conclusion of the chapter *The Window on the West* in *The Two Towers*. To a rough synopsis of the essay he gave the title *Dwarves and Men*, which I have adopted.

The text was begun in manuscript, but after three and a half pages becomes typescript for the remainder of its length (28 pages in all). It was written on printed papers supplied by Allen and Unwin, of which the latest date is September 1969. A portion of the work was printed in *Unfinished Tales*, Part Four, Section 1, *The Drúedain*, but otherwise little use of it was made in that book. Unhappily the first page of the text is lost (and was already missing when I received my father's papers), and takes up in the middle of a sentence in a passage discussing knowledge of the Common Speech.

In relation to the first part of the essay, which is concerned with the Longbeard Dwarves, I have thought that it would be useful to print first what is said concerning the language of the Dwarves in the two chief antecedent sources. The following is found in the chapter on the Dwarves in the *Quenta Silmarillion* as revised and enlarged in 1951 (XI.205, §6):

> The father-tongue of the Dwarves Aulë himself devised for them, and their languages have thus no kinship with those of the Quendi. The Dwarves do not gladly teach their tongue to those of alien race; and in use they have made it harsh and intricate, so that of those few whom they have received in full friendship fewer still have learned it well. But they themselves learn swiftly other tongues, and in converse they use as they may the speech of Elves and Men with whom they deal. Yet in secret they use their own speech only, and that (it is said) is slow to change; so that even their realms and houses that have been long and far sundered may to this day well understand one another. In ancient days the Naugrim dwelt in many mountains

of Middle-earth, and there they met mortal Men (they say) long ere the Eldar knew them; whence it comes that of the tongues of the Easterlings many show kinship with Dwarf-speech rather than with the speeches of the Elves.

The second passage is from Appendix F, *Dwarves* (with which cf. the original version, p. 35, §15).

But in the Third Age close friendship still was found in many places between Men and Dwarves; and it was according to the nature of the Dwarves that, travelling and labouring and trading about the lands, as they did after the destruction of their ancient mansions, they should use the languages of men among whom they dwelt. Yet in secret (a secret which, unlike the Elves, they did not willingly unlock, even to their friends) they used their own strange tongue, changed little by the years; for it had become a tongue of lore rather than a cradle-speech, and they tended it and guarded it as a treasure of the past. Few of other race have succeeded in learning it. In this history it appears only in such place-names as Gimli revealed to his companions; and in the battle-cry which he uttered in the siege of the Hornburg. That at least was not secret, and had been heard on many a field since the world was young. *Baruk Khazâd! Khazâd ai-mênu!* 'Axes of the Dwarves! The Dwarves are upon you!'

Gimli's own name, however, and the names of all his kin, are of Northern (Mannish) origin. Their own secret and 'inner' names, their true names, the Dwarves have never revealed to any one of alien race. Not even on their tombs do they inscribe them.

Here follows the text of the essay which I have called *Of Dwarves and Men*.

... only in talking to others of different race and tongue, the divergence could be great, and intercommunication imperfect.[1] But this was not always the case: it depended on the history of the peoples concerned and their relations to the Númenórean kingdoms. For instance, among the Rohirrim there can have been very few who did not understand the Common Speech, and most must have been able to speak it fairly well. The royal house, and no doubt many other families, spoke (and wrote) it correctly and familiarly. It was in fact King Théoden's native language: he was born in Gondor, and his father Thengel had used the Common Speech in his own home even after his return to Rohan.[2] The Eldar used it with the care and skill that they applied to all linguistic matters, and being longeval and retentive in memory they tended indeed, especially when speaking formally or on important matters, to use a somewhat archaic language.[3]

The Dwarves were in many ways a special case. They had an ancient language of their own which they prized highly; and even when, as among the Longbeard Dwarves of the West, it had ceased to be their native tongue and had become a 'book-language', it was carefully preserved and taught to all their children at an early age. It thus served as a *lingua franca* between all Dwarves of all kinds; but it was also a written language used in all important histories and lore, and in recording any matters not intended to be read by other people. This Khuzdul (as they called it), partly because of their native secretiveness, and partly because of its inherent difficulty,[4] was seldom learned by those of other race.

The Dwarves were not, however, skilled linguists – in most matters they were unadaptable – and spoke with a marked 'dwarvish' accent. Also they had never invented any form of alphabetic writing.[5] They quickly, however, recognized the usefulness of the Elvish systems, when they at last became sufficiently friendly with any of the Eldar to learn them. This occurred mainly in the close association of Eregion and Moria in the Second Age. Now in Eregion not only the Fëanorian Script, which had long become a mode of writing generally used (with various adaptations) among all 'lettered' peoples in contact with the Númenórean settlements,[6] but also the ancient 'runic' alphabet of Daeron elaborated [> used] by the Sindar was known and used. This was, no doubt, due to the influence of Celebrimbor, a Sinda who claimed descent from Daeron.[7] Nonetheless even in Eregion the Runes were mainly a 'matter of lore' and were seldom used for informal matters. They, however, caught the fancy of the Dwarves; for while the Dwarves still lived in populous mansions of their own, such as Moria in particular, and went on journeys only to visit their own kin, they had little intercourse with other peoples except immediate neighbours, and needed writing very little; though they were fond of inscriptions, of all kinds, cut in stone. For such purposes the Runes were convenient, being originally devised for them.

The Longbeard Dwarves therefore adopted the Runes, and modified them for their own uses (especially the expression of Khuzdul); and they adhered to them even far into the Third Age, when they were forgotten by others except the loremasters of Elves and Men. Indeed it was generally supposed by the unlearned that they had been invented by the Dwarves, and they were widely known as 'dwarf-letters'.[8]

Here we are concerned only with the Common Speech. Now

the Common Speech, when written at all, had from its beginning been expressed in the Fëanorian Script.[9] Only occasionally and in inscriptions not written with pen or brush did some of the Elves of Sindarin descent use the Runes of Daeron, and their spelling was then dependent on the already established usages of the Fëanorian Script. The Dwarves had originally learned the Common Speech by ear as best they could, and had no occasion to write it; but in the Third Age they had been obliged in the course of trade and other dealings with Men and Elves to learn to read the Common Speech as written, and many had found it convenient to learn to write it according to the then general customs of the West. But this they only did in dealings with other peoples. For their own purposes they (as has been said) preferred the Runes and adhered to them.

Therefore in such documents as the Book of Mazarbul – not 'secret' but intended primarily for Dwarves, and probably intended later to provide material for chronicles[10] – they used the Runes. But the spelling was mixed and irregular. In general and by intention it was a transcription of the current spelling of the Common Speech into Runic terms; but this was often 'incorrect', owing to haste and the imperfect knowledge of the Dwarves; and it was also mingled with numerous cases of words spelt phonetically (according to the pronunciation of the Dwarves) – for instance, letters that had in the colloquial pronunciation of the late Third Age ceased to have any function were sometimes omitted.[11]

In preparing an example of the Book of Mazarbul, and making three torn and partly illegible pages,[12] I followed the general principle followed throughout: the Common Speech was to be represented as English of today, literary or colloquial as the case demanded. Consequently the text was cast into English spelt as at present, but modified as it might be by writers in haste whose familiarity with the written form was imperfect, and who were also (on the first and third pages) transliterating the English into a different alphabet – one that did not for instance employ any letter in more than one distinct value, so that the distribution of English *k, c — c, s* was reduced to *k — s*; while the use of the letters for *s* and *z* was variable since English uses *s* frequently as = *z*. In addition, since documents of this kind nearly always show uses of letters or shapes that are peculiar and rarely or never found elsewhere, a few such features are also introduced: as the signs for the English vowel pairs *ea*, *oa*, *ou* (irrespective of their sounds).

This is all very well, and perhaps gives some idea of the kind of text Gandalf was trying to read in great haste in the Chamber of Mazarbul. It also accords with the general treatment of the languages in *The Lord of the Rings*: only the actual words and names of the period that are in Elvish languages are preserved in what is supposed to have been their real form.[13] Also, this treatment was imposed by the fact that, though the actual Common Speech was sketched in structure and phonetic elements, and a number of words invented, it was quite impossible to translate even such short extracts into its real contemporary form, if they were visibly represented. But it is of course in fact an erroneous extension of the general linguistic treatment. It is one thing to represent all the dialogue of the story in varying forms of English: this must be supposed to be done by 'translation' – from memory of unrecorded sounds, or from documents lost or not printed, whether this is stated or not, whenever it is done in any narrative dealing with past times or foreign lands. But it is quite another thing to provide *visible* facsimiles or representations of writings or carvings supposed to be of the date of the events in the narrative.[14]

The true parallel in such a case is the glimpse of Quenya given in Galadriel's Farewell – either in a transcription into our alphabet (to make the style of the language more easily appreciated) or in the contemporary script (as in *The Road Goes Ever On*) – followed by a translation. Since, as noted, the provision of a contemporary text in the actual Common Speech was not possible, the only proper procedure was to provide a translation into English of the legible words of the pages hastily examined by Gandalf.[15] This was done in the text; and short of a construction of the actual Common Speech sufficient to allow the text to be in its contemporary form, all that can legitimately be done.

A special difficulty is presented by the inscription on Balin's tomb. This is effective in its place: giving an idea of the style of the Runes when incised with more care for a solemn purpose, and providing a glimpse of a strange tongue; though all that is really necessary for the tale is the six lines on I.334[16] (with the translation of the inscription in bigger and bolder lettering). The actual representation of the inscription has however landed in some absurdities.[17]

The use in the inscription of the older and more 'correct'

values and shapes of the *Angerthas*, and not the later 'usage of Erebor', is not absurd (though possibly an unnecessary elaboration); it is in accord with the history of the Runes as sketched in the Appendix E. The older Runes would be used for such a purpose, since they were used in Moria before the flight of the Dwarves, and would appear in other inscriptions of like kind – and Balin was claiming to be the descendant and successor of the former Lords of Moria. The use of the Dwarf-tongue (Khuzdul) is possible in so short an inscription, since this tongue has been sketched in some detail of structure, if with a very small vocabulary. But the names *Balin* and *Fundin* are in such a context absurd. The Dwarves, as is stated in III.411,[18] had names in their own language; these they only used among themselves (on solemn occasions) and kept strictly secret from other peoples, and therefore never spelt them out in writing or inscriptions meant for or likely to be seen by strangers. In times or places where they had dealings, in trade or friendship, with their neighbours, they adopted 'outer names' for convenience.[19] These names were in form generally suited to the structure of the Common Speech [> the structure of the language from which they were derived]. Very frequently they had recognizable meanings in that language, or were names current in it; sometimes they were names [> current in it, being names] used by neighbouring Men among whom they dwelt, and were derived from the local Mannish language in which they might have a still known meaning, though this was not often the case [*this phrase struck out*].[20] Whether the adopted names that had meanings were selected because these meanings had some relation to their secret 'inner' names cannot be determined. The adopted names could be and sometimes were changed – usually in consequence of some event, such as the migration of either the Dwarves or their friends that separated them.

The case of the Dwarves of Moria was an example of adoption of names from Mannish languages of the North, not from the Common Speech.[21] It might have been better in that case to have given them in their actual forms. But in carrying out the theory (necessary for the lessening of the load of invention of names in different styles of language), that names derived from the Mannish tongues and dialects of the West historically related to the Common Speech should be represented by names found (or made of elements found in) languages related to English, the Dwarvish names were taken from Norse: since the

Mannish language from which they were adopted was closely related to the more southerly language from which was derived the language of Rohan (represented as Old English, because of its greater archaism in form as compared with those elements in the Common Speech derived from the languages of the same kinship). In consequence such names as *Balin*, etc. would not have appeared in any contemporary inscription using actual Khuzdul.[22]

Relations of the Longbeard Dwarves and Men[23]

In the Dwarvish traditions of the Third Age the names of the places where each of the Seven Ancestors had 'awakened' were remembered; but only two of them were known to Elves and Men of the West: the most westerly, the awakening place of the ancestors of the Firebeards and the Broadbeams; and that of the ancestor of the Longbeards,[24] the eldest in making and awakening. The first had been in the north of the Ered Lindon, the great eastern wall of Beleriand, of which the Blue Mountains of the Second and later ages were the remnant; the second had been Mount Gundabad (in origin a Khuzdul name), which was therefore revered by the Dwarves, and its occupation in the Third Age by the Orks of Sauron was one of the chief reasons for their great hatred of the Orks.[25] The other two places were eastward, at distances as great or greater than that between the Blue Mountains and Gundabad: the arising of the Ironfists and Stiffbeards, and that of the Blacklocks and Stonefoots. Though these four points were far sundered the Dwarves of different kindreds were in communication, and in the early ages often held assemblies of delegates at Mount Gundabad. In times of great need even the most distant would send help to any of their people; as was the case in the great War against the Orks (Third Age 2793 to 2799). Though they were loth to migrate and make permanent dwellings or 'mansions' far from their original homes, except under great pressure from enemies or after some catastrophe such as the ruin of Beleriand, they were great and hardy travellers and skilled road-makers; also, all the kindreds shared a common language.[26]

But in far distant days the Dwarves were secretive [*struck out:* – and none more so than the Longbeards –] and had few dealings with the Elves. In the West at the end of the First Age the dealings of the Dwarves of the Ered Lindon with King Thingol ended in disaster and the ruin of Doriath, the memory of which still poisoned the relations of Elves and Dwarves in after ages. At that time the migrations of Men from the East and South had brought advance-guards into Beleriand; but they were not in great numbers, though further east in Eriador and Rhovanion (especially in the northern parts) their kindred must already have occupied much of the land. There dealings between Men and the Longbeards must soon have begun. For the Longbeards, though the proudest of the seven kindreds, were also the wisest and the most farseeing. Men held them in awe and were eager to learn from them; and the Longbeards were very willing to use Men for their own purposes. Thus there grew up in those regions the economy, later characteristic of the dealings of Dwarves and Men (including Hobbits): Men became the chief providers of food, as herdsmen, shepherds, and land-tillers, which the Dwarves exchanged for work as builders, roadmakers, miners, and the makers of things of craft, from useful tools to weapons and arms and many other things of great cost and skill. To the great profit of the Dwarves. Not only to be reckoned in hours of labour, though in early times the Dwarves must have obtained goods that were the product of greater and longer toil than the things or services that they gave in exchange – before Men became wiser and developed skills of their own. The chief advantage to them was their freedom to proceed unhindered with their own work and to refine their arts, especially in metallurgy, to the marvellous skill which these reached before the decline and dwindling of the Khazâd.

This system developed slowly, and it was long before the Longbeards felt any need to learn the language of their neighbours, still less to adopt names by which they could be known individually to 'outsiders'. This process began not in barter and trade, but in war; for the Longbeards had spread southward down the Vales of Anduin and had made their chief 'mansion' and stronghold at Moria; and also eastward to the Iron Hills, where the mines were their chief source of iron-ore. They regarded the Iron Hills, the Ered Mithrin, and the east dales of the Misty Mountains as their own land. But they were under attack from the Orks of Morgoth. During the War of the Jewels and the Siege of Angband, when Morgoth needed all his strength, these attacks ceased; but when Morgoth fell and Angband was destroyed hosts of the Orks fled eastwards seeking homes. They were now masterless and without any general leadership, but they were well-armed and very numerous, cruel, savage, and reckless in assault. In the battles that followed the Dwarves were outnumbered, and though they were the most redoubtable warriors of all the Speaking Peoples they were glad to make alliance with Men.[27]

The Men with whom they were thus associated were for the most part akin in race and language with the tall and mostly fair-haired people of the 'House of Hador', the most renowned and numerous of the Edain, who were allied with the Eldar in the War of the Jewels. These Men, it seems, had come westward until faced by the Great Greenwood, and then had divided: some reaching the Anduin and passing thence northward up the Vales; some passing between the north-eaves of the Wood and the Ered Mithrin. Only a small part of this people, already very numerous and divided into many tribes, had then passed on into Eriador and so come at last to Beleriand. They were brave and loyal folk, truehearted, haters of Morgoth and his servants; and at first had regarded the Dwarves askance, fearing that they were under the Shadow (as they said).[28] But they were glad of the alliance, for they were more vulnerable to the attacks of the Orks: they dwelt largely in scattered homesteads and villages, and if they drew together into small townships they were poorly defended, at best by dikes and wooden fences. Also they were lightly armed, chiefly with bows, for they had little metal and the few smiths among them had no great skill. These things the Dwarves amended in return for one great service that Men could offer. They were tamers of beasts and had learned the mastery of horses, and many were skilled and fearless riders.[29] These would often ride far afield as scouts and keep watch on movements of their enemies; and if the Orks dared to assemble in the open for some great raid, they would gather great force of horsed archers to surround them and destroy them. In these ways the Alliance of Dwarves and Men in the North came early in the Second Age to command great strength, swift in attack and valiant and well-protected in defence, and there grew up in that region between Dwarves and Men respect and esteem, and sometimes warm friendship.

It was at that time, when the Dwarves were associated with Men both in war and in the ordering of the lands that they had secured,[30] that the Longbeards adopted the speech of Men for communication with them. They were not unwilling to teach their own tongue to Men with whom they had special friendship, but Men found it difficult and were slow to learn more than isolated words, many of which they adapted and took into their own language. But on one point the Longbeards were as rigidly secretive as all other Dwarves. For reasons which neither Elves nor Men ever fully understood they would not reveal any personal names to people of other kin,[31] nor later when they had acquired the arts of writing allow them ever to be carved or written. They therefore took names by which they could be known to their allies in Mannish forms.[32] This custom endured among the Longbeards into the Fourth Age and beyond the view of these histories. It would appear that when speaking to Men with whom they had close friendship, and would speak together of the histories and memories of their peoples, they also gave similar names to Dwarves remembered in their annals long before the meeting of Dwarves and Men. But of these ancient times only one name was in the Third Age preserved: *Durin*, the name they gave to the prime ancestor of the Longbeards and by which he was known to Elves and Men. (It appears to have been simply a word for 'king' in the language of the Men of the North of the Second Age.)[33] The names of the Longbeards otherwise are not known in lists going back before the ruin of Moria (Khazad-dûm), Third Age 1980; but they are all of the same kind, sc. in a long 'dead' Mannish language.

This can only be explained by supposing that these names from the early Second Age had been adopted by the Dwarves, and preserved with as little change as their own language, and continued to be given (and often repeated) for something like four thousand years or more since the Alliance was destroyed by the power of Sauron! In this way they soon became to later Men specially Dwarvish names;[34] and the Longbeards acquired a vocabulary of traditional names peculiar to themselves, while still keeping their true 'inner' names completely secret.

Very great changes came to pass as the Second Age proceeded. The first ships of the Númenóreans appeared off the coasts of Middle-earth about Second Age 600, but no rumour of this portent reached the distant North. At the same time, however, Sauron came out of hiding and revealed himself in fair form. For long he paid little heed to Dwarves or Men and endeavoured to win the friendship and trust of the Eldar. But slowly he reverted again to the allegiance of Morgoth and began to seek power by force, marshalling again and directing the Orks and other evil things of the First Age, and secretly building his great fortress in the mountain-girt land in the South that was afterwards known as Mordor. The Second Age had reached only the middle of its course (c. Second Age 1695) when he invaded Eriador and destroyed Eregion, a small realm established by the Eldar migrating from the ruin of Beleriand that had formed an alliance also with the Longbeards of Moria. This marked the end of the Alliance of the Longbeards with Men of the North. For though Moria remained impregnable for many centuries, the Orks reinforced and commanded by servants of Sauron invaded the mountains again. Gundabad was re-taken, the Ered Mithrin infested and the communication between Moria and the Iron Hills for a time cut off. The Men of the Alliance were involved in war not only with Orks but with alien Men of evil sort. For Sauron had acquired dominion over many savage tribes in the East (of old corrupted by Morgoth), and he now urged them to seek land and booty in the West. When the storm passed,[35] the Men of the old Alliance were diminished and scattered, and those that lingered on in their old regions were impoverished, and lived mostly in caves or in the borders of the Forest.

The Elvish loremasters held that in the matter of language the changes in speech (as in all the ways of their lives) of the Speaking Peoples were far slower in the Elder Days than they later became. The tongue of the Eldar changed mainly by design; that of the Dwarves resisted change by their own will; the many languages of Men changed heedlessly in the swift passing of their generations. All things changed in Arda, even in the Blessed Realm of the Valar; but there the change was so slow that it could not be observed (save maybe by the Valar) in great ages of time. The change in the language of the Eldar would thus have been halted in Valinor;[36] but in their early days the Eldar continued to enlarge and refine their language, and to change it, even in structure and sounds. Such change, however, to remain uniform required that the speakers should remain in communication. Thus it came about that the languages of the Eldar that remained in Middle-earth diverged from the language of the High Eldar of Valinor so greatly that neither could be understood by speakers of the other; for they had been separated for a great age of time, during which even the Sindarin, the best preserved of those in Middle-earth, had been subject to the heedless changes of passing years, changes which the Teleri were far less concerned to restrain or to direct by design than the Ñoldor.

II

The Atani and their Languages[37]

Men entered Beleriand late in the First Age. Those with whom we are here concerned and of whose languages some records later were preserved belonged mostly to three peoples, differing in speech and in race, but known in common to the Eldar as the *Atani* (Sindarin *Edain*).[38] These *Atani* were the vanguard of far larger hosts of the same kinds moving westwards. When the First Age ended and Beleriand was destroyed, and most of the Atani who survived had passed over sea to Númenor, their laggard kindred were either in Eriador, some settled, some still wandering, or else had never passed the Misty Mountains and were scattered in the lands between the Iron Hills and the Sea of Rhûn eastward and the Great Forest, in the borders of which, northward and eastward, many were already settled.

The Atani and their kin were the descendants of peoples who in the Dark Ages had resisted Morgoth or had renounced him, and had wandered ever westward from their homes far away in the East seeking the Great Sea, of which distant rumour had reached them. They did not know that Morgoth himself had left Middle-earth;[39] for they were ever at war with the vile things that he had bred, and especially with Men who had made him their God and believed that they could render him no more pleasing service than to destroy the 'renegades' with every kind of cruelty. It was in the North of Middle-earth, it would seem, that the 'renegades' survived in sufficient numbers to maintain their independence as brave and hardy peoples; but of their past they preserved only legends, and their oral histories reached no further back than a few generations of Men.

When their vanguards at last reached Beleriand and the Western Shores they were dismayed. For they could go no further, but they had not found peace, only lands engaged in war with Morgoth himself, who had fled back to Middle-earth. 'Through ages forgotten,' they said, 'we have wandered, seeking to escape from the Dominions of the Dark Lord and his Shadow, only to find him here before us.'[40] But being people both brave and desperate they at once became allies of the Eldar, and they were instructed by them and became ennobled and advanced in knowledge and in arts. In the final years of the War of the Jewels they provided many of the most valiant warriors and captains in the armies of the Elvish kings.

The Atani were three peoples, independent in organisation and leadership, each of which differed in speech and also in form and bodily features from the others – though all of them showed traces of mingling in the past with Men of other kinds. These peoples the Eldar named the Folk of Bëor, the Folk of Hador, and the Folk of Haleth, after the names of the chieftains who commanded them when they first came to Beleriand.[41] The Folk of Bëor were the first Men to enter Beleriand – they were met in the dales of East Beleriand by King Finrod the Friend of Men, for they had found a way over the Mountains. They were a small people, having no more, it is said, than two thousand full-grown men; and they were poor and ill-equipped, but they were inured to hardship and toilsome journeys carrying great loads, for they had no beasts of burden. Not long after the first of the three hosts of the Folk of Hador came up from southward, and two others of much the same strength followed before the fall of the year. They were a more numerous people; each host was as great as all the Folk of Bëor, and they were better armed and equipped; also they possessed many horses, and some asses and small flocks of sheep and goats. They had crossed Eriador and reached the eastern feet of the Mountains (Ered Lindon) a year or more ahead of all others, but had not attempted to find any passes, and had turned away seeking a road round the Mountains, which, as their horsed scouts reported, grew ever lower as they went southwards. Some years later, when the other folk were settled, the third folk of the Atani entered Beleriand.[42] They were probably more numerous than the Folk of Bëor, but no certain count of them was ever made; for they came secretly in small parties and hid in the woods of Ossiriand where the Elves showed them no friendship. Moreover they had strife among themselves, and Morgoth, now aware of the coming of hostile Men into Beleriand, sent his servants to afflict them. Those who eventually moved westward and entered into friendship and alliance with the Eldar were called the Folk of Haleth, for Haleth was the name of their chieftainess who led them to the woods north of Doriath where they were permitted to dwell.

The Folk of Hador were ever the greatest in numbers of the Atani, and in renown (save only Beren son of Barahir descendant of Bëor). For the most part they were tall people, with flaxen or golden hair and blue-grey eyes, but there were not a few among them that had dark hair, though all were fair-skinned.[43]

Nonetheless they were akin to the Folk of Bëor, as was shown by their speech. It needed no lore of tongues to perceive that their languages were closely related, for although they could understand one another only with difficulty they had very many words in common. The Elvish loremasters[44] were of opinion that both languages were descended from one that had diverged (owing to some division of the people who had spoken it) in the course of, maybe, a thousand years of the slower change in the First Age.[45] Though the time might well have been less, and change quickened by a mingling of peoples; for the language of Hador was apparently less changed and more uniform in style, whereas the language of Bëor contained many elements that were alien in character. This contrast in speech was probably connected with the observable physical differences between the two peoples. There were fair-haired men and women among the Folk of Bëor, but most of them had brown hair (going usually with brown eyes), and many were less fair in skin, some indeed being swarthy. Men as tall as the Folk of Hador were rare among them, and most were broader and more heavy in build.[46] In association with the Eldar, especially with the followers of King Finrod, they became as enhanced in arts and manners as the Folk of Hador, but if these surpassed them in swiftness of mind and body, in daring and noble generosity,[47] the Folk of Bëor were more steadfast in endurance of hardship and sorrow, slow to tears or to laughter; their fortitude needed no hope to sustain it. But these differences of body and mind became less marked as their short generations passed, for the two peoples became much mingled by intermarriage and by the disasters of the War.[48]

The Folk of Haleth were strangers to the other Atani, speaking an alien language; and though later united with them in alliance with the Eldar, they remained a people apart. Among themselves they adhered to their own language, and though of necessity they learned Sindarin for communication with the Eldar and the other Atani, many spoke it haltingly, and some of those who seldom went beyond the borders of their own woods did not use it at all.[49] They did not willingly adopt new things or customs, and retained many practices that seemed strange to the Eldar and the other Atani, with whom they had few dealings except in war. Nonetheless they were esteemed as loyal allies and redoubtable warriors, though the companies that they sent to battle beyond their borders were small. For they were and remained to their end a small people, chiefly concerned to protect their own woodlands, and they excelled in forest warfare. Indeed for long even those Orks specially trained for this dared not set foot near their borders. One of the strange practices spoken of was that many of their warriors were women, though few of these went abroad to fight in the great battles. This custom was evidently ancient;[50] for their chieftainess Haleth had been a renowned amazon with a picked bodyguard of women.

> At this point a heading is pencilled on the typescript: III *The Drúedain (Púkel-men)*; after this there are no further divisions with sub-titles inserted. Together with the concluding paragraph of section II printed above, the account of the Drúedain that now follows is given in *Unfinished Tales*, pp. 377–82, concluding with the story called *The Faithful Stone*; and there is no need to repeat this here.[51] At the end of the story is a passage contrasting Drûgs and Hobbits, which since it was given in curtailed form in *Unfinished Tales* (p. 382) is printed here in full; the present text then continues to the end, or rather abandonment, of the essay.

This long account of the Drúedain has been given, because it throws some light on the Wild Men still surviving at the time of the War of the Ring in the eastern end of the White Mountains, and on Merry's recognition of them as living forms of the carved Púkel-men of Dun Harrow. The presence of members of the same race among the Edain in Beleriand thus makes another backward link between *The Lord of the Rings* and *The Silmarillion*, and allows the introduction of characters somewhat similar to the Hobbits of *The Lord of the Rings* into some of the legends of the First Age (e.g. the old retainer (Sadog) of Húrin in the legend of Túrin).[52]

The Drûgs or Púkel-men are not however to be confused with or thought of as a mere variant on the hobbit theme. They were quite different in physical shape and appearance. Their average height (four feet) was only reached by exceptional hobbits; they were of heavier and stronger build; and their facial features were unlovely (judged by general human standards). Physically they shared the hairlessness of the lower face; but while the head-hair of the hobbits was abundant (but close and curly), the Drûgs had only sparse and lank hair on their heads and none at all on their legs and feet. In character and temperament they were at times merry and gay, like hobbits, but they had a grimmer side to their nature and could be sardonic and ruthless; and they had or were credited with strange or magical powers. (The tales, such as 'The Faithful Stone', that speak of their transferring part of their 'powers' to their artefacts, remind one in miniature of Sauron's transference of power to the foundation of the Barad-dûr and to the Ruling Ring.)[53] Also the Drûgs were a frugal folk, and ate sparingly even in times of peace and plenty, and drank nothing but water. In some ways they resembled rather the Dwarves: in build and stature and endurance (though not in hair); in their skill in carving stone; in the grim side of their character; and in 'strange powers'. Though the 'magic' skills with which the Dwarves were credited were quite different; also the Dwarves were much grimmer; and they were long-lived, whereas the Drûgs were short-lived compared with other kinds of Men.

The Drûgs that are met in the tales of the First Age – cohabiting with the Folk of Haleth, who were a woodland people – were content to live in tents or shelters lightly built round the trunks of large trees, for they were a hardy race. In their former homes, according to their own tales, they had used caves in the mountains, but mainly as store-houses only occupied as dwellings and sleeping-places in severe weather. They had similar refuges in Beleriand to which all but the most hardy retreated in times of storm and bitter weather; but these places were guarded and not even their closest friends among the Folk of Haleth were welcomed there.

Hobbits on the other hand were in nearly all respects normal Men, but of very short stature. They were called 'halflings'; but this refers to the normal height of men of Númenórean descent and of the Eldar (especially those of Ñoldorin descent), which appears to have been about seven of our feet.[54] Their height at the periods concerned was usually more than three feet for men, though very few ever exceeded three foot six; women seldom exceeded three feet. They were not as numerous or variable as ordinary Men, but evidently more numerous and adaptable to different modes of life and habitat than the Drûgs, and when they are first encountered in the histories already showed divergences in colouring, stature, and build, and in their ways of life and preferences for different types of country to dwell in (see the Prologue to *The Lord of the Rings*, p. 12). In their unrecorded past they must have been a primitive, indeed 'savage' people,[55] but when we meet them they had (in varying degrees) acquired many arts and customs by contact with Men, and to a less extent with Dwarves and Elves. With Men of normal stature they recognized their close kinship, whereas Dwarves or Elves, whether friendly or hostile, were aliens, with whom their relations were uneasy and clouded by fear.[56] Bilbo's statement (*The Lord of the Rings* I.162)[57] that the cohabitation of Big Folk and Little Folk in one settlement at Bree was peculiar and nowhere else to be found was probably true in his time (the end of the Third Age);[58] but it would seem that actually Hobbits had liked to live with or near to Big Folk of friendly kind, who with their greater strength protected them from many dangers and enemies and other hostile Men, and received in exchange many services. For it is remarkable that the western Hobbits preserved no trace or memory of any language of their own. The language they spoke when they entered Eriador was evidently adopted from the Men of the Vales of Anduin (related to the Atani, / in particular to those of the House of Bëor [> of the Houses of Hador and of Bëor]); and after their adoption of the Common Speech they retained many words of that origin. This indicates a close association with Big Folk; though the rapid adoption of the Common Speech in Eriador[59] shows Hobbits to have been specially adaptable in this respect. As does also the divergence of the Stoors, who had associated with Men of different sort before they came to the Shire.

The vague tradition preserved by the Hobbits of the Shire was that they had dwelt once in lands by a Great River, but long ago had left them, and found their way through or round high mountains, when they no longer felt at ease in their homes because of the multiplication of the Big Folk and of a shadow of fear that had fallen on the Forest. This evidently reflects the troubles of Gondor in the earlier part of the Third Age. The increase in Men was not the normal increase of those with whom they had lived in friendship, but the steady increase of invaders from the East, further south held in check by Gondor, but in the North beyond the bounds of the Kingdom harassing the older 'Atanic' inhabitants, and even in places occupying the Forest and coming through it into the Anduin valley. But the shadow of which the tradition spoke was not solely due to human invasion. Plainly the Hobbits had sensed, even before the Wizards and the Eldar had become fully aware of it, the awakening of Sauron and his occupation of Dol Guldur.[60]

On the relations of the different kinds of Men in Eriador and Rhovanion to the Atani and other Men met in the legends of the First Age and the War of the Jewels see *The Lord of the Rings* II.286–7 [in the chapter *The Window on the West*]. There Faramir gives a brief account of the contemporary classification in Gondor of Men into three kinds: High Men, or Númenóreans (of more or less pure descent); Middle Men; and Men of Darkness. The Men of Darkness was a general term applied to all those who were hostile to the Kingdoms, and who were (or appeared in Gondor to be) moved by something more than human greed for conquest and plunder, a fanatical hatred of the High Men and their allies as enemies of their gods. The term took no account of differences of race or culture or language. With regard to Middle Men Faramir spoke mainly of the Rohirrim, the only people of this sort well-known in Gondor in his time, and attributed to them actual direct descent from the Folk of Hador in the First Age. This was a general belief in Gondor at that time,[61] and was held to explain (to the comfort of Númenórean pride) the surrender of so large a part of the Kingdom to the people of Eorl.

The term Middle Men, however, was of ancient origin. It was devised in the Second Age by the Númenóreans when they began to establish havens and settlements on the western shores of Middle-earth. It arose among the settlers in the North (between Pelargir and the Gulf of Lune), in the time of Ar-Adûnakhôr; for the settlers in this region had refused to join in the rebellion against the Valar, and were strengthened by many exiles of the Faithful who fled from persecution by him and the later Kings of Númenor. It was therefore modelled on the classification by the Atani of the Elves: the High Elves (or Elves of Light) were the Ñoldor who returned in exile out of the Far West; the Middle Elves were the Sindar, who though near kin of the High Elves had remained in Middle-earth and never seen the light of Aman; and the Dark Elves were those who had never journeyed to the Western Shores and did not desire to see Aman. This was not the same as the classifications made by the Elves, which are not here concerned, except to note that 'Dark Elves' or 'Elves of Darkness' was used by them, but in no way implied any evil, or subordination to Morgoth; it referred only to ignorance of the 'light of Aman' and included the Sindar. Those who had never made the journey to the West Shores were called 'the Refusers' (*Avari*). It is doubtful if any of the Avari ever reached

Beleriand[62] or were actually known to the Númenóreans.

In the days of the earlier settlements of Númenor there were many Men of different kinds in Eriador and Rhovanion; but for the most part they dwelt far from the coasts. The regions of Forlindon and Harlindon were inhabited by Elves and were the chief part of Gil-galad's kingdom, which extended, north of the Gulf of Lune, to include the lands east of the Blue Mountains and west of the River Lune as far as the inflow of the Little Lune.[63] (Beyond that was Dwarf territory.)[64] South of the Lune it had no clear bounds, but the Tower Hills (as they were later called) were maintained as an outpost.[65] The Minhiriath and the western half of Enedhwaith between the Greyflood and the Isen were still covered with dense forest.[66] The shores of the Bay of Belfalas were still mainly desolate, except for a haven and small settlement of Elves at the mouth of the confluence of Morthond and Ringló.[67] But it was long before the Númenórean settlers about the Mouths of Anduin ventured north of their great haven at Pelargir and made contact with Men who dwelt in the valleys on either side of the White Mountains. Their term Middle Men was thus originally applied to Men of Eriador, the most westerly of Mankind in the Second Age and known to the Elves of Gil-galad's realm.[68] At that time there were many men in Eriador, mainly, it would seem, in origin kin of the Folk of Bëor, though some were kin of the Folk of Hador. They dwelt about Lake Evendim, in the North Downs and the Weather Hills, and in the lands between as far as the Brandywine, west of which they often wandered though they did not dwell there. They were friendly with the Elves, though they held them in awe and close friendships between them were rare. Also they feared the Sea and would not look upon it. (No doubt rumours of its terror and the destruction of the Land beyond the Mountains (Beleriand) had reached them, and some of their ancestors may indeed have been fugitives from the Atani who did not leave Middle-earth but fled eastward.)

Thus it came about that the Númenórean term Middle Men was confused in its application. Its chief test was friendliness towards the West (to Elves and to Númenóreans), but it was actually applied usually only to Men whose stature and looks were similar to those of the Númenóreans, although this most important distinction of 'friendliness' was not historically confined to peoples of one racial kind. It was a mark of all kinds of Men who were descendants of those who had abjured the

Shadow of Morgoth and his servants and wandered westward to escape it – and certainly included both the races of small stature, Drûgs and Hobbits. Also it must be said that 'unfriendliness' to Númenóreans and their allies was not always due to the Shadow, but in later days to the actions of the Númenóreans themselves. Thus many of the forest-dwellers of the shorelands south of the Ered Luin, especially in Minhiriath, were as later historians recognized the kin of the Folk of Haleth; but they became bitter enemies of the Númenóreans, because of their ruthless treatment and their devastation of the forests,[69] and this hatred remained unappeased in their descendants, causing them to join with any enemies of Númenor. In the Third Age their survivors were the people known in Rohan as the Dunlendings.

There was also the matter of language. It was six hundred years after the departure of the survivors of the Atani oversea to Númenor that a ship came first to Middle-earth again out of the West and passed up the Gulf of Lune.[70]

> The story that follows, recounting the meeting of the Númenórean mariners with twelve Men of Eriador on the Tower Hills, their mutual recognition of an ancient kinship, and their discovery that their languages though profoundly changed were of common origin, has been given in *Unfinished Tales*, pp. 213–14.[71] Following the conclusion of that extract (ending with the words 'they found that they shared very many words still clearly recognizable, and others that could be understood with attention, and they were able to converse haltingly about simple matters') the essay continues as follows.

Thus it came about that a kinship in language, even if this was only recognizable after close acquaintance, was felt by the Númenóreans to be one of the marks of 'Middle-men'.[72]

The loremasters of later days held that the languages of Men in Middle-earth, at any rate those of the 'unshadowed' Men, had changed less swiftly before the end of the Second Age and the change of the world in the Downfall of Númenor. Whereas in Númenor owing to the longevity of the Atani it had changed far more slowly still. At the first meeting of the Shipmen and the Men of western Eriador it was only six hundred years since the Atani went oversea, and the Adûnaic that they spoke can hardly have changed at all; but it was a thousand years or more since the Atani who reached Beleriand had parted from their kin. Yet even now in a more changeful world languages that have been separated for fifteen hundred years and longer may be recognized as akin by those unlearned in the history of tongues.

As the long years passed the situation changed. The ancient Adûnaic of Númenor became worn down by time – and by neglect. For owing to the disastrous history of Númenor it was no longer held in honour by the 'Faithful' who controlled all the Shorelands from Lune to Pelargir. For the Elvish tongues were proscribed by the rebel Kings, and Adûnaic alone was permitted to be used, and many of the ancient books in Quenya or in Sindarin were destroyed. The Faithful, therefore, used Sindarin, and in that tongue devised all names of places that they gave anew in Middle-earth.[73] Adûnaic was abandoned to unheeded change and corruption as the language of daily life, and the only tongue of the unlettered. All men of high lineage and all those who were taught to read and write used Sindarin, even as a daily tongue among themselves. In some families, it is said, Sindarin became the native tongue, and the vulgar tongue of Adûnaic origin was only learned casually as it was needed.[74] The Sindarin was not however taught to aliens, both because it was held a mark of Númenórean descent and because it proved difficult to acquire – far more so than the 'vulgar tongue'. Thus it came about that as the Númenórean settlements increased in power and extent and made contact with Men of Middle-earth (many of whom came under Númenórean rule and swelled their population) the 'vulgar tongue' began to spread far and wide as a *lingua franca* among peoples of many different kinds. This process began in the end of the Second Age, but became of general importance mainly after the Downfall and the establishment of the 'Realms in Exile' in Arnor and Gondor. These kingdoms penetrated far into Middle-earth, and their kings were recognized beyond their borders as overlords. Thus in the North and West all the lands between the Ered Luin and the Greyflood and Hoarwell[75] became regions of Númenórean influence in which the 'vulgar tongue' became widely current. In the South and East Mordor remained impenetrable; but though the extent of Gondor was thus impeded it was more populous and powerful than Arnor. The bounds of the ancient kingdom contained all those lands marked in maps of the end of the Third Age as Gondor, Anórien, Ithilien, South Ithilien, and Rohan (formerly called Calenardhon) west of the Entwash.[76] On its extension at the height of its power, between the reigns of Hyarmendacil I and Rómendacil II (Third Age 1015 to 1366) see *The Lord of the Rings* Appendix A p.325.[77] The wide lands between Anduin and the Sea of Rhûn were however never effectively settled or occupied, and the only true north boundary of the Kingdom east of Anduin was formed by the Emyn Muil and the marshes south and east of them. Númenórean influence however went far beyond even these extended bounds, passing up the Vales of Anduin to its sources, and reaching the lands east of the Forest, between the River Celon[78] (Running) and the River Carnen (Redwater).

Within the original bounds of the Kingdoms the 'vulgar speech' soon became the current speech, and eventually the native language of nearly all the inhabitants of whatever origin, and incomers who were allowed to settle within the bounds adopted it. Its speakers generally called it Westron (actually *Adûni*, and in Sindarin *Annúnaid*). But it spread far beyond the bounds of the Kingdoms – at first in dealings with 'the peoples of the Kingdoms', and later as a 'Common Speech' convenient for intercourse between peoples who retained numerous tongues of their own. Thus Elves and Dwarves used it in dealings with one another and with Men.

The text ends here abruptly (without a full stop after the last word, though this may not be significant), halfway down a page.

NOTES

1 A notable case is that of the conversation between Ghân chieftain of the Wild Men and Théoden. Probably few if any of the Wild Men other than Ghân used the Common Speech at all, and he had only a limited vocabulary of words used according to the habits of his native speech.
2 The Kings and their descendants after Thengel also knew the Sindarin tongue – the language of nobles in Gondor. [Cf. Appendix A (II), in the list of the Kings of the Mark, on Thengel's sojourn in Gondor. It is said there that after his return to Rohan 'the speech of Gondor was used in his house, and not all men thought that good.']
3 The effect on contemporary speakers of the Common Speech of Gondor being comparable to that which we should feel if a foreigner, both learned and a skilled linguist, were when being courteous or dealing with high matters to use fluently an English of say about 1600 A.D., but adapted to our present pronunciation.
4 Structurally and grammatically it differed widely from all other

languages of the West at that time; though it had some features in common with Adûnaic, the ancient 'native' language of Númenor. This gave rise to the theory (a probable one) that in the unrecorded past some of the languages of Men – including the language of the dominant element in the Atani from which Adûnaic was derived – had been influenced by Khuzdul.

5   They had, it is said, a complex pictographic or ideographic writing or carving of their own. But this they kept resolutely secret.

6   Including their enemies such as Sauron, and his higher servants who were in fact partly of Númenórean origin.

7   [Like Gil-galad, Celebrimbor was a figure first appearing in *The Lord of the Rings* whose origin my father changed again and again. The earliest statement on the subject is found in the post-*Lord of the Rings* text *Concerning Galadriel and Celeborn*, where it is said (cf. *Unfinished Tales* p. 235):

> Galadriel and Celeborn had in their company a Noldorin craftsman called Celebrimbor. He was of Noldorin origin, and one of the survivors of Gondolin, where he had been one of Turgon's greatest artificers – but he had thus acquired some taint of pride and an almost 'dwarvish' obsession with crafts.

He reappears as a jewel-smith of Gondolin in the text *The Elessar* (see *Unfinished Tales* pp. 248 ff.); but against the passage in *Concerning Galadriel and Celeborn* just cited my father noted that it would be better to 'make him a descendant of Fëanor'. Thus in the Second Edition (1966) of *The Lord of the Rings*, at the end of the prefatory remarks to the Tale of Years of the Second Age, he added the sentence: 'Celebrimbor was lord of Eregion and the greatest of their craftsmen; he was descended from Fëanor.'

On one of his copies of *The Return of the King* he underlined the name *Fëanor* in this sentence, and wrote the following two notes on the opposite page (the opening of the first of these means, I think: 'What then was his parentage? He must have been descended from one of Fëanor's sons, about whose progeny nothing has been told').

> How could he be? Fëanor's only descendants were his seven sons, six of whom reached Beleriand. So far nothing has been said of their wives and children. It seems probable that *Celebrinbaur* (silverfisted, > *Celebrimbor*) was son of Curufin, but though inheriting his skills he was an Elf of wholly different temper (his mother had refused to take part in the rebellion of Fëanor and remained in Aman with the people of Finarphin). During their dwelling in Nargothrond as refugees he had grown to love Finrod and ^ his wife, and was aghast

at the behaviour of his father and would not go with him. He later became a great friend of Celeborn and Galadriel.

The second note reads:

> Maedros the eldest appears to have been unwedded, also the two youngest (twins, of whom one was by evil mischance burned with the ships); Celegorm also, since he plotted to take Lúthien as his wife. But Curufin, dearest to his father and chief inheritor of his father's skills, was wedded, and had a son who came with him into exile, though his wife (unnamed) did not. Others who were wedded were Maelor, Caranthir.

On the form *Maelor* for *Maglor* see X.182, §41. The reference in the first of these notes to the wife of Finrod Felagund is notable, since long before, in the *Grey Annals*, the story had emerged that Felagund had no wife, and that 'she whom he had loved was Amárië of the Vanyar, and she was not permitted to go with him into exile'. That story had in fact been abandoned, or forgotten, but it would return: see the note on Gil-galad, p. 350.

These notes on Celebrimbor son of Curufin were the basis of the passages introduced editorially in the published *Silmarillion*, p. 176 (see V.300-1), and in *Of the Rings of Power, ibid.* p. 286. But in late writing (1968 or later) on the subject of Eldarin words for 'hand' my father said this:

> Common Eldarin had a base KWAR 'press together, squeeze, wring'. A derivative was *kwāra : Quenya *quár*, Telerin *pār*, Sindarin *paur*. This may be translated 'fist', though its chief use was in reference to the tightly closed hand as in using an implement or a craft-tool rather than to the 'fist' as used in punching. Cf. the name *Celebrin-baur > Celebrimbor*. This was a Sindarized form of Telerin *Telperimpar* (Quenya *Tyelpinquar*). It was a frequent name among the Teleri, who in addition to navigation and ship-building were also renowned as silver-smiths. The famous Celebrimbor, heroic defender of Eregion in the Second Age war against Sauron, was a Teler, one of the three Teleri who accompanied Celeborn into exile. He was a great silver-smith, and went to Eregion attracted by the rumours of the marvellous metal found in Moria, Moria-silver, to which he gave the name *mithril*. In the working of this he became a rival of the Dwarves, or rather an equal, for there was great friendship between the Dwarves of Moria and Celebrimbor, and they shared their skills and craft-secrets. In the same way *Tegilbor* was used for one skilled in calligraphy (*tegil* was a Sindarized form of Quenya *tekil* 'pen', not known to the Sindar until the coming of the Noldor).

When my father wrote this he ignored the addition to Appendix B in the Second Edition, stating that Celebrimbor 'was descended from Fëanor'; no doubt he had forgotten that that theory had appeared in print, for had he remembered it he would undoubtedly have felt bound by it. – On the statement that Celebrimbor was 'one of the three Teleri who accompanied Celeborn into exile' see *Unfinished Tales*, pp. 231–3.

Yet here in the present essay, from much the same time as that on Eldarin words for 'hand' just cited, a radically different account of Celebrimbor's origin is given: 'a Sinda who claimed descent from Daeron'.]

8 They did not, however, appear in the inscriptions on the West Gate of Moria. The Dwarves said that it was in courtesy to the Elves that the Fëanorian letters were used on that gate, since it opened into their country and was chiefly used by them. But the East Gates, which perished in the war against the Orks, had opened upon the wide world, and were less friendly. They had borne Runic inscriptions in several tongues: spells of prohibition and exclusion in Khuzdul, and commands that all should depart who had not the leave of the Lord of Moria written in Quenya, Sindarin, the Common Speech, the languages of Rohan and of Dale and Dunland.

[In the margin against the paragraph in the text at this point my father pencilled:

N.B. It is actually said by Elrond in *The Hobbit* that the Runes were *invented* by the Dwarves and written with silver pens. Elrond was half-elven and a master of lore and history. So either we must tolerate this discrepancy or modify the history of the Runes, making the actual *Angerthas Moria* largely an affair of Dwarvish invention.

In notes associated with this essay he is seen pondering the latter course, considering the possibility that it was in fact the Longbeard Dwarves who were the original begetters of the Runes; and that it was from them that Daeron derived the idea, but since the first Runes were not well organised (and differed from one mansion of the Dwarves to another) he ordered them in a logical system.

But of course in Appendix E (II) he had stated very explicitly the origin of the Runes: 'The Cirth were devised first in Beleriand by the Sindar'. It was Daeron of Doriath who developed the 'richest and most ordered form' of the Cirth, the Alphabet of Daeron, and its use in Eregion led to its adoption by the Dwarves of Moria, whence its name *Angerthas Moria*. Thus the inconsistency, if inconsistency there was, could scarcely be removed; but in fact there was none. It was the 'moon-runes' that Elrond declared (at the end of the chapter *A Short Rest*) to have been invented by the Dwarves and written by them with silver pens, not the Runes as an alphabetic form – as my father at length noted with relief. I mention all this as an illustration of his intense concern to avoid discrepancy and inconsistency, even though in this case his anxiety was unfounded. – For an earlier account of the origin of the Runes see VII.452–5.]

9   [At this point the text in manuscript ends, and the typescript takes up.]

10 As things went ill in Moria and hope even of escaping with their lives faded the last pages of the Book can only have been written in the hope that the Book might be later found by friends, and inform them of the fate of Balin and his rash expedition to Moria – as indeed happened.

11 Cases were the reduction of double (long) consonants to single ones medially between vowels, or the alteration of consonants in certain combinations. Both are exemplified in the Third Age colloquial *tunas* 'guard', i.e. a body of men acting as guards. This was a derivative of the stem TUD 'watch, guard' + *nas* 'people': an organized group or gathering of people for some function. But *tudnas*, though it was often retained in 'correct' spelling, had been changed to *tunnas* and usually was so spelt: *tunas* which occurred in the first line of the preserved three pages was 'incorrect' and represented the colloquial. (Incidentally this *nas* is probably an example of the numerous loanwords from Elvish that were found in Adûnaic already and were increased in the Common Speech of the Kingdoms. It is probably < Quenya *nossë* or Sindarin *nos*, 'kindred, family'. The short o of Elvish became *a* in such borrowed words.)

12 [The three pages were reproduced in *Pictures by J. R. R. Tolkien*, 1979, no.23 (second edition, 1992, no.24).]

13 Exceptions are a few words in a debased form of the Black Speech; a few place-names or personal names (not interpreted); the warcry of the Dwarves. Also a few place-names supposed to be of forgotten origin or meaning; and one or two personal names of the same kind (see Appendix F, p. 407).

14 The sherd of Amenartas was in Greek (provided by Andrew Lang) of the period from which it was supposed to have survived, not in English spelt as well as might be in Greek letters. [For the sherd of Amenartas see H. Rider Haggard, *She*, chapter 3.]

15 The first song of Galadriel is treated in this way: it is given only in translation (as is all the rest of her speech in dialogue). Because in this case a verse translation was attempted, to represent as far as possible the metrical devices of the original – a considered composition no doubt made long before the coming of Frodo and independent of the arrival in Lórien of the One Ring. Whereas the Farewell was addressed direct to Frodo, and was an extempore outpouring in free rhythmic style, reflecting the overwhelming increase in her regret and longing, and her personal despair

after she had survived the terrible temptation. It was translated accurately. The rendering of the older song must be presumed to have been much freer to enable metrical features to be represented. (In the event it proved that it was Galadriel's abnegation of pride and trust in her own powers, and her absolute refusal of any unlawful enhancement of them, that provided the ship to bear her back to her home.) [Cf. the passage in a letter from my father of 1967 cited in *Unfinished Tales*, p. 229; *Letters* no.297, at end.]

16 [This refers to the last six lines (which include the interpretation of the inscription on the tomb) of the chapter *A Journey in the Dark*, beginning '"These are Daeron's Runes, such as were used of old in Moria," said Gandalf', which in the three-volume hardback edition of *The Lord of the Rings* alone appear on that page.]

17 Possibly observed by the more linguistically and historically minded; though I have received no comments on them.

18 [This refers to the end of Appendix F, I ('Gimli's own name ...'), cited above, p. 296.]

19 In later times, when their own Khuzdûl had become only a learned language, and the Dwarves had adopted the Common Speech or a local language of Men, they naturally used these 'outer' names also for all colloquial purposes. [*Khuzdûl* is in this case spelt with a circumflex accent on the second vowel.]

20 [At the same time as the alterations shown were made to the text of this passage my father wrote in the margin: 'But see on this below – they were derived from a long lost Mannish language in the North.' See pp. 303–4, and note 23 below.]

21 The references (in Appendix A [beginning of III, *Durin's Folk*]) to the legends of the origin of the Dwarves of the kin known as Longbeards (Khuzdul *Sigin-tarâg*, translated by Quenya *Andafangar*, Sindarin *Anfangrim*) and their renowned later 'mansions' in Khazad-dûm (Moria) are too brief to make the linguistic situation clear. The 'deeps of time' do not refer (of course) to geological time – of which only the Eldar had legends, derived and transmuted from such information as their loremasters had received from the Valar. They refer to legends of the Ages of Awakening and the arising of the Speaking Peoples: first the Elves, second the Dwarves (as they claimed), and third Men. Unlike Elves and Men the Dwarves appear in the legends to have arisen in the North of Middle-earth. [This note continued as follows, but the continuation was subsequently struck out.] The most westerly point, the place of the birth or awakening of the ancestor of the Longbeards, was in the traditions of the Third Age a valley in the Ered Mithrin. But this was in far distant days. It was long before the migrations of Men from the East reached the North-western regions. And it was long again before the

Dwarves – of whom the Longbeards appear to have been the most secretive and least concerned to have dealings with Elves or Men – still felt any need to learn any languages of their neighbours, still less to take names by which they could be known to 'outsiders'.

22 [My father's point was that *Balin* and *Fundin* are actual Old Norse names used as 'translations' for the purpose of *The Lord of the Rings*. What he should have done in a visual representation of the tomb-inscription was to use, not of course their 'inner' names in Khuzdul, but their *real* 'outer' names which in the text of *The Lord of the Rings* are represented by *Balin* and *Fundin*.]

23 [It seems that it was when my father reached this point in the essay that he made the alterations to the text on p. 300 with the marginal observation given in note 20, and struck out the latter part of note 21.]

24 He alone had no companions; cf. 'he slept alone' (III.352). [The reference is to the beginning of Appendix A, III. The passage in the text is difficult to interpret. My father refers here to four places of awakening of the Seven Ancestors of the Dwarves: those of 'the ancestors of the Firebeards and the Broadbeams', 'the ancestor of the Longbeards', 'the Ironfists and Stiffbeards', and 'the Blacklocks and Stonefoots'. (None of these names of the other six kindreds of the Dwarves has ever been given before. Since the ancestors of the Firebeards and the Broadbeams awoke in the Ered Lindon, these kindreds must be presumed to be the Dwarves of Nogrod and Belegost.) It seems that he was here referring to Durin's having 'slept alone' in contrast to the other kindreds, whose Fathers were laid to sleep in pairs. If this is so, it is a different conception from that cited in XI.213, where Ilúvatar 'commanded Aulë to lay the fathers of the Dwarves severally in deep places, each with his mate, save Durin the eldest who had none.' On the subject of the 'mates' of the Fathers of the Dwarves see XI.211–13. – In the margin of the typescript my father wrote later (against the present note): 'He wandered widely after awakening: his people were Dwarves that joined him from other kindreds west and east'; and at the head of the page he suggested that the legend of the Making of the Dwarves should be altered (indeed very radically altered) to a form in which other Dwarves were laid to sleep near to the Fathers.]

25 [In the rejected conclusion of note 21 the place of the awakening of the ancestor of the Longbeards was 'a valley in the Ered Mithrin' (the Grey Mountains in the far North). There has of course been no previous reference to this ancient significance of Mount Gundabad. That mountain originally appeared in the chapter *The Clouds Burst* in *The Hobbit*, where it is told that the

OF DWARVES AND MEN 323

Goblins 'marched and gathered by hill and valley, going ever by tunnel or under dark, until around and beneath the great mountain Gundabad of the North, where was their capital, a vast host was assembled'; and it is shown on the map of Wilderland in *The Hobbit* as a great isolated mass at the northern end of the Misty Mountains where the Grey Mountains drew towards them. In *The Lord of the Rings*, Appendix A (III), Gundabad appears in the account of the War of the Dwarves and Orcs late in the Third Age, where the Dwarves 'assailed and sacked one by one all the strongholds of the Orcs that they could [find] from Gundabad to the Gladden' (the word 'find' was erroneously dropped in the Second Edition).]

26 According to their legends their begetter, Aulë the Vala, had made this for them and had taught it to the Seven Fathers before they were laid to sleep until the time for their awakening should come. After their awakening this language (as all languages and all other things in Arda) changed in time, and divergently in the mansions that were far-sundered. But the change was so slow and the divergence so small that even in the Third Age converse between all Dwarves in their own tongue was easy. As they said, the change in Khuzdul as compared with the tongue of the Elves, and still more with those of Men, was 'like the weathering of hard rock compared with the melting of snow.'

27 The Dwarves multiplied slowly; but Men in prosperity and peace more swiftly than even the Elves.

28 For they had met some far to the East who were of evil mind. [This was a later pencilled note. On the previous page of the typescript my father wrote at the same time, without indication of its reference to the text but perhaps arising from the mention (p. 301) of the awakening of the eastern kindreds of the Dwarves: 'Alas, it seems probable that (as Men did later) the Dwarves of the far eastern mansions (and some of the nearer ones?) came under the Shadow of Morgoth and turned to evil.']

29 No Dwarf would ever mount a horse willingly, nor did any ever harbour animals, not even dogs.

30 For a time. The Númenóreans had not yet appeared on the shores of Middle-earth, and the foundations of the Barad-dûr had not yet been built. It was a brief period in the dark annals of the Second Age, yet for many lives of Men the Longbeards controlled the Ered Mithrin, Erebor, and the Iron Hills, and all the east side of the Misty Mountains as far as the confines of Lórien; while the Men of the North dwelt in all the adjacent lands as far south as the Great Dwarf Road that cut through the Forest (the Old Forest Road was its ruinous remains in the Third Age) and then went North-east to the Iron Hills. [As with so much else in this account, the origin of the Old Forest Road in 'the Great Dwarf

324   THE PEOPLES OF MIDDLE-EARTH

Road', which after traversing Greenwood the Great led to the Iron Hills, has never been met before.]

31 Only the personal names of individuals. The name of their race, and the names of their families, and of their mansions, they did not conceal.

32 Either actual Mannish names current among the Northern Men, or names made in the same ways out of elements in the Mannish tongue, or names of no meaning that were simply made of the sounds used by Men put together in ways natural to their speech.

33 [My father might seem to write here as if *Durin* was the 'real' Mannish name of the Father of the Longbeards; but of course it is a name derived from Old Norse, and thus a 'translation'.]

34 Somewhat similar to the way in which the 'runes' of Elvish origin were widely regarded by Men in the Third Age as a Dwarvish mode of writing.

35 Sauron was defeated by the Númenóreans and driven back into Mordor, and for long troubled the West no more, while secretly extending his dominions eastward.

36 Though such changes and divergence as had already occurred before they left Middle-earth would have endured – such as the divergence of the speech of the Teleri from that of the Ñoldor.

37 [This and the subsequent section-heading, together with their numbers, were pencilled in later. The title of section I is lost with the loss of the first page of the essay.]

38 The name is said to have been derived from *atan* 'man, human being as distinct from creatures', a word used by that kindred which the Eldar first encountered in Beleriand. This was borrowed and adapted to Quenya and Sindarin; but later when Men of other kinds became known to the Eldar it became limited to Men of the Three Peoples who had become allies of the Eldar in Beleriand.

[A typewritten draft for the page of the essay on which this second section begins is preserved (though without the section-heading or number, see note 37): in this draft the present note begins in the same way, but diverges after the words 'adapted to Quenya and Sindarin' thus:

> It was however associated by the Eldar with their own word *atar (adar)* 'father' and often translated 'Fathers of Men', though this title, in full *atanatar*, properly belonged only to the leaders and chieftains of the peoples at the time of their entry into Beleriand. In Sindarin *adan* was still often used for 'man', especially in names of races with a preceding prefix, as in *Dún-adan*, plural *Dúnedain*, 'Men of the West', Númenóreans; *Drû-edain* 'Wild-men'.

The statement here that *Atani* was derived from a word in the

Bëorian language, *atan* 'man', contradicts what was said in the chapter *Of the Coming of Men into the West* that was added to the *Quenta Silmarillion*, XI.219, footnote: '*Atani* was the name given to Men in Valinor, in the lore that told of their coming; according to the Eldar it signified "Second", for the kindred of Men was the second of the Children of Ilúvatar'; cf. *Quendi and Eldar*, XI.386, where essentially the same is said (the devising of the name *Atani* is there ascribed to the Ñoldor in Valinor).]

39 [This refers to Morgoth's captivity in Aman. See X.423, note 3.]

40 [Cf. the words of Andreth, X.310, and of Bereg and Amlach, XI.220, §18).]

41 [Haleth was not the name of the chieftain who commanded the Folk of Haleth when they first came to Beleriand: see XI.221–2 and the genealogical tree, XI.237. But this is probably not significant, in view of what is said at the end of the paragraph: these people 'were called the Folk of Haleth, for Haleth was the name of their chieftainess who led them to the woods north of Doriath where they were permitted to dwell.' On the other hand, the statement that Hador was the name of the chieftain who led the Folk of Hador into Beleriand seems to ignore that greatly enlarged and altered history that had entered in the chapter *Of the Coming of Men into the West* (cf. note 38), according to which it was Marach who led that people over the Mountains, and Hador himself, though he gave his name to the people, was a descendant of Marach in the fourth generation (see XI.218–19 and the genealogical tree, XI.234). In that work the division of the Folk of Hador into three hosts, referred to a little later in the present paragraph, does not appear – indeed it was said (XI.218, §10) that Bëor told Felagund that 'they are a numerous people, and yet keep together and move slowly, being all ruled by one chieftain whom they call Marach.']

42 [In other accounts the Folk of Haleth were the second kindred of the Edain to enter Beleriand, not the last; thus in QS §127 (V.275), when Haleth was still Haleth the Hunter and had not been transformed into the Lady Haleth, 'After Bëor came Haleth father of Hundor, and again somewhat later came Hador the Goldenhaired', and in *Of the Coming of Men into the West* §13 (XI.218) 'First came the Haladin ... The next year, however, Marach led his people over the Mountains'. In that text (§10) Bëor told Felagund that the people of Marach 'were before us in the westward march, but we passed them', and there is no suggestion of the story told here that they reached Eredlindon first of all the Edain, but that 'seeking a road round the Mountains' they 'came up from southward' into Beleriand. – Of internal strife among the Folk of Haleth, referred to a few lines later in this paragraph, there has been no previous mention.]

43 No doubt this was due to mingling with Men of other kind in the past; and it was noted that the dark hair ran in families that had more skill and interest in crafts and lore.

44 With a knowledge of the language of the Folk of Bëor that was later lost, save for a few names of persons and places, and some words or phrases preserved in legends. One of the common words was *atan*. [With the last sentence cf. note 38.]

45 [With this is perhaps to be compared what my father wrote elsewhere at this time (p. 373, note 13) concerning the long period during which the 'Bëorians' and the 'Hadorians' became separated in the course of their westward migration and dwelt on opposite sides of a great inland sea.]

46 Beren the Renowned had hair of a golden brown and grey eyes; he was taller than most of his kin, but he was broad-shouldered and very strong in his limbs.

47 The Eldar said, and recalled in the songs they still sang in later days, that they could not easily be distinguished from the Eldar – not while their youth lasted, the swift fading of which was to the Eldar a grief and a mystery.

48 [With this account of the Folk of Bëor and the Folk of Hador may be compared the description that my father wrote many years before in the *Quenta Silmarillion*, V.276, §130.]

49 [On the alteration of the relationship between the three languages of the Atani, whereby that of the Folk of Haleth replaced that of the Folk of Hador as the tongue isolated from the others, see p. 368 and note 4.]

50 Not due to their special situation in Beleriand, and maybe rather a cause of their small numbers than its result. They increased in numbers far more slowly than the other Atani, hardly more than was sufficient to replace the wastage of war; yet many of their women (who were fewer than the men) remained unwed.

51 [Apart from some slight and largely unnecessary modifications to the original text (in no case altering the sense) there are a few points to mention about that printed in *Unfinished Tales*. (1) The spelling *Ork(s)* was changed to *Orc(s)*, and that of the river *Taiglin* to *Teiglin* (see XI.228, 309–10). (2) A passage about the liking of the Drûgs for edible fungus was omitted in view of my father's pencilled note beside it: 'Delete all this about funguses. Too like Hobbits' (a reference of course to Frodo and Farmer Maggot's mushrooms). This followed the account of the knowledge of the Drûgs concerning plants, and reads:

> To the astonishment of Elves and other Men they ate funguses with pleasure, many of which looked to others ugly and dangerous; some kinds which they specially liked they caused to grow near their dwellings. The Eldar did not eat these things. The Folk of Haleth, taught by the Drúedain, made

some use of them at need; and if they were guests they ate what was provided in courtesy, and without fear. The other Atani eschewed them, save in great hunger when astray in the wild, for few among them had the knowledge to distinguish the wholesome from the bad, and the less wise called them ork-plants and supposed them to have been cursed and blighted by Morgoth.]

52 [See *Unfinished Tales*, p. 386, note 8. Elsewhere Húrin's serving-man is named *Sador*, not *Sadog*.]
53 [This sentence is cited in *Unfinished Tales*, p. 387, note 11.]
54 See the discussion of lineal measurements and their equation with our measures in the legend of *The Disaster of the Gladden Fields*. [This discussion (which, with the work itself, belongs to the very late period – 1968 or later) is found in *Unfinished Tales*, pp. 285 ff., where a note on the stature of Hobbits is also given.]
55 In the original sense of 'savage'; they were by nature of gentle disposition, neither cruel nor vindictive.
56 Of different kinds: Dwarves they found of uncertain temper and dangerous if displeased; Elves they viewed with awe, and avoided. Even in the Shire in the Third Age, where Elves were more often to be met than in other regions where Hobbits dwelt or had dwelt, most of the Shire-folk would have no dealings with them. 'They wander in Middle-earth,' they said, 'but their minds and hearts are not there.'
57 ['Nowhere else in the world was this peculiar (but excellent) arrangement to be found': opening of the chapter *At the Sign of the Prancing Pony*. This observation is here attributed to Bilbo as the ultimate author of the Red Book of Westmarch.]
58 Indeed it is probable that only at Bree and in the Shire did any communities of Hobbits survive at that time west of the Misty Mountains. Nothing is known of the situation in lands further east, from which the Hobbits must have migrated in unrecorded ages.
59 When they entered Eriador (early in the second century of the Third Age) Men were still numerous there, both Númenóreans and other Men related to the Atani, beside remnants of Men of evil kinds, hostile to the Kings. But the Common Speech (of Númenórean origin) was in general use there, even after the decay of the North Kingdom. In Bilbo's time great areas of Eriador were empty of Men. The desolation had begun in the Great Plague (soon after the Hobbits' occupation of the Shire), and was hastened by the final fall and disappearance of the North Kingdom. In the Plague it would seem that the only Hobbit communities to survive were those in the far North-west at Bree and in the Shire. [The opening sentence of this note, placing the entry of the Hobbits into Eriador 'early in the second century of the

Third Age', is plainly a casual error: presumably my father intended 'millennium' for 'century' (in Appendix B the date of the coming of the Harfoots is given under Third Age 1050, and that of the Fallohides and the Stoors under 1150).]

60 The invasions were no doubt also in great part due to Sauron; for the 'Easterlings' were mostly Men of cruel and evil kind, descendants of those who had served and worshipped Sauron before his overthrow at the end of the Second Age.

61 Though the native traditions of the Rohirrim preserved no memories of the ancient war in Beleriand, they accepted the belief, which did much to strengthen their friendship with Gondor and their unbroken loyalty to the Oath of Eorl and Cirion. [In relation to this note and to the passage in the text to which it refers my father wrote in the margin of the typescript:

> It may have been actually true of those Men in Middle-earth whom the returning Númenóreans first met (see below); but other Men of the North resembling them in features and temper can only have been akin as descending from peoples of which the Atani had been the vanguard.]

62 [In *Quendi and Eldar* (XI.377) there is a reference to Avari 'who had crept in small and secret groups into Beleriand from the South', and to rare cases of an Avar 'who joined with or was admitted among the Sindar'; while in that essay Eöl of Nan Elmoth was an Avar (XI.409 and note 33).]

63 [The Little Lune was first marked on the third and last of my father's general maps of the West of Middle-earth (that on which my original map published with *The Lord of the Rings* was closely based), but this appears to be the first time that it has been named.]

64 [With this statement that the region beyond the inflow of the Little Lune was 'Dwarf territory' cf. Appendix A (I, iii), where it is told that Arvedui, the last king of Arthedain, 'hid in the tunnels of the old dwarf-mines near the far end of the Mountains'.]

65 Gil-galad's people were mainly Ñoldorin; though in the Second Age the Elves of Harlindon were mainly Sindarin, and the region was a fief under the rule of Celeborn. [In the prefatory note to the annals of the Second Age in Appendix B it is said: 'In Lindon south of the Lune dwelt for a time Celeborn, kinsman of Thingol'; see *Unfinished Tales* p. 233 and note 2, where the present note is referred to.]

66 [See *Unfinished Tales*, pp. 262–3 (extract from a late essay on the names of the rivers and beacon-hills of Gondor). – The name was typed *Enedwaith* with the *h* added subsequently, but later in this essay (note 76) the form typed is *Enedhwaith*; so also in that on river-names just mentioned, although in the extracts given in

OF DWARVES AND MEN

Unfinished Tales I printed *Enedwaith* for agreement with published texts.]

67 This according to the traditions of Dol Amroth had been established by seafaring Sindar from the west havens of Beleriand who fled in three small ships when the power of Morgoth overwhelmed the Eldar and the Atani; but it was later increased by adventurers of the Silvan Elves seeking for the Sea who came down the Anduin. The Silvan Elves were Middle Elves according to the Númenórean classification, though unknown to the Atani until later days: for they were like the Sindar Teleri, but were laggards in the hindmost companies who had never crossed the Misty Mountains and established small realms on either side of the Vales of Anduin. (Of these Lórien and the realm of Thranduil in Mirkwood were survivors in the Third Age.) But they were never wholly free of an unquiet and a yearning for the Sea which at times drove some of them to wander from their homes. [On this haven (Edhellond) see *Unfinished Tales*, pp. 246–7 and note 18 on p. 255.]

68 The first sailings of the Númenóreans to Middle-earth were to the lands of Gil-galad, with whom their great mariner Aldarion made an alliance.

69 As the power of Númenor became more and more occupied with great navies, for which their own land could not supply sufficient timber without ruin, their felling of trees and transportation of wood to their shipyards in Númenor or on the coast of Middle-earth (especially at Lond Daer, the Great Harbour at the mouth of the Greyflood) became reckless. [See *Unfinished Tales*, p. 262, on the tree-felling of the Númenóreans in Minhiriath and Enedhwaith. Of the kinship of the forest-dwellers of those regions with the People of Haleth there is no suggestion elsewhere (see also note 72 below). With the following sentence in the text, 'In the Third Age their survivors were the people known in Rohan as the Dunlendings' cf. *Unfinished Tales*, p. 263: 'From Enedhwaith they [the native people fleeing from the Númenóreans] took refuge in the eastern mountains where afterwards was Dunland'.]

70 [This was the voyage of Vëantur the Númenórean, grandfather of Aldarion the Mariner: see *Unfinished Tales*, pp. 171, 174–5.]

71 [At the words in the text printed in *Unfinished Tales* 'as if addressing friends and kinsmen after a long parting' there is a note in the essay which I did not include:

> The Atani had learned the Sindarin tongue in Beleriand and most of them, especially the high men and the learned, had spoken it familiarly, even among themselves: but always as a learned language, taught in early childhood; their native

language remained the Adûnaic, the Mannish tongue of the Folk of Hador (except in some districts of the west of the Isle where the rustic folk used a Bëorian dialect). Thus the Sindarin they used had remained unchanged through many lives of Men.

With this cf. *Unfinished Tales*, p. 215 note 19. I do not know how the mention here of 'a Bëorian dialect' surviving in the west of Númenor is to be related to the total loss of the language of the Folk of Bëor referred to in note 44; see also p. 368 and note 5.]

72 This may have been one of the reasons why the Númenóreans failed to recognize the Forest-folk of Minhiriath as 'kinsmen', and confused them with Men of the Shadow; for as has been noted the native language of the Folk of Haleth was not related to the language of the Folks of Hador and Bëor.

73 And those that they adopted from older inhabitants they usually altered to fit the Sindarin style. Their names of persons also were nearly all of Sindarin form, save a few which had descended from the legends of the Atani in the First Age.

74 It thus became naturally somewhat corrupted from the true Sindarin of the Elves, but this was hindered by the fact that Sindarin was held in high esteem and was taught in the schools, according to forms and grammatical structure of ancient days.

75 The Elf-realm became diminished in the wars against Sauron, and by the establishment of Imladris, and it no longer extended east of the Ered Luin.

76 The Enedhwaith (or Central Wilderness) was shared by the North and South Kingdoms, but was never settled by Númenóreans owing to the hostility of the Gwathuirim (Dunlendings), except in the fortified town and haven about the great bridge over the Greyflood at Tharbad. [The name *Gwathuirim* of the Dunlendings has not occurred before.]

77 [It was said in Appendix A (I, iv) that at the height of its power the realm of Gondor 'extended north to Celebrant', and a long note in the essay at this point, beginning 'But for "Celebrant" read "Field of Celebrant"', is an exposition of the significance of the latter name (*Parth Celebrant*). This note is given in *Unfinished Tales*, p. 260.]

78 [The River Running is named *Celduin* in Appendix A, III (RK p. 353). *Celon* was the river that in the First Age rose in the Hill of Himring and flowed past Nan Elmoth to join the Aros; and since *Celduin* as the name of the River Running appears in the very late text *Cirion and Eorl* (*Unfinished Tales* p. 289) *Celon* here is presumably no more than a casual confusion of the names.]

XI
THE SHIBBOLETH OF FËANOR
With an excursus on the name of
the descendants of Finwë

In all my father's last writings linguistic history was closely intertwined with the history of persons and of peoples, and much that he recounted can be seen to have arisen in the search for explanations of linguistic facts or anomalies. The most remarkable example of this is the following essay, arising from his consideration of a problem of historical phonology, which records how the difference in pronunciation of a single consonantal element in Quenya played a significant part in the strife of the Noldorin princes in Valinor. It has no title, but I have called it *The Shibboleth of Fëanor*, since my father himself used that word in the course of the essay (p. 336).

Like *Of Dwarves and Men*, it was written (composed in typescript throughout) on paper supplied by Allen and Unwin, in this case mostly copies of a publication note of February 1968; and as in that essay there are very many notes interpolated into the body of the text in the process of composition. Appended to it is a lengthy excursus (half as long again as the essay from which it arose) on the names of Finwë's descendants, and this I give also; but from both *The Shibboleth of Fëanor* proper and from this excursus I have excluded a number of notes, some of them lengthy, of a technical phonological nature. The work was not finished, for my father did not reach, as was his intention, discussion of the names of the Sons of Fëanor; but such draft material as there is for this part is given at the end of the text. All numbered notes, both my father's and mine, are collected on pp. 356 ff.

This work was scarcely used in *Unfinished Tales* except for a passage concerning Galadriel, which is here repeated in its original context; but elements were used in the published *Silmarillion*.

The Shibboleth of Fëanor
The case of the Quenya change of þ to s[1]

The history of the Eldar is now fixed and the adoption of Sindarin by the Exiled Ñoldor cannot be altered. Since Sindarin made great use of þ, the change þ > s must have occurred in Ñoldorin Quenya in Valinor before the rebellion and exile of the Ñoldor, though not necessarily long before it (in Valinorian reckoning of time). The change cannot therefore be explained as a development (that is a sound-substitution of *s* for an unfamiliar *þ*) in Quenya of the Third Age: either due to the Elves themselves, since they were familiar with *þ*; or to such people as the Númenórean scholars in Gondor, since *þ* occurred in the Common Speech, and also in the Sindarin which was still used as a spoken language among the upper classes, especially in Minas Tirith.

The use by Galadriel, as reported in *The Lord of the Rings*, must therefore be normal. It is not however an obstacle to the use of *þ* in representing the classical book-Quenya, pre-Exilic or post-Exilic, in grammars, dictionaries or transcripts. It is in fact desirable, since the older *þ* was always kept distinct in writing from original *s*. This in Exilic conditions, which made necessary the writing down anew from memory of many of the pre-Exilic works of lore and song,[2] implies a continuing memory of the sound *þ*, and the places in which it had previously occurred; also probably a dislike of the change to *s* in the colloquial Quenya on the part of the scholars. It is in any case impossible to believe that any of the Ñoldor ever became unfamiliar with the sound *þ* as such. In Valinor they dwelt between the Vanyar (Ingwi) and the Teleri (Lindar),[3] with whom they were in communication and sometimes intermarried. The Vanyar spoke virtually the same language (Quenya) and retained *þ* in daily use; the Teleri spoke a closely related language still largely intelligible to the Ñoldor,[4] and it also used *þ*. The Ñoldor were, even compared with other Eldar, talented linguists, and if *þ* did not occur in the language that they learned in childhood – which could only be the case with the youngest generations of those who set out from Aman – they would have had no difficulty in acquiring it.

The change *þ* > *s* must therefore have been a conscious and deliberate change agreed to and accepted by a majority of the Ñoldor, however initiated, after the separation of their dwellings from the Vanyar. It must have occurred after the birth of Míriel, but (probably) before the birth of Fëanor. The special connexion of these two persons with the change and its later history needs some consideration.

The change was a general one, based primarily on phonetic 'taste' and theory, but it had not yet become universal. It was attacked by the loremasters,[5] who pointed out that the damage this merging would do in confusing stems and their derivatives that had been distinct in sound and sense had not yet been sufficiently considered. The chief of the linguistic loremasters at that time was Fëanor. He insisted that þ was the true pronunciation for all who cared for or fully understood their language. But in addition to linguistic taste and wisdom he had other motives. He was the eldest of Finwë's sons and the only child of his first wife Míriel. She was a Ñoldorin Elda of slender and graceful form, and of gentle disposition, though as was later discovered in matters far more grave, she could show an ultimate obstinacy that counsel or command would only make more obdurate. She had a beautiful voice and a delicate and clear enunciation, though she spoke swiftly and took pride in this skill. Her chief talent, however, was a marvellous dexterity of hand. This she employed in embroidery, which though achieved in what even the Eldar thought a speed of haste was finer and more intricate than any that had before been seen. She was therefore called *Perindë* (Needlewoman) – a name which she had indeed already been given as a 'mother-name'.[6] She adhered to the pronunciation þ (it had still been usual in her childhood), and she desired that all her kin should adhere to it also, at the least in the pronunciation of her name.

Fëanor loved his mother dearly, though except in obstinacy their characters were widely different. He was not gentle. He was proud and hot-tempered, and opposition to his will he met not with the quiet steadfastness of his mother but with fierce resentment. He was restless in mind and body, though like Míriel he could become wholly absorbed in works of the finest skill of hand; but he left many things unfinished. Fëanáro was his mother-name, which Míriel gave him in recognition of his impetuous character (it meant 'spirit of fire'). While she lived she did much with gentle counsel to soften and restrain him.[7] Her death was a lasting grief to Fëanor, and both directly and by its further consequences a main cause of his later disastrous influence on the history of the Ñoldor.

The death of Míriel Þerindë – death of an 'immortal' Elda in the deathless land of Aman – was a matter of grave anxiety to the Valar, the first presage of the Shadow that was to fall on Valinor. The matter of Finwë and Míriel and the judgement that the Valar after long debate finally delivered upon it is elsewhere told.[8] Only those points that may explain the conduct of Fëanor are here recalled. Míriel's death was of free will: she forsook her body and her *fëa* went to the Halls of Waiting, while her body lay as if asleep in a garden. She said that she was weary in body and spirit and desired peace. The cause of her weariness she believed to be the bearing of Fëanor, great in mind and body beyond the measure of the Eldar. Her weariness she had endured until he was full grown, but she could endure it no longer.

The Valar and all the Eldar were grieved by the sorrow of Finwë, but not dismayed: all things could be healed in Aman, and when they were rested her *fëa* and its body could be reunited and return to the joy of life in the Blessed Realm. But Míriel was reluctant, and to all the pleas of her husband and her kin that were reported to her, and to the solemn counsels of the Valar, she would say no more than 'not yet'. Each time that she was approached she became more fixed in her determination, until at last she would listen no more, saying only: 'I desire peace. Leave me in peace here! I will not return. That is my will.'

So the Valar were faced by the one thing that they could neither change nor heal: the free will of one of the Children of Eru, which it was unlawful for them to coerce – and in such a case useless, since force could not achieve its purpose. And after some years they were faced by another grave perplexity. When it became clear at last that Míriel would never of her own will return to life in the body within any span of time that could give him hope, Finwë's sorrow became embittered. He forsook his long vigils by her sleeping body and sought to take up his own life again; but he wandered far and wide in loneliness and found no joy in anything that he did.

There was a fair lady of the Vanyar, Indis of the House of Ingwë. She had loved Finwë in her heart, ever since the days when the Vanyar and the Ñoldor lived close together. In one of his wanderings Finwë met her again upon the inner slopes of Oiolossë, the Mountain of Manwë and Varda; and her face was lit by the golden light of Laurelin that was shining in the plain of Ezellohar below.[9] In that hour Finwë perceived in her eyes the love that had before been hidden from him. So it came to pass that Finwë and Indis desired to be wedded, and Finwë sought the counsel of the Valar.

The long debate that they held on the matter may be passed over briefly. They were obliged to choose between two courses: condemning Finwë to bereavement of a wife for ever, or allowing one of the Eldar to take a second wife. The former seemed a cruel injustice, and contrary to the nature of the Eldar. The second they had thought unlawful, and some still held to that opinion.[10] The end of the Debate was that the marriage of Finwë and Indis was sanctioned. It was judged that Finwë's bereavement was unjust, and by persisting in her refusal to return Míriel had forfeited all rights that she had in the case; for either she was now capable of accepting the healing of her body by the Valar, or else her *fëa* was mortally sick and beyond their power, and she was indeed 'dead', no longer capable of becoming again a living member of the kindred of the Eldar.

'So she must remain until the end of the world. For from the moment that Finwë and Indis are joined in marriage all future change and choice will be taken from her and she will never again be permitted to take bodily shape. Her present body will swiftly wither and pass away, and the Valar will not restore it. For none of the Eldar may have two wives both alive in the world.' These were the words of Manwë, and an answer to the doubts that some had felt. For it was known to all the Valar that they alone had the power to heal or restore the body for the re-housing of a *fëa* that should in the later chances of the world be deprived; but that to Manwë also was given the right to refuse the return of the *fëa*.

During the time of his sorrow Finwë had little comfort from Fëanor. For a while he also had kept vigil by his mother's body, but soon he became wholly absorbed again in his own works and devices. When the matter of Finwë and Indis arose he was disturbed, and filled with anger and resentment; though it is not recorded that he attended the Debate or paid heed to the reasons given for the judgement, or to its terms except in one point: that Míriel was condemned to remain for ever discarnate, so that he could never again visit her or speak with her, unless he himself should die.[11] This grieved him, and he grudged the happiness of Finwë and Indis, and was unfriendly to their children, even before they were born.

How this ill will grew and festered in the years that followed is the main matter of the first part of *The Silmarillion*: the Darkening of Valinor. Into the strife and confusion of loyalties in that time this seemingly trivial matter, the change of *þ* to *s*, was caught up to its embitterment, and to lasting detriment to the Quenya tongue. Had peace been maintained there can be no doubt that the advice of Fëanor, with which all the other loremasters privately or openly agreed, would have prevailed. But an opinion in which he was certainly right was rejected because of the follies and evil deeds into which he was later led. He made it a personal matter: he and his sons adhered to *þ*, and they demanded that all those who were sincere in their support should do the same. Therefore those who resented his arrogance, and still more those whose support later turned to hatred, rejected his shibboleth.

Indis was a Vanya, and it might be thought that she would in this point at least have pleased Fëanor, since the Vanyar adhered to *þ*. Nonetheless Indis adopted *s*. Not as Fëanor believed in belittlement of Míriel, but in loyalty to Finwë. For after the rejection of his prayers by Míriel Finwë accepted the change (which had now become almost universal among his people), although in deference to Míriel he had adhered to *þ* while she lived. Therefore Indis said: 'I have joined the people of the Ñoldor, and I will speak as they do.' So it came about that to Fëanor the rejection of *þ* became a symbol of the rejection of Míriel, and of himself, her son, as the chief of the Ñoldor next to Finwë. This, as his pride grew and his mood darkened, he thought was a 'plot' of the Valar, inspired by fear of his powers, to oust him and give the leadership of the Ñoldor to those more servile. So Fëanor would call himself 'Son of the *Þerindë*', and when his sons in their childhood asked why their kin in the house of Finwë used *s* for *þ* he answered: 'Take no heed! We speak as is right, and as King Finwë himself did before he was led astray. We are his heirs by right and the elder house. Let them *sá-sí*, if they can speak no better.'

There can thus be no doubt that the majority of the Exiles used *s* for *þ* in their daily speech; for in the event (after Morgoth had contrived the murder of Finwë) Fëanor was deprived of the leadership, and the greater part of the Ñoldor who forsook Valinor marched under the command of Fingolfin, the eldest son of Indis. Fingolfin was his father's son, tall, dark, and proud, as were most of the Ñoldor, and in the end in spite of the enmity between him and Fëanor he joined with full will in the rebellion and the exile, though he continued to claim the kingship of all the Ñoldor.

The case of Galadriel and her brother Finrod is somewhat different.[12] They were the children of Finarfin, Indis' second son. He was of his mother's kind in mind and body, having the golden hair of the Vanyar, their noble and gentle temper, and their love of the Valar. As well as he could he kept aloof from the strife of his brothers and their estrangement from the Valar, and he often sought peace among the Teleri, whose language he learned. He wedded Eärwen, the daughter of King Olwë, and his children were thus the kin of King Elwë Þindikollo[13] (in Sindarin Elu Thingol) of Doriath in Beleriand, for he was the brother of Olwë; and this kinship influenced their decision to join in the Exile, and proved of great importance later in Beleriand. Finrod was like his father in his fair face and golden hair, and also in noble and generous heart, though he had the high courage of the Ñoldor and in his youth their eagerness and unrest; and he had also from his Telerin mother a love of the sea and dreams of far lands that he had never seen. Galadriel was the greatest of the Ñoldor, except Fëanor maybe, though she was wiser than he, and her wisdom increased with the long years.

Her mother-name was Nerwen 'man-maiden', and she grew to be tall beyond the measure even of the women of the Ñoldor; she was strong of body, mind, and will, a match for both the loremasters and the athletes of the Eldar in the days of their youth. Even among the Eldar she was accounted beautiful, and her hair was held a marvel unmatched. It was golden like the hair of her father and her foremother Indis, but richer and more radiant, for its gold was touched by some memory of the star-like silver of her mother; and the Eldar said that the light of the Two Trees, Laurelin and Telperion, had been snared in her tresses. Many thought that this saying first gave to Fëanor the thought of imprisoning and blending the light of the Trees that later took shape in his hands as the Silmarils. For Fëanor beheld the hair of Galadriel with wonder and delight. He begged three times for a tress, but Galadriel would not give him even one hair. These two kinsfolk, the greatest of the Eldar of Valinor,[14] were unfriends for ever.

Galadriel was born in the bliss of Valinor, but it was not long, in the reckoning of the Blessed Realm, before that was dimmed; and thereafter she had no peace within. For in that testing time amid the strife of the Ñoldor she was drawn this way and that. She was proud, strong, and self-willed, as were all the descendants of Finwë save Finarfin; and like her brother Finrod, of all her kin the nearest to her heart, she had dreams of far lands and dominions that might be her own to order as she would without tutelage. Yet deeper still there dwelt in her the noble and generous spirit (*órë*) of the Vanyar, and a reverence for the Valar that she could not forget. From her earliest years she had a marvellous gift of insight into the minds of others, but judged them with mercy and understanding, and she withheld her good will from none save only Fëanor. In him she perceived a darkness that she hated and feared, though she did not perceive that the shadow of the same evil had fallen upon the minds of all the Ñoldor, and upon her own.

So it came to pass that when the light of Valinor failed, for ever as the Ñoldor thought, she joined the rebellion against the Valar who commanded them to stay; and once she had set foot upon that road of exile, she would not relent, but rejected the last message of the Valar, and came under the Doom of Mandos. Even after the merciless assault upon the Teleri and the rape of their ships, though she fought fiercely against Fëanor in defence of her mother's kin, she did not turn back. Her pride was unwilling to return, a defeated suppliant for pardon; but now she burned with desire to follow Fëanor with her anger to whatever lands he might come, and to thwart him in all ways that she could. Pride still moved her when, at the end of the Elder Days after the final overthrow of Morgoth, she refused the pardon of the Valar for all who had fought against him, and remained in Middle-earth. It was not until two long ages more had passed, when at last all that she had desired in her youth came to her hand, the Ring of Power and the dominion of Middle-earth of which she had dreamed, that her wisdom was full grown and she rejected it, and passing the last test departed from Middle-earth for ever.

The change to *s* had become general among the Ñoldor long before the birth of Galadriel and no doubt was familiar to her. Her father Finarfin, however, loved the Vanyar (his mother's people) and the Teleri, and in his house *þ* was used, Finarfin being moved by Fëanor neither one way or the other but doing as he wished. It is clear nonetheless that opposition to Fëanor soon became a dominant motive with Galadriel, while her pride did not take the form of wishing to be different from her own people. So while she knew well the history of their tongue and all the reasons of the loremasters, she certainly used *s* in her own daily speech. Her Lament – spoken before she knew of the pardon (and indeed honour) that the Valar gave her – harks back to the days of her youth in Valinor and to the darkness of the years of Exile while the Blessed Realm was closed to all the

Ñoldor in Middle-earth. Whatever she may have done later, when Fëanor and all his sons had perished, and Quenya was a language of lore known and used only by the dwindling remnant of the High Elves (of Ñoldorin descent), she would in this song certainly have used *s*.

The *s* was certainly used in Beleriand by nearly all the Ñoldor.[15] And it was in this form (though with knowledge of its history and the difference in spelling) that Quenya was handed on to the loremasters of the Atani, so that in Middle-earth it lingered on among the learned, and a source of high and noble names in Rivendell and in Gondor into the Fourth Age.

The essay is followed by three 'notes'. Note 1 is a substantial development of the words in the essay (p. 332) 'The change was ... based primarily on phonetic "taste" and theory', which is here omitted. Note 2, given below, is an account of Elvish name-giving that differs in some important respects from the earlier and far more complex account in *Laws and Customs among the Eldar*, X.214–17. Note 3 is the long account of the names of Finwë's descendants.

Note on Mother-names

The Eldar in Valinor had as a rule two names, or *essi*. The first-given was the father-name, received at birth. It usually recalled the father's name, resembling it in sense or form; sometimes it was simply the father's name, to which some distinguishing prefix in the case of a son might be added later when the child was full-grown. The mother-name was given later, often some years later, by the mother; but sometimes it was given soon after birth. For the mothers of the Eldar were gifted with deep insight into their children's characters and abilities, and many had also the gift of prophetic foresight.

In addition any of the Eldar might acquire an *epessë* ('after-name'), not necessarily given by their own kin, a nickname – mostly given as a title of admiration or honour. Later some among the exiles gave themselves names, as disguises or in reference to their own deeds and personal history: such names were called *kilmessi* 'self-names' (literally names of personal choice).[16]

The 'true names' remained the first two, but in later song and history any of the four might become the name generally used and recognized. The true names were not however forgotten by the scribes and loremasters or the poets, and they might often be introduced without comment. To this difficulty – as it proved to those who in later days tried to use and adapt Elvish traditions of the First Age as a background to the legends of their own heroes of that time and their descendants[17] – was added the alteration of the Quenya names of the Ñoldor, after their settlement in Beleriand and adoption of the Sindarin tongue.

The names of Finwë's descendants

Few of the oldest names of the Eldar are recorded, except those of the four leaders of the hosts on the Great Journey: *Ingwë* of the Vanyar; *Finwë* of the Ñoldor; and the brothers *Elwë* and *Olwë* of the Teleri. It is not certain that these names had any 'meaning', that is any intentional reference to or connexion with other stems already existing in primitive Eldarin; in any case they must have been formed far back in the history of Elvish speech. They consist each of a stem (*ing-*, *fin-*, *el-*, *ol-*) followed by a 'suffix' *-wë*. The suffix appears frequently in other Quenya names of the First Age, such as *Voronwë*, generally but not exclusively masculine.[18] This the loremasters explained as being not in origin a suffix, though it survived in Quenya only as a final element in names, but an old word for 'person', derivative of a stem EWE. This took as a second element in a compound the form *wē*; but as an independent word *ewē*, preserved in Telerin as *evë* 'a person, somebody (unnamed)'. In Old Quenya it survived in the form *eo* (< *ew* + the pronominal suffix -ŏ 'a person, somebody'), later replaced by *námo*; also in the Old Quenya adjective *wéra*, Quenya *véra* 'personal, private, own'.

The first elements were often later explained as related to Quenya *inga* 'top, highest point' used adjectivally as a prefix, as in *ingaran* 'high-king', *ingor* 'summit of a mountain'; to Common Eldarin PHIN 'hair', as in Quenya *finë* 'a hair', *findë* 'hair, especially of the head', *finda* 'having hair, -haired'; and to the stem *el*, *elen* 'star'. Of these the most probable is the relation to *inga*; for the Vanyar were regarded, and regarded themselves, as the leaders and principal kindred of the Eldar, as they were the eldest; and they called themselves the *Ingwer* – in fact their king's proper title was *Ingwë Ingweron* 'chief of the chieftains'. The others are doubtful. All the Eldar had beautiful hair (and were especially attracted by hair of exceptional loveliness), but the Ñoldor were not specially remarkable in this respect, and there is no reference to Finwë as having had hair of exceptional length, abundance, or beauty beyond the measure of his people.[19] There is nothing known to connect Elwë more closely with the stars than all the other Eldar; and the name seems invented to go as a pair with Olwë, for which no 'meaning' was suggested. OL as a simple stem seems not to have occurred in Eldarin, though it appears in certain 'extended' stems, such as *olos/r* 'dream', *olob* 'branch' (Quenya *olba*); neither of which seems to be old enough, even if suitable in sense, to have any connexion with the name of the Ciriáran (mariner king) of the Teleri of Valinor.[20]

It must be realized that the names of the Eldar were not necessarily 'meaningful', though composed to fit the style and structure of their spoken languages; and that even when made or partly made of stems with a meaning these were not necessarily combined according to the normal modes of composition observed in ordinary words. Also that when the Eldar arrived in Aman and settled there they had already a long history behind them, and had developed customs to which they adhered, and also their languages had been elaborated and changed and were very different from their primitive speech as it was before the coming of Oromë. But since they were immortal or more properly said 'indefinitely longeval' many of the oldest Eldar had names devised long before, which had been unchanged except in the accommodation of their sounds to the changes observed in their language as compared with Primitive Eldarin.

This accommodation was mainly of the 'unheeded' kind: that is, personal names being used in daily speech followed the changes in that speech – though these were recognized and observed. The changes from the Quenya names of the Ñoldor to Sindarin forms when they settled in Beleriand in Middle-earth were on the other hand artificial and deliberate. They were made by the Ñoldor themselves. This was done because of the sensitiveness of the Eldar to languages and their styles. They felt it absurd and distasteful to call living persons who spoke Sindarin in daily life by names in quite a different linguistic mode.[21]

The Ñoldor of course fully understood the style and mode of Sindarin, though their learning of this difficult language was swift; but they did not necessarily understand the detail of its relation to Quenya. At first, except in the few words which the great changes in the Sindarin form of Telerin in Middle-earth had left unaltered or plainly similar, none of them understood or were yet interested in the linguistic history. It was at this early period that the translation of most of their Quenya names took place. In consequence these translations, though fitted entirely to Sindarin in form and style, were often inaccurate: that is, they did not always precisely correspond in sense; nor were the equated elements always actually the nearest Sindarin forms of the Quenya elements – sometimes they were not historically related at all, though they were more or less similar in sound.

It was, however, certainly the contact with Sindarin and the enlargement of their experience of linguistic change (especially the much swifter and more uncontrolled shifts observable in Middle-earth) that stimulated the studies of the linguistic loremasters, and it was in Beleriand that theories concerning Primitive Eldarin and the interrelation of its known descendants were developed. In this Fëanor played little part, except in so far as his own work and theories before the Exile had laid the foundations upon which his successors built. He himself perished too early in the war against Morgoth, largely because of his recklessness, to do more than note the differences between the dialects of North Sindarin (which was the only one he had time to learn) and the Western.[22]

The learning of the loremasters was available to all who were interested; but as the hopeless war dragged on, and after its earlier and deceptive successes passed through defeats and disasters to utter ruin of the Elvish realms, fewer and fewer of the Eldar had opportunity for 'lore' of any kind. An account of the years of the Siege of Angband in chronicle form would seem to leave neither place nor time for any of the arts of peace; but the years were long, and in fact there were intervals as long as many lives of Men and secure places long defended in which the High Eldar in exile laboured to recover what they could of the beauty and wisdom of their former home. All peace and all strongholds were at last destroyed by Morgoth; but if any wonder how any lore and treasure was preserved from ruin, it may be answered: of the treasure little was preserved, and the loss of things of beauty great and small is incalculable; but the lore of the Eldar did not depend on perishable records, being stored in the vast houses of their minds.[23] When the Eldar made records in written form, even those that to us would seem voluminous, they did only summarise, as it were, for the use of others whose lore was maybe in other fields of knowledge,[24] matters which were kept for ever undimmed in intricate detail in their minds.

Here are some of the chief names of Finwë and his descendants.

1. *Finwë* for whom no other names are recorded except his title *Ñoldóran* 'King of the Ñoldor'. His first wife was *Míriel* (first name) *Perindë* (mother-name). The names of her kin are not recorded. Her names were not translated. His second wife was *Indis*, which means 'great or valiant woman'. No other names are recorded. She is said to have been the daughter of King Ingwë's sister.

2. The only child of Míriel was afterwards usually called *Fëanor*. His first name was *Finwë (minya)*, afterwards enlarged when his talents developed to *Kurufinwë*. His mother-name was in Quenya, as given by Míriel, *Fëanáro* 'spirit of fire'. *Fëanor* is the form nearly always used in histories and legends, but is as it stands only half Sindarized: the genuine Sindarin form was *Faenor*; the form *Fëanor* (the ë is only a device of transcription, not needed in the original) probably arose through scribal confusion, especially in documents written in Quenya, in which *ea* was frequent but *ae* did not normally occur.[25]

3. Finwë had four children by Indis: a daughter *Findis*, a son, a daughter *Írimë*, and a son.[26] *Findis* was made by combining the names of her parents. Little is said of her in *The Silmarillion*. She did not go into exile, but went with her mother after the slaying of Finwë and they abode among the Vanyar in grief until such time as it seemed good to Manwë to restore Finwë to life.[27] His second daughter was named *Írien*[28] and her mother-name was *Lalwendë* (laughing maiden). By this name, or in shortened form *Lalwen*, she was generally known. She went into exile with her brother Fingolfin, who was most dear to her of all her kin; but her name was not changed, since *Lalwen* fitted the style of Sindarin well enough.[29]

To his sons Finwë gave his own name as he had done to Fëanor. This maybe was done to assert their claim to be his legitimate sons, equal in that respect to his eldest child *Kurufinwë Fayanáro*, but there was no intention of arousing discord among the brothers, since nothing in the judgement of the Valar in any way impaired Fëanor's position and rights as his eldest son. Nothing indeed was ever done to impair them, except by Fëanor himself; and in spite of all that later happened his eldest son remained nearest to Finwë's heart.

As with Fëanor, Finwë later added prefixes to their name: the elder he called Ñolofinwë, and the younger Arafinwë. Ñolo was the stem of words referring to wisdom,[30] and Ara, ar- a prefixed form of the stem Ara- 'noble'. Fëanor felt aggrieved both by the use of his father's name for his two younger brothers, and again by the prefixes that were added; for his pride was growing and clouding his reason: he thought himself not only the greatest master of Kurwë (which was true) but also of Nolmë (which was not true, save in matters of language), and certainly the noblest of the children of Finwë (which might have proved true, if he had not become the proudest and most arrogant).

The Ñoldor in exile as a rule chose one only of their names to be given a Sindarin shape; this was the name, usually, which each preferred (for various reasons), though the ease of 'translation' and its fitting into Sindarin style was also considered.

On Fëanor, Faenor see above. Ñolofinwë (one of the first to be changed) was given the form Fingolfin, that is Finwë Ñolofinwë was given a Sindarin style in sounds, and combined in one name. A most unusual procedure, and not imitated in any other name.[31] It was not a translation. The element Quenya ñolo- was merely given its equivalent Sindarin form gol. Finwë was simply reduced to fin in both places; thus was produced a name very much in Sindarin style but without meaning in that language. (If Finwë had been treated as a word of this form would have been, had it occurred anciently in Sindarin, it would have been Finu – but in the Northern dialect Fim, as in Curufim.)[32] Fingolfin had prefixed the name Finwë to Ñolofinwë before the Exiles reached Middle-earth. This was in pursuance of his claim to be the chieftain of all the Ñoldor after the death of Finwë, and so enraged Fëanor[33] that it was no doubt one of the reasons for his treachery in abandoning Fingolfin and stealing away with all the ships. The prefixion in the case of Finarfin was made by Finrod only after the death of Fingolfin in single combat with Morgoth. The Ñoldor then became divided into separate kingships under Fingon son of Fingolfin, Turgon his younger brother, Maedros son of Fëanor, and Finrod son of Arfin; and the following of Finrod had become the greatest.

4. The children of Fingolfin. Fingolfin's wife Anairë refused to leave Aman, largely because of her friendship with Eärwen wife of Arafinwë (though she was a Ñoldo and not one of the Teleri).

But all her children went with their father: *Findekáno, Turukáno, Arakáno,* and *Írissë* his daughter and third child; she was under the protection of Turukáno who loved her dearly, and of *Elenwë* his wife.[34] Findekáno had no wife or child;[35] neither had Arakáno.

These names were probably father-names, though *Arakáno* had been the mother-name of Fingolfin. *Káno* meant in Quenya 'commander', usually as the title of a lesser chief, especially one acting as the deputy of one higher in rank.[36] The Sindarizing of these names as *Fingon* and *Turgon* shows knowledge of the sound-changes distinguishing Sindarin from Telerin, but disregards meaning. If these names had actually been ancient Sindarin names they would at the time of the coming of the Exiles have taken the forms *Fingon* and *Turgon,* but they would not have had their Quenya meanings, if interpretable at all. Possibly they would have conveyed 'Hair-shout' and 'Master-shout' [see note 36]. But this did not matter much since old Sindarin names had by that time frequently become obscured by sound-changes and were taken as names and not analysed. With regard to *Findekáno / Fingon* it may be noted that the first element was certainly Quenya *findë* 'hair' – a tress or plait of hair[37] (cf. *findessë* a head of hair, a person's hair as a whole), but this is not conclusive proof that the name *Finwë* was or was thought to be derived from this stem. It would have been sufficient for Fingolfin to give to his eldest son a name beginning with *fin-* as an 'echo' of the ancestral name, and if this was also specially applicable it would have been approved as a good invention. In the case of Fingon it was suitable; he wore his long dark hair in great plaits braided with gold.

Arakáno was the tallest of the brothers and the most impetuous, but his name was never changed to Sindarin form, for he perished in the first battle of Fingolfin's host with the Orks, the Battle of the Lammoth (but the Sindarin form *Argon* was often later given as a name by Ñoldor and Sindar in memory of his valour).[38]

Írissë who went ever with the people of Turgon was called *Íreth*,[39] by substitution of Sindarin *-eth* (< *-ittā*) frequent in feminine names for Quenya *-issë.* Elenwë her mother had no Sindarin name, for she never reached Beleriand. She perished in the crossing of the Ice; and Turgon was thereafter unappeasable in his enmity for Fëanor and his sons. He had himself come near to death in the bitter waters when he attempted to save her and his daughter *Itaril*, whom the breaking of treacherous ice had cast into the cruel sea. Itaril he saved;[40] but the body of Elenwë was covered in fallen ice.

Itaril, or in longer form *Itarillë*, was the only child in the third generation from Finwë to go with the exiles, save only Arothir son of Angrod brother of Finrod.[41] Both have renown in the legends of the *Silmarillion*; but Itaril had a great destiny, for she was the mother of Ardamir Eärendil. Her name in Sindarin form was *Idril*, but this also was only an alteration of form, for neither of the Quenya stems that the name contains were found in Sindarin.[42]

5. The children of Finarfin. These were named: *Findaráto Ingoldo*; *Angaráto*; *Aikanáro*; and *Nerwendë Artanis*, surnamed *Alatáriel*. The wife of *Angaráto* was named *Eldalótë*, and his son *Artaher*. The most renowned of these were the first and the fourth (the only daughter), and only of these two are the mother-names remembered. The names of Sindarin form by which they were usually called in later song and legend were *Finrod*, *Angrod* (with wife *Eðellos* and son *Arothir*), *Aegnor*, and *Galadriel*.

The names *Findaráto* and *Angaráto* were Telerin in form (for Finarfin spoke the language of his wife's people); and they proved easy to render into Sindarin in form and sense, because of the close relationship of the Telerin of Aman to the language of their kin, the Sindar of Beleriand, in spite of the great changes that it had undergone in Middle-earth. (*Artafindë* and *Artanga* would have been their more natural Quenya forms, *arta-* the equivalent of *aráta-* preceding, as in *Artanis* and *Artaher*.)[43] The order of the elements in compounds, especially personal names, remained fairly free in all three Eldarin languages; but Quenya preferred the (older) order in which adjectival stems preceded, while in Telerin and Sindarin the adjectival elements often were placed second, especially in later-formed names, according to the usual placing of adjectives in the ordinary speech of those languages. In names however that ended in old words referring to status, rank, profession, race or kindred and so on the adjectival element still in Sindarin, following ancient models, might be placed first. Quenya *Artaher* (stem *artahēr-*) 'noble lord' was correctly Sindarized as *Arothir*.

Eðellos translated *Eldalótë* according to sense: 'Elven-flower'. *Angaráto* became naturally *Angrod*. It is probable that both brothers first received the name *Aráto*, later differentiated.

The *Find-* in *Findaráto* referred to hair, but in this case to the golden hair of this family derived from Indis. The *Ang-* in *Angaráto* was from Common Eldarin *angā* 'iron' (Quenya, Telerin *anga*, Sindarin *ang*). Angrod early developed hands of great strength and received the *epessë Angamaitë* 'iron-handed', so that *ang-* was used by Finarfin as a differentiating prefix.

Aikanáro was called by his father *Ambaráto*. The Sindarin form of this would have been *Amrod*; but to distinguish this from *Angrod*, and also because he preferred it, he used his mother-name[44] (which was however given in Quenya and not Telerin form). *Aika-nār-* meant 'fell fire'. It was in part a 'prophetic' name; for he was renowned as one of the most valiant of the warriors, greatly feared by the Orks: in wrath or battle the light of his eyes was like flame, though otherwise he was a generous and noble spirit. But in early youth the fiery light could be observed; while his hair was notable: golden like his brothers and sister, but strong and stiff, rising upon his head like flames. The Sindarin form *Aegnor* that he adopted was however not true Sindarin. There was no Sindarin adjective corresponding to Quenya *aika* 'fell, terrible, dire', though *aeg* would have been its form if it had occurred.[45]

Galadriel was chosen by Artanis ('noble woman') to be her Sindarin name; for it was the most beautiful of her names, and, though as an *epessë*, had been given to her by her lover, Teleporno of the Teleri, whom she wedded later in Beleriand.[46] As he gave it in Telerin form it was *Alatāriel(lë)*. The Quenyarized form appears as *Altariel*, though its true form would have been *Ñaltariel*. It was euphoniously and correctly rendered in Sindarin *Galadriel*. The name was derived from the Common Eldarin stem ÑAL 'shine by reflection'; **ñalatā* 'radiance, glittering reflection' (from jewels, glass or polished metals, or water) > Quenya *ñalta*, Telerin *alata*, Sindarin *galad*, + the Common Eldarin stem RIG 'twine, wreathe', **rīgā* 'wreath, garland'; Quenya, Telerin *ría*, Sindarin *rî*, Quenya, Telerin *riellë*, *-ríel* 'a maiden crowned with a festival garland'. The whole, = 'maiden crowned with a garland of bright radiance', was given in reference to Galadriel's hair. *Galad* occurs also in the *epessë* of Ereinion ('scion of kings') by which he was chiefly remembered in legend, *Gil-galad* 'star of radiance': he was the last king of the Eldar in Middle-earth, and the last male descendant of Finwë[47] except Elrond the Half-elven. The *epessë* was given to him because his helm and mail, and his shield overlaid with silver and set with a device of white stars, shone from afar like a star in sunlight or moonlight and could be seen by Elvish eyes at a great distance if he stood upon a height.

There were other descendants of Finwë remembered in legend who may be noted here, though their names were given in Sindarin or in Quenya at later times when Sindarin was the daily language of the Noldor, and they do not offer the problems of translation or more formal adjustment which are presented by the Quenya names given before the Exile.

Itarildë (Idril)[48] daughter of Turgon was the mother of Eärendil; but his father was a Man of the Atani, of the House of Hador: Tuor son of Huor.[49] Eärendil was thus the second of the Pereldar (Half-elven),[50] the elder being Dior, son of Beren and Lúthien Tinúviel daughter of King Elu Thingol. His names were, however, given in Quenya; for Turgon after his foundation of the secret city of Gondolin had re-established Quenya as the daily speech of his household. Eärendil had this name as father-name, and as mother-name he was called *Ardamírë*. In this case both names were 'prophetic'. Tuor in his long journey by the west shores of Beleriand, after his escape from captivity, had been visited by the great Vala Ulmo in person, and Ulmo had directed him to seek for Gondolin, foretelling that if he found it he would there beget a son ever afterwards renowned as a mariner.[51] Improbable as this seemed to Tuor, since neither the Atani nor the Noldor had any love of the sea or of ships, he named his son in Quenya 'sea-lover'. More purely prophetic was the name *Ardamírë* 'Jewel of the World'; for Itarildë could not foresee in her waking mind the strange fate that brought at last the Silmaril into the possession of Eärendil, and enabled his ship to pass through all the shadows and perils by which Aman was at that time defended from any approach from Middle-earth. These names were not given Sindarin forms in legend,[52] though Sindarin writers sometimes explained that they meant *mír n'Arðon* and *Seron Aearon*. By the marriage of Eärendil to Elwing daughter of Dior son of Beren the lines of the Pereldar (Pereðil) were united. Elros and Elrond were the sons of Eärendil. Elros became the first king of Númenor (with the Quenya title *Tar-Minyatur*, 'high first-ruler'). Elrond was received into the company and life-span of the Eldar, and became esquire and banner-bearer of Ereinion Gil-galad. When in later days he wedded Celebrían, daughter of Galadriel and Celeborn, the two lines of descent from Finwë, from Fingolfin and Finarfin, were united and continued in Arwen their daughter.[53]

The names *Elros* and *Elrond*, the last of the descendants of Finwë born in the Elder Days, were formed to recall the name of their mother *Elwing*. The meaning of *wing* is uncertain, since it occurs in no other personal name, nor in the records of either Sindarin or Quenya. Some of the loremasters, remembering that after their return to a second life Beren and Lúthien dwelt in Ossiriand,[54] and that there Dior dwelt after the fall of Doriath among the Green Elves of that forest country, have supposed that *wing* is a word of the tongue of the Green Elves; but little was preserved of that tongue after the destruction of Beleriand, and the interpretation of *wing* as meaning 'foam, spume, spindrift' as of water blown by the wind, or falling steeply over rocks, is but a likely guess. It is supported, however, by the fact that Ossiriand was a land cloven by seven rivers (as its name signifies), and that these fell steeply and very swift from the Mountains of Ered Lindon. Beside one great waterfall, called in Sindarin *Lanthir Lamath* ('waterfall of echoing voices'), Dior had his house. Moreover the name *Elros* (in Quenya form *Elerossë*) means 'star foam', sc. starlit foam.[55]

The numbered notes to the preceding text are given on pp. 356 ff., but the following editorial notes on Gil-galad and Felagund are most conveniently placed here.

The parentage of Gil-galad

My father originally supposed that Gil-galad was the son of Felagund King of Nargothrond. This is probably first found in a revision to the text FN II of *The Fall of Númenor* (V.33); but it remained his belief until after the completion of *The Lord of the Rings*, as is seen from the major early text of the Tale of Years (p. 173), and from *Of the Rings of Power*, where in the published text (*The Silmarillion* p. 286) *Fingon* is an editorial alteration of *Felagund*. In additions of uncertain date made to the *Quenta Silmarillion* (XI.242) it is told that Felagund sent away his wife and his son Gil-galad from Nargothrond to the Havens of the Falas for their safety. It is to be noted also that in the text of the Tale of Years just referred to not only was Gil-galad the son of Felagund but Galadriel was Gil-galad's sister (and so Felagund's daughter): see pp. 174 and 185 note 10.

It emerged, however, in the *Grey Annals* of 1951 (XI.44, §108) that Felagund had no wife, for the Vanya Amárië whom he loved had not been permitted to leave Aman.

Here something must be said of Orodreth, son of Finarfin and brother of Felagund, who became the second King of Nargothrond (for intimations of the decline in importance of Orodreth in earlier phases of the *legendarium* see III.91, 246, V.239; also *Unfinished Tales* p. 255 note 20). In the genealogical tables of the descendants of Finwë, which can be dated to 1959 but which my father was still using and altering when he wrote the excursus to *The Shibboleth of Fëanor* (see note 26), the curious history of Orodreth can be traced. Put as concisely as possible, Finrod (Felagund) was first given a son named *Artanáro Rhodothir* (so contradicting the story in the *Grey Annals* that he had no wife) the second King of Nargothrond, and father of Finduilas. Thus 'Orodreth' was now moved down a generation, becoming Finrod's son rather than his brother. In the next stage my father (recalling, apparently, the story in the *Grey Annals*) noted that Finrod 'had no child (he left his wife in Aman)', and moved Artanáro Rhodothir to become, still in the same generation, the son of Finrod's brother Angrod (who with Aegnor held the heights of Dorthonion and was slain in the Battle of Sudden Flame).

The name of Angrod's son (still retaining the identity of 'Orodreth') was then changed from *Artanáro* to *Artaresto*. In an isolated note found with the genealogies, scribbled at great speed but nonetheless dated, August 1965, my father suggested that the best solution to the problem of Gil-galad's parentage was to find him in 'the son of Orodreth', who is here given the Quenya name of *Artaresto*, and continued:

> Finrod left his wife in Valinor and had no children in exile. Angrod's son was Artaresto, who was beloved by Finrod and escaped when Angrod was slain, and dwelt with Finrod. Finrod made him his 'steward' and he succeeded him in Nargothrond. His Sindarin name was *Rodreth* (altered to *Orodreth* because of his love of the mountains .. .. His children were Finduilas and Artanáro = Rodnor later called Gil-galad. (Their mother was a Sindarin lady of the North. She called her son Gil-galad.) Rodnor Gil-galad escaped and eventually came to Sirion's Mouth and was King of the Ñoldor there.

The words that I cannot read contain apparently a preposition and a proper name, and this latter could be *Faroth* (the High Faroth west of the river Narog). – In the last of the genealogical tables *Artanáro (Rodnor) called Gil-galad* appears, with the note that 'he escaped and dwelt at Sirion's Mouth'. The only further change was the rejection of the name *Artaresto* and its replacement by *Artaher*, Sindarin *Arothir*; and thus in the excursus (note 23) Arothir [Orodreth] is named as Finrod's 'kinsman and steward', and (note 47) Gil-galad is 'the son of Arothir, nephew of Finrod'. The final genealogy was:

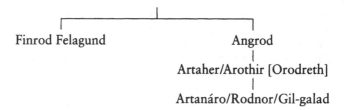

Since Finduilas remained without correction in the last of the genealogies as the daughter of Arothir, she became the sister of Gil-galad.

There can be no doubt that this was my father's last word on the subject; but nothing of this late and radically altered conception ever touched the existing narratives, and it was obviously impossible to introduce it into the published *Silmarillion*. It would nonetheless have been very much better to have left Gil-galad's parentage obscure.

I should mention also that in the published text of *Aldarion and Erendis* (*Unfinished Tales* p. 199) the letter of Gil-galad to Tar-Meneldur opens 'Ereinion Gil-galad son of Fingon', but the original has 'Finellach Gil-galad of the House of Finarfin' (where *Finellach* was changed from *Finhenlach*, and that from *Finlachen*). For the name *Ereinion* see p. 347 and note 47. So also in the text of *A Description of the Island of Númenor* (*Unfinished Tales* p. 168) I printed 'King Gil-galad of Lindon' where the original has 'King Finellach Gil-galad of Lindon'; I retained however the words 'his kinswoman Galadriel', since Fingon and Galadriel were first cousins. There is no trace among the many notes and suggestions written onto the genealogical tables of a proposed descent of Gil-galad from Finarfin; but in any case *Aldarion and Erendis* and the closely related *Description of Númenor* preceded by some time (I would now be inclined to date them to about 1960) the making of Gil-galad into the grandson of Angrod, with the name Artanáro Rodnor, which first appears as a new decision in the note of August 1965 given above. Much closer analysis of the admittedly extremely complex material than I had made twenty years ago makes it clear that Gil-galad as the son of Fingon (see XI.56, 243) was an ephemeral idea.

The Dwarvish origin of the name Felagund

Among the notes accompanying the Elvish genealogies and dated December 1959 (see note 26) the following should be recorded. I have mentioned (XI.179) that against the name *Felagund* in the chapter *Of the Siege of Angband* in the *Quenta Silmarillion* (where it was said that 'the Gnomes of the North, at first in jest, called him ... Felagund, or "lord of caverns"') my father noted on the late typescript: 'This was in fact a Dwarfish name; for Nargothrond was first made by Dwarves as is later recounted.' The statement in the 1959 notes is as follows:

The name *Felagund* was of Dwarvish origin. Finrod had help of Dwarves in extending the underground fortress of Nargothrond. It is supposed originally to have been a hall of the Petty-dwarves (*Nibinnogs*), but the Great Dwarves despised these, and had no compunction in ousting them – hence Mîm's special hatred for the Elves – especially for great reward. Finrod had brought more treasure out of Túna than any of the other princes.

Felagund: Dwarvish √*felek* hew rock, *felak* a tool like a broad-bladed chisel, or small axe-head without haft, for cutting stone; to use this tool. √*gunud* equivalent of Eldarin *s-rot*:[56] *gundu* underground hall. *felakgundu, felaggundu* 'cave-hewer'. This name was given because of Finrod's skill in lighter stone-carving. He cut many of the adornments of the pillars and walls in Nargothrond. He was proud of the name. But it was often by others Eldarized into *Felagon*, as if it had the same ending (*-kānō*) as in *Fingon, Turgon*; and the first element was associated with Sindarin *fael* 'fair-minded, just, generous', Quenya *faila* (? from √*phaya* 'spirit', adjectival formation meaning 'having a good *fëa*, or a dominant *fëa*').

This note is the basis of the brief statement in the index to the published *Silmarillion*, entry *Felagund*.

The names of the Sons of Fëanor with the legend of the fate of Amrod

My father did not fulfil his intention to give in the 'excursus' an account of the names of the Sons of Fëanor (see note 32), but some pages of initial drafting are extant. The text begins legibly in ink, but at the end of the list of 'mother-names' changes to ball-point pen, and the legend of Amrod and Amras would be too illegible to reproduce had not my father gone over it and glossed the worst parts more clearly. There are many experimental etymological notes on the Eldarin words referring to red colour and copper, and on the names of the twin brothers, which are here omitted. In the first list I have added the Sindarin names for clarity.

(1) [Maedros] *Nelyafinwë* 'Finwë third' in succession.[57] *(Nelyo)*

(2) [Maglor] *Kanafinwë* 'strong-voiced or ?commanding'. *(Káno)*[58]

(3) [Celegorm] *Turkafinwë* 'strong, powerful (in body)'. *(Turko)*

(4) [Curufin] *Kurufinwë* Fëanor's own name; given to this, his favourite son, because he alone showed in some degree the same temper and talents. He also resembled Fëanor very much in face. *(Kurvo)*

(5) [Caranthir] *Morifinwë* 'dark' – he was black-haired as his grandfather. *(Moryo)*
(6) [Amrod] *Pityafinwë* 'Little Finwë'. *(Pityo)*[59]
(7) [Amras] *Telufinwë* 'Last Finwë'. *(Telvo)*[60]

Their 'mother-names' are recorded (though never used in narrative) as:

(1) *Maitimo* 'well-shaped one': he was of beautiful bodily form. But he, and the youngest, inherited the rare red-brown hair of Nerdanel's kin. Her father had the *epessë* of *rusco* 'fox'. So Maitimo had as an *epessë* given by his brothers and other kin *Russandol* 'copper-top'.[61]
(2) *Makalaurë* Of uncertain meaning. Usually interpreted (and said to have been a 'prophetic' mother-name) as 'forging gold'. If so, probably a poetic reference to his skill in harping, the sound of which was 'golden' (*laurë* was a word for golden light or colour, never used for the metal).
(3) *Tyelkormo* 'hasty-riser'. Quenya *tyelka* 'hasty'. Possibly in reference to his quick temper, and his habit of leaping up when suddenly angered.
(4) *Atarinkë* 'little father' – referring to his physical likeness to Fëanor, later found to be also seen in his mind.
(5) *Carnistir* 'red-face' – he was dark (brown) haired, but had the ruddy complexion of his mother.
(6) *Ambarto*[62]
(7) *Ambarussa*

These two names of [the] twins *(i·Wenyn)* were evidently meant to begin similarly. *Ambarussa* 'top-russet' must have referred to hair: the first and last of Nerdanel's children had the reddish hair of her kin. Around the name Ambarto [> Umbarto] – which one might expect to begin with an element of the same sense as (7) – much legend and discussion gathered. The most authentic seems to be thus:

The two twins were both red-haired. Nerdanel gave them both the name *Ambarussa* – for they were much alike and remained so while they lived. When Fëanor begged that their names should at least be different Nerdanel looked strange, and after a while said: 'Then let one be called [*Ambarto* >] *Umbarto*, but which, time will decide.'

Fëanor was disturbed by this ominous name ('Fated'), and changed it to *Ambarto* – or in some versions thought

Nerdanel had said *Ambarto*, using the same first element as in *Ambarussa* (sc. *amba* + Quenya *arta* 'exalted, lofty'). But Nerdanel said: '*Umbarto* I spoke; yet do as you wish. It will make no difference.'

Later, as Fëanor became more and more fell and violent, and rebelled against the Valar, Nerdanel, after long endeavouring to change his mood, became estranged. (Her kin were devoted to Aulë, who counselled her father to take no part in the rebellion. 'It will in the end only lead Fëanor and all your children to death.') She retired to her father's house; but when it became clear that Fëanor and his sons would leave Valinor for ever, she came to him before the host started on its northward march, and begged that Fëanor should leave her the two youngest, the twins, or one at least of them. He replied: 'Were you a true wife, as you had been till cozened by Aulë, you would keep all of them, for you would come with us. If you desert me, you desert also all of our children. For they are determined to go with their father.' Then Nerdanel was angry and she answered: 'You will not keep all of them. One at least will never set foot on Middle-earth.' 'Take your evil omens to the Valar who will delight in them,' said Fëanor. 'I defy them'. So they parted.

Now it is told how Fëanor stole the ships of the Teleri, and breaking faith with Fingolfin and with those faithful to him sailed away in them to Middle-earth, leaving the rest of his host to make their way on foot with great travail and loss. The ships were anchored off the shore, in the Firth of Drengist, and all the host of Fëanor went on land and camped there.

In the night Fëanor, filled with malice, aroused Curufin, and with him and a few of those most close to Fëanor in obedience he went to the ships and set them all aflame; and the dark sky was red as with a terrible dawn. All the camp was roused, and Fëanor returning said: 'Now at least I am certain that no faint-heart or traitor among you will be able to take back even one ship to the succour of Fingolfin and his folk.' But all save few were dismayed, because there were many things still aboard that they had not yet brought ashore, and the ships would have been useful for further journeying. They were still far north and had purposed to sail southward to some better haven.

In the morning the host was mustered, but of Fëanor's seven sons only six were to be found. Then Ambarussa (6) went pale with fear. 'Did you not then rouse Ambarussa my brother (whom you called Ambarto)?' he said. 'He would not come ashore to sleep (he said) in discomfort.' But it is thought (and no doubt Fëanor guessed this also) that it was in the mind of Ambarto to sail his ship back [?afterwards] and rejoin Nerdanel; for he had been much [?shocked][63] by the deed of his father.[64]

'That ship I destroyed first,' said Fëanor (hiding his own dismay). 'Then rightly you gave the name to the youngest of your children,' said Ambarussa, 'and *Umbarto* "the Fated" was its true form. Fell and fey are you become.' And after that no one dared speak again to Fëanor of this matter.[65]

For the mention, in a note on the typescript of the *Annals of Aman*, of the story of the death of one of the twin-brothers in the burning of the ships at Losgar see X.128, §162; and for the account of Nerdanel and her estrangement from Fëanor in late rewriting of the *Quenta Silmarillion* see X.272–3, 279.

The material concerning the names of the twin brothers is confused and confusing, clearly because it was only as my father worked on them that the strange and sinister story emerged. It seems to me very probable that when he gave the mother-names *(6) Ambarto* and *(7) Ambarussa* it had not yet arisen, nor yet when he began the note that follows the list of the mother-names, saying that 'the first and last of Nerdanel's children had the reddish hair of her kin' – that is Maedros with his nickname *Russandol* and the younger of the twins *Ambarussa* (Amras).

The story first emerged, I think, with the words 'The most authentic seems to be thus: The two twins were both red-haired. Nerdanel gave them both the name *Ambarussa* ...' It was then, no doubt, that my father changed the name *Ambarto* to *Umbarto* in the list and reversed the names of the twin brothers (see note 62), so that *Ambarussa* becomes the elder of the two and *Ambarto/Umbarto* the youngest of Fëanor's children, as he is in the legend told here.

At the head of the first page of this text concerning the names of the Sons of Fëanor my father wrote, when the story was now in being:

All the sons save Curufin preferred their mother-names and were ever afterwards remembered by them. The twins called each other *Ambarussa*. The name *Ambarto/Umbarto* was used by [?no one]. The twins remained alike, but the elder grew darker in hair, and was more dear to his father. After childhood they [?were not to be] confused. ...

Thus in the legend 'Ambarussa (6)' asked Fëanor whether he had not roused 'Ambarussa my brother' before setting fire to the ships.

NOTES

1 [This heading is derived from the opening sentence of the essay, which is in fact 'The case of þ > s is more difficult.' I have not been able to discover the reference of this. The typescript is extant as a separate whole, paginated consecutively from A to T.]

2 Few of these can have been carried from Valinor, and fewer still can have survived the journey to Middle-earth; but the memory of the loremasters was prodigious and accurate.

3 [The term *Ingwi* seems not to have been used since the *Lhammas* of the 1930s, where '*Ingwelindar* or *Ingwi*' appears as the name of the house and people of Ingwë, chief among the First Kindred of the Elves (then called the *Lindar*), V.171. For the much later application of the term *Lindar* see XI.381–2.]

4 Without special study. But many of the Ñoldor could speak Telerin and *vice versa*. There were in fact some borrowings from one to another; of which the most notable was the general use of the Telerin form *telpë* 'silver' for pure Quenya *tyelpë*. [For the substitution of *telpë* see *Unfinished Tales* p. 266.]

5 They continued to deplore it, and were able to insist later that the distinction between older þ and s should at least always be preserved in writing.

6 [See the Note on Mother-names at the end of the essay, p. 339. It is not stated elsewhere that *Serindë* was Míriel's 'mother-name'.]

7 [It had been said several times in the later *Quenta Silmarillion* texts that *Fëanáro* was a 'name of insight' given to him by Míriel at his birth; moreover in the story of Míriel when it first appeared her spirit passed to Mandos soon after Fëanor was born, and it is expressly said in *Laws and Customs among the Eldar* that he never saw his mother (X.217). The story has now been altogether changed in this aspect: Míriel named him with this name 'in recognition of his impetuous character'; 'while she lived she did much with gentle counsel to soften and restrain him'; and subsequently 'her weariness she had endured until he was full grown, but she could endure it no longer'. After Míriel's 'death' or departure 'for a while he also had kept vigil by his mother's body, but soon he became wholly absorbed again in his own works and devices' (p. 335).]

8 [A full account of other texts bearing on this matter is given in X.205–7, 225–7, 233–71. These texts are substantially earlier than the present essay (see X.300), which is by no means entirely congruent with them.]

9 [Elsewhere *Ezellohar* is the name not of the plain but of the Green Mound on which grew the Two Trees (X.69, etc.); while in *Quendi and Eldar* (XI.399, 401) *Korollairë* is said to be a translation of the Valarin name *Ezellohar*, of which the first element

ezel, ezella meant 'green'. But perhaps by 'the plain of Ezellohar' my father meant 'the plain in which stood the mound of
Ezellohar'.]

10 Doubting that the test of a few years could show that the will of
any one of the Children was fixed immovably; and foreboding
that breaking the law would have evil consequences.

11 Death by free will, such as Míriel's, was beyond his thought.
Death by violence he thought impossible in Aman; though as is
recorded in *The Silmarillion* this proved otherwise.

12 [With a necessary change in the opening sentence, the following
passage, as far as 'and passing the last test departed from Middle-
earth for ever' on p. 338, was printed in *Unfinished Tales*, pp.
229–31 – since it is of great importance in the history of Galadriel
– but with no indication of its context: it seems desirable therefore to give it again here.]

13 [Elwë's name *Pindikollo* (elsewhere *Sindikollo, Sindicollo*) was
omitted from the text in *Unfinished Tales*.]

14 Who together with the greatest of all the Eldar, Lúthien Tinúviel,
daughter of Elu Thingol, are the chief matter of the legends and
histories of the Elves.

15 It is not even certain that all Fëanor's sons continued to use *þ*
after his death and the healing of the feud by the renowned deed
of Fingon son of Fingolfin in rescuing Maedhros [> Maedros]
from the torments of Morgoth.

16 [The wholly different account of 'Chosen Names' in *Laws and
Customs among the Eldar* (X.214–15) appears to have been
abandoned.]

17 As is seen in *The Silmarillion*. This is not an Eldarin title or work.
It is a compilation, probably made in Númenor, which includes
(in prose) the four great tales or lays of the heroes of the Atani,
of which 'The Children of Húrin' was probably composed
already in Beleriand in the First Age, but necessarily is preceded
by an account of Fëanor and his making of the Silmarils. All however are 'Mannish' works. [With this cf. X.373 and p. 390, note
17 in this book.]

18 Notably in *Manwë*, the Quenya name of the 'Elder King', the
chief of the Valar. This is said to have been of the same age as the
names *Ingwë*, etc., and to contain the Valarin element *aman, man*
'blessed, holy' learned from Oromë, and of course unconnected
with the Eldarin interrogative element *ma, man*. [See XI.399.]

19 He had black hair, but brilliant grey-blue eyes.

20 Connexion with Telerin *vola* 'a roller, long wave', which was
sometimes made by the Teleri themselves, was not a serious
'etymology' but a kind of pun; for the king's name was not
normally *Volwë* (Common Eldarin **wolwē*) but Olwë in Telerin
as in Quenya, and *w* was not lost before *o* in Telerin as it was

in Quenya. Also the connexion of the Teleri with sea-faring developed long after the naming of Olwë.

21 It was otherwise in written histories (which were by the Ñoldor in any case mostly composed in Quenya). Also the names of 'foreign persons' who did not dwell in Beleriand and were seldom mentioned in daily speech were usually left unaltered. Thus the names of the Valar which they had devised in Valinor were not as a rule changed, whether they fitted Sindarin style or not. The Sindar knew little of the Valar and had no names for any of them, save Oromë (whom all the Eldar had seen and known); and Manwë and Varda of whose eminence they had been instructed by Oromë; and the Great Enemy whom the Ñoldor called Melkor. For Oromë a name had been made in Primitive Eldarin (recalling the sound of his great horn) of which *Oromë* was the Quenya form, though in Sindarin it had become *Araw*, and by the Sindar he was later more often called *(Aran) Tauron* 'the (king) forester'. Manwë and Varda they knew only by the names 'Elder King' and 'Star-queen': *Aran Einior* and *Elbereth*. Melkor they called *Morgoth* 'the Black Enemy', refusing to use the Sindarin form of *Melkor*: *Belegûr* 'he that arises in might', save (but rarely) in a deliberately altered form *Belegurth* 'Great Death'. These names *Tauron, Aran Einior, Elbereth*, and *Morgoth* the Ñoldor adopted and used when speaking Sindarin.

[For the association of the name *Oromë* with that of his great horn see XI.400–1. – The names *Belegûr, Belegurth* have been mentioned in the index to the published *Silmarillion*, which here derives from the present note. Very many years before, the name *Belegor* is found as an ephemeral name of Morgoth in *The Lay of the Children of Húrin* (III.21, note 22).]

22 His sons were too occupied in war and feuds to pay attention to such matters, save Maglor who was a poet, and Curufin, his fourth and favourite son to whom he gave his own name; but Curufin was most interested in the alien language of the Dwarves, being the only one of the Ñoldor to win their friendship. It was from him that the loremasters obtained such knowledge as they could of the Khuzdûl.

23 Nor were the 'loremasters' a separate guild of gentle scribes, soon burned by the Orks of Angband upon pyres of books. They were mostly even as Fëanor, the greatest, kings, princes and warriors, such as the valiant captains of Gondolin, or Finrod of Nargothrond and Rodothir [> Arothir] his kinsman and steward. [For Arothir see the note on the parentage of Gil-galad, pp. 349–51.]

24 And as some insurance against their own death. For books were made only in strong places at a time when death in battle was likely to befall any of the Eldar, but it was not yet believed that

Morgoth could ever capture or destroy their fortresses.

25 [In an addition to the *Annals of Aman* Fëanor's first name is given as 'Minyon First-begotten' (X.87); in *Laws and Customs among the Eldar* his first name was *Finwë*, in the second version *Finwion* (X.217 and note 20). For previous references to *Kurufinwë* see the index to Vol.X (*Curufinwë*); and with the mention here of the form *Faenor* cf. X.217, footnote.]

26 [In *The War of the Jewels* I referred to a set of Elvish genealogies with a clear resemblance to those of the Edain given in that book: see XI.229, where I noted that the former are followed by notes expressly relating to them and dated December 1959. These genealogies are almost exclusively concerned with the descendants of Finwë, and are set out in four separate tables, all apparently belonging to much the same time, and showing the same sort of development in stages as is seen in those of the houses of the Edain. At least eight years and probably more divide them from the present 'excursus', whose date is fixed as not earlier than February 1968; but my father clearly had them in front of him when he wrote this, and alterations made to the latest of the four agree with statements made in it. In all these tables there are still three daughters of Finwë and Indis: *Findis*, *Faniel*, and *Írimë* (see X.207, 238, and also X.262, where *Finvain* appears for *Írimë*), and no correction was made. In the excursus *Faniel* has disappeared, and the younger daughter appears both as *Írimë* and *Írien* (see note 28).]

27 If he ever did so. Little has been ever heard in Middle-earth of Aman after the departure of the Ñoldor. Those who returned thither have never come back, since the change of the world. To Númenor in its first days they went often, but small part of the lore and histories of Númenor survived its Downfall. [With the words in the text at this point concerning Indis cf. *Laws and Customs among the Eldar* (X.249 and note 17), where Finwë in Mandos said to Vairë: 'But Indis parted from me without death. I had not seen her for many years, and when the Marrer smote me I was alone. ... Little comfort should I bring her, if I returned.']

28 [It is strange that my father should give the name of the second daughter of Finwë as both *Írimë* and *Írien* within the space of a few lines. Possibly he intended *Írien* at the first occurrence but inadvertently wrote *Írimë*, the name found in all the genealogies (note 26).]

29 But the true equivalent in Sindarin was *Glaðwen* (Common Eldarin stem *g-lada-* > Quenya *lala-*, Telerin *glada*, Sindarin *glað-*).

30 'Wisdom' – but not in the sense 'sagacity, sound judgement (founded on experience and sufficient knowledge)'; 'Knowledge'

would be nearer, or 'Philosophy' in its older applications which included Science. Ñolmë was thus distinct from Kurwë 'technical skill and invention', though not necessarily practised by distinct persons. The stem appeared in Quenya (in which it was most used) in forms developed from Common Eldarin ñgol-, ñgōlo-, with or without syllabic ñ: as in *Ñgolodō > Quenya Noldo (Telerin golodo, Sindarin goloð) – the Noldor had been from the earliest times most eminent in and concerned with this kind of 'wisdom'; ñolmë a department of wisdom (science etc.); Ingolë (ñgōlē) Science/Philosophy as a whole; ñolmo a wise person; ingólemo one with very great knowledge, a 'wizard'. This last word was however archaic and applied only to great sages of the Eldar in Valinor (such as Rúmil). The wizards of the Third Age – emissaries from the Valar – were called Istari 'those who know'.

The form Ingoldo may be noted: it is a form of Ñoldo with syllabic ñ, and being in full and more dignified form is more or less equivalent to 'the Ñoldo, one eminent in the kindred'. It was the mother-name of Arafinwë [Finarfin], and like the name Arakáno 'high chieftain' that Indis gave to Nolofinwë [Fingolfin] was held to be 'prophetic'. Eärwen gave this name [Ingoldo] to her eldest child Artafindë (Finrod), and by it he was usually called by his brothers and sister who esteemed him and loved him. It was never Sindarized (the form would have been Angoloð). The name spread from his kin to many others who held him in honour, especially to Men (the Atani) of whom he was the greatest friend among the Eldar. Thus later it became frequent as a given name in Númenor, and continued to be so in Gondor, though reduced in the Common Speech to Ingold. One such Ingold appears in The Lord of the Rings as the commander of the guard of the North Gate into the Pelennor of Gondor.

[In earlier texts (see X.265 note 10) the name Ingoldo was the mother-name of Ñolofinwë (Fingolfin), 'signifying that he came of both the kin of the Ingar and of the Noldor'; while the mother-name of Arafinwë (Finarfin) was Ingalaurë 'for he had the golden hair of his mother's people'. Apart from the first one, the genealogical tables give Fingolfin and Finarfin the mother-names Arakáno and Ingoldo as here.]

31 Except for Finarfin as the name of his younger brother. This was also the only name of a Ñoldo who did not come into exile to receive a Sindarin form. This was because Arafinwë's children had a special position among the exiles, especially in relation to King Thingol of Doriath, their kinsman, and were often referred to collectively by the Sindar as 'the children of Finarfin' or the Nothrim [> Nost] Finarfin, 'the house/family of Finarfin'.

32 [In the text at this point there is a reference forward to discussion of the names of the Sons of Fëanor, but this was not reached

in the typescript before it was abandoned; see pp. 352 ff.]
33 As he said with some justice: 'My brother's claim rests only upon a decree of the Valar; but of what force is that for those who have rejected them and seek to escape from their prison-land?' But Fingolfin answered: 'I have not rejected the Valar, nor their authority in all matters where it is just for them to use it. But if the Eldar were given free choice to leave Middle-earth and go to Aman, and accepted it because of the loveliness and bliss of that land, their free choice to leave it and return to Middle-earth, when it has become dark and desecrated, cannot be taken away. Moreover I have an errand in Middle-earth, the avenging of the blood of my father upon Morgoth, whom the Valar let loose among us. Fëanor seeks first his stolen treasures.'

[It is said in the text at this point that Fingolfin claimed to be 'the chieftain of all the Ñoldor after the death of Finwë', and the same was said in the essay proper (p. 336). All the texts agree that after the banishment of Fëanor from Tirion, and the departure of Finwë with him to Formenos, Fingolfin ruled the Ñoldor in Tirion; and it was said in the *Quenta Silmarillion* (see IV.95, V.235) that afterwards, when the Flight of the Ñoldor began, those of Tirion 'would not now renounce the kingship of Fingolfin'. On the other hand, in the final story of the events leading to the Flight, when Fëanor and Fingolfin had become half-brothers, they were reconciled 'in word' before the throne of Manwë at the fateful festival; and in that reconciliation Fingolfin said to Fëanor: 'Thou shalt lead and I will follow' (see X.197, 287).]

34 [On *Anairë* wife of Fingolfin and *Elenwë* wife of Turgon see XI.323, §12; and on *Arakáno*, Sindarin *Argon*, see note 38.]
35 [In all the genealogical tables Fingon's Quenya name is *Finicáno* except in the last, in which it is *Findicáno* (altered to *Findecáno*). In all the tables he is marked as having a wife, though she is not named; in the first, two children are named, *Ernis* and *Finbor*, *Ernis* subsequently becoming *Erien*, but in the final table they were struck out, with the note that Fingon 'had no child or wife'.]
36 It was a derivative of Common Eldarin KAN 'cry, call aloud', which developed divergent meanings (like 'call' in English or the Germanic stem *hait-*) depending on the purposes for which a loud voice would be used: e.g. to take an oath, make a vow or promise; to announce important news, or messages and orders; to issue orders and commands in person; to 'call for' – to name a thing or person desired, to summons; to call a person by name, to name. Not all of these were found in any one of the later languages (Quenya, Telerin, Sindarin). In Quenya the sense *command* had become the usual one: to issue orders in person, whether by

derived authority or one's own; when applied to things it meant *demand*. In archaic language the older and simplest agental form **kānō > káno* still had the sense 'crier, or herald', and *kanwa* 'an announcement' as well as 'an order' – later *terkáno* (one *through* whom orders or announcements are made) was used for 'herald'. In Telerin *cāno* meant 'herald', and the verb *can-* was mostly used in the sense 'cry aloud, call', but also 'to summons or name a person'. In Sindarin *can-* was used for 'cry out, shout, call', with implications supplied by the context; it never meant either 'order' or 'name'; *caun* (**kānā*) meant 'outcry, clamour', often in plural form *conath* when referring to many voices, and often applied to lamentation (though not as English 'cry' to weeping tears): cf. *naergon* 'woeful lament'.

37 Common Eldarin **phini-* a single hair, **phindē* a tress; Sindarin *fîn; find, finn-*.

38 When the onset of the Orks caught the host at unawares as they marched southwards and the ranks of the Eldar were giving way, he sprang forward and hewed a path through the foes, daunted by his stature and the terrible light of his eyes, till he came to the Ork-captain and felled him. Then though he himself was surrounded and slain, the Orks were dismayed, and the Ñoldor pursued them with slaughter.

[The third son of Fingolfin, Arakáno (Argon), emerged in the course of the making of the genealogies. A pencilled note on the last of the four tables says that he fell in the fighting at Alqualondë; this was struck out, and my father noted that a preferable story was that he perished in the Ice. It is curious that this third son, of whom there had never before been any mention, entered (as it seems) without a story, and the manner of his death was twice changed before the remarkable appearance here of 'the first battle of Fingolfin's host with the Orks, the Battle of the Lammoth', in which he fell. In the account in the *Grey Annals* (XI.30) Fingolfin, after the passage of the Helkaraxë, 'marched from the North unopposed through the fastness of the realm of Morgoth, and he passed over Dor-Daedeloth, and his foes hid beneath the earth'; whereas in the present note his host was attacked in Lammoth 'at unawares as they marched southwards' (see the map, XI.182).]

39 [All the genealogical tables give the name of Fingolfin's daughter as *Írissë (Írith)*; in the last of them *Írith* was changed to *Íreth*, the form found here, but later still both names were struck out and replaced by *(Ar)Feiniel* 'White Lady' (on this see XI.317–18, and 409 with note 34).

There is a strange confusion in this paragraph. Above, my father said that Írissë was 'under the protection of' Turukáno (Turgon) her brother and his wife Elenwë; but here Írissë is the *daughter* of Elenwë who perished in the Ice. This cannot be rectified by the substitution of the correct name (*Anairë* for *Elenwë*, or *Itaril* for *Írissë*, *Íreth*), because he was expressly writing of Elenwë and expressly writing of Írissë.]

40 [Turgon's saving of his daughter Idril Celebrindal from death in the Helkaraxë has not been referred to before.]

41 [Arothir has been named earlier (note 23) as the 'kinsman and steward' of Finrod; see also note 47.]

42 (1) *it* in *itila* 'twinkling, glinting', and *íta* 'a flash', *ita-* verb 'to sparkle'. (2) *ril-* 'brilliant light': cf. *silmaril(lë)*, the name given by Fëanor to his three Jewels. The first was especially applied to the bright lights of the eyes, which were a mark of all the High Eldar who had ever dwelt in Valinor, and at times in later ages reappeared in their descendants among mortal men, whether from Itaril or Lúthien.

43 **arat-* was an extended form of the stem *ara-* 'noble'. The derivative *arātā* was much used as an adjective in Telerin and Sindarin (Telerin *arāta*, Sindarin *arod*). In Quenya it had become specialized, and mainly used in *Aratar* 'the Exalted', the Nine of the chief Valar. It was however still used in noble names.

44 [On p. 346 my father said that of the children of Finarfin the mother-names were remembered only in the cases of Finrod (*Ingoldo*) and Galadriel (*Nerwendë*); he omitted to mention *Aikanáro*.]

45 Quenya *aika* was derived from a Common Eldarin stem GAYA 'awe, dread'; but the adjectival form *gayakā from which *aika* descended was not preserved in Telerin or Sindarin. Other derivatives were *gāyā 'terror, great fear': Telerin *gāia*, Sindarin *goe*, Quenya *áya*. Adjectives formed on this, Telerin *gāialā*, Sindarin *goeol*, replaced Quenya *aika*. In a name of this sort in Sindarin the noun would most naturally have been used, producing *goenaur* > *Goenor*. Also **Gayar-* 'the Terrifier', the name made for the Sea, the vast and terrifying Great Sea of the West, when the Eldar first came to its shores: Quenya *Eär*, *Eären*, Telerin *gaiar*; Sindarin *gaear*, *gae(a)ron*, *Belegaer*. This word is also found in the Quenya name *Eärendil*, the mariner (sea-lover); see p. 348.

The stem acquired in Quenya a specially high and noble sense – except in *eär*, though that was also majestic in its vastness and power; and *aika*, though that was seldom applied to evil things. Thus Quenya *áya* meant rather 'awe' than 'fear', profound reverence and sense of one's own littleness in the presence of things or persons majestic and powerful. The adjective *aira* was the nearest equivalent to 'holy'; and the noun *airë* to 'sanctity'. *Airë* was used by the Eldar as a title of address to the Valar and the greater Máyar. Varda would be addressed as *Airë Tári*. (Cf. Galadriel's Lament, where it is said that the stars trembled at the sound of the holy queen's voice: the prose or normal form of which would have been *tintilar lirinen ómaryo Airë-tário*.) This change, though possible to have occurred (as it has in our 'awe') without extraneous influence, was said by the loremasters to have been partly due to the influence of the Valarin language, in which *ayanu-* was the name of the Spirits of Eru's first creation. [With the last sentence of this note cf. XI.399.]

46   [On the remarkable change whereby Celeborn (Teleporno) became a Telerin Elf of Aman see *Unfinished Tales* pp. 231–3, where the present passage is cited. The etymology of *Galadriel* that follows in the text was used for the account of the name in the Appendix to *The Silmarillion*, entry *kal-*.]

47   He was the son of Arothir, nephew of Finrod. [See the note on the parentage of Gil-galad, pp. 349 ff. – From this work was derived Gil-galad's name *Ereinion* introduced into *The Silmarillion*.]

48   [Earlier (p. 346) the name is *Itarillë*; *Itarildë* appears in the first three genealogical tables, but the fourth has *Itarillë*.]

49   These names were given in the language of that kindred of the Atani (Edain) – but adapted to Sindarin – from which in the main the Adûnaic or native Atanic language of Númenor was descended. Their explanation is not here attempted.

50   [The term *Pereldar* 'Half-eldar' was originally used of the Nandor or Danas (see V.200, 215), but it is here used as is the Sindarin form *Peredhil* in Appendix A (I, i) of Elrond and Elros; cf. *i·Pheredhil* p. 256, *Pereðil* p. 348.]

51   [In the account of Ulmo's words to Tuor on the coast at Vinyamar in the later *Tale of Tuor* the Vala did indeed allude prophetically to Eärendil, but in a manner far more veiled and mysterious: 'But it is not for thy valour only that I send thee, but to bring into the world a hope beyond thy sight, and a light that shall pierce the darkness' (*Unfinished Tales* p. 30).]

52   Forms affected by Sindarin in manuscripts, such as *Aerendil*, *Aerennel*, etc. were casual and accidental.

53   When Aragorn, descended in long line from Elros, wedded Arwen in the third union of Men and Elves, the lines of all the Three Kings of the High Elves (Eldar), Ingwë, Finwë, and Olwë and Elwë were united and alone preserved in Middle-earth. Since Lúthien was the noblest, and the most fair and beautiful, of all the Children of Eru remembered in ancient story, the descendants of that union were called 'the children of Lúthien'. The world has grown old in long years since then, but it may be that their line has not yet ended. (Lúthien was through her mother, Melian, descended also from the Máyar, the people of the Valar, whose being began before the world was made. Melian alone of all those spirits assumed a bodily form, not only as a raiment but as a permanent habitation in form and powers like to the bodies of

the Elves. This she did for love of Elwë; and it was permitted, no doubt because this union had already been foreseen in the beginning of things, and was woven into the *Amarth* of the world, when Eru first conceived the being of his children, Elves and Men, as is told (after the manner and according to the understanding of his children) in that myth that is named The Music of the Ainur.)

[As is said in the text at this point Arwen was descended from Finwë both in the line of Fingolfin (through Elrond) and in the line of Finarfin (through Celebrían); but she was also descended from Elwë (Thingol) through Elrond's mother Elwing, and through Galadriel's mother Eärwen from Olwë of Alqualondë. She was not directly descended from Ingwë, but her fore-mother Indis was (in earlier texts) the sister of Ingwë (X.261–2, etc.), or (in the present work, p. 343) the daughter of his sister. It is hard to know what my father had in mind when he wrote the opening of this note.]

54 Until they died the death of mortal Men, according to the decree of the Valar, and left this world for ever.

55 [Here the typescript stops, not at the foot of a page; and at this point my father wrote:

Alter this to: *Wing*. This word, which the loremasters explained as meaning 'foam, spindrift', only actually occurs in two names of the Eärendil legend: *Elwing* the name of his wife, and (in Quenya form) *Vingilótë* (translated in Adûnaic as *Rothinzil*) 'Foam-flower', the name of Eärendil's ship. The word is not otherwise known in Quenya or Sindarin – nor in Telerin despite its large vocabulary of sea-words. There was a tradition that the word came from the language of the Green Elves of Ossiriand.]

56 [Elsewhere in these notes the stem *rot, s-rot* is given the meaning 'delve underground, excavate, tunnel', whence Quenya *hróta* 'dwelling underground, artificial cave or rockhewn hall', *rotto* 'a small grot or tunnel'.]

57 ['Finwë third': his grandfather was *Finwë*, and his father *Kurufinwë*, first named *Finwë* also (p. 343).]

58 [*Káno*: see note 36.]

59 [The P of *Pityafinwë*, but not of the short form *Pityo*, was changed to N.]

60 [*Pityafinwë* and *Telufinwë* are bracketed with the words 'Twins   *Gwenyn*'.]

61 [On a separate page written at the same time is a note on the father of Nerdanel (Fëanor's wife):

Nerdanel's father was an 'Aulendil' [> 'Aulendur'], and became a great smith. He loved copper, and set it above gold.

His name was [*space; pencilled later* Sarmo?], but he was most widely known as *Urundil* 'copper-lover'. He usually wore a band of copper about his head. His hair was not as dark or black as was that of most of the Ñoldor, but brown, and had glints of coppery-red in it. Of Nerdanel's seven children the oldest, and the twins (a very rare thing among the Eldar) had hair of this kind. The eldest also wore a copper circlet.

A note is appended to *Aulendur*:

'Servant of Aulë': sc. one who was devoted to that Vala. It was applied especially to those persons, or families, among the Ñoldor who actually entered Aulë's service, and who in return received instruction from him.

A second note on this page comments on the name *Urundil*:

√RUN 'red, glowing', most often applied to things like embers, hence adjective *runya*, Sindarin *ruin* ' "fiery" red'. The Eldar had words for some metals, because under Oromë's instruction they had devised weapons against Morgoth's servants especially on the March, but the only ones that appear in all Eldarin languages were iron, copper, gold and silver (ANGA, URUN, MALAT, KYELEP).

Earlier Nerdanel's father, the great smith, had been named *Mahtan* (see X.272, 277), and he was so called in the published *Silmarillion*. For earlier statements concerning the arming of the Eldar on the Great Journey see X.276-7, 281.]

62 [*Ambarto* was changed to *Umbarto*, and the positions of Umbarto and Ambarussa were reversed: see p. 355.]

63 ['shocked' was an uncertain interpretation on my father's part of the illegible word.]

64 [The deed of his father: the treacherous taking of all the Telerian ships for the passage of the Fëanorians to Middle-earth.]

65 [The text ends with brief notes on the 'Sindarizing' of the Quenya names of the Sons of Fëanor, but these are too rapid, elliptical, and illegible to be reproduced. It may be mentioned, however, that Sindarin *Maedros* is explained as containing elements of Nelyafinwë's mother-name *Maitimo* (Common Eldarin *magit*- 'shapely', Sindarin *maed*) and of his *epessë Russandol* (Common Eldarin *russā*, Sindarin *ross*); and also that the Sindarin form of *Ambarussa* (numbered 6, i.e. the elder twin) is here *Amros*, not *Amras*.]

XII
THE PROBLEM OF *ROS*

In his last years my father attached the utmost importance to finding explanations, in historical linguistic terms, of names that went far back in the 'legendarium' (see for example his discussion of the very old names *Isfin* and *Eöl* in XI.317–18, 320), and if such names had appeared in print he felt bound by them, and went to great pains to devise etymologies that were consonant with the now minutely refined historical development of Quenya and Sindarin. Most taxing of all was the case of the name *Elros*, and others associated with it either in form or through connection in the legends; but, equally characteristically, his writings on this matter contain many observations of interest beyond the detail of phonological history: for the linguistic history and the 'legendarium' became less and less separable.

In the long excursus on the names of the descendants of Finwë given in the last chapter he had said (p. 349) that *Elros* and *Elrond* were 'formed to recall the name of their mother *Elwing*', and he had noted that the element *wing* occurs only in that name and in the name of Eärendil's ship *Vingilótë* (p. 365, note 55): he referred to a speculation of loremasters that *wing* was a word of the tongue of the Green-elves of Ossiriand, whose meaning was guessed with some probability to be 'foam, spindrift'. The name *Elros* he stated there without hesitation to mean 'star(lit) foam', in Quenya form *Elerossë* (but earlier, in *Quendi and Eldar* (XI.414), he had said that the meaning was 'star-glitter', while *Elrond* meant 'star-dome', as still in the present essay).

But this was not the last of his speculations on the matter, and there are several typewritten texts that return to the problem (all of them belonging to the same period, 1968 or later, as *The Shibboleth of Fëanor*, but certainly following that work). The most notable of these I give in full. It has no title, but begins with a statement defining the content:

> The best solution of the difficulty presented by the name *Elros*, fixed by mention in *The Lord of the Rings*, and the names of the sons of Fëanor: *Maedros*, the eldest, and *Amros*, now proposed as the name of both the twins (sixth and seventh) – to which a story is attached that it is desirable to retain.

This is a reference to the very rough manuscript text (appended to the list of father-names and mother-names of the Sons of Fëanor) in which the extraordinary story of the twin brothers is told (pp. 353–5); for the form *Amros* (not *Amras*) see p. 366, note 65.

The typescript was made very rapidly (with the usual number of interspersed notes, among them two of great interest), and it has required some editing, of a very minor kind, for the sake of clarity.

The one *-ros* was supposed (at its adoption) in *Elros* to contain a Sindarin stem **ross-* from base ROS 'spray, spindrift' (as scattered by a wind from a fountain, waterfall, or breaking waves).[1] The other is supposed to be a colour word, referring to the red, red-brown hair of the first, sixth, and seventh sons of Fëanor, descending to them from their maternal grandfather, father of Nerdanel, Fëanor's wife, a great craftsman, devoted to the Vala Aulë.

It is difficult to accept these two homophonic elements – of unconnected, indeed unconnectable, meanings – as used in Sindarin, or Sindarized names.[2] It is also unfortunate that the first appears too reminiscent of Latin *rōs* ['dew'] or Greek *drosos*, and the latter too close to well-known modern European 'red' words: as Latin *russus*, Italian *rosso*, English *russet*, *rust*, etc. However, the Elvish languages are inevitably full of such reminiscences, so that this is the lesser difficulty.

Proposed solution. Associate the name *Elros* with that of his mother *Elwing*: both contain final elements that are isolated in the legendary nomenclature (see note on *wing* in the discussion of the Sindarizing of the Ñoldorin heroic names).[3] But instead of deriving them from the Nandorin (or Green-elvish) of Ossiriand, it would be an improvement to derive them from the Mannish tongues: the language of Beren father of Dior; both **ros* and **wing* could thus be removed from Eldarin. The Adûnaic of Númenor was mainly derived from that of the most powerful and numerous people of 'the House of Hador'. This was related to the speech of Bëor's people who first entered Beleriand (probably about as nearly as Ñoldorin Quenya to Telerin of Valinor): communication between the two peoples was possible but imperfect, mainly because of phonetic changes in the Bëorian dialect. The language of the Folk of Haleth, so far as it was later known, appears to have been unrelated (unless in remote origin) and unintelligible to the other two peoples.[4]

The folk of Bëor continued to speak their own tongue among themselves with fair purity, though many Sindarin words were borrowed and adapted by them.[5] This was of course the native tongue of Beren, lineal descendant of Bëor the Old. He spoke Sindarin after a fashion (probably derived from North Sindarin); but his halting and dialectal use of it offended the ears of King Thingol.[6] But it was told in the legend of Beren and Lúthien that Lúthien learned Beren's native tongue during their long journeys together and ever after used it in their speech together. Not long before they came at last back to the borders of Doriath he asked her why she did so, since her own tongue was richer and more beautiful. Then she became silent and her eyes seemed to look far away before she answered: 'Why? Because I must forsake thee, or else forsake my own people and become one of the children of Men. Since I will never forsake thee, I must learn the speech of thy kin, and mine.' Dior their son, it is said, spoke both tongues: his father's, and his mother's, the Sindarin of Doriath. For he said: 'I am the first of the *Pereðil* (Half-elven); but I am also the heir of King Elwë, the *Eluchíl*.'[7]

He gave to his elder son the name *Eluréd*, that is said to have the same significance, but ended in the Bëorian word *rêda* 'heir'; to his second son he gave the name *Elurín*,[8] but his daughter the name *Elwing*. For she was born on a clear night of stars, the light of which glittered in the spray of the waterfall by which his house was built.[9] The word *wing* was Bëorian, meaning fine rain or the spray from fountains and waterfalls blown by a wind; but he joined this to Elvish *el-* 'star' rather than to the Bëorian,[10] because it was more beautiful, and also went with the names of her brothers: the name *Elwë* (Sindarin *Elu*) was believed to be and probably was derived from *el* 'star'.[11]

Eluréd and Elurín, before they came to manhood, were both slain by the sons of Fëanor,[12] in the last and most abominable deed brought about by the curse that the impious oath of Fëanor laid upon them. But Elwing was saved and fled with the Silmaril to the havens of the surviving Eldar at the Mouths of Sirion. There she later wedded Eärendil, and so joined the two Half-elven lines. Her sons she named *Elros* and *Elrond*; and after the manner of her brothers the first ended in a Bëorian word, and the second in an Elvish. *Elros* was indeed close in meaning to her own name: it contained the Bëorian word for 'foam' and the white crest of waves:[13] *rôs*. Its older form [was] *roth (róþ)*. This was used in Adûnaic songs and legends concerning the coming of the Atani to Númenor in a translation of the name of Eärendil's ship. This they called *Rothinzil*.[14] Also in Númenor their first king was usually given the name *Elroth*. The word *wing(a)* was not known in Adûnaic. It was maybe an invention of the Lesser Folk,[15] for in their steep shores there had been waterfalls, whereas in the wooded land of the Greater Folk that went down in gentle slopes there had been none.

In this way also may be explained the name that Eärendil gave to his ship in which he at last succeeded in passing over the Great Sea. He himself called it *Wingalótë*, which like his own names were Quenya in form; for Quenya was his childhood's speech, since in the house of his mother's father, Turukáno (Turgon), King of Gondolin, that speech was in daily use.[16] But *Vinga-* was not a Quenya word: it was a Quenyarized form of the Bëorian *wing* that appeared in *Elwing* the name of his spouse. The form given to this name in Sindarin was *Gwingloth*, but as said above it was in the Adûnaic of Númenor translated as *Rothinzil*.

In the havens of refuge, when Morgoth's conquest was all but complete, there were several tongues to be heard. Not only the Sindarin, which was chiefly used, but also its Northern dialect; and among the Men of the Atani some still used their Mannish speeches; and of all these Eärendil had some knowledge. It is said that before Manwë he spoke the errand of Elves and Men first in Sindarin, since that might represent all those of the suppliants who had survived the war with Morgoth; but he repeated it in Quenya, since that was the language of the Ñoldor, who alone were under the ban of the Valar; and he added a prayer in the Mannish tongues of Hador and Bëor,[17] pleading that they were not under the ban, and had aided the Eldar only in their war against Morgoth, the enemy of the Valar. For the Atani had not rebelled against the Valar; they had rejected Morgoth and fled Westward seeking the Valar as the representatives of the One. This plea Manwë accepted, and one voice alone spoke aloud the doubt that was in the hearts of all the Valar. Mandos said: 'Nonetheless they are descendants of Men, who rejected the One himself. That is an evil seed that may grow again. For even if we under Eru have the power to return to Middle-earth and cast out Morgoth from the Kingdom of Arda, we cannot destroy all the evil that he has sown, nor seek out all his servants – unless we ravaged the whole of the Kingdom and made an end of all life therein; and that we may not do.'

The names *Elros* and *Elrond* that Elwing gave to her sons were held prophetic, as many mother-names among the Eldar.[18]

For after the Last Battle and the overthrow of Morgoth, when the Valar gave to Elros and Elrond a choice to belong either to the kin of the Eldar or to the kin of Men, it was Elros who voyaged over sea to Númenor following the star of Eärendil; whereas Elrond remained among the Elves and carried on the lineage of King Elwë.[19] Now *Elrond* was a word for the firmament, the starry dome as it appeared like a roof to Arda; and it was given by Elwing in memory of the great Hall of the Throne of Elwë in the midst of his stronghold of Menegroth that was called the *Menelrond*,[20] because by the arts and aid of Melian its high arched roof had been adorned with silver and gems set in the order and figures of the stars in the great Dome of Valmar[21] in Aman, whence Melian came.

But alas! This explanation fell foul of a small fact that my father had missed; and it was fatal. He noted on the text that 'most of this fails', because of the name *Cair Andros* (a Sindarin name, as were virtually all the place-names of Gondor), the island in the Anduin north of Minas Tirith, of which it had been said in Appendix A (RK p. 335, footnote) that it 'means "Ship of Long-foam"; for the isle was shaped like a great ship, with a high prow pointing north, against which the white foam of Anduin broke on sharp rocks.' So he was forced to accept that the element *-ros* in *Elros* must be the same as that in *Cair Andros*, the word must be Eldarin, not Atanic (Bëorian), and there could be no historical relationship between it and the Númenórean Adûnaic *Rothinzil*.[22]

Evidently following this is another note, from which it emerges that he still held to the view that the word *wing* ('spray, spindrift') was of Bëorian origin; and while noting that the name Wingalótë [> Wingelótë] of Eärendil's ship had not appeared in print, he observed that it 'must be retained, since it is connected with the name *Elwing*, and is in intention formed to resemble and "explain" the name of Wade's ship Guingelot.'[23] On *Guingelot* and *Wingelot* see my discussion in III.142–4 (in which I overlooked this remarkable statement). Concerning *wing* he said again that Eärendil named his ship in Quenya form, since that language had been his childhood speech, and that he intended its meaning to be 'Foam-flower'; but he adopted the element *wing* from the name of Elwing his wife. That name was given to her by her father Dior, who knew the Bëorian tongue (cf. p. 369).[24]

NOTES

1 [Cf. the *Etymologies*, V.384, stem ROS[1], 'distil, drip': Quenya *rossë* 'fine rain, dew', Noldorin *rhoss* 'rain', seen also in *Celebros*

'Silver-rain' (when *Celebros* was the name of the waterfall rather than the stream, XI.151).]

2 [Added in the margin: 'Though *Maedros* is now so long established that it would be difficult to alter'. In a later note, however, my father declared that he would change *Maedros* to *Maedron*.]

3 [See p. 365, note 55.]

4 This was the reason, in addition to their admiration of the Eldar, why the chieftains, elders, and wise men and women of the Atani learned Sindarin. The Halethian language was already failing before Túrin's time, and finally perished after Húrin in his wrath destroyed the small land and people. [Cf. *Of Dwarves and Men*, pp. 307–8 and note 49. In the chapter *Of the Coming of Men into the West* added to the *Quenta Silmarillion* Felagund learned from Bëor that the Haladin (the Folk of Haleth) 'speak the same tongue as we', whereas the People of Marach (the 'Hadorians') were 'of a different speech' (XI.218, §10). This was changed in the published *Silmarillion*: see XI.226. – With what is said here of the decline of the 'Halethian' language cf. *The Wanderings of Húrin* (XI.283 and note 41): 'the old tongue of the Folk which was now out of daily use'.]

5 Not necessarily confined to names of things that had not before [been] known. In the nomenclature of later generations assimilation to the Eldarin modes, and the use of some elements frequent in Eldarin names, can be observed. [It has been stated many times that the 'Bëorians' forsook their own language in Beleriand: see V.275 (footnote), XI.202, 217 (first footnote), 226; *Unfinished Tales* p. 215, note 19.]

6 He [Thingol] had small love for the Northern Sindar who had in regions near to Angband come under the dominion of Morgoth, and were accused of sometimes entering his service and providing him with spies. The Sindarin used by the Sons of Fëanor also was of the Northern dialect; and they were hated in Doriath.

7 [*Eluchíl* (Thingol's Heir): see XI.350.]

8 'Remembrance of Elu': containing Sindarin *rîn* from Common Eldarin *rēnē* < base REN 'recall, have in mind'. [These names *Eluréd* and *Elurín* replace *Eldún* and *Elrún* (originally *Elboron* and *Elbereth*); and the story that Dior's sons were twins had been abandoned (see XI.300, 349–50). From this passage and note were derived the names in the published *Silmarillion* and the statements in the index concerning them.]

9 [Cf. *The Shibboleth of Fëanor*, p. 349: 'Beside one great waterfall, called in Sindarin *Lanthir Lamath* ("waterfall of echoing voices"), Dior had his house.' From these passages the reference in the published *Silmarillion* (p. 235) was derived.]

10 Which is not recorded, but was probably similar to the Adûnaic *azar*. [In *The Notion Club Papers*, IX.305, the Adûnaic name of

Eärendil, *Azrubêl*, was said to be 'made of *azar* "sea" and the stem *bel-* (*azra*, IX.431).]

11 [This opinion is referred to in *The Shibboleth of Fëanor* (pp. 340–1), but regarded as improbable.]

12 [The original story was that Dior's sons 'were slain by the evil men of Maidros' host' (see IV.307). Subsequently they were 'taken captive by the evil men of Maidros' following, and they were left to starve in the woods' (V.142); in a version of the Tale of Years the perpetrators were 'the cruel servants of Celegorn' (XI.351).]

13 The Atani had never seen the Great Sea before they came at last to Beleriand; but according to their own legends and histories the Folk of Hador had long dwelt during their westward migration by the shores of a sea too wide to see across; it had no tides, but was visited by great storms. It was not until they had developed a craft of boat-building that the people afterwards known as the Folk of Hador discovered that a part of their host from whom they had become separated had reached the same sea before them, and dwelt at the feet of the high hills to the south-west, whereas they [the Folk of Hador] lived in the north-east, in the woods that there came near to the shores. They were thus some two hundred miles apart, going by water; and they did not often meet and exchange tidings. Their tongues had already diverged, with the swiftness of the speeches of Men in the 'Unwritten Days', and continued to do so; though they remained friends of acknowledged kinship, bound by their hatred and fear of the Dark Lord (Morgoth), against whom they had rebelled. Nonetheless they did not know that the Lesser Folk had fled from the threat of the Servants of the Dark and gone on westward, while they had lain hidden in their woods, and so under their leader Bëor reached Beleriand at last many years before they did.

[There has of course never been any previous trace or hint of this story of the long sojourn of the 'Bëorians' and the 'Hadorians' ('the People of Marach', a name not mentioned in this essay, see p. 325, note 41) by the shores of a great inland sea. In this account of their dwellings my father first wrote 'south-east' and 'north-west', changing them at once; and the particularity of this suggests that he had a specific geographical image in mind. This must surely be the Sea of Rhûn, where (features going back to the First Map to *The Lord of the Rings*, VII.305) there are hills on the south-western side and a forest coming down to the north-eastern shores; moreover the distance of two hundred miles across the sea agrees with the map. – It is said here that the 'Bëorians' reached Beleriand 'many years' before the 'Hadorians'. According to the later *Quenta Silmarillion* chapter *Of the Coming of Men into the West* Felagund met Bëor in Ossiriand in

310, and the People of Marach came over the Blue Mountains in 313 (XI.218, §13 and commentary). In *Of Dwarves and Men* (p. 307) 'the first of the three hosts of the Folk of Hador' came into Beleriand 'not long after' the Folk of Bëor, having in fact reached the eastern foothills of the Ered Lindon first of all the kindreds of the Edain. In that text there is mention of an opinion that a long period of separation between the two peoples would account for the divergence of their languages from an original common tongue (p. 308 and note 45).]

14 [The name *Rothinzil* 'Flower of the Foam' appeared in *The Drowning of Anadûnê*, IX.360 (*Rôthinzil*).]

15 ['The Lesser Folk': the People of Bëor. This sentence refers to the content of note 13.]

16 Though for most of its people it had become a language of books, and as the other Ñoldor they used Sindarin in daily speech. In this way there arose several blended forms, belonging strictly to neither language. Indeed, the name of the great city of Turgon by which it was best known in legend, *Gondolin(d)*, is an example. It was given by Turgon in Quenya *Ondolindë*, but generally its people turned it towards Sindarin, in which Eldarin **gon*, **gondo* 'stone, rock' had retained the g- lost in Quenya. [See XI.201.]

17 The language of the Folk of Haleth was not used, for they had perished and would not rise again. Nor would their tongue be heard again, unless the prophecy of Andreth the Wise-woman should prove true, that Túrin in the Last Battle should return from the Dead, and before he left the Circles of the World for ever should challenge the Great Dragon of Morgoth, Ancalagon the Black, and deal him the death-stroke.

[This remarkable saying has long roots, extending back to the prophecy at the end of the old *Tale of Turambar* (II.115-16), where it was told that the Gods of Death (Fui and Vefántur) would not open their doors to Túrin and Nienóri, that Úrin and Mavwin (Húrin and Morwen) went to Mandos, and that their prayers

> came even to Manwë, and the Gods had mercy on their unhappy fate, so that those twain Túrin and Nienóri entered into Fôs'Almir, the bath of flame, even as Urwendi and her maidens had done in ages past before the first rising of the Sun, and so were all their sorrows and stains washed away, and they dwelt as shining Valar among the blessed ones, and now the love of that brother and sister is very fair; but Turambar indeed shall stand beside Fionwë in the Great Wrack, and Melko and his drakes shall curse the sword of Mormakil.

In the *Sketch of the Mythology* or 'earliest Silmarillion' of the

1920s the prophecy with which it ends (IV.40) declares that when Morgoth returns, and 'the last battle of all' is fought,

> Fionwë will fight Morgoth on the plain of Valinor, and the spirit of Túrin shall be beside him; it shall be Túrin who with his black sword will slay Morgoth, and thus the children of Húrin shall be avenged.

The development of this in the *Quenta* (IV.165) tells that in the day of the last battle, on the fields of Valinor,

> Tulkas shall strive with Melko, and on his right shall stand Fionwë and on his left Túrin Turambar, son of Húrin, Conqueror of Fate; and it shall be the black sword of Túrin that deals unto Melko his death and final end; and so shall the children of Húrin and all Men be avenged.

And the final passage of the *Quenta*, concerning the prophecy of the recovery of the Two Trees, ends with the words (*ibid.*):

> But of Men in that day the prophecy speaks not, save of Túrin only, and him it names among the Gods.

These passages reappear in the revised conclusion of the *Quenta* that belongs with the *Quenta Silmarillion* of 1937 (see V.323–4, 333), with two changes: Túrin in the Last Battle is said to be 'coming from the halls of Mandos', and in the final sentence concerning the prophecy 'no Man it names, save Túrin only, and to him a place is given among the sons of the Valar.' In the cursory corrections that my father made much later to this conclusion (see XI.245–7) he changed 'Túrin ... coming from the halls of Mandos' to 'Túrin ... returning from the Doom of Men at the ending of the world', and against the concluding passage (including the reference to Túrin as 'a son of the Valar') he placed a large X.

Another reference is found in the *Annals of Aman* (X.71, 76), where it is said of the constellation Menelmakar (Orion) that it 'was a sign of Túrin Turambar, who should come into the world, and a foreshowing of the Last Battle that shall be at the end of Days.'

In this last reappearance of the mysterious and fluctuating idea the prophecy is put into the mouth of Andreth, the Wise-woman of the House of Bëor: Túrin will 'return from the Dead' before his final departure, and his last deed within the Circles of the World will be the slaying of the Great Dragon, Ancalagon the Black. Andreth prophesies of the Last Battle at the end of the Elder Days (the sense in which the term 'Last Battle' is used shortly afterwards in this text, p. 371); but in all the early texts (the *Quenta*, IV.160; the *Annals of Beleriand*, IV.309, V.144; the *Quenta Silmarillion*, V.329) it was Eärendil who destroyed Ancalagon.]

18 They had no other names that are recorded; for Eärendil was nearly always at sea in many fruitless voyages, and both his sons were born in his absence.
19 And also that of Turgon; though he preferred that of Elwë, who was not under the ban that was laid on the Exiles.
20 *Menelrond*: 'heaven-dome'.
21 [On the Dome of Varda above Valinor see X.385–8.]
22 [Another note among these papers derives the Adûnaic word *roth* (as in *Rothinzil*) from a stem RUTH, 'not originally connected to foam. Its basic sense was "scar, score, furrow", and yielded words for plough and ploughing; when applied to boats it referred to their track on water, especially to the curling water at the prow (*obroth* "fore-cutting", whereas the wake was called *nadroth* "hind-track", or the smooth *roth*).']
23 [He also said here that though *Rothinzil* had not appeared in print he wished to retain it.]
24 [This 'Bëorian' explanation of *wing* seems to have been abandoned also, since in what seems to be the latest among these discussions my father said that both elements in *Elwing* were Sindarin: he proposed an etymology whereby Quenya *wingë*, Sindarin *gwing* 'appears to be related' to the Quenya verb *winta* 'scatter, blow about' (both transitive and intransitive), comparing Quenya *lassewinta* as a variant of *lasselanta*, 'leaf-fall, autumn'.]

XIII
LAST WRITINGS
Of Glorfindel, Círdan, and other matters

There is a small collection of very late manuscripts, preserved together, closely similar in appearance, and all written on the blank sides of publication notices issued by Allen and Unwin. Most of these are copies of the same notice dated 19 January 1970 (used also by my father for his late work on the story of Maeglin, XI.316), but one of these writings was stated by him to be developed from a reply to a correspondent sent on 9 December 1972, and another is dated by him 20 November 1972. I think it very probable that the whole collection belongs to that time, the last year of his life: he died on the second of September, 1973, at the age of eighty-one. There are clear evidences of confusion (as he said at one point, 'my memory is no longer retentive'); but there are elements in them that are of much interest and should be recorded.

Though writing in manuscript he retained his practice of interspersing notes into the body of the text, distinguishing them by a different (italic) script. All the numbered notes, authorial and editorial, are collected at the end of the chapter.

GLORFINDEL

In the summer of 1938, when my father was pondering *The Council of Elrond* in *The Lord of the Rings*, he wrote: 'Glorfindel tells of his ancestry in Gondolin' (VI.214). More than thirty years later he took up the question of whether Glorfindel of Gondolin and Glorfindel of Rivendell were indeed one and the same, and this issued in two discussions, together with other brief or fragmentary writings closely associated with them. I will refer to these as '*Glorfindel I*' and '*Glorfindel II*'. The first page of *Glorfindel I* is missing, and the second page begins with the words 'as guards or assistants.' Then follows:

An Elf who had once known Middle-earth and had fought in the long wars against Melkor would be an eminently suitable companion for Gandalf. We could then reasonably suppose that Glorfindel (possibly as one of a small party,[1] more probably as a sole companion) landed with Gandalf–Olórin about Third Age 1000. This supposition would indeed explain the air of special power and sanctity that surrounds Glorfindel – note how the Witch-king flies from him, although all others (such as King Eärnur) however brave could not induce their horses to face him (Appendix A (I, iv), RK p. 331). For according to accounts (quite independent of this case) elsewhere given of Elvish nature, and their relations with the Valar, when Glorfindel was slain his spirit would then go to Mandos and be judged, and then would remain in the Halls of Waiting until Manwë granted him release. The Elves were destined to be by nature 'immortal', within the unknown limits of the life of the Earth as a habitable realm, and their disembodiment was a grievous thing. It was the duty, therefore, of the Valar to restore them, if they were slain, to incarnate life, if they desired it – unless for some grave (and rare) reason: such as deeds of great evil, or any works of malice of which they remained obdurately unrepentant. When they were re-embodied they could remain in Valinor, or return to Middle-earth if their home had been there. We can therefore reasonably suppose that Glorfindel, after the purging or forgiveness of his part in the rebellion of the Ñoldor, was released from Mandos and became himself again, but remained in the Blessed Realm – for Gondolin was destroyed and all or most of his kin had perished. We can thus understand why he seems so powerful a figure and almost 'angelic'. For he had returned to the primitive innocence of the First-born, and had then lived among those Elves who had never rebelled, and in the companionship of the Maiar[2] for ages: from the last years of the First Age, through the Second Age, to the end of the first millennium of the Third Age: before he returned to Middle-earth.[3] It is indeed probable that he had in Valinor already become a friend and follower of Olórin. Even in the brief glimpses of him given in *The Lord of the Rings* he appears as specially concerned for Gandalf, and was one (the most powerful, it would seem) of those sent out from Rivendell when the disquieting news reached Elrond that Gandalf had never reappeared to guide or protect the Ring-bearer.

The second essay, *Glorfindel II*, is a text of five manuscript pages which undoubtedly followed the first at no long interval; but a slip of paper on which my father hastily set down some thoughts on the matter presumably came between them, since he said here that while Glorfindel might have come with Gandalf, 'it seems far more likely that he was sent in the crisis of the Second Age, when Sauron invaded Eriador, to assist Elrond, and that though not (yet) mentioned in the annals recording Sauron's defeat he played a notable and heroic part

LAST WRITINGS 379

in the war.' At the end of this note he wrote the words 'Númenórean ship', presumably indicating how Glorfindel might have crossed the Great Sea.

This name is in fact derived from the earliest work on the mythology: *The Fall of Gondolin*, composed in 1916–17, in which the Elvish language that ultimately became that of the type called Sindarin was in a primitive and unorganized form, and its relation with the High-elven type (itself very primitive) was still haphazard. It was intended to mean 'Golden-tressed',[4] and was the name given to the heroic 'Gnome' (Ñoldo), a chieftain of Gondolin, who in the pass of Cristhorn ('Eagle-cleft') fought with a Balrog [> Demon], whom he slew at the cost of his own life.

Its use in *The Lord of the Rings* is one of the cases of the somewhat random use of the names found in the older legends, now referred to as *The Silmarillion*, which escaped reconsideration in the final published form of *The Lord of the Rings*. This is unfortunate, since the name is now difficult to fit into Sindarin, and cannot possibly be Quenyarin. Also in the now organized mythology, difficulty is presented by the things recorded of Glorfindel in *The Lord of the Rings*, if Glorfindel of Gondolin is supposed to be the same person as Glorfindel of Rivendell.

As for the former: he was slain in the Fall of Gondolin at the end of the First Age, and if a chieftain of that city must have been a Ñoldo, one of the Elf-lords in the host of King Turukáno (Turgon); at any rate when *The Fall of Gondolin* was written he was certainly thought to be so. But the Ñoldor in Beleriand were exiles from Valinor, having rebelled against the authority of Manwë supreme head of the Valar, and Turgon was one of the most determined and unrepentant supporters of Fëanor's rebellion.[5] There is no escape from this. Gondolin is in *The Silmarillion* said to have been built and occupied by a people of almost entirely Ñoldorin origin.[6] It might be possible, though inconsistent, to suppose that Glorfindel was a prince of Sindarin origin who had joined the host of Turgon, but this would entirely contradict what is said of Glorfindel in Rivendell in *The Lord of the Rings*: most notably in *The Fellowship of the Ring*, p. 235, where he is said to have been one of the 'lords of the Eldar from beyond the furthest seas ... who have dwelt in the Blessed Realm.' The Sindar had never left Middle-earth.

This difficulty, far more serious than the linguistic one, may be considered first. At any rate what at first sight may seem the simplest solution must be abandoned: sc. that we have merely a reduplication of names, and that Glorfindel of Gondolin and Glorfindel of Rivendell were different persons. This repetition of so striking a name, though possible, would not be credible.[7] No other major character in the Elvish legends as reported in *The Silmarillion* and *The Lord of the Rings* has a name borne by another Elvish person of importance. Also it may be found that acceptance of the identity of Glorfindel of old and of the Third Age will actually explain what is said of him and improve the story.

When Glorfindel of Gondolin was slain his spirit would according to the laws established by the One be obliged at once to return to the land of the Valar. Then he would go to Mandos and be judged, and would then remain in the 'Halls of Waiting' until Manwë granted him release. Elves were destined to be 'immortal', that is not to die within the unknown limits decreed by the One, which at the most could be until the end of the life of the Earth as a habitable realm. Their death – by any injury to their bodies so severe that it could not be healed – and the disembodiment of their spirits was an 'unnatural' and grievous matter. It was therefore the duty of the Valar, by command of the One, to restore them to incarnate life, if they desired it. But this 'restoration' could be delayed[8] by Manwë, if the *fëa* while alive had done evil deeds and refused to repent of them, or still harboured any malice against any other person among the living.

Now Glorfindel of Gondolin was one of the exiled Ñoldor, rebels against the authority of Manwë, and they were all under a ban imposed by him: they could not return in bodily form to the Blessed Realm. Manwë, however, was not bound by his own ordinances, and being still the supreme ruler of the Kingdom of Arda could set them aside, when he saw fit. From what is said of Glorfindel in *The Silmarillion* and *The Lord of the Rings* it is evident that he was an Elda of high and noble spirit: and it can be assumed that, though he left Valinor in the host of Turgon, and so incurred the ban, he did so reluctantly because of kinship with Turgon and allegiance to him, and had no part in the kinslaying of Alqualondë.[9]

More important: Glorfindel had sacrificed his life in defending the fugitives from the wreck of Gondolin against a Demon out of Thangorodrim,[10] and so enabling Tuor and Idril daughter of Turgon and their child Eärendil to escape, and seek refuge at the Mouths of Sirion. Though he cannot have known the importance of this (and would have defended them even had they been fugitives of any rank), this deed was of vital importance to the designs of the Valar.[11] It is therefore entirely in keeping with the general design of *The Silmarillion* to describe the subsequent history of Glorfindel thus. After his purging of any guilt that he had incurred in the rebellion, he was released from Mandos, and Manwë restored him.[12] He then became again a living incarnate person, but was permitted to dwell in the Blessed Realm; for he had regained the primitive innocence and grace of the Eldar. For long years he remained in Valinor, in reunion with the Eldar who had not rebelled, and in the companionship of the Maiar. To these he had now become almost an equal, for though he was an incarnate (to whom a bodily form not made or chosen by himself was necessary) his spiritual power had been greatly enhanced by his self-sacrifice. At some time, probably early in his sojourn in Valinor, he became a follower, and a friend, of Olórin (Gandalf), who as is said in *The Silmarillion* had an especial love and concern for the Children of Eru.[13] That Olórin, as was possible for one of the Maiar, had already visited Middle-earth and had become acquainted not only with the Sindarin Elves and others deeper in Middle-earth, but also with Men, is likely, but nothing is [> has yet been] said of this.

Glorfindel remained in the Blessed Realm, no doubt at first by his own choice: Gondolin was destroyed, and all his kin had perished, and were still in the Halls of Waiting unapproachable by the living. But his long sojourn during the last years of the First Age, and at least far into the Second Age, no doubt was also in accord with the wishes and designs of Manwë.

When did Glorfindel return to Middle-earth? This must probably have occurred *before* the end of the Second Age, and the 'Change of the World' and the Drowning of Númenor, after which no living embodied creature, 'humane' or of lesser kinds, could return from the Blessed Realm which had been 'removed from the Circles of the World'. This was according to a general ordinance proceeding from Eru Himself; and though, until the end of the Third Age, when Eru decreed that the Dominion of Men must begin, Manwë could be supposed to have received the permission of Eru to make an exception in his case, and to have devised some means for the transportation of Glorfindel to Middle-earth, this is improbable and would make Glorfindel of greater power and importance than seems fitting.

We may then best suppose that Glorfindel returned during the Second Age, before the 'shadow' fell on Númenor, and while the Númenóreans were welcomed by the Eldar as powerful allies. His return must have been for the purpose of strengthening Gil-galad and Elrond, when the growing evil of the intentions of Sauron were at last perceived by them. It might, therefore, have been as early as Second Age 1200, when Sauron came in person to Lindon, and attempted to deceive Gil-galad, but was rejected and dismissed.[14] But it may have been, perhaps more probably, as late as c.1600, the Year of Dread, when Barad-dûr was completed and the One Ring forged, and Celebrimbor at last became aware of the trap into which he had fallen. For in 1200, though he was filled with anxiety, Gil-galad still felt strong and able to treat Sauron with contempt.[15] Also at that time his Númenórean allies were beginning to make strong permanent havens for their great ships, and also many of them had actually begun to dwell there permanently. In 1600 it became clear to all the leaders of Elves and Men (and Dwarves) that war was inevitable against Sauron, now unmasked as a new Dark Lord. They therefore began to prepare for his assault; and no doubt urgent messages and prayers asking for help were received in Númenor (and in Valinor).[16]

The text ends here, with no indication that it was unfinished, although the 'linguistic difficulty' referred to on p. 379 was not taken up.

Written at the same time as the 'Glorfindel' texts is a discussion of the question of Elvish reincarnation. It is in two versions, one a very rough draft (partly written in fact on the manuscript of *Glorfindel I*) for the other. This text is not included here,[17] except in its concluding part, which concerns the Dwarves' belief in the rebirth or reappearance of their Fathers, most notably Durin. I give this passage in the form that it has in the original draft. It was written at a speed (with punctuation omitted, and variant forms of phrases jostling one another) that the printed form that follows does not at all convey; but it is a record of emerging thought on a matter concerning which very little is to be found in all my father's writings.

It is possible that this false notion[18] was in some ways connected with the various strange ideas which both Elves and Men had concerning the Dwarves, which were indeed largely derived by them from the Dwarves themselves. For the Dwarves asserted that the spirits of the Seven Fathers of their races were from time to time reborn in their kindreds. This was notably the case in the race of the Longbeards whose ultimate forefather was called Durin, a name which was taken at intervals by one of his descendants, but by no others but those in a direct line of descent from Durin I. Durin I, eldest of the Fathers, 'awoke' far back in the First Age (it is supposed, soon after the awakening of Men), but in the Second Age several other Durins had appeared as Kings of the Longbeards (Anfangrim). In the Third Age Durin VI was slain by a Balrog in 1980. It was prophesied (by the Dwarves), when Dáin Ironfoot took the kingship in Third Age 2941 (after the Battle of Five Armies), that in his direct line there would one day appear a Durin VII – but he would be the last.[19] Of these Durins the Dwarves reported that they retained memory of their former lives as Kings, as real, and yet naturally as incomplete, as if they had been consecutive years of life in one person.[20]

How this could come to pass the Elves did not know; nor would the Dwarves tell them much more of the matter.[21] But the Elves of Valinor knew of a strange tale of Dwarvish origins, which the Ñoldor brought to Middle-earth, and asserted that they had learned it from Aulë himself. This will be found among the many minor matters included in notes or appendices to *The Silmarillion*, and is not here told in full. For the present point it is sufficient to recall that the immediate author of the Dwarvish race was the Vala Aulë.[22]

> Here there is a brief version of the legend of the Making of the Dwarves, which I omit; my father wrote on the text: 'Not a place for telling the story of Aulë and the Dwarves.'[23] The conclusion then follows:

The Dwarves add that at that time Aulë gained them also this privilege that distinguished them from Elves and Men: that the spirit of each of the Fathers (such as Durin) should, at the end of the long span of life allotted to Dwarves, fall asleep, but then lie in a tomb of his own body,[24] at rest, and there its weariness and any hurts that had befallen it should be amended. Then after long years he should arise and take up his kingship again.[25]

> The second version is very much briefer, and on the question of the 'rebirth' of the Fathers says only: '... the reappearance, at long intervals, of the person of one of the Dwarf-fathers, in the lines of their kings – e.g. especially Durin – is not when examined probably one of

rebirth, but of the preservation of the *body* of a former King Durin (say) to which at intervals his spirit would return. But the relations of the Dwarves to the Valar and especially to the Vala Aulë are (as it seems) quite different from those of Elves and Men.'

THE FIVE WIZARDS

Another brief discussion, headed 'Note on the landing of the Five Wizards and their functions and operations', arose from my father's consideration of the matter of Glorfindel, as is seen from the opening words: 'Was in fact Glorfindel one of them?' He observed that he was 'evidently never supposed to be when *The Lord of the Rings* was written', adding that there is no possibility that some of them were Eldar 'of the highest order of power', rather than Maiar. The text then continues with the passage given in *Unfinished Tales*, p. 394, beginning 'We must assume that they were all Maiar ...'; but after the words with which that citation ends ('... chosen by the Valar with this in mind') there stands only 'Saruman the most powerful', and then it breaks off, unfinished. Beside these last words is a pencilled note: 'Radagast a name of Mannish (Anduin vale) origin – but not now clearly interpretable' (see *Unfinished Tales* p. 390 and note 4).

On the reverse of the page are some notes which I described in *Unfinished Tales* as uninterpretable, but which with longer scrutiny I have been largely able to make out. One of them reads as follows:

No names are recorded for the two wizards. They were never seen or known in lands west of Mordor. The wizards did not come at the same time. Possibly Saruman, Gandalf, Radagast did, but more likely Saruman the chief (and already over mindful of this) came first and alone. Probably Gandalf and Radagast came together, though this has not yet been said. ... (what is most probable) ... Glorfindel also met Gandalf at the Havens. The other two are only known to (have) exist(ed) [*sic*] by Saruman, Gandalf, and Radagast, and Saruman in his wrath mentioning five was letting out a piece of private information.

The reference of the last sentence is to Saruman's violent retort to Gandalf at the door of Orthanc, in which he spoke of 'the rods of the Five Wizards' (*The Two Towers* p. 188). Another note is even rougher and more difficult:

The 'other two' came much earlier, at the same time probably as Glorfindel, when matters became very dangerous in the Second Age.[26] Glorfindel was sent to aid Elrond and was (though not yet said) pre-eminent in the war in Eriador.[27] But the other two Istari were sent for a different purpose. Morinehtar and

Rómestámo.[28] Darkness-slayer and East-helper. Their task was to circumvent Sauron: to bring help to the few tribes of Men that had rebelled from Melkor-worship, to stir up rebellion ... and after his first fall to search out his hiding (in which they failed) and to cause [?dissension and disarray] among the dark East ... They must have had very great influence on the history of the Second Age and Third Age in weakening and disarraying the forces of East ... who would both in the Second Age and Third Age otherwise have ... outnumbered the West.

At the words in the citation from this text in *Unfinished Tales* (p. 394) 'Of the other two nothing is said in published work save the reference to the Five Wizards in the altercation between Gandalf and Saruman' my father wrote: 'A note made on their names and functions seems now lost, but except for the names their general history and effect on the history of the Third Age is clear.' Conceivably he was thinking of the sketched-out narrative of the choosing of the Istari at a council of the Valar (*Unfinished Tales* p. 393), in which the Two Wizards (or 'the Blue Wizards', *Ithryn Luin*) were named Alatar and Pallando.

CÍRDAN

This brief manuscript is also associated with the discussion of Glorfindel: rough drafting for it is found on the verso of one of the pages of the text *Glorfindel II*.

This is the Sindarin for 'Shipwright',[29] and describes his later functions in the history of the First Three Ages; but his 'proper' name, sc. his original name among the Teleri, to whom he belonged, is never used.[30] He is said in the Annals of the Third Age (c.1000) to have seen further and deeper into the future than anyone else in Middle-earth.[31] This does not include the Istari (who came from Valinor), but must include even Elrond, Galadriel, and Celeborn.

Círdan was a Telerin Elf, one of the highest of those who were not transported to Valinor but became known as the Sindar, the Grey-elves;[32] he was akin to Olwë, one of the two kings of the Teleri, and lord of those who departed over the Great Sea. He was thus also akin to Elwë,[33] Olwë's elder brother, acknowledged as high-king of all the Teleri in Beleriand, even after he withdrew to the guarded realm of Doriath. But Círdan and his people remained in many ways distinct from the rest of the Sindar. They retained the old name Teleri (in later Sindarin[34] form *Telir*, or *Telerrim*) and remained in many ways a separate folk, speaking even in later days a more archaic language.[35] The Ñoldor called them the *Falmari*, 'wave-folk', and the other Sindar *Falathrim* 'people of the foaming shore'.[36]

It was during the long waiting of the Teleri for the return of the floating isle, upon which the Vanyar and Ñoldor had been transported over the Great Sea, that Círdan had turned his thoughts and skill to the making of ships, for he and all the other Teleri became impatient. Nonetheless it is said that for love of his kin and allegiance Círdan was the leader of those who sought longest for Elwë when he was lost and did not come to the shores to depart from Middle-earth. Thus he forfeited the fulfilment of his greatest desire: to see the Blessed Realm and find again there Olwë and his own nearest kin. Alas, he did not reach the shores until nearly all the Teleri of Olwë's following had departed.

Then, it is said, he stood forlorn looking out to sea, and it was night, but far away he could see a glimmer of light upon Eressëa ere it vanished into the West. Then he cried aloud: 'I will follow that light, alone if none will come with me, for the ship that I have been building is now almost ready.' But even as he said this he received in his heart a message, which he knew to come from the Valar, though in his mind it was remembered as a voice speaking in his own tongue. And the voice warned him not to attempt this peril; for his strength and skill would not be able to build any ship able to dare the winds and waves of the Great Sea for many long years yet. 'Abide now that time, for when it comes then will your work be of utmost worth, and it will be remembered in song for many ages after.' 'I obey,' Círdan answered, and then it seemed to him that he saw (in a vision maybe) a shape like a white boat, shining above him, that sailed west through the air, and as it dwindled in the distance it looked like a star of so great a brilliance that it cast a shadow of Círdan upon the strand where he stood.

As we now perceive, this was a foretelling of the ship[37] which after apprenticeship to Círdan, and ever with his advice and help, Eärendil built, and in which at last he reached the shores of Valinor. From that night onwards Círdan received a foresight touching all matters of importance, beyond the measure of all other Elves upon Middle-earth.

This text is remarkable in that on the one hand nothing is said of the history and importance of Círdan as it appears elsewhere, while on the other hand almost everything that is told here is unique. In the *Grey Annals* it was said (XI.8, §14):

> Ossë therefore persuaded many to remain in Beleriand, and when King Olwë and his host were embarked upon the isle and passed over the Sea they abode still by the shore; and Ossë returned to them, and continued in friendship with them. And he taught to them the craft of shipbuilding and of sailing; and they became a folk of mariners, the first in Middle-earth ...

But of Ossë there is now no mention; shipbuilding on the coasts of Beleriand is said to have begun in the long years during which the Teleri awaited Ulmo's return, and is indeed spoken of (see note 29) as the further evolution of a craft already developed among the Teleri during the Great Journey.

Other features of this account that appear nowhere else (in addition of course to the story of Círdan's desire to cross the Sea to Valinor, and his vision of the white ship passing westward through the night above him) are that the Teleri delayed long on the shores of the Sea of Rhûn on the Great Journey (note 29; cf. p. 373, note 13); that Círdan was the leader of those who sought for Elwë Thingol, his kinsman; and that Eärendil was 'apprenticed' to Círdan, who aided him in the building of Vingilot.

NOTES

1   It may be noted that *Galdor* is another name of similar sort and period of origin, but he appears as a messenger from Círdan and is called Galdor of the Havens. *Galdor* also appeared in *The Fall of Gondolin*, but the name is of a more simple and usual form [than *Glorfindel*] and might be repeated. But unless he is said in *The Fall of Gondolin* to have been slain, he can reasonably be supposed to be the same person, one of the Ñoldor who escaped from the siege and destruction, but fled west to the Havens, and not southwards to the mouths of Sirion, as did most of the remnant of the people of Gondolin together with Tuor, Idril, and Eärendil. He is represented in *The Council of Elrond* as less powerful and much less wise than Glorfindel; and so evidently had not returned to Valinor, and been purged, and reincarnated.

[See note 3. – The words 'the name [Galdor] is of a more simple and usual form [than Glorfindel] and might be repeated' show that on the lost first page my father had discussed (as he would do in the following text) the possibility that there were two distinct persons named Glorfindel, and had concluded that it was too improbable to be entertained. – 'But unless he is said in *The Fall of Gondolin* to have been slain': my father would probably have been hard put to it to lay his hand on *The Fall of Gondolin*, and without consulting it he could not say for certain what had been Galdor's fate (this, I take it, is his meaning). In fact, Galdor was not slain, but led the fugitives over the pass of Cristhorn while Glorfindel came up at the rear (II.191-2), and in the 'Name-list to *The Fall of Gondolin*' (II.215) it is said that he went to Sirion's mouth, and that 'he dwelleth yet in Tol Eressëa'. He was the lord of the people of the Tree in Gondolin, and of him it was said in the old tale that he 'was held the most valiant of all the Gondothlim save Turgon alone' (II.173).]

2 That angelic order to which Gandalf originally belonged: lesser in power and authority than the Valar, but of the same nature: members of the first order of created rational beings, who if they appeared in visible forms ('humane' or of other kind) were self-incarnated, or given their forms by the Valar [*added later*: and who could move/travel simply by an act of will when not arrayed in a body – which they could assume when they reached the places that ... *(illegible)*.]

3 Galdor in contrast, even in the brief glimpses we have in the Council, is seen clearly as an inferior person, and much less wise. He, whether he appears in *The Silmarillion* or not, must be either (as his name suggests) a Sindarin Elf who had never left Middle-earth and seen the Blessed Realm, or one of the Ñoldor who had been exiled for rebellion, and had also remained in Middle-earth, and had not, or not yet, accepted the pardon of the Valar and returned to the home prepared for them in the West, in reward for their valour against Melkor. [The view of Galdor expressed in this note and in note 1 seems hardly justified by the report of his contributions to the Council of Elrond; and if he were indeed Galdor of Gondolin he had had long ages in which to acquire wisdom in the hard world of Middle-earth. But there is no reason to suppose that when my father wrote the chapter *The Council of Elrond* he associated Galdor of the Havens with Galdor of Gondolin.]

4 [For the original etymology of *Glorfindel*, and the etymological connections of the elements of the name, see II.341.]

5 [In the *Annals of Aman* (X.112, §135) it is told that following the Oath of the Fëanorians 'Fingolfin, and his son Turgon, therefore spoke against Fëanor, and fierce words awoke'; but later (X.118, §156), when it is told that even after the utterance of the Prophecy of the North 'all Fingolfin's folk went forward still', it is said that 'Fingon and Turgon were bold and fiery of heart and loath to abandon any task to which they had put their hands until the bitter end, if bitter it must be.']

6 [The original conception that Gondolin was peopled entirely by Ñoldor was changed in many alterations to the text of the *Grey*

Annals (see the Index to *The War of the Jewels*, entry *Gondolin*, references under 'population'): it is stated indeed (XI.45, §113) that when Turgon sent all his people forth from Nivrost to Gondolin they constituted 'a third part of the Noldor of Fingolfin's House, and *a yet greater host of the Sindar*'. The statement here that Gondolin was 'occupied by a people of almost entirely Ñoldorin origin' obviously runs entirely counter to that conception.]

7 [In the margin of the page my father asked subsequently: 'Why not?' The question seems to be answered, however, in the following sentence of the text – where the emphasis is of course on the word 'Elvish': 'no other major character in the *Elvish* legends ... has a name borne by another *Elvish* person of importance.' It would indeed have been open to him to change the name of Glorfindel of Gondolin, who had appeared in no published writing, but he did not mention this possibility.]

8 Or in gravest cases (such as that of Fëanor) withheld and referred to the One.

9 Though he [Glorfindel] is not yet named in the unrevised part of *The Silmarillion* treating of this matter, it is recorded that many of the Noldor of Turgon's following were in fact grieved by the decision of their king, and dreaded that evil would soon result from it. In the Third Host, that of Finarfin, so many were of this mind that when Finarfin heard the final doom of Mandos and repented, the greater part of that host returned to Valinor. Yet Finrod son of Finarfin, noblest of all the Ñoldor in the tales of Beleriand, also went away, for Turgon had been elected supreme lord of the Ñoldorin hosts.

[In the *Annals of Aman* (X.113, §138) there was no suggestion that Finrod (= Finarfin) led a separate 'Third Host': 'Thus at the last the Noldor set forth divided in two hosts. Fëanor and his following were in the van; but the greater host came behind under Fingolfin'; and the same was said in the *Quenta Silmarillion* (V.235, §68, not changed later). But this note carries an extreme departure from the tradition, in the entire omission of Fingolfin. This has in fact been encountered before, in my father's very late work – of this same period – on the story of Maeglin, where relationships are distorted on account of a defective genealogy making Turgon the son of Finwë (XI.327); but here, in a central story of *The Silmarillion*, Turgon is called 'king', and 'supreme lord of the Ñoldorin hosts', and Fingolfin disappears. Of course it is not to be thought that my father actually intended such a catastrophic disruption of the narrative structure as this would bring about; and it is reassuring to see that in a reference elsewhere in these papers Fingolfin reappears.]

10   [In the margin, and written at the same time as the text, my father noted: 'The duel of Glorfindel and the Demon may need revision.']
11   This is one of the main matters of *The Silmarillion* and need not here be explained. But in that part of *The Silmarillion* as so far composed it should not be left to appear that Ulmo, chiefly concerned in the coming of Tuor to Gondolin, in any way acted contrary to the Ban, against Manwë or without his knowledge. [My father perhaps had in mind Ulmo's words to Tuor on the shore at Vinyamar, *Unfinished Tales* p. 29.]
12   This implies that Glorfindel was natively an Elda of great bodily and spiritual stature, a noble character, and that his guilt had been small: sc. that he owed allegiance to Turgon and loved his own kindred, and these were his only reasons for remaining with them, although he was grieved by their obstinacy, and feared the doom of Mandos.
13   [Cf. the *Valaquenta* (*The Silmarillion*, p. 31): 'In later days he was the friend of all the Children of Ilúvatar, and took pity on their sorrows ...']
14   No doubt because Gil-galad had by then discovered that Sauron was busy in Eregion, but had secretly begun the making of a stronghold in Mordor. (Maybe already an Elvish name for that region, because of its volcano Orodruin and its eruptions – which were not made by Sauron but were a relic of the devastating works of Melkor in the long First Age.) [See note 15.]
15   [This passage concerning Gil-galad and Sauron in the year 1200 of the Second Age, with the express statement that 'Sauron came in person to Lindon', seems to conflict with what is said in *Of the Rings of Power* (*The Silmarillion* p. 287), that 'Only to Lindon he did not come, for Gil-galad and Elrond doubted him and his fair-seeming', and would not admit him to the land.]
16   For the Valar were open to the hearing of the prayers of those in Middle-earth, as ever before, save only that in the dark days of the Ban they would listen to one prayer only from the Ñoldor: a repentant prayer pleading for pardon.
17   [My father here discussed again the idea that Elvish reincarnation might be achieved by 'rebirth' as a child, and rejected it as emphatically as he had done in the discussion called 'Reincarnation of Elves', X.363–4; here as there the physical and psychological difficulties were addressed. He wrote here that the idea 'must be abandoned, or at least noted as a false notion, e.g. probably of Mannish origin, since nearly all the matter of *The Silmarillion* is contained in myths and legends that have passed through Men's hands and minds, and are (in many points) plainly influenced by contact and confusion with the myths, theories, and legends of Men' (cf. p. 357, note 17).

My discussion of this matter in X.364 must be corrected. I said there that the idea that the 'houseless' *fëa* was enabled to rebuild its *hröa* from its memory became my father's 'firm and stable view of the matter', 'as appears from very late writing on the subject of the reincarnation of Glorfindel of Gondolin'. This is erroneous. This last discussion of Elvish reincarnation refers only to the 'restoration' or 'reconstitution' of the former body by the Valar, and makes no mention of the idea that it could be achieved by the 'houseless *fëa*' operating of itself.]

18 [The 'false notion' is that of Elvish rebirth as a child: see note 17.]
19 ['Durin VII & Last' is shown in the genealogical table in Appendix A, III as a descendant of Dáin Ironfoot. Nothing is said of him in that Appendix; but see p. 278 in this book.]
20 Yet it is said that their memories were clearer and fuller of the far-off days.
21 That the Elves ever came to know so much (though only at a time when the vigour of both their races was declining) is thought to be due to the strange and unique friendship which arose between Gimli and Legolas. Indeed most of the references to Dwarvish history in Elvish records are marked with 'so said Legolas'.
22 Who was sometimes called *Návatar*, and the Dwarves *Auleönnar* 'children of Aulë'.
23 [This brief version ends with these remarkable words: 'But Eru did not give them the immortality of the Elves, but lives longer than Men. "They shall be the third children and more like Men, the second."']
24 The flesh of Dwarves is reported to have been far slower to decay or become corrupted than that of Men. (Elvish bodies robbed of their spirit quickly disintegrated and vanished.)
25 [A note at the end of the text without indication for its insertion reads:] What effect would this have on the succession? Probably this 'return' would only occur when by some chance or other the reigning king had no son. The Dwarves were very unprolific and this no doubt happened fairly often.
26 [These notes go with the text *Glorfindel II*, when my father had determined that Glorfindel came to Middle-earth in the Second Age, probably about the year 1600 (p. 382).]
27 [With this reference to Glorfindel's part in the war in Eriador cf. the note cited on pp. 378–9.]
28 [Elsewhere on this page this name is written *Róme(n)star*.]
29 Before ever they came to Beleriand the Teleri had developed a craft of boat-making; first as rafts, and soon as light boats with paddles made in imitation of the water-birds upon the lakes near their first homes, and later on the Great Journey in crossing rivers, or especially during their long tarrying on the shores of the 'Sea of Rhûn', where their ships became larger and stronger. But

in all this work Círdan had ever been the foremost and most inventive and skilful. [On the significance of the Sea of Rhûn in the context of the Great Journey see XI.173–4.]

30 Pengoloð alone mentions a tradition among the Sindar of Doriath that it was in archaic form *Nōwē*, the original meaning of which was uncertain, as was that of Olwë. [On the meaning of *Olwë* see p. 341 and note 20.]

31 [Cf. Appendix B (head-note to the Third Age): 'For Círdan saw further and deeper than any other in Middle-earth' (said in the context of his surrender of Narya, the Ring of Fire, to Mithrandir). The statement here that this is said 'in the Annals of the Third Age (c.1000)' is puzzling, but is presumably to be related to the words in the same passage of Appendix B 'When maybe a thousand years had passed ... the *Istari* or Wizards appeared in Middle-earth.']

32 A Quenya name given by the exiled Ñoldor, and primarily applied to the folk of Doriath, people of Elwë Grey-cloak.

33 [That Círdan was a kinsman of Elwë is mentioned in *Quendi and Eldar* (XI.384 and note 15).]

34 This is used as a general term for the Telerian dialect of Eldarin as it became in the changes of long years in Beleriand, though it was not entirely uniform in its development.

35 [Cf. *Quendi and Eldar*, XI.380: 'The *Eglain* became a people somewhat apart from the inland Elves, and at the time of the coming of the Exiles their language was in many ways different.' (The *Eglain* are the people of Círdan.)]

36 [For *Falathrim* see *Quendi and Eldar*, XI.378; and with *Falmari* cf. X.163, §27: 'The Sea-elves therefore they became in Valinor, the Falmari, for they made music beside the breaking waves.']

37 *Vingilótë*, 'Sprayflower'. [Beside 'Spray' my father subsequently wrote 'Foam', and noted also: '*wingë*, Sindarin *gwing*, is properly a flying spume or spindrift blown off wavetops': see p. 376, note 24.]

PART THREE

TEACHINGS OF PENGOLOÐ

XIV
DANGWETH PENGOLOÐ

This work, example and record of the instruction of Ælfwine the Mariner by Pengoloð the Wise of Gondolin, exists in two forms: the first ('A') a good clear text with (apart from one major exception, see note 6) very few changes made either in the act of writing or subsequently, and the second ('B') a superb illuminated manuscript of which the first page is reproduced as the frontispiece of this book. This latter, together with the brief text *Of Lembas*, was enclosed in a newspaper of 5 January 1960, on which my father wrote: 'Two items from the lore of Pengoloð', and also '*Danbeth* to question. How/Why did Elvish language change? Origin of *Lembas*.' On a cardboard folder enclosing the newspaper he wrote: 'Pengoloð items. §*Manen lambë Quendion ahyanë* How did the language of Elves change? §*Mana i·coimas Eldaron* What is the "*coimas*" of the Eldar?'

Above the *gw* of *Dangweth* on the illuminated manuscript he lightly pencilled *b*; but on an isolated scrap of paper found with the two texts are some jottings of which the following are clear: 'Keep *Dangweth* "answer" separate from *-beth* = *peth* "word"'; '√*gweth* "report, give account of, inform of things unknown or wished to be known"'; and '*Ndangwetha* S[indarin] *Dangweth*'.

The *Dangweth Pengoloð* cannot be earlier than 1951, while from the date of the newspaper (on which the two texts are referred to) it cannot be later than the end of 1959. I would be inclined to place it earlier rather than later in the decade; possibly the second manuscript B is to be associated with the fine manuscript pages of the Tale of Years of the First Age (see X.49), one of which is reproduced as the frontispiece to *Morgoth's Ring*.

Version B follows A very closely indeed for the most part (which is probably an indication of their closeness in time): a scattering of very minor changes (small shifts in word-order and occasional alterations in vocabulary), with a very few more significant differences (see the notes at the end of the text). That it was a work of importance to my father is evident from his writing it again in a manuscript of such elegance; and an aspect of his thought here, in respect of the conscious introduction of change by the Eldar on the basis of an understanding of the phonological structure of their language in its entirety, would reappear years later in *The Shibboleth of Fëanor* (see p. 332 and note 3 to the present essay).

The text that follows is of course that of Version B, with alteration of a few points of punctuation for greater clarity.

Dangweth Pengoloð
the Answer of Pengolod
to Aelfwine who asked him how came it that the tongues of the Elves changed and were sundered

Now you question me, Ælfwine, concerning the tongues of the Elves, saying that you wonder much to discover that they are many, akin indeed and yet unalike; for seeing that they die not and their memories reach back into ages long past, you understand not why all the race of the Quendi have not maintained the language that they had of old in common still one and the same in all their kindreds. But behold! Ælfwine, within Eä all things change, even the Valar; for in Eä we perceive the unfolding of a History in the unfolding: as a man may read a great book, and when it is full-read it is rounded and complete in his mind, according to his measure. Then at last he perceives that some fair thing that long endured: as some mountain or river of renown, some realm, or some great city; or else some mighty being, as a king, or maker, or a woman of beauty and majesty, or even one, maybe, of the Lords of the West: that each of these is, if at all, all that is said of them from the beginning even to the end. From the spring in the mountains to the mouths of the sea, all is Sirion; and from its first upwelling even to its passing away when the land was broken in the great battle, that also is Sirion, and nothing less. Though we, who are set to behold the great History, reading line by line, may speak of the river changing as it flows and grows broad, or dying as it is spilled or devoured by the sea. Yea, even from his first coming into Eä from the side of Ilúvatar, and from the young lord of the Valar in the white wrath of his battle with Melkor unto the silent king of years uncounted that sits upon the vanished heights of Oiolosse and watches but speaks no more: all that is he whom we call Manwë.

Now, verily, a great tree may outlive many a Man, and may remember the seed from which it came ere all the Men that now walk the earth were yet unborn, but the rind upon which you lay your hand, and the leaves which overshadow you, are not as that seed was, nor as the dry wood shall be that decays into the mould or passes in flame. And other trees there are that stand about, each different in growth and in shape, according to the chances of their lives, though all be akin, offspring of one yet older tree and sprung therefore from a single seed of long ago.[1] Immortal, within Eä, are the Eldar, but since even as Men they dwell in forms that come of Eä, they are no more changeless than the great trees, neither in the forms that they inhabit, nor in the things that they desire or achieve by means of those forms. Wherefore should they not then change in speech, of which one part is made with tongues and received by ears?

It hath been said by some among our loremasters that, as for Men, their elders teach to their children their speech and then soon depart, so that their voices are heard no more, and the children have no reminder of the tongue of their youth, save their own cloudy memories: wherefore in each brief generation of Men change may be swift and unrestrained. But this matter seemeth to me less simple. Weak indeed may be the memories of Men, but I say to you, Ælfwine, that even were your memory of your own being as clear as that of the wisest of the Eldar, still within the short span of your life your speech would change, and were you to live on with the life of the Elves it would change more, until looking back you would perceive that in your youth you spake an alien tongue.

For Men change both their old words for new, and their former manner of speaking for another manner, in their own lifetimes, and not only in the first learning of speech; and this change comes above all from the very changefulness of Eä; or if you will, from the nature of speech, which is fully living only when it is born, but when the union of the thought and the sound is fallen into old custom, and the two are no longer perceived apart, then already the word is dying and joyless,[2] the sound awaiting some new thought, and the thought eager for some new-patterned raiment of sound.

But to the changefulness of Eä, to weariness of the unchanged, to the renewing of the union: to these three, which are one, the Eldar also are subject in their degree. In this, however, they differ from Men, that they are ever more aware of the words that they speak. As a silversmith may remain more aware than others of the tools and vessels that he uses daily at his table, or a weaver of the texture of his garments. Yet this makes rather for change among the Eldar than for steadfastness; for the Eldar being skilled and eager in art will readily make things new, both for delight to look on, or to hear, or to feel, or for daily use: be it in vessels or raiment or in speech.

A man may indeed change his spoon or his cup at his will, and need ask none to advise him or to follow his choice. It is other indeed with words or the modes and devices of speech. Let him bethink him of a new word, be it to his heart howsoever fresh and fair, it will avail him little in converse, until other men are of like mind or will receive his invention. But among the Eldar there are many quick ears and subtle minds to hear and appraise such inventions, and though many be the patterns and devices so made that prove in the end only pleasing to a few, or to one alone, many others are welcomed and pass swiftly from mouth to mouth, with laughter or delight or with solemn thought – as maybe a new jest or new-found saying of wisdom will pass among men of brighter wit. For to the Eldar the making of speech is the oldest of the arts and the most beloved.

Wherefore, Ælfwine, I say to you: whereas the change that goes long unperceived, as the growth of a tree, was indeed slow of old in Aman ere the Rising of the Moon, and even in Middle-earth under the Sleep of Yavanna slower far than it is now among Men, yet among the Eldar this steadfastness was offset by the changes that come of will and design: many of which indeed differ little in outward seeming from those of unwitting growth. Thus the Eldar would alter the sounds of their speech at whiles to other sounds that seemed to them more pleasant, or were at the least unstaled. But this they would not do at haphazard. For the Eldar know their tongue, not word by word only, but as a whole: they know even as they speak not only of what sounds is that word woven which they are uttering, but of what sounds and sound-patterns is their whole speech at one time composed.*[3] Therefore none among the Eldar would change the sounds of some one word alone, but would rather change some one sound throughout the structure of his speech; nor would he bring into one word only some sound or union of sounds that had not before been present, but would replace

---

*And these are for the most part few in number, for the Eldar being skilled in craft are not wasteful nor prodigal to small purpose, admiring in a tongue rather the skilled and harmonious use of a few well-balanced sounds than profusion ill-ordered.

some former sound by the new sound in all words that contained it – or if not in all, then in a number selected according to their shapes and other elements, as he is guided by some new pattern that he has in mind. Even as a weaver might change a thread from red to blue, either throughout his web, or in such parts thereof as were suitable to the new pattern, but not randomly here and there nor only in one corner.[4]

And lo! Ælfwine, these changes differ little from like changes that come in the speeches of Men with the passing of time. Now as for the Eldar we know that such things were done of old by choice, full-wittingly, and the names of those who made new words or first moved great changes are yet often remembered. For which reason the Eldar do not believe that in truth the changes in the tongues of Men are wholly unwitting; for how so, say they, comes the order and harmony that oft is seen in such changes? or the skill both in the devices that are replaced and the new that follow them? And some answer that the minds of Men are half asleep: by which they mean not that the part whereof Men are unaware and can give no account slumbers, but the other part. Others perceiving that in nothing do Men, and namely those of the West,[5] so nearly resemble the Eldar as in speech, answer that the teaching which Men had of the Elves in their youth works on still as a seed in the dark. But in all this maybe they err, Ælfwine, for despite all their lore least of all things do they know the minds of Men or understand them.[6]

And to speak of memory, Ælfwine: with regard to the Elves – for I know not how it is with Men – that which we call the *coirëa quenya*, the living speech, is the language wherethrough we think and imagine; for it is to our thought as the body to our spirit, growing and changing together in all the days of our being.[7] Into that language therefore we render at once whatsoever we recall out of the past that we heard or said ourselves. If a Man remembers some thing that he said in childhood, doth he recall the accents of childhood that he used in that moment long ago? I know not. But certainly we of the Quendi do not so. We may know indeed how children not yet accomplished in speech, and how the 'fullspoken', as we say, spake at times long ago, but that is a thing apart from the images of life-memory, and is a matter of lore. For we have much lore concerning the languages of old, whether stored in the mind or in writings; but we hear not ourselves speak again in the past save with the language that clothes our thought in the present. Verily, it may chance that in the past we spake with strangers in an alien tongue, and remember what was then said, but not the tongue that was used. Out of the past indeed we may recall the sounds of an alien speech as we may other sounds: the song of birds or the murmur of water; but that is but in some cry or brief phrase. For if the speech were long or the matter subtle then we clothe it in the living language of our present thought, and if we would now relate it as it was spoken, we must render it anew, as it were a book, into that other tongue – if it is preserved still in learned lore. And even so, it is the alien voices that we hear using words in our memory, seldom ourselves – or to speak of myself, never. It is true indeed that the Eldar readily learn to use other tongues skilfully, and are slow to forget any that they have learned, but these remain as they were learned, as were they written in the unchanging pages of a book;*[8] whereas the *coirëa quenya*, the language of thought, grows and lives within, and each new stage overlies those that went before, as the acorn and the sapling are hidden in the tree.

Wherefore, Ælfwine, if thou wilt consider well all that I have said to thee at this time, not only what is plainly expressed, but also what is therein to be discovered by thought, thou wilt now understand that, albeit more wittingly, albeit more slowly, the tongues of the Quendi change in a manner like to the changes of mortal tongues. And that if one of the Eldar survives maybe the chances of fifty thousand of your years, then the speech of his childhood will be sundered from the speech of his present, as maybe the speech of some city or kingdom of Men will be sundered in the days of its majesty from the tongue of those that founded it of old.

In this last point also our kindreds are alike. Greater as is the skill of the Quendi to mould things to their will and delight, and to overcome the chances of Eä, yet they are not as the Valar, and with regard to the might of the World and its fate, they are but weak and small. Therefore to them also severance is severance, and friends and kin far away are far away. Not even the Seeing

* Save only in the strange event of the learning by one whole people of an alien speech, that thereafter they take into living and daily use, which will then change and grow with them, but their own former tongue pass away or become but a matter of lore. This has happened only once in the history of the Eldalië, when the Exiles took up the speech of Beleriand, the Sindarin tongue, and the Noldorin was preserved among them as a language of lore.

Stones of the craftsmen of old could wholly unite those that were sundered, and they and the masters that could make them were few. Therefore change, witting or unwitting, was not even long ages ago shared, nor did it proceed alike save among those that met often and had converse in labour and in mirth. Thus, swifter or slower, yet ever inescapably, the far-sundered kindreds of the Quendi were sundered also in speech: the Avari from the Eldar; and the Teleri from the other Eldar; and the Sindar, who abode in Middle-earth, from the Teleri that came at last unto Aman; and the Exiles of the Noldor from those that remained in the land of the Valar. And so still it goes in Middle-earth.

Yet long since, Ælfwine, the fashion of the World was changed; and we that dwell now in the Ancient West are removed from the circles of the World, and in memory is the greater part of our being: so that now we preserve rather than make anew. Wherefore, though even in Aman – beyond the circles of Arda, yet still with Eä – change goes ever on, until the End, be it slow beyond perceiving save in ages of time, nonetheless here at last in Eressëa our tongues are steadfast; and here over a wide sea of years we speak now still little otherwise than we did – and those also that perished – in the wars of Beleriand, when the Sun was young.

Sin Quente Quendingoldo
Elendilenna

NOTES

1 The end of this sentence, from 'offspring of one yet older tree', is not found in version A.
2 'dying or dead' A.
3 In the note to *The Shibboleth of Fëanor* which I have omitted (p. 339) my father wrote:
> The Eldar had an instinctive grasp of the structure and soundsystem of their speech as a whole, and this was increased by instruction; for in a sense all Eldarin languages were 'invented' languages, art-forms, not only inherited but also material engaging the active interest of their users and challenging awarely their own taste and inventiveness. This aspect was evidently still prominent in Valinor; though in Middle-earth it had waned, and the development of Sindarin had become, long before the arrival of the Ñoldorin exiles, mainly the product of unheeded change like the tongues of Men.

4   Version A has here a footnote omitted in B:
    Thus it was that when the name *Banyai* of old was changed to *Vanyar* this was done only because the sound *b* was changed to *v* throughout the language (save in certain sequences) – and this change, it is recorded, began among the Vanyar; whereas for the showing of many the new device of *r* was brought in and used in all words of a certain shape – and this, it is said, was begun among the Noldor.
5   *namely* is used here in the original but long lost sense of the word, 'especially, above all'. The phrase is absent in A, which reads simply: 'Or some answer that the teaching ...'
6   Here version A, as originally written, moves at once to the concluding paragraphs of the *Dangweth*, from 'But in this point at least our kindreds are alike ...' (p. 400) to its ending in the words 'we speak now still little otherwise than they did who fought in Beleriand when the Sun was young.' These paragraphs were struck out, and all the intervening matter (from 'And to speak of memory, Ælfwine ...') introduced, before they were reached again, somewhat changed in expression but not in content, and now virtually identical to the form in version B.
7   This sentence, from 'for it is to our thought ...', is absent in A.
8   The footnote here is absent in A.

XV
OF LEMBAS

For the association of this brief work, extant in a single manuscript, with the *Dangweth Pengoloð* see p. 395. It is a finely written text of two pages, in style like that of the fine manuscript of the *Dangweth* which it accompanies, but not of the same quality, and on thin paper. My father introduced some illumination at its beginning in red ball-point pen, and with the same pen wrote at the head of the first page, above the title *Of Lembas*: '*Mana i·coimas in·Eldaron?*' *maquente Elendil* (the same question as appears on the cardboard folder enclosing the two texts, p. 395). At the same time he added quotation marks at the beginning and end of the text, showing that it is the answer of Pengoloð to Ælfwine's question, 'What is the *coimas* of the Eldar?' It seems possible that these additions in ball-point pen were added later, to make the text into a companion piece to the *Dangweth*; but there is in any case no evidence for date, beyond the limits of 1951 and 1959 (p. 395).

Of Lembas

'This food the Eldar alone knew how to make. It was made for the comfort of those who had need to go upon a long journey in the wild, or of the hurt whose life was in peril. Only these were permitted to use it. The Eldar did not give it to Men, save only to a few whom they loved, if they were in great need.*

The Eldar say that they first received this food from the Valar in the beginning of their days in the Great Journey. For it was made of a kind of corn which Yavanna brought forth in the fields of Aman, and some she sent to them by the hand of Oromë for their succour upon the long march.

---

* This was not done out of greed or jealousy, although at no time in Middle-earth was there great store of this food; but because the Eldar had been commanded to keep this gift in their own power, and not to make it common to the dwellers in mortal lands. For it is said that, if mortals eat often of this bread, they become weary of their mortality, desiring to abide among the Elves, and longing for the fields of Aman, to which they cannot come.

Since it came from Yavanna, the queen, or the highest among the elven-women of any people, great or small, had the keeping and gift of the *lembas*, for which reason she was called *massánie* or *besain*: the Lady, or breadgiver.[1]

Now this corn had in it the strong life of Aman, which it could impart to those who had the need and right to use the bread. If it was sown at any season, save in frost, it soon sprouted and grew swiftly, though it did not thrive in the shadow of plants of Middle-earth and would not endure winds that came out of the North while Morgoth dwelt there. Else it needed only a little sunlight to ripen; for it took swiftly and multiplied all the vigour of any light that fell on it.

The Eldar grew it in guarded lands and sunlit glades; and they gathered its great golden ears, each one, by hand, and set no blade of metal to it. The white haulm was drawn from the earth in like manner, and woven into corn-leeps[2] for the storing of the grain: no worm or gnawing beast would touch that gleaming straw, and rot and mould and other evils of Middle-earth did not assail it.

From the ear to the wafer none were permitted to handle this grain, save those elven-women who were called *Yavannildi* (or by the Sindar the *Ivonwin*),[3] the maidens of Yavanna; and the art of the making of the *lembas*, which they learned of the Valar, was a secret among them, and so ever has remained.'

Lembas is the Sindarin name, and comes from the older form *lenn-mbass* 'journey-bread'. In Quenya it was most often named *coimas* which is 'life-bread'.[4]

Quente Quengoldo.

NOTES

1 In the story of Túrin it is said of Melian's gift of *lembas* to Beleg the Bowman (*The Silmarillion* p. 202) that it was 'wrapped in leaves of silver, and the threads that bound it were sealed at the knots with the seal of the Queen, a wafer of white wax shaped as a single flower of Telperion; for according to the customs of the Eldalië the keeping and giving of *lembas* belonged to the Queen alone. In nothing did Melian show greater favour to Túrin than in this gift; for the Eldar had never before allowed Men to use this waybread, and seldom did so again.'

With '*massánie* or *besain*' cf. the entry in the *Etymologies*, V.372, stem MBAS 'knead': Quenya *masta*, Noldorin *bast*, 'bread'; also the words *lembas, coimas,* explained at the end of the present text as 'journey-bread' and 'life-bread'. Above the *ain* of *besain* is faintly pencilled *oneth.* sc. *besoneth.*

In using the word *Lady* here my father no doubt had an eye to its origin in Old English *hlǣf-dīġe*, of which the first element is *hlāf* (modern English *loaf*) with changed vowel, and the second a derivative of the stem *dīg-* 'knead' (to which *dough* is ultimately related); cf. *lord* from *hlāf-weard* 'bread-keeper'.

2 *haulm*: the stalks of cultivated plants left when the ears or pods have been gathered; *corn-leeps*: *leep (leap)* is an old dialect word for a basket (Old English *lēap*).

3 *Ivonwin*: the Noldorin (i.e. later Sindarin) form *Ivann* for *Yavanna* appears in the *Etymologies*, V.399, stem YAB 'fruit'.

4 This was written at the same time as the rest of the manuscript, but set in as printed, and was excluded from the quotation marks added later to the body of the text. The words *Quente Quengoldo* ('Thus spoke Pengoloð') also belong to the time of writing.

PART FOUR

UNFINISHED TALES

XVI
THE NEW SHADOW

This story, or fragment of a story, is now published for the first time, though its existence has long been known.[1] The textual history is not complicated, but there is a surprising amount of it.

There is, first, a collection of material in manuscript, beginning with two sides of a page carrying the original opening of the story: this goes no further than the recollection of the young man (here called Egalmoth)[2] of the rebuke and lecture that he received from Borlas[3] when caught by him stealing apples from his orchard as a boy. There is then a text, which I will call 'A', written in rapid but clear script, and this extends as far as the story ever went (here also the young man's name is Egalmoth). This was followed by a typescript in top copy and carbon 'B', which follows A pretty closely and ends at the same point: there are a great many small changes in expression, but nothing that alters the narrative in even minor ways (the young man, however, now bears the name Arthael). There is also an amanuensis typescript derived from B, without independent value.[4]

Finally, there is another typescript, 'C', also with carbon copy, which extends only to the point in the story where the young man – here named Saelon[5] – leaves Borlas in his garden 'searching back in his mind to discover how this strange and alarming conversation had begun' (p. 416). This text C treats B much as B treats A: altering the expression (fairly radically in places), but in no way altering the story, or giving to it new bearings.

It seems strange that my father should have made no less than three versions, each showing very careful attention to improvement of the text in detail, when the story had proceeded for so short a distance. The evidence of the typewriters used suggests, however, that C was made very substantially later. The machine on which B was typed was the one he used in the 1950s before the acquisition of that referred to in X.300, while the italic script of A could with some probability be ascribed to that time; but the typewriter used for C was his last.[6]

In his *Biography* (p. 228) Humphrey Carpenter stated that in 1965 my father 'found a typescript of "The New Shadow", a sequel to *The Lord of the Rings* which he had begun a long time ago but had abandoned after a few pages. ... He sat up till four a.m. reading it and thinking about it.' I do not know the source of this statement; but further evidence is provided by a used envelope, postmarked

8 January 1968, on the back of which my father scribbled a passage concerning Borlas, developing further the account of his circumstances at the time of the opening of the story (see note 14). This is certain evidence that he was still concerned with *The New Shadow* as late as 1968; and since the passage roughed out here would follow on from the point reached in the typescript C (see note 14) it seems very likely that C dates from that time.

Such as the evidence is, then, the original work (represented by the manuscript A and the typescript B) derives from the 1950s. In a letter of 13 May 1964 (*Letters* no.256) he wrote:

> I did begin a story placed about 100 years after the Downfall [of Sauron], but it proved both sinister and depressing. Since we are dealing with *Men* it is inevitable that we should be concerned with the most regrettable feature of their nature: their quick satiety with good. So that the people of Gondor in times of peace, justice and prosperity, would become discontented and restless – while the dynasts descended from Aragorn would become just kings and governors – like Denethor or worse. I found that even so early there was an outcrop of revolutionary plots, about a centre of secret Satanistic religion; while Gondorian boys were playing at being Orcs and going round doing damage. I could have written a 'thriller' about the plot and its discovery and overthrow – but it would be just that. Not worth doing.

From the evidence given above, however, it is seen that his interest in the story was subsequently reawakened, and even reached the point of making a new (though incomplete) version of what he had written of it years before. But in 1972, fifteen months before his death, he wrote to his friend Douglas Carter (*Letters* no.338):

> I have written nothing beyond the first few years of the Fourth Age. (Except the beginning of a tale supposed to refer to the end of the reign of Eldarion about 100 years after the death of Aragorn. Then I of course discovered that the King's Peace would contain no tales worth recounting; and his wars would have little interest after the overthrow of Sauron; but that almost certainly a restlessness would appear about then, owing to the (it seems) inevitable boredom of Men with the good: there would be secret societies practising dark cults, and 'orc-cults' among adolescents.)

To form the text that now follows I print C so far as it goes, with the sinister young man given the name Saelon; and from that point I give the text of B, changing the name from Arthael in B to Saelon.

THE NEW SHADOW

This tale begins in the days of Eldarion, son of that Elessar of whom the histories have much to tell. One hundred and five years had passed since the fall of the Dark Tower,[7] and the story of that time was little heeded now by most of the people of Gondor, though a few were still living who could remember the War of the Ring as a shadow upon their early childhood. One of these was old Borlas of Pen-arduin. He was the younger son of Beregond, the first Captain of the Guard of Prince Faramir, who had removed with his lord from the City to the Emyn Arnen.[8]

'Deep indeed run the roots of Evil,' said Borlas, 'and the black sap is strong in them. That tree will never be slain. Let men hew it as often as they may, it will thrust up shoots again as soon as they turn aside. Not even at the Feast of Felling should the axe be hung up on the wall!'

'Plainly you think you are speaking wise words,' said Saelon. 'I guess that by the gloom in your voice, and by the nodding of your head. But what is this all about? Your life seems fair enough still, for an aged man that does not now go far abroad. Where have you found a shoot of your dark tree growing? In your own garden?'

Borlas looked up, and as he glanced keenly at Saelon he wondered suddenly if this young man, usually gay and often half mocking, had more in his mind than appeared in his face. Borlas had not intended to open his heart to him, but being burdened in thought he had spoken aloud, more to himself than his companion. Saelon did not return his glance. He was humming softly, while he trimmed a whistle of green willow with a sharp nail-knife.

The two were sitting in an arbour near the steep eastern shore of Anduin where it flowed about the feet of the hills of Arnen. They were indeed in Borlas's garden and his small grey-stone house could be seen through the trees above them on the hillslope facing west. Borlas looked at the river, and at the trees in their June leaves, and then far off to the towers of the City under the glow of late afternoon. 'No, not in my garden,' he said thoughtfully.

'Then why are you so troubled?' asked Saelon. 'If a man has a fair garden with strong walls, then he has as much as any man can govern for his own pleasure.' He paused. 'As long as he keeps the strength of life in him,' he added. 'When that fails, why trouble about any lesser ill? For then he must soon leave his garden at last, and others must look to the weeds.'

Borlas sighed, but he did not answer, and Saelon went on: 'But there are of course some who will not be content, and to their life's end they trouble their hearts about their neighbours, and the City, and the Realm, and all the wide world. You are one of them, Master Borlas, and have ever been so, since I first knew you as a boy that you caught in your orchard. Even then you were not content to let ill alone: to deter me with a beating, or to strengthen your fences. No. You were grieved and wanted to improve me. You had me into your house and talked to me.

'I remember it well. "Orcs' work," you said many times. "Stealing good fruit, well, I suppose that is no worse than boys' work, if they are hungry, or their fathers are too easy. But pulling down unripe apples to break or cast away! That is Orcs' work. How did you come to do such a thing, lad?"

'*Orcs' work!* I was angered by that, Master Borlas, and too proud to answer, though it was in my heart to say in child's words: "If it was wrong for a boy to steal an apple to eat, then it is wrong to steal one to play with. But not more wrong. Don't speak to me of Orcs' work, or I may show you some!"

'It was a mistake, Master Borlas. For I had heard tales of the Orcs and their doings, but I had not been interested till then. You turned my mind to them. I grew out of petty thefts (my father was not too easy), but I did not forget the Orcs. I began to feel hatred and think of the sweetness of revenge. We played at Orcs, I and my friends, and sometimes I thought: "Shall I gather my band and go and cut down his trees? Then he will think that the Orcs have really returned." But that was a long time ago,' Saelon ended with a smile.

Borlas was startled. He was now receiving confidences, not giving them. And there was something disquieting in the young man's tone, something that made him wonder whether deep down, as deep as the roots of the dark trees, the childish resentment did not still linger. Yes, even in the heart of Saelon, the friend of his own son, and the young man who had in the last few years shown him much kindness in his loneliness.[9] At any rate he resolved to say no more of his own thoughts to him.

'Alas!' he said, 'we all make mistakes. I do not claim wisdom, young man, except maybe the little that one may glean with the passing of the years. From which I know well enough the sad truth that those who mean well may do more harm than those who let things be. I am sorry now for what I said, if it roused hate in your heart. Though I still think that it was just:

untimely maybe, and yet true. Surely even a boy must understand that fruit is fruit, and does not reach its full being until it is ripe; so that to misuse it unripe is to do worse than just to rob the man that has tended it: it robs the world, hinders a good thing from fulfilment. Those who do so join forces with all that is amiss, with the blights and the cankers and the ill winds. And that was the way of Orcs.'

'And is the way of Men too,' said Saelon. 'No! I do not mean of wild men only, or those who grew "under the Shadow", as they say. I mean all Men. I would not misuse green fruit now, but only because I have no longer any use for unripe apples, not for your lofty reasons, Master Borlas. Indeed I think your reasons as unsound as an apple that has been too long in store. To trees all Men are Orcs. Do Men consider the fulfilment of the life-story of a tree before they cut it down? For whatever purpose: to have its room for tilth, to use its flesh as timber or as fuel, or merely to open the view? If trees were the judges, would they set Men above Orcs, or indeed above the cankers and blights? What more right, they might ask, have Men to feed on their juices than blights?'

'A man,' said Borlas, 'who tends a tree and guards it from blights and many other enemies does not act like an Orc or a canker. If he eats its fruit, he does it no injury. It produces fruit more abundantly than it needs for its own purpose: the continuing of its kind.'

'Let him eat the fruit then, or play with it,' said Saelon. 'But I spoke of slaying: hewing and burning; and by what right men do such things to trees.'

'You did not. You spoke of the judgement of trees in these matters. But trees are not judges. The children of the One are the masters. My judgement as one of them you know already. The evils of the world were not at first in the great Theme, but entered with the discords of Melkor. Men did not come with these discords; they entered afterwards as a new thing direct from Eru, the One, and therefore they are called His children, and all that was in the Theme they have, for their own good, the right to use – rightly, without pride or wantonness, but with reverence.[10]

'If the smallest child of a woodman feels the cold of winter, the proudest tree is not wronged, if it is bidden to surrender its flesh to warm the child with fire. But the child must not mar the tree in play or spite, rip its bark or break its branches. And the good husbandman will use first, if he can, dead wood or an old tree; he will not fell a young tree and leave it to rot, for no better reason than his pleasure in axe-play. That is orkish.

'But it is even as I said: the roots of Evil lie deep, and from far off comes the poison that works in us, so that many do these things – at times, and become then indeed like the servants of Melkor. But the Orcs did these things at all times; they did harm with delight to all things that could suffer it, and they were restrained only by lack of power, not by either prudence or mercy. But we have spoken enough of this.'

'Why!' said Saelon. 'We have hardly begun. It was not of your orchard, nor your apples, nor of me, that you were thinking when you spoke of the re-arising of the dark tree. What you were thinking of, Master Borlas, I can guess nonetheless. I have eyes and ears, and other senses, Master.' His voice sank low and could scarcely be heard above the murmur of a sudden chill wind in the leaves, as the sun sank behind Mindolluin. 'You have heard then the name?' With hardly more than breath he formed it. 'Of Herumor?'[11]

Borlas looked at him with amazement and fear. His mouth made tremulous motions of speech, but no sound came from it.

'I see that you have,' said Saelon. 'And you seem astonished to learn that I have heard it also. But you are not more astonished than I was to see that this name has reached you. For, as I say, I have keen eyes and ears, but yours are now dim even for daily use, and the matter has been kept as secret as cunning could contrive.'

'Whose cunning?' said Borlas, suddenly and fiercely. The sight of his eyes might be dim, but they blazed now with anger.

'Why, those who have heard the call of the name, of course,' answered Saelon unperturbed. 'They are not many yet, to set against all the people of Gondor, but the number is growing. Not all are content since the Great King died, and fewer now are afraid.'

'So I have guessed,' said Borlas, 'and it is that thought that chills the warmth of summer in my heart. For a man may have a garden with strong walls, Saelon, and yet find no peace or content there. There are some enemies that such walls will not keep out; for his garden is only part of a guarded realm after all. It is to the walls of the realm that he must look for his real defence. But what is the call? What would they do?' he cried, laying his hand on the young man's knee.

'I will ask you a question first before I answer yours,' said Saelon; and now he looked searchingly at the old man. 'How have you, who sit here in the Emyn Arnen and seldom go now even to the City – how have you heard the whispers of this name?'

Borlas looked down on the ground and clasped his hands between his knees. For some time he did not answer. At last he looked up again; his face had hardened and his eyes were more wary. 'I will not answer that, Saelon,' he said. 'Not until I have asked you yet another question. First tell me,' he said slowly, 'are you one of those who have listened to the call?'

A strange smile flickered about the young man's mouth. 'Attack is the best defence,' he answered, 'or so the Captains tell us; but when both sides use this counsel there is a clash of battle. So I will counter you. I will not answer you, Master Borlas, until you tell me: are you one of those who have listened, or no?'

'How can you think it?' cried Borlas.

'And how can *you* think it?' asked Saelon.

'As for me,' said Borlas, 'do not all my words give you the answer?'

'But as for me, you would say,' said Saelon, 'my words might make me doubtful? Because I defended a small boy who threw unripe apples at his playmates from the name of Orc? Or because I spoke of the suffering of trees at the hands of men? Master Borlas, it is unwise to judge a man's heart from words spoken in an argument without respect for your opinions. They may be meant to disturb you. Pert maybe, but possibly better than a mere echo.[12] I do not doubt that many of those we spoke of would use words as solemn as yours, and speak reverently of the Great Theme and such things – in your presence. Well, who shall answer first?'

'The younger it would have been in the courtesy of old,' said Borlas; 'or between men counted as equals, the one who was first asked. You are both.'

Saelon smiled. 'Very well,' he said. 'Let me see: the first question that you asked unanswered was: *what is the call, what would they do?* Can you find no answer in the past for all your age and lore? I am young and less learned. Still, if you really wish to know, I could perhaps make the whispers clearer to you.'

He stood up. The sun had set behind the mountains; shadows were deepening. The western wall of Borlas's house on the hill-side was yellow in the afterglow, but the river below was dark. He looked up at the sky, and then away down the Anduin. 'It is a fair evening still,' he said, 'but the wind has shifted eastward. There will be clouds over the moon tonight.'

'Well, what of it?' said Borlas, shivering a little as the air chilled. 'Unless you mean only to warn an old man to hasten indoors and keep his bones from aching.' He rose and turned to the path towards his house, thinking that the young man meant to say no more; but Saelon stepped up beside him and laid a hand on his arm.

'I warn you rather to clothe yourself warmly after nightfall,' he said. 'That is, if you wish to learn more; for if you do, you will come with me on a journey tonight. I will meet you at your eastern gate behind your house; or at least I shall pass that way as soon as it is full dark, and you shall come or not as you will. I shall be clad in black, and anyone who goes with me must be clad alike. Farewell now, Master Borlas! Take counsel with yourself while the light lasts.'

With that Saelon bowed and turned away, going along another path that ran near the edge of the steep shore, away northward to the house of his father.[13] He disappeared round a bend while his last words were still echoing in Borlas's ears.

For some while after Saelon had gone Borlas stood still, covering his eyes and resting his brow against the cool bark of a tree beside the path. As he stood he searched back in his mind to discover how this strange and alarming conversation had begun. What he would do after nightfall he did not yet consider.

He had not been in good spirits since the spring, though well enough in body for his age, which burdened him less than his loneliness.[14] Since his son, Berelach,[15] had gone away again in April – he was in the Ships, and now lived mostly near Pelargir where his duty was – Saelon had been most attentive, whenever he was at home. He went much about the lands of late. Borlas was not sure of his business, though he understood that, among other interests, he dealt in timber. He brought news from all over the kingdom to his old friend. Or to his friend's old father; for Berelach had been his constant companion at one time, though they seemed seldom to meet nowadays.

'Yes, that was it,' Borlas said to himself. 'I spoke to Saelon of Pelargir, quoting Berelach. There has been some small disquiet down at the Ethir: a few shipmen have disappeared, and also a small vessel of the Fleet. Nothing much, according to Berelach.

'"Peace makes things slack," he said, I remember, in the voice of an under-officer. "Well, they went off on some ploy of their own, I suppose – friends in one of the western havens, perhaps – without leave and without a pilot, and they were drowned. It serves them right. We get too few real sailors these days. Fish are more profitable. But at least all know that the west coasts are not safe for the unskilled."

'That was all. But I spoke of it to Saelon, and asked if he had heard anything of it away south. "Yes," he said, "I did. Few were satisfied with the official view. The men were not unskilled; they were sons of fishermen. And there have been no storms off the coasts for a long time."'

As he heard Saelon say this, suddenly Borlas had remembered the other rumours, the rumours that Othrondir[16] had spoken of. It was he who had used the word 'canker'. And then half to himself Borlas had spoken aloud about the Dark Tree.

He uncovered his eyes and fondled the shapely trunk of the tree that he had leaned on, looking up at its shadowy leaves against the clear fading sky. A star glinted through the branches. Softly he spoke again, as if to the tree.

'Well, what is to be done now? Clearly Saelon is in it. But is it clear? There was the sound of mockery in his words, and scorn of the ordered life of Men. He would not answer a straight question. The black clothes! And yet – why invite me to go with him? Not to convert old Borlas! Useless. Useless to try: no one would hope to win over a man who remembered the Evil of old, however far off. Useless if one succeeded: old Borlas is of no use any longer as a tool for any hand. Saelon might be trying to play the spy, seeking to find out what lies behind the whispers. Black might be a disguise, or an aid to stealth by night. But again, what could I do to help on any secret or dangerous errand? I should be better out of the way.'

With that a cold thought touched Borlas's heart. Put out of the way – was that it? He was to be lured to some place where he could disappear, like the Shipmen? The invitation to go with Saelon had been given only after he had been startled into revealing that he knew of the whispers – had even heard the name. And he had declared his hostility.

This thought decided Borlas, and he knew that he was resolved now to stand robed in black at the gate in the first dark of night. He was challenged, and he would accept. He smote his palm against the tree. 'I am not a dotard yet, Neldor,' he said; 'but death is not so far off that I shall lose many good years, if I lose the throw.'

He straightened his back and lifted his head, and walked away up the path, slowly but steadily. The thought crossed his mind even as he stepped over the threshold: 'Perhaps I have been preserved so long for this purpose: that one should still live, hale in mind, who remembers what went before the Great Peace. Scent has a long memory. I think I could still smell the old Evil, and know it for what it is.'

The door under the porch was open; but the house behind was darkling. There seemed none of the accustomed sounds of evening, only a soft silence, a dead silence. He entered, wondering a little. He called, but there was no answer. He halted in the narrow passage that ran through the house, and it seemed that he was wrapped in a blackness: not a glimmer of twilight of the world outside remained there. Suddenly he smelt it, or so it seemed, though it came as it were from within outwards to the sense: he smelt the old Evil and knew it for what it was.

Here, both in A and B, *The New Shadow* ends, and it will never be known what Borlas found in his dark and silent house, nor what part Saelon was playing and what his intentions were. There would be no tales worth the telling in the days of the King's Peace, my father said; and he disparaged the story that he had begun: 'I could have written a "thriller" about the plot and its discovery and overthrow – but it would be just that. Not worth doing.' It would nonetheless have been a very remarkable 'thriller', and one may well view its early abandonment with regret. But it may be that his reason for abandoning it was not only this – or perhaps rather that in saying this he was expressing a deeper conviction: that the vast structure of story, in many forms, that he had raised came to its true end in the Downfall of Sauron. As he wrote (*Morgoth's Ring* p. 404): 'Sauron was a problem that Men had to deal with finally: the first of the many concentrations of Evil into definite power-points that they would have to combat, *as it was also the last of those in "mythological" personalized (but non-human) form.*'

NOTES

1 It has also been read publicly, by myself (Sheldonian Theatre, Oxford, 18 August 1992). At that time, not having studied the papers with sufficient care, I was under the impression that text B was the latest, and it was this that I read – the young man's name being therefore Arthael.

2   In the original draft of the opening of the story (preceding A) the name was first written *Almoth*, but changed immediately to Egalmoth. The original *Egalmoth* was the lord of the people of the Heavenly Arch in Gondolin; it was also the name of the eighteenth Ruling Steward of Gondor.

3   *Borlas* was the name of the eldest son of Bór the Easterling, later changed to *Borlad* (XI.240); he was slain in the Battle of Unnumbered Tears, faithful to the Eldar.

4   The first page of this was typed on the machine that my father first used about the end of 1958 (X.300), and the remainder on the previous one (that used for text B).

5   The name *Saelon* is found in drafting for the *Athrabeth Finrod ah Andreth* as a name of the wise-woman Andreth of the Edain, who debated with Finrod; in the final text this became *Saelind*, translated 'Wise-heart' (X.305, 351-2).

6   This is the machine on which the very late 'historical-etymological' essays were typed, and which I use to this day.

7   A puzzling question is raised by this dating, concerning the historical period in which the story is set. In the opening paragraph the original draft (preceding A) has:

It was in the days of Eldarion, son of that Elessar of whom ancient histories have much to tell, that this strange thing occurred. It was indeed less than one hundred and twenty years since the fall of the Dark Tower ...

The first complete text, the manuscript A, has: 'Nearly one hundred and ten years had passed since the fall of the Dark Tower', and this is repeated in B. My father typed the opening page of the late text C in two closely similar forms, and in the first of these he retained the reading of A and B, but in the second (printed here) he wrote 'One hundred and five years'. In the letter of 1964 cited on p. 410 he said 'about 100 years after the Downfall', and in that of 1972 (*ibid.*) 'about 100 years after the death of Aragorn'. We thus have, in chronological order of their appearance, the following dates after the fall of the Dark Tower:

less than 120 years (original opening of the story);
nearly 110 years (A and B);
about 100 years (letter of 1964);
nearly 110 years (first copy of the opening page of C, c.1968);
105 years (second copy of the opening page of C).

The fall of the Dark Tower took place in the year 3019 of the Third Age, and that Age was held to have been concluded at the end of 3021; thus the dates from the fall of the Tower (in the same order, and making them for brevity definite rather than approximate) are Fourth Age 118, 108, 98, 108, 103. Thus every date given in the texts (and that in the letter of 1964) places the story *before* the death of Aragorn – which took place in Fourth Age

120 = Shire Reckoning 1541 (Appendix B, at end); yet every one of the texts refers it to the days of his son Eldarion.

The solution of this must lie in the fact that in the First Edition of *The Lord of the Rings* (*ibid.*) Aragorn's death was placed twenty years earlier, in Shire Reckoning 1521, i.e. Fourth Age 100. The date given in the letter of 1964 ('about 100 years after the Downfall') is indeed too early even according to the dating of the First Edition, but that is readily explained as being a rough approximation appropriate in the context. More puzzling are the dates given in the two versions of the first page of the late text C, which do not agree with the date of Aragorn's death in the Second Edition (1966). The first of these ('nearly 110 years') can be explained as merely taking up the reading of text B, which my father was following; but in the second version he evidently gave thought to the date, for he changed it to '105 years': that is, Fourth Age 103. I am at a loss to explain this.

In the letter of 1972 he gave a much later date, placing the story in about Fourth Age 220 (and giving to Eldarion a reign of at least 100 years).

8   See *The Return of the King* (chapter *The Steward and the King*), p. 247.
9   Both A and B have 'sons' for 'son', and they do not have the words 'in his loneliness'. With the latter difference cf. the last sentence of the C text and its difference from B (note 14).
10 This passage in the argument was expressed rather differently in B (which was following A almost exactly):

> 'A man,' said Borlas, 'who tends a tree and guards it from blights, and eats its fruit – which it produces more abundantly than its mere life-need; not that eating the fruit need destroy the seed – does not act like a canker, nor like an Orc.
>
> 'But as for the cankers, I wonder. They live, it might be said, and yet their life is death. I do not believe that they were part of the Music of the Ainur, unless in the discords of Melkor. And so with Orcs.'
>
> 'And what of Men?' said Arthael.
>
> 'Why do you ask?' said Borlas. 'You know, surely, what is taught? They were not at first in the Great Music, but they did not enter with the discords of Melkor: they came from Ilúvatar himself, and therefore they are called the Children of God. And all that is in the Music they have a right to use – rightly: which is with reverence, not with pride or wantonness.'

11 The name *Herumor* is found in *Of the Rings of Power and the Third Age* (*The Silmarillion* p. 293) as that of a renegade Númenórean who became powerful among the Haradrim in the time before the war of the Last Alliance.

12 B (exactly repeating A) has here: 'No, Master Borlas, in such a matter one cannot judge words by the shape they are spoken in.'
13 A has here 'his father Duilin'. This, like Egalmoth, is another name from the story of Gondolin: Duilin was the leader of the people of the Swallow, who fell from the battlements when 'smitten by a fiery bolt of the Balrogs' (II.178). It was also the original name of the father of Flinding, later Gwindor, of Nargothrond (II.79, etc.): Duilin > Fuilin > Guilin.
14 At this point C comes to an end, at the foot of a page. B has here: 'He had not been in good health since the spring; old age was gaining upon him' (see note 9). From here onwards, as noted earlier, I follow text B, changing the name Arthael to Saelon. – The passage written on an envelope postmarked 8 January 1968, referred to on pp. 409–10, would follow from this point in C; it reads (the last phrases being very difficult to make out):

> For he lived now with only two old servants, retired from the Prince's guard, in which he himself had once held office. Long ago his daughter had married and now lived in distant parts of the realm, and then ten years ago his wife had died. Time had softened his grief, while Berelach [his son] was still near home. He was his youngest child and only son, and was in the King's ships; for several years he had been stationed at the Harlond within easy reach by water, and spent much time with his father. But it was three years now since he had been given a high command, and was often long at sea, and when on land duty still held him at Pelargir far away. His visits had been few and brief. Saelon, who formerly came only when Berelach [? ... been his old friend] was with Borlas, but had been most attentive when he was in Emyn Arnen. Always in to talk or bring news, or [?run] any service he could

For the site of 'the quays and landings of the Harlond' see *The Return of the King* (chapter *Minas Tirith*), p. 22.

15 Borlas is described at the beginning of the story as the younger son of Beregond, and he was thus the brother of Bergil son of Beregond who was Pippin's companion in Minas Tirith. In A Borlas gave the name *Bergil* to his own son (preceded by *Berthil*).
16 For *Othrondir* A has *Othrondor*.

XVII
TAL-ELMAR

The tale of Tal-Elmar, so far as it went, is preserved in a folded paper, bearing dates in 1968, on which my father wrote the following hasty note:

> Tal-Elmar
>
> Beginnings of a tale that sees the Númenóreans from the point of view of the Wild Men. It was begun without much consideration of geography (or the situation as envisaged in The Lord of the Rings). But either it must remain as a separate tale only vaguely linked with the developed Lord of the Rings history, or – and I think so – it must recount the coming of the Númenóreans (Elf-friends) *before the Downfall*, and represent their choice of permanent havens. So the geography must be made to fit that of the mouths of Anduin and the Langstrand.

But that was written thirteen years after he had abandoned the story, and there is no sign that he returned to it in his last years. Brief as it is, and (as it seems) uncertain of direction, such a departure from all other narrative themes within the compass of Middle-earth will form perhaps a fitting conclusion to this History.

The text is in two parts. The first is a typescript of six sides that breaks off in the middle of a sentence (p. 432); but the first part of this is extant also in a rejected page, part typescript and part manuscript (see note 5). Beyond this point the entire story is in the first stage of composition. The second part is a manuscript on which my father wrote 'Continuation of Tal-Elmar' and the date January 1955; there is no indication of how long a time elapsed between the two parts, but I believe that the typescript belongs also to the 1950s. It is remarkable that he should have been working on it during the time of extreme pressure between the publication of *The Two Towers* and that of *The Return of the King*. This manuscript takes up the story from the point where it was left in the typescript, but does not complete the unfinished sentence; it becomes progressively more difficult, and in one section is at the very limit of legibility, with some words uninterpretable. Towards the end the narrative breaks up into experimental passages and questionings. With a few exceptions I do not record corrections to the text and give only the later reading; and in one or two cases I have altered inconsistent uses of 'thou' and 'you'.

TAL-ELMAR

In the days of the Dark Kings, when a man could still walk dry-shod from the Rising of the Sun to the Sea of its setting, there lived in the fenced town of his people in the green hills of Agar an old man, by name Hazad Longbeard.[1] Two prides he had: in the number of his sons (seventeen in all), and in the length of his beard (five feet without stretching); but his joy in his beard was the greater. For it remained with him, and was soft, and ruly to his hand, whereas his sons for the most part were gone from him, and those that remained, or came ever nigh, were neither gentle nor ruly. They were indeed much as Hazad himself had been in the days of his youth: broad, swarthy, short, tough, harsh-tongued, heavy-handed, and quick to violence.

Save one only, and he was the youngest. Tal-elmar Hazad his father named him. He was yet but eighteen years of age, and lived with his father, and the two of his brothers next elder. He was tall, and white-skinned, and there was a light in his grey eyes that would flash to fire, if he were wroth; and though that happened seldom, and never without great cause, it was a thing to remember and be ware of. Those who had seen that fire called him Flint-eye, and respected him, whether they loved him or no. For Tal-elmar might seem, among that swart sturdy folk, slender-built and lacking in the strength of leg and neck that they praised, but a man that strove with him soon found him strong beyond guess, and sudden and swift, hard to grapple and harder to elude.

A fair voice he had, which made even the rough tongue of that people more sweet to hear, but he spoke not over much; and he would stand often aloof, when others were chattering, with a look on his face that men read rightly as pride, yet it was not the pride of a master, but rather the pride of one of alien race, whom fate has cast away among an ignoble people, and there bound him in servitude. For indeed Tal-elmar laboured hard and at menial tasks, being but the youngest son of an old man, who had little wealth left save his beard and a repute for wisdom. But strange to say (in that town) he served his father willingly, and loved him, more than all his brothers in one, and more than was the wont of any sons in that land. Indeed it was most often on his father's behalf that the flint-flash was seen in his eyes.

For Tal-elmar had a strange belief (whence it came was a wonder) that the old should be treated kindly and with courtesy, and should be suffered to live out their life-days in such ease as they could. 'If ye must gainsay them,' he said, 'let it be done with respect; for they have seen many years, and many times, maybe, have they faced the evils which we come to untried. And grudge not their food and their room, for they have laboured longer than have ye, and do but receive now, belatedly, part of the payment that is due to them.' Such plain folly had no effect on the manners of his people, but it was law in his house; and it was now two years since either of his brothers had dared to break it.[2]

Hazad loved this youngest son dearly, in return for his love, yet even more for another cause which he kept in his heart: that his face and his voice reminded him of another that he long had missed. For Hazad also had been the youngest son of his mother, and she died in his boyhood; and she was not of their people. Such was the tale that he had overheard, not openly spoken indeed, for it was held no credit to the house: she came of the strange folk, hateful and proud, of which there was rumour in the west-lands, coming out of the East, it was said. Fair, tall, and flint-eyed they were, with bright weapons made by demons in the fiery hills. Slowly they were thrusting towards the shores of the Sea, driving before them the ancient dwellers in the lands.

Not without resistance. There were wars on the east-marches, and since the older folk were yet numerous, the incomers would at times suffer great loss and be flung back. Indeed little had been heard of them in the Hills of Agar, far to the west, for more than a man's life, since that great battle of which songs were yet sung. In the valley of Ishmalog it had been fought, the wise in lore told, and there a great host of the Fell folk had been ambushed in a narrow place and slaughtered in heaps. And in that day many captives were taken; for this had been no affray on the borders, or fight with advance guards: a whole people of the Fell Folk had been on the move, with their wains and their cattle and their women.

Now Buldar, father of Hazad, had been in the army of the North King[3] that went to the muster of Ishmalog,[4] and he brought back from the war as booty a wound, and a sword, and a woman. And she was fortunate; for the fate of the captives was short and cruel, but Buldar took her as his wife. For she was beautiful, and having looked on her he desired no woman of his own folk. He was a man of wealth and power in those days, and did as he would, scorning the scorn of his neighbours. But when his wife, Elmar, had learned at length enough of the speech of her new kin, she said to Buldar on a day: 'I have much to thank thee for, lord; but think not ever to get my love so. For thou hast torn me from my own people, and from him that I loved and from the child that I bore him. For them ever shall I yearn and grieve, and give love to none else. Never again shall I be glad, while I am held captive among a strange folk that I deem base and unlovely.'

'So be it,' said Buldar. 'But it is not to be thought that I should let thee go free. For thou art precious in my sight. And consider well: vain is it to seek to escape from me. Long is the way to the remnant of thy folk, if any still live; and thou wouldst not go far from the Hills of Agar ere thou met death, or a life far worse than shall be thine in my house. Base and unlovely thou namest us. Truly, maybe. Yet true is it also that thy folk are cruel, and lawless, and the friends of demons. Thieves are they. For our lands are ours from of old, which they would wrest from us with their bitter blades. White skins and bright eyes are no warrant for such deeds.'

'Are they not?' said she. 'Then neither are thick legs and wide shoulders. Or by what means did ye gain these lands that ye boast of? Are there not, as I hear men say, wild folk in the caves of the mountains, who once roamed here free, ere ye swart folk came hither and hunted them like wolves? But I spoke not of rights, but of sorrow and love. If here I must dwell, then dwell I must, as one whose body is in this place at thy will, but my thought far elsewhere. And this vengeance I will have, that while my body is kept here in exile, the lot of all this folk shall worsen, and thine most; but when my body goes to the alien earth, and my thought is free of it, then in thy kin one shall arise who is mine alone. And with his arising shall come the end of thy people and the downfall of your king.'

Thereafter Elmar said no more on this matter; and she was indeed a woman of few words while her life lasted, save only to her children. To them she spoke much when none were by, and she sang to them many songs in a strange fair tongue; but they heeded her not, or soon forgot. Save only Hazad, the youngest; and though he was, as were all her children, unlike her in body, he was nearer to her in heart. The songs and the strange tongue he too forgot, when he grew up, but his mother he never forgot; and he took a wife late, for no woman of his own folk seemed desirable to him that knew what beauty in a woman might be.[5]

Not that many were his for the wooing, for, even as Elmar had spoken, the people of Agar had waned with the years, what with ill weathers and with pests, and most of all were Buldar and his sons afflicted; and they had become poor, and other kindreds had taken their power from them. But Hazad knew naught of the foreboding of his mother, and in her memory loved Tal-elmar, and had so named him at birth.

And it chanced on a morning of spring that when his other sons went out to labour Hazad kept Tal-elmar at his side, and they walked forth together and sat upon the green hill-top above the town of their people; and they looked out south and west to where they could see far away the great bight of the Sea that drove in on the land, and it was shimmering like grey glass. And the eyes of Hazad were growing dim with age, but Tal-elmar's were keen, and he saw as he thought three strange birds upon the water, white in the sun, and they were drifting with the west wind towards the land; and he wondered that they sat upon the sea and did not fly.

'I see three strange birds upon the water, father,' he said. 'They are unlike any that I have seen before.'

'Keen may be thine eyes in youth, my son,' said Hazad, 'but birds on the water thou canst not see. Three leagues away are the nearest shores of the Sea from where we sit. The sun dazzles thee, or some dream is on thee.'

'Nay, the sun is behind me,' said Tal-elmar. 'I see what I see. And if they be not birds, what are they? Very great must they be, greater than the Swans of Gorbelgod,[6] of which legends tell. And lo! I see now another that comes behind, but less clearly, for its wings are black.'

Then Hazad was troubled. 'A dream is on thee, as I said, my son,' he answered; 'but an ill dream. Is not life here hard enough, that when spring is come and winter is over at last thou must bring a vision out of the black past?'

'Thou forgettest, father,' said Tal-elmar, 'that I am thy youngest son, and whereas thou has taught much lore to the dull ears of my brethren, to me thou hast given less of thy store. I know nothing of what is in thy mind.'

'Dost thou not?' said Hazad, striking his brow as he stared out towards the Sea. 'Yes, mayhap it is a long while since I spoke of it; it is but the shadow of a dream in the back of my thought. Three folk we hold as enemies. The wild men of the mountains and the woods; but these only those who stray alone need fear.

The Fell Folk of the East; but they are yet far away, and they are my mother's people, though, I doubt not, they would not honour the kinship, if they came here with their swords. And the High Men of the Sea. These indeed we may dread as Death. For Death they worship and slay men cruelly in honour of the Dark. Out of the Sea they came, and if they ever had any land of their own, ere they came to the west-shores, we know not where it may be. Black tales come to us out of the coast-lands, north and south, where they have now long time established their dark fortresses and their tombs. But hither they have not come since my father's days, and then only to raid and catch men and depart. Now this was the manner of their coming. They came in boats, but not such as some of our folk use that dwell nigh the great rivers or the lakes, for ferrying or fishing. Greater than great houses are the ships of the Go-hilleg, and they bear store of men and goods, and yet are wafted by the winds; for the Sea-men spread great cloths like wings to catch the airs, and bind them to tall poles like trees of the forest. Thus they will come to the shore, where there is shelter, or as nigh as they may; and then they will send forth smaller boats laden with goods, and strange things both beautiful and useful such as our folk covet. These they will sell to us for small price, or give as gifts, feigning friendship, and pity for our need; and they will dwell a while, and spy out the land and the numbers of the folk, and then go. And if they do not return, men should be thankful. For if they come again it is in other guise. In greater numbers they come then: two ships or more together, stuffed with men and not goods, and ever one of the accursed ships hath black wings. For that is the Ship of the Dark, and in it they bear away evil booty, captives packed like beasts, the fairest women and children, or young men unblemished, and that is their end. Some say that they are eaten for meat; and others that they are slain with torment on the black stones in the worship of the Dark. Both maybe are true. The foul wings of the Sea-men have not been seen in these waters for many a year; but remembering the shadow of fear in the past I cried out, and cry again: is not our life hard enough without the vision of a black wing upon the shining sea?'

'Hard enough, indeed,' said Tal-elmar, 'yet not so hard that I would leave it yet. Come! If what you tell is good sooth we should run to the town and warn men, and make ready for flight or for defence.'

'I come,' said Hazad. 'But be not astonished, if men laugh at me for a dotard. They believe little that has not happened in their own days. And have a care, dear son! I am in little danger, save to starve in a town empty of all but the crazed and the aged. But thee the Dark Ship would take among the first. Put thyself not forward in any rash counsel of battle.'

'We will see,' answered Tal-elmar. 'But thou art my chief care in this town, where I have and give little love. I will not willingly part from thy side. Yet this is the town of my folk, and our home, and those who can are bound to defend it, I deem.'

So Hazad and his son went down the hill-side, and it was noon; and in the town were few people, but crones and children, for all the able-bodied were abroad in the fields, busy with the hard toil of spring. There was no watch, for the Hills of Agar were far from hostile borders where the power of the Fourth King[7] ended. The town-master sat by the door of his house in the sun, dozing or idly watching the small birds that gathered scraps of food from the dry beaten mud of the open place in the midst of the houses.

'Hail! Master of Agar!' said Hazad, and bowed low; but the master, a fat man with eyes like a lizard, blinked at him, and did not return his greeting.

'Sit hail, Master! And long may you sit so!' said Tal-elmar, and there was a glint in his eye. 'We should not disturb your thought, or your sleep, but there are tidings that, maybe, you should heed. There is no watch kept, but we chanced to be on the hill-top, and we saw the sea far off, and there – birds of ill omen on the water.'

'Ships of the Go-hilleg,' said Hazad, 'with great wind-cloths. Three white – and one black.'

The master yawned. 'As for thee, blear-eyed carl,' he said, 'thou couldst not tell the sea itself from a cloud. And as for this idle lad, what knows he of boats or wind-cloths, or all the rest, save from thy crazed teaching? Go to the travelling knappers[8] with thy crone-tales of Go-hilleg, and trouble me not with such folly. I have other matters of more weight to ponder.'

Hazad swallowed his wrath, for the Master was powerful and loved him not; but Tal-elmar's anger was cold. 'The thoughts of one so great must needs be weighty,' said he softly, 'yet I know not what thought of more weight could break his repose than the care of his own carcase. He will be a master without people, or a bag of bones on the hillside, if he scorns the wisdom of Hazad son of Buldar. Blear eyes may see more than those lidded with sleep.'

The fat face of Mogru the Master grew dark, and his eyes were blood-shot with rage. He hated Tal-elmar, yet never before had the youth given him cause, save that he showed no fear in his presence. Now he should pay for that and his new-found insolence. Mogru clapped his hands, but even as he did so he remembered that there were none within call that would dare to grapple with the youth, nay, not three together; and at the same time he caught the glint of Tal-elmar's eye. He blanched, and the words that he had been about to speak, 'Slave's son and your brat', died on his lips. 'Hazad uBuldar, Tal-elmar uHazad, of this town, speak not so with the master of your folk,' he said. 'A watch is set, though ye who have not the ruling of the town in hand may know it not. I would wait till I have word from the watchers, whom I trust, that anything ill-boding has been seen. But if ye be anxious, then go summon the men from the fields.'

Tal-elmar observed him closely as he spoke and he read his thought clearly. 'Now I must hope that my father errs not,' he said in his heart, 'for less peril will battle bring me than the hate of Mogru from this day forth. A watch! Yea, but only to spy on the goings and comings of the townsfolk. And the moment I go forth to the field, a runner will go to fetch his servants and club-bearers. An ill turn have I done to my father in this hour. Well! He who begins with the hoe should wield it to the row's end.' He spoke therefore still in wrath and scorn. 'Go you to the knappers yourself,' he said, 'for you are wont to use these sly folk, and heed their tales when they suit you. But my father you shall not mock while I stand by. It may well be that we are in peril. Therefore you shall come now with us to the hill-top, and look with your own eyes. And if you see there aught to warrant it, you shall summon the men to the Moot-hill. I will be your messenger.'

And Mogru also through the slits of his eyelids watched the face of Tal-elmar as he spoke, and guessed that he was in no danger of violence if he gave way for this time. But his heart was filled with venom; and it irked him also not a little to toil up the hill. Slowly he rose.

'I will come,' he said. 'But if my time and toil be wasted, I shall not forgive it. Aid my steps, young man; for my servants are in the fields.' And he took the arm of Tal-elmar and leaned heavily upon him.

'My father is the elder,' said Tal-elmar; 'and the way is but short. Let the Master lead, and we will follow. Here is your staff!' And he released himself from the grasp of Mogru, and gave him his staff which stood by the door of his house; and taking the arm of his father he waited until the Master set out. Sidelong and black was the glance of the lizard-eye, but the gleam of the eye of Tal-elmar that it caught stung like a goad. It was long since the fat legs of Mogru had made such speed from house to gate; and longer since they had heaved his belly up the slippery hill-sward beyond the dike. He was blown, and panting like an old dog, when they came to the top.

Then again Tal-elmar looked out; but the high and distant sea was now empty, and he stood silent. Mogru wiped the sweat from his eyes and followed his gaze.

'For what reason, I ask, have ye forced the Master of the town from his house, and brought him hither?' he snarled. 'The sea lies where it lay, and empty. What mean ye?'

'Have patience and look closer,' said Tal-elmar. Away to the west highlands blocked the view of all but the distant sea; but rising to the broad cap of the Golden Hill they fell suddenly away, and in a deep cleft a glimpse could be seen of the great inlet and the waters near its north shore. 'Time has passed since we were here before, and the wind is strong,' said Tal-elmar. 'They have come nearer.' He pointed. 'There you will see their wings, or their wind-cloths, call them what you will. But what is your counsel? And was it not a matter that the Master should see with his own eyes?'

Mogru stared, and he panted, now with fear as much as for the labour of walking uphill, for bluster as he might he had heard many dark tales of the Go-hilleg from old women in his youth. But his heart was cunning, and black with anger. Sidelong he looked first at Hazad, and then at his son; and he licked his lips, but he let not his smile be seen.

'You begged to be my messenger,' he said, 'and so shalt thou be. Go now swiftly and summon the men to the Moot-hill! But that will not end thy errand,' he added, as Tal-elmar made ready to run. 'Straight from the fields thou shalt go with all speed to the Strand. For there the ships, if ships they be, will halt, most likely, and set men ashore. Tidings thou must win there, and spy out well what is afoot. Come not back at all, unless it is with news that will help our counsels. Go and spare thyself not! I command thee. It is time of peril to the town.'

Hazad seemed about to speak in protest; but he bowed his head, and said naught, knowing it vain. Tal-elmar stood one moment, eyeing Mogru, as one might a snake in the path. But he saw well that the Master's cunning had been greater than his. He had made his own trap, and Mogru had used it. He had declared a time of peril to the town, and he had the right to command any service. It was death to disobey him. And even if Tal-elmar had not named himself as messenger (desiring to prevent any secret word being passed to servants of the Master), all would say that the choice was just. A scout should be sent, and who better than a strong bold youth, swift on his feet? But there was malice, black malice, in the errand nonetheless. The defender of Hazad would be gone. There was no hope in his brothers: strong louts, but with no heart for defiance, save of their old father. And it was likely enough that he would not return. The peril was great.

Once more Tal-elmar looked at the Master, and then at his father, and then his glance passed to Mogru's staff. The flint-flash was in his eyes, and in his heart the desire to kill. Mogru saw it and quailed.

'Go, go!' he shouted. 'I have commanded thee. Thou art quicker to cry wolf than to start on the hunt. Go at once!'

'Go, my son!' said Hazad. 'Do not defy the Master. Not where he has the right. For then thou defiest all the town, beyond thy power. And were I the Master, I would choose thee, dear though thou be; for thou hast more heart and luck than any of this folk. But come again, and let not the Dark Ship have thee. Be not over-bold! For better would be ill tidings brought by thee living than the Sea-men without herald.'

Tal-elmar bowed and made the sign of submission, to his father and not to the Master, and strode away two paces. And then he turned. 'Listen, Mogru, whom a base folk in their folly have named their master,' he cried. 'Maybe I shall return, against thy hope. My father I leave in thy care. If I come, be it with word of peace, or with a foe on my heel, then thy mastership will be at an end, and thy life also, if I find that he has suffered any evil or dishonour that thou couldst prevent. Thy knife-men and club-bearers will not help thee. I will wring thy fat neck with my bare hands, if needs be; or I will hunt thee through the wilds to the black pools.' Then a new thought struck him, and he strode back to the Master, and laid hands on his staff.

Mogru cringed, and flung up a fat arm, as if to ward off a blow. 'Thou art mad today,' he croaked. 'Do me no violence, or thou wilt pay for it with death. Heardest thou not the words of thy father?'

'I heard, and I obey,' said Tal-elmar. 'But first errand is to the men, and there is need now of haste. Little honour have I among them, for they know well thy scorn of us. What heed will they pay, if the Slave's bastards, as thou namest us when I am not by, comes[9] crying the summons to the Moot-hill in thy name without token. Thy staff will serve. It is well known. Nay, I will not beat thee with it yet!'

With that he wrested the staff from Mogru's hand and sped down the hill, his heart yet too hot with wrath to take thought for what lay before him. But when he had declared the summons to the startled men in the acres on the south slopes and had flung down the staff among them, bidding them hasten, he ran to the hill's foot, and out over the long grass-meads, and so came to the first thin straggle of the woods. Dark they lay before him in the valley between Agar and the downs by the shore.

It was still morning, and more than an hour ere the noon, but when he came under the trees he halted and took thought, and knew that he was shaken with fear. Seldom had he wandered far from the hills of his home, and never alone, nor deep into the wood. For all his folk dreaded the forest[10]

Here the typescript text breaks off, not at the foot of a page, and the manuscript 'Continuation of Tal-Elmar' (as the name is now written) begins (see p. 422).

It was swift for the eye to travel to the shore, but slow for feet; and the distance was greater than it seemed. The wood was dark and unwholesome, for there were stagnant waters between the hills of Agar and the hills of the shoreland; and many snakes lived there. It was silent too, for though it was spring few birds built there or even alighted as they sped on to the cleaner land by the sea. There dwelt in the wood also dark spirits that hated men, or so ran the tales of the people. Of snake and swamp and wood-demon Tal-Elmar thought as he stood within the shadow; but it needed short thought to come to the conclusion that all three were less peril than to return, with lying excuse or with none, to the town and its master.

So, helped a little perhaps by his pride, he went on. And the thought came to him under the shadow as he sought for a way through swamp and thicket: What do I know, or any of my people, even my father, of these Go-hilleg of the winged boats? It might well be that I who am a stranger in my own people should find them more pleasing than Mogru and all others like him.

With this thought growing in him, so that at length he felt rather as a man who goes to greet friends and kinsmen than as one who creeps out to spy on dangerous foes, he passed unhurt through the shadow-wood, and came to the shore-hills, and began to climb. One hill he chose, because bushes clambered up its slope and it was crowned with a dense knot of low trees. To this cover he came, and creeping to the further brink he looked down. It had taken him long, for his way had been slow, and now the sun had fallen from noon and was going down away on his right towards the Sea. He was hungry, but this he hardly heeded, for he was used to hunger, and could endure toil day-long without eating when he must. The hill was low, but ran down steeply to the water. Before its feet were green lands ending in gravels, beyond which the waters of the estuary gleamed in the westering sun. Out in the midst of the stream beyond the shoals three great ships – though Tal-Elmar had no such word in his language to name them with – were lying motionless. They were anchored and the sails down. Of the fourth, the black ship, there was no sign. But on the green near the shingles there were tents, and small boats drawn up near. Tall men were standing or walking among them. Away on the 'big boats' Tal-Elmar could see [?others] on watch; every now and then he caught a flash as some weapon or arms moved in the sun. He trembled, for the tales of the 'blades' of the Cruel Men were familiar to his childhood.

Tal-Elmar looked long, and slowly it came to him how hopeless was his mission. He might look until daylight failed, but he could not count accurately enough for any use the number of men there were; nor could he discover their purpose or their plans. Even if he had either the courage or the fortune to come past their guards he could do nothing useful, for he would not understand a word of their language.

He remembered suddenly – another of Mogru's schemes to be rid of him, as he now saw, though at the time he had thought it an honour – how only a year ago, when the waning town of Agar was threatened by marauders from the village of Udul far inland,[11] all men feared that an assault would come, for Agar was a drier, healthier, and more defensible site (or so its townsmen believed). Then Tal-Elmar had been chosen to go and spy out the land of Udul, as 'being young, bold, and better versed in the country round'. So said Mogru, truly enough, for the townsfolk of Agar were timid and seldom went far afield, never daring to be caught by dark outside their homes. Whereas Tal-Elmar often, if he had chance and no labour called (or if it did, sometimes), would walk far afield, and though (being so taught from babyhood) he feared the dark, he had more than once been benighted far from the town, and was even known to go out to the watch-hill alone under the stars.

But to creep into the unfriendly fields of Udul by night was another and far worse thing. Yet he had dared to do it. And he had come so close to one of the huts of watchmen that he could hear the men inside speaking – in vain. He could not understand the purport of their speech. The tones seemed mournful and full of fear[12] (as men's voices were at night in the world as he knew it), and a few words he seemed to recognize, but not enough for understanding. And yet the Udul-folk were their near neighbours – indeed though Tal-Elmar and his people had forgotten it, as they had forgotten so much, their near kin, part of the same people in past and better years. What hope then was there that he would recognize any single word, or even interpret rightly the tones, of the tongue of men alien from his own since the beginning of the world? Alien from his own? My own? But they are not my people. Only my father. And again he had that strange feeling, coming from where he knew not to this young lad, born and bred in a decaying half-savage people: the feeling that he was not going to meet aliens but kinsmen from afar and friends.

And yet he was also a boy of his village. He was afraid, and it was long before he moved. At last he looked up. The sun on his right was now going down. Between two tree-stems he caught a glimpse of the sea, as the great round fire, red with the light sea-mist, sank level with his eye, and the water was kindled to fiery gold.

He had seen the sun sink into the sea before, yet never before had he seen it so. He knew in a flash (as if it came from that fire itself) that he had seen it so, [? he was called,][13] that it meant something more than the approach of the 'King's time', the dark.[14] He rose and as if led or driven walked openly down the hill and across the long sward to the shingles and the tents.

Could he have seen himself he would have been struck with wonder no less than those who saw him now from the shore. His naked skin – for he wore only a loin-cloth, and little cloak of ... fur cast back and caught by a thong to his shoulder – glowed golden in the [? sunset] light, his fair hair too was kindled, and his step was light and free.

'Look!' cried one of the watchmen to his companion. 'Do you see what I see? Is it not one of the Eldar of the woods that comes to speak with us?'

'I see indeed,' said the other, 'but if not some phantom from the edge of the [? coming] dark [? in this land accursed] it cannot be one of the Fair. We are far to the south, and none dwell here. Would indeed we were [? north away near to (the) Havens].'

'Who knows all the ways of the Eldar?' said the watchman. 'Silence now! He approaches. Let him speak first.'

So they stood still, and made no sign as Tal-Elmar drew near. When he was some twenty paces away his fear returned, and he halted, letting his arms fall before him and opening his palms outwards to the strangers in a gesture which all men could understand.

Then, as they did not move, nor put hand to any weapon so far as he could see, he took courage again and spoke, saying: 'Hail, Men of the sea and the wings! Why do you come here? Is it in peace? I am Tal-Elmar uHazad of the folk of Agar. Who are you?'

His voice was clear and fair, but the language that he used was but a form of the half-savage language of the Men of the Dark, as the Shipmen called them. The watchman stirred. 'Elda!' he said. 'The Eldar do not use such a tongue.' He called aloud, and at once men tumbled out of the tents. He himself drew forth a sword, while his companion put arrow to bowstring. Before Tal-Elmar had time even to feel terror, still less to turn and run – happily, for he knew nothing of bows and would have fallen long before he was out of bowshot – he was surrounded by armed men. They seized him, but not with harsh handling, when they found he was weaponless and submissive, and led him to a tent where sat one in authority.

Tal-Elmar feels the language to be *known* and only veiled from him.

The captain says Tal-Elmar must be of Númenórean race, or of the people akin to them. He must be kindly treated. He guesses that he had been made captive as a babe, or born of captives. 'He is trying to escape to us,' he says.

'A pity he remembers nothing of the language.' 'He will learn.' 'Maybe, but after a long time. If he spoke it now, he could tell us much that would speed our errand and lessen our peril.'

They make Tal-Elmar at last understand their desire to know how many men dwell near; are they friendly, are they like he is?

The object of the Númenóreans is to occupy this land, and in alliance with the 'Cruels' of the North to drive out the Dark People and make a settlement to threaten the King. (Or is this while Sauron is absent in Númenor?)

The place is on estuary of Isen? or Morthond.

Tal-Elmar could count and understand high numbers, though his language was defective.

Or does he understand Númenórean? [*Added subsequently*: Eldarin – these were Elf-friends.] He said when he heard the men speak to one another: 'This is strange for you speak the language of my long dreams. Yet surely now I stand in my own land and do not sleep?' Then they were astonished and said: 'Why did you not speak so to us before? You spoke like the people of the Dark who are our enemies, being servants of our Enemy.' And Tal-Elmar answered: 'Because this tongue has only returned to my mind hearing you speak it; and because how should I have known that you would understand the language of my dreams? You are not like those who spoke in my dreams. Nay, a little like; but they were brighter and more beautiful.'

Then the men were still more astonished, and said: 'It seems that you have spoken with the Eldar, whether awake or in vision.'

'Who are the Eldar?' said Tal-Elmar. 'That name I did not hear in my dream.'

'If you come with us you may perhaps see them.'

Then suddenly fear and the memory of old tales came upon Tal-Elmar again, and he quailed. 'What would you do to me?' he cried. 'Would you lure me to the black-winged boat and give me to the Dark?'

'You or your kin at least belong already to the Dark,' they answered. 'But why do you speak so of the black sails? The black sails are to us a sign of honour, for they are the fair night before the coming of the Enemy, and upon the black are set the silver stars of Elbereth. The black sails of our captain have passed further up the water.'

Still Tal-Elmar was afraid because he was not yet able to imagine black as anything but the symbol of the night of fear. But he looked as boldly as he could and answered: 'Not all my kind. We fear the Dark, but we do not love it nor serve it. At least so do some of us. So does my father. And him I love. I would not be torn from him not even to see the Eldar.'

'Alas!' they said. 'Your time of dwelling in these hills is come to an end. Here the men of the West have resolved to make their homes, and the folk of the dark must depart – or be slain.'

Tal-Elmar offers himself as a hostage.

There is no more. At the foot of the page my father wrote 'Tal-Elmar' twice, and his own name twice; and also 'Tal-Elmar in Rhovannion', 'Wilderland', 'Anduin the Great River', 'Sea of Rhûn', and 'Ettenmoors'.

NOTES

1 In the rejected version of the opening section of the text the story begins: 'In the days of the Great Kings when a man could still walk dryshod from Rome to York (not that those cities were yet built or thought of) there lived in the town of his people in the hills of Agar an old man, by name *Tal-argan* Longbeard', and Tal-argan remained the name without correction in the rejected page. The second version retained 'the Great Kings', the change to 'the Dark Kings' being made later on.
2 This paragraph was later placed within square brackets.
3 Both versions had 'the Fourth King', changed on the second to 'the North King' at the same time as 'the Great Kings' was changed to 'the Dark Kings' (note 1).
4 In the rejected version the father of Tal-argan (Hazad) was named *Tal-Bulda*, and the place of the battle was the valley of *Rishmalog*.
5 At this point the rejected first page ends, and the text becomes primary composition. A pencilled note at the head of the replacement page proposes that Buldar father of Hazad should be cut out, and that it should be Hazad himself who wedded the foreign woman Elmar (who is unnamed in the rejected version).
6 The name typed was *Dur nor-Belgoth*, corrected to *Gorbelgod*.
7 'the Fourth King' was not corrected here: see note 3.
8 *knappers*: a 'knapper' was one who broke stones or flints. This word replaced 'tinkers', here and at its occurrence a little later.
9 I have left the text here as it stands.

10 A marginal note here says that Tal-elmar had 'no weapon but a casting-stone in a pouch'.

11 The text as written had 'far inland, and all men feared', corrected to 'far inland. All men feared'. I have altered the text to provide a complete sentence, but my father (who was here writing at great speed) doubtless did not intend this, and would have rewritten the passage had he ever returned to it.

12 In the margin my father wrote that the village of Udul was dying of a pestilence, and the marauders were in fact seeking food in desperation.

13 The conclusion of the text is in places in excruciatingly difficult handwriting, and the words I have given as 'he was called' are doubtful: but I can see no other interpretation of them.

14 Against the words on p. 434 'never daring to be caught by dark outside their homes' my father wrote: 'Dark is "the time of the King".' As is seen from a passage on p. 436, the King is Sauron.

INDEX

The very great number of names occurring in this book, and the frequency of reference in many cases, would require an index much larger than those of the previous volumes if the same pattern were followed; and I have therefore reduced it by omitting three categories of names. Each of these is concentrated in a small part of the book, and in the case of the second and third it seems to me that, even apart from considerations of overall length, the utility of detailing alphabetically such complex material is very doubtful.

(1) *Hobbit names*. The number of names of individual Hobbits, including all the recorded changes, is so large (about 370) that I have restricted the references to the entry *Hobbit-families*. Here all the family-names are listed, with references to every page (including all the geneaological tables) where the name of the family, or of any member of the family, occurs. Exceptions to this are Bilbo and Frodo Baggins, Sam Gamgee, Meriadoc Brandybuck, and Peregrin Took, who are entered separately in the index on account of the large number of references to them.

(2) *The Calendars*. All page-references for the names of the *months* and the *days of the week* in the different languages are collected under those entries. Under *Calendars* are listed the entries in the index concerning the matter of Chapter IV, and references to the Elvish names and terms are given under *Calendars* and *Seasons*.

(3) *The Common Speech*. References are given under *Common Speech* and *Hobbit families* to all pages where 'true' names (supposed to underlie the 'translated' names) appear, these being only exceptionally included in the index.

The entries *Second Age*, *Third Age*, *Fourth Age* and *Shire-reckoning* do not include simple references to dates. Some names spelt with initial C in *The Lord of the Rings* will be found under K: *Calimehtar, Calimmacil, Calmacil, Castamir, Cemendur, Cirith Ungol, Ciryaher (Ciryahir), Ciryandil*.

Adrahil Twenty-first Prince of Dol Amroth. 32, 36, 206, 220–1, 223, 240; earlier *Agrahil* 220
Adûnaic 31–2, 34, 55, 63–5, 75, 79, 140, 146, 155, 157–8, 314–15, 317, 320, 330, 364–5, 368–72, 376. See *Númenórean*.

Adûni; Adúnar, Andúnar See *Common Speech*.
Aegnor Son of Finarfin. 346–7, 350; other names *Aikanáro* 346–7, 363, *Ambaráto (Amrod)* 347
Ælfwine 142–3, 153, 156–9, 395–403; named *Elendil* 401, 403
Afterworld, The 243, 246
Agar, Hills of Agar The town and land of Tal-elmar. 423–6, 428, 432–5, 437
Aglahad Nineteenth Prince of Dol Amroth. 223
Aglarrâma The ship of Ar-Pharazôn. 156. See *Alkarondas*.
Aikanáro See *Aegnor*.
Ainur (364); see *Music of the Ainur*.
Akallabêth 'The Downfallen' (not as title of work). 157–8.
Alatar One of the Blue Wizards. 385
Alatáriel See *Galadriel*.
Aldamir Twenty-third King of Gondor. 199, 214
Aldarion and Erendis (title of work). 141, 155, 351. See *Tar-Aldarion*.
Aldor the Old Third King of Rohan. 271
Alkarin 198, 212. See *Atanatar II*.
Alkarondas The ship of Ar-Pharazôn. 156. See *Aglarrâma*.
Alliance of Dwarves and Men 303–5.
Alphros Twenty-fourth Prince of Dol Amroth. 221, 223
Alqualondë 362, 365, 380
Aman 157, 312, 317, 325, 332–4, 341, 344, 346, 348–50, 357, 359, 361, 364, 371, 398, 401, 403–4. See *Blessed Realm*.
Amandil Father of Elendil. 156, 159–63, 165, 175, 183, 186–7, 191, 257. (Replaced *Valandil* (2).)
Amárië Vanya, beloved of Felagund. 318, 349
Amarth Doom. 365
Ambaráto See *Aegnor*.
Ambarto See *Amrod*.
Ambarussa (1) Amras. 353, 355. (2) Name given to both the twin sons of Fëanor. 353–5 (see *Amros*). On the twins (*i·Wenyn* 353, *Gwenyn* 365) see 355, 366.
Amin See *Estel*.
Amlach A leader of dissension in Estolad. 325
Amlaith of Fornost First King of Athedain. 193, 208, 228, 253
Amon Amarth 176, 186. See *Mount Doom*.
Amon Sûl Weathertop (most references are to the *palantír*). 176, 189, 191, 193–4, 208–10, 229–30, 245
Amras Son of Fëanor, twin of Amrod. 352–3, 355, 366, 368; other names *Amros* 366, 368, *Telufinwë, Telvo* 353, 365, and see *Ambarussa*.
Amrod Son of Fëanor, twin of Amras. 352–3; other names *Ambarto, Umbarto* 353–5, 366, *Pityafinwë, Pityo* 353, 365, and see *Ambarussa*.

INDEX

Amros = *Ambarussa* as the name of both the twin sons of Fëanor. 367
Amroth King of Lórien. 36, 65, 82, 206, 222–3, 294
Amrothos Third son of Imrahil of Dol Amroth. 221, 223
Anairë Wife of Fingolfin. 344, 361, 363
Anardil Sixth King of Gondor. 197, 212
Anárion 32, 157, 169–70, 172, 176–7, 188, 191–2, 195, 197–8, 207–8, 210, 212, 218, 227, 232–3, 254, 257
Anárioni Heirs of Anárion. 196
Ancalagon The Black Dragon. 374–5
Andafangar 321. See *Longbeards*.
Anderson, Douglas 117
Andor The Land of Gift, Númenor. 144; *the Gift* 144
Andreth 'Wise-woman' of the Edain. 325, 374–5, 419; other names *Saelon, Saelind* 419
Anduin (including *sources, vale(s), mouths* of Anduin; *Upper, Middle, Lower Anduin*) 10, 32, 34, 38, 49–50, 56–7, 65, 74–5, 122, 152, 167, 174–7, 183, 186, 192, 197–200, 204–7, 214, 229–30, 233, 235–6, 238, 242, 251, 258–9, 267, 272–3, 302–3, 311, 313, 316, 329, 371, 384, 411, 416, 422, 437; see *Great River*.
Andúnië (chiefly in *Lord(s) of Andúnië*) 145, 152, 154, 156, 159–62, 164–5, 257
Anfalas Fief of Gondor. 34
Anfangrim 321, 383. See *Longbeards*.
Angaráto See *Angrod*.
Angband 302, 342, 358, 372
Angelimir Twentieth Prince of Dol Amroth. 220–3; *Angelimar* (erroneous) 222
Angerthas (Runes) 300; *Angerthas Moria* 319. See *Cirth*.
Angle, The Land between Hoarwell and Loudwater. 66–7, 250
Angmar 9, 66–7, 189, 193–5, 201, 209–10, 217–18, 230, 232, 242, 254, 256, 258, 283
Angomaitë Corsair of Umbar. 199, 215, 231, 248; later *Angamaitë* 215. See also *Angrod*.
Angrenost See *Isengard*.
Angrod Son of Finarfin. 346–7, 350–1; other names *Angaráto, Angamaitë* 346–7, *Artanga* 346
Annals of Aman 62, 79, 142, 147–8, 185, 190, 355, 359, 375, 388–9. *Annals of Beleriand* 375; see *Grey Annals*.
Annúminas 167, 169, 176, 191–3, 195, 208, 210, 228, 258, 268. See *Dunhirion, Tarkilion*.
Annúnaid See *Common Speech*.
Anórien 45, 315
Arador Fourteenth Chieftain of the Dúnedain. 196, 211, 238, 258, 263, 268; former name *Arvoreg*(?) 211

Ar-Adûnakhôr Twentieth Ruler of Númenor. 154, 165, 312. See *Herunúmen*.
Arafinwë See *Finarfin*.
Araglas Sixth Chieftain of the Dúnedain. 196, 211; former name *Arallas* 211
Aragorn I Fifth Chieftain of the Dúnedain. 196, 211
Aragorn II 32, 42–3, 65, 70, 167, 196, 202, 206, 211, 220, 226, 238–43, 253–4, 258, 262–70, 364, 410, 419–20. See *Elessar, Thorongil*.
Aragost Eighth Chieftain of the Dúnedain. 196, 211; former name *Arandost* 211
Arahad I Seventh Chieftain of the Dúnedain. 196, 211
Arahad II Tenth Chieftain of the Dúnedain. 196, 211; former name *Arangar* 211
Arahail Second Chieftain of the Dúnedain. 196, 211; former name *Aranhantil* 211
Arakáno Son of Fingolfin. 345, 361–2; Sindarin form *Argon* 345, 361–2. See also *Fingolfin*.
Aranarth First Chieftain of the Dúnedain. 196, 211, 232, 253
Arantar Fifth King of Arnor. 192
Aranuir Third Chieftain of the Dúnedain. 196, 211; former name *Aranuil* 211
Araphant Fourteenth King of Arthedain. 195, 201, 209–10, 215–16, 232
Araphor Ninth King of Arthedain. 194, 209, 230; former name *Malvegil II* 209
Arassuil Eleventh Chieftain of the Dúnedain. 196, 211; earlier *Arasuil* 211
Aratan Second son of Isildur. 208. (Replaced *Eärnur* (1).)
Aratar 'The Exalted', the chief Valar. 363
Arathorn I Twelfth Chieftain of the Dúnedain. 196, 211
Arathorn II Fifteenth Chieftain of the Dúnedain. 32, 196, 202, 211, 226, 238, 263–6
Araval Thirteenth King of Arthedain. 195, 209–10; former name *Arvallen* 209
Aravir Fourth Chieftain of the Dúnedain. 196, 211
Aravorn Ninth Chieftain of the Dúnedain. 196, 211
Araw (Sindarin) Oromë. 204, 219, 358
Ar-Balkumagān Adûnaic name of Tar-Kiryatan. 151
Archet Village of the Bree-land. 39, 81
Arciryas Brother of Narmakil II of Gondor. 216
Arda 149–50, 157, 305, 323, 370–1, 380; *the Circles of Arda* 401
Ardamir, Ardamírë Mother-name of Eärendil. 346, 348
Ar-Feiniel Daughter of Fingolfin. 362. See *Írissë*.
Argeleb I Seventh King of Arthedain. 189, 194, 208–9, 230; former name *Celebrindol* 209

Argeleb II Tenth King of Arthedain. 9, 15, 194, 209, 231, 254; former name *Arveleg* 209
Ar-Gimilzôr Twenty-third Ruler of Númenor. 154–5, 159
Argon See *Arakáno*.
Argonath, Gates of, Pillars of 198, 259
Argonui Thirteenth Chieftain of the Dúnedain. 196, 211
Arkenstone, The 281
Armenelos City of the Kings in Númenor. 145–6, 148, 160–1, 164. *Arminalêth* (Adûnaic) 145, 147–8, 154, 164. See *Númenos, Tar Kalimos*.
Arnor 66, 170–1, 176, 186, 189, 191–4, 196, 202, 208, 226–8, 230–1, 239, 243–4, 247, 253–4, 265–6, 269, 315. See *Arthedain*.
Aros, River In Beleriand. 330
Arothir Son of Angrod; Father of Gil-galad. 346, 350–1, 358, 363–4; Quenya *Artaher* 346, 350–1. See *Orodreth*.
Ar-Pharazôn, Pharazôn 149, 151, 153–7, 159–65, 175–8, 181–3, 186(–7), 262. See *Tar-Kalion*.
Artaher See *Arothir*.
Artamir Son of Ondohir King of Gondor. 201, 215, 232
Artanáro See *Gil-galad*. *Artanis* See *Galadriel*.
Arthael See *Saelon*.
Arthedain (1) Earlier name of Arnor. 9, 167, 169, 171–2, 188, 207–8, 211; *Artheden* 167. (2) One of the divisions of earlier Arnor. 193–5, 227–8, 232, 254, 256, 328
Arthur, King 44
Arvedui 'Last-king' of Arthedain. 190, 195, 201, 204, 208–10, 215–16, (225–6), 232, 248, 253–4, 256, 258, 328
Arvegil Eleventh King of Arthedain. 194, 209, 254
Arveleg I Eighth King of Arthedain. 189, 194, 209–10, 230; former name *Beleg II* 209
Arveleg II Twelfth King of Arthedain. 194, 209; former name *Argeleb* 209
Ar-Zimraphel Queen of Ar-Pharazôn. 154–5, 159; earlier *(Ar-)Zimrahil* 155, 157, 159–62. See *Tar-Míriel*.
Arwen Also ~ *Undómiel, Evenstar*. 196, 202, 211, 234–5, 239–41, 243–4, 246–7, 249, 258, 262, 265–70, 349, 364–5. See *Finduilas* (2).
Ash Mountains 258
Atalantë 'The Downfallen'. 157–8. See *Akallabêth*.
Atanamir See *Tar-Atanamir*.
Atanatar I Tenth King of Gondor. 197
Atanatar II Sixteenth King of Gondor. 198–9, 212–14, 229, 231, 259–60; named *Alkarin* 198, 212
Atanatári 54, 62, and see 324–5. See *Fathers of Men*.
Atani Men of the Three Houses. 31, 34, 54, 63, 65, 173, 198,

306–8, 311–14, 317, 324–30, 339, 348, 357, 360, 364, 369–70, 372–3; *Atanni* 54, 62; *Atanic* 311, 364, 371; origin of the name 324–5. See *Edain*.
Athrabeth Finrod ah Andreth 419
Atlantis 158
Aulë 295, 322–3, 354, 366, 368, 383–4; *Aulendil, Aulendur* 'Servant of Aulë' 365–6; *Aulëonnar* 'Children of Aulë' 391. See *Návatar*.
Avallon 144, 146–7, 173, 175–8, 185, 189, 191, 244. See *Eressëa*.
Avallónë (1) Eressëa. 146–7, 157. (2) Haven in Eressëa. 144, 146–7, 157–8, 185
Avari (and singular *Avar*) 29, 174, 312, 328, 401; *the Refusers* 312. See *East-elves*.
Azanulbizar 275; *Battle of* ~ (278)–9, 286–7. See *Dimrill Dale, Nanduhirion*.
Azog Orc of Moria, slayer of Thrór. 278, 284
Azrubêl (Adûnaic) Eärendil. 373

Bag End 4, 48, 83, 87, 91–2, 113, 288–9; true Hobbit name 48, 83
Baggins, Bilbo 3–5, 7, 10–13, 15, 19, 25, 29, 36, 39–40, 43–4, 50, 54, 56, 58, 60, 69, 72, 86–7, 89–93, 99–101, 109–12, 123–4, 129, 131, 169, 220, 226, 238–9, 241, 243, 251, 255, 282–3, 288–9, 311, 327; his farewell party 85–7, 89, 94, 99, 102, 106, 118, 124, 131, 226, 241, 289; true Hobbit name 46, 50
Baggins, Frodo 13, 19, 25, 36, 42, 50, 52, 60, 69, 86–92, 94–7, 100–1, 104–5, 109–11, 124, 166, 168, 226, 241–3, 255, 282, 288–9, 320, 326; *Frodo of the Nine Fingers* 242; true Hobbit name 50, 59
Baldor Son of Brego King of Rohan. 236, 270–1
Balin Companion of Thorin Oakenshield. 240, 279–80, 293, 299–301, 320, 322
Balrog (the Balrog of Moria) 222, 233, 249, 275, 277–8, 286, 383; 379, 421. *Demon* 379–80, 390
Barad-dûr 121, 129, 132–3, 153, 168–70, 174, 176–80, 182, 192, 206, 240, 243, 252, 265, 310, 323, 382. See *Dark Tower*.
Barahir (1) Father of Beren One-hand. 307. (2) Eighth Ruling Steward. 204
Baranduin, River 9, 39–40, 54, 56, 67, 70, 72, 83, 86, 193–4, 196, 209, 225, 228, 231, 248; *Branduin* 67. See *Brandywine, Malevarn*.
Barazinbar 275. See *Caradras, Redhorn*.
Bard of Esgaroth 239
Barrow Downs 194, 208, 228. See *Tyrn Goerthaid*.
Battle of Bywater See *Bywater*.
Battle of Five Armies 239, 276–7, 288, 383
Battle of (the) Greenfields 8–11, 15, 211, 236

Battle of Sudden Flame 350
Battle of Unnumbered Tears 419
Bede 137
Belecthor I Fifteenth Ruling Steward. 205, 219
Belecthor II Twenty-first Ruling Steward. 205, 220, 238, 250
Beleg (1) Beleg the Bowman. 404. (2) Second King of Arthedain. 193, 208
Belegaer The Great Sea. 363
Belegorn Fourth Ruling Steward. 204, 219; former names *Bardhan, Belgorn* 219
Belegost Dwarf-city in Ered Lindon. 185, 275, 322
Belegûr, Belegurth (Sindarin) Melkor. 358; *Belegor* 358
Beleriand 73–6, 78, 146, 163, 174, 185, 223, 301–3, 305–7, 309–10, 313–14, 317, 319, 324–6, 328–9, 337, 339–41, 345–9, 357–8, 368, 372–4, 379, 385, 387, 389, 391–2, 400–2; *East Beleriand* 307
Belfalas Fief of Gondor. 220–2; *Bay of Belfalas* 183, 313
Bëor (the Old) 63, 146, 307–8, 325, 368, 370, 372–3; *House, Folk, People of Bëor* 294, 307–8, 311, 313, 326, 330, 368, 374–5; *Bëorians* 326, 372–3; *Lesser Folk* 370, 373–4
Bëorian (language) 325, 330, 368–71, 376
Bëorn 72; *Bëornings* 34, 71, 272
Bereg A leader of dissension in Estolad. 325
Beregond (1) Twentieth Ruling Steward. 205–6, 220; former name *Baragond* 220. (2) Man of Minas Tirith, father of Bergil and Borlas. 411, 421
Berelach Son of Borlas of Pen-arduin. 416–17, 421; rejected names *Berthil, Bergil* 421
Beren (1) Beren son of Barahir. 307, 326, 348–9, 368–9. (2) Nineteenth Ruling Steward. 205, 220, 248, 274
Bergil Son of Beregond (2); brother of Borlas (2). 421
Bifur Companion of Thorin Oakenshield. 279
Big Folk Men (as seen by Hobbits). 311
Bilbo See *Baggins.*
Black Captain Lord of the Ringwraiths. 207, 241–2
Black Gate 242, 271. See *Morannon.*
Blacklocks One of the kindreds of the Dwarves. 301, 322
Black Riders 241; *Lord of the Black Riders* 267
Black Speech 65, 83 (cited), 320
Black Years The Second Age. 166–8. See *Dark Years.*
Blanco Hobbit, first settler of the Shire, with his brother Marcho. 6, 17, 87. (Replaced *Cavallo.*)
Blessed Realm 130, 144, 146, 305, 334, 337–8, 378–81, 386, 388. See *Aman.*
Blue Mountains (including *the Mountains*) 31, 173, 185, 279, 287, 301, 307, 313, 325, 328, 374. See *Ered Lindon, Ered Luin.*

Blue Wizards   See *Wizards*.
Bofur   Companion of Thorin Oakenshield. 279
Bombur   Companion of Thorin Oakenshield. 279
Book of Mazarbul   See *Mazarbul*.
Book of the Kings   25, 191, 253; ~ *and Stewards* 255, 261
Bór the Easterling   419
Borin   Brother of Dáin I. 276, 279, 288. (Replaced *Nár* (1).)
Borlas   (1) Son of Bór the Easterling, later *Borlad*. 419.   (2) Borlas of Pen-arduin. 409–18, 420–1.
Boromir   (1) Eleventh Ruling Steward. 205, 219, 235.   (2) Son of Denethor II. 32, 206–7, 219, 221, 240–2.
Bounders   Border-guards of the Shire. 6
Brandybuck, Meriadoc (Merry)   7, 39, 49–50, 59, 69, 80–1, 83, 87, 95–7, 99, 102, 104–7, 109–11, 117, 261, 273, 283–4, 309; true Hobbit name 50, 59, 69, 81, 83; his title 102, 105; and see *Holdwine*.
Brandy Hall   87, 103, 105–6
Brandywine Bridge   (9), 17, 93, 117, 258
Brandywine, River   6, 9, 39–40, (48), 54, 67, 72, 86, 105, 225, 231, 235, 238, 313; history of the Hobbit name 39–40, 54, 72, 83–4
Bree   9–10, 34, 39, 52, 56, 80–1, 119, 121–3, 125, 127, 129, 131, 193, 208, 225, 228, 230–1, 281, 287–8, 311, 327; *Bree-land* 248; *Bree-folk, Men of Bree*, &c. 10, 34, 39, 52, 70, 81, 123, 230; *the Old Home* 9–10
Brego   Second King of Rohan, son of Eorl the Young. 236, 270–1
Bridgefields   Region of the Shire. 93, 117
British   (Celtic) 81
Broadbeams   One of the kindreds of the Dwarves. 301, 322
Bruinen, River   56, 193, 208. See *Loudwater*.
Brytta   Eleventh King of Rohan. 274; earlier *Léof* 274
Bucca of the Marish   First Shire-thain. 232, 248
Buckland   10, 17, 50, 57, 80, 99, 104–5, 112, 235, 255; *East March* 17, 112
Budgeford   In Bridgefields. 88, 93, 96–7, 117
Buldar   Father of Hazad Longbeard. 424–6, 429, 437; earlier *Tal-Bulda* 437
Butterbur, Barnabas   51–2, 60, 70, *Barney* 52; later name *Barliman* 70; his true name 52, 60
Bywater   114–16; *Battle of Bywater* 9
Byzantium   102

Cair Andros   Island in Anduin. 206, 371
Calenardhon   Province of Gondor, afterwards Rohan. 273, 315; earlier spelling *Calenardon* 205, 219, 236, 272
Calendars   See *Days of the week, Months, Seasons; Moon, Sun; Old*

Year, New Year, Yule, Midyear('s) Day, Lithe, Overlithe; New Era. For terms employed in the Eldarin calendar see 125–7, 131–2, 134–5, 137
Camelot 44
Caradras 69. See *Barazinbar, Redhorn.*
Caranthir Son of Fëanor. 318, 353; other names *Morifinwë, Moryo, Carnistir* 353
Caras Galadon 36, 65, 82
Cardolan One of the divisions of earlier Arnor. 193–5, 208–10, 228, 230
Carnen, River The Redwater, flowing from the Iron Hills. 316
Carpenter, Humphrey *Biography.* 409
Carrock, The Bëorn's rock in Anduin. 38, 57
Cavallo Earlier name of the Hobbit Blanco. 6, 9–10, 17, 86–7, 209, 225
Celduin, River 330; erroneously *Celon* 316. See *(River) Running.*
Celeborn (1) The White Tree of Eressëa. 148. (2) Lord of Lórien. 36–7, 79, 174, 222–3, 234, 317–19, 328, 348, 364, 385; *Teleporno* 347, 364
Celebrant, River 198. *Field, Battle of Celebrant* 205, 219, 236, 271–2, 330; *Parth Celebrant* 330. See *Silverlode.*
Celebrían Wife of Elrond. 226, 234–6, 243, 247, 249, 264–6, 268, 348, 365
Celebrimbor Great craftsman of Eregion. 179, 297, 317–19, 382; origin of the name 179, 317–18
Celebrindor Fifth King of Arthedain. 193, 208; former names *Celebrindol* 193, 208–9, *Celemenegil* (?) 208–9
Celebros 'Silver-rain', waterfall in Brethil. 371–2
Celegorm Son of Fëanor. 318, 352; *Celegorn* 373; other names *Turkafinwë, Turko* 352, *Tyelkormo* 353
Celepharn Fourth King of Arthedain. 193
Celon, River In Beleriand, tributary of Aros. 330. See *Celduin.*
Celtic 46, 50, 80
Cerin Amroth 240, 244; *Kerin ~* 265–6, 269
Chetwood Forest of the Bree-land. 39, 81
Chieftain(s) of the Dúnedain 188, 192–3, 195, 197, 202, 210–11, 215, 232, 238, 254, 263–4; *Lord(s) ~* 253, 263
Children of Ilúvatar 325, 390; *~ of Eru* 334, 364–5, 381, 413; *~ of God* 420; *the Children* 357; *Elder Children of the World* 23, 77; *the Second Children* (Men) 391; *the Third Children* (Dwarves) 391. See *Eruhîn.*
Children of the Valar 143. See *Sons of the Valar.*
Chronology *(of composition: external dating)* 3, 6–7, 14–16, 18, 28, 54, 61–2, 68, 119, 140–1, 148, 158, 163, 177, 188, 190, 222, 226, 246, 259, 293, 295, 318, 331, 350–1, 359, 367, 377, 395, 403, 409–10, 422

448   THE PEOPLES OF MIDDLE-EARTH

Circles of the World, The   77, 150, 157, 257, 374–5, 381, 401; and see *Arda*.
Círdan   145, 179, 194–5, 228, 232, 243, 281, 385–7, 392; called *Círdan of Lune* 195, 232; his original Telerin name *Nōwë* 392
Ciriáran   See *Olwë*.
Cirion   Twelfth Ruling Steward. 205, 219, 236, 272–3, 328; former name *Hador* 219; *Cirion and Eorl* (title of work) 293, 330; *Oath of* ~ 328
Cirth   (Runes) 22, 75–6, 81–2, 319; *Short Cirth of Dale and the Mark* 76, *Long Cirth of Moria* 76. See *Angerthas, Daeron, Runes*.
Ciryon   Third son of Isildur. 208. (Replaced *Vëandur*.)
Coldfells   Region north of Rivendell. 263
Combe   Village of the Bree-land. 53, 81
Common Speech, Common Tongue   16–17, 20–2, 24, 28, 32–9, 41–5, 48–52, 54–5, 57–60, 63–5, 68, 70–4, 76, 78–9, 81–2, 120, 122, 128–9, 133, 203, 295–301, 311, 316, 319–21, 327, 332, 360. Other names: *Adûni* 316, *Andúnar, Adúnar* 32, *Annúnaid* 316, *Undúna* 55, *Yandúnë* 32; *Falathren* 32, 55; *Sóval Phárë* 32, 55; and see *Westnish, Westron*.
   Common Speech and related names and words (not 'translated') cited: 44–54, 58–61, 68–9, 76, 78, 81, 83–4; and see 299.
Company of the Ring   242, 265
Corsairs of Umbar   199–200, 203, 205, 214, 218, 220, 222, 231, 236, 242
Cristhorn   'Eagle-cleft', in the mountains about Gondolin; later name *Cirith Thoronath*. 379, 388
Curufin   Son of Fëanor. 317–18, 352, 354–5, 358; his wife 317–18; other names *Kurufinwë, Kurvo* 352, *Atarinkë* 353
Curunír   Saruman. 228–9, 233, 235, 249.

Daeron (of Doriath)   (and earlier *Dairon*) 76, 297, 319; *Alphabet, Runes of* ~ 75–6, 297–8, 319, 321
Dagorlad   The Battle Plain. 169, 176, 192, 200
Dáin I   Father of Thrór. 275–7, 279
Dáin II (Ironfoot)   35, 237, 239, 250, 276–8, 281, 284, 286, 288, 383, 391
Dale   21–3, 34–5, 38–9, 41, 53–4, 57, 60, 65, 70, 73, 75–6, 81, 122, 236–9, 319
Danians   Nandor. 75–6; *Danian Elves* 76; *Danas* 76, 364
Dark(ness), The   182–3, 427, 436–7, *Nether Darkness* 149; *Men of* ~ , *People of* ~ 312, 435–6, *Servants of* ~ 373
Dark Ages   306
Dark Elves   312; *Elves of Darkness* 312
Dark Lord   (references to Morgoth and Sauron) 31, 35, 65, 200, 215, 245–6, 264, 306, 373, 382; *Dark Power* (Morgoth) 78

INDEX

Dark Tower 83, 173, 242, 265, 411, 419. See *Barad-dûr*.
Dark Years 32, 65, 74, 173–4, 178
Days of Dearth 17
Days of Flight 168, 174
Days of the week Hobbit names 123–5, 130, 137; Quenya names 130, 133, 138; Noldorin (Sindarin) names 125, 130, 138
Dead Marshes 201
Déagol 38, 53, 57, 81, 166, 168–9, 172, 225, 233, 247
Deathless Land 158
Denethor I Tenth Ruling Steward. 204–5, 219, 235, 249
Denethor II Twenty-sixth Ruling Steward. 32, 43, 68, 206–7, 220–1, 240–2, 258, 410
Dimrill Dale 275; *Battle of* ~ 237. See *Azanulbizar, Nanduhirion*.
Dior (1) Thingol's Heir. 223, 348–9, 368–9, 371–2; his sons 373. See *Eluchíl*. (2) Ninth Ruling Steward. 204, 219, 235, 249
Dirhael Grandfather of Aragorn II. 196, 238, 263; changed to *Dirhoel* 238, 263
Dís Sister of Thorin Oakenshield. 277, 285
Dol Amroth 36, 206–7, 220–3, 240, 244, 329
Dol Dûgul See *Dol Guldur*.
Dol Guldur Sauron's dwelling in Mirkwood. 193, 229, 234–5, 237, 239, 247, 249–50, 252, 276–7, 280, 283–4, 287–8, 311; former name *Dol Dûgul* 225, 247, *Dol Dúghul, Dol Dúgol* 247
Dome of Valmar 371; *Dome of Varda* 376
Dor-Daedeloth The land of Morgoth. 362
Dor Haeron Land between Entwash and Isen. 273
Dori Companion of Thorin Oakenshield. 279
Doriath 76, 174, 185, 301, 307, 319, 325, 337, 349, 360, 369, 372, 385, 392
Dorthonion 68, 185, 350
Downfall of Númenor See *Númenor*.
Dragons 72, 227, 252, 275; drakes 374. See *Ancalagon, Smaug*.
Drengist, Firth of 354
Drowning of Anadûnê (title of work) 64, 140–5, 147, 149–50, 154–6, 158, 164, 171, 183, 374; (not as title) 157
Drúadan Forest 65
Drúedain Wild Men of the White Mountains. 293, 309, 324, 326
Drûgs Drúedain. 309–10, 314, 326
Duilin (1) A lord of Gondolin. 421. (2) Original name of the father of Gwindor of Nargothrond. 421. (3) Father of Saelon (1). 421.
Dúnedain 31–4, 36, 38, 40, 55, 63, 68, 74, 119–20, 122–3, 125, 127–31, 145–6, 149, 193–5, 213, 225, 227, 230, 232, 245, 253, 258, 260, 263, 267, 324; *Dúnadan* 324; *Dúnedein* 31, 55. See also *Chieftains of the Dúnedain*.

Dunharrow 53, 236, 271, 309
Dunhirion Rejected name of Annúminas. 167. See *Tarkilion*.
Dunland 11, 34, 38, 65–7, 229, 250, 271, 279, 319, 329; *Dunlandish* (language) 38; *Dunlanders* 271; *Dunlendings* 34, 65, 205, 314, 329–30 (see *Gwathuirim*).
Durin (the Deathless) 173, 185, 237, 275–7, 279, 286, 304, 322, 324, 382–3; his awakening 301, 321–2. *Durin's Folk, House, Line, Race* 227, 233, 236–7, 275–6, 278, 281–6, 288
  Later kings named *Durin* 275, 284, 383–4; *Durin III* 275, 277, 279, 284, 286, > *Durin VI* 284, 383; *Durin VII and Last* 278–9, 383, 391
Durin's Bane 286
Dwalin Companion of Thorin Oakenshield. 279–80, 288
Dwarrowdelf Moria. 24, 44, 58; Westron *Phuru-nargian* 44, 76, 78 (earlier forms 58).
Dwarves (and *Dwarf*; also many compounds, as *Dwarf-boots, -mines, -cities*) 4, 7–8, 10, 15, 21–4, 26, 31, 35–6, 44, 46, 54–6, 58, 60, 70–1, 73, 76, 81–2, 173–4, 184–5, 205, 220, 222–3, 227, 230, 233, 235–40, 244, 246, 249–50, 252, 261, 275–6, 278, 280–1, 283–5, 288, 295–8, 300–5, 310–11, 313, 316, 318–23, (324), 327–8, 351–2, 358, 382–4, 391. Names of the Dwarves 22, 35, 54, 60, 71, 73, 81, 296, 300, 304, 321–2
Dwarvish (of language and writing) 44, 81, 279, 286, 297, 300, 304, 319, 324, 351–2; (with other reference) 301, 317, 383, 391; *Dwarfish* 351

Eä 396–7, 400–1
Eagles 239
Eälótë Eärendil's ship. 143. See *Rothinzil, Vingilot*.
Eär The Great Sea. 363
Eärendil (1) 143, 145, 152, 158, 173–5, 179, 346, 348, 363–5, 367, 369–71, 373, 375–6, 381, 386–7; *Eärendel* 168, 170; *Lay of* ~ 163; *Heir of* ~ (King of Númenor) 154–5. See *Ardamir*.
Eärendil (2) Fifth King of Gondor. 197, 212. (3) Tenth and last King of Arnor. 32, 64, 189, 208, 247. (Replaced by *Eärendur* (2).)
Eärendur (1) Fifteenth Lord of Andúnië. 159, 164. (2) Tenth King of Arnor. 64, 189, 193, 208, 227–8, 247, 253. (Replaced *Eärendil* (3).)
Earliest Days 8, 15. See *Elder Days*.
Eärnil I Thirteenth King of Gondor. 197, 213
Eärnil II Thirty-second King of Gondor. 201, 204, 212, 216–18, 232–3, 245, 248, 252, 254, 256, 262
Eärnur (1) Second son of Isildur. 191, 208. (Replaced by *Aratan*.) (2) Thirty-third King of Gondor. 201–2, 204, 212, 217, 225–6, 233–4, 245, 247, 256, 378

Eärwen   Daughter of Olwë, wife of Finarfin. 337, 344, (346), 360, 365
East, The   75, 149, 154, 194, 200, 229, 231, 233–4, 240, 242, 264, 305–6, 323; references to Men of the East 79, 197, 200, 205, 215, 232, 258, 272, 302, 305–6, 311, 321, 424, 427, and see *Easterlings*.
East-elves   Avari. 73, 174; *Eastern Elves* 79
Easterlings   197–8, 213–14, 219, 228, 230, 236, 258, 271–2, 296, 328
Eastfold   Region of Rohan. 274
East March   See *Buckland*.
East Road   93, 117. See *Great Road*.
Ecthelion I   Seventeenth Ruling Steward. 205, 219–20, 236, 249. *Ecthelion's Tower* 205, 236
Ecthelion II   Twenty-fifth Ruling Steward. 206, 220, 240, 258
Edain   Men of the Three Houses. 31–2, 62, 64, 74–6, 143–6, 149, 159, 162, 173, 181, 203, 258, 269, 303, 306, 309, 325, 359, 364, 374, 419. See *Atani*.
Edhellond   Elf-haven north of Dol Amroth. (313), 329
Egalmoth   (1) A lord of Gondolin. 419, 421.   (2) Eighteenth Ruling Steward. 205, 219–20, 419.   (3) See *Saelon*.
Eglain   The people of Círdan. 392
elanor   Golden flower of Lórien. 266
Elbereth   (1) 'Star-queen', Varda. 358, 437.   (2) Son of Dior (see *Elurín*). 223, 372.   (3) Son of Elrond (replaced by *Elrohir*). 224
Elboron   (1) Son of Dior (see *Eluréd*). 223, 372.   (2) Son of Elrond (replaced by *Elladan*). 224.   (3) Second Prince of Ithilien, son of Faramir. 221, 223
Eldakar   (1) Fourth King of Arnor. 192.   (2) Twenty-first King of Gondor. 199, 205, 213–14, 231, 255, 260–2. See *Vinitharya*.
Eldalië   The people of the Eldar. 400, 404
Eldalótë   Wife of Angrod. 346; Sindarin *Eðellos* 346
Eldamar   'Elvenhome' in Aman. 78
Eldar   (and singular *Elda*) 29–33, 36, 55, 61, 64–5, 77–8, 82, 120, 122–3, 125–6, 129, 143, 145–9, 152, 157–8, 174, 176, 178–80, 191, 193, 202–3, 227–9, 243–4, 249, 256, 296–7, 303–8, 310–11, 321, 324–6, 329, 331–5, 337, 339–42, 347–8, 357–8, 360–4, 366, 368–72, 379–82, 384, 390, 395, 397–401, 403–4, 419, 435–7; *High Eldar* 305, 342, 363; *the Fair* 435. *Laws and Customs among the Eldar* (title of work) 356–7, 359
Eldarin   (of language; also *Primitive, Common Eldarin*) 30, 145, 152, 157, 318–19, 340–2, 346–7, 352, 357–63, 366, 368, 371–2, 374, 392, 401, 436; verb '*Eldarize*' 352; (with other reference) 124, 127, 131, 137–8, 153, 357
Eldarion   Son of Aragorn and Arwen. 202, 217–18, 244–6, 410, 419–20

Elder Days 8, 15, 23, 143, 147, 156, 173, 184–5, 202, 233, 243, 263, 268–70, 275, 305, 338, 349, 375; on different meanings see 173, 184–5, 263, 268–9

Eldest Tree, Elder Tree 123, 130, 147–8. See *Galathilion, Silpion, Telperion; Two Trees*.

Eldûn Son of Dior. 372. See *Elboron, Eluréd*.

Elendil (1) *the Tall* 32–4, 39, 74, 156–7, 163–4, 166, 169–71, 175–7, 183, 188–9, 191–3, 196–7, 201–3, 207, 212, 217–18, 253, 257, 267; his sword 186, 195, 227, 239, 263, 266. See *Nimruzîr; Narsil*.

Elendil (2) Ælfwine. 401, 403

Elendili Elf-friends of Númenor. 151, 155, 160, 185; *Elendilli* 151. See *Elf-friends, (The) Faithful, Nimruzîrim*.

Elendur (1) Eldest son of Isildur. 208. (Replaced *Kiryandil* (1).) (2) Ninth King of Arnor. 193

Elenna 'Starwards', Númenor. 145

Elentir Brother of Amandil, lover of Zimrahil. 159–63, 165

Elenwë Wife of Turgon. 345–6, 361–3

Elessar (1) Rejected name of King Eärnur of Gondor. 247

Elessar (2) Aragorn II. 32, 132, 196, 202–3, 207, 211, 217, 243–4, 246, 253, 255, 258, 261, 268, 410, 419; *the Elfstone* 243; *the Great King* 414; *Annals, Chronicles of the House of Elessar* 243, 245

Elf-friends (of Númenor) 151–2, 155, 161, 163, 174–5, 191, 203, 234, 422, 436. See *Elendili*.

Elfhild of Eastfold Wife of Théoden. 274

Elfstone See *Elessar* (2).

Elfwine the Fair Nineteenth King of Rohan, son of Éomer. 221

Elladan and Elrohir Sons of Elrond. 196, 224, 226, 234–6, 238–9, (243), 249, 264, 273. See *Elboron, Elbereth*.

Elmar Mother of Hazad Longbeard. 425–6, 437

Elrohir See *Elladan and Elrohir*.

Elphir Twenty-third Prince of Dol Amroth. 221, 223

Elrond 79, 146, 163, 168, 174, 179, 192, 195–6, 202, 207, 211, 224–6, 228–9, 232, 234–5, 238–44, 247, 249, 253, 256–7, 262–7, 269, 273, 319, 347–9, 364–5, 367, 369–71, (376), 378, 382, 384–5, 388, 390; the name 371; doom of the children of Elrond 234–5, 256–7, 265

Elros 144–6, 150–1, 153–4, 160, 164, 166, 168–71, 173, 178, 202, 256–7, 348–9, 364, 367–71, (376); *Elerossë* 349, 367, *Elroth* 369. *The Line of Elros* (title of work) 151, 155, 163, 165, 184. See *Tar-Minyatur*.

Elrûn Son of Dior. 372. See *Elbereth, Elurín*.

Eluchíl 'Thingol's Heir', name of Dior. 369, 372

Eluréd 'Heir of Elu (Thingol)', son of Dior. 369, 372. Earlier names *Elboron, Eldûn*.

INDEX

Elurín 'Remembrance of Elu (Thingol)', son of Dior. 369, 372. Earlier names *Elbereth, Elrûn.*

Elu Thingol See *Elwë, Thingol.*

Elven-, Elf- -blood 206, 226, 247; -folk 29, 206; -kind 257; -king 176; kingdom(s) 36, 211; -lady 221; -lords 379; -lore 32; -name 222; -peoples 78; -race 234; -realm(s) 196, 330; -rings 13; -speech 29; -tongue(s) 36, 41, 146, 164, 174; -towers 17; -wise 240; -women 404

Elvenhome 20, 22, 63. See *Eldamar.*

Elven-latin, Elf-latin Quenya. 30, 41, 62

Elves (and *Elf*) 8, 19–21, 23, 29–33, 35–6, 42, 46, 54–5, 58, 62–3, 65, 73–4, 76–7, 79, 82, 127–8, 139, 144, 152–3, 168–9, 172–4, 177–80, 220–1, 227–9, 234, 240, 244, 257, 264–5, 275, 285, 295–8, 301–2, 304, 307, 311–13, 316–17, 319, 321–3, 326–8, 330, 332, 352, 356–7, 364–5, 370–1, 377–8, 380–6, 388, 390–2, 395–7, 399, 403. *Elves of Light* 312; and see *East-elves, Middle Elves, Western Elves, Woodland Elves.*

Elvish (of language and writing) 20, 22, 24, 29–31, 34, 36, 39–45, 54, 58, 63–5, 67–9, 70–5, 78–9, 82, 125, 138, 151, 157, 164, 193, 297, 299, 315, 320, 324, 340, 348, 368–9, 379, 390, 395; (with other reference) 4, 29–30, 61, 73, 75, 119–20, 125, 133, 144–5, 294, 305–6, 308, 339–40, 342, 351, 359, 378, 380, 382, 389–91

Elwë Thingol of Doriath. 333, 340–1, 357, 364–5, 369, 371, 376, 385–7, 392. See *Sindikollo, Thingol.*

Elwing 348–9, 365, 367–71, 376

Emyn Arnen Hills in Ithilien. 207, 220, 411, 415, 421; *hills of Arnen* 411

Emyn Beraid 176, 186, 191, 195, 210, 231; *Emyn Gwahaedir, Emyn Hen Dúnadan* 186. See *Gwahaedir, Tower Hills.*

Emyn Muil 198, 205, 259, 316

End, The 401; *the end of the world* 265, 335, 375

Enedhwaith Lands between Greyflood and Isen. 313, 328–30; *Enedwaith* 294, 328–9

Enemy, The 21, 24, 267, 436; *the Great Enemy* 358

England 26, 45, 50, 52, 82; *ancient England* 22, 49, (143)

English (language) 20–1, 27, 41–7, 49–50, 52–4, 58, 60–1, 70–1, 81–2, 103, 137, 298–300, 316, 320, 361–2, 368, 405. *Old English* (also 'ancient', 'ancestral', 'archaic' English) 15, 21, 27, 41, 44, 50–3, 58, 60–1, 70–1, 76, 82 (people), 83, 125, 137, 274, 301, 405

Entwash, River 53, 273, 315

Eöl 'The Dark Elf', father of Maeglin. 328, 367

Éomer Eighteenth King of Rohan. 53, 65, 207, 221, 240, 244, 246, 271–3; named *Éadig* 244

Éomund Father of Éomer and Éowyn. 240, 242, 244, 273

Eönwë Herald of Manwë. 143, 163. See *Fionwë*.
Eorlings The Rohirrim. 34; *Eorlingas* 272
Eorl the Young First King of the Mark. 21, 26, 50, 205, 219, 236, 261, 271–3, 312, 328; *Oath of Eorl and Cirion* 328
Éothéod 'Horse-folk' and 'Horse-land' (53). 34, 53, 81, 205, 236, 271–3; earliest name *Irenland* 271
Éowyn Sister of Éomer. 39, 43, 53, 68, 181, 207, 221, 240, 242, 244, 246, 273
Epilogue (to *The Lord of the Rings*) 68, 112
Eradan Second Ruling Steward. 204
Erchirion Second son of Imrahil of Dol Amroth. 221, 223
Erebor 236–42, 244, 246, 249–50, 252, 275–8, 280–1, 284, 288, 300, 323; *The Quest of Erebor* (title) 282, 288–9. See Lonely Mountain.
Ered Lindon 34, 301, 307, 322, 325, 349, 374. See *Ered Luin*; Blue Mountains, Mountains of Lune.
Ered Luin 78, 184, 281–2, 314–15, 330. See *Ered Lindon*.
Ered Mithrin 302–3, 305, 321–3. See Grey Mountains.
Eregion 79, 168–9, 174, 177–80, 297, 305, 317–19, 390. See Hollin.
Ereinion See Gil-galad.
Eressëa 31, 33, 144, 146–9, 152, 157–8, 163, 173, 177–8, 185, 189, 386, 401; *Tol Eressëa* 143, 158, 388; *Lonely Isle* 158. See Avallon, Avallónë (1).
Eriador 10–11, 33–4, 36–40, 56, 66–7, 119, 125, 153, 174, 179–80, 185, 195–6, 220, 227, 229–31, 235–6, 248, 250, 263–4, 281, 293, 302–3, 305–7, 311–14, 327, 378, 384, 391
Erien Daughter of Fingon (rejected). 361; earlier name *Ernis* 361
Eru 364–5, 370, 381, 391, 413; *Eru Ilúvatar* 270. See Children of Ilúvatar, (The) One.
Eruhîn (Children of Eru), Númenóreans. 149
Esgaroth 34, 38, 65, 239; *Lake Town* 72
Estel 'Hope', name of Aragorn II in his youth. 269–70; earlier *Amin* 269
Ethir (Anduin) The Mouths of Anduin. 416
Ethraid Erui The Crossings of Erui (river of Gondor). 199
Ettenmoors Troll-fells north of Rivendell. 437
Etymologies, The In *The Lost Road*. 68–9, 158, 371, 404–5
European 41, 61, 368
Evendim, Lake In Arnor. 313. See *Nenuial*.
Exile, The (of the Noldor) 185, 337–9, 342–4, 348, 360; *Exilic* 332
Exiles, The (also *Exiled Noldor*) 20, 30–1, 36, 62, 65, 73, 78, 146, 173, 331, 336, 339, 344–6, 360, 376, 379–80, 392, 400–1. Exiles of Númenor 158, 312
Ezellohar The Green Mound of the Trees in Valinor. 356; *the plain of Ezellohar* 334, 357

INDEX 455

Fading Years The Third Age. 227
Faithful, The (of Númenor) 160, 162, 176, 182, 257, 312, 315. See *Elendili, Elf-friends.*
Faithful Stone, The A tale of the Drúedain. 309–10.
Falas, Havens of the (329), 349
Falastur Name taken by Tarannon, twelfth King of Gondor. 197–8, 213
Falathren 'Shore-language': see *Common Speech.*
Falathrim Elves of the Falas. 386, 392. See *Eglain, Falmari* (2).
Fallowhides 10, 15, 37, 40, 47, 54, 56–9, 66, 229–30, 328; *Fallowhides* 248; *Fallohidish* 57
Falmari (1) The Teleri of Valinor, *Sea-elves.* 392. (2) Elves of the Falas. 386, 392
Faniel Daughter of Finwë and Indis. 359
Faramir (1) Son of Ondohir King of Gondor. 201, 215, 232. (2) Son of Denethor II; Prince of Ithilien. 16, 43, 63–5, 67–8, 73, 181, 206–7, 220–1, 223, 240, 244, 246, 295, 312, 411; *the Prince* 421
Far Downs 17, 112
Farin Father of Fundin father of Balin. 279
Farthings 17, 112; the word 45, 58; *East Farthing* 10, 56–7, 122, 129, *East-farthingers* 122; *North Farthing* 9, 115, 236
Fastred (1) Son of King Folcwine of Rohan. 206, 238, 274; earlier name *Folcwalda* 271, 274. (2) See *Fengel.*
Fathers of Men 23, 31–2, 34, 39, 54–5, 62, 64–5, 168, 173, 324; *Fathers of the Three Houses* 63–4; *the Fathers* 77. See *Atanatári.*
fëa The indwelling spirit of an incarnate being. 333–5, 352, 380, 391
Fëanor 30, 256, 317(–18)–19, 331–9, 342–5, 352–9, 361, 363, 368–9, 379, 388–9; *alphabet of* ~ 22. Other names and forms *Fëanáro* 333, 343, 356, *Fayanáro* 343, *Faenor* 343, 359; *Finwë* 359, 365, *Finwë minya* 343, *Finwion* 359, *Minyon* 359; *Kurufinwë (Curufinwë)* 343, 352, 359, 365. See *Sons of Fëanor.*
Fëanorian (alphabet, script) 40–1, 76, 82, 297–8, 319. *Fëanorians* 366, 388
Felagund Name used alone or with Finrod: see *Finrod* (2). Origin of the name 351–2; *Felagon* 352
Felaróf The horse of Eorl the Young. 274
Fell Folk of the East (in the tale of Tal-elmar) 424, 427
Fell Winter (Third Age 2911) 238
Fengel Fifteenth King of Rohan. 270–1, 273–4; ephemeral names *Fastred, Felanath* 274
Fenmarch Region of Rohan. 53
Fili Companion of Thorin Oakenshield. 277, 285
Finarfin 77, 317 *(Finarphin)*, 336–8, 344, 346–7, 349, 351, 360, 363, 365, 389; *Nothrim, Nost* ~ the house of Finarfin 360. Other

names *Arafinwë* 344, 360, *Arfin* 344; *Ingoldo* 360, *Ingalaurë* 360. See *Finrod* (1).
Finbor Son of Fingon (rejected). 361
Findaráto See *Finrod* (2). *Findekáno* See *Fingon*.
Findis Daughter of Finwë and Indis. 343, 359
Finduilas (1) of Nargothrond. 350–1. (2) Earlier name of Arwen. 226, 247. (3) of Dol Amroth, wife of Denethor II. 36, 206, 220–1, 240
Finellach See *Gil-galad*.
Fingolfin 336, 343–5, 348, 354, 357, 360–2, 365, 388–9; other names *Nolofinwë* 344, 360; *Arakáno* 345, 360; *Ingoldo* 360
Fingon 344–5, 349, 351–2, 357, 361, 388; other names *Findekáno* 345, 361, *Finicáno*, *Findicáno* 361
Finrod (1) Earlier name of Finarfin. 77, 79, 389
Finrod (2) Finrod Felagund. (References include *Finrod* and *Felagund* used alone) 77, 173–4, 185, 307–8, 317–18, 325, 336–7, 344, 346, 349–52, 358, 360, 363–4, 372–3, 389, 419; *Friend of Men* 307. Other names *Findaráto* 346–7, *Artafindë* 346, 360; *Ingoldo* 346, 360, 363. His wife 317–18, 349–50. See *Felagund*.
Finvain Daughter of Finwë and Indis. 359
Finwë 77, 293, 331, 333–7, 339–40, 343–50, 359, 361, 364–5, 367, 389; his title *Noldóran* 343
Fionwë Son of Manwë. 142–3, 163, 166, 172, 185, 374–5. See *Eönwë*.
Firebeards One of the kindreds of the Dwarves. 301, 322
Fíriel Daughter of King Ondohir, wife of King Arvedui. 195, 201–2, 215–16, 232
First Age 62, 65, 78, 143, 163, 168, 172–3, 185, 187, 256, 275, 301, 304, 306, 308–10, 312, 330, 340, 357, 378–9, 381, 383, 390, 395
Firstborn, The The Elves. 147, 150, 378
First Kindred of the Elves 356
Folca Thirteenth King of Rohan. 274
Folcred Son of King Folcwine of Rohan. 206, 238, 271, 274
Folcwalda See *Fastred*.
Folcwine Fourteenth King of Rohan. 206, 238, 271, 274
Forgotten Men The Dead Men of Dunharrow. 267
Forlindon Lindon north of the Gulf of Lune. 313
Formenos Stronghold of the Fëanorians in Valinor. 361
Fornost 5, 9, 20, 39, 186, 193–5, 208–10, 225, 228, 230, 232, 253; *Battle of Fornost* 232. See *Norbury*.
Forochel 195, 232; *Bay of* ~ 32; *Snowmen of* ~ (*Lossoth*) 210, 258
Fôs Almir The Bath of Flame (I.187, II.138). 374
Foster, Robert *The Complete Guide to Middle-earth*. 117, 278
Fourth Age 133, 172–3, 185, 202, 211, 223, 278, 304, 339, 410
Frankish 46–7

Fréalaf Tenth King of Rohan. 237 (~ *Hildeson*), 271
Fréawine Fifth King of Rohan. 53
Free Fair, The On the White Downs. 6
French 52
Frerin Brother of Thorin Oakenshield. 276, 281, 287
Frodo See *Baggins*.
Frór Brother of Thrór. 276
Fui Death-goddess (Nienna). 374
Fundin Father of Balin and Dwalin. 279, 281, 287, 300, 322

Galador First Lord of Dol Amroth. 220–2
Galadriel 36–7, 74, 77, 79, 82, 174, 185, 226, 234–5, 239, 243–4, 264–6, 293, 317–18, 320–1, 331–2, 336–8, 346–9, 351, 357, 363–5, 385; her 'Lament' 299, 320, 338, 363; as daughter of Felagund and sister of Gil-galad 174, 185, 349. Other names *Alatáriel(lë)* 346–7, *Altariel* 347; *Artanis* 346–7; *Nerwen(dë)* 337, 346, 363
Galadwen Sindarin name of Vidumavi. 260
Galathilion Name of the White Tree (1) of Valinor 147–8; (2) of Tirion (Túna), *Galathilion the Less* 147–8; (3) of Eressëa 147–8
Galdor (1) of Goldolin. 387–8. (2) of the Havens 387–8
Gamgee, Sam(wise) 6, 13, 25, 42–4, 48, 51, 63, 68, 87, 108, 111–16, 120, 126, 131, (242), 268–9; *Sam Gardner* 139; his true Hobbit name 51, 60, 83; *the Great Red Book of Samwise* 19
Gamling the Old Man of Rohan. 65
Gamwich Village of the Shire. 112, 115–16
Gandalf 4, 7, 12–14, 38, 42, 57, 66, 68, 148, 157, 206, 228, 234–5, 237–8, 240–2, 251, 276, 282–3, 287–8, 299, 321, 377–8, 381, 384–5, 388. See *Mithrandir, Olórin*.
Garman Father of Eorl the Young. 272–3. (Replaced by *Léod*.)
Gates of Morning 149
Germanic 47, 50, 94, 361
Ghân(-buri-Ghân) 316
Giants 46, 58
Gilbarad Father of Ivorwen. 263, 270
Gildor (Inglorion) 36
Gil-galad 78, 150, 152–3, 168–9, 173–4, 176, 179, 185, 189, 192, 313, 317–18, 328–9, 347–51, 358, 364, 382, 390; other names *Ereinion* 'Scion of Kings' 347–8, 351, 364; *Finellach, Finhenlach, Finlachen* 351; *Artanáro, Rodnor* 350–1
Gilmith Sister of Galador, first Lord of Dol Amroth. 221
Gilrain (1) River of Gondor. 294. (2) Mother of Aragorn. 196, 238, 263, 268, 270; *Gilraen* 269–70
Gimilkhâd Father of Ar-Pharazôn. 154, 159, 161–2, 164
Gimli 242, 244, 246, 261, 270, 285–6, 296, 391
Girdle of the Earth 150

Gladden Fields 38, 57, 177, 192, 227, 233, 238, 251. *The Disaster of the* ~ (title of work) 207–8, 293, 327
Gladden, River 38, 57, 66–7, 230, 280, 323
Glóin (1) Son of Thorin I. 275–7. (2) Companion of Thorin Oakenshield. 242, 244, 276–7, 279, 287
Glorfindel (of Gondolin and Rivendell) 67, 377–82, 384–5, 387–91
Gnome(s) Noldor. (23), 24, 63, 76–7, 81–2, 351, 379
Gnomish 20, 23–4, 71, 74–7
Goblins 4, 21, 23, 249–50, 323
God(s) 148, 306 (of Morgoth), 312, 374–5; *God* (Eru Ilúvatar) 157, 420
Go-hilleg Númenóreans (in the tale of Tal-elmar). 427–8, 430, 433
Golden Hall 71, 236. See *Meduseld*.
Golden Tree The *mallorn* planted by Sam Gamgee. 139
Golfimbul Orc-chief slain by Bandobras Took. 236
Gollum 3–5, 7, 11–14, 38, 54, 57, 66, 112, 167–9, 225, 227, 233, 239, 241, 248, 251. See *Sméagol*.
Gondolin 317, 348, 358, 370, 374, 377–81, 387–91, 395, 419, 421; *The Fall of Gondolin* (title of work) 379, 387–8; *Ondolindë* 374
Gondor 6, 20–2, 25, 32, 34, 38, 42–3, 45, 53, 63, 68, 74, 120–2, 124, 128, 132–3, 136, 163, 167, 169–71, 176, 188, 190–2, 194–207, 210–20, 225–33, 235–6, 238–45, 247–50, 252–5, 258–60, 265–7, 269, 271–4, 283, 293–4, 296, 311–12, 315–16, 328, 330, 332, 339, 360, 371, 410–11, 414, 419; *Gondorian* 138, 410; *Council of Gondor* 203, 256; early name *Ondor* 71
Gondothlim Old name of the people of Gondolin. 388
Gorbelgod, Swans of In the tale of Tal-elmar. 426, 437; earlier *Dur nor-Belgoth* 437
Gorgoroth 176
Great Battle At the end of the First Age. 142–3, 163, 166–8, 172, 177, 187
Great Dwarf Road 323. See *Old Forest Road*.
Greater Folk See *Hador*.
Great Journey (of the Eldar to the Sea) 340, 366, 387, 391–2, 403; the (Great) *March* 76, 366, 403
Great Lands Middle-earth. 72, 149, 175
Great River 56, 238, 311, 437; the *River* 66, 177, 183, 218, 239, 248, 259. See *Anduin*.
Great Road 193. See *East Road*.
Great Sea See *(The) Sea*.
Greek 46, 69, 103, 320, 368
Green-elves 349, 365, 367; *Green-elvish* 368. See *Danians, Nandor*.
Greenfields See *Battle of (the) Greenfields*.
Greenholm On the Far Downs. 112
Greenwood (the Great) 79, 174, 193, 229, 244, 258–9, 303, 324; the *Wood*, the (Great) *Forest* 303, 305–6, 323. See *Mirkwood*.

Grey Annals 62, 79, 142, 146, 185, 190, 318, 349–50, 362, 387, 388–9
Grey Company 267
Grey-elves 78–9, 221, 385; see *Sindar*. *Grey-elven* (language) 78–9, 145; see *Sindarin*.
Greyflood, River 198, 229, 271, 273, 313, 315, 329–30; see *Gwathló*.
Grey Havens 36, 168, 173–4, 178–80, 236, 243, 257, 264; *the Havens* 228, 384, 387–8, 435
Grey Mountains 233, 322–3. See *Ered Mithrin*.
Grishnákh 83
Gróin Father of Óin and Glóin. 279
Grór Brother of Thrór. 277
Guardians, The The Valar 181 (~ *of the World*), 182
Guingelot The ship of Wade. 371
Gundabad, Mount 301, 305, 322–3
Gwahaedir The *Palantíri*. 186; *Emyn Gwahaedir*, the Tower Hills, 186. See *Emyn Beraid*.
Gwathló, River 198, 294. See *Greyflood*.
Gwathuirim Dunlendings. 330
Gwingloth See *Vingilot*.

Hador (1) 'Father of Men'. 63, 144, 146, 308, 325, 370; *House, Folk, People of Hador* 294, 303, 307–8, 311–13, 325–6, 330, 348, 368, 373–4; *Hadorians* 326, 372–3; *Greater Folk* 370
Hador (2) Seventh Ruling Steward. 204, 219; former name *Cirion* 219
Haladin The people of (the Lady) Haleth. 325, 372
Haleth (1) Haleth the Hunter. 63, 325. (2) The Lady Haleth. 307, 309, 325; *Folk, People of Haleth* 307–8, 310, 314, 325–6, 329–30, 368, 372, 374; *Halethian* (language) 372. See *Haladin*.
Haleth (2) Son of Helm of Rohan. 274; earlier *Haeleth* 271, 274
Half-elven 256, 319, 347–8, 369. See *Peredhil, Pereldar*.
Halfling(s) 10, 133, 196, 229, 231, 242–3, 265, 285, 310
Halifirien Beacon-hill of Gondor. 53
Hallas Thirteenth Ruling Steward. 205
Halls of Waiting 333, 378, 380–1
Háma Son of Helm of Rohan. 271
Harad Lands of the South. 79, 175, 197–9, 201, 206, 213–14, 216, 232, 271; *Near Harad* 198
Haradrim People of the Harad. 201, 206, 229, 238, 420
Harfoots 10–11, 15, 37, 54, 56–7, 59, 66, 229–30, 247, 328
Harlindon Lindon south of the Gulf of Lune. 313, 328
Harlond The harbour of Minas Tirith. 421
Harnen, River 197–8
Hasufel Horse of Rohan. 53

Havens See *Grey Havens, Falas.*
Hazad Longbeard Father of Tal-elmar. 423–31, 435, 437; earlier *Tal-argan* 437
Heavens, Sky (in name of a day of the week) 123, 130
Hebraic 51, 70
Helkaraxë 362–3; *the Ice* 345, 362–3
Helm Hammerhand Ninth King of Rohan. 236–7, 271–2, 274
Helm's Deep 53, 236, 271, 274
Henneth Annûn 206
Herion Third Ruling Steward. 204
Herumor (1) 'Black Númenórean', a lord of the Haradrim. 420. (2) In *The New Shadow*. 414
Herunúmen Quenya name of Ar-Adûnakhôr. 164
High-elven (language) 20, 22–3, 30, 36, 77–8, 193, 219, 228, 234, 253, 379; *High-elvish* 63
High Elves 31, 73, 78, 174, 221, 246, 256–7, 312, 339, 364; *High Eldar*, see *Eldar*.
High Faroth The highlands above Nargothrond. 350
High Men Númenóreans. 312; *High Men of the Sea* 427
Hild Sister of Helm of Rohan. 271
Himring, Hill of 330
Hoarwell, River 67, 229, 250, 315
Hobbit families References include all occurrences of members of families (women by maiden name, not married name) except for *Bilbo, Frodo, Meriadoc, Peregrin, Samwise*, which are separately entered. For the true names (not referenced here) of families and individuals see 45–51, 58–60, 68–9, 81, 83.
  Baggins 5, 85–98, 100–1, 103–7, 109–11
  Banks 108
  Boffin 5, 15, 88–92, 94, 96–101, 106, 108–11, 117–18
  Bolger 40, 51, 61, 70, 87–111, 117–18
  Bracegirdle 89–92, 99–101, 103, 105
  Brandybuck 40, 47, 57, 59, 69, 80, 89–92, 95–7, 99–106, 108–11, 117
  Brockhouse 100–1
  Brown 114–16
  Brownlock 88
  Bunce 88, 91–2
  Burrows 86, 88–90, 92, 94, 99–103, 105–6
  Chubb 86, 88, 90–2, 109–11; *Chubb-Baggins* 88, 92, 94, 97
  Cotton 44, 68, 108, 112–16, 118
  Diggle 94, 97
  Drinkwater 102
  Fairbairn 25, 112–13, 116
  Gamgee (including *Gardner, Greenhand, Roper*) 45, 83, 108, 111–16

Gaukroger 87–8, 91–2, 94, 96
Goldworthy 103
Goodbody 88, 97
Goodchild 114–15
Goodenough 100–1
Goold 102–3, 105
Grubb 88–92, 100–1
Headstrong 103
Hogpen 102–3, 105
Hornblower 6, 17, 51, 69–70, 88–92, 94, 97
Lightfoot 94, 97
Noakes 86
Oldbuck 40, 80, 83, 102–3, 105–6, 232, 235
Proudfoot 86, 88–92
Sackville 89–92
Sackville-Baggins 69, 86–92, 94, 99–101, 118
Sandyman 86
Smallburrow 6
Smygrave 69
Took 5–7, 10–11, 15–18, 40, 47, 85–6, 89–92, 97–102, 104–11, 115–18, 121, 226, 235–8, 243, 249–50, 283, 288; *Took-Bolger* 106; *Took-Brandybuck* 105–6; *North-tooks of Long Cleeve* 108
Whitfoot 112, 115
Hobbiton 85, 89–92, 112–13, 116, 118, 241; ~ Hill 98; *the Hill* 98, 288
Hobbit(s) (Often used attributively, as *Hobbit legend*, ~ *year*) 3, 5–8, 10, 13–20, 24–5, 27–9, 37–61, 66–7, 69–74, 86, 94, 102, 119, 121–5, 127–33, 136–7, 168, 209, 211, 225, 229, 236, 245, 247, 253, 262, 268, 283, 288, 302, 309–11, 314, 326–7; true Westron words for 'Hobbit' 83; *wild Hobbits* 10, 121, 127; *western Hobbits* 37–8, 311; *Shire-Hobbits* 126. See *Halflings, Periannath*.
    Language of Hobbits 8, 10, 15, 17, 20, 27, 37–9, 43, 45, 48–55, 57–8, 67, 72–3, 311; the word *Hobbit* (etymology and 'translation') 10, 49–50, 53, 59–60, 69, 83
Hobbit, The (title) 3, 7, 10, 12, 15, 18, 25, 29, 53, 71–2, 76, 81–2, 249, 283, 286, 288, 319, 322–3
Holdwine Meriadoc's name in Rohan. 261, 273
Hollin 76, 79, 168, 174, 248. See *Eregion*.
Hornburg 296
Hornpipe Twist A variety of pipeweed. 6, 18; ~ *Cake* 18
Houses of Healing 68
hröa The body of an incarnate being. 391
Hundor Son of Haleth the Hunter. 325
Huor Father of Tuor. 348

Húrin (1)   Húrin of Dor-lómin. 144, 309, 327, 372, 374–5; *The Children of Húrin* 357–8; old form *Úrin* 374. *The Wanderings of Húrin* (title) 372
Húrin (2)   Steward to King Minardil. 202–3. (3) *Húrin I*. Fifth Ruling Steward. 204. (4) *Húrin II*. Fourteenth Ruling Steward. 205. (5) *Húrin of the Keys* (of Minas Tirith). 271
Hurinionath   Descendants of Húrin (2). 202–3, 218
Hyarmendakil I   Name taken by Kiryahir, fifteenth King of Gondor. 197–8, 210, 212–13, 260, 315; translated *South-slayer* 198, 213
Hyarmendakil II   Name taken by Vinyarion, twenty-fourth King of Gondor. 199, 214

Ice, The   See *Helkaraxë*.
Idril   Also ~ *Celebrindal*. 82, 346, 348, 363, 380, 387; *Itaril* 346, 363, *Itarillë* 346, 364, *Itarildë* 348, 364
Ilmarë   Daughter of King Ondohir (rejected name; see *Fíriel*). 210, 216
Ilúvatar   150, 157, 322, 396, 420; *Eru* ~ 270. See *Children of Ilúvatar*.
Imladris   Rivendell. 36, 44, 58, 79, 83, 168–9, 174, 176, 179–80, 184, 186, 192–3, 195–6, 207–8, 225, 228, 232, 235, 239, 241, 263–5, 267, 330; earlier *Imladrist* 36, 44, 168, 184, 209; Westron *Karningul* 68, 83 (earlier forms 44, 58, 68, 76, 83)
Imrahil   Twenty-second Prince of Dol Amroth. 32, 36, 221, 223, 244, 271
Imrazôr the Númenórean   Father of Galador first Lord of Dol Amroth. 220–3
Indilzar   Elros. 164
Indis   Second wife of Finwë. 77, 334–7, 343, 347, 359, 365
Ingold   Man of Minas Tirith. 360
Ingoldo   See *Finarfin, Fingolfin, Finrod* (2).
Ingwë   King of the Vanyar. 334, 340, 343, 356–7, 364–5; *Ingwë Ingweron* 340
Ingwer, Ingwi   Vanyar. 332, 340, 356. *Ingwi, Ingwelindar*, house and people of Ingwë, 356; *Ingar* 360
Inklings, The   19–20, 25, 140
Inland Sea   258, 294, 326, 373. See *Rhûn*.
Inner Lands   (of Middle-earth) 185. *Inner Seas* 149
Inziladûn   154, 159–60, 162. See *Tar-Palantir*.
Inzilbêth   Queen of Ar-Gimilzôr. 159–60, 162
Irenland   See *Éothéod*.
Íreth, Írith   See *Írissë*.
Írimë   Daughter of Finwë and Indis. 343, 359; other names *Írien* 343, 359; *Lalwen(dë)* 343, (*Glaðwen* 359)
Írissë   Daughter of Fingolfin. 345, 362–3; Sindarin *Íreth, Írith* 345, 362–3. See *Ar-Feiniel*.

INDEX 463

Ironfists One of the kindreds of the Dwarves. 301, 322
Iron Hills 233, 237, 239, 250, 276, 282, 286, 302, 305–6, 323–4
Isen, River 271, 273, 313, 436. *The Battles of the Fords of Isen* (title) 293
Isengard 7, 69, 191, 229, 233, 238, 241–2, 248, 251, 262, 267; *Angrenost* 191
Isfin Original name of Fingolfin's daughter Írissë, Íreth. 367
Ishmalog, valley of In the tale of Tal-elmar. 424; earlier *Rishmalog* 437
Isildur 32, 157, 163, 166–70, 172, 176–7, 186, 189, 191–2, 194–6, 198, 202, 208–9, 225–8, 230–3, 237–8, 247, 253, 257, 263–4, 266–7; *Isildur's Bane* 241
Isildurioni Heirs of Isildur. 192, 208
Istari 228–9, 247, 360, 384–5, 392. See *Ithryn Luin, Wizards.*
Italian 368
Itaril See *Idril.*
Ithilien 45, 200–1, 204–7, 215–16, 219, 233, 235, 238, 244, 250, 262, 315; *North* ~ 206, 218; *South* ~ 201, 206, 216–17, 238, 315; *Prince of* ~ 207, 223, 244
Ithryn Luin Blue Wizards. 385
Ivonwin See *Yavannildi.*
Ivorwen Mother of Gilrain. 263, 270; earlier *Evorwen* 263
Ivriniel Daughter of Adrahil of Dol Amroth. 221, 223

Jewels, War of the 163, 302–3, 306, 312; *the (Great) Jewels*, the Silmarils, 30, 78, 363

Kalimehtar (1) Younger brother of Rómendakil II. 199, 213. (2) Thirtieth King of Gondor. 200, 212, 215–16, 232
Kalimmakil Son of Narmakil II, father of Siriondil (2). 201, 216
Kalmakil Eighteenth King of Gondor. 198–9, 212–13, 259–60; *Calmacil* 259
Karma-kundo Title of Minalkar as Regent of Gondor. 260
Kastamir 'The Usurper', twenty-second King of Gondor. 199, 213–14, 231, 248
Kemendur Fourth King of Gondor. 197, 212
Kerin Amroth See *Cerin Amroth.*
Khand Land south-east of Mordor. 79
Khazâd The Dwarves. 24, 296, 302
Khazad-dûm 24, 44, 278, 286, 304, 321. See *Dwarrowdelf, Moria.*
Kheled-zâram Mirrormere. 275, 281, 286
Khuzdul, Khuzdûl The language of the Dwarves. 297, 300–1, 317, 319, 321–3, 358
Kibil-nâla Silverlode. 279, 286; (Mirrormere, see 275, 286). See *Zigil-nâd.*
Kili Companion of Thorin Oakenshield. 277, 285

King's Men (in Númenor) 151–3; *King's Folk* 151, 174–5
Kings of Men Númenóreans. 31, 55, 261, 263, 270
King's Reckoning 128, 131–3, 138; *Kings' Reckoning* 132
King under the Mountain 236, 239, 275–7, 286
Kin-strife (of Gondor) 190, 198–9, 213–14, 230, 254–5, 258–60, 262
Kirith Ungol 201
Kiryahir Fifteenth King of Gondor (see *Hyarmendakil I*). 198, 210, 212; *Ciryahir, Ciryaher* 210. See also *Kiryandil* (2).
Kiryandil (1) Eldest son of Isildur. 191, 208. (Replaced by *Elendur*(1).) (2) Fourteenth King of Gondor. 197, 212–13; former name *Kiryahir* 212. (3) Father of Eärnil II King of Gondor (rejected). 216
Kiryatan See *Tar-Kiryatan*.
Korollairë The Green Mound of the Two Trees. 356
Kurufinwë See *Curufin, Fëanor*.

Lake Town See *Esgaroth*.
Lammoth Region north of Drengist. 362; *Battle of the Lammoth* 345, 362
Langstrand Coastal fief of Minas Tirith. 422
Lanthir Lamath Waterfall in Ossiriand. 349, 372; cf. 369
Last Alliance (also the *Alliance*) 166, 169–70, 176, 192, 420
Last Battle (at the end of the First Age) 371, 375; ('at the end of Days') 374–5
Latin 46–7, 52, 69, 88, 102–3, 368
Laurelin 130, 334, 337
Lebennin 45, 199, 238
Legolas 36, 64, 79, 82, 220, 242, 244, 246, 286, 391
Lembas The 'waybread' of the Eldar; Quenya *coimas*. 395, 403–4
Lemberi Early name for the Sindar. 62; *Lemberin* (language) 30, 36, 41, 62, 65, 73
Lembi Earlier term for Lemberi. 30, 61–2, 76
Léod Father of Eorl the Young. 273–4. (Replaced *Garman*.)
Léof See *Brytta*.
Lesser Folk See *Bëor*.
Letters of J. R. R. Tolkien, The 7, 15, 18, 26, 69, 80, 158, 190, 321, 410; other letters 71–3, 88, 246
Lewis, W. H. 140
Lhammas The 'Account of Tongues'. 62, 356
Lhothland, Lhothlann Plain east of Dorthonion. 68
Limlight, River 259
Lindar (1) The Vanyar. 30, 62, 356; *Lindarin* (language) 30. (2) The Teleri. 332, 356
Lindon Lands west of the Blue Mountains. 36, 78, 168–9, 173–4, 179, 183, 193–5, 209, 230, 246, 328, 351, 382, 390

Lindórië   Sister of Eärendur (1), Lord of Andúnië. 159
Lithe, The; Lithedays   The three Summerdays in the Shire Calendar. 6, 15, 121-2, 124, 128-9, 131-2, 136. See *Overlithe.*
Little Folk   Hobbits. 311; *Little People* 9
Little Lune   Tributary of the River Lune. 313, 328
Lond Daer   Great Númenórean haven at mouth of the Greyflood. 329
Lonely Isle   See *Eressëa.*
Lonely Mountain   (also *the Mountain*) 35, 39, 73, 124, 131, 236, 275-6, 281-2; *the Great Hall* (within the Mountain) 281. See *Erebor.*
Longbeards   Durin's Folk. 295, 297, 301-5, 319, 321-4, 383. See *Andafangar, Anfangrim; Sigin-târag.*
Longbottom   Village in the South Farthing. 6, 18
Long Cleeve   Home of the North-tooks. 108
Long Lake   34
Long Winter   (Third Age 2758-9) 17, 205, 220, 236, 271
Lord of the Rings, The   (References specifically to the First and Second Editions) 11-12, 17, 24-6, 66, 98, 112, 117, 190, 210, 215, 247, 249, 255-6, 258-9, 261, 274, 317-18, 323, 420
Lords of the West   144, 152, 175-6, 181, 244, 396
Loremasters   55, 158, 203, 297, 305, 308, 314, 321, 332-3, 335, 337-40, 342, 349, 356, 358, 363, 365, 367, 397
Lórien   36, 65-6, 70, 73-4, 79, 82, 174, 206, 221-3, 226, 234-5, 239-40, 264-6, 273, 283, 320, 323, 329. See *Lothlórien.*
Losgar   Place of the burning of the ships by Fëanor. 355
Lossarnach   238
Lossoth   210, 258. See *Forochel.*
Lost Road, The   140, 156
Lothíriel   Daughter of Imrahil; wedded King Éomer. 221, 244, 271
Lothlórien   82, 244, 266. See *Lórien.*
Loudwater, River   38, 56, 67, 250. See *Bruinen.*
Lowdham, Arundel   Member of the Notion Club. 158
Lune   (River and Gulf) 312-15, 328; see *Little Lune. Círdan of Lune* 195, 232. *Mountains of Lune* 78; see *Ered Lindon.*
Lúthien   Also ~ *Tinúviel.* 211, 226, 234, 243, 265, 318, 348-9, 357, 363-4, 369; *Children of Lúthien* 364

Maedros   Son of Fëanor. 318, 344, 352, 355, 357, 366-7, 372; *Maedhros* 357; *Maidros* 224, 373; *Maedron* 372. Other names *Nelyafinwë* 352, (365)-6, *Nelyo* 352; *Maitimo* 353, 366; *Russandol* 353, 355, 366
Maeglin   377, 389
Maggot, Farmer   326
Maglor   Son of Fëanor. 318, 352, 358; *Maelor* 318. Other names *Kanafinwë, Káno,* 352; *Makalaurë* 353

Mahtan   Father of Nerdanel, Fëanor's wife. 366. See *Urundil*.
Maiar   378, 381, 384, (388); *Máyar* 363–4
Malbeth the Seer   Foreteller of the fate of Arvedui. 256
Malevarn   Rejected Elvish name of the Brandywine, changed by Hobbits to *Malvern*. 39, 67
Mallor   Third King of Arthedain. 193, 208
Malvegil   Sixth King of Arthedain. 193, 208–9
Mandos   356, 359, 370, 374–5, 378, 380–1; *Doom of Mandos* 338, 389–90
Mannish   29, 32, 34, 37–9, 41–2, 54, 61, 63–5, 67, 71, 73, 75, 141, 296, 300–1, 304, 321, 324, 330, 357, 368, 370, 384, 390
Manwë   142–4, 152, 157, 334–5, 343, 357–8, 361, 370, 374, 378–81, 390, 396; *Aran Einior, the Elder King* 357–8
Marach   Leader of the third host of the Edain. 325; *People of Marach* 372–4
Marcho   Hobbit, brother of Blanco. 6, 17, 87; earlier *Marco* (brother of *Cavallo*) 6, 9–10, 17, 86–7, 209, 225
Mardil   'The Good Steward', first Ruling Steward of Gondor. 132, 201–4, 217–19, 225, 233; ~ *Voronwë* 204, 219
Marish, The   10, 15, 56, 103, 232, 248
Mark (of Rohan), The   See *Rohan*.
Mar-nu-Falmar   'Land under the waves', Númenor. 157
Marrer, The   Morgoth. 359
mathom   8, 39, 53, 81
Mazarbul, Book of   22, 26, 293, 295, 298, 320; *Chamber of* ~ 299
Meduseld   236, 271. See *Golden Hall*.
Melian   185, 364–5, 371, 404 (see especially 364–5).
Melkor   358, 377, 385, 388, 390, 396, 413–14, 420; old form *Melko* 374–5. See *Belegûr*.
Menegroth   'The Thousand Caves' in Doriath. 371
Meneldil   Son of Anárion; third King of Gondor. 170, 177, 191–2, 197, 208, 212
Meneldur   See *Tar-Meneldur*.
Menelmakar   Orion. 375
Menelmindon   See *Meneltarma*.
Menelrond   'Heaven-dome', Hall of the Throne in Menegroth. 37, 376
Meneltarma   The Pillar of Heaven in Númenor. 145–6, 153, 158; earlier *Menelmin, Menelmindon*, &c. 146
Meriadoc (Merry)   See *Brandybuck*.
Michel Delving   15, 89–91
Middle-earth   12, 20–2, 25–33, 55, 61, 64–5, 71, 73–5, 78–9, 82, 119–20, 124, 144–6, 149, 151–4, 156–7, 159, 164, 168–73, 175–6, 178, 180–3, 187–8, 191–2, 227–8, 234, 236, 243–4, 254, 257, 263–5, 296, 304–6, 312–15, 321, 323–4, 327–9, 338–9, 341–2, 344, 346–8, 354, 356–7, 359, 361, 364, 366, 370, 377–9,

INDEX

381–3, 386–8, 390–2, 398, 401, 403–4, 422; Maps 187, 328, 373

Middle Elves 312, 329. *Middle Men* 312–14

Midyear('s) Day 121, 128–9, 131–5, 288; *Midyear Days* 128, 131; *Midyear* 135–6

Mîm The Petty-dwarf. 352

Minalkar Regent, and later the nineteenth King of Gondor (Rómendakil II). 259–60; *Minalcar* 259

Minardil Twenty-fifth King of Gondor. 199–200, 202–3, 214–15, 231

Minas Anor 163, 170, 176–7, 191–2, 199–201, 213, 215–18, 228, 231–3

Minas Ithil 176, 191, 195, 201, 215–17, 233, 240; *Stone of Ithil*, ~ *-stone* 206, 217, 240–1

Minas Morgul 195, 201, 203, 207, 215–18, 233–4; *Morgul* 204–5, 217–19, 241, *Lord of* ~ 233

Minastan Son of Minardil. 200

Minastir See *Tar-Minastir*.

Minas Tirith 74, 157, 181, 201–2, 204–5, 207, 215–17, 233, 236, 238, 240–3, 265, 267, 271, 274, 282, 332, 371, 421; *the City* 43, 411–12, 415. See *Mundburg*.

Mindolluin, Mount 148, 414

Minhiriath Lands between Brandywine and Greyflood. 294, 313–14, 329–30

Míriel (1) First wife of Finwë, mother of Fëanor. 332–6, 342, 356–7; named *Perindë* 333, 336, 342, *Serindë* 356. (2) See *Tar-Míriel*.

Mirkwood (including *the Forest*) 10, 34, 36, 65, 73–4, 82, 166, 193, 198, 208, 214, 219, 225, 229, 234, 239, 242, 244, 248, 272, 275, 280, 311, 316, 329. See *Greenwood*.

Mirrormere 275, 286. See *Kheled-zâram*.

Misty Mountains (including *the Mountains*) 4, 9, 34–6, 38, 56, 65–6, 72, 174, 176, 193, 196, 205, 219–20, 225–6, 229–30, 233, 235, 237, 239, 241, 248, 264, 272, 275–6, 278, 302, 305–6, 311, 323, 327, 329

Mithrandir 206, 228, 240, 243, 251, 265, 281–2, 287, 392. See *Gandalf*.

Mithrellas Companion of Nimrodel, mother of Galador. 220–2

mithril 184, 233, 244, 275, 318; *true-silver* 233, *Moria-silver* 318

Mogru Master of Agar (tale of Tal-elmar). (428), 429–34

Months Hobbit names 9, 16, 122, 125, 129, 136–8; Quenya names 134–6, 138; Noldorin (Sindarin) names 135–6, 138

Moon, The 119, 121, 123, 125, 127, 130, 137, 398. For 'Moon's day' see 123, 130, 137

Morannon 200, 215, 265. See *Black Gate*.

Mordor 83, 153, 168–9, 174, 176, 178–9, 182, 191, 196, 200–2,

204, 206, 215, 217, 226, 231–3, 240–3, 251–2, 256, 265–7, 283, 305, 315, 324, 384, 390
Morgoth 65, 142–4, 163, 166, 168, 173, 181–2, 185, 256, 275, 302–7, 312, 314, 323, 325, 327, 329, 336, 338, 342, 344, 357–9, 361–2, 366, 370–5, 404; *the Black Enemy* 358. See *Melkor*.
Morgul See *Minas Morgul*.
Moria 24, 45, 58, 76, 78–9, 173–4, 179, 184–5, 221, 223, 227, 233, 235, 237, 240, 246, 249–50, 261, 275–9, 281, 286, 293, 297, 300, 302, 304–5, 318–21; *Gates of Moria* 79, 179, 237, 278, 319; *Lord(s) of* ~ 300, 319. See *Dwarrowdelf, Khazad-dûm; mithril*.
Morinehtar One of the Blue Wizards. 384
Mormakil Túrin Turambar. 374
Morthond, River 313, 436
Morwen (1) Wife of Húrin of Dor-lómin. 374; old name *Mavwin* 374. (2) Sister of Orodreth Steward of Gondor. 205, 219–20. (3) Daughter of Húrin of the Keys. 271
Mountain of Fire 174, 178. See *Orodruin*.
Mountains of Lune See *Lune*.
Mount Doom 176, 206, 240, 242, 267. See *Amon Amarth*.
múmak Great elephant of the Harad. 79
Mundburg, Mundberg Minas Tirith. 274
Music of the Ainur 365, (413, 415), 420

Náin (1) *Náin I*. Slain by the Balrog of Moria. 252, 275, 277, 288. (2) *Náin II*. Grandfather of Thrór. 276, 284, 288. (3) *Náin* father of Dáin Ironfoot. 277
Nandor 76, 364; *Nandorin* (language) 368. See *Danians, Green-elves*.
Nanduhirion, Battle of 237, 281. See *Azanulbizar, Dimrill Dale*.
Nan Elmoth Forest in Beleriand. 328, 330
Nár (1) Brother of Dáin I. 276–7, 279. (Replaced by *Borin*.) (2) Companion of Thrór to Moria. 276, (278)
Nargothrond 185, 317, 349–52, 358, 421
Narmakil I Seventeenth King of Gondor. 198, 212–13, 259–60
Narmakil II Twenty-ninth King of Gondor. 200–1, 215–16
Narog, River 350
Narsil The sword of Elendil. 195, 227, 239. See *Elendil*.
Narya The Ring of Fire. 392
Naugrim The Dwarves. 27, 174, 295. Earlier name *Nauglir* 23, 26
Návatar A name of Aulë. 391
Nazgûl 178, 217. See *Úlairi*.
Near Harad See *Harad*.
Nen Hithoel Lake in Anduin. 259
Nenuial Lake in Arnor. 192. See *Evendim*.
Nerdanel Wife of Fëanor. 353–5, 365–6, 368

Nerwen(dë) See *Galadriel.*
Nether Darkness 149
New Era (of Calendar) 132–6, 202, 243
New Year 121, 128–9, 133, 139; *New Year's Day* 121, 127, 129, *Yearsday* 121, 129
Nibinnogs Petty-dwarves. 352
Nienóri Old form of Niënor, sister of Túrin Turambar. 374
nifredil White flower of Lórien. 266
Nimloth Name of the White Tree (1) of Eressëa 147–8; (2) of Númenor 147–8
Nimrodel Elf of Lórien, beloved of Amroth. 36, 65, 82, 221–3, 294
Nimruzîr Elendil the Tall. 164
Nimruzîrim Elf-friends. 151, 164
Nine Rings See *Rings of Power.*
Nine Walkers 242. See *Company of the Ring.*
Nivrost Earlier form of Nevrast, region of Beleriand. 389
Nogrod Dwarf-city in Ered Lindon. 185, 275, 322
Noldor (and singular *Noldo*) 23, 30–1, 33, 36, 62–3, 65, 73–9, 143, 145–7, 163, 173–4, 185, 203, 293, 305, 312, 318, 324–5, 331–4, 336–45, 348, 350, 356, 358–62, 366, 370, 374, 378–80, 383, 386–90, 392, 401–2; *Flight of the Noldor* 361. See *Exiles, Gnomes.*
Noldorin (of language; in almost all cases = later Sindarin) 20, 22, 26, 30–4, 36, 39–41, 45, 52–5, 61–3, 65, 68–9, 74–5, 125, 130, 133, 135–6, 138, 146, 189, 193, 203, 217, 219, 228, 234, 371, 400, 404–5; Noldorin Quenya 331, 368, 400; (with other reference) 36, 40, 76–7, 79, 310, 317, 328, 331, 333, 339, 368, 379, 389, 401. See *Gnomish.*
Nolofinwë See *Fingolfin.*
Norbury 5, 7, 39, 47, 103; *Northburg, Northbury* 5; *Northworthy* 5, 7, 15, 225, 247. See *Fornost.*
Nori Companion of Thorin Oakenshield. 279
Norse 27, 41, 54, 60, 70–1, 81, 278, 300, 322, 324
North, The (References to Men of the North) 21, 30, 39, 64, 71, 303–5, 323–4, 328
Northburg, Northbury See *Norbury*
North Downs 313
Northern (of language) 21–2, 34–5, 49, 53–4, 60, 260, 296
Northern Line The Heirs of Isildur. 32, 64, 188–90, 192, 207–8, 216, 254–5, 257, 279
North Kingdom (Arnor and Arthedain) 38, 40, 121, 125, 127–9, 171–2, 176, 186, 193, 195, 201, 208, 210, 227–8, 230–2, 254, 258, 268–9, 327, 330
Northmen 198–9, 205, 214, 230, 258–60
Northope Village north of Hobbiton. 98. (Replaced by *Overhill.*)
Northworthy See *Norbury.*

470 THE PEOPLES OF MIDDLE-EARTH

Notion Club Papers 140, 146, 158, 372
Nōwë See *Círdan*.
Númendil Seventeenth Lord of Andúnië. 159, 161–2, 165
Númenor (including references to the Downfall or Drowning of Númenor, not as title of work) 31–3, 55, 63–5, 71, 74–5, 123, 128, 130, 140–1, 144–55, 157–8, 160–1, 163, 166–78, 180–3, 185, 187–8, 191, 193, 202–3, 208, 234, 239, 244, 246, 249, 256–7, 263, 306, 312–15, 317, 329–30, 348, 357, 359–60, 364, 368–71, 381–2, 422, 436. *A Description of Númenor* (title) 141, 144, 351. See *Westernesse*.
Númenórean (language; see *Adûnaic*) 31–2, 64–5, 75, 145, 151–2, 158, 163, 174, 327, 371, 436; (with other reference) 34, 36, 65, 74, 124, 131–2, 141, 151, 153, 156, 169, 172, 179–80, 186, 188, 191, 199, 203–4, 206, 211, 214, 218, 234, 293–4, 296–7, 310, 312–17, 329, 332, 379, 382, 435
Númenórean(s) 31, 33, 55, 63–4, 74–5, 138, 146–7, 149–50, 152–6, 160, 164, 167–70, 173–5, 178–82, 184, 186, 194, 196, 198, 206, 209, 220–3, 225, 227, 230, 267, 304, 312–14, 323–4, 327–30, 382, 420, 422, 436
Númenos Early name of Armenelos. 145, 147

Ohtar Esquire of Isildur. 227
Oiolossë Mount Everwhite. 334, 396
Óin (1) Father of Náin II. 276, 284. (2) Companion of Thorin Oakenshield. 240, 276–7, 279
Old English See *English*.
Old Forest 235; *the Forest* 194.
Old Forest Road (in Mirkwood) 323. See *Great Dwarf Road*.
Old Home See *Bree*.
Old World 30; *ancient world* 55, 257
Old Year 121, 128–9; *Old Year's Day* 121, 127, 129, *Yearsend* 121, 129, 133–4, 136
Olog-hai Race of Trolls. 79; earlier forms *Horg-hai* 79, *Olg-hai* 79–80
Olórin Gandalf's name in Valinor. 377–8, 381
Olwë Brother of Elwë; Lord of Alqualondë. 76, 337, 340–1, 357–8, 364–5, 385–7, 392; *Ciriáran* (mariner king) 341
Ondohir Thirty-first King of Gondor. 195, 200–4, 210, 212, 215–16, 218, 232, 245, 254, 256; *Ondonir* 195, 200–2, 210, 216; final form *Ondoher* 210
Ondolindë See *Gondolin*. *Ondor* See *Gondor*.
One, The 182, 370, 380, 389, 413. See *Eru*.
Orc(s) (including many compounds, as *Orc-chief, -holds*) 9, 21, 24, 35–6, 42, 65, 70, 75, 80, 83, 177, 192–3, 196, 204–6, 211, 219–20, 223, 225–7, 230, 235–9, 242–3, 249–50, 264, 271–3, 276–8, 280, 323, 326, 410, 412–15, 420; *Orks* 301–5, 309, 319,

326, 345, 347, 358, 362; *ork-plants* (fungi) 327; *Orkish* 35, 414
Ori   Companion of Thorin Oakenshield. 240, 279
Orion   375. See *Menelmakar*.
Ornendil   Son of Eldakar King of Gondor. 199, 214
Orodreth   (1) Originally brother of Felagund and second King of Nargothrond. Later names and genealogical history 349–51; finally son of Angrod and father of Gil-galad, see *Arothir*. (2) Sixteenth Ruling Steward. 205, 219
Orodruin   168, 174, 176, 179, 240, 242, 390. See *Mountain of Fire*.
Oromë   341, 357–8, 366, 403; his horn 358. See *Araw, Tauron*.
Oromet   The hill of Tar Minastir's tower, near Andúnië. 164
Orthanc   176, 191, 205–6, 229, 233, 240–1, 248, 384
Osgiliath   169, 179, 191–2, 197, 199–200, 203–4, 207, 215, 217–19, 231, 235, 238
Ossë   387
Ossiriand   76, 307, 349, 365, 367–8, 373
Ostohir   (1) Seventh King of Gondor. 197, 210, 213, 228; *Ostonir* 197, 210, 213; final form *Ostoher* 210. (2) *Ostohir II* (rejected), see 212, 215
Othrondir   Man of Gondor. 417, 421; earlier *Othrondor* 421
Overhill   Village north of Hobbiton. 98, 113–15. (Replaced *Northope*.)
Overlithe   121, 124, 129, 130–1; *Leapday* 124, 130

Palantir, Palantíri   176, 186, 191, 193–5, 199–201, 206, 208–10, 217, 230, 232–3, 240, 245. See *Gwahaedir, Seven Stones*.
Pallando   One of the Blue Wizards. 385
Paracelsus   Physician and visionary theorist of the sixteenth century. 23, 76
Parth Celebrant   See *Celebrant*.
Paths of the Dead   265, 267, 270
Pelargir   City and port on Anduin. 32, 65, 74–5, 79, 152–3, 175, 183, 197, 199–200, 206, 215, 231, 312–13, 315, 416, 421
Pelendur   Steward to King Ondohir. 203–4, 215–18, 232, 248, 256
Pelennor Fields   360; *Battle of the* ~ 242, 265, 267
Pen-arduin   The dwelling of Borlas in the Emyn Arnen. 411
Pengoloð (the Wise)   143, 152–3, 392, 395–6, 403, 405; *Quendingoldo* 401, *Quengoldo* 404–5
Peredhil, Pereðil   348, 364, 369; *i·Pheredhil* 256. See *Pereldar, Half-elven*.
Peregrin (Pippin)   See *Took*.
Pereldar   348, 364. The Half-elven (see *Peredhil*); old sense, the Nandor, 364
Periannath   193–4, 196, 229–32, 236, 247–8. See *Haflings, Hobbits*.
Petty-dwarves   352. See *Nibinnogs; Mîm*.
Pharazôn   See *Ar-Pharazôn*.

Pictures by J. R. R. Tolkien 26, 320
Pipeweed 6–7, 16–17, 69; *tobacco* 6, 16; *sweet galenas* 6
Plague, The (Great) 17, 194, 200, 203, 209, 231, 254–5, 327
Poros, River 198
Powers, The The Valar. 29–30, 130, 149, 183; *the Great* 149, *the Rulers* 30, 123; *the evil Power* 36, 83, *the Dark Power* 78
Prancing Pony, The 70; *the Pony* 52, 60
Prophecy of the North 388
Púkel-men 309

Quendi Elves. 29, 31, 77, 295, 395–6, 399–401. *Quendi and Eldar* (title) 325, 328, 356, 367, 392
Quendingoldo, Quengoldo See *Pengoloð*.
Quenta Silmarillion 27, 61–2, 76, 142–3, 147–8, 190, 285, 295, 325–6, 349, 351, 355–6, 361, 372–3, 375, 389; *Quenta Noldorion* 30, 62
Quenta, The *(Quenta Noldorinwa)* 27, 374–5
Quenya 30–2, 36–7, 41, 52, 55, 62, 69, 78, 126, 129–30, 133, 135, 138, 154, 164, 193, 210, 217, 219, 234, 299, 315, 318–21, 324, 331–2, 335, 339–49, 352–4, 356–61, 363, 365–8, 370–1, 374, 376, 392, 404; *Quenyarin* 379; verb *'Quenyarize'* 347, 370

Radagast 384
Rangers 195, 225
Rateliff, John 140
Rauros 206, 242
Realms in Exile 188–91, 225, 245, 254, 256, 263, 268, 279, 315
Red Book of Westmarch 12, 25; *the Red Book* 12, 25, 29, 35, 41, 47–8, 52, 61, 123–4, 126, 130–1, 217, 243–4, 253, 255, 262, 282, 327; *Great ~ of Samwise* 19
Redhorn Mountain 275; *Redhorn Pass* 229, 248, 250. See *Caradras*.
Redwater, River 316. See *Carnen*.
Rhovan(n)ion 198, 213–14, 259, 262, 280, 302, 312–13, 437; *Róvannion* 214. See *Wilderland*.
Rhudaur One of the divisions of earlier Arnor. 193–4, 208–9, 228, 230
Rhûn, Sea of 204, 294, 306, 316, 373, 387, 391–2, 437; *fields of Rhûn* 219; *Sea of Rhúnaer* 198, 229 (*Rúnaer* 198)
Rían Sister of Dior Steward of Gondor. 204, 219, 249.
Rider Haggard 320
Riders of Rohan 34, 52, 71, 272–3. See *Rohirrim*.
Ring, The (including references to the *Great Ring, One Ring, Ruling Ring*) 3–5, 7, 11, 13, 15, 19, 25, 29, 33, 124, 131, 153, 166–70, 172–4, 177–80, 186, 225, 233, 237–43, 247–8, 251, 264–7, 282–3, 310, 320, 338, 382. See *Company, War of the Ring*.
Ringbearer(s) 242–3, 246, 265, 267, 378

Ringló, River 313
Rings of Power 79, 168, 172, 174, 177–9, 235, 237, 251–2; *Elven-rings* 13. The Three Rings of the Elves 33, 179–80, 227, 243, 265. The Seven Rings of the Dwarves 237, 250, 252, 276, 280, 283; *the Ring-wearer* 286; the Ring of Thrór and Thráin 250, 252, 276, 280–1, 283–4. The Nine Rings of Men 175–230.
Ringwraiths 153, 175, 177, 193, 200–2, 207, 215–16, 230, 233–4, 240–1, 245, 252, 265; *Chief, Lord of the Ringwraiths* 195, 201, 217, 230, 233, 242, 245. See *Nazgûl, Úlairi; Black Captain, Witch-king*.
Rivendell 36, 44, 76, 79, 168, 174, 177, 225, 239–42, 246, 253, 255, 269–70, 273, 283, 339, 377–80. See *Imladris*.
Road Goes Ever On, The 299
Rodnor See *Gil-galad*.
Rohan 10, 21, 34, 38–9, 41, 49–50, 52–4, 58–60, 65, 68–71, 81, 83, 122, 157, 205–7, 219–21, 236–40, 242, 244, 255, 261, 267, 271–4, 296, 301, 314–16, 319, 329; *Rochann* 53, 236, *Rohann* 60; *Gap of* ~ 271, 273, *Wold of* ~ 205, 271; and see *Riders of Rohan*.
   Mark of Rohan, the Mark 49, 52–3, 76, 81, 261, 270, 272, 274, 316
Rohirrim 34, 38, 41, 49, 52–3, 60, 65, 71, 75, 82, 236, 238–9, 242, 245, 271–2, 296, 312, 328; earlier name *Rohiroth* 71; *Horse-lords* 272. See *Riders of Rohan, Eorlings*.
Rómendakil I Name taken by Tarostar, eighth King of Gondor. 197, 213, 228; translated *East-slayer* 197, 213, 228, *East-victor* 213
Rómendakil II Name taken by Minalkar, Regent and later the nineteenth King of Gondor. 198, 213–14, 258–60, 315
Rómenna Great haven in the east of Númenor. 151–2, 160, 162
Rómestámo One of the Blue Wizards. 385; *Róme(n)star* 391
Rothinzil Adûnaic name of Vingilot. 143, 163, 365, 369–71
Rúmil The sage of Tirion. 360; *alphabet of Rúmil* 22
Runes 22, 72, 75–6, 81, 297–300, 319–20, 324; *moon-runes* 319; *dwarf-letters* 297. Runic 297–8, 319. See *Angerthas, Cirth*.
Running, River 259, 316, 330. See *Celduin*.

Sador Old servant of Húrin of Dor-lómin. 327; *Sadog* 309, 327
Saelon (1) Young man of Gondor. 409–18, 421; earlier names *Almoth, Egalmoth* 409, 419, *Arthael* 409–10, 418, 420. (2) See *Andreth*.
Sam(wise) See *Gamgee*.
Sangahyanda Corsair of Umbar. 199, 215, 231, 248; later *Sangahyando* 215
Sarmo Father of Nerdanel. 366. See *Urundil*.
Saruman 83, 205–6, 227–8, 233, 235, 237–42, 248–9, 251, 262, 267, 274, 283–4, 384–5. See *Curunír*.

474   THE PEOPLES OF MIDDLE-EARTH

Sauron   31–3, 65, 74, 79, 129, 133, 150–4, 158, 163, 166–84, 191–3, 196, 200–2, 206, 208, 211, 215, 219, 225–9, 234–5, 237–40, 242–3, 249–52, 257, 264–7, 280, 283–4, 287, 301, 304–5, 310–11, 317–18, 324, 328, 330, 378, 382, 385, 390, 410, 418, 436, 438; *Eye of* ~ 266, *Messenger of* ~ 68; called *the King* in the tale of Tal-elmar 434, 436, 438. See *(The) Sorcerer*.
Scandinavian   53–4, 61
Scary   Village in the East Farthing. 117
Sea, The   21, 30–3, 62, 64, 73–4, 78–9, 153, 156–8, 163, 173–4, 176, 178–9, 183, 191, 235–6, 238, 244, 251, 265–7, 313, 329, 363, 379, 387, 423–4, 426–7, 430, 433–4; *the Great Sea* 61, 145, 306, 363, 370, 373, 379, 385–6; Elvish names 363. For 'Sea's day' see 123, 125, 130, 138
Sea-kings   Kings of Númenor. 153, 155; *King of the Sea* 156
Seasons   (of the Calendars) *Spring* 121, 127, 133–5; *Spring-days* 133–5. *Summer* 133–7; *Summer-day(s)* 121–2, 124, 128, 131–2, 136, and see *Lithe*. *Harvest* 121, 123–4, 127, 131–3, 137; *Autumn* 133–5. *Winter* 123, 129, 133–7. *Stirring* 133–5; *Stirring-days* 133–4. For Elvish names see 134–5.
Second Age   74, 78, 140, 150, 166–73, 177–8, 184–6, 188, 192, 208, 225–6, 246, 256, 262, 293–4, 297, 301, 303–5, 312–15, 317–18, 323, 328, 378, 381–5, 391
Seven Fathers (of the Dwarves), the Fathers   322–3, 382–3, *Seven Ancestors* 301, 322; *Seven Kindreds* 302 (for names of the kindreds see 301).
Seven Rings   See *Rings of Power*.
Seven Stones   The *Palantíri*. 176, 191; *Seeing Stones* 400–1; other references to *the Stone(s)* 176, 195, 206, 209–10, 217, 232, 240–1, 245
Shadow, The   (in various applications) 68, 143, 145, 150, 152, 154, 174, 177, 180, 193, 228–9, 234–5, 240, 248, 262, 264–5, 267, 269–70, 303, 306, 311, 314, 323, 333, 338, 382, 413; *Men of the Shadow* 330; *unshadowed Men* 314
Shadowfax   53, 157
Shelob   251
Ship-kings   (of Gondor) 198
Shire, The   (Often used attributively, as *Shire word*) 5–6, 8–10, 12, 15–17, 20, 36–7, 40, 42–3, 45–56, 58–60, 69–70, 83, 87, 112, 118–19, 121–31, 136, 138, 168, 209, 220, 225–6, 231–2, 235–6, 238–9, 241, 243, 248, 251, 255, 268, 281–3, 287, 289, 311, 327; true name of the Shire *Sûza* 45, 58; Maps 11, 18, 93, 98, 117
Shire-reckoning   6, 9, 85–6, 106, 119, 121, 125, 128–9, 131, 133–4, 138, 225, 231, 247–8, 270. *Shire-reform* (of the Calendar) 121–2, 129, 133
Shire-records, Note on the   14, 261

Shirking Original name of the Thain of the Shire. 5–7, 11, 87, 107–8, 111, 248–9; *Shire-king* 6, 107, 248–9
Shirriffs 6, 9, 14; *Shirriff* < *Shire-reeve* 6
Sigin-tarâg 321. See *Longbeards*.
Silmarien Ancestress of the Lords of Andúnië. 154–5, 257
Silmarillion, The (1) Author's references. 14, 190, 295, 309, 335, 343, 346, 357, 379–81, 383, 388–90; origin of the work 357. (2) The published work. 82, 140, 142–3, 153, 183, 294, 318, 331, 349, 351–2, 358, 364, 366, 372, 390, 404, 420. See *Quenta Silmarillion*.
Silmaril(s) 256, 337, 348, 357, 369; *Silmarillë* 363, *Silmarilli* 30. See *Jewels*.
Silpion 130. See *Eldest Tree*.
Silvan Elves 223, 329; *Silvan* 66, 221; *woodland race*, ~ *tongue* 79
Silverlode, River 279, 286. See *Celebrant*; *Kibil-nâla*, *Zigil-nâd*.
Silvertine 279. See *Zirak-zigil*.
Sindar (and singular *Sinda*) 62, 78, 223, 297, 312, 318–19, 328–9, 345–6, 358, 360, 379, 385–6, 389, 392, 401, 404; *Northern Sindar* 372. See *Grey-elves*.
Sindarin (of language) 61–2, 65–6, 78–9, 125, 136, 138, 143, 146, 189, 210, 260, 305–6, 308, 315–16, 318–21, 324, 329–32, 337, 340–50, 352, 358–72, 374, 376, 379, 385, 392, 395, 400–1, 404–5; *North Sindarin* 342, 344, 369–70, 372; verb '*Sindarize*' 318, 343, 345–6, 360, 366, 368. See *Grey-elven*, *Lemberin*, *Noldorin*.
    (with other reference) 79, 298, 328, 348, 350, 379, 381, 388
Sindikollo, Sindicollo Elwë (Thingol). 357; *Þindikollo* 337, 357; *Greycloak* 78, 392
Sirion, River 396; *Mouth(s) of Sirion* 350, 369, 381, 387–8
Siriondil (1) Eleventh King of Gondor. 197. (2) Father of Eärnil II, King of Gondor. 201, 216
Sketch of the Mythology 374–5
Smaug (including references to *the Dragon*) 35, 39, 54, 57, 72, 237, 239, 276–7, 281–3
Sméagol 38–9, 53, 57, 81, 166, 225, 233, 239, 251. See *Gollum*.
Smial(s) 11, 14, 39, 53, 58, 81, 111; *Great Smials* 106, 108, 235
Snowmen of Forochel See *Forochel*.
Sons of Fëanor 294, 317, 331, 336, 339, 345, 352–5, 357–8, 360, 366–9, 372
Sons of the Valar 163, 172, 375. See *Children of the Valar*.
Sorcerer, The Sauron. 193, 234–5, 237, 239, 252, 276–7.
Sorcerer-king, The 209–10, 215–17. See *Witch-king*.
South, The 149, 152–3, 194, 229, 240, 242, 328; *Men of the South* 187, 302
Southern Line The Heirs of Anárion. 188, 190, 196, 210–11, 217–18, 222, 255

Southern Star A variety of pipeweed. 6
South Kingdom Gondor. 170, 177, 230–2, 330; *the Kingdom* 311, 316
Sóval Phárë See *Common Speech*.
Starkhorn Mountain above Dunharrow. 53
Stars, The 123, 127, 130. For 'Stars' day' see 123–4, 130. *The Star (of Eärendil)* 144
Stewards of Gondor 43, 128, 132, 188, 202–7, 217–18, 220, 222, 225–6, 234, 245. *Roll of, House of, the Stewards* (records) 191, 253, and see *Book of the Kings; Tomb of the* ~ 207
Steward's Reckoning 128, 132–4, 138; *Stewards'* ~ 132
Stiffbeards One of the kindreds of the Dwarves. 301, 322
Sting 11
Stock Village of the Marish. 98
Stonefoots One of the kindreds of the Dwarves. 301, 322
Stones, The See *Seven Stones*.
Stoors 10–11, 15, 37–8, 54, 56–7, 66–7, 81, 227, 229–31, 233, 248, 250, 311, 328; *Stoorish* 56–7; the name *Stoor* 39, 53
Strider 189
Summer-days See *Seasons*.
Sun, The 123, 127, 130, 374, 401–2, 423; sun-rounds *(coranári)*, years, 120, 126–8, 131. For 'Sun's day' see 123, 130, 137

Tal-elmar 422–4, 426–38
Taniquetil 157
Tar-Aldarion, Aldarion Sixth Ruler of Númenor, 'the Mariner'. 155, 329
Tar-Ankalimë Daughter of Tar-Aldarion and Erendis; seventh Ruler of Númenor. 155
Tar-Ankalimon (-Ancalimon) Fourteenth Ruler of Númenor, son of Atanamir. 150–2, 186.
Tarannon Twelfth King of Gondor (see *Falastur*). 197, 213
Tar-Atanamir, Atanamir Seventh and later thirteenth Ruler of Númenor. 149–53, 164, 170–1, 177, 180, 184, 186
Tar-Elendil Fourth Ruler of Númenor. 154–5, 257
Tar Kalimos Earlier name of Armenelos. 145–6
Tar-Kalion (-Calion) Quenya name of Ar-Pharazôn. 151, 153, 155, 164, 169–72, 175
Tarkil Sixth King of Arnor. 192
Tarkilion Rejected name of Annúminas. 167. See *Dunhirion*.
Tarkiryan Brother of Tarannon (Falastur), King of Gondor. 197, 213
Tar-Kiryatan (-Ciryatan) Eighth and later twelfth Ruler of Númenor, 'the Shipbuilder'; also *Kiryatan, Ar-* ~. 150–2, 171, 180. See *Ar-Balkumagān*.
Tar-Meneldur, Meneldur Fifth Ruler of Númenor, father of Aldarion. 155, 351

INDEX 477

Tar-Minastir Eleventh Ruler of Númenor. 153; *King Minastir* 164
Tar-Minyatur Elros. 257, 348 ('high first-ruler').
Tar-Míriel, Míriel Daughter of Tar-Palantir, queen of Ar-Pharazôn. 154–5, 157, 159–61, 165, 181. See *Ar-Zimraphel*.
Tarondor (1) Seventh King of Arnor. 192. (2) Twenty-seventh King of Gondor. 198, 200, 215, 231
Tarostar Eighth King of Gondor (see *Rómendakil I*). 197, 228
Tar-Palantir Twenty-fourth Ruler of Númenor; Adûnaic *Inziladûn*. 154, 159–62, 164, 181
Tauron Oromë; *(Aran) Tauron* 'the (king) forester'. 358
Teiglin, Taiglin, River 326
Teleporno See *Celeborn* (2).
Telemnar Twenty-sixth King of Gondor. 200, 203, 215, 231, 254
Teleri (and singular *Teler*) 30, 73, 76, 82, 305, 318–19, 324, 329, 332, 337–8, 340–1, 344, 347, 354, 357–8, 385–7, 391, 401; Sindarin *Telir, Telerrim* 385
Telerian (of language) 30, 36, 65, 73–4, 392; (with other reference) 174, 366
Telerin (of language) 318, 340–1, 345–7, 356–7, 359–63, 365, 368; (with other reference) 337, 364, 385
Telperion 147–8, 337, 404. See *Eldest Tree*.
Telumehtar Twenty-eighth King of Gondor (see *Umbardakil*). 200, 215.
Thain (of the Shire) 6, 11, 14–15, 107–8, 116, 118, 232, 235–7, 250, 268–9; *Shire-thain* 232; earlier *Elder* 11, *Thane* 11, 14, 87. See *Shirking*.
Thangorodrim 143, 163, 172, 233, 380
Tharbad 11, 38, 66, 330 (great bridge of Tharbad).
Thengel Sixteenth King of Rohan. 239, 270, 272, 296, 316
Théoden Seventeenth King of Rohan. 7, 21, 26, (49), 53, 59–60, 69, 81, 83, 239–40, 242, 244, 270–4, 296, 316; called *Edniwe, Ednew* 'Renewed' 274
Théodred Son of Théoden. 242, 274
Théodwyn Sister of Théoden. 240, 271
Thingol 76, 78, 301, 328, 360, 365, 369, 372, 387; *Elu* ~ 337, 348, 357, *Elu* 369, 372. See *Elwë, Sindikollo*.
Third Age 12, 25–7, 29, 33, 37, 65–6, 73, 75, 79, 140, 166–71, 173, 177–8, 192, 195–6, 201–2, 208, 211, 223, 225–7, 233–4, 236, 243, 246–7, 265, 275, 285, 293, 296–8, 301, 304, 311, 314–15, 320–1, 323–4, 327–9, 332, 360, 378, 380–1, 383, 385, 392, 419
Thorin I Son of Thráin I. 275–7
Thorin II (Oakenshield) 35, (53, 81), 237–9, 249–50, 276–7, 279–89
Thorin III (Stonehelm) 277–9
Thorondir Twenty-second Ruling Steward. 206

Thorongil Name taken by Aragorn II in Gondor. 258
Thráin I Son of Náin I. 252, 275–7, 286, 288
Thráin II Son of Thrór. 237–8, 249–50, 252, 276–81, 283–4, 286–8
Thranduil King of the Elves of Mirkwood. 36, 79, 82, 174, 239, 242, 244, 329
Three Houses (of Men, of the Fathers of Men, of the Edain) 31–2, 55, 62–4, 146; *Three Peoples* 324
Three Kindreds (of the Elves) 23, 77
Three Rings See *Rings of Power*.
Thrór 236–8, 249–50, 252, 275–8, 280–1, 284–6; Thrór's Map 284, 286
Tighfield Village of the Shire. 112, 114–16
Tirion 147, 361. See *Túna*.
Tol Eressëa See *Eressëa*.
Tolfalas Island in the Bay of Belfalas. 183, 187
Tookland 115
Took, Peregrin (Pippin) 11, 15, 43, 51, 59, 69, 83, 85, 87, 90–2, 107–8, 110–11, 115–16, 118, 157, 255, 261, 268–9, 421; true Hobbit name 51, 59
Tower Hills 17, 112, 176, 186, 313–14; *the Towers* 112, *Elf-towers* 17. See *Emyn Beraid*.
Treebeard 36–7, 55
Trolls 35–6, 75, 79–80, 82, 196, 235, 238, 263; *Stone-trolls* 80. See *Olog-hai*.
Trollshaws 208
Tuckborough Chief place of the Tookland. 11, 110–11. *Great Writ of ~* 40, 123, 137, *Yearbook of ~* 67, 137; see *Yellowskin*.
Tulkas 375
Túna 147–9, 352. See *Tirion*.
Tuor 348, 364, 380, 387, 390
Turambar Ninth King of Gondor. 197, 228. See also *Túrin (Turambar)*.
Turgon (1) King of Gondolin. 317, 344–5, 348, 352, 361–3, 370, 374–5, 379–81, 388–90; *Turukáno* 345, 362, 370, 379
Turgon (2) Twenty-fourth Ruling Steward. 206, 220, 248
Túrin (1) *Turambar* 309, 372, 374–5, 404; *Tale of Turambar* 374
Túrin (2) *Túrin I*. Sixth Ruling Steward. 204, 219. (3) *Túrin II*. Twenty-third Ruling Steward. 206, 220, 238, 250
Turukáno See *Turgon (1)*.
Two Trees 123, 130, 147, 337, 356, 375. See *Eldest Tree*; and for 'Tree day', 'Tree's day' see 123, 125, 130.
Tyrn Goerthaid The Barrow-downs. 194

Udul Village in the tale of Tal-elmar. 433–4, 438
Uglúk 83

Úlairi Ringwraiths. 153, 175, 177–8, 193, 200–1, 208, 215–17, 233–4, 241; *Chief, Lord of the Úlairi* 193, 217

Ulmo 348, 364, 387, 390

Umbar 151, 153, 155–6, 175, 178, 182–3, 186, 197–200, 205, 213–14, 218, 220, 222, 231, 236, 242, 262. See *Corsairs of Umbar.*

Umbardakil Name taken by Telumehtar, twenty-eighth King of Gondor. 200

Umbarto See *Amrod.*

Undúna See *Common Speech.*

Undying Lands 147

Unfinished Tales 141, 144, 151, 154–5, 159, 163–5, 184, 186, 208, 210, 222–3, 282, 287–8, 293–5, 309, 314, 317, 319, 321, 326–31, 349, 351, 356–7, 364, 372, 384–5, 390

Unwin, Sir Stanley 7, 15, 18; *Unwin, Rayner* 80, 190, 246

Urundil Father of Nerdanel, Fëanor's wife. 366. Other names *Sarmo, Mahtan* 366; unnamed 353–4, 368

Urwendi The Sun-maiden. 374

Vairë 'The Weaver', wife of Mandos. 359

Valakar Twentieth King of Gondor. 198–9, 213–14, 230–1, 260–1; *Valacar* 259

Valandil (1) First Lord of Andúnië. 160, 164. (2) Earlier name of Amandil, father of Elendil. 156, 163, 175, 186, 189, 191. (3) Youngest son of Isildur; third King of Arnor. 186, 191–2, 207–8, 227–8

Valandur Eighth King of Arnor. 193

Valaquenta (title) 143, 390

Valar (and singular *Vala*) 123, 130, 143, 145, 150, 152, 154, 158–9, 174–5, 180–1, 305, 312, 321, 323, 333–8, 343, 348, 354, 357–8, 360–1, 363–6, 368, 370–1, 374, 378–81, 383–6, 388, 390–1, 396, 400–1, 403–4; *People of the Valar* (Maiar) 364. *Ban of the Valar* (on the Númenóreans) 149, 175, (on the Exiled Noldor) 370, 376, 380, 390. See *Children, Sons of the Valar; Guardians, Powers.*

Valarin (language) 356–7, 363

Valinor 30–1, 123, 130, 144, 146–8, 173, 175–6, 183, 305, 325, 331–3, 336–9, 341, 350, 354–6, 358, 360, 363, 368, 375–6, 378–83, 385–7, 389, 392, 401; *Host of* ~ 163, *Darkening of* ~ 335

Valinórean, Valinorian 30, 331

Valmar, Dome of 371. See *Varda.*

Vanyar (and singular *Vanya*) 62, 77, 82, 318, 332, 336–8, 340, 343, 349, 386, 402; *Banyai* 402. *Vanyarin* 77

Varda 334, 358, 363(–4); *Airë Tári* 363–4; *Dome of Varda* 376. See *Elbereth.*

Variags The people of Khand. 79
Vëandur Third son of Isildur. 191, 208. (Replaced by *Ciryon*.)
Vëantur Númenórean navigator. 329
Vefántur Mandos. 374
Vidugavia King of Rhovanion. 198, 259–60, 262; rejected name *Vinitharya* 262
Vidumavi Daughter of Vidugavia; wife of Valakar. (198, 213–14, 259), 260. See *Galadwen*.
Vingilot 'Foamflower', Eärendil's ship. 143, 163, 387; *Vingilótë* 365, 367, 392; *Wingelot, Wingelótë* 371, *Wingalótë* 370–1; Sindarin *Gwingloth* 370. See *Eälótë, Rothinzil; Guingelot*.
Vinitharya Name in the language of the Northmen of Eldakar, King of Gondor. 199, 260–2; *Vinthanarya* 214
Vinyamar The house of Turgon in Nevrast (Nivrost). 364, 390
Vinyarion Twenty-fourth King of Gondor (see *Hyarmendakil II*). 199, 214
Völuspá Poem of the Old Norse *Edda*. 71, 278
Vorondil Son of Pelendur; Steward to King Eärnil II. 204, 218–19
Voronwë See *Mardil*.

Wade 371 (see III.142–4).
Wainriders 195, 200–1, 215–16, 218, 232, 254–5
Walda Twelfth King of Rohan. 274
Wales 50
War of the Dwarves and Orcs 205, 220, 237, 249–50, 276–8, 301, 319, 323
War of the Elves and Sauron 168–9, 172, 174, 177–8, 180
War of the Jewels See *Jewels*.
War of the Ring 25, 137, 173, 196, 242, 244–5, 253, 255, 257, 261–3, 265–9, 282, 309, 411
Watchful Peace 234–5, 249
Water, The 117
Weather Hills 189, 193–4, 209, 313
Weathertop 56, 189, 229. See *Amon Sûl*.
Welsh 50, 81
West, The (the lands beyond the Great Sea, ancient West, Far ~ , Uttermost ~ , and the West of Middle-earth (cf. *Westlands*), or in more general sense) 16, 20, 30, 32–3, 55, 72, 149, 164, 173, 176, 183, 211, 228–9, 235, 242–3, 252, 257, 264, 266, 271, 294, 297–8, 300–1, 305, 312–15, 317, 324, 328, 363, 385–6, 388, 399, 401; and see *Lords of the West*. Men of the West 21, 64, 189, 324, 437, *Western Men* 62
Western Elves 70, 73, 78
Westernesse Númenor. 21, 31, 64, 74, 79, 152, 173, 181
Westfold 65
Westlands (of Middle-earth) 12, 32, 35–6, 39, 55, 61, 78, 119, 125,

133, 146, 172–3, 176, 179, 191, 196, 204, 228, 240, 242, 244–5, 255, 267, 287, 424
Westmarch   17, 25, 112; and see *Red Book*.
Westnish   Term preceding *Westron*. 55, 57, 64; *Western language* 72
Westron   17, 28, 32–9, 44, 55, 57–8, 64–5, 68–9, 72, 76, 78, 81–3, 316. See *Common Speech*.
White Council   (also *the Council*) 204, 226, 235, 237–9, 241, 248–9, 251, 283
White Downs   6, 112, 115
White Mountains   34, 205, 235–6, 244, 267, 272, 274, 309, 313, (415)
White Tower   (in Minas Tirith) 200, 205–6, 215, 232, 236, 238. See *Ecthelion I*.
White Tree   (1) of Tirion/Túna. 147–9; *Galathilion the Less* 147–8. (2) of Eressëa. 147–8, 176, 191; *Nimloth* 147–8, *Galathilion* 147–8, *Celeborn* 148. (3) of Númenor. 130, 147–8; *Nimloth* 147–8. (4) of Minas Ithil. 176, 191–2. (5) Of Minas Anor, Minas Tirith. 163, 170, 177, 192, 200, 204, 206, 217, 220, 231, 234, 238, 243
Whitfurrows   Village in the East Farthing. 98, 117
Wilderland   38, 56, 66–7, 214, 230, 250, 323, 437; map of ~ 323. See *Rhovan(n)ion*.
Wild Men   (of Drúadan Forest) 65, 309, 316, 324; (out of the East) 197, 205, 272, 413, 422, 426
Winchester   44
Wingelot   See *Vingilot*.
Wise, The   229, 234, 238, 249, 264–5
Witch-king   (of Angmar) 193–5, 201, 209–10, 230, 232–3, 241–2, 248, 256, 258, 378. See *Sorcerer-king*.
Wizards   228, 245, 311, 360, 392; *the Five Wizards* 384–5; *the Two Wizards (Blue Wizards)* 384–5; *Wise Men* 228. See *Istari*.
Woodhall   Village in the East Farthing. 93, 95, 118
Woodland Elves, Elves of the Woods   (in various applications) 20, 22, 26, 75–6, 185; *Wood-elves* 70
Woodmen of Mirkwood   34, 71
Woody End   93, 118
World, The   References to the change of the world. 156, 176, 244, 257, 266, 270, 275, 314, 359, 381, 401. See *Circles of the World, (The) End*.
Wulf   (of Rohan) 271

Yale, The   Region of the Shire. 88, 97–8, 100–1
Yandúnë   See *Common Speech*.
Yavanna   147–8, 403–5; *Sleep of Yavanna* 398; *Ivann* 405
Yavannildi   'Maidens of Yavanna' 404; Sindarin *Ivonwin* 404–5
Year of Dread   382

Yearsday, Yearsend See *New Year, Old Year.*
Yellowskin 40, 67. See *Tuckborough.*
Yule 121, 127; *Yuletide* 129; *Yuleday(s)* 121, 124, 128–9, 131–2, 138

Zigil-nâd Silverlode. 279, 286. See *Kibil-nâla.*
Zimrahil See *Ar-Zimraphel.*
Zirak-zigil Silvertine. 279